CODEX DERYNIANUS II

Population Per Square Mile = 87

Et tenuit nostras numerosus Horatius aures,
Dum ferit Ausonia carmina culta lyra.
Virgilium vidi tantum: nec amara Tibullo
Tempus amicitiæ fata dedere meæ.

CODEX DERYNIANUS II

Being a Comprehensive Guide to the Peoples, Places, & Things
Of the Derynye & the Human Worlds of the XI Kingdoms:
Including Historyes of the Major & Minor States & the
Occurrences Which Have Been of Most Importance to Them:
With Compleat Biographyes of the Prominent Personages & Holy
Saints of Gwynedd, Torenth, Meara, Bremagne, Mooryn, Howicce,
Llannedd, The Connait, R'Kassi, Orsal & Tralia, Fallon, Byzantyun,
The Forcinn Buffer States, & the Other Countryes of This Region
From the Birth of Our Lord Jesus Christ unto *Anno Domini* MCXXX:
Together with a Detail'd Chronological Historye of the
Great Sovereign Kingdom of Gwynedd and All Her Neighbours:
Also Including a Liturgical Calendar of the Saints of Gwynedd:
With Many Lists of the Patriarchs, Primates, Kings, Princes,
Dukes, Earls, Counts, & Other Nobles & Notables of These States:
With Much True Opinions & Observations Regarding Same.

All Compiled & Edited & Translated & Occasionally Penn'd
by Those Most Trustworthy & Wholly Dedicated *Auteurs*:

Ye Honourable KATHERINE KURTZ
Lady of Holybrook Hall

and

Ye Honourable ROBERT REGINALD
Brother of Saint Bernardine's

Who Have Consulted Many Rare & Unusual Sources to
Uncover These Facts & Stories, Many of Which Have
Not Been Previously Related in Volume Form.

Maps by Amy Harlib

UNDERWOOD BOOKS
Nevada City, California
MMV

Copyright © 1998, 2005 by Katherine Kurtz & Robert Reginald
Maps © 2005 by Amy Harlib
All rights reserved. No part of this book may be
reproduced in any form without the expressed
written consent of the authors. Other than the Deryni,
none of the characters herein are based
on any real person, living or dead.

Library of Congress Cataloging-in-Publication Data

Kurtz, Katherine.
  Codex derynianus II : being a comprehensive guide to the peoples, places & things of the Derynye & the human worlds of the XI Kingdoms ... / all compiled & edited & translated & occasionally penn'd by Katherine Kurtz and Robert Reginald.
    p. cm.
  Includes bibliographical references and index.
  ISBN-13: 978-1-887424-96-7 (pbk.)
  ISBN-10: 1-887424-96-2 (pbk.).
  1. Kurtz, Katherine—Handbooks, manuals, etc. 2. Fantastic fiction, American—Handbooks, manuals, etc. 3. Deryni (Fictitious characters)—Handbooks, manuals, etc. 4. Gwynedd (Imaginery place)—Handbooks, manuals, etc. I. Reginald, R. II. Title.
PS3561.U69Z468 2005
813'.54—dc22   2005-15755

UNDERWOOD BOOKS
P.O. Box 1919
Nevada City, CA 95959

Editio Secunda

10 9 8 7 6 5 4 3 2 1

ARGUMENTUM/CONTENTS

In Memoriam: Whitney Louise Rogers 6

Proœmium: The Second *Codex* 7

Introductio: Uncovering the *Codex* 11

Præfatio: *Gaudeamus!* 17

Codex Derynianus II 19

Ordo Temporum: A Chronology of the XI Kingdoms 262

Calendarium Liturgicum XI Regnorum: A Liturgical Calendar of the XI Kingdoms 342

De Auctoribus et Bibliographia Librorum 345

Genealogiæ Familiarum Regiarum XI Regnorum: Genealogies of the Royal Families
    of the XI Kingdoms 348

Tabulæ XI Regnorum: Maps of the XI Kingdoms, by Amy Harlib 354

IN MEMORIAM

WHITNEY LOUISE ROGERS

(6 July 1986 – 9 November 2001)
Ætat. XV

*A daughter of the Gods,
And most divinely fair.*

Neptis Michælis Burgi Auctoris

*"La feuille tombe à terre,
Ainsi tombe la beauté"*

PROŒMIUM

At vos incertam, mortale, funeris horam
Quæritis, et qua sit mors aditura via;
Quæritis et cœlo Phœnicum inventa sereno,
Quæ sit stella homini commoda, quæque mala.

PROŒMIUM

The Second *Codex*

It has often been observed that one great archaeological find will quickly lead to another, and so it has been with the *Codex Derynianus*. Three years after the original discovery of this amazing manuscript in the R'Kassi desert, a second copy has now been unearthed in the ruins beneath Grecotha. During excavations for the new underground tramway being constructed near Saint Kilian's Cathedral, a partially collapsed room was uncovered by one of the work crews, and when the wall markings suggested a structure that dated back to the time of the Free City, Professor Menville was immediately called to the site. The many amazing artifacts that he found during the following months need not be described in detail here, for they were the subject of much media attention at the time; who, for example, can forget the published accounts of Menville's final breakthrough into the treasure room, and his famous response to the question of what he saw in there: "Marvelous things. Wonderful, wonderful things!" (Those wishing to read a more detailed account of these findings, and to view a selection of the astonishing color photographs taken during the year-long excavation, should seek out Professor Menville's own enchanting account of his expedition, *Glorious Grecotha*.)

In the third of the rooms excavated, which was evidently employed as a *bibliotheca* and study room, Menville found evidence that at least part of the facility was in limited use for a far longer period than indicated by the other physical evidence. Scattered throughout the shelves, some of which had collapsed, dumping their contents onto piles of mildewed incunabula, were a number of tomes dating from later centuries, including several hitherto unknown, among them Dewi's *Historia Nova Derynianorum Gwyneddi*, *Les Mélodies de Mélissande*, the *Pompœ Aureolœ Susianœ*, and others. And there, standing upright in the midst of these marvelous volumes, was a beautifully bound copy of the *Codex Derynianus*.

Dr. Ezra Werner has postulated, in an article published recently in *The Journal of the Gwyneddan Historical Society*, that this was, in fact, the author's own copy, basing his conclusion on the many corrections and updates jotted in the margins of the manuscript; but since we have no clear evidence that will identify the writer, and no name other than that given in the work itself—Theophilus—and no firm location with which the author is associated, this treatise has not been universally accepted. Indeed, Rev. Abner Davis states in his response in *Acta Derynianorum* that a more likely candidate is Count Berrhones, a key figure in the Torenthi Court during this period, or even his literary archrival, Campbell de Broun, both of whom are mentioned in the *Codex* as well-known writers of their time.

What *can* we infer about the author of the *Codex*? He—or according to Professor Jamison Houle, *she*—was a creature of his (or her) time, very well educated and read, with connections in both the Torenthi and Gwyneddan courts, as well as personal access to many of the key players of the period, and was also knowledgeable about both history and politics. Houle believes that the author had to be one of the women behind the throne of Gwynedd during Kelson's reign, pointing to Princess Rothana as the likeliest prospect. Her background and education, her connections with East and West, her closeness to both Kelson and the rulers of the Forcinn States, make her the perfect choice, in his estimation.

Dr. Lewin L. Levin, however, believes we should take the author at his word, that "Theophilus" is not, as many critics believe, a pseudonym, although it may be a religious name; and thus he regards Fra Théophile de Chardin, Grand Master of the Order of St. Willibrord, as the obvious writer. Why else would Théophile be mentioned by name, he asks, when in the context of the rest of the manuscript he is clearly out of place? We know very little about the historical Théophile, indeed, no more than the bare particulars of his position: he was ordained into the Order in the year 1111, and elected its Grand Master in 1122, a very short time in which to rise so far. He died in the year 1155. Since it was the practice of the members of this Order to be given a religious name upon taking monastic vows, his baptismal name is unknown. His surname is relatively common in the Forcinn States, and a barony of that name also existed at that time in Fallon, as part of the County of Enghieux.

Dr. Avery Barrett, on the other hand, holds that "Theophilus" is the joint pseudonym of a group of writers, that no one individual could possibly have known or have had access to all of the information recorded in the *Codex*, that either a group of Deryni mages or a religious house compiled the material over a period of years, perhaps under the guidance of an editor. Barrett points out that the name Theophilus appears in the New Testament as the probably fictitious person ("Lover of God") to whom some of the letters of Saint Paul are directed. The author(s) of the *Codex* knew his (or their) audience, and knew also that the readers would catch the reference, as an intentional nod to the Almighty.

Whatever the case, the result is a marvelous compendium of extraordinarily rich materials about the early development of the Deryni in the XI Kingdoms. However, the scholars who had been involved in editing and preparing the original *Codex* for publication soon noted some differences between the two versions. The second *Codex* clearly was finished some years after the first, incorporating four more years of chronological data, as well as mentioning events, persons, and places from the *Nupta Kelsoni Regis*. There were other, more subtle differences. Some errors of fact in the original volume were corrected (see Sr. Prof. Rudolfo Aguilar's intriguing analysis, "*Codex* Below Decks: Errata Desiderata," in *The Journal of Deryni Archaeology*), and some additional general entries were added, including one on healers. The note in the first version that a copy had been delivered to King Kelson was carefully amended in the second to state that a copy had been "sent" to Kelson, implying that it had never been received. This matches the known historical record somewhat better, for there is no evidence in other sources that King Kelson or anyone else in his court had any knowledge of the precise role that Camber Earl of Culdi had played in the preservation of Deryni heritage two centuries earlier. There is also no colophon in the second book.

Both *Codices* also display some intriguing lacunæ, failing to mention, for example, the published Deryni chronicles and epics on Orin and Jodotha, Duke Alaric Morgan, King Owain Haldane, or the events surrounding the Battle of Killingford. One can only presume that these accounts had not yet been written in the year 1130, when the second *Codex* comes to an end. On the other hand, the compiler evidently had access to many other sources which have not survived the ravages of the centuries, and for which the *Codex* remains the only known source. Indeed, Prof. Alford Barron Vassilakos believes many of these to be fictitious, citing, in his essay "The *Codex* De-Codexed," instances of what he regards as embellishments created by the writer to justify his accounts of certain events, although Dr. Jesmyn Hunt, in her rather pointed response, "*Codex Vindex*," effectively demolishes Campbell's arguments. Most observers do believe that there were some embellishments, in accordance with the literary norms of the day, but that these were provided only to bridge small gaps in the records, and not intentionally to deceive. There is a strong undercurrent of faith and truth in both manuscripts, and the writer seems to have made a serious attempt to adhere to the historical record, good or bad. His own feelings only rise to the surface when he comments on such figures as Hubert MacInnis, and these judgments are very evident to the reader.

Once again we are pleased to offer this new version of the *Codex Derynianus* to a broader audience, with the hope that it will engender as much excitement and pleasure as the original. We also wish to thank those readers who have provided commentary on and suggestions for improving the first edition, including the following individuals (in alphabetical order):

Dom Aelred (Father Scott), Tony Ahrens, Donna Beard, Robb Belak, Bernadette Crumb, Matt Cushing, Felan (Leanne Phillips), Debnor (Richard Sheaves-Bein), Sid Gale, Anuj Goel, Celia Grey, Keith Glaeske, Joyce Haslam, Dennis Higbee, Melissa Houle, Roberta Johnson, Kyri (Tania Ryan), P. Winslowe Lacesso, Donald Lantzke, Anne Leckie, Julie Lim, Lisa E., John McLaughlin, Marion Moebus (Snuffybear), Pat Nolan and Thumper (of course), Artemis OakGrove, Brom O'Berin (Darryl Secord), A. Leigh Ann Paige, Russ Paris, Lori (Laura) Perrelet, Martin Pilkington, Andrew Priestley, Irina Rempt, Sianny Schira, Carolyn and Mark Shilts (with *pax*), Steven H. Silver, Julie Stampnitzky, Linda Stuckenschneider-Epstein, Toni Sydor, Julianne Toomey, Tim Underwood, Sara VanLooy, Susan Werner, and Robert A. Woodward, among many others.

In particular, we give very especial thanks to **Rebecca L. Davis** for her errata lists, her advice, and her positive criticism.

Our blessings to each and every one of you for reading and listening—and for just being there.

—Basil Jerome Westerling, Hist. Phil. Dr. Emeritus
Libraria Pfausolea Antiquitatum, Universitas Sancti Bernardini
15.III.1999 et 19.VI.2005

¿Qué es la vida? Un frenesi
¿Qué es la vida? Una illusion
Una sombra, una ficción,
Y el major bien es pequeño;
Que toda la vida es sueño,
Y los sueños sueño son.

INTRODUCTIO

Et quisquam ingenuas etiamnum suspicit artes,
Aut tenerum dotes carmen habere putat?
Ingenium quondam fuerat pretiosius auro;
At nunc barbaries grandis, habere nihil.

INTRODUCTIO

UNCOVERING THE *CODEX*

The discovery three years ago of a virtually complete copy of the *Codex Derynianus* in the R'Kassi Desert created a great surge of excitement in the scholarly world, and we are pleased finally to offer a definitive English-language translation of the Latin original. Although the existence of this book had been known from its mention in the *Annales Kelsoni Regis*, most of the original copies had been presumed lost in the Great Fire of Rhemuth in 1366, which destroyed so much of the original architectural and cultural heritage of the city, including the Royal Archives and Library, and the collections of the University of Gwynedd and of the Archbishop of Rhemuth. Indeed, were it not for the survival of numerous copies of the *Deryni Chronicles*, our contemporaneous sources for the history of Gwynedd during this period would depend almost completely on foreign-language accounts, particularly those of Torenth, plus the miscellaneous documents surviving in such regional centers as Coroth, and the handful of singed tomes remaining in the Great Royal Library of Valoret after the Siege of 1543.

Only a few fragments of the *Codex* had surfaced previously, just enough to validate its existence, including the fortunate discovery thirty-five years ago of two leaves of the original work that had been used to stiffen the internal binding of a thirteenth-century psalter. Evidently, the volume was produced in several different versions (the number is unknown) between about 1126-1138, and then supplanted about 1145 by Boden the Clerk's immensely popular *Lives of the Kings of Gwynedd*, which was widely distributed. We can speculate that the somewhat abstruse text of the *Codex* limited its circulation to the King and his family and major councilors, and to the major royal and ecclesiastical libraries in Valoret, Rhemuth, and Grecotha.

Professor Menville has written widely of the astonishing archaeological finds at oasis Wadi-Ghubrail, so I shall not elaborate on them here. Suffice it to say that no one in the scholarly world, least of all Dr. Menville himself, expected to find a copy of this or any other document buried in what amounted to a medieval trashheap, and there has been much speculation as to the agencies that might have brought it to that site. When the *Codex* was first uncovered, Dr. Menville, Dr. Cameron, and the other members of the dig immediately secured the site, and made certain that every effort was made scientifically to analyze the stratigraphy and to ensure that nothing at the site had been disturbed since the deposit of the artifact. In addition, the carbon-14 analysis of the vellum on which the document was written, together with studies of the dye used and style of writing, indicated a period of origin that does not contradict the date that appears in the book itself, the fifth or sixth year of the reign of King Kelson. We are fortunate indeed that the dry desert climate preserved the discarded text during the ensuing seven and one-half centuries. How, then, did a copy of this obscure document come to be left at a forgotten oasis in R'Kassi?

We can only speculate. It is clear from the Deryni Chronicles that King Kelson I was under siege during the early years of his reign from a wide variety of potential suitors, both domestic and foreign, all of them offering their eligible female relations as prospective brides for the unmarried monarch. These efforts intensified following the death of the King's first bride at the hands of her brother in 1124. Indeed, the accounts in the *Nupta* make clear that, following the initial stabilization of his regime and the end of the series of insurrections which inaugurated his reign, the monarch's frustration with the constant emphasis on his need to produce an heir to the throne prompted ever-increasing and ever-lengthening absences on his part from both his advisers and his capital city, including at least one incident in which he nearly lost his throne to his ambitious first cousin. One can sympathize with his plight. During this period the chief ministers continued to send and receive an exceptionally large number of embassies from foreign powers, ostensibly regarding the marriage prospects of the King; many of these were undoubtedly legitimate, while others, as events later made clear, had somewhat more sinister purposes.

It is entirely possible that an official delegation from or to Gwynedd and one of the Forcinn or border states was in the late 1120s ambushed while camping at Wadi-Ghubrail, then a shrine to Saint Gabriel, the party being scattered or massacred. The bandits would likely have found very little value in an illuminated manuscript other than its gilded front cover (which was missing), and would have quickly tossed the remnant away; or it may possibly have been dropped while the ambassadors were fleeing for their lives. In either event, a sand storm may well have covered the evidence of a skirmish very quickly and buried it under several feet of insulating soil, not to be disturbed again for hundreds of years. The area where the book was found was located several hundred meters to the East of the oasis, and had evidently been used as a dump by wayfarers. By the time the excavation was begun, the site had become a mound composed of fifty meters of alternating layers of sand and debris.

Physically, the *Codex* measures 30.45 centimeters in height and 21.85 centimeters in width. The binding has cracked and peeled badly, with the front cover apparently torn away; what remains of the leather exterior is dark and plain and unadorned. There is a remnant of a clasp fitting located on the middle edge of the back cover. The cover has one obvious wormhole on the spine, and in fact the dessicated body of a larva was located within; the parchment text itself is undamaged, however. The title page, if the incunabulum ever had one, is missing. The initial letters of King Kelson's name and several other major figures in Gwynedd's history are illuminated, but otherwise the book appears to have been designed for utilitarian use and not for mere display.

Although the bulk of the text is in Latin, there are scattered words in Greek and in Gwyneddan and Torenthi dialects, indicating that the compiler was familiar with a variety of languages and expected his audience to be the same. Unusually for this period, the basic work is organized in alphabetical order by main entry. The compiler evidently drew very heavily on the *Chronicles of the Deryni* and the *Chronicles of Saint Camber*, with which he was intimately familiar, and skimmed over those parts of the history of the Eleven Kingdoms which were less interesting to him. His intent here was clearly to champion the Deryni, and one may speculate that he himself belonged to that race. However, the *Codex*'s chief importance lies in its many quotations from other sources which have not survived the ravages of time, and while there are no great revelations here, the book does provide numerous amendations and variations to our knowledge of two key periods in the history of Gwynedd, specifically surrounding the reigns of King Cinhil I and King Kelson.

Throughout the text the editor uses a series of abbreviations which he obviously expects the reader to know and understand, and these have generally been explicated in full here. Some of these, such as the "R." following Kelson's name or the "D." following Alaric, are obvious (*e.g.*, Kelsonus R.=Kelson the King); others are much more obscure, clearly requiring a cultural context now lacking in order to interpret them properly. The reader should also understand that much of the text is formulaic in nature, with the compiler using a set of standard formats and repeated language from which he deviates only rarely. On the final page of the volume is a small, square, boxed colophon, also abbreviated:

> Cod^{x}Dery^{s}Fec^{t}ThPh^{Sr}
> Ord^{o}Pen^{ts}+Wllb^{d}Val^t
> Bib^{a}Reg^{a}Rhem^{a}AKR^{v-}

which might be interpreted: *"Codex Derynianus* made by Theophilus Brother of the Order of the Penitents of Saint Willibrord of Valoret at the Royal Library of Rhemuth in the fifth year of King Kelson" (*i.e.*, 1125/26; the end of the date is smudged and might also read "vi" [i.e., 1126/27]). This monk may have been the actual author of the work or just a copy scribe attached to the Royal Archives; in any event, nothing is known of him beyond his name. Indeed, Menville believes that the attribution is entirely pseudonymous, that the "God-Loving" author of the *Codex* was deliberately attempting to conceal his (or her) identity; or that the author was so well known at Court that he was using the pen name to make some sort of statement whose significance is now lost; or that the Reg^a somehow refers to the King himself or to one of the members of his immediate family. We may never know for sure. A "Théophile" is mentioned in the text, but he may or may not be the author.

Inscribed at the bottom of this final leaf is a quotation from Lucretius in a precise, square hand: "Tantum religio potuit suadere malorum" ("Such evil deeds could religion prompt"); the note is ini ailed "KD." Below that is an unsigned line adapted from Catullus in a third, smaller, more cursive hand: "Vivamus, meus Rex, atque amemus" ("Let us live, my King, and love"). Whether the "KD" refers to King Kelson I is unknown, since no validated sample of his handwriting or signature survives, nor is it clear what the letter "D" might signify in any case.

The authors have done a masterful job of translating the original text of the *Codex* into the modern-day vernacular while retaining the flavor of the original text. This popular edition of the book is being released at the same time as the scholarly version, and is identical to it except for the absence of footnotes and other editia. We believe it will become an important and even entertaining addition to the growing literature of Deryniana.

—Basil Jerome Westerling, Hist. Phil. Dr.
Libraria Pfausolea Antiquitatum, Universitas Sancti Bernardini
1.v.1996

Primum Graius homo mortaleis tollere contra
Est oculos ausus, primusque obsistere contra.
Quem neque fama deum, nec fulmina, nec minitanti
Murmure compressit cœlum: sed eo magis acrem
Irritat animi virtutem, effringere ut arta
Naturæ primus portarum claustra cupiret.
Ergo vivida vis animi pervicit, et extra
Processit longe flammantia mœnia mondi:
Atque omne immensum peragravit mente animoque;
Unde refert nobis victor, quid possit oriri,
Quid nequeat: finita potestas denique quoique
Quanam sit ratione, atque alte terminus hærens.
Quare relligio pedibus subjecta, vicissim
Obteritur, nos exæquat victoria cælo.

CODEX DERYNIANUS II

All Kings, and all their favorites,
All glory of honors, beauties, wits,
The sun itself, which makes times, as they pass,
Is elder by a year, now, than it was
When thou and I first one another saw:
All other things, to their destruction draw,
Only our love hath no decay;
This, no tomorrow hath, nor yesterday,
Running, it never runs from us away,
But truly keeps his first, last, everlasting day.

Non possidentem multa vocaveris
Recte beatum. Rectius occupat
Nomen beati, qui Deorum
Muneribus sapienter uti,
Duramque callet pauperiem pati,
Pejusque let flagitium timet;
Non ille pro caris amicis
Aut patria timidus perire.

PRÆFATIO

Signa te, signa; temere me tangis et angis:
Roma tibi subito motibus ibit amor.

GAUDEAMUS!

Insofar as Our Lord God Jesus Christ has seen fit to restore our Lord and Master Kelsonus Primus, *Rex Gwyneddi et Dominus XI Regnorum, Liberator Deryniorum* (Deliverer of the Deryni), to his throne and to his people unharmed, and to overthrow the usurper Conallus *Princeps Interrex*, cursèd be his name, let us rejoice in our Master's deliverance from the bowels of the earth and the clutches of thrice-damned Satanas.

To champion the King's name we have dedicated ourselves to setting down the truth of what we know about the good and the evil of those days which have passed since the beginning of our history, and especially those events which have affected the fate of the Deryni people and the Great House of the Haldani. These are the people and these are the places which the Land has well known. These are the mighty and these are the small among God's children who have made a difference in our world.

To those great kings who are to come, blessèd be he who preserves this record, blessèd be he who copies it for another, blessèd be he who renews this book and repairs its bindings, blessèd be he who causes it to be read in the churches and the schools. Blessèd are the tellers of tales who sing the songs of the great deeds enscribed herein. For if we speak the truths of these words often enough, they will not be forgotten, they will not be hidden, they will shine throughout the ages, forever and ever. Amen.

All places that the eye of heaven visits
Are to a wise man ports and happy havens.
Teach thy necessity to reason thus;
There is no virtue like necessity.
Think not the king did banish thee,
But thou the king.

CODEX DERYNIANUS

Abbeyford. This town in Gwynedd is located next to the ruins of the Michaeline stronghold at New Argoed on a major ford of the River Lendour. It is particularly known for its important wool and mutton markets. [*The King's Justice*].

Abel, son of John the Goldsmith, later called Brother Benedict. He was received into the *Ordo Verbi Dei* and took the name Benedict in the year 874, and was later cloistered at the Priory of Saint Illtyd's. [*Camber of Culdi*].

Adelicia *of Horthness*, Countess of Sheele, Lady. She was born on the VIIIth day of November in the Year of Our Lord 913, being the second daughter of Rhun Earl of Sheele and Kristin Lady MacNeill. She intermarried with Tambert I Duke of Cassan on the XXIst day of May in the year 929, and by him she had children: the Hereditary Duke Tammaron later Duke of Cassan; the Lord Flynn; the Lady Eldona; the Lady Annetta. She was serving as a companion to Michaela Queen of Gwynedd in the Summer of the year 928. She died on the XVIIth day of March in the year 955, aged XLI years. R.I.P. [*King Javan's Year*; *The Bastard Prince*].

Adreana *Calder of Sheele MacArdry*, Countess of Transha. She was born on the IXth day of June in the Year of Our Lord 1070, being the only surviving daughter of Thomas Earl Calder of Sheele and Yvetta Lady Howard. She intermarried with Caulay MacArdry Earl of Transha on the IXth day of June in the year 1086, and by him she had children: the Tanist Ardry, dead at age XIX; the Tanist Michael, dead at age XXIX; the Lady Maryse, who secretly intermarried with Lord Duncan second son of the Duke of Cassan, and by him had one child, the Lord Dhugal, who was raised by his grandmother as if he were her own child, and was generally believed to be; the Lady Yvette, who intermarried with Peray Lord Howard; the Lady Ianna, dead at age X of the yellow skin; the Lord Arthur, the Lady Giolla, the Lord Cullen, the Lady Bernine, all born still or dead as infants; the Lady Caldreana, who was raised as a twin of Lord Dhugal, and who intermarried with Philo Hereditary Count of Pelagog. The Countess Adreana died on the IVth day of November in the year 1118, aged XLVIII years. R.I.P. [*The Deryni Archives*; *The Bishop's Heir*].

Adrian *MacLean*, Hereditary Count and Master of Kierney, Lord. He was born on the XXIst day of December in the Year of Our Lord 888, being the only son and heir of Iain II Earl of Kierney and Catriona Lady of Mar, and grandson of Aislinn Lady MacRorie sister to Camber Earl of Culdi. He intermarried with Mairi Lady of Nyford on the XIIth day of June in the year 905, and by her he had children: the Lord Camber Allin called "Camlin"; the Lord Leicester, born still; the Lord Adamnan, dead at the age of VII days; the Lady Ownah, who perished aworm at age II. He also served as foster father to Aidan Thuryn. He was brutally murdered at Trurill by the Regents on the XXXIst day of December in the year 917 with Aidan Thuryn and others, being forced to watch the soldiers crucify his son before himself being killed. He was XXIX years of age at his death. R.I.P. [*Camber the Heretic*; *The Harrowing of Gwynedd*; *The Bastard Prince*].

Adrian *MacRorie*, Hereditary Count and Master of Culdi. He was born on the XVth day of January in the Year of Our Lord 842, being the eldest son and heir of Ballard II MacRorie Earl of Culdi and Ardis Lady Drummond. He died of the Black Death on the XXXIst day of March in the year 856, aged XIV years, and was succeeded as Master of Culdi by his younger brother, Lord Angus. R.I.P. [*Camber of Culdi*; *Saint Camber*].

Agapitos *ho Hieromonachos*, Archbishop of Beldour, Saint. This monk of Byzantyun was elevated to the new see of Beldour by Keladión Patriarch of Kónstantinopolis in the year 355. He made great strides in converting the heathen tribes of Torenth, and undertook a pilgrimage to the Anvil of the Lord and Rûm in the year 362. He died in the year 368, and was succeeded by his auxiliary, Bishop Taurasios. His feastday is the XVIth day of March. *Tempora mutantur, nos et mutamur in illis.*

Agatha. She was serving as a maid for Queen Michaela at Rhemuth Castle in June of the year 928. [*The Bastard Prince*].

Agnes *de Barra*, Lady. She was serving as a lady-in-waiting to Queen Jehana in the year 1125. She elicited much interest from the young men at court, although her brother watched over her rather closely. [*Deryni Checkmate*; *The Quest for Saint Camber*].

Agnes *Murdoch*, Lady. She was born on the IVth day of January in the Year of Our Lord 900, being the eldest child and only daughter of Murdoch Earl of Carthane and Elaine Lady de Fintan. She intermarried as his second wife with Rhun Earl of Sheele on the Xth day of January in the year 918, and by him she had children: the Hereditary Count Isarn later Earl of Sheele; the Lady Émeraude later Baroness of Horthness in her own right, who intermarried with Lord Quiric Fitz-Arthur. She died of a growth in the breast on the IXth day of January in the year 940, aged XL years. R.I.P. [*The Harrowing of Gwynedd*].

Ahern *Jernian de Corwyn*, Hereditary Duke of Corwyn, later Earl of Lendour. He was born on the Ist of February in the Year of Our Lord 1071, being the son and heir of Keryell Earl of Lendour and Stevana Heiress of Corwyn. He was knighted by King Donal Blaine II at Twelfth Night Court in the Year of Our Lord 1089, and was also then confirmed in his office as Earl of Lendour; he campaigned with the King that year in Meara. On his deathbed, he intermarried with Zoë Bronwyn Morgan, eldest daughter of Sir Kenneth Morgan and his Ist wife, Anya Almaris, on the VIIth day of June in the Year of Our Lord 1089, but the marriage was never consummated, owing to his much lamented and lamentable passing on that same evening from the aching bowels. *E compie' mia giornata innanzi sera.* R.I.P.

Ahmed. He was a grain merchant from the East who appeared at Rhemuth in July of the year 1124. [*The King's Justice*].

Aidan (III) Alexander *Haldane*, King of Gwynedd. He was born on the XIIth day of October in the Year of Our Lord 627, being the eldest son and heir of Augarin King of Gwynedd and Rosemaryn Lady MacLean. He intermarried with the Princess Sinead daughter of Lulach Sovereign Prince of Kheldour and Sigrid Lady of Normarch Ley, on the I[st] day of July in the year 659, and by her he had children: the Princess Bethany, who intermarried with Barghash ibn Hassan al-Khideri, Nabil of Salah Reis, and secondly with Imre I King of Torenth, leaving issue; the Prince Augustin, dead at age VI of flux; the Princess Moira Roselynn, who intermarried with Aleksy Prince of Torenth and Count of Altorf and Vorarl, and by him had a child, the Princess Rocasta, who intermarried with Rhori Mór Prince of Kheldour and ancestor of the House of MacRorie, leaving issue; the Princess Usheen; the Princess Kiloran; the Hereditary Prince Kelvin, dead at age VIII of the bloody lungs; the Princess Hyacinthe; the Hereditary Prince Ifor, who died shortly after his father.

The Prince Aidan succeeded his father on the XXVIIIth day of February in the year 673, and was crowned by Archbishop Gisenod at Valoret as Aidan III (the only time that style was used) on the XIth day of April in that year. In a series of military campaigns he greatly expanded the boundaries of his Kingdom into Transflumenia and The Purple March, more than doubling the size of Gwynedd. He defeated the Count of Cashien in the year 675 and the Count of Carbury in the year 679, taking the subsidiary title, "Lord of the Purple March." The town of Grecotha, formerly a free city, was captured in the year 678, and the *scholae* there were formed into a major university in the year 682 by Queen Sinead, who championed the cause of education. Further expansion to the North was blocked by a series of Gwyneddan defeats at the hands of the Counts of Eastmarch and Southmarch in the 680s. King Aidan died at the Battle of Ebor in combat with Torv Count of Eastmarch on the VIIth day of July in the year 698, aged LXX years; his only surviving son, Prince Ifor, was severely wounded at the same time, and never reigned. Aidan was succeeded after an interregnum of II months by his half-brother, the Prince Llarik. R.I.P. [*Saint Camber*].

Aidan Alroy Camber *Haldane*, Prince of Gwynedd. He was born on the XVIIIth day of October in the Year of Our Lord 904, being the eldest son and heir of Cinhil I King of Gwynedd and Megan Lady de Cameron. But God having need of more angels, he was killed by poisoned salt provided by the evil presbyter Humphrey at his baptismal ceremony on the VIth day of November in that year, aged I month, and taken into the Heavens as one of God's saints, to sit at His right hand. His godparents were Rhys Lord Thuryn and Evaine MacRorie his wife; he was baptized by his father. He was buried in a tomb in the floor of the Haven's chapel II days after his death. R.I.P. [*Camber of Culdi*; *King Javan's Year*; "The Priesting of Arilan"].

Aidan Augarin Ifor *Haldane*, Prince of Gwynedd, also called "Daniel Draper." He was born on the IXth day of February in the Year of Our Lord 820, being the fourth son of Ifor King of Gwynedd and Nuala Lady Udaut, and the only child of his parents to survive the Festillic *coup d'état* of the year 822. He intermarried with Avis de Burgeys on the XXXth day of May in the year 842, and by her he had children: the Hereditary Prince Alroy also known as Royston Draper; the Princess Margret also called Gretta Draper, dead at age VI of the rosy fever; the Princess Isabel also called Belle Draper, who intermarried with the trader Maelor ap Tewdwr, leaving issue unknown.

As a child of II the Prince Aidan was smuggled out of Rhemuth Castle during the chaos of King Festil's *coup* by a servant of the palace, Jasper Draper, and was raised by him and his wife, Ingaret *née* Fullman, as Draper's bastard son together with their other children. The child was given the name Daniel Draper, and the family moved to Valoret shortly thereafter.

Daniel was a successful merchant and trader in woolen goods and cloth on Fullers' Alley in the city of Valoret. In old age, after the death of his wife and son, he became one of Rhys Thuryn's first patients on the IVth day of August in the year 897. On the XXVIIth day of September in the year 903, he revealed to Rhys his true identity, and had him verify his claim by allowing Rhys to sift through his memories. He died later that day, aged LXXXIII years. After the restoration of the monarchy, he was reburied in the year 918 in the family crypt of the Haldanes at Rhemuth. He had the traditional grey Haldane eyes. R.I.P. [*Camber of Culdi*; *Camber the Heretic*].

Aidan Camber *Thuryn*. He was born on the VIth day of January in the Year of Our Lord 907, being the eldest son of Rhys Lord Thuryn and Evaine Lady MacRorie. By the year 917 he had been fostered to Adrian Lord MacLean at his estate in Trurill, not far from Cor Culdi. Having been mistaken for Camlin MacLean at Trurill, he was tortured and killed by Manfred's men on the XXXIst day of December in the year 917, aged X years. R.I.P. [*Camber the Heretic*; *The Harrowing of Gwynedd*; *The Bastard Prince*].

Aidan Owain Jashan *Haldane*, Prince of Gwynedd, Duke of Valoret. He was born on the XXXIst day of December in the Year of Our Lord 999, being the third son of Urien King of Gwynedd and Jaroni Princess of R'Kassi. He had formed an attachment with Étiennette Countess du Roringe at the time of his death, and was even said by some to have been engaged to her, but because no vows had been spoken and no bans announced, their child, Perrin, who was born VIII months after the Prince's death on the XIth day of February in the year 1021, was declared bastard, without dynastic rights. However, his Uncle, the King Malcolm, later took pity on the boy and gave him a small estate, the Barony of Kilchon in Southern Carthmoor, whereupon he became a well-known vintner and winemonger, and achieved great fame by perfecting the so-called Perrinine *rosé*. The Baron Perrin du Roringe intermarried with his cousin, the Lady Justyna daughter of Maximilian Earl of Carthane, and died on his LXXXth birthday on the XIth day of February in the year 1101, leaving issue: the Lady Aidana, who intermarried with Moncure Gillispie Earl of Danoc; the Lord Étienne later Baron of Kilchon; the Lady Uriena, who at the age of XVI years went with her sister to see the fair held each Summer at Nyford, and became enamoured of a juggler there; she ran off with him when the performers went on to the next town on their circuit, and was not heard from again.

The Prince Aidan was trained in the martial arts at an early age, and having excelled at them, was named Subcommander of one-half of the Northern Army by his father the King on the XVIth day of June in the year 1018. Abruzzès says that "...in my thirty years at court I spoke to a dozen courtiers and servants who still remembered the Prince Aidan, calling him fair in hair and skin, well-muscled, with curly mustachios and a square chin, not truly handsome but having an attraction to women that was obvious in their response to him. He was manly, courteous, quick to laugh and to make jokes, easy in society, and he was liked and even loved by the men and women around him.

"The portrait of him which hangs in the Palace library displays him in all his military finery, complete with sword and great axe, and the fierceness evident even in his painted eyes reflects the other half of his personage, which was the vileness of his temper. Friend or foe, he would turn upon them in an instant if they opposed him or impressed him as discourteous, and the eruption, once started, could never be put back into the mountain. And this is what killed him, for although he won many a duel and tussle, often over trivialties, he could not win them all."

The Prince Aidan died at Grecotha on the XVIIIth day of June in the year 1020, aged XX years, and was returned to Rhemuth for burial in the family crypt beneath Saint George's Cathedral. He was greatly mourned. R.I.P.

Ailin *MacGregor*, Archbishop Primate of Valoret and All Gwynedd, sometime Auxiliary Bishop of Valoret. He was born on the VIIIth day of September in the Year of Our Lord 874. He early expressed interest in the Church, and was ordained priest at All Saints' Cathedral on the XXth day of October in the year 893. He was elected an itinerant Bishop on the IXth day of March in the year 916, serving as Auxiliary Bishop of Valoret under both Archbishop Jaffray and Archbishop Hubert. Being devoted to the memory of the late Archbishop Jaffray, he abstained from the rigged vote of the XXVIth day of December in the year 917 for Archbishop Hubert MacInnis. He assisted in the Candlemas services at Valoret Cathedral on the IInd day of February in the year 918. He attended the coronation of King Javan on the XXXIst day of July in the year 921.

The Bishop Ailin was sympathetic to the aims of the new Regency of King Owain, having been courted for several years by the exiled Bishop Dermot. He lodged one of the original copies of the new codicil to the late King Rhys Michael's will in the archives of the Cathedral of All Saints, and aided the Kheldour Lords in their passage from Eastmarch through Valoret to Rhemuth on the IVth day of July in the year 928, supplying them with fresh horses, XXX ecclesiastical knights, and the presence of his own person. Following the success of the *coup* against the former Regents, Bishop Ailin was elected Archbishop Primate of Valoret and All Gwynedd on the XIth day of July in succession to the deposed Archbishop Hubert. He died on the XXth day of October in the year 941, aged LXVII years. R.I.P. *Pro aris et focis*. [*Saint Camber*; *Camber the Heretic*; *The Harrowing of Gwynedd*; *King Javan's Year*; *The Bastard Prince*].

Ainslie, Lord Argoed, Lord Regent of Gwynedd. He was born on the XIXth day of October in the Year of Our Lord 873, being the eldest son and heir of Philibert d'Argent Lord Argoed and Jeronima Lady Corteskin. He intermarried with Eilidh Lady Ballingmore on the VIth day of July in the year 900, and by her he had children: the Hereditary Lord Robert called "Robin"; the Lady Philadelphia called "Delphay." This Baron had his estates at Old Argoed in Western Gwynedd near its border with Rhendall. He was appointed Deputy Commissioner for Grecotha by King Javan on the Ist day of September in the year 921, and was sent from Rhemuth to make the rounds of several of the local courts. He was severely wounded in the supposed attack on Prince Rhys Michael on the XXXIst day of October in that year, and was taken to the palace of Bishop Edward MacInnis at Grecotha for recovery. He was well enough a week later to assume direction of the search for the "kidnapped" Prince Rhys Michael. He was named to the new Regency Council of King Owain on the IInd day of August in the year 928.

Ten years later, on the Ist day of March in the year 938, when King Owain attained his majority and the Regency Council was disbanded, the Lord Ainslie announced his retirement from the King's service, and returned to his estates in Argoed, saying that he had served King and Country for all of his years, and now would serve his cows. There he remained for the next XXXV years. He attained his Cth birthday on the XIXth day of October in the Year of Our Lord 973, an event which caused great comment at the time, and died at Argoed V days later, saying that he had served his cows sufficiently well, and that it was now time to serve his Lord. He was buried there with high honours, with King Uthyr and all of his family and the Great Lords coming to Old Argoed to attend his funeral, and was interred in the family crypt there. He was succeeded by his grandson, Sir Javyl. R.I.P. [*King Javan's Year*; *The Bastard Prince*].

Airsid. Of this ancient Deryni brotherhood very little is now known by the brethren. According to the *Legends*, the *Airsid* constructed the complex used by the Camberian Council, "hidden beneath a high, rock-girt plateau of the Rhendall Moutains, almost within sight of the sea. They claimed credit for the *keeill* itself, and apparently had at least started work on the chamber which now housed the Council, but they had disappeared before it could be finished—no one knew why." Marquion called Orin "the last of the Airsid," but Stavroula hé Bibliothékaria has suggested that the

Airsidi dwell among us even unto the present day. [*Camber the Heretic*; *The Harrowing of Gwynedd*].

Aislinn Kethevan *MacRorie MacLean*, Dowager Countess of Kierney. She was born on the XXIVth day of April in the Year of Our Lord 851, being the youngest daughter of Ballard II Earl of Culdi and Ardis Lady Drummond, and the sister of Camber Earl of Culdi. She intermarried with Iain I Earl of Kierney on the IVth day of June in the year 869, and by him she had children: the Hereditary Count Iain *Junior* later Earl of Kierney; the Lord Geoffrey; the Lord Angus, ancestor of the noble McLain family; the Lady Ardissa. She was killed by the Regents at her estate of Trurill on the XXXIst day of December in the year 917. R.I.P. [*Camber the Heretic*; *The Harrowing of Gwynedd*].

Alan *Sommerfield*, Sir. He was a seasoned captain of the elite McLain lancers during the Mearan War in June of the year 1124. [*The King's Justice*].

Alana *Destaing d'Oriel*. This Deryni was born on the XXIInd day of October in the Year of Our Lord 899. She intermarried with Lord Oriel de Bourg on the IInd day of June in the year 916, and by him she had one daughter: the Lady Karis, who intermarried with Tieg Thuryn. She was imprisoned with her daughter at Rhemuth Castle in the year 917 to compel her husband to work for the Regents. During the *coup d'état* by the former Regents on the XIth day of May in the year 922, her husband was killed, but in the confusion she and her daughter were taken to the former Michaeline Haven by Étienne Titular Baron de Courcy, and they survived the troubles of this period. She died on the XVIIIth day of November in the year 963, aged LXIV years. [*The Harrowing of Gwynedd*; *King Javan's Year*; *The Bastard Prince*].

Alaric Anthony *Morgan*, VIIth Duke of Corwyn, Earl of Lendour, King's Champion, Lord Protector of the South, Hereditary Knight and Laird of Morganhall, Sir. He was born on the XXIXth day of September in the Year of Our Lord 1091, being the eldest son and heir of Sir Kenneth Kai Morgan and Alyce Lady de Corwyn, and heir general through his Deryni mother to the Duchy of Corwyn and County of Lendour. He intermarried with Richenda daughter of Richard FitzEwan Baron of Rheljan and Michendra Princess of Andelon, and widow of Bran Coris Earl of Marley, on the Ist day of May in the year 1122, and by her he had children: the Countess Briony Bronwyn; the Hereditary Duke Kelric Alain Earl of Lendour; the Countess Sophonisba Alyca Richenda. He also raised Brendan Borisov Coris Earl of Marley, his wife's son by her first marriage.

He succeeded at birth as Earl of Lendour and Duke of Corwyn. On the Ist day of November in the year 1095, in the absence of the Hereditary Prince Prince Brion, King Donal Blaine gave the IV-year-old Deryni boy the means to induce the Haldane potential in Brion should the need ever arise. On the IIIrd day of August in the year 1100 he was playing with the II McLain brothers at Culdi when he fell out of a tree and broke his arm; the witch-woman Bethane set the fracture. After the death of his father on the XXIVth day of September in that year, he succeeded him in his small holding of Morganhall, and was sent to Court as a royal page, and met Brion King of Gwynedd for the first time at Christmas Court on the XXIVth day of December; he became a squire at age XII. On the XIIIth day of June in the year 1105 he accompanied King Brion on his expedition to put down the rebellion of Rorik III Earl of Eastmarch, and a few days later, on the XXIst day instant, helped him to attain his Haldane potential to fight the Festillic pretensions of Hogan Gwernach Duke of Marluk. He was officially confirmed as Duke of Corwyn at Michaelmas in that same year, the day he attained his majority, and was knighted on the IIIrd day of March in the year 1110.

On the Ist day of May in the year 1115 he was present at the annual Horse Fair in Rhelledd, where he first met Sean Earl Derry; later that month, on the XIth day of May, he witnessed the knighting of the said Earl Derry in Rhemuth and made him his aide. On the XVIIth day of April in the year 1118 he questioned an itinerant swordsmith named Ferris, who had been accused of murder and rape in the town of Kiltuin, and found him innocent of the crime. On the XVIth day of September in the year 1120 he was sent by the King to the City of Cardosa, which was being pressed by Wencit King of Torenth, to report on the military situation there. He was called back to Rhemuth on learning of the death of King Brion, and attended the coronation of King Kelson on the XVth day of November in the year 1120, being named the King's Champion there.

Ostracized by many because of his Deryni blood, he was satirized early in the year 1121 by a scurrilous ballad then being circulated in Corwyn about the so-called "Duke Cirala," his name spelt backwards. He used the pseudonym "Alain the Hunter" during his visit to Saint Torin's Shrine at Dhassa on the XXVIIIth day of March in the year 1121, where he was attacked and drugged by Warin de Grey and Lawrence Gorony. Later that year he served in the expedition mounted by the King against Wencit King of Torenth, and took part in the final duel arcane on the IInd day of July in that year, in which Wencit and his III allies were killed.

As a youth he was wont to dress in black, until Thomas Cardiel Archbishop of Rhemuth upbraided him in the year 1123 for mimicking the Devil, at which point he adopted more colourful garb appropriate to his high rank. On the XXIIIrd day of January in the year 1123 he was named Lord Protector of the South by King Kelson. He was present at the Synod which elected Henry Istelyn Bishop of Meara on the XXVIth day of November in that same year, and accompanied the King a few weeks later on his lightning raid to Ratharkin in Meara on the VIIIth day of December.

In the year 1125 he refused to acknowledge that the King and Dhugal Earl of Transha had actually died at Grelder Creek on the XXIst day of March, and kept searching for them with his cousin, Duncan Duke of Cassan, in the Lendour Mountains. He helped to enable the Haldane potential of Duke Nigel on the XVth day of May in the year 1124 and that of Nigel's son Prince Regent Conall on the IVth day of April in the year 1125. Later, when he and Duncan finally found the King near Saint Kyriell's in the Lendour Mountains on the XIIth

day instant, he was one of the main instruments of stability in restoring order to the Kingdom. King Kelson was present at the baptism of Alaric's eldest son in Coroth on the Xth day of June in that same year.

In June of the year 1128, he accompanied the Torenthi emissaries from Coroth to Desse on his ship *Rhafallia*, and thence to Rhemuth. He returned to Corwyn a few days later, where he hosted a banquet in his ducal palace at Coroth on the IInd day of July. On the following day, he sailed to Orsal with King Kelson, and was informed at that point of the King's intended marriage to the Lady Araxie Haldane. He then accompanied the King's party to Torenth, arriving at Beldour on the VIIIth day instant. With King Kelson and King Liam, he visited the Nikolaseum in Torenthály, and was shown the portal there.

He took part in King Liam's first Council on the XVIth day of the month, but returned to Rhemuth with King Kelson later that evening, and transported back and forth on the King's business between the capitals for the next several days. On the XXth day instant, he met the *Rhafallia* at Desse, and escorted his wife and her party back to Rhemuth on the following day. He accompanied King Kelson and the Archbishops of Gwynedd on an inspection of the new Chapel of Saint Camber in the Basilica of Rhemuth Castle. He was among the party of dignitaries welcoming the Servants of Saint Camber to Rhemuth on the XXXth day of July. Later that evening, he agreed to the request by the King to give Mátyás Duke d'Arjenol the coordinates of the portal in the Cathedral.

He witnessed the double royal wedding at Saint George's Cathedral in Rhemuth on the following day. He also defended Duke Mátyás against the attack of Count Teymuraz, and assisted Duke Dhugal in healing the Torenthi's knife wound.

He is described in the *Chronicles* as having "...wide grey eyes in an oval face, hair glistening gold, cropped to only a few inches for ease of care in the battle field; full wide mouth above the squared-off chin; long sideburns accentuating the lean cheek bones." His arms are: *sable*, a gryphon segreant *vert* within a double tressure flory-counter-flory *or*. *Fortis et fidelis*. ["Swords Against the Marluk"; "Legacy"; "The Priesting of Arilan"; "The Knighting of Derry"; "Trial"; *Deryni Rising*; *Deryni Checkmate*; *High Deryni*; *The Bishop's Heir*; *The King's Justice*; *The Quest for Saint Camber*; *Deryni Magic*; *King Kelson's Bride*].

Albanya. This duchy of Csodala is situate in the Albanyan Hills on the Southeastern border of Torenth, abutting on the County of Vechta. The Duchy has few resources other than its own people, whom it exports as mercenaries to the nations surrounding it. The ruler in the year 1130 is Azlan Beg.

Albin Nigel Brion Hakim *Haldane*, Prince of Gwynedd, Hereditary Duke of Carthmoor. He was born posthumously on the IIIrd day of February in the Year of Our Lord 1126, being the only son and heir of Conall Prince Regent of Gwynedd and Hereditary Duke of Carthmoor and Rothana Nabila of Nur Hallaj. He was disinherited at birth by his grandfather, the Duke Nigel, from any right of succession to the Duchy of Carthmoor, but he retained his princely title at the specific behest of King Kelson, being next in line to the Gwyneddan throne after his grandfather.

After his birth, Prince Albin was taken by Rothana to Nur Hallaj to meet his grandparents. His mother intended him for the life of the cloister, but he was reinstated as heir to the Duchy of Carthmoor on the XXXth day of July in the year 1128, at the specific request of King Kelson and with the agreement of Duke Nigel and Princess Rothana. He had fair skin, pale eyes, and night-black hair worn in a *g'dula*. [*The Quest for Saint Camber*; *King Kelson's Bride*].

***Alcara* or *al-Qarrah*.** This small independent Sheikhdom consists of XXIV oases located in the extreme Northwestern part of the Anvil of the Lord, surrounded by the Principality of Jáca to the Northeast, the fortress of Djellarda to the East, the Principality of Autun to the West, the Autuni Mountains to the North, and the great wastelands to the South, including the Emirate of Sarqif.

The history of this region is obscure, for the Arabi language which is spoken here had no written form until the coming of the Prophet Muhammad, and no records survive from the early centuries of al-Qarrah save for mentions of raids by its warriors in the chronicles of other states, especially Bremagne and Fallon or even Gwynedd. *The Great Book of Djellarda* mentions one Shahrukh ibn Nasr al-Din al-Qarrah as reigning Sheikh during the year 721 at the height of the Muslim Wars, and it is said that the Sheikh of al-Qarrah then controlled all of the Great Desert to a point hundreds of miles South, and West unto the port city of Kharthat, even venturing forth into the Atalantic Ocean with his fleet of fast, single-banked galleys. But when the Sheikh Shahrukh was killed by Bearand King of Gwynedd on the xth day of July in the year 752 at the Battle of the Jamin Straits, the power of the Sheikhs was broken forever, and little is said about them in any source during the next C years.

However, some of the Sheikhs are said to have become mercenaries, and to have sold their warriors for a price to the highest bidder, seeing no other way in which to attain either their own honour or the coin with which to buy additional high-quality weapons. In particular, the Kings of Torenth came to rely on these desert fighters as an integral part of their army, for the Qarrahi men were highly trained both as swordsmen and as horsemen, and also were frequently skilled in the art and science of Deryni magick. Thus, it is not surprising that a contingent of desert warriors from al-Qarrah accompanied the Prince Festil when he invaded Gwynedd in June of the year 822. The survivors of that adventure were given prominent places in the new establishment created by the Festils; several received titles of nobility reflecting their origins, including the noble family called Alcara, descended from a younger son of Faisal then Sheikh of al-Qarrah.

The winters of al-Qarrah are mild, but the summers are fiercely hot and dry, and the unsuspecting traveler can be marooned for days by the seemingly endless sandstorms that can blow forth at any time. The region is also known for the lush sweet *madjool* dates that it exports, and for the fine Arabi horses that it breeds.

The well-known traveler Campbell de Broun notes laconically in his diary: "There is not much to see in al-Qarrah." See also: Jebediah.

SHEIKHS OF AL-QARRAH

House of al-Qarrah

Qarrah ibn Firuz	680?
Nasr al-Din (son)	700?
Shahrukh (son)	720?-752
Hafif (son)	752-780?
Ghulam (cousin)	780?-790?
Sa'ad (son)	790?-795
Firuz (brother)	795-802
Jalal (brother)	802-816
Faisal (grandson)	816-871
Ghiyas al-Din (son)	871-880
Ali (cousin)	880-903
Qutb al-Din (son of Ghiyas)	903-922
Ghitrif (son)	922-948
Ghasan (nephew)	948-979
Tahir (son)	979-1000
Mu'addil (2nd cousin)	1000-1004
Tahir (restored)	1004-1008
Khalaf (son)	1008-1021
Talhah (brother)	1021-1038
Tughan (son)	1038-1066
Tajj al-Din (uncle)	1066-1069
Faruq (brother)	1069-1074
Arslan (son)	1074-1088
Hamid (son of Khalaf)	1088
Rub'al (son of Faruq)	1088-1122
Hamza (son)	1122-1127
Turan (brother)	1127-1130+

Aldred I Arkady *Furstán*, called "The Great," King of Torenth. He was born on the Ist day of June in the Year of Our Lord 645, being the eldest son and joint heir of Tamás King of Torenth and the Princess Iouliana daughter of Kallistos Grand Prince of Byzantyun. He intermarried with Bertradis daughter of Augarin King of Gwynedd and Caldora Lady de la Marche on the VIIIth day of June in the year 666, and by her he had children: the Hereditary Prince Imre later Count of Tolán later Imre I King of Torenth; the Prince Wenzel Sylvist later Count of Sostra; the Prince Nikon later Count of Tolán by cession from his brother; the Princess Kyrilla, who intermarried with Philoxenos Sebastokratór of Nateras; the Princess Pelagia, who intermarried with Mériadec Roi de Bremagne; the Princess Acacia, who intermarried with Hovakim Great Prince of the Kodratsi; the Prince Marek later Count of Nakkar; the Prince Tamás, who died acroupy at age V.

By the terms of his father's will, the Prince Aldred succeeded to the throne jointly with his brother Prince László on the XVIIth day of June in the year 677, and was girded with the sword by Patriarch Meletios I on the Ist day of January in the year 678; he reigned alone after his brother died on the VIIIth day of March in the year 681. This Great King expanded the borders of Torenth beyond the Fertile Crescent circumscribed by the River Beldour, and moved North along the mountains, conquering Tolán-by-the-Sea on the XXXth day of August in the year 677, when he defeated and killed Zvonimir Herzog von Tolán at the Battle of Elderon. His conquests nearly doubled the size of his realm. He died on the XXIInd day of October in the year 701, aged LVI years, being succeeded by his eldest son, and was buried with his forefathers in the family crypt at TorentháIy. R.I.P.

Aldred II Andre Nimur Rurik *Furstán*, King of Torenth. This parricide was spawned of the Devil on the XVth day of July in the Year of Our Lord 1090, being the only son and heir of Carolus III King of Torenth and Erzsébet Countess von Mourom. He was betrothed to Charissa Pretender of Gwynedd, daughter of Hogan Gwernach Duke of Tolán and Larissa Heiress de Marluk, on the XXIXth day of September in the year 1105, and intermarried with her on the XIVth day of June in 1106, and by her he had children: the Princess Marcissa, dead at age II of a fall suffered while playing with her father; the Hereditary Prince Gejza Taksóny, who was born and died on the XXXIst day of March in 1110.

According to Desiderius Callan, in the early months of 1110, after King Carolus III had made public his plans to meet with Brion King of Gwynedd to secure a peace between the II realms, "...Prince Aldred and his wife conceived a plan to place themselves on the throne of Torenth, for Princess Charissa feared the loss of her birthright if a treaty was signed. They decided to hold a banquet in the King's name on the evening before his departure, and to poison him there. At great expense the Princess secured a packet of Fenneli figs from the Forcinn Buffer States, and after dipping them in honey and ground nuts, inserted the poison powder into the largest and ripest of the fruits. When the feast was nearing its end, she herself carried the platter of sugared treats to the King, saying, 'Wouldst my Father care for a sweet?,' positioning the tray so that he would see the plumpest fruit there before his eyes. As she expected, he plucked it from the dish and popped it entire into his mouth. He died three hours later in great agony." However, other writers have blamed the King's death on the scheming of his ambitious brother, the Prince Wencit, or on the chronic distress of the belly to which he was prone.

The Prince Aldred was proclaimed King on the XIth day of February in the year 1110, but was never girded with the sword at Iób. Although he had to this point maintained a certain discretion in his actions, this evil prince unleashed the bounds of licentiousness following his accession, much to the despair of his nobles and the clergy. One of his favourites, Count Guye de Nevins, was made High Chancellor, and many other Council members were displaced by the King's sycophants. Meetings of the Great Council ceased to be held regularly, save to witness the executions of those who opposed the new regime. Although the King was Deryni, he had never become proficient at the magical arts, and preferred instead the science of tyranny, which he practiced with equal competence.

Berrhones says that when Queen Charissa attempted to intercede with her husband, being pregnant with her IInd child, "she was dragged forth and beaten nearly to death while the King stood by laughing," causing her to lose her baby II days later and rendering her permanently barren. She left her sickbed after II weeks to seek out her uncle, the Prince Wencit, telling him, "I must be rid of this man." On the XVth day of April in the year 1110 the Prince Wencit and his men burst into the King's bedchambers and seized the King and his favourite, declaring Aldred deposed. Nevins was attainted, tortured, disemboweled, and drawn and quartered in the public square; his estates were seized by the crown. The former King was tried before a jury of nobles and churchmen for the murder of his unborn son and for his other unnatural acts, and was convicted, attainted, sentenced to death, and decapitated on the XVIIIth day of April while his wife and the new King watched. His body was thrown into the river, his name removed from the rolls of the House of Furstán, and the beginning of Wencit's reign as King backdated to February. His widow renounced her title as Dowager Queen, and resumed the style Duchess of Tolán.

Count Berrhones says of this Prince that he "...was inattentive to his wife, preferring to keep the society of young men." Pavlovsky adds that "he was thin, delicate, easily led, uninterested in affairs of state, and entirely self-absorbed." Aba Sámuil wryly notes his proclivity for "fancy dress, fancy parties, and fancy men." The *Chronicles* call him "callow, with sweaty palms." The Prince Aldred was XIX years of age when he was sent to roast like a ripened, cracked chestnut in the fiery furnaces of Hell. He is omitted from many of the king lists of Torenth. ["Legacy"].

Alduin. This extensive forest lies near the ruined manor house of Tor Caerrorie on the estate once inhabited by Camber MacRorie Earl of Culdi. The well-known explorer Campbell de Broun was once lost in this region, and wryly noted in his reminiscences, *A Wanderer's Diary*, that:

"Last night it began to rain very heavy and continued this morning, in consequence of which we did not start but remain encamped. Some of our party, including my Nell, went into the tent and stayed there. The sick horse that I thought was dying the day before yesterday was still alive but very far spent. He staggered as he swayed, and about the IXth hour of the clock last evening he died, which added yet another item to our misfortunes. It brought past scenes fresh to my memory. Our situation was most unpleasant, the day gloomy and reflections discoloured, and I could see no prospect of much earthly pleasure. Misfortunes of the severest kind have already overtaken us, and what more still awaits us I cannot know. That we have difficulties to encounter is certain in this wooded wilderness where scarce a ray of comfort pierces its gloomy shadows, but those reflections remain painful. It ceased raining just after the noon hour, and we dried some of our plunder and cut strips of tough meat from the carcass of our deceased companion, cooking and salting them to carry with us on our journey. The trails were filled with roots and limbs and were very treacherous to our surviving mounts. I shall thank God and all his angels most heartily when we have finally left this dreary place." *Præfervidum ingenium Alduinorum*. [*The Bishop's Heir*].

Alexander. A scout for the MacArdry Clan in November of the year 1123, he spotted the party of ex-Archbishop Edmund Loris landing near Transha, and reported same to his Earl. [*The Bishop's Heir*].

Alexander II *Darby*, Archbishop of Rhemuth. He was born on the XXVIth day of October in the Year of Our Lord 1044. He trained as a physician, and practiced that art for many years before deciding to enter holy orders in the middle years of life. His *De Natura Deryniorum*, written as a thesis when he was a seminarian at the University of Grecotha in the year 1081, was required study for all aspiring clergy in Gwynedd during the ensuing IV decades. He was ordained priest on the XVIth day of June instant, and after serving at a number of parishes in central Gwynedd, was appointed pastor of Saint Mark's Church near the *Arx Fidei* Seminary near Valoret on the XIVth day of April in the year 1104, which was considered a sign of his rapidly rising prominence.

On the Ist day of August in that year he accompanied Archbishop Oliver to the Abbey Church of the Paraclete at *Arx Fidei* to take part in the ordination of the newly graduated seminarians there. He was elected an itinerant Bishop on the XIIth day of April in the year 1107, and was named Archbishop of Rhemuth on the Xth day of May in the year 1108 in succession to Archbishop James de Varagh. He ordained Duncan Lord McLain as priest on the Xth day of April in the year 1113. He died on the IIIrd day of February in the year 1117, aged LXXII years, and was buried in the crypt of Saint George's Cathedral. He was succeeded later that year by Bishop Patrick Corrigan. R.I.P. ["The Priesting of Arilan"; *The Quest for Saint Camber*].

Alfred *of Woodbourne*, Archbishop of Rhemuth, sometime Auxiliary Bishop of Rhemuth. He was born on the XXVIIth day of November in the Year of our Lord 874. He was ordained priest on the XVth day of May in the year 893, and immediately gained the attention of his superiors with his intelligence and faith. On the IIIrd day of January in the year 905 Father Alfred was appointed official Confessor to Cinhil I King of Gwynedd. In July of that year he advised Guaire to consider the priesthood as a possible future vocation. By the year 917 he had become the official Confessor to the new King Alroy and his II younger brothers, and was present at Alroy's coronation in May. He was elected an itinerant Bishop by the Synod of Bishops at Valoret on the XIIth day of November in that year, being named Auxiliary Bishop of Rhemuth. He was given the care of Prince Javan's religious training on the VIIth day of March in the year 918. He attended the coronation of King Javan on the XXXIst day of July in the year 921. He was chosen Archbishop of Rhemuth on the XIth day of July in the year 928 in succession to Archbishop Robert Oriss. He died of the poxy plague on the IVth day of April in the year 948, aged LXXIII years, and was succeeded by Bishop Rostaing d'Ancézune. His death from a new major outbreak of this hideous disease prompted an anti-Deryni uprising in Valoret. R.I.P. [*Saint Camber*; *Camber the Heretic*; *The Harrowing of Gwynedd*; *King Javan's Year*; *The Bastard Prince*].

Alister Camber Donal *Haldane*, Prince of Gwynedd. He was born on the Ist day of August in the Year of Our

Lord 907, being the fifth son of Cinhil I King of Gwynedd and Megan Lady de Cameron, and was named for Bishop Alister Cullen. He died of the oversleeping on the XIIIth day of November of the same year, aged III months, and was buried in the crypt of All Saints' Cathedral in Valoret. His body was later moved to the family crypt of the Haldanes at Saint George's Cathedral in Rhemuth. R.I.P. [*Camber the Heretic*].

Alister *Cullen*, Archbishop Primate of Valoret and All Gwynedd, Lord Regent of Gwynedd, sometime Bishop of Grecotha, Chancellor of Gwynedd, sometime Vicar General of the Order of Saint Michael. This Deryni prelate was born on the IXth day of August in the Year of Our Lord 858, being the son of Sir Ambrose Cullen and Alda Lady Eskill. He trained first at Saint Liam's Abbey School as a child, then at Saint Neot's between 870 and 872, where he was taught classics by Dom Eleric, and then at the Michaeline commanderie at Cheltham from 872. He was ordained on the IVth day of March in the year 877 by his maternal uncle, Raymond Prince-Bishop of Dhassa, and joined the Michaelines in the year 879. He was elected Vicar General of the Order of Saint Michael on the XXXth day of October in the year 901. On the XIth day of June in the year 905 he was elected Bishop of Grecotha, and was to have been consecrated in August. He participated in the War Council held on the XXIIIrd day of June at the Great Hall in Valoret Palace. He was killed at Iomaire II days later in mortal combat with the Pretender Ariella. He was XLVI years of age at his death; his shape and identity were assumed on the battlefield by Camber MacRorie Earl of Culdi.

Wearing the shape-shifted face of Alister Cullen, Camber became Bishop of Grecotha in 905, Chancellor of Gwynedd, and, briefly, Archbishop Primate of Valoret and All Gwynedd in 917. Alister's body, which had been given the semblance of Camber Earl of Culdi, was buried in the MacRorie family crypt at Tor Caerrorie on the IVth day of July in the year 905, but was moved to the Michaeline Haven on the IInd day of September following, being buried next to the infant Prince Aidan in the chapel there. His gravestone read: "Lord, now lettest Thou Thy servant depart in peace."

He is described in the *Legends* as having "eyes that glittered like sea ice, and heavy brows nearly meeting on his forehead. His hair was steel grey. He was tall, and wore a blue cassock." R.I.P. [*Camber of Culdi*; *Saint Camber*; *Camber the Heretic*; *The Harrowing of Gwynedd*].

Alix *Orexis*, Saint. She was born of noble parents in IVth-century Rûm, and at first led a frivolous life. After IX weeks of overindulgence in figs and dandelion wine, a most potent combination, she gave herself entirely to God and founded an order devoted to the teaching of good manners and proper decorum to the children of the poor. This great mystic later became entirely mute, believing that it is better to say nothing at all than to defame the Name of the Lord. She was appropriately described by one of her spiritual daughters as "a child of silent suffering," and she made certain, through her gestures and the written word, that everyone knew it. Her sister, Saint Anne Orexis, succeeded her, but not for long. The Countess Ringgöld, who took the name of Sister Zabel, was a penitent of this Order. Her feastday is the IXth day of January.

All-Father. He was the chief god of the heathen religion of Eistenfalla, being the head of the Old Ones. Some of his followers were persecuted in later times by the Christian folk living there. ["Trial"].

All Saints' Cathedral. This great church is the seat of the Archbishop Primate of Valoret and All Gwynedd, and was the first cathedral constructed in Gwynedd, its cornerstone having been laid on the VIIIth day of June in the year 646. The great structure of the original edifice was completed some IV years later, with the dedication ceremony being conducted on the IIIrd day of September in the year 650. It was here that King Alroy was crowned on the XXVth day of May in the year 917. Beneath the church lies a large crypt where the Festillic Kings of Gwynedd and the Archbishops of Valoret are buried. [*Camber of Culdi*; *Saint Camber*; *Camber the Heretic*; *The Quest for Saint Camber*].

Allah. This heathen God of the Moors was invoked by Al-Rasoul ibn Tarik, ambassador of Torenth, in his visit to Rhemuth on the IIIrd day of March in the year 1125. [*The Quest for Saint Camber*].

Aloysius, Father. He was serving as a canon priest at All Saints' Cathedral in Valoret during the year 918. He escorted Prince Javan to Archbishop Hubert's quarters on the IXth day of February of that year. [*The Harrowing of Gwynedd*].

Alpheios I *apo Kouinkiou* (secular name, Jonathan de Quincy), Patriarch of Beldour and All Torenth, sometime Metropolitan of Netterhaven, Lord. He was born in Tralia on the VIIth day of March in the Year of Our Lord 1071, being the son of Kenton Sieur de Quincy in Tralia and Albinette Lady des Thibeaux. He intermarried with Fathria bint Ismail Abu Shakhbut on the IVth day of August in the year 1090, and was ordained a parish priest on the IXth day of March in the year 1095. After his wife's death in the year 1098, *sans postérité*, he entered the Abbey of Saint-Sasile in Southern Torenth, and was given the monastic name of Alpheios by Metropolitan Gamalinos. He was elected an itinerant Bishop on the XXIst day of March in the year 1108, and Metropolitan of Netterhaven on the XVIIth day of October in the year 1116.

At the death of the Thrice Holy Patriarch Aristarchos I on the VIIIth day of August in the year 1123, the Holy Synod chose Metropolitan Alpheios as his successor on the XIIth day of September following, and he was enthroned at Saint Constantine's Church in Beldour on the XXXth day instant. He girded King Liam Lajos II with the sword on New Year's Day in the year 1124, and a year later blessed the enameled cross that was sent as a gift by the Regent Mahael II Duke d'Arjenol to Kelson King of Gwynedd.

On the Xth day of July in the year 1128, he participated in the rehearsals for the *killijálay* ceremony formally to install King Liam Lajos II with his full powers. Two days later, at the request of the Torenthi monarch, he asked King Kelson to substitute for Count Czalsky in the ceremony, after the latter's body had been discovered. On the XVIth day instant he presided over the actual *killijálay*, and helped defend King Liam Lajos from the attack of his uncle, Duke Mahael. That evening, he took part in the new King's first Council. He presided over the funeral of Morag late Dowager Duchess d'Arjenol, Regent of Torenth, and mother of the King on the IInd day of August. Later that year, he proposed to King Liam Lajos a series of reforms of the Torenthi clergy, including the forced retirement of any bishop attaining his LXXXth year, and the expansion of the Holy Synod to include all of the hierarchy with the rank of Metropolitan, Archbishop, or Presiding Abbot of an Order. He chaired a commission to determine the facts surrounding the death of Alroy Arion II late King of Torenth. This powerful Deryni had a long, grey beard, and spoke in a rich basso voice. An ornate pectoral cross and several *panagia* adorned his breast. [*The Quest for Saint Camber*; *King Kelson's Bride*].

Alroy Alexander *Haldane*, Prince of Gwynedd. He was born on the IXth day of October in the Year of Our Lord 809, being the second son of Ifor King of Gwynedd and Nuala Lady Udaut. He was murdered with his family by the soldiers of King Festil I on the XXIst day of June in the year 822, aged XII years. R.I.P. [*Camber of Culdi*].

Alroy Arion II Arkady Aldred *Furstán d'Arjenol*, King of Torenth, Hereditary Duke d'Arjenol, Duke of Beldouria. He was born on the XIIth day of May in the Year of Our Lord 1109, being the eldest son and heir of Lionel II Duke d'Arjenol and the Princess Morag daughter of Nimur II King of Torenth, and an VIIIth-generation descendant in the male line of Torval I Duke d'Arjenol youngest son of Nimur I King of Torenth.

The Prince Alroy was created Duke of Beldouria on the IVth day of March in the year 1120, under the terms of the Edict of Succession issued by King Wencit on that day. At the simultaneous deaths of the Hereditary Duke's father, the Duke Lionel, and his uncle, Wencit King of Torenth, the Prince Alroy was proclaimed the latter's successor on the IInd day of July in the year 1121, with his mother and his uncle, Mahael II Duke d'Arjenol, acting as co-Regents. As his forename was deemed too Western to be acceptable, he was girded with the sword by Patriarch Aristarchos I under the name Arion II on New Year's Day in the year 1122, and sent homage to his Overlord, Kelson King of Gwynedd, later that year. He attained his majority on the XIIth day of May in the year 1123, and the Council of Regency was disbanded; his regirding ceremony, in which power would be transferred from Duke Mahael II to the new King, was set for the XVth day of July.

On the Ist day of June the King was invited on a hunting expedition by his uncle Mahael. While riding alone in the woods on the IXth day of June in the year 1123, the King fell from his horse when his cinch snapped and broke his back. Since his paralysis could not be cured, he refused to be healed, saying "it is not meet for a King to be seen by his people as a cripple." He lingered for III days before expiring on the XIIth day of June, aged XIV years, and was buried with his ancestors in the family crypt at Torenthály. His death was popularly believed in Torenth to have been caused by Kelson King of Gwynedd, to prevent the King from acting in his majority, and a cult formed around Alroy's name shortly after his death. He was succeeded as King by his younger brother, the Prince Liam Duke of Nördmarcke later Lajos II King of Torenth.

Count Berrhones was present at this King's funeral, and wrote of it in his *Memoirs*: "It was one of the saddest days this old courtier can remember. The entire population of Beldour, it seemed, made the trip upriver to Torenthály that afternoon, waiting for the *caïque* of state to arrive at the *Quai de l'Amirauté*. The barge was draped all in black, the King's cedar coffin resting under the canopy in the place of honour. The day was hot, and there was a hint of cloud in the distance. Six of the *Derviche* guard loaded the body on a simple litter, and then carried it up the *Avenue des Rois*, the King-to-Be Liam following behind with his head hung down, holding the lead of Alroy's riderless steed. The crowd surrounding the procession was immense, numbering perhaps fifty thousand people, maybe more. There were angry murmurings on all sides as the *cortège* neared Saint Iób's, where the Most Holy Aristarchos was waiting. The Patriarch seemed particularly weary that day: to have buried II monarchs in as many years was more than even that great man could bear, and indeed, he did not survive his King by much more than a month.

"I heard one man shout: 'D--n the Haldanes!' and others broke in with similar threats and curses, so that the Holy Patriarch had to hold up his hands and plead with the crowd for quiet. 'Peace,' he said. 'A good man passes this way, and we should honour his memory with respect and dignity, not enmity and hate.' Then he motioned for the procession to enter his Church.

"The coffin was gently laid on top of King Furstán's tomb in the nave of the Church, and the mourners took their places to either side. I saw the King's mother, the Princess Morag, together with both her surviving sons, the King-to-Be and the Hereditary Prince-to-Be, occupying the Royal box. Standing behind them were the Great Lords in order of rank: the Dukes Mahael d'Arjenol, Vidar d'Arkadia, Ignácz of Sasovna, Erdödy of Jándrich, Káspár of Truvorsk, Václáv of Östmarcke, and Antonije of Altorf; and the Counts Teymuraz of Brustarkia, Hermann of Tarvejak, Kristóf of Medras, Termöd of Vechta, Marek-Nimur of Tigre, Benedek of Netterhaven, Róry of Kulnán, Emil of Hohensax, Branyng of Sostra, Julián of Querben, Geréndy of Göttsland, Ungnad of Fajardô, Rufim of Fathane, László of Czalsky, and many other Lords besides.

"The great Sword of Furstán, a scimitar as long as a man is tall, was carried in by VI husky Albani guards, who set it on a table in front of Furstán-Mögila, carefully removed the jewel-encrusted scabbard without touching the metal, and then left. A Simplician monk opened the coffin to reveal King Alroy's unlined face. Earlier that day the King's corpse had been washed in rosewater and aloes by III monks of Saint Simplicius, to purify it both physically and psychically. In accordance with tradition the late King's hands were laid on his breast, crossed one over the other; his nose, mouth, and ears were stuffed with cloves of garlic and plugs of linen to keep away evil spirits and intrusions of magic; and the body was wrapped in a shroud made from a single piece of raw white silk, save for the head, which was left uncovered. The coffin was overlaid with cloth-of-gold emblazoned with the black leaping hart of the King's House, and also with a belt of diamonds signifying his rank.

"'Let us pray,' intoned the Patriarch, being seconded by the Holy Synod—the Metropolitans Alpheios, Adam, Damianos, Eustathios, Kyrillos, Élias, Neophytos, Prokopios, Dabid, Phélix, Ephraim, and Iób, and the Archbishops Gabriél, Modestos, Anthimos, Gerbasios, Maximos, and Loukas. The solemn mass began. I took my place II rows behind the Grand Vizier and Chief Minister, since I still deserved a measure of respect for my former position at Court. Clouds of incense swirled in the air above us, and II choirs of monks chanted portions of the liturgy back and forth across the Church. I happened to stand next to Ferencz Lord Pány, an old gossip if ever there was one, and as the rite droned on into its IIIrd hour, I muttered to him something about the bunions on my toes and my fallen arches. He nudged me back and whispered in my ear, 'You know that Arjenol kept it secret for a week.' I was shocked; the first I had heard of the King's passing was the Patriarch's public announcement in Constantine Square IV days earlier.

"'Ay, 'tis true,' he continued. 'The Duke invited the young King out on a hunting trip to celebrate his coming-of-age, and that was where he met his, uh, unfortunate accident. Supposedly his back was broken and he survived for some days, but I hear his physician was later strangled. Why do this unless they had something to hide?' He quickly looked around, and dropped his voice even lower: 'One of the guards said that the King's body was preserved by magic and the corpse kept propped up for days in his tent, eyes glued wide open, cheeks reddened with henna, hair tinted with tar.' 'But surely people would have known,' I replied. 'Arjenol signed for every message and sent the replies in the King's name, saying the King was indisposed. Meals were served on schedule, the food being hidden later. When the tents were struck, *at night*, Mahael put Alroy in a carriage where his features could barely be seen by his men as they headed back to Beldour.' 'Is all this true?' I asked. He paused, then snorted, running his hand over his greying beard: 'Who knows? All I hear these days is rumours and rumours of rumours. Half the Court is convinced the Haldane killed Alroy, and most of the people agree. But I always ask myself: who stands to gain?'

"By this time the Archbishops had begun giving out the Eucharist, the bread and wine representing the body and blood of Christ, and most of the mourners got in line, but I noticed as I moved forward that Duke Mahael was staying in his place. He had never been a religious man, but this was too much! I saw young Liam glance quickly over his shoulder at his uncle, and he returned the look with venom. When I reached my place again, the service had begun winding to its conclusion.

"The Patriarch then moved to the head of the bier, with the Holy Synod standing in II lines flanking the coffin; lifting his hands in supplication, he said: 'Whereas it hath pleased Almighty God to gather into Heaven our Sovereign King and Lord, the High and Mighty King Alroy Arion the Second, let there be remembrance of his name for thrice times XXX generations, let the Metropolitans and the Lords and all the children of the Church cherish his memory from generation to generation for ever and ever.' 'Amen,' echoed those present. 'We beseech the Archangels Gabriél, Michaél, Raphaél, and Ouriél to escort Our King to his rightful place at the feet of the Almighty. May God receive our brother Alroy Arion and welcome him into His family.' 'Amen.' 'He has put aside the things of this world, he has need of them no more. Therefore, Alroy Arion Arkady Aldred Furstán d'Arjenol, we take from thee thy riches, for they mean nothing in the Kingdom of Heaven.' A monk removed the belt of diamonds from atop the coffin. 'We take from thee thy titles and thy honours, for thou art mere clay before the majesty of God.' The emblazoned cloth-of-gold was taken away. 'We take from thee thy sight, thy breath, and thy speech, for thou dost not need them in Heaven.' The Holy Aristarchos traced the sign of the cross in chrism on the late King's forehead, nose, and lips. 'And we take from thee thy power, for it is not thine to keep, but belongs to another.' The Patriarch closed his eyes and placed his left hand on the dead King's breast and the right on the sword, and then a glow began to engulf them both, running quickly through the spectrum of colours. I saw the Most Holy's face change and briefly assume the form of Ancient Furstán's, and then the light swept down the King's body, draining from it through Furstán/Aristarchos into the Great Sword just beyond. There was a collective sigh from everyone in the Church. It was over. Job's Complaint began sounding its mournful dirge as we sadly filed out.

"After the late King's body had been carried out to its temporary resting place, there to remain under a Circassian guard until a formal tomb should be constructed, I stood again in front of Saint Iób's, listening to the rumble of thunder in the distant skies interspersed with the tolling of XIV years for Good King Alroy. Old Pány brushed my arm, clearly agitated: 'Berrhones...,' he said. 'Think nothing of it,' I replied. 'I have become remarkably deaf in my old age.' But there was nothing wrong with my ears or my mind, and I recalled his words most vividly in latter days."

After the installation of King Liam Lajos II in the year 1128, the new monarch ordered an investigation into the circumstances of his royal brother's death, and appointed a commission headed by Count Berrhones, and including Patriarch Alpheios, Mátyás Duke d'Arjenol, Káspár Duke of Truvorsk, Róry Count of Kulnán, and Radu Count of Marrast as judges. The Gwyneddans were exonerated from any blame whatsoever in the murder of King Alroy, but Mahael II late Duke d'Arjenol and his brother, Teymuraz former Count of Brustarkia, were charged with the crime and tried on the IVth day of March in the year 1129. The body of Duke Mahael was exhumed for the trial, and propped upright next to a seated scarecrow representing the absent Count Teymuraz, shards of flesh still clinging to the corpse. Both men were found guilty of regicide on the XIth day instant, excommunicated from the Church of Torenth by the Patriarch, and condemned to death. The body of Duke Mahael was paraded through the streets of Beldour, and then quartered, with pieces being displayed in the chief cities of the realm. Count Teymuraz was declared pariah and outlaw, with no man being allowed to give him sanctuary under the pain of instant excommunication and death by the pole. R.I.P. [*High Deryni*; *The Bishop's Heir*; *The King's Justice*; *King Kelson's Bride*].

Alroy Bearand Brion *Haldane*, King of Gwynedd. He was born on the XXVth day of May in the Year of Our Lord 905, being the second but eldest surviving son of Cinhil I King of Gwynedd and Lady Megan de Cameron, and the elder twin of Prince Javan. He never married.

His Haldane potential was set by the King on the Ist day of February in the year 917. He succeeded his father on the following day under the rule of the V Regents, and presided over his first Council meeting on the IIIrd day of February. He supported the Regents in their *coup* against Archbishop Alister Cullen on the XXVth day of December in the year 917. He attained his majority on the XXVth day of May in the year 919.

Always a sickly lad, he was kept continually medicated and sedated by the Regents. His health began to decline once again in the last year of his reign, due to a persistent cough that would not be healed. He called for his brother Prince Javan to be brought to him in the early morning hours of the XXIIIrd day of June in the year 921, and passed him the Eye of Rom as acknowledgment of Javan's status as Heir Presumptive to the throne of Gwynedd. King Alroy died of the consumptive complaint later that day, and was succeeded by his twin brother. He lay in state at Saint Hilary's Basilica in the Palace at Rhemuth, and was buried with his ancestors on the XXVIth day of June, with Great George being tolled XVI times, one for each year of his life. He had the traditional grey eyes and jet black hair typical of the Haldanes. R.I.P. [*Saint Camber*; *Camber the Heretic*; *The Harrowing of Gwynedd*; *King Javan's Year*].

Alroy Bearand Ifor *Haldane*, Prince of Gwynedd. He was born on the XXVIIIth day of December in the Year of Our Lord 843, being the only son and heir of Aidan Prince of Gwynedd and Avis de Burgeys. He intermarried with Nellwyn de Menville on the XVth day of June in the year 859, and by her he had one child: the Prince Cinhil later King of Gwynedd, also called Nicholas Draper.

This Prince used the name of Royston John Draper in everyday life, and worked with his father in the latter's woolen trade in Valoret. He died in the Great Plague on the XXIInd day of September in the year 878, aged XXXIV years, and was buried in Saint John's Church cemetery in Valoret. His body was exhumed and brought to the family crypt in Rhemuth in the year 918, where it was buried with all of the honours due a Prince of the royal blood. R.I.P. [*Camber of Culdi*].

Alta Jorda. The seat of the Jordanet family in Joux, the estate of Alta Jorda is situate in the hill country of that Duchy, not far from its border with Vézaire and Thuria, and was the home of the Lady Vivienne, a long-serving member of the Camberian Council. A portal was located there. [*King Kelson's Bride*].

Alver. This sovereign duchy is located Southeast of the Kingdom of Bremagne and West of the Anvil of the Lord, sandwiched between the Autuni Mountains and the River Rampante. It was founded on the XVIth day of July in the year 821 by Alver Lord Firüz, and has remained in his family ever since. Each male in his line bears the name Alver, based on a vow made by Firüz to his patron at *gros jeu de puce*, Alveos. The capital city, Alverville, is located on the coast of the Atalantic Ocean where the River Rampante meets the sea; it lies across the River delta from the great Free Port of Kharthat. The Duchy acts as a conduit for much of the trade that flows between East and West, and is also known for being a place of refuge for individuals not welcome elsewhere in the XI Kingdoms. Alver's arms feature a green frog rampant. *A Kharthatti ti vidi, a Alvervilla ti connobbi!* [*King Kelson's Bride*].

DUCS D'ALVER

HOUSE OF ALVER

Alver I Firüz	821-844
Alver II Mandavil (son)	844-877
Alver III Damien (son)	877-898
Alver IV Louÿs (brother)	898-911
Alver V Georges (son)	911-940
Alver VI Jehan (son)	940-971
Alver VII Bertrand (grandson)	971-1027
Alver VIII Victor (brother)	1027-1035
Alver IX Alain (son)	1035-1059
Alver X Hoël (son)	1059-1084
Alver XI Jacques (son)	1084-1106
Alver XII Henri (son)	1106-1130+

Alvis, Dom. This Healer was serving as a master of the prenovice students at Saint Neot's Abbey during the year 917. ["First Session"].

Alwyne. He was a soldier serving in the army of King Brion in June of the year 1105, and had the temerity to question the King about his assumption of his Haldane potential. He had earlier served with King Donal Blaine II. ["Swords Against the Marluk"].

Alyce Javana *de Corwyn de Morgan*, Heiress of Corwyn. She was born on the IInd day of February in the Year of Our Lord 1070, being the eldest child of Keryell Earl of Lendour and Stevana Heiress de Corwyn, and the elder twin sister of Vera Howard. She intermarried with Sir Kenneth Kai Morgan on the XVIIIth day of June in the year 1090, and by him she had children: Alaric Anthony later Duke of Corwyn; Bronwyn Rhetice, who was betrothed to Kevin Earl of Kierney at the time of her death. This noble lady, through whom passed the right of succession to the Duchy of Corwyn and the County of Lendour, died of the milk fever on the XXIXth day of December in the Year of Our Lord 1095, aged XXV years. She was buried in Saint Teilo's Church at Castle Culdi in a sarcophagus bearing her life-sized effigy in alabaster. R.I.P. [*Deryni Checkmate*].

Amaury Herbin Vaïlo *Makróry*, Hereditary Count Kulnán. He was born on the XXIst day of December in the Year of Our Lord 1098, being the eldest son and heir of Róry II Count Kulnán and the Countess Talienne daughter of Zimri Duke of Truvorsk. He intermarried with the Countess Ginesta daughter of Count Maksian late Heir Presumptive to the Duchy of Sasovna, on the Ist day of June in the year 1118, and by her he had children: the Countess Róryne; the Count Maurin Lord Ézion; the Count Laurion; the Countess Tamsyn; the Countess Nolána.

On the IXth day of July in the year 1128, he attended a state banquet at Beldour honouring King Kelson and his party, together with King Liam Lajos II, Amaury's cousin, Káspár Duke of Truvorsk, Mátyás Count of Komnénë, and Erdödy Duke of Jándrich, among other members of the Torenthi nobility. He was ordered by King Liam on the XXVIIth day instant to help ward all known portals in Beldour and Torenthály against the intrusion of Count Teymuraz. After King Liam's installation, Count Amaury continued to serve the Torenthi state as a statesman and adviser to the new monarch. [*King Kelson's Bride*].

Amaury of Rhelledd, Bishop. Father Amaury was elected an itinerant Bishop of Gwynedd on the XIXth day of January in the year 1122 at the Council of Rhemuth. [*Deryni Magic*].

Ambert Aloysius *Quinnell*, Sovereign Prince of Cassan. He was born on the XXIVth day of November in the Year of Our Lord 853, being the eldest son and heir of Audebert Prince of Cassan and Marianna Lady duBois. He intermarried with Duvessa Lady Sinclair on the XVth day of July in the year 897, and by her he had children: the Princess Anne, who intermarried with Fane Earl Fitz-Arthur; the Princess Devika; the Princess Quenelda; the Hereditary Prince Antiochus, dead at age III when he fell from a wall; the Prince Aloys, dead at III days of the milk sickness. He succeeded his father on the XIIth day of March in the year 909. On the XXIInd day of September in the year 916 he signed a treaty with Cinhil I King of Gwynedd whereby he acknowledged the King as Overlord, and agreed that at his death, the Principality of Cassan would become a Duchy of Gwynedd under his daughter and son-in-law; a codicil added in 918 shifted the succession of the Duchy to his grandson, the Lord Tambert, and to the heirs of Tambert's body whatsoever. He died after a long illness on the XXIst day of May in the year 921, aged LXVII years, and was succeeded by his grandson as Duke of Cassan. His final will and testament was officially presented at Court on the XXXth day of July in that same year, and Cassan was formally annexed to Gwynedd on that date. R.I.P. [*The Harrowing of Gwynedd*; *King Javan's Year*].

Ambros de Nolane, Father. He was a chaplain serving Jehana Dowager Queen of Gwynedd in the year 1124. The adept Azim introduced a compulsion in his mind on the XXXth day of June in that year to preach a sermon of tolerance to Dowager Queen Jehana. He accompanied her to Rhemuth on the XXIXth day of June in the year 1128. [*The King's Justice*; *The Quest for Saint Camber*; *King Kelson's Bride*].

Amyot of Morland, Lord. This Deryni baron was killed in the attempted assassination of the Princes Javan and Rhys Michael on the XXVIIIth day of September in the year 917. His cousin, Lord Trefor, also perished there. [*Camber the Heretic*].

Andelon. This sovereign principality, a Southern neighbour of the Forcinn States, is situate in the Southern portion of the Andell Mountains and the adjoining highlands, and is bordered by Logréine to the North, Jáca to the West, Nur Hallaj on the River Thuria to the East, and the Anvil of the Lord to the South. It was founded on the VIIIth day of July in the year 735 by the Count Khoren Vastouni. On the IInd day of April in the year 897 the Count Suleiman proclaimed himself Ist Prince of Andelon. The last male descendant of this family, the Prince Mikhail, died on the XIIth day of December in the year 1112, and was succeeded by his elder daughter, Princess Sofiana. Her heir is her eldest son, Prince Kamil. The capital of the Principality, Rhanamé, is situate at the juncture of the Rivers Bhutti and Thuria, and is known for its quaint, crooked streets and double-storey'd houses. Exports include crafts of all kinds, among them tapestries, intricate carvings from dark, rare woods and precious stones, and ambers containing the images of insects and mythical beasts. [*King Kelson's Bride*].

COUNTS AND PRINCES OF ANDELON

HOUSE OF VASTOUNI OR SULEIMANI

Khoren	735-774
Isa (son)	774-799
Rashid (son)	799-815
Abdallah (son)	815-844
Da'ud (son)	844-877
Yusuf (son)	877-897
Suleiman I (son; Prince 897)	897-922
Shukr Allah (brother)	922-925
Jirjis (son)	925-948
Afram I (son)	948-955
Yuhanna (nephew)	955-988
Suleiman II (son)	988-1011
Butrus (cousin)	1011
Suleiman II (restored)	1011-1013
Sim'an (brother of Butrus)	1013-1014
Suleiman II (restored)	1014-1018
Ya'qub (son)	1018-1022
Afram II (son)	1022-1055
Antun (son)	1055-1081
Mikhail (son)	1081-1112
Sofiana (daughter)	1112-1130+

Andrew. This Fiannan was serving as auxiliary helmsman aboard the Duke of Corwyn's ship *Rhafallia* in March of the year 1121. He imbibed a slow poison before attempting to assassinate the Duke; but Richard Lord FitzWilliam took the blow meant for his master, thereby saving Alaric. Andrew died in agony on the XXVth day of that month. [*Deryni Checkmate*].

Andrew, son of James, later Brother Benedict. He was born in the Year of Our Lord 858, being the son of James and grandson of James the Elder. He was received into the *Ordo Verbi Dei* and took the name Benedict in the year 877, and was cloistered at the Priory of Saint Piran's. He was the second "Benedict" that Camber and his family investigated while searching for some trace of Prince Cinhil Haldane. He was terminally ill with consumption when interviewed by Joram and Rhys Thuryn in November of the year 903. R.I.P. [*Camber of Culdi*].

Andrew *of Senan*, Saint and Martyr. This holy man of the IVth century was executed by the pagan King Aurelio, who covered him with mud and baked him over a slow flame. After VI long hours the King inquired whether Saint Andrew was done with his God, and he is said to have replied, "Not done yet. Best add another fagot to the fire." He is the patron saint of bakers and stokers. His feastday is celebrated on the VIIIth day of March. [*The Bishop's Heir*]. SEE ALSO: Saint Senan's Cathedral.

Andrew *the Smith*. This farrier at Grecotha in October of the year 905 was observed by Alister/Camber on the last day of that month, who liked his work so well that he asked Andrew to check all of the shoes on his own horses. [*Saint Camber*].

Angelica, Mother. She was serving as a midwife near the village at Lochalyn Castle during June of the year 928. She was brought to the fortress by the Lady Sudrey in that month to assist in the establishment of an infirmary, and treated the injured hand of Rhys Michael King of Gwynedd with the herb *tacil* on the XXIVth day instant. She was "an ample old woman dressed in the simple homespun and tweeds of the local folk. Her mother used to work with the Healer there in the old days." [*The Bastard Prince*].

Angelus *de Lacey*, Bishop of Stavenham. He was born on the XVIIIth day of January in the Year of Our Lord 1043. This prelate initially supported the Archbishops' party during the Interdict Schism of 1121, but later backed Bishops Thomas Cardiel and Denis Arilan of the King's faction, and rode with the Royal Army despite his advanced age. He died of pneumonia on the XVIth day of January in the year 1122 during the Council of Rhemuth, aged LXXVIII years, and was buried with great honours. R.I.P. [*Deryni Checkmate*; *High Deryni*; *The Bishop's Heir*]

Angus Fearchair *MacEwan*, Sir, Hereditary Duke of Claibourne, Earl of Kheldour. He was born on the XVth day of May in the Year of Our Lord 1110, being the eldest son and heir of Graham III Duke of Claibourne and Mistral Lady Leslie. He intermarried with Dimity Lady Houlgate, daughter of Sanborne de Traherne Baron Houlgate and Heir Presumptive to the Earldom of Rhendall, on the XVth day of October in the year 1129. Lord Angus was knighted by King Kelson on the VIth day of January in the year 1128. On the XXth day of July in that year he accompanied Alaric Morgan Duke of Corwyn to Desse to meet Morgan's ship, *Rhafallia*, which was carrying the Duchess Richenda and her party from Coroth, and returned with them to Rhemuth on the next day. He succeeded his father as Earl of Kheldour on the XIIIth day of December in the year 1129. [*King Kelson's Bride*].

Angus *MacLean*, Lord, Sir. He was born on the XIth day of January in the Year of Our Lord 875, being the youngest son of Iain I Earl of Kierney and Aislinn Lady MacRorie. He intermarried with Ardis Lady Drummond daughter of Henry Lord Drummond on the XXXIst day of May in the year 893, and by her he had children: Sir Charles MacLean, who changed the spelling of his name to McLain and was the direct ancestor in the male line of the later McLain Earls of Kierney and Dukes of Cassan; the Lady Alathea; the Lord Henry; the Lady Astrid. He died on the XIIth day of March in the year 904, aged XXIX years. R.I.P.

Angus *MacRorie*, Hereditary Count and Master of Culdi. He was born on the Vth day of April in the Year of Our Lord 844, being the second son and heir of Ballard II Earl of Culdi and Ardis Drummond. He was betrothed to Meriel Lady McClung at the time of his death. He became Master of Culdi on the death of his elder brother, the Lord Adrian, in the year 856, but died unmarried of the Plague on the XVIIIth day of August in the year 862, aged XVIII years. He was succeeded as heir by his younger brother, the Lord Camber. R.I.P. [*Camber of Culdi*; *Saint Camber*].

Annalind Afreca Malise *Quinnell*, Sovereign Prince and Pretender of Meara. She was born on the XXIIIrd day of January in the Year 1008, being the second daughter of Jolyon II Prince of Meara and Princess Urracca daughter of Faucon Hereditary Prince of Bremagne, and the a twin to Princess Roisian. She was betrothed to Prince Adolphus Titular Duke of Eastmarch on the Ist day of January in the year 1025, and after his death was further betrothed to Prince Marek *Junior* son of Marek II Pretender of Gwynedd, but both of her intended husbands died before a marriage could take place. She then intermarried with Rhiryd Kincaid Earl of Kilarden on the XVth day of September in the year 1041, and by him she had children: the Prince Judhael Pretender of Meara; the Princess Jorice, who died an infant in August of the year 1045 following the defeat of her mother's army.

Following her sister Roisian's marriage to Malcolm King of Gwynedd in the year 1025, Annalind's mother, the Princess Urracca, maintained that the Princess Annalind had an equal right to the throne of Meara under the laws of that country, and that Roisian had abdicated her throne by leaving Laas without permission of the Great Lords. Princess Annalind was declared her successor on the Xth day of July in that year, and crowned at Laas on the XVIIIth day instant. She ruled for II years without much opposition.

In the year 1027 King Malcolm made the first of his several expeditions to Meara to hunt for Urracca, Annalind, and their supporters, but only succeeded in capturing and executing one of their captains, Loren Kincaid Earl of Kilarden. However, Annalind and her mother escaped to The Connait. In the year 1041 the

Princess Annalind married said Earl's successor in contravention of the laws of Gwynedd, the House of Quinnell having been placed by King Malcolm under the ægis of the Royal Marriages Act in the year 1025.

Three years later, on the Ist day of December in the year 1044, Annalind was again proclaimed Sovereign Prince of Meara at Laas, and began organizing an army to defend her country. King Malcolm invaded in July of the year 1045, and the II forces fought a pitched battle near the capital city of Laas on the VIth day of August following. The Princess and her husband were captured as her army was fleeing, and she was ordered to produce her son and heir, the III-year-old Prince Judhael, who had been hidden by the Earl of Cloome, in order to save her own life. When she refused, she and her husband were tried and executed with several supporters on the VIIIth day of August in the year 1045, aged XXXVII years; her bones were later reinterred in the family crypt at Laas. Her son Prince Judhael inherited her pretensions. R.I.P. *La dignité de la femme est d'être ignorée, sa gloire est dans l'estime de son mari, ses plaisirs sonts dans le bonheur de sa famille.* [*The Bishop's Heir*; *The King's Justice*].

Anne Varvara *Quinnell*, Princess and Regent of Cassan. This great Lady was born on the IIIrd day of May in the Year of Our Lord 899, being the eldest child of Ambert Sovereign Prince of Cassan and Duvessa Lady Sinclair. She intermarried with Fane Earl Fitz-Arthur on the XXIInd day of September in the year 916, and by him she had children: the Lord Tambert later Duke of Cassan; the Lady Anne *Junior*, who intermarried with Owain King of Gwynedd; the Lady Nieve; the Lord Eldon; the Lady Ophelia; the Lady Duvessine; the Lord Nolan. She became co-Regent of Cassan for her eldest son at the death of her father on the XXIst day of May in the year 921, and presented her father's final will and testament at the Court of Rhemuth on the XXXth day of July in that same year. The Principality of Cassan was formally annexed to Gwynedd at that time. This beauteous lady died in the fullness of her years, well respected and greatly honoured, on the XVIIIth day of September in the year 982, aged LXXXIII years. According to the *Heirs*, "She had a slender figure gowned and veiled in murrey silk, with jet black hair. Her voice was low and melodious, her dark-lashed eyes a clear blue-grey in the pale perfection of her face." R.I.P. [*The Harrowing of Gwynedd*; *King Javan's Year*].

Anscom *of Trevas*, Archbishop Primate of Valoret and All Gwynedd. This Deryni monk was born at Trevas on the XXIInd day of February in the Year of Our Lord 848. In his youth he attended the monastery school at Saint Neot's, where he met and became friends with Robert Orris, later Archbishop of Rhemuth. He joined the Gabrilite Order in the year 869, and served as a subdeacon and student for II years with Camber Hereditary Count of Culdi at the seminary of the University of Grecotha. He presided over the marriage of Camber to his wife in the year 871, and later baptized all of his children. Anscom was elected Archbishop Primate of Valoret and All Gwynedd on the IIIrd day of March in the Year 891 in succession to Archbishop William II. He presided over the marriage of Prince Cinhil Haldane to Lady Megan de Cameron on the XXIVth day of December in the year 903.

Anscom participated in the War Council held in the Great Hall of Valoret Palace on the XXIIIrd day of June in 905. He was also present on the Ist day of July in the year 905 when the victorious Gwyneddan army returned to Valoret, and presided II days later over the funeral of Camber Earl of Culdi. He was named to the Royal Council on the VIth day of November in 905. In later years he was partial to goat's milk to alleviate pains in the stomach. He died of a cancer in the belly on the Ist day of September in the year 906, aged LVIII years, and was buried II days later in the crypt of the Archbishops beneath All Saints' Cathedral. R.I.P. [*Camber of Culdi*; *Deryni Challenge*; *Saint Camber*; *The Harrowing of Gwynedd*].

Ansel Irial *MacRorie*, Lord, *de jure* IXth Earl of Culdi. This Deryni was born on the XXIIIrd day of March in the Year of Our Lord 900, being the second son of Cathan MacRorie Hereditary Count of Culdi and Elinor Lady Howell, and brother of Davin Earl of Culdi. He intermarried with Fiona Lady MacLean on the XIVth day of May in the year 929, and by her he had children: the Lady Katrin; the Lady Davina; the Lord Stuart Cathan later called Stuart MacAthan. He was present at the coronation of King Alroy in Valoret on the XXVth day of May in the year 917. Following the death of his brother Davin on the XXVIIIth day of September in that year, he should have succeeded to the Earldom of Culdi, but the title was attainted by the Regents. He used the disguise of "Brother Lorcan," a Michaeline lay scribe, to return with his grandfather and uncle to Grecotha later that evening. He attended the Synod of Bishops held at Valoret in November and December of 917 as an aide to his grandfather.

The Lord Ansel was inducted into the Camberian Council on the VIIIth day of January in 918. He met with Joram at Dhassa II days later. He and Tavis mounted an expedition for the Camberian Council into Valoret Castle on the XXIst day instant, to block the Deryni powers of the Drummonds, and was severely injured by a guard while leaving; he was then healed by Tavis and Sylvan. By Spring of 918 he had become a prime mover in the resistance against the Regents, using his network of agents in the Valoret region to watch the movements of their enemies.

He was blamed by the former Regents for the supposed kidnapping of Prince Rhys Michael in November of 921 and the murder of King Javan on the XIth day of May in the year 922, but both plots were actually engineered by the High Council. By the year 928 he was living in the former Michaeline Haven. In June of that year he brought a contingent of disguised Michaeline knights to aid Sudrey Dowager Countess of Eastmark, and was present on the XXIst day of that month when King Rhys Michael arrived with his army.

He died in the year 948, aged XLVIII years. His descendants, in whom are vested the right to petition for the restoration of the title of the Earldom of Culdi, use the surname MacAthan. He had pale golden hair, but dyed it darker during several months in 917 to avoid identification by the Regents' men; later, he strongly resembled his more famous uncle, Father Joram MacRorie. R.I.P. [*Camber of Culdi*; *Saint Camber*; *Camber the Heretic*; *The Harrowing of Gwynedd*; *King Javan's Year*; *The Bastard Prince*].

Anselm, Father. He served as chaplain to the Duke of Corwyn's mother, the Lady Alyce de Morgan de Corwyn, in the 1090s, and later became pastor of the parish church of Saint Teilo in Culdi. He performed the last rites on the bodies of Lady Bronwyn de Morgan and Lord Kevin McLain on the XXIXth day of March in the year 1121. [*Deryni Checkmate*].

Anvil of the Lord. This large desert region is situate to the Southeast of the Kingdom of Bremagne on the Atalantic Ocean, and sits astride the known routes to the Holy Land, being bounded on the North and Northeast by the Kingdom of R'Kassi and the Forcinn Buffer States, on the Northwest by Jáca, Autun, Alver, Bremagne, and Fallon, on the West by the Atalantic Ocean, the Sea of Sighs, and the Jamin Strait, and on the East by the Kingdom of Libania and the Holy Lands. It is inhabited by a mixture of Christian Beduins and Muslim Moors, who occupy a number of oases scattered throughout the barren desert wastes, loosely organized into a confederation of XXI Sheikhdoms, Sultanates, and Emirates, the chief and most prosperous among them being the Sheikhdom of Alcara or al-Qarrah at the far North end of the Anvil. The main port of the region, and the only town with a harbour, is the Free City of Kharthat, which lies across the River Rampante from Alverville in the Duchy of Alver; it was once called the "Scourge of the West" when Moorish raiders used it as a base for their maritime operations. The city and its port were burned on the XVIIth day of August in the year 755 by Bearand King of Gwynedd.

On the Northern border between the Anvil and the Kingdom of R'Kassi is situate the old Michaeline fortress of Djellarda, the seat of the small independent Christian state of that name. It was thence that the knights of this Order retreated in September of the year 917. By the year 1124 they had become the Knights of the Anvil. [*Camber the Heretic*; *The King's Justice*; *King Kelson's Bride*].

Aquineas, Earl and Baron de Fintan. He was born on the IXth day of April in the Year of Our Lord 855, being the eldest son and heir of Virgil Baron de Fintan and Hebe Lady Clonmel. He intermarried with Lettice Lady Laughill on the XXIVth day of May in the year 875, and by her he had children: the Hereditary Count Ovid later Earl de Fintan; the Lord Phineas later Earl de Fintan; the Lady Elaine, who intermarried with Murdoch Earl of Carthane; the Lord Castor later Earl de Fintan; the Lady Ornat.

He succeeded his father as Baron on the XIVth day of January in the year 864, and was created Earl by King Cinhil I on the VIIth day of July in the year 905, being appointed to the Royal Council on the VIth day of November in the same year. He later served on the military staff of Jebediah of Alcara Earl Marshal of Gwynedd. He was sent by King Cinhil I with Earl Tammaron on the IInd day of July in the year 906 to patrol the border between Eastmarch and Torenth in the Rheljan Mountains. He died on the IInd day of August in the year 910, aged LV years, and was succeeded by his eldest son, Lord Ovid. R.I.P. [*Saint Camber*].

Araxie Léan *Haldane*, Queen of Gwynedd, Baroness Dunluce. She was born on the XVIIIth day of December in the Year of Our Lord 1109, being the second daughter of Prince Richard Haldane Duke of Carthmoor and Earl of Culdi and Sivorn von Horthy Princess of Orsal and Tralia. She intermarried with Kelson King of Gwynedd on the VIIth day of August in the year 1128, and by him she had children: the Princess Araxandra Louise Sivorn Cécile; the Princess Rhuÿs Jehane Silvé Richelle, a twin to her sister; the Hereditary Prince Javan Uthyr Richard Urien.

After the death of her father in the year 1114, the Princess Araxie was created Baroness Dunluce in her own right by King Brion. Several years later, she was removed to Orsal and Tralia by her mother, the Dowager Countess Sivorn, who remarried Savile Baron Kishknock in the year 1116, and spent most of the ensuing years in that land. She was trained by Azim in the Deryni arts, and by her uncle, Létald Hort of Orsal, in politics, and was also counseled by Princess Rothana, with whom she became acquainted when the latter traveled to Nur Hallaj in the year 1126. By the year 1127, common gossip had linked her name to Prince Cuan Heir Presumptive to the Throne of Howicce as a prospective bride, although Cuan actually preferred his cousin, Princess Gwenlian of Llannedd.

By the summer of the year 1128, Araxie had been convinced by Princess Rothana that her destiny was intertwined with that of King Kelson. Correspondingly, she met with him on the IIIrd day of July at Orsal, following a state banquet there, and accepted his proposal of marriage. Their betrothal was avowed before Bishop Arilan later that same night in a private ceremony, but not made public until later that summer. When the escaped assassin Count Teymuraz took ship from Saint-Sasile on the XVIth day instant, thereby posing a threat to the royal women at Orsal, Araxie and her family were transported to Rhemuth for their safety before sunrise on the following morning. The engagement of Araxie and Kelson was announced to the Privy Council of Gwynedd later that same day.

On the XXIst day instant, Princess Araxie proposed to her future husband that he present Sir Jolyon Ramsay a ducal title, thereby solving a potential difficult political situation. Five days later, she worked with Duchess Meraude to bring the late Prince Conall's daughter, Conalline Amelia, back to court and to gain Duke Nigel's acceptance of both his grandchildren.

Araxie was present on the XXXth day of that month at the presentation of the Servants of Saint Camber, and was instrumental in convincing Rothana to accept King Kelson's terms for her appointment as an assistant to Bishop Duncan and for the reinstatement of Prince Albin as heir to the Duchy of Carthmoor. On the following day, she attended the double Mearan wedding at Saint George's Cathedral, and assisted in saving Mátyás Duke d'Arjenol from the attack by Count Teymuraz, and in removing the compulsion from the mind of Sean Earl Derry. Her formal engagement to King Kelson was announced publicly that evening.

She was crowned Queen of Gwynedd by Archbishop Bradene on the day of her wedding, with a brief image of Saint Camber appearing during the ceremony. Queen Araxie had grey eyes and a slim figure. She was tall and fair, with golden hair, a combination without compare. *Beata gli occhi che la vider viva.* [*King Kelson's Bride*].

Arban *Howell*, Earl of Eastmarch, Baron of Iomaire. He was born on the XXXth day of June in the year 1061, being the eldest surviving son and heir of Rory Howell Baron of Iomaire and Felicia Lady O'Flynn, and a direct descendant in the male line of Kennet Howell Earl of Eastmarch. He intermarried with Crispina Baroness de Vali on the XVIth day of November in the year 1088, and by her he had children: the Hereditary Lord and Count Ian later Earl of Eastmarch; the Lady Maire Heiress of Eastmarch, who intermarried with Burchard Baron de Varian later Earl of Eastmarch.

The Lord Arban succeeded his father as Baron of Iomaire on the XXIXth day of December in the year 1084. In May of the year 1105 the Baron Arban supported the King against the rebellion of his IInd cousin, Rorik III Earl of Eastmarch, and attacked the Earl with his own forces, defeating and capturing him and killing his son and heir Kennet on the XIIIth day of June following. As a reward for his services he was created Earl of Eastmarch in his cousin's place by Brion King of Gwynedd on the XXth day instant, the previous Earl having been attainted, tried, and executed earlier that morning. He died on the XVth day of December in the year 1115, aged LIV years, and was succeeded by his only son, Ian, who turned traitor in the year 1120. R.I.P. ["Swords Against the Marluk"].

Archer *of Arrand*, Bishop of Dhassa. This human theologian was a member of the *Ordo Verbi Dei*. He began preaching on the ungodliness of the Deryni race in the Spring of the year 917. On the XIIth day of November in that year he was elected an itinerant Bishop of Gwynedd by the Synod in Valoret. He was elected Bishop of Dhassa on the XXVIIth day of December following, but could not take possession of his see until the IIIrd day of February of the year 918, when Rhun Earl of Sheele forcibly ousted his predecessor, the deposed Deryni Bishop Niallan. [*Camber the Heretic*].

Ardis (I) *Drummond MacRorie*, Countess of Culdi. She was born on the last day of November in the Year of Our Lord 811, being the eldest child of David Lord Drummond and Anna Lady Cappell. She intermarried with Ballard II MacRorie Earl of Culdi on the IVth day of May in the year 839, and by him she had children: the Lady Elspeth later Abbess of Saint Hilda's; the Hereditary Count Adrian dead at age XIV; the Hereditary Count Angus dead at age XVIII; the Hereditary Count Camber later Earl of Culdi; the Lady Aislinn, who intermarried with Iain I Earl of Kierney. She died on the XXIXth day of March in the year 882, aged LXX years, and was buried in the crypt of the MacRories at Tor Caerrorie. R.I.P.

Ardis (II) *Drummond MacLean*, Lady. She was born on the XIIth day of August in the Year of Our Lord 876, being the youngest child of Henry Lord Drummond and Amalia Lady MacNiall. She intermarried with Angus Lord MacLean on the XXXIst day of May in the year 893, and by him she had children: Sir Charles, who changed the spelling of his name and was the direct ancestor in the male line of the later McLain Earls of Kierney and Dukes of Cassan; the Lady Alathea; the Lord Henry Drummond; the Lady Astrid. She died in the year 948, aged LXIX years. R.I.P.

Ardry *MacArdry*, Tanist of Clan MacArdry and Hereditary Count of Transha. He was born on the I[st] day of September in the Year of Our Lord 1087, being the eldest son and heir of Caulay Earl of Transha and Adreana Lady Calder of Sheele. He never married. He was killed in a drunken brawl with a McLain retainer on the XXIInd day of March in the year 1107, aged XIX years, and was succeeded as Tanist by his younger brother, Lord Michael. R.I.P. [*The Bishop's Heir*; *The King's Justice*].

Argoed or *New Argoed*. There were II Michaeline establishments of this name, called Old Argoed and New Argoed to distinguish them from each other. The original Argoed was built on the ruins of an old silver mine, Argentarium, located on the Eastern slope of the Rhendall Mountains. When the vein was exhausted circa the year 700, the site was abandoned, but was deeded by Bearand King of Gwynedd in the year 789 to Rowland Ballintree Grand Master of the Order of Saint Michael to establish the IInd of the new Order's monasteries there. But the water supply was tainted by the leachings from the old mine, and eventually proved inadequate to sustain a large community over a long period of time. Therefore, the Order petitioned Festil II King of Gwynedd to exchange the site with another plot more suitably located, and he did so on the XVIth day of August in the year 850, giving them an estate at Mollingford. The original land was then deeded by King Festil III as a fief to Sir Philibert d'Argent (now created Lord Argoed) on the I[st] day of May in the year 858 to reward him for services rendered to the Crown.

The name Argoed was re-established by the Order on the XVIth day of January in the year 905 to designate their new Commanderie situate at the South tip of the Lendour Mountains on the River Lendour. The Abbey at New Argoed was abandoned on the XVIIth day of September in the year 917, when the Michaeline Order completed its evacuation from the Kingdom of Gwynedd. [*Saint Camber*; *Camber the Heretic*].

Argostino, Father. This Llanneddi was ordained at *Arx Fidei* Seminary with Denis on the IInd day of February in the year 1105. ["The Priesting of Arilan"].

Ariella I Festila Nimura *Furstána-Festila*, Princess and Titular Queen of Gwynedd. This evil witch was born on the IXth day of October in the Year of Our Lord 875, being the second daughter and fourth child of Blaine I King of Gwynedd and Pasqualetta Contessa di Barbarico di Torenti. She was engaged to marry Aleksandar Baron d'Zenevis at the time of her father's death in the year 900, but renounced the union shortly thereafter with the permission of her brother, King Imre.

To gain power she entered into an incestuous union with her brother Imre King of Gwynedd after his accession to the throne, and by him she had one son: the Hereditary Prince Mark also called Marek in Torenth, whom she had legitimatized by her cousin, Nimur I King of Torenth, and the Beldouri Patriarch Sergios II after Marek's birth in January of the year 905. After King Imre's suicide on the IInd day of December in the year 904, she escaped from the palace at Valoret through a secret passageway, used a transfer portal to travel to Beldour, and declared herself Queen of Gwynedd.

She bore her child on the last day of January in the year 905, and then began plotting actively against King Cinhil I. She used magic to create unseasonable rains in Gwynedd in June of that year to cover the movements of her invading army. On the XXVth day of June the two armies met at Iomaire, and Ariella was defeated and killed by Bishop Alister Cullen, whom she mortally wounded in return. She was XXIX years of age at her death. Her body was cut into pieces and sent to the four corners of Gwynedd to be posted on the gates of all major cities, her head being reserved for a pike on the main keep at Valoret. She does not appear on the official king lists of Gwynedd.

The *Legends* describe her as "...every inch the match of [King] Imre in beauty and sheer visual splendor. Her hair was a tumble of chestnut curls, and her quick hazel eyes missed nothing. She was gowned in dark brown velvet stamped with gold, the perfection of her form was captured in a supple flow of colour from neck to wrist to slippered toe, save where the neckline made a plunging vee to caress the curve of her breasts. A tawny jewel lay a-tremble in the hollow of the cleft." [*Camber of Culdi*; *Saint Camber*; *The Harrowing of Gwynedd*; *The Bastard Prince*; *King Kelson's Bride*].

Ariella II Athénodóra Amaranda *Furstána-Festila*, Princess and Titular Queen of Gwynedd. She was born on the IIIrd day of March in the Year of Our Lord 971, being the eldest child of Mark-Imre Hereditary Prince of Gwynedd and Maryam daughter of Simon Count Tsérétéli. She intermarried with the Count Rogan younger son of Termöd II Duke d'Arjenol on the XVIIth day of May in the year 987, and by him had one daughter: the Countess Charis-Tamara, dead of *la cholérique* at age X. Berrhones also attributes to her an infant son, the Count Mekhitar, a stone for whom, he says, he once espied in the family crypt in Arzh.

On the XXVIth day of June in the year 1025 she was resident at her *dacha* in Tolán, when she heard the awful news of the great debacle at Killingford and the deaths of her brother, the former Pretender Imre III, and his heirs King Marek II, Hereditary Prince Festil, and Prince Marek *Junior*, her family having been extinguished unto the fourth generation save for the Lady Salentina, who was said to have had no dynastic rights. This event made her the new Festillic Queen of Gwynedd, but she renounced her rights on the VIIIth day of July in favour of her younger sister, Princess Imriella. She spent the next II decades ministering to the cripples of Killingford, but in her later years retired as a lay sister to the Convent of Saint Catulina in the Duchy of Joux. She died at Trebaçeaux on the IXth day of December in the year 1045, aged LXXIV years, when the elder branch of the House of Festil became extinct, and the representation of the family passed to the descendants of her aunt and namesame, Princess Ariella wife of Duchad Mór. R.I.P.

Arien Esmeralda Carola *Furstána*, Princess of Torenth, Hereditary Duchess and Princess Regent d'Arjenol. This illustrious lady was born on the I^st day of December in the Year of Our Lord 996, being the eldest daughter and second child of Kyprian II King of Torenth and the Grand Princess Polyxena daughter of Démétrios II Autokratór of Byzantyun. She intermarried with Averil Hereditary Duke d'Arjenol on the XVth day of May in the year 1010, and by him she had one son: the Hereditary Duke Torval later Torval II Duke d'Arjenol called "The Posthumous."

After her husband's untimely passing on the IVth day of November in the year 1010, Arien remained in Arzh until 1025, serving as Regent for her underaged son from the XXIst day of April in the year 1020 through the XIVth day of February in the year 1025, when the Duke Torval II attained his majority. Shortly thereafter she successfully petitioned her father to allow her to return permanently to Beldour. After her brother King Arkady's accession to the throne later that year, she became a close companion and advisor to him for the next III decades. There she embarked in her middle years upon a great history of her family, entitled *Lives of the XII Kings of Torenth*, which is one of the chief sources of material about the House of Furstán and the rulers of Torenth from the time of King Festil to King Arkady II.

Berrhones says of this Princess that "...contrary to some of her family, she was fair-skinned and in her youth had fine blonde hair sweeping back across her shoulders, with a face whose features could have been sculpted from pink Carollan marble. When I first came to court I remember hearing the older servants and courtiers speak with respect of this lovely lady, as if she were yet alive, since in their minds she still abided; and of how knowing and kind she was to them, how gracious for one carrying the blood royal. She would not have them do for her what she could do herself. In old age she suffered greatly from aching joints and bad legs, which eventually left her incapable of walking, but still she kept a cheery aspect about her, and would not be glum. 'I have no time,' she said, 'to waste on being sorry for myself, for I am the luckiest of women.' It was during this time that she wrote her histories, which are the best legacy any of her family could have left to the nation."

The Princess Arien died on the XVIIIth day of January in the year 1059, aged LXII years, and was buried with her ancestors in the family crypt at Torenthály. R.I.P.

Arik. He was serving as a guard in the household of Rhys and Evaine Thuryn in the year 917, and traveled with Evaine's party from Sheele to Trurill at the end of December in that year. [*Camber the Heretic*].

Arion I Mátyás Imre *Furstán*, King of Torenth. This Great King was born on the XIVth day of February in the Year of Our Lord 900, being the eldest son and heir of Nimur I King of Torenth and Katalin Countess of Festil-Mnata. He intermarried with the Kniazhna Pavela Heiress of Jándrich and daughter of Ygor Sovereign Kniaz' of Jándrich on the XXVIIth day of May in the year 917, and by her he had children: the Hereditary Prince Károly, who died before his father, leaving issue (among VIII others), the Hereditary Prince Malachy; the Prince Ysarn later Duke of Marluk, who intermarried with his Ist cousin, the Princess Imriella daughter of Marek I Pretender of Gwynedd and the Princess Charis Duchess of Tolán, on the XXIIIrd day of July in the year 944, leaving issue; the Prince Sigard later Count of Göttsland later Duke of Jándrich; the Princess Thomaïs, who intermarried with Szilárd Count Apalfaya; the Prince Vidar later Duke of Truvorsk later Sovereign Prince-Bishop of Podébrad later Prince Regent of Torenth, who died unmarried and *sans postérité* on the IInd day of December in the year 1015, aged LXXXIX years.

The Prince Arion succeeded his father on the Ist day of April in the year 917, being girded with the sword by Patriarch Antiochos I on New Year's Day in the year 918. A cautious man, he moved slowly when dealing with Gwynedd, for he feared the magical potentialities of the Haldane Kings. He dispatched his younger brother, the Prince Miklós, to represent the Crown at the coronation of King Javan in the year 921, but only tacitly supported the efforts of his brother to restore their cousin, Prince Marek, to the throne of Gwynedd. Late in that year he sent letters to his newly rediscovered cousin, Sudrey Countess of Eastmarch, but she responded that she would not assist Torenth. On the XVIIth day of July in the year 927 the King arranged for the marriage of his widowed sister, the Princess Charis, to Prince Marek, giving her the Duchy of Tolán as a dowry.

But when the King's brother, the Prince Miklós, challenged Rhys Michael King of Gwynedd to a duel arcane on the XXIInd day of June in the year 928, and was killed by his magic, then did the Healer Cosim alter the memory of the nefarious Prince Marek, Festillic Pretender to the throne of Gwynedd, in order to keep the true nature of his cousin's death from King Arion. Thus, the King Arion had no more knowledge of the Haldane potential than before, and to avoid immediate war, he ordered the Festil to cease his machinations until his line was firmly established.

On the VIIth day of March in the year 929 the old Kniaz' of Jándrich died, and by the treaty of marriage which Arion had made in the year 917, that land became part of Torenth, in recognition whereof the King's second son, the Prince Sigard, was then created Duke of Jándrich. For the next II decades Arion contented himself with rectifying the new borders that his father had moved to the East and pacifying the native tribes there. He constructed well-paved and -guarded roads throughout his kingdom to provide quick and easy access for his messengers, governors, and armies to every part of Torenth. It was said by Princess Arien in her *Lives of the XII Kings of Torenth* that "one could walk at midnight in any of the great cities of the land during King Arion's reign, and never fear for the safety of oneself or one's friends or family. It was this King's proudest boast that 'an honest man is honestly treated in Torenth'." *Compendiaria res improbitas, virtusque tarda.*

In Spring of the year 948 the Pretender Marek made his move into Gwynedd. Although the King provided the Festil with supplies and weapons, he would not muster out his army, or mount a full-scale invasion of Gwynedd, for he said to the Prince: "You must win your throne yourself, as did King Festil." When the campaign collapsed later that year in Iomaire, King Arion had neither lost face nor the lives of his followers, but continued to provide a refuge in his kingdom for the Pretender, his family, and his followers.

In the year 960 the Hereditary Prince Károly lay abed with the consumptive disease, and wasted away before the eyes of his family, dying late in the year on the XXIIIrd day of November. This brought a great sorrow into the heart of the King his father, who was often heard to lament, according to Hannibalis de Gallarate, that "It is a terrible thing to have lived so long that I have seen my children die before me." And although he reigned another XII years, the King was never again the same man as before, and gradually delegated away many of the routine affairs of state to his grandson and heir, the Prince Malachy.

King Arion was well versed in both the magical and mundane arts, enjoyed the theatre and literature and music, and himself was an artist of note, painting portraits of many of his immediate family. He passed from this world at the IIIrd hour on the IInd day of March in the Year 972, aged LXXII years, and was succeeded by his grandson, the Hereditary Prince Malachy. The old King was buried with great honours with his ancestors in the family crypt at Torenthály. He is said to have had shoulder-length, fair hair in his early years. According to the *Heirs*, "He had more mastery of his power than Marek expected he would ever wield. Miklós had been powerful, but casual in his use of his magic; Arion was all focus and steely will." R.I.P. [*The Harrowing of Gwynedd*; *King Javan's Year*; *The Bastard Prince*].

Arjenol. This Duchy of Torenth is situate in the far Eastern part of the country, being located East of the Duchy of Östmarcke, Northeast of the Duchy of Lorsöl, North of the Duchy of Vorna, South of the Norselands, and West of the Sovereign Grand Duchy of Érskeburg and the Sovereign Principality of West Veskitsa.

The Principality of Arjenol was founded in the year 645 by Lord Braïdik, whose origins are veiled in the clouds, but who conquered the city of Arzh on the XIth day of October in that year and proclaimed himself Prince. In the year 801 the Hereditary Prince Kálmán of Torenth led an expedition against Svarnik Prince of Arjenol to punish him for his raids against Torenthi settlers moving up the River Brust. Svarnik was killed on the XIIth day of June in that year, and Arzh was burned. Arjenol regained its independence II years later under Prince Hernik. In the year 896 Nimur I King of Torenth defeated and killed Prince Thrasarik on the XVIIth day of July, and replaced him with a distant relative, the Prince Zdanik, who was forced to swear fealty to the House of Furstán. When that Prince attempted to revolt some XX years later, King Nimur invaded for a second time, utterly crushing the Arjenol forces on the

XXIst day of October in the year 916. The Prince was captured and forced to watch the torture and execution of every member of his family save his youngest daughter, who was married at the age of I year to the King's youngest son Torval. Prince Torval was named the Ist Duke d'Arjenol on the XXVth day instant. The Prince Zdanik was then buried up to his neck in front of the King's palace, with passers-by being encouraged to give him small drinks of water. He lingered for more than a week, dying on the VIth day of November following. Duke Torval I's VIIth-generation descendant is Duke Mahael II Prince Regent of Torenth.

Campbell de Broun once traveled in Southern Arjenol, which he described in his diary as follows: "We started very early in the morning by crossing the Faupas River, which had a deep channel and steep banks; the bridge across it not being safe, we forded it and had a hard pull up the other side. An Orsalian team that fell in with us yesterday stalled here and we helped him up. Soon after crossing the river we entered a very extensive plain, the greatest we had yet seen; it was one continuous expanse with scarce a tree to relieve the sight. The day was a little cloudy and very calm, and the smoke, settled down very close, obscured the sun. The prospect here was dreary rather than otherwise: nothing to be seen but a dusky horizon on every side. After crossing the prairie, which was many leagues wide, we entered some woodland and shortly thereafter arrived at the Little Wash, which had some good bottom. After leaving it we entered another, more extensive prairie composed of elevated or sloping plains. The first part on this end was partly right level, some XII leagues through. We came then II leagues through the wood and encamped at Hedgehog Creek, which contained no water but just muddy puddles.

"The next day we crossed the Salt River onto another flat. This prairie reminded me of the deserts of R'Kassi, being one extended plain and not a stick of timber to be seen; it was a drear place. We made do with a couple of wild chickens for our supper. The bugs are very bad tonight. How I long again to see the hills of Cloome, where the water runs clear and cold and the forests are full of game." *Adieu, plaisant pays d'Arjénole! O ma patrie la plus chérie, qui as nourri ma jeune enfance!* [*High Deryni*; *The Bishop's Heir*; *The King's Justice*; *King Kelson's Bride*].

SOVEREIGN PRINCES OF ARJENOL

HOUSE OF BRAÏDIK

Braïdik	645-662
Ardrik (son)	662-704
Ringan I (grandson)	704-734
Lionel I (son)	734-761
Ringan II (son)	761-777
Franzik (son)	777-795
Svarnik (grandson of Lionel I)	795-801
INTERREGNUM	
Hernik (grandson of Ringan II)	803-848
Ringan III (son)	848-851
Termöd I (brother)	851-855
Thrasarik (brother)	855-896
Zdanik (great-grandson of Svarnik)	896-916
Braïda (daughter)	916-993

DUKES OF ARJENOL

HOUSE OF FURSTÁN D'ARJENOL

Torval I (husband of Braïda)	916-981
Termöd II (grandson)	981-992
Ringan IV (son)	992-1020
Torval II (grandson)	1020-1092
Mahael I (son)	1092-1100
Lionel II (son)	1100-1121
Mahael II (brother)	1121-1128
Mátyás (brother)	1128-1130+

Arkadia. This ancient County and Duchy of Torenth is located Northwest of the city of Beldour, South of the Beldour River and the Duchy of Truvorsk, East of the Duchy of Sasovna, North of the Duchy of Altorf, and Northwest of the Crown Duchy of Beldouria. It was established as a County in the year 600 by Kassian Count Vorarl to honour his first-born son, Prince Aldred. Prince Pál was the Ist titleholder to be called Duke. The Honour was regranted at different times to various branches of the Royal House of Furstán.

COUNTS AND DUKES OF ARKADIA

HOUSE OF FURSTÁN D'ARKADIA

Aldred	600-639
Tamás (son)	639-655
Melchior (son)	655-720
Festil I (cousin)	720-748
INTERREGNUM	
Maksim (grandson)	769-824
Mátyás I (son)	824-859
Festil II (son)	859-880
Mátyás II (son)	880
Pál (cousin; Duke)	882-901
Dmitri (brother)	901-933
Imre (son)	933-955
Marek (cousin)	956-962
Menander (brother)	962-982
Kyprian (nephew)	984-1012
Nikola I (son)	1012-1025
Kirill (brother)	1025-1079
Nikola II (son)	1079-1111
Vidar (son)	1111-1130+

Arkady II Árpád Aloys André *Furstán*, King of Torenth. This illustrious Prince came into this world on the last day of November in the Year of Our Lord 995, being the eldest son and heir of Kyprian II King of Torenth and Grand Princess Polyxena daughter of Démétrios II Autokratór of Byzantyun. He intermarried with the Grafina Dura daughter of Arsieu II Sovereign Prince of Jáca on the IInd day of May 1015, and by her he had children: the Princess Grigoryna Györgyna, who, being forced to marry a man not of her choosing, Balthazar Count von Maultasche, took her own life by throwing herself off the battlements of her father's castle on the XXIVth day of June in the year 1037; the Hereditary Prince Arion Nikola; the Prince Sigard Andrósz; the Princess Nummela Favila; the Hereditary Prince István Imre; the Princess Mladena Amelda; the Hereditary Prince Nimur Dénes later Nimur II King of Torenth. All but the eldest and youngest of these children died tragically within weeks of each other of the typhoidous grippe in July of the year 1032.

The Prince Arkady commanded the right wing of his father's army at Killingford in the year 1025, and was saved from death only by the sacrifice of his next younger brother, Prince Nikola, who threw himself in front of an axe intended for the other. He is said to have mourned the loss of his most-beloved brother for the rest of his life. According to his sister, Arien Dowager Duchess d'Arjenol, who wrote her *Lives of the XII Kings of Torenth* in the year 1055, "He was heard to lament after his succession that Nikola would have made the better King, that Nikola should have been King, that Nikola would have walked his own road, but that he, Arkady, was doomed forever to follow in his father's footsteps." King Arkady built the VII-tiered Nikolaseum at Torenthály to honour his brother's memory, beginning in the year 1026; after its dedication on the XVIth day of June in the year 1030, the tomb justly became regarded as one of the great wonders of the world. He also began construction of the great stone span of Saint Basil's Bridge in Beldour in the year 1031, and completed it XI years later in the year 1042; it was regarded as a technological and engineering marvel of the time, being one of the largest bridges in the known world. The dedication of this structure, on the XVIth day of June in the year 1042, was an occasion for great jubilee in Torenth, for it finally linked together Old and New Beldour with a permanent crossing that would not be swept away by the periodic Spring floods to which the River Beldour is so susceptible.

The Prince Arkady succeeded his father on the XXIst day of July in the year 1025, and was girded with the sword by the Patriarch Timotheos II on the New Year's Day following, as is the custom in old Torenth. He immediately set out to rebuild the army and the nobility, for many of his officers and noblemen had died in the war, and many families were left without grown men to manage their estates. He reformed the laws governing the transmission of land, allowing the widows of these men legally to manage their own properties, and to pass them to their surviving children and other heirs. The batchelors of the realm under the age of XLV years he ordered to marry within the year, under penalty of conscription into the army (if freedmen) or of heavy levies (if nobility). He organized a marriage ceremony presided over by the Patriarch himself at old Beldour in June of the year 1026, a celebration that is said to have joined D couples together, and personally gave each of the freedmen the deed to their land and a single gold korona as dowry.

He encouraged his younger sister the Princess Arien to marry her cousin, Averil Hereditary Duke d'Arjenol, in the year 1010; after her son's coming of age in the year 1025, she returned to Beldour that Spring, and became a close companion and advisor to her brother for the next III decades. His father the former King Kyprian he made Grand Duke of Furstán, and situated him in great style in a manor house at Torenthály; but when some VIII years later the former monarch attempted to regain the throne, King Arkady put him away in a monastery under the close guard of the austere military order of Saint Sviatoslav, telling the Abbot to treat his royal guest no differently than the meanest new recruit to the Order. And so it was done as the King said.

In his relations to the neighbouring state of Gwynedd this King followed the policies of his ancestors, tacitly supporting the aspirations of the Festillic and Mearan Pretenders. He campaigned in the Northeastern part of his realm in the years 1044 and 1053, adding several small states to his suzerainty, and generally strengthening the line of border defenses against the heathen barbarians of the North. He started the fortification there which later became known as the Arkadian Wall, stretching between the Great North Sea and the mountains to the East, and blocking access to the nomadic savages which dwelled in that place. But after the death of his sister Princess Arien in the year 1059 he made no further expeditions anywhere.

Princess Arien describes her brother in these terms: "The King was slight in stature, with flaxen hair that gradually darkened with age, a comely face, intense eyes, and a quick intelligence. He was not a man to suffer fools lightly. Despite the great personal tragedies and betrayals that he suffered in his lifetime, he remained kind toward his fellow man, and was never hesitant to give alms to the poor, particularly when he could do so incognito. Having attained through inheritance all the stature of the world that other men so envied, still he cared not much for his position, and would have gladly given it up, I believe, in exchange for a simpler life. That he was King was evident in both his demeanor and his breeding, but arrogance was never a part of his character. He cared for his servants and his staff, and always thanked them even for the most ordinary of services, presenting them with gifts on all the major feastdays. Indeed, he was the best of Kings that this old land has yet seen."

This great and good monarch died in his LXXXVth year on the XIIth day of May in the year 1080, and was buried in the family crypt at Torenthály, next to his beloved sister, the Princess Arien. He had intense blue eyes, light brown hair, and a close-cropped, reddish beard. R.I.P. [*King Kelson's Bride*].

Armagh, Master. He was serving as weapons master to King Imre in the year 903, being one of only a few men allowed to spar with that monarch. He had a scar across one forearm. [*Camber of Culdi*].

Armand, Sir. He was a legendary hero of the Eleven Kingdoms, and became the subject of many ballads, including one sung at Court on the IIIrd day of March in the year 1125 during the celebration to commemorate King Kelson's knighting. [*The Quest for Saint Camber*].

Arnaud, Sieur de Vali, Sir. He was born on the XXXth day of January in the year 1096, being the son of Sir Marcel de Vali and Arna Lady Howell. He married Elspeth Lady Derry on the XVIIIth day of July in the year 1122, and by her he had children: the Hereditary Lord Derry; the Lady Marcelline. He was knighted with Sean Earl Derry by King Brion on the XIth day of May in the Year of 1115, with Alaric Duke of Corwyn acting as his sponsor. Sir Arnaud de Vali succeeded his cousin, Proulx Sieur de Vali, on the IIIrd day of February in the year 1119. On the XXVth day of March in the year 1121 his manor house in Northeastern Corwyn was burned by Warin de Grey's raiders. His home had been rebuilt and fortified by March of the year 1125. [*Deryni Checkmate*; *High Deryni*; *The Quest for Saint Camber*].

Arnham. This region was located in The Purple March, and was associated with the Barony of Marlor. Its best-known citizen was Edward MacInnis Bishop of Grecotha. [*The Harrowing of Gwynedd*].

Arnold, Brother. This monk from a local parish church helped guide King Kelson and Dhugal to the ruins of Tor Caerrorie on the XXth day of March in the year 1125. [*The Quest for Saint Camber*].

Arnulf, Father. He was the aged household chaplain of the d'Eirial estate in the year 977. He delivered Baron Radulf's coronet to the new Lord, Gilrae, after the former's death. ["Vocation"].

Árpád Imre *Furstán*, King of Torenth, Count of Southmarcke. This wicked Prince was born on the VIth day of June in the Year of Our Lord 821, being the only son and heir of Kyprian Prince of Torenth and Lady Arabella daughter of Azelin Count Miz'na. He intermarried with the Princess Kadhloha daughter of Theimuraz Prince of Autun on the Vth day of July in the year 856, but she proved barren.

The Prince Árpád succeeded his father as Count of Southmarcke on the IVth day of August in the year 827, and his grandfather, Lajos I, as King of Torenth on the XXth day of March in the year 845, and was girded with the sword at Iób on the New Year's Day following by Patriarch Stephanos IV. The XXVI years of his reign were spent in the pursuit of the pleasures of the flesh, for which God severely punished him by giving him sores on his private parts, which eventually rotted and fell off in middle age. He then became wantonly cruel, sponsoring endless rounds of games which pitted man against man and beast against beast in every possible combination. For this some people loved him. Yet he retained an equal cunning in his placement of his courtiers and Great Lords, so that none dared raise hand to him lest they have it chopped off by the ambitions of another. Thus, when finally he lost his reason in the year 871, it was his own cousin the Prince Malachy who finally deposed him, on the I[st] day of May in that year. The former King Árpád was sent to the Monastery of Sankt Pëtr in Arkadia, and died there on his birthday, the VIth day of June in the year 872, aged LI years.

Arranal Canyon. This strategic Northern passage lies Southeast of the city of Marbury on the River Arran, providing a natural gateway through the high mountains connecting Torenth and Marley in Gwynedd. In the Summer of the year 905 the Pretender Ariella brought M armed men through this canyon from Tolán as part of her invasion of Gwynedd. In June of the year 928 the *Custodes* knights of Lord Joshua were sent here to get them away from Lochalyn Castle. In the Spring of the year 1121 Ewan III Duke of Claibourne stationed a small Gwyneddan army here to repel any invasion from the East or South by the forces of Wencit King of Torenth.

Campbell de Broun described his journey through this region thus: "It rained this morning, then began to thunder; the appearance of a storm prevented us from starting on our way, and it poured very heavily till the noon hour. We then fixed up and started with the road quite rough, this being mostly hilly land and the bottom filled with small, white-and-black timbers. We soon entered a kind of barrens with but little growth save brush and some scrubby white oaks and a great quantity of pale flinty rocks. We crossed several streams of pure water, the most considerable being a branch of the Glenkeen called Rock Creek; it is closely confined by the naked barren ranges on each side, with little or no bottom land, and whatever was rich cut to pieces with the freshets. We saw even more hills in the distance; here and there were little groves and thickets of underbrush which resembled cultivated spots in a wilderness. This area had a romantically wild appearance, not disagreeable to the eyes of this weary traveler (only as he estimated the distance he had yet to go), as hill rose over hill and mountain over mountain. We continued till late in the evening, reaching a way station on the waters of the Glenkeen; and, on account of its continual storming, we did not pitch our tent there but lay about in a shed nearby.

"The next morning the sky was clear, and we proceeded ever upward. The road was better here, but its muddy spots were treacherous, with patches of snow lying in the hollows even in June. The air was cold and crisp. Pines covered the lower slopes, bare rocks above. Near the top we espied a peak called 'The Castle' from its pointed spires; I did not see much of a hold in it myself. We encamped in a hollow just the other side of the top, having plenty of game and fresh, cold water right at hand. That night I could have reached out and touched God Himself." [*Saint Camber*; *The Bastard Prince*; *High Deryni*].

Arrand. This small port town is located in Llannedd on the River Eirian, a few miles South of its junction with the River Llanarfon. Its best-known citizen was Archer Bishop of Dhassa. See also: Archer.

Arran River. This rapidly-flowing stream has its headwaters in Loch Derrig in the foothills of the Rheljan Mountains, several miles North of Lochalyn Castle in the County of Eastmarch; thence it runs Northeast through the Arranal Canyon before turning due North, where it exits at the village of Mayfair into the Gulf of Normarch. The Arran forms a natural border for part of its length between the Duchy of Tolán in Torenth and the Earldom of Marley in Gwynedd. Its major Northern branch, the River Glenkeen, has its headwaters in Lake Guitane near the city of Marbury in Marley, whence it runs Southeast to join the Arran River just before the combined streams enter the Arranal Canyon.

Arx Fidei Abbey (*Citadel of the Faith*). This former establishment of the *Custodes Fidei* was located III hours' ride North of Rhemuth on the West bank of the River Eirian. It was here that Prince Javan spent III years as a lay brother of the *Ordo Custodum Fidei* between the years 918 and 921, before he succeeded to the throne of Gwynedd. The Abbot in the latter year was Father Halex. The Abbey was disbanded in the year 928 after the accession of Owain King of Gwynedd. [*King Javan's Year*].

Arx Fidei Seminary (Citadel of the Faith). This establishment of the *Custodes Fidei* is located on the South side of the River Eirian just East of the city of Valoret near Saint Mark's Parish Church, having been founded in the year 948 as a successor monastery to the original *Arx Fidei* Abbey near Rhemuth. It was here that Father Jorian de Courcy was ordained on the Ist day of August in the year 1104, but his Deryni nature having been discovered, he was later burnt at the stake. A few months later Denis Arilan was successfully ordained priest in the Church of the Paraclete at *Arx Fidei* without his Deryni nature being discovered on the IInd day of February in the Year of Our Lord 1105. ["The Priesting of Arilan"].

Asaph, Saint. This ancient Mearan saint of the VIth century excelled as a coppersmith, and some remarkable specimens of his religious handiwork still surface from time to time in the border towns throughout that region. Alas, his great masterpiece, *The Apocalpyse of Saint John*, constructed at the top of Mount Sgagach in Northeastern Meara and comprising several interlocking panels XX feet high which together formed a pyramid depicting the entire story of that most Holy Book on its several faces, was destroyed by lightning on the day of its dedication, taking its creator with it. Saint Asaph's feastday is celebrated on the XXIst day of June, and a great Cathedral dedicated to his name is situate in central Laas.

Ascelin, Father. This *Custodes* priest replaced the deceased Father Boniface at Saint Hilary's Basilica in Rhemuth late in the year 920. He later served as Father Faelan's designated replacement during those times when Faelan was absent at *Arx Fidei*. He accompanied the Royal Expedition to Eastmarch in June of the year 928, and gave Lord Albertus the last rites after his death on the XXth day of that month. [*King Javan's Year*; *The Bastard Prince*].

Aubrey *Gillispie*, Earl of Danoc. He was born on the XIIIth day of August in the Year of Our Lord 1071, being the eldest surviving son and heir of Moncure Gillispie Earl of Danoc and Aidana Lady Perrin. He never married. He succeeded his father on the XXXth day of June in the year 1097. He was one of the Lords present at the War Council chaired by King Kelson at Dhassa on the XXIXth day of June in the year 1121, and also at the War Council held on the XXVth day of December in the year 1123 to discuss the developing Mearan crisis. In the year 1130 the Earl Aubrey's heir was his younger brother, the Lord Perrey. [*High Deryni*; *The Bishop's Heir*].

Augarin (II) Alexander *Haldane*, King of Gwynedd, Count of Haldane, *Pater Gwyneddi*. He was born on the XXVIIth day of July in the Year of Our Lord 611, being the second son of Bearand II Count of Haldane and the Princess Gertrudis daughter of Prangins King of Mooryn. He intermarried with Rosemaryn Lady MacLean on the XXIVth day of May in the year 626, and by her he had children: the Hereditary Prince Aidan later King of Gwynedd; the Prince Cinhil, dead at age XI; the Prince Bearand later Count of Haldane by cession of his father later Protector of the Throne of Gwynedd (*i.e.*, Regent). After his first wife's death in childbirth on the VIIIth day of July in the year 632, he intermarried secondly with Caldora Lady de la Marche on the IInd day of September in the year 646, and by her he had children: the Princess Bertradis, who intermarried with Aldred I King of Torenth; the Prince Donal later Count of Desse; the Prince Llarik later Count of Rhemuth later Protector of the Throne of Gwynedd later King of Gwynedd; the Prince Halbert later Halbert II Count of Haldane in succession to his brother; the Princess Isobelle; the Princess Casmen, who intermarried with Murtagh Consul of the Nigh Ford; the Prince Auran later Count of Valoret.

The Lord Augarin succeeded his brother, the Count Aidan II, on the XIth day of March in the year 640, under the title Count Augarin II. From the beginning of his reign he led the fight to free the Holy Church from the outside control of the tyrannical Patriarch Johannes III of Bremagne, and to establish a national religious hierarchy centered at his capital of Valoret. When the Counts of Carthane and Lendour opposed his efforts, he raised an army and enlisted the support of his brother, Father Aurelius Haldane, and Sixtus the Prince-Bishop of Dhassa. He conquered Jamish Count of Lendour in the year 643, and Rubik Count of Carthane on the XXth day of April in the year 645. On the Ist day of May in the year 645 he proclaimed himself High King of Haldane. He deposed the last Bremagni Archbishop of Valoret, Servilius, and arranged for the election of his younger brother, Aurelius Haldane, as the first independent Archbishop of Valoret, on the Xth day of that month. On the XXth day instant the Archbishop Aurelius crowned his brother King at Valoret. The King issued a proclamation on the Ist day of January in the year 647 changing the name of the state to Gwynedd. He spent his years consolidating his regime, and fighting off invasions from Bremagne in the years 649 and 655, and from the Herkos raiders beyond the seas in the 660s.

According to Xerxes Hellenikos, "he was a short man, thin where his brothers were fat, with a hook nose, a ragged scar on one cheek from a fight at age XV, and not much hair left on his head, even in his youth. His eyes were steady grey, and he often used his small hands to gesture as he spoke. His voice would resonate even through the farthest reaches of a large room. He could judge a man's character within a moment of speaking to him. I remember seeing him once at some everyday Court function, and marveling how everyone else there, including his sons and brothers, seemed but a pale imitation or shadow of this great man. His sheer presence immediately commanded one's attention. In my life as an emissary I have met the Kings and Princes of two dozen states, and they were as nothing compared to this man." The Great King Augarinus Primus, *Pater Gwyneddi*, died much lamented on the XXVIIIth day of

February in the year 673, aged LXI years, and was buried in the crypt of the Haldanes at Valoret. R.I.P. *Augescunt aliæ gentes, aliæ minuuntur.* [*Camber the Heretic*].

Aurelian, Dom. He was a young Gabrilite Healer who took refuge with Gregory Earl of Ebor at Trevalga. He was present at the Haven on the XXIst day of January in the year 918, when he helped heal Ansel MacRorie. He wore his hair in a traditional Gabrilite braid. [*The Harrowing of Gwynedd*].

Aurelius Albin *Haldane***, Prince, Archbishop Primate of Valoret and All Gwynedd.** He was born on the XVIIIth day of August in Year of Our Lord 613, being the third son of Bearand II Count of Haldane and the Princess Gertrudis daughter of Prangins King of Mooryn. He was originally christened Aurel by his father, but used the Latinate form of his name from the time he entered the Church in the year 628. He was ordained priest on the XIIth day of June in the year 633. From his earliest years he was a leader of the movement to free his Church from the bonds of foreign interference, and supported his brother's aspirations to become the first King of the united lands of the Eirian Crescent.

On the XVIth day of March in the year 645 he was secretly consecrated Bishop of Valoret by Sixtus Prince-Bishop of Dhassa and Honoratus Abbot-Bishop of Concaradine, and with them proclaimed the independence of the Church on the XIIth day of April following. His brother, Count Augarin II, conquered Carthane on the XXth day instant, and deposed Eulogius Bishop of Nyford. Following the proclamation of the monarchy on the Ist day of May, he quietly organized the new structure of the Church with the support of the King, and was himself elected Ist independent Archbishop of Valoret on the Xth day of that month; new Bishops were elected for Nyford and Rhemuth, plus IV itinerant Bishops. He crowned King Augarin X days later, and presided at the King's marriage to Caldora Lady de la Marche on the IInd day of September in the year 646. He tirelessly worked for the benefit of his congregation, spreading the word of God throughout the land. He died of prostration on the VIth day of June in the year 666, aged LII years, and was buried in the crypt of All Saints' Cathedral in Valoret. His passing was greatly mourned by his Royal brother and the people. He was succeeded by Bishop Higerius. R.I.P. *Divina natura dedit agros, ars humana ædificavit urbes.*

Autun. This small principality is located in the Autuni Mountains between Bremagne to the West and the Anvil of the Lord to the East, with the small Duchy of Alver lying to the South. The headwaters of the River Rampante originate in central Autun. The country was originally headed by an elected Prince-Bishop, from the time of Cassian in the year 314. The secular state was founded on the Ist day of April in the year 804 by Giorgi Count of Nebroth, and has remained in his family ever since. The capital of this state is Saint Cassian's. Although exports are few, the hair of the Autuni tricorned goat produces a fabric which is highly prized by those fortunate enough to possess it, so soft and supple, it is said, that even *"Dii laneos pedes habent."*

PRINCES OF AUTUN

HOUSE OF NEBROTH

Giorgi I	804-845
Derok (son)	845-856
Kartham (son)	856-889
Pharsman I (son)	889-911
Mirdat I (son)	911-933
Bakur (son)	933-949
Swimon (brother)	949-960
Artchil (son)	960-992
Giorgi II (son)	992-1013
Vakhtang (nephew)	1013-1044
Giorgi III (son)	1044-1056
Konstantiné (cousin)	1056-1059
Davit (brother)	1059-1065
Bagrat (son)	1065-1088
Mirdat II (brother)	1088-1104
Irakli (brother)	1104-1109
Pharsman II (son)	1109-1130+

Avis *de Burgeys* **Draper.** She was born on the XXIInd day of June in the Year of Our Lord 825, being the daughter of Edward de Burgeys and Sari Hews. She intermarried with Prince Aidan Haldane (Daniel Draper) on the XXXth day of May in the year 842, and by him she had children: the Hereditary Prince Alroy also known as Royston Draper; the Princess Margret also called Gretta Draper, dead at age VI of the rosy fever; and the Princess Isabel also called Belle Draper, who intermarried with the trader Maelor ap Tewdwr, leaving issue unknown. She died on the XXIst day of March in the year 875, aged XLIX years, and was buried in Saint John's Church cemetery in Valoret. R.I.P.

Aynbeth Araxie *von Horthy***, Princess d'Orsal and Tralia.** She was born on the XXXIst day of October in the Year of Our Lord 1121, being the third daughter of Létald Hort of Orsal and Prince of Tralia and Husniyya Sharifa of R'Kassi. [*King Kelson's Bride*].

Azim ibn Qais ibn Hassan *ar-Rafiq***, Nabil or Prince of Nur Hallaj, Sir.** He was born on the VIIth day of January in the year 1079, being the third son of Qais ibn Hassan Emir of Nur Hallaj and Kamila daughter of Athbi Sultan of Gonj, and brother of Hakim Emir of Nur Hallaj. This high-ranking master of the magical arts became a preceptor of the Knights of the Anvil, the successors of the Michaelines (the main abbey of which was located at Djellarda near the Anvil of the Lord), joining the Order in the year 1099. He also taught and trained a number of promising Deryni adepts, including Richenda Duchess of Corwyn and Araxie Queen of Gwynedd.

In May of the year 1124 he sent Richenda an interesting scroll dating from the 900s which gave details concerning the death of Camber Earl of Culdi at Iomaire. He visited her on the XXXth day of June in that year using the alias of "Ludolphus the Peddler," carrying correspondence from his niece-in-law, the Princess Rohays. He also introduced a compulsion in the mind of Father Ambros, Chaplain to Dowager Queen Jehana, on that same day, instructing the priest to preach a sermon of tolerance to Jehana.

He was elected to the Camberian Council on the XIth day of February in the year 1128, replacing the Lady Kyri. On the IIIrd day of July in that year he discussed the political situation in Torenth with King Kelson, Duke Dhugal, and Duke Alaric Morgan, informing them that he believed that Mahael Duke d'Arjenol was plotting to kill and remove King Liam Lajos, in order to retain his power as Regent. That same night, Azim was chastised by Bishop Arilan for not consulting sufficiently with the Camberian Council.

Azim represented his brother, Hakim II Prince of Nur Hallaj, at the inauguration of King Liam Lajos later that month. On the XIth day instant he accompanied King Kelson's party on a ride into the Torenthi countryside; there he informed Kelson that King Liam Lajos II has asked Kelson to replace the murdered Count Czalsky in the *killijálay* ceremony, and offered to help train him. Four days later he met with the Camberian Council.

King Kelson learned of Azim's membership on the Council on the XVIth day instant, being informed by Bishop Arilan. Azim attended King Liam's first Crown Council later that day. Afterwards, he met privily with King Kelson and his companions, and pledged to do everything in his power to locate Count Teymuraz; he also reveals that the Hort probably has a portal which could provide an avenue of safety for the bridal party still resident in Orsal. He departed for Orsal on the next day, and was instrumental in getting both the Torenthis and Gwyneddans to reveal mutual portal sites in their countries. He again met with the Camberian Council later that day to select a new coadjutor to replace Lady Vivienne.

On the XXVIIth day of that month, Azim transported briefly from Beldour to Rhemuth, where he and Arilan gave King Kelson the news of Morag's death, returning later that evening. Four days later, following the double Mearan wedding, Azim cleansed Sean Earl Derry's mind of the magical compulsion which had been placed in it many years before by Wencit King of Torenth, and later reinforced by Morag and Teymuraz. He returned to Djellarda later that same day. He was tall, had black eyes, a long aquiline nose, and close-clipped black beard, and often wore a black *keffiyeh*. [*The King's Justice*; *King Kelson's Bride*].

Bahadur Khan I ibn Qabus al-Duala *al-Muttalib*, King of R'Kassi. He was born on the XVIth day of May in the Year of Our Lord 1084, being I of the XI sons of Qabus al-Duala King of R'Kassi and Princess Ripsimé daughter of Shahrukh the Grand Khalifah of Libania and the Lady Jelenia Princess of Grecia. He intermarried with the Sultana Gaïana daughter of Ziyaeddin Sultan of Gonj on the XVIIth day of July in the year 1114, and by her he had children: the Princess Raba'a; the Princess Hanuf; the Princess Badria; the Hereditary Prince Mubarak Khan; the Prince Timur Mirza; the Prince Khusrow Bahman; the Princess Izzet; the Prince Qahraman al-Hasan.

He succeeded his brother, the King Abd al-Ilah, on the Xth day of December in the year 1112. He was a guest at the reception held to honour King Liam Lajos II in the Hanging Gardens of Furstánály Palace on the IXth day of July in the year 1128, and was also present at the *killijálay* and subsequent feast held on the XVIth day instant. [*King Kelson's Bride*].

Baldwin. This soldier of the Rhemuth garrison "attacked," with Nevell, the Healer Oriel on the XXth day of March in the year 922. In reality, his will had been subverted by the Deryni Sitric at the instigation of the former Regents. He was questioned II days later by Lord Jerowen and the recovered Healer Oriel, but had only confused memories of the event. He was murdered by Dimitri on the next day following, his death being made to look like a suicide, and was buried in a potter's field. R.I.P. [*King Javan's Year*].

Ballard II *MacRorie*, VIth Earl of Culdi. He was born on the Vth of October in the Year of Our Lord 808, being the eldest son and heir of Adrian Earl of Culdi and Jessamyn Lady de la Roché. He intermarried with Ardis Lady Drummond on the IVth day of May in the year 839, and by her he had children: the Lady Elspeth later Abbess of Saint Hilda's; the Hereditary Count Adrian, who died before his father; the Hereditary Count Angus, who died before his father; the Hereditary Count Camber later Earl of Culdi; the Lady Aislinn, who intermarried with Iain MacLean Earl of Kierney, leaving issue. He died on the VIIIth day of June in the year 871, aged LXII years, and was succeeded by his IIIrd but only surviving son, Lord Camber. His tomb was discovered at Tor Caerrorie by King Kelson on the XXth day of March in the year 1125. R.I.P. [*King Javan's Year*; *The Quest for Saint Camber*].

Ballard Rory *MacRorie*, Lord. He was born on the XIIth day of September in the Year of Our Lord 877, being the second son of Camber Earl of Culdi and Jocelyn Lady de la Marche. He died of the same fever which took his sister Jerusha on the VIth day of March in the year 888, aged X years, and was buried at Tor Caerrorie. His tomb was discovered by King Kelson on the XXth day of March in the year 1125. R.I.P. ["Catalyst"; *King Javan's Year*; *The Quest for Saint Camber*].

Ballymar. This town is located just East of Uiskin on the Northern tip of the Duchy of Cassan. In the year 1122 it was erected into a new coastal see under Bishop Lachlan de Quarles, who was succeeded by Bishop Hugh de Berry in the year 1125. [*The Bishop's Heir*; *The King's Justice*; *The Quest for Saint Camber*].

Balmoric, Brother. He was a monk at Saint Torin's Shrine near Dhassa in the year 1121, and a supporter of Warin de Grey. He held the keys to one locked room at the shrine, and used his access to help capture the Duke of Corwyn in March of that year. *Triumpho morte tam vita*. [*Deryni Checkmate*].

Barrett Ross *de Laney*, Earl Barstowe, Titular Lord de Laney. He was born in the Purple March on the XVIth day of November in the Year of Our Lord 1050, being the eldest son and heir of Barstowe Lord de Laney and Modesta Lady Bannock. He intermarried with Jehana Dowager Queen of Gwynedd on the XVth day of October in the year 1128, and by her he had a child: the Hereditary Countess Arÿole Rosaura Modeste.

The Lord Barrett de Laney was trained at an early age by the Deryni master, Michon Titular Baron de Courcy. On the Vth day of April in the year 1068 he intervened to save a score of condemned Deryni children from the soldiers who would have killed them, and was blinded before he could himself be rescued by Darrell Romsey. He should have succeeded his father on the XVth day of March in the year 1078, but could never seek the official recognition of the King, now that his Deryni nature had been revealed, and his estate in Gwynedd, being without management, eventually decayed and was confiscated for nonpayment of taxes in the year 1083. He then spent some years as the guest of various Deryni friends in other countries, before finally purchasing a house on the Southern coast of Alver.

He was appointed to the Cambrian Council about the year 1080, and served as a Coadjutor of that body from at least the year 1121. He was one of IV arbiters of the duel arcane held between Wencit King of Torenth and Kelson King of Gwynedd and their followers at Llyndruth Meadows on the IInd day of July in the year 1121. He met with the Cambrian Council on the XXVIIIth day of June in the year 1128 to discuss possible brides for King Kelson. On the IVth day of July following, he was discovered by Dowager Queen Jehana doing research in the secret library annex, which had been constructed by King Kelson to house certain Deryni texts. Over the subsequent weeks, she became a student of Barrett, who discussed with her and Father John Nivard some of the finer points of Deryni philosophy, as expounded by the ancient masters.

He attended another Council meeting on the XVth day instant, and again II days later, when a new Coadjutor was chosen to replace Lady Vivienne. He attended the latter's funeral in Alta Jorda on the XIXth day of July. He transported Jehana to his home on the coast of Alver on the XXIVth day following, to show her his garden, and to allow him to see through her eyes.

His relationship with Jehana eventually led to a closer liaison, which union was celebrated in the presence of King Kelson and his Court the following October. At the same time, the King created Barrett Earl Barstowe in memory of the new peer's father, with remainder to any heirs of his body whatsoever, and confirmed him in his original title of Lord de Laney, granting him estates in the Purple March to replace those he had lost so many years before. His marriage with the Dowager Queen of Gwynedd was blessed by God the following year. The couple maintained abodes in both Gwynedd and Alver, alternating between them from season to season. Earl Barrett was bald in his latter years, and had bright emerald eyes. ["Bethane"; *High Deryni*; *The Bishop's Heir*; *The King's Justice*; *The Quest for Saint Camber*; *King Kelson's Bride*].

Bartholomew. He was a guard in Rhys and Evaine Thuryn's household in the year 917. At the end of December in that year he accompanied Evaine and her family from Sheele to Trurill. [*Camber the Heretic*].

Barwicke. This tiny village is located near the source of the River Eirian Northeast of Valoret, at the Southwestern edge of the plain of Iomaire. Saint Jarlath's Monastery is situate nearby. The region is II hours' ride Northeast of Saint Liam's Abbey. It was here that a mob of humans burned a Deryni monastic school on the XVIth day of February in the year 917. [*Camber of Culdi*; *Camber the Heretic*].

Basil, Saint. This courageous IVth-century defender of the faith was a native of Cæsarea in Kappadokia. After his studies at Kónstantinopolis, he visited several monastic colonies in the Far East, and founded one there himself on the River Iris in Pontius, for which he wrote his *Rules*, still the standard work of its kind. In the year 370 he was made Metropolitan of Cæsarea, and at once entered upon his brave fight against the Moors, who had the support of the imperial authorities at Byzantyun. Through his efforts Saint Basil saved the whole of Kappadokia for the faith. He was also known as a preacher and writer of long doctrinal works, including his *De Spiritu Sancto Indiviso*, which was published in LVII volumes and XXIII *Supplementi*. His work is unsurpassed in all Christendom, forming as it does a bridge between the old and the new. Indeed, on the XVIth day of June in the year 1042 Saint Basil's Bridge was dedicated in his honour by King Arkady II of Torenth as a permanent link between Old and New Beldour. His feastday is the IInd day of January.

Bayvel *de Cameron*, Lord Farnham. He was born on the XXIIIrd day of December in the Year of Our Lord 861, being the second surviving son of Gutor Lord Farnham and Leoline Lady MacTyre, and an uncle of Megan Queen of Gwynedd. He intermarried with Ulicia Lady de Bonham on the XXXth day of September in the year 886, and by her he had children: the Hereditary Lord Leonidas later Baron Farnham; the Lady Bonita; the Lord Bonham, a twin with his sister; the Lady Felicia. He succeeded to the Barony on the death of his older brother, Yorke Lord Farnham, on the XXIIIrd day of December in the year 891. He participated in the War Council held on the XXIIIrd day of June in 905 at the Great Hall in Valoret Palace, and was present at the Battle of Iomaire II days later. He died on the IXth day of March in the year 926, aged LXIV years, and was succeeded by his son, Lord Leonidas. R.I.P. [*Saint Camber*].

Bearand Llarik Donal *Haldane* called "The Great," King of Gwynedd, *Defensor Regni*, Saint. He was born on the VIIth day of September in the Year of Our Lord 720, being the eldest son and heir of Ryons King of Gwynedd and Raphaela Princess of Torenth. He intermarried with Iona Lady de Vali on the XXVIIth day of May in the year 740, and by her he had children: the Hereditary Prince Augarin, dead at age IX of the weak limb; the Prince Bearand *Junior*, dead at birth; the Princess Karissa, who never married and died at age XXV of chills; the Prince Donal, who died colicky at age II months; the Princess Jestyna, dead at birth; the Princess Valeria and the Hereditary Prince Valerian, twins who died within III days of their birth; the Hereditary Prince Ryanik, dead at age VII of *la grippe*. Following the death of his first wife on the XIVth day of November in the year 776, King Bearand intermarried secondly with Aisling Lady Kincaid of Kilarden on the XVIth day of June in the year 777, and by her he had children: the Hereditary Prince Ifor later King of Gwynedd; the Princess Aurora, who intermarried with Gwalchmai Baron Carrach, leaving issue; the Princess Petrea; the Princess Angharad.

The Prince Bearand succeeded his father on the XIXth day of August in the year 736, at a time when the Kingdom of Gwynedd was under severe pressure from foreign raiders and barbarian incursions. He was crowned by Archbishop Lantelm on the XXIXth day of September following at Valoret. According to the *Legends*, "he pushed the Moorish invaders back into the sea and broke the back of their naval power forever. Their legions have never dared to cross the great wastes or to sail the Southern Seas again." The Moorish armada was destroyed in the Battle of the Jamin Straits on the Xth day of July in the year 752. He followed his victory there with a decisive raid on the infidels' chief port of Kharthat on the XVIIth day of August in the year 755 that burned much of that town and sank or damaged LIV enemy ships, forever ending their threat to the West. For these efforts he was known as "Saint Bearand" even during his own lifetime, and was awarded the title *Defensor Regni* by Adon Archbishop Primate of Valoret. He died in the arms of God and all of his archangels on the XIIth day of December in the year 794, aged LXXIV years. He was canonized on the Cth anniversary of his birth on the VIIth day of September in the year 820 by Archbishop William I, and his feastday was established on that date.

On the XXXIst day of July in the year 921 the Torenthi Prince Miklós, acting as a representative of his government, presented the newly crowned King Javan of Gwynedd with an ancient illuminated scroll detailing the life of King Bearand. An abbey dedicated to his Holy Name is located at the foot of the High Grelder Pass, near Caerrorie. R.I.P. [*Camber of Culdi*; *The Harrowing of Gwynedd*; *King Javan's Year*; *The Quest for Saint Camber*].

Beck. This boy of Twilham Green in the Purple March fell into a river and was rescued by Geordie Drummond in April of the year 905. [*Deryni Challenge*].

Belden *of Erne*, Bishop of Cashien. He was born on the XXVIth day of November in the Year of Our Lord 1063. He was ordained priest on the XVIIIth day of July in the year 1081, and was elected Bishop of Cashien on the Xth day of June in the year 1112. He supported Edmund Loris ex-Archbishop of Valoret in 1121 and again in 1123, when Loris tried to reinstate himself. Following Loris's capture and execution by Kelson King of Gwynedd on the XIIth day of July in the year 1124, Bishop Belden was suspended from his priestly functions for his part in the Mearan Rebellion, and was formally degraded from his see and imprisoned for life by the Synod of Valoret on the XVIIIth day of March in the year 1125. [*The Bishop's Heir*; *The King's Justice*; *The Quest for Saint Camber*].

Beldour. This capital city of Torenth is one of the great wonders of the world, having been called by Ingwar Ingwarsson "that great shining place, old friend Beldour," and by Colgon mac Lorcan "blue-black Beldour, my mistress of the night." The original town site was founded in the Year of Our Lord 224 by the Autokratór Basileios, who made it the central focus of his plans for expansion of the Byzantyun Empire in the West, calling the place Démos Belteros. Although the meaning of this name is self-evident to any student of the Greek tongue, legend holds that Belteros actually refers to the indigenous people of the region, the Beldourynoi, a small tribe of whom had migrated there from Kheldour some L or C years earlier. The Great Basileios also began construction of a huge Greek church, the Cathedral of Saint Constantine of Beldour, which was completed in the year 232, but was largely destroyed by the great earthquake which struck the city on the XIVth day of March in the year 1008, an event which sent great terror into the hearts of King and subjects alike, for they all believed that the Millennium had finally come, strange as this might seem.

Reconstruction of the edifice was begun immediately in even grander style than before, and this largest church in the Western world was consecrated after nearly II decades of construction on the XIVth day of March in the year 1022, the anniversary day of the disaster, by the Patriarch Abraam IV. The nave of the Cathedral is exceeded in size only by that of Holy Sophia herself in Kónstantinopolis.

The King's Palace is noted for its opulence and its hanging gardens, a rooftop array of exotic plants brought from the four quarters of the world. Not to be missed by any visitor to the capital city is the Queen's Zoo, which includes examples of creatures from the IV quarters of the world, as well as the legendary "wild man" of Torenth, who was captured in the mountains of Arjenol, and brought to Beldour in chains III inches thick, there to be put on display for all to see.

The city proper consists of II distinct parts, these being Old Beldour, or that section of the town which occupies the left bank of the River Beldour, and includes the old city walls, the King's Palace, the Cathedral of Saint Constantine and the Patriarch's chancellery, the Abbey of Saint Theophanés, the Keep of Legalsó Vár (the "Hole") and its Chapel of Saint Ambrosios the Base, Saint Ptolemy's House (the official State Archives of Torenth), Saint Alexios's House (the official Church Archives of Torenth), and the *Megalé tou Genous Scholé* (the chief training school for Deryni); and New Beldour, or that section of the town which occupies the right bank of the River Beldour, and includes the Queen's Zoo, the Great Marketplace, the University of Beldour, and most of the residences of the Great Lords. The diverse sections of the city are linked by the great stone span of Saint Basil's Bridge, one of the largest in the known world, which was constructed by the King Arkady II and completed and dedicated on the XVIth day of June in the year 1042. [*King Kelson's Bride*].

PATRIARCHS OF BELDOUR AND ALL TORENTH

Saint Agapitos ho Hieromonachos	355-368
Taurasios Andropompos	368-375
Euphaës apo Anzas	375-377
Paulos I apo Heilandou	377-384

Démétrios apo Labernou	384-388
Symeón I apo Temmekoulas	388-399
Saint Ióannés I apo Kouachellas	399-401
Barsés apo Polykaón	401
León I apo Phelanou	401-432
Prótogenés apo Barstou	432-433
Stratonikos apo Kabazonis	433-438
Ióannés II ho Neleus	438-440
León II apo Phintas	440-451
Kónstantinos apo Heméthou	451-454
Abraam I apo Hespeirias	454-469
Daniél apo Chinou	469-477
Audaxios I apo Cheiriballeiou	477-482
Sóphronios Pontos	482-485
Paulos II ho Adelphos	486-497
Thómas I Lakestadés	497-501
Damianos apo Kalimésas	501-507
Paulos III Agesipolis	507-511
Barrhadadés apo Ioukaipas	511-513
Kelsos apo Beirlakou Megalou	513
Saint Stephanos I apo Belokephaleias	513-544
Eudoxios I Balsamón	544-546
Héliadés ho Phourstanos	546-555
Sabinianos apo Morongou	555-558
Aphthonios apo Eindiou	559-560
Bassos I apo Ioukkas	561-566
Ióannés III Meltasios	566-581
Euorkios apo Déboras	581-591
Eustathios Alexandridés	591-600
Gamalinos I apo Rialtas	600-619
Athanasios I Agobardos	619-620
Markos I apo Bómontou	620-625
Dabid Xanthopoulos	625-633
Paulos IV Boukolión	633-634
Patrikios apo Banninou	634-651
Stylianos ho Leuis	651-666
Meletios Metaxakés apo Phontanas	666-678
Marinianos apo Kóltonis	679-680
Ouranios apo Bernardeinou	680-694
Marión apo Ratotou	694-698
Antónios I Epizélos	698-703
Akouilinos Homogalax	703-711
Kandidos Pléktron	711-718
Kosmas Arkteios	719-725
Stephanos II Laudikianos	725-734
Theodotos Klaudianos	734-752
Philotheos Stauroulés	752-754
Theodóros I Zemuros	754-777
Timotheos I apo Malbinou	777-779
Euphratión Subikos	779-781
Alexandros Zakchaios	781-790
Panolbios Tancheus	791-799
Ióannés IV Arabianos	799-815
Stephanos III Hérakleidés	815-818
Kyrión I Bubékos	818-822
Philoxenos I h'Opoi	822-834
Theodóros II apo Arzenolou	834-838
Stephanos IV Ouiboullios	838-862
Syrikios apo Kaloxou	862-863
Augaros ho Phérentios	863-865
Asterios ho Phourstanos	865-868
Isidóros ho Karlobichos	868-875
Theodóritos apo Tolánou	875-890
Ióannés V Phlabios	890-893
Sergios I Perseus apo Kalexikou	893-898
Porphyrios I Trósidamas	898-901
Sergios II apo Ouilliersou	901-905
Antiochos apo Khannibalou	905-922
Eusebios I Phourstanos-Sittichos	922-935
Eunomios apo Beldourou	935-942
Loukas apo Derkou	943-944
Andreas Bezprémios	944-948
Rhouphinos apo Phrangipaniou	948-961
Eusebios II Morlaios apo Perris	961-966
Abraam II Zacharias	966-969
Abraam III Prémyslabos	969-975
Archelaos Ungnados	976-988
Olympios Gutkéledos	988-994
Kyrión II Baksos apo Alkantrou	994-1003
Markos II ho Phourstanos	1003-1016
Abraam IV Kórbinos	1016-1025
Timotheos II huios Rhouphinou	1025-1033
Athanasios II Hokhanémsos	1033-1048
Philoxenos II Góritzos	1048
Symeón II Leónardés	1049-1054
Eudoxios II Inzagios	1055-1059
Stephanos V ho Phourstanos	1059-1066
Ióannés VI apo Adelphiou	1066-1070
Thómas II apo Beldourou	1071-1077
Bassos II apo Porteris	1077-1081
Antónios II apo Ortenbourgou	1081-1086
Audaxios II Héliadés	1086-1088
Ióannés VII Babenbourgos	1088-1098
Athanasios III huios Ollamkhou	1098-1106
Gamalinos II apo Ouiegdegou	1106-1113
Porphyrios II apo Iphphou	1113-1121
Aristarchos apo Bonaldou	1121-1123
Alpheios apo Kouinkiou (de Quincy)	1123-1130+

Bened. He was *cyann* or chief of the hill people at Saint Kyriell's, and a member of the Quorial. He took King Kelson and Dhugal Duke of Cassan prisoner when they emerged from the string of underground tombs beneath the Lendour Mountains on the xth day of April in the year 1125. *Quem sæpe transit casus aliquando invenit*. [*The Quest for Saint Camber*].

Benedict, Abbot and Saint. This early monk was born in the vth century A.D. in the County of Nersia in Rûm, and about the year 500 joined a community of like-minded individuals near Affilia. Finding even the company of such holy men confining, he retired to a cave near Sybiako to live the hermit's traditional life. But he could not escape the rumours of his own sanctity, which drew supplicants by the hundreds, forcing him to organize them into a dozen communities to save them from starvation and the elements and their own natures. Eventually he created his Holy Rule of III rings to bind them all under his wise tutelage. He died while standing in prayer before the altar of his Grand Abbey at Monte Cassan, and was buried vertically, the inscription on his tomb reading, "I stand for God." His symbol is a raven holding a piece of consecrated bread in its beak. His feastday is the xi^{th} day of July.

Benedict, Brother. This was the name used by Prince Cinhil Haldane when he became a monk of the *Ordo Verbi Dei* in the year 879. It was also the religious name of several other possible candidates investigated in the year 903 by Rhys Thuryn and Father Joram MacRorie. These included: Abel, Andrew, Henricus, John, Josephus, Matthew, Robert, and Rolf. [*Camber of Culdi*; *Saint Camber*].

Benjamin, Father. He was a seminarian at the *Arx Fidei* establishment who was ordained with Denis Arilan on the IInd day of February in the year 1105. His elderly mother was present at the ceremony. ["The Priesting of Arilan"].

Bennett. He was serving as a sergeant with Bran Coris Earl of Marley in June of the year 1121. *Ajutati, che Dio l'ajuti*. [*High Deryni*].

Benoît *Ralson d'Evering*, **Lord, Auxiliary Bishop of Valoret.** He was born on the IIIrd day of March in the year 1078, being the second son of Anselme Ralson Baron d'Evering and Guarine Lady Meulent. He was a candidate for the office of Bishop of Meara in November of 1123, but was passed over in favor of Henry Istelyn. However, he was elected Auxiliary Bishop of Valoret at the Synod of Valoret on the XXIst day of March in the year 1125, and was saying mass at the Cathedral there II days later when the survivors of the King's quest returned to the city. [*The Bishop's Heir*; *The Quest for Saint Camber*].

Beren, Sir. This Michaeline knight was present at the Battle of Iomaire on the XXVth day of June in the year 905. [*Saint Camber*].

Berrhones Neilos Ambrosiou *von Shandis*, **Count Castlerodh.** He was born on the XXIInd day of January in the Year of Our Lord 1055, being the youngest son of Ambrosios Neilou Graf von Shandis and Niké Lady Kallithrix. He intermarried with the Lady Hybla daughter of Sillón Lord Makróry, on the XIIth day of October in the year 1081, and by her he had children: the Hereditary Count Neilos, whose children include Lord Raduslav; the Lord Aristobolos; the Lord Misaél; the Lady Kallimaché; the Lady Démétria; the Lady Athénaïs; the Lord Sisyphos.

Lord Berrhones came to court at Beldour as a young man in the year 1074, where he soon attached himself to the King's Chief Minister, Hésychios Prótomenés. When Nimur II succeeded to the throne on the XIIth day of May in the year 1080, Berrhones became part of that monarch's inner circle of advisors, and remained at the center of Torenthi politics for a half century. He participated in the *killijálay* of King Nimur on the Ist day of January in the year 1081. He served as Vizier of the Duchy of Beldouria from the Vth day of June in the year 1085 through the middle of 1095, as Chancellor of the Exchequer of the Kingdom of Torenth from the XIIth day of July in the year 1095 through the end of the reign of King Carolus III, and Grand Vizier of the Kingdom of Torenth from the Ist day of April in the year 1111 through the end of the reign of King Wencit. He was created Count Castlerodh by King Nimur II in appreciation of his services to the Crown on the XIIth day of January in the year 1105, his estate being located in the Duchy of Sasovna.

After the death of King Wencit on the IInd day of July in the year 1121, he retired from state service to write his history, the first volume of which was published as *Memoirs of Fifty Years at Court* in 1122. A IInd book, *The Life of King Nimur II*, appeared in the year 1125, and a IIIrd volume, *The Life of King Wenzel II*, in 1129. *Ficus ficus, ligonem ligonem vocat*.

Campbell de Broun has called these books "...very useful when one is journeying. They have often given me a laugh where I least expected to find one, and have kept the rain off my head in the most depressing of climes; I have found them especially helpful when dealing with the traveler's complaint." However, Eustathios apo Oinou has called them "...the most important contemporary treatises on the inner workings of the Torenthi monarchy."

In the year 1128 he was brought out of retirement by the Regent Mahael II to act as Master of Ceremonies at the *killijálay* for King Liam Lajos II, scheduled to be held on the XVIth day of July in that year. On the XIth day previous, Count Czalsky, who was to represent the Western quarter for the installation ceremony, was found foully murdered, and King Kelson was asked to replace him. Count Berrhones was instrumental in helping to train Kelson for his participation.

In March of the year 1129 he chaired a commission at the request of King Liam Lajos to investigate the death of King Alroy Arion II. He later wrote another book about his experiences, *Regents' Regicide Revealed*, which was issued in the Fall of that year and widely circulated in the XI Regni, to much acclaim and comment. [*King Kelson's Bride*].

Bertie *MacArdry*. This young borderman was wounded in a skirmish with outlaws at Trurill on the XXIVth day of November in the year 1123, and was then tended by Dhugal Lord MacArdry. *Les hommes sonts rares*. [*The Bishop's Heir*].

Bertrand *de Ville*, **Sir**. He was born on the XVIIIth day of February in the Year of Our Lord 901, being the son of Sir Bernard de Ville and Astoria Lady Sacheverell. He was serving as a squire to Prince Javan in the year 917, and was sent by Tavis to bring Rhys Thuryn to heal the Prince on the XXIVth day of December in that year. On the XXIIIrd day of June in the year 921 he accompanied Sir Charlan as one of the knights sent by King Alroy to fetch Prince Javan back to Court. He was present at Alroy's death later that day, and was ordered by the new King Javan to bring the Healer Oriel to him. He attended the coronation of King Javan on the XXXIst day of July in the year 921. He was sent North by King Javan on the XXIst day of April in the year 922 to confirm the report that Master Revan had return to his baptizing on the River Eirian, and was himself baptized; he reported back to the Council before the end of that month. He was slain with his monarch by the former Regents on the XIth day of May in the year 922, aged XXI years. R.I.P. [*Camber the Heretic*; *King Javan's Year*].

Bethane *Romsey*. She was born in the Year of Our Lord 1051. She intermarried with Darrell Master Romsey, a teacher of mathematics at the University of

Grecotha, and by him she had a child who was born still; he was killed on the Vth day of April in the year 1068 defending Deryni children from persecution. She saw the IV McLain and Morgan children playing together near Culdi on the IIIrd day of August in the year 1100, and helped set Alaric's broken arm after he fell out of a tree. Later she lived as a witch-woman and shepherdess in a cave in the hills above Culdi. She had some small inkling of Deryni magic, but her misbegotten love spell, purchased by the architect Rimmell, went sadly awry and accidentally killed the Lady Bronwyn and her betrothed, Kevin McLain, on the XXIXth day of March in the year 1121. The King ordered that a search be made for her after this incident, but she was never found. According to the *Chronicles*, "...She was an ancient crone in tattered rags. Her face was seamed and weathered, surrounded by a mane of matted grey hair once dark. Her black eyes flashed, her teeth were yellow and rotted, her breath foul." ["Bethane"; *Deryni Checkmate*; *King Kelson's Bride*].

Bethenar. The banners of this ancient Gwyneddan Barony were present in the army of Kelson King of Gwynedd in June of the year 1121. [*High Deryni*].

Bevan *de Torigny*, Bishop of Culdi, sometime Abbot of the *Ordo Vox Dei*. He was born on the XXIXth day of February in the Year of Our Lord 1060. He joined the *Ordo Vox Dei* in the year 1072, and was elected Abbot of the Order on the XIIth day of May in the year 1099. He was also known as a respected lecturer at the University of Grecotha. He was consecrated an itinerant Bishop of Gwynedd on the XIXth day of January in the year 1122, and was elected to the see of Culdi at the Synod of Valoret on the XVIIIth day of March in the year 1125. He was celebrating mass at All Saints' Cathedral later that same day when Duncan arrived at Valoret with news of Tiercel's death. He assiduously supported King Kelson and the restoration of the cult of Saint Camber. *Conscientia mille testes.* [*The Quest for Saint Camber*].

Bevis *de Clyde*, Father. This monk was sent from Saint Iveagh's Abbey to inform Kelson King of Gwynedd of the escape of ex-Archbishop Edmund Loris from his prison cell in November of the year 1123. [*The Bishop's Heir*].

Birgit *Subalter* O'Carroll. She was born on the Xth day of March in the Year of Our Lord 897. She intermarried with Ursin O'Carroll on the XIIth day of June in the year 916, and by him she had one son: Carrollan. She was imprisoned with her child beginning in the year 917 to act as hostages for her Deryni husband's service to the Regents, and was still being held captive in March of the year 922. She and her child were rescued from the massacre at the River Eirian on the XIth day of May in that year. Her date of death is unknown. [*King Javan's Year*].

Blaine I Godomar Radislaus *Furstán-Festil*, King of Gwynedd, Duke of Rhemuth. The fourth King of the House of Festil was born on the XVIIIth day of December in the Year of Our Lord 842, being the third son and fourth child of Festil III King of Gwynedd and Dionysia daughter of Andronikos Thópis, Stratégos and Despotés of Esklavonia. He intermarried with Pasqualetta Contessa di Barbarico di Torenti on the IVth day of September 868, and by her he had children: the Hereditary Prince and Duke Festil, dead at age V from the yellow mouth; the Prince Rubin, dead at VI weeks of the running sores; the Princess Bartolommea, who married a gardener without her father's permission (by whom she had a daughter, Andronika, whose fate is unknown), and was shut away in a convent, dying there of grief at age XXII; the Princess Ariella later Queen of Gwynedd; the Princess Laudamia, who intermarried with Klaudios III Autokratór of Byzantyun; the Hereditary Prince Imre later Duke of Rhemuth later King of Gwynedd.

As the IIIrd son of his father, the Prince Blaine was destined for the Church, and was ordained priest on the IXth day of March in the year 860 and consecrated Bishop on the XXXIst day of May in the year 862. On the XXIst day of May in the year 867 he was elected Archbishop of Rhemuth, but resigned his see and renounced his priestly vows with the permission of Thomas Archbishop Primate of Gwynedd on the IIIrd day of June in the following year. For the Prince's elder brother, the Hereditary Prince and Duke Imre, had forsaken his wife, being besotted by the beauteous male concubine, Antinoös "the God." Since the King Festil's only grandson had died young, the Prince Blaine agreed to marry forthwith and produce an heir.

The Prince Blaine was created Duke of Rhemuth on the Xth day of April in the year 872. He succeeded his father on the VIth day of March in the year 885, and was crowned on the Ist day of May following by Archbishop Ursul. One of his first acts as King was to have his Gabrilite confessor create a new transfer portal at the Basilica in Rhemuth. He traveled to Beldour to render homage to Imre II King of Torenth in August of that year, and spent a month there visiting with his cousins. While he was absent from Gwynedd his uncle, Rudolf von Festil-Carthmoor Archbishop of Rhemuth, suddenly died of the spotted pox, prompting a protest by the population of that town in favour of the native clergy. The uprising quickly spread throughout the region to support the restoration of the Haldane monarchy in the person of Cathyr Baron Carrach, a descendant of the old human dynasty, being the eldest son of Gwyddno the son of Calatin the son of Gwalchmai Baron Carrach and the Princess Aurora daughter of King Bearand Haldane. King Blaine rushed back from Beldour in September accompanied by CC men, rallied his troops at Valoret, and defeated the upstart's army XX leagues North of Rhemuth on the XXVIth day of September. The Pretender Cathyr was executed together with all of his family on the Xth day of October, and the King ordered the abandonment of Rhemuth and the destruction of the Cathedral there. In October of the year 888 King Blaine visited Tor Caerrorie, and was hunting with Camber Earl of Culdi and Countess Jocelyn when the estate was attacked by bandits.

Guigues describes this monarch as "...stern, unsmiling, a hard taskmaster, whose belief in the strictures of the Old Testament was far stronger than his use for the New. He was loved neither by his family nor his people." Bonifacio di Musachi comments, however, "...that for all his sternness, he was at heart a fair man, decrying injustice wherever he found it. He kept a tight watch on the treasury, and punished the more outrageous elements of the Deryni nobility whenever he found them. Alas, he did not go looking very often, particularly in his later years."

King Blaine's health began to decline halfway through his reign, and he developed a cancer in his belly in the Fall of the year 899. After suffering through VI months of increasing agony, only partially mitigated by drugs and Healers, he passed from this world on the XXVIIIth day of February in the year 900, aged LVII years. He is said to have stated on the day before his death that "he was now paying for his sins on earth, that he never should have renounced his vocation, which was a true one, that he had never wanted to be King, but had done the best that he could with what he was given, and that he hoped God would forgive him." He was buried with great honours in the crypt of his ancestors in All Saints' Cathedral at Valoret. He was succeeded by his only surviving son, Prince Imre. R.I.P. ["Catalyst"; *Camber of Culdi*; *The Harrowing of Gwynedd*].

Boggy Hillman or "Boghill." This Kheldour strongman and giant challenged Geordie Lord Drummond in April of the year 905. He lost. [*Deryni Challenge*].

Boniface, Father. This priest, calligrapher, and illuminator at Saint Hilary's Basilica in Rhemuth was appointed confessor to Prince Javan on the VIIth day of March in the year 918. Although human, he had made a study of the ancient Deryni authors, and over the years had collected a number of rare scrolls authored by them which he kept in his private library in the chapel of the Basilica. He died on the VIth day of November in the year 920, and was replaced by Father Ascelin. R.I.P. [*The Harrowing of Gwynedd*; *King Javan's Year*].

Bonner II *Sinclair*, **Earl of Tarleton.** He was born on the VIth day of September in the Year of Our Lord 899, being the only son and heir of Peter Earl of Tarleton and Saskia Lady O'Conor. He intermarried with Virbena Lady Spriggans on the IInd day of September in the year 918, and by her he had children: the Hereditary Count Tudur later Baron Sinclair; the Lady Paulina; the Lord Albert; the Lady Dauphine.

On the XXIXth day of January in the year 918 he succeeded to the title on his father's resignation, and occasionally sat in for him on the Royal Council of Gwynedd. On the XXVth day of May in that year he presented King Alroy and Prince Javan with a pair of ferrets for their birthday celebration. On the XXVth day of June in the year 928 he was asked to join the Royal Council for the meeting called by Archbishop Hubert on that day, and there he first heard the news of his father's death. He died in the year 948, aged XLVIII years; his title was attainted and reverted to the Crown, but his eldest son was allowed to retain the older family title of Baron Sinclair. R.I.P. [*The Harrowing of Gwynedd*; *King Javan's Year*; *The Bastard Prince*].

Borg. He was serving as an archer in the service of Manfred Earl of Culdi during June of the year 928. He was called by his master to examine the injury to the hand of King Rhys Michael on the XXIInd day of that month, and then gave the monarch his horse. [*The Bastard Prince*].

Bors. This Gwyneddan soldier was serving Coel Lord Howell in November of the year 903. By order of his master he followed Father Joram MacRorie to Saint John's Church. [*Camber of Culdi*].

Botolph. This Forcinni was serving as a horse-keeper at Valoret Castle in the year 917. The Princes Javan and Rhys Michael bought him a fine cambric shirt embroidered with the odd geometric cross-stitching of his homeland at the fair held in Valoret on the XXVIIIth day of May in that year. [*Camber the Heretic*].

Bradene *de Tourz*, **Archbishop Primate of Valoret and All Gwynedd, sometime Bishop of Grecotha.** This learned primate was born in Fallon on the IVth day of November in the Year of Our Lord 1067, being the third son of Bernardin Sieur de Tourz and Mahaut Lady Tonnère. He entered the Church in Bremagne, and was ordained there by Patriarch Philippus II on the XXIVth day of October in the year 1085. He came to Gwynedd in the year 1088 to study at the University of Grecotha, and soon became known as one of the chief scholars of the realm. Father Bradene was elected an itinerant Bishop on the Xth day of May in the year 1108, and was advanced to the See of Grecotha on the XXIIIrd day of March in the year 1117, serving with great distinction. He remained neutral during the Interdict Schism of the year 1121.

At the Council of Rhemuth on the XIIth day of January in the year 1122 Bishop Bradene was elected Archbishop of Valoret and Primate of All Gwynedd to replace the deposed Archbishop Edmund Loris. He remained faithful to the Crown of Gwynedd during the troubles that marked the early years of King Kelson, and became the rock on which the Church structure was ultimately rebuilt. He annointed Princess Araxie as Queen after her marriage to King Kelson on the VIIth day of August in the year 1128. *Deus hæc fortasse benigna reducet in sedem vice*. [*Deryni Checkmate*; *High Deryni*; *The Bishop's Heir*; *The King's Justice*; *King Kelson's Bride*].

Bran Borisov *Coris*, **Earl of Marley.** He was born on the XVIth day of October in the Year 1095, being the eldest surviving son and heir of Ryan Earl of Marley and Forisa Lady Howell. He intermarried with Richenda Lady of Rheljan on the XIIth day of June in the year 1116, and by her he had children: the Hereditary Count Brendan Borisov later Earl of Marley; the Lady Ysabeau Rhiannon, dead of the black mouth at age I.

Bran Coris succeeded his father on the IIIrd day of January in the year 1114. In the year 1121 he initially supported Kelson King of Gwynedd, and took a force of MM men to protect the region below Cardosa from the invasion of Wencit King of Torenth. He sent his wife and child for protection to the Free City of Dhassa. However, he allowed himself to be subverted by Wencit's magic during the Summer of that year, and was eventually killed in the duel arcane between Kelson

King of Gwynedd and King Wencit at Llyndruth Meadows on the IInd day of July in the year 1121. He was XXV years of age at his death. Although Bran was ajudged traitor, his young son was allowed to succeed as Earl, and his widow intermarried with Alaric Morgan Duke of Corwyn on the Ist day of May in the year 1122.

He is described in Volumen III of the *Chronicles* as a "...good tactician and leader of men, and extremely generous to those who supported him. He has gold brown eyes and a certain set to the handsome mouth which betokened stubborness and determination." [*Deryni Rising*; *High Deryni*; *The Bishop's Heir*; *The King's Justice*; *The Quest for Saint Camber*; *King Kelson's Bride*].

Branyng II Dioniz Albrecht *von Furstán-Sostra*, Count of Sostra. He was born on the Vth day of May in the Year of Our Lord 1098, being the second but eldest surviving son of Branyng I Count of Sostra and the Countess Janka daughter of Passarion Duke of Jándrich. He never married. The Count Branyng succeeded his father on the XVth day of June in the year 1126, and quickly established himself at the Torenthi Court as one of the favorites of Mahael II Duke d'Arjenol and Regent of Torenth. On the IXth day of July in the year 1128 he and Rasoul gave Kelson King of Gwynedd a tour of the city of Beldour. He became involved in the *Killijálay* Conspiracy against King Liam Lajos II, and was killed while participating in the psychic attack upon the king on the XVIth day instant. He was branded a traitor, but his cousin, Duke Yoánn, was allowed to succeed to the title, subject to payment of a tithe to the Crown for a period of X years. At the time of his death, he was courting Princess Morag. He had braided sidelocks. [*King Kelson's Bride*].

Brecon Jolyon Jameson *Ramsay-Quinnell*, Earl of Kilarden, Earl of Culdi *jure uxoris*, Hereditary Duke of Laas, Sir. He was born on the XIIth day of June in the Year of Our Lord 1103, being the eldest son and heir of Sir Jolyon Ramsay later Duke of Laas and Oksana Lady d'Enghieux. He was betrothed to the Princess Richelle Haldane Countess of Culdi in the Summer of the year 1127, and intermarried with her on the XXXIst day of July in the year 1128, and by her he had a child: the Lord Richard Albert Jolyon Hereditary Count of Kilarden and Culdi.

Sir Brecon Ramsay was created Earl of Kilarden on the day of his wedding in the year 1128, the title being called out of abeyance in his favour by King Kelson. On the Ist day of September in that year, he publicly and irrevocably renounced before an assembly of the Mearan nobility at Laas all pretensions to the throne of Meara for himself and his descendants. He was of middling height, with sandy hair tied behind his head, and dark eyes. [*King Kelson's Bride*].

Bremagne. The region which later comprised the Kingdom of Bremagne was conquered by the Byzantyun Emperor Augoustos I in the year 9 B.C., who called his new province Britannia Magna and his capital city Augoustopolis. The original Byzantyun settlements were located along the coast of the Southern Sea, but gradually expanded inland to the Autuni Mountains. By the year 200 the Province included most of the states now known as Bremagne, Fallon, and Jáca. The Byzantyun Empire began to disintegrate at the beginning of the Vth century, when Haldane and Carthmoor were progressively and rapidly abandoned. Fallon was evacuated in the year 433, and the last Byzantyun coastal outposts were withdraw to the East in the year 466, with the remaining settlers left to fend for themselves.

Different regions quickly began quarreling with each other, and a half dozen small states gradually came into being, the largest of these being the County of Magne. The Counts of this state gradually subsumed the others, until Erispoé Méen declared himself Roi de Bremagne on the Ist day of December in the year 555. The succession passed to the cadet line of Faucon in the year 793.

In the year 842 rebellion broke out in the Northern Province of Fallon, and after a year of fighting, that state declared its independence under its first King, Hennequin d'Albéric, on the XXVIIth day of July in the year 843, with the boundary line being set at the River Laval.

The Kingdom of Bremagne is known for its mild, wet climate and gentle sea breezes. Like Gwynedd, Bremagne and Fallon were christianized by missionaries from Rûm, and they use the Latin language in their liturgies. The Head of the Bremagni Church is the Patriarch, who resides at the old capital of Augusteville, but the Kings of Bremagne removed their secular government to a new capital at Rémigny in the year 910. King Théofrid II later built a beautiful summer palace, Millefleurs, on the Baie des Fleurs. The rolling green pastures of Bremagne support many different crops and herds, and the Kingdom has remained consistently prosperous over the centuries.

As Campbell de Broun once said, "The land itself is lovely, covered with forests and well-kept fields of crops, but the people of Bremagne are very rude to foreigners. We stopped one night at a little café near Millflower [sic], and asked the boorish proprietor for a bottle of wine and loaf of bread. He would not accept our good Mearan coin, and threw us out without so much as a cup of water. He had the bad grace to curse us as we left, hungry and without shelter for the night. It began to rain. It rains every day in Bremagne. Plainly, this is not Cloome." [*King Kelson's Bride*].

KINGS OF BREMAGNE

HOUSE OF ERISPOÉ

Erispoé Méen	555-577
Hoël le Magne (son)	577-598
Meyric I (son)	598-609
Gurmhaillon (son)	609-635
Judicaël (nephew)	635-645
Chilperich (brother)	645-651
Pléon (brother)	651-673
Mériadec (son)	673-680
Ursion I (brother)	680-701
Gisloald (cousin)	701-722
Adalbéron I (son)	722-762
Ursion II (son)	762-777
Ryol I (son)	777-793

HOUSE OF FAUCON

Faucon I (second cousin)	793-820
Déodat (son)	820-822
Faucon II (brother)	822-841
Gérard (nephew)	841-855
Quintin (uncle)	855
Enguerrand (grandson)	855-886
Théofrid I (brother)	886-893
Adalbéron II (brother)	893-894
Manassès (son)	894-919
Leothéric (son)	919-942
Valentin (son)	942-944
Joscerand I (brother)	944-947
Théofrid II (brother)	947-977
Raculphe I (grandson of Manassès)	977-989
Harduin (grandson)	989-1006
Théofrid III (brother)	1006-1031
Otton (uncle)	1031-1033
Joscerand II (son)	1033-1050
Théofrid IV (son)	1050-1055
Raculphe II (brother)	1055-1076
Charibert (nephew)	1076-1107
Meyric II (brother)	1107-1118
Ryol II (son)	1118-1130+

Bren Tigan. This ancient Deryni dance was performed at Michaelmas by the King Imre and his sister the Princess Ariella in the year 903. *Nous dansons sur un volcan.* [*Camber of Culdi*].

Brendan Borisov *Coris*, Earl of Marley. He was born on the IInd day of June in the Year of Our Lord 1117, being the eldest son and heir of Bran Earl of Marley and Richenda Lady of Rheljan. He was sent with his mother to Dhassa for safety in the Spring of the year 1121. His treacherous father was killed in a duel arcane on the IInd day of July in that year; even so, Lord Brendan was confirmed as Earl in July of the year 1123 by King Kelson, and became the ward of his stepfather, Alaric Duke of Corwyn, with his mother serving as Regent of Marley. He served as page to his Morgan during the Mearan expedition in the year 1124, and accompanied him in March of the year 1125 when Alaric returned to Coroth from Rhemuth. He traveled with his stepfather and Saer Earl of Rhendall to Desse in June of the year 1128, where he participated in escorting the emissaries from Torenth, Rasoul and Count Mátyás, from the port of Desse to Rhemuth. He also accompanied King Kelson to Beldour in Torenth in early July of that year. His arms are: *or*, an eagle displayed *azure*. [*The Bishop's Heir*; *The King's Justice*; *The Quest for Saint Camber*; *King Kelson's Bride*].

Brice *de Paor*, Baron of Trurill. He was born on the IInd day of December in the Year of Our Lord 1082, being the eldest surviving son of Brothen Baron of Trurill and Calocera Lady Briel. He intermarried with Merwenna Lady MacThorlac on the XXXth day of April in the year 1107, and by her he had children: the Hereditary Lord Bronach; the Lady Briella; the Lady Bridget; the Lord Brioc. He succeeded his father on the XXIst day of June in the year 1110. In the year 1123 this border Lord was correctly suspected by King Kelson of supporting the pretensions of Caitrin Princess of Meara in her rebellion against Gwynedd. The Baron Brice escorted Edmund Loris ex-Archbishop of Valoret to Ratharkin after the latter's escape from Saint Iveagh's Abbey in November of that year. He was detailed to harass and delay the main Gwyneddan army during the Mearan Rebellion of 1124, and developed a scorched earth policy to deprive the invaders of any food or usable goods. He ravaged the convent at Saint Brigid's Abbey on the XVth day of June in that year, and burned Ratharkin on the XXIXth day instant. He was captured and executed for his crimes at Talacara on the IInd day of July in the year 1124, aged XLI years. His title was subsequently attainted by King Kelson. His arms were: two swords in saltire over a third in pale, all on an *azure* field. [*The Bishop's Heir*; *The King's Justice*].

Brigid *of Droghera*, Saint. She was born circa the year 450 at Droghera in the Culdi Highlands. She took the veil in her youth and founded the *Couvent de la Vacherie* in Logréine, later relocating it to Meara when a milk tax was imposed by a local baron. Every day she would stand in the front of her establishment and ring the cowbells to call her herds home for the milking. Hundreds of the local poor would also respond, eagerly awaiting the rounds of cheese which she would cheerfully hand out to anyone who looked sufficiently hungry and decrepit. Saint Brigid is often represented holding a *croix flambée* over her head, sometimes with a cow, and for her good works she has often been regarded as the protectress of those engaged in dairy work. She is greatly venerated in the border areas, almost as much, it is said, as the great Saint Patrick himself. Her feast is the IInd day of February.

The Convent of Saint Brigid was sacked by Brice Baron of Trurill and Ithel Prince of Meara during the Mearan Rebellion on the XVth day of June in the year 1124. Rothana Princess or Nabila of Nur Hallaj was serving there as a novice, and she provided information to King Kelson that resulted in Prince Ithel's execution for his crimes. *Guerre aux châteaux, paix aux chaumières.* [*The Quest for Saint Camber*].

Brion Donal Cinhil Urien *Haldane*, King of Gwynedd, Sir. He was born on the XXIst of June in the Year of Our Lord 1081, being the eldest son and heir of Donal Blaine II King of Gwynedd and Richeldis Princess of Howicce and Llannedd. He intermarried at Rémigny with the Princess Jehana daughter of Meyric II Roi de Bremagne and Rosaura Princess of Logréine on the VIth day of January in the year 1104, and by her he had children: the Hereditary Prince Kelson later Prince of Meara later King of Gwynedd; the Princess Rosane Marie Élisabeth Jaÿne, dead shortly after birth of the blue skin.

The Prince Brion succeeded his father on the XIVth day of November in the year 1095, and due to ill weather was not crowned until XXIVth day of March in the year 1096 by Archbishop Paul III. He was knighted by his uncle, Richard Duke of Carthmoor, on the VIth day of January in the year 1099. Subsequently he made several state visits to the United Kingdom of Howicce and Llannedd in the year 1102, and to the Kingdoms of Fallon and Bremagne during the following year; he met his future wife at Millefleurs in the Summer of the year 1103.

On the XIIIth day of June in the year 1105 he mounted an expedition to put down the rebellion of Rorik III Earl of Eastmarch. He was challenged by Hogan Gwernach the Marluk, Festillic Pretender of Gwynedd and Duke of Tolán, on the XXIst day of that month, and was then assisted by Alaric Morgan Duke of Corwyn to attain his Haldane Potential. He defeated and killed the Marluk in a duel arcane later that same day. The Queen Jehana left the King on the Vth day of July following to go into religious retreat at Saint Giles's Abbey in the Rheljan Mountains of Eastmarch, and did not return to Rhemuth until fetched by the King on the VIth day of February in the year 1106. On the I^st day of December in that year King Brion led his forces into Meara to put down a rebellion there by the Pretender Judhael, and succeeded in capturing Prince Judhael's II sons-in-law, Derek Delaney Earl of Sommerdale and Michael Lord MacDonald, plus Miran Lord Kincaid; they were executed by the King for treason on the I^st day of January following. On the XIth day of May in the year 1115 Brion knighted Sean Earl Derry and Arnaud Sieur de Vali at Rhemuth, and later that day witnessed Sean's profession of service to Alaric Morgan Duke of Corwyn.

King Brion was slain on the plain of Candor Rhea near Rhemuth by the nefarious magic of the Festillic Pretender Charissa on the I^st day of November in the year 1120, and was buried in the crypt of his ancestors at Saint George Cathedral in Rhemuth. He was XXXIX years of age at his death, and was succeeded by his son, Prince Kelson.

In *Volumen I* of the *Chronicles of the Deryni*, he is described as "...dark, lean, with a just a touch of grey beginning to show at his temples, precise black beard...wide grey eyes...[that] glittered with shrewd intelligence and wit,...with the hands of a fighting man." R.I.P. ["Swords Against the Marluk"; "Legacy"; "The Knighting of Derry"; "The Priesting of Arilan"; *Deryni Rising*; *The Bishop's Heir*; *King Kelson's Bride*].

Briony Bronwyn *de Morgan*, Lady, called "Poppin." She was born on the XXXIst day of January in the Year of Our Lord 1123, being the eldest child of Alaric Morgan Duke of Corwyn and Richenda Lady of Rheljan. She was present on the docks of Coroth to greet her father and King Kelson on their arrival there on the IInd day of July in the year 1128, and later that month traveled to Rhemuth for the royal weddings and for the official establishment of the Chapel of Saint Camber in Rhemuth Castle. She had bright blonde hair. [*The Bishop's Heir*; *The King's Justice*; *King Kelson's Bride*].

Bronwyn Rhetice *de Morgan*, Lady. She was born on the XIIth day of December in the Year of Our Lord 1095, being the only daughter of Sir Kenneth Kai Morgan and Alyce Heiress de Corwyn, and sister of Alaric Morgan Duke of Corwyn. She was with her brother Alaric at Culdi on the IIIrd day of August in the year 1100 when the latter fell out of a tree and broke his arm. She was betrothed to Kevin McLain Earl of Kierney in the Fall of the year 1120, but was killed with him at Culdi by the magic of the witch-woman Bethane on the XXIXth day of March in the year 1121. She was XXV years of age at her death, and was buried with Kevin at Saint Teilo's Church in Culdi. R.I.P. [*Deryni Rising*; *Deryni Checkmate*; *The Bishop's Heir*].

***Brotherhood of Saint Joric* (*Fraternitas Sancti Jorici*).** This Order, also called the Children of the Flowers of God (*Pueri Florum Dei*), was founded on the XIXth day of September in the year 777 by Adon newly elected Archbishop Primate of Valoret to honour the memory of Saint Joric the Gardener, his ancestor. One Chapterhouse was established at Rosemount on the Eirian River, and the grounds of this establishment became so beautiful that even the Kings of Gwynedd would make pilgrimages to stop and smell the roses there. This abbey remains one of the great scenic wonders of the Eleven Kingdoms, being filled with no less than LIV varieties of roses, plus many other flowers besides. The postulants of this Order wear robes of many hues, except for the Abbot, whose habit is green. In the year 905 the Vicar General of this Order, Father Theopompus, attended the consecration at Valoret of Alister Cullen as Bishop of Grecotha and Robert Oriss as Archbishop of Rhemuth on the IXth day of July. [*Saint Camber*].

Brustarkia. This town and the County of the same name are located in Northwestern Arjenol in Eastern Torenth. A Michaeline House-Minor was situate here in the year 917; it was I of III "outside" houses to which the Michaelines retreated in August and September. The County of Brustarkia was an appendage of the Dukes d'Arjenol, passing through a number of branches in that family. Count Teymuraz was created Count of Brustarkia by King Carolus III on the Vth day of April in the year 1109, but lost the title when he was tried *in absentia* and attainted on the Xth day of August in the year 1128. The honour was then presented by King Liam Lajos II to Mátyás Duke d'Arjenol. [*Camber the Heretic*; *King Kelson's Bride*].

Burchard, Earl of Eastmarch, Baron de Varian, General. He was born on the XVIIIth day of December in the year 1085, being the eldest son of Branwell Baron de Varian and Amaryllis Lady Udaut. He intermarried with the Lady Maire Heiress of Eastmarch and daughter of Arban Earl of Eastmarch and Crispina Baroness de Vali on the XVIth day of May in the year 1107, and by her he had children: the Hereditary Count Burwell; the Hereditary Lord Bassey; the Lady Mairyllis; the Lord Barnaby; the Lady Arbana; the Lord Crispin.

General Burchard was serving in the Gwyneddan Army under Jared Duke of Cassan in the year 1121, but together with General Gloddruth barely escaped the slaughter at Rengarth on the XXVIIIth day of June. He was created Earl of Eastmarch on the VIth day of January in the year 1122 as reward for his services in the war against Torenth, and in the right of his wife, the Heiress of Eastmarch. He was present at the Christmas Council of 1123, and again served as General in the Cassani Army during the invasion of Meara by Duncan McLain Duke of Cassan in May of the year 1124. He succeeded his father as Baron de Varian on the XXIXth day of January in the year 1126, and with the approval of King Kelson immediately designated his IInd son as heir to that title. [*High Deryni*; *The Bishop's Heir*].

Burton, Father. He was a priest of the *Custodes Fidei* in the year 918, and was present at the questioning of the Drummonds on the XXIInd day of January in that year. [*The Harrowing of Gwynedd*].

Byzantyun. She is the mother of lands, the empire of empires, the maker of civilizations. Great Byzantyun lies XXV days' journey to the South and East of Arjenol. Once on a time the Autokratores of Byzantyun controlled a mighty realm that spanned much of the known world, but by the year 430 most of the lands that now comprise the Eleven Kingdoms and Torenth had been lost to the men from the sea and the savage tribes of the North, and by the year 466 Bremagne had gone as well. But the Empire continued, albeit much reduced in land and even more in numbers; and the Great King of Kings, the Autokratór, the Mighty King, the King of the IV Parts of the World, still presides from his gold-encrusted throne in Kónstantinopolis; and the Hieropatriarchés, the Protector of the Holy Lands, the Custodian of the Sacred Chrism and the True Cross of Christ, continues to proclaim his sacred status as first among equals of the XII autocephalous sees of the True Church. Byzantyun shall live forever!

KAISARES AND AUTOKRATÓRES OF BYZANTYUN

HOUSE OF IOULIOS

Ioulios I "Basileios"	45-17
Augoustos I "Huios" (son)	17 BC-17
Tiberios I "Iaspis" (stepson)	17-42
Klaudios I "Progeneios" (nephew)	42-58
Britannikos I "Talaurinos" (son)	58-79
Ioulios II "Gnóstos" (son)	79-84
Bespasianos I "Locheos" (brother)	84-111
Ioulios III "Pannychis" (son)	111-138
Adrianos "Hyderos" (cousin)	138-145
Antóninos "Zomos" (son)	145-167
Markos I "Xouthos" (son)	167-188
Klaudianos I "Phthegma" (nephew)	188-212
Philippos I "Médos" (brother)	212-218
Ióannés I "Pomphos" (brother)	218-223
Basileios I "Megas" (son)	223-262
Ioulios IV "Hyperorios" (son)	262-263
Ioulianos "Parnops" (brother)	263-288
Ioustos "Démopithékos" (brother)	288-301
Ióannés II "Paróos" (son)	301-318
Augoustos II "Thlikos" (son)	318-345
Ióannés III "Polykteanos" (son)	345-363
Britannikos II "Epaktór" (son)	363-404
Klaudios II "Lispos" (son)	404-406
Ioustinos "Proponos" (uncle)	406-410
Augoustos III "Harpagmos" (grandson)	410-443
Markos II "Antónios" (son)	443-459
Basileios II "Eusebés" (brother)	459-468
Markos III "Borypus" (son)	468-488
Kosmas I "Psellos" (brother)	488-491
Basileios III "Physa" (brother)	491-506
Titos "Hypobléden" (son)	506-539
Philippos II "Metaboulos" (usurper)	539
Titianos or Titos II "Gelós" (son of Titos)	539-545
Klaudianos II "Thiasótés" (son)	545-581
Markianos I "Polykaés" (brother)	581-591
Markos IV "Markianidés" (son)	591-599
Stephanos "Diabolos" (brother)	599-606
Michaél "Nikétór" (cousin)	606-651
Kypriana "Euetéria" (daughter)	651-652
Aimilianos "Philométor" (son)	652-666
Markos V "Philadelphos" (brother)	666-678
Markos VI "Philopatór" (son)	678-699
Bespasianos II "Kallinikos" (son)	699-728
Kosmas II "Belos" (son)	728-733
Augoustos IV "Karyon" (nephew)	733-759
Démétrios I "Ptóchikos" (son)	759-786
Augoustos V "Tetrax" (son)	786-808
Pausanias "Pythikos" (cousin)	808-811
Antiochos "Magos" (son)	811-830
Markos VII "León" (grandson of Démétrios)	830-837
Ioulios V "Enkyklos" (brother)	837-852
Kónstantios "Leirion" (son)	852-875
Klaudios III "Eutornos" (son)	875-898
Amoena "Boukolé" (wife)	898
Basileios IV "Chalkenchés" (son)	898-933
Klaudios IV "Zacholos" (son)	933-944
Démétrios II "Eumenés" (son)	944-978
Démétrios III "Hustryx" (son)	978-995
Angelos I "Anthrédón" (son)	995-1010
Kónstas "Oreiocharés" (brother)	1010-1018
Angelos II "Melanossos" (son)	1018-1056
Augousta "Thea" (daughter)	1056-1070
Andronikos "Mikros" (husband)	1070-1087
Angelos III "Demosios" (son)	1087-1089
Markianos II "Kachrys" (brother)	1089-1116
Tiberios II "Ornithogonos" (son)	1116-1130+

Caball MacArdry, Lord, Tanist of Clan MacArdry. He was born on the IVth day of June in the Year of Our Lord 1088, being the eldest son of Autry Lord MacArdry and Gwladys Lady of Ballymar, and great-grandson of Ardal Earl of Transha and Malya Lady McLain youngest daughter of Sir Roger McLain. He was serving as Castellan of Castle Transha in November of the year 1123, and was the next Tanist to the Clan's chieftainship after Dhugal MacArdry Earl of Transha. After the death of Clan Chief Caulay MacArdry Earl of Transha on the I[st] day of December in that year, and in the absence of the old Earl's heir, Dhugal MacArdry, Caball assumed temporary command of Castle Transha. *O bone custos, salve: columen vero familiæ*. [*The Bishop's Heir*].

Caeriesse. According to the troubadour Lord Llewelyn, this was the XIth part of the Eleven Kingdoms, which sank beneath the sea about the year 525. Accurate records describing the fate and even the location of Caeriesse are scarce. It may have lain off Kierney in the Gulf of Kheldour, or in the Atalantic Ocean to the West. [*Camber of Culdi*].

Caerrorie, Tor. This was the principal residence of Camber Earl of Culdi, being located a few hours' ride Northeast of Valoret. Following the attainder of the MacRorie clan in the year 917, it later served briefly as the seat of Manfred MacInnis, before he built a new manor house to the West. It passed through II families before becoming the property of the Earls of Carcashale, and belonged to Earl Thomas in the year 1125. King Kelson visited the ruins of Tor Caerrorie in March of that year on his quest for the relics of Saint Camber, and examined the ruined burial chamber there. [*Camber of Culdi*; *Saint Camber*; *Camber the Heretic*; *The Harrowing of Gwynedd*; *The Quest for Saint Camber*].

Caitrin Caren Urracca *Quinnell,* **called "Cate," Sovereign Prince and Pretender of Meara, Queen of Meara and Cassan.** This notorious Princess was born on the XXVIIIth day of December in the Year of Our Lord 1065, being the eldest daughter and heir of Judhael III Prince and Pretender of Meara and the Princess Aude daughter of Fergus King of Howicce. She intermarried with Derek Delaney Earl of Somerdale on the Ist day of May in the year 1100, and by him she had one son: the Hereditary Prince Jolyon, dead acroupy at age I. After her husband was executed by Brion King of Gwynedd on the Ist day of January in the year 1107, she intermarried secondly with the Lord Sicard MacArdry son of Arthur Earl of Transha on the IXth day of March in that year, and by him she had children: the Hereditary Prince Ithel, hanged for his crimes in the year 1124; the Prince Llewell, beheaded in the year 1124 for murdering his sister; the Princess Sidana, who intermarried with Kelson King of Gwynedd, and was murdered on her wedding day in the year 1124 by her brother Prince Llewell.

The Princess Caitrin, called "Cate" by her family, succeeded to the pretensions of her father at his death on the XIVth day of February in the year 1109. During the year 1123 she plotted to reestablish Meara as an independent principality, and began a rebellion against Kelson King of Gwynedd in December of that year, declaring herself Queen of Meara and Cassan on the XVIIth day of that month. She laid claim to the latter territory under an ancient treaty of mutual succession made between the two branches of the House of Quinnell in the year 770. When in the following year her IInd husband was killed and his army routed on the IIIrd day of July in the year 1124, and all of her children had died as a result of her actions, together with her nephew, Bishop Judhael, she was deposed on the XIIth day of that month, and sent to Saint Giles's Abbey for the rest of her days to contemplate her many sins. She died there on the XXIst day of October in the year 1127, aged LXI years. [*The Deryni Archives*; *The Bishop's Heir*; *The King's Justice*; *The Quest for Saint Camber*].

Calam. This sovereign Grand Duchy is located on the central coast of The Connait, surrounding the Bay of the same name, having been founded in the year 956 by Branly MacClyde, *soi-disant* Baron of Calamty. There is no truth to the story that the Grand Duke had formerly been a pirate in the Southern Sea, or that he sought refuge in The Connait to escape the punishment of hanging that had been imposed by the courts of XXII different lands (only III such states had contemned him). To the North of Calam lies the Duchy of Cyby, to the east the Principality of Arbroath and the County of Réomay, and to the South the Republic of Little Fenwick. The capital of Calam, the town of Calamaine, has been rebuilt on many separate occasions following its destruction by severe winter storms and massive tidal bores. Campbell de Broun once visited here, noting: "I first saw the calamity which is Calamaine on the Calends of April. Fortuitously, it was my last viewing of the subject, since I departed the place on the very next day, accompanied by Marigold, Meander, and dear Brother Théo." [*King Kelson's Bride*].

GRAND DUKES OF CALAM

HOUSE OF MACCLYDE

Branly I MacClyde	956-986
Gron I (son)	986-1004
Georgie (son)	1004-1038
Gron II (son)	1038-1048
Clyde (brother)	1048-1071
Destin (brother)	1071-1072
Branson (son)	1072-1092
Branly II (son)	1092-1109
Gron III (brother)	1109-1130+

Calbert, Abbot. This learned and holy man was serving as head of the *Arx Fidei* Seminary in Gwynedd during the years 1104 and 1105. ["The Priesting of Arilan"].

Caleb. He was serving as a guard of Bishop Alister Cullen's household in January of the year 917. He was assigned by Cullen to stay with Manfred's party, which had just been assaulted by rogue Deryni nobles, until help arrived. [*Camber the Heretic*].

Calvagh, Dom. He was a Healer and teacher at Saint Neot's in the year 905. His pupil, Brother Ulric, killed him in a fit of madness on the IInd day of May in that year. Both bodies were then dissected for the instruction of the other novices. R.I.P. ["The *Examen*"].

Camber Allin *MacLean,* **called "Camlin," Lord,** *de jure* **VIIth Earl of Kierney, Saint.** He was born on the XXth day of March in the Year of Our Lord 906, being the only son and heir of Adrian MacLean Master of Kierney and Mairi Lady of Nyford. On the XXXIst day of December in the year 917 his father's castle at Trurill was sacked and burned by Manfred's men, and his father and grandmother killed. He was himself tortured and crucified, but was found by Evaine and Ansel on the following day, and was healed by her with the help of her infant son, Tieg. However, the healing was imperfect, leaving his wrists too weak to wield a sword. He should have succeeded his grandfather Iain II Earl of Kierney at his death on the XIXth day of March in the year 918, but he was believed dead by the Regents, and the title was settled instead on his cousin, Lady Richeldis.

He received Deryni instruction during the 920s from Dom Rickart, Dom Queron, Father Joram MacRorie, and Bishop Niallan. By the year 928 he had become part of Joram's underground movement to save the Deryni, and resided with him at the old Michaeline Haven. He later went into exile, and is said to have married and had children. He died in the year 948, aged XLII years. He greatly resembled his cousin, Father Joram MacRorie, in appearance. R.I.P. [*Camber the Heretic*; *The Harrowing of Gwynedd*; *The Bastard Prince*].

Camber Kyriell *MacRorie*, VIIth Earl of Culdi, Archbishop Primate of Valoret and All Gwynedd, sometime Lord Chancellor of Gwynedd, sometime Lord Regent of Gwynedd, sometime Bishop of Grecotha, called *Defensor Hominum* and Kingmaker, Saint. He was born on the IIIrd day of August in the Year of Our Lord 846, being the third son of Ballard II Earl of Culdi and Ardis Lady Drummond. He intermarried with Jocelyn Lady de la Marche on the XVIIIth day of May in the year 871, and by her he had children: the Hereditary Count and Master Cathan, who was murdered by King Imre at the age of XXX years, leaving issue; the Lady Jerusha, dead at XII of the Frissian Fever; the Lord Ballard, dead at age XI of the Frissian Fever; the Lord Joram later a Michaeline priest; the Lady Ardissa, born still; the Lady Evaine, who intermarried with the Healer Rhys Thuryn.

As the IIIrd son of his father, the Lord Camber was intended for the Church, and was sent in the year 861 to the University of Grecotha, where he studied with some of the greatest minds in the realm. In religion he used the name Brother Kyriell. However, the death of his next older brother before he could take final vows made him heir to the County of Culdi, and he was asked to put his religious career aside on the XVIIIth day of August in the year 862. On the Ist day of December in the year 875 he was appointed by King Festil III to the Royal Council, and served the old King and his son, the King Blaine I, until the latter's death in the year 900. On the VIth day of January in the year 886 he was appointed Chancellor of the Kingdom of Gwynedd. On the XIth day of October in the year 888 he was out hunting with his wife Jocelyn and King Blaine I when bandits attacked his estate at Caerrorie.

He retired from active service to the Crown with the accession of King Imre on the XXVIIIth day of February in the year 900, and returned to his estates at Tor Caerrorie. On the XIVth day of November in the year 903 he traveled under the name of Kyriell with Rhys Thuryn to investigate the last of the "Brothers Benedict," and discovered and confirmed the location of the Haldane heir, Prince Cinhil, at Saint Foillan's Abbey. After the Restoration he became part of the new King's inner circle. In this capacity he participated in the War Council held on the XXIIIrd day of June in 905 at the Great Hall in Valoret Palace, being named Commander of the Culdi levies. He was believed killed II days later at Iomaire, but actually survived, taking on the guise and role of the deceased Vicar General Father Alister Cullen.

As Cullen he was secretly ordained a priest at the Michaeline Haven in the early morning hours of the IXth day of July in the year 905, and was publicly consecrated Bishop of Grecotha at Valoret later the same day, serving until 917. King Cinhil I had a special set of vestments created for him on the occasion of his consecration. He was summoned to Court on the XXXIst day of October in the year 905, and stayed there until Twelfth Night of the year 906. He was also appointed to the Royal Council and again named Chancellor of Gwynedd on the VIth day of November in the year 905. On the Ist day of August in the year 914 he baptized his grandson Tieg Joram Thuryn, a Healer, at Sheele in a special magical ceremony. As Camber he was canonized on the XIVth day of November in the year 906, and given the title *Defensor Hominum* (*Defender of Men*) and Kingmaker, being named the patron saint of Deryni magic; but his sainthood was rescinded by the Council of Ramos in the year 917.

As Cullen he was named one of the V Regents of King Alroy on the IInd day of February in the year 917, but was deposed the next day and replaced by Sighere Duke of Claibourne; he was also removed at that time from his office of Lord Chancellor. He attended the Synod of Bishops held at Valoret in November and December of 917. He was elected Archbishop Primate of Valoret and All Gwynedd on the XXIVth day of December in the year 917, being officially installed and then illegally deposed by the Regents on Christmas Day. He was attainted and outlawed by the Regents on the XXVIIth day of December. He was killed on the VIth day of January in the year 918 by the Regents' men, but was able to cast a spell, later reinforced by his daughter Evaine, that placed him in a suspended state between this world and the next. He seemed to appear at the empowerment of King Javan on the XXVIth day of June in the year 921, and also over the next II centuries in spirit form to selected individuals to influence their conduct for the positive.

According to Talbot's *Lives of the Saints*, which also included a portrait, "Toward the end of the Interregnum, Camber discovered that under controlled conditions, in select individuals, the full scope of Deryni power could be acquired by humans. He it was who assisted the heirs of the old human rulers to acquire this power, and later led the revolt which crushed the Deryni Interregnum for good." Also: "Rumours persist that Camber's alleged death in 905 never occurred, that he went into hiding to wait for a chance to reappear and again work his deeds of magic." A shrine dedicated to this saint was located at Saint Neot's in the Lendour hills, but was destroyed with that abbey in December of the year 917 by Rhun and the Regents.

Camber's status as a Saint was restored by the Church of Gwynedd in the year 1125, although no shrines were erected to his memory until King Kelson inaugurated the Chapel of Saint Camber in Rhemuth Castle on the XXXth day of July in the year 1128, under the tutelage of the Servants of Saint Camber. Bishop Duncan McLain was made rector of the establishment.

An account of Holy Camber's life is given in the *Acta Sancti Camberi*, penned shortly after his death by Holbein of Hastur; this book was allowed to be copied once again during the reign of King Kelson. Camber's arms were: per pale *gules* and *azure*, a sword proper enfiled of an Earl's coronet of the same. He is usually portrayed as grey-haired and wearing a monk's cowl. R.I.P. ["Catalyst"; *Camber of Culdi*; *Saint Camber*; "Healer's Song"; *Camber the Heretic*; *The Harrowing of Gwynedd*; *King Javan's Year*; *The Bastard Prince*; *Deryni Rising*; *High Deryni*; *The Bishop's Heir*; *King Kelson's Bride*].

Camberian Council. This group was established on the XVth day of April in the year 909 by the following individuals: Bishop Alister Cullen (*i.e.*, Camber Earl of Culdi), Father Joram MacRorie, Lady Evaine MacRorie Thuryn, Lord Rhys Thuryn, and Earl Jebediah of Alcara. The Council was intended to police the ranks of the Deryni, to keep the peace between the races, to conduct research into magical practices, and to regulate the use of magic by Deryni, including establishing codes of conduct for duels arcane and other confrontations between Deryni. Traditionally, II members were elected as Coadjutors of the Camberian Council, to provide guidance and direction for the others.

According to the *Legends*, the Council Chamber used by the group "was hidden beneath a high, rock-girt plateau of the Rhendall Moutains, almost within sight of the sea. An ancient Deryni brotherhood known only as the Airsid claimed credit for the *keeill* itself, and apparently had at least started work on the chamber which now housed the Council, but they had disappeared before it could be finished—no one knew why. Neither *keeill* nor Council chamber were now accessible except by transfer portal, and no one could even guess how the first one might have been placed there. Even the existence of the complex had been discovered only by accident, from a chance reference in one of the ancient manuscripts which still occupied most of Evaine's leisure time. After that, many more months had passed before they were confident enough of their visualizations of the described portal there to risk an actual transfer. Eventually they had done it, though; and discovery of the then only partially completed Council chamber and *keeill* had given them both a secure meeting place and a sanctuary for ritual workings. They had felt at home immediately." It sported a great purple dome, and was completely inaccessible by land. Some scholars believe that the Airsid will one day return to claim their home.

On the XXIst day of December in the year 910 the following members were added to the Council's ranks: Archbishop Jaffray of Carbury, Gregory Earl of Ebor, and Dom Turstane; Dom Emrys declined a position. Shortly thereafter Jaffray coined the name Camberian Council, feeling it appropriate as a reminder of the ideals the group strove to uphold. On the XXIst day of May in the year 916 Dom Turstane died in an accident; when his seat was not immediately filled, Jebediah began calling it "Saint Camber's Siege," in which form it remained unfilled. The membership of the Council was set thereafter at VII. On the VIth day of March in the year 917 the Council approved a plan to "block" the powers of selected Deryni if the officially-sanctioned human persecution continued.

Although Davin Earl of Culdi was being considered for membership in the year 917, he was killed on the XXVIIIth day of September before a decision could be reached. Less than a month later, on the XVth day of October, Archbishop Jaffray was killed, reducing the Council to VI. Ansel MacRorie was selected to replace Jaffray, but before he could be formally inducted, III more deaths reduced the Council's ranks still further: Rhys Thuryn on Christmas Day of 917, and Earl Jebediah and Cullen/Camber on Twelfth Night of 918. Ansel was inducted with reduced formality on the VIIIth day of January in the year 918, with Jesse Hereditary Count of Ebor following on the Xth day and Dom Queron Kinevan on the XIth day instant. Tavis O'Neill and Bishop Niallan Trey were added on the XIIth day of February. Evaine Thuryn's death on the I[st] day of August in 918 reduced the Council to VII members once again.

In the XIIth century the Council's membership included: Michon Titular Baron de Courcy and Stanzar (born 1030, appointed 1067, died 1097); Lady Vivienne de Jordanet (born 1050, appointed circa 1080, Coadjutor from 1121 to replace Stefan Coram, died 1128); Barrett de Laney (born 1050, appointed before 1104 and perhaps as early as 1080, Coadjutor by 1120); Lord Rhydon Pretender of Eastmarch (born 1068, appointed in November 1091, expelled in 1105); Stefan Coram (born 1076, appointed before 1104, perhaps in 1098 to replace Michon, killed July 1121, Coadjutor from before 1120); Sofiana Sovereign Princess of Andelon (born 1080, appointed circa 1105, possibly to replace Lord Rhydon, resigned in 1112, appointed to replace her replacement, Thorne Hagen, in August 1123, Coadjutor in 1128); Sir Jamyl Arilan (born 1079, appointed in 1100, died in 1107); Baron Laran ap Pardyce (born 1065, appointed in 1102, a physician); Bishop Denis Arilan (born 1083, appointed before 1120, possibly to replace his brother in 1107); Thorne Hagen (appointed February 1113 to replace Sofiana, resigned in September 1121); Lady Kyri of the Flame (born 1093, appointed shortly before 1120, resigned 1127); Tiercel de Claron (born 1098, appointed by 1120, killed in March 1125); Sir Sion Benet (appointed November 1127 to replace Tiercel); Azim ibn Qais (appointed February 1128 to replace Kyri).

In the year 1120 the Council warned Charissa Pretender of Gwynedd not to interfere with the government of that country, but she chose to ignore their admonitions, to her ultimate destruction. The next year the Council voted to make Father Duncan McLain and Alaric Morgan Duke of Corwyn liable for magical challenge, and was forced to receive the pair in the Council chambers together with Kelson King of Gwynedd, when Bishop Denis Arilan brought them there on the I[st] day of July. On the next day the Council adjudicated the duel arcane between Wencit King of Torenth and his III supporters and King Kelson and his III followers.

In the year 1128 the Council considered the issue of King Kelson's marriage on the XXVIIIth day of June, and also met several times in July to discuss the rapidly unfolding events in Torenth. [*Camber the Heretic*; *The Harrowing of Gwynedd*; *King Javan's Year*; *The Bastard Prince*; *Deryni Rising*; *High Deryni*; *The Bishop's Heir*; *The King's Justice*; *The Quest for Saint Camber*; *Deryni Magic*; *King Kelson's Bride*].

Campbell Sigan *de Broun*, Sir. This itinerant explorer and traveler was born near Cloome in Meara on the Vth day of May in the year 1065, being the eldest son of Sir Alexander de Broun and Margaret Lady Campbell, who was a granddaughter of Taine Earl of Cloome. He several times mentions a wife in his diary, but often by a different name, including Nell, Susan, Tess, and Mollie, and it is not known whether these are really the same person, or represent wholly different individuals. He is known to have sired several children, among them Sir Taine de Broun, who became a Captain of Cavalry in the service of the Prince of Pardiac, Reginald de Broun, called by Berrhones "*theophilés kai theomantis*," and a daughter named Katherine, a writer like her father, who retired to Erin to pen many fanciful romances of elden life (some of them in rhymed iambic pentameter), and garnered a most devoted following.

Campbell de Broun claimed to have visited much of the civilized and barbarian world in a lifetime of journeying. His experiences were published in the popular travelogue, *A Wanderer's Diary*, published in the year 1114, which included several amusing and wry anecdotes of some of the most (and least) memorable places in the Eleven Kingdoms; and *More Dialogues from a Wandering Penman*, published in 1128. He was knighted by the Duke of Laas in the following year.

Count Berrhones, author of *Memoirs of Fifty Years at Court*, called Campbell's Ist book "...without merit, obviously invented by the author, wholly useless as a guidebook, of interest only to old ladies with too much time on their hands. He should have stayed in Cloome." His harsh comment perhaps derived from the fact that Campbell described a well-known mountain near Lendour as having a "...crown as bare and shiny as Berrhones's head, with a fringe of trees round the edge. We climbed to the top, but found nothing of interest there, like so much of the author's work."

While visiting the bleaker parts of the Kheldish Riding, the author wrote of himself: "Then did I cast a thought towards home, and looked forward to those happier days when, far distant from here, I might read this and reflect where once I was. How vain was the thought that I should ever see those days of felicity when I could review my past life with any degree of pleasure, and retrace as in a map the voyager, his course, and the wanderings of his ways through many years. But it is the nature of man to lay up happiness for the future. He never enjoys the present moment, but ponders on the past or future—both beyond his reach. Yet still I enjoyed the present moment, although I was wet and cold—and so I started once again to correct my lines." *Comes facundus in via pro vehiculo est.*

Candlemas. This feast of the Purification of the Blessed Virgin Mary is celebrated in Gwynedd on the IInd day of February. The candles used in ecclesiastical services throughout the rest of the year are blessed on this day. King Cinhil I died on Candlemas in the year 917. One year later on this date the new religious order, the *Custodes Fidei*, was proclaimed by Archbishop Hubert. [*The Harrowing of Gwynedd*].

Candor Rhea. This rolling plain is located just North of Rhemuth and East of the River Eirian. In the late Summer of the year 917 the III royal princes—Alroy, Javan, and Rhys Michael—spent much time here hunting, racing their horses, hawking, and playing. It was here that Brion King of Gwynedd was treacherously slain by the Pretender Charissa Duchess of Tolán on the Ist day of November in the year 1120. A sacred well is also situate at this site. *Revenons à nos moutons.* [*Camber the Heretic*; *Deryni Rising*; *The Bishop's Heir*; *The King's Justice*].

Caprus *Donivald*, Baron d'Eirial. He was born in on the XVIth day of April in the Year of Our Lord 960, being the second surviving son of Radulf Donivald Baron d'Eirial but the first by his second wife, Zillah Lady Davison. He intermarried with Ardentia Lady d'Albi on the XVIIth day of June in the year 982, and by her he had children: the Hereditary Lord Dalbin, who died before his father, leaving issue; the Lord Arden; the Lady Radulphine; the Lord Gilrae; the Lady Renée. The Lord Caprus succeeded his brother Gilrae Baron d'Eirial on the latter's renunciation of his title on the XXIVth day of December in the year 977. He died at Killingford on the XVIth day of June in the year 1025, aged LXV years, and was succeeded by his grandson, the Hereditary Lord Davis. He had bright yellow curls in his youth. R.I.P. ["Vocation"].

Cara Mia *Hagen*. She was born on the IInd day of August in the Year of Our Lord 1106, being the only daughter of Thorne Hagen and Laloie de Saint-Étienne. She died of the pox on the XIXth day of October in the year 1116, aged X years. She was somber and had night-black hair. R.I.P. [*High Deryni*].

Carbury. This strategic port town is located on the Gulf of Kheldour directly North of Grecotha, and serves as a central trading crossroads for goods being shipped between Claibourne, Kierney, Meara, and Gwynedd, both by land and by sea. Originally the domain of the sovereign Count of Carbury, it was incorporated into the Kingdom of Gwynedd by King Aidan on the XXIVth day of August in the year 679. Carbury was created an episcopal see on the XVIIIth day of October in the year 1025 in the person of Bishop Heber, specifically to minister to the great fishing fleets of the Gulf of Kheldour. The see was disestablished on the XVth day of January in the year 1122, being then deemed unnecessary by its close proximity to the older see of Grecotha, and its Bishop Creoda transferred to the newly re-established Bishopric of Culdi. Saint Stefan's Priory is also located here. Elinor Lady MacRorie's parents lived in Carbury during the IXth century. The town of Carbury is well known for its narrow, cobbled streets that wind over its hills, and its quaint houses tiled with stones to ward off the frequent storms that blow in from the Kheldour Gulf.

Campbell de Broun once noted that "I found myself more seasick in traveling up and down the hilly ways of Carbury than I ever got at sea." [*Camber of Culdi*; *Camber the Heretic*; *The Bishop's Heir*; *The King's Justice*]. See also: Creoda, Jaffray, Saint Stefan's Priory.

Carcashale. This earldom is located in the Lendour Mountains of Northeastern Gwynedd, being situate East of Valoret, North of Corwyn, and South of Eastmarch. Its territory also includes the ruined manor houses of Tor Caerrorie and Dolban, with the present seat of the Earl located near the latter structure. Carcashale was created from remnants of the old County of Southmarch on the VIIIth day of June in the year 823 by King Festil I as a reward for service rendered by his friend and comrade, Sir Valen Kanabos. The title was attainted at the restoration of the Haldane monarchy in the year

904, and was regranted a year later to Zachary Baron Genlis. The estate of Caerrorie was presented to Theophilus Earl of Carcashale by King Malcolm in the year 1025 for his service in the recent war. In the year 1125 King Kelson visited Thomas Earl of Carcashale. See also: Thomas.

EARLS OF CARCASHALE

HOUSE OF KANABOS

Valen Kanabos	823-866
Varak (son)	866-888
Veronik (son)	888-901
Vitalik (son)	901-904

HOUSE OF GENLIS

Zachary	905-933
Zebedee (son)	933-948
Zeno (brother)	948-955
Theodelphus (nephew)	955-982
Titus (son)	982-1006
Zion (son)	1006-1025
Theophilus (cousin)	1025-1044
Tobias (son)	1044-1066
Theobald (son)	1066-1101
Thomas (son)	1101-1130+

Carcashal. This small town is located in Northwestern Gwynedd near Transha, on a direct line between Ratharkin and the Transha coast. Dhugal Lord MacArdry was captured here in December of the year 1123 by the Mearan rebels, Brice Baron of Trurill and Edmund Loris ex-Archbishop of Valoret. [*The Bishop's Heir*; *The Quest for Saint Camber*].

Cardosa. This oft-disputed walled city lies on the border between Gwynedd and Torenth, being located near the Southern end of the Rheljan Mountains on a high plateau of sheer-faced rock some MMMM feet above the Eastmarch plain. To the West lies the Earldom of Eastmarch, to the Southwest the Duchy of Corwyn, to the Northeast the Duchies of Tolán and Truvorsk in Torenth, and to the East and Southeast the Duchy of Sasovna in Torenth.

Cardosa was occupied on the IXth day of June in the year 905 by Ariella Pretender of Gwynedd. Two hundred years later, on the XVIth day of September in the year 1120, Alaric Morgan Duke of Corwyn was sent here by King Brion to assess the military situation. The fortress fell to the siege of Wencit King of Torenth on the VIth day of May in the year 1121, before it could be relieved by soldiers from Gwynedd. Following the death of King Wencit on the IInd day of July in that year, the city was definitively awarded to Gwynedd. It was created a new episcopal see on the XVth day of January in the year 1122 under Bishop Siward. [*Saint Camber*; *Deryni Rising*; *Deryni Checkmate*; *High Deryni*; *The Bishop's Heir*].

Cardosa Defile. This pass through the Rheljan Mountains serves as a transit point between Sasovna in Torenth and Eastmarch, with the city of Cardosa being located near the top of the Defile. On the XXIIIrd day of June in the year 905 the Pretender Ariella brought DCCC of her men through the Defile to the foot of the mountains at Llyndruth Meadows. [*Saint Camber*; *High Deryni*].

cardounet. This game of strategy, similar to chess, was played on a inlaid board of light and dark woods with men carved of ebony and ivory. An especially fine *cardounet* set was owned by King Cinhil I, who enjoyed playing the game with Bishop Alister Cullen. His sons, particularly the Princes Javan and Rhys Michael, also fancied the contest. A fine board made of ebony and olivewood and inlaid with mother of pearl and semi-precious gems was presented to King Alroy and Prince Javan at their XIIIth birthday celebration by Étienne Baron de Courcy on the XXVth day of May in the year 918. [*Camber the Heretic*; *The Harrowing of Gwynedd*; *King Javan's Year*].

Carle. He was serving the Earl Maldred in November of the year 903. [*Camber of Culdi*].

Carloman, Lord Thornton. He was born on the Ist day of February in the Year of Our Lord 862, being the eldest son and heir of Carantock Lord Thornton and Mazota Lady Tay. He intermarried with Foi Lady Mobeoc on the Xth day of June in the year 882, and by her he had children: the Lady Silvina; the Hereditary Lord Justus; the Lady Carrega; the Lord Flannan; the Lord Castul. He succeeded his father on the XVth day of January in the year 867. This treacherous Baron had his holding on the coast of Northern Kheldour, not far from Stavenham, in the year 905. His manor house was sunk into solid rock, with the foundation resting directly on bare cliff. He was the chief sponsor and benefactor of the human rebel priest, the Gryphon of God. He had red hair and beard intermixed with tufts of grey. He was killed by anti-Deryni partisans supporting the Regents on the XIIIth day of December in the year 917, aged LX years, his title being attainted II weeks later. [*Deryni Challenge*].

Carolus II, *i.e.*, **Károly II Káspár Kálmán** *Furstán*, **called "Bold Carolus," King of Torenth, Duke of Székaly**. He was born on the IVth day of November in the Year of Our Lord 966, being the second son of Malachy II King of Torenth and Ianthe Princess of Salonique. He intermarried with Richardis Baroness de Kluwas on the XVth day of April in the year 984, but she was barren. He was created Duke of Székaly on his coming of age in the year 980. In the campaign of the year 984 he commanded the rear guard of the Festillic Prince Imre II's army when the latter invaded Gwynedd, and in the military disaster which followed, was severely wounded while trying to protect the retreating Torenthi forces. His father the King and his elder brother the Hereditary Prince having been killed on the field on the IIIrd day of August, he succeeded to the throne, although he was never girded with the sword at Iób. Through his heroic efforts he managed to save a IIIrd of the army and recover the bodies of his relatives. Suffering from multiple injuries and worn out by his exertions, he died just V days later on the VIIIth day of August 984, while on the return trek to Torenth. He was aged XVII years at his death, and was buried with his ancestors at Torenthály. A statue in his honour was later erected at Old Beldour by his brother and successor, Kyprian II. He is omitted from some king lists of Torenth, and is not included in Princess Arien's *Lives of the XII Kings of Torenth*. R.I.P. *Fremdes Pferd und eigene Sporen haben bald den Wind verloren.*

Carolus III, *i.e.*, **Károly III Kyprian Konstantin Kirill** *Furstán*, **called "Young Carolus," King of Torenth, Duke of Nördmarcke.** He was born on the XIXth day of May in the Year of Our Lord 1070, being the fifth child and third son and heir of Nimur II King of Torenth and Charis Rochelle Princess of Festil. He intermarried with Erzsébet Countess von Mourom on the XXVIIth day of October in the year 1089, and by her he had children: the Hereditary Prince Aldred later Aldred II King of Torenth; the Princess Kunegunda Ophelia, who was mauled and killed by a dog in the year 1096 at the age of IV. According to Angelos Lord de Courtenay, Princess Erszébet "died of grief the following year, for she blamed herself for allowing the child to wander away, and would not be consoled." Following the death of Hogan Gwernach Duke of Tolán on the XXIst day of June in the year 1105, the Prince Carolus also adopted the former's daughter and heir, the Princess Charissa Duchess of Tolán and Festillic pretender to the throne of Gwynedd, and married her to his son and heir several years later.

The Prince Carolus was created Duke of Nördmarcke on his coming of age in the year 1084, and became heir to the throne on the VIth day of January in the year 1095, after his eldest brother the Hereditary Prince Nimur had died and his next elder brother Prince Torval had been put aside by their father for imbecility. On the XXIInd day of November in the year 1106, the Prince succeeded to the throne of his father, and was girded with the sword under the reign name of Károly III by Patriarch Gamalinos II on the New Year's Day following. On this occasion he announced a general amnesty of prisoners and a reduction of the estate levy, and these actions were widely hailed.

On the IInd day of January in the year 1110, following a skirmish at Fathane on the XIth day of December in the previous year between the forces of Torenth and Gwynedd, King Carolus sent emissaries to Brion King of Gwynedd to arrange a meeting in which the monarchs might discuss a possible treaty of peace between the states and a permanent settlement of the Festillic claims to Gwynedd, for, according to Halitch, "he saw no reason that two nations with so much in common should continue in a state of war."

Then, states Berrhones, "The Princess Charissa being enraged at the possible loss of her heritage, she persuaded her husband to plot against their father. During a banquet held on the night before the King was to depart, Charissa took to her Father a platter of the Fenneli figs he so dearly loved, the fruit of which she had secured at great expense. He smiled and began to eat, but within moments started to choke and gasp as if a bone had stuck in his throat. He died before the court Healer could arrive." However, other authorities put his death at the feet of his ambitious brother, Prince Wencit, who, however, was absent from Court at this time, or merely state that it was according to "God's will," for he was well known to overindulge himself at the banquet table.

Capellis notes that "Prince Carolus was fat even as a young man, and grew ever stouter with age. He loved his games and horses, and while attentive to his duties, was of no better than average wit. He was easy to please and pleasant even to his servants, a man whose shortcomings were readily forgiven by those who knew him well."

King Carolus passed from this earth on the XIth day of February in the year 1110, aged XXXIX years, and was buried with his ancestors at Torenthály. He was succeeded by his only son, Prince Aldred. R.I.P. ["Legacy"].

Carrega *Thornton*, **Lady**. She was born on the XIIth day of May in the year 888, being the daughter of Carloman Lord Thornton and Foi Lady Mobeoc. She lived near Stavenham, and had red hair and green eyes. [*Deryni Challenge*].

Carrollan *O'Carroll*. This Deryni was born on the IXth day of July in the year 917, being the only child of Ursin O'Carroll and Birgit Subalter. He was imprisoned with his mother beginning in the year 917 to act as hostages for his Deryni father's service to the Regents, and was still being held captive in March of the year 922. He was visited by King Javan and at his command tested with *merasha* in that month, which proved him to be Deryni. His powers were later blocked. He was rescued from the massacre at the River Eirian on the XIth day of May in that year, but his subsequent fate is unknown. His hair was dark with glints of red. [*King Javan's Year*].

Carsten, Bishop of Meara. He was born on the Ist day of February in the Year of Our Lord 1044. This elderly prelate originally sided with Archbishop Edmund Loris in the Interdict Schism of the year 1121, but, when it became evident that Loris and Archbishop Patrick Corrigan would lose the battle with Kelson King of Gwynedd, he later assumed a neutral stance. He died during on the XXth day of July in the year 1123, aged LXXIX years, precipitating the Mearan Crisis. R.I.P. [*Deryni Checkmate*; *High Deryni*; *The Bishop's Heir*].

Carthane. This small Earldom lies in the South of Gwynedd, being situate in the pocket of land formed by the lower reaches of River Eirian, the River Lendour, and the River Carthane. The Crown Duchy of Haldane lies to the North. Nyford is its capital city.

This region was conquered by Basileios I Autokratór of Byzantyun, with Carthanus Province being established in the year 249. Carthane was evacuated by the Easterners in the year 444, and the area was divided amongst the local barons. In the year 466 Isik Lord Nyford conquered several of his neighbours and proclaimed himself Count of Carthane. His descendant, Count Rubik, was defeated and killed on the XXth day of April in the year 645 by Augarin II Count of Haldane, and Carthane was incorporated into the new Kingdom of Gwynedd. The title was awarded to King Augarin's cousin, Lord Auran Haldane, and the latter's eldest daughter, the Countess Riona, succeeded her father and married King Llarik. At her death in the year 697, her IInd son, Prince Jestyn, inherited the title, but it reverted to the Crown II years later.

The region was then divided by King Llarik into several baronies, including one called Carthane, which was given to Murvyn grandson of King Augarin. The last Baron of Carthane, Urbic, was attainted by King Festil I in the year 822. His great-grandson, Murdoch *de jure* Baron Carthane, was restored to his title by King Cinhil I in the year 905, and created Earl of Carthane on the Ist day of December in the year 907. His grandson, Earl Cashel, was attainted in the year 948. The honour was then regranted to Prince Cluim Haldane later King of Gwynedd in the year 953. Upon his succession to the throne, Cluim granted the title to his youngest son, Prince Michael Rhys, who renounced his rights to the throne of Gwynedd for himself and his descendants and settled in the Kingdom of Howicce. Thence the title passed by grant to the latter's IInd son, Earl Godwyn Pirek-Haldane, and from him in direct descent down to modern times.

The standard of this Earldom at the time of Earl Murdoch included black aurochs on a crimson field, but was later modified to incorporate a quartered Haldane arms. [*The Harrowing of Gwynedd*; *King Javan's Year*; *The Quest for Saint Camber*].

COUNTS OF CARTHANE

HOUSE OF CRESCENS

Isik Crescens	466-480
Clarent (son)	480-509
Bernin (son)	509-528
Julin (son)	528-555
Alkim (son)	555-570
Marcelin (son)	570-602
Emerit (brother)	602-608
Rubik (nephew)	608-645

HOUSE OF HALDANE

Auran (cousin of King Augarin)	645-679
Riona (daughter)	679-697
Jestyn (son)	697-699

BARONS AND EARLS OF CARTHANE

HOUSE OF MURDOCH

Murvyn (1st cousin)	705-733
Dann (son)	733-756
Murfree (son)	756-788
Oswy (son)	788-798
Urbic (brother)	798-822
Osmond (son)	822-851
Murlyn (brother)	851-858
Osgar (nephew)	858-881
Osmael (son)	881-905
Murdoch (son; Earl 907)	905-921
Richard (son)	921-948
Cashel (son)	948

HOUSE OF PIREK-HALDANE

Cluim	953-985
Michael I Rhys (son)	985-1011
Godwyn (son)	1011-1036
Maximilian (son)	1036-1046
Arthyr (brother)	1046-1077
Innis (nephew)	1077-1098
Quentin (brother)	1098-1100
Michael II Cluim (son)	1100-1130+

Carthmoor. This duchy of Gwynedd is situate in the extreme Southeast portion of the Kingdom, bordering the Earldom of Carthane and the Royal Honour of Haldane to the North, the Kingdom of Llannedd to the West, the Southern Sea to the South, and an assortment of lesser Earldoms and Baronies lying between it and the Duchy of Corwyn to the East.

Originally part of the Kingdom of Mooryn, Carthmoor was split from that state when Mooryn was annexed to Gwynedd in the year 835, and the Duchy then descended successively through various branches of the House of Festil and the House of Haldane. The Festillic title was deeded to Count Bogdan the morganatic younger son of King Festil III; Bogdan Duke of Carthmoor was allowed to retain his ducal title by King Cinhil I, since he had no right to the Festillic succession. Duke Bogdan's son, the Duke Rudolf II, was dispossessed by the Regents on the XXVIIth day of December in the year 917. The Duchy of Carthmoor was then regranted by King Alroy to his brother, the Prince Rhys Michael, the Prince Javan having entered a religious house.

The title became traditional with the IInd sons of the House of Haldane, passing only in the male line, and often being vested in the Crown; the Prince Nigel, the incumbent at the time of King Kelson, is only the IIIrd Haldane holder of the title to have surviving male heirs. The Princes Jashan and Richard also bore the subsidiary title of Earl of Culdi, the latter of which descended to Richard's eldest daughter the Countess Richelle at his death on the XVth day of October in the year 1114. In the year 1125 Duke Nigel disinherited his grandson, Prince Albin, after the treason of Conall Hereditary Duke of Carthmoor, but Albin was restored to the succession III years later. *Divina natura dedit agros, ars humana ædificavit urbes*. [*The Bishop's Heir*; *The King's Justice*; *King Kelson's Bride*].

DUKES OF CARTHMOOR

HOUSE OF FURSTÁN-FESTIL

Festil	826-839
Rudolf I (son)	839-885
Bogdan (nephew)	885-908
Rudolf II (son)	908-917

HOUSE OF HALDANE

Rhys Michael	920-928
Uthyr (son)	929-948
Cinhil (son)	949-962

INTERREGNUM

Quinnell (nephew)	975-977
Jashan (cousin)	978-1055
Richard (great-nephew)	1055-1114
Nigel (nephew)	1114-1130+

Cashel *Murdoch*, **Lord, Sir.** He was born on the XXVIth day of January in the Year of Our Lord 904, being the third son of Murdoch Earl of Carthane and Elaine Lady de Fintan. He never married. By Martina Knickere, a woman who claimed to be his wife though she could not prove the relationship, Sir Cashel sired several children: Sir Murdoch FitzCashel, who claimed the Earldom of Carthane in the year 948 after the death of his cousin, Earl Cashel *Junior*, but was unsuccessful in establishing his right to that title; Hagan FitzCashel; Rintha FitzCashel; Alfred FitzCashel later Charlton.

The Lord Cashel was present at the death of King Alroy on the XXIIIrd day of June in the year 921, and a month later saw his father killed by Hrorik Earl of Eastmarch on the Ist day of August. Cashel was knighted by King Javan on the VIth day of January in the year 922. He was absent from the capital during the *coup d'état* of July in the year 928, and never returned to the city. During his subsequent wanderings he learned of Jesse Lord MacGregor's impending marriage to Tiarna MacMurray, daughter of Captain Murray, at Lochalyn Castle in Eastmarch on the XIIth day of April in the year 930, and determined to disrupt the ceremony and challenge Jesse to a duel, in order to restore his own name by killing the attainted Deryni. But for the Ist time in his career he misjudged his opponent, and was killed in a fair fight, aged XXVI years. He was not much missed. In the *Heirs* he is described as "a burly bully who was constantly spoiling for a fight, and was good enough to win most of them." [*King Javan's Year*; *The Bastard Prince*].

Cashien. This ecclesiastical see and town of Travlum is located in Gwynedd near its border with The Connait, directly West of Rhemuth, on the East side of the Mughdorna Mountains. The town was conquered by King Aidan on the XIIth day of July in the year 675. At the time of the accession of Cinhil I King of Gwynedd in the year 904, Dermot O'Beirne was Bishop, and was succeeded in the year 917 by Abbot Zephram of Lorda. Two hundred years later, in the year 1121, Belden of Erne was Bishop, and was succeeded in the year 1125 by Father James MacKenzie. [*The Harrowing of Gwynedd*; *King Javan's Year*; *The Bishop's Heir*; *The King's Justice*; *The Quest for Saint Camber*].

Cassan. This Duchy of Northwestern Gwynedd lies North of Meara on the Gulf of Kheldour. Cassan was originally part of the Principality of Meara, but split from that nation on the XVIth day of November in the year 762 when Prince Janus died, leaving a young son, Prince Alphonse. Janus's younger brother, Prince Armon, assumed the throne, while the young Alphonse fled with his mother, the Dowager Princess Ostrythe, to her native city of Ballymar in Cassan. There she raised the standard of revolt, declaring her son the rightful Prince of Meara. But she lacked the military strength to dislodge her husband's brother, and he could not touch his sister-in-law in her stronghold. After VIII years of intermittent warfare both parties signed a treaty on the VIth day of August in the year 770 recognizing the independent status of Cassan, but including a provision that, should either branch of the family become extinct in the male line, the other would have succession rights. However, at the death of the last Sovereign Prince, Ambert Quinnell, on the XXIst day of May in the year 921, Prince Ambert's grandson, Tambert Fitz-Arthur Quinnell, became the Ist Duke of Cassan under terms of an irrevocable agreement that had been signed between Cassan and Gwynedd on the XXIInd day of September in the year 916, despite the official protest of Austin Sovereign Prince of Meara. The final will and testament of the Sovereign Prince Ambert was officially presented at Court on the XXXth day of July in the year 921, and Cassan was formally annexed to Gwynedd on that date. At the extinction of Tambert's House in the year 1025, the Duchy passed through the female line to the House of McLain, and further passed by cession on the XXIst day of May in the year 1125 to the House of MacArdry McLain. Cassan was briefly claimed by the Pretender of Meara, the Princess Caitrin, in the year 1124. [*The Harrowing of Gwynedd*; *King Javan's Year*; *Deryni Rising*; *Deryni Checkmate*; *High Deryni*; *The Bishop's Heir*; *The King's Justice*; *King Kelson's Bride*].

SOVEREIGN AND CLIENT PRINCES OF CASSAN

HOUSE OF QUINNELL

Alphonse (son of Prince Janus of Meara)	762-789
Audic (son)	789-795
Jensic (brother)	795-823
Amalric (nephew)	823-846
Jerome (son)	846-866
Jolyon (brother)	866-868
Antiochus (son)	868-891
Audebert (son)	891-909
Ambert (son)	909-921

DUKES OF CASSAN
HOUSE OF FITZ-ARTHUR QUINNELL

Tambert I (grandson)	921-948
Tammaron (son)	948-994
Fane (son)	994-1016
Tambert II (son)	1016-1025

TITLE IN ABEYANCE

HOUSE OF [MACARDRY] MCLAIN

Andrew (grandson)	1034-1099
Jared (son)	1099-1121
Duncan (son; abdicated)	1121-1125
Dhugal *MacArdry McLain* (son)	1125-1130+

Cassian, Prince-Bishop of Autun, Saint. This IVth-century prelate was elected Prince-Bishop of Autun in the 314, and died in the year 350. Brother Cassian is said to have originated from the East, and came to the Autuni Mountains to convert the savages there. He forbade the presence of women in his principality, and relied upon a constant stream of new followers to replenish the ranks of his knights. This policy was overturned shortly after his death, due to a lack of enthusiasm on the part of potential postulants. A *Custodes Fidei* Abbey dedicated to his name is located on the Plain of Iomaire in Gwynedd. His feastday is the Vth day of August. R.I.P. [*The Bastard Prince*].

Castleroo. This Mearan town lies on the coast of the Atalantic Ocean at Kilarden Bay in the Northwestern part of this province. It provided many soldiers to the Mearan Rebellion in the year 1124. [*The King's Justice*].

Cathan Adrian *MacRorie*, Hereditary Count and Master of Culdi. He was born on the XXXth day of August in the Year of Our Lord 873, being the eldest son and heir of Camber Earl of Culdi and Jocelyn Lady de la Marche. He intermarried with Elinor Lady Howell on the XXVIth day of May in the year 897, and by her he had children: the Lord Davin Elathan later Earl of Culdi; the Lord Ansel Irial, ancestor of the MacAthan family.

He was home sick with a cold on the XIth day of October in the year 888, and helped dispatch some bandits who raided Tor Caerrorie then. He was appointed to the Royal Council by Imre King of Gwynedd on the latter's coronation on the XXVth day of March in the year 900, and served in that capacity for III years; he was also appointed a Royal Commissioner of the Tariff Court on the VIth day of January in the year 901. On the XXIXth day of September in the year 903 he petitioned King Imre for the lives of the hostages taken in reprisal for Lord Rannulf's murder near Caerrorie earlier that month, and the King granted him one life only of his choosing out of the L peasants being held. He selected the boy Revan, a carpenter's apprentice of XIII years who was one of the more promising students of Lord Cathan's sister, Evaine Lady MacRorie. After the execution of the remaining hostages, he retreated to Saint Liam's Abbey in October, but was greatly depressed at the political situation. He returned to Court in November. He was unjustly accused by his brother-in-law, Coel Lord Howell, of the murder of Earl Maldred on the Ist day of December in the Year 903, and was killed by King Imre for suspected treason. His body was returned to Tor Caerrorie for burial in the family crypt on the next day. He was XXX years of age at his death, and was succeeded as Hereditary Count by his son, Lord Davin.

He was described in the *Legends of Camber of Culdi* as "not so tall as Camber, and a little darker of hair and eye and skin than his illustrious sire, yet he was still unmistakably a MacRorie, and many looked to him now as a voice of reason to the headstrong young king." R.I.P. ["Catalyst"; *Camber of Culdi*; *Saint Camber*; *The Harrowing of Gwynedd*].

Cathan Cinhil *Drummond*, Lord Regent of Gwynedd, Sir. He was born on the XXIIIrd day of March in the Year of Our Lord 910, being the eldest son and heir of James "Jamie" Lord Drummond and Elinor Lady Howell, and the brother of Michaela Queen of Gwynedd, half-brother of Lord Ansel MacRorie, and the brother-in-law of Rhys Michael King of Gwynedd. He intermarried with Jerusha Thuryn on the XXXth day of April in the year 937, and by her he had children: the Lady Kyriella, who intermarried with Stuart Lord MacAthan son of Ansel Lord MacRorie later MacAthan; the Lord Corwin; the Lady Evalina.

His powers were blocked by Tavis on the XXIst day of January in the year 918. He was questioned by the Regents on the next day following about the events of the previous night, when Tavis and Ansel had mounted an expedition into Valoret Castle to block the Deryni powers of the Drummonds. He was made a royal squire by February of that year. He was serving as a junior aide to Prince Rhys Michael by June of the year 921, but was named squire to King Javan in July, replacing Sir Charlan. He continued in that role when Rhys Michael succeeded to the throne a year later.

He was taken prisoner by the former Regents during their coup of the XIth day of May in the year 922, but was allowed to remain in the Royal household, albeit partially drugged, and was released from confinement later that Summer. He was knighted on the VIth day of January in the year 928, and was officially appointed an aide to King Rhys Michael on the same day. He dined with his sister the Queen and the King on the XIVth day of June in that year; later that evening his Deryni powers were restored by Tieg Thuryn, who removed the block placed years before by Tavis. He then participated in the empowerment of the King later that evening.

He saved the new King Owain's life by slaying Rhun the Ruthless on the Vth day of July in the year 928, and was named to the new Regency Council of King Owain on that same day. He died on the XVIIIth day of October in the year 957, aged XLVII years. R.I.P. [*The Harrowing of Gwynedd*; *King Javan's Year*; *The Bastard Prince*].

Catulina, Saint. This VIth-century saint originally served as a maid of honour for Lady Saliba of R'Kassi. At the age of XIII years, she joined a religious community in Thuria, and was later appointed Novice Mistress of a convent at Trebaçeaux in Joux, where an Order dedicated to her name was eventually established. Here she spent her life praying for the many sinners she saw around her, and was favoured by God with the most amazing visions of Heaven and Hell and the Megas Factors, in which she endlessly re-enacted the scenes of our Lord's passion. Uncounted thousands flocked to her convent annually to seek her advice. Her mystical experiences were set down by Brother Nathan Robertson in his *Vita de Catulina Insulsa*, which was published in IX volumes in the Xth century. Her feastday is the XIVth day of February.

Caulay *MacArdry*, called "The Old MacArdry," Chief of Clan MacArdry, Earl of Transha. He was born on the XXIVth day of August in the Year of Our Lord 1061, being the eldest surviving son and heir of Arthur MacArdry Earl of Transha and Alannah Lady O'Beirne. He intermarried with Adreana Lady Calder of Sheele on the IXth day of June in the year 1086, and by her he had children: the Tanist Ardry, dead at age XIX, *sans postérité*; the Tanist Michael, dead at age XXIX, *sans postérité*; the Lady Maryse, who secretly intermarried with Duncan Lord McLain later Duke of Cassan, and died at age XVI giving him one child, the Lord Dhugal, who was raised by his grandfather as if he were his own child and was generally believed to be; the Lady Yvette, who intermarried with Peray Lord Howard; the Lady Ianna, dead at age X of the yellow skin; the Lord Arthur, the Lady Giolla, the Lord Cullen, the Lady Bernine, all born still or dead as infants; the Lady Caldreana, who was raised as a twin of Lord Dhugal, and who intermarried with Philo Hereditary Count of Pelagog.

The Lord Caulay succeeded his father on the XXVIIth day of December in the year 1080. On the XXVth day of November in the year 1123 Kelson King of Gwynedd visited the old Earl in his castle of Transha on the Gulf of Kheldour, where he paid the ailing Chief the respect due to him as a clan chief. A week later, on the Ist day of December, the Earl of Transha collapsed and died of pains in his chest when he heard of the capture of his grandson by Brice of Trurill and the Mearan rebels. He was LXII years of age at his death, and was succeeded by his foster son, Lord Dhugal, as Clan Chief and Earl of Transha. R.I.P. [*The Bishop's Heir*; *The King's Justice*; *The Quest for Saint Camber*].

Cecile, Sister. This nun of the Sisters of Saint Perpetua was serving as a companion to Jehana Dowager Queen of Gwynedd in the year 1124. She accompanied the Queen when she returned to Rhemuth for the royal weddings in June of the year 1128. [*The King's Justice*; *The Quest for Saint Camber*; *King Kelson's Bride*].

Centule Barnabe Zezayer *de Vésan*, Prince of Vézaire. He was born on the XXXth day of May in the Year of Our Lord 1104, being the second son of Centule V Grand Duc du Vézaire and the Countess Victoire daughter of Gaspard Sovereign Count of Fianna. He intermarried with the Princess Lérida daughter of Isarn II Sovereign Prince of Logréine on the XIXth day of March in the year 1129, and by her he had a child: the Prince Ysarnot Comte du Panthé. He served as an official representative of his father to the installation ceremony of Torenthi King Liam Lajos II, and was honoured at a reception in the Hanging Gardens of Furstánály Palace on the XIth day of July in the year 1128. [*King Kelson's Bride*].

Charis Scarlamonde *Furstána*, Princess of Torenth, Duchess of Tolán. This beauteous lady was born on the IXth day of December in the Year of Our Lord 901, being the eldest daughter and second child of Nimur I King of Torenth and Katalin Countess of Festil-Mnata, and sister of Arion I King of Torenth. She intermarried with Ursion Graf von Brosswick on the XVIIIth day of July in the year 917, and by him she had one child: the Hereditary Lord Burchardus later Margraf von Brosswick. After her first husband's death of the spotted pox on the last day of August in the year 919, she returned to the Court of her brother to raise her son.

But for reasons of state the King Arion I intermarried her secondly with the Hereditary Prince Marek Pretender to the throne of Gwynedd on the XVIIth day of July in 927, and by him she had children: the Hereditary Prince Imre later Imre II Titular King of Gwynedd; the Princess Imriella, who intermarried with her Ist cousin, the Prince Ysarn Duke of Marluk and son of Arion I King of Torenth, on the XXIIIrd day of July in the year 944, leaving issue; the Princess Ysolte, who was born dead; the Prince Arim-Miklós later Count of Moyrenc, dead of the consumptive complaint at the age of XVI years; the Princess Chariella, who intermarried with her Ist cousin, the Prince Rogan Hereditary Duke d'Arjenol, on the XIIth day of May in the year 949, leaving issue; the Princess Bernardine, who died a hydrophobe at age V; the Princess Ætherien, who took the veil under the name Sister Ragenfride of the Order of Saint Catulina and died in the year 978, aged XL years.

The Duchess Charis and her infant son Imre were sent by her husband back to Tolán in June of the year 928 a few days before the events that resulted in the death of Miklós Prince of Torenth on the XXIInd day of that month. This worthy Dame was known for her good works and kindliness towards the poor and unfortunate, but she also acted as an adviser to her Royal Husband and Brother, urging caution in their relations with the House of Haldane. She died of the leprous scurvy on the VIth day of July in 981, aged LXXIX years, and was buried with her ancestors at Torenthály. R.I.P. [*The Bastard Prince*].

Charissa Aymarine Festiliana *Furstána-Festila-mac Tadhg*, called "The Shadowed One," "The Shadowed Lady of the North," and "The Lady of the Silver Mists," Titular Queen and Princess of Gwynedd, sometime Queen of Torenth, Duchess of Tolán and Marluk, Countess of Gwernach. This spawn of the Devil was born on the XIIIth day of May in the Year of Our Lord 1094, being the only surviving child and heir of Hogan Gwernach Duke of Tolán and Titular King of Gwynedd and Larissa Heiress de Marluk. She was betrothed to her cousin, the Hereditary Prince Aldred later Aldred II King of Torenth, on the XXIXth day of September in the year 1105, and intermarried with him on the XIVth day of June in the year 1106, and by him she had children: the Princess Marcissa, dead at age II of a fall suffered while playing with her father; the Hereditary Prince Gejza Taksony, who was born and died on the XXXIst day of March in 1110.

The Princess Charissa was devoted to her father, and when he decided at the instigation of Prince Wencit to challenge Brion King of Gwynedd for the throne of that country in June of the year 1105, she supported his decision. After her father was slain on the XXIst day of that month, the Princess Charissa was adopted by Carolus III Hereditary Prince and King of Torenth, who immediately proclaimed her Queen of Gwynedd with himself as Regent, and then betrothed her to his own son and heir a few months later. She attained her majority on the XIIIth day of May in the year 1108, when the Regency was formally dissolved, but was never girded with the sword at Iób, the girding of women being contrary to Torenthi custom. Nonetheless, she plotted to restore her line to the throne of Gwynedd from her early years, and is said by Berrhones to have poisoned her foster father, the King Carolus, on the XIth day of February in the year 1110, when he sought a reconciliation with Brion King of Gwynedd.

However, her husband, the new King Aldred II, abused her most brutally, and when he caused her to lose her only son on the last day of March in that year, she schemed with her uncle-in-law, the Prince Wencit, to remove this nefarious monarch from the throne of Torenth. The King Aldred was deposed on the XVth day of April in the year 1110 and executed III days later. With the permission of King Wencit, Charissa renounced her title of Dowager Queen of Torenth and resumed the style Duchess of Tolán. Eight months later she signed a last will and testament on the VIIth day of January in the year 1111, naming the King Wencit, his children, and his sister the Princess Morag Duchess d'Arjenol her next heirs-at-law after any issue of her own body.

The Princess Charissa was officially warned by the Camberian Council in the year 1120 not to interfere in the politics of Gwynedd, an admonition that she ignored to her ultimate destruction. On the I[st] day of November in that year she finally avenged her father by murdering Brion King of Gwynedd with magic on the field of Candor Rhea near Rhemuth. She met Alaric Morgan Duke of Corwyn in the Library at Rhemuth Palace on the XIVth day instant, having transported to the portal there, and in a discussion with him there she falsely denied having participated in Brion's death. She was killed by the new King Kelson in a duel arcane held on the next day in Saint George's Cathedral at Rhemuth, her body being utterly consumed by crimson flames.

Berrhones further states: "Like most of her line, she was wholly obsessed with power and vengeance and her supposed heritage, which was so far removed in her case, to the IXth degree, that it would have been almost meaningless to anyone else. The only power that the Festils ever wielded after 904 was their power to shape the destiny of the Torenthi state, and that always adversely. She was the last of her line, and we are well rid of them all." Alaric Morgan Duke of Corwyn wrongly believed that Charissa had developed the drug *merasha*.

Lord Desiderius Callan notes her as being "...petite, well dressed, even comely, although too intense by far to be regarded by most men as pretty or desirable. She herself was almost wholly uninterested in the opposite sex except as a means to an end; the only love of her life outside of herself was the memory of her deceased father, which she cherished like a prized fruit one has bought at the fair, but discovers at first bite that it has rotted inside. There was always an aura of inevitable tragedy about her, as if she knew from the start that, like some pagan god cursed by the fates, she was doomed to repeat the actions of her predecessors over and over again until the drama had played itself out to its predestined and utterly horrible end. No one who ever met her will forget the hard little eyes and utterly cheerless face of the twelve-year-old woman in a child's body. And no one who knew her would have ever wanted to trade places with her." Volumen I of the *Chronicles of the Deryni* describes her as having "...a slight pale figure, delicate hands folded primly in her lap,...[with] pale blue eyes." She had fair hair that fell well past her waist.

At her death the Duchy of Tolán and the Festillic pretensions to the throne of Gwynedd were inherited by her *cousin germain*, Wencit King of Torenth, who claimed them through his mother, the Princess Charis Rochelle daughter of the Princess Chriselle Duchess of Tolán and Pretender of Gwynedd; the border County of Gwernach went into abeyance between two co-heiresses, and by an ancient treaty was claimed for administration by the Kingdom of Gwynedd; and the Duchy of Marluk escheated to the Torenthi Crown.

Charissa's arms were: ermine, two lion's jambes *gules*, clawed *or*, in chief dancetty *gules* a jewelled coronet *or*. *Aperte mala quum est mulier, rum demum est bona.* ["Legacy"; *Deryni Rising*; *Deryni Checkmate*; *High Deryni*; *The Bishop's Heir*; *King Kelson's Bride*].

Charlan Kai *Morgan*, Hereditary Knight and Laird of Morganhall, Sir. This distinguished knight was born on the XXIIIrd day of October in the year 902, being the eldest son and heir of Sir Peregrine Kai Morgan and Charlandra Lady Dye. He succeeded his father as Hereditary Knight and Laird of Morganhall on the VIth day of June in the year 917. He was made squire to Prince Javan by the year 918, and was required by the Regents to watch him at all times, being interrogated by them weekly. The Prince early took steps to ensure that incriminating information should not be reported, by blocking Charlan's memory of certain events. On the IXth day of February in that year Charlan accompanied the Prince to Archbishop Hubert's quarters, and was cloaked by Javan with his mantle in the chapel there as a disguise. He left the Prince's service when the latter took temporary vows on the I[st] day of August in that year. Thereafter he served in the King's household for II years, and was knighted by King Alroy on the IIIrd day of December in the year 920.

He was sent by King Alroy on the XXIIIrd day of June in the year 921 to fetch Prince Javan back to Court. After Javan's accession to the throne on that same day, he resumed his former duties as squire to the new King, and then was named his chief aide in July. At this time King Javan also restored his memories of Javan's previous tampering with his mind, and asked him for his voluntary loyalty. Sir Charlan agreed, but also asked that his memory continue to be blurred for his own safety and that of his monarch. He attended the coronation of King Javan on the XXXIst day of July in the year 921.

This good and faithful knight was slain with his monarch by the former Regents on the XIth day of May in the year 922, aged XIX years, and was succeeded by his younger brother, Sir Kailan Eustache Morgan. He was kind and clever and had sandy hair. R.I.P. [*The Harrowing of Gwynedd*; *King Javan's Year*; *The Bastard Prince*].

Charles, Brother. He was formerly a baker in the village of Caerrorie, and testified before the Council of Bishops at Valoret on the XXIVth day of October in the year 906 that he himself had seen Camber Earl of Culdi buried in the family crypt on his estate of Tor Caerrorie. He later became a Servant of Saint Camber at Dolban, and died there in the year 917, killed by the Regents. [*Saint Camber*; *Camber the Heretic*].

Charles *FitzMichael*, Father. This priest was ordained at the *Arx Fidei* establishment with Denis Arilan on the IInd day of February in the year 1105. He was Denis Arilan's chief competitor for top academic honours at the Seminary. ["The Priesting of Arilan"].

Cheltham. This town is located on the River Eirian Northeast of Saint Liam's Abbey on the South side of the river, not far from Tor Caerrorie. During the VIIIth and IXth centuries it was the site of the Commanderie of the Order of Saint Michael. It was destroyed by Imre King of Gwynedd on the XVth day of December in the year 903. [*Camber of Culdi*; *Saint Camber*].

Chriselle Carola Carmina *Furstána-Festila-Mór*, **Titular Queen of Gwynedd, Duchess of Tolán and Truvorsk.** She was born on the Vth day of July in the year 1010, being the second daughter and third child of AriElinora Titular Queen of Gwynedd and Manuel Graf von Spire. She intermarried with the Prince Zimri Duke of Truvorsk and son of Kyprian II King of Torenth on the XIXth day of June in the year 1027, and by him she had children: the Princess Demetria, dead of biliousity at age III; the Princess Camille, who took the veil with the Order of the Blessed Virgin under the name Mary Beatrice, and died in the year 1101; the Prince Blaine, born still; the Princess Ariel, who died of the shaking disease at age V; the Princess Charis Rochelle, also called Charchelle, who intermarried with her cousin, Nimur II King of Torenth, leaving issue; the Hereditary Prince Marcus also called Marek, who intermarried with Jonelle Heiress of Gwernach and died at age XVIII of a pain in his belly, which was caused, according to popular belief, by poison supplied by the Haldanes, leaving issue, the Prince Hogan Duke of Tolán and Truvorsk and Count of Gwernach.

The Princess Chriselle succeeded her mother on the XXXth day of September in the year 1050, but she did little to advance her cause and was never formally installed, the Patriarch Symeón II refusing to admit a woman, and placed all of her hopes on her young son, the Hereditary Prince Marcus. Following his untimely death on the XXVIth day of October in the year 1060 she grew most melancholy, and sought to make a pilgrimage to the Holy Shrine of Saint Sava of the East in Jáca, where a hermit reportedly could speak with the dead; but, having progressed just halfway on her journey, she suddenly took ill and died after II days of suffering, eaten up with a fever, perishing on the XIth day of August in the year 1061, aged LI years. She was packed in brine and returned to Torenthály for burial with her family. R.I.P.

Christophle Urbanus, secular name Dafydd Urban *Ramsay-Quinnell*, **Brother.** He was born on the IVth day of April in the Year of Our Lord 1110, being the second son of Sir Jolyon Ramsay later Duke of Laas and Oksana Lady d'Enghieux. He entered the Order of Saint Cyran on the XIth day of July in the year 1125, taking the religious name of Christophle. He arrived at Rhemuth for the Royal weddings on the XXIXth day of July in the year 1128. Together with his father and elder brother, he renounced all rights to the Throne of Meara on the Ist day of September in that year. [*King Kelson's Bride*].

Church, Holy and Apostolic. The Holy and Apostolic Church was founded by our Lord Jesus Christ, Who died for our sins, and Who gave unto His XII apostles the power and the right and the duty to spread the Word of God and to convert all of the pagan folk. Corresponding to the XII apostles are the sees of the XII autocephalous churches, which in order of their precedence are these:

Kónstantinopolis and All Byzantyun, headed by the Hieropatriarch Zebinos I, first among equals of all the hierarchs;
Iskandria and All Aigyptos, headed by the Papiarch Shukrallah III;
Rûm and All Etruskia, headed by the Pontifex Maximus Papiarch Zacharias IV;
Antukhia and All Asshyr, headed by the Autiarch Makkikha II;
Hierosalem the Holy City and All Samisrael, headed by the Custodiarch Kallandión II;
Beldour and All Torenth, headed by the Patriarch Alpheios I;
Augusteville and All Bremagne and Fallon, headed by the Patriarch Benedictus VII;
Thenë and All Grecia, headed by the Metropolitan Kyrillos IV;
Nychosy and All Kibris, headed by the Metropolitan Grégorios III;
Valoret and All Gwynedd and Meara, headed by the Archbishop Primate Bradene I;
Sirhowy and All Howicce and Llannedd and The Connait, headed by the Archbishop Primate Aicard I, which jurisdiction once also included the Church of Meara;
Tralia and All Orsal and Forcinn, headed by the Hieropiscop Avitus II.

Church of the Paraclete. This adjunct establishment of the *Arx Fidei* Seminary is located just East of the city of Valoret on the South side of the River Eirian. ["The Priesting of Arilan"].

Ciard *O Ruane*. He was Dhugal MacArdry's faithful middle-aged gillie, having been appointed to that role by Caulay MacArdry Earl of Transha shortly after Dhugal's birth in the year 1108. Ciard was a member of the party comprising King Kelson, Dhugal, and others when they visited Castle Transha on the XXVth day of November in the year 1123. He accompanied his master on the invasion of Meara from the North in May and June of the year 1124. He assisted Dhugal in contacting Kelson after the debacle at the Dorna Plain on the IInd day of July of that year. He accompanied Dhugal to Rhemuth for the latter's knighting on the IIIrd day of March in the year 1125, and further attended him on his quest for the relics of Saint Camber later that month. [*The Bishop's Heir*; *The King's Justice*; *The Quest for Saint Camber*].

Cieran, Brother. He was a lay brother at Saint Piran's Priory during the year 903, having been a member of that establishment for at least X years previous. [*Camber of Culdi*].

Cinhil I Donal Ifor *Haldane*, **King of Gwynedd.** He was born on the XXVIIth day of April in the Year of Our Lord 860, being the only son and heir of Prince Alroy Haldane (Royston Draper) and Nellwyn de Menville. He intermarried with Megan Lady de Cameron on the XXIVth day of December in the year 903, and by her he had children: the Hereditary Prince Aidan Alroy Camber, murdered at the age of III weeks; Hereditary Prince Alroy later King of Gwynedd; the Prince Javan later King of Gwynedd; the Prince Rhys Michael later Duke of Carthmoor later King of Gwynedd; the Prince Alister, dead at the age of III months.

As a youth he used the name of Nicholas Gabriel Draper, and participated in his grandfather's woolen business in Valoret. After his father's death on the XXIInd of September during the Great Plague of the year 878, he was sent on the XVIIth day of April in the year 879 to Saint Foillan's Abbey, where he joined the *Ordo Verbi Dei* and became the priest and monk Brother Benedict. On the XIVth day of November in 903 he was found there by Camber Earl of Culdi and Rhys Thuryn, and was informed of his grandfather's death. He was kidnapped from the cloister on the IVth day of December in that year by Joram MacRorie and Rhys Thuryn, and put forward as the Haldane candidate for the throne of Gwynedd. He was given a dispensation from his vows, and married the ward of Camber Earl of Culdi.

He spent a year at the underground Michaeline Haven near Dhassa. He baptized his infant son Aidan there on the VIth day of November in the year 904, and when the child was poisoned by Father Humphrey that same day, himself killed the priest with his magic. He defeated Imre King of Gwynedd in a duel arcane on the IInd day of December following, and also defeated Imre's sister Princess Ariella and her army at the Battle of Iomaire on the XXVth day of June in the year 905.

On the IInd day of July he witnessed Camber's assimilation of Alister Cullen's memories, and espied what he believed was Camber's ghost at Valoret Castle. At the same time he also noticed Camber's daughter Evaine, who had temporarily assumed the shape of the Michaeline "Brother John." To commemorate Cullen's installation as Bishop of Grecotha on the IXth day of July at Valoret, the King had a special set of vestments created for the new prelate. He was called as a reluctant witness before the hearings held by Archbishop Jaffray on the XXIVth day of October in the year 906 to validate the miracles attributed to "Saint Camber." He visited the shrine of the new Saint on the IInd day of January following.

This great King died of the consumptive complaint on the IInd day of February in the year 917, aged LVI years. His body lay in state in the chapel of Valoret Castle, and his funeral was held on the IXth day instant. His body was buried temporarily in a crypt beneath the Cathedral of All Saints in Valoret, near the Festillic kings, but was later removed and reinterred in the family crypt of the Haldanes at Rhemuth. He seemed to appear at the empowerment of King Javan on the XXVIth day of June in the Year 921.

The *Legends* describe him as having "glossy black hair silvered at the temples, the clear grey Haldane eyes, sage and serene in the lean, handsome face; the slender hands, smooth through years of prayer, but strong, capable of whatever the man should will." R.I.P. *Saint ne peut, si Dieu ne veut.* [*Camber of Culdi*; *Saint Camber*; *Camber the Heretic*; *The Harrowing of Gwynedd*; *King Javan's Year*; *The Bastard Prince*; *King Kelson's Bride*].

Cinhil II Aymeric Nygel *Haldane*, Hereditary Prince and King of Gwynedd, called "The Uncrown'd King." He was born on the XIVth day of March in the Year of Our Lord 989, being the eldest son and heir of Urien King of Gwynedd and the Princess Jaroni daughter of Bhair al-Salah King of R'Kassi. He intermarried with the Lady Micole of Dhassa on the IIIrd day of May in the year 1019, and by her he had children: the Princess Rhetice; the Prince Aldan, born still; and the Princess Albina, dead ahjvey at age II. His wife perished in childbirth on the IInd day of August in the year 1024.

On the IVth day of February in the year 1025 Urien King of Gwynedd named Prince Cinhil Commander of the Royal Army, then being assembled to oppose the expected invasion of Gwynedd by Marek II Pretender of Festil, Kyprian II King of Torenth, and Jolyon II Prince of Meara. He defeated Prince Jolyon on the XXIXth day of May, then moved his forces to the Falling Water River. There he successfully met the challenge of King Kyprian and Prince Marek at Killingford, destroying the elder branch of the Festils.

His father the King Urien having perished on the final day of battle, the Hereditary Prince Cinhil succeeded to the throne of Gwynedd, and immediately began Herculean efforts to save what he could of his injured army. For VII days he laboured mightily, seeming never to sleep, but on the last of these, he suddenly collapsed and died. Although no wounds appeared on his body, it was later thought that he had suffered some grievous wrong to his spirit, one that could not be cured by the physicians of this world. He passed from this life on the XXIVth day of June in the year 1025, aged XXXVI years, and was returned for burial in the family vault at Rhemuth. His younger brother the Prince Malcolm succeeded him as King.

Cornaro has called this Prince "...a most perfect gentleman, kind with those around him but never weak, an excellent judge of character, quick to learn and quick to forgive, a good soldier and commander of men, devoted to his wife and daughters, one of the best kings the Haldanes have yet produced. His loss was a tragedy of the first rank." Because he was never crowned, he is not included on some of the king lists of Gwynedd. R.I.P.

"Cirala," Duke. This name, an anagram for Alaric Morgan Duke of Corwyn, appeared in an anti-Morgan ballad which was repeated to Alaric by the troubadour Gwydion in March of the year 1121. [*Deryni Checkmate*].

Circassia. This ancient emirate is situate in the southeastern quarter of the Kingdom of Libania. It is known primarily for the well-trained mercenaries it hires out to other lands, payment being accepted only in bars of gold. [*King Kelson's Bride*].

Claibourne. Originally part of the Principality of Kheldour, this Northern duchy was split from old Kheldour in the year 906, following the annexation of the Deryni monarchy by Sighere Earl of Eastmarch. Sighere was created I[st] Duke of Claibourne by King Cinhil I on the XXVIth day of August in that year. Claibourne is bounded on the East by the Kheldish Riding, Marley, and Eastmarch, on the North by the Atalantic Ocean, on the West by the Gulf of Kheldour, and on the South by Gwynedd. The duchy is long and narrow, being circumscribed on its Eastern flank by the Rhendall Mountains. Its principal cities include Claibourne Town, the capital, and Rhorau. The former includes the Castle of the Duke of Claibourne and the wondrous Pillars of Rothnall. The principal export of Claibourne is smoked fish. [*Saint Camber*; *The Harrowing of Gwynedd*; *King Javan's Year*; *King Kelson's Bride*].

DUKES OF CLAIBOURNE

HOUSE OF MACEWAN

Sighere	906-917
Ewan I (son)	917-918
Graham I (son)	918-948
Ewan II (grandson)	948-984
Angus (son)	984-1012
Tresham (son)	1012-1025
Keene (son)	1025-1054
Fychan (brother)	1054-1056
Graham II (son)	1056-1078
Ursic (son)	1078-1095
Ewan III (son)	1095-1129
Graham III (son)	1129-1130+

Claret, Widow. This carline found part of the body of the Deryni Lord Rannulf on her land near Tor Caerrorie on the XXVIth day of September in the year 903, and promptly went into hysterics. [*Camber of Culdi*].

Cloome. This town, the seat of the Earldom of the same name, lies on the coast of the Atalantic Ocean at the Southernmost point of the Principality of Meara. It provided many men for the rebel army during the Mearan Rebellion of the year 1124. This was also the seat of the Earls of Cloome, who often supported the Pretenders of Meara. The first of this illustrious line was Ramsay mac Taine, who was created Earl of Cloome by Prince Ithel in the year 972.

Campbell de Broun claimed Cloome as his home, and wrote about it at the end of his diary: "We stopped at Lockeridge Plantation and fed, then proceeded on up Knapps Creek to Master Muir's, where we encamped. We started early the next morning, stopping near the old cabins to feed, then crossed the mountain. Every part of the road has now become quite familiar. We reached the Back Creek about midday, and stopped at Frederick the Buyer's. The final morning was a little cloudy with some appearance of rain. We proceeded on after breakfast, full of the idea of home, and that this was our last day's travel after so long a journey. We stopped at the Master Wood's; him and his lady attended us. They had previously heard of us, and had put the house in order for our reception. We reached it about afternoon. The place looked somewhat desolate, the house being unoccupied and the garden grown up with weeds. I have seen in my wanderings all that the world has to offer. I have suffered many hardships and found the occasional joy. Yet in all this great world, I can truly say that there is no place quite like Cloome." *Clooma dominum emit*. [*The King's Justice*; *King Kelson's Bride*].

EARLS OF CLOOME

HOUSE OF RAMSAY

Ramsay mac Taine	972-999
Taine I (son)	999-1018
Lere (son)	1018-1025
James (brother)	1025-1048
Gaudry (son)	1048-1066
Norbert (nephew)	1066-1096
Taine II (son)	1096-1098
Nolen (brother)	1098-1110
Lloyd (brother)	1110-1122
Macassar (son)	1122-1130+

Cloyce de Clarendon, Sir. This *Custodes* knight was serving as one of Lord Albertus's aides in June of the year 928 during the Expedition to Eastmarch. He helped guard Sir Cathan Drummond on the return trip to Rhemuth. [*The Bastard Prince*].

Cluim Michael Reginaud Haldane, King of Gwynedd, Earl of Carthane. He was born on the XXIVth day of April in the Year of Our Lord 953, being the third surviving son of Uthyr King of Gwynedd and Grania MacInnis Countess of Culdi. He intermarried with the Lady Swynbeth daughter of Tammaron Duke of Cassan on the IXth day of May in the year 972, and by her he had children: the Hereditary Prince Urien later King of Gwynedd; the Princess Tiphanelle, who intermarried with Gosbert King of Howicce; the Prince Jashan later Duke of Carthmoor and Earl of Culdi later Archbishop of Rhemuth and Valoret, who died *sans postérité*; the Princess Ysyllt, who intermarried with Jolyon II Prince of Meara; the Prince Michael Rhys later Earl of Carthane, who renounced his rights to the throne of Gwynedd for himself and his descendants in the year 1009 and intermarried with Mithradita Heiress of the Duchy of Pirek in Howicce, becoming Duke *jure uxoris* and changing his surname by deed poll to Pirek-Haldane, his title of Carthane in Gwynedd being deeded to his IInd son, Earl Godwyn, ancestor of the later Counts of this line; the Princess Michaelina Rhyssa, a twin with her brother, who intermarried with Amandus Count de Prözh in Howicce.

This noble Prince was created Earl of Carthane shortly after his birth, but deeded away this title upon his succession to the throne of Gwynedd to his youngest son, the Prince Michael Rhys. The Prince Cluim served for II years in the Gwyneddan army during the wars with the Festils and Torenth between the years 983 and 985. He succeeded his brother, the King Jasher, on the latter's death in battle on the IInd day of July in the year 985, and successfully brought the war to a conclusion. He was crowned by William III Archbishop of Valoret on the VIIth day of September on that year. The major interest of this Prince was securing peace in his time, and to this end he made a number of important embassies to and alliances with the Kingdoms of Howicce and Llannedd, the Principality of Meara, and others. He died of the stytche on the XVIIIth day of December in the year 994, aged XLI years, and was succeeded by his eldest son, Prince Urien. R.I.P. [*King Javan's Year*].

Coamer* or *Kómar Mountains. This range, called the Kómar Mountains in Torenth, serves as the Southern border between the sovereign kingdoms of Torenth and Gwynedd. To the West lies the Rengarth Plain, and to the East the Medras Steppes. The headwaters of the Western River rise at Kingslake in these mountains. In the Southern part of the range lie the vast Veldur Forests, a major hunting and trapping region. Winters are harshest in the Northernmost part of the range, and the passes there can remain blocked with snow and ice from late November through March. Spring thaws and freshets then flood the caverns and crevices, making passage dangerous for man and beast alike. This great natural barrier between the II kingdoms has protected each from invasion, and has, at the same time, discouraged a more normal commerce, which may be one reason why Torenth and Gwynedd have remained so separate during their histories. [*High Deryni*].

Coel *Howell*, Lord. He was born on the last day of January in the Year of Our Lord 871, being the eldest son and heir of Michael Lord Howell and Gobinet of Vourney, and a half-brother to Elinor Lady Howell and Melissa Lady Howell, each sired of a different mother. He was appointed to the Royal Council of Gwynedd by King Imre on the XXVth day of March in the year 900, and to the Court of Crown Commissioners on the VIth day of January in the year 901. He advised the King on the XXXth day of September in the year 903 to increase his reprisals against the Willimites, who were suspected of having slain Lord Rannulf. On the XXIXth day of November in that year he sent his agents Bors and Fulk to spy on the activities of Father Joram MacRorie and Lord Rhys Thuryn.

He led his rival, Earl Maldred, into an ambush on the day following, and used the murder to accuse Lord Cathan MacRorie of treason. He then found traces of the Draper family records at Saint John's Church in Valoret, and brought the material to the King. He was arrested and executed for treason by Cinhil I King of Gwynedd on the Xth day of January in the year 905, aged XXXIII years. *Écrasez l'infâme.* [*Camber of Culdi*; *Saint Camber*].

Colblaine. This small town was located near Transha in Northwestern Gwynedd. [*The Bishop's Heir*].

Coldoire Pass. This gap through the Rheljan Mountains lies South of the Arranal Canyon, forming a natural passageway between Lochalyn Castle in Eastmarch and the Duchy of Tolán in Torenth, and is defended on its Eastern end by Culliecairn Castle. The Coldoire River (called the Kóldór in Torenth) drains from the cut Eastward into Torenth, and then turns South, where it eventually meets the River Beldour. In June of the year 905 part of the Pretender Ariella's army encamped near here. On the VIIth day of June in the year 928 the forces of Prince Miklós occupied the Castle of Culliecairn at the head of the pass, prompting a reponse from Hrorik Earl of Eastmarch, who was killed in the skirmish that followed. The Barony of Coldoire was established in the year 929 by King Owain, who with the advice of his Regents awarded the title to Riocard of Fearn. Later Barons included the notorious rebel, Rhydon Titular Earl of Eastmarch. [*Saint Camber*; *The Bastard Prince*; "Legacy"].

Colin Périgord Arnaud *d'Auxerre*, Lord of Fianna. He was born on the XIIth day of April in the Year of Our Lord 1102, being the younger son of Gezelin Sovereign Count of Fianna and the Princess Mélusine daughter of Donat King of Fallon. In the Fall of the year 1120 he contrived with Charissa Pretender of Gwynedd to kill Brion King of Gwynedd, and gave the latter a flask of Fiannan wine tainted by *merasha* on the Ist day of November in that year. He was sent with Lord Ralson on that evening to fetch Alaric Duke of Corwyn back to Rhemuth, but was severely wounded in ambush near Valoret on the VIIth day of November in the year 1120, dying there of his injuries on the next day following, aged XVIII years. His body was held temporarily at Saint Mark's Abbey before being returned to his ancestral crypt at Truyère in Fallon for burial. *Accipe nunc Fiannanum insidias, et crimine ab uno disce omnes.* [*Deryni Rising*; *The Quest for Saint Camber*].

Collos. He was the alleged Vézairean brother of Dimitri, the Deryni "sniffer" employed by Paulin of Ramos. Paulin and his men encountered Collos and his brother at sea in the Summer of the year 921, and saved Collos from dying of a fever. In gratitude, Dimitri offered himself in service to Paulin, with Collos being held captive as a surety in Carthmoor. After the death of Dimitri in the year 928, the new Regents sent for Collos to interrogate him regarding his supposed brother's activities, but he could not be found. [*King Javan's Year*].

Col(l)umcille, Father. He was serving as a priest at Lochalyn Castle in Eastmarch during June of the year 928. [*The Bastard Prince*].

Colman II Rodrick Aodh Domnic *MacFaolan-Gruffud*, King of Howicce and Llannedd, Duke of Morganvawr. He was born on the IVth day of May in the Year of Our Lord 1093, being the second son of Illann II King of Howicce and Llannedd and the Princess Célestine, daughter of Ursion Duc du Parmentier and sometime Heir Presumptive of the Kingdom of Bremagne and the Princess Maisie daughter of Donat King of Fallon. He was betrothed in the year 1123 to the Princess Janniver daughter of Pons Sovereign Prince of Pardiac, but when her innocence was violated by Ithel Hereditary Prince of Meara in the year 1124, he denounced her as unclean and lascivious, and she was forced upon the mercy of the King of Gwynedd. Later, he is said to have entered into an understanding with Lucilia Lady Taino, widow of Mineon Count Taino, about the year 1126, but this proposed connection never took place. He also made offers for the hands of several ladies affiliated with the royal houses lying across the Southern Sea, but to no avail, his reputation having preceded him.

The Prince Colman was created Duke of Morganvawr by his brother, King Ronan IV, on the IVth day of May in the year 1107. He succeeded his brother on the VIIIth day of December in the year 1119. Barring any future issue from his own loins, the King Colman's heirs are his cousin, Prince Cuan, to the Kingdom of Howicce, and his younger half-sister, Princess Gwenlian, to the Kingdom of Llannedd. [*King Kelson's Bride*].

Company of Royal Foot. This elite group of Gwyneddan soldiers formed an honour guard in February of the year 917 around the bier of King Cinhil I as he lay in state in Valoret. [*Camber the Heretic*].

Conall Blaine Cluim Uthyr *Haldane*, Hereditary Duke of Carthmoor, Prince Regent of Gwynedd, Sir. This wicked Prince was born on the IIIrd day of March in the Year of Our Lord 1107, being the eldest son and heir of Nigel Duke of Carthmoor and Meraude Lady de Traherne, and Ist cousin to Kelson King of Gwynedd. He intermarried with Rothana Nabila of Nur Hallaj on the XIth day of April in 1125, and by her he had one son: the Prince Albin Nigel Brion Hakim, born posthumously in the year 1126, who was disinherited at the time of his birth by his grandfather from succeeding to the Duchy of Carthmoor, but was reinstated in the year 1128. By his mistress, Vanissa 't-Serclaes, the Prince Conall also had a bastard girlchild, Conalline Amelia, born posthumously on the VIth day of August in the year 1125; she was adopted by her grandfather and given the surname of Haldane in the year 1128, but without dynastic rights.

On the XXVth day of June in the year 1121 he was sent under flag of truce to Warin de Grey to seek a parley. On the XXVth day of November in the year 1123 he accompanied the King Kelson to Trurill and then to Castle Transha, where he objected publicly to the austere accomodations, much to the embarrassment of the King. On the VIIIth day of December following he was included in the King's party during their lightning raid into Meara, and he himself captured the rebel Prince Llewell on the IXth day instant. He accompanied the King's army as it swept into Meara on the XXth day of May in the year 1124, but returned to Rhemuth on the XVIIth day of June as commander of an escort for the ravaged nuns and novices of Saint Brigid's Abbey.

By the Winter of the year 1124 he had begun receiving instruction from the renegade Deryni, Tiercel de Claron, in assuming his Haldane potential. On the IIIrd day of March of the year 1125 he was knighted by his father, Prince Nigel Duke of Carthmoor. Five days later, after having been instructed by Tiercel in the use of the transfer portals in Rhemuth Castle, he killed his mentor in a pique of temper, and hid the remains. The next day he left with Kelson's party on a quest for the remains of Saint Camber, and nearly fell into the flood of the Grelder Creek that swept away the King and Earl Dhugal on the XXIst day instant, but was barely saved and returned to Rhemuth.

On the XXVIth day of March, when he realized that his father was beginning to guess his secret, he attacked Duke Nigel with his magic and put him into a deep coma, assuming power as the new Prince Regent of Gwynedd. He then approached Archbishop Thomas Cardiel on the IInd day of April, and convinced him that Lady Rothana's request for a dispensation from her religious vows, originally dispatched before Kelson's disappearance, was intended to enable Conall and Rothana to marry. Two days later he was again brought to his Haldane potential by Bishop Duncan, Duke Alaric, and Bishop Denis Arilan. He was deposed as Prince Regent on the return of King Kelson to Valoret on the XIXth day of April, and was tried, convicted, and beheaded for his crimes on the IIIrd day of May in the year 1125, aged XVIII years. He was buried with his ancestors in the crypt of the Haldanes beneath Saint George's Cathedral.

He is described in *The Histories of King Kelson* as having a silky mustache and short-cropped black hair, and being slender and slightly taller than his father. His gold ring bore the arms of a IInd son's eldest son: a bordured and crescent-charged Haldane lion overlaid with a label of III points. [*High Deryni*; *The Bishop's Heir*; *The King's Justice*; *The Quest for Saint Camber*; *King Kelson's Bride*].

Conalline Amelia *Haldana't-Serclaes*, later Amelia *Haldane*, Lady. She was born posthumously on the VIth day of August in the Year of Our Lord 1125 to Conall Prince Regent of Gwynedd and Vanissa 't-Serclaes, his former mistress. She was brought to Court with her mother on the XXVIth day of July in the year 1128 under the name Amelia, where she met her grandfather, Nigel Duke of Carthmoor, and became a companion to Nigel's daughter, Princess Eirian. She was formally adopted by Duke Nigel on the VIIIth day of October following, in order to provide her with a name, education, and standing at Court, and was created Baroness Whitney by King Kelson, but without dynastic rights. She had light brown, curly hair and grey eyes. [*King Kelson's Bride*].

Concaradine, Free Port of. This merchant city is located on the West bank of the River Eirian at the point where it joins the River Llanarfon, on the border of Gwynedd with Llannedd. Concaradine was founded as the Byzantyuni fort Concurrandum during the IIIrd century. It quickly prospered, and established its autonomy following the Byzantyuni withdrawal several hundred years later. Famous for its gold and jewel artisans, Concaradine also serves as the turnaround point for the great Southern fleets, such as Morgan's Caralighters. It was the site of a great University in elder days, called the Conlegium Concurrandum. Traditionally, this city has always been free from the levy of taxes by the Kings of Gwynedd, except during the reign of King Imre. It was from here that Monsignor Lawrence Gorony took a merchant ship on the XXth day of March in the year 1121 to deliver the interdict message of the Archbishops to Bishop Tolliver at Coroth. [*Deryni Rising*; *Deryni Checkmate*].

Conlan, Bishop of Stavenham. He was born on the VIth day of May in the Year of Our Lord 1084. He was ordained priest on the Vth day of April in the year 1104, and was elected an itinerant Bishop of Gwynedd on the XIXth day of August in the year 1120. In the Interdict Schism he initially sided with Edmund Loris Archbishop Primate of Valoret, but later supported the

King's Party. He was elected Bishop of Stavenham on the XIXth day of January in the year 1122 to replace Bishop Angelus de Lacey. [*High Deryni*; *The Bishop's Heir*; *The Quest for Saint Camber*].

The Connait. This region lies to the West of Gwynedd, to the North of Howicce, and to the South of Meara, and consists of a number of sovereign states acknowledging no other Overlord, including the Principalities of Pardiac and Arbroath, the Grand Duchy of Calam, the Duchies of Llangan, Cyby, and Gaël, the independent Bishopric of Tyburn, the Free Republic of Fenwick, and the counties of Trevalga, Taino, Saint-Sabinian, and Réomay, plus XVI other autonomous Counties (among them Marchmont) and Baronies, and a handful of independent Abbeys, numbering *in toto* XXXI distinct sovereignties. There has ever been much contentiousness between and among these separate territories over their respective boundaries and fiefdoms, and this constant strife has molded many generations of experienced fighting men. Consequently, this region is especially known for its mercenaries, which it cheerfully hires out in great numbers to any outside state that has need of them, including the so-called Principality of Meara during the Rebellion of the year 1124, when CCC soldiers were leased by Edmund Loris ex-Archbishop of Valoret from Pons Prince of Pardiac. On those few occasions when an outside state such as Howicce has tried to invade the region, the loosely-organized Council of Sovereign Princes has elected a Supreme Warlord to drive them out. In the Summer of the year 1128 the Council delegated Gron III Grand Duke of Calam to represent them in Beldour at the inauguration of Liam Lajos II King of Torenth.

The Connait has a warm, dry climate, with little rain falling in the summer months on its rolling, brown hills. Its relatively poor economy is based mainly around sheep farming and salmon fishing and the exportation of its fighting men. The coat-of-arms of the Council of Sovereign Princes of The Connait displays: ermine, two salmon haurient addorsed *gules*. [*The Harrowing of Gwynedd*; *The King's Justice*; *King Kelson's Bride*].

Connor. This guard at Valoret Castle was serving the Regents in the year 918. He was questioned by Prince Javan about the events of the night of the XXIst day of January in that year, when Tavis and Ansel invaded the Castle to block the Deryni powers of the Drummond family. [*The Harrowing of Gwynedd*].

Conquhare, Baron Campbell. He was born on the Vth day of January in the Year of Our Lord 1079, being the eldest son and heir of Cuchulainn II Baron Campbell and Ossiana Lady Morchoe. He intermarried with Renny Lady Higgins on the IVth day of May in the year 1099, and by her he had children: the Hereditary Lord Crohoore; the Lady Constance; the Lord Columban; the Lady Cossian; the Lord Celsus; the Lord Carthy. He succeeded his father on the XVIIth day of November in the year 1104. This Lord of Eastmarch was a longtime retainer to the family of the Earl of Marley. He was serving as an aide to Bran Coris the traitor Earl during June of the year 1121, but was not held responsible by the King for his master's actions. [*High Deryni*].

Constance, Sister. She was a nun at Saint Brigid's Abbey in Meara in the year 1124. She was killed in the attack by the Prince Ithel's men on the XVth day of June in that year. R.I.P. [*The King's Justice*].

Cor Culdi. This hereditary ancestral seat and fortress of the Earls of Culdi is located near the town of the same name in the Purple March, near the border between Gwynedd and Meara. [*Camber of Culdi*].

Cor Ramet. On this field in Corwyn near Dol Shaia the King Kelson of Gwynedd and the rebel Bishops agreed to rendezvous on the XVIIIth day of June in the year 1121. [*High Deryni*].

Corban *Howell*, Earl of Eastmarch *jure uxoris*, Lord Howell. He was born on the XIXth day of November in the Year of Our Lord 900, being the eldest son and heir of Cellach Lord Howell and Phyllida Lady Rebais, and the Ist cousin of Coel Lord Howell. He intermarried with Stacia Heiress of Eastmarch on the XXIInd day of May in the year 927, and by her he had children: the Hereditary Count Kennet later Earl of Eastmarch; the Lady Ferelithe; the Lord Jago; the Lady Joslin; the Lady Sudrette; the Lord Corbik.

The Lord Corban became Earl of Eastmarch *jure uxoris* on the VIIth day of June in the Year 928, and was confirmed in his rank by King Rhys Michael on the XXIVth day instant. After the Torenthi occupation of Culliecairn Castle in early June of that year, he rode to Marley to seek the assistance of his uncle-in-law, the Earl Sighere, and sent letters to his wife's cousin, Graham I Duke of Claibourne, and also to King Rhys Michael, seeking military assistance. He became a strong supporter of the Haldane monarchy. He died on the IXth day of December in the year 968, aged LXVIII years, and was succeeded by his son, Lord Kennet. According to the *Heirs*, "he was a darkly handsome young man with a close-clipped black beard and kind eyes." R.I.P. [*The Bastard Prince*].

Corbet *Mathiesen*, Bishop. He was born on the XVIth day of October in the Year of Our Lord 1086. He was ordained priest on the IIIrd day of July in the year 1105, and was elected an itinerant Bishop of Gwynedd on the XIXth day of January in the year 1122. [*Deryni Magic*].

Cordan. He was serving as chief surgeon to Bran Coris Earl of Marley in June of the year 1121. [*High Deryni*].

Corinne Cassandaria *Furstána-Festila*, Princess of Gwynedd. She was born on the XXXth day of April in the Year of Our Lord 841, being the eldest daughter and third child of Festil III King of Gwynedd and Lady Dionysia daughter of Andronikos Thópis, Strátegos and Despot of Esclavonia. She died of the creeping cramps on the last day of March in the year 854, aged XII years, and was buried with her family at All Saints' Cathedral in Valoret. Of this sad little girl, whose portrait still hangs in the old Palace at Valoret, Dom Alexius wrote:

"She never walked nor talked." R.I.P. [*King Javan's Year*].

Cormac *Hamberlyn*. This border chieftain was outlawed by Brion King of Gwynedd on the Ist day of January in the year 1107, and became a brigand in the hills above Ratharkin. He later supported Caitrin Princess of Meara during the Mearan Rebellion of the years 1123 and 1124, but escaped the King's dragnet when the uprising collapsed. [*The King's Justice*].

Coroth. This capital city of the Duchy of Corwyn is located in Southeastern Gwynedd on Coroth Bay at the mouth of the Twin Rivers. Because of the siroccos which blow down the Rengarth Plain during the Fall months, the fort was originally called Caurus or Corus by the Byzantyuni invaders who arrived there circa the year 200. It quickly became a thriving port town that continued to grow even after the departure of the Easterners in the year 486. Thus, Maximianus *Gubernator* established his independence shortly thereafter, and gradually expanded his realm to incorporate his neighbouring states, calling himself *Comes Cauri* by the year 500. Maxime I d'Estavaye IVth Count of Coroth proclaimed himself King of the new Kingdom of Mooryn on the Ist day of September in the year 561.

Coroth's location on the Bay of that name provides it with a sheltered port and a mild climate year round, and ships from the Eleven Kingdoms, Torenth, the Forcinn States, Fallon, and Bremagne call there constantly throughout the year. The city is protected by II forts with lighthouses situate on the crescent points of the Bay, and by the great iron chain Restrainer strung between the twin granite jetties during times of war. Upper Corwyn also includes areas of dense forest that provide the basis for a thriving lumber industry. The city includes such splendors as the magnificent Palace, the well-endowed Ducal Library, the Castle Gardens, Saint Matthew's Gate, and Saint Matthew's Cathedral.

Campbell de Broun once arrived here by sea, and noted: "I shall never travel by ship again. The food was bad, the company worse, and I was sick the entire voyage. The vision of Coroth rising up from the right-hand side of its Bay was a welcome sight to this weary trav'ler. We disembarked on the quay, and crossed Old Dominic Prospect to the Great Dragon Inn. Although the cost of a night's lodging was usurious, I paid the gold Crown gladly to have a tasty meal and a fine feather'd bed, for I had heard about this place on my travels. Nor was I disappointed. This inn catered to a better custom than usual, and the company was gentle and the eatery warm and clean and pleasant on this Spring ev'ning. The seafood here was the best I have tasted outside of Cloome itself, fresh from the Bay, and the wine was Fiannan, not as good as Mearan, but certainly passable. My bed was soft and bug-free, and the women accomodating. If I can afford the passage, I might even return here one day." *Mais dans ce monde, il n'y a rien d'assuré que la mort et les impôts.* [*The Bishop's Heir*; *The Quest for Saint Camber*; *King Kelson's Bride*].

Coroth Bay. This harbor provides an all-weather anchorage for ships reaching the city of Coroth. On the upper entrance to the Bay, at Eskill Head, lies Great Roderick, the largest lighthouse in Mooryn, which shines the way for ships coming from both North and South to enter the sheltered harbor. [*The Quest for Saint Camber*; *King Kelson's Bride*].

Corund, Sir. This knight was ordered to guard the Princes Javan and Rhys Michael at the fair in Valoret during May of the year 917. Corund was killed in the assassination attempt on the princes on the XXVIIIth day of September in that year, while defending his charges, and was buried with high honours. R.I.P. [*Camber the Heretic*; *King Javan's Year*].

Corwode. This manor of the Corwyn estates was given by Brion King of Gwynedd to Sir Kenneth Kai Morgan on the XXIXth day of December in the year 1095. It was to have been part of Bronwyn de Corwyn's dowry on her marriage to Kevin McLain in March of the year 1121, but it reverted to the Duchy on her death, to be held in reserve for the eventual marriage of Duke Alaric's daughter, Lady Briony. *Cineres credis curare sepultos?* [*Deryni Checkmate*].

Corwyn. This duchy, one of the largest in Gwynedd, is located in the far Southeastern portion of the country. The Western River forms its Northeastern border with Torenth, the Lendour Mountains its Western border with the Crown Duchy of Haldane. Its Northern border touches at different points on the Earldom of Derry, the old Prince-Bishopric of Dhassa, and the Earldom of Lendour, as well as several lesser estates. To the South lies the Southern Sea and the Twin Rivers, and to the Southwest the Duchy of Carthmoor. The capital of Corwyn is the old city of Coroth, which also served as the seat of the defunct Kingdom of Mooryn.

Historically, the Duchy is one of the successor states to the old Kingdom of Mooryn. The first Duke, Sieur Dominic du Joux, eldest son and heir of Lord Richard du Joux and grandson of Réginald Duc du Joux, was created Duke of Corwyn on the XXIst day of October in the year 826 by King Festil I II months after the marriage of the Hereditary Prince Festil *Junior* to Brionne Heiress of Mooryn, to honour the contributions of Dominic's father, Lord Richard, who had died establishing Festil I on this throne. Corwyn's autonomous status remained unchanged until the time of Duke Jernian and the invasion of Gwynedd by the Pretender Imre II. At the death of the last Duke in the direct line, Sir Stiofan Anthony de Corwyn, in the year 1068, whose only son Airlie had predeceased him, the title fell into abeyance, passing successively through his granddaughter, Stevana Countess of Lendour, and great-granddaughter, Lady Alyce de Corwyn de Morgan, before being reinstated in the present titleholder, Duke Alaric, the Ist male heir in IV generations. During the Interregnum the Duchy was administered by various Crown-appointed Governors. The arms of this duchy are: *sable*, a gryphon segreant *vert* within a double tressure flory-counter-flory *or*. *A Corvinia chi vi nasce, mal vi si pasce*. [*Deryni Rising*; *Deryni Checkmate*; *High Deryni*; *The Bishop's Heir*; *The Quest for Saint Camber*; *King Kelson's Bride*]. See also: Alyce, Alaric, Briony, Kelric, Vera.

DUKES OF CORWYN

HOUSE OF CORWYN

Dominic	826-872
Artorius (grandson)	872-904
Taysan (son)	904-935
Arion (son)	935-978
Jernian (son)	978-1026
Stiofan Anthony (son)	1026-1068

TITLE IN ABEYANCE

HOUSE OF MORGAN

Alaric (great-great-grandson)	1091-1130+

Cosim. He was serving as personal Healer to Miklós Prince of Torenth during June of the year 928, and examined the body of his master on the XXIInd day of that month. He then altered the memories of Prince Marek, at the pretender's request, to keep the knowledge of the nature of Miklós's death hidden from Arion I King of Torenth. He was a striking-looking Deryni with piercing eyes and silver highlights at his temples, and he wore the high-collared, dark green tunic of a military Healer. [*The Bastard Prince*].

Council of Ramos. This Great Church Council was held from December of the year 917 through Spring of the year 918 at the village of Ramos West of Valoret. Initially called to overturn the election of Bishop Alister Cullen as new Archbishop Primate of Valoret and All Gwynedd and to install Bishop Hubert MacInnis as his successor, it quickly metamorphosed into a wide-ranging examination of the status of the Deryni minority in the Kingdom of Gwynedd. It was this Council that initiated the bans against the Deryni serving in Holy Orders and, indeed, in any position of authority. The Council promulgated as its final acts a code of laws and practices popularly known as the Ramos Conventions. Some of these were overturned in July of the year 928, but most remained in force until King Kelson ordered their wholesale re-examination and rescission in the Summer of the year 1125. [*Camber the Heretic*; *The Harrowing of Gwynedd*; *The King's Justice*; *The Quest for Saint Camber*].

Council, Royal Council, Privy Council, or High Council of Gwynedd. This governing body of Gwynedd advises the King or his Regents on matters of state. Members of the Council may be appointed by the King in his majority or by his Regents in his minority, and the King or his designee always sits on the Council. By custom, the legally-designated Regents of Gwynedd also serve on the Council, as do the Archbishops of Valoret and Rhemuth.

In the year 903, the penultimate year of King Imre, members included: Cathan MacRorie Master of Culdi; Coel Lord Howell; Anscom Archbishop Primate of Valoret and All Gwynedd; Earl Santare; Maldred Earl Kirwan; Torcuill Baron de la Marche; Dothan Lord of Erne.

In the year 905, the Ist year of King Cinhil I, the membership of the Council included: Alister Cullen Bishop of Grecotha; Jebediah of Alcara, Earl Marshal of Gwynedd; Anscom Archbishop Primate of Valoret and All Gwynedd; Robert Archbishop of Rhemuth; Hildred Baron Nagapple, Master of Horse of Gwynedd; Torcuill Baron de la Marche; Aquineas Earl Fintan; Murdoch Earl of Carthane. Sighere Duke of Claibourne was appointed in the year 906. Earl Fintan died in the year 910, and was replaced by Bishop Kai Descantor.

In the year 916, the XIIth year of King Cinhil I, the members included: Jaffray Archbishop Primate of Valoret and All Gwynedd; Robert Archbishop of Rhemuth; Alister Cullen Bishop of Grecotha; Darius Earl Udaut; Jebediah Earl Marshal of Gwynedd; Hildred Baron Nagapple, Master of Horse of Gwynedd; Torcuill Baron de la Marche; Bishop Kai Descantor; Sighere Duke of Claibourne; Murdoch Earl of Carthane.

On the IInd day of February in the year 917, which was also the Ist year of King Alroy, the Regents assumed power, and on the next day dismissed Alister Cullen, Kai Descantor, Jebediah, and Torcuill. The members then included: Hubert Auxiliary Bishop of Rhemuth; Jaffray Archbishop Primate of Valoret and All Gwynedd; Robert Archbishop of Rhemuth; Murdoch Earl of Carthane; Rhun Earl of Sheele; Darius Earl Udaut, High Constable of Gwynedd; Sighere Duke of Claibourne; Hildred Baron Nagapple, Master of Horse of Gwynedd. Duke Sighere died in July of 917, and was replaced by his son, Ewan I Duke of Claibourne. Archbishop Jaffray died in October of that year. Following the murder of Duke Ewan in 918, Manfred Earl of Culdi was named Earl Marshal in his place, and Fane, new Deputy Regent of Kheldour, and Bishop Paulin were was also added to the Council. Earl Manfred resigned as Earl Marshal in 919, and was replaced by Brother Albertus, Grand Master of the *Equites Custodum Fidei*.

In June of the year 921, the Ist year of King Javan, the Council included: Murdoch Earl of Carthane; Rhun Earl of Sheele; Hubert Archbishop Primate of Valoret and All Gwynedd; Robert Archbishop of Rhemuth; Darius Earl Udaut, High Constable of Gwynedd; Tammaron Earl Fitz-Arthur; Manfred Earl of Culdi; Rhys Michael Prince of Gwynedd; Brother Albertus, Grand Master of the *Equites Custodum Fidei* and Earl Marshal of Gwynedd; Bishop Paulin, Vicar General of the *Custodes Fidei*; Hildred Baron Nagapple, Master of Horse of Gwynedd; Fane Lord Fitz-Arthur; and Bonner II Earl of Tarleton. Fane Lord Fitz-Arthur became Regent of Cassan in May, and was removed from the Council in July, being replaced by Lord Jerowen as Vice Chancellor of Gwynedd. Murdoch died in August, and was replaced by his son, Richard Murdoch Earl of Carthane. Jerowen and Hildred were killed in May of 922.

In June of the year 928, the VIIth year of King Rhys Michael, the members included: Richard Murdoch Earl of Carthane; Rhun Earl of Sheele; Hubert Archbishop Primate of Valoret and All Gwynedd; Robert Archbishop of Rhemuth; Darius Earl Udaut, High Constable of Gwynedd; Tammaron Earl Fitz-Arthur; Manfred Earl of Culdi; Brother Albertus, Grand Master of the *Equites Custodum Fidei* and Earl Marshal of Gwynedd; Bishop Paulin, Vicar General of the *Custodes Fidei*; and Bonner II Earl of Tarleton.

In July of the year 928, the Ist year of King Owain, following the *coup d'état* by the new Regents, the members included: Graham I Duke of Claibourne; Sighere Earl of Marley; Sir Cathan Drummond; Ainslie Lord Argoed; Sir Robert Ainslie; Alfred Archbishop of Rhemuth; Ailin Archbishop Primate of Valoret and All Gwynedd; Michaela Dowager Queen of Gwynedd.

Two centuries later, in the year 1120, the XXVIth year of Brion King of Gwynedd, the membership included: Nigel Duke of Carthmoor; Jared McLain Duke of Cassan; Kevin McLain Earl of Kierney; Ewan III MacEwan Duke of Claibourne; Bran Coris Earl of Marley; Rogier Earl Fallon; Bishop Denis Arilan; Ian Howell Earl of Eastmarch; Patrick Corrigan Archbishop of Rhemuth; Edmund Loris Archbishop Primate of Valoret and All Gwynedd; Gérard Lord Ralson; and Alaric Morgan Duke of Corwyn. After the deaths of Ralson and Brion in November of 1120, Jehana Dowager Queen Gwynedd replaced the King as Regent. She in turn was replaced by Sean O'Flynn Earl Derry (appointed by Kelson for the deceased Ralson) and King Kelson on the XIVth day instant. Rogier was killed later that evening by Ian. Kevin, Jared, Bran, Ian, and Patrick Corrigan all died by the year 1121.

By the year 1124, the Vth year of King Kelson, the Royal Council consisted of: Ewan III MacEwan Duke of Claibourne; Duncan McLain Duke of Cassan; Bradene Archbishop Primate of Valoret and All Gwynedd; Alaric Morgan Duke of Corwyn; Thomas Cardiel Archbishop of Rhemuth; Dhugal MacArdry Earl of Transha; Saer de Traherne Earl of Rhendall; Sean O'Flynn Earl Derry; Jodrell Baron Ardglass; Denis Arilan Bishop of Dhassa; and Nigel Duke of Carthmoor. [*Deryni Rising*; *Deryni Checkmate*; *High Deryni*; *The Bishop's Heir*; *The King's Justice*].

Creoda, Bishop of Carbury, later Bishop of Culdi. He was born on the XVIIth day of July in the Year of Our Lord 1054. He was ordained priest on the XIIth day of December in the year 1073. He was elected an itinerant Bishop of Gwynedd on the Xth day of May in the 1108, Auxiliary Bishop of Rhemuth on the XXIIIrd day of March in the year 1117, and Bishop of Carbury on the XIth day of April in the year 1119. During the Interdict Schism of the year 1121 he initially sided with the Archbishops; however, when it became clear that Edmund Loris Archbishop of Valoret would lose his struggle against Kelson King of Gwynedd, he adopted a neutral stance. His see was dissolved on the XVth day of January in the year 1122, and he was moved to the newly re-established see of Culdi. In November of the year 1123 the Bishop Creoda connived to bring Loris back to power, forming an alliance with several dissident Bishops, including Prince Judhael of Meara. He was promised the Patriarchate of Meara in return. After the rebellion failed in July of the year 1124 and Loris was executed, Bishop Creoda was formally degraded from his see and imprisoned for life by the action of the Synod of Valoret on the XVIIIth day of March in the year 1125. [*Deryni Checkmate*; *High Deryni*; *The Bishop's Heir*; *The King's Justice*; *The Quest for Saint Camber*].

Crevan *Allyn*, Vicar General of the Order of Saint Michael. He was born on the XXIXth day of December in the Year of Our Lord 861. He joined the Michaeline Order in the year 875, and was ordained priest on the XXth day of October in the year 881. He became one of the principal organizers of the Michaeline retreat underground before the onslaught of King Imre's forces at the end of the year 904. He was picked by Camber to succeed Alister Cullen as Vicar General of the Order on the VIth day of July in the year 905, and was elected and formally installed II days later. He attended the consecration of Alister Cullen as Bishop of Grecotha and Robert Oriss as Archbishop of Rhemuth on the IXth day of July in the year 905 at Valoret. On the XXIIIrd day of October in the year 906 he participated in the first consistory of Archbishop Jaffray. In August of the year 917 he began the preparations for an orderly secret withdrawal of the Michaelines from Gwynedd, and gave the order for the evacuation on the IInd day of September of that year. He died in exile at Djellarda on the XIIth day of May in the year 932, aged LXX years. According to the *Legends*, "he had that sort of intuition and perspective which allowed him to move with the times, flexible in the lesser things while remaining true to what could not be compromised, no matter what the temptation." R.I.P. [*Saint Camber*; *Camber the Heretic*].

Crinan. He was serving as a squire to Cathan Hereditary Count of Culdi in September of the year 903. He brought the news of Cathan's death to Tor Caerrorie on the Ist day of December in that year. On the next day he doubled for Rhys Thuryn under a shape-changing spell to prevent King Imre's soldiers from arresting Camber and his family. *Die Schönen Tage in Kärrörie sind nun zu Ende.* [*Camber of Culdi*; *Camber the Heretic*].

Cronin, Abbot of Saint Mary's in the Hills. He was serving as head of Saint Mary's in the Hills near Culdi monastery in January of the year 918. [*The Harrowing of Gwynedd*].

Crooked Dragon Inn. This rather dowdy hostelry is located in the Torenthi border town of Fathane. It was here that Sean Earl Derry stayed on the XXIInd day of March in the year 1121, when he was spying for Alaric Duke of Corwyn on the movements of Torenthi forces in the area.

Campbell de Broun has said of this establishment that "...It squats like a bedbug in the central part of Fathane. That evening the fog was very thick as we made our way slowly into town, and we could hear the bells of the river boats ringing dully over the waterfront. Everything, including us, was dripping with damp. A few persons watched us but most just shied away. We became hungry for real food and clean beds and our horses were completely played out. But the ale was watery, the beds full of lumps and bugs, and our wretched mounts had better to eat than we poor travelers. How good it will be to sleep in our own beds again!" [*Deryni Checkmate*].

Cuan Culen Cressing Coel *MacFaolan-Gruffud*, Heir Presumptive to the Throne of Howicce, Duke of Maigh. He was born on the IInd day of February in the Year of Our Lord 1110, being the son of the Prince Cormac Duke of Maigh and the Countess Mélovée daughter of Branly II Grand Duke of Calam. He succeeded his father on IVth day of October in the year 1122. He became Heir Presumptive to the Throne of Howicce after the deaths of King Ronan IV in the year 1119, and of Duke Cormac III years later. His name has been romantically linked with that of his cousin, the Princess Gwenlian, Heir Presumptive to the Throne of Llannedd. [*King Kelson's Bride*].

Cùilteine. This Marcher holding South of Droghera was considered as a potential site for the new Michaeline Commanderie in the year 905. Although passed over in favour of New Argoed, a minor Michaeline House was established here at this time, and existed for XII years, until evacuated in September of the year 917. It was located near Saint Brigid's Abbey in Western Gwynedd, on the border with Meara. [*Saint Camber; Camber the Heretic; The Bishop's Heir; The Quest for Saint Camber*].

Cùilteine Road. Dhugal Earl of Transha traversed this highway with his captive, the Princess Sidana, while escaping from Ratharkin and the Mearan rebels on the IXth day of December of the year 1123. [*The Bishop's Heir*].

Culdi. This walled town in the Honour of Culdi, once the seat of the Earl of Culdi, is located in Gwynedd in the mountains which form the border between Meara and Gwynedd. The title was created on the XXIInd day of July in the year 822 by King Festil I for his sword-companion, Ballard MacRorie, and descended in his family through Davin MacRorie, who was attainted in the year 917. The County of Culdi was re-erected on the Ist day of October in that same year for Manfred MacInnis Baron Marlor. In the year 982, at the death of Earl Manfred's granddaughter, Grania Countess of Culdi and Dowager Queen of Gwynedd, the Earldom of Culdi escheated to the Crown, and was regranted on the XXXth day of November in that same year to Prince Jasher Haldane, and after his death to Prince Jashan Haldane, and then to Prince Richard Haldane at his birth in the year 1055. However, the town of Culdi, its castle and environs, were donated by the King of Gwynedd to the Duchy of Corwyn in the year 1092, perhaps because of its ancient associations with the Deryni Saint Camber of Culdi. Buried at Culdi are Lady Alyce de Corwyn de Morgan, who died in the year 1095, her daughter, Lady Bronwyn, and Bronwyn's fiancé, Kevin McLain Earl of Kierney, the latter II dying there on the XXIXth day of March in the year 1121. Culdi was also the site of the Synod which met in November of the year 1123 to elect a new Bishop of Meara, Henry Istelyn. [*Camber of Culdi; Deryni Rising; Deryni Checkmate; High Deryni; The Bishop's Heir; The King's Justice; The Quest for Saint Camber*].

EARLS OF CULDI

HOUSE OF MACRORIE

Ballard I	822-824
Angus (brother)	824-826
Cathan (son)	826-827
Joram (brother)	827-828
Adrian (brother)	828-838
Ballard II (son)	838-871
Camber (son)	871-905
Davin (grandson)	905-917

HOUSE OF MACINNIS

Manfred	917-928
Iver (son)	928-948
Grania (daughter)	948-982

HOUSE OF HALDANE

Jasher (son)	982-985
Jashan (nephew)	985-1055
Richard (great-nephew)	1055-1111
Cinric (son)	1111-1114
Richard (2nd time)	1114
Richelle (daughter)	1114-1130+

Culdi Highlands. These hills are located South of Culdi and North of Droghera. It was here that the hidden abbey of Saint Mary's in the Hills was located in the Xth century. [*Camber the Heretic*].

Culliecairn. This Haldane stronghold is located near the Gwyneddan border with Torenth at the head of the Coldoire Pass between Eastmarch and the Duchy of Tolán, and comprises a castle, small town, and permanently-occupied garrison. On the VIIth day of June in the year 928 the fortress was taken by Prince Miklós, brother of the King of Torenth, prompting a skirmish in which Hrorik II Earl of Eastmarch lost his life. The Torenthi forces withdrew on the XXIIIrd day of that month at the order of Prince Marek, following the death of their commander, Prince Miklós. *Bellum ita suscipiatur, ut nihil aliud nisi pax quæsita videatur.* [*The Bastard Prince*].

Custodes Fidei (The Guardians of the Faith), **also called *Ordo Custodum Fidei*.** This religious Order was founded by Paulin Sinclair of Ramos on the IInd day of February in the year 918 as a successor to the Little Brothers of Saint Ercon. The Order was originally created to reform ecclesiastical education in Gwynedd in such a way that all Deryni would be excluded from Holy Orders. It was given complete authority over all education in Gwynedd, including supervision of examinations for entry into the priesthood. All seminaries in the land were immediately made over to the new Order, and all ordinations were halted until Lammastide (the Ist day of August following), by which time the Order was asked to issue an approved list of seminaries. Its mandate was later expanded to ferret out and eliminate members of the Deryni race by whatever means possible.

The military arm of the Order, called the *Equites Custodum Fidei (The Knights of the Guardians of the Faith)*, was intended to replace the Michaelines, and to defend the Church from its Deryni enemies. Peter former Earl of Tarleton was named the first Grand Master of the Order under the religious name of Albertus. Also appointed were Marcus Concannon as Chancellor General in charge of the seminaries, Brother Serafin as Inquisitor General, and Father Lior as Serafin's assistant. Paulin Sinclair of Ramos was named first Vicar General. Chapters were established in all cathedrals in Gwynedd. The Order's principal seminary, the *Arx Fidei* Abbey (*Citadel of Faith*), was originally located just North of Rhemuth in the year 918, but was disbanded X years later and re-established in the year 948 at a new site across the River Eirian from Valoret, near the associated Abbey Church of the Paraclete.

On the XIIth day of July in the year 928 the *Custodes* were ordered by Ailin Archbishop Primate of Valoret and All Gwynedd to reform their practices, and the *Equites* section of the Order was completely disbanded, as were individual *Custodes* establishments at Ramos and Rhemuth.

Brothers of the Order wore a cincture of braided Haldane red and gold knotted over a black cassock, which was a symbol of the Order's mandate to unify holy and secular law; their black mantles were faced with Haldane crimson to signify the special patronage of the Crown of Gwynedd. The Grand Master was invested with a wide scarlet sash, tying over it the cincture plaited of Haldane scarlet and gold cords; his black mantle was lined with scarlet, clasped with a pair of haloed lion heads at the throat, and bore a larger version of the haloed-lion badge *appliquéd* over the left shoulder. The Order's arms were: *gules*, a winged golden lion sejant guardant, its head ennobled with a halo, holding in its dexter paw an upraised sword. *Tantum religio potuit suadere malorum.* [*The Harrowing of Gwynedd*; *King Javan's Year*; "The Priesting of Arilan"]. See also: Paulin, *Equites Custodum Fidei.*

Cyric, Brother. He was a monk at Saint Stefan's abbey in April of the year 905. [*Deryni Challenge*].

Cyric Olivier Fabian Donus von Horthy, Hereditary Horthness and Prince of Tralia. He was born on the VIIIth day of March in the Year of Our Lord 1106, being the eldest son and heir of Létald Hort of Orsal and Prince of Tralia and the Sharifa Husniyya daughter of Rauf al-Zaman King of R'Kassi and the Shaikha Zekiye daughter of Abd al-Mejid II Emir of Tôrtous. He accompanied his father, Kelson King of Gwynedd, and Liam Lajos II King of Torenth from Orsal upriver to Beldour, beginning on the IVth day of July in the year 1128. He discussed his own possibilities for marriage with King Kelson some III days later, urging that monarch to pick a bride soon, so that the field would be opened for other prospective bridegrooms. On the XVIIth day instant, following the installation of King Liam Lajos, he took command of his father's ships on their return trip downriver to Orsal. He entered the service of Bahadur Khan King of R'Kassi later in that year. He was tall and fair. [*King Kelson's Bride*].

Czalsky. This County of Torenth is situate North of Arjenol and East of Jándrich in Torenth, South of Avarsland, and west of the sovereign Grand Duchy of Érskeburg on the border of that country with Torenth. The region was annexed by King Arion I in the year 956, who amalgamated together several autonomous lordships and granted them all under I title to his IInd cousin, Bogdan Graf von Süzdal, under the title Count Czalsky. [*King Kelson's Bride*].

COUNTS CZALSKY

HOUSE OF FURSTAN-SÜZDAL-CZALSKY

Bogdan I	956-971
Dytryk (son)	971-999
Oleg (brother)	999-1002
Gur'yan (son)	1002-1024
Bogdan II (son)	1024-1025
Bazhen (brother)	1025
Kiryak (cousin)	1025-1029
Silyan (grandson)	1029-1076
Bogdan III (son)	1076-1101
Maryav (nephew)	1101-1119
László (son)	1119-1128
Bertil (brother)	1128-1130+

Daffreen River. This stream serves as the natural boundary between the Duchy of Claibourne on the West and the Kheldish Riding on the East for the bottom half of its course. Its headwaters lie in the Kheldish Mountains of the Kheldish Riding, and it ultimately empties into the Atalantic Ocean just East of Stavenham. The Daffreen is particularly known for its fine salmon fishing, and for the spectacular vista of the Leumuisge, a great waterfall that drops some CL feet from the Cregganside.

Dafydd *Leslie*, Lord. He was born on the XVIth day of May in the Year of Our Lord 894, being the son of Jonatan Lord Leslie and Rolanda Lady Healy, and a nephew of Jowerth Lord Leslie. He wrote to Ansel MacRorie informing him of King Cinhil I's death on the IInd day of February in the year 917. He was arrested on the XVIth day of August in the year 917 by the Regents' soldiers, and brought to Rhemuth for questioning. Rather than betray his colleagues, during an interrogation by Tavis O'Neill he died there on the XXIst day instant of self-induced convulsions, aged XXIII years. A month later, on the XXVIIIth day of September, his foster brother, Trefor Lord of Morland, attempted to avenge him by attacking the Princes Javan and Rhys Michael. R.I.P. [*Camber the Heretic*].

Daíthi, Father. This *Custodes* priest was appointed as Chaplain to King Javan at Rhemuth in succession to Father Faelan on the IVth day of October in the year 921. He made daily appeals to Faelan to return to *Arx Fidei* Abbey. [*King Javan's Year*].

Damon. He was serving as a guard in Rhys and Evaine Thuryn's household in the year 917. At the end of December in that year he accompanied Evaine and her family on her trip from Sheele to Trurill. He found and rescued the tortured Camlin Lord MacLean at Trurill on the Ist day of January following. [*Camber the Heretic*].

Danoc. This Gwyneddan earldom is located South of the County of Jenas on the River Llanarfon, at the corner which forms the border between Gwynedd and Howicce and Llannedd. The first Earl, Gillis Gillispie, was elevated from Baron to Earl by King Malcolm on the XIXth day of November in the year 1025 in recognition of his valour at Killingford. [*High Deryni*; *The Bishop's Heir*].

EARLS OF DANOC

HOUSE OF GILLISPIE

Gillis	1025-1038
Canody (son)	1038-1062
Galen (brother)	1062-1066
Moncure (son)	1066-1097
Aubrey (son)	1097-1130+

Darius, Baron and Earl Udaut, Lord Constable of Gwynedd. He was born on the XXXIst day of March in the Year of Our Lord 869, being the eldest son and heir of Cyrus Baron Udaut and Philomena Lady Bourquin. He intermarried with Pema Lady MacInnis on the XIIIth day of May in the year 903, and by her he had children: the Hereditary Count Moray later Earl Udaut; the Lady Lirin, who intermarried with Richard Earl of Carthane; the Lady Ermengarde; the Lord Avon later Baron Varagh.

The Lord Udaut succeeded his father as Baron on the IVth day of March in the year 884. On the VIth day of November in the year 905 this human Baron was appointed by King Cinhil I to the Royal Council and named Lord Constable of Gwynedd, maintaining that position for some XXIII years. He was then sent later that day with Baron Torcuill de la Marche to seek an alliance with Sighere Earl of Eastmarch and Warlord of Kheldour, in which mission they were successful. On the IVth day of February in the year 917 he was created Earl by King Alroy acting on the advice of his Regents. As Constable Lord Udaut attended the trial of the Deryni assassins on the XXVIIIth day of September in that year. He was present at the death of King Alroy on the XXIIIrd day of June in the year 921, and gave his oath to the new King Javan later that same day.

On the VIIth day of September in that year he was given a new set of land warrants to be distributed throughout Gwynedd. On the IInd day of December following he had the bodies of the V alleged members of Ansel's so-called bandit party drawn and quartered, their parts being distributed for display throughout Gwynedd. However, he betrayed his oath and supported the former Regents during their *coup d'état* of the XIth day of May in the year 922.

In June of the year 928 he was delegated to remain in Rhemuth in his role as Lord Constable. However, as he was escorting the King Rhys Michael and his Haldane levies on their way out of the city on the XVth day of that month, his horse was deliberately spooked by the Deryni double agent, Dimitri. Earl Udaut was thrown from his seat and killed, his back being broken by the fall, and his arm mangled and leg broken. He was LXIX years of age at his death, and was succeeded by his eldest son, Lord Moray. He was buried with Honours at Saint Hilary's Basilica. [*Saint Camber*; *Camber the Heretic*; *The Harrowing of Gwynedd*; *King Javan's Year*; *The Bastard Prince*].

Darrell *Romsey*. He was a teacher of mathematics at the University of Grecotha in the year 1068. He intervened to rescue Lord Barrett de Laney after the latter had been blinded by the King's soldiers while rescuing Deryni children, but was killed by the guards' arrows in retaliation on the Vth day of April in that year. His pregnant wife Bethane, who soon miscarried, became an old witch-woman in the hills; many decades later she accidentally caused the deaths of Bronwyn de Morgan and Kevin McLain with a misguided love charm sold to the architect Rimmell. R.I.P. ["Bethane"; *Deryni Checkmate*; *King Kelson's Bride*].

Davet *Nevan*, Bishop. He was born on the XXIst day of November in the Year of Our Lord 868, being the son of Sir Marius Nevan and Procla Lady Teltown. He was ordained priest on the Vth day of June in the year 888, and was consecrated an itinerant Bishop of Gwynedd on the XIIth day of August in the year 900. He attended the consecration of Father Alister Cullen as Bishop of Grecotha and Vicar General Robert Oriss as Archbishop of Rhemuth on the IXth day of July in the year 905 at Valoret. He attended the Synod of Bishops held at Valoret in November and December of 917, but was kicked by a horse and died on the XXVth day of December when the Regents illegally overturned the election of Alister Cullen as Archbishop of Valoret. He was XLIX years of age at his death. R.I.P. [*Saint Camber*; *Camber the Heretic*; *The Harrowing of Gwynedd*].

Davin Elathan *MacRorie*, VIIIth Earl of Culdi. He was born on the XIIIth day of April in the Year of Our Lord 898, being the eldest son and heir of Cathan MacRorie Hereditary Count and Master of Culdi and Elinor Lady Howell. He never married. He succeeded his father as Hereditary Count of Culdi on the Ist day of December in the year 903, and his grandfather as Earl of Culdi after his grandfather Camber's supposed death on the XXVth day of June in the year 905; he was confirmed in the latter title by King Cinhil I on the VIIth day of July following, under the regency of his mother and uncle, Father Joram MacRorie. He attained his majority on the XIIIth day of April in the year 912. He was present at the coronation of King Alroy at Valoret on the XXVth day of May in the year 917.

On the Ist day of June in that year he volunteered to act as a spy for the Camberian Council at the Court of King Alroy, and was shape-shifted into the form of the soldier Eidiard, his powers being blocked so his Deryni nature could not be detected by the Regents. He went with the princes to Rhemuth, and was assigned guard duty under the supervision of Sir Piedur. He was kicked by a horse in August of that year, and healed by Tavis. He was paralyzed in the assassination attempt on the princes on the XXVIIIth day of September in the year 917, and died shortly thereafter from his injuries, aged XIX years. His true face was then restored and his identity confirmed. Davin should have been succeeded by his younger brother, Lord Ansel MacRorie, but the Earl was posthumously outlawed by the Regents, his title attainted, and his body drawn and quartered. R.I.P. *Spesso da un gran male, nasce un gran bene*. [*Camber of Culdi*; *Saint Camber*; *Camber the Heretic*; *King Javan's Year*].

Davis. One of Bishop Thomas Cardiel's men-at-arms, he assisted in the "capture" of Alaric Morgan Duke of Corwyn and Father Duncan McLain at Dhassa on the XIXth day of June in the year 1121. [*High Deryni*].

Davoran O'Dell. He was born on the XIth day of November in the Year of Our Lord 1111, being the younger son of the Honourable Raemon O'Dell, Esquire, and Amphissa Hiberner. He was serving as a squire to King Kelson in the year 1128. On the XXth day of July in that year, he rode with Alaric Duke of Corwyn and Sir Angus MacEwan from Rhemuth to Desse to meet the Duke's ship *Rhafallia*. [*King Kelson's Bride*].

Dawkin. This master cobbler questioned by Alaric Morgan Duke of Corwyn and Father Duncan McLain on the Dhassa Road on the XIXth day of June in the year 1121, concerning the possibility of a back route into the city of Dhassa. [*High Deryni*].

Declan *Carmody*. This Deryni was born on the IVth day of September in the Year of Our Lord 887. He intermarried with Honoria Lettermore on the IInd day of September in the year 909, and by her he had children: Darragh; Donagh. He was impressed into the service of the Regents in the year 917 as a "sniffer," his wife and II small sons being held hostage for his good behaviour. He was present with Rhun Earl of Sheele at the sack of Saint Neot's Abbey on the XXIVth day of December in that year, acting as a mental messenger between Rhun's forces and the Deryni Oriel at Court, and truth-read Sir Rondel for the Regents at the state wedding banquet at Valoret on the Xth day of January in the year 918. On the XXIInd day instant he was forced to question the Drummonds about the events at Valoret Castle of the night before, and collapsed from the strain. He then underwent several months of rehabilitation. On the XXVth day of May in 918 he refused to rip the Regent Ewan's mind, and slashed his own wrists; before he was allowed to die, he was forced to watch his wife and II young sons strangled at the Regents' orders. He was XXX years of age at his death. R.I.P. [*The Harrowing of Gwynedd*; *King Javan's Year*].

Deegan. He was serving as a retainer of Wencit King of Torenth at Esgair Ddu in June of the year 1121. [*High Deryni*].

Deiniol, Brother. He was serving as an assistant to Brother Polidorus at Saint Cassian's Abbey in Iomaire in June of the year 928. He fetched a basin of hot water to clean King Rhys Michael's injured hand on the XXVth day of that month. [*The Bastard Prince*].

Delrae, Captain Sir. He was the captain of Dowager Queen Jehana's Bremagni honour guard in June of the year 1124. [*The King's Justice*].

Denis Michael *Arilan*, Bishop of Dhassa, sometime Auxiliary Bishop of Rhemuth. He was born on the XXVIIIth day of December in the Year of Our Lord 1083, being the second son of Sir Michael Sextus Arilan and Stephania Lady Jeffries. On the Ist day of August in the year 1104 he was a student at the *Arx Fidei* Seminary near Valoret, where he witnessed the disgrace and arrest of his Deryni friend, Father Jorian de Courcy, whose Deryni nature had been betrayed by *merasha* in the sacramental wine. He later saw Jorian burnt at the stake in November, and attempted to have untainted wine substituted at his own ordination. Although the substitution could not be made, he was nonetheless successfully ordained priest on the IInd day of February in the year 1105 at the Church of the Paraclete, being the first Deryni to have achieved ordination without discovery in almost CC years.

He was appointed Confessor to King Brion on the XVIIIth day of March in the year 1115, being promoted to Monsignor. He rose rapidly through the ecclesiastical ranks thereafter, being consecrated Auxiliary Bishop of Rhemuth on the XXIInd day of May in the year 1118, and elected Bishop of Dhassa on the XIVth day of January in the year 1122. He also served secretly as a member of the Camberian Council, having been appointed to that group circa the year 1107, in succession to his brother, Sir Jamyl. He was appointed to the High Council by King Brion on the same day that he was consecrated Bishop. On the IVth day of April in the year 1125 he acted with Duncan and Alaric to activate Prince Conall's Haldane potential.

On the IInd day of July in the year 1128, Arilan was present at Castle Coroth to welcome King Kelson and Duke Alaric, and met with them later that evening to discuss possible brides for the monarch. On the following day he met with Azim. He was present in the King's party on the voyage up river to Beldour during the next week. On the XVth day instant he transported from Beldour to Rhendall, where he discussed Kelson's betrothal to Princess Araxie with his fellow Camberian Council members. On the following day, he informed King Kelson that the Council believed that an assassination attempt would be made against King Liam Lajos II at the *killijálay* ceremony. Later that day, he attended Liam's first council meeting in Beldour. King Kelson then asked Arilan to remain in Beldour as Gwynedd's ambassador to that country, and to provide further guidance to King Liam. On the XVIIth day of July, he transported to Orsal, and then back to Beldour. Ten days later, he was informed by Duke Mátyás of Princess Morag's death, and transported to Rhemuth with Azim to inform King Kelson of this event. He then returned to his post in Beldour.

Bishop Denis has ever been a good and faithful servant to the Crown of Gwynedd. He has blue-violet eyes. ["The Priesting of Arilan"; "The Knighting of Derry"; *Deryni Rising*; *The Bishop's Heir*; *The King's Justice*; *The Quest for Saint Camber*; *King Kelson's Bride*].

Denys, Lord Collier. He was born on the XXVIIIth day of September in the Year of Our Lord 1099, being the second son of Fergananym Baron Collier and Withypoll Lady Dresternagh. He never married. This Gwyneddan nobleman was captured with Jared Duke of Cassan at Rengarth on the XXVIIIth day of June in the year 1121, and was executed with him by Wencit King of Torenth at Llyndruth Meadows on the Ist day of July following, aged XX years. R.I.P. [*High Deryni*].

Denzil *Carmichael*, Lord. He was born on the VIth day of January in the Year of Our Lord 887, being the fourth son of Avery Baron Carmichael and Pristeen Lady Gortnahù. This Deryni bowman attempted to assassinate the Princes Javan and Rhys Michael on the XXVIIIth day of September in the year 917. He was captured by the Princes' guards, and died later that same day, aged XXX years, during an interrogation conducted by Oriel at the order of the Regents. [*Camber the Heretic*].

Derah, Al-. This black R'Kassi stallion was owned by Alaric Morgan Duke of Corwyn in November of the year 1106, at the time when he visited the ruins of Saint Neot's Abbey with Brion King of Gwynedd. [*Deryni Checkmate*].

Derfel, Father. This priest was serving as Chaplain of Lochalyn Castle in Eastmarch in June of the year 928. On the XXIVth day instant he performed a great service to the Crown of Gwynedd by witnessing the signatures of the principals to the codicil of King Rhys Michael's will. He had a beard and ginger hair, and was of middle years. "The man exuded an air of kindness, and was utterly trustworthy." [*The Bastard Prince*].

Dermot *O'Beirne*, Bishop of Cashien, later Auxiliary Bishop of Valoret, later Archbishop Primate of Valoret and All Gwynedd. He was born on the XXVIth day of October in the Year of Our Lord 875, being the son of Sir Dionys O'Beirne and Lucretia Lady Sharpe. This human prelate succeeded his uncle, Eacharn O'Beirne, as Bishop of Cashien on the XIIth day of July in the year 903; it was rumoured in some quarters that his predecessor was actually his father. He attended the consecration of Father Alister Cullen as Bishop of Grecotha and Robert Oriss as Archbishop of Rhemuth on the IXth day of July in the year 905 at Valoret. On the XXIIIrd day of October in the year 906 he participated in the first consistory of Archbishop Jaffray, and responded to Guaire's petition for the canonization of Camber MacRorie by asking for a confirmation from a Deryni probe of Guaire's mind. He attended the Synod of Bishops held at Valoret in November and December of 917, and fancied occupying the office of Archbishop himself. He was attainted and outlawed by the Regents on the XXVIIth day of December, and went into exile.

He met with Joram at Dhassa on the Xth day of January in the year 918. He was later restored to his office as Bishop and named Auxiliary Bishop to Archbishop Ailin on the XIth day of July in the year 928. He succeeded Ailin as Archbishop Primate of Valoret and All Gwynedd on the Ist day of December in the year 941. He died in the year 948, aged LXXII years. R.I.P. [*Saint Camber*; *Camber the Heretic*; *The Harrowing of Gwynedd*; *The Bastard Prince*].

Derry. This small Earldom is situate along the Western face of the Coamer Mountains between Rengarth and Kingslake, extending Westward to the River Duncapall, just North of the Lendour Range. Castle Derry lies in the foothills just South of the great fortress of Rengarth. The Honour was first granted on the IVth day of July in the year 953 by King Uthyr to Lord Flynn Fitz-Arthur Quinnell, second son of Tambert I Duke of Cassan, in recognition of his services to the Crown. Sir Sean Seamus O'Flynn was Earl in the year 1128. ["The Knighting of Derry"; *King Kelson's Bride*].

EARLS DERRY

HOUSE OF O'FLYNN

Flynn	953-997
Lanark (son)	997-1021
Tamlynn (son)	1021-1025
Mellish (uncle)	1025-1029
Meyler (son)	1029-1055
Meyrich (son)	1055-1072
Airich (son)	1072-1101
Seamus (son)	1101-1106
Sean (son)	1106-1130+

Derverguille, Lady. This beauteous Lady was commemorated in the ballad bearing her name which was composed by the Lord Llewelyn. She was supposedly killed by the cruel Lord Gerent in the IXth century. [*Deryni Checkmate*].

***Deryni* (or *Derynii* or *Dourynoi* or *Les Dérynois*).** Some scholars say that this race of men originated from the lost land of Caeriesse, which sank beneath the waves about the year 525; in the surviving legends of that place, the Deryni are mentioned as being children and descendants of the old pagan Gods. Gifted with extraordinary powers of perception and adeption, the Deryni have long been feared and persecuted by the human majority in the Eleven Kingdoms. During the years of the Byzantyun occupation of Gwynedd the Rûman chronicles of Prochorus mention a race of men living to the Northwest called the Heldurnii, their nation being termed Heldurnia (later Kheldour). These "sea people" or "dark men" came from the West and settled along the coast of that rugged land before the year 200, but kept mostly to themselves, having little intercourse with their neighbours. The one attempt by the Byzantyun Empire to move Northwest of the River Eirian met with disaster in the year 253, when the Heldurnii utterly destroyed III legions and their auxiliaries sent by Byzantyun Autokratór Basileios the Great, thereby halting any further expansion by the Empire in that direction. However, the Kheldourynoi (as the Easterners called them) are infrequently mentioned in the histories of the Eleven Kingdoms until the VIth century of the Christian Era, following the disappearance of Caeriesse. The early chronicles of Torenth also note a well-established Deryni colony, Beldouria, near Torenthály.

The Deryni mages were instrumental in the establishment of the Kingdom of Gwynedd and an independent Church of Valoret, and as a reward for their service, the Great King Augarin Haldane awarded them many lands and titles in his new Kingdom. But there were those of this ancient race who began to stray from the path of righteousness, seeking to expand their powers at the expense of base-born men and consorting with the dark powers of Satan. It was the infamous Gilles Lord Friern who first broke with his betters and formed a group of adepts dedicated to the pursuit of pleasure and personal power. Although this coven of evil sorcerers was finally broken by Orin, greatest of all the Deryni mages, Friern's chief disciple, Malyon Mac Madach, escaped into the East, where he continued his researches and gathered about him a brotherhood of like-minded individuals sometimes called the "dark-haired men." Some say that he uncovered the secrets of life itself, and that he or his heirs continue to flourish somewhere in the Moorish lands even to this day.

Persecution of the Deryni increased greatly during the last year of Cinhil I King of Gwynedd, and after his death, the human Regents used their powers to suppress and torment and murder Deryni men, women, and children. During the CC years of the Deryni Holocaust, tens of thousands perished, some from the most horrible torture instruments that man has ever devised. Many innocents, human and Deryni alike, were condemned by the Regents or their followers merely to obtain title to their lands or property. God will severely punish all the wicked men who participated in these despicable acts.

Outside of Gwynedd the Deryni survived, but never in the numbers that they had reached before. Only in Torenth did the Deryni Lords remain in power, and there the balance was ever a precarious one, for they were outnumbered by their human subjects by a number of almost X to I. Fortunately, the most noble Kings Arion I and Arkady II of Torenth were just and capable men, who treated Deryni and humans alike with dignity and with honour.

The Deryni shall live again. The Great King Kelson, like Lazarus newly risen from his grave, blessed by God with a nature half Deryni and half human, restored to his throne through the blessings of our Lord, shall lead us out from the desert into a new Earthly paradise. The Deryni shall endure forever.

Deryni Plague. This disease, originally called the Spotted Plague, first appeared during a heat wave that affected all Gwynedd in the Summer of the year 917. Humans were more severely affected than Deryni, with the very young and very old being particularly vulnerable. Among the first to die was old Sighere Duke of Claibourne on the IInd day of July in that year. The disease abated with the easing of the hot weather in September, but returned again in mid-October of that year during a IInd period of heat, by which time it was being called the Deryni Plague. The unrest sparked by this affliction led indirectly to the assassination of Archbishop Jaffray on the XVth day of October in that year. [*Camber the Heretic*].

Desse. This port town of Gwynedd lies V miles South of Rhemuth on the East bank of the River Eirian and the North bank of the River Molling, and is frequently used by travelers leaving for the Southern Sea. Just North of Desse lie the first shallows of the Eirian, making further travel upriver difficult save for low barges and small boats. In olden days Desse was a Crown County, sometimes placed in the Haldane family, but later became a Barony under the House of Ahearne after the Restoration of King Cinhil I. Blake Ahearne Baron of Desse attended King Alroy's funeral services at Rhemuth on the XXVIth day of June in the year 921. Two hundred years later Alaric Morgan Duke of Corwyn debarked from this port for Coroth on the Xth day of March in the year 1125. *La gotera dando hace señal en la piedra.* [*King Javan's Year*; *The Quest for Saint Camber*; *King Kelson's Bride*]. See also: William.

Deveril, Lord Grangegaeth. He was born on the Ist day of October in the Year of Our Lord 1077, being the eldest son and heir of Duff Lord Grangegaeth and Divinity Lady Clonty. He intermarried with Bronea Lady O'Caom on the IXth day of April in the year 1099, and by her he had children: the Hereditary Lord Deasun; the Lady Dominica; the Lord Dé; the Lord Daivi; the Lady Daireen. He succeeded his father on the IInd day of November in the year 1083. He was serving as Seneschal to Jared Duke of Cassan in August of the year 1100, and was still lodged in that post (albeit somewhat older) in March of the year 1121. He was fair-haired. ["Bethane"; *Deryni Checkmate*].

Devlin. He was a gleeman of Clan MacArdry in November of the year 1123. [*The Bishop's Heir*].

Dhassa. This holy city of Gwynedd lies directly East of Rhemuth and Southeast of Valoret in the Lendour Mountains, being situate on the Northwest end of Lake Jashan. The mountains surrounding Dhassa are covered with great trees and filled with plentiful game, and the numerous streams and lakes teem with fish of all kinds, but there is little native stone accessible. Thus, the city is known particularly for its woodcraft, and most of its buildings, unlike the other cities of Gwynedd, are constructed out of wood. The wooden shrines of its patron saints, Torin and Ethelburga, guard its approaches to the South and the North, respectively.

During the Byzantyun period a small Greek trading station, Dasea, was established on the present site of Dhassa, the name reflecting the plethora of forests in the area. Later, the physical isolation of the place promoted its autonomy from its neighbours. The IIIrd Bishop of Dhassa, Fandilas, declared his independence from the Kingdom of Mooryn on the Ist day of May (Rudemas) in the year 597, cutting the Southern road into his city and changing his title to Prince-Bishop. From this date Dhassa was an independent free state which controlled the immediate territory from the mountain passes to either side of Lake Jashan, including the surrounding areas of the Lendour Mountains extending to at least X miles North and South of the Gunury Valley.

Sixtus Prince-Bishop of Dhassa was instrumental in the establishment of the independent Church of Gwynedd in the year 645, providing with Honoratus Abbot-Bishop of Concaradine the means by which a legally constituted hierarchy was elected there. The autonomy of Dhassa could only be maintained while II different states controlled the territory flanking the opposite ends of the Gunury Pass. When the Kingdom of Mooryn was subsumed into Gwynedd in the year 835, the city's independence became increasingly untenable. Finally, the last Prince-Bishop, Raymond, signed a treaty with Festil III King of Gwynedd on the XXIInd day of October in the year 879, agreeing that upon his death or retirement, Dhassa would legally become part of Gwynedd, while retaining its tax-exempt status as a free city of the realm. Accordingly, at Raymond's death on the IXth day of August in the year 903, Dhassa was formally incorporated into the Kingdom of Gwynedd, and Raymond's successor, Bishop Niallan Trey, bore an ecclesiastical title only.

It was to this city that Rhys Thuryn and Joram MacRorie took the captive Prince Cinhil on the Vth day of December in the year 903. The Bishop Niallan of Dhassa was attainted and outlawed on the XXVIIth day of December in the year 917, after he had sheltered refugees from various Deryni establishments. The Regent Rhun began a siege of the city in January of the year 918, and Niallan was forced to leave his post on the IIIrd day of February following. He was deposed from his post and Archbishop Hubert's Synod appointed a successor, Bishop Archer.

Dhassa's central location makes it an ideal meeting place for the Gwyneddan Curia. Because the Bishop of Dhassa is traditionally neutral in politics, he often possesses considerable influence over the affairs of both church and state. A conclave of the Bishops of Gwynedd was held here at the Cathedral on the XXVIIIth day of March in the year 1121 to pronounce a bill of excommunication against Alaric Morgan Duke of Corwyn and Father Duncan McLain Earl of Kierney. Bishop Denis Arilan was elected Bishop of Dhassa on the XIVth day of January in the year 1122.

Campbell de Broun, on his brief journey through Dhassa, noted that this place, more than any other, reminded him of his native Cloome, except that it was somewhat colder and damper; but he objected to the payment of a toll to enter the city, saying that old Saint Silas of Cloome was a poor man when he lived and a poor man when he died, and that he would never have required his penitents to gild the priests at *his* church. [*Camber of Culdi*; *The Harrowing of Gwynedd*; *King Javan's Year*; *Deryni Checkmate*; *High Deryni*; *The Bishop's Heir*; *King Kelson's Bride*]. See also: Ruadan.

(PRINCE-) BISHOPS OF DHASSA

Æmilius Discolor	548-575
Petronius Pyrrhus	575-588
Fandilas Porcus (Prince-Bishop 597)	588-618
Urbanus I Amplitudo	618-622
Licerius Charon	622-639
Sixtus Os	639-655
Pappio Petaso	655-660
Æternus Rapulum	660-670
Ignatius Definitivus	670-676
Celsinus Synedrus	677-691
Linus Consessor	691-702
Audax Auceps	702-711
Vincentius Effector	712-722
Tarniscus Refugus	722-732
Felix I Pellitus	732-738
Verus Amor	738-752
Aural Cavum	752-766
Humbert Umbratilis	766-780
Berlion du Berdou	780-782
Agislus Flebilis	783-794
Quintin de Bremagne	794-811
Bernouin de Bremagne (brother)	811-815
Urban II Facinus	815-833
Claude le Bon	833-841
Wannic McTyr	841-847
Premon Johnsson	848-862
Raymond Eskill (last Prince-Bishop)	862-903
Niallan Trey (nephew of Raymond)	903-918
Archer of Arrand	918-936
Piers Caradawg	936-948
Hagan FitzCashel	948
Barthes MacDann	948-955
Soffred de Pons	955-964
Domitian d'Albesque du Lienne	964-971
Stephen Alexander	971-976
Joab di Cybò	976-998
Arsen MacLaris	998-1011
Leontius Quadratus	1011-1025
Gerald de Morgan	1025-1028
Briand of Meara	1028-1030
Cyril de Montine	1030-1062
Felix II MacKinnon	1062-1063
Valens de Marga	1064-1087
Neil O'Beirne	1088-1103
Petros Béssarion de Romanis	1103-1105
Travis Traherne	1105-1116
Thomas Cardiel	1116-1122
Denis Arilan	1122-1130+

Dhugal Ardry *MacArdry McLain*, **Chief of Clan MacArdry, Duke of Cassan, Earl of Transha and Kierney, Lord Lieutenant of Meara, Sir.** He was born on the IIIrd day of January in the Year of Our Lord 1108, being the only son of Duncan McLain Duke of Cassan and Maryse Lady MacArdry, and the grandson of Caulay MacArdry Earl of Transha; the Lord Dhugal was raised as the Earl Caulay's son and eventual heir, and did not learn of his actual parentage until the age of XVI years, when the truth was first discovered by his father. He became Tanist of the Clan MacArdry and Master of Transha after the death of his uncle, Michael Lord MacArdry, on the XXIVth day of October in the year 1119. He was a foster and blood brother to Kelson King of Gwynedd, and used that connection to the King's advantage when he introduced the monarch to his grandfather, Caulay Earl of Transha, on the XXVth day of November in the year 1123 at Castle Transha. He was captured a week later on the I[st] day of December by the rebel Baron Brice of Trurill, and taken to Ratharkin.

The news of his capture caused his grandfather to die of pains in his chest on that day, at which point Dhugal became Clan Chief and Earl of Transha, although unbeknownst to him. On the IXth day instant he escaped from Ratharkin following the consecration of Prince Judhael as Bishop, taking the Princess Sidana captive as he fled the city. He was formally invested as Earl of Transha on Christmas Day in the year 1123.

He participated in the invasion of Meara on the XVIth day of May in the year 1124 as one of the commanders of the Cassani Army in the North. On the IInd day of July following he escaped the field of Dorna with the help of his father, and was able to contact the King that evening through psychic means. He arranged for the surrender of his aunt, the Pretender Caitrin, X days later, and was named Lord Lieutenant of Meara by King Kelson. He was knighted by his father on the IIIrd day of March in the year 1125. He accompanied the King on his quest for the relics of Saint Camber later that month, and fell into Grelder Creek on the XXIst day instant, being swept underground with the King. Several weeks later he emerged from the depths beneath the Lendour Mountains with the King by finding his way through a series of caverns. He discovered in the interim, *mirabile dictu*, that he had inherited his father's healing powers, and was able to cure both his own injuries and those of the King.

Earl Dhugal succeeded as Duke of Cassan by cession from his father on the XXIst day of May in the year 1125. On the XXVIIIth day of June in the year 1128 he attended the wedding between Princess Janniver and Sir Jatham Kilshane. Later that evening, King Kelson revealed to him the newly established secret annex to the royal library in Rhemuth Castle. On the next day, Dhugal met with Kelson and Duke Nigel to discuss Rory's attraction to Lady Noelie. On the IInd day of July in that year, he met with Kelson and others in Coroth to discuss recent developments. He then traveled with the King to Orsal. On the IIIrd day instant, Dhugal healed the slight wounds incurred by the King from an assassination attempt on the road to Horthánthy Castle. That evening, he discussed the day's events with Kelson and Duke Alaric, and assisted the King in melting down the late Queen Sidana's wedding ring.

He accompanied the royal party heading upriver to Beldour, and on the IVth day of July linked with Kelson and Morgan to discuss the Torenthis. On the Xth day instant, he was present when King Liam Lajos II and Count Mátyás showed the royal party the great Nikolaseum in Torenthály. That evening, he met with Kelson to review the events of the day. On the following day, he joined Kelson, Azim, and Derry for a ride into the nearby hills. On the XVIth day of July, he was present at the *killijálay* and the attempted assassination of King Liam, and attended the latter's initial council meeting that evening. Still later, he met privily with Liam, Mátyás, Azim, Arilan, and Kelson to plan strategy.

On the following day, he and Morgan transported back and forth between Orsal and Beldour, carrying information between the II monarchs, and thence to Rhemuth, where he attended the Privy Council meeting presided over by King Kelson. He supped privily with the King on the XXth day instant. On the XXVIth day of July, he was part of the royal party inspecting the new Chapel of Saint Camber in the basilica of Rhemuth Castle. On the XXXth day instant, he formed part of the official welcoming party for the Servants of Saint Camber. On the following day, he attended the dual royal wedding in Rhemuth, and assisted Morgan in healing the wounds incurred by Duke Mátyás in an assassination attempt.

Duke Dhugal wore his long, copper-bronze hair drawn to the nape of his neck in border fashion and plaited in a short braid tied with a leather thong, and by the year 1125 also sported a bushy red mustache. He was ever a true friend and companion to King Kelson. *Contre fortune bon cœur*. [*The Bishop's Heir*; *The King's Justice*; *The Quest for Saint Camber*; *King Kelson's Bride*].

Dickon *Kirby*. He was born in the year 1113, being the son of Henry Kirby Captain of the Duke of Corwyn's good ship *Rhafallia*, on which he was serving as cabin boy in March of the year 1121. [*Deryni Checkmate*].

Dickon *Thompson*. This baker was the target of a suit brought to Court by Master Gilbert the Silversmith on the XXIVth day of December in the year 917, alleging that Dickon's son had got Gilbert's daughter with child. The pair were ordered by the Regents to wed. [*Camber the Heretic*].

Dimitri, Master. This Deryni master was born, probably in Eastern Torenth or Arjenol, on the XXIst day of November in the Year of Our Lord 879. He was recruited by Paulin as a "sniffer" on the XIth day of June in the year 921. According to Paulin, as quoted in Volumen II of the *Heirs*, "a party of his knights returning from the Forcinn encountered Dimitri and his brother Collos on a ship outbound from Fianna. Collos was gravely ill with a fever, so one of the battle surgeons attended him. Once the crisis was past, and it was clear that Collos would live, it emerged that the two were Deryni, and that Dimitri, the other brother, had been an undersheriff in Vézaire, allegedly deposed for malfeasance and misappropriation of funds. He, of course, maintained that he was framed—which may or may not be true.... The two were destitute. Collos almost certainly would have died if my battle surgeon had not intervened.... Dimitri let it be known that, while he eventually hoped to return and take revenge on those who had accused him falsely, his gratitude to those who had saved his brother's life impelled him to offer them his service for pay."

King Javan and his allies first learned of his existence through the testimony of Father Faelan in July of the year 921. His name was also mentioned by Father Joram to Bishop Niallan and Jesse MacGregor in their questioning of Brother Serafin and Father Lior on the XXIXth day of that month. He murdered Baldwin and Nevell at Paulin's behest on the XXIIIrd day of March in the year 922, having shaved his beard and infiltrated the Palace at Rhemuth in the guise of a *Custodes* knight. After King Javan's murder in May of that year, he remained in service with Paulin. Despite the best efforts of Joram, Dimitri managed to avoid contact during the next VI years with any members of the Deryni underground resistance movement.

On the XIVth day of June in the year 928 he was present at the Council meeting which received the ambassador from Prince Miklós, but was actually working as a double agent for that Prince, maintaining regular contact with him by using the mind and body of the guard Iosif to transmit his mental messages. Later that evening, as he was returning to his quarters in the Palace, he accidentally encountered Father Joram and Tieg Thuryn near the Royal Library, and they overcame him by surprise and quickly determined the depth of his betrayal of Gwynedd. They took him through the portal there to the former Michaeline Haven.

His mind was then altered by Joram and his allies to make him their weapon against the former Regents, and he was returned to Rhemuth Palace. His first target was the Constable Udaut, who was killed when his horse spooked while he escorted the royal expedition to Eastmarch out of the city on the following day. Dimitri then summoned a swarm of bees to attack Lord Albertus on the XVIIIth day of June, and killed Albertus and mind-ripped his brother Paulin II days later, being captured after saving King Rhys Michael. Dimitri was tortured by Rhun and Manfred, and died later that night as a suicide when a mental death trigger was tripped, but not before reporting mentally to Prince Miklós. He died on the XXth day of June, aged XLVIII years. His body was burned as a heretic's corpse on the next morning in the yard of Saint Cassian's Abbey.

He is described in the *Heirs* as having "dark eyes above a neatly trimmed beard and mustache of a mousy brown flecked with grey, greyer hair cut just below his ears, one of which—the right—was pierced through the lobe by a slender golden hoop, the diameter of a man's thumb. His high-collared tunic was black, buttoned at the shoulder like a soutane, but it was not a cleric's attire—not with all that heavy silk braid lavished across collar and cuffs and shoulders. The design had a foreign feel to it, Eastern perhaps." He had a wide knowledge of Deryni-specific drugs. [*King Javan's Year*; *The Bastard Prince*].

Diniz, Lord Varney. He was born on the VIIIth day of August in the Year of Our Lord 1076, being the second son of Julius Lord Varney and Zinnia Lady Mello. This Torenthi nobleman operated a business selling and shipping wine and other spirits near Fathane in March of the year 1121. [*Deryni Checkmate*].

Djellarda. This original Mother House and Commanderie of the Order of Saint Michael was located at the tip of the Forcinn Buffer States, overlooking the Anvil of the Lord, and was thus sometimes called "The Gate of the Anvil." It was one of the III "external" houses to which the Michaelines retreated from Gwynedd in September of the year 917, under the leadership of Grand Master Crevan Allyn. Here the Order gradually evolved over the next CC years into the Knights of the Anvil, by which name it was known in the year 1124, when Azim was a preceptor there and Rocail the Order's Grand Master. [*Camber the Heretic*; *The King's Justice*].

Dobbs. He was serving as an advance scout in King Kelson's army in Eastmarch in June of the year 1121. [*High Deryni*].

Dolban. This partially ruined fortified manor was located on the South side of the River Eirian East of Valoret on the main road between Valoret and Caerrorie. It was purchased by Guaire d'Arliss and Dom Queron Kinevan on the IVth day of June in the year 906 to serve as the Mother House for the newly established order, the Servants of Saint Camber. The main House was sacked on the XXVIIIth day of December in the year 917 by the Regents, and LX followers of the Saint were burned at the stake in its courtyard.

It was eventually rebuilt in the year 966 by the Order of Saint Jerome, under a grant from King Uthyr. Dolban was visited some CC years later on the XVIth day of March in the year 1125 by King Kelson, who was looking for traces of Saint Camber. Located near here at this time was the manor house of Thomas Earl of Carcashale, also owner of the then-ruined manor at Tor Caerrorie. [*Saint Camber*; *Camber the Heretic*; *The Harrowing of Gwynedd*; *The Quest for Saint Camber*].

Dolfin. He was born on the XXIInd day of June in the year 1110, and was serving as senior squire to Kelson King of Gwynedd in the year 1125. He went with the King in March of that year on his quest for relics of Saint Camber, and fell into the Grelder Creek with the King, Dhugal, and others on the XXIst day of that month. Although battered, he survived with a broken wrist and several cracked ribs, and returned to service later that year. [*The Quest for Saint Camber*].

Dolon Kensell *Haldane,* **Hereditary Prince of Gwynedd.** This wretched prince was born on the XXIVth day of November in the Year of Our Lord 675, being the eldest son and heir of the wicked Llarik King of Gwynedd and Riona Countess of Carthane. Although his father had christened him Dolon, he disliked the name intensely and preferred to be called "Kensell." He was betrothed to the Princess Lucinda daughter of Ottonin King of Mooryn at the time of his death. He was arrested with his brother, the Prince Jestyn, by their father the King on the VIth day of October in the year 699, and both were charged with treason and unnatural acts. He was beheaded with his brother on the XVIth day of that month, aged XXIII years, and was buried in the crypt of his ancestors beneath Saint George's Cathedral in Rhemuth. The II brothers were popularly believed to have been innocent of any crime. Some blamed the King's new wife, the Princess Sidonie, for their deaths, saying that she had made advances toward them and when spurned, had them killed from spite; but others have stated that the brothers were themselves at fault, that one or both seduced the young Princess after her marriage, and that the son she bore in the following year was the product of this incestuous union. [*The Harrowing of Gwynedd*; *The Bishop's Heir*].

Dol Shaia. This area in Carthmoor is located in the Southern foothills of the Lendour Mountains near that Duchy's border with Corwyn. It was here that Kelson King of Gwynedd encamped on the XVIIIth day of June in the year 1121, where he was met by the Duke of Corwyn, Sean Earl Derry, and Nigel Duke of Carthmoor, and also received the homage of the rebel Bishops. [*High Deryni*; *The Bishop's Heir*].

Dominic, Brother. This monk was serving as infirmarian at Saint Mary's in the Hills Abbey in January of the year 918. He attended Evaine Lady Thuryn upon her arrival there on the IInd day of that month. [*Camber the Heretic*].

Dominic *Buyenne,* I[st] **Duke of Corwyn, Sieur du Joux.** He was born on the XXVIIIth day of August in the Year of Our Lord 800, being the eldest son and heir of Richard Lord du Joux and the Countess Tayce von Furstán-Fathane, and grandson of Réginald Duc du Joux on his father's side and of the Prince Imre Elgar Count of Fathane on his mother's side. He intermarried with Angélique Countess of Jacance on the IInd day of August in the year 824, and by her he had children: the Hereditary Duke al-Imre, who died before his father in the year 867, aged XLII years, having intermarried with Evania MacRhori Lady Cullanan, and by her leaving issue, the Lord Artorius later Duke of Corwyn; the Lady

Carola; the Lady Felicity; the Lord Julick; the Lady Fionnuala; the Lady Mugaine; the Lord Melgar Imre.

The Sieur Dominic was created Duke of Corwyn by Festil I King of Gwynedd on the XXIst day of October in the year 826, both to honour his own services to the Crown as well as the exploits of his father, who had perished IV years earlier during the invasion of Gwynedd, courageously taking a fatal blow meant for his cousin the King. In addition, the placement of one of the King's own relations in Mooryn helped secure the flanks of Festil's new kingdom. After an illustrious reign of nearly L years, the great Duke Dominic died on the XVIth day of November in the year 872, aged LXXII years, and was succeeded by his grandson, the Lord Artorius. His black marble sarcophagus tomb is located in the Grotto of the Hours on the grounds of Castle Coroth. R.I.P. [*Deryni Checkmate*].

Dominic, Father. This Michaeline priest was serving at Saint Liam's Abbey near Tor Caerrorie, and taught Joram MacRorie and Rhys Thuryn there beginning in the year 888. He was still resident at Saint Liam's on the XXVIIIth day of September in the year 903, when he was visited by his former pupil Rhys. [*Camber of Culdi*].

Donal Alroy *Haldane*, Prince of Gwynedd, Count of Desse. He was born on the XIXth day of August in the Year of Our Lord 649, being the fourth son of Augarin King of Gwynedd, but the first by his second wife, Caldora Lady de la Marche. He was created Count of Desse on his coming of age in the year 663. This comely and intelligent Prince died unmarried on the Xth day of March in the year 673, aged XXIII years, shot through the eye with an arrow in an alleged hunting accident near Dolban. Some writers aver that the new King Aidan had arranged for his half-brother's most convenient passing, since there was an old intimation at Court that the King Augarin had never properly intermarried with his first wife, and that his children by that union were thus made bastards. The Prince Donal was much mourned by his younger brother, the Prince Llarik, who accused his elder half-siblings of connivance in his brother's murder. R.I.P.

Donal Blaine II Aidan Cinhil *Haldane*, King of Gwynedd. He was born on the VIIth day of May in the Year of Our Lord 1030, being the eldest son and heir of Malcolm King of Gwynedd and Roisian Princess of Meara. At the age of VI years he was betrothed by his father to the Lady Dulchesse daughter of Nivelon IV Grand Duc du Vézaire, and he married that Lady at Côte d'Alban on the XVIIIth day of July in the Year 1046, but this union proved barren. After his first wife's death on the VIth day of May in the year 1078, he intermarried secondly with the Princess Richeldis MacFaolan daughter of Colman I King of Howicce and Gwenaël Sovereign Queen of Llannedd on the IIIrd day of September in the year 1080, and by her he had children: the Hereditary Prince Brion later King of Gwynedd; the Prince Blaine Richard Colman Emanuel, dead at age X of the consumptive complaint; the Princess Xenia Iona Esmeralda Rosa, who intermarried with Sigismund Graf von Golzców, but died in childbirth on the XXVIth day of February in the year 1104 with her stillborn daughter, Dorothea Dulchesse; the Prince Nigel later Duke of Carthmoor; the Princess Silke Anne Gwenaël Lizabeth later Infirmarian of the Convent of Saint Dymphna at Grecotha and a great patroness of the arts and learning; the Prince Joachim Roy Walter Cinhil, who was trampled to death by a horse at age IV.

King Donal Blaine II is also known to have fathered several natural children by various ladies of his court, III of whom he acknowledged and legitimated in the months before his death (but without dynastic rights): Cyana daughter of Lady Bellafane Pálffy; Desideria daughter of Elyse Baronne du Mont-Jésus; Ferdinand later Baron Highcastle, whose mother is unknown.

This Prince succeeded his father on the IIIrd day of March in the year 1074, and was crowned King of Gwynedd by Michael of Kheldour Archbishop Primate of Valoret and All Gwynedd on the XXIIIrd day of April following. On the IInd day of May in the year 1076 he mounted an expedition against Meara to hunt Judhael III Pretender of that Principality, but returned home empty-handed a month later. He launched a second expedition to Meara on the XXXth day of April in the year 1089, and hounded to death the Princess Onora on the XVIth day of May following, also capturing and executing Robard Lord Kincaid and Francis Lord Sommerdale brother of Derek Delaney Earl of Sommerdale and husband of Princess Caitrin on the XXVth day of June instant. He returned to Rhemuth on the IInd day of June following. On the XVIIIth day of May in the year 1090, the King sent a raiding party into Sasovna in Torenth under the command of his brother Duke Richard to retaliate for the Torenthi raids against Corwyn during the preceding year, but withdrew to Gwynedd after several weeks. On the Ist day of November in the Year 1095 he set the Haldane potential for his absent son in the person of the IV-year-old Deryni, Alaric Morgan Duke of Corwyn. He died of heart pangs on the XIVth day of November in the year 1095, aged LXV years, and was buried in the crypt of his ancestors beneath Saint George's Cathedral in Rhemuth. R.I.P. ["Swords Against the Marluk"; *Deryni Rising*; *The Bishop's Heir*; *King Kelson's Bride*].

Donal Dongal *Haldane*, Prince of Gwynedd. He was born on the XXIVth day of March in the Year of Our Lord 818, being the third son of Ifor King of Gwynedd and Nuala Lady Udaut. He was murdered together with his brothers and sisters by the soldiers of Festil I King of Gwynedd on the XXIst day of June in the year 822, aged IV years. R.I.P. [*Camber of Culdi*].

Donal, Master. He was working as a scribe and lay scholar at Rhemuth Castle in June of the year 928. He was enamored of Rhysel Thuryn, who liked but did not love him. Donal was somewhat gangly, with short, dark hair. [*The Bastard Prince*].

Donneral. These ducal estates owned by the Duchy of Corwyn were to have been the dowry of Bronwyn Lady Morgan. William the Reeve gave an account of them to Alaric Duke of Corwyn in March of the year 1121.

After the Lady Bronwyn's death in that same month, they were later placed in trust for Duke Alaric's young daughter, the Lady Briony, until such time as she should marry. [*Deryni Checkmate*].

Dorn. He was serving as a squire to Prince Javan in the year 917, and was killed defending his master from a Deryni ambush on the XXVIIIth day of September in that year. R.I.P. [*Camber the Heretic*].

Dorna Plain. It was here, South of the town of Kilarden in Meara, that Duncan McLain Duke of Cassan finally found Sicard Lord MacArdry's army, which had laid a trap for him, on the IInd day of July in the year 1124. On the next day King Kelson's army overwhelmed the Mearans, and Lord Sicard was slain by the King. [*The King's Justice*].

Dothan, Lord of Erne. He was born on the XVIIth day of March in the Year of Our Lord 856, being the eldest son and heir of Anrai Lord of Erne and Cairbreanna Lady Arboe. He intermarried with Dulcie Lady Carrigaline on the XVth day of August in the year 877, and by her he had children: the Lady Nesta; the Hereditary Lord Hywel; the Lady Zinna Heiress of Erne. He was appointed to the Royal Council on the XXVth day of March in the year 900 by King Imre. He was arrested and held for trial by Cinhil I King of Gwynedd on the Xth day of January in the year 905. His son and daughter, Lord Hywel and Lady Nesta, were killed in an assassination attempt on the King on the XXIInd day of June in that year. Lord Dothan was tried, condemned, attainted, and executed on the XVth day of July following, aged XLIX years. His surviving daughter was married to one of King Cinhil's supporters, Sir Destry MacAnnan, who was created Baron of Erne in the year 906. [*Saint Camber*].

Dov, Lord. He was serving as a Gabrilite Healer at Saint Neot's Abbey on the IIIrd day of May in the year 905, when he assisted in the dissection of the bodies of Dom Calvagh and Brother Ulric. He was later slain by Rhun's men on the XXIVth day of December in the year 917. R.I.P. ["The *Examen*"; *Camber the Heretic*].

Draper. The surname used by the Haldane family during the Interregnum. See also: Avis, Aidan, Daniel, Nellwyn, Royston, Nicholas. [*Camber of Culdi*].

Drellingham. This small town is located in Northern Corwyn at the edge of the Lendour Mountains. It was here that General Gloddruth agreed to meet King Kelson and his army *en route* from Dhassa to Cardosa in June of the year 1121. [*High Deryni*].

Droghera. This Marcher holding was located on the Meara-Gwynedd border just South of Culdi. Alaric Morgan Duke of Corwyn and Kelson King of Gwynedd discussed strategy here on the XXIIIrd day of November in the year 1123. [*The Bishop's Heir*]. See also: Brigid, Gillebert.

Drogo *de Palance*, Sir. He was serving as castellan to Rhun Earl of Sheele in the year 928. He joined the Royal Expedition to Eastmarch on the XVIIIth day of June in that year, bringing with him some provisions and an additional XX knights. [*The Bastard Prince*].

***Drummond*, House of.** The House of Drummond was founded by Sir Drummond Christopherson, a knight of Howicce, who wandered into Gwynedd seeking service with King Bearand Haldane about the year 750. He saved the King's life in battle and was ennobled by him in recognition of his outstanding service to the Crown on the VIIIth day of January in the year 760, with all of his male heirs in the direct line being granted the unusual privilege of carrying the title Lord for as long as the family should exist. His only son, Lord Christopher Drummond, is the common ancestor of all the Drummond lines. The latter's son, Lord David, was the father of Lord John, Lord James, and Lady Ardis, who intermarried with Ballard II Earl of Culdi. See also: Ardis, Cathan, Elinor, Geordie, Henry, James, Jamie, Jerusha, John, Lydia, Michaela.

Dualta *Jarriot*, Lord. He was born on the IIIrd day of February in the Year of Our Lord 872, being the younger son of Jeremias Lord Jarriot and Parca Lady Partridge. He joined the Michaelines in the year 893, and was serving Alister Cullen in July of the year 905. With King Cinhil I he interrupted the integration of Cullen's memories by Camber on the IInd day of that month, and later espied what he believed was Camber's ghost. On the next day he attended the Grand Chapter meeting of the Michaelines at Valoret. He was sent by the King with Lord Hildred on the VIth day of November in the year 905 to survey the horse studfarms of Gwynedd. He testified before the Council of Bishops at Valoret on the XXIVth day of October in the year 906 that he had witnessed the miracle of Camber's appearance and Cullen's resuscitation the year before. [*Saint Camber*].

Duchad *Mór*, Count of Tigre. He is also called "Durchad" in some records. He was born in Torenth on the XVIIth day of April in the Year of Our Lord 952, being the eldest son and heir of Angus I Mór Count of Tigre and Messalina Lady Rhorau, and a ninth-generation descendant in the male line from Rhori Mór Prince of Kheldour through his second son, Lord Diarmid, who continued to use the surname Mór to distinguish his family from the elder branch, the MacRhoris. Lord Duchad Mór intermarried with the Princess Ariella daughter of Imre II Pretender of Gwynedd on the XXXIst day of May in the year 966, and by her he had identical twin sons: the Hereditary Prince Festil Angus later Count of Tigre, who was betrayed and murdered at Marbury on the penultimate day of August in the year 994 by his jealous mistress, Amandine Lady d'Alver, who mistook his brother for Festil and killed him first, and then poisoned Festil and herself in despair—by this Lady the Prince Festil sired a bastard son, Festus Baron d'Amandine, who later married and left issue, but without dynastic rights; and the Prince Blaine Imre, murdered with his brother, who intermarried with Corvina Lady Zevenden, and by her had one surviving child: the Countess AriElinora later Duchess of Tolán and titular Queen of Gwynedd in succession to her *cousine germaine*, the Princess Imriella.

After his wife died in childbirth on the XXIInd day of March in the year 967, Duchad intermarried secondly with Saraid Lady Aileach on the XVth day of October in that year, and by her he had children: the Lord Angus Duchad later Angus II Count of Tigre in succession to his half-brother, Prince Festil; the Lady Niamhessa; the Lord Magogue; the Lord Rhori; the Lady Samhaoir.

The Lord Duchad succeeded his father as Count of Tigre in Torenth on the VIIIth day of May in the year 979. In the year 985 the Pretender Imre II enlisted his son-in-law for a IIIrd try at the throne of Gwynedd, and named Duchad Mór Commander of an army then being assembled in Eastmarch. Mercenaries were sought from the IV quarters of the world, including the Forcinn States, Orsal, The Connait, and others. The Count of Tigre had developed a new theory of warfare, whereby he assembled an elite corps of highly armored infantry which would be held in reserve to strike at the weakest part of the enemy lines once they had been softened through repeated charges of the cavalry and the massive use of spears and arrows, or, if necessary, used to defend the Festil's own line if its center should rupture. The city of Rengarth, Imre's capital in Eastern Gwynedd, was fortified with a moat, pits, and stakes. The Pretender's grandson and heir, Prince Imre III, was declared of age a year ahead of his time, then knighted and ennobled as Duke of Eastmarch and sent home to Torenth for his own safety.

The advancing Gwyneddan army was spotted on the XXXth day of May in that year. The first clash between the II forces took place on the plain in front of the city on the IInd day of June. The Haldane's main attack was stopped by Duchad's armored infantry, but when the Count's cinch suddenly broke, causing him to fall and be trampled in the melée, his army ran for the safety of the town. The Count was XXXIII years of age at his death, and was succeeded in Tigre by his eldest son, the Prince Festil. R.I.P. ["Swords Against the Marluk"].

Duncan Howard *McLain*, sometime Duke of Cassan, Earl of Kierney, and Viceroy of Meara, Auxiliary Bishop of Rhemuth, Rector of the University of Saint Camber, Provost of the Basilica of Saint Camber, Sir. He was born on the IInd day of February in the Year of Our Lord 1092, being the second son of Jared McLain Duke of Cassan, but the first by his second wife, Vera Lady Howard (Corwyn); he was also a first cousin to Alaric Morgan Duke of Corwyn. He secretly intermarried with the Lady Maryse MacArdry daughter of Caulay Earl of Transha on the XXVth day of March in the year 1107, and by her he had one son, long unbeknownst to him: the Lord Dhugal, who was raised as a son of his maternal grandfather and eventually succeeded him as Earl of Transha.

The Lord Duncan was playing near Culdi with his brother Kevin and his foster siblings, Lady Bronwyn and Alaric Lord Morgan, when the latter broke his arm on the IIIrd day of August in the year 1100. Another boyhood friend was Hugh de Berry. Upon learning of the death of his wife on the IIIrd day of January in the year 1108, aged XVII years, the Lord Duncan continued his studies for the priesthood, and was ordained on the Xth day of April in the year 1113 by Alexander Darby Archbishop of Rhemuth. He was brought to Rhemuth by Father Denis Arilan as his secretary and assistant on the IVth day of May in the year 1116, and became a tutor to Hereditary Prince Kelson on the XXIst day of June following. He was appointed Chaplain and Confessor to Prince Kelson on the Ist day of December in the year 1117, and promoted to Monsignor on the VIth day of January following. He was elected Auxiliary Bishop of Rhemuth on the XXth day of November in the year 1123, although not actually consecrated until the XVIth day of December following.

The Lord Duncan succeeded his brother Kevin as Earl of Kierney and Hereditary Duke of Cassan on the XXIXth day of March in the year 1121, and his father as Duke of Cassan on the Ist day of July following.

He was ordered by the King on the XVIth day of May in the year 1124 to raise the Cassani and Kierney armies and to invade Meara from the North. He and his army were trapped South of Kilarden on the Dorna Plain on the IInd day of July by the Mearan Army under the command of Lord Sicard MacArdry husband of the pretender Caitrin. Duncan was captured and tortured by ex-Archbishop Edmund Loris and Monsignor Lawrence Gorony, but was rescued by the King on the following day. He was named Viceroy of Meara on the XIIth day of July in the same year.

He was knighted by King Kelson on the IIIrd day of March in 1125, and then himself immediately knighted his own son, revealing himself publicly as Deryni for the first time. He agreed to remove himself from the public eye until the question of his right to exercise his priestly duties was resolved by the Synod of Valoret, and remained in Rhemuth when King Kelson went on his quest a few days later. On the XVth day of March he discovered the body of Tiercel de Claron, and left the next morning to report this to Bishop Denis Arilan in Valoret, arriving there on the XVIIIth day of March; he pretended to be a courier named "John" during his III-day trip. On the XXVth day of March he left Rhemuth for Coroth via portal to Dhassa to tell Alaric Morgan Duke of Corwyn of King Kelson's supposed death. He helped empower Prince Regent Conall's Haldane potential on the IVth day of April following.

Duncan and Alaric found King Kelson and Dhugal on the XIIth day of April in that year, and helped restore the King to his throne. Duncan ceded his secular titles to his son, the Earl Dhugal, on the XXIst day of May in the year 1125. On the XXVIIIth day of June in the year 1128, he was present at the wedding of Princess Janniver and Sir Jatham Kilshane. He remained in Rhemuth while King Kelson traveled to Corwyn, Orsal, and Torenth.

After the King returned to Rhemuth, on the XXth day of July, he helped transport Brendan, Payne, and Derry from Orsal to Rhemuth. He then met with Kelson later that day in the library of Rhemuth Castle. On the following day, he dined with Kelson, Dhugal, Morgan, and Richenda. On the XXVIth day instant, he was asked by the King to accept an appointment as Rector of the new *schola* for Deryni studies to be established in Rhemuth. On the XXXth day of that month, he was named by King Kelson to the newly established post of Provost of the Basilica of Saint Camber. On the VIIth

day of August in that year, he presided over the wedding between King Kelson and Princess Araxie.

He had striking blue eyes, and was ever a friend to King Kelson and Alaric Morgan Duke of Corwyn. ["Bethane"; *Deryni Rising*; *Deryni Checkmate*; *High Deryni*; *The Bishop's Heir*; *The King's Justice*; *The Quest for Saint Camber*; *The Deryni Archives*; *King Kelson's Bride*].

Dunstan. He was a cobbler living at Rengarth in the year 903, and grandfather to John son of Daniel, one of the "Brothers Benedict" at Saint Piran's Abbey. [*Camber of Culdi*].

Durin, Master. This Gwyneddan Healer served at the Battle of Iomaire in June of the year 905. [*Saint Camber*].

Duvessa Alpina *Sinclair Quinnell*, Princess of Cassan. She was born on the XIVth day of February in the Year of Our Lord 870, being the youngest daughter of Tudur Earl of Tarleton and Paulina Lady Kilshane, and sister of Bonner I Earl of Tarleton. She intermarried with Ambert Sovereign Prince of Cassan on the XVth day of July in the year 897, and by him she had children: the Princess Anne, who intermarried with Fane Earl Fitz-Arthur; the Princess Devika; the Princess Quenelda; the Hereditary Prince Antiochus, dead at age III; the Prince Aloys, dead at III days. She appeared at Court in Rhemuth on the XXXth day of July in the year 921 to bear witness to her husband's last will and testament, at which time the Principality of Cassan was formally annexed to Gwynedd. She died on the IInd day of October in the year 932, aged LII years. R.I.P. [*The Harrowing of Gwynedd*; *King Javan's Year*].

Dylan *ap Thomas*, Lord. This Deryni was born on the XIth day of March in the Year of Our Lord 879, being the seventh son of Thomas Baron Coolhill and Buan Lady Laghy. He was killed while trying to assassinate the Princes Javan and Rhys Michael on the XXVIIIth day of September in the year 917. [*Camber the Heretic*].

Dymphna, Saint. This worthy was the daughter of the VIth-century Mearan laird Cyfrudd, who opposed her conversion to the Christian faith and tried to marry her to a local pagan chieftain, Lord Portraine. She escaped over the mountains to Grecotha with her devoted chaplain, Saint Jeroboam of Sauternes, where they hid in caverns housing the old Rûman baths. Their relics were discovered together there in the IXth century, extraordinarily well preserved. Since then numberless cases of insanity, fits, and the shaking palsy have been cured there. A *lavabrum* was soon built over the site by Mother Matilda Montesque du Breuil, founder of the Sisters of the Holy Water, who believed in the efficacy of repeated immersions at their shrine, and also maintained an asylum near the site for the demented, the witless, and the hopelessly confused. Saint Dymphna is often invoked as the patroness of lunatics and dipsomaniacs. Her feastday is the XVth day of May.

Eamonn *MacDara*. This Mearan Deryni poet lived about the year 700; he is best known as the author of "The Ghosting of Ardal L'Étrange," which alludes to a spell for defying death. Evaine mentioned him while doing her research in the year 918. She finally found a copy of his work in Father Boniface's private library at the Basilica at Rhemuth on the XIIIth day of April in that year. [*The Harrowing of Gwynedd*].

Eastmarch. This long narrow County is flanked on the East by the Rheljan Mountains and on the West by the Plain of Iomaire; its Northern boundary is the Earldom of Marley, and its Southern reaches extend to Llyndruth Meadows West of Cardosa.

The early history of Eastmarch is shrouded in obscurity. The savage tribes which occupied the plain of Iomaire during the Byzantyun occupation of Gwynedd helped keep the Easterners from ever establishing a permanent presence on the Northern side of the River Eirian. In the year 508 the pagan chief Knut invaded from the Northern Sea, moving Southwest along the Arran River into the Rheljan Mountains, and finally into the plains of Iomaire, where he established himself as the hereditary Margrave of The Marches.

His grandson, the Margrave Alöf, conquered vast stretches of land to the South and West. He died in the year 592, and his last will and testament divided The Marches among his IV sons, to wit: Ion Count of Northmarch, Thrond Count of Westmarch, Eirik I Count of Southmarch, and Einarr Count of Eastmarch. The Count Thrond died without male issue in the year 630, and his domains were divided amongst the other III realms. The County of Southmarch was conquered in the year 823 by Festil I King of Gwynedd, and this state was divided between the new Honours of Culdi, Carcashale, and others. The County of Northmarch or Normarch Ley or Marley, as it was later called, merged with Eastmarch when the Heiress of Normarch Ley, Ulrika, married her cousin, Magnus I Count of Eastmarch, in the year 715. Eastern Marley was annexed to Torenth in the year 755.

In the year 905 Sighere Earl of Eastmarch invaded and conquered the independent Principality of Kheldour, but being unable to pacify and hold all the parts of that large state, sought aid from Cinhil I King of Gwynedd, and became his vassal. Sighere was thereupon created Duke of Claibourne (the new name for old Kheldour), and he gave Eastmarch to his IInd son, the Earl Hrorik II, and Marley to his IIIrd son, the Earl Sighere *Junior*, which was thereafter split off again from Eastmarch. The latter Earl married Sudrey Heiress of Kheldour and Rhorau, and in this line is vested the right to claim the old titles. Their daughter, Stacia Countess of Eastmarch, married Corban Lord Howell, the ancestor of this family.

In the year 1105 the Earl Corban's direct descendant, Earl Rorik III, supported the aspirations of Hogan Gwernach Festillic Pretender of Gwynedd, and was deposed and killed by his cousin, Arban Lord Howell. Arban's son and successor, the Earl Ian, took up the cause of Charissa Duchess of Tolán in her attempt to seize the Gwyneddan throne in November of the year 1120, and was killed by Alaric Morgan Duke of Corwyn. Eastmarch was then given by the King to Earl Ian's brother-in-law, Burchard Lord de Varian, who had remained loyal.

The standard of the County at the time of Hrorik II Earl of Eastmarch included golden suns and a silver saltire on an *azure* field. *Nichtswürdig ist die Nation, die nicht ihr Alles freudig setzt an ihre Ehre.* [*Saint Camber*; *The Harrowing of Gwynedd*; *The Bastard Prince*; *Deryni Rising*; *The Bishop's Heir*; *King Kelson's Bride*].

MARGRAVES OF THE MARCHES

HOUSE OF HALFDAN

Knut	508-534
Halfdan (son)	534-552
Alöf (son)	552-592

DIVIDED INTO FOUR STATES

COUNTS OF NORTHMARCH OR NORMARCH LEY

Ion (son of Alöf)	592-601
Haakon (son)	601-622
Eysteinn (son)	622-652
Erlend (brother)	652-655
Valldar (son)	655-682
Sveinn (son)	682-711
Ulrika (daughter; wife of Magnus I)	711-715

MERGED WITH EASTMARCH

COUNTS OF WESTMARCH

Thrond (son of Alöf)	592-630

COUNTS OF SOUTHMARCH

Eirik I (son of Alöf)	592-624
Grimr (son)	624-630
Olaf (son)	630-683
Dalf (nephew)	683-693
Eirik II (son)	693-719
Thorkall (son)	719-741
Hrafn (cousin)	741-777
Flein (grandson)	777-822
Eirik III (cousin)	822-823

CONQUERED BY GWYNEDD

COUNTS AND EARLS OF EASTMARCH

Einarr (son of Alöf)	592-613
Harald I (son)	613-633
Thorfinn (nephew)	633-666
Sverri (son)	666-680
Torv (son)	680-703
Magnus I (grandson)	703-744
Yngvarr (son)	744-761
Hrorik I (son)	761-796
Björn (nephew)	796-804
Magnus II (brother)	804-815
Ivarr I (son)	815-822
Harald II (cousin)	822-838
Hrolf I (son)	838-862
Ewan (son)	862-889
Hlodver (son)	889-891
Sighere I (brother)	891-906
Hrorik II (son)	906-928
Stacia (daughter)	928-967

HOUSE OF HOWELL

Corban I Howell (husband)	928-968
Kennet (son)	968-973
Sighere II (son)	973-983
Rolf II (brother)	983-984
Colwyn (brother)	984-999
Ivarr II (son)	999-1025
Custus (son)	1025-1038
Faudell (brother)	1038-1055
Corban II (son)	1055-1088
Rorik III (son)	1088-1105
Arban (cousin)	1105-1115
Ian (son)	1115-1120

HOUSE OF VARIAN

Burchard (brother-in-law)	1122-1130+

Ebor. This small Earldom was located North of Valoret, being flanked on the South by Sheele, on the East by the Lendour Mountains, on the North by Iomaire, and on the West by the Purple March. The Honour was granted by King Festil III to his Deryni friend and comrade-in-arms, Sir Rhygan MacDinan, youngest son of Dinan last Sovereign Prince of Kheldour, on the Vth day of December in the year 851. Earl Gregory MacDinan was attainted by the Regents on the XXVIIth day of December in the year 917, and the title slipped into abeyance after he removed his family to Trevalga in The Connait. His son, Jesse MacGregor Hereditary Count of Ebor and Sovereign Count of Trevalga was instrumental in aiding Father Joram MacRorie to preserve the Deryni heritage in Gwynedd. The right to petition for restoration of this Honour is currently vested in the Counts of Trevalga in The Connait. [*Camber the Heretic*; *The Harrowing of Gwynedd*; *King Javan's Year*].

EARLS OF EBOR

HOUSE OF MACDINAN

Rhygan MacDinan	851-875
Rhirid (son)	875-888
Gregory (son)	888-917

Edgar, Baron of Mathelwaite. He was born on the IVth day of November in the Year of Our Lord 1083, being the eldest son and heir of Quale Baron of Mathelwaite and Tamella Lady Slievenagriddle. He never married. He succeeded his father on the last day of February in the year 1115. In November of the year 1120 he was persuaded by the traitor Ian Howell Earl of Eastmarch that Alaric Morgan Duke of Corwyn should be assassinated. With II accomplices, he overpowered the guard outside the King's room and discovered that Kelson was missing from his chamber on the evening of the XIVth day of that month. He challenged the Duke of Corwyn and Father Duncan McLain when they returned the unconscious King to his room through a secret door. He tried to claim that Alaric had used him to attempt to kill the King, but eventually admitted that his real target was Morgan. Lord Edgar was under a magical compulsion to kill himself rather than reveal Ian's part in the plot against Kelson, and so he took his own life. He was XXXVII years of age at his death, and was succeeded by his younger brother, Lord Edwin. He is described in the *Chronicles* as a "dimwitted vassal of the Duke of Corwyn." [*Deryni Rising*].

Edmond I, Archbishop Primate of Valoret and All Gwynedd. He was born in Travlum about the year 705. He was elected Bishop of Grecotha in the year 752, and was named successor to Symphorian Archbishop of Valoret on the XXIst day of November in the year 766. He preached a great crusade against the Moors in the year 770. He died on the Vth day of May in the year 777, and was succeeded by Bishop Adon. [*Camber the Heretic*].

Edmund II Alfred *Loris*, Archbishop Primate of Valoret and All Gwynedd. This black-hearted cleric was born on the XXIIIrd day of December in the Year of Our Lord 1064, being the son of Alvyn Loris and Yanata Gipson. He was ordained priest on the XIIth day of April in the year 1084 by Michael Archbishop of Valoret, and was elected Bishop of Stavenham on the XXIVth day of March in the year 1101, where he became known for his efforts to seek out and destroy Deryni. He was elected Archbishop Primate of Valoret and All Gwynedd on the XXth day of February in the year 1115 in succession to Archbishop Oliver de Nore, who had died the previous December.

At the death of Brion King of Gwynedd on the Ist day of November in the year 1120 he supported the Queen Jehana in her efforts to maintain her regency and attaint Alaric Morgan Duke of Corwyn, and was successful in gaining the backing of his colleague, Patrick Corrigan Archbishop of Rhemuth, and a majority of the Bishops. His attempts to excommunicate Alaric and Father Duncan McLain and to place an interdict on the Duchy of Corwyn on the XXth day of March in the year 1121 resulted in a split of his curia, with VI Bishops forming their own independent Synod at Dhassa. When his campaign threatened the continued rule of Kelson King of Gwynedd, that monarch removed him from office and placed him under arrest for crimes against the state on the XXVIth day of June in that year. He was officially stripped of his rank and privileges by his fellow Bishops sitting in council on the Xth day of January in the year 1122, and exiled to a secluded cell at Saint Iveagh's Abbey on the coast of Claibourne.

However, with the help of Jeroboam and his former aide Monsignor Lawrence Gorony, he escaped his captivity on the XXIXth day of November in the year 1123, and traveled by boat and horse to Ratharkin in Meara. There he embraced the cause of the rebel Queen Caitrin of Meara, and formed his own Synod of renegade Bishops, calling himself Primate of Meara. He deposed Henry Istelyn Bishop of Meara on the Vth day of December following, and executed him on the XVIIIth day instant. When Kelson King of Gwynedd invaded Meara and defeated the Pretender's army during June and July of the year 1124, he captured the former Archbishop and his supporters on the IIIrd day of July at Dorna. They were taken under close arrest to Laas in Meara, where they were tried as traitors and executed by hanging on the XIIth day instant. Edmund Loris was LIX years of age at his death, and was buried in an unmarked grave in a potter's field.

Loris is described in the *Chronicles* as having blue eyes and grey hair fringing a balding pate: "He was an impressive looking man. His body was lean and fit beneath the rich violet cassock he wore, and the fine silvery hair formed a whispy halo effect around the magenta skull cap covering his clerical tonsure. The bright blue eyes were hard and cold, and the gaunt hawk-face was anything but beneficent." ["The Knighting of Derry"; *Deryni Rising*; *Deryni Checkmate*; *High Deryni*; *The Bishop's Heir*; *The King's Justice*; *The Quest for Saint Camber*].

Edmund *Lyle*. He was a Torenthi spy killed by Sean Earl Derry in Fathane on the XXIVth day of March in the year 1121. [*Deryni Checkmate*].

Edouard, Dom. The Deryni author of a work on the occult arts, *Haut Arcanum*, which was consulted by Evaine Thuryn in the year 918. She found a copy of this book in Father Boniface's private library in the chapel of the Basilica at Rhemuth on the XIIIth day of April in that year. [*The Harrowing of Gwynedd*].

Edulf. He was serving as an ostler to the House of Culdi in the year 903, and was one of the L peasants executed in September at the command of Imre King of Gwynedd in retribution for the death of Lord Rannulf. He read the names of the hostages to Lord Cathan MacRorie to help him pick the one life he had been granted by the King to save. R.I.P. [*Camber of Culdi*].

Edward *de Broun of Cloome*, Bishop. This native of Cloome in Meara was born on the XVIIIth day of August in the Year of Our Lord 1083, being the son of Sir Heywood de Broun and Oonagh Lady Bawnfune, and a nephew of Campbell de Broun. He was ordained priest on the VIIIth day of July in the year 1102, and elected an itinerant Bishop of Gwynedd, without fixed see, on the XIXth day of January in the year 1122. [*Deryni Magic*].

Edward, Father. He was the priest who baptized Nicholas Draper (Prince Cinhil Haldane) in the year 860. [*Camber of Culdi*].

Edward, Lord Macanter. He was born on the XXIVth day of November in the Year of Our Lord 1084, being the eldest son and heir of Emmet Lord Macanter and Ida Lady Grillagh. He intermarried with Gyleena Lady Drummuck on the IIIrd day of July in the year 1104, and by her he had children: the Lady Teine; the Hereditary Lord Drumm; the Lady Grilla; the Lady Emmetta; the Lady Emer; the Lord Ward. He succeeded his father on the XVth day of December in the year 1113. This border Baron had often ridden with Ian Howell Earl of Eastmarch during the IInd decade of the XIIth century. [*High Deryni*].

Edward Lucius *Ramsay*, Lord, Sir. He was born on the XXXIst day of March in the Year of Our Lord 1005, being the younger son of James Earl of Cloome and Susana Lady Crewe. He intermarried with the Lady Magrette Princess of Meara, daughter of Jolyon II Sovereign Prince of Meara, on the XIIth day of May in the year 1035, and by her he had children: the Lord

Colin; the Lady Alcinda; the Lady Lucinda, a twin with her sister; the Lord Thomas, who died childless; the Lord Edgar; the Lord Samuel; the Lord Matthew, who died young; the Lord Alexander; the Lady Laurel; the Lady Maureen, a twin to her sister, later a nun of Saint Brigid's Abbey under the name Sister Hosanna.

After the Lord Edward and Princess Magrette renounced any rights to the throne of Meara for themselves, they retreated to the relative safety and security of Cloome, where they raised their large family relatively untouched by the periodic uprisings of the followers of Magrette's sister Princess Annalind and her descendants. He died in Cloome on the XVIIth day of August in the year 1078, aged LXXIII years. R.I.P. [*King Kelson's Bride*].

Edward *MacInnis*, Baron Arnham, Bishop of Grecotha. He was born at Arnham on the IIIrd day of December in the Year of Our Lord 897, being the younger son of Manfred Earl of Culdi and Estellan Lady Buckleigh, and a nephew to Hubert MacInnis Archbishop Primate of Valoret and All Gwynedd. He was ordained priest on the XIIth day of September in the year 916, elected an itinerant Bishop of Gwynedd on the XXVIth day of December in the year 917, and was created Bishop of Grecotha, succeeding Bishop Alister Cullen, on the day following. He assisted at his brother Iver's marriage with Richeldis Lady MacLean on the Vth day of March in the year 918. He attended the coronation of King Javan on the XXXIst day of July in the year 921. He died on the XXIIIrd day of July in the year 956, aged LVIII years. R.I.P. [*Camber the Heretic*; *The Harrowing of Gwynedd*; *King Javan's Year*].

Egbert, Brother. He was a monk of the *Ordo Verbi Dei* at Saint Jarlath's Monastery in Barwicke. He brought Father Joram MacRorie and Rhys Thuryn dry clothing when they visited there on the XXVIIIth day of September in the year 903. He later took them to the library where the lists of postulants were kept. [*Camber of Culdi*].

Eidiard *of Clure*. He was a soldier in the Palace Guard who had accepted an assignment to guard the Princes Javan and Rhys Michael, but had not yet assumed his duties in June of the year 917. He was replaced by the shape-changed Davin Earl of Culdi to enable the Camberian Council to receive reports on events occurring in the inner Palace circles. The real Eidiard was taken back to New Argoed by the Michaelines. He is described in the *Legends* as being "...a slender young Highland man of Davin's approximate colouring and build." [*Camber the Heretic*].

Eirian Elspeth Sidana *Haldane*, Princess of Gwynedd, future Queen of Torenth. She was born on the XVIIth day of June in the Year of Our Lord 1124, being the fourth child and eldest daughter of Nigel Prince of Gwynedd and Meraude Lady de Traherne. She was betrothed to Liam Lajos II King of Torenth on the XIVth day of November in the year 1128, the marriage scheduled to take place in the year 1138. *Aves piacevol viso, abito onesto.* [*The Quest for Saint Camber*; *King Kelson's Bride*].

Eirian, River. This watercourse, the longest river in Gwynedd, arises near Saint Jarlath's Abbey Northeast of Caerrorie, and after joining with several lesser streams, gradually turns West toward Valoret. The River bends South and West thereafter, and due South at Candor Rhea, passing through the capital of Rhemuth. At Desse it turns Southeast, gradually widening out below this point, until it reaches several miles in width between Carthmoor and Llannedd. The River Eirian is freely navigatible North to Desse, which acts as the port of nearby Rhemuth, and partially navigatible thereafter by shallow barges and small boats. Major tributaries include: the River Lendour joining at Nyford, the River Llanarfon at Concaradine, the River Molling at Desse, the River Cleyde at Tarleville, the Falling Water or Red River East of Valoret, the Grelder Creek in the Lendour Mountains. *Rura mihi et rigui placeant in vallibus amnes, flumina amem sylvasque inglorius*.

Eistenfalla. This city, the capital of Eistenmark, is located in the cold country far to the North of Torenth on the coast of the Northern Sea. It is inhabited by the barbarian tribes who still follow a god called the All-Father, chief of the so-called Old Ones, statues of whom are displayed in the main temple there. In the year 997 a priest of the All-Father, Dyggvi Bolverksson, led his people into a lengthy war with Torenth, before finally being killed in the year 1009. Eistenfalla was then briefly occupied by the forces of Kyprian II King of Torenth before that monarch withdrew from the land. One of Eistenfalla's citizens in later times, the master swordsmith Ferris, came to Kiltuin in Corwyn on the XVIth day of April in the year 1118 to sell his weapons.

The Kings of Eistenmark are elected for life by the Thinge, an assembly of the people, which also has the power to depose the monarch if he loses their confidence. The climate is cold and inhospitable much of the year; during the brief Summer, which lasts only II or III months, the sun may shine all the day round. In the dead of Winter, there are days when no sun is seen at all. *Dygghvie fit la guerre à la liberté; Dygghvie n'est plus*. ["Trial"].

Eithne. She was serving as a maid at Rhemuth Castle in June of the year 928. [*The Bastard Prince*].

Ekaterina Évariste Sisine *de Mont-Volcan*, Princess of Jáca. She was born on the XXVth day of February in the Year of Our Lord 1111, being the eldest child of Rotrou II Sovereign Prince of Jáca and Kemala Shaikha of al-Qarrah. A notable beauty of her day, she was mentioned in the year 1128 as being a potential bride for King Kelson and other noblemen of a suitable age and position. Her father brought her with him to the inauguration of Liam Lajos II King of Torenth in July of that year. She had dark eyes. [*King Kelson's Bride*].

Elaine *de Fintan*, Countess of Carthane, Lady. She was born on the XIIIth day of May in the Year of Our Lord 880, being the daughter of Aquineas Earl de Fintan and Lettice Lady Laughill. She intermarried with Murdoch Earl of Carthane on the VIth day of March in the year 899, and by him she had children: the Lady

Agnes, who intermarried as his second wife with Rhun Earl of Sheele; the Hereditary Lord Richard later Earl of Carthane; the Lord Jason, dead at age III; the Lord Cashel *Senior*. At the tournament following the coronation of King Alroy on the XXVIIth day of May in the year 917 she bestowed a chaplet of wildflowers upon Prince Javan when he won second place in pole-bending. She was also present at the state wedding in Valoret of her only daughter on the Xth day of January in 918. She witnessed her husband's death at the hands of Hrorik Earl of Eastmarch on the I[st] day of August in the year 921. She later served as a lady at Court during the reign of Rhys Michael King of Gwynedd. She died on the XXIst day of October in the Year of Our Lord 970, aged XC years. Prince Javan was once heard to call her Murdoch's "bitch of a wife." *Scilicet expectas, ut tradat mater honestos atque alios mores, quam quos habet?* R.I.P. [*Camber the Heretic*; *The Harrowing of Gwynedd*; *King Javan's Year*].

Elaine *MacInnis McLain*, Countess of Kierney. She was born on the IInd day of April in the Year of Our Lord 1072, being the daughter of Manfred Baron MacInnis and Signe Lady Calder of Sheele. She intermarried with Jared Earl of Kierney on the XXXth day of June in the year 1087, and by him she had one son: Lord Kevin Douglas later Earl of Kierney. She died from the complications of childbirth on the XXVth day of May in the year 1088, aged XVI years. R.I.P. [*Deryni Checkmate*].

Elas, Lord Bicester, General. He was born on the XXIVth day of March in the Year of Our Lord 1072, being the younger son of Helias Baron Bicester and Tarba Lady Ferrer. He intermarried with Zoë Lady Willcox on the Vth day of May in the year 1093, and by her he had children: the Lady Lassie; the Lady Radegund; the Lord Elleher; the Lord Elvan; the Lady Zoïba. This Gwyneddan General was present at the War Council held at Dhassa on the XXIXth day of June in the year 1121, and later at the Council held on the XXVth day of December of 1123 discussing the Mearan rebellion. [*High Deryni*; *The Bishop's Heir*].

Elderon, originally Muhammad *al-Darun*, Saint. This Moor was converted to the Christian faith in the year 788, and joined the Knights of Saint Michael at Djellarda. During an assault on that fortress by Faisal King of R'Kassi X years later, he died heroically defending a small gate that would have given access to the Abbey by the infidels. A Michaeline Abbey dedicated to his name is located in Tolán on the coast of the Northern Sea near the Eastmarch border with Torenth. His feastday is the XXXIst day of January. [*Camber the Heretic*].

Eleric, Dom. He was a Gabrilite priest who taught classics at Saint Neot's Abbey in the early 870s. One of his students there was Alister Cullen later Bishop of Grecotha. [*Saint Camber*].

Eleven Kingdoms (*XI Regni*). This ancient name for the fair lands surrounding and including Gwynedd antedates all written records. Although many writers have made their own lists of the realms comprising the Eleven Kingdoms, Berrhones and Callan agree on these names: Gwynedd, Howicce, The Connait, Meara, Torenth, Tolán, Kheldour, Llannedd, Mooryn or Corwyn, Eastmarch, and Carthmoor. Some earlier writers, however, such as Lord Llewelyn, substitute the lost land of Caeriesse for Carthmoor. *My library was dukedom large enough.* [*Camber of Culdi*; *King Kelson's Bride*].

Elfrida, Dame. She was a witch-woman near Culdi who cast a spell on Rimmell about the year 1100 which made his hair turn white; she was run out of her village shortly thereafter. [*Deryni Checkmate*].

Elgin, Captain. This soldier accompanied Corban Earl of Eastmarch to Marley in June of the year 928. [*The Bastard Prince*].

Elgin *de Torres*, Father. He was a seminarian and subdeacon at the *Arx Fidei* establishment who was ordained with Denis Arilan on the IInd day of February in the year 1105. He slept in the same dormitory as Arilan, and was questioned by him on the IXth day of August in the year 1104 regarding the uncovering of Father Jorian de Courcy's Deryni nature. ["The Priesting of Arilan"].

El Ha'it. This estate located on lake Hor Ya'qub in Andelon is owned by Richenda Duchess of Corwyn. [*The King's Justice*].

Elinor Elisabedd *Howell MacRorie Drummond*, Lady. She was born on the I[st] day of June in the Year of Our Lord 880, being the daughter of Michael Lord Howell and Mary Lady MacLean, and half-sister to Coel Lord Howell and Melissa Lady Howell, each being sired of a different mother. She intermarried firstly with Cathan MacRorie Hereditary Count of Culdi on the XXVIth day of May in the year 897, and by him she had children: the Hereditary Count Davin Elathan later Earl of Culdi; the Lord Ansel Irial, the ancestor of the MacAthan line. After her husband's death on the I[st] day of December in the year 903, she intermarried secondly with James "Jamie" Lord Drummond on the XVIIth day of July in the year 906, and by him she had children: the Lady Michaela Jocelyne, who intermarried with Rhys Michael King of Gwynedd; the Lord Cathan Cinhil, also called Cathal, who intermarried with Jerusha Evaine Jodotha Thuryn, daughter of Rhys Lord Thuryn and Evaine Lady MacRorie.

In late September of the year 903 she was visiting her parents in Carbury, whom she had not seen for II years. She was present on the I[st] day of July in the year 905 when the victorious Gwyneddan army returned to Valoret. In the year 918 she returned to court with her wards, Lady Giesele MacLean and Lady Richeldis MacLean, and attended the state wedding banquet on the Xth day of January. Her powers were blocked by Tavis on the XXIst day instant. On the next day she was closely questioned by the Regents about the events of the night before. After her husband's death, she was sent into forced retirement to Saint Dymphna's Convent at Grecotha. She died on the XXVIth day of October in the year 957, aged LXXVII years, of apoplexy suffered when she received the unexpected news of her son Cathan's death. R.I.P. [*Camber of Culdi*; *Saint Camber*; *The Harrowing of Gwynedd*; *King Javan's Year*].

Elinora, *i.e.*, **AriElinora Imrietta** *Furstána-Festila-Mór*, **Titular Queen of Gwynedd, Duchess of Tolán.** She was born on the XXIVth day of September in the year 985, being the only surviving child and heir of Blaine Imre Prince of Furstán-Festil-Tigre and Corvina Lady Zevenden, and granddaughter of Duchad Mór Count of Tigre and Princess Ariella daughter of Imre II Pretender of Gwynedd. She intermarried with Manuel Graf von Spire on the XIIth day of May in the year 1005, and by him she had children: the Prince Blaine Manuel, dead at age XII of eating wolfshirr; the Princess AriElandra, dead at age IV of the variable vesicance; the Princess Chriselle later Pretender of Gwynedd and Duchess of Tolán, who intermarried with the Prince Zimri Duke of Truvorsk son of Kyprian II King of Torenth; the Princess Markella, who intermarried with Torval II Duke d'Arjenol.

The Princess Elinora succeeded her *cousine germaine*, the Princess Imriella, on the XIVth day of February in the year 1038, but, other than arranging the marriage of her II surviving daughters to prominent members of the Torenthi royal house, she made no effort to press her claim to the throne of Gwynedd. She was never formally installed. Elinora is the ancestress of the Junior branch of the House of Furstán-Festil. She is perhaps best known for her collection of poetic laments, *Woe Is Unto Me*, issued in IV volumes after her death, concerning which Berrhones said, "'Ραγες ομφακίζουσι μάλα." She died on the XXXth day of September in the year 1050, aged LXV years, and was buried with her family at Torenthály. R.I.P.

Elroy, Father. In March of the year 1125 this priest was serving as a chamberlain to Bradene Archbishop Primate of Valoret and All Gwynedd. He announced King Kelson to the General Synod of Bishops held at Valoret on the XVth day instant. He was a courtly cleric of middle years. [*The Quest for Saint Camber*].

Elspeth. She was serving as a maid at Rhemuth Castle in June of the year 928, and shared sleeping quarters with Liesel (Rhysel Thuryn). [*The Bastard Prince*].

Elspeth *MacRorie*, **Lady, Abbess of Saint Hilda's.** She was born on the XVIth day of March in the Year of Our Lord 840, being the eldest daughter of Ballard II Earl of Culdi and Ardis Lady Drummond, and elder sister of Camber Earl of Culdi. She early expressed an interest in the Church, and entered the Convent of Saint Hilda's in the year 858, being elected Abbess of that establishment on the XXVIIth day of June in the year 889. She was killed by the forces of the Regents on the XIVth day January in the year 918, aged LXXVII years; her body was later recovered and buried with full honours in the Abbey cemetery. R.I.P.

Elvira, Lady. She was serving as a lady-in-waiting to Jehana Queen of Gwynedd in November of the year 1120. *Bella femmina che ride, vuol dir, borsa che piange.* [*Deryni Rising*].

Embert, Brother. He was serving as a monk and physician of the *Custodes Fidei* in June of the year 928. He was directed to keep Sir Cathan Drummond sedated on the XXIXth day of that month. [*The Bastard Prince*].

Emrys, Abbot of Saint Neot's Abbey, Dom. This renowned Gabrilite adept and Healer was born on the Vth day of September in the Year of Our Lord 835. He joined the Order of Saint Gabriel in the year 856, and was elected Abbot of Saint Neot's Abbey on the XIIIth day of July in the year 888. He killed Brother Ulric on the IInd day of May in the year 905, after the latter went berserk during his training to become a Healer, and later used Ulric's body as an example of how to treat war wounds. He attended the consecration of Father Alister Cullen as Bishop of Grecotha and Vicar General Robert Oriss as Archbishop of Rhemuth on the IXth day of July in the year 905 at Valoret.

He came to Valoret in the Summer of the year 906 to complain to King Cinhil I of encroachments on his Abbey's lands. On the XXIIIrd day of October in that year he participated in the Ist consistory of Archbishop Jaffray. On the XXIst day of December in the year 910 he declined a position on the Camberian Council on account of age. On the VIth day of March in the year 917 he was enlisted by the Council to find additional Healers who had the "blocking" talent, and met with Rhys and Camber at Saint Neot's Abbey on the XVIth day of April. He was present at the coronation of King Alroy at Valoret on the XXVth day of May. On the XXIVth day of December in that year he was slain while destroying the portal at Saint Neot's Abbey, defending it against the incursion of Rhun the Ruthless and his men. He was LXXXII years of age at his death.

He is described in the *Legends* as being a "white-haired, white-robed shadow of a man, gliding wraith-like in the invisible mantle of his Deryniness." His last psychic message at the abandoned portal of Saint Neot's Abbey noted that "The humans kill what they do not understand." R.I.P. [*Saint Camber*; "First Session"; "The *Examen*"; *Camber the Heretic*; *The Harrowing of Gwynedd*].

Episcopal Sees of Gwynedd. These are the chief sees of the Archbishops and Bishops of Gwynedd: Valoret (All Saints' Cathedral); Rhemuth (Saint George's Cathedral); Dhassa (Saint Andrew's Cathedral); Coroth (Saint Matthew's Cathedral); Grecotha (Saint Luke's Cathedral); Cashien (Saint Bridget's Cathedral); Stavenham (Christ Church Cathedral); Marbury (Saint Stephen's Cathedral); Meara (Saint Uriel and All Angels' Cathedral); Cardosa (Saint Mary's Cathedral); Carbury (Saint Peter's Cathedral, disestablished 1122); Nyford (Saint Joseph's Cathedral); Rhorau (Saint Columba's Cathedral, suspended 1118); Cardosa (Saint Anne's Cathedral).

Equites Custodum Fidei **(*Knights of the Guardians of the Faith*)**. This military arm of the *Custodes Fidei* was founded as a Suborder on the IInd day of February in the year 918, under the leadership of its Ist Grand Master,

Lord Albertus formerly Peter Sinclair Earl of Tarleton, as a replacement for the Order of Saint Michael. Over C knights were given the title of *Eques Custodum Fidei* on that day. The Order was given the infamous "Benediction of the Sword," which absolved all of the *Equites* from malicide, or any justifiable killing of the wicked, specifically the Deryni. Commanderies were sited in all of the cathedral cities in Gwynedd, and other Priories were scattered throughout the Kingdom. The Suborder was ordered disbanded for its crimes against God and man by Ailin Archbishop Primate of Valoret and All Gwynedd on the XIIth day of July in the year 928.

The knights of this Suborder sported black surcoats bearing a red moline cross charged with a haloed lion's head, white sashes fringed with red, braided cinctures of scarlet and gold worn as a cordon around the left shoulder, and black mantles faced with scarlet. [*The Harrowing of Gwynedd*; *King Javan's Year*].

Ercon, Saint. This well-known scholar and historian flourished shortly after the reign of Bearand King of Gwynedd in the VIIIth century. He was the elder brother of the martyred Saint Willim, and was himself killed while trying to locate his brother's murderers. He later became the patron saint of the Little Brothers of Saint Ercon, founded by Paulin Sinclair of Ramos on the XXXth day of April in the year 912. The Mother House of this order was located in Ramos on the River Eirian. His feastday is the XXXth day of April. [*Camber the Heretic*; *The Harrowing of Gwynedd*].

Erdic, Father. This old priest was chaplain to the d'Eirial family in the 960s, when Gilrae was a small boy, but had died by the year 977. R.I.P. ["Vocation"].

Erdödy Radulf Rostov Varfolomei *Furstán-Jándrich*, **Duke of Jándrich, Count of Sympheropol**. He was born on the XXXth day of December in the Year of Our Lord 1094, being the eldest son and heir of Radyslav Count of Sympheropol and the Countess Neolina daughter of Philoktémon Sovereign Duke of Mörovsky. He intermarried with the Lady Bogdana daughter of Maryav Count Czalsky, and by her he had children: the Hereditary Duke Nimur; the Countess Passariona; the Countess Olympiada; the Count Yevtei; the Countess Aëlita.

He succeeded his father as Count of Sympheropol on the IIIrd day of January in the year 1108, and his first cousin once removed, the Duke Sigard III, as Duke of Jándrich on the IVth day of November in the year 1114. On the XXXth day of June in the year 1123, he attended the funeral of King Alroy Arion II. With other Torenthi notables, he attended a state dinner in Beldour honouring King Liam Lajos II and King Kelson on the IXth day of July in the year 1128. [*King Kelson's Bride*].

Erena. This Willimite disciple's sick child had a fever which was "cured" by the prayers of Revan and Queron on the IXth day of February in the year 918. [*The Harrowing of Gwynedd*].

Eric. He was serving as a page to Bran Coris Earl of Marley in June of the year 1121. [*High Deryni*].

Esgair Ddu. Also called "The Black Cliff," this is the fortress prison of Cardosa Castle in the Rheljan Mountains. Sean Lord Derry was briefly held captive there by King Wencit on the XXIst day of June in the year 1121. [*High Deryni*].

Estellan *Buckleigh MacInnis*, **Countess of Culdi, Lady**. She was born on the XXVIth day of January in the Year of Our Lord 875, being the daughter of Sir Cyr Buckleigh and Engadine Lady Malreux. She intermarried with Manfred Earl of Culdi on the Ist day of April in the year 895, and by him she had children: the Hereditary Count Iver later Earl of Culdi; the Lord Edward later Baron Arnham and Bishop of Grecotha. She was serving as a companion to Queen Michaela in June of the year 928, and helped her dress for the period of mourning beginning on the IInd day of July in that year. She died on the XXIXth day of August in the year 946, aged LXXI years. R.I.P. [*The Harrowing of Gwynedd*; *The Bastard Prince*].

Esther, Lady. This lady-in-waiting to Jehana Dowager Queen of Gwynedd was sent to summon King Kelson to his Ist Council meeting on the XIVth day of November in the year 1120. She later interrupted the King and Alaric Morgan Duke of Corwyn on that same day just after they killed the stenrect in the Palace garden. She was plump, flighty, and excitable. [*Deryni Rising*].

Ethelburga, Saint. This IVth-century martyr, daughter of a trader in Dasea (the old name of Dhassa), suffered from illness as a child, but promised to convert her family to the Christian faith if ever she recovered her health. On the day that she finally rose from her bed, she convinced her father, Burghard, and her IV sisters, Sexburga, Kyneburga, Hemburga, and Withburga, to be baptized by the local priest. Although twice married, she remained a virgin all her life, saying that she had given herself only to Christ and that he was a jealous husband. Late in life she joined a Mooryn religious order consisting of her sisters and other like-minded individuals, and they spent their days in prayer and sharing the ecstatic visions to which they were prone. However, a local Lord ordered them to pay taxes, and when Ethelburga refused, he had her seized, stripped of her clothes, and given to his men. Her despoiled body was returned to the community on the next day, a beatific smile etched permanently on her face. Her body remained incorrupt, and can still be seen near Saint Bodo's Church at the village of Gunury, where it is displayed once annually on the Gunury carriage, endlessly circling the village green from sunrise until sundown, at which point IV bells are rung, I in memory of each of her sisters, and Saint Ethelburga is finally returned to her resting place. She was later adopted as Patroness of the holy city of Dhassa, where a shrine dedicated to her name guards the Northern approach to that town. Her feastday is the XIIth day of October. [*Deryni Checkmate*; *The Bishop's Heir*].

Étienne, Baron de Courcy. This Deryni Lord was born on the XXIInd day of November in the Year of Our Lord 873, being the eldest surviving son and heir of Léopard Baron de Courcy and the Duchesse Cygnette daughter of Reynard II Duc du Joux. After immigrating to Northern Carthmoor in the year 890, he intermarried with Kenza Lady Stiofan on the XXIIIrd day of June in the year 891, and by her he had children: the Hereditary Lord Guiscard, who died before his father, leaving issue; the Lord Huon; the Lady Élvienne; the Lady Fleurette. He succeeded his father on the IXth day of October in the year 901, and was appointed a Law Lord by King Cinhil I in the year 905. He maintained an estate in the far South of Gwynedd near its border with Carthmoor. He gave a *cardounet* board as a gift to King Alroy and the Prince Javan on their XIIIth birthday in the year 918. He was sent by Joram MacRorie in the year 920 to infiltrate the Haldane Court in preparation for King Javan's accession.

He was present at the death of King Alroy on the XXIIIrd day of June in the year 921, and was the Ist peer of Gwynedd to acknowledge Prince Javan as the new King. He was soon named the King's Confidential Secretary, and attended the coronation of King Javan on the XXXIst day of July in that year. He moved to the antechamber of the new library in Rhemuth Palace a few days later, and was given the responsibility of guarding the new portal there and maintaining contact with the Michaeline Haven.

On the XIth day of May in the year 922 the former Regents overthrew and killed King Javan and his allies. Étienne initially escaped the soldiers, and was able to spirit away the wife and daughter of the Healer Oriel to the former Michaeline Haven. There he quickly gave Tieg Thuryn a mental history of the events leading up to the *coup*; his memories were later transcribed by Tieg for Bishop Niallan's history of the Haldane family after the Restoration. He then chose to return to Rhemuth with his powers blocked, and submitted to torture by the former Regents rather than give away the secret of the portal that he had so jealously guarded. He was tried, attainted, and executed on the XXth day of May in the year 922, aged XLVIII years; his body was exhumed in the year 929 by the Regents of King Owain and he was reburied with honours in the crypt of Saint George's Cathedral. At that time, the attainder was overturned, and his grandson, Lord Alphard, was given the Barony of Stanzar in lieu of Courcy.

He is described in the *Heirs* as "a dark, hook-nosed man in burgundy, wearing a baron's coronet and a chain of minor office. He looked to be in his late forties, clean-shaven, but with grey threaded through the jet-black hair; a powerful man, still in his prime." He had previously sported a beard and mustache. R.I.P. [*The Harrowing of Gwynedd*; *King Javan's Year*; *The Bastard Prince*].

Etruskia. This ancient land lies East of R'Kassi, being situate on a long peninsula surrounded by the Median Sea. The capital of this place is the Holy City of Rûm, built upon VII mounds called hills, through which weaves the River Tyger. The natives speak a language called Latino, the older form of which is termed Latin, and is still being used by the Etruskian Church headed by the Papiarch, and by many of the churches of the West.

This old republic is governed by a Grand Consul, who is elected by the Senate to rule for I year only. During the time of Christ one Julio attempted to make himself King, but was quickly cut down by the people, who now dislike all pretensions of monarchy.

According to Campbell de Broun, who once visited this place, "...the climate is mild in the winter, with no snow or ice, but the summers are like an inferno, being hot and damp and full of bugs. The people here are short and dark and speak too quickly to be understood. They eat their main meals in the middle of the day and nap in the afternoons, closing down their shops and offices until evening. This seemed very strange to us until we felt the weight of the heat ourselves. The rich retreat to their villas by the sea or in the mountains which form the spine of this land, but the common folk just endure. There are violent storms in the summer, but little enough rain overall. The main roads are paved with close-fitted stone, making them the best this weary traveler has yet seen. We came upon inns spaced regularly every XV leagues or so, and found them both clean and cheap, and the food very filling. Were it not for the sun, this would be a most pleasant place to spend one's days."

Eugen *von Roslov*, Graf. This Deryni was sent by Prince Miklós of Torenth on the XIVth day of June in the year 928 to Rhys Michael King of Gwynedd in Rhemuth, being presented to him at Rhemuth. He then read an ultimatum from his master demanding that the King appear for the Pretender Marek's son's christening at Culliecairn later that month. He then threw down a gauntlet in front of the King, challenging him before his Council. According to Volumen III of the *Heirs*, "the man's dark hair was cut short around his long face, the severity emphasizing high cheekbones and slightly canted dark eyes above a thin mustache and a small, close-clipped beard." [*The Bastard Prince*].

Eustace *of Fairleigh*, Bishop. This itinerant Bishop attended the consecration of Alister Cullen as Bishop of Grecotha and Robert Oriss as Archbishop of Rhemuth on the IXth day of July in the year 905 at Valoret. On the XXIIIrd day of October in the year 906 he participated in the Ist consistory of Archbishop Jaffray. He attended the Synod of Bishops held at Valoret in November and December of 917, but abstained from the rigged vote of the XXVIth day of December for Archbishop Hubert MacInnis. He was the only itinerant prelate to retain his rank after the Council of Ramos. He was wiry thin, and was noted for his wry sense of humour. [*Saint Camber*; *Camber the Heretic*].

Evaine Elspeth Jessamyn *MacRorie Thuryn*, Lady. She was born on the VIth day of October in the Year of Our Lord 882, being the only surviving daughter of Camber Earl of Culdi and Jocelyn Lady de la Marche. She intermarried with Rhys Lord Thuryn on the VIth day of January in the year 904, and by him she had children: the Lord Aidan Camber, dead at age X; the Lady Rhysel Jocelyn, who intermarried with Sir Robin Ainslie; the Lord Tieg Joram, who intermarried with

Karis d'Oriel; the Lady Jerusha Evaine Jodotha, who intermarried with Sir Cathan Drummond.

After her mother's death she served as chatelaine of Tor Caerrorie for her father. Like her father she was a scholar and student of the old Deryni scrolls; on the XXVIIth day of September in the year 903 she attempted with him to translate an ancient scroll of Pargan Howiccan. She served as godmother to Prince Aidan Haldane at his baptism on the VIth day of November in the year 904. She was present on the I[st] day of July in the year 905 when the victorious Gwyneddan army returned to Valoret. On the next day she assisted her father in integrating the memories of Alister Cullen, and gained access to his bedchamber by assuming the form of a Michaeline monk, "Brother John."

She was a founding member of the Camberian Council on the XVth day of April in the year 909. She participated in a special magical ceremony baptizing her IIIrd child, Tieg, on the I[st] day of August in the Year 914 at her manor house of Sheele North of Valoret. On the IVth day of February in the year 917 she was used by her husband as an example of Rhys's newfound ability to "turn off" Deryni powers. She spent much of the year 918 researching obscure Deryni texts to help restore her father's spirit. She used the guise of "Brother John" a IInd time to meet Prince Javan at Rhemuth on the Xth day of April in that year. She died on the I[st] day of August in the year 918, aged XXXV years, while attempting to restore her father from a suspension spell. She seemed to appear at the empowerment of King Javan on the XXVIth day of June in the year 921. *Amar a Deus é a maior das virtudes, ser amado de Deus, é a maior das felicidades.* R.I.P. ["Catalyst"; *Camber of Culdi*; *Saint Camber*; "Healer's Song"; *Camber the Heretic*; *The Harrowing of Gwynedd*; *King Javan's Year*; *The Bastard Prince*].

Evans, Father. He was serving as secretary to Thomas Cardiel Bishop of Dhassa in March of the year 1121. [*Deryni Checkmate*].

Evering. This Barony of Gwynedd is located on the coast of the Southern Sea between the Duchies of Corwyn and Carthmoor. It was founded by Sir Ralson de Cosnac, a knight of Vézaire, who took service with Owain King of Gwynedd in the year 946, and was ennobled by King Uthyr on the XVth day of November in the year 948 for his valor at the Battle of Laxalt. On the VIIth day of November in the year 1120 Gérard Ralson Baron d'Evering was killed while returning from Coroth to Rhemuth after fetching Alaric Morgan Duke of Corwyn following King Brion's death. [*Deryni Rising*]. See also: Benoît, Gérard.

BARONS D'EVERING

HOUSE OF RALSON DE COSNAC

Ralson de Cosnac	948-955
Amédée (son)	955-984
Gonthard (brother)	984-1019
Humbert (son)	1019-1025
Desmond (nephew)	1025-1046
Vincent (son)	1046-1071
Anselme (son)	1071-1109
Gérard (son)	1109-1120
Torsin (son)	1120-1130+

Ewan I *MacEwan*, **Duke of Claibourne, Viceroy of the Kheldish Riding, Earl of Rhendall, sometime Hereditary Count of Eastmarch, Lord Regent and Earl Marshal of Gwynedd.** He was born on the XIVth day of April in the Year of Our Lord 881, being the eldest son and heir of Sighere Duke of Claibourne and Synolda Lady de Lacey, and brother of Hrorik Earl of Eastmarch and Sighere *Junior* Earl of Marley. He intermarried with Mary Lady Graham on the XIVth day of March in the year 906, and by her he had children: the Hereditary Duke and Earl Graham later Duke of Claibourne; the Lord Hrorik later Earl Feradach; the Lady Marian; the Lord Bromhall later Baron Parslaw; the Lord Brecon later Baron Tencin; the Lady Oenone.

As the heir and representative of his father he participated in the War Council held on the XXIIIrd day of June in the year 905 at the Great Hall in Valoret Palace, and was created Earl of Rhendall on the XXVIth day of August in the year 906 by King Cinhil I. On the IIIrd day of February in the year 917 he was appointed Acting Regent to young King Alroy in his father's stead. He was present at the coronation of King Alroy on the XXVth day of May in that year.

Earl Ewan succeeded his father as Duke on the IInd day of July in the year 917, and at that time was also named Lord Regent and Earl Marshal of Gwynedd and Commander of the Royal Army. He reorganized the Gwyneddan forces and sent a portion of them to Rhemuth under the command of Murdoch Earl of Carthane, Tammaron Earl Fitz-Arthur, and Manfred Earl of Culdi; the IInd force stayed at Valoret to hold military exercises. He was present at the official state wedding banquet held at Valoret on the Xth day of January in the year 918. However, he was treacherously deposed from his office by his fellow Regents and then stabbed by Murdoch on the XXVth day of May in the year 918, aged XXXVII years. Declan Carmody was ordered to rip Ewan's mind before he could die, but instead gave the Duke the *coup de grâce*. His body was returned to Kheldour for burial, and he was succeeded by his son, Earl Graham. R.I.P. [*Saint Camber*; *Camber the Heretic*; *The Harrowing of Gwynedd*; *King Javan's Year*].

Ewan III Kenzie *MacEwan*, **Duke of Claibourne, Hereditary Lord Marshal of the Royal Council of Gwynedd.** He was born on the IXth day of August in the Year of Our Lord 1066, being the eldest son and heir of Ursic Duke of Claibourne and Eugenia Lady d'Annibale. He intermarried with Eustachea Marchesa de' Assemani in Southern Bremagne on the XXXth day of June in the year 1088, and by her he had children: the Hereditary Duke and Earl Graham Ewan later Graham III Duke of Claibourne; the Lady Anastasia; the Lord Martin Hrorik later Earl of Moramar; the Lady Efigenia; the Lady Almarica; the Lord Alistair Ursic later Baron Burgess.

The Duke Ewan succeeded his father on the IIIrd day of February in the year 1095, and proved a stalwart supporter of the new King Brion from the beginning of his reign. He accompanied Brion on his expedition to

Eastmarch in the year 1105. He also joined him on his venison hunt at Candor Rhea on the Ist day of November in the year 1120; thus, he was present when the King was foully murdered by the magic of the Pretender Charissa on that day. As Hereditary Earl Marshal of Gwynedd, he called into session the Ist meeting of the Royal Council following the King's death on the XIVth day instant. He commanded the Northernmost of Kelson's III border armies during the war with Torenth in the year 1121.

He rode with Kelson King of Gwynedd to Trurill in November of the year 1123. He was present in Rhemuth at Kelson's knighting on the IIIrd day of March in the year 1125. In his later years many of his duties were assumed by his son and heir. He died of *la grippe* at Claibourne on the XIIIth day of December in the year 1129, aged LXIII years, and was succeeded by his eldest son, Earl Graham.

He is described in the *Chronicles* as having shaggy reddish hair and beard, and being a lover of dogs. *Potentissimus est qui se habet in potestate.* R.I.P. [*Deryni Rising*; *Deryni Checkmate*; *High Deryni*; *The Bishop's Heir*; *The King's Justice*; *The Quest for Saint Camber*; *King Kelson's Bride*].

Eye of Rom. One of the paraphernalia belonging to the monarch of Gwynedd, the Eye consists of a large cabochon ruby the size of a man's little finger tip, set in the claws of a red-gold mounting terminating in a slender gold wire that enables the wearer to use it as an earring. It originally belonged to Camber Earl of Culdi, who gave it to Cinhil I King of Gwynedd and endowed it with certain magical powers to enable the so-called Haldane potential in the King and his descendants.

It was passed by Cinhil I to his son, King Alroy, and by Alroy to his brother, King Javan, and by Javan to his brother, King Rhys Michael, and thence to each successive heir of the family. King Kelson had to retrieve the gem from his father's grave on the XIVth day of November in the year 1120. It was feared lost again when King Kelson was swept underground on the XXIst day of March in the year 1125, but his reappearance a month later restored the Eye to its proper place.

According to Volumen I of the *Legends*, "legends say that it fell from the stars on the night of our Savior's birth, and was brought by the Magi as a gift to the Child. It has been in the MacRorie family for XII generations, and we have endowed it with certain characteristics which will be useful to [the Haldanes]." Its name suggests that the gem had spent some centuries in the city of Rûm in Etruskia. *E il Sol montava in su con quelle stelle.* [*Camber of Culdi*; *Camber the Heretic*; *King Javan's Year*; *The Bastard Prince*; *Deryni Rising*; *The Quest for Saint Camber*].

Fabius, Brother. This *Custodes* monk from Saint Cassian's Abbey was sent with dispatches from Father Lior and Rhun Earl of Sheele to Archbishop Hubert at Rhemuth, arriving at dusk on the XXVth day of in June in the year 928. He also told Hubert and Secorim the news of Albertus's death and Paulin's incapacitation, relaying his information on that same evening at the residence of Robert Oriss Archbishop of Rhemuth. [*The Bastard Prince*].

Faelan, Father. He was born on the last day of October in the Year of Our Lord 898. He joined the *Custodes Fidei* Order in the year 918, and was assigned to the *Arx Fidei* Abbey near Rhemuth, where he became friendly with Prince Javan. He was appointed King Javan's confessor on the XVIIIth day of July in the year 921 at the new monarch's specific request. Father Faelan was required by his superiors to report monthly to *Arx Fidei* about the King's activities, but he also provided Javan and his allies with information about the workings of the *Custodes*, including the revelation that Paulin had acquired a new Deryni "sniffer," Master Dimitri. At times Faelan showed signs of torture at Paulin's hand.

He attended the coronation of King Javan on the XXXIst day of July in the year 921. Fearing further torture, he refused to return to *Arx Fidei* on the IInd day of October in that year, and II days later was excommunicated by Paulin when he defied the latter's command to return. He was strangled by Lord Albertus at Paulin's orders on the Xth day instant, aged XXII years, his death being made to look like suicide by hanging. He was buried in a potter's field outside Rhemuth. R.I.P. [*King Javan's Year*; *The Bastard Prince*].

Falainn. This was Bishop Alister Cullen's favorite dun mare at Grecotha in October of the year 905; she was shod by Andrew the Smith. [*Saint Camber*].

Fallon. This sovereign Kingdom lies on the coast of the Southern Sea between the Kingdom of Bremagne and the County of Fianna. The region was conquered by the Byzantyun Emperor Augoustos I in the year 9 B.C., who called the new province Britannia Magna and established his capital city at Augoustopolis on the River Laval. By the year 200 the Province included most of the states now known as Bremagne, Fallon, and Jáca. The Byzantyun Empire began to disintegrate at the beginning of the Vth century. Fallon was evacuated in the year 433, and became a sovereign County centered at the coastal city of Truyère on the Northern side of the River Laval. It was subsumed into Bremagne in the year 555.

In the year 842 rebellion broke out in Fallon, and that state declared its independence under its first King, Hennequin d'Albéric, on the XXVIIth day of July in the year 843, with the boundary line between the two countries being drawn at the River Laval. The lovely city of Truyère again became its capital city.

Fallon has a mild climate moderated year-round by breezes from the Southern Sea. It is particularly known for its fine wines and cheeses, and for the comeliness of its women. The Earl Rogier of Gwynedd derived from Fallon. *"La Fallon marche à la tête de la civilisation."* [*Deryni Rising*; *King Kelson's Bride*]. See also: Rogier.

KINGS OF FALLON

HOUSE OF ALBÉRIC

Hennequin d'Albéric	843-861
Ermessin le Génie (son)	861-892
Ayméri (son)	892-906
Philibert (nephew)	906-930

Matfred (son)	930-955
Manrique (son)	955-977
Albéric I (son)	977-998
Mathieu (brother)	998-1001
Bérenger (son)	1001-1018
Tancrède (son)	1018-1052
Albéric II (son)	1052-1066
Donat (brother)	1066-1068
Mayeul (son)	1068-1090
Albéric III (cousin)	1090-1104
Cixilane (son)	1104-1130+

Fane *Fitz-Arthur*, Earl Fitz-Arthur, Deputy Regent of Kheldour, Lord Regent of Gwynedd, Regent of Cassan. He was born on the XIVth day of December in the Year of Our Lord 895, being the second but eldest surviving son and heir of Tammaron Earl Fitz-Arthur and Nieve Lady O Nuaillan. He intermarried with the Princess Anne Heiress of Cassan and daughter of Ambert Quinnell Sovereign Prince of Cassan on the XXIInd day of September in the year 916, and by her he had children: the Hereditary Duke Tambert later Duke of Cassan; the Lady Anne *Junior*, who intermarried with Owain King of Gwynedd; the Lady Nieve; the Lord Eldon later Earl Fitz-Arthur; the Lady Ophelia; the Lady Duvessine; the Lord Nolan.

Upon his marriage he was made co-heir to the new Duchy of Cassan which would be established at the death of his father-in-law. On the IVth day of June in the year 918 he was named Deputy Regent of Kheldour by the Regents, and appointed to the Royal Council of Gwynedd, and the succession to the Duchy of Cassan was shifted to his eldest son, Tambert. He succeeded as co-Regent of Cassan at the death of Prince Ambert on the XXIst day of May in the year 921. After the succession of King Javan a month later, he was removed by the new monarch from the Council of Gwynedd on the XXVIIth day of June following, on the grounds that he could not successfully fulfill his obligations to both offices.

The Lord Fane succeeded his father as Earl on the Vth day of July in the year 928. He died in the year 948, aged LII years, and by his letters testimentary was succeeded in the County of Fitz-Arthur by his IInd son, Lord Eldon. R.I.P. *Es lebt, ein Gott zu strafen und zu rächen.* [*The Harrowing of Gwynedd*; *King Javan's Year*; *The Bastard Prince*].

Farone, Abbot and Reverend Father. He was the head of Saint Stefan's Monastery near Carbury in April of the year 905. [*Deryni Challenge*].

Fathane. This Torenthi port town is located on the Eastern bank of the Western River, just North of the Twin Rivers Sound. According to the *Chronicles*, "Ships from Torenth and Corwyn traded there regularly, and it was also a point of departure for hunters and trappers going farther upriver to the great Veldur Forests. This combination of interests made Fathane a very lively town." It was here that Sean Earl Derry spent a night at the Crooked Dragon Inn and the Jack Dog Tavern on the XXIVth day of March in the year 1121. This city was also used as a staging area for Torenthi raids on Corwyn that Spring.

The County of Fathane was granted to the Prince Imre Elgar second surviving son of King Mátyás at his coming of age on the IVth day of May in the year 779, but he died without heirs male on the XXth day of January in the year 795; by his second surviving daughter, the Countess Tayce, he was the grandfather of Dominic Ist Duke of Corwyn. The Honour of Fathane was then given to Count Imre's nephew, the Prince Festil son of Kálmán II King of Torenth, on the XIIth day of August in that same year, and was deeded by him upon his succession to the Gwyneddan throne to his IIIrd son, Prince Rufim, and thence to Rufim's brother, Prince Károly, in whose family the title has descended to the present day. This family is the only extant direct male line remaining from the issue of Festil I King of Gwynedd. [*Deryni Checkmate*].

COUNTS OF FATHANE

HOUSE OF FURSTÁN-FESTIL-FATHANE

Imre Elgar (son of Torenthi King Mátyás)	779-795
Festil I (nephew)	795-822
Rufim I (son)	822-868
Károly (brother)	868-875
Rufim II (son)	875-902
Festil II (brother)	902-909
Kálmán (nephew)	909-938
István (son)	938-961
Damián (son)	961-988
Rufim III (son)	988-1019
Mihály (cousin)	1019-1022
Lipóld (son)	1022-1060
Flóránt (son)	1060-1087
Emmerick (son)	1087-1111
Rufim IV (son)	1111-1130+

Fergus, Lord. This heavyset Baron was a vassal of Jared Duke of Cassan. He executed the murderer Rimmell at Culdi on the XXIXth day of March in the year 1121 in obedience to the Duke's command. [*Deryni Checkmate*].

Ferris. He was a master swordsmith from Eistenfalla, a country far North of Torenth, and a follower of the pagan god, the "All-Father." He came to Kiltuin in Corwyn on the XVIth day of April in the year 1118 to peddle weapons, but quickly got into trouble due to his inability to speak the local language. He was attacked while drinking at the Green Man Tavern there, and then arrested and accused of murdering a woman called Lillas. At his trial by Bishop Ralf Tolliver on the following day, Alaric Morgan Duke of Corwyn questioned Ferris and declared him innocent of the crime. He was then released by the Bishop. He later fashioned a special sword for the Duke in gratitude, and joined Morgan's service. ["Trial"].

Festil I Ferencz *Furstán*, called "The Conqueror," King of Gwynedd, Margraf of Medras, Count of Fathane. The first of the Festillic Kings of Gwynedd was born at Beldour on the VIIIth day of June in the Year of Our Lord 780, being the second son and third child of Kálmán II King of Torenth and Grand Princess Démétria daughter of Augoustos IV Autokratór of

Byzantyun. He intermarried with Maire Duchess of Phtheus in Grecia on the XIVᵗʰ day of April in the year 799, and by her he had children: the Hereditary Graf Festil later Hereditary Prince of Gwynedd and Earl of Lendour later Festil II King of Gwynedd; the Princess Arielle, who intermarried with Konrád Graf von Lustnau und Weckesser; the Prince Imre later Earl of Rhemuth and Archbishop of Valoret, who died in the year 839, *sans postérité*; the Prince Rufim later Count of Fathane by cession of his father later Patriarch of Beldour under his religious name, Asterios I, who died in the year 868, *sans postérité*; the Prince Lipóld, dead of the trembling ague at age VIII; the Prince Ottókar István later Earl of Rhemuth by cession from his brother later Sovereign Prince of Nyford by inheritance from his sister, and who died unmarried in the year 867 at the age of LVII of a fall from his horse, when his titles escheated to the crown; the Princess Andruine, who intermarried with Evrard Count of Rhorau-Harpenberg; the Prince Károly also called Carolus later Count of Altorf later Count of Fathane by inheritance from his brother, created Earl of Haldane *ad personam* by his brother, King Festil II, founder of the House of Furstán-Festil-Fathane, who left issue, III sons and III daughters, and died in the year 875, aged LXI years; the Princess Yolande later Sovereign Princess of Nyford, her father's favourite child, a renowned beauty of her day who was popularly called the "Festil Virgin," and who, although she received many suits of marriage from princes throughout the region, rejected them all and died unmarried in the year 863 of a swelling in her breast, aged XLVII years, saying, according to Guigues, that "she would serve as mistress to no man"; she was returned for burial at the family crypt in Valoret, and was succeeded by her older brother, Prince Ottókar.

The Great King Festil I was created Count of Fathane by his grandfather on the XIIᵗʰ day of August in the year 795, and Margraf of Medras by his father on the VIIᵗʰ day of June in the year 818. As a youth he trained with his father's army, and acted as the Commander of a Thousand in his father's expedition to Arjenol in the year 801; he was appointed General of the Torenthi Army in the year 818. In the Spring of the year 822 he convinced his ailing father that he could conquer Gwynedd with a lightning strike across the border during the Festival of First Fruits, and organized a brigade of CCC highly-trained attack troops, relying on a long-standing claim to the throne of Gwynedd deriving from his descent from Aidan King of Gwynedd, his great-great-great-grandfather.

Riding by night, keeping to the back trails of the mountains and valleys, and breaking his force into X units of XXX men each, Festil was able to gather his small army outside the gates of Rhemuth during the early morning hours of the XXIˢᵗ day of June in that year. He infiltrated his soldiers into the city disguised as monks and peasants, then attacked through the open doors of the palace with deadly force. Before the guard could react, the King and his family and major advisors were dead. In the chaos, a launderer named Jasper Draper hid the II-year-old Prince Aidan in a clothing sack, and bundled him away before the invaders gained sufficient control of the palace to block all the exits, thereby preserving the Haldane Dynasty.

Although troops loyal to the Haldanes had rallied from around the city by the noon hour, and had put the palace under siege, they lacked a unified command, and the Torenthi King and his army were already pouring across the border to support the usurper. The arrival a week later of the invading soldiers sealed the fate of the Haldane monarchy, and resistance soon collapsed. All members of the Haldane family and many from the major noble houses were executed or attainted and exiled. King Festil I took the oath on the IIIʳᵈ day of July, and was crowned according to Gwyneddan custom on the XXIIⁿᵈ day instant by Emerick Archbishop Primate of Valoret and All Gwynedd, but also swearing allegiance to his father as suzerain of Gwynedd. King Kálmán II returned to Torenth within the week and died at Torenthály on the XXVIIIᵗʰ day of November in that year.

During his XVII-year reign the King Festil I extensively reorganized the nobility, moved his capital to Valoret closer to the border with Torenth, began building an elaborate palace there, established a standing army to protect his regime, ordered a comprehensive survey and codification of the laws of Gwynedd, eliminated obsolete edicts and issued new ones as necessary, ordered a revamping of the tax system of the state, established a permanent office of clerks to manage and organize royal decrees, messages, and other papers, and promulgated a bull of tolerance towards the native humans and Deryni, deliberately appointing several Gwyneddan advisers to his first High Council.

Guigues calls him "...large, well-muscled, big-boned, with a lined, chunky face on a thick neck topped by a mop of uncombed and shaggy grey hair; he looked like an ox but spoke with the honey-sweetened tones of a statesman. His vision of his adopted country, of a realm in which the best of human and Deryni could sit down and work together without prejudice, was unmatched by that of any of his successors, and although he was forced by circumstance to give many of the choicest plums in his kingdom to his Deryni soldiers and supporters and to make obeisance to his father and brother, he adopted an increasingly independent posture as the years went by. Had he lived another decade, the Haldanes would never have been restored."

This Great King died of the weak limb after II years of suffering on the Vᵗʰ day of November in the year 839, aged LIX years, and was buried in the newly established family crypt beneath All Saints' Cathedral at Valoret. He was succeeded by his eldest son, Prince Festil. R.I.P. [*Camber of Culdi*; *Camber the Heretic*].

Festil II Avgust Fyödor *Furstán-Festil*, **called "The Lame," King of Gwynedd, Duke of Carthmoor, Earl of Lendour.** The second Festillic King was born at Fathane on the XXIIIʳᵈ day of February in the Year of Our Lord 800, being the eldest son and heir of Festil I King of Gwynedd and Maire Duchess of Phtheus. He intermarried with Chiara Marchesa de' Arabbia on the XVIIᵗʰ day of September in 817, and by her he had one child: the Hereditary Prince Festil later Festil III King of Gwynedd.

His wife having died in childbirth on the Vᵗʰ day of July in the year 818, he intermarried secondly on the

XVIIth day of August in the year 826 with the Princess Brionne called "Briona" after her marriage, daughter of Nanthelme King of Mooryn, and by her he had children: the Princess Mariamne, who intermarried with Gérard Roi de Bremagne; the Prince Rudolf later Duke of Carthmoor and Archbishop of Rhemuth, who died in the year 885, aged LVI years, *sans postérité*, precipitating the rebellion of the Haldane Pretender, Cathyr Baron Carrach; the Princess Lovise, who intermarried with Danilo Burgraf von Oldenbourg in Tolán; the Princess Delilah, who intermarried with Sergei Count of Mnata.

His second wife having died on the IVth day of October in the year 835, the King Festil II intermarried thirdly with a commoner, Agharat widow of Rhodri Kadell, on the XXIIIrd day of June in the year 836, and she died on the IIIrd day of January following, leaving issue: Lord Marek, born still. He intermarried fourthly with Jornanda Countess of Zrin on the XIIth day of March in the year 837, but she was barren.

The Prince Festil was created Earl of Lendour shortly after his father's succession to the throne of Gwynedd, on the IIIrd day of July in the year 822, and Duke of Carthmoor on the XVIIth day of August in the year 826 on his marriage to Brionne Heiress of Mooryn; he ceded the former title, but elevated to the status of a Duchy, to his elder son, and the latter title to his younger son, Prince Rudolf, shortly after Festil II's accession to the throne of Gwynedd on the Vth day of November in the year 839. He was crowned on the Ist day of April in the year 840 by Mallenus Archbishop Primate of Valoret and All Gwynedd. He traveled to Beldour on the Ist of May in the year 840 to acknowledge his cousin, Lajos I King of Torenth, as Overlord; but the King being absent at Kors, the King Festil gave his oath to Prince Regent Konrád instead. On the XXIInd day of April in the year 849 a massive raid by the infidels destroyed much of Nyford, but the King hesitated to respond.

Two years later, much dissipated through his overindulgence in spirits, King Festil II was killed when his carriage overturned on the way from Valoret to Rhemuth, on the XXIXth day of April in 851. He was LI years of age at his death, and was succeeded by his eldest son, Prince Festil. His body was buried at the Royal Crypt of his ancestors at Valoret. Guigues hints that the royal carriage had been sabotaged by unnamed conspirators, but other writers have pointed out that such accidents were not uncommon during this time, and that a flash of lightning striking a nearby tree probably caused the horses to bolt.

In his history *The Five Festils*, Guigues calls this monarch "...as comely as any of this family, with finely wrought features and a full head of carefully coiffed hair, but timid in his decisions, and more interested by far in the gaudy social events he could muster than in matters of state. His one great initiative was the expansion of his palace at Valoret, for which he spared no expense. The finest artisans were brought from Bremagne and Forcinn and even further distances, and he levied a special I-year tax in the year 848 to finance the project." R.I.P. [*Camber of Culdi*].

Festil III István *Furstán-Festil*, called "Greybeard," King of Gwynedd, Duke of Lendour. The third Festillic King was born at Torenthály on the Vth day of July in the Year of Our Lord 818, being the eldest son and heir of Festil II King of Gwynedd and Chiara Marchesa de' Arabbia. He intermarried with Dionysia daughter of Andronikos Thópis, Stratégos and Despot of Esclavonia, on the XXIIIrd day of June in the year 836, and by her he had children: the Hereditary Prince and Duke Festil Ferdinand, dead of the noxious wilt at age I; the Hereditary Prince Imre Lajos later Duke of Rhemuth, who drowned in the River Slieven at age XXXIII, without surviving male issue; the Princess Corinne, who died of the crippling cramps at age XII; the Prince Blaine later Archbishop of Rhemuth later Duke of Rhemuth later Blaine I King of Gwynedd.

After his first wife passed from this world on the XXVIth day of February in the year 851, the King Festil intermarried secondly with Hélène the widow of Élias Kantakouz on the VIIth day of August in the year 852, and had further issue, without dynastic rights: Lord Bogdan later Duke of Carthmoor by inheritance from his uncle, Archbishop Rudolf; Lord Roman later Count of Dacia in Torenth; Lord Stephan later Count of Kantakouz in Torenth; Lady Stephane, a twin with her brother, who intermarried with Miloš Lord Crnević.

The Prince Festil was created Duke of Lendour on the Vth day of November in the year 839 after his father's accession to the throne of Gwynedd. He succeeded his father on the XXIXth day of April in the year 851, and was crowned by Odilbert Archbishop Primate of Valoret and All Gwynedd on the XXVIIIth day of May following. He made the trip to Beldour in July of that year to acknowledge the suzerainty of Árpád King of Torenth. He traveled to Bremagne in the year 853 to meet King Gérard, and signed with him a treaty of friendship and alliance against the infidels on the XXVIIth day of July. On the IIIrd day of April in the year 856 he met with Lludd I King of Llannedd to discuss their joint defense against the barbarians, for the raiders were very troublesome that year, coming North by the river as far as Desse, and once attacking Rhemuth overland from that port. Much of his reign was spent in strengthening the Southern defenses of the kingdom against the black-haired folk.

On the XVIIth day of October in the year 878 the King was struck down by paralysis during a Council meeting, and although he later recovered his tongue, he remained for the rest of his life partially lame and slurry of speech. During this period he relied very heavily upon the wise counsel of Camber Earl of Culdi to help govern the Kingdom. The Great King Festil III passed from this world on the VIth day of March in the year 885, aged LXVI years, and was buried in the family crypt at Valoret. He was succeeded by his eldest surviving son, Prince Blaine.

Guigues calls this monarch "...a handsome and dignified man, with carefully-trimmed grey beard and curled mustachios, much concerned with his appearance, but also very conscious of his duties and responsibilities. It is said that he knew when a rat squeaked in Valoret, and that if he squeaked without the King's permission, he had better give a good explanation for it. No one in Gwynedd looked the part of the King any more than the King himself, which was just as well, since he would tolerate no disrespect and no backtalk from any of his subjects, be they high- or low-born. When questioned by one petitioner about his decision in a particular case, the King responded that he believed in the headright system of justice; and when asked just what the headright system was, he smiled one of his rare smiles, and spoke further that the respondent should gaze upon the pikes affixed high on the city walls, and see the right of any man to have his own head displayed thereon. And he gave that man a closer look than he would have liked." R.I.P. [*Camber of Culdi*; *Camber the Heretic*].

Festil Ferdinand Lajos *Furstán-Festil*, **Prince of Gwynedd**. He was born on the XVIIth of March in the Year of Our Lord 837, being the eldest son of Festil III King of Gwynedd and Dionysia daughter of Andronikos Thópis, Stratégos and Despot of Esclavonia, and died of the noxious wilt in March of the year 838, date unknown but after his birthday, aged I year. R.I.P.

Festil Filipp László *Furstán-Festil*, **Prince of Gwynedd**. He was born on the VIIIth of January in the Year of Our Lord 869, being the eldest son of Blaine King of Gwynedd and Pasqualetta Contessa di Barbarico di Torenti, and died of the yellow mouth on the XXth day of January in 874, aged V years. He was buried in the family crypt at Valoret. R.I.P.

Festil Ottó *Furstán*, **King of Torenth, Count of Arkadia**. He was born on the XXVth day of May in the Year of Our Lord 699, being the third son and fifth child of Imre I King of Torenth and Bethany Lady Haldane widow of Barghash ibn Hassan al-Khideri, Nabil of Salah Reis, and daughter of Aidan King of Gwynedd. He intermarried with Princess Iphigénie daughter of Ursion I Roi de Bremagne on the VIIIth day of June in the year 724, and by her he had children: the Princess Jaya, who died young; the Princess Kálmána, who intermarried with Usman ibn Badlay al-Hakk, Shaikh of Kumala; the Princess Ottilia, who intermarried with Démétrios I Autokratór of Byzantyun; the Hereditary Prince Mátyás Imre later King of Torenth.

This bloodthirsty Prince was created Count of Arkadia in the year 720. He challenged and defeated his cousin King Radislaus in personal combat on the Vth day of December in the year 738, and succeeded him over the protests of his older brothers, and also murdered his predecessor's sons and siblings. He was girded with the sword by Patriarch Theodotos I on the Ist day of January following. During the next X years he concerned himself with maintaining and expanding his own power, killing or imprisoning anyone who dared to speak against him. During the III-day New Year's celebration of the year 748, the King joked about murdering the rest of his family, and the Prince Wenzel Sylvist Count of Sostra, who was not amused, gathered together his surviving cousins with the King's brothers and son-in-law, and waited until the King was in his cups at the banquet that evening. Then they drowned the monarch in a vat of his ale in the early morning hours of the IInd day of January in the year 748. The King Festil was XLVIII years of age at his death, and was succeeded by his minor son, the Prince Mátyás Imre, under the regency of Prince Wenzel Sylvist. His body was interred in the family vault of the Furstáns at Torenthály.

Festus, Earl of Legain. He was born on the Xth day of May in the Year of Our Lord 820, being the son of Sir Havil Legain and Artegalla Lady Moyle. He intermarried with Redmonda Lady Teemore on the IXth day of May in the year 840, and by her he had children: the Hereditary Count Crispus later Earl of Legain; the Lady Fabia; the Lord Antonius; the Lady Gloriana; the Lord Henricus, who was received into the *Ordo Verbi Dei* and took the name Benedict in the year 876. Sir Festus was created Earl of Legain by King Festil II on the XVIIth day of November in the year 847. He died on the Ist day of January in the year 888, aged LXVII years, and was succeeded by his son, Lord Crispus. [*Camber of Culdi*].

Fianna. This small sovereign County lies across the Southern Sea from Carthmoor, between Logréine and the Kingdom of Fallon. It achieved its independence during the breakup of the old Bremagni state on the XXVIIth day of July in the year 843, under its Ist ruler, Hervé Baron d'Auxerre. The capital city, also called Fianna, is located on the South bank of the Eau-de-Vin River where it enters the Southern Sea. Among its best-known exports are its sweet wines, which due to the temperate climate and generous rainfall are unparalleled in the Eleven Kingdoms. Colin Lord of Fianna, a younger son of Count Gezelin, conspired with the Pretender Charissa to kill Brion King of Gwynedd in the year 1120. [*Camber of Culdi*; *Camber the Heretic*; *Deryni Rising*; *Deryni Checkmate*; *The Bishop's Heir*; *King Kelson's Bride*]. See also: Colin.

COUNTS OF FIANNA

HOUSE OF AUXERRE

Hervé d'Auxerre	843-888
Auxer (son)	888-890
Guillaume I (son)	890-912
Béraud (brother)	912-916
Arnaud (brother)	916-927
Guillaume II (nephew)	927-960
Périgord (son)	960-986
Guillaume III (son)	986-1008
Otton (cousin)	1008-1023
Guillaume IV (son)	1023-1049
Arlebaud (son)	1049-1050
Guillaume V (nephew)	1050-1066
Collin (brother)	1066
Antoine I (brother)	1066-1088
Gaspard (son)	1088-1101
Gezelin (son)	1101-1130
Antoine II (son)	1130-1130+

Field of Kings, or Nekrodocheion Basilikon. Situate in Torenthály in Torenth, this is the final resting place of the monarchs and princes of the House of Furstán. Prominent among the monuments there is the VII-tiered Nikolaseum, erected by King Arkady II to honour the heroic death at Killingford of his younger brother, Prince Nikola. On the XVIth day of July in the year

1128, by order of King Liam Lajos II, Mahael Duke d'Arjenol and Branyng II Count of Sostra were impaled on stakes at the entrance of the cemetery, as a warning to evildoers everywhere. The bodies were removed on the XVIIIth day instant. [*King Kelson's Bride*].

Finella. This Sheeleán was chosen by the Camberian Council to be Revan's "love interest." She supposedly died on the VIth day of March in the year 917, despite the efforts of Rhys Thuryn; Revan used her "passing" as an excuse to join the Willimites, an anti-Deryni group, later that year. [*Camber the Heretic*].

Fintan. This Earldom was located in the far Southwestern portion of Gwynedd in Travlum. The Barony of Fintan was first granted to Sir Martial de Fintan by King Festil I on the VIth day of December in the year 825 to honour his exploits in the war of succession during the preceding III years. The Baron Aquineas was elevated to Earl by King Cinhil I on the VIIth day of July in the year 905. The Honour became extinct during the great war with Torenth on the IIIrd day of September in the year 983, when Pliny Earl de Fintan was killed at the Battle of Argoed, and the Earldom escheated to the Crown. See also: Aquineas, Elaine.

BARONS AND EARLS DE FINTAN

HOUSE OF FINTAN

Martial	825-844
Virgil (son)	844-864
Aquineas (son; Earl 905)	864-910
Ovid (son)	910-931
Phineas (brother)	931-936
Castor (brother)	936-940
Cicero (son)	940-966
Pliny (son)	966-983

Fiona *MacLean*. She was born on the XVIth day of December in the Year of Our Lord 892, being the second child of Iain II Earl of Kierney and Catriona Lady of Mar, and the younger sister of Adrian MacLean Hereditary Count of Kierney. She intermarried with Ansel Lord MacRorie on the XIVth day of May in the year 929, and by him she had children: the Lady Katrin; the Lady Davina; the Lord Stuart Cathan later called Stuart MacAthan. She survived the attack of Manfred's men on Trurill Castle on the XXXIst day of December in the year 917 by climbing down a garderobe shaft after her attackers torched the keep. She was rescued the next day by Evaine's party, and was later brought to the Haven. She assisted with the healing of Ansel MacRorie on the XXIst day of January in the year 918, and formed an attachment with him. By the Spring of the year 918 she had been given the care of the Thuryn children, and later took them to the safety of Trevalga in The Connait. She died in the year 948, aged LV years. She was small, dark, and quick. R.I.P. [*Camber the Heretic*; *The Harrowing of Gwynedd*].

Flann. He was a radical Willimite serving Revan in February of the year 918. This firebrand of a youth had wild black eyes and a mane of curly black hair. [*The Harrowing of Gwynedd*].

Foillan, Abbot and Saint. The Bremagni Abbot was dabbed with rotten figs and wild honey by infidel soldiers and stung to death by his own bees circa the year 450. His brothers were Saint Ultan, who succeeded him as Abbot, and Saint Fursey. An *Ordo Verbi Dei* abbey dedicated to his name is located about III days' ride Southeast of Valoret in the Lendour Mountains; it was here that Camber and Rhys first found Prince Cinhil Haldane. His feastday is the XXXIst day of October, and he is the patron saint of beekeepers. [*Camber of Culdi*].

Forcinn Buffer States. This group of V independent Principalities is located across the Southern Sea from Gwynedd, lying Southeast of Orsal along the Eastern coast of that gulf, and encompassed by the River Tralia on the North and East, and the Andell Mountain Range to the South. Although nominally under the Overlordship of the Hort of Orsal and Prince of Tralia, the States have at times exercised considerable independence. The Forcinn States include the following nations: the Duchy of Joux, the Grand Duchy of Vézaire, the Principality of Logréine, the Principality of Thuria, and the Principality of Nur Hallaj, although some commentators also add the Principality of Andelon. The Forcinn states are famous for their exports of leather goods and for their lush Fenneli figs. [*Deryni Rising*; *Deryni Checkmate*; *The Bishop's Heir*; *The Quest for Saint Camber*; *King Kelson's Bride*].

Fratres Sancti Simplicii (**Brothers of Saint Simplicius**), or *Ordo Fratrum Sancti Simplicii*. This Order was founded in the year 655 by Gerland de Torannan to honour the memory of Saint Simplicius, and maintains I large establishment, the Holy Icons Monastery, in Arjenol. It was here that the imbecilic Torval Prince of Torenth and Duke of Lorsöl was sent in the year 1095 to live out his days as a gardener, which he did most contentedly.

Fratres Silentii (**Brothers of Silence**), or *Ordo Fratrum Silentii*. This contemplative Order, whose penitents are not allowed to speak except under the most extraordinary circumstances, was founded on the XXIXth day of February in the year 900 by Frater Felix Fortenoe, who adopted as his motto, "Silence speaketh louder than words," and further said, "We must show by our quiet example how loudly speaketh our unspoken faith." He adopted as the *Ordo*'s patron saint the holy martyr Iveagh, who had given his life to proselytize the faith in early Howicce. Frater Felix established the Mother House of this Order, aptly called Saint Iveagh's Abbey or the Halls of Iveagh, on an isolated section of the Southwestern coast of Kheldour. The members of this Order wore sea blue robes to commemorate, it is said, the appearance of Saint Iveagh's relick'd tongue preserved in the main altar there, and which, it is said, speaks out once every IV years on the anniversary of the day of the blessed martyr's demise, also being the XXIXth day of February. It was the *Fratres Silentii* who were given the assignment of guarding Hubert MacInnis ex-Archbishop Primate of Valoret in the year 928, and Edmund Loris ex-Archbishop Primate of Valoret in January of the year 1122. In the latter task they failed. *C'est une grande misère que de n'avoir pas assez* *d'esprit pour bien parler, ni assez de jugement pour se taire*. [*The Bishop's Heir*; *The Bastard Prince*].

Frizell, Baron Lovat. This Deryni Lord was born on the XXVIth day of March in the Year of Our Lord 845, being the eldest surviving son of Leofric Baron Lovat and Severa Lady Ludlow. He intermarried with Germaine Lady Fezenze on the XVIIth day of May in the year 871, and by her he had children: the Hereditary Lord Arkell; the Lady Bonne; the Lady Margotta; the Lord Trumwin; the Lord Ivo. He succeeded his father on the IVth day of December in the year 870. His youngest son, Lord Ivo, was executed by the Regents on the XXVIIIth day of September in the year 917 for his attempted assassination on the lives of the Princes Javan and Rhys Michael. He was himself attainted with the other Deryni nobles of Gwynedd on the XXVIIth day of December following. He escaped with his family to the Kingdom of Llannedd a few days later, and died near Arrand on the IInd day of March in the year 920, aged LXXIV years. In his descendants is vested the right to petition for the restoration of the ancient Barony of Lovat. *Vox audita perit, litera scripta manet*. [*Camber the Heretic*].

Frostling. This albino horse, the favourite mount of Cinhil I King of Gwynedd, was ridden by him during the campaign against the Pretender Ariella in June of the year 905. [*Saint Camber*].

Fulbert *de Morrisey*, **Lord**. This Deryni nobleman was born on the IIIrd day of July in the Year of Our Lord 888, being a younger son of Jonah Baron de Morrisey and Frédérice Lady Bermond. He never married. He attempted to assassinate the Princes Javan and Rhys Michael on the XXVIIIth day of September in the year 917. He was captured, tried, and executed by the Regents on the same day, aged XXIX years. [*Camber the Heretic*].

Fulk. This soldier was serving Coel Lord Howell in the year 903. At his master's order he followed Rhys Lord Thuryn to Valoret Castle on the XXVIIIth day of November in that year. [*Camber the Heretic*].

Fulk ap Anticyre. He was a boyhood friend and blood-brother of Michael MacArdry Tanist of Clan MacArdry, serving him in about the year 1100. [*The Bishop's Heir*].

Fulk, Baron FitzWilliam. He was born on the XIIth day of December in the Year of Our Lord 1062, being the eldest son and heir of Feories Baron FitzWilliam and Mailsi Lady Finn. He intermarried with Jemma Lady Behy on the XXVIth day of August in the year 1095, and by her he had children: the Lady Feora; the Lady Jemima; the Lady Fenella; the Hereditary Lord Richard, killed in the year 1121, *sans postérité*. The Lord Fulk succeeded his father on the XIIth day of May in the year 1093. His small Barony was located in the Kheldish Riding. He died on the XXXIst day of January in the year 1124, aged LXI years, and was succeeded by his younger brother, Lord Finn. R.I.P. [*Deryni Checkmate*].

Fulk *Fitz-Arthur*, **Baron Viskin, Lord and Sir**. He was born on the XVIIIth day of July in the Year of Our Lord 907, being the third son of Tammaron Earl Fitz-Arthur and Nieve Lady O Nuallain, and a brother of Fane Deputy Regent of Kheldour. He intermarried with Niamh Lady Ballymar on the Xth day of May in the year 930, and by her he had children: the Lord Fane, killed at Laxalt in the year 948, *sans postérité*; the Hereditary Lord Redmond later Baron Viskin; the Lady Moina; the Lord Nolan; the Lady Mabbina; the Lord Laoghaire. In the year 921 Lord Fulk was serving as a junior squire to King Alroy. By June of the year 928 he had become a senior aide to King Rhys Michael, with one of his duties being to report to the Council anything untoward said by the King or his Queen. He was dark-haired and -eyed, and very obliging to the King, although his first loyalty was clearly to his father, the Earl; but his allegiance was changed by Rhysel Thuryn when she took over his mind on the XIVth day of June in that year. He rode out with his monarch on the XVth day instant for Eastmarch, and was present at his master's death on the XXVIIIth day of June. On the next day he was sent under house arrest to his older brother's estates in Cassan, but was recalled on the Xth day of August in that year to testify against the King's murderers. He was then appointed a Royal Equerry. He was created Baron Viskin on the XVth day of November in the year 948. He died on the VIIth day of December in the year 984, aged LXXVII years, and was succeeded by his eldest surviving son, Lord Redmond. R.I.P. [*King Javan's Year*; *The Bastard Prince*].

Fullers' Alley. On this small backstreet of Valoret lived and worked Daniel Draper and others of the clothing trade. Located near here was Saint John's Parish Church. [*Camber of Culdi*].

Fursey, Abbot of Lagny, Saint. This brother of Saint Foillan and of Saint Ultan established several monasteries in Ratmat and Yarmut circa the year 440, and later founded Saint Maccul's Abbey, also called the Maccularium, at Lagny in Bremagne. Unlike his II brothers, however, he did not keep bees, but he did promote the study of birds, publishing that most curious work, *De Vocibus Cornicum*, in which he promoted the idea that birds are the messengers of God, and if one could only understand their language, one could speak with the angels. In consequence thereof, he organized at his monasteries huge feeding troughs mounted on the apices of each roof and steeple, and indeed it appeared at times as if the very sills were alive with the sound of music. His feastday is the XVIth day of January. He is the patron saint of birdwatchers, translators, and custodians. [*Camber of Culdi*].

Furstán (III) *Torenthály*, **King of Torenth, Duke of Beldouria**. He was born on the IXth day of January in the Year of Our Lord 509, being the eldest surviving son and heir of Thüring Doux Beldouris and Cornelia Lady Arktoxidés. He intermarried with Judentha Lady d'Arzh (or Darzhov) on the XIIth day of May in the year 545, and by her he had children: the Hereditary Prince Arkady later Arkady I King of Torenth; the Prince Miklós later Miklós I King of Torenth; the Princess

Roschianör, who intermarried with Augarin I Count of Haldane; the Princess Reginwice, who intermarried with Damien Comte de Bavón; the Prince Wenzel later Wenzel I King of Torenth; the Prince Kázmér later Count of Sostra.

This illustrious Prince succeeded his father as Duke on the Vth day of June in the year 537, being anointed by the Archbishop Stephanos I on the New Year's Day following. In a series of campaigns beginning the next year, he conquered several smaller states to the West and Southwest, including Medras, Sostra, and Fathane, and on the XXVIIth day of September in the year 545 he declared himself King of the newly established state of Torenth, which was named for the chief seat of his family near Beldour.

He was the first King of Torenth to be girded with the sword at Iób, by the Archbishop Eudoxios I on New Year's Day in the year 546, having devised the ceremony in order to empower his descendants with the special magical traits they needed to defend themselves; and then he promptly deposed the Primate, replacing him with his own creature in the person of his first cousin, Ödön Count Fabinyi later Bishop Héliadés, now elevated to the title of Patriarch. In September of the year 566 Klaudianos Autokratór of Byzantyun sent an army into Eastern Torenth, seeking to conquer that region a IInd time. The King Furstán rallied his army near Beldour, and defeated Klaudianos on the IXth day of October in that year, but was himself seriously injured. He died of the rotting disease on the XIXth day of October in the year 566, aged LVII years, and was succeeded by his eldest son, Prince Arkady. His body was returned for burial in the Church of Sankt Iób at Torenthály, where it remains the focal point for the *killijálay* ceremony inaugurating each new Torenthi monarch at the beginning of his reign.

The monument is described thusly in *Bride*: "The top peaked along its length like the roof of a long narrow house. Rough hewn from a matte-black granite, the sarcophagus itself was encased in a framework of fretted silver inlaid with bits of onyx, delicate tracery as fine and fragile as a spider's web." R.I.P. [*King Kelson's Bride*].

Furstán, House of. The Royal House of Furstán, which includes Kings of both Torenth and Gwynedd as well as other noble and ducal lines, was founded in the year 388 by Furstán I, Rex Vicis or Viceroy of Byzantyun and Comes Beldouris, who claimed to be the grandson or great-grandson of the Deryni mage Mahael of Kheldour, although no such connection has ever been proven. The Viceroy's descendant, Furstán III Torenthály Duke of Beldouria, declared himself King of Torenth on the XXVIIth day of September in the year 545, and was girded by the Archbishop Eudoxios I on the New Year's Day following.

The main branches of this family all spring from the loins of this King and his sons and grandsons, including the First House of Furstán, overthrown in the year 655; the Second House of Furstán (Furstán-Tamásy), which succeeded to the throne of Torenth in the year 655 and became extinct in the male line in the year 1121; the House of Furstán-Festil, an offshoot of the previous family, which succeeded to the throne of Gwynedd in the year 822, and merged with the Second House in the year 1120; the House of Furstán d'Arjenol, also known as the Third House of Furstán, which succeeded to the throne of Torenth in the year 1121; the House of Furstán-Jándrich, descended from the Prince Sigard son of King Arion I; the House of Furstán d'Arkadia, descended from the Prince Kirill son of King Kyprian II; the House of Furstán Torvály or Furstán-Sostra, descended from Torval Count of Sostra son of Ringan IV Duke d'Arjenol; the House of Furstán-Festil-Fathane, descended from Festil I King of Gwynedd; and many others besides, including princes and princesses who intermarried into other royal and princely families, among them the House of Haldane itself in ancient times, concerning whose succession rights the law is obscure.

The law of succession of the House of Furstán, which applies to all of its branches of the family save that of the House of Furstán-Festil (which, once it had attained royal status, conformed itself to the laws of Gwynedd), provides that only male heirs may inherit the throne or other noble dignities, but that should a family become extinct in the male line for at least II generations, the female descendant nearest in degree to the last male heir of her branch may then transmit the honour to her most senior male descendant or descendants; however, she may not herself exercise that dignity or its rights or responsibilities, although she may serve as Regent to an underaged son, provided that some other male who has reached his majority is associated with her in the regency. Mere illegitimacy has never been a bar to inheritance in the Kingdom of Torenth, although most royal bastards have been acknowledged and legitimated by their fathers and then disinherited by giving them lesser titles of nobility.

Should a male line fail completely, a female representative who has no heirs male herself may become sovereign or ennobled, provided, however, that her husband (should she have one) shall share her power and dignities from the date that she marries, and provided also that, should she have only daughters as heirs of her body, the eldest of them shall succeed her.

The title borne by the heir apparent to the Throne of Torenth has always been Duke of Beldouria since the time of King Imre II; more distant heirs have sometimes been given other ducal titles.

The arms of the House include a leaping hart emblazoned in black on a roundel of silver, this on an orange field. *Dos linajes solo hay en el mundo, el tener y el no tener.* [*High Deryni*; *The Bastard Prince*; *The King's Justice*; *King Kelson's Bride*]. See also: Aldred, Alroy, Ariella, Arien, Arion, Arkady, Árpád, Blaine, Carolus, Charis, Charissa, Chriselle, Corinne, Elinora, Festil, Hogan, Imre, Imriella, Kálmán, Károly, Kennet, Kyprian, Lajos, László, Liam, Lionel, Mahael, Malachy, Marek, Marek-Imre, Mátyás, Miklós, Morag, Nikola, Nimur, Radislaus, Ronal, Stanisha, Sudrey, Tamás, Termöd, Teymuraz, Torenth, Torval, Wencit, Zimri.

Furstánály Palace. This is the chief seat of the Kings of Torenth in the city of Beldour. The central portion of the building was constructed, according to legend, by Furstán I Duke of Beldouria circa the year 400, but was rebuilt several times in ever more elaborate motifs, particularly by Duke Thüring and his son, King Furstán I. Additional wings were added by King Kálmán I circa the year 600, by King Tamás beginning in the year 666, and King Mátyás I, who constructed the Hanging Gardens in the 780s to please his IVth wife, Queen Landizábel. These have justly been regarded as one of the VII architectural wonders of the world, being irrigated by a sophisticated system of pipes and pumps, and kept green throughout the year by the judicious application of highly refined weather spells. The gardens include a maze in the shape of a Furstáni *tughra*, at the center of which is a statue of Landizábel herself. Other notable features of the Palace include Queen Brisquayne's Gallery, where the extraordinary tapestries of the ancient Deryni mage Jaél are kept permanently on display, the Obsidian Throne of King Furstán in the Great Hall of the People, the Bibliothéké Ariénaia, which includes the largest collection of codices and manuscripts in the XI Regni, and the Loutroi Kyanoi or Blue Baths, kept heated throughout the year for the use of royalty, nobleman, and commoner alike. [*King Kelson's Bride*].

Furstánán. This town is situate in Southern Torenth on the north bank of the River Beldour, near the Twin Rivers Strait. The city is known for its many domes and cupolas, particularly the large church and monastery of Saint-Sasile. [*King Kelson's Bride*].

Gabriel, Saint. Also called "The Herald," he is one of the archangel protectors called upon to ward a magical circle in certain ceremonies, his quarter being the West and his sign being a white crescent. His name in the Moorish tongue is Jibrail or Ghubriyal or Ghubrail, and his name means "God is my strength." His element is water. Wadi-Ghubrail, located in one of the Forcinn border states, was a shrine to Saint Gabriel. His feastday is the XXIVth day of March. [*Saint Camber*; *Camber the Heretic*; *The Harrowing of Gwynedd*; *King Javan's Year*; *The King's Justice*; *The Bastard Prince*].

Gabrilites (*Ordo Sancti Gabrielis* or *Order of Saint Gabriel*). This all-Deryni esoteric Order was based in the South Lendour Mountains at Saint Neot's Abbey. The Brotherhood was founded on the XXIVth day of March in the year 745 by Brother Junius Pollansus, and incorporated elements of earlier pagan Deryni movements that eventually died out by the Xth century. The Order was especially noted for its teaching and training of would-be Healers, and was generally considered to provide the most thorough instruction available in these arts. Members of the Order wore cowled white robes with white cinctures and white mantles, and were sworn to non-violence; however, unlike monks of other orders, Gabrilites never used the tonsure as a sign of their devotion, but wore their uncut hair in a IV-stranded braid called a *g'dula*. When circumstances required that they cut this braid, a special ceremony was required to burn the hair and purge the celebrant of any ill effects thereof.

On the XXIVth day of December in the year 917 the Order was suppressed by Rhun the Ruthless acting under the orders of the Council of Regents of Gwynedd, and many of the Order's brethren were slain, although some escaped through the portal at Saint Neot's Abbey's to Dhassa, and thence abroad. The badge of the Order was a circled cross with flared ends, usually white or pale blue. Healers of the Order displayed a badge of a couped right hand, *vert* pierced in the palm by a white star of VIII points, being the reverse of the standard secular Healer's badge. Prominent members of this Order included Dom Emrys, the last Abbot of Saint Neot's, and Dom Queron. [*Camber of Culdi*; "First Session"; "*The Examen*"; *Camber the Heretic*; *The Harrowing of Gwynedd*].

Gaetan. This retainer of the Hort of Orsal tried to kill King Kelson on the IIIrd day of July in the year 1128, and fell to his death from the winding road leading to the Hort's castle. It was later determined that his mind had been altered and will subverted, probably by Mahael II Duke d'Arjenol. [*King Kelson's Bride*].

Galiardi, *the Merchant.* The father of Josephus, later Brother Benedict of the *Ordo Verbi Dei*. [*Camber of Culdi*].

Gallard *de Breffni*, Sir. He was born on the VIth day of February in the Year of Our Lord 886, being the son of Sir August de Breffni and Celta Lady Fosseux. He joined the *Equites Custodum Fidei* in the year 918 shortly after the Order's inauguration. On the XXXIst day of October in the year 921 this *Custodes* knight was one of those who abducted Prince Rhys Michael during his supposed kidnapping by Ansel Lord MacRorie. He killed Sir Tomais in the Council chamber on the XIth day of May in the year 922 during the *coup d'état* by the former Regents in Rhemuth. He accompanied the Royal Expedition to Eastmarch in June of the year 928, and was summoned by Rhun Earl of Sheele to interrogate and torture the Deryni double agent, Dimitri, on the XXth day instant. Two days later he tested the Torenthi envoy, Hombard, with *merasha*. He was killed by Ansel MacRorie during the *coup d'état* against the former Regents on the Vth day of July in that year, aged XLII years. [*The Bastard Prince*].

Garish *de Brey*. He was a Torenthi spy killed by Sean Lord Derry at Fathane in March of the year 1121. [*Deryni Checkmate*].

Garon. He was serving as a squire to Wencit King of Torenth in June of the year 1121. [*High Deryni*].

Garwode. This mountain village is located near Saint Torin's Shrine on the side of Lake Jashan, not far from Dhassa. [*High Deryni*].

Gavin *Lecarrow*, Sir. He was born on the IVth day of March in the Year of Our Lord 902, being the son of Godwin Lord Lecarrow and Mathilde Lady Châlit. In February of the year 917 he was serving as squire to the Hereditary Prince (later King) Alroy, and was drugged by Rhys Lord Thuryn on the I[st] day of that month. He was knighted by the King Alroy on the IIIrd day of December in the year 920. On the XXIIIrd day of June in the year 921 he was ordered by the new King Javan to head an honour guard escorting King Alroy's body to lie in state at Saint Hilary's Basilica. He attended the coronation of King Javan on the XXXIst day of July in that year. Several days later on the IInd day of August, he was sent by Javan to Nyford to report on conditions there. He was later ordered by Javan to become the Healer Oriel's personal bodyguard. He was killed by Sitric and his men on the orders of the former Regents on the XXth day of March in the year 922, while defending Oriel. He was XX years of age at his death, and was buried with all due ceremony in the crypt of the Cathedral at Rhemuth. R.I.P. [*Camber the Heretic*; *King Javan's Year*].

g'dula. It is the special braid of hair worn as a badge by the Gabrilite order, who never cut their locks. The *g'dula* consists of IV interwoven strands which have a special symbolism. [*The Harrowing of Gwynedd*].

Gellis *de Cleary*, Father. He was the Acting Preceptor of the Order of Saint Michael (the Michaelines) in July of the year 905. [*Saint Camber*].

Gelric, Brother. This former Llanneddi courtier became a monk at Saint Bearand's Abbey. He guided King Kelson and his party toward the High Grelder Pass above Saint Bearand's Abbey. He fell into Grelder Creek on the XXIst day of March in 1125 with King Kelson, and drowned with his mount. He was a garrulous, thin individual who rode a shaggy piebald pony. R.I.P. [*The Quest for Saint Camber*].

Gendon. He was serving as a sergeant for Brice Baron of Trurill in November of the year 1123. [*The Bishop's Heir*; *The King's Justice*].

Geoffrey *MacLean*, Lord. He was born on the XIIIth day of May in the Year of Our Lord 872, being the second son of Iain I Earl of Kierney and Aislinn Lady MacRorie. He intermarried with Laura Lady Wynford on the XXXth day of April in the year 899, and by her he had children: the Lady Laurette, dead at age V; the Lady Richeldis later Countess of Kierney, who intermarried with Iver Earl of Culdi; the Lady Giesele, murdered at age XII by the Regents. He died in a hunting accident on the XXIst day of November in the year 911, aged XXXIX years; the wardship of his family was then given to James Lord Drummond. R.I.P. [*The Harrowing of Gwynedd*].

Geordie. This reformed Deryni joined the Willimite Order as a disciple of Revan in February of the year 918. [*The Harrowing of Gwynedd*].

Geordie *Drummond*, Lord. This Deryni nobleman was born on the XXVIIIth day of February in the Year of Our Lord 887, being the third son of Henry Lord Drummond and Lydia Lady McBain, and the nephew of James "Jamie" Lord Drummond. In April of the year 905 he was sent by Camber Earl of Culdi on a mission to Kheldour to investigate the dealings of a rebel human priest who called himself the Gryphon of God. After many adventures, he successfully slew the Gryphon and returned to Culdi. On his travels he used the alias of Geordie Drumm, a textile merchant from Rhemuth, to enter Grecotha. He later vanished on a voyage to the West across the Atalantic Ocean to seek traces of the lost Caeriesse, and was never heard from again. R.I.P. [*Deryni Challenge*].

George, Martyr and Saint. This holy martyr suffered death at Luddaît in the Anvil of the Lord in about the year 450. He was generally regarded as a model of knighthood and the avenger of women, and so naturally became the patron saint of Gwynedd. He is said to have slain the worm Verticosus at Malmsley. A cathedral dedicated to his name is the Seat of the Archbishop of Rhemuth. His feastday is the XXIIIrd day of April. [*The Bishop's Heir*].

Georgius, Brother. This boyhood friend of Vicar General Paulin Sinclair was serving as a monk at *Arx Fidei* Abbey in the Fall of the year 921; at that time he was terminally ill, and presumably died shortly thereafter. R.I.P. [*King Javan's Year*].

Gérard *Ralson*, Baron d'Evering. He was born on the Vth day of April in the Year of Our Lord 1076, being the eldest son and heir of Anselme Ralson Baron d'Evering and Guarine Lady Meulent. He intermarried with Clotilde Lady Aydie on the XIth day of October in the year 1096, and by her he had children: the Hereditary Lord Torsin later Baron d'Evering; the Lord Vézian; the Lord Frédélon; the Lady Mascarose. He was serving with King Brion's troops in June of the year 1105 during the Eastmarch Rebellion and the battle with Hogan Gwernach the Marluk. He was one of the soldiers who witnessed the King being brought to his Haldane potential, and questioned the King about the incident. Later he was appointed by Brion to the Gwyneddan Royal Council, and was sent to fetch Alaric Morgan Duke of Corwyn after the death of Brion King of Gwynedd on the Ist day of November in the year 1120. He was killed in ambush near Valoret on the VIIth day instant, aged XLIV years, and was succeeded by his eldest son, Lord Torsin. R.I.P. ["Swords Against the Marluk"; *Deryni Rising*].

Gerent, Lord. He was supposedly a cruel Baron of Interregnum times, responsible for the death of Mathurin and Derverguille in the early IXth century, as commemorated in the popular ballad composed by Lord Llewelyn. [*Deryni Checkmate*].

Gideon, Sir. He served as Castellan at Nyford for Murdoch Earl of Carthane and his son and successor, Richard Earl of Carthane. He accompanied the latter Lord on his return to Rhemuth in May of the year 922. [*King Javan's Year*].

Giesele *MacLean*, Co-Heiress of Kierney, Lady. She was born on the XXXth day of November in the Year of Our Lord 905, being the daughter of Geoffrey Lord MacLean and Laura Lady Wynford, and a niece of Iain II Earl of Kierney. When her father died in the year 911, she was made a ward of her cousin, James Lord Drummond. At the murder of another cousin, Lord Adrian MacLean, and the presumed death of his son,

Lord Camber MacLean, on the XXXIst day of December in the year 917, she and her surviving sister became co-heiresses to the Earldom of Kierney. She was smothered to death at the order of the Regents on the XXIst day of January in the year 918, aged XII years, to make her older sister Richeldis the sole heir. R.I.P. [*The Harrowing of Gwynedd*; *King Javan's Year*].

Gifford. He was serving as a manservant to Rhys Lord Thurys in the year 903. [*Camber of Culdi*].

Gilbert *Desmond*, Bishop. He was born on the XIXth day of April in the Year of Our Lord 1066, being a son of Sir Rabaut Desmond and Pagerie Lady Bréard. He was ordained priest on the XXXth day of July in the year 1086, and was consecrated an itinerant Bishop of Gwynedd on the XVIth day of May in the year 1103. In the year 1121 he supported Bishops Thomas Cardiel and Denis Arilan during the Interdict Crisis. However, he followed Edmund Loris ex-Archbishop of Valoret in his attempt to restore himself to the position of Primate of Gwynedd during the Mearan Rebellion of the years 1123 and 1124. After Loris's execution in July of that year he was subsequently suspended as Bishop on the XVIIIth day of March in the year 1125, but was allowed to continue functioning as a priest under close supervision. [*Deryni Checkmate*; *High Deryni*; *The Bishop's Heir*; *The King's Justice*; *The Quest for Saint Camber*].

Gilbert, Master. He was serving as the battle-surgeon for Radulf Baron d'Eirial in December of the year 977. He had brown eyes and a compassionate nature. ["Vocation"].

Gilbert *the Silversmith*, Master. This worker of silver brought a suit against Dickon Thompson before the Regents on the XXIVth day of December in the year 917, alleging that Dickon's son had got a child by Gilbert's daughter. The Regents ordered the pair to wed. [*Camber the Heretic*].

Giles. He was serving as chief body squire to Kelson King of Gwynedd in November of the year 1120. He brought the regalia of the King's Champion to Alaric Morgan Duke of Corwyn for Kelson's coronation held on the XVth day of that month. He was still squire in the year 1124. [*Deryni Rising*; *The Bishop's Heir*].

Giles, Saint. Many legends have been woven around the memory of this VIIIth-century Connaiti martyr. He was a borderman by birth, and as a youth was seduced into a brotherhood of black sorcerers practicing necromancy and other hideous magical arts. He was saved from a life of certain damnation by an accident which felled him while hunting. As he lay there helpless with his leg broken, the deer which he had been stalking suddenly appeared before him, saying, "Giles, Giles, why dost thou slay me?" He then took a mighty oath to God that should he survive his ordeal he would dedicate his life to the path of Light and the preservation of all the wild things on this good green Earth. A woodsman found him the next day, and carried him to safety. The emblem of this holy man is a hind, which is often depicted as accompanying him; he is also sometimes shown with an arrow piercing his breast or leg.

A convent dedicated to his name is located in the lake region of Shannis Meer near the Eastmarch border, and is much frequented as a place of pilgrimage. It was here that Queen Jehana went into retreat in the year 1105 and again after King Kelson's coronation in the year 1120. His feastday is the Ist day of September. He became one of the most popular saints in the Eleven Kingdoms, being venerated as the patron saint of cripples, beggars, and blacksmiths. *On donne des conseils, mais on n'inspire point de conduite.* [*Deryni Checkmate*; *The Bishop's Heir*].

Gillebert *of Droghera*. This Willimite became the first Deryni "cleansed" of his affliction by the baptismal ministry of Revan on the IXth day of June in the year 918. The Earl Manfred later had him tested with *merasha*, and confirmed that his Deryni powers had indeed miraculously been lost. [*The Harrowing of Gwynedd*].

Gillis, Brother. This Gabrilite monk was slain at Saint Neot's Abbey by Rhun's men on the XXIVth day of December in the year 917. R.I.P. [*Camber the Heretic*].

Gilrae *Donivald*, sometime Baron d'Eirial, Archbishop of Rhemuth. He was born on the XIIth day of January in the Year of Our Lord 957, being the eldest son and heir of Radulf Baron d'Eirial and Eanswith Lady Fenwick. He was knighted by Uthyr Haldane King of Gwynedd on the Ist day of April in the year 977. That Summer he fell from his horse, and the injury to his arm grew into a cancer. He briefly succeeded his father as Baron on the XXIVth day of December in the year 977, but, having been healed by the hermit Simonn, he immediately resigned his barony on the same day to his half-brother and heir, the Lord Caprus. He then pursued a vocation as a priest, and was ordained on the XIth day of August in the year 979. He was elected Archbishop of Rhemuth on the XXIVth day of March in the year 995, and served with distinction. He died of the shivering ague on the anniversary of his resignation, the XXIVth day of December in the year 998, aged XLI years, and was buried with great ceremony with his predecessors in the crypt of the Archbishops at Saint George's Cathedral in Rhemuth. R.I.P. ["Vocation"].

Gloddruth *Godreddson*, General. He was born on the XXth day of November in the Year of Our Lord 1079, being the eldest son of Captain Godredd Colbertson and Leofeva his wife. He intermarried with Horla Felbrigg about the year 1100, and by her he had children: Gerbert; Hunna; Ludd; Sidwine; Ieva. He was serving as one of Jared Duke of Cassan's generals in the year 1121, and managed to escape the slaughter of Jared's army at Rengarth on the XXVIIIth day of June in that year. He later became a military aide to Kelson King of Gwynedd. He was present at the Christmas Council of the year 1123 to discuss the Mearan crisis, and served with the main Gwyneddan Army during the invasion of Meara in May of the year 1124. *Probitas laudatur et* *alget.* [*High Deryni*; *The Bishop's Heir*; *The King's Justice*].

Godwin *Godreddson*, General. He was born on the XIth day of October in the Year of Our Lord 1081, being the second son of Captain Godredd Colbertson and Leofeva his wife. Godwin was serving as an officer in the Gwyneddan Army in the year 1121, and was present at the Dhassa war council on the XXIXth day of June in that year. He also participated in the Christmas Council of the year 1123 to discuss the Mearan crisis. [*High Deryni*; *The Bishop's Heir*; *The King's Justice*].

Graham. A sergeant in the army of Bran Coris Earl of Marley in June of the year 1121. [*High Deryni*].

Graham I Donal Angus *MacEwan*, Duke of Claibourne, Lord Regent of Gwynedd. He was born on the XXXth day of January in the Year of Our Lord 907, being the eldest son and heir of Ewan I Duke of Claibourne and Mary Lady Graham, and a nephew of Hrorik II Earl of Eastmarch and Sighere Earl of Marley. He intermarried with Nicola Lady Spenser on the XXXIst day of May in the year 922, and by her he had one son and heir: the Hereditary Duke Hrorik Ewan Earl of Rhendall, who married Janeltis MacInnis Baroness Marlor and died before his father, leaving issue, the Hereditary Duke Ewan later Ewan II Duke of Claibourne, and the Lady Gillian later Countess of Rhendall in her own right by the will of her grandfather.

He served as a page at the official state weddings in Valoret of Rhun Earl of Sheele and Richard Lord Murdoch on the Xth day of January in the year 918. After his father's murder on the XXVth day of May in the same year, he came to Rhemuth in early June with his II uncles and Regents, Earls Hrorik and Sighere, to claim his honours, but was denied the title of Viceroy of Kheldour borne by his late father. Thereafter no member of his family came to Court until they attended the coronation of King Javan on the XXXIst day of July in the year 921, and in the procession he bore a slender ivory sceptre encrusted with gold on a crimson cushion.

The Duke Graham attained his majority on the XXXth day of January in the year 921, when his Regency was disbanded. His cousin-in-law, Corban Earl of Eastmarch, sought his aid in June of the year 928 to repulse the forces of Torenth from Culliecairn, and he was present at Lochalyn Castle on the XXIst day of that month to greet King Rhys Michael and his army. He was named to the new Regency Council of King Owain on the XXVIIIth day of June in the year 928. He died in the year 948, aged XLI years, and was succeeded by his grandson, the Hereditary Duke Ewan II, in Claibourne, and his granddaughter, the Lady Gillian, in the County of Rhendall.

According to the *Heirs*, he was "clean shaven, but sporting a wiry border clout a good deal lighter than the rich shades of auburn that marked all the other male descendants of the first Sighere." R.I.P. [*The Harrowing of Gwynedd*; *King Javan's Year*; *The Bastard Prince*].

Graham III Nectan *MacEwan*, Duke of Claibourne, Earl of Kheldour. He was born on the VIth day of March in the Year of Our Lord 1089, being the eldest son and heir of Ewan III Duke of Claibourne and Eustachea Marchesa de' Assemani. He intermarried with Mistral Lady Leslie daughter of Sir Iorg Leslie on the XXIIIrd day of April in the year 1109, and by her he had children: the Hereditary Count Angus later Earl of Kheldour; the Lord Tresham; the Lord Sigardh; the Lady Sigarette, a twin to her brother; the Lady Tiparilla; the Lord Lloghis; the Lady Llivia; the Lady Nectane. He succeeded his father as Duke of Claibourne on the XIIIth day of December in the year 1129, at which point his eldest son, Lord Angus, succeeded to the secondary title of Kheldour. [*King Kelson's Bride*].

Great George. This huge bell atop Saint George's Cathedral in Rhemuth is the largest of its kind in the Eleven Kingdoms, having been installed as the final component of the Cathedral's renovation in the year 919. It was first rung on the XXIst day of April in that year. Later it tolled the death of King Alroy on the XXIIIrd day of June in the year 921, and was rung again at the King's funeral III days later. It also tolled on the morning of King Rhys Michael's funeral on the Vth day of July in the year 928. Its peal could be heard throughout the entire city of Rhemuth. [*King Javan's Year*; *The Bastard Prince*].

Great Plague. The Black Death was first seen in the year 875 in the Anvil of the Lord. By the following year it had spread to Bremagne, and by the year 877 to the Kingdom of Llannedd and the Forcinn Buffer States. In March of the year 878 plague was reported in the Gwyneddan port city of Concaradine, and rapidly spread upriver into Rhemuth and Valoret and thence throughout the Kingdom. Thousands died before the pestilence dissipated with the Winter months. During the following year Meara was hit, then Kheldour, and then Northern Torenth. Local outbreaks in the Eleven Kingdoms were noted in the years 880, 884, and 891. Another major outbreak occurred in the year 948, beginning with the death of Alfred of Woodbourne Archbishop of Rhemuth, whose passing prompted an anti-Deryni uprising in Gwynedd. [*Camber of Culdi*].

Grecotha. This ancient city is located Northwest of Valoret near the border of Gwynedd with Kheldour. It was the former site of the Varnarite School, and now houses the University of Grecotha, the greatest establishment of higher education in Gwynedd. It was also one of the earliest dioceses of Gwynedd.

Formerly a free city acknowledging the Count of Carbury as Overlord, the town of Grecotha was conquered on the XIth day of July in the year 678 by Aidan King of Gwynedd, who incorporated it into his realm. On the XXIXth day of May in the year 682 the various *scholae* located at Grecotha were formed into a University by Queen Sinead, who championed the cause of education. The city was sacked by the Norsemen on the XIIth day of July in the year 705, and by raiders from Torenth on the IIIrd day of June in the year 767. The great Battle of Grecotha between Torenth and Gwynedd was fought here on the IIIrd day of August in the year 984, but the Torenthi army was defeated and forced to withdraw after the death of King Malachy II.

Among the better-known prelates to have derived from this town were Alister Cullen later Archbishop Primate of Valoret and All Gwynedd, and Alexander Darby later Archbishop of Rhemuth. [*Camber of Culdi*; *Saint Camber*; "The Priesting of Arilan"; *Deryni Checkmate*; *High Deryni*; *The Bishop's Heir*].

Green Man Tavern. This establishment was located in Kiltuin on the Corwyn side of the border between Corwyn and Torenth. It was here that Ferris the swordsmith was attacked on the XVIth day of April in the year 1118. ["Trial"].

Green Tower. One of the V spires of Castle Coroth, it has VII bars of green glass set in its high walls; its IV companions are called the Black Tower, the Vermillion Tower, the Gold Tower, and the Blue Tower, reflecting both tradition and the differing colours of the panes of glass once used in each.

The origins of these Towers are shrouded in antiquity, for they were constructed by the early Dukes of Corwyn on the foundations of older structures dating back to before the Byzantyun occupation. In the mid-XIth century the Deryni scholar Lord Lewys ap Norfal studied the placement of the Towers in an effort to ascertain their mathematical and magical significance, but is reported to have come away with more questions than answers. Through his excavations he was able to determine that each of the Towers rested on a single slab of cut granite inscribed with strange runes of the old tongue, which he was not able to decipher. Moreover, his calculations revealed that a line drawn from each Tower to every other Tower formed a grid that intersected at a point below the Barrough Garden in the central courtyard of Castle Coroth. He then conducted a IInd excavation in the Barrough, which revealed an ancient burial site containing the skeletal remains of an elden chieftain, complete with sword, spear, armor, magical implements of unknown design and use, and the bodies of several retainers and a horse.

Etched on the wall of the tomb was a diagram of V Towers similar in design to those attached to Castle Coroth, but each of them limned with a different colour. At Lewys's suggestion, his patron Stiofan Anthony Duke of Corwyn remodeled the existing Towers in the year 1051, inserting coloured panes of glass into each to match the hues shown in the ancient diagram, which also corresponded, curiously enough, to the colours of the V *Protocols* of Orin; for Lord Lewys believed that the arrangement and names of each Tower were not accidental, that they represented the remnants of a magical tradition which had not survived except in certain secret societies which practised the black arts. He determined to conduct an experiment to see if the forces accessed by the Towers could be harnessed and put to proper use, ignoring several warnings from the Camberian Council not to proceed.

At sunrise on the XXIst day of March in the year 1052, which is the Vernal Equinox, Lord Lewys conducted a magical working in the Barroughyard near the center of the Castle grounds, erecting a large *shiral* crystal there. As the light of the sun touched the window of the Green Tower, it reflected to the garden, each subsequent Tower adding its light to the focal point as the sun continued to rise. When the last Tower, which had windows of black obsidian glass, was touched by the rays of light, the crystal suddenly flashed white, temporarily blinding all of the observers. When their vision cleared, the mage was nowhere to be seen. He was never heard from again, but in the absence of any remains, was assumed to have been transported to some other place or time beyond human ken.

The Duke "Stanthony" boarded up the Towers and removed the glass from them, except for the Green his favourite, and never allowed anyone else to enter them again during his lifetime, for he blamed himself for the loss of his friend. Legend holds that Lord Lewys will eventually return to the exact spot from which he vanished.

The room at the top of the Green Tower was serving as a retreat for the Duke of Corwyn in March of the year 1121. [*Deryni Checkmate*].

Gregory Siannon *MacDinan*, **Earl of Ebor, Count of Trevalga.** He was born on the XVIth day of January in the Year of Our Lord 875, being the eldest son and heir of Rhirid Earl of Ebor and Sibylla Lady Vansholt, and a great-grandson in the male line of Dinan last Sovereign Prince of Kheldour of the House of MacTyre. He intermarried with Eloise Lady de Mauzé on the XIIth day of August in the year 895, and by her he had children: the Hereditary Count Jesse *de jure* Earl of Ebor later Count of Trevalga; the Lord Geoffrey; the Lord Hilary; the Lady Mireille; the Lady Seanna, said to have intermarried with Sir Aldin McCarthy.

This Deryni Lord succeeded his father on the XIIth day of December in the year 888. He was made a member of the Camberian Council on the XXIst day of December in the year 910. He was appointed Warden of the Western Marches on the IInd day of December in the year 915 by King Cinhil I. On the XXXth day of January in the year 917 he was thrown from his horse and suffered a dislocation of his shoulder and a fracture of his collarbone; the Healer Rhys Lord Thuryn was sent by the King to his aid. In the process of trying to control Gregory, Rhys discovered how to turn off the Earl's Deryni powers. The Earl was present at the coronation of King Alroy at Valoret on the XXVth day of May in the year 917.

Gregory purchased a small, isolated estate at Trevalga in The Connait that Summer, and moved his family there on the Ist day of October in that year. His title of Ebor was attainted by the Regents on the XXVIIth day of December, but Gregory continued to use the title Count in The Connait, and it was confirmed by the Council of Sovereign Princes there on the Ist day of December in the year 918, who admitted him to full membership II years later. His particular interest in the genealogy of the nobility was almost encyclopedic. He is described in Volumen III of the *Legends* as having "a high forehead and reddish-blond hair and beard, with pale eyes." A few years later, according to the *Heirs*, his "reddish-blond hair had gone to nearly colourless. The pale blue eyes burned with an almost feverish brightness beneath the high noble brow." He died on the Xth day of February in the year 932, aged LVII years, and was succeeded in the County of Trevalga by his eldest son, Lord Jesse. R.I.P. *Magnos hominos virtute metimur, non fortuna*. [*Camber the Heretic*; *The Harrowing of Gwynedd*; *King Javan's Year*].

Gregory *of Arden*, Abbot of Saint Jarlath's. Father Gregory was serving as head of Saint Jarlath's Abbey, the Mother House of the *Ordo Verbi Dei*, when Father Joram MacRorie and Rhys Lord Thuryn visited there on the XXVIIIth day of September in the year 903. He gave them permission to examine the registry of postulants. [*Camber of Culdi*].

Grelder Creek. This fast-running mountain stream runs through the Southern end of the High Grelder Pass, terminating in a spectacular waterfall. The water then pools at the base of the falls, where it forms a whirlpool that is partially carried away underground. The level of this waterway is particularly high and the flow most turbulent during the Spring months. It was here that Kelson King of Gwynedd and Dhugal Earl of Transha were swept away underground on the XXIst day of March in the year 1125. [*The Quest for Saint Camber*].

Grelder Pass, High. This passageway through the mountains leads from Saint Bearand's Abbey, Northeast of Caerrorie, to the Iomaire Plain below. It was near here that Kelson King of Gwynedd and Dhugal Earl of Transha fell into the Grelder Creek and were swept away underground on the XXIst day of March in the year 1125.

Campbell de Broun describes his travels through this country in like manner: "We crossed one branch of the creek going North, and it began to rain. The cliffs on the North side made a very grand and sublime appearance: they were composed of a hard flinty rock and rose a M feet high in places, nearly perpendicular. At a distance they appeared perfectly smooth, and resembled a vast stone wall. We clambered thro' crevices of rock and slipped down the trees to the foot. A sudden bend of the river threw it again in our course in the same mile. On the one side as before there was a high cliff, but lying on the opposite side of the creek. By this time the rains were very heavy. We were thoroughly wet but we stopped under a projecting rock of the cliff and sheltered till the rain abated a little, by which time we were chilled and shivering with the cold. We waded a freshet about waist deep and continued our journey. In the evening it cleared up, and we touched a bend of the river again. There we set up camp by a fine blackberry patch. Finally we were partly dry again and dinner was fine, a little jerky with fresh fruit and clean water. We traveled just III and one-half leagues today." [*The Quest for Saint Camber*].

Grigor *of Dunlea*, Baron. He was born on the IInd day of August in the Year of Our Lord 1074, being the eldest son and heir of Wynric Baron of Dunlea and Bodina Lady Fécamp. He intermarried with Roberta Lady Snaring on the XVIIth day of May in the year 1096, and by her he had children: the Hereditary Lord Merlesveinn; the Lady Mereswith, a twin to her brother; the Lady Modgeva; the Lord Modwyn. This neighbour Lord to Brice Baron of Trurill supported Caitrin Princess of Meara during the Rebellion of the years 1123 and 1124. One of his soldiers was captured by Kelson's army in late May of the year 1124, but died before he could reveal more than his master's name. He was attainted in July of that year. [*The King's Justice*].

Groggin. This robber, a companion to Lothan, confronted Geordie Drummond at Twilham Green in April of the year 905. [*Deryni Challenge*].

Gron III Comyn *MacClyde*, Sovereign Grand Duke of Calam. He was born on the XIXth day of October in the Year of Our Lord 1075, being the second surviving son of Branson Grand Duke of Calam and the Princess Jannequine daughter of Poncet II Sovereign Prince of Pardiac. He intermarried with Polichinelle Countess of Réomay on the IInd day of March in the year 1101, and by her he had children: the Lady Poncetine; the Hereditary Grand Duke Branson; the Lord Purly; the Lady Placidia; the Lord Gabin; the Lady Aspasie. The Lord Gron succeeded his brother, Grand Duke Branly II, on the XVIth day of November in the year 1109. In the year 1128 he was sent by the Connaiti Council of Sovereign Princes to represent The Connait at the installation of King Liam Lajos II. Together with several other foreign dignitaries, he was fêted at a banquet held in his honour on the IXth day of July in that year in the Hanging Gardens of Furstánály Palace. [*King Kelson's Bride*].

Grotto of the Hours. Located in the gardens surrounding Castle Coroth, this dim, cavernous recess served as a private retreat for the Corwyn Dukes. It also featured the black marble sarcophagus of Dominic Ist Duke of Corwyn. [*Deryni Checkmate*].

Gryphon of God. He was a warped human sorcerer-priest operating North of Stavenham on the jagged coast of Kheldour in April of the year 905. He was raised as an orphan; his mother had been a witch who was burned as a heretic. He had a cruel, dominating mien but a charismatic voice. Geordie Lord Drummond put a quick end to him. [*Deryni Challenge*].

Guaire *d'Arliss*, Lord, Sir. He was born on the Vth day of June in the Year of Our Lord 880, being the eldest son and heir of Gui Lord d'Arliss and Minsmere Lady Adolphe. He began his career as an officer at the Court of Imre King of Gwynedd in the year 903, having previously served more than a year under the command of Lord Santare, who dismissed him for lechery. He later served as a knight and soldier for the notorious Earl Maldred. He also was a close friend of Cathan Hereditary Count of Culdi and Minister to the King. After Cathan's death he accompanied the King's burial party to Tor Caerrorie, and there spoke with Camber Earl of Culdi on the IInd day of December. Two days later he received orders from the King to arrest Camber and his family, but instead helped them to escape, being injured in the process. He was taken with them to their Haven near Dhassa.

After the restoration of the Haldane monarchy on the IInd day of December in the year 904, he became one of the central group of advisers to the new King. He was serving as an aide to Camber Earl of Culdi in the year 905, and in that capacity participated in the

War Council held on the XXIIIrd day of June at the Great Hall in Valoret Palace. He brought a small levy of men from Arliss to the Battle of Iomaire II days later, but placed them under the command of Camber Earl of Culdi before the latter's "death" there. After praying before the body of Camber on the evening of the IIIrd day of July at Valoret, he saw an image of the late Earl, who urged him to become Father Alister Cullen's aide.

He followed Camber's advice and then became an assistant to the new Bishop. On the IInd day of February in the year 906 he petitioned Cullen to allow him to found the Servants of Saint Camber. He attended the Ist consistory held by Archbishop Jaffray on the XXIIIrd day of October in the year 906 to recognize the new Order and to canonize Camber. His petition was granted on the XIVth day of November following. He was killed in the massacre of the Servants at Dolban by the Regents' men on the XXVIIIth day of December in the year 917, aged XXXVII years. R.I.P. [*Camber of Culdi*; *Saint Camber*; *The Harrowing of Gwynedd*].

Guiscard *de Courcy*, Sir. This Deryni Lord was born on the IVth day of March in the Year of Our Lord 892, being the eldest son of Étienne Baron de Courcy and Kenza Lady Stiofan. He intermarried with Jael Lady Coanuy on the XIVth day of June in the year 919, and by her he had children: Sir Alphard later Baron Stanzar and *de jure* Baron de Courcy; the Lady Shellyn.

He was sent by Father Joram MacRorie in the year 920 to infiltrate the Haldane Court in preparation for the accession of King Javan. He was one of a group of young knights who had prepared a set of legal documents in anticipation of the succession of King Javan, and was present at the death of King Alroy on the XXIIIIrd day of June in the year 921. He took Javan through the portal in Rhemuth to meet Joram on the following day, and was named as an aide to King Javan late in July of that year.

Sir Guiscard attended the coronation of King Javan on the XXXIst day of July in the year 921. He was slain with his monarch by the former Regents on the XIth day of May in the year 922, aged XXX years, and his title attainted. According to the *Heirs*, he was hook-nosed and had dark eyes. "He was a seasoned fighting man, but ink stains on the first two fingers of his right hand proclaimed him a man of letters as well." R.I.P. [*King Javan's Year*; *The Bastard Prince*].

Gulf of Kheldour. This great body of salt water is connected to the Atalantic Ocean on the North, and flanks the Duchy of Claibourne on the East, the Purple March on the South, the Earldoms of Transha and Kierney on the West, and the Duchy of Cassan on the Northwest. It is a major fishing area for sardines and whitefish, and also serves as a primary waterway between and among Cassan, Carbury, and Claibourne.

Gunury Pass. This Southern gateway to the shrine of Saint Torin's and the Holy City of Dhassa lies in the Lendour Mountains on the road from Coroth to Dhassa. [*Deryni Checkmate*].

Guthrie. He was a sergeant serving in Bishop Alister Cullen's household guard in January of the year 917. He wanted to pursue the renegade Deryni nobles, but was stopped by Cullen. He was instructed by his master to stay with Manfred Baron Marlor's party, which had just been assaulted by the renegades, until help arrived. [*Camber the Heretic*].

Gwenlian Leonilla Guntara Barnaba *MacFaolan-Gruffud*, Hereditary Princess of Llannedd. She was born on the last day of February in the Year of Our Lord 1109, being the only daughter of Illann II King of Howicce and Llannedd by his second wife, Amielle Countess of Zaria. She became Heir Presumptive to the throne of Llannedd on the death of her half-brother, King Ronan IV, on the VIIIth day of December in the year 1119. Her name has been associated romantically with her Ist cousin, Prince Cuan, Heir Presumptive to the Kingdom of Howicce. [*King Kelson's Bride*].

Gwernach. This small County of Torenth is situate along the Eastern side of the Rheljan Mountains, in the long valley formed by the Northern Branch of the Beldour River, also called the Belnorth, on the border of Torenth with Eastmarch. The Honour was first granted by Malachy II King of Torenth to Sir Kirion Andrássy and the legitimate heirs whatsoever of his flesh in the year 984. On the death of his direct descendant, Princess Charissa Duchess of Tolán and Pretender of Gwynedd, in the year 1120, the title fell into abeyance between several co-heiresses descended from the Lady Valeria younger sister of Countess Artemis. Kelson King of Gwynedd claimed the right of administration of Gwernach until the issue was resolved. See also: Charissa, Hogan.

COUNTS OF GWERNACH

HOUSE OF ANDRÁSSY

Kirion Andrássy	984-1008
Alexis (son)	1008-1025
Gorace (son)	1025
Jelève (aunt)	1025-1028
Artemis (niece)	1028-1045
Jonelle (daughter)	1045-1091
Hogan (son)	1091-1105
Charissa (daughter)	1105-1120

TITLE IN ABEYANCE

Gwydion *ap Plennadd*. This well-known troubadour was attached to the Court of the Duke of Corwyn in the year 1121. According to the *Chronicles*, "...He sang the finest ballads in the Eleven Kingdoms." He was a small wiry man with dark features who dressed in flamboyant clothing and played a round-bellied lute with fretted fingerboard slung by a golden cord. [*Deryni Checkmate*].

Gwyllim, Captain. He was an officer and personal companion to Bran Earl of Marley in June of the year 1121. [*High Deryni*].

Gwynedd. The ancient Kingdom of Gwynedd is situate at the heart of the Eleven Kingdoms, being surrounded by the Kheldish Riding on the North, Torenth in the East, the Southern Sea in the South, and Meara, The

Connait, and the United Kingdoms of Howicce and Llannedd in the West and Southwest.

Gwynedd was occupied by Basileios I Λutokratór of Byzantyun in the year 249, although that Empire never reached any further North than the line formed by the River Eirian. The region was called Provincia Quinta (the Fifth Province), which later became Gwynedd in the local tongue. When the Byzantyuni soldiers withdrew from Old Gwynedd in the year 408, the local chieftains there declared their independence, becoming Counts of Haldane, Carthane, Lendour, Molling, and Rhemuth. The boundaries and even the identities of these states changed greatly over the next II centuries, shifting back and forth until Augarin II Count of Haldane was able to subdue Carthane on the XXth day of April in the year 645. He declared himself King of the new unified state of Haldane on the Ist day of May in that year, changing it to Gwynedd on the Ist day of January in the year 647. Simultaneously, Aurelius Bishop of Haldane and brother to King Augarin secured the independence of the Church of Gwynedd from the Patriarchate of Bremagne with the assistance of Sixtus Prince-Bishop of Dhassa and Honoratus Abbot-Bishop of Concaradine.

The original boundaries of Gwynedd were encompassed by the Rivers Eirian and Lendour, but under Augarin's son and successor, King Aidan, they quickly expanded to include Transflumenia and The Purple March, almost doubling the size of the realm. The town of Grecotha, formerly a free city, was captured on the XIth day of July in the year 678, and the *scholae* there were unified into a major university on the XXIXth day of May in the year 682 by Queen Sinead, who championed the cause of education. Further expansion to the North was blocked by a series of Gwyneddan defeats at the hands of the Counts of Eastmarch and Southmarch in the 680s and 690s. King Aidan was killed at the Battle of Ebor in combat with Torv Count of Eastmarch on the VIIth day of July in the year 698, his son and heir, Prince Ifor, being severely wounded.

During the VIIIth century Gwynedd and its neighbours were severely ravaged from the South by the Moorish fleets of Tarik ibn Fadl al-Qaradh and his successor, Hamid ibn Tarik al-Muzzan. On the XXXth day of May in the year 733 the raiders even besieged the city of Rhemuth, before King Ryons arrived with a relief force from the North on the VIth day of June. However, Ryons was himself killed by the Moors at the Battle of Nyford on the XIXth day of August in the year 736. It was his son and successor, the King and Saint Bearand, who finally destroyed the main Moorish armada in the Battle of the Jamin Straits on the Xth day of July in the year 752; he followed his victory there with a decisive raid on the infidels' chief port of Kharthat on the XVIIth day of August in the year 755 that burned much of that town and sank or damaged LIV enemy ships, forever ending their threat to the West.

On the XXIst day of June in the year 822 Bearand's son, King Ifor, was killed with all of his family except young Prince Aidan by the invading forces of King Festil I, a younger son of the King of Torenth, whose family had an ancient claim to the Gwyneddan throne through Princess Bethany daughter of King Aidan. During these years Southmarch was added to the realm, and several other neighbours became client states. The House of Furstán-Festil ruled for V generations, troubled only by the revolt of Cathyr Baron Carroch in the year 885. King Imre was finally overthrown on the IInd day of December in the year 904 by the last male descendant of the Haldanes, King Cinhil I.

Under King Cinhil I and his successors, the power of the throne was often shared with the Great Lords, who used the threat of the Deryni minority to secure their power, and who established a persecution of the Deryni that lasted II centuries. In the early years of the re-established Haldane rule Kheldour, Eastmarch, and Cassan were all incorporated into the Kingdom of Gwynedd, nearly doubling its size.

The increase in the boundaries of the state promoted an almost constant state of conflict during the next CC years with Torenth and the Festillic Pretenders who resided there, and with its natural ally, the Principality Meara, in the West. Torenth tolerated and even championed its Deryni Lords and mages, and both states feared the territorial ambitions of the human peers of Gwynedd. Meara was defeated by Gwynedd in the year 1025 during the course of the bloodiest conflict that the Eleven Kingdoms have ever seen, and conquered II years later, but its rugged terrain forced the Kings of Gwynedd to send a continual series of armies over the next century to pacify the region.

The best hope of ending the seemingly eternal cycle of war and retaliation and revenge came to be centered on one man, Kelson King of Gwynedd, whose half-Deryni heritage made possible for the first time a future in which both human and Deryni might reconcile their differences, in which the conflict with Torenth might finally cease.

We pray to God Almighty that He in all of His wisdom will grant this our one wish, that there be peace in our time between all the nations and races of men on Earth. See also: Charissa, Chriselle, Cinhil, Cluim, Conall, Corinne, *Council of Gwynedd*, Dolon, Donal, Eirian, Elinora, Ewan, Festil, Hogan, Hubert, Ifor, Imre, Imriella, Jashan, Jasher, Javan, Jebediah, Jehana, Jestyn, Kelson, Llarik, Maire, Malcolm, Mark, Megan, Michaela, Murdoch, Nigel, Nuala, Nygel, Oliver, Owain, Payne, Rhetice, Rhun, Rhys Michael, Richard, Richeldis, Roisian, Rory, Rothana, Ryons, Sidana, Sinead, Tammaron, Urien, Uthyr, Wencit, Ysabeau.

KINGS OF GWYNEDD

HOUSE OF HALDANE

Augarin (II)	645-673
Aidan (III) (son)	673-698
Llarik (brother)	698-719
Ryons (son)	719-736
Bearand (son)	736-794
Ifor (son)	794-822

HOUSE OF FURSTÁN-FESTIL

Festil I "The Conqueror" (great-great-great-grandson of Aidan)	822-839
Festil II "The Lame" (son)	839-851
Festil III "Greybeard" (son)	851-885
Blaine I (son)	885-900
Imre I "The Last" (son)	900-904

HOUSE OF HALDANE

Cinhil I "The Restorer" (great-grandson of Ifor)	904-917
Alroy (son)	917-921
Javan (brother)	921-922
Rhys Michael (brother)	922-928
Owain (son)	928-948
Uthyr (brother)	948-980
Nygel (son)	980-983
Jasher (brother)	983-985
Cluim (brother)	985-994
Urien (son)	994-1025
Cinhil II "The Uncrown'd King" (son)	1025
Malcolm (brother)	1025-1074
Donal Blaine II (son)	1074-1095
Brion (son)	1095-1120
Kelson (son)	1120-1130+

PRETENDERS OF THE HOUSE OF FURSTÁN-FESTIL

Ariella I (sister of Imre I)	904-905
Marek I (son; abdicated)	905-975
Imre II (son)	975-985
Imre III (grandson; abdicated)	985-1024
Marek II (son)	1024-1025
Marek III (son)	1025
Ariella II (sister of Imre III; abdicated)	1025
Imriella (sister)	1025-1038
Elinora (cousin)	1038-1050
Chriselle (daughter)	1050-1061
Hogan Gwernach "The Marluk" (grandson)	1061-1105
Charissa (daughter)	1105-1120

PRETENDERS OF THE HOUSE OF FURSTÁN TAMÁSY

Wencit (cousin of Charissa)	1120-1121
Morag (sister)	1121-1128
Teymuraz (cousin)	1129-1130+

Hakim II ibn Qais ibn Hassan *ar-Rafiq*, Emir of Nur Hallaj. This Deryni master was born on the XIXth day of August in the year 1074, being the eldest surviving son and heir of Qais ibn Hassan Emir of Nur Hallaj and the Sayyida Kamila daughter of Athbi Sultan of Gonj. He intermarried with Fabrissa Princess of R'Kassi on the IXth day of May in the year 1090, and by her he had children: the Nabila Osheh, who intermarried with Ibrahim ibn Isa Shaikh of Abu Hashar; the Nabil Qabus, who died young; the Nabila Williama, who intermarried with Kamil Hereditary Prince of Andelon; the Hereditary Nabil Sulen; the Nabil Saqr later Wali of Qalbat; the Nabil Dalmak later Wali of Wadi Sultanah; the Nabila R'thana (later Rothana), who intermarried with Conall Prince Regent of Gwynedd, leaving issue; the Nabil Bhutti, who died young.

The Great Hakim succeeded his noble father on the IIIrd day of June in the year 1111. His most distinguished brothers included the Nabil Azim and the Nabil Hassan, the latter of which served as tactician to Hogan Gwernach Pretender of Gwynedd in June of the year 1105. [*The King's Justice*].

Haldane. This royal Duchy comprises the Northern part of central Gwynedd, lying South of the River Eirian, and is traditionally held directly by the King. Originally founded by Halbert the Dane, called "Haldane," on the XXXth day of June in the year 411, the County of Haldane gradually expanded at the expense of its neighbours, until Augarin II conquered Carthane in the year 645. He then proclaimed himself King of Gwynedd. The title of Haldane was granted first to his son, Count Bearand, and then to a younger son, Count Halbert II, whose son and successor, Count Aurelian, was attainted and executed by King Llarik in the year 705. Aurelian's third son, Lord Auric, escaped the purge and fled the country, never to return. King Llarik then named his heir, Prince Ryons, Duke of Haldane, a title that remained associated with the heir to the throne until the Festillic Interregnum.

COUNTS OF HALDANE

HOUSE OF HALDANE

Halbert I the Dane	411-433
Hansoc (son)	433-461
Guerric (son)	461-465
Jestyn (brother)	465-466
Jesric (brother)	466-506
Aidan I (son)	506-522
Cinhil I (son)	522-544
Bearand I (nephew)	544-559
Cinhil II "The Short" (brother)	559-572
Augarin I (son)	572-601
Kensell (son)	601-609
Bearand II "The Long" (son)	609-631
Aidan II "The Fat" (son)	631-640
Augarin II "The Great" (brother; King 645)	640-645
Bearand III (son)	645-698
Halbert II (brother)	698-705
Aurelian (son)	705

Haldane Archers' Corps. This unit of the Gwyneddan army was commanded by Nigel Duke of Carthmoor in the year 1121. Each of the archers is partnered with a foot soldier holding a spear and shield, whose duty it is to protect the archer during a rain of enemy bowfire. All men in the regiment wear the green and violet feather cockades of the Haldane Archers' Corps on the front of their hard leather fighting caps. Accompanying them are the regimental drummers, garish in their lowland dress of green and violet stripes. [*High Deryni*].

Haldane, House of. This royal family of Gwynedd was traditionally founded by Halbert the Dane, called Haldane, who proclaimed himself Ist Comes Haldani on the XXXth day of June in the year 411. An ancient legend recounted by Orin holds that Halbert fled from old Kheldour after his brother, a Prince of that country, unjustly accused him of making advances to his wife. Count Augarin II proclaimed himself King of Gwynedd on the Ist day of May in the year 645. The Haldane Kings were displaced between the years 822 and the IInd day of December in the year 904 by the Festils of Torenth, but were restored in December of the latter year by King Cinhil I. The present Head of the House is King Kelson.

The laws of succession of the House provide that only male members of the family may inherit the throne, unless and until the legitimate male line becomes extinct, when the nearest female heir may succeed *ad personam*. Those born out of wedlock are forever barred from succession, even when legitimated after the fact. Also barred from the throne are male members of the royal houses of foreign states. The next heirs to the throne of Gwynedd in the year 1130 in order of succession are: Javan Hereditary Prince of Gwynedd; Nigel Duke of Carthmoor, his grandson and his surviving children; the daughters of Richard late Duke of Carthmoor, Richelle Countess of Culdi and Araxie Baroness Dunluce; the Princess Rhetice and her heirs, if any; the Princess Suibhne and her heirs. The arms of the House are: *gules*, a lion rampant gardant *or*. See also: Aidan, Albin, Alister, Alroy, Araxie, Augarin, Aurelius, Bearand, Brion, Cinhil, Cluim, Conall, Conalline, Dolon, Donal, Eirian, Ifor, Jashan, Jasher, Javan, Jestyn, Kelson, Llarik, Maire, Malcolm, Michael, Michaela, Nigel, Nygel, Owain, Payne, Rhetice, Rhys Michael, Richard, Richelle, Rory, Ryons, Urien, Uthyr, Ysabeau.

Halex, Abbot of the *Arx Fidei* Abbey, Father. This member of the *Custodes Fidei* Order was serving as Abbot of the *Arx Fidei* Monastery North of Rhemuth in June of the year 921. He was a strict priest and did not approve of any divergence from the discipline and regimentation expected of his seminarians. [*King Javan's Year*].

Hamilton, Lord Falkenham, Hereditary Seneschal of the Duchy of Corwyn. He was born on the xth day of September in the Year of Our Lord 1055, being the eldest surviving son and heir of Hambert Lord Falkenham and Kathra Lady Saint-Valéry. He intermarried with Dulce Lady Guerche on the xxix^{th} day of July in the year 1075, and by her he had children: the Lady Valéry; the Hereditary Lord Hamric; the Lord Gwerch; the Lady Iva; the Lady Ermine. He succeeded his father as Seneschal of Coroth Castle on the xviii^{th} day of September in the year 1096. In the year 1121 he commanded the local troops in defense of Coroth and its environs during his master's absence. He had a difference of opinion with the troubadour Gwydion in March of that year. According to the *Chronicles*, "...He was a warrior not a courtier, and his close association with Gwydion and other more cultured personages had been nerve-wracking. He was now in his element as he herded his contingent aboard ship." [*Deryni Checkmate*; *High Deryni*; *The Bishop's Heir*].

Hanfell. This was the site of a shrine to Saint Camber in the year 917. [*Camber the Heretic*].

Harold *Fitzmartin*, Lord. He was born on the iv^{th} day of August in the Year of Our Lord 1079, being the third son of Harth Baron Fitzmartin and Heloise Lady Snook. He intermarried with Almunda Lady Ulcombe on the xxi^{st} day of May in the year 1099, and by her he had children: the Lord Harold *Junior*; the Lord Harth *Junior*; the Lord Almund; the Lord Ulcomb; the Lord Omer; the Lord Brice. On the xiv^{th} day of November in the year 1120 he was one of the III vassals of Alaric Morgan Duke of Corwyn who was persuaded by Ian Howell Earl of Eastmarch that Morgan should be assassinated. To this end he invaded King Kelson's apartments, but was killed by Father Duncan McLain in the ensuing skirmish. [*Deryni Rising*].

Harold *Martham*. This vassal of Alaric Morgan Duke of Corwyn was fined for allowing his animals to graze on another's lands in March of the year 1121. [*Deryni Checkmate*].

Hassan ibn Qais ibn Hassan *ar-Rafiq*, Nabil of Nur Hallaj. He was born on the xvii^{th} day of December in the Year of Our Lord 1076, being the second son of Qais ibn Hassan Emir of Nur Hallaj and Kamila daughter of Athbi Sultan of Gonj, and brother of Hakim II Emir of Nur Hallaj. He was a military adviser to Hogan Gwernach Pretender of Gwynedd in June of the year 1105, and later acted as aide to Princess Charissa, Hogan's daughter and successor. He was attending her when she killed Brion King of Gwynedd on the I^{st} day of November in the year 1120. He returned to Nur Hallaj after Charissa's death on the xv^{th} day instant. He customarily wore black robes and a keffiyeh drawn over the lower half of his face. ["Legacy"].

Haut Eirial. This Abbey of the Michaeline knights was located in the Southern Lendour Mountains of Gwynedd. It was ravaged by the forces of King Imre in December of the year 903. Having been rebuilt under Good King Cinhil I, although never fully restored, it was given by the Order to the local Bishop in the Summer of the year 917. The new house was destroyed by Rhun the Ruthless, who thought it still housed the Michaelines, on the xxiv^{th} day of December in that year. The land surrounding the Abbey was then made over to the new Baron, Cyril Longarm, who called himself d'Eirial after his new estate. [*Saint Camber*; *Camber the Heretic*].

Haut Vermelior. This was the site of a shrine to Saint Camber in the year 917; it was destroyed by the Regents during the following year. [*Camber the Heretic*].

Haven (or Sanctuary), Michaeline. This place of refuge was constructed in the Lendour Mountains near Dhassa by the Michaeline Order during the ix^{th} century, and was used by Camber Earl of Culdi to hide members of his own family and Prince Cinhil Haldane and his entourage between December of the year 903 and December of the year 904. It was here that Cinhil I married Megan Lady de Cameron; in the chapel therein were buried Prince Aidan Haldane and his murderer, Father Humphrey.

The Haven was reopened at the end of the year 917 to provide a refuge for displaced Deryni. By early in the year 918 Lady Evaine Thuryn and her family were living there, as were a number of the Gabrilites who had escaped the massacre at Saint Neot's Abbey the month before, with refugees who had fled the sack of Dhassa in February. In the year 921 it was still being used by members of the Camberian Council, with some messages being exchanged to and from Trevalga via carrier pigeon. King Javan visited there on the xxiv^{th} day of June in that year to meet Father Joram MacRorie and Bishop Niallan; on the following night, Javan returned to have his Haldane potential activated. Its fate after the *coup d'état* of the year 928 which deposed the former Regents is unknown. [*Camber of Culdi*; *Camber the Heretic*; *The Harrowing of Gwynedd*; *King Javan's Year*].

Healers. The origins of the healing arts are lost in the mists of history. The early chronicles of the XI Kingdoms speak of certain "wandering saints" who, by laying their hands upon the heads of the afflicted and calling on the Lord's sweet power, could heal the sick and wounded, assuage the pains of those who could not be cured, and sometimes raise the dead from their eternal sleep. But it was not until the time of Saint Varnar of Bassettdale, who lived during the time of Jesric Count of Haldane, that an attempt was made to organize a *schola* where this and the other Deryni arts might be studied and enhanced.

Holy Varnar, who is said to have been a natural son of Lord Alric Haldane and Count Jesric's younger brother, first established his *Conlegium Artium Derynianarum* in the city of Valoret, but having become involved in a dispute with the Count, the exact nature of which remains obscure, he removed himself and his followers to the free city of Grecotha in about the year 500. There he purchased an old storehouse just inside the city walls, and began remaking it with the aid of his brethren. This establishment became the nucleus of the several *scholae* which later became the University of Grecotha.

The *Schola Artis Salutaris* was among the 1st of these schools to be established. From the beginning, Saint Varnar insisted that the healing talent was a gift from God that should be both nurtured and properly developed. To this end he is said to have written the *Adsum Domine*, although other scholars attribute this hymn to Orin, and to have formulated the rules of practice and theories of operation of the healing arts; and he began sending the few acolytes who had completed their studies out into the world, attaching them to the great lords temporal and spiritual in the region, where they could use their influence for good to search for additional potential students in the larger cities of the land.

Soon, news of the *schola* had spread far and wide, and those who believed they had the talent began finding their respective ways to Grecotha from counties and kingdoms throughout the XI Regni. When good Saint Varnar was taken into Heaven in the year 524, his deputy, Lord Aylmar Haldane, a nephew of the late Count Jesric, succeeded him as *Magister Magisterii*, and this practice of anointing one's successor continued unabated for II more centuries. Within XXX years of Varnar's death, his followers had successfully petitioned the Patriarch Æmelius for his canonization, and had established an Order to honour his name, comprised both of lay persons and religious brethren in equal numbers. In 634 the great teacher Orin, a former pupil of the *schola*, established the *Templum Archangelorum* in the County of Haldane to provide a *conlegium* in that region to train Deryni and healers, but that institution was suppressed circa the year 710 by King Llarik, who so thoroughly destroyed the abbey that its site cannot now be located, although many wise men have tried.

In the year 743, the Grandmaster Godfredus passed from this earth, and was succeeded in the usual fashion by his deputy, the Grandmaster Leowulf. But when the Honourable Leowulf also perished some III months later of the pox, without having named a successor, the *Ordo Sancta Varnari* was divided into II factions upon the question of who among them should exercise the authority. The 1st of these groups, consisting mostly of the laymen in the Order, demanded that an election be held, and that the voice of every member be heard. But the other part, comprising most of the priests and brethren, insisted that the ancient rule be followed, and that the most senior religious person among them should become Grandmaster.

For II years they debated the issue, the peace being kept by the elders among them. But at last, when no agreement could be reached that was acceptable to more than half, Frater Junius Pollansus, the designated candidate of the priestly faction, declared that he and his followers would withdraw from the community and found their own Order, to be called the Gabrilites. The property of the community was fairly divided under the ægis of the Bishop of Grecotha, Bernardus Saquetus, and the newly-created *Ordo Santi Gabrielis* trekked far to the south, finally settling in the Lendour Mountains, where they built an establishment called the Monastery of Saint Neot. The Varnarites also moved their *schola* to a new location on the opposite side of Grecotha from where they had previously been located, for by this time it was clear that, even with the departure of the Gabrilites, they needed larger quarters.

Both *scholae* prospered, and the Gabrilites founded a second branch at Thuria in the year 800, at the invitation of Count Émilien II, and a third branch at Netterhaven in Jándrich in the year 835, at the behest of Prince Gremislav. But, alas, the Thurian house was destroyed shortly thereafter, when Kronburg was attacked during the invasion of Léonard Duc du Joux in the year 812; the Mother House at Saint Neot's was sacked by the Regents at the end of 917, who greatly oppressed the Deryni throughout the Kingdom of Gwynedd; and the Jándrichan branch was decimated and its *conlegium* burned when the city of Netterhaven was overrun by the Norsemen in the year 997.

Similarly, the Varnarites were arrested and pressed into the service of the Gwyneddan Regents at the end of 917, with their families being held hostage for their behaviour, and those who would not agree were slaughtered on the spot and buried in unhallowed ground; and the buildings of the *schola* in Grecotha were confiscated and given over to the Church.

Following the final victory over the Norsemen by Kyprian II King of Torenth in the year 1023, an attempt was made by him to gather together the surviving healers, all of them then being in their middle years or beyond, and to re-establish the *schola* in the ruins of Netterhaven; but this effort was halted when war broke out again in the year 1025, and the healers were sent West to assist the Torenthi soldiers. Most perished at the Battle of Killingford, trying to alleviate the pain and suffering of their fellow men, and the remainder were too few in number to reconstitute the *schola*.

Later, good King Arkady II of Torenth attempted to import sufficient healers from Byzantyun and Asshyr to rebuild the ancient centers of learning during the 1030s, but the ways of these foreigners were strange and their tongues *outrés*, and not many wished to make the long overland journey from the East, or to remain more than a few years in far-off Torenth once they had earned their fortunes. Thereafter, the use of healers in the West was kept to the fortunate few who were wealthy or powerful enough to import them.

Indeed, by the time of King Kelson, healers had become so uncommon in the West that even most of the Deryni masters there had never experienced them, and many refused to believe even that they existed, calling the stories of their supposed workings the babbling of old women. In Torenth, the use of healers in the XIIth century was restricted to the Royal Court, where they were deliberately hidden from the eyes of others. For "all knowledge is power," sayeth the great Orinus, "and those there are who would keep such learning unto themselves, and benefit thereby."

But there shall come a day when we shall see the Deryni walking openly upon the Earth, and the balm of Gilead shall again be made ready to sooth the sick and the wounded and those who are greatly injured. Let anyone who loves God and honours His truth strive to make the circle whole once more. Amen.

Heloise, Mother. She was serving as Abbess of Saint Brigid's Abbey during the ravage of that cloister by Brice Baron of Trurill and Ithel Hereditary Prince of Meara on the XVth day of June in the year 1124. She returned to Rhemuth with Prince Conall later that month. She witnessed the relinquishment of Rothana's vows as a novice of the Order of Saint Brigid on the Xth day of April in the year 1125 at Rhemuth. Γυναικι κόσμος 'ο τρόπος, ου τα χρυσία. [*The King's Justice; The Quest for Saint Camber*].

Henricus, later Brother Benedict. He was born on the XXVIth day of December in the Year of Our Lord 849, being the youngest son of Festus Earl of Legain and Redmonda Lady Teemore. He was received into the *Ordo Verbi Dei* and took the name Benedict in the year 876. He died on the XXIst day of August in the year 911, aged LXI years. [*Camber of Culdi*].

Henry, Baron de Vere. He was born on the XXXIst day of August in the Year of Our Lord 1069, being the youngest son of Herlwin Baron de Vere and Tatty Lady Clotworthy. He intermarried with Glasna Lady Lislea on the IXth day of May in the year 1088, and by her he had children: the Lady Concepta; the Lady Bríd; the Lady Æthna; the Lady Rólanna; the Lady Darerca; the Hereditary Lord Beineon. He succeeded his elder brother, the Lord Heremon, on the XVIth day of March in the year 1121. This nobleman from the Duchy of Corwyn was accused in July of the year 1124 of not paying his tithe to the town of Abbeyford. [*Deryni Checkmate; The King's Justice*].

Henry Drummond, Lord. He was born on the last day of September in the Year of Our Lord 842, being the eldest son and heir of James Lord Drummond and Afreca Lady MacCathal. He intermarried with Amalia Lady MacNiall on the Vth day of July in the year 864, and by her he had children: the Lord Henry *Junior*; the Lord James *Senior*, who died at age VIII of a fall from his horse; the Lord James *Junior* called "Jamie," named for his deceased brother; the Lady Ardis, who intermarried with Angus Lord MacLean. He died on the XVIIIth day of December in the year 899, aged LVII years. R.I.P. *Laborum dulce lenimen.*

Henry *Drummond Junior*, Lord. He was born on the Xth day of August in the Year of Our Lord 865, being the eldest son of Henry Lord Drummond and Amalia Lady MacNiall. He intermarried with Lydia Lady McBain on the XXIst day of April in the year 884, and by her he had children: the Lord Richard; the Lord Hamish; the Lord Geordie. He died on the XIIth day of February in the year 905, aged XXXIX years. R.I.P. [*Deryni Challenge*].

Henry *Istelyn*, Bishop of Meara, Lord, Martyr and Saint. He was born on the XXIVth day of May in the year 1072, being the son of Hugues Comte d'Istelyn in Bremagne and Renée Demoiselle de Vannes. He early sought a life in the Church, and came to Gwynedd to study at the University of Grecotha. He was ordained priest on the XVth day of September in the year 1096 by Paul III Tollendal Archbishop Primate of Valoret. He was consecrated an itinerant Bishop on the XXIIIrd day of March in the year 1117. Although he was not present at the meeting of the Synod at Dhassa in March of the year 1121, he sided with Bishops Thomas Cardiel and Denis Arilan against the Archbishops' faction. He appeared at Dol Shaia on the XVIIIth day of June in that year to attach himself to King Kelson's staff and to minister to the Gwyneddan army. On the XIXth day of January in the year 1122 he was elected Auxiliary Bishop of Valoret and assistant to Archbishop Bradene, and on the XXVIth day of November of the year 1123 he was chosen Bishop of Meara, being installed at Ratharkin by the Synod IV days later. He was deposed by the rebel Archbishop Loris on the Vth day of December following, but when he refused to acknowledge Loris's authority over him, was subsequently tried, condemned, hanged, drawn, and quartered on the XVIIIth day instant. He was LIII years of age at his death. He was declared martyr and officially canonized by the Synod of Valoret on the XVIIth day of April in the year 1125. His feastday is the XVIIIth day of December. *Nequam illud verbum 'st, nisi qui bene facit.* R.I.P. [*High Deryni; The Bishop's Heir; The King's Justice; The Quest for Saint Camber*].

Henry *Kirby*, Captain. He was serving as master of Alaric Morgan Duke of Corwyn's good ship *Rhafallia* in March of the year 1121, and ferried his Grace the Duke to and from Orsal on the XXVth day of that month. According to the *Chronicles*, he was "...a tall man, in well-worn brown leather breeches and jerkin, muffled by a rough wool cloak of faded crimson. He wore the peaked leather cap of a ship's master, with the green cockade of Morgan's sea service jutting gaily from the brim. His bushy, rust-coloured mustache and beard bristled when he talked." His young son, Dickon, served as cabin boy aboard his vessel. [*Deryni Checkmate*].

Henry *of Rutherford*, Sir. This knight was serving Rhun Earl of Sheele in June of the year 928. He brought the message of Prince Miklós's death and King Rhys Michael's injury to the Royal Council at Rhemuth on the XXVIth day of that month. [*The Bastard Prince*].

High Gods. They dominated the pantheon of the old Deryni legends, being celebrated in a poem by Pargan Howiccan. Their servant was Makurias-in-Glory, who was beseeched by Lord Johanan to allow him to cast out the Lleassi, the Lords of the Dark Places, from the orb of Earth. Ἀθανάτους μεν πρωτα θεους, νόμω 'ως διάκειται, τίμα. [*Camber of Culdi*].

Hilary, Bishop of Arliss, Saint. He was born in Logréine in the Vth century, and while still a pagan, he gained high office in the Byzantyun government. He was later baptized at Lérins and joined the monastic community there. He then became an assistant to his uncle, Honorarius Bishop of Arliss, and eventually succeeded him in the see. He was a zealous worker for the Lord, but not always prudent in his actions. An ancient royal basilica dedicated to his name is located within the walls of Rhemuth Castle, of which Monsignor Duncan McLain was rector in the year 1123. His feastday is the Vth day of May. [*The Bishop's Heir*].

Hilda, Abbess of Saint Ostrythe's, Saint. This native of Normarch Ley was baptized as a child by Saint Paulin, and at the age of XXXIII joined the Convent of Saint Ostrythe. She was elected Abbess there in the year 828, and later taught at Grecotha. It is said that V of her postulants became Bishops, and she was much revered as a patron of learning and culture. She died in the year 839; shortly after her death, an Abbey dedicated to her name was founded near Grecotha. Her feastday is the XVIIth day of November.

Hildred, Baron Nagapple, Master of Horse of Gwynedd, Sir. He was born on the VIth day of March in the Year of Our Lord 865, being the son of one Aled, a horse trainer and breeder from Travlum, and his wife, Unity. He intermarried with Máda Lady de Léis on the XIXth day of October in the year 905, and by her he had children: the Hereditary Lord DeLacey later Baron Nagapple; the Lady Delilah, a twin with her brother; the Lord Aldred; the Lady Dervorgilla; the Lady Decla. Hildred Nagapple was knighted by King Cinhil I on the VIth day of January in the year 905, and was created Baron Nagapple on the VIIth day of July following, being appointed to the Royal Council on the VIth day of November. Then he was sent by King Cinhil I to survey the horse breeding stock throughout Gwynedd, for he was a well-known expert on the subject. He did such a good job that he was later appointed Master of Horse of Gwynedd. Hildred was still serving on the Council in June of the year 921, when King Javan ascended the throne, and supported the new monarch. He attended King Alroy's funeral on the XXVIth day of that month, and spent the months which followed at Rhemuth helping to retrain the King as a rider. He was severely wounded by the former Regents during their coup of the XIth day of May in the year 922, and retired from politics. He died of the lingering affects of his injuries on the XIVth day of September in the year 923, aged LVIII years, and was succeeded by his son, Lord DeLacey. According to the *Heirs*, "he was a bandy-legged little man far more interested in his horses than in politics." R.I.P. [*Saint Camber*; *King Javan's Year*].

Hillary *Fougères*, Lord. He was born in Logréine on the IVth day of April in the Year of Our Lord 1077, being the fourth son of Sir Pasqual Fougères and Havoise Demoiselle d'Avaugour. He intermarried with Berthe Lady Donzie on the IInd day of July in the year 1096, and by her he had children: the Lord Hillary Junior; the Lord Berthold; the Lord Argant; the Lady Caprice. He early determined on a military career, and joined the Corwynian army in the year 1095. He rose rapidly through the ranks, and was ennobled *ad personam* by Alaric Morgan Duke of Corwyn with the sanction of King Brion on the XXIVth day of November in the year 1119. He was serving as Commander of the Castle garrison for the Duchy of Corwyn at Coroth from at least the year 1121, and was still in that position IV years later. [*Deryni Checkmate*; *High Deryni*; *The Bishop's Heir*; *The Quest for Saint Camber*].

Hoag. This Haldane Lancer was serving with the Gwyneddan Army during its invasion of Meara in June of the year 1124. On the IIIrd day of July in that year he was used by Raif as a medium to establish contact with Sofiana Sovereign Princess of Andelon and with the Camberian Council. [*The King's Justice*].

Hoël *le Magne*, IInd Roi de Bremagne. He was born on the IInd day of August in the Year of Our Lord 547, being the eldest son of Erispoé the Ist Roi de Bremagne and the Princess Roschia daughter of Thüring Duke of Beldouria. He intermarried with Ermessinde Comtesse du Bigerre on the XIth day of June in the year 568, and by her he had children: the Hereditary Prince Meyric later Meyric I Roi de Bremagne; the Princess Dodone; the Prince Otton; the Prince Astanove; the Princess Béatrix; the Prince Eskivat. The Prince Hoël succeeded his father on the XXth day of January in the year 577. During his youth he wrote the well-known religious hymn, "Veni Creator," which was sung at the coronation of Alroy King of Gwynedd on the XXVth day of May in the year 917 and at that of King Javan on the XXXIst day of July in the year 921. He died on the XXVth day of November in the year 598, aged LI years, and was succeeded by his son, Prince Meyric. *Divina particula auræ*. R.I.P. [*Camber the Heretic*; *King Javan's Year*].

Hogan Zimri Marek Gwernach *Furstán-Festil mac Tadhg*, called "The Marluk," Titular King of Gwynedd, Duke of Tolán and Truvorsk, Duke of Marluk *jure uxoris*, Count of Gwernach. This mighty Prince was born into this world on the IIIrd day of April in the Year of Our Lord 1060, being the only child of Marcus Hereditary Festillic Prince of Gwynedd and the Lady Jonelle Countess of Gwernach. Contrary to his mother's wishes he undertook a form of matrimony with Kethevan von Soslán-Davit on the XIth day of October in the year 1076, but although the marriage was annulled on the Vth day of December in that year by his uncle Nimur II King of Torenth, he continued to live with this lady in sin until he was reconciled with his mother in the year 1090.

By this union he had children, all without dynastic rights, whom he legitimated on the VIIIth day of August in the year 1099: Zimarek later Count of Tarkhan; Miriani, who intermarried with Hamman Lord Astajan; Mikael later Count of Sankt-Irakli; Shoshani, found dead in her bed at the age of II years, for no cause which physician or priest could ever determine, save that Almighty God desired another soul in Heaven.

The Duke Hogan then intermarried with the sanction of the King to the Lady Larissa Duchess and Heiress de Marluk on the XXVIIth day of May in the year 1093, the ceremony being conducted by the Patriarch Ióannés VII at the Cathedral of Saint Constantine in Beldour, and by her he had twin daughters: the Hereditary Princess and Duchess Clarissa later Duchesss of Marluk, who died at the age of IV days; the Hereditary Princess and Duchess Charissa later Duchess of Marluk and Tolán and Countess of Gwernach, who intermarried with Aldred II King of Torenth, and died without surviving issue in the year 1120. His second wife having died on the XVIth day of May in the year 1094 of the effects of childbirth, the Duke Hogan remarried his first wife, the Lady Kethevan, on the VIIIth day of August in the year 1099 and created her Countess of Soslán. She died on the XIXth day of June in the year 1103, aged XLIII years.

The Pretender Hogan succeeded his grandmother, the Duchess Chriselle, on the XIth day of August in the year 1061, and was girded with the spur and sword and couped with *colée* on New Year's Day in the year 1075 by Patriarch Thómas II. He succeeded his grandfather as Duke of Truvorsk on the XXIIIrd day of November in the year 1078, and his mother as Count of Gwernach on the XIIth day of March in the year 1091. Berrhones says of this Prince that "...he would have been well enough content to remain on his several estates and play the gentleman farmer, for he had no great desire for either war or politics. He dressed informally at home, and stayed away from Court as much as possible, taking great interest in agricultural pursuits and the breeding of horses.

"But the Prince Wencit had realized after the death of his eldest brother and the putting away of the second in the year 1095 that his own prospects had suddenly been raised by a very large measure, not only in Torenth, where he was IIIrd in succession after his brother and nephew, but also in the Festillic succession, for Duke Hogan's only direct heir was an infant daughter. If she should not survive childhood, and if Hogan fell attempting to secure his birthright, the Festillic pretensions would be reunited with the Torenthi crown, and pass to Wencit's brother, Carolus, Hereditary Prince of Torenth, to Carolus's son Aldred, and then perhaps to Wencit himself. And even if Hogan should succeed in winning the crown of Gwynedd, there would be opportunities aplenty for a Torenthi prince in the new regime.

"So Wencit encouraged his father and brother to push the Marluk into asserting his claim, firstly, he said, because Duke Hogan was the first male representative of the Festils to survive and prosper in IV full generations, and secondly because only a man in his prime would be able to defeat the Haldane, and he should not therefore wait over long. But in this the Prince Wencit was not wholly truthful or successful, for the Duke Hogan was unwilling to move until he was certain that his daughter would survive the trials of childhood, although move he finally did."

In Spring of the year 1105 Hogan Gwernach Pretender of Gwynedd prepared to challenge Brion King of Gwynedd in a contest of arms and magic. They met at the Llegoddin Canyon Trace, where their soldiers clashed, and this battle being indecisive, the II commanders then fought a duel arcane to the death. The Duke Hogan was defeated and killed on the XXIst day of June in that year, aged XLV years, and his body was returned to Beldour for burial at Torenthály. He was succeeded in his pretensions by his only surviving child, the Princess and Duchess Charissa, who vowed vengeance for her father's untimely passing; but at Hogan's death the Duchy of Truvorsk passed to his next male heir, his half-uncle, the Lord Lóránt, and thence to the present Duke, Lord Káspár. R.I.P. ["Swords Against the Marluk"; "Legacy"; *Deryni Rising*; *The Bishop's Heir*; *King Kelson's Bride*].

Holy Icons Monastery. This secluded refuge located in the Arjenoli Mountains was dedicated to the *Fratres Sancti Simplicii* (*Brothers of Saint Simplicius*), who devoted their lives and energies to caring for the mentally deficient. It was here that the imbecile Torval Prince of Torenth and Duke of Lorsöl was sent in the year 1095 to live out his days toiling in the rose gardens of the monastery. There he was often visited by his sister, Morag Duchess d'Arjenol, who was much devoted to him.

Holy Shrine of Saint Sava of the East. Situate near the Principality of Jáca between the Kingdom of R'Kassi and the Anvil of the Lord, this shrine honours the memory of the Blessed Saint Sava. It is said that in the mid-XIth century there resided at the Shrine a scabrous hermit who could speak with the dead. The Princess Chriselle Duchess of Tolán and Pretender of Gwynedd had grown most melancholy following the untimely death of her son, the Hereditary Duke and Prince Marcus, in the year 1060, and made a pilgrimage to the Holy Shrine, for she swore to have one final word with her deceased son. But, while still halfway on her journey in the deserts of R'Kassi, she suddenly took ill and died II days later at an oasis, eaten up with the Frissian fever. Her soul was taken into Heaven, and she was reunited with her son.

Hombard *of Tarkent*, **Sir**. This human envoy from Torenth presented himself before Lochalyn Castle on the XXIInd day of June in the year 928, giving the terms of Prince Miklós's proposed parley with King Rhys Michael. He was immediately tested with *merasha* by Master Stevanus and Sir Gallard de Breffni. The Prince Marek later assumed Hombard's form to deceive Rhys Michael and his allies at their subsequent meeting. According to the *Heirs*, "he was a tough-looking man of middle years clad in riding leathers with Miklós's badge on his shoulder, wearing a steel cap but no weapons of any kind. Grey threaded the hair, and his eyes were blue." [*The Bastard Prince*].

Honoria *Lettermore Carmody*. This Deryni lady intermarried with Declan Carmody on the IInd day of September in the year 909, and by him she had children: Darragh; Donagh. She was imprisoned at Rhemuth Castle with her children to compel her husband to work for the Regents. When he rebelled on the XXVth day of May in the year 918, all III were strangled before Declan's eyes before he himself was murdered. R.I.P. [*The Harrowing of Gwynedd*; *King Javan's Year*].

Horthánthy. This is the town and harbour of the Île d'Orsal. There Turpion von Horthy built a wondrous III-tiered summer palace which he called Horthánthy, all coated in verdigris and surrounded by lush gardens filled with plants imported from the IV quarters of the world, and a rooftop park partially patterned after the Hanging Garden of Furstánály Palace in Beldour. The entrance to the great harbour of Orsal is guarded by a pharos built high into the sky in corkscrew fashion, striped in emerald and ivory, which provides warning to the ships approaching the shallows there, as well as giving warning to His Hortic Majesty concerning all boat traffic coming and going on the Twin Rivers Strait, and serves also as a beacon by night or day. It communicates with a similar tower situate on the mainland opposite Orsal, part of a chain of such signal posts reaching well into the heart of Tralia.

Access to the Palace is restricted to single-person traffic by use of a narrow roadway winding back and forth up the side of Zöldhegy or Montvert, the great hill of Orsal, and by the banning of horses from the official residence. Much of the transportation on the island is conducted by hand-drawn carts or *jinrikisha*, which are easily accomodated to the narrowly turning streets of the town. A lost work of Kitron is said to have commented on the occult significance of the arrangement of these byways, although Ely de l'Ouse considered the notion mere nonsense. According to the *Nuptis Kelsoni Regis*, it has "an exuberant array of graceful open arches and slightly domed roofs, soft verdigris against the chalk white summit." However, Campbell de Broun, on his sole visit there, remarked to his companions: "We are surely not in Cloome any more." [*King Kelson's Bride*].

Horthness. This small Barony is located in the central part of the Purple March, having been granted by King Festil II to Sir Remig von Horthy on the VIth day of June in the 846. Baron Remig claimed to be a descendant of Rogan the Hort of Orsal and Prince of Tralia, although most genealogists give this statement little credence. His grandson was Rhun called the Ruthless, later Earl of Sheele. On the XIVth day of June in the year 943 the title was given as a dowry to the Lady Émeraude daughter of Rhun Earl of Sheele, who intermarried on that date with Lord Quiric Fitz-Arthur, in whose line the title continues. Their son was Ulvar Baron of Horthness. The banners of Horthness were represented in the army of Kelson King of Gwynedd in June of the year 1121. [*The Harrowing of Gwynedd*; *High Deryni*]. See also: Adelicia, Juliana.

Howicce. The Kingdom of Howicce is located Southwest of Gwynedd, and is bordered by Gwynedd on the Northeast, Llannedd on the East, The Connait on the North, and the Great Atalantic Ocean everywhere else. The first King, Aed mac Faolan, established his rule on the Ist day of June in the Year of Our Lord 651 by subduing the petty states of the region. On the VIth day of July in the year 792 the King Bresal I conquered The Connait, but lost the region XII years later on the XVth day of September in the year 804. Several attempts were made by subsequent monarchs to re-establish their control over this land, but none were successful for more than brief periods. Incursions were also made during the mid-800s into Southwestern Gwynedd and into Llannedd, but these were quickly repulsed. On the XXVth day of May in the year 918 the Prince Cormac of Howicce attended the birthday celebrations of King Alroy and Prince Javan in Rhemuth, presenting them with a pouch of freshwater pearls.

On the Xth day of May in the year 1055 Colman I King of Howicce married Gwenaël Sovereign Queen of Llannedd, and their son, Illann II, united the II realms under the rule of I monarch when he succeeded his mother on the XXVIth day of July in the year 1082, having already acceded to the throne of Howicce on the XVth day of December in the year 1071. However, both states still maintain their governments separately to this day, and being joined together only through the person of the same monarch, could readily split again in the future. The laws which govern each country are variant, allowing the succession of women to the throne in Llannedd but not in Howicce; thus, the present heir to King Colman II in the Kingdom of Howicce, barring any future issue of his own flesh, is his Ist cousin, the Prince Cuan son of the late Prince Cormac, but his heir in the Kingdom of Llannedd is his young half-sister, the Princess Gwenlian. King Colman II was betrothed in the year 1123 to the Princess Janniver, but her honour being soiled by the hideous violation of Ithel Hereditary Prince of Meara on the XVth day of June in the year 1124, he did forsake her.

The capital of Howicce is Sirhowy, a city of some fifty thousand souls situate on the River Llinmari where it enters the Southern Sea, which River also serves as the boundary line between the United Kingdoms. Here is located the Palace of the King, as well as the residence of the Archbishop Primate of Howicce and Llannedd, the great Cathedral of Saint Eloff or Eliphius the Martyr, the grand spires of that renowned institution of higher learning, the University of Sirhowy, and that most curious of structures, the Octagon House, seat of the Supreme of Howicce, which has VIII doors and VIII windows, each side being daubed in a different colour.

The *numerus* VIII possesses a certain mystical significance to the Howiccans, and they fear its import most tremendously. Although many have scoffed at such notions, the wise men of Howicce will point to the history of their land, and how the VIIIth King thereof, Aed II, was murdered just a week after his father's death, and how the XVIth, the King Cormac, was poisoned by his wife after little more than a year on his throne, and that the XXIVth, the King Fergus, was married V times before he begat an heir, each wife living but a short time after her marriage (even the last), and that he suffered from boils and chilblains all of his days and frequently lamented his fate and wished that he could die sooner, although of course he did not.

Over the centuries a number of younger sons of the great houses of Gwynedd have settled in Howicce, the most prominent among them being the Prince Michael Rhys Haldane later Earl of Carthane, who renounced his rights to the throne of Gwynedd for himself and his descendants on the XVIIth day of August in the year 1009 and intermarried with Mithradita Heiress of the Duchy of Pirek in Howicce, becoming Duke *jure uxoris* and changing his surname by deed poll to Pirek-Haldane, his title of Carthane in Gwynedd being deeded to his IInd son, Earl Godwyn, ancestor of the later Counts of this line. His descendants have included some of the most respected peers of the Kingdom, including the present representative, Rhys Cinhil Duke of Pirek.

Campbell de Broun journeyed through the central plains of Howicce at the very beginning of his travels: "We left Lord Traylock's in the morning, crossing the skirt of the prairie to the Crooked River, about III leagues, where we ferried ourselves over. The weather was extremely hot and sultry. There was some appearance of rain, but, not withstanding, we entered the big prairie through which it was more than XXX leagues to the Runt House. We had not proceeded more than VIII leagues, and had left the track through the prairie to go by the Round Grove, when it began to rain on us. The timber in it was tolerable thick, but on account of the angry cloud that was hanging over us, from which the lightning almost continously flashed, we thought it imprudent to enter the Grove and kept out on the plain. We now had no track to follow, but took the course as near as we could.

"The rain now poured down in such torrents that we could see no more than C yards around us. We soon lost sight of the Round Grove and had nothing now to guide us. We began to be fearful that we might have taken a wrong course, and should it be towards the Northwest it would lead us into the Grand Prairie before we could reach any settlement. The wind now blew with great violence and beat the rain in our faces; the thunder rolled with an awful suddenness around us, sometimes bursting just over our heads in such dreadful peals that the earth trembled with terror. The lightning flashed so frequently that we were continually enveloped in the blaze which presented an awful constrast to the gloomy darkness that hung around us. It appeared as if the cloud, being surcharged with weight, had come down, was resting on the plain, and then discharging itself in torrents.

"The awful peals of thunder, the violence of the wind driving the torrents of rain before it, and the continued blaze and horrible glare of the lightning, altogether presented a scene so terrible that it seemed as if the elements were at war with each other or were combined and raging with dreadful fury, just ready to destroy us. In all this rage and elemental war, who but would reflect how terrible is God when He clothes himself in the majesty of His power, when He puts on His terror, or frowns in anger? From the hollow of His hand He lets loose the thunder and from His eyes flash the dread lightning—who but would look beyond the effect to the more terrible cause? Or who would wish to provoke the anger of Him, who when He speaks in thunder, puts on not half His terrors?

"I am not naturally afraid of thunder—it generally awakens emotions sublime and pleasing—but I must confess that those awakened by this storm were rather more awful. It continued with unabating violence for many hours; we kept on the one course as near as we could. We had nothing to direct us, and we could not discern a tree. All around us the extended plain was covered with clouds and thick darkness. This plain is so level that the rain drains off it but slowly, and our horses had literally to wade the prairie. The storm a little abating, and the clouds rising finally from off the plain, we could see at some distance around us; on ascending a small barrow or burial mound, we looked out for the timber as eagerly as ever the tempest-beaten mariner, who, long absent from the land, looked for it when he expected he was near; and soon after we discovered, at a great distance before us, the West Grove.

"We hurried on then to cross the Quenda before it should rise; on arriving, we found it considerably swelled. We expected to swim it but on entering found we could ford the river. We crossed II forks of it and put up at one McGann's. That night, lying alone in the farmer's loft, scratching myself where the hay poked through the blanket, I pondered upon our day's adventures, and wondered if I should ever again see my home in Cloome. I had been on the road now for lo these past III months, and I regretted most deeply my intemperate words. What a fool I had been. Papa, wilt thou ever forgive me?"

The coat-of-arms of the United Kingdom combine lozenges alternating in violet and green, representing the contrasting colours of both monarchies. [*Saint Camber*; *The Harrowing of Gwynedd*; *Deryni Rising*; *King Kelson's Bride*].

KINGS OF HOWICCE

HOUSE OF MACFAOLAN-(GRUFFUD)

Aed I mac Faolan	651-677
Illann I Festus (son)	677-703
Ronan I (son)	703-718
Rodrick (son)	718-720
Cuan (uncle)	720-735
Becc (nephew)	735-766
Madagan (son)	766-788
Aed II (son)	788
Daigh (brother)	788-789
Bresal I Consentaneus (brother)	789-821
Aed III (son)	821-859
Braon (cousin)	859-860
Ronan II (son of Aed III)	860-888
Aed IV (son)	888-906
Ronan III (son)	906-944
Cormac (brother)	944-946
Carlus I (grandson)	946-949
Aed V (uncle)	949-955
Roen (son)	955-966
Finghin (son)	966-971
Gosbert (2nd cousin)	971-998
Carlus II (son)	998-1016
Bresal II (brother)	1016-1028

Fergus (son)	1028-1047
Colman I (son)	1047-1071
Illann II (son; abdicated)	1071-1099
Ronan IV (son)	1099-1119
Colman II (brother)	1119-1130+

Hrorik II, Earl of Eastmarch. He was born on the XXVIIth day of December in the Year of Our Lord 882, being the second son of Sighere Duke of Claibourne and Synolda Lady de Lacey. He intermarried with the Countess Sudrey Heiress of Rhorau on the XVth day of May in the year 908, and by her he had children: the Lady Stacia later Countess of Eastmarch, who intermarried with Corban Lord Howell later Earl of Eastmarch *jure uxoris*; the Lady Swan, who died an infant; the Lady Shine, dead at age III of the rosy crawlies.

On the XXVIth day of August in the year 906 the Lord Hrorik was ceded his father's title of Earl of Eastmarch, with confirmation being made by Cinhil I King of Gwynedd. He was present at Valoret at the coronation of King Alroy on the XXVth day of May in the year 917. He rode to Rhemuth on the IVth day of June in the year 918 with his brother, Sighere *Junior* Earl of Marley, and their nephew, Graham the new Duke of Claibourne, to confirm the latter's titles.

He attended the coronation of King Javan on the XXXIst day of July in the year 921, and at the state banquet held later that evening he accused Murdoch Earl of Carthane of murdering both his brother, Ewan Duke of Claibourne and Ewan's aide, Sir Kennet of Rhorau. Murdoch pulled his sword and attacked Hrorik, but was forced by King Javan to withdraw. Then the Earl Hrorik challenged the Earl Murdoch to trial by combat, which was seconded by King Javan, and on the next day killed Murdoch Earl of Carthane in fair battle, God having made his judgment plain to all. In this contest he suffered severe injuries himself, from which he eventually recovered.

On the XXXth day of May in the year 928 he rode out to the Coldoire Pass when he received news of a Torenthi incursion, and spent a week there harrying the much larger enemy force. He agreed to a parley with Prince Miklós of Torenth, but was killed in front of Culliecairn Castle when the flag of truce was dishonoured, on the VIIth day of June in the year 928. His body was returned to his seat of Lochalyn Castle on the day following. He was XLV years of age at his death.

Since the Earl Hrorik had no sons, he was succeeded by his only surviving daughter as Countess of Eastmarch. Among the descendants of this family is vested the right to petition for the restoration of the Earldom of Rhorau. The Eastmarch standard includes golden suns and a silver saltire on an *azure* field. R.I.P. [*Saint Camber*; *Camber the Heretic*; *The Harrowing of Gwynedd*; *King Javan's Year*; *The Bastard Prince*].

Hubert John William Valerian *MacInnis*, Archbishop Primate of Valoret and All Gwynedd, sometime Lord Regent of Gwynedd. This evil cleric was born on the IVth day of November in the Year of Our Lord 876, being the second son of Colquhoun Manfred MacInnis *de jure* Baron Marlor and Clayre Lady MacLanaghan, and brother to Manfred Earl of Culdi and uncle of Edward Bishop of Grecotha. He early determined upon a life in the clergy, and was ordained priest by Archbishop Anscom on the XIVth day of March in the year 896. He attached himself to the household of Murdoch Baron of Carthane, serving as his personal chaplain during the next IX years, but through the influence of his patron he was able to secure consecration as an itinerant Bishop of Gwynedd on the XIIIth day of October in the year 909. He was elected Auxiliary Bishop of Rhemuth on the XVIIIth day of October in the year 916, and was assigned by King Cinhil I to oversee the education of the Hereditary Prince Alroy in his study of the Scriptures.

He was named one of the V Regents of King Alroy on the IInd day of February in the year 917, at which time he also became a member of the Royal Council. He was present at the trial of the Deryni assassins on the XXVIIIth day of September in that year. On the XVth day of October, following the death of Archbishop Jaffray, Hubert was chosen by the Regents as their candidate for the vacant office, and attended the Synod of Bishops held at Valoret in November and December of 917. Although Bishop Alister Cullen emerged as the compromise candidate following numerous deadlocked votes, his installation as Archbishop Primate on the XXVth day of December was curtailed through the connivance of Bishop Hubert, who was illegally elected Archbishop Primate by a rump council of Bishops, and enthroned in Cullen's place II days later.

Archbishop Hubert promulgated the abomination called the *Ordo Custodum Fidei* at the Candlemas celebrations held at All Saints' Cathedral in Valoret on the IInd day of February in the year 918. He presided at the marriage of Iver Lord MacInnis with Richeldis Lady MacLean on the Vth day of March in the year 918. On the XXVth day of May in that year he presented Prince Javan on his birthday with a silver chalice, paten, and chasuble that had once belonged to King Cinhil I. He was present at the death of King Alroy on the XXIIIrd day of June in the year 921. Hubert attended the coronation of King Javan on the XXXIst day of July in the year 921, and placed the crown on the new monarch's head.

He was present at the residence of the ailing Robert Oriss Archbishop of Rhemuth when he received news of the death of Lord Albertus on the XXVth day of June in the year 928, and at that time declared himself responsible for Albertus's death and Paulin's incapacitation, saying that he had recruited the Deryni Dimitri many years before. He was captured in July of that year, tried by the Council of Bishops, and deposed from office on the XIth day of that month; he was then banished to Saint Iveagh's Abbey, where he was held in close confinement and subjected to a regimen of fasting and penance for his many sins of omission and commission. He died on the XXXth day of November in the year 929, reportedly much reduced in size. He was aged LIII years at his death, and went straight to Hell, where the Devil had prepared a special receptacle for his wretched soul. *Adulandi gens prudentissima laudat sermonem indocti, faciem deformis amici.*

He is described in the *Legends* as having "enough bulk to make up for several men, [with a] blue-eyed and blond-fringed cherubic face belying the hypocrisy which lurked beneath the wine-cassocked breast. Hubert had managed to endear himself to all three of the young princes, and they liked him perhaps best of all five regents—which was unfortunate, because Hubert MacInnis was not a nice man." He had tiny rosebud lips, and grew ever more mountainous in size with the years: "...perhaps it was the sheer expanse of purple cassock, unbroken by the extra layers of episcopal attire with which the Archbishop usually was wont to adorn his ample person." [*Camber the Heretic*; *The Harrowing of Gwynedd*; *King Javan's Year*; *The Bastard Prince*].

Hugh *de Berry*, Bishop of Ballymar. This native of Cassan was born on the XXIVth day of November in the Year of Our Lord 1091, being the son of Sir Jarnithin de Berry and Audrenne Lady Porhoët. One of his boyhood friends was Duncan Lord McLain, with whom he maintained a lifelong friendship. Later he and Duncan both entered holy orders within months of each other, and they were ordained priests together at Saint George's Cathedral on the Xth day of April in the year 1113 by Alexander Archbishop of Rhemuth. He was then assigned as personal secretary to Patrick Corrigan Archbishop of Rhemuth.

On the XXth day of March in the year 1121 he was the first person to warn King Kelson of the conspiracy then being devised by the Archbishops against Alaric Morgan Duke of Corwyn and Father Duncan McLain. As a reward for his loyalty, he was consecrated an itinerant Bishop on the XIXth day of January in the year 1122, and was then elevated to the see of Ballymar in Kierney by the Synod of Valoret on the XVIIIth day of March in the year 1125. He spoke in defense of Duncan McLain at the Synod conducted on the XVIIIth day of April following. According to the *Chronicles*, he had thinning brown hair, and was bright, honest, discreet, and loyal. [*Deryni Checkmate*; *High Deryni*; *The Bishop's Heir*; *The King's Justice*; *The Quest for Saint Camber*].

Humphrey *of Gallareaux*, Father. This Deryni Michaeline priest was captured by King Imre's men and interrogated on the XIXth day of December in the year 903. He was later freed, and attached himself to Archbishop Anscom's staff. But his will had been forcibly subverted by the King Imre, and he poisoned the infant Prince Aidan at Imre's instigation on the VIth day of November in the year 904. He was immediately killed by Prince Cinhil Haldane through magic, and was buried in the Michaeline Haven. R.I.P. [*Camber of Culdi*; *Saint Camber*; *King Javan's Year*].

Hurd *de Blake*. This landowner in the Duchy of Corwyn had IV acres burned out by Warin de Grey's men in March of the year 1121. [*Deryni Checkmate*].

Husniyya "Niyya" bint Rauf al-Zaman bint Qabus al-Duala *al-Muttalib*, Princess and Sharifa of R'Kassi and Tralia. She was born on the XVth day of December in the Year of Our Lord 1088, being the daughter of Rauf al-Zaman King of R'Kassi and the Shaikha Alyendra Noor al-Vézaire. She intermarried with Létald Hort of Orsal and Prince of Tralia on the XXXIst day of May in the year 1105, and by him she had children: His Hereditary Horthness the Prince Cyric; the Princess Rezza; the Prince Rogan; the Prince Marcel; the Princess Marcelline, a twin with her brother; the Princess Aynbeth; the Prince Oswin; the Prince Kelliam; the Princess Péadora, a twin to her brother. [*King Kelson's Bride*].

Hywel *of Erne*, Lord. He was born on the XIth day of December in the Year of Our Lord 880, being the eldest son and heir of Dothan Lord of Erne and Dulcie Lady Carrigaline. He never married. He attempted with his sister the Lady Nesta to assassinate King Cinhil I by sorcery on the XXIInd day of June in the year 905 in retaliation for the imprisonment of his father, Lord Dothan of Erne. The King immediately killed him with magic. Hywel was XXIV years of age at his death. [*Saint Camber*].

Iain I *MacLean*, Vth Earl of Kierney. He was born on the XIth day of April in the Year of Our Lord 832, being the eldest son and heir of Brennan Earl of Kierney and Ebora of Transha. He intermarried with Aislinn Lady MacRorie, sister of Camber Earl of Culdi, on the IVth day of June in the year 869, and by her he had children: the Hereditary Count Iain *Junior* later Iain II Earl of Kierney; the Lord Geoffrey ancestor of the later Earls of Kierney; the Lord Angus ancestor of the McLain family; the Lady Ardissa. The Lord Iain succeeded his father on the XIIIth day of December in the year 860. He died on the XXIInd day of December in the year 895, aged LXIII years, and was succeeded by his eldest son, Lord Iain *Junior*. R.I.P.

Iain II *MacLean*, VIth Earl of Kierney. He was born on the XVth day of April in the year 870, being the eldest son and heir of Iain I Earl of Kierney and Aislinn Lady MacRorie. He intermarried with Catriona Lady of Mar on the IIIrd day of October in the year 887, and by her he had children: the Hereditary Count Adrian, who was murdered by the Regents at Trurill, leaving issue; the Lady Fiona. The Lord Iain succeeded his father on the XXIInd day of December in the year 895. He was slain by the Regents in an alleged hunting accident on the XIXth day of March in the year 918, aged XLVII years, at which point his title should have been inherited by his grandson, Lord Camber Allin MacLean; but, since the latter was believed by the Regents to have been killed at Trurill with his father, the Hereditary Count Adrian, the Earldom passed instead to the Lady Richeldis MacLean MacInnis, eldest surviving daughter of Earl Iain's deceased brother, the Lord Geoffrey MacLean. R.I.P. [*The Harrowing of Gwynedd*].

Ian *Calder of Sheele*, Bishop and Lord. He was born on the XXXth day of December in the Year of Our Lord 1072, being the third son of Thomas Earl Calder of Sheele and Yvetta Lady Howard, and a great-uncle of Dhugal MacArdry Duke of Cassan and Earl of Kierney. He early entered the service of the Church, and was ordained priest on the Xth day of May in the year 1091. He was consecrated as an itinerant Bishop of Gwynedd on the XXth day of February in the year 1115 by Edmund Loris Archbishop Primate of Valoret. It is not surprising, then, that he supported Loris in the latter's attempt in December of the year 1123 to restore himself to his former position as Primate of Gwynedd, but was arrested when the rebellion collapsed in the following year. He was stripped of his rank on the XVIIIth day of March in the year 1125, but was allowed to continue functioning as a priest under close supervision. [*The Bishop's Heir*; *The King's Justice*].

Ian *Howell*, Earl of Eastmarch. This nefarious peer was born on the IVth day of July in the Year of Our Lord 1089, being the only son and heir of Arban Earl of Eastmarch and Crispina Baroness de Vali. He never married. He succeeded his father as Earl on the XVth day of December in the year 1115. In the year 1120 this Deryni renegade allied himself with Charissa Duchess of Tolán and Pretender of Gwynedd, having been promised the Duchy of Corwyn by her, and he worked to restore the House of Festil to the throne of Gwynedd. He assisted her in the assassination of Brion King of Gwynedd on the Ist day of November in that year. A few weeks later he murdered several guards at Rhemuth Palace and instigated attacks on the King and his allies, in the hope of discrediting Alaric Duke of Corwyn, but without much success. He acted as his patroness's champion at Kelson's coronation on the XVth day of November in the year 1120, and was severely wounded in single combat by Alaric Morgan Duke of Corwyn; he was given the *coup de grâce* by the Lady Charissa. He was XXXI years of age at his death, and was attainted traitor, his estates being forfeit to the crown. His title was ultimately given to his brother-in-law, Burchard de Varian, a loyal supporter of both the Kings Brion and Kelson.

He is described in the *Chronicles of the Deryni* as having chestnut hair and brown eyes, a meticulously tended beard and mustache, a thin mouth, high cheek bones, and round eyes. His arms were: *azure*, a saltire *argent* between two suns in pale *or*. [*Deryni Rising*; *The Bishop's Heir*].

Iddin, *i.e.*, Nuriddin *de Vesca*. This Deryni guard officer of the Hort of Orsal also served as a spy for Teymuraz Count of Brustarkia. When, on the XVIIth day of July in the year 1128, he noted that the Hort's women guests had departed, he took over the guard Luric's mind, and used him to uncover the Hort's secret portal. He then sent this information to Teymuraz, warning him not land at Orsal. [*King Kelson's Bride*].

Ifor Augarin Niall *Haldane*, also called Niall Lord Kincaid, King of Gwynedd. He was born on the IXth day of April in the Year of Our Lord 778, being the only surviving son of Bearand King of Gwynedd and Aisling Lady Kincaid. He intermarried with Nuala Lady Udaut on the VIIIth day of November in the year 806, and by her he had children: the Hereditary Prince Jashan later Earl of Valoret; the Prince Alroy; the Princess Maire; the Prince Donal; the Prince Aidan later called Daniel Draper; the Princess Michaela; the Princess Ysabeau.

The Prince Ifor succeeded his father on the XIIth day of December in the year 794, and was crowned by Valatonius Archbishop Primate of Valoret on the VIIIth day of March in the year 795. As a young man of XVIII years he decided that his education concerning the outside world was somewhat lacking, and traveled incognito to the old realms of Bremagne, Rûm, Byzantyun, and other points in the East during the year 797 and again in the year 799, using the *nom d'emprunt* of Niall Lord Kincaid. There he acquired much learning and acquainted himself with the many wondrous sights of the great world, and also with the latest advances in the technology of war and the science of farming. Upon his return, he used this new knowledge to effect many reforms in the administration of government and to improve the horticulture of the Kingdom. He also brought back several bins of cuttings, including trees, vines, and fruits, some of which were successfully cultivated in subsequent seasons. In the year 808 he took ship to the Anvil of the Lord, where he made a pilgrimage to the Holy Places to give thanks for the birth of his son and heir.

On the XXIst day of June in the year 822 Prince Festil of Torenth abruptly invaded Gwynedd, and murdered the King with all of his family except the II-year-old Prince Aidan. The latter was secreted in a bundle of laundry and removed from Rhemuth Castle by Jasper Draper, who took him to Valoret and raised the Prince as his own son. The King Ifor was XLIV years of age at his death; his body was exhumed II years after his death and given a quiet but honourable burial by his successor, King Festil I. The *Legends* describe him as "slender and dark, with black hair and beard and mustache silvered with middle age, grey eyes direct, clear, but unable to foresee the fate which had awaited him but a few years after he sat for the portrait." R.I.P. [*Camber of Culdi*].

Ifor, Bishop of Marbury. He was born on the XXVIth day of August in the Year of Our Lord 1076. He was ordained priest on the IInd day of July in the year 1094, consecrated an itinerant Bishop of Gwynedd on the XIXth day of October in the year 1109, and elected Bishop of Marbury on the XIIth day of March in the year 1120. He sided with Archbishops Loris and Corrigan during the Interdict Schism of the year 1121, but later became neutral when it became obvious that the Archbishops would lose their battle with Kelson King of Gwynedd, and was allowed to retain his position by the new Synod of Bishops. [*Deryni Checkmate*; *High Deryni*; *The Bishop's Heir*].

Illan *de Bourges*, Lord. He was born on the VIIIth day of February in the Year of Our Lord 874, being the son of Felician Baron Bourges and Elgiva Lady Birdsey. He joined the Order of Saint Michael in the year 891. This Michaeline knight was stationed at Valoret Castle in the year 905, when he was awakened by Lord Dualta and asked to relieve him from duty on the IInd day of July. He escaped to Djellarda in the year 917 when the Michaelines evacuated from Gwynedd, and was killed by the Moors on the XXXth day of December in the year 926, aged LII years. R.I.P. [*Saint Camber*].

Illtyd, Abbot and Saint. One of the most celebrated saints in the Eleven Kingdoms, he is said to have embraced the monastic life at an early age and to have founded the Abbey of Llan-Illrut or Llantwit in

Llannedd in about the year 525. According to some writers, the original structure of this establishment was located on Caldey Island in the center of the River Llanarfon near the Free Port of Concaradine; but others place the Abbey on the Southern bank of the same River near its source in the Mughdorna Mountains. He received a vision in old age directing him to the East, where he discovered the body of Saint Neot in the Anvil of the Lord in the year 555, an event which is commemorated annually by the *Lavage de Saint-Néot* in Jáca. He died not long thereafter, worn out by his exertions. An *Ordo Verbi Dei* Abbey dedicated to his name is located on the River Eirian near Nyford. His feastday is the VIth day of November. [*Camber of Culdi*].

Ilona, Saint. This VIIIth-century saint was the daughter of a wealthy merchant in Beldour. At the age of XV years she was given in marriage to a colleague of her father's, but her betrothed died of pains in his chest on their wedding night, much to her dismay. The distraught widow then persuaded her father to build for her an obelisk to commemorate her *époux perdu*, and there she constructed a nunnery some X miles outside the city gates of Beldour, where she gathered about her a lively group of young widows and other sympathetic souls, who dedicated themselves to pray for their deceased husbands and lost companions. She proved a most generous benefactress. The Princess Jessamyn, who took the veil at age XIV under the religious name of Sophia, entered the Convent of Saint Ilona in the Year of Our Lord 794, dying there LVI years later. Saint Ilona's feastday is the XXIVth day of December.

Imre I István Ingwar *Furstán-Festil*, called "The Last," King of Gwynedd, Duke of Rhemuth, Overlord of Meara and Mooryn. This Spawn of the Devil came into this world on the last day of December in the Year of Our Lord 881, being the third son and sixth child of Blaine I King of Gwynedd and Pasqualetta Contessa di Barbarico di Torenti. He never legally married, but entered into an incestuous relationship with his witch of a sister, the Princess Ariella, and by her he had one posthumous son: the Hereditary Prince and Duke Mark later called Marek in Torenth. According to Guigues in *The Five Festils*, King Imre was doted upon by his parents as a child, his elder brothers having died young, and also babied by his elder sisters. He was an indifferent student, uninterested in politics or the military arts, and followed a path of total dissipation and leisure.

The Prince Imre was deeded the Duchy of Rhemuth on the XVIth day of March in the year 885. He succeeded his father on the XXVIIIth day of February in the year 900, and immediately began replacing King Blaine's Council with a mix of young and inexperienced sycophants and supporters, although he did promote Lord Cathan MacRorie. The state treasury, which had been carefully conserved during his father's reign, was spent lavishly on state parties and elaborate celebrations, beginning with his own coronation on the XXVth day of March in that same year. To raise additional funds for his treasury, and to build a new capital at the small town of Nyford in Southern Gwynedd, he issued a proclamation on Twelfth Night in the year 901 that levied a new tax on all landowners in Gwynedd, amounting to one-sixth of their holdings, and also required that all other freeholders pay a head tax or provide their own bodies as labour in lieu of payment.

He declined to make the trip to Beldour to pay homage to his cousin, Nimur I King of Torenth, until II years after his accession on the XXIIIrd day of May in the year 902, stating that he first had to put his father's house in order; and when he approached the old King of Torenth, the King Imre insisted that he be given a chair on an equal level with that of his Overlord before he would proceed with the formal installation and the swearing of oaths. This caused much ill comment at that time. Still, his official engagement to his cousin's daughter, the Princess Lajosha, was announced on the XIIth day of June in that year, before he departed Torenth for Valoret.

Upon his return, he traveled to Nyford to oversee the initial phases of construction of his new Palace there. No expense was spared, with artisans being brought from as far away as Byzantyun itself to work on the structure. At about this time or shortly thereafter, those at Court noticed that the Princess Ariella had begun to exert an unhealthy influence on her brother, eventually convincing him to postpone his forthcoming marriage to the Princess Lajosha, which had been scheduled to take place by Matthewmas in the year 902. The matrimonials were again postponed in the year 903, and the Princess suddenly died of the palsied paralysis on the I[st] day of March in the year 904. Some say that there was no paralysis at all, but that the Princess had opened the veins of her wrists in her bath and bled herself to death.

During the IVth year of King Imre's reign there was much discontent abroad in the country, and support for the King and his policies began to diminish very rapidly. The discovery of a hitherto unknown Haldane heir, Prince Cinhil, precipitated the crisis. In a swift coup that was reminiscent of Festil I's assumption of power in the year 822, the Haldane Prince and his chief supporters confronted the King in his own bedchambers. Having been defeated in a test of magic with Cinhil, the cowardly Imre took his life and condemned himself to eternal damnation on the IInd day of December in the year 904, but his pregnant sister Ariella escaped. Imre was XXII years of age at his death. His head was put on a pike above the city walls for all to see, but his body was eventually interred in the family crypt of the Festils at Valoret.

The *Legends* describe him as "a striking young man, for all that he was of small stature and relatively few years, shorter by half a head than most of the men in the room, yet he still cut a regal figure. His hair was of a deep chestnut hue, cropped shoulder length, surrounding lively brown eyes which bulged slightly in a pleasant, albeit somewhat vacant, face. He wore a short, skin-tight tunic of brown velvet which revealed every line of the hard young body, and emphasized a pair of well-turned legs encased in brown silken hose, with leather dancing slippers on his feet. A gold-and-amber cloak lined with red fox brushed the floor behind him." *Assiduus in oculis hominum fuerat, quæ res minus verendos magnos homines ipsa satietate facit.*

[*Camber of Culdi*; *Saint Camber*; *The Harrowing of Gwynedd*; *The Bastard Prince*; *King Kelson's Bride*].

Imre II Nimur Tamás *Furstán-Festil*, called "The Young Pretender," King of Gwynedd at Rengarth, Duke of Tolán. He was born on the XXIIIrd day of May in the Year of Our Lord 928, being the eldest son and heir of Marek I Hereditary Prince and Titular King of Gwynedd and the Princess Charis Duchess of Tolán and daughter of Nimur I King of Torenth. He intermarried with Tamara Countess of Netterhaven on the XIIth day of December in the year 948, and by her he had children: the Hereditary Prince Mark-Imre, ancestor of the senior branch of the house of Furstán-Festil, who died before his father, with issue; the Princess Ariella, who intermarried with Duchad Mór Count of Tigre, and by him had twin sons: the Prince Festil later Count of Tigre, and the Prince Blaine, ancestor of the junior branch of the House of Furstán-Festil, who left issue; the Princess Charissa, dead at age V of the poisoned blood; the Prince Markáspár, dead at age IV of unknown causes; the Princess Anastasia, who intermarried with Makonnen Hort of Orsal and Prince of Tralia; plus II unnamed stillborn children.

The occasion of the christening of Prince Imre on Saint John's Eve in the year 928 was used as an excuse by Prince Miklós of Torenth to occupy the fortress of Culliecairn on the Coldoire Pass on the VIIth day of June in that year. However, the infant Prince and his mother were sent by his father back to Tolán before the confrontation with Rhys Michael King of Gwynedd that killed Prince Miklós of Torenth on the XXIInd instant.

The Prince Imre was well educated in the military and political arts at Beldour and Torenthály, and participated in several Torenthi military expeditions to the Southeast. He succeeded to his father's pretensions on the latter's abdication on the IVth day of February in the year 975, and immediately determined to press his claim to the throne of Gwynedd. He sought the aid of Malachy II King of Torenth, but when the former proved hesitant in committing men and materiel to the cause, he eventually befriended the latter's son, the Hereditary Prince Nimur, gradually convincing him that the time was ripe for a full-scale invasion of their joint enemy. There being no Patriarch in Beldour in the year 976, the Pretender Imre II delayed his formal investiture as the Festillic heir until New Year's Day in the year 977, when he was girded with spur and sword by Patriarch Archelaos I according to Torenthi custom and couped with *colée*, being declared *de jure* King of Gwynedd.

The Prince Imre had quietly gathered an army of some 10,000 men by the Summer of the year 983, hiding them in the Eastern valleys of the Rheljan Mountains, and naming his son Mark-Imre Commander of the expeditionary force. The initial attack at Marbury on the XIIth day of August in that year took the Gwyneddans completely by surprise, and the Torenthi quickly occupied Marley and killed Brian Earl of Marley. Nygel King of Gwynedd responded with a hastily-gathered force of knights and levies, and met the enemy army near Old Argoed on the IIIrd day of September in that year. The King was killed and his army defeated, the Gwyneddan forces falling back towards Grecotha. Eastmarch was overrun by Imre's forces, and the Pretender proclaimed himself King as Imre II on the XXIInd day of September, with his Court being established first at Cardosa and then at Rengarth a few weeks later. The early arrival of Winter storms in November abruptly halted the invasion, but also prevented any meaningful response by Jasher the new Haldane King of Gwynedd until the Spring.

That Winter was one of the severest ever recorded in the history of Gwynedd. A quarter of the Festillic army starved, froze, or died of disease before the snows and ice had retreated sufficiently to allow supply trains finally to reach their camp. Even the highborn were not immune: the Prince Mark-Imre lost part of his left foot to frostbite. Half of the army was forced back to Torenth in February of the year 984 to be refitted and rebuilt by Malachy II King of Torenth at Medras.

A relief force under the command of Hereditary Prince Nimur left Beldour on the XVIIIth day of June in that year, and joined with his father's army at Medras and the remnants of Imre's army at Rengarth III weeks later. The combined expedition then moved North into Carcashale and Iomaire on the XVIIth day of July, being constantly harassed by small groups of Gwyneddan soldiers attacking from ambush, but never finding the enemy's main army. On the afternoon of the IInd day of August, the Torenthis appeared before the walls of Grecotha and demanded the surrender of that city. In a council of war held that evening the Princes Mark-Imre and Nimur urged a frontal assault on the Gwyneddan fortress, while Imre and King Malachy counseled caution. However, the II young Princes carried the day, and at dawn the Festillic banners moved forward.

But Jasher the new King of Gwynedd had redeployed his forces during the night, and when the Torenthi army breached the Eastern gate of the city, they found no one inside, for the Gwyneddans were attacking them from the rear. The small cluster of Torenthi noblemen and officers directing the battle behind the lines were quickly overrun, the Princes Mark-Imre and Nimur and the King Malachy being killed almost immediately. The remaining Torenthis broke ranks and fled East. The new King Carolus II and the Young Pretender organized a retreat, but both were wounded in the fighting, Carolus dying during the following week of his injuries. Only Prince Imre survived. Kyprian II the new King of Torenth being a minor, no further support from that quarter could be expected.

However, Southern Eastmarch and Rengarth still remained in Imre's hands, and he maintained a Court there through the Winter of the year 985. Believing that the Haldane would have to move against him by Summer or lose Eastmarch forever, the Young Pretender enlisted his son-in-law, Duchad Mór Count of Tigre, for a IIIrd try at the throne of Gwynedd. Mercenaries were brought from Forcinn, Orsal, the Connait, and other sources, and a new army assembled under the Count's command. Duchad Mór's armored infantry would be held in reserve to strike at the weakest part of the enemy lines, or to repulse any Gwyneddan soldiers that broke through. Rengarth was heavily fortified and a moat dug around the city. The Pretender's grandson and heir, the

Prince Imre III, was declared of age a year ahead of time, and then knighted and ennobled as Duke of Eastmarch; he was promptly sent to Beldour to rally volunteers for the cause, and also to remove him from the scene in case of disaster.

The Gwyneddan army was spotted on the XXXth day of May in the year 985. The first clash between the II forces took place on the plain in front of the city on the IInd day of June. The Haldane's attack was broken by Duchad Mór's armored infantry, but the Count fell from his horse when his cinch suddenly broke, and he was trampled to death in the melée. The Pretender's army was forced back into Rengarth, and a lengthy siege commenced. The Prince Imre believed that volunteers from Torenth would soon arrive to relieve him, and determined to hold out until then. Gwyneddan siege engines began battering the walls of Rengarth day and night, and an assault was conducted on the city on the XXIXth day of June, but failed, and again on the IInd day of July through a breach in the Southern wall.

Jasher King of Gwynedd was killed in the melée but the city was overrun, and Prince Imre committed suicide by throwing himself from the palace wall. His body was then taken to Valoret, where it was excommunicated, desecrated, disemboweled, and quartered, with pieces being sent for display throughout the kingdom. His head was placed on a pike at the same spot his grandfather's had been displayed some LXXX years before. Thus ended the life of Imre II sometime King of Eastmarch and Rengarth but never of Gwynedd. He was LVII years of age at his death, and was succeeded in his pretensions by his grandson, the Prince Imre III. [*The Bastard Prince*].

Imre III Festil Nimur *Furstán-Festil*, **called "The New Pretender," Titular King of Gwynedd, Duke of Tolán, Titular Duke of Eastmarch**. This nefarious prince was born on the IVth day of January in the Year of Our Lord 972, being the eldest son and heir of Marek-Imre Hereditary Prince of Gwynedd and the Countess Maryam daughter of Simon Count Tsérétéli. He intermarried with the Princess Torvalla daughter of Malachy II King of Torenth on the last day of May in the year 989, and by her he had children: the Hereditary Prince Mark later Marek II Titular King of Gwynedd; the Prince Adolphus later Titular Duke of Eastmarch by cession from his father, who was killed on the XXXth day of January in the year 1025, leaving a natural son, Giorgi Count Thannen, without dynastic rights; the Prince Konstantiné later Earl of Cardosa, who was killed in a duel in the year 1016, aged XXII years, *sans postérité légitime*, leaving a natural son, Sir Allás Naum, without dynastic rights; the Princess Agrafena, dead at age XI of paralysis; the Princess AriEmilia, dead at age V of the spotted pox; the Prince Pavel, dead of the slimy slough not long after his baptism.

The Prince Imre III was declared of age by his grandfather the Young Pretender and created Duke of Eastmarch on the Ist day of May in the year 985. He was sent to Beldour the next day to rally volunteers for the cause, and also to remove him from danger in case of disaster, but had only gathered some MMM men before he received the news in mid-July of his grandfather's death. He then proclaimed himself Imre III King of Gwynedd, but having no resources of his own, remained at Court in Beldour, cultivating the friendship of the young King Kyprian II. He was girded with spur and sword and couped with *colée* on New Year's Day in the year 986 by Patriarch Archelaos I. He sought to take advantage of the death of Cluim King of Gwynedd on the XVIIIth day of December in the year 994, and began assembling an army early in the following year in Western Torenth; but the severe heat and drought which affected the Eleven Kingdoms in June and July of the years 995 and 996 made such an expedition impossible, and the force was ultimately incorporated into the Torenthi army when the latter was forced to respond to a major barbarian incursion from the Norselands. King Kyprian II would provide no support to Prince Imre during the next III decades.

In the year 1024 the King Imre and King Kyprian resolved their differences, and agreed to join with Jolyon II Sovereign Prince of Meara in an attack on Gwynedd the following year. King Kyprian II ordered the assembly of the largest force of armed men ever seen in Torenth. To secure Kyprian's cooperation, Imre agreed to abdicate his rights on the XXXIst day of December in the year 1024 in favour of his son, the Prince and Duke Marek II. But the element of surprise had been lost, and the King of Gwynedd began gathering his own army near Valoret under the command of his son and heir, the Hereditary Prince Cinhil.

In the first weeks of May of the year 1025 the armies began to move. The soldiers of Torenth occupied Rengarth on the XXth day of that month, and Marek II was proclaimed rightful King of Gwynedd. The Festillic army of Tolán invaded Northern Eastmarch under Imre's command, and joined with King Kyprian's forces just West of Cardosa on the XIth day of June in that year.

The two enemies met on the XVth day of June at a crossing of the Falling Water River called Schillingford. After III days of stalemate, after the deaths of untold thousands of soldiers and noblemen, the Prince Imre and his family, yea, unto the IVth generation, all perished on the XVIIth day of June in the year 1025. The former Pretender was carried off to Hell at the age of LIII years, there to roast in flames for all eternity for the useless deaths of so many valiant men; and perishing with him were the Pretender Marek II, and Marek's son, the Hereditary Prince Festil. Prince Marek *Junior* was captured and executed a week later.

The remains of the Prince Imre and his sons and grandsons were returned to Beldour and buried in the family vault at Torenthály, save for that of Prince Marek *Junior*, whose body was ritually disemboweled and quartered, parts being sent to all the major cities of Gwynedd. The Princes Imre and Marek were succeeded in their pretensions by Imre's youngest sister, the Princess Imriella, after the eldest, the Princess Ariella II, had declined the honour. Prince Imre sported a grey beard, and was becoming somewhat forgetful in his final years. [*The Deryni Archives*].

Imre Ingwar Jöns *Furstán-Festil*, **Prince of Gwynedd, Earl of Rhemuth, Archbishop Primate of**

Valoret and All Gwynedd, sometime Bishop of Grecotha. He was born on the XIth day of October in the Year of Our Lord 805, being the third child and second son of Festil I King of Gwynedd and Marie Duchess of Phtheus. He was early destined for the Church, and was ordained priest on the XXIst day of September in the year 821 by the Torenthi Patriarch Kyrión I. He was created Prince of Gwynedd and Earl of Rhemuth by his father on the XIIth day of August in the year 822, but Father Imre gave all the revenues from his estates to the Church. He was elected Bishop of Grecotha on the XIth day of July in the year 823, and Archbishop Primate of Valoret and All Gwynedd on the XXIIIrd day of May in the year 834, and served capably in that capacity until his death from piles and the putrid bowel on the I[st] day of December in the year 839. He was said by Amador Guigues to have been enormously fat, but he had a kindly disposition and loved little children and animals. He was also renowned for his musical ability, displaying a fine baritone voice which he used to good effect during Sunday services. He was chiefly responsible during his short tenure for reforming choir practice in all the major cathedrals and religious orders, stating in an encyclical letter issued to his Bishops and Abbots just a few months before his death that "they should raise up their voices in song to the Lord." He was XXXIV years of age at his death, and was buried in the crypt of the Archbishops beneath All Saints' Cathedral at Valoret. He was succeeded as Archbishop by Mallenus Auxiliary Bishop of Beldour. R.I.P.

Imre Lajos Conant *Furstán-Festil*, Hereditary Prince of Gwynedd, Duke of Rhemuth. He was born on the XXXIst day of March in the Year of Our Lord 839, being the second son and heir of Festil III King of Gwynedd and the Lady Dionysia daughter of Andronikos Lord Thópis, Stratégos and Despot of Esclavonia. He intermarried with Marie-Juhèle Comtesse du Charpigny on the XXVIIth day of July in the year 859, and by her he had children: the Princess Nimurella, who intermarried with Alver III Damien Duc d'Alver; the Prince Andronic, dead at age VI of the sweating sickness; the Princess Yamina, who intermarried with Eudes Prince de Bremagne.

The Hereditary Prince Imre was created Duke of Rhemuth on the IIIrd day of May in the year 851. He abandoned his wife in the year 867, being besotted by the beauteous Antinoös "the God," whom he married in a ceremony contrary to the laws of God and man. A collector of obscure tomes on the magical arts, he was traveling to Grecotha to peruse a new manuscript when he was swept away and drowned in the River Slieven on the IVth day of April in the year 872. He was XXXIII years of age at his death, and was succeeded as Hereditary Prince by his brother, Prince Blaine. His body was returned for burial in the family crypt at Valoret. His widow intermarried in 875 with Alver II Mandavil Duc d'Alver, father of her daughter's husband, and following his death II years later, intermarried with Giorgios Duke of Naxos in the year 881.

Imre I Zsolt *Furstán*, King of Torenth. He was born on the VIIIth day of November in the Year of Our Lord 667, being the eldest son and heir of Aldred I King of Torenth and the Princess Bertradis daughter of Augarin King of Gwynedd. He intermarried with his first cousin the Princess Bethany widow of Barghash ibn Hassan al-Khideri, Nabil of Salah Reis, and daughter of Aidan King of Gwynedd on the XIVth day of April in the year 685, and by her he had children: the Hereditary Prince Aldred, murdered on the VIIth day of December in the year 722 by his cousin the King Radislaus, leaving issue; the Prince Zsolt later Count of Medras; the Princess Arkadia, who intermarried with Thaddæus Maksim Count von Dikt; the Princess Damura, who died a spinster at age LXXXIX; the Prince Festil later Count of Arkadia later King of Torenth; the Prince Kálmán later Count of Csölgasz, dead at age XIX of wounds received in a duel over a gambling debt; the Princess Goswina, who intermarried with Alram Count Goggish; the Prince Porphyry later Count of Truvorsk, who died unmarried and childless at the age of LXI; the Princess Raphaela, who intermarried with Ryons King of Gwynedd.

The Prince Imre succeeded his father King Aldred on the XXIInd day of October in the year 701, and was girded with the sword by Patriarch Antónios I on the New Year's Day following. He was a notorious miser who denied any luxuries to his wife and children, and continually raised the taxes on his nobles. Some historians have said that it was a conspiracy of the nobility with his I[st] cousin, the Prince Radislaus, that poisoned him at a banquet on the Vth day of December in the year 722, aged LV years; but others have attributed his demise to the poor quality of his food, for he always had his cooks buy the cheapest measures of everything; and still others say that the absence of heating in the great hall of the main palace contributed to the making of a minor cough into a major fitte. In any event, the Prince Radislaus immediately proclaimed himself King and killed the Hereditary Prince Aldred II days later; the rest of Imre's sons were exiled for life. The King Imre I was buried in the vault of his ancestors at Torenthály. R.I.P.

Imre II Tamás *Furstán*, King of Torenth, Blessed. He was born on the XVIIIth day of July in the Year of Our Lord 842, being the eldest son and heir of Malachy I King of Torenth and the Princess Fabiana daughter of Hennequin King of Fallon. He intermarried with the Grand Princess Kónstantia daughter of Tiberios the Grand Prince of Byzantyun on the XVIIIth day of July (his natal day) in the year 865, and by her he had children: the Hereditary Prince Nimur later Nimur I King of Torenth; the Princess Imriette, who intermarried with Basileios IV Autokratór of Byzantyun; the Prince Pál later Duke of Arkadia who, having renounced his ducal title and his rights to the throne of Torenth, intermarried with Camille Heiress du Joux and succeeded as Paulard Sovereign Duc du Joux; the Princess Rurikana, who intermarried with Uriel Hort of Orsal and Prince of Tralia; the Princess Petra, who intermarried with Darylle Comte Frôme du Malette in Joux; the Prince Dmitri later Duke Kálmányi and Arkadia, who, having renounced his ducal titles and his rights to the throne of Torenth, intermarried with the Lady Auxentiana daughter of Aimilianidés Sebastrokratór of Tagros, and later succeeded his father-in-law as Démétrios II Sovereign

Sebastrokratór of Tagros. The Queen Kónstantia having died on the XVIth day of March in the year 880, the King intermarried secondly with Chantal de Meulent widow of Gaspar Gorodnik on the XVth day of April in the year 881, and by her he had further children, without dynastic rights: the Lady Barbaranna, who intermarried with Hugues Comte du Bault in Joux; the Lord Émilien later Baron Lavéene in Vézaire.

The Prince Imre succeeded his father on the IInd day of November in the year 877, and was girded with the sword on New Year's Day in the year 878 by Patriarch Theodóritos I. A profoundly religious man, he financed the construction of an addition to the Cathedral of Saint Constantine and an adjoining convent to honour his first wife's memory on the IIIrd day of May in the year 880, and completed it III years later, the structure being reconsecrated on the XIIth day of October in the year 883. His hundreds of melodious hymns and chants were collected into the book, *Songs unto God*, which appeared a year after his death, and he also wrote a major philosophical treatise, *De Caritate Dei*, and a philosophical guide to the art and science of government, *Rex Justus*. The good King Imre II passed from this earth on the Vth day of December in the year 891, aged XLIX years, much mourned by his family and his subjects, and was buried with his ancestors at Torenthály. He was succeeded by his eldest son, Prince Nimur. King Imre was beatified by the Patriarch Andreas I on the VIIth day of May in the year 945. R.I.P. *Duos qui sequitur lepores, neutrum capit.*

Imriella Elizabeth *Furstána-Festila*, **Titular Queen of Gwynedd, Duchess of Tolán**. She was born on the XXVth day of July in the Year of Our Lord 975, being the third child of Mark-Imre Hereditary Prince of Gwynedd and the Countess Maryam daughter of Simon Count Tsérétéli. At the death of her brother Prince Imre III and his son, Prince Marek II, on the XVIIth day of June in the year 1025, her elder sister, Princess Ariella II, renounced her rights on the VIIIth day of July in that year, and the Princess Imriella then succeeded to the Duchy of Tolán and the titular throne of Gwynedd. She was not installed at Saint Constantine's, the Patriarch Timotheos II having refused to countenance a woman receiving the accolades of a Christian knight. On the XXVth day of December in the year 1026, she intermarried with Swithven Count of Langendoss, but had no children by him.

Lech Bötha ascribes to her a natural son, Marek-Emar, born to her in her XVIth year and taken from her by her brother to be raised in a monastery under some other name, and this bastard supposedly became a mercenary in the Forcinn and later took service with the King of Bremagne; but he is unmentioned in any other source, and Berrhones discounts his existence altogether. A passing reference in Princess Arien's chronicle mentions Imriella's love of cats and music, and says that "...she became a curiosity in my Brother's court, a delightful old lady with a cherubic face who loved children and would tell them by the hour such marvelously evocative stories of the history of her family, but who reacted violently to any mention of the word 'Haldane.' Towards the end of her life she was visited on her estate in Tolán by a handsome young courtier from the South, and was seen weeping shortly after he left. She passed on only a few months later."

The Princess Imriella died of paralysis on the XIVth day of February in the year 1038, aged LXII years, and was buried near her home at Tolán, specifically declining to be buried with her cousins at Torenthály. The Princess Imriella was succeeded in her pretensions by her *cousine germaine*, the Princess Elinora, although some old loyalists to the family still regarded Imriella's elder sister, the Princess Ariella II as the rightful heir, despite her renunciation. Ariella, who refused to visit her sister during the last years of her life, when she pretended to be the Queen of Gwynedd, made a secret pilgrimage to her gravesite a year after she died, and planted a yew bush there, saying that "it would stay green forever with its scarlet berries, and remind the passers-by of the *joie de vivre* that my sister once had." When the Princess Ariella II herself died some VII years later in Trebaçeaux, on the IXth day of December in the year 1045, aged LXXIV years, the elder branch of the House of Furstán-Festil became extinct. R.I.P.

Inn of the Seven Friars. This hostelry was located in Grecotha. Geordie Lord Drummond stayed here in April of the year 905 while on his way to Stavenham. [*Deryni Challenge*].

Interdict. This official Church sanction against a state or region prohibits the celebration of the sacraments or the holy mass in that country. It is intended to force a ruler or politician or people to change his or their immoral conduct to conform with official Church teachings. An interdict was levied against the Duchy of Corwyn on the XXth day of March in the year 1121 and later against the entire Kingdom of Gwynedd, but was soon lifted when the King's Party overthrew the Archbishops Edmund Loris and Patrick Corrigan on the XXVIth day of June in that year. [*Deryni Checkmate*; *High Deryni*].

Interdict Schism. This rift in the Gwyneddan Church took place in the year 1121, having been precipitated by the interdict promulgated against the Duchy of Corwyn on the XXth day of March in that year, and the excommunication levied against Alaric Morgan Duke of Corwyn and Father Duncan McLain Earl of Kierney at the Council of Dhassa shortly thereafter. Two factions emerged from the split: the so-called "Archbishops' Party," which extended the interdict to the entire Kingdom of Gwynedd, supported the Archbishops Edmund Loris and Patrick Corrigan in their efforts to reinstate civil and religious sanctions against all Deryni; and the so-called "King's Party," which followed Bishops Thomas Cardiel and Denis Arilan and professed tolerance for humans and Deryni alike. When King Kelson and his supporters prevailed on the XXVIth day of June in that year, the Archbishops and their supporters were deposed, and Bishop Thomas Cardiel and his followers promoted. The schism re-emerged when the former Archbishop Loris was freed from his imprisonment at Saint Iveagh's on the XXIXth day of November in the year 1123 and proclaimed himself autocephalous Primate of Meara, but after the latter's execution on the XIIth day of July in the year 1124, the rebellion collapsed and the breach in the Church was finally healed. [*Deryni Checkmate*; *High Deryni*; *The Bishop's Heir*; *The King's Justice*].

Interregnum. In theory, any period of non-rule occurring between the reigns of II monarchs or II church primates; in Gwynedd, the term specifically refers to the rule of the V Festillic Kings between the years 822 and 904. [*High Deryni*].

Iomaire. Located on the great Plain of Iomaire, this small Barony was once an appendage of the noble House of Howell, having been granted by King Malcolm on the XIXth day of November in the year 1025 to Lord Kennet Howell IInd son of Colwyn Howell Earl of Eastmarch. His great-grandson, Arban Howell Baron of Iomaire, surprised and routed the forces of his traitor cousin, Rorik III Earl of Eastmarch, on the XIIIth day of June in the year 1105, capturing the Earl and killing his heir. Arban was then named Earl of Eastmarch by King Brion on the XXth day instant. At the death of his only son, Ian Howell Earl of Eastmarch, in the year 1120, the latter was attainted and the Earldom given to Ian's brother-in-law, Burchard de Varian, but Sir Colson Howell, a grandson of Lord Kennet's IInd son, Sir Colman Howell, was allowed by King Kelson to inherit the Barony of Iomaire. ["Swords Against the Marluk"].

BARONS OF IOMAIRE

HOUSE OF HOWELL

Kennet	1025-1032
Jonas (son)	1032-1059
Rory (son)	1059-1084
Arban (son)	1084-1115
Ian (son)	1115-1120
Colson (2nd cousin)	1120-1127
Colman (son)	1127-1130+

Iomaire, Plain of. This vast pastureland stretches from the Northernmost slopes of the Lendour Mountains into the borders of Eastmarch and Gwynedd to the West of the Rheljan Mountains. It was here on the XXVth day of June in the year 905 that the Pretender Ariella was defeated and killed by the forces of Cinhil I King of Gwynedd. A shrine was later erected marking the place where Camber MacRorie Earl of Culdi supposedly fell in battle. The forces of Rhys Michael King of Gwynedd passed through here in June of the year 928. [*Saint Camber*; *The Bastard Prince*; *The Quest for Saint Camber*].

Iosif. He was serving as a guard at Rhemuth Castle during June of the year 928. His mind and body were used repeatedly by the Deryni double agent, Dimitri, to transmit messages to Dimitri's master, Prince Miklós. In return Dimitri gave him powerful erotic dreams. He was large, full-featured, and powerfully built, with a mop of curly, black hair. [*The Bastard Prince*].

Irenæus or Eirénaios, secular name Anphim *von Kotlas*, Father, later Titular Bishop of Rensk. He was born in Jándrich on the IVth day of September in the Year of Our Lord 1082, being the third son of Boyan Lord Kotlas and Andya Lady Tsiolkova. He joined the Order of Saint Kosmas in the year 1100, and was ordained priest on the Xth day of August in the year 1102 at the Monastery of Saint Trifon. He later studied at the *Megalé tou Genous Scholé* in Beldour. This Torenthi hieromonk and priest was attached to King Liam Lajos II during his later years in Rhemuth, to provide the young monarch with spiritual instruction in the Orthodox religion. He accompanied his King back to Beldour in the year 1128, and there helped prepare him for the *killijálay* ceremony in July of that year. He also assisted King Kelson to prepare for his part in the installation on the XIIIth day of July. He became a friend and close adviser to the new King. As a reward for his services, he was created Titular Bishop of Rensk on the XVIth day of May in the year 1129. He was tall and dark-eyed, with a florid complexion and grey streaking his dark hair and beard. [*King Kelson's Bride*].

Isarn II Anaclète Jehan Flocon *d'Avoine*, Sovereign Prince of Logréine. He was born on the IInd day of October in the Year of Our Lord 1080, being the second son of Isarn I Prince of Logréine and the Lady Jordana daughter of Tiraquell Sieur de Jordanet and Countess Murielle du Joux, who was the youngest daughter of Régnier I Sovereign Duc du Joux. He intermarried with the Princess Élée daughter of Dragonet Sovereign Prince of Jáca and the Princess Perpenna daughter of Bagrat Sovereign Prince of Autun, on the XVth day of November in the year 1107, and by her he had children: the Princess Lérida, who intermarried with the Prince Centule second son of Centule V Grand Duc du Vézaire; the Hereditary Prince Pépin; the Prince Mâcon; the Princess Hesceline; the Princess Pylade; the Prince Orcival; the Prince Parthène.

The Prince Isarn succeeded his father on the IIIrd day of December in the year 1109, his elder brother Prince Grigor having perished before him *sans postérité légitime*. In the year 1128 he attended the installation of Liam Lajos II as King of Torenth, being officially welcomed at a *fête* held on the IXth day of July in that year in the Hanging Gardens of Furstánály Palace. *Fortier est qui se, quam qui fortissima mœna vincit.* [*King Kelson's Bride*].

Ithel Jolyon Ælfred Berenger *MacArdry Quinnell*, Hereditary Prince of Meara, Sir. He was born on the IInd day of December in the Year of Our Lord 1107, being the eldest son and heir of Caitrin Princess and Pretender of Meara and Sicard Lord MacArdry son of Arthur Earl of Transha. With the death of Jared McLain Duke of Cassan on the Ist day of July in the year 1121 and the succession of his son Father Duncan Earl of Kierney to the title, the Prince Ithel became heir presumptive to the Earldom of Kierney, although that claim (and others) have been disputed by Lady Davisba La Crèce in her classic tome, *L'Étude des Droits Réservés de la Maison des Mac-Laines*. The Pretender Caitrin intended that Prince Ithel should succeed to the Earldom when she had killed the incumbent, and also contemplated awarding him the Duchy of Cassan under an ancient treaty of mutual succession between the two main branches of the House of Quinnell.

The Prince Ithel was knighted by his father on the IInd day of November in the year 1123, when his mother began plotting against Kelson King of Gwynedd to make Meara an independent principality. He was said to be scheming for the death of his mother in November of that year, but this statement by the Earl of Transha may have been mere rumour. The Prince Ithel participated in the rape and pillage of the nuns at Saint Brigid's on the XVth day of June in the year 1124. Two weeks later on the IInd day of July in that year, he was captured at Talacara near Ratharkin in Meara, and promptly tried and condemned by King Kelson for his crimes. He was hanged by the neck until dead from the nearest tree; his body was later returned for burial in the family crypt of the Quinnells at Laas. He was XVI years of age at his death. [*The Bishop's Heir*; *King Kelson's Bride*].

Iveagh, Saint. This martyr of IVth-century Howicce was converted to Christianity at the age of XXVII. He proselytized unceasingly on behalf of his new faith and would not be silenced. Finally, the local pagan ruler, Rinkon Count Oughtagh, ordered Iveagh arrested and his tongue torn out, and then released him back on the streets, saying, "Finally we will have one good night of sleep." But *mirabile dictu!*, on the morrow there was Holy Iveagh preaching once again on the streets of Oughtagh, and he would not be silenced. Whereupon the Count Rinkon ordered him killed, saying, "We must have peace." On the next day, when the Count awoke from his sleep, God had made him dumb, so that thereafter he could only make signs with his hands.

Saint Iveagh's sterling example inspired the founding on the XXIXth day of February in the year 900 of an order of contemplative monks called the *Fratres Silentii* (that is, the Brothers of Silence), whose Mother House is located on the coast of Southern Kheldour. His feastday is the XXIXth day of February, at which time, it is said, his relick'd tongue speaks out once every IV years to give testimony to his unswerving faith. [*The Bishop's Heir*].

Iver *MacInnis*, Earl of Culdi, Baron Marlor, Earl of Kierney *jure uxoris*, Sir. He was born on the XXIst day of January in the Year of Our Lord 896, being the eldest son and heir of Manfred Baron Marlor later Earl of Culdi and Estellan Lady Buckleigh. He intermarried with Richeldis Lady MacLean and Heiress of Kierney on the Vth day of March in the year 918, and by her he had children: the Lady Janeltis later Baroness Marlor in her own right, who intermarried with Hrorik Ewan Hereditary Duke of Claibourne and Earl of Rhendall; the Hereditary Count Hobard later Earl of Kierney; the Lady Grania later Countess of Culdi in her own right, who intermarried with Uthyr King of Gwynedd.

Lord Iver traveled with his father from Culdi to Valoret in the year 918, arriving in time to attend the official state wedding on the Xth day of January in that year, and was introduced there to his future wife. He became Earl of Kierney *jure uxoris* on the death of Iain II Earl of Kierney on the XIXth day of March in the year 918. He was present at the death of King Alroy on the XXIIIrd day of June in the year 921. In the intervening years he spent much of his time managing his estates in Kierney. In the year 928 he brought his L lancers to join the King's Expedition to Eastmarch, meeting them at Ebor on the XIXth day of June in that year. He succeeded his father as Earl on the Vth day of July following. He died in the year 948, aged LII years, and was succeeded by his son, Count Hobard. In his youth he had a pimply face, and was not much liked at Court. [*The Harrowing of Gwynedd*; *King Javan's Year*; *The Bastard Prince*].

Ivo *Hepburn*. He was born on the IInd day of February in the year 1113, being the son of Sir Lalo Hepburn and Catherine Tweed. He was serving as a junior squire to Kelson King of Gwynedd in March of the year 1125. He briefly served in the same capacity for Prince Regent Conall during the latter's usurpation of the throne in April of the year 1125. He was still serving as a squire in the year 1128. He had dark curly hair. [*The Quest for Saint Camber*; *King Kelson's Bride*].

Ivo, Lord Lovat. He was born on the XXIInd day of August in the year 888, being the youngest son of Frizell Baron Lovat and Germaine Lady Fezenze. This Deryni Lord attempted to assassinate the Princes Javan and Rhys Michael on the XXVIIIth day of September in the year 917. He was captured, tried, and executed by the Regents on the same day, aged XXIX years. [*Camber the Heretic*].

Jáca. This small sovereign principality lies between the Kingdom of Fallon to the North and West and the Anvil of the Lord to the South, with Andelon situate just to the Northeast. Originally part of the Kingdom of Fallon, Jáca declared its independence on the Ist day of May in the year 901 under Arsieu Comte de Mont-Volcan, incorporating the Counties of Jacance and Mont-Volcan and the Barony of Pixière. Except for a brief period between the years 931 and 933, when Fallon was able to re-establish control, Jáca has maintained its autonomy ever since.

Located on a high plateau and surrounded on III sides by the Autuni and the Andel Mountains, Jáca has a pleasant summer climate, but is frequently isolated by winter snows during the months of December through March. The country lies on the main trade route between Alcara in the Anvil of the Lord and Fallon and Andelon. The Holy Saint Sava is said to have derived from this region, and a shrine in his honour is located at the capital town of Jachère. [*King Kelson's Bride*].

PRINCES OF JÁCA

HOUSE OF MONT-VOLCAN

Arsieu I	901-929
Huart (son)	929-931
INTERREGNUM	
Dévot (brother)	933-944
Rotrou I (brother)	944-959
Randon (nephew)	959-988
Gédéon (son)	988-990
Arsieu II (brother)	990-1022
Onan (son)	1022-1048
Yves (son)	1048-1077
Ebles (son)	1077

Dragonet (grandson)	1077-1129
Rotrou II (son)	1129-1130+

Jack Dog Tavern. This was Sean Earl Derry's favourite drinking spot in the Torenthi port of Fathane, which he frequented while spying on the Torenthi army on the XXIVth day of March in the year 1121. [*Deryni Checkmate*].

Jaffray *of Carbury*, Archbishop Primate of Valoret and All Gwynedd. This Deryni cleric was born at Carbury on the XVIth day of October in the Year of Our Lord 861, being the son of Francis the Jarman. He joined the Gabrilite Order at the age of XIV years, and was ordained priest on the XIIth day of June in the year 879. He was elected an itinerant Bishop of Gwynedd on the XXXth day of March in the year 902, and preached primarily in the Purple March, not far from his home in Carbury. He was chosen by Archbishop Anscom to succeed him, and the selection was ratified by the King and the Council of Bishops on the VIIth day of September in the year 906, which was also the date he was enthroned.

The Archbishop Jaffray called his first consistory on the XXIIIrd day of October in that year. He became a member of the Camberian Council on the XXIst day of December in the year 910. He presided over the coronation of King Alroy at All Saints' Cathedral in Valoret on the XXVth day of May in the year 917. He was present at the trial of the Deryni assassins on the XXVIIIth day of September following. He was killed on the XVth day of October in that same year while leading his ecclesiastical knights to put down an anti-Deryni riot by the townspeople in Valoret. He was aged LV years at his death, and was buried with high honours on the I[st] day of November following at All Saints' Cathedral, with Bishop Alister Cullen presiding. He was well known as a compromiser and conciliator. R.I.P. *Rien ne trouble sa fin: c'est le soir d'un beau jour.* [*Saint Camber*; *Camber the Heretic*; *The Harrowing of Gwynedd*].

James. He was serving as one of Warin de Grey's sergeants in June of the year 1121. [*High Deryni*].

James, Brother. This monk was serving as a copy clerk in Archbishop Patrick Corrigan's chancery office during March of the year 1121. At the behest of Father Hugh de Berry he copied the interdict letter from the Archbishops to Father Duncan McLain. [*Deryni Checkmate*].

James *Drummond* (I), Lord. He was born on the IXth day of August in the Year of Our Lord 818, being the second son and third child of David Lord Drummond and Anna Lady Cappell, and the uncle of Camber MacRorie Earl of Culdi. He intermarried with Afreca Lady MacCathal on the Vth day of June in the year 841, and by her he had children: the Lord Henry; the Lady Aasa; the Lady Margretha; the Lady Adele; the Lady Moira; the Lord Geoffrey; the Lord Harald. He died on the IVth day of January in the year 876, aged LVII years. R.I.P. [*Deryni Challenge*].

James *Drummond* (II), Lord. He was born on the XIIIth day of December in the Year of Our Lord 866, being the second son of Henry Lord Drummond and Amalia Lady MacNiall. He died on the XXIst day of August in the year 875 when he was thrown from a horse, aged VIII years. R.I.P.

James "Jamie" *Drummond* (III), Lord. He was born on the VIIIth day of May in the Year of Our Lord 876, being the youngest son of Henry Lord Drummond and Amalia Lady MacNiall. He was christened in honour of his older brother of the same name. He intermarried with Elinor Lady Howell widow of Cathan MacRorie Hereditary Count of Culdi on the XVIIth day of July in the year 906, and by her he had children: the Lady Michaela, who intermarried with Rhys Michael King of Gwynedd; the Lord Cathan Cinhil called "Cathal," who intermarried with Jerusha Lady Thuryn.

He was staying with Camber Earl of Culdi at Tor Caerrorie in September of the year 903. In November of that year he was present at Court in Valoret. On the I[st] day of December in the year 904 he led one of the contingents of Michaeline soldiers which assaulted the city of Valoret. As commander of the Drummond levies, he participated in the War Council held on the XXIIIrd day of June in the year 905 at the Great Hall in Valoret Palace. After the death of his cousin, Geoffrey Lord MacLean, on the XXIst day of November in the year 911, Lord James Drummond was made guardian of Geoffrey's II surviving daughters, Lady Richeldis and Lady Giesele.

He returned to Court on the VIth day of January in the year 918, and his powers were blocked on the XXIst day of that month by Tavis. On the next day he was closely questioned by the Regents about the Deryni incursion into the Palace and the murder of Giesele Lady MacLean. He gave the Lady Richeldis away at her marriage to Iver Lord MacInnis on the Vth day of March in that year. He was supposedly killed by highway robbers while on a mission for the Regents on the XXIIIrd day of October in the year 918, aged XLII years, but many suspected that the Regents themselves had arranged for his most convenient murder. R.I.P. [*Camber of Culdi*; *Deryni Challenge*; *Saint Camber*; *The Harrowing of Gwynedd*; *King Javan's Year*].

James *MacKenzie*, Bishop of Cashien. He was born on the XIIth day of January in the year 1088, being the son of Sir Horatio MacKenzie and Dashielle Lady Horne. He was ordained priest on the Vth day of August in the year 1106, and became a well-known scholar at the University of Grecotha. He was elected an itinerant Bishop of Gwynedd on the XIXth day of January in the year 1122, and was elevated to the see of Cashien on the XVIIIth day of March in the year 1125. [*The Quest for Saint Camber*].

James, Master. He was serving as a physician to the Court of Gwynedd during August of the year 921. On the I[st] day of July in the year 928 he prepared a sleeping draught for Queen Michaela after she was informed of her husband's death. [*The Bastard Prince*; *King Javan's Year*].

James *the Blacksmith*. He was working as a smithy at Castle Coroth in the Duchy of Corwyn during March of the year 1121. [*Deryni Checkmate*].

Jamyl Sextus *Arilan*, Laird of Tre-Arilan, Sir. This most noble Deryni Lord was born on the XXVIIth day of February in the Year of Our Lord 1079, being the eldest son and heir of Sir Michael Sextus Arilan and Stephania Lady Jeffries, and the brother of Bishop Denis Arilan. He intermarried with Alix Baronne de Haut-Léon on the XVIIth day of May in the year 1102, and by her he had children: the Hereditary Laird Seisyll; the Lady Javana; the Lady Jashana; the Lord Sextus. Secretly trained as a Deryni master by Michon Baron de Courcy, he served as a member of the Camberian Council from the year 1100 until his death. He came to court and was knighted by Duke Richard Haldane in the year 1097, and was quickly recognized for his political acumen by the young Brion King of Gwynedd, soon becoming his friend and confidant. He succeeded his father as Laird of Tre-Arilan on the IIIrd day of August in the year 1103, and was appointed to the Royal Council on the Xth day of December in that year.

In August of the year 1104, at a time when his younger brother Denis Arilan was a seminarian at the *Arx Fidei* Abbey East of Valoret, Sir Jamyl became involved in an attempt to thwart the efforts of Archbishop Oliver de Nore to uncover and burn all Deryni applicants for the priesthood. Although his own efforts in this regard were unsuccessful, his brother was ordained without discovery, a ceremony Sir Jamyl witnessed on the IInd day of February in the year 1105. He participated in the lightning strike on Meara conducted by Brion King of Gwynedd on the I[st] day of December in the year 1106, and was seriously wounded in a skirmish with Mearan rebels II days later. He died of his lingering injuries on the IInd day of February in the year 1107, aged XXVII years, and was succeeded by his young son, the Laird Seisyll.

The family estate, Tre-Arilan, was located near Rhemuth; a transfer portal was situated in the ritual chamber at the end of a secret passageway opening beside the fireplace there. According to the *Chronicles*, Sir Jamyl had deep blue-violet eyes. Οψει δε με περι Φιλίππους. R.I.P. ["The Priesting of Arilan"; *King Kelson's Bride*].

Jándrich. This great duchy of Torenth is situate in the Northeastern part of that Kingdom, being bordered on the North by the Northern Sea and Eistenmarcke, on the West by Tolán and Tigre, on the South by Nördmarcke, and on the East by Czalsky. Once an independent Principality, Jándrich was partially conquered by Aldred I the Great King of Torenth on the XXIXth day of July in the year 698, the Kniaz' Ulick falling on his sword in despair. Later holders of the title paid tribute to the Kings of Torenth, until King Arion I married Pavela Heiress of Jándrich in the year 917. At her father's death on the VIIth day of March in the year 929, the Principality became part of Torenth, and the title was then given to Arion's IIIrd son, the Prince Sigard Count of Göttsland. The chief city and capital of Jándrich is Netterhaven, a thriving trading port on the Northern Sea, which was destroyed by the invasion of the Norsemen in the year 997, but was rebuilt by the successive efforts of Duke Ygor II, Duke Ladislav II, and King Arkady II between 1015-1035. The Zaydar Steppe, a great treeless plain covered with coarse grass and gorse, occupies the Northern half of Jándrich, while the Southern section is known for its fine apple orchards and dairy farms. The fruit is widely exported in whole and dried form to the other parts of the XI Kingdoms. [*King Kelson's Bride*].

SOVEREIGN PRINCES OF JANDRICH

HOUSE OF MIRAKSOVICH

Abdon Miraksovich	577-593
Kallimakh (grandson)	593-626
Romil (son)	626-655
Dimas (nephew)	655-667
Miloslav (son)	667-690
Ulick (son)	690-698
Filetep (brother)	698-711
Maksian (brother)	711-713
Ippolit (cousin)	713-714
Maksian (2nd time)	714
Vilen (usurper)	714-715
Maksian (3rd time)	715
Vilen (2nd time)	715-717
Tverdislav (son of Ulick)	717-719
Maksian (4th time)	719-720
Satornil (son of Ippolit)	720-744
Natan (son)	744-779
Miraks (son)	779-802
Ladislav I (brother)	802-804
Gremislav (son)	804-850
Briachislav (son)	850-861
Valerian (nephew)	861-897
Ygor I (son)	897-929

DUKES OF JÁNDRICH

HOUSE OF FURSTÁN-JÁNDRICH

Sigard I (son of Arion I of Torenth)	929-992
Nimur (son)	992-1011
Ygor II (son)	1011-1025
Ladislav II (brother)	1025-1044
Sigard II (son)	1044-1075
Passarion (nephew)	1075-1099
Sigard III (son)	1099-1114
Erdödy (cousin)	1114-1130+

Janniver Jorice *MacClung*, Princess of Pardiac. She was born on the XXIInd day of December in the year 1104, being the only surviving daughter of Pons Sovereign Prince of Pardiac in The Connait and Perronelle Countess Douars. She intermarried with Sir Jatham Kilshane later Baron Kilshane on the XXVIIIth day of June in the year 1128, and by him she had a child: the Hereditary Lord Aldus.

She had previously been betrothed on the IVth day of April in the year 1124 to Colman II King of the United Kingdoms of Howicce and Llannedd, but never actually married him. After she was violated by Ithel Hereditary Prince of Meara on the XVth day of June in the year 1124 during his pillage of Saint Brigid's Abbey, where she was staying briefly while on route to

Llannedd, she was disavowed by her intended groom. She was then escorted to the safety of Rhemuth in Gwynedd by Prince Conall II days later, but, her virginity having been stolen by the loathsome Prince Ithel, she was later rejected by both her betrothed and her father. King Kelson gave her permanent sanctuary at his Court that same year. She was a devoted friend and confidante to Rothana Princess Regent of Gwynedd.

She was described in *Bride* as wearing a wedding gown of silver samite; "a rose wreath crowned her mane of golden curls." [*The King's Justice*; *The Quest for Saint Camber*; *King Kelson's Bride*].

János *Sokrat*, Tanár. He was born on the XXIInd day of August in the Year of Our Lord 1064, being the son of Tanár Bulcsú Sokrat and Tünde Lady Virsli. This Torenthi adviser to King Liam Lajos II assisted in the training of King Kelson for the *killijálay* ceremony, on the XIIIth day of July in the year 1128. On the XXVIIth day of that month, Mátyás Duke d'Arjenol ordered him together with Amaury Hereditary Count Kulnán to help ward all known portals in Beldour and Torenthály against the possible intrusion of Count Teymuraz. Sokrat was blinded in his old age by the eyescales, and had to used a young boy to help guide his feet. [*King Kelson's Bride*].

Jared Douglas *McLain*, Duke of Cassan, Earl of Kierney, Lord of Leanshire. He was born on the XVth day of September in the Year of Our Lord 1064, being the eldest surviving son and heir of Andrew McLain Duke of Cassan and Jesma Lady McLain daughter of Aneas Lord McLain. He intermarried firstly with Elaine Lady MacInnis on the XXXth day of June in the year 1087, and by her he had one son: the Lord Kevin Douglas later Earl of Kierney, who died before his father, *sans postérité*. The Earl Jared's first wife having died of the effects of childbirth on the XXVth day of May in the year 1088, he intermarried secondly to Vera Lady Howard on the IXth day of May in the year 1090, and by her he had children: the Lord Duncan Howard later Earl of Kierney later Duke of Cassan later Auxiliary Bishop of Rhemuth; the Lady Isabet Anna, born still; the Lady Alicia Jesma Isabet, dead at age III of the roseola. After his second wife's death of the wasting wheezes on the XXXIst day of January in the year 1115, the Duke Jared intermarried thirdly with Margaret Neuve widow of Raymond Sinclair on the XXVIth day of September in the year 1116, but had no children by her.

The Earl Jared succeeded his father as Duke of Cassan on the I[st] day of August in the year 1099, and served in the Mearan campaign of Brion King of Gwynedd in the year 1106. He later commanded part of the army of King Kelson in Eastmarch in the year 1121, where he was betrayed by Bran Coris Earl of Marley at Rengarth and captured by Wencit King of Torenth on the XXVIIIth day of June. This noble Duke was executed at Llyndruth Meadows on the I[st] day of July in that year, aged LVI years, and was succeeded by his only surviving son, Father Duncan. He was ever a friend to the House of Haldane. His arms were: *argent*, three roses *gules*; on a chief *azure* a lion dormant *argent*. *Je plie, et ne romps pas*. R.I.P. [*Deryni Rising*; *Deryni Checkmate*; *High Deryni*; *The Bishop's Heir*; *The King's Justice*].

Jarlath, Abbot and Bishop, Saint. This VIth-century Bishop of Meara was a somewhat timid disciple of Jesus Christ until the day he was struck by lightning. When he came to his senses, still smoking from God's touch and reeling from the vision he had received, he actively began preaching the Word, telling one and all that they must follow his example. To promote his teachings he founded the *Ordo Verbi Dei* (*The Order of the Word of God*) in the year 564, serving as the first Abbot of this dedicated group. The Mother House of the Order, which is dedicated to his name, is located at Barwicke II hours' ride Northeast of Saint Liam's Abbey on the upper reaches of the River Eirian, at the Southwestern edge of the Plain of Iomaire. His feast-day is the VIth day of June, the date of his death in the year 588. *Orandum est ut sit mens sana in corpore sano*. [*Camber of Culdi*; *The Bastard Prince*].

Jarmuth *Rhydon*. This Deryni Healer masqueraded as a common glazier while serving as a companion to Geordie Lord Drummond in April of the year 905. He had a high-pitched, reedy voice. [*Deryni Challenge*].

Jashan Jestyn Dolon *Haldane*, Hereditary Prince of Gwynedd, Earl of Valoret. He was born on the XIIth day of October in the Year of Our Lord 807, being the eldest son and heir of Ifor King of Gwynedd and Nuala Lady Udaut. He attained his majority in the Fall of the year 821, when he was made Earl of Valoret, but was murdered VIII months later with his family by the soldiers of King Festil I on the XXIst day of June in the year 822. He was aged XIV years at his death, and was later buried with his family in the crypt beneath All Saint's Cathedral in Valoret. *Permitte Deo cætera*. R.I.P. [*Camber of Culdi*].

Jashan Nygel Ifor Eadwig *Haldane*, Prince of Gwynedd, Duke of Carthmoor, Earl of Culdi, High Chancellor of Gwynedd, sometime Bishop of Grecotha, sometime Archbishop of Rhemuth, Archbishop Primate of Valoret and All Gwynedd. He was born on the Xth day of July in the Year of Our Lord 978, being the second son of Cluim King of Gwynedd and Swynbeth Lady Fitz-Arthur Quinnell. He was created Duke of Carthmoor at birth by his uncle, the King Nygel, and succeeded his uncle, the King Jasher, as Earl of Culdi on the IInd day of July in the year 985, in accordance with the latter's last will and testament. He was intended for the clergy from an early age, and was ordained priest on the IVth day of August in the year 998 by Gilrae d'Eirial Archbishop of Rhemuth, who blessed the boy with a benediction that repeated the words of Jesus Christ our Saviour: "Come, follow me," an admonition later widely interpreted as a prophecy that Lord Jashan would one day occupy his seat. He was elected Bishop of Grecotha on the VIIth day of March in the year 1019, Archbishop of Rhemuth on the XVth day of April in the year 1034, and Archbishop Primate of Valoret and All Gwynedd on the XXXth day of October in the year 1044.

In the year 1025 he helped organize the defenses of Grecotha against a possible attack by Jolyon II Prince of Meara, who was invading from the West, and accompanied the Prince Cinhil's army to Killingford in June of that year. Following the great slaughter there, he ministered to the fallen soldiers on the battlefield, giving many of them the last rites, and helped to organize the care of the wounded. He became an adviser both to King Cinhil II and his brother King Malcolm when they succeeded to the throne after King Urien's death at Killingford. He was appointed Lord High Chancellor of Gwynedd by King Malcolm on the Ist day of July in the year 1025, and was instrumental in guiding Gwynedd in its recovery from the great war. Later that year he established a charity, the Fellowship of King Jasher (*Societas Jasheris Regis*), dedicated to supporting the widows and the orphaned children of the deceased soldiers, and was joined in this effort by many scions of the great houses of Gwynedd.

Following his election as Archbishop of Valoret, he ordered a systematic codification and reorganization of the canon law of Gwynedd, and sought to overturn some of the more reprehensible elements of the remaining Statutes of Ramos, although with little success. The revenues from his estates at Carthmoor and Culdi were dedicated completely to aiding the poor of Gwynedd. According to Bellay, he was a passionate *dévot* of *cardounet*, organizing several matches between well-known players and offering small prizes to the winners. His greatest earthly honour, he said, was finally to beat the grandmaster Rohan Soubize in a game of *cardounet* after losing XVII straight matches to him. After a lifetime of service to Church and State, this noble Primate died on the IInd day of September in the year 1055, aged LXXVII years, and was buried with high honours in the Crypt of the Archbishops beneath All Saints' Cathedral. He was much mourned by King and country alike. R.I.P.

Jashan, Lake. This long narrow lake, the largest and deepest in all Gwynedd, lies in the Lendour Mountains Southeast of Valoret. At the Northwest end of the lake is the Holy City of Dhassa, and at its Southwest end is situate the shrine of Saint Torin's, which guards the Southern approaches to the city. The lake is only passable by ferry boat after travelers have honoured the Saint's name at the shrine. The River Lendour has its headwaters here, issuing from the South end of the Lake.

An old legend maintains that a great green serpent inhabits the cold, murky depths of Lake Jashan, but nonesuch has ever been captured, although many claim to have seen it. According to Campbell de Broun, who once stopped at the Lake to test his angling skills, "All I ever caught on Lake Jashan was a minnow, a cloud of *no-see-ums*, and a bad case of the grippe." [*Deryni Checkmate*; *High Deryni*].

Jasher Owain Cinhil *Haldane*, King of Gwynedd, Earl of Culdi, Sir. He was born on the IInd day of October in the Year of Our Lord 951, being the second surviving son of Uthyr King of Gwynedd and Grania MacInnis Countess of Culdi. He never married, but a year after his death a young man came forward calling himself Arthur Jasher Haldane, and claiming to be the natural son of the King Jasher and one Ennis Drim; but being unable to provide any documentary proof of either his birth or his parents' marriage, and despite the corroborating testimony of Mistress Drim, Arthur was unable to establish his right to a portion of his supposed father's material estate or to the County of Culdi, his petition being denied by the High Council and the King sitting in judgment. It is said that this "Arthur Haldane" later settled in Torenth and was given a small fief therein by the Duke of Tolán, and that his descendants continue to flourish in that place to this very day.

The Prince Jasher was early intended for the Church, but declined to take Holy Orders, instead becoming a lay knight of the Order of Saint Willibrord on the XXIXth day of September in the year 970. By the last will and testament of his mother, Grania Countess of Culdi, he succeeded her as Earl thereof at her death on the XXXth day of November in the year 982. He succeeded his elder brother, King Nygel, as monarch when the latter was killed at the Battle of Argoed against Imre II Pretender of Gwynedd on the IIIrd day of September in the year 983, and was crowned at Valoret by Archbishop William III on the Ist day of December following.

After King Nygel's death, the King Jasher organized a systematic withdrawal of the Gwyneddan forces from Eastmarch, Iomaire, and Rhendall, concentrating his army in II groups, the first being situate just North of a line between Carbury and Grecotha, and the IInd under command of his brother and heir, Prince Cluim, at Ebor just North of Valoret. The advancing Torenthi army was defeated at Shanbogh on the Xth day of October in that year, and it retreated to Cardosa and Rengarth in Eastmarch. That Winter was one of the harshest on record in the history of Gwynedd, and the cold temperatures and heavy snows prevented any further military action during that year by either side.

By the Spring of the year 984 the King Jasher had reorganized his army and was prepared to meet the invaders. He again concentrated his major forces in II groups at Grecotha and Ebor to defend Gwynedd's major cities, but created a IIIrd small group of marauders to harass the enemy train. The Festillic army appeared outside the walls of Grecotha on the IInd day of August in that year, and attacked on the next day. During the night King Jasher redeployed his forces, and at first light caught the Torenthi soldiers from behind as they were scaling the walls. Malachy II King of Torenth, Nimur Hereditary Prince of Torenth, and Mark-Imre Hereditary Prince of Festil, were all killed in the assault. The enemy army withdrew into Torenth, taking with them the bodies of their leaders.

In the IIIrd year of the war, the King Jasher was prepared to take the offensive. Gathering his troops at Valoret, he marched North and then East to attack the Pretender Imre II at his hideaway in Rengarth, which had been heavily fortified over the Winter months. He reached the Pretender's citadel on the XXXth day of May in the year 985. In a battle before the city on the IInd day of June following, the Pretender's son-in-law, Duchad Mór Count of Tigre, was killed, and the Festillic army forced back into the citadel. A lengthy siege commenced.

The initial assault on the walls of Rengarth on the XXIXth day of June failed. Three days later a IInd attack was made, led by the King himself. King Jasher was killed as he topped the walls, but his assault on the city was successful. The Pretender Imre II, seeing that all was lost, threw himself from the walls of his castle. King Jasher was XXXIII years of age at his death, and was succeeded by his younger brother, Prince Cluim, as King, and, in accordance with his last will and testament, by his nephew, the Prince Jashan, as Earl of Culdi. His body was packed in brine and returned to Rhemuth for his funeral, which was held on the XXIst day of July. The entire nation mourned the passing of the Saviour of Gwynedd. R.I.P.

Jason Brown. He worked as an apprentice for Daniel Draper (the mundane name of Prince Aidan Haldane), and inherited Draper's woolen and clothing business after his master's death on the XXVIIth day of September in the year 903. [*Camber of Culdi*].

Jason Dunquin, Sir. He was born on the VIIIth day of October in the Year of Our Lord 882, being the son of Sir Jauncey Dunquin and Malise Lady Bantry. He intermarried with Gillian Lady Erskine on the VIIth day of June in the year 902, and by her he had children: Sir Janner; Sir Jenkin; Sir Jersey; the Lady Joicette. He was the senior knight assigned to guard the Princes Javan and Rhys Michael during the fair held at Valoret to celebrate the coronation of King Alroy in May of the year 917, and was present at the assassination attempt on the Princes on the XXVIIIth day of September in that year. He remained loyal to King Javan when the latter inherited the throne, and paid homage to him at his accession on the XXIIIrd day of June in the year 921; he brought the King a white leather belt as a gift, and secretly knighted Javan on that same day. He was one of a group of loyal barons and young knights who secretly prepared a set of legal documents in anticipation of the succession of King Javan.

He attended the coronation of King Javan on the XXXIst day of July in the year 921, and had a set of supple white boots made for the King on this occasion. He was appointed Deputy Commissioner for Grecotha on the XIXth day of September following, and was specifically given the responsibility for Prince Rhys Michael's safety and discipline. He was killed defending the Prince on the XXXIst day of October in that year, aged XXXIX years, when an arrow struck him in the back, and his body was returned for burial at Rhemuth. He was short and dark, burly, bearded, and slightly grey, and he enjoyed playing dice. R.I.P. [*Camber the Heretic; King Javan's Year*].

Jasper Miller, Father. He was serving as a noncombatant Michaeline priest in December of the year 903. He attended Bishop Alister Cullen at the Battle of Iomaire in the year 905, and was slain there by the magic of the Pretender Ariella on the XXVth day of June. R.I.P. [*Camber of Culdi*].

Jass MacArdry, Sir. He was born on the Xth day of November in the Year of Our Lord 1104, being the son of Sir Judd MacArdry and Sebastiana Lady Kadoorie. This loyal MacArdry man served as a retainer to Dhugal Earl of Transha during the invasion of Meara by the Cassani Army in June of the year 1124. He assisted Dhugal in contacting King Kelson after the debacle at Dorna Plain on the IInd day of July following. He was knighted by Kelson on the IIIrd day of March in the year 1125, and accompanied him on his quest for the relics of Saint Camber. He was briefly captured by Prince Regent Conall and held hostage by him on the XIXth day of April in that year, before being freed by the King. [*The King's Justice; The Quest for Saint Camber*].

Jatham Kilshane, Baron of Kilshane, Sir. He was born on the XIth day of October in the Year of Our Lord 1107, being the son of Sir Manus Kilshane and Amaryllis Lady Macosquin. He intermarried with the Princess Janniver daughter of Pons Sovereign Prince of Pardiac, on the XXVIIIth day of June in the year 1128, and by her he had a child: the Hereditary Lord Aldus. Jatham was trained as a page by Nigel Duke of Carthmoor, and later served as a squire to Kelson King of Gwynedd. He was part of the King's entourage during the latter's visit to Trurill in November of the year 1123.

He was knighted by the King on the IIIrd day of March in the year 1125, and accompanied him on his quest for the relics of Saint Camber. As a wedding present, King Kelson created him Baron Kilshane, in the revival of an ancient extinct honour, on the XXIXth day of June in the year 1128. He had dark hair. *Proximus sum egomet mihi.* [*Deryni Rising; The King's Justice; The Quest for Saint Camber; King Kelson's Bride*].

Javan Jashan Urien Haldane, King of Gwynedd. He was born on the XXVth day of May in the Year of Our Lord 905, being the third but second surviving son of Cinhil I King of Gwynedd and Megan Lady de Cameron, and the younger twin brother of King Alroy. He never married. He was born with a clubbed right foot, but learned to cope with his disability remarkably well. He was treated by the Healer Tavis O'Neill through part of his adolescence.

Prince Javan's Haldane potential was set by his royal father on the Ist day of February in the year 917. He won IInd place in pole-bending at the tournament held to celebrate his brother's coronation in May of that year, and received a chaplet of wildflowers from Elaine Countess of Carthane. He had developed mental shields by that Summer and had begun to truth-read by October of that year. The Healer Tavis encouraged him in the development of his powers, and coached him until forced to leave Court. By then the Prince had met with the exiled Archbishop Alister Cullen (Camber Earl of Culdi), and had established contacts with the Camberian Council. He began blurring the memories of his squire, Charlan, at about this time.

After the last accessible transfer portal in Valoret Castle was closed on the XXIInd day of January in the year 918, he deliberately encouraged the Regents to believe that he had a religious vocation by showing excessive devotion to prayer. On the XXXth day of March in that year he read King Alroy's mind, but was interrupted by the Healer Oriel, who realized that Javan had shields and other powers. Both henceforward pledged to work together towards a common goal. On the Ist day of August in the year 918 he voluntarily entered the *Arx Fidei* Seminary near Rhemuth after his Ist profession of temporary vows in the *Custodes Fidei*, and spent nearly III years there in contemplation.

He succeeded his twin brother, the King Alroy, on the XXIIIrd day of June in the year 921, and was crowned on the XXXIst day of July following by Archbishop Hubert, being the Ist monarch to be crowned at Rhemuth since King Ifor in the year 795. His Haldane potential was activated on the XXVIth day of June in that year. Although he attempted to reform the government and clergy, he was ultimately unsuccessful in curbing the power of the former Regents. His major accomplishment was the codification and indexing of the laws passed during the reigns of his father and elder brother, and a major revision and reissuing of the land warrants of the Kingdom. He was murdered by the High Lords of Gwynedd during a *coup d'état* conducted by them on the XIth day of May in the year 922, aged XVI years, and was succeeded by his younger brother, Prince Rhys Michael. His body was returned to Rhemuth on the XXVth day of that month, the anniversary of his birth, and was buried in the crypt of his ancestors in Saint George's Cathedral II days later. He had the grey eyes and black hair common to his family. R.I.P. [*Saint Camber*; *Camber the Heretic*; *The Harrowing of Gwynedd*; *King Javan's Year*; *The Bastard Prince*].

Jebediah, Earl of Alcara, Earl Marshal of Gwynedd, Grand Master of the Order of Saint Michael, Sir. This Michaeline knight was born on the XVIIIth day of July in the Year of Our Lord 861, being the third son of Obadiah Lord Alcara and Thamar Lady Mkheidze, and a cousin of Sir Sion Benét, whose domain was a day's ride from Nyford. As a young man he determined to find his own way in the world, and joined the Order of Saint Michael as a lay knight on the XIIth day of June in the year 879. He was elected Grand Master of the Knights of the Order of Saint Michael on the IIIrd day of August in the year 902, ranking IInd only to the Vicar General. On the Ist day of December in the year 904 he led one of the contingents of Michaelines stationed at Dhassa in their assault on Valoret, bringing them into the Castle through the transfer portals therein. He was subsequently made Acting Commander of King Cinhil I's army by the Summer of the year 905, and participated in the War Council of the XXIIIrd day of June at the Great Hall in Valoret Palace.

He accompanied the army to Iomaire, and took part in the great battle there against the Pretender Ariella II days later. He attended the Grand Chapter meeting at Valoret on the IIIrd day of July following. He was named Earl Marshal of Gwynedd and Field Commander of the Royal Armies on the VIth day of November in the year 905 and was appointed to the Royal Council with the life rank of Earl of Alcara. On the IInd day of July in the year 906 he joined the King on his Summer campaign with Earl Sighere to quiet the Festillic partisans still roaming the Rhendall hills.

On the XXIIIrd day of October in the year 906 he participated in the Ist consistory of Archbishop Jaffray. He was a founding member of the Camberian Council on the XVth day of April in the year 909. He participated in a special magical ceremony to baptize Tieg Joram Thuryn at Sheele on the Ist day of August in the Year 914. He was sent by Rhys from Ebor to Camber on the XXXIst day of January in the year 917.

He was dismissed from his position as Earl Marshal and Commander of the Armies of Gwynedd and member of the Council by the Regents of King Alroy on the IIIrd day of February in that year. On the following day Rhys Lord Thuryn used him to demonstrate the newly-discovered technique of "turning off" Deryni powers. He made his farewells to his Michaeline brethren in late September of that year. He was attainted and outlawed by the Regents on the XXVIIth day of December. Jebediah was killed defending Alister/Camber on the VIth day of January in the year 918, aged LVI years. His body was brought first to Saint Mary's in the Hills Abbey near Culdi, and then transported to the Michaeline Haven, where it was laid to rest in the chapel there. His grave marker bore the words: "With the blessed Archangel, he shall stand at the right side of the altar of incense, defending the Light." R.I.P. [*Camber of Culdi*; *Saint Camber*; "Healer's Song"; *Camber the Heretic*; *The Harrowing of Gwynedd*].

Jehana, *i.e.*, **Jehane-Julienne-Adélaïde *de Besançon*, Princesse de Bremagne, sometime Lord Regent of Gwynedd, Dowager Queen of Gwynedd, Lady Barstowe.** She was born on the XXVIIth day of October in the Year of Our Lord 1088, being the second child and eldest daughter of Meyric II Roi de Bremagne and the Princess Rosaura daughter of Isarn I Sovereign Prince of Logréine and Jordana Lady de Jordanet, and a great-grandniece of Lord Lewys ap Norfal du Joux. She was betrothed on the XIth day of August in the year 1103 to Brion King of Gwynedd, and intermarried with him on the VIth day of January in the year 1104, and by him she had children: the Hereditary Prince Kelson later King of Gwynedd; the Princess Rosane Marie Élisabeth Jaÿne, who perished a few days after her birth of the blue skin. After the death of King Brion in the year 1120, Queen Jehana intermarried secondly with Barrett de Laney Earl Barstowe on the XVth day of October in the year 1128, and by him she had a child: the Hereditary Countess Arÿole Rosaura Modeste.

The Princess Jehane was educated at the Convent of Saint-Élie near Millefleurs; the Abbess of this establishment, one Mother Rohane, was a notorious Deryni-hater. She met her husband-to-be during his state visit to the Kingdom of Bremagne during May of the year 1103, and was immediately captivated by him, and he by her. After their marriage at Millefleurs, she returned with him to Rhemuth, but had some difficulty in adjusting to life there.

Following the return of her husband and Alaric Morgan Duke of Corwyn from their battle with Hogan Gwernach Duke of Marluk in the Summer of the year 1105, she was horrified to discover that magic had been used on both sides, and blamed the Duke for seducing her husband into the Deryni ways. She subsequently entered into seclusion at the Abbey of Saint Giles near Shannis Meer in Eastmarch on the Vth day of July in the year 1105. She was reconciled with her husband on the VIth day of February in the year 1106, when he came and took her away from Saint Giles. Thereafter she became pregnant almost immediately with her I[st] child, and came to enjoy her life in Gwynedd. However, she never trusted Alaric Morgan, and blamed him for everything that went wrong in her life, including the death of her infant daughter.

She girded Sean Earl Derry with the white belt of knighthood on the XIth day of May in the year 1115. At the sudden murder of her husband the King Brion on the I[st] day of November in the year 1120, she briefly served as Regent of the Kingdom of Gwynedd, but was displaced when her only son Prince Kelson declared himself of age on the XIVth day instant. She returned to Shannis Meer on the XIIIth day of March in the year 1121, and remained there in seclusion and prayer until the XVth day of May in the year 1124, when she abruptly returned to Rhemuth. She returned to Bremagne to visit her brother, King Ryol II, in the summer of 1127, seeing him for the I[st] time in X years; she also traveled to Fallon in the Fall of that year, and then spent the winter months in Orsal with Sivorn Lady Kishknock.

Her life-long aversion to all things Deryni only began to ameliorate after she returned to Rhemuth on the XXVIth day of June in the year 1128 to take up her duties as part of the Regency Council being assembled to govern Gwynedd during her son's pending absence. She discovered the secret annex to the Palace Library on the IVth day of July, meeting the Deryni mages, Barrett de Laney and Laran ap Pardyce, and eventually began to take instruction from the former. On the next day she accompanied the Duchess Meraude to visit the latter's granddaughter, Conalline, hoping to devise a plan to bring the latter to court.

Over the ensuing weeks, and with the assistance of Barrett, she gradually came to change her outlook regarding the Deryni, and became enamoured of the gentleman. She allowed him to transport her to his abode on the coast of Alver on the XXIVth day instant. Two days later, she helped inspect the new Chapel of Saint Camber. Also on this day, she connived with Meraude for Duke Nigel to meet his granddaughter for the I[st] time. On the XXXth day of July, she was part of the official group that welcomed the Servants of Saint Camber to Rhemuth. She attended the double royal wedding on the following day, and the wedding of her son a week later.

In Volumen I of the *Chronicles of the Deryni*, she is noted as having "...hair coiled in a long auburn braid at the back of her head and secured with a pair of filigreed pins, [with] high cheek bones, slightly squared jaw line, and smoky green eyes." By the year 1128 she usually wore white, nun-like robes, until her meeting with Barrett, and had a frosting of grey hair at her temples. ["The Knighting of Derry"; *Deryni Rising*; *Deryni Checkmate*; *High Deryni*; *The Bishop's Heir*; *The King's Justice*; *The Quest for Saint Camber*; *King Kelson's Bride*].

Jelsin. This bay mare was Geordie Lord Drummond's personal horse; because she was so winded, he left her behind at Cor Culdi before beginning his quest in April of the year 905. *Omnia mea mecum porto*. [*Deryni Challenge*].

Jemet. This R'Kassan scout was serving in the main army of Kelson King of Gwynedd during the Mearan campaign in June of the year 1124. [*The King's Justice*].

Jenas. This earldom of Gwynedd is located in the extreme Western part of the country, just South of Cashien at the foot of the Mughdorna Mountains. The title was originally granted by King Malcolm to Sir Piran ap Coran on the XIXth day of November in the year 1025. [*The Bishop's Heir*].

EARLS OF JENAS

HOUSE OF PIRAN

Piran ap Coran	1025-1041
Jenan (son)	1041-1077
Rowan (son)	1077-1101
Ninian (son)	1101-1121
Roger (son)	1121-1130+

Jennan Vale. This little village in Northeast Corwyn situate near its border with Torenth was the site of a skirmish between the troops of Nigel Duke of Carthmoor and the rebel peasants of Warin de Grey on the XVIIth day of June in the year 1121. [*High Deryni*].

Jeroboam. This preacher monk was directly responsible for helping Edmund Loris former Archbishop of Valoret to escape from his prison cell at Saint Iveagh's Abbey on the XXIXth day of November in the year 1123. He was later captured, tried, and sent back to Saint Iveagh's to take the Archbishop's place under close confinement for the rest of his days. [*The Bishop's Heir*].

Jerome, Brother. He was an elderly sacristan in charge of the vestments at the Cathedral of Saint George in Rhemuth in November of the year 1120, when he told Father Duncan McLain that rumours implicated Alaric Morgan Duke of Corwyn in a possible assassination plot against King Kelson. He was still serving there IV years later. He had been associated with the Church since the year 1075. [*Deryni Rising*; *The Bishop's Heir*].

Jerowen *Reynolds*, Vice Chancellor of Gwynedd, Lord. He was born on the Vth day of November in the Year of Our Lord 855, being the son of Sir Jasper Reynolds and Alethea Lady Mexborough. He intermarried with Lepella Lady Joly on the XXXth day of May in the year 876, and by her he had children: Sir Rodney; the Lady Tessa; the Lady Skye; Sir Æneas; the Lady Sylvy; Sir Slaney; the Lady Cælia; the Lady Sibylla; Sir Yuke; the Lady Rencie. This Law Lord was one of a group of Barons and knights who had prepared a set of legal documents in the year 921 in anticipation of the succession of King Javan. He was appointed by the King to the Royal Council on the IInd day of July in that year, replacing Fane Regent of Cassan, and was also named Vice Chancellor of Gwynedd. He attended the coronation of King Javan on the XXXIst day of July following. On the XXIIIrd day of August he began preparing at the King's order a new set of land warrants to be distributed throughout Gwynedd; these were completed on the VIIth day of September following. He then was ordered to begin compiling a comprehensive index covering the records of legislation issued during the reigns of Kings Cinhil I and Alroy, in order to codify the laws of the Haldanes, but he found that the papers from the latter period, particularly during the Regency, were wanting in many respects. He was murdered by the former Regents during their *coup d'état* of the XIth day of May in the year 922, aged LXVI years. He was a silver-haired gentleman of distinction, and was said to have had a fine legal mind. R.I.P. [*King Javan's Year*].

Jerusha Evaine Jodotha *Thuryn Drummond*, **Lady.** This Healer was born on the I[st] day of January in the Year of Our Lord 918, being the second surviving daughter of Rhys Lord Thuryn and Evaine Lady MacRorie. She intermarried with Sir Cathan Drummond on the XXXth day of April in the year 937, and by him she had children: the Lady Kyriella, who intermarried with Stuart Lord MacAthan; the Lord Corwin; the Lady Evalina. After her mother's death on the I[st] day of August in the year 918, she was raised by her cousin, Fiona Lady MacLean. This venerable and revered Lady died on the VIIth day of January in the year 1001, aged LXXXIII years. R.I.P. [*The Harrowing of Gwynedd*].

Jerusha Lile *MacRorie*, **Lady**. She was born on the I[st] day of February in the Year of Our Lord 876, being the eldest daughter of Camber Earl of Culdi and Jocelyn Lady de la Marche. She died of the Frissian fever with her brother Ballard on the VIth day of March in the year 888, aged XII years, and was buried with her family at Tor Caerrorie. The remains of her tomb were discovered by King Kelson on the XXth day of March in the year 1125. R.I.P. ["Catalyst"; *King Javan's Year*; *The Quest for Saint Camber*].

Jervis. He was serving as a household steward for Sudrey Dowager Countess of Eastmarch at Lochalyn Castle on the VIIIth day of June in the year 928. He was ordered by his mistress to prepare an infirmary in the Great Hall to care for the wounded following the Torenthi attack on Culliecairn. [*The Bastard Prince*].

Jesse *MacGregor*, **Hereditary Count and Master of Ebor, Sovereign Count of Trevalga, Sir.** He was born on the XIXth day of January in the Year of Our Lord 901, being the eldest son and heir of Gregory Earl of Ebor and Eloise Lady de Mauzé. He intermarried with Tiarna MacMurray on the XIIth day of April in the year 930, and by her he had children: the Lord Murray later Count of Trevalga; the Lady Maible; the Lord Maelis; the Lady Malvina; the Lord Matadin; the Lord Macrory; the Lady Moyra. After his father's accidental fall on the XXXth day of January in the year 917, Jesse sent a message to the King asking for the aid of the Healer, Rhys Thuryn. He attended a meeting of the Camberian Council on the IIIrd day of February in that year, and linked with Camber to identify the young Deryni marauders who had attacked Manfred's party a week earlier. He was attainted with his father by the Regents on the XXVIIth day of December in the year 917, but removed with him to Trevalga in The Connait.

He became a member of the Camberian Council on the Xth day of January in the year 918. By the year 921 he had become the liaison between Joram and Ansel. He received a message via carrier pigeon at the Haven on the XXIInd day of June in that year indicating that King Alroy was dying. He met the new King Javan at the Haven on the XXIVth day of that month. On the XXVIIIth day of July following he assumed the disguise of a *Custodes* monk to visit the King at Rhemuth and to examine the new portal site being established in the room off the library there. During the next decade he became an agent for the Deryni underground of Father Joram MacRorie, using the former Michaeline Haven as a base of operations. On the XVIIth day of June in the year 928 he helped Ansel MacRorie bring a contingent of disguised former Michaeline knights to aid Sudrey Dowager Countess of Eastmarch, and was present on the XXIst day of that month when King Rhys Michael arrived at Lochalyn Castle with his army. He succeeded his father as Count of Trevalga on the Xth day of February in the year 932, and was confirmed in his title by the Council of Sovereign Princes of The Connait on the IVth day of April following. He died on the VIIIth day of October in the year 981, aged LXXX years, and was succeeded by his son, Lord Murray. Among his descendants is vested the right to petition the Crown of Gwynedd for the restoration of the Earldom of Ebor.

He is described in the *Legends* as being "a husky, olive-skinned youth. He was a quiet but intense young man. He was trim and muscled, holding himself with the feline grace and precision of an experienced fighting man." In the *Heirs* it is further noted that "he was not a tall man, but his compact frame was muscled and hard. At twenty he had been a warrior almost half his life. Flecks of gold stirred in the depths of brown eyes that missed very little. The sun had bronzed his olive skin and put brassy lights in the brown hair tied back in a queue." R.I.P. [*Camber the Heretic*; *The Harrowing of Gwynedd*; *King Javan's Year*; *The Bastard Prince*].

Jestyn Werril *Haldane*, **Prince of Gwynedd, Count of Carthane**. He was born on the VIIIth day of September in the Year of Our Lord 680, being the second son of Llarik King of Gwynedd and Riona Countess of Carthane. He never married.

The Prince Jestyn inherited his mother's title at her death on the XVIth day of November in the year 697. He was arrested with his brother, the Prince Dolon Kensell, by their father the King on the VIth day of October in the year 699, and both were charged with treason and unnatural acts. He was beheaded with his brother on the XVIth day of that month, aged XIX years, and was buried in the crypt of his ancestors beneath Saint George's Cathedral in Rhemuth. The II brothers were popularly believed to have been innocent of any crime; many blamed the King's new wife, the Princess Sidonie, for their deaths, saying that she had made advances towards them, and that when they refused, she had them killed out of spite; but others have stated that the brothers were themselves at fault, having seduced the young Princess after her marriage, and that the son born to her the following year was the product of an incestuous union. *Araignée au matin, chagrin; araignée au midi, espoir.* R.I.P. [*The Harrowing of Gwynedd*; *The Bishop's Heir*].

Jilyan, Mother. She was a *ban-aba* or Abbess among the hill folk of Saint Kyriell's in April of the year 1125, and also served on the town Quorial. She came to Rhemuth with the newly constituted Servants of Saint Camber on the XXXth day of July in the year 1128, and agreed to King Kelson's proposal to establish a *schola* of Deryni learning there. [*The Quest for Saint Camber*; *King Kelson's Bride*].

Joachim, Brother. This weathered and emaciated Willimite became Revan's chief disciple in the year 917, and had become his staunchest supporter a year later. According to the *Legends*, "his voice held the clipped lilt of the Mooryn highlands." [*Camber the Heretic*; *The Harrowing of Gwynedd*].

Jocelyn de la Marche MacRorie, Countess of Culdi, Lady. She was born on the XXIst day of July in the Year of Our Lord 848, being the daughter of Evan Baron de la Marche and Brio Lady Gillaspie. She intermarried with Camber MacRorie Earl of Culdi on the XVIIIth day of May in the year 871, and by him she had children: the Hereditary Count and Master Cathan, who was murdered at age XXX by King Imre, leaving issue; the Lady Jerusha, dead at age XII of the Frissian fever; the Lord Ballard, dead at XI on the same day and of the same ailment which killed his sister; the Lord Joram later a Michaeline priest; the Lady Ardissa, born still; the Lady Evaine, who married with Rhys Lord Thuryn.

In the year 888 the Lady Jocelyn was pleased to learn that her son Joram intended to pursue the priesthood. She was out hunting with her husband on the XIth day of October in that year when bandits attacked their estate at Tor Caerrorie. She died on the XIIth day of December in the year 896, aged XLVIII years, and was buried in the family crypt at Caerrorie. After her death her daughter Evaine served as Chatelaine of the manor. R.I.P. ["Catalyst"; *Camber of Culdi*].

Jodoc d'Armaine, Lord, Bishop. He was born on the XXIst day of October in the Year of Our Lord 1087, being the younger son of Philippot Sieur d'Armaine and Eugénie Demoiselle Maintenon. He was ordained priest on the IVth day of November in the year 1107, and was being considered for consecration as an itinerant Bishop by the Synod of Valoret on the XIXth day of March in the year 1125. Bishop Siward questioned him closely concerning his qualifications. He was elected Bishop on the next day. [*The Quest for Saint Camber*].

Jodotha of Carnedd. This great Deryni Healer was born in the Year of Our Lord 655. She became an accomplished adept at an early age, being trained at the *Templum Archangelorum*, and later studied under the Deryni Master Orin. Some of the lectures that she gave at the Varnarite University in Grecotha, plus an extract of a paper she had written on memory, bearing the sigil of the long-vanished Healers' *Schola* at Portree, were later consulted by the Lady Evaine Thuryn. According to legend, she attempted to save the lives of the II sons of King Llarik in the year 699, and perished with them on the XVIth day of October in that year, aged XLIV years.

Two centuries later on the XIXth day of April in the year 918 the Lady Evaine and Father Joram MacRorie found the body of Orin in the ruins beneath Grecotha; grasped in his hand was a medallion containing a lock of Jodotha's hair and her portrait. Nearby was the body of Jodotha herself, lying beside the bier. According to the *Heirs*, "She had rich red hair framing delicate but lively looking features. The chin was pointed, the mouth firm but curved in just the suggestion of a smile. The eyes were dark, with a depth that seemed to transcend the medium of mere painter's pigment." She wore a violet silk gown, a torque of twisted gold around her throat, and lay on a mantle of scarlet. In her portrait she was holding the symbols of a deacon of the Church. Her body collapsed into dust when it was touched by Evaine. Beneath it was her ring, which read: "Jodotha, *serva De[or]um*"; *i.e.*, Servant of the Gods. R.I.P. [*The Harrowing of Gwynedd*].

Jodrell, Baron Ardglass, General. He was born on the IXth day of August in the Year of Our Lord 1096, being the eldest son and heir of Junanan Baron Ardglass and Dulcinea Lady Tincurragh. He succeeded his father on the Ist day of September in the year 1121. He married Portia Lady Lemaire in the year 1122. This young lieutenant of Duncan McLain Duke of Cassan in Kierney was appointed to the High Council of Gwynedd at the latter's suggestion on the XIVth day of April in the year 1122. He was part of King Kelson's entourage during his progress through Meara in the Summer of the year 1123. He later accompanied the King during his lightning raid to Ratharkin on the VIIIth day of December in that year. He served as a General in the Cassani army that invaded Northern Meara in May of the year 1124. [*The Bishop's Heir*; *The King's Justice*; *The Quest for Saint Camber*].

Johanan, Lord. This legendary Deryni hero was the subject of Canto IV of a work by Pargan Howiccan. According to myth Johanan besought Makurias-in-Glory for permission to lay siege to the Lleassi, the Lords of the Dark Places, and to cast them out from Earth. [*Camber of Culdi*].

Johannes, Brother. This lay Michaeline monk had just recently joined the service of Father Alister Cullen in June of the year 905, and was present at the Battle of Iomaire on the XXVth day instant. He assisted Rhys Lord Thuryn in treating the supposed injuries of Cullen (actually the shape-changed Camber Earl of Culdi), and returned to Valoret with the victorious army. [*Saint Camber*].

John. He was the factor who bought the old manor house of Dolban for the newly established Order of the Servants of Saint Camber on the IVth day of June in the year 906. [*Saint Camber*].

John, Abbot of Athelingay, Saint. This holy man was invited by Bearand King of Gwynedd to restore religion and learning in the churches of Gwynedd after the devastating raids of the Moors in the VIIIth century. The King appointed him Abbot of Athelingay, and John worked zealously in furthering Bearand's wishes. Two monks of his own community murdered him one night in his church, before he could call them to account for their supposed theft of votive offerings left in the Church. A parish church dedicated to his name is located near Fullers' Alley in Valoret, where the Draper family records were kept. His feastday is the XXIInd day of February. R.I.P. [*Camber of Culdi*].

John *Drummond*, Lord. He was born on the XXVIIIth day of April in the Year of Our Lord 813, being the eldest son and second child of David Lord Drummond and Anna Lady Cappell, and the uncle of Camber Earl of Culdi. He intermarried with So-Domina Lady Dreenan on the IVth day of June in the year 829, and by her he had children: the Lord John *Junior*; the Lady Mary; the Lady Phyllis; the Lord Douglas; the Lady Anne; the Lord David. He died on the Vth day of May in the year 876, aged LXIII years. His descendants still thrive in the borders of the Purple March. R.I.P. [*Deryni Challenge*].

John *FitzPadraic*, Bishop of Meara. He was born on the XIIth day of October in the Year of Our Lord 1082. He was ordained priest on the XXth day of July in the year 1110, was elected an itinerant Bishop of Gwynedd on the XIXth day of January in the year 1122, and was elevated to the see of Meara on the XVIIIth day of March in the year 1125 in succession to the martyred Bishop Henry Istelyn. He was a level-headed and moderate churchman of proven loyalty to the legitimate ecclesiastical hierarchy and the Crown. [*The Quest for Saint Camber*].

John *Nivard*, Father. He was born on the XXVIth day of September in the Year of Our Lord 1102, being the son of Master Julian Nivard and Cinna de Clary. This young Deryni seminarian was undergoing a crisis of faith when he was discovered by Denis Arilan Bishop of Dhassa in the year 1121. He was ordained by Arilan on the XIIth day of October in the year 1124, and was serving the Bishop as his chaplain in March of the year 1125. He was used by Alaric Morgan Duke of Corwyn and Bishop Duncan McLain Duke of Cassan as the IIIrd part of a mind link to try locating the missing King Kelson and Dhugal MacArdry Earl of Kierney on the XXIXth day of that month.

He presided over the wedding between Sir Jatham Kilshane and the Princess Janniver on the XXVIIIth day of June in the year 1128. By this time he had been appointed guardian of the Royal Library in Rhemuth Palace, and had access to the secret annex that had recently been created there by King Kelson. On the Vth day of July he was confronted by Dowager Queen Jehana, who demanded that he provide her with details of the annex. On the XVIth day instant, he was among the officials who met with King Kelson when he returned from Beldour. Four days later, he helped transport Brendan, Derry, and Payne from Orsal to Rhemuth. He was asked by King Kelson to say masses for the repose of the soul of Morag Dowager Duchess d'Arjenol on the XXVIIth day of July. Short in stature but steady as a rock from Arilan's training, he had green eyes and a head of crisp, dark curls springing from around his tonsure. [*The Quest for Saint Camber*; *King Kelson's Bride*].

John *of Elsworth*. This guard in Rhemuth Palace was used by Ian Howell Earl of Eastmarch as a medium to communicate with the Pretender Charissa on the XIVth day of November in the year 1120. [*Deryni Rising*].

John, son of Daniel, later Brother Benedict. He was born in the Year of Our Lord 861, being the grandson of Dunstan, a poor cobbler living in Rengarth. He was received into the *Ordo Verbi Dei* and took the name Benedict in the year 882, being cloistered at the Priory of Saint Piran's. He was the first "Benedict" that Camber and his family investigated while searching for some trace of Prince Cinhil Haldane. [*Camber of Culdi*].

John the Baptist, Saint. The life of this biblical figure was used by the Camberian Council in the year 917 as a model to develop Master Revan into a charismatic Willimite preacher who could facilitate the "blocking" of Deryni powers while dunking his followers in the River Eirian. His feastday is the XXIVth day of June. [*Camber the Heretic*; *The Bastard Prince*].

Jokal *of Tyndour*. This Deryni Healer and poet is said to have lived in VIIIth century Kheldour, and was especially noted for having penned a long poetic work, the *Joci Jokali*, that included several passages on healing. Rhys Lord Thuryn was surprised by some of the procedures described therein. Barrett de Laney later commented to Dowager Queen Jehana that Kitron and Jokal both credited Orin with the creation of the Healer's *Adsum Domine*, although Barrett himself discounted their remarks, believing the verse to have had an earlier existence. The precise location of Tyndour has yet to be determined; it is believed to have been burned during the early Regency period of King Alroy. [*The Harrowing of Gwynedd*; *King Kelson's Bride*].

Jolyon Edward Archambald *Ramsay-Quinnell*, Duke of Laas, Sir. He was born on the IIIrd day of December in the year 1077, being the eldest son of Sir Dafydd Ramsay of Cloome and Noa Lady Armengol. He intermarried with Oksana Lady d'Enghieux on the XXIInd day of May in the year 1102, and by her he had children: Brecon Jolyon Jameson later Hereditary Duke of Laas and Earl of Kilarden and Culdi, who intermarried with the Princess Richelle Haldane Countess of Culdi; Judhael Jubal, dead at age V of the slimy slough; Noelie Quintilla, who intermarried with Prince Rory Haldane later Duke of Ratharkin; Dafydd Urban, who entered the Order of Saint Cyran in the year 1125 under the name Brother Christophle Urbanus; Taxila Oksana, who perished at age III of vescicance; Edwyn Colin, dead at age VI of the morning miasma. He traveled to Rhemuth with his family in the Summer of the year 1127 for the betrothal of his eldest son to Princess Richelle Haldane, and again for the dual wedding of his son and daughter on the XXXIst day of July in the year 1128. To give him appropriate rank as a member of the royal family of Gwynedd, he was created Duke of Laas by King Kelson on the preceding evening. On the Ist day of September following, he irrevocably renounced all rights to the throne of Meara for himself and his descendants before an assemblage of the nobility and notables of that land, thereby ending the final titular claims to that honour. He was tall and dark-eyed, and had whispy, fair hair going grey at the temples. [*King Kelson's Bride*].

Jolyon II Justinian Jedediah *Quinnell*, Sovereign Prince of Meara. This Prince was born on the VIIth day of March in the Year of Our Lord 970, being the second surviving son of Joël Sovereign Prince of Meara and Faustina Contessa di Cebà. He intermarried firstly with the Princess Ysyllt daughter of Cluim King of Gwynedd on the VIth day of June in the year 999, and by her he had a child: the Princess Camilla-Louise, called the Millennium Child, who was born on the XXIVth day of January in the year 1000, but would not suckle and died II days after her birth. After his first wife's death on the XIIth day of October in the year 1006, he intermarried secondly with the Princess Urracca daughter of Faucon Hereditary Prince of Bremagne on the XXth day of April in the year 1007, and by her he had children: the Princess Roisian later Sovereign Prince of Meara, who intermarried with Malcolm King of Gwynedd; the Princess Annalind later Prince and Pretender of Meara, a twin with her sister, who intermarried with Rhiryd Lord Kincaid, leaving issue; the Hereditary Prince Joël, dead at age II of the stoney relick; the Hereditary Prince Jubal, dead at age VI of a fall; the Princess Judit, tainted with cambique at the age of VIII; the Princess Jorianna, a twin with her sister, dead at age II of the frothing mouth; the Princess Magrette, who intermarried with Edward Lord Ramsay son of the Earl of Cloome, leaving issue; the Hereditary Prince Job, who died shortly after birth.

The Prince Jolyon succeeded his brother, the Sovereign Prince Judhael II, on the XXIInd day of October in the year 1001. With the death of his last surviving son, the Hereditary Prince Job, on the VIth day of July in the year 1018, the Prince Jolyon began to worry about the future of his state, for he had but one heir male yet surviving, his bachelor uncle Quinn Count of Ithelthorn, and under the laws of Meara, each of Jolyon's III surviving daughters possessed an equal right to inherit the Amethyst Throne. Therefore, as the Princesses began to approach the age where they might be considered for the state of holy matrimony, he sought husbands for them whom he could test as possible successors to his throne. He considered proposals from many different quarters, but ultimately decided on an alliance of convenience with Torenth and Tolán, for these lands were far distant from his own, and he feared the ambitions of Gwynedd.

The Prince Jolyon agreed to support the plans of Kyprian II King of Torenth and Imre III Pretender of Festil to invade Gwynedd in the year 1025, and to that end gathered his forces at Ratharkin in the Winter and Spring following. On the XXIIIrd day of May in that year he occupied the walled city of Culdi, and proclaimed himself Prince of Cassan and Lord of the Purple March. But he was surprised and killed at the Cleyde on the XXIXth day instant, aged LV years, when the direct male line of the House of Quinnell became extinct. Under the terms of his last will and testament, the Princess Roisian was immediately proclaimed Sovereign Prince of Meara, and was soon taken as bride by Malcolm King of Gwynedd, thereby precipitating a century of war between the Mearan partisans and the House of Haldane. R.I.P. [*The Bishop's Heir*; *The King's Justice*].

Jonas, Father. This old parish priest was serving the MacRorie family at Tor Caerrorie in the year 903. He conducted the funeral service for Cathan MacRorie Hereditary Count of Culdi on the IInd day of December in that year. [*Camber of Culdi*].

Joram Angus *MacRorie*, Lord, Sir, and Father. This illustrious priest was born on the XXIIIrd day of November in the Year of Our Lord 878, being the third son of Camber Earl of Culdi and Jocelyn Lady de la Marche. He was sent with his foster brother Rhys Lord Thuryn to Saint Liam's Abbey near Caerrorie to attend school there in late October of the year 888. Like his father before him, he early professed interest in the Church. After being knighted by Blaine I King of Gwynedd on the Ist day of December in the year 896, he entered the Militant Order of Saint Michael the following Spring, also taking up seminary training for the priesthood. He was ordained on the XVth day of May in the year 899 by Anscom Archbishop Primate of Valoret and All Gwynedd.

In September of the year 903 he was serving as a Master at Saint Liam's Abbey near Caerrorie. It was here that Rhys Thuryn visited him on the XXVIIIth day of that month to inform him of Rhys's discovery of Prince Aidan Haldane, who had died the day before in Valoret after revealing the existence of a grandson and heir, Prince Cinhil. They traveled North on the same day to Saint Jarlath's Abbey to examine the records of the postulants, and then returned to Tor Caerrorie to report to Camber Earl of Culdi on Michaelmas.

Father Joram participated in the War Council held on the XXIIIrd day of June in 905 at the Great Hall in Valoret Palace. He attended the Grand Chapter meeting of the Michaelines in Valoret on the IIIrd day of July in that year. He left Saint Liam's and was appointed confidential secretary to Bishop Alister Cullen (*i.e.*, Camber Earl of Culdi) in the year 905. He opposed the canonization of Camber, but was unable to stop it.

He was a founding member of the Camberian Council on the XVth day of April in the year 909. He was present at the baptism of his nephew and namesake, Tieg Joram Thuryn, at Sheele on the Ist day of August in the year 914. He attended the Synod of Bishops held at Valoret in November and December of 917 as an aide to his father, but was outlawed with the other Deryni Lords by the Regents on the XXVIIth day of December. He later coordinated resistance to the Regents and assisted Prince Javan to realize his full Haldane powers on the XXVIth day of June in the year 921. On the XXIXth day of July in that year he transported through the new portal into Rhemuth to question Father Lior and Brother Serafin, who had been captured by the Deryni resistance.

After the murder of King Javan by the former Regents on the XIth day of May in the year 922, he lost contact with the new King, Rhys Michael, who was kept under close guard by the Council. Even so, over the next few years Joram and his underground Deryni began making plans for a *coup d'état* that would eventually overthrow the brutal rule of the former Regents, with a target date of early in the year 929. The challenge of Prince Miklós and Prince Marek to the King in June of the year 928 forced him to accelerate his plans. On the XIVth day of June in that same year, he participated in enabling the Haldane potential of King Rhys Michael, together with Queen Michaela, and Rhysel and Tieg Thuryn.

After the death of King Rhys Michael on the XXVIIIth day of June, and the appointment of a new Regency for IV-year-old King Owain, Joram and his allies finally began their own *coup d'état* a week later. The new Regents were established on the Vth day of July in the year 928 in accordance with the last will and testament of King Rhys Michael, and the High Lords of the previous regime were either killed or deposed.

Father Joram MacRorie died in the year 948, aged LXIX years. He was lean and fit, and blond like his father, although by the reign of King Rhys Michael his hair had turned grey and was receding at the temples, and his face had become almost ascetic in appearance. He was among the noblest men of his generation, being eclipsed in stature only by his more famous father. R.I.P. ["Catalyst"; *Camber of Culdi*; *Saint Camber*; "Healer's Song"; *Camber the Heretic*; *The Harrowing of Gwynedd*; *King Javan's Year*; *The Bastard Prince*].

Jorevin of Cashel. This ancient Deryni mystic was best known as author of the *Tomes*. His works were consulted by Evaine Lady Thuryn in the year 918. [*The Harrowing of Gwynedd*].

Jorian *de Courcy*, Lord, Father. This Deryni was born the XXVIth day of December in the year 1083, being a younger son of Alcime Baron de Courcy and Guinimande Lady Dembrun. He was ordained priest at the *Arx Fidei* Seminary on the Ist day of August in the year 1104, but was uncovered as Deryni through the *merasha* placed in the communion wine. He was arrested and taken to Valoret for trial before the Archbishops' Tribunal on the Ist day of September following. Father Jorian was condemned, excommunicated, imprisoned, and then burned at the stake at *Arx Fidei* on the XIth day of November following (that is, Martinmas). He was later cited by his friend Bishop Denis Arilan as the example of a Deryni showing greater courage than Arilan himself possessed. R.I.P. ["The Priesting of Arilan"; *The Quest for Saint Camber*].

Joric *the Gardener*, Saint. This VIIth-century holy man believed in spreading the word of the Lord by disseminating throughout the land the seeds of roses, lilacs, and other beauteous flowers, saying: "A rose by any other name is not the same." After his death, so the legend goes, a rose bush grew out of his mouth, and the name of Saint Mary miraculously appeared on the leaves of one of the roses. An Order dedicated to his name, the Brotherhood of Saint Joric, was founded by Adon Archbishop Primate of Valoret on the XIXth day of September in the year 777, and a monastery erected at Rosemount on the River Eirian. This establishment remains one of the great scenic wonders of the Eleven Kingdoms, being filled with no less than LIV varieties of roses, plus many other flowers besides. His feastday is the XXXth day of June.

Joseph. He was serving Earl Maldred in November of the year 903. [*Camber of Culdi*].

Joseph. He was serving as a clerk to Bran Coris Earl of Marley in the year 1121. [*High Deryni*].

Josephus, son of Master Galiardi the Merchant, later Brother Benedict. He was received into the *Ordo Verbi Dei* and took the name Benedict in the year 876, and was later cloistered at the Priory of Saint Ultan's. [*Camber of Culdi*].

Joshua *Delacroix*, Acting Grand Master of the *Equites Custodum Fidei*, Lord, Captain. He was born on the XVIIIth day of February in the Year of Our Lord 889, being a younger son of Averil Lord Delacroix and Tamsin Lady Firren. He joined the *Custodes Fidei* soon after its founding in the year 918, and was serving as an officer at the *Arx Fidei* Abbey in the year 921. He commanded the group of soldiers who opposed Prince Javan leaving the Abbey on the XXIIIrd day of June in that year. Seven years later he and the LXXX knights he commanded joined the Royal Expedition to Eastmarch at Valoret on the XVIIIth day of June in the year 928. After the death of Lord Albertus II days later, he was named Acting Grand Master of the *Equites Custodum Fidei* and was sent North to the Arranal Canyon to watch for the Torenthi forces on the XXXth day of June in that year. He served briefly as Captain-General of the Order at Ramos, but the *Equites* were disbanded the following month, and he left the Order to return to his father's estate. He died there on the XXIIIrd day of December in the year 945, aged LVI years. [*King Javan's Year*; *The Bastard Prince*].

Joshuic Foot. This unit of the Gwyneddan Army consisted of a squad of ecclesiastical soldiers under the direct command of Thomas Cardiel then Bishop of Dhassa in June of the year 1121. Their banners were violet, their shields shaped like kites. [*High Deryni*].

Joux. This small sovereign Duchy of the Forcinn Buffer States lies South of the Hort of Orsal and Principality of Tralia on the South side of the River Thuria, and is further bordered by the Grand Duchy of Vézaire to the South, the Principality of Thuria to Southeast, and the Twin Rivers Strait of the Southern Sea to the West. Joux was founded on the XIth day of November in the year 661 by the Duc Béraud Buyenne, a son-in-law of Rogan Hort of Orsal, who received his estate as part of his wife's dowry. His son Reynard I greatly expanded Joux's boundaries, conquering several smaller Muslim states to the South and throwing off the suzerainty of Orsal and Tralia. The Duchy eventually encompassed much of what is now called the Forcinn, but successive rulers of Joux gradually lost control of the outlying regions during the VIIIth and IXth centuries.

On the XXXIst day of January in the year 931 Duc Reynard III died without heirs male, and was succeeded jointly by his daughter, the Duchesse Camille, with her husband, the Duc Paulard formerly Prince Pál of Torenth, under the terms of a Treaty between the Hort of Orsal and the King of Torenth by which Tralia re-established its suzerainty over Joux. Reynard's IInd daughter, the Duchesse Violette, succeeded simultaneously as Princess of Thuria, which was then split off from Joux. Another offshoot of the House of Buyenne is the Ducal House of Corwyn, whose founder, the Ist Duke Dominic, was the eldest son of Lord Richard, the IIIrd son of Réginald Duc du Joux.

The capital of Joux is the quaint seaside town of Trebaçeaux, situate on the Southern bank of the River Thuria opposite the Île d'Orsal. It is said that the cafés here serve the best *gâteaux des crabes* and *potage de la mer* in the entire Eleven Kingdoms. Each year at the Fête du Joueurs the lutists gather from around the XI Kingdoms, instruments in hand, to lure the fairies from out their lairs, or so 'tis said. The Côte d'Aurore, as the coast of the Southern Sea is commonly known, is renowned for the beauty of its coves and inlets, and for its fine sandy beaches. [*King Kelson's Bride*].

DUCS DU JOUX

HOUSE OF BUYENNE

Béraud Buyenne	661-699
Reynard I (son)	699-728
Arnaud (son)	728-740
Baudouin (brother)	740-755
Réginald (nephew)	755-782
Bouchard (son)	782-811
Bernard (son)	811-812
Léonard (cousin)	812-844
Reynard II (son)	844-871
Rémy I (son)	871-888
Reynard III (son)	888-931
Camille (daughter)	931-951

HOUSE OF BUYENNE-FURSTÁN

Paulard of Torenth (husband)	931-942
Éméry-Rémy II (son)	942-959
Reynard IV (son)	959-987
Gaspard (brother)	987-988
Gérard (nephew)	988-1019
Régnier I (cousin)	1019-1040
Talière (son)	1040-1047
Geoffroi (brother)	1047-1089
Régnier II (son)	1089-1119
Richard (son)	1119-1130+

Jowan *Griffith*. He was serving as squire to Conall Prince of Gwynedd in the years 1124 and 1125, and accompanied him on King Kelson's quest for the relics of Saint Camber. He fell into the Grelder Creek on the XXIst day of March in the year 1125, and was drowned, aged XV years. R.I.P. [*The King's Justice*; *The Quest for Saint Camber*; *King Kelson's Bride*].

Jowerth, Lord Leslie. This Deryni Baron was born on the IInd day of October in the Year of Our Lord 868, being the eldest son of Eoghan Lord Leslie and Poilina Lady Morchoe, and an uncle of Dafydd Lord Leslie. He married Siany Lady Taaffe on the Ist day of July in the year 893, and by her he had children: the Lady Mairona; the Lady Paili; the Hereditary Lord Jambert; the Lady Regina; the Lady Edana. The Lord Jowerth succeeded his father on the IVth day of December in the year 894. He was appointed a minister to King Imre on the XXVth day of March in the year 900, and was named to the Court of Crown Commissioners on the VIth day of January in the year 901. He was reaffirmed to the Council of the new King Cinhil I on the VIth day of January in the year 905, and was present at the War Council held on the XXIIIrd day of June to discuss the Pretender Ariella's impending invasion of Gwynedd. He died of pains in his chest on the VIIIth day of August in the year 915, aged XLVI years, and was succeeded by his son, Lord Jambert. R.I.P. [*Camber of Culdi*; *Saint Camber*; *Camber the Heretic*].

Jubal, Brother. A monk at Saint Foillan's Abbey in December of the year 903. [*Camber of Culdi*].

Judhael (III) Amyas Jolyon *Quinnell-Kincaid*, **Prince and Pretender of Meara, Earl of Kilarden.** He was born on the XIXth day of June in the Year of Our Lord 1042, being the only son and heir of Rhiryd Kincaid Earl of Kilarden and the Princess Annalind Sovereign Prince and Pretender of Meara, and grandson of Jolyon II Sovereign Prince of Meara. He intermarried with the Princess Aude daughter of Fergus King of Howicce and Lissa Lady McLain, elder daughter of Tairchell Earl of Kierney, on the XXIInd day of May in the year 1060 at Sirhowy, and by her he had children: the Hereditary Prince Jolyon, dead of the morbid fever at age III; the Princess Caitrin later Pretender of Meara, who intermarried with Derek Lord Delaney, and secondly with Sicard Lord MacArdry, leaving issue; the Princess Sorcha, dead at age II of the flux; the Princess Onora, a twin with her sister Sorcha, who intermarried with Michael Lord MacDonald, and by him had I surviving son, the Prince Judhael (IV); the Hereditary Prince Jason, dead of the scarlet pox at age I; the Hereditary Prince Joris, dead of the musty mewls at age II.

On the XXIInd day of July in the year 1045 Malcolm King of Gwynedd mounted an expedition into Meara to put down a rebellion by the Princess Annalind, who had reiterated her rights as Sovereign Prince of that country, and he succeeded in capturing the Pretender, her husband, and several other members of her family. But Annalind's III-year-old son and heir, the Prince Judhael, had been hidden away by the Earl of Cloome, one of her supporters, in order to preserve the cause in the event of her death. When she refused to produce the little boy, the Princess Annalind and her husband were tried and executed for treason with several of their supporters on the VIIIth day of August in the year 1045. She was succeeded in her pretensions by the Prince Judhael, who was proclaimed Sovereign Prince of Meara by the rebel forces under the title Judhael III on the XIIIth day instant; he simultaneously succeeded his father as Earl of Kilarden.

The Prince Judhael was sent to the Kingdom of Howicce to be educated at the University of Sirhowy, and spent several decades there. He returned to his native land in April of the year 1076, and once again raised the banners of rebellion against Gwynedd. Donal Blaine II King of Gwynedd entered the Principality of Meara on the IInd day of May in that year, and defeated the Pretender's army on the XXth day of that month, but the Prince escaped South into The Connait, and remained abroad in Howicce until March of the year 1089. King Donal Blaine returned to Meara on the XXXth day of April in the year 1089, and hounded to death the Princess Onora on the XVIth day of May following, capturing and executing on the XXVth day instant Robard Lord Kincaid and Francis Lord Sommerdale, the latter being the brother of Derek Delaney Earl of Sommerdale and husband of Princess Caitrin. Again the Prince Judhael escaped to the South.

The birth of the Hereditary Prince Kelson to Brion King of Gwynedd on the XIVth day of November in the year 1106, and Kelson's creation as Prince of Meara, prompted the final rebellion of Prince Judhael, who sent his letter of defiance to Rhemuth on the XXth day instant. On the Ist day of December following Brion King of Gwynedd mounted a surprise expedition into Meara to put down this revolt by the Prince Judhael, and succeeded in capturing the Pretender's II sons-in-law, Derek Earl of Sommerdale and Michael Lord MacDonald, and also his cousin, Miran Lord Kincaid, all of whom were tried, condemned, and executed by the King on the Ist day of January in the year 1107. The Prince Judhael escaped into the hills above Ratharkin with his eldest daughter, Princess Caitrin, and her infant son, Prince Jolyon, who died acroupy II days later. Prince Judhael died in exile on the XIVth day of February in the year 1109, aged LXVI years, and by the terms of his last will and testament was succeeded in his pretensions by his elder daughter, the Princess Caitrin, and as Earl of Kilarden by his cousin, Ros Lord Kincaid.

Sir Murrough Cornaro has called this Prince "...a lost soul, a man who clearly was more comfortable researching the antecedents of his House and the history of Meara than in prosecuting any political aims. He was bracketed by II strong women—his mother and his daughter—who scoffed at his unwillingness to put himself forward and assert his claims. He blamed himself for the deaths of his relatives, saying, 'Had we stay'd in Sirhowy, we would not have been a Prince, mayhap, but happier would we be: Old Meara had no need of me.' On his deathbed he urged his daughter Caitrin to leave her pretensions behind, saying, 'We fear that you will live long enough to see your ambitions reduced to dust, and your menfolk along with them.' Following the deaths of his sons-in-law and grandson, he began to wander in his mind, and would speak to the servants as if they were one of his lost relatives. He died a broken man. His one abiding legacy was a genealogical history of the Quinnell family, *A House Divided*, which was published after his passing." R.I.P. [*The Deryni Archives*].

Judhael (IV) Michael Richard Jolyon *MacDonald Quinnell*, Hereditary Prince of Meara, Bishop of Ratharkin. He was born on the XVIth day of August in the Year of Our Lord 1085, being the only surviving son of Michael Lord MacDonald and Onora Princess of Meara. He was early destined for the Church, having no desire to pursue the political aspirations of his House, and was ordained priest on the Xth day of March in the year 1105. He was considered for the office of Bishop of Meara in the Conclave of Bishops held at Culdi on the XXIIIrd day of November in the year 1123, but was passed over due to his family connections and the impending crisis in Meara. As a result, he became embittered at his situation, and was readily seduced by the offer of Edmund Loris ex-Archbishop Primate of Valoret to be illegally consecrated as Bishop of Ratharkin on the IXth day of December in that year. He was briefly heir presumptive to the Mearan Pretender Caitrin after the execution of the latter's son, the Hereditary Prince Ithel, on the IInd day of July in the year 1124, but was himself beheaded by the order of Kelson King of Gwynedd on the XIIth day instant for the danger that he posed to the throne. He was XXXVIII years of age at his death; having repented most earnestly of his sins, he sought the forgiveness of both King and Archbishop, which was graciously granted, and he was honourably interred with his ancestors at Laas. He is described in the *Chronicles* as having a ramrod-straight carriage and prematurely silver hair, with pale blue eyes. *Semen est sanguis Christianorum.* R.I.P. [*The Bishop's Heir*; *The King's Justice*; *The Quest for Saint Camber*; *King Kelson's Bride*].

Juliana *of Horthness*, Countess of Marley, Lady. She was born on the XXVIIIth day of May in the Year of Our Lord 904, being the elder daughter of Rhun Earl of Sheele and Kristin Lady MacNeill. She was being groomed for possible marriage to Alroy King of Gwynedd in the year 918, when she attended Candlemas services at Valoret on the IInd day of February in that year, and was later matched by the Regents with King Javan, who, however, declined her hand. She intermarried with Sean Coris Earl of Marley on the VIth day of May in the year 929, and by him she had children: the Hereditary Count Brian later Earl of Marley; the Lord Daryl; the Lady Tanya; the Lord Reiner; the Lady Artemis. She died on the IXth day of November in the year 979, aged LXXV years. She was described in her youth as "a bold, dark-eyed beauty." R.I.P. [*The Harrowing of Gwynedd*; *King Javan's Year*].

Julius *ben David*. This Jewish dealer in horseflesh was present at the Rhelledd Horse Fair on the Ist day of May in the year 1115. He tried to drive a hard bargain with Sean O'Flynn Earl Derry, but failed. ["The Knighting of Derry"].

Juris, Dom. This Gabrilite Healer and priest was serving at Saint Neot's Abbey on the IIIrd day of May in the year 905, when he assisted in the dissection of the bodies of Dom Calvagh and Brother Ulric. After the destruction of that monastery by the Regents on the XXIVth day of December in the year 917, he escaped to

Dhassa through a portal and temporarily found refuge in Bishop Niallan Trey's household. He had transferred to the Michaeline Haven by January of the year 918. ["The *Examen*"; *Camber the Heretic*; *The Harrowing of Gwynedd*].

Kai *Descantor*, Bishop. This Deryni cleric was born on the VIIth day of March in the Year of Our Lord 859, being the son of Sir Morton ap Kai Descantor and Munya McQuilkin. He was ordained priest on the XXIXth day of July in the year 879, and was consecrated as an itinerant Bishop of Gwynedd on the XXXth day of March in the year 902. He attended the consecration of Father Alister Cullen as Bishop of Grecotha and Vicar General Robert Oriss as Archbishop of Rhemuth on the IXth day of July in the year 905 at Valoret. He was appointed to the Royal Council by King Cinhil I on the Ist day of December in the year 910, but was dismissed from that position by the Regents of King Alroy on the IIIrd day of February in the year 917. He spent the Summer of that year in Kheldour, and then attended the Synod of Bishops held at Valoret in November and December. He was murdered by the Regents' men while destroying the Portal at the sacristy of All Saints Cathedral in Valoret on the XXVth day of December in the year 917 during the chaos following the illegal deposition of Archbishop Primate Alister Cullen. He was LVIII years of age at his death. R.I.P. [*Saint Camber*; *Camber the Heretic*; *The Harrowing of Gwynedd*].

Kale *Pemberly*, Lord Pemberly, Deputy Chamberlain of Gwynedd. He was born on the XXIXth day of July in the Year of Our Lord 1087, being the son of Cos Lord Pemberly and Lettice Lady Carroway. He intermarried with Sativa Lady Kress on the XIIth day of April in the year 1110, and by her he had children: the Hereditary Lord Brockleigh; the Lady Aubregine; the Lady Aubretta; the Lord Crispim; the Lord Parsleigh; the Lady Moestra. The Lord Pemberly succeeded his father on the Vth day of May in the year 1124. He was appointed to the post of Deputy Chamberlain of Gwynedd by King Kelson in the following year. [*King Kelson's Bride*].

Kálmán II Imre *Furstán*, called "The Carollan," King of Torenth. He was born on the VIIth day of March in the Year of Our Lord 756, being the eldest surviving son and heir of Mátyás King of Torenth and the Princess Jessandra daughter of François Prince of Bremagne. He intermarried with Grand Princess Démétria daughter of Augoustos IV Autokrátor of Byzantyun on the XIth day of May in the year 774, and by her he had children: the Hereditary Prince Lajos later Lajos I King of Torenth; the Princess Lætitia, who intermarried with Edwy Baron LaSalle; the Prince Festil later Count of Fathane later Margraf of Medras later Festil I King of Gwynedd; the Princess Jessamyn, who took the veil at age XIV under the religious name of Sister Sophia at the Convent of Saint Ilona in Westmarcke, dying there LVI years later; the Princess Cassandra, who died from a pain in her belly at age IV; the Prince Termöd later Termöd I Sovereign Prince of Kheldour and Count of Rhorau; the Prince Imreály later Count of Netterhaven; the Prince Károlyman, dead of the whoop at age II; the Prince Vassily later Count of Altorf, lost in a sandstorm in the R'Kassi Desert, *ætatis* XIX, unmarried; the Princess Alysona, who intermarried with Jacques Comte du Dézzarette in Tralia.

The Prince Kálmán was trained as a soldier and General in his father's army. He was appointed Commander of the Torenthi Royal Army on the XIVth day of April in the year 801, and led an expedition on the IInd day of June in that year into the Arjenoli Mountains, following complaints by Torenthi settlers on the River Brust that they were being harassed by raiding parties from Arzh. On the XIIth day instant he defeated the army of Svarnik Sovereign Prince of Arjenol, killing that ruler, and then proceeded up the River Brust to Arzh, which he sacked and burned. Members of Prince Svarnik's family were tortured and violated, Mstyslav Bishop of Arzh was crucified upside down in the nave of his own Church, and the leading citizens of Arjenol were impaled on stakes lining the main thoroughfare of the city, their bodies being covered with honey and leaves. Concerning these atrocities, the Prince Kálmán was heard to remark, "It takes a good farmer from Beldour to grow a green forest in Arzh." It is said that his sons learned much from their father's example.

The Prince Kálmán succeeded his father on the XVIIIth day of December in the year 808, and was girded with the sword at Iób by Patriarch Ióannés IV on the New Year's Day following. He continued the policies of King Mátyás by pressing the frontiers of the Kingdom continually outward.

In April of the year 822, although already ill unto death with the wasting sickness, he was convinced by his IInd son Festil Margraf of Medras to support a strike into Gwynedd during that country's Festival of First Fruits. When the Prince Festil killed Ifor King of Gwynedd on the XXIst day of June in that year, Kálmán King of Torenth traveled to Valoret in slow stages, and crowned his son King of Gwynedd on the XXIInd of July, acting as Overlord of that country, thereby establishing a pattern that continued for V generations. He returned to Beldour within a month, and died there on the XXVIIIth day of November in the year 822, aged LXVI years. He was buried in the crypt of his ancestors at Torenthály, and was succeeded by his son, Prince Lajos.

His cognomen derived from a statement by one of his many enemies that "the King Kálmán had a face that could have been planed from Carollan marble, with eyes set in stone like little blue sapphires, hard and cruel and utterly without mercy." *Feindlich ist die Welt und falsch gesinnt! Es liebt ein jeder nur sich selbst.*

Kamil ibn Reyhan *Vastouni*, Hereditary Prince of Andelon. He was born on the IVth day of March in the Year of Our Lord 1097, being the eldest son and heir of Sofiana Sovereign Princess of Andelon and Reyhan Lord Séchelles. He intermarried with the Nabila Williama daughter of Hakim II Sovereign Prince of Nur Hallaj and Fabrissa Princess of R'Kassi, on the VIIth day of September in the year 1116, and by her he had children: the Princess Rutha; the Princess Ysa; the Hereditary Prince Ya'qub; the Prince Mikhail-Kamil; the Princess Kaya. *Siamo tutti figli d'Adamo.* [*King Kelson's Bride*].

Karis d'Oriel, Lady. This Deryni Lady was born on the XIVth day of July in the Year of Our Lord 917, being the only child of Oriel Lord de Bourg and Alana Lady Destaing. She intermarried with Tieg Lord Thuryn on the XXVth day of August in the year 935, and by him she had children: the Lady Madelon, who intermarried with Jürgen Lord Leslie; the Lady Aine; the Lord Jacuth; the Lady Lassa. In the year 921 she visited briefly with her father: she was then "rosy-faced, wide-eyed and innocent, beneath a tangle of red-gold curls." During the *coup d'état* by the former Regents which took place on the XIth day of May in the year 922, her father was killed, but in the confusion she and her mother were saved and taken to the Michaeline Haven by Étienne Baron de Courcy. She died in the year 948, aged XXXI years. R.I.P. [*King Javan's Year*; *The Bastard Prince*].

Károly, Father. This Torenthi Orthodox priest was asked by the Torenthi Patriarch on the Xth day of July in the year 1128 to explain to the visiting King Kelson the meaning of the *killijálay* ceremony. After Kelson was substituted for the deceased Count Czalsky, on the XIIth day instant, Father Károly delivered to the King the robe that he would use in the installation of Torenthi King Liam Lajos II. He was promoted Archpriest shortly thereafter. [*King Kelson's Bride*].

Károly Krikor Ottó *Furstán*, Hereditary Prince of Torenth, Duke of Beldourja, Blessed. This holy Prince was born on the XXIVth day of July in the Year of Our Lord 918, being the eldest son and heir of Arion I King of Torenth and the Kniazhna Pavela daughter of Ygor Sovereign Kniaz' of Jándrich. He intermarried with the Nabila Zubayda bint Abdallah Emir of Tôrtous on the XIth day of March in the year 939, and by her he had children: the Prince Malachy later Malachy II King of Torenth; the Prince Marek later Duke of Arkadia later Markos II Patriarch of Beldour and All Torenth, who died in the year 1016, aged LXXIV years; the Princess Márisa, who intermarried with Chingiz Sultan of Jama'a in the Anvil of the Lord, and had XVII children; the Prince Mátyás later Duke of Sostra, thrown from a horse and crippled at the age of XV, who never married and died childless at the age of XXX; the Princess Margitella, who intermarried with Harduin Roi de Bremagne; the Princess Mikhailina, who intermarried with Demokrit Graf von Achaika; the Prince Miroslav, who died young of the clipp'd ptomainia; the Prince Menander later Duke of Arkadia by cession from his brother; the Princess Mösza, who reached the age of reason, but concerning whom nothing further is said in the chronicles. The Dowager Princess Zubayda later served as Regent of Torenth for her grandson, King Kyprian II.

In the year 948 the Prince Károly volunteered to serve with the Pretender Marek when the latter invaded Gwynedd, and was severely wounded in the Battle of Laxalt, losing his left arm when the rot set in. When the surgeon was preparing to amputate, he was heard to remark, "Cut away, doctor. I have another yet to spare." But during this campaign he gained much trouble in his bowels that afflicted him adversely in later life, and probably also the consumption that eventually killed him.

By the year 960 it was clear that the Prince Károly could not outlive his father the King, and so he called together his surviving children, and told them: "I go soon to meet my Maker. You must never forget that there will come a day when Almighty God will call you to account for your actions, and that, since you have been born upon a higher plane, you also shall be held to a higher standard." With the blessing of the Patriarch Rhouphinos, he died calling upon the name of Jesus Christ on the XXIIIrd day of November in the year 960, aged XLII years, much mourned by his father and his sons, and was buried with his ancestors in the family crypt at Torenthály. He was beatified by the Patriarch Markos II, his own son, on the XXIVth day of July in the year 1004. R.I.P.

Káspár Lóránt Vilmos Ryszart *Furstán-Truvorsk*, Duke of Truvorsk. He was born on the XXIVth day of August in the Year of Our Lord 1093, being the eldest son and heir of Lóránt Duke of Truvorsk and the Princess Cyrice eldest daughter of Sobbon Hort of Orsal and Prince of Tralia and Maya Princess of Thuria. He intermarried with the Lady Ivoirie daughter of Gezelin Sovereign Count of Fianna and Mélusine Princess of Fallon on the XXIXth day of August in the year 1115, and by her he had children: the Countess Ismène; the Hereditary Duke Rügen; the Count Teleman; the Count Vidar; the Countess Brenta.

The Duke Káspár succeeded his father on the IIIrd day of April in the year 1122. He dined with King Liam Lajos and King Kelson in Furstánály Palace on the IXth day of July in the year 1128, as part of the preliminary festivities leading to the former's installation as ruler of Torenth. [*King Kelson's Bride*].

Kedrach. This Llanneddi stallion was owned by Brion King of Gwynedd in the year 1106 when he visited the ruins of Saint Neot's Abbey with Alaric Morgan Duke of Corwyn. [*Deryni Checkmate*].

Keeill. Located beneath the chambers used by the Camberian Council, and originally constructed by an ancient Deryni brotherhood, the *Airsid*, this room is described in the *Legends* as being "heavy and massive, the walls curved instead of faceted-in-eight. Roughly-dressed ashlar pillars, twelve of them, stood flush against the perimeter, with enough space between for a person to stand. The single bronze door in the Northern quarter opened between two of them. Four bronze cressets held torches which gave smoky, wavering life to the four quarters, thrusting vague, dancing shadow-shapes in and among the recesses of the pillars. The ceiling was somewhat more finely finished, having geometric vaulting of a blue-grey stone that glittered slightly in the torchlight.

"A dais of grey-black slate occupied most of the center of the room, the first of its seven shallow steps starting only an armspan from the heavy mass of the pillars. Precisely in the center of the dais was a square of stark white marble, an armspan on each edge and a hand's-breadth thick." [*Camber the Heretic*].

Kelric Alain *Morgan*, Hereditary Duke of Corwyn, Earl of Lendour. He was born on the IIIrd day of May in the Year of Our Lord 1125, being the eldest son and heir of Alaric Morgan Duke of Corwyn and Richenda Lady of Rheljan. He succeeded to the courtesy title of Earl of Lendour at birth. He was baptized on the Xth day of June following by Bishop Duncan McLain, in the presence of Kelson King of Gwynedd, who served as his godfather. [*The Quest for Saint Camber*; *King Kelson's Bride*].

Kelson Cinhil Rhys Anthony *Haldane*, King of Gwynedd, Overlord of Torenth, Prince of Meara, Duke of Haldane, Lord of the Purple March, Guardian of Gwernach, Sir. He was born at the IIIrd hour of the afternoon on the XIVth day of November 1106, being the only son and heir of Brion King of Gwynedd and the Princess Jehana daughter of Meyric II Roi de Bremagne. He proposed to Sidana Princess of Meara on Christmas Day in the year 1123, and intermarried with her on the VIth day of January following, but she was murdered by her brother Prince Llewell moments after the recitation of their vows, *sans postérité*. He entered into an informal betrothal of marriage with Rothana Nabila of Nur Hallaj on the VIIIth day of March in the year 1125, but in the following month, believing Kelson dead, she intermarried with the King's Ist cousin, Prince Regent Conall. He intermarried secondly with the Princess Araxie Haldane Baroness Dunluce on the VIIth day of August in the year 1128, and by her he had children: the Princess Roxelane Louise Sivorn Cécile; the Princess Rhuÿs Jehane Siloë Richelle, a twin to her sister; the Hereditary Prince Javan Uthyr Richard Urien, created Prince of Meara at birth.

The Prince Kelson was created Prince of Meara at birth by King Brion. According to Alaric Morgan Duke of Corwyn, Kelson was trained to ride from the time that he could sit upon a steed unaided. "His fencing masters were the finest to be found. His skill with lance and bow were prodigious. He studied military history and strategy, languages, philosophy, mathematics, and medicine. He even touched on the occult arts in defiance of his mother's wishes. He sat at his father's side in the Council chambers, where he acquired the rudiments of rhetoric and logic that were Brion's trademark."

The Prince Kelson was present at the knighting of Sean O'Flynn Earl Derry on the XIth day of May in the year 1115. The Prince succeeded his father on Ist day of November in the year 1120 under the regency of his mother, and attained his majority II weeks later on the XIVth day of November. He defeated and killed Princess Charissa the Festillic Pretender in a duel arcane on the XVth day instant, and was then crowned King at Saint George's Cathedral by Archbishop Edmund Loris. Under an ancient treaty with Torenth, Kelson claimed guardianship over the border County of Gwernach, which went into abeyance at Charissa's death. The King later defeated the rebellious Loris on the XXVIth day of June in the year 1121, setting the stage for the reform of the Gwyneddan clergy. He faced Wencit King of Torenth in a duel arcane on the IInd day of July following, and the Torenthi monarch and his chief supporters were killed. King Kelson became Overlord of Torenth on this date.

The King conducted a progress through Meara in the Summer of the year 1123, and after the outbreak of rebellion by the Princess Caitrin on the XXIVth day of November in that year, he saved his friend Dhugal Earl of Transha and captured Sidana Princess of Meara and her brother Prince Llewell in a lightning raid from Rhemuth to Ratharkin on the IXth day of December following.

He led the Gwyneddan army into Meara on the XXth day of May in the year 1124, and within VI weeks had reached the city of Ratharkin. On the IInd day of July he captured and executed the Hereditary Prince Ithel and Brice Baron of Trurill for their crimes, and on the following day came to the rescue of Father Duncan McLain Duke of Cassan and his army on the plain of Dorna. There he himself killed the Mearan commander, Lord Sicard MacArdry husband of the Pretender Caitrin, with an arrow through his eye when Sicard refused to submit. He executed Prince-Bishop Judhael the Pretender's cousin, ex-Archbishop Edmund Loris, and Monsignor Lawrence Gorony at Laas on the XIIth day instant, ending the Mearan rebellion. The Pretender Caitrin was sent under close confinement to a nunnery.

The King was knighted by his uncle, Nigel Duke of Carthmoor, on the IIIrd day of March in the year 1125. He left on a quest for the relics of Saint Camber on the IXth day instant, and investigated the ruins of Tor Caerrorie on the XXth day of that month. He and his friend Dhugal MacArdry Earl of Transha and Kierney fell into the High Grelder Creek on the next day following, and were swept away underground by the flood, with Kelson fracturing his skull. His injury was healed by Dhugal a few days later. They followed the river's course through a series of underground chambers until they were stopped by an artificially constructed wall. Breaking through the barrier, they entered a series of tombs, each newer than the last, until they finally emerged from underground at Saint Kyriell's on the Xth day of April.

King Kelson returned to Valoret on the XVIth day instant, and to Rhemuth on the XIXth day following. On that day the King confronted his rebellious cousin Prince Regent Conall in a duel arcane, and defeated him when the image of Saint Camber miraculously appeared. He visited Corwyn on the Xth day of June following for the christening of his godson, Kelric Alain Earl of Lendour.

In the year 1128 the question of the King's marriage, which had been festering within the body politic for some years, finally erupted into open debate among Kelson's councillors. Many possible candidates were suggested: the Lady Noelie daughter of Sir Jolyon Ramsay Titular Pretender of Meara, the Princess Ekaterina of Jáca, the Princess Elisabet or Princess Marcelline of Orsal and Tralia, the Princess Gwenlian of Llannedd, and the Princess Ursula of Howicce, among others.

The King himself still preferred the Princess Rothana, but she irrevocably refused him on the XXVIIIth day of June, following the marriage of Princess Janniver and Sir Jatham Kilshane earlier that day. However, she suggested to him on this occasion that he consider his I^st cousin once removed, the Princess Araxie Haldane Baroness Dunluce, daughter of Kelson's late great-uncle, the Prince Richard.

Accordingly, he met with Araxie in Orsal on the IIIrd day of July, and reached an agreement of betrothal with her, which was formalized that evening before Bishop Denis Arilan. Arilan informed the Camberian Council of Kelson's intentions on the evening of July XVth. On the following day, after Kelson and his friends had transported to Orsal, he informed the Hort of Orsal and his family of the betrothal; and later that evening Kelson transported to Rhemuth, and told his mother and his immediate family of the forthcoming marriage. On the XVIIth day instant, Princess Araxie joined him in Rhemuth, and Kelson informed the Privy Council of the proposed union during his noon meeting with them. The I^st public announcement of the marriage was made on the evening of the last day of July, and the ceremony itself took place a week later, being presided over by Bishop Duncan McLain.

Liam Lajos II King of Torenth had attained his majority in April of the same year, and the great lords of both countries had agreed on the necessity of King Liam assuming the burden of state as quickly as possible, to foil the ambitions of Mahael II Duke d'Arjenol and late Regent of Torenth. Accordingly, preparations were made to return King Liam to Torenth in early July of the year 1128. They sailed from Desse on the XXXth day of June, reaching Coroth on the IInd day of July. Kelson and his party crossed the channel to Orsal on the following day, where an attempt was made on the King's life by II Deryni assassins.

On the IVth day instant, the II Kings and their party sailed up the River Beldour towards the city of that name, arriving there amid great fanfare some IV days later. That same evening King Kelson met the IV participants in the *killijálay* or installment ceremony. King Liam showed Kelson the great monument which is called the Nikolaseum on the Xth day instant. On the following day, the body of Count Czalsky was found strangled, and King Liam asked Kelson to replace him in the *killijálay*, to which the latter readily agreed. He began practicing immediately, being trained by Azim, Father Irenæus, Father Károly, and János Sokrat.

On the XVIth day of July King Liam Lajos II was formally installed as monarch of Torenth. During the ceremony Mahael Duke d'Arjenol and his brother Count Teymuraz attacked Liam, but Mahael was defeated by Kelson, Count Mátyás, and Patriarch Alpheios. Teymuraz was taken prisoner, but escaped soon thereafter. King Kelson then relinquished his overlordship over Torenth, and was asked to participate in King Liam's I^st Royal Council that evening. He decided to return at once to Orsal to remove the Hort's womenfolk and Araxie and her kin from any danger from Teymuraz, and from there transported directly to Rhemuth.

On the XVIIth day instant, Kelson called his Privy Council into session to discuss recent events, and to announce his betrothal to Princess Araxie. On the XXVIth day of July, the King announced that he was creating Prince Rory Duke of Ratharkin and Viceroy of Meara, Sir Jolyon Ramsay Duke of Laas, and Brecon Ramsay Earl of Kilarden, and that Prince Albin was being restored to his rightful position as Hereditary Duke of Carthmoor. He also asked Bishop Duncan McLain to become Rector of the new Deryni *schola* he planned to create in Rhemuth. That afternoon, the King, the II Archbishops of Gwynedd, and others inspected the new Chapel of Saint Camber established in the basilica of Rhemuth Palace.

On the XXXth day of the month, Kelson and his Court welcomed the arrival of the Servants of Saint Camber to Rhemuth. He also persuaded Princess Rothana to accept the position of lay assistant to the Rector of the new Deryni *schola*. That afternoon the new chapel was formally consecrated, and that evening, Sir Jolyon Ramsay was created Duke of Laas. King Kelson attended the dual royal wedding between Brecon Ramsay and Princess Richelle and Prince Rory and Noelie Ramsay on the following day, and helped thwart an attack by Count Teymuraz on his younger brother, Count Mátyás. At Kelson's own wedding ceremony, a week later, Princess Araxie was crowned Queen of Gwynedd by Archbishop Bradene. On the XIVth day of November, King Kelson celebrated his natal day by hosting King Liam Lajos II of Torenth at Rhemuth. At the celebratory dinner held that day, he announced an affiliation of family between the Royal Houses of Haldane and Furstán, and by revealed that the Queen was with child.

He is described in the *Chronicles* as having the traditional grey eyes and black hair of the Haldane line, with a lean but muscular build. By the year 1128 he wore his hair long and braided, doubled back on itself with a wrapping of gold for special ceremonies. His arms are: *gules*, a lion rampant guardant *or*. ["The Knighting of Derry"; *Deryni Rising*; *Deryni Checkmate*; *High Deryni*; *The Bishop's Heir*; *The King's Justice*; *The Quest for Saint Camber*; *King Kelson's Bride*].

Kennet *Furstán-Kheldour*, sometime Count of Rhorau and Iowerth and *de jure* Prince of Kheldour, Captain, Sir. He was born on the XIIth day of December in the Year of Our Lord 891, being the only surviving son and heir of Kemal Furstán-Kheldour Count Iorwerth and Bathsheba Lady of Claibourne, and a nephew of Termöd II Prince of Kheldour and brother to Sudrey Countess of Eastmarch. He never married.

The Lord Kennet was raised by his uncle Termöd following his parents' early demise. After his uncle's murder by Willimite partisans on the IXth day of July in the year 904, and the execution and attainder of Termöd's son, Prince Tomlin, on the XVIIIth day of September in the year 905, Sir Kennet succeeded his cousin as Count of Rhorau and *de jure* Prince of Kheldour, although he never formally claimed or used the latter title. He was only XIV years of age, but he continued to hold the fortress of Rhorau against Sighere Earl of Eastmarch for nearly a year until it fell on the XVth day of August in the year 906, when he was captured with his sister, Lady Sudrey. Both were made hostages of Sighere Duke of Claibourne, who gave them into the wardenship of his son and heir, Ewan Earl of Rhendall later Duke of Claibourne.

The Earl Ewan made Kennet his squire, and was said to have loved him like his own son; he knighted Kennet on the IInd day of April in the year 911. By the time that Ewan succeeded his father as Duke on the IInd day of July in the year 917, Sir Kennet was serving as a Captain of Ewan's mounted cavalry.

Sir Kennet's titles of Rhorau and Kheldour were attainted in the year 906, although he was allowed his life and ultimately his liberty; he was unsuccessful in petitioning King Cinhil I in the year 915 for a restoration of his former honours. He was killed by Murdoch Earl of Carthane while defending his master, Ewan Duke of Claibourne, on the XXVth day of May in the year 918, aged XXVI years, and should have been succeeded in his various titles by his sister and heir, Sudrey Countess of Eastmarch.

The Torenthi Prince Miklós inquired about the fate of Sir Kennet and his sister at the coronation banquet of King Javan on the XXXIst day of July in the year 921, which query precipitated a mortal combat between Hrorik II Earl of Eastmarch and Murdoch Earl of Carthane, when the former accused the latter of murdering his brother Ewan. R.I.P. [*Saint Camber*; *King Javan's Year*; *The Bastard Prince*].

Kennet *Howell*, Earl of Eastmarch. He was born on the XXXth day of May in the Year of Our Lord 928, being the eldest son and heir of Stacia Countess of Eastmarch and Corban Lord Howell. He intermarried with his cousin, Tanya Lady Marley, on the IXth day of June in the year 947, and by her he had children: the Hereditary Count Sighere later Earl of Eastmarch; the Lady Susanta, who intermarried with Nygel King of Gwynedd; the Lord Rolf later Rolf II Earl of Eastmarch; the Lord Colwyn later Earl of Eastmarch; the Lady Deline. He succeeded his mother on the IInd day of April in the year 967, and his father on the IXth day of December in the year 968. He died on the XXIIIrd day of August in the year 973, aged XLV years, and was succeeded by his eldest son, Lord Sighere. R.I.P. [*The Bastard Prince*].

Kenneth Kai *Morgan*, Hereditary Knight and Laird of Morganhall, Sir. He was born on the VIIth day of October in the Year of Our Lord 1046, being the eldest surviving son and heir of Sir Kai Anthony Morgan and Madonna Lady McLain, second daughter of Arnall Earl of Kierney. He intermarried with Anya Lady Almaris in 1067, and by her he had issue: Master Kai Kennis, who died fibroidy at age III; Master Kailan Lain, born dead; Mistress Zoë Bronwyn; Mistress Geill; Mistress Alazais. After the death of his wife, he intermarried with the Lady Alyce Heiress de Corwyn on the XVIIIth day of June in the year 1090, and by her he had further children: Sir Alaric Anthony later Duke of Corwyn and Earl of Lendour; the Lady Bronwyn Rhetice, who was betrothed to Kevin McLain Earl of Kierney at the time of her death in the year 1121.

Sir Kenneth succeeded his father as Hereditary Knight and Laird of Morganhall on the XXth day of March in the year 1076. He attached himself to the Court of his mentor King Donal Blaine II on the latter's succession to the Gwyneddan throne in the year 1074, and participated in the Mearan expedition which the King mounted II years later. Indeed, it was the King himself who arranged for Sir Kenneth's brilliant marriage to the beautiful and wealthy Lady Alyce de Corwyn. On the XXIXth day of December in the year 1095 Brion King of Gwynedd awarded Sir Kenneth the estate called Corwode, to be passed by him to his heirs-at-law, and which was later allotted as part of the dowry of Lady Bronwyn Morgan. Sir Kenneth died on the XXIVth day of September in the year 1100, aged LIII years, and was succeeded as Hereditary Laird and Knight of Morganhall by his son, Duke Alaric. R.I.P. ["Swords Against the Marluk"; *Deryni Checkmate*].

Kenric, Dom. This experienced Gabrilite Healer was serving as a monk at Saint Neot's Abbey when the forces of Rhun Earl of Sheele attacked there on the XXIVth day of December in the year 917. He escaped the conflagration by taking the transfer portal to Dhassa, and sought refuge temporarily in Bishop Niallan Trey's household. By January of the year 918 he had moved to the Michaeline Haven. [*Camber the Heretic*; *The Harrowing of Gwynedd*].

Kevin Douglas *McLain*, Earl of Kierney, Hereditary Duke of Cassan, Sir. He was born on the XXIInd day of May in the Year of Our Lord 1088, being the eldest son and heir of Jared McLain Duke of Cassan and Elaine Lady MacInnis. He was betrothed to Lady Bronwyn Countess de Morgan in the Fall of the year 1120; they were to be married in March of the year 1121.

As heir to his father's estates, he succeeded to the courtesy title of Earl of Kierney on the Ist day of August in the year 1099. On the IIIrd day of August in the year 1100 he was playing with his friends at Culdi when Alaric Morgan Duke of Corwyn fell out of a tree and broke his arm. At that time he met the witch-woman known as Bethane, who set the injured boy's limb. He was knighted by King Brion on the XVIth day of November in the year 1106, and participated in the King's Mearan expedition a month later. He was killed at Culdi together with his betrothed by the misplaced magic of that same witch-woman on the XXIXth day of March in the year 1121, aged XXXII years, and was buried in Saint Teilo's Church at Castle Culdi. After his death his half-brother, Father Duncan McLain, succeeded him as Earl and heir to the Duchy of Cassan. R.I.P. [*Deryni Rising*; *Deryni Checkmate*; *High Deryni*; *The Bishop's Heir*].

Kharthat, Free Port of. This city, the only town in the Anvil of the Lord, is situate on the South side of the River Rampante where it meets the Atalantic Ocean, on the opposite bank of the River from the city of Alverville capital of the Duchy of Alver. It serves as the major trading port for the Anvil of the Lord, providing the only safe harbour for hundreds of miles to the South along Le Sable Noir. It was here that Bearand King of Gwynedd conducted a raid on the Moors then plaguing the Eleven Kingdoms on the XVIIth day of August in the year 755, burning much of the town and its port and sinking or damaging LIV enemy ships, forever ending the Muslim threat to the West. Thorne Hagen first found his companion Moira in the marketplace here in February of the year 1115. This was also the spot from which Azim's galley sailed to Gwynedd in June of the year 1124; he later reboarded the ship South of Rhemuth on the River Eirian, and used it to exit Gwynedd after delivering his warning to Richenda of an impending Torenthi assassination plot against Nigel Duke of Carthmoor. [*High Deryni*; *The King's Justice*].

Kheldish Riding. This Northeastern portion of the old Principality of Kheldour is held directly by the King of Gwynedd, having been split from Kheldour after the latter's annexation by Cinhil I King of Gwynedd on the XXVIth day of August in the year 906, and made into a separate Viceregality. Located East of Claibourne and North of Marley, the Riding is bounded on the North by the Atalantic Ocean and on the East by the Northern Sea, and encompasses the Kheldish Mountains. Its capital is Stavenham. The Kheldish Riding is particularly known for the high quality of its woolen goods, especially the plaids and tartans woven by the many highlanders there. [*The Harrowing of Gwynedd*; *The Bishop's Heir*].

Kheldour. Located in the far Northwest of Gwynedd on the Atalantic Ocean, this ancient principality included the lands now known as Claibourne, Rhorau, the Kheldish Riding, and Rhendall. The coast of Kheldour was settled at a time before recorded history by the Sea People, who are called the Heldurnii in the old Rûman chronicles of Prochorus. The Byzantyun annals of the early Christian Era speak of the "Kheldourynoi," who "came from the West in their long ships and established a Commonwealth of villages..." at least a century before the Easterner conquerors themselves arrived in the year 249. According to Kallinikos apo Mókiou, "These people practiced many strange and barbarous rites, and did not mix with other folk. Their magi could touch minds and make men see things that were not real."

The Autokratór Basileios sent an army against them in the year 253, seeking to extend his Empire beyond the River Erinys, but VI weeks later only IV soldiers out of the five thousand who had left Rhombuticum returned home, sick and exhausted and trembling with fear. They spoke of being attacked by devils from Hell with green fire. The Great King did not move North again." The only direct source for the early history of this nation, Mahael's *History of Kheldour* (*Historia Kheldourias*), was apparently lost after the Haldane Restoration, although copies may yet exist in some distant archive.

Some centuries later, the Principality of Kheldour was proclaimed on the IIIrd day of June in the year 555 by the Count Cùnard MacTyre, who had systematically conquered all of his neighbours. By the year 600 the ruler of this rapidly expanding state was calling himself "Princeps Kheldouri." The last Deryni ruler of the House of MacTyre was Prince Dinan, who was killed on the XXth day of July in the year 823 by King Festil I of Gwynedd and his Torenthi allies; Festil then gave Kheldour to his younger brother, Count Termöd I, who became the I[st] autonomous Prince of Festillic Kheldour on the XIVth day of August following, acknowledged King Festil as Overlord. His descendants ruled the Principality until the fall of the House of Furstán-Festil.

In the year 905 Kheldour was invaded and quickly conquered by Sighere Earl of Eastmarch, and the last Prince, Tomlin, was captured and executed on the XVIIIth day of September. Kheldour was then annexed to Eastmarch, but Tomlin's young cousin, Kennet Count of Rhorau and *de jure* Prince of Kheldour, continued to resist for another year in his fortress in the Rhendall Mountains. In the year 906 Earl Sighere made obeisance to Cinhil I King of Gwynedd, and was raised to the rank of Duke of Claibourne and Viceroy of Kheldour on the XXVIth day of August in the year 906, with Kheldour becoming part of Gwynedd. Sighere gave his other lands in Marley and Eastmarch to his younger sons; Claibourne passed to his eldest son Ewan in the year 917.

The Viceregality of Kheldour was offically dismantled by the Regency Council of King Alroy on the IVth day of June in the year 918, but the title of Earl of Kheldour was awarded to Angus MacEwan Hereditary Duke of Claibourne by King Uthyr Haldane on the IXth day of March in the year 966, and has been maintained as a secondary title for the heir to the Duchy ever since. Kheldour is particularly noted for its fine textiles and carpets, and for the plenitude of great fish lurking off its coast. [*Camber of Culdi*; *Saint Camber*; *The Harrowing of Gwynedd*; *King Javan's Year*; *King Kelson's Bride*]. See also: Kennet, Sudrey, Termöd.

PRINCES AND EARLS OF KHELDOUR

HOUSE OF MACTYRE

Cùnard MacTyre	555-581
Lingen (son)	581-589
Madog (brother)	589-611
Dewar (brother)	611-629
Lulach (son)	629-655
Balliol (son)	655-682
Ednyfed (cousin)	682-701
Ieuan (son)	701-716
Iorwerth (nephew)	716-743
Maelgwn (son)	743-777
Rhygyfarch (cousin)	777-799
Goronwy (brother)	799-804
Ruck (son)	804-820
Dinan (son)	820-823

HOUSE OF FURSTÁN-KHELDOUR

Termöd I (son of Kálmán II of Torenth)	823-845
Tarquin (son)	845-877
Termöd II (nephew)	877-904
Tomlin (son)	904-905

HOUSE OF MACEWAN

Angus I (Earl)	966-984
Tresham (son)	984-1012
Geoffrey (son)	1012-1025

IN ABEYANCE

Graham I (grandson of Tresham)	1054-1056
Ursic (son)	1056-1078
Ewan II (son)	1078-1095
Graham II (son)	1095-1129
Angus II (son)	1129-1130+

Kierney. The Earldom of Kierney is situate in the Northwestern part of Gwynedd, being bordered by the Duchy of Cassan to the North, the Gulf of Kheldour to the East, the Earldoms of Transha and Culdi to the

South, and the Principality of Meara to the West. Originally part of the Principality of Cassan, it was conquered by Festil I King of Gwynedd on the XIIth day of September in the year 822, and given to one of the King's close companions and comrade-in-arms, Iolo Lord MacLean, and to the heirs general of his body. On the supposed extinction of the male line on the XIXth day of March in the year 918, the title passed through the late Geoffrey Lord MacLean to his daughter, the Countess Richeldis and her husband, Iver Lord MacInnis. The death of Richard MacInnis at Killingford on the XVIth day of June in the year 1025 again produced the extinction of the direct male line, and the title passed to his daughter Glorian and then to her son, Arnall Lord McLain son of Roger Lord McLain. On the IXth day of January in the year 1076 the Earldom became a secondary holding of the Dukes of Cassan. In the year 1124, during the war between Gwynedd and Meara, Prince Ithel Quinnell, heir to the Pretender Caitrin, claimed the Earldom of Kierney as next legal heir to that title. Bishop Duncan McLain resigned his titles on the XXIst day of May in the year 1125 in favour of his son, the Duke and Earl Dhugal MacArdry Earl of Transha, a close companion of King Kelson. His heir in the year 1130 is Alaric Duke of Corwyn. [*The Harrowing of Gwynedd*; *Deryni Rising*; *Deryni Checkmate*; *High Deryni*; *The Bishop's Heir*; *King Kelson's Bride*].

EARLS OF KIERNEY

HOUSE OF MACLEAN

Iolo MacLean called "The Lean"	822-830
Mowbray (son)	830-842
Bennet (brother)	842-844
Bethune (brother)	844-855
Brennan (brother)	855-860
Iain I (son)	860-895
Iain II (son)	895-918
Richeldis (niece)	918-1000

HOUSE OF MACINNIS

Iver (husband)	918-948
Hobard (son)	948
Richard (son)	948-1025
Glorian (daughter)	1025-1033

HOUSE OF MCLAIN

Arnall (son)	1033-1076
Andrew (son)	1076
Jared (son)	1076-1099
Kevin (son)	1099-1121
Duncan (brother; abdicated)	1121-1125

HOUSE OF MACARDRY MCLAIN

Dhugal (son)	1125-1130+

Kilarden. This Earldom, with its the walled town of the same name, lies near the Northern border of Meara with Cassan at the headwaters of the Kilarden River on Blue Lake. The Earldom was first granted to Darin Lord Kincaid by Justin Sovereign Prince of Meara on the XIIth day of October in the year 856. Judhael III Pretender of Meara bore the subsidiary title Earl of Kilarden, which he inherited from his father; at his death in the year 1109 it passed to his cousin, Earl Ros. The Earldom provided many men to the army of Meara during the Rebellion of 1123 and 1124. At the death on the IXth day of February in the year 1127 of Earl Ros, who was kept under close confinement during the last III years of his life, the title went into abeyance among the descendants of the II female co-heiresses of Earl Miran, the Ladies Inez and Nío. The abeyancy was resolved by King Kelson in favour of Sir Brecon Ramsay, a descendant of Lady Inez of the elder line, on the XXXIst day of July in the year 1128. [*The King's Justice*; *King Kelson's Bride*].

EARLS OF KILARDEN

HOUSE OF KINCAID

Darin Kincaid	856-877
Rhydion (son)	877-902
Sabin (son)	902-918
Rosin (brother)	918-933
Varin (son)	933-972
Miran (son)	972-997
Loren (son)	997-1027
Rhiryd (son)	1027-1045
Judhael (son)	1045-1109
Ros (cousin)	1109-1127

TITLE IN ABEYANCE

HOUSE OF RAMSAY-QUINNELL

Brecon (cousin)	1128-1130+

Kilchon. This small Barony is situate in the Southern part of Carthmoor, just West of the Barony and Port of Dunluce. From antiquity it belonged to the family of Sainte-Beuve, which became extinct in the year 856. The holding was then given to the Baron Dunluce, but he was deprived of his estates by the Regents in the year 917, and the title passed to Rhys Michael Duke of Carthmoor later King of Gwynedd. It was granted by King Malcolm to Perrin the natural son of the Prince Aidan late Duke of Valoret on the XVIIth day of August in the year 1036. Kilchon is known for its vintage wines, the finest in all Gwynedd. Lord Perrin achieved great fame by perfecting the Perrinine *rosé* over a XXX-year period, sending the Ist samples to his patron the King in the year 1069.

BARONS OF KILCHON

HOUSE OF PERRIN DU RORINGE

Perrin	1036-1101
Étienne (son)	1101-1125
Caidin (son)	1125-1130+

Kilian *MacShane*, Dom. This Gabrilite Healer was serving at Saint Neot's Abbey in the year 905. As a junior student he witnessed the killing of Dom Ulric by the Abbot, Dom Emrys, after the former went berserk on the IInd day of May in that year. By the year 917 he was a master Healer himself, being assigned the responsibility for the initial training of junior novices in the art and science of the healing arts. One of his students on the XVIth of April in that year, just VIII months before the destruction of the monastery by the Regents, was Simonn. ["The *Examen*"; "First Session"; *Camber the Heretic*].

Killijálay is the ceremony of installation for the Kings of Torenth, having been devised by King Furstán to provide for the Torenthi people and nation a visible demonstration of the powers of the Furstáni, but also to enhance the magical abilities of the monarchs of Torenth so that they might prevail over those enemies who would seek to overturn the will of God. The *killijálay* has always taken place on the New Year's Day following the succession of a Torenthi monarch, except when there has been a vacancy in the office of Patriarch, or when the occupant of the Obsidian Throne has not yet attained his majority under law. In the latter case, a more abbreviated ceremony is scheduled when King has passed his XIVth year, to transfer the actual power of Furstán to the adult monarch.

The *killijálay* is presided over by the Patriarch of Beldour and All Torenth, who having symbolically depowered the deceased King, then draws upon the energy poured by Furstán into the tomb of the Church of Sankt Iób in Torenthály, and infuses it into the new Padishah. The invigorated monarch must then demonstrate his capabilities by lifting the great Sword of State, which normally requires the strength of VI adult males to move from its stand, and with it create a magical display visible to all his countrymen, Deryni and non-Deryni alike. Only then can he be regarded as a true King. Εν μύρτου κλαδι το ξίφος φορήσω. [*King Kelson's Bride*].

***Killingford*, originally *Schillingford*.** Located on the Falling Water or Red River Northeast of Ebor, this ford was the scene of the largest battle in the history of the XI Kingdoms, in which thousands of Torenthi and Gwyneddan soldiers perished. The armies of the II nations became engaged at the village of Schilling on the XVth day of June in the year 1025, and continued to struggle over its site for II more days. No accurate accounting of the casualties has ever been attempted, but the devastation to the nobility of both countries was so great that many titles were rendered extinct or passed to distant branches of their respective families. Two Kings of Gwynedd perished as a result of the Great War, as it came to be called, and the King of Torenth abdicated shortly after returning to Beldour.

Eugenia Lady Campbell wrote the following account of the initial engagement, based upon the memoirs of Browning Lord Campbell: "Father rode onto the field of battle that day upon his favourite mount, a sturdy little R'Kassi mare named 'Luziana.' She was tawny in colour, like unto that of the golden chess-nut; she sported a pure white blazen on her fore head, and her dainty feet were tipped with white, as if, it seemed, she had been dip't in fine white sugar. Father elicited much scorn from his comrades-in-arms, as he rode into combat on such a tiny steed, a playtoy really, she seem'd.

"Then disaster struck; the mighty Torenthian marauders rolled over our lines, as if they were made of nothing but flimsy tinder sticks. Father's comrades fell about him, struck down by blows and arrows alike. Many lay dead, many more were wounded most painfully. Screaming and shouting to each other, our soldiers, in confusion now, retreated as best they could, back towards the hills that marked our Highland home.

"Father was hit; he suffered a great blow upon the head and a sabre slashed his thigh. His mount struggled onward until she was caught in an onslaught of arms, a churning sea of blades and bows. She was struck in the nigh rear leg by an arrow, a near-mortal wound which should have felled the mightiest destrier. She slipped, then staggered a-foot once more. Father clung for his life to her golden mane, and urged her forward with shouts of fear and encouragement.

"The 'Little Lucy,' for that was what she was called, ran for IV miles on III legs, and carried Father to safety that fateful day. She and he survived their wounds, but went a-warring no more. His next-born child, my youngest sister but one, was named Luziana—but we all called her 'Little Lucy' in honour of the plucky mare who had saved Father's life." [*King Kelson's Bride*].

***Kilshane*.** This ancient coastal Earldom bordered Transha on the South and Cassan on the North. The town of Kilshane, the former capital of this County, lies on the Northern coast of Kierney on the Gulf of Kheldour. It was the home of the "Bonnie Earl of Kilshane," the subject of many border ballads; supposedly, he rode day and night for nearly a week to warn an early Chief of the Clan MacArdry of an invasion by sea. The honour was created by Alphonse Sovereign Prince of Cassan for his friend and supporter Bellagh Lord Kilshane on the XXXth day of April in the year 786. The title became extinct at the death of Earl Banbhan in the year 948. In a revival of the title, Sir Jatham Kilshane was created Baron Kilshane by King Kelson on the XXIXth day of June in the year 1128, the day after his wedding to Janniver Princess of Pardiac. *Ein Kaiserwort soll man nicht dreh'n, noch deuteln.* [*The Quest for Saint Camber*; *King Kelson's Bride*]. See also: Jatham, Jathan.

EARLS OF KILSHANE

HOUSE OF KILSHANE

Bellagh Kilshane	786-809
Beolagh (son)	809-818
Beanon (brother)	818-835
Blathmac (son)	835-861
Ballin (nephew)	861-888
Berghet (son)	888-916
Baethan (son)	916-944
Beelybhob (cousin)	944
Banbhan (son)	944-948

TITLE EXTINCT

SECOND HOUSE OF KILSHANE

Jatham (Baron)	1128-1130+

***Kiltuin*.** This port town of Northeastern Corwyn, a fief of the Bishop of Coroth, is located on the Western River on the Corwyn side of the border just South of Fathane. It was here that the swordsmith Ferris was tried for murder by Bishop Ralf Tolliver on the XVIIth

day of April in the year 1118. He was ultimately found innocent. ["Trial"].

Kimball, Abbot. This *Custodes* priest was serving as head of Saint Cassian's Abbey on the Iomaire Plain in June of the year 928. He exorcised King Rhys Michael and all of the surviving Great Lords on the XXIst day of that month, supposedly to remove the taint of the renegade Deryni Dimitri. [*The Bastard Prince*].

King's Rangers. This elite constabulary was organized in the reign of King Cluim to patrol those regions of Gwynedd outside of the towns and cities. They had broad-based powers to investigate crimes and restore order. One of their number in the year 1118 was called Stalker. ["Trial"].

Kingslake. This village in Northeast Corwyn is located at the head of the Kingslake Water, which forms the headwaters of the Western River. The town was visited by Warin de Grey and Sean O'Flynn Earl Derry on the XXVth day of March in the year 1121. The Royal Tabard Inn is located here. [*Deryni Checkmate*].

Kinkellyan. This old songsmith was serving as clan bard at Castle Transha when Kelson King of Gwynedd visited there on the XXVth day of November in the year 1123. He wore white robes and brandished II evergreen boughs in salute. [*The Bishop's Heir*].

Kirkon. This R'Kassi native was serving as a scout in the service of Kelson King of Gwynedd during the Mearan invasion during June of the year 1124. [*The King's Justice*].

Kisah. This giant live cheetah was draped like a cloak around the shoulders and down the back of the Torenthi ambassador al-Rasoul ibn Tarik when he visited the Court of Rhemuth on the IIIrd day of March in the year 1125. Dhugal MacArdry Earl of Transha and Kierney found her most congenial. [*The Quest for Saint Camber*].

Kitron *of Csodala*. He was the Deryni author of that classic guide to the occult, *Principia Magica*, parts of which are written in code. He is said to have derived from the Duchy of Petchora in Csodala, being the son of Kåndahar the Mage, or, according to some sources, of Kayler Graf von Dalénka. In the year 1128 Barrett de Laney discussed with Jehana Dowager Queen of Gwynedd a recently-discovered manuscript by Kitron on the healing arts, *De Natura Sanationis Deryniana*. Campbell de Broun claimed, in his *More Dialogues from a Wandering Penman*, to have shared a pleasant evening of eating and drinking with a descendant of Kitron, Lord Rubroek von Kübbe, near the town of Sztürm in the Csodalan Province of Drangh. "Rubroek," he said, "spoke highly of his ancestor, but noted that Kitron rejected the classical values of Deryni magic in favour of artistic creativity." [*The Harrowing of Gwynedd*; *Deryni Magic*; *King Kelson's Bride*].

Knights of the Anvil (Equites Incudis). This militant religious Order was founded by refugees from the Order of Saint Michael, which was dispersed from Gwynedd after the death of King Cinhil I in the year 917 and relocated its Mother House at Djellarda in the Anvil of the Lord, East of the Kingdom of Bremagne. The Order was renamed on the I[st] day of January in the Year of Our Lord 923. Two centuries later, in the year 1124, Rocail was serving as Grand Master and Azim was a preceptor for the Order. [*The King's Justice*].

Komnénë. This small rural County of Torenth is located in Southwestern Arjenol. It was erected as a Lordship by King Wencit to honour Mátyás son of Mahael I Duke d'Arjenol on the IIIrd day of January in the year 1115, and was raised to a County on the XVIth day of September in the year 1125 by King Liam Lajos II. After Count Mátyás became Duke d'Arjenol in the year 1128, the Honour was deeded to his IInd son, Count Lóránt Lajos Kalinik, at the latter's birth on the IInd day of February in the year 1130. *Lumen in Komnenna*. [*King Kelson's Bride*].

Kulnán, or Cullanan. This small County of Western Torenth is situate in the Eastern foothills of the Rheljan Mountains, being demarcated on II sides by the Northern Beldour River and the Kóldór River, and by the Duchy of Truvorsk on the East, the County of Tigre and the Duchy of Nördmarcke on the North, the County of Gwernach on the West, and the Duchy of Sasovna on the South. The Honour was given by Torenthi King Imre I to Lord Siebert Makróry on the IInd day of March in the year 712, and has remained in his family ever since. The capital of the County is Kulnánberg. [*King Kelson's Bride*].

COUNTS OF KULNÁN

HOUSE OF MAKRÓRY

Siebert I MacRhori	712-769
Maurin I (son)	769-791
Amaury I (brother)	791-819
Siebert II (son)	819-823
Kámbor (son)	823-855
Dávin (son)	855-882
Siebert III (son)	882-899
Alvin (brother)	899
Jóry (son)	899
Eldin (cousin)	899-917
Kelvin (son)	917-944
Róry I (son)	944-975
Lélin (nephew)	975-998
Kólbert (brother)	998-1006
Maurin II (son)	1006-1023
Dónan (son)	1023-1025
Maurin III (cousin)	1025-1066
Amaury II (son)	1066-1078
Dáris (brother)	1078-1091
Armin (son)	1091-1104
Róry II (son)	1104-1130+

Kyla, Lady. This VIIIth-century poet was a well-known writer from Mooryn. The Lady Rhysel fetched a volume of Kyla's verse for Michaela Queen of Gwynedd on the XIVth day of June in the year 928. [*The Bastard Prince*].

Kylan. This archer from Saint Kyriell's village in Eastern Gwynedd was serving on the town Quorial in April of the year 1125. [*The Quest for Saint Camber*].

Kyprian II Könyves Káspár Kirill *Furstán*, King of Torenth, Grand Duke of Furstán, Duke of Arkadia, called "Nikétés" or "Conqueror." This evil Prince was spawned on the XIIIth day of October in the Year of Our Lord 975, being the third son and sixth child of Malachy II King of Torenth and Ianthe Princess of Salonique. He intermarried with Grand Princess Polyxena daughter of Démétrios II Autokratór of Byzantyun, on the XXIXth day of June in 994, and by her he had children: the Hereditary Prince Arkady later Arkady II King of Torenth; the Princess Arien later Regent d'Arjenol, who intermarried with Averil Hereditary Duke d'Arjenol, leaving issue; the Prince Nikola later Duke of Arkadia by cession of his father, slain at Killingford, *sans postérité*; the Prince Zimri later Duke of Truvorsk; the Prince Kirill later Duke of Arkadia in succession to his brother; the Princess Kónstanza, who died young; the Prince Andruin later Duke of Lorsöl later Stephanos V Patriarch of Beldour, who died in the year 1066, *sans postérité*; the Princess Sachette, who was blinded in an accident at the age of XIII and sent to a nunnery, where she died of the consumptive disease, aged XXXIII years and VII days.

In the Summer of the year 984 Malachy II King of Torenth supported the pretensions of the Festillic Prince Imre II to the throne of Gwynedd, and mustered an army to invade that realm; the Prince Kyprian was created Duke of Arkadia on the XVIIIth day of June and left at home. In the disastrous campaign which followed, the King Malachy II and the Hereditary Prince Nimur were killed, and Malachy's second son, Prince Carolus, briefly succeeded his father as King Károly II before himself dying on the VIIIth day of August 984. Prince Kyprian then became King under the joint regency of his grandmother, the Dowager Princess Zubayda, and his great-uncle, the Prince Vidar Duke of Truvorsk and Prince-Bishop of Podébrad. He attained his majority on the XIIIth day of October in the year 989, and was girded with the sword by Patriarch Olympios I on the New Year's Day following.

According to the Princess Arien, writing in her *Lives of the XII Kings of Torenth*, "The King Kyprian was ever driven by a need to avenge himself upon the Haldanes, whom he blamed for the deaths of his father and brothers, and he spent all the days of his life seeking to defeat the illegitimate Kings of Gwynedd. For this was the truth of the matter, that he hated the scions of Halbert the Dane and believed them an aberration of the Devil to be cleansed wholly from the Earth. He was fond of saying that the world could support either the Haldanes or the Furstáns, but not both."

King Kyprian's contemporary, Count Gábor Tököly, said of this Prince that he was "intense even as a lad, a man driven by demons he scarcely knew or controlled." Pabóly Count d'Altorf has stated: "The King was not a handsome man, being somewhat burly and thick through the chest, yet he commanded the respect of his peers with the force of his will, and one did not counter him lightly. He had a temper that would burst upon a questioner with great vehemence, often with little provocation and to ill effect. Many of his chief advisers were ultimately executed, imprisoned, or exiled over seemingly minor faults, and then were not available when he had great need of them. The man who served him least was himself."

In the Spring of the year 995 the King Kyprian joined with Imre III the Festillic Pretender to assemble a force that would invade Gwynedd in the Summer, but the army was disbanded when severe heat and drought struck Gwynedd and Torenth during the months of June and July, bringing great hardship upon the land.

In the Spring of the year 997, King Kyprian was Ist honoured with the appelation Conqueror by his newly-appointed Court astrologer, Melantro later Lord Birgol. On the XVIth day of May in that year the city of Netterhaven in the Duchy of Jándrich was unexpectedly attacked and burnt by the Northern hordes of Eistenmark and Tretelgia. Three days later the Michaeline establishment at Brustarkia was overrun. King Kyprian received news of the attacks at Medras, where he was gathering a new army to invade Gwynedd. He immediately assumed control of the Pretender Imre's force, joined it with his own, and marched Northeast on the XXth day instant.

Two days later the city of Arzh in Arjenol was besieged by the barbarians of Dyggvi Bolverksson, priest and leader of the Eistenmark hordes. Kyprian relieved Arzh on the XXVIth day of May, and fought an indecisive battle at Portis on the day following. The King split his forces, leaving a portion to protect Arzh, and taking the rest to Netterhaven on the XXXth day of May. On the IInd day of June he fought a battle at Kálmár, defeating a IInd horde of barbarians from Tretelgia. On the VIIth day of that month the reserve Torenthi force was massacred at Arzh and the city was burnt. The Eistenmark forces then departed Arjenol for the East.

During the following year King Kyprian took an expedition East to hunt the Eistenmark hordes, but was unsuccessful. In the year 1002 Kyprian marched North to Eistenmark, being defeated at Roslów on the XVIIth day of July and losing a IIIrd part of his army; he was forced to retreat. In the next year the hordes again attacked Netterhaven, but were repulsed. A great earthquake struck central and Southern Torenth on the XIVth day of March in the year 1008, destroying much of Beldour and causing giant waves on the Twin Rivers and the Northern Sea. On the XIth day of June in that year Dyggvi now King of Eistenmark struck South into Torenth, burning and looting farms and small towns for II weeks before withdrawing. On the XVIIIth day of June in the year 1009 King Kyprian II took a large army North into Eistenmark, defeating and killing Dyggvi on the XXVIIIth day instant, and occupying Eistenfalla, the capital city, II days later. The Torenthi forces withdrew on the IIIrd day of September in that year.

In the year 1012 the King Kyprian traveled East to Byzantyun on the Ist official visit there from Torenth in hundreds of years. He met with Kónstas Autokratór of Byzantyun on the XXIInd day of June in that year, and signed a mutual treaty of defense against the Northern barbarians. On the IVth day of June in the following year a joint expeditionary force from Byzantyun and

Torenth proceeded North against the barbarians of Avarsland; a IInd expedition took place in the year 1014. On the IIIrd expedition, the Autokratór Kónstas was killed at the Battle of Boldù on the XVIth day of August in the year 1018, and his army withdrew. On the IIIrd day of August in the year 1023 King Kyprian destroyed the barbarians at their capital city of Avargorod, finally ending the Northern threat.

The King was persuaded to turn his eyes West again in the year 1025, when he supported a move by Imre III former Pretender of Gwynedd and his son Marek II to invade Gwynedd. The II armies met at Schillingford (later Killingford) on the XVth day of June. After III days of battle, the Torenthis withdrew the remnants of their exhausted and depleted army back across the border. The King abdicated on the XXIst day of July in 1025. His son and successor, the King Arkady II, honoured his father with the new title of Grand Duke of Furstán, and settled him in a manor house at Torenthály, with a separate income and retainers.

In the year 1033 the former King Kyprian attempted to regain his throne, but was ultimately unsuccessful. He was deprived of his title, stripped of his servants and estates, and sent under close confinement to the Monastery of Saint Sviatoslav in Jándrich. The former King Kyprian II, now the blind monk Pantaleón, died there on the last day of the year 1037, a very old man at the age of LXII years. His body was initially placed with those of his deceased brethren at Saint Sviatoslav's, but his bones were disinterred and returned for burial at Torenthály by his grandson, King Nimur II, in the year 1088.

Kyri *de Róiste*, called "Kyri of the Flame," Lady. This Deryni noblewoman was born in The Connait on the VIth day of December in the Year of Our Lord 1093, being the second daughter of Liam Lord de Róiste and Jacinta Lady O Coileáin. She intermarried with Martel Lord Nykorik on the XXIXth day of July in the year 1127, and by him she had a child: the Hereditary Lord Karloman. She was appointed to the Camberian Council about the year 1115, but resigned her position on the IIIrd day of November in the year 1127, when she realized she was with child. [*High Deryni*; *The Bishop's Heir*; *The King's Justice*; *The Quest for Saint Camber*; *King Kelson's Bride*].

Kyriell. It was Camber Earl of Culdi's name in religion; hence, he is sometimes referred to as Saint Kyriell. A long-lost village of this name is located in the hills North and East of Tor Caerrorie, where some of the Servants of Saint Camber went into voluntary exile after the enforcement of the Statutes of Ramos in the year 918. [*Camber of Culdi*; *The Harrowing of Gwynedd*; *The Quest for Saint Camber*].

Laas. This coastal city on the Bay of Laas was the ancient capital of the sovereign Principality of Meara, but following the incorporation of that realm into Gwynedd in the year 1027, the administrative capital of the new Province of Meara was moved to the city of Ratharkin in the following year. The city was again made the center of the nation following the rebellion of the Mearan pretender Princess Caitrin in the year 1123, but was displaced by King Kelson on the XIIth day of July in the year 1124. The city is best known for the old Palace of the Princes of Meara, which has remained a center of veneration by the common folk of this land. It is here that the Hereditary Prince of Gwynedd has been brought since the year 1030 to be declared and anointed "Prince of Meara." In addition, the great stone Cathedral of Saint Asaph includes a spire covered with reddish tile to resemble the copper which that holy man used to create his most famous constructions.

In ancient times the Heir Apparent to the Throne of Meara often bore the title Count (later, Duke) of Laas, the last official holder of this Honour being Jubal Hereditary Prince of Meara. However, King Kelson revived the title on the XXXth day of July in the year 1128 for Sir Jolyon Ramsay, last heir to the pretensions of the old princely line, who thereupon renounced all rights to the Mearan throne for himself and his descendants. [*The Bishop's Heir*; *The King's Justice*; *King Kelson's Bride*].

Lachlan *de Quarles*, Bishop of Ballymar. He was born on the Ist day of January in the Year of Our Lord 1081, being the fourth son of Sir Misael de Quarles and Yosea Lady Paige. He was ordained priest on the XXXIst day of May in the year 1101, and was consecrated an itinerant Bishop of Gwynedd on the XXth day of February in the year 1115. He remained neutral in the Interdict Crisis of the year 1121. He was elected Bishop of Ballymar in Cassan by the Synod on the XVth day of January in the year 1122, but supported Edmund Loris ex-Archbishop of Valoret in his attempt to reinstate himself as Primate on the Vth day of December in the year 1123. After the latter's capture and execution by Kelson King of Gwynedd on the XIIth day of July in the year 1124, Bishop Lachlan was suspended for his part in the Mearan Rebellion, and was formally degraded from his see and imprisoned for life by the action of the Synod of Valoret on the XVIIIth day of March in 1125. [*The Bishop's Heir*; *The King's Justice*; *The Quest for Saint Camber*].

Lael, Father. He was serving as chaplain and battle-surgeon to Thomas Cardiel Archbishop of Rhemuth during the invasion of Meara by the Gwyneddan Army on the XXth day of May in the year 1124. He accompanied King Kelson on his quest for the relics of Saint Camber on the IXth day of March in the year 1125. [*The King's Justice*; *The Quest for Saint Camber*].

Lajos I Kis *Furstán*, King of Torenth. He was born on the XVIIth day of February in the Year of Our Lord 775, being the eldest son and heir of Kálmán II King of Torenth and Grand Princess Démétria daughter of Augoustos IV Autokratór of Byzantyun. He intermarried with Amoena Grafina von Thys on the XXIInd day of May in the year 794, and by her he had children: the Hereditary Prince Mátyás, killed fighting R'Kassi raiders on the XIIth day of April in the year 831, *sans postérité*; the Prince Kyprian later Count of Southmarcke, dead of the *peste bubonique* on the IVth day of August in the year 827, leaving issue III children, the Hereditary Prince Árpád Imre later Count of Southmarcke, who succeeded his grandfather, *sans postérité*, the Prince Lajos Péter later Count of Nördmarcke, and the Princess Eufemia; the Prince Tamás later Count of Östmarcke, killed in a tournament in the year 816, aged XVII years, *sans postérité*; the Prince Konrád later Graf or Count von Westmarcke and Prince Regent of Torenth, who died on the XVIth day of January in the year 863, leaving issue, the Count Malachy later Malachy I King of Torenth; the Prince Boleslav, dead of the blue ticke at age IX; the Princess Merregard, who intermarried with Tigran King of R'Kassi; the Princess Déodate, who intermarried with Heinrich Graf von Saxhold; the Prince Vólmar later Count of Truvorsk; the Prince Imrad later Count Quérben; the Princess Engelbertina, who intermarried with Yves Lord de Voss; the Prince György, dead at age III of the speckled spleen; the Princess Eilika, who took the veil as Sister Agatha of the Little Mothers of Perpetual Sorrow; the Prince Endre later Count of Medras, *sans postérité*. Queen Amoena died of the Black Death on the Ist day of August in the year 827.

The Prince Lajos was trained in the military arts at an early age, and served his father in Marley and Northern Gwynedd during the Ist decades of the IXth century. He succeeded his father on the XXVIIIth day of November in the year 822, and was girded with the sword on the Ist day of January in the year 823 by Patriarch Philoxenos I. Although he had supported his brother King Festil I's incursion into Gwynedd in June of the preceding year, and had accepted his fealty and that of a IIIrd brother, Termöd I Sovereign or Autonomous Prince of Kheldour, the King Lajos gradually came to mistrust both of these siblings, and maintained a strict watch on the Gwyneddan army lest it be used against him.

The premature deaths of the King's III eldest sons and his wife, II of them by plague, seemed to remove all the joy from his life, and he became in later years increasingly morose, pessimistic, and suspicious of plots among his courtiers and other family members. After the death in battle of his son and heir, the Prince Mátyás, the King Lajos undertook a retaliatory expedition against the Kingdom of R'Kassi in the year 832, killing the R'Kassi King Timur on the XVIIth day of July in that year. Lajos replaced Timur with the latter's cousin, Prince Tigran, as client King, and married him to his daughter the Princess Merregard.

Not long thereafter, the King Lajos retired to the oasis of Kors in R'Kassi, naming his son Konrád as Prince Regent, and he remained there for XI years, despite the many entreaties of his Lords and children to return home. It is said that he sought to find peace in a place where no one could disturb him without his permission, where he could find the truth of his existence in tranquility. The Old King returned each year to Beldour to conduct the traditional New Year *celebratio*, in which the King blessed all of the Land and the People of Torenth, and each of his surviving children and grandchildren and the Great Lords, and was himself blessed by the Patriarch to give them all good fortune for the coming year. King Lajos I died at Kors on the XXth day of March in the year 845, aged LXX years, and was succeeded by his grandson, the Prince Árpád. He was buried with his ancestors at Torenthály. R.I.P.

Lambert *MacArdry*. He was serving as a retainer to Dhugal MacArdry Earl of Transha during the invasion of Meara in July of the year 1124. He assisted Dhugal in contacting Kelson after the debacle at Dorna Plain on the IInd day instant. [*The King's Justice*].

Laran *ap Pardyce*, XVIth Baron Pardyce. This Deryni Lord was born at Pardyceum in the Mughdorna Mountains of Howicce on the XIVth day of March in the Year of Our Lord 1065, being the eldest son and heir of Pardyce ap Laoghaire Baron Pardyce and Honoria Lady Redmond. He was trained as a physician and a scholar, and was considered a master of the magical arts. He was appointed to the Camberian Council on the Vth day of October in the year 1090, and was still serving in that capacity in the year 1130. He met with Sir Jamyl and Denis Arilan on the XVIIIth day of November in the year 1104 to discuss Denis's upcoming ordination. He was one of IV arbiters of the duel arcane held between Wencit King of Torenth and Kelson King of Gwynedd and their followers at Llyndruth Meadows on the IInd day of July in the year 1121.

On the IVth day of July in the year 1128, he was surprised to meet Barrett de Laney and Jehana Dowager Queen of Gwynedd in the library of Rhemuth Palace. Eleven days later, he transported to Alta Jorda to help console his friend and colleague, Lady Vivienne de Jordanet, who had been afflicted with the paralysis. She perished II days later. In his youth, he had reddish-brown hair (which later turned to grey) and dark brown eyes, and often displayed a serious expression on his lean, angular face; ink smudges often covered the Ist and IInd fingers of his right hand. He wore scholar's robes over an expensive undertunic. ["The Priesting of Arilan"; *High Deryni*; *The Bishop's Heir*; *The King's Justice*; *The Quest for Saint Camber*; *King Kelson's Bride*].

László Gheorghe Viljem Dytrik *von Furstán-Süzdal-Czalsky*, Count Czalsky. He was born on the XVIth day of June in the Year of Our Lord 1101, being the eldest son and heir of Maryav Count Czalsky and the Countess Dyvina, daughter of Prince Berlår Duke of Albanya and second son of Henze King of Csodala, and the Princess Praya of Szátmár. He was betrothed at the time of his death to the Princess Sahura daughter of Prince Diokletián of Rus', but the marriage was never formalized; she later married his younger brother. After his death, several women came forward to make claims against his estate on behalf of their bastard children, whom he had never legitimized, which claims were later upheld by a Court of Tribunal.

Count László succeeded his father on the XXth day of December in the year 1119, and soon was spending most of his time in Beldour, courting the "new men" who came to power in the wake of King Wencit's death in the year 1121. He quickly became attached to the Regent Mahael II Duke d'Arjenol, and participated with him in the conspiracy to kill King Liam Lajos II in the year 1128, Count Czalsky being designated to serve as a member of the Moving Ward to protect the innocent monarch. On the VIIIth day of July in that year, he met with Duke Mahael and his brothers in Beldour to discuss recent events, and to finalized their plans.

Three days later, at the instigation of Count Mátyás, he was murdered and his body thrown into the River Beldour, where it was discovered the next day. He had a reputation for pursuing the ladies. He was succeeded by his younger brother, Count Bertil. [*King Kelson's Bride*].

László Vak *Furstán*, King of Torenth, Count Molnar. He was born on the VIth day of November in the Year of Our Lord 647, being the second son and joint heir of Tamás King of Torenth and the Princess Iouliana daughter of Kallistos Grand Prince of Byzantyun. He intermarried with the Lady Charitóna daughter of Dionysios Despot of Morias on the XVth day of September in the year 665, and by her he had children: the Prince Radislaus later King of Torenth; the Prince Tamósz later Count Molnar by cession from his father; the Princess Gabriela; the Princess Izabella; the Princess Zosima.

The Prince László succeeded his father jointly with his brother Aldred I on the XVIIth day of June in the year 677, and was girded with the sword by Patriarch Meletios I on the I[st] day of January in the year 678. The King László is said to have been a skilled musician, playing the lute and harp as well as any traveling bard. However, he had a weak heart, and died of pains therein on the VIIIth day of March in the year 681, aged XXXIII years, although Szapolyai asserts that the King was poisoned by his brother. The King László was taken to Torenthály for burial in the family vault, his brother King Aldred then becoming sole King of Torenth. R.I.P.

Laughlin, Father. This priest was serving with King Kelson's army during the invasion of Meara in July of the year 1124. [*The King's Justice*].

Lauren, Sir. This Michaeline knight was slain at the Battle of Iomaire on the XXVth day of June in the year 905. His place in the Grand Chapter was taken by Lord Dualta. R.I.P. [*Saint Camber*].

Lawrence Edward *Gorony*, Monsignor. This evil priest was born in Llannedd on the XIIth day of September in the Year of Our Lord 1072. He was ordained priest on the IInd day of July in the year 1094, and was appointed Chaplain to Oliver de Nore Archbishop Primate of Valoret and All Gwynedd on the XIIIth day of February in the year 1104. After the latter's death in the year 1114, he became an aide to his successor, Archbishop Edmund Loris. He was promoted by Loris to Monsignor on the XXIIIrd day of March in the year 1117. He was fervently anti-Deryni. As Loris's aide he helped Warin de Grey capture Alaric Morgan Duke of Corwyn at Saint Torin's Shrine in Dhassa on the XXVIIIth day of March in the year 1121, and later arranged for the escape of Loris from his captivity at Saint Iveagh's Abbey on the XXIXth day of November in the year 1123. He participated in the Mearan rebellion, and was captured with the Archbishop on the IIIrd day of July in the year 1124 by Kelson King of Gwynedd. He was tried for treason by the King, convicted, and hanged for his crimes in the Great Hall at Laas on the XIIth day instant, aged LI years. His body was interred in a potter's field. ["The Priesting of Arilan"; *Deryni Checkmate*; *High Deryni*; *The Bishop's Heir*; *The King's Justice*; *The Quest for Saint Camber*].

Lawrence, Lord Welch. He was born on the XXIInd day of August in the Year of Our Lord 1098, being a younger son of Myron Baron Welch and Janette Lady Lennon. He intermarried with Roberta Lady Floren on the IIIrd day of July in the year 1118, and by her he had children: the Lord Leary; the Lady Peggie, born posthumously. In November of the year 1120 he was one of the III vassals of the Duke of Corwyn who was persuaded by Ian Howell Earl of Eastmarch that Duke Alaric Morgan should be assassinated. To this end he invaded the King's apartments on the XIVth day of that month, and was taken prisoner in the ensuing *melée*. He was tried, convicted, and executed on the XIIIth day of December following, aged XXII years. [*Deryni Rising*].

Lendour. This small mountain Earldom is situate Southeast of Valoret and Northeast of Dhassa, being surrounded by the Earldom of Eastmarch on the North, the Duchy of Corwyn on the South, the Earldom of Derry on the East, and the Royal Duchy of Haldane on the West. The Honour was first granted to Prince Festil *Junior*, son and heir of King Festil I, on the IIIrd day of July in the year 822, and merged with the Crown in the year 839. King Festil II then created his own son, Prince Festil, Duke of Lendour later that year, and it again merged with the Crown in the year 851. Lord Cynfyn ap Dauyd, a friend and supporter of Festil III King of Gwynedd, was created Earl of Lendour on the XVIIth day of December in the year 856. The title became extinct in the male line in the person of his direct descendant, the crippled Earl Ahern ap Keryell, who succeeded his father in the year 1086, and died unmarried and childless on the XVIIth day of November in the year 1090. The Earldom then passed through Ahern's elder sister, Lady Alyce de Corwyn de Morgan, to her son, Alaric Morgan Duke of Corwyn, who inherited the Honour at birth. The Earldom became a courtesy title for Alaric's son, Lord Kelric, at the latter's birth in the year 1125. [*King Kelson's Bride*].

EARLS OF LENDOUR

HOUSE OF FURSTÁN-FESTIL

Festil I (son of King Festil I of Gwynedd)	822-839
Festil II (son; Duke)	839-851

HOUSE OF CYNFYN

Cynfyn ap Dauyd	856-888
Iliff (son)	888-911
Merrik (son)	911-933
Weir (brother)	933-956
Erwin (son)	956-979
Muir (son)	979-1011
Euan (son)	1011-1025
Walther (cousin)	1025-1029
Taillefer (nephew)	1029-1055
Keryell (son)	1055-1086
Ahern (son)	1086-1090

HOUSE OF MORGAN

Alaric (nephew)	1091-1125

Kelric (son) 1125-1130+

Lendour Mountains. This range is born in a region of hills situate Northeast of Valoret, and runs South down the spine of Gwynedd to the Duchy of Carthmoor, serving as the boundary line separating Carthmoor, Corwyn, Lendour, Carcashale, and Eastmarch from the Haldane Crown Lands. Located within the Lendours are the city of Dhassa, the Gunury Pass, the High Grelder Pass, the village of Saint Kyriell's, and such Abbeys as Saint Torin's, Saint Neot's, Saint Foillan's, Haut Eirial, and many other places besides, both known and unknown.

The distinguished traveler Campbell de Broun traversed many different parts of the Lendour Range on occasion, and recorded his observations from one of these ventures in his diary: "This morning I started in good spirits, thinking I was over the worst road. We came III or IV leagues to a little rill called Wolfpen Creek, which was somewhat of a curiosity on account of its channel. It was a deep ravine in a solid rock near XX feet deep, and almost perpendicular on both sides. It was not over XX feet across; the road crossed on a wooden bridge which was built on a crib in the bottom of the creek. There were the remains of a tub mill just below the bridge, built on one of the falls in the rock which afforded a good pitch for the water on the wheel. The road from the creek was very steep and rocky for some distance, very difficult for the wagons coming this way, the rocks in some places near II feet high spreading across roads so that horses couldn't slow up to pull hard. We got up our horses with some difficulty and came on to this place, Laurel Creek, where we encamped a few hours before night to dry our baggage and to rest our horses before we tried Cotton Hill. I thought that this was the worst part, but the next day's travel proved me wrong. Although lush and green in parts, this was a hard country, unforgiving to man and beast, and I was heartily glad to be rid of it." [*Deryni Checkmate*; *The Bishop's Heir*].

Lester, Lord Trillick. He was born on the VIIth day of September in the Year of Our Lord 1066, being the son of Lorne Lord Trillick and Etain Lady Greene. He intermarried with Pippa Lady Cartwright on the XXIXth day of April in the year 1085, and by her he had children: the Hereditary Lord Adam; the Lord Hosea; the Lord Joseph; the Lady Nanza; the Lord Benjamin. He succeeded his cousin, Lord Luther, on the IInd day of February in the year 1112. He was captured with Jared McLain Duke of Cassan at Rengarth on the XXVIIIth day of June in the year 1121, and was executed with him by King Wencit on the Ist day of July following. He was aged LIV years at his death, and was succeeded by his eldest son, Lord Adam. R.I.P. [*High Deryni*].

Létald Sobbon Jubal Josse *von Horthy*, Hort of Orsal and Sovereign Prince of Tralia, Overlord of the Forcinn States. This representative of an ancient and noble line was born on the XIIth day of November in the Year of Our Lord 1077, being the eldest son and heir of Sobbon Hort of Orsal and Prince of Tralia and the Princess Maya daughter of Raimond Prince of Thuria. He intermarried with the Sharifa Husniyya daughter of Rauf al-Zaman King of R'Kassi on the XXXIst day of May in the year 1105, and by her he had children: His Hereditary Horthness the Prince Cyric; the Princess Rezza; the Prince Rogan; the Prince Marcel; the Princess Marcelline, a twin with her brother; the Princess Aynbeth; the Prince Oswin; the Prince Kelliam; the Princess Péadora, a twin with her brother.

The Prince Létald succeeded his father on the XXVIIth day of October in the year 1101. Due to the Hort's troubled relations with the Kingdom of R'Kassi in November of the year 1120, this "old sea lion" sent his eldest son, Prince Cyric, to represent him at the coronation of Kelson King of Gwynedd on the XVth day of that month. He himself met with Alaric Duke of Corwyn on the XXVth day of March in the year 1121 to discuss the developing military situation with Torenth, and he sent his IInd son, the Prince Rogan, back with the Duke to be trained as a squire and a knight.

On the IIIrd day of July in the year 1128, Kelson King of Gwynedd arrived with all of his party at Horthánthy, the summer capital of Orsal and Tralia, there to be greeted by the Hort and his family. On the next day, Létald took King Kelson and King Liam Lajos II of Torenth on board his own ship, the *Niyyana*, to make the voyage upriver to Beldour, where the Torenthi monarch would be formally invested as King. They reached Beldour some IV days later, and Létald met with official observers from the Forcinn States on the IXth day instant.

After the *killijálay* ceremony on the XVIth day of July and the attempted assassination of King Liam in Torenthály, the Hort agreed to allow King Kelson and some of his entourage to transport to a hidden portal at Orsal, in order to protect and secure the royal womenfolk in residence there from the potential depredations of the escaped Count Teymuraz. In return, Létald required Gwynedd and Torenth to provide him reciprocal access to a portal in each of those countries, and the Kings agreed.

On the XVIIth day instant, the Hort transported again to Beldour, and thence back to Orsal. Later that day, Létald's ships departed Beldour under the command of his eldest son, Prince Cyric, and they arrived at Orsal III days later. He and his sons later attended the several royal weddings held in Gwynedd in July and August of that year.

Count Berrhones once noted that Prince Létald's bloodlines encompassed the best and worst of the heritages of East and West, so that he could "justly claim that he was related to every royal and major noble family in the XI Kingdoms, many times over." Linus Calamarius once said of the Hort, "*Aut insanit homo, aut versus facit.*" He had a moon-shaped face, green eyes, a well-fed torso, and a fringe of close-trimmed grey-speckled hair. He sported rings on every finger of his hands. The Hort's arms are: *vert-de-mer*, a sea lion with raised tail *argent*. *L'Hort est L'Hort, par nécessité*. [*Deryni Rising*; *Deryni Checkmate*; *King Kelson's Bride*].

Leutiern. This ancient Deryni mystic is best known as the author of the *Tomes de Sagesse*. His works were consulted by Evaine Lady Thuryn in Spring of the year 918. [*The Harrowing of Gwynedd*].

Leviticus, Brother. He was serving as vestiarian at Saint Foillan's Abbey in the year 903, and discovered on the VIth day of December in that year that II robes were missing from the monastery's clothing supply after the kidnapping of Brother Benedict (Prince Cinhil Haldane). [*Camber of Culdi*].

Lewys *ap Norfal*, originally Louÿs Régnier Gaspard de Buyenne-Furstán, Lord du Joux. He was born on the IInd day of March in the Year of Our Lord 1015, being the third son of Régnier I Duc du Joux and Jolanthe Princess of Fallon, and a great-grand-uncle of Jehane Queen of Gwynedd. He assumed his surname in honour of his Deryni instructor, the master Norfal ap Ailfrid. He intermarried with the Countess Ilde daughter of Boris Count d'Arjenol on the VIIth day of May in the year 1038, and by her he had children: the Count Morian ap Lewys; the Countess Jessamy, who intermarried with Sief MacAthan. The Lord Lewys was a well-known master of the arcane arts, who became notorious after he rejected the authority of the Camberian Council in the year 1049. He disappeared on the XXIst day of March in the year 1052, aged XXXVII years, when an experiment in the occult that he was conducting at Coroth Castle went seriously awry. [*High Deryni*; *The Bishop's Heir*; *The King's Justice*].

Liam, Saint. This holy monk was born about the year 730 in Concaradine. He was early trained as a soldier and knight, and later became a well-known scholar of the Church, penning many learned treatises on philosophy and theology, including the *Crepusculum Hominis* and *Mercennarius Dei*, his autobiography. He founded several abbeys in Gwynedd, including the *Monasterium Scientiae Arcanae*, a Deryni establishment in Travlum which was abandoned in the year 917. Liam died about the year 780, and was canonized in the year 823. A Michaeline abbey and monastic school dedicated to his name was located near Tor Caerrorie IV hours' ride Northeast of Valoret; Father Alister Cullen, Father Joram MacRorie, and Rhys Lord Thuryn were educated there, and Joram later taught there briefly, but the monastery was closed in the year 905; the school continued under different supervision for another XL years. Saint Liam, the patron of teachers, has his feastday celebrated on the IVth day of July. [*Camber of Culdi*; *Camber the Heretic*].

Liam Lajos II Lionel László *Furstán d'Arjenol*, called "Laje," King of Torenth, Duke of Nördmarcke. He was born on the IIIrd day of April in the Year of Our Lord 1114, being the third son and fourth child of Lionel II Duke d'Arjenol and Morag Princess of Torenth. He was betrothed to the Princess Eirian daughter of Nigel Duke of Carthmoor on the XIVth day of November in the year 1128, the marriage to take place in the year 1138, when Eirian would come of age.

The Prince Liam was created Duke of Nördmarcke by King Wencit on the IVth day of March in the year 1120. He succeeded his brother, the King Alroy Arion II, on the XIIth day of June in the year 1123, and received a titular girding of the sword on the New Year's Day following by Patriarch Alpheios I; his forename being deemed too Western, he was given the official reign name of Lajos II. The Regency that had served his brother before him was immediately reactivated, with his mother, Morag Dowager Duchess d'Arjenol and Princess of Torenth, and his uncle, Mahael II Duke d'Arjenol, appointed to serve as Regents until he should come of age. He traveled to Rhemuth to swear homage to Kelson King of Gwynedd as Overlord of Torenth on the XIXth day of May in the year 1124, and was detained there at Court during the Mearan campaign. The following Spring, in conjunction with the knighting of Kelson King of Gwynedd on the IIIrd day of March in the year 1125, the young King Liam was made squire to Nigel Duke of Carthmoor so that he might learn the art and science of statecraft requisite for a future monarch.

The King Liam Lajos II attained his majority on the IIIrd day of April in the year 1128, and the Regency was dissolved, the final act of the II Regents being a request sent to Kelson King of Gwynedd and Overlord of Torenth to return their monarch to Beldour for his official empowerment at the *killijálay* ceremony scheduled for mid-July. However, the former Regent Mahael II Duke d'Arjenol was plotting with his brother, Teymuraz Count of Brustarkia, and others to overthrow the young King, and to set his underaged brother, the Prince Ronal Rurik, in his place.

King Kelson agreed to restore Torenth's rightful monarch to his throne. On the XXIXth day of June in that year II emissaries from Torenth, Mátyás Count of Komnéné and al-Rasoul ibn Tarik, arrived at Rhemuth, bringing with them robes of state and an ancient Torenthi crown. On the next day King Liam departed with King Kelson and his party from Desse for Coroth, arriving there on the IInd day of July. They traveled to Orsal on the following day, finding there a fleet of Torenthi war galleys waiting to provide a suitable escort. On the winding road up to the Hort of Orsal's palace, the II Kings were attacked by a pair of rogue Deryni, but managed to save themselves.

On the next day, the brother monarchs and their entourages departed Orsal for Beldour, spending IV days traveling up that great river. King Liam Lajos was greeted with great enthusiasm by his countrymen at Furstánán, the Ist Torenthi settlement that they reached, where the lights of Saint-Sasile played over the many domed buildings of church and town. On the VIIth day of the month, a myriad of small boats from Südmarcke surrounded their small fleet, the townsmen singing songs to their King come home again.

King Liam and his entourage arrived in Beldour on the VIIIth day of July. On the following day he met with his mother, uncles, and surviving brother, and later hosted a reception for the royal guests from the XI Kingdoms. He dined that evening with King Kelson, Count Mátyás, and others of the Royal Court. On the Xth day instant he began rehearsals for the *killijálay* ceremony. That afternoon he introduced Kelson and Dhugal to the Nikolaseum in Torenthály, and Mátyás suggested that a plot to overthrow Liam was being countenanced by Duke Mahael and Count Teymuraz. On the next day, King Liam asked King Kelson to replace the deceased Count Czalsky in the installation ceremony.

The *killijálay* took place on the XVIth day of July, amid great pomp and circumstance at the Church of Sankt Iób in Torenthály. During the crucial moment of the ceremony, when the young King was most vulnerable, he was suddenly and viciously attacked by his uncle, Mahael II Duke d'Arjenol, with the assistance of Mahael's brother Teymuraz Count of Brustarkia, and Liam was nearly overthrown. But the Thrice Holy Patriarch Alpheios I, together with Mátyás Count of Komnéně, Morag Dowager Queen of Torenth (the King's mother), and Kelson King of Gwynedd, came to his aid and defeated Duke Mahael, who was impaled on a stake and left to rot in the sun on that same day. Count Teymuraz was arrested, but escaped his captors through the portal of the Nikolaseum. King Kelson then released King Liam from his vassaldom, and restored the independence of the Torenthi monarchy.

That evening, the new King conducted his first Crown Council, with the participation of his friends from Gwynedd, and made Count Mátyás Duke d'Arjenol. Later that day, he met privily with Kelson and his entourage and Létald Hort of Orsal, and they agree to establish reciprocal portal locations in all III states. Liam then transported briefly to Orsal and back again, in order to learn the address of the portal there.

On the XXVIIth day of July he received word of his mother's foul murder at the hands of Teymuraz her brother. Three days later he requested permission on behalf of himself and his uncle Mátyás to attend the royal weddings to be held at Saint George's Cathedral in Rhemuth, and transported there the next day. He was then introduced by King Kelson to Princess Araxie, Kelson's betrothed. Duke Mátyás was attacked by his brother Teymuraz later that day, and after he was healed, he and the King returned to Beldour. They returned a week later for King Kelson's own wedding. Liam had night-black eyes and bronze glints shining through his clubbed black hair. [*The Bishop's Heir*; *The King's Justice*; *The Quest for Saint Camber*; *King Kelson's Bride*].

***Liber Ricae* (Book of the Veil).** This rare Deryni text dealt with various obscure matters of the occult arts. Evaine Lady Thuryn attempted to locate the work in Spring of the year 918, but was unsuccessful. A copy was said to have been housed in the old Varnarite Library in Grecotha, but may now be lost. [*The Harrowing of Gwynedd*; *Deryni Magic*].

Licken, General Fingal. He was serving as a military adviser for Wencit King of Torenth in June of the year 1121. [*High Deryni*].

Lillas. This comely lass was well-bred, of good family and reputation, convent-educated, and the *fiancée* of the ranger Stalker. When she was raped and murdered on the XVIth day of April in the year 1118 by IV ruffians in the city of Kiltuin, the itinerant foreign swordsmith Ferris was accused of the crime, but was later proved innocent by Alaric Morgan Duke of Corwyn. R.I.P. ["Trial"].

Lindestark. The County of Lindestark is situate in the Northernmost part of the Duchy of Claibourne, lying along the rugged coastline Northeast of Claibourne Town. The Honour was granted by Sighere Sovereign Earl of Eastmarch to his comrade-in-arms, Sir Linden FitzOsberne, in the year 905 for his services in the recent war against Kheldour. Unique to the peerage of Gwynedd, the titleholder of Lindestark is called Count, not Earl, and swears allegiance first to the Duke of Claibourne, successor peer to the Earl of Eastmarch in Kheldour, and only then to the King of Gwynedd. The banners of Lindestark were represented in the army of Kelson King of Gwynedd in June of the year 1121. [*High Deryni*].

COUNTS OF LINDESTARK

HOUSE OF LINDESTARK OR FITZOSBERNE

Linden FitzOsberne	905-929
Osberne I (son)	929-961
Linnell I (son)	961-983
Ossian (son)	983-984
Linus (brother)	984
Horne (cousin)	984-987
Osberne II (son)	987-1004
Lionnet (brother)	1004-1006
Osberne III (son)	1006-1025
Allen (cousin)	1025-1042
Linnell II (grandson)	1042-1088
Osman (son)	1088-1119
Greville (son)	1119-1130+

Lionel II Torval Bolomir *Furstán d'Arjenol*, Duke d'Arjenol. He was born on the VIIth day of August in the Year of Our Lord 1087, being the eldest son and heir of Mahael I Duke d'Arjenol and the Princess Jaïne daughter of Isarn I Prince of Logréine, and a direct descendant in the male line of Torval I Prince of Torenth and Duke d'Arjenol. He intermarried with the Princess Morag daughter of Nimur II King of Torenth on the XXVIth day of September in the year 1107, and by her he had children: the Countess Jaïnette, dead at age VI months of the runny bowels; the Hereditary Duke Alroy later Arion II King of Torenth; the Prince Averil, drowned at age VI while playing in the River Beldour; the Prince Liam later Duke of Nördmarcke later Lajos II King of Torenth; the Prince Ronal Rurik later Duke of Lorsöl later Heir Presumptive to the throne of Torenth; the Princess Stanisha, born posthumously VII months after her father's death.

The Duke Lionel received training from an early age as both a statesman and as an adept, but his Deryni talents were slight in comparison to those of his half-brothers, and rarely employed, so that some commentators have called him human. He succeeded his father as Duke on the XVIth day of May in the year 1100 under the joint Regency of his uncle Pépinot Count of Logréine and his cousin Wencit Duke of Vorna later King of Torenth. He attained his majority on the VIIth day of August in the year 1101, when the Regency was dissolved.

On the XXVIIIth day of November in the year 1119 the King Wencit of Torenth, Duke Lionel's brother-in-law, lost his only grandchild and male heir, and by letters testamentary signed on the IVth day of March in the year 1120, the King made the Duke's III sons the next heirs to the throne of Torenth after any heirs of his own flesh, and he also removed them from succession to the Duchy of Arjenol, naming Lionel's younger half-brother, Lord Mahael, as Hereditary Duke d'Arjenol. On the XVIIIth day of June in the year 1121 the Duke Lionel gave himself as hostage to Bran Coris Earl of Marley so that Coris could meet with King Wencit, and was given a sleeping potion by the Earl so that he could not use his Deryni powers. Some weeks later he was killed in the duel arcane between King Wencit and his supporters and Kelson King of Gwynedd at Llyndruth Meadows, perishing on the IInd day of July in the year 1121, aged XXXIII years. His body was returned for burial in the family crypt at Arzh in the Great Hall of the Ancestors.

He is described in the *Chronicles* as being "...tall, with a vaguely foreign air about him, a lean, bearded face. His hair was long and black, and caught in the back in a silver clasp. He was resplendent in a black brocaded cloak and crimson tunic, a black plumed helmet, and he was carrying a flame-bladed dagger of silver thrust casually through his rich silk sash, worn to be drawn from the left. Other than that he appeared to be unarmed. He was riding a bay charger." His arms were: per pale, *or* and *argent*, three crescents counterchanged. R.I.P. [*High Deryni*; *The Bishop's Heir*; *The King's Justice*; *King Kelson's Bride*].

Lior, Grand Master and Inquisitor General of the *Custodes Fidei*, Father. This evil priest was born on the XIIIth day of August in the Year of Our Lord 875. He was ordained priest on the XVIIth day of March in the year 894, and was involved in the founding of the *Custodes Fidei*, being named assistant to the Inquisitor General Serafin on the IInd day of February in the year 918. During the early Summer of the year 921 he worked with Master Dimitri in Carthmoor. He and Brother Serafin were taken prisoner and questioned by King Javan and Sir Guiscard de Courcy on the XXIXth day of July in the year 921. Lior was promoted to Inquisitor General after Serafin's untimely death.

Father Lior accompanied the Royal Expedition to Eastmarch in June of the year 928. He was summoned by Rhun Earl of Sheele to interrogate and torture the Deryni double agent, Dimitri, on the XXth day instant, and was then named Acting Vicar General of the *Custodes Fidei*. He was wounded in the coup of the Vth day of July in the year 928, and died of his injuries II days later, aged LII years, before he could be brought to trial for his many crimes. He was buried in a potter's field outside Rhemuth, but his body was exhumed in the night by persons unknown, and was never recovered. [*The Harrowing of Gwynedd*; *King Javan's Year*; *The Bastard Prince*].

Lirel, Dame. This old woman served as the nurse for the royal Princes of Gwynedd until the year 916. Prince Javan and Prince Rhys Michael bought her a length of blue ribbon at the fair held in Valoret on the XXVIIIth day of May in the year 917. [*Camber the Heretic*].

Lirin Daria *Udaut Murdoch*, Countess of Carthane. She was born on the VIIIth day of December in the Year of Our Lord 906, being the eldest daughter of Darius Lord Udaut and Pema Lady MacInnis. She intermarried with Richard Earl of Carthane on the Xth day of January in the year 918, but being underaged, she remained in her father's house for II more years; and by her husband she had children: the Hereditary Count Cashel *Junior* later Earl of Carthane, who died shortly after his father, *sans postérité*; the Lord Jason, killed in a border skirmish in the year 945, *sans postérité*; the Lord Evert, who died young; the Lady Persephone; the Lady Elana, who died young; the Lord Ludovic, a monk of Saint Boniface's under the name Brother Gedeon; the Lady Margot, who intermarried with Flynn Fitz-Arthur Quinnell Earl Derry; the Lady Pemella, who died young; the Lord Murdoch *Junior*, who died young. The Lady Lirin was present at the dying of her father-in-law, Murdoch Earl of Carthane, on the Ist day of August in the year 921. She was serving as a companion to Michaela Queen of Gwynedd in June of the year 928, but was sent home after the countercoup in July. She died on the VIIth day of May in the year 972, aged LXV years. R.I.P. [*The Harrowing of Gwynedd*; *King Javan's Year*; *The Bastard Prince*].

Little Brothers of Saint Ercon (*Fratres Parvi Sancti Erconis*). The teaching Order of the Erconites was founded at Ramos on the XXXth day of April in the year 912 by Father Paulin Sinclair, to honour the name of an anti-Deryni saint who had been a scholar and historian of some repute. Among its aims were the suppression of the Deryni from all religious orders. The Mother House of this Order was located at Ramos on the River Eirian. The Erconites were incorporated into the *Custodes Fidei* on the IInd day of February in the year 918. [*Camber the Heretic*].

Llanarfon River. This branch of the Great Eirian River splits from its mother at Concaradine, tending due West to where it rises in the Mughdorna Mountains in Howicce. It forms the Northern boundary of the Kingdom of Llannedd, separating it from the Kingdom of Gwynedd.

Llannedd. This Great Kingdom is located to the Southwest of Gwynedd, and is bordered by the Duchy of Carthmoor and the Duchy of Carthane in Gwynedd on the East and Northeast, being separated from them by the great River Eirian; the small Free Port of Concaradine, and the Duchy of Travlum and the Earldom of Danoc in Gwynedd on the North, being separated from them by the River Llanarfon; the Kingdom of Howicce on the West, being separated from it by the River Maigh and the Mughdorna Mountains; and the Southern Sea to the South.

The first sovereign Prince of Llannedd, Cadell ap Gruffud, established himself on the IIIrd day of May in the Year of Our Lord 677. The Prince Cynan I declared himself King on the same date in the year 729. On several occasions the Kings of Llannedd attempted to conquer Concaradine and Transflumenia (Travlum) North of the Llanarfon River, but they were always opposed by the Kings of Gwynedd, and gradually came to an acceptance of the status quo with those monarchs.

On the XXXth day of November in the year 1041 Madawc King of Llannedd died without heirs male, and was succeeded by his elder daughter, the Princess Gwenaël. Her marriage on the xth day of May in the year 1055 to Colman I King of Howicce united the II countries under the personal rule of their son, the Prince Illann, who succeeded his mother in Llannedd on the xxvith day of July in the year 1082. However, each state remains under the separate administration of its own government, and, since the Kingdom of Llannedd allows the succession of females while Howicce does not, the countries could split again should the male line fail. Indeed, the heir to the Throne of Llannedd is the present King's young sister, the Princess Gwenlian, but King Colman II's heir in Howicce is his cousin, the Prince Cuan. Queen Richeldis of Gwynedd was a Princess of Llannedd.

The capital of Llannedd, Pwyllheli, lies near the mouth of the River Eirian where it enters the Southern Sea; the town was burned several times by Moorish raiders during the VIIIth century, but was quickly rebuilt on each occasion. Much of Llannedd is flat and fertile, with just the Northwestern corner of the country encompassing part of the Mughdorna Highlands. One of the great wonders of this country is the Crystalline Cathedral of Saint Gruffud at Pwyllheli, which was constructed by Queen Gwenlian, a most pious lady, beginning in the year 915. Also situate at Pwyllheli are the magnificent Royal Tombs, including the III-tiered Elenesium, built by Gwenlian to honour the memory of her saintly sister, the Queen Elen, who drowned in Cuas Bay while fishing. Gwenlian's grandson, King Lludd II, built the great Lighthouse called Lisnick at Enniston, which has guided ships away from the rocks there for over a century.

Campbell de Broun noted in his travels that: "We took a *pirogue* down the Llanarfon River; it rose about III feet last night, much against us. We waded chiefly in the water and got about III miles, and then encamped on a bank. It was cloudy and like for rain. We dried our things, supped on fish, and made a bed of cane, spreading our blankets and sleeping soundly and comfortably until day. On the next morrow we left the water and proceeded on through the cane, leaving part of our wet plunder at Ramsey's place. Then I discovered a small streak of black cloud rising up the River in the Northwest; it was just above the horizon when first seen, and advanced slowly. One of our hands, a sailor named Stoto, said we should have a storm. He had frequently observed such clouds on the Southern coast and near the Western Islands, and said that they were always certain forerunners of frequently dreadful hurricanes.

"I observed this cloud to advance or rise steadily till it was nearly over us, getting ever more dark and gloomy. The foremost edge was a black streak, behind which the clouds were dark and rain-like, but not so black as the stripe which reached from East to West as far as we could see, which to me was novel and seemed awfully sublime and grand. Our sailor said it was a wind cloud; indeed, we could hear the wind roaring at a distance, and when the cloud had advanced nearly over us, it commenced blowing very hard where we were. Soon after began a rain which was driven by the wind and beat through Ramsey's house, in which we had taken shelter. After the storm was over, we continued on down to Jaffrey's, the hands all anxious to get some spirits. We pitched our tent on the bank in the same place where it was a week ago. We were wet through, and it rained again all night. I thought this evening of my home in Cloome, secure and dry and very far away from here. I wonder if I shall ever see it again." [*Saint Camber*; *The Harrowing of Gwynedd*; *Deryni Rising*; *King Kelson's Bride*].

PRINCES AND KINGS OF LLANNEDD

HOUSE OF GRUFFUD

Cadell I ap Gruffud	677-706
Cynan I (son; King 729)	706-732
Coel (son)	732-744
Cador (brother)	744-766
Caswall (son)	766-784
Crydion (son)	784-811
Casnar (son)	811-840
Lludd I (nephew)	840-868
Catwallawn (brother)	868
Maredudd (cousin)	868-889
Cynan II (son)	889-905
Elen (daughter)	905-907
Gwenlian (sister)	907-944
Reith (husband and cousin)	910-931
Cystennyn (son)	944-956
Lludd II (son)	956-991
Cadell II (son)	991-1009
Llary (brother)	1009-1033
Madawc (cousin)	1033-1041
Gwenaël (daughter)	1041-1082

HOUSE OF MACFAOLAN-GRUFFUD

Illann (II) (son; abdicated)	1082-1099
Ronan (IV) (son)	1099-1119
Colman (II) (brother)	1119-1130+

Llarik Broccan *Haldane*, King of Gwynedd, Count of Rhemuth, sometime Protector of the Throne of Gwynedd, called "The Cruel." This evil King was born on the IXth day of March in the Year of Our Lord 651, being the fifth son of Augarin King of Gwynedd, but the second by his second wife, Caldora Lady de la Marche. He intermarried with his cousin, Riona Haldane Countess of Carthane, on the xxxth day of June in the year 674, and by her he had children: the Hereditary Prince Dolon Kensell, killed by his father at age XXIV; the Princess Bertrana; the Prince Jestyn, killed by his father at age XIX; the Prince Augarin, dead of the grippe at age X; the Princess Maryrose; the Prince Caldor, who died an infant; the Princess Llarica; the Princess Marlys. After the death of his first wife on the XVIth day of November in the year 697, the King Llarik intermarried secondly with the Princess Sidonie daughter of Mear Prince of Meara on the IInd day of August in the year 699, and by her he had children: the Hereditary Prince Ryons; the Princess Laheen; the Prince Llywarch, who died young; the Prince Aural later Prince-Bishop of Dhassa; the Princess Fideilme.

The Prince Llarik was created Count of Rhemuth by his father on his coming of age in the year 665. The Great King Augarin died in the year 673, and was succeeded by his elder son, the Hereditary Prince

Aidan. But the Prince Donal elder brother of Llarik challenged the Prince Aidan's right to the throne, saying that his father's Ist marriage had never been properly registered, and also that Aidan's mother had been legally betrothed to another at the time of her marriage, and was therefore not free to enter into the bonds of matrimony. But the Prince Aidan called together Gisenod the newly elected Archbishop Primate of Valoret and several other clerics as an ecclesiastical court, and they ruled that the marriage was valid in the eyes of the Church. A few days later, on the Xth day of March in that year, the Prince Donal was found dead in the forest of Candor Rhea with an arrow through his eye. The Prince Llarik, younger brother of Prince Donal, accused his half-brothers of murder, and brooded over this injustice for the next quarter century.

The King Aidan died on the VIIth day of July in the year 698 at the Battle of Ebor in combat with Torv Count of Eastmarch. His only surviving son, the Hereditary Prince Ifor, was severely wounded in the same encounter, losing an arm and a leg, and was like to die of the rot, or at least to remain crippled for the rest of his days. The Prince Bearand, younger brother of King Aidan and himself advanced in years, therefore declared himself Protector of the Throne on the XVIth day instant, and ordered a convening of the High Council on the Ist day of August to discuss the succession.

But the Hereditary Prince Ifor would not die, nor would he renounce his rights to the throne, and the Council was split over who should rule as King, or even whether the Prince Bearand had the right to be Protector. On the next day following, the Prince Llarik again raised the issue of the legitimacy of King Augarin's Ist marriage, and the Prince Bearand became so angry that he began shouting at his brother and suddenly turned very red in the face, and he collapsed in front of the Great Lords of the Council. On the IIIrd day of the month the Prince Llarik appeared again before the Council and declared himself Protector of the Throne, since the Prince Bearand was no longer able to fulfill the obligations of his office. But the Council could not agree while the Prince Ifor still lived.

According to Lord Loughlin mac More, "What followed is uncertain, for the records of this period are mostly silent about the events of the next month. Some say that the Princes Bearand and Ifor did die of natural causes, and that the Prince Llarik then made himself King of the Realm, and had the Ist marriage of King Augarin annulled, making Llarik the only legitimate male heir to the throne. But others say that the Prince Bearand was smothered in his bed, that Prince Ifor was allowed gradually to starve to death, and that Bearand's son Prince Jashan disappeared from his room and was never seen again. Still others say that the Prince Jashan, fearing the fate that awaited him in Gwynedd, left Rhemuth in the dead of night and took boat downstream to Llannedd, and thence to Bremagne, where he found refuge, dying there in old age. In any event, by the beginning of September the Prince Llarik was master of the Kingdom of Gwynedd."

The Prince Llarik was proclaimed King of Gwynedd on the IInd day of September in the year 698. He arrested half of the old Council, charging them with treason, and replaced those whom he considered disloyal with some of his own friends. On the VIth day of October in the year 699 he ordered the arrest of his own II sons and heirs, and had them executed X days later for high treason, claiming that they coveted his wife and his throne and were plotting with the exiled Prince Jashan. Some have hinted of scandals in the Palace, saying that the King's beautiful young wife, the Princess Sidonie, whom he had married just II months earlier, became involved with I or both of the handsome Princes, and that the heir that she bore the following Spring was actually the child of her stepson.

But the King by this time had grown distrustful of everyone, and he ordered the execution of many of the officials and peers of Gwynedd. No one was safe. This was a dark period in the history of the Realm, with the failure of the *Pax Rûmanum* inspiring attacks by the barbarian hordes on the South and North of Gwynedd beginning in the year 702. Grecotha was sacked on the XIIth day of July in the year 705, and Nyford was burned by Moorish raiders on the XXXIst day of May in the year 707. The King had little military training, and was forced to rely on his generals, whom he attempted to play off one against another. As a result, the Kingdom was ill-served in its defense, and the people suffered greatly.

Lord Loughlin states: "In old age the King would not let himself be seen in public, and refused to attend even the meetings of the Great Council. He kept to his rooms, and communicated with the world through II advisers, one of whom had been a slave, the other a commoner. He insisted that half of his meals be eaten by someone else before he would touch them. He would not cut his hair or trim his nails. It is said that he had already written out the orders to have his surviving son, Prince Ryons, arrested and executed, when the latter was secretly informed by a member of the guard, and took the necessary steps. What is known for certain is that the King Llarik fell from his window to the stones below, either dying by his own hand or by the hand of another."

The King Llarik died on the XIth day of January in the year 719, aged LXVII years, and was succeeded by his eldest surviving son, the Prince Ryons. He was not much mourned. *Quicunque turpi fraude semel innotuit, etiamsi verum dicit, amittit fidem.* [*The Harrowing of Gwynedd*].

Lleassi. They were the Lords of the Dark Places in the old Deryni mythology; their sphere was the orb of Earth, and they were exceedingly powerful. According to the tales of Pargan Howiccan, the Deryni Lord Johanan sought to cast them out with the permission of Makurias-in-Glory. *Dies iræ, dies illa, sæclum solvet in favilla, teste David cum Sibylla.* [*Camber of Culdi*].

Llegoddin Canyon Trace. This winding, treacherous canyon is located about an hour's ride from the Rustán Cliffs in the Rheljan Mountains, North of Cardosa. It was here that Brion King of Gwynedd defeated and killed the Festillic pretender Hogan Gwernach on the XXIst day of June in the year 1105. *Con todo el mondo guerra, y paz con Gwyneddo.* ["Swords Against the Marluk"; "Legacy"].

Llentieth. This Deryni school was located in the Mughdorna Mountains North of Cashien close by the Connaiti border in the year 917. [*Camber the Heretic*].

Llew ab Blew. He was serving as a guard in Bishop Alister Cullen's household in January of the year 917. [*Camber the Heretic*].

Llewell Sicard Judhael Drogon *MacArdry Quinnell*, Prince of Meara. This sororicide was born on the IXth day of September in the Year of Our Lord 1108, being the second son of Sicard Lord MacArdry and Caitrin Princess and Pretender of Meara. He was captured on the IXth day of December in the year 1123 while chasing Dhugal MacArdry Earl of Transha, who had taken captive his sister, Princess Sidana. He opposed the betrothal of Sidana to Kelson King of Gwynedd, and then murdered her most foully moments after her wedding to the King on the VIth day of January in the year 1124. He was tried for this crime, convicted, and beheaded on the IInd day of February following, aged XV years. His body was later disinterred and returned to Laas for burial in the Quinnell family crypt. [*The Bishop's Heir*; *The King's Justice*; *The Quest for Saint Camber*; *King Kelson's Bride*].

Llewel(l)yn ap Turlough, Lord. He was born about the year 780 in Mooryn, being the eldest son of Lord Turlough ap Ladislas. He succeeded his father on the IInd day of February in the year 796. Having been blinded by the smallpox at the age of XVIII years, the Lord Llewelyn turned to the wire-strung Deryni harp for solace, studying it for III years under the tutelage of Breton ap Dhomhnaill. He abandoned his heritage as a peer of the realm, deeding his title to his younger brother, Lord Lludd ap Turlough, on the Ist day of April in the year 801, and set out on the road as an itinerant musician, one who would soon compose many haunting melodies of shimmering grace and elegance. He became the best-known troubadour of his day, producing many of his finer works for Risteard Lord Reynnells. In later years he served as court bard to Nanthelme High King of Mooryn, and later to Dominic Duke of Corwyn. His works include the classic "Ballad of Mathurin and Derverguille," and "Éíníní Caeriesse," which celebrates the lost land which sank beneath the sea hundreds of years earlier. These were collected with other works into the *Lays of the Lord Llewelyn*. He died at Coroth on the XVIth day of April in the year 850, aged about LXX years. R.I.P. [*Camber of Culdi*; *The Harrowing of Gwynedd*; *Deryni Checkmate*].

Llyndruth Meadows and Plain. These grasslands are located at the foot of the Cardosa Defile in the Rheljan Mountains. They were the site of the final confrontation between Kelson King of Gwynedd and Wencit King of Torenth on the IInd day of July in the year 1121. The Plain of Llyndruth is known for its wild antelope, and the Meadows attract deer, bear, and other animals down from the mountains.

Of this area Campbell de Broun speaks very highly in his diaries: "We crossed a little creek called Parmers Branch, along which there was a grove of timber to its source in the Bluffs not more than a league off. On crossing this branch we again entered the prairie, which was level and rich, being the River bottom, and appeared to be well-calculated for cultivation. There was a skirt of timber all along the River on the left, and on the right we discovered the Rheljan Bluffs rising above the Llyndruth Plain and covered with timber, which had a very striking and beautiful appearance. They presented to the view many handsome sites for building and looked as if nature formed it expressly for that purpose, with the rich, open Plain in front stretching far and wide and bordering on the River. It required but little aid of the fancy to convert every one of those sites into a gentleman's seat, with groves, orchards, meadows, etc. This prairie reached to the Grande River with very little difference in its appearance." [*High Deryni*; *The Bishop's Heir*].

Lochalyn Castle. This ancient stronghold and seat of the Earls of Eastmarch was erected by the Count Magnus I in the year 730 in the Northern foothills of the Rheljan Mountains. It was here that Rhys Michael King of Gwynedd came with his army in June of the year 928 to provide support for Sudrey Dowager Countess of Eastmarch and her daughter, Stacia Countess of Eastmarch. On the XXIVth day instant King Rhys Michael here signed a codicil to his last will and testament, setting in place new provisions for a Regency Council for his son, Hereditary Prince Owain.

Two centuries later, in November of the year 1104, Rorik III Earl of Eastmarch rallied his forces here against Brion King of Gwynedd, and proceeded South; however, he was soon overthrown by his cousin, Arban Baron of Iomaire later Earl of Eastmarch, who occupied the Castle in the year 1105. The village of Lochalyn is located nearby. [*The Bastard Prince*; "Swords Against the Marluk"].

Logréine. This small sovereign Principality, one of the Forcinn states, lies on the coast of the Southern Sea, being bordered by Fianna on the West, Vézaire on the East, Andelon on the South, and the Southern Sea on the North. The state includes much of the Andel Range to the Eau-de-Vin River, which forms the boundary line between Logréine and Fianna. The capital city, Lognac, is located on the Baie des Chameaux.

The Principality of Logréine was founded on the VIIth day of August in the year 755 by Prince Flocon I, who declared his independence from Réginald Duc du Joux, while the latter was occupied with defending himself from Moorish raiders. The Prince Dreux extended Logréine's borders to the River Thuria in the year 915, but was driven back a few years later by the Prince of Andelon. In recent decades the ruling House has made several significant marital connections with the Kings of Bremagne and Torenth.

Logréine exports peat and marshberries from its coastal bogs, oats and pork from its central plain, and cedar wood from the Andel Mountains which cover the Western half of its territory. Although only a small portion of the country is arable, the Principality does produce several varieties of ale, mead, wine, and other spirits; indeed, a "bottle or two of Logréine," according to Campbell de Broun, will move the traveler "a goodly far distance down the road, even in bad weather." *Quæ venit ex tuto, minus est accepta voluptas.* [*King Kelson's Bride*].

Princes of Logréine

House of d'Avoine

Flocon I d'Avoine	755-788
Brunon (son)	788-811
Conon (son)	811-834
Bobon (usurper)	834
Simon I (son)	834-852
Limon (brother)	852-871
Flocon II (son)	871-899
Hescelin (cousin)	899-901
Dreux Le Grand (son)	901-955
Drunon (son)	955-966
Josselin (son)	966-984
Flocon III (son)	984-1003
Simon II (nephew)	1003-1038
Pépin I (son)	1038-1044
Simon III (brother)	1044-1056
Flocon IV (brother)	1056-1059
Lancelin (son)	1059-1088
Pépin II (cousin)	1088-1089
Isarn I (son)	1089-1109
Isarn II (son)	1109-1130+

Lóránt Zimri Kyprian Károly *Furstán-Truvorsk*, Duke of Truvorsk, Sir. He was born on the Ist day of June in the Year of Our Lord 1063, being the third son of Zimri Duke of Truvorsk, but the first by his second wife, the Lady Dauphine natural daughter of Talière Duc du Joux by the Lady Tintorette de Nemours. He intermarried with the Lady Cyrice, eldest daughter of Sobbon Hort of Orsal and Prince of Tralia and Maya Princess of Thuria, on the XXth day of March in the year 1090, and by her he had children: the Countess Vidarra, who intermarried with Lord Lewys ap Halloran ap Morian ap Lewys ap Norfal; the Hereditary Duke Káspár later Duke of Truvorsk; the Count Zimri Lóránt; the Count Vólmar; the Countess Karla; the Countess Hoganna; the Countess Ariberta.

The Duke Lóránt was trained by many a master of Deryni lore, having originally been fostered at the Court of Geoffroi Duc du Joux in the year 1073. In the year 1083 he took a caravan across the great desert to the Holy Lands, on a journey taking LIX days, and is said to have visited Kibris and the fabled city of Rûm and many other places besides, before returning to Torenth in the year 1088.

He succeeded his nephew, the Duke Hogan Gwernach, on the XXIst day of June in the year 1105, and immediately set about reforming and restoring the ancient Truvorski Court, which had been allowed to languish by Duke Hogan, who preferred spending his days in the cooler highlands of Marluk and Gwernach. He rebuilt those parts of his seat of Neumarck which had been allowed to fall into ruin, and re-established justice throughout the land. The Duke Lóránt had by this time also gained a reputation as a master of the Deryni arts and sciences, and he fostered a number of promising young men sent to him for that purpose by King Nimur II and King Wencit, among them Mátyás Count of Komnéné and Duke d'Arjenol.

In the year 1120 he began showing signs of the wasting disease which is sometimes seen among the scions of the House of Furstán, and within a year he could no longer walk, but had to be carried everywhere by servants. But he maintained his good spirits unto the end, saying that he was the luckiest man alive to have had such a decent father and mother and such a loving wife and excellent children; and he died, beloved by all who knew him and bathed in the light of the Lord, on the IIIrd day of April in the year 1122, aged LVIII years. He was interred with many of his ancestors in Saint Václáv's Church on the family estate of Neumarckburg. R.I.P. [*King Kelson's Bride*].

Lorcan, Sir. This knight was serving as seneschal to the Baron d'Eirial in December of the year 977. He had a fierce loyalty to the d'Eirials. ["Vocation"].

Lorenzo, Brother. A bookbinder at Rhemuth Palace in June of the 928, he repaired a volume of Kyla's verse for Queen Michaela. [*The Bastard Prince*].

Lorsöl. This Duchy of Torenth is situate Southeast of the Beldour River, Southeast of the Duchy of Marluk, South of Arjenol, West of Vorna, and Northwest of Vechta. Originally an independent Principality, Lorsöl was conquered in the year 892 by Nimur I King of Torenth, the last Graf, Eckehardt III, submitting and surrendering his sovereignty on the XVIIIth day of September in that year. He was then formally acknowledged as Count of Lorsöl, but military governors responsible only to Beldour actually ruled the territory for many years. On the extinction of the ancient line in the year 1039, the Honour was given by Arkady II King of Torenth to his younger brother, Prince Andruin later Stephanos V Patriarch of Beldour, and thence to Prince Torval his great-nephew. The title was regranted by King Wencit to his nephew, Prince Ronal Rurik, in the year 1120. [*King Kelson's Bride*].

Grafs von Lorsöl

House of Haberlingen

Haberlin	661-688
Eckehardt I (son)	688-713
Lasko (son)	713-731
Moserlin (brother)	731-734
Eckehardt II (son)	734-777
Sesson (cousin)	777-788
Bernhardt I (son of Eckehardt II)	788-806
Grimoald (son)	806-832
Wilhelm-Ernst (son)	832-845
Bernhardt II (brother)	845-854
Eckehardt III (son)	854-895
Bernhardt III (son)	895-922
Georg-Gaimardt (nephew)	922-950
Karel-Mainhardt I (son)	950-976
Max-Eckehardt IV (son)	976-999
Hans-Reinhardt (brother)	999-1003
Boris-Bardöl (usurper)	1003
Max-Eckehardt V (son of Hans)	1003-1025
Paul-Bernhardt IV (uncle)	1025-1028
Karel-Mainhardt II (brother)	1028-1033
Franz-Eberhardt (brother)	1033-1039

DUKES OF LORSÖL

HOUSE OF FURSTÁN
Andruin (son of Kyprian II of Torenth)	1039-1066
Torval (great-nephew)	1066-1119
Ronal Rurik (nephew)	1120-1130+

Lothan. This robber, a companion to Groggin, confronted Geordie Lord Drummond at Twilham Green in April of the year 905. [*Deryni Challenge*].

Loyall, Father. He was serving as the Abbot's chaplain at the *Arx Fidei* seminary in the year 1104. ["The Priesting of Arilan"].

Luke, Saint. This Evangelist is often depicted in art in the guise of a physician, sometimes accompanied by a winged ox. A passage from Chapter IX of his *Gospel* was quoted by Hubert MacInnis Archbishop Primate of Valoret and All Gwynedd to King Javan at Rhemuth in November of the year 921; Javan quoted part of the scripture back to him. His feastday is the XVIIIth day of October. [*King Javan's Year*].

Luke, Sister. She was the nun assigned from Bishop Thomas Cardiel's staff to assist the Countess Richenda at Llyndruth Meadows in July of the year 1121. [*High Deryni*].

Luric *Visoux*. He was a guard in the service of the Hort of Orsal in the year 1128. His mind and will were subsumed by the traitor Iddin de Vesca on the XVIIth day of July in that year, who used him to uncover the secret of the Hort's portal. [*King Kelson's Bride*].

Lydia *McBain Drummond*. She was born on the Vth day of January in the Year of Our Lord 866, being the daughter of Gordon Lord McBain and Louise Lady Reynnells. She intermarried with Henry Lord Drummond *Junior* on the XXIst day of April in the year 884, and by him she had children: the Lord Richard; the Lord Hamish; the Lord Geordie. She died on the XXXth day of August in the year 908, aged XLII years. R.I.P. [*Deryni Challenge*].

Macaire. He was serving as a scout in the party of Kelson King of Gwynedd during the latter's visit to Trurill on the XXIVth day of November in the year 1123. [*The Bishop's Heir*].

MacArdry, House of. The ancestor of this noble House of Gwynedd, Sir Ardry mac Graith, is mentioned in a 792 chronicle of Cassan as a border Laird on the coast of the Gulf of Kheldour. Ardry's direct descendant, the Clan Chief and Laird Egan MacArdry, was elevated to the Earldom of Transha on the XIIth day of October in the year 926 by King Rhys Michael. On the XXIst day of May in the year 1125 Dhugal MacArdry Earl of Transha also inherited the Duchy of Cassan. "*Prend-moi tel que je suis.*" [*The Bishop's Heir*; *The King's Justice*; *The Quest for Saint Camber*]. See also: Adreana, Ardry, Bertie, Caball, Caulay, Dhugal, Ithel, Jass, Lambert, Llewell, Maryse, Matthias, Michael, Sicard, Sidana.

LAIRDS OF CARTHCART & CHIEFS OF MACARDRY

HOUSE OF MACARDRY
Ardry mac Graith mac Ardry	792?-811
Graith MacArdry (son)	811-837
Buagh (son)	837-843
Brone (brother)	843-881
Rolann (son)	881-902
Egan (son)	902-931

SEE EARLS OF TRANSHA FOR LATER LAIRDS

Maccul, Bishop and Saint. This IVth-century holy man began life as a simple pagan fisherman in the village of Uiskin in Cassan. He was out in his boat one day during a particularly poor season, when he stood up in his craft and called into the skies: "I have heard the priests talking about you, Oh Lord, and I did not believe what they said. Send me now a sign and I will follow you the rest of my days." And with his next cast, his net was filled so full of fish that he could hardly draw it in. He immediately went to the local priest and was baptized. He later became Bishop of Lusk in Northwestern Howicce. It was on his feastday, the XXVIIth day of April, that Royston Draper was baptized. He is patron of fishermen and lost causes. [*Camber of Culdi*].

MacEwan, House of. The earliest known progenitor of this ancient noble house was Knut, who proclaimed himself Sovereign Margrave of the Marches in the year 508. His direct descendant, Sighere Earl of Eastmarch, was created Duke of Claibourne in the year 906 by Cinhil I King of Gwynedd. Sighere's son and successor was Duke Ewan I, whence the family derives its name. See also: Ewan, Graham, Hrorik, Sean, Sighere, Stacia.

MacGregor, House of. This surname was adopted by Jesse son of Gregory MacDinan Earl of Ebor to honour his father's name. [*King Javan's Year*]. See also: Gregory, Jesse, Seanna.

MacInnis, House of. The first known member of this noble House was Inis mac Raphoe Lord Marlor, who is noted in a tax record of Llarik King of Gwynedd in the year 704; the date of his elevation to the title is unknown. Dallan Baron Marlor was attainted on the VIth day of July in the year 822 after the successful invasion of Gwynedd by King Festil I, but the Honour was reinstated on the VIIth day of July in the year 905 by King Cinhil I in the person of Dallan's great-grandson, Sir Manfred MacInnis. The latter was created Earl of Culdi on the Ist day of October in the year 917, and Earl Manfred's son, the Hereditary Count Iver, married Richeldis MacLean Heiress of Kierney on the Vth day of March in the year 918. The titles of Marlor and Culdi were deeded as dowries to his daughters by Earl Iver, and the County of Kierney inherited by his son, Earl Hobard. With the death of Hobard's son Earl Richard at Killingford on the XVIth day of June in the year 1025, the House of MacInnis became extinct in the male line. See also: Edward, Elaine, Estellan, Hubert, Ivor, Manfred, Richeldis.

MacLean, House of. The founder of this Gwyneddan noble House was Sir Iolo MacLean also called "The

Lean," who was created Earl of Kierney by King Festil I on the XIIth day of September in the year 822. He may have been a son or younger brother of the Ion or Iern mac Lean of Marley who is mentioned in a surviving deed of Sir Iolo in the year 831. The title of Kierney passed to the MacInnis family on the XIXth day of March in the year 918, when the elder branch of the MacLean family became extinct, but returned to the cadet line of McLain on the XIth day of November in the year 1033. See also: Adrian, Aislinn, Angus, Ardis, Camber Allin, Fiona, Geoffrey, Giesele, Iain, Kierney, Mairi, Richeldis, Trurill, as well as the cognate House of McLain.

Maclyn. He was a handler of horses employed by Julius at the Rhelledd Horse Fair on the I[st] day of May in the year 1115. ["The Knighting of Derry"].

Macon, Master. He was serving as battle-surgeon for Jared McLain Duke of Cassan in August of the year 1100. ["Bethane"].

MacRorie, House of. The progenitor of this Torenthi and Gwyneddan family was Rhori Mór Prince of Kheldour, who was born on the XIIth day of June in the Year 683, being a son of Morolt MacTyre Prince of Kheldour and Paili Lady Tinnascart, a nephew of Ieuan MacTyre Sovereign Prince of Kheldour, and a brother of Iorwerth Sovereign Prince of Kheldour. He was fostered in the year 693 to Aldred I King of Torenth, and intermarried on the VIIth day of May in the year 711 with the Princess Rocasta daughter of Aleksy Prince of Torenth and the Princess Moira Roselynn daughter of Aidan King of Gwynedd. The dowry of Princess Rocasta was the estate of Cullanan or Kulnán in the Northern Rheljan foothills adjoining the Duchy of Tolán.

Their eldest son, Lord Siebert MacRhori, was born on the IInd day of March in the Year of Our Lord 712, and was created I[st] Count Cullanan at birth; he intermarried with Mhari Lady d'Arjenol, a Deryni, on the XIXth day of June in the year 729, and by her he had children: the Hereditary Count Maurin later Count Cullanan, born in the year 730; the Lady Rosamhari; the Lady Regan; the Lady Downett; the Lady Ashling; the Lord Amaury later Count Cullanan, born in the year 740. The Count Maurin having only daughters, his brother Amaury succeeded him as IIIrd Count in the year 791.

The Count Amaury intermarried with Zarya Countess von Furstán-Altorf on the IInd day of August in the year 759, and by her he had children: the Hereditary Count Siebert later Siebert II Count of Cullanan, born in the year 760, in whose family the Torenthi title of Cullanan continues to descend; the Lord Ballard later I[st] Earl of Culdi, born in the year 765; the Lord Camber, a priest of the Order of Saint Yevdokim in Torenth, born in the year 768; the Lord Angus later Baron MacRorie later Earl of Culdi, born in the year 769.

The Lords Ballard and Angus accompanied Prince Festil in June of the year 822 on his invasion of Gwynedd; for his loyalty, Lord Ballard was created Earl of Culdi on the XXIInd day of July in that year, with remainder to his heirs male whatsoever, his lands being situate near the border with Meara. Lord Angus received a small castle near Valoret and the title Baron MacRorie. Upon the Earl Ballard's death without male issue on the XVIIth day of December in the year 824, his title passed to his younger brother, Baron Angus, who died II years later on the XIIth day of March in the year 826, leaving issue III sons, the Lords Cathan, Joram, and Adrian, each of whom succeeded to the title in turn. The best-known member of this family was Camber MacRorie VIIth Earl of Culdi, Chancellor of the Kingdom of Gwynedd in the reign of King Blaine I, and later canonized Saint.

The current representative of the Torenthi branch of the family is Rhori MacRhori Count Cullanan (or Róry Makróry Count Kulnán, as he is called in Torenth); his eldest son, the Hereditary Count Amaury, is resident at Court in Beldour, and Rhori's daughter Iris and son-in-law Rodulf Lord Murdoch manage his estates, with the assistance of Lord Amaury's wife and several grandchildren.

The arms of this house are blazoned: per pale *gules* and *azure*, in pale a sword proper enfiled of an Earl's coronet of the same. [*Camber of Culdi*]. See also: Adrian, Aislinn, Angus, Ansel, Ardis, Ballard, Camber, Cathan, Culdi, Davin, Elinor, Elspeth, Evaine, Jerusha, Jocelyn, Joram, *Tor Caerrorie*.

Magan, Father. This young *Custodes* priest was serving as an assistant to Father Lior in June of the year 928. He refined the technique of "Deryni pricking" by applying *merasha* directly into the navel, where it slowly leeched into the victim's blood. He was summoned by Rhun Earl of Sheele to interrogate and torture the Deryni double agent, Master Dimitri, on the XXth day instant. He was tried, convicted, and hanged on the XVth day of July in that year for his crimes during the "Regency" period. [*The Bastard Prince*].

Magrette Adeliza Alexa *Ramsay-Quinnell*, Princess of Meara, Lady of Cloome. She was born on the XXIIIrd day of December in the year 1015, being the third surviving daughter of Jolyon II Sovereign Prince of Meara and the Princess Urracca daughter of Faucon Hereditary Prince of Bremagne. She intermarried with Lord Edward Ramsay son of the Earl of Cloome on the XIIth day of May in the year 1035, and by him she had children: the Lord Colin; the Lady Alcinda; the Lady Lucinda, a twin with her sister; the Lord Thomas, who died childless; the Lord Edgar; the Lord Samuel; the Lord Matthew, who died young; the Lord Alexander; the Lady Laurel; the Lady Maureen, a twin to her sister, later a nun of Saint Brigid's Abbey under the name Sister Hosanna.

In the year 1035 the Princess Magrette sought an audience with her brother-in-law, Malcolm King of Gwynedd, and begged him to allow her to marry the Lord Edward, whom she loved dearly, for she was sickened in her heart by the tragic deaths of her kin and the estrangements between her sisters. He agreed to her petition. In return she relinquished any pretensions to the Throne of Meara for herself *ad personam*, swearing lifelong fealty to King Malcolm and her sister, the Princess and Queen Roisian, even though these oaths had the consequence of separating her from her other sister, the Princess Annalind Pretender of Meara, and from her mother, the Dowager Princess Urracca. Then she and her husband retreated to the relative safety of Cloome, where the Lady Magrette chose to bear her children and tend her home and hearth under the protection of her husband's family, rather than spend a precarious existence in exile, constantly fearing for her life and for the safety of those she loved.

The Lady Magrette was as lovely in form as the fabled Hélène de Troi, as can be seen from the portrait of her that survives in the Great Hall of the Earls of Cloome; and she had a reputation for being sane and just and secure in all her dealings with those who served her. Indeed, it was said by those in Cloome that, had she chosen to pursue her legitimate pretensions to the Principate, she would have had ample support from the Highlanders of the Cloome Mountains. Her elder sister Annalind and all of that family were more often feared than respected, and many of the Southern clans of Meara had grown utterly weary of the constant bickering and fighting between Annalind and her supporters and detractors, and longed only for an end to the bloodshed.

In later years the Honourable Campbell de Broun, who claimed clanship with the Ramsays on his mother's side, and was thus related *per matrimonium* to the Princess, was wont to say of this fine Lady, whom he had met whilst still a lad, that she "had been fashioned of a finer cut of tartan than the rest of her clan, and displayed far, far nobler aspirations upon her sainted brow than the Grand High Princes of Meara." This revered Lady died on the VIIth day of March in the year 1079, aged LXIII years. R.I.P. [*King Kelson's Bride*].

Mahael *Phóstéridés*. This ancient Deryni historian lived about the year 300, being among the earliest known writers of his race. He is called by some early Torenthi scholars Makhaél apo Beldourias or Phóstéridés (which is to say, "Mahael son of the Light-Bringer" in the Byzantyun tongue). Several works are attributed to him, but none are known to have survived into modern times save the oddly-titled *History of Kheldour* (*Historia Heldourniae*), a grimoire used by the Camberian Council and others to explore archaic Deryni lore. Copies of this work may still exist in Torenth and Byzantyun, and may have been used, according to Athanasios Hokhanémsos, to find the lost Isle of Loryùppa. In the legends of Torenth, Mahael is called the direct ancestor of the House of Furstán and the Kings of Torenth, through his son Salathiel, his grandson Elemér, and great-grandson Mahael ho Phourstanos, but this claim has never been proven. [*Camber the Heretic*].

Mahael I Averil Oskar *Furstán d'Arjenol*, Duke of Arjenol. He was born on the IIIrd day of March in the Year 1035, being the eldest son and heir of Torval II Duke d'Arjenol and the Princess Markella daughter of the Princess AriElinora Titular Queen of Gwynedd and Duchess of Tolán and Manuel Graf von Spire. He intermarried with the Princess Jaïne, daughter of Isarn I Sovereign Prince of Logréine and Lady Jordana daughter of Tiraquell Sieur de Jordanet, on the XVIth day of April in the year 1085, and by her he had children: the Countess Raïsa, who entered into an unseemly relationship with her uncle, Grigor Prince of Logréine, and by him had a natural son, the Lord Ivor, without dynastic rights; the Hereditary Duke Lionel later Lionel II Duke d'Arjenol, who intermarried with the Princess Morag Heiress of Torenth, and had IV sons, II of them becoming Kings of Torenth; the Countess Nadezhda, who intermarried with Roman Kniaz' of Kier; the Countess Tatyana, a twin with her sister, who intermarried with Boltar Graf Kobrinsky.

After his first wife's death in childbirth on the VIIth day of March in the year 1089, the Duke Mahael intermarried secondly with Daniela Grafina von Ryndziak on the IVth day of November in the year 1090, and by her he had further children: the Count Mahael *Junior* later Count Amassy later Mahael II Duke d'Arjenol; the Count Pavel, who died at age II after tumbling down a staircase; the Count Teymuraz later Count of Brustarkia later Heir Presumptive and Regent of the Duchy d'Arjenol later Grand Duke of Phourstania; the Countess Marina, who intermarried with Eduardo Conde de Callisto; the Countess Natalya, a twin with her sister Marina, who died young; the Countess Friederike, a nun of Saint Triduana's under the name Sister Thyra; the Count Mátyás surnamed the Posthumous, later Lord and Count Komnéné, Count of Brustarkia, and Duke d'Arjenol.

The Hereditary Duke Mahael succeeded his father on the XXXth day of April in the year 1092. He was not a strong man at the time of his accession to the Duchy, and his health declined rapidly during his last II years, so that he was unable to provide more than token direction to the affairs of state. It is said that he would sit for long hours in an easy chair in the solar at the back of his palace, a cane crossed over his legs, and if his children ventured too close, without warning he would give them a switch across their posteriors, saying it was good for their discipline. He died of the shaking sickness on the XVIth day of May in the year 1100, aged LXV years, and was buried in the Great Hall of the Ancestors at Arzh. He was succeeded by his eldest son, the Hereditary Duke Lionel. R.I.P. *Quam veterrumu 'st tam homini optumu 'st amicus.*

Mahael II Termöd Aëlla Walcher *Furstán d'Arjenol*, Count Amassy, Duke of Arjenol, Prince of Torenth, Co-Regent of Torenth. He was born on the XIXth day of July in the Year of Our Lord 1091, being the second son of Mahael I Duke d'Arjenol, but the first by his second wife, Daniela Grafina von Ryndziak, and a younger half-brother of Lionel II Duke d'Arjenol. He was betrothed to the Princess Eufemia daughter and heir of Wencit King of Torenth in the year 1110, and intermarried with her on Xth day of June in the year 1115, and by her he had one child: the Hereditary Prince of Torenth Malachy Mátyás Mahael Nimur, who died at the age of II days, his mother also dying of the effects of childbirth on the XXVIth day of November in the year 1119. By Lodève Mirza Mörovskaya, he also sired a natural child who was legally acknowledged in his will, one Kirill Mahaelovich, born about the year 1111, to whom he gave the estate of Faupásy in Southern Arjenol, which bequest was allowed to stand by King Liam Lajos II, but without dynastic rights.

Count Mahael was created Count Amassy by King Nimur II on the XIXth day of July in the year 1105. He succeeded his brother as Duke d'Arjenol by the terms of King Wencit's last will and testament at the death of Lionel II on the IInd day of July in the year 1121, Lionel's own sons having been designated heirs to the throne of Torenth. Together with the Dowager Duchess Morag Princess of Torenth, the Duke Mahael II was named co-Regent to the young King Alroy Arion II, and after that monarch's death on the XIIth day of June in the year 1123, which he was later believed to have instigated, he also became co-Regent for Alroy's brother and successor, the King Liam Lajos II. He sent agents to Rhemuth on the IInd day of July in the year 1124 to assassinate Nigel Prince Regent of Gwynedd, and to seize the Princess Morag and her son, Liam King of Torenth, who were then being held against their will at the Court of Gwynedd, but his men were discovered and thwarted.

His regency was ended with the coming-of-age of his nephew on the IIIrd day of April in the year 1128. He then conspired with his younger brother, Teymuraz Count of Brustakia, to murder the King and to assume the throne of Torenth at the *killijálay* ceremony scheduled for the XVIth day of July in that year. His plot was uncovered by his youngest brother, Mátyás Count of Komnénë, and he was defeated by the combined powers of King Liam Lajos, King Kelson, Count Mátyás, Princess Morag, Patriarch Alpheios, and Count Teymuraz, who turned on him in the end; his mind was taken by King Liam Lajos, and his body impaled upon a stake in the Field of Kings, being allowed to rot there in the sun for III days and III nights, so that all men might observe the price of his treason.

The Duke Mahael II was XXXVI years of age at his death; his titles and honours were posthumously attainted and given unto his brother, Count Mátyás, save for the bequest made to his natural son, which, under the laws of Torenth, was an evil necessary to remove the child from the succession. Mahael is described in *Bride* as having a "close-clipped black beard [and] dark eyes heavy lidded." He sported a "massive, murky bloodstone seal-ring on his left forefinger." He wore his black hair in a long braid. As Harrington saith, "Treason doth never prosper, what's the reason? Why if it prosper, none dare call it treason." *Et quando uberior vitiorum copia? Quando maior avaritiæ patuit sinus? Alea quando hos animos?* [*The Bishop's Heir*; *The King's Justice*; *The Quest for Saint Camber*; *King Kelson's Bride*].

Maia *Campbell de Cameron*, Lady Farnham. She was born on the IVth day of February in the Year of Our Lord 869, being the daughter of Hector Lord Campbell and Mirabel Lady O'Malley. She intermarried with Yorke de Cameron Lord Farnham on the XXth day of December in the year 886, and by him she had one surviving child: the Lady Megan, who intermarried with Cinhil I King of Gwynedd. She and her husband both died on the XXIIIrd day of December in the year 891 when their carriage overturned, and their daughter was shortly thereafter made a ward of Camber Earl of Culdi. She was XXII years of age at her death. R.I.P. [*Camber of Culdi*].

Maire Alice *Haldane*, Princess of Gwynedd. She was born on the XXIst day of January in the Year of Our Lord 812, being the eldest daughter of Ifor King of Gwynedd and Nuala Lady Udaut. She was murdered with the rest of her family by the soldiers of King Festil I on the XXIst day of June in the year 822. R.I.P. [*Camber of Culdi*].

Mairi *of Nyford MacLean*, Lady. She was born on the XXVIIth day of July in the Year of Our Lord 890, being the daughter of Cairbre Baron of Nyford and Oona Lady Chaplin. She intermarried with Adrian MacLean Hereditary Count and Master of Kierney on the XIIth day of June in the year 905, and by him she had children: the Lord Camber Allin called "Camlin"; the Lord Leicester, born still; the Lord Adamnan, dead at the age of VII days; the Lady Ownah, who perished aworm at age II. She survived the attack of Manfred's men on Trurill Castle on the XXXIst day of December in the year 917 by climbing down a garde-robe shaft after her attackers had torched the keep. She was rescued on the next day by Evaine Lady Thuryn's party, but by the Spring of the year 918 she had begun losing her wits to the effects of grief and depression. To save what was left of her mind, her Deryni powers were blocked and she was sent to Saint Mary's in the Hills. She died there on the Xth day of October in the year 919, aged XXIX years. R.I.P. [*Camber the Heretic*; *The Harrowing of Gwynedd*].

Makurias-in-Glory. This being was the Servant of the High Gods in the old Deryni mythology. According to the tales of Pargan Howiccan, Lord Johanan beseeched Makurias-in-Glory to allow Johanan to cast out the Lleassi. [*Camber of Culdi*].

Malachi *de Bruyn*. He was born on the XIth day of June in the Year of Our Lord 1087, being the son of Sir Shadrach de Bruyn and Ailis Lady Lovecraft. This Cloomean, a distant cousin of Campbell de Broun, was serving as a junior seminarian at the *Arx Fidei* establishment near Valoret in the year 1105. He assisted with the ceremony that ordained Denis Arilan priest on the IInd day of February in that year. ["The Priesting of Arilan"].

Malachy I Mihály Emrich *Furstán*, King of Torenth, Graf von Westmarcke. He was born on the XXIXth day of September in the year 823, being the eldest son and heir of the Prince Regent Konrád Graf von Westmarcke and the Princess Richardis daughter of Prince Imre Elgar Count of Fathane. He intermarried with the Princess Fabiana daughter of Hennequin later Ist King of Fallon on the XIVth day of July in the year 841, and by her he had children: the Hereditary Graf and Prince Imre later Imre II King of Torenth; the Prince Konrád later Konrád II Graf von Westmarcke by cession from his father, dead at age XXXVI of worms, *sans postérité*; the Prince Miklós later Graf von Westmarcke in succession to his brother Konrád II later Sovereign Count of Medras in succession to his sister Mérode; the Princess Petronella, who intermarried with Brenn Count Vernich; the Princess Mérode later Sovereign Countess of Medras, who died at age XLVII.

The Prince Malachy succeeded his father as Graf von Westmarcke on the XVIth day of January in the year 863. In the year 871 the Graf Malachy, when he saw the debauchery into which his cousin the King Árpád had fallen, called together a Council of the Great Lords and the surviving members of the House of Furstán, and said, "He is not fit to rule." To this statement both Council and Church agreed, and deposed the King from his high place, sending the Prince Árpád to the Monastery of Sankt Pëtr near Medras. The Prince Malachy being the next heir in succession, he assumed the throne on the Ist day of May in the year 871, and was girded with the sword by Patriarch Isidóros I on the New Year's Day following. During this King's short reign he curbed the expenses of the state and rebuilt the treasury which had been depleted by his predecessor. He died of the *angina pectoris* on the IInd day of November in the year 877, aged LIV years, much mourned by his people, and was succeeded by his eldest son, the Prince Imre. He was buried with high honours in the crypt of his ancestors at Torenthály. R.I.P.

Malachy II Miklós Mátyás *Furstán*, King of Torenth. He was born on the XIXth day of April in the Year of Our Lord 940, being the eldest son and heir of Károly Hereditary Prince of Torenth and the Shaikha Zubayda bint Abdallah Emir of Tôrtous. He intermarried with Ianthe Princess of Salonique on the XIth day of July in the year 964, and by her he had children: the Hereditary Prince Nimur, killed in the Battle of Grecotha in the year 984, *sans postérité*; the Prince Carolus later Duke of Székaly later Károly II King of Torenth; the Princess Arien, dead of the stoney relique at age V; the Princess Torvalla, who intermarried with Imre III Pretender of Gwynedd, leaving issue; the Princess Genthia, who intermarried with Ringan IV Duke d'Arjenol, leaving issue; the Prince Kyprian later Duke of Arkadia later Kyprian II King of Torenth.

After the Queen Ianthe died of the consumptive complaint on the XXth day of December in the year 978, the King intermarried secondly with Brisquayne Baronne du Haut-Dossory on the Ist day of June in the year 979, and by her he had children: the Prince Marek-Rethel, dead of the flurious flux at age II; the Princess Adeléonore, who intermarried with Lancelme Soubize Comte d'Enghieux; the Princess Abyssinthe, a twin to her sister, who intermarried with Manassès Soubize Sieur d'Enghieux, a twin brother of the Comte Lancelme. The King Malachy also acknowledged several bastard children.

The Prince Malachy succeeded as Hereditary Prince of Torenth on the death of his father, the Prince Károly, on the XXIIIrd day of November in the year 960. From this date forward he was carefully trained by his grandfather to assume the reins of state, and was given both minor and major responsibilities during the ensuing VIII years. He conducted several successful military campaigns against the barbarian tribes of the Norseland beginning in the year 962.

The Prince succeeded his grandfather, the King Arion I, on the IInd day of March in the Year 972, and was girded with the sword at Iób on the New Year's Day following by Patriarch Abraam III. His own experience led him to associate his eldest son, the Hereditary Prince Nimur, in the government from the year 979. This young Prince had long been friendly with Marek-Imre Hereditary Prince of Festil, grandson of the Old Pretender of Gwynedd, and was persuaded by him and in turn persuaded his father to fund a Festillic invasion of Gwynedd in the year 983.

Although the campaign began well enough in the Fall of that year, with Nygel King of Gwynedd being killed in one of the Ist engagements, followed by the disorderly retreat of the Gwyneddan army before a superior force, the severe winter weather which arrived in November halted the movement of the invaders, forcing them to encamp for III months. A Vth part of the Festillic army starved, froze, or died of disease before the snows retreated sufficiently to allow the expedition to return to Torenth. It was then that the King Malachy made his crucial decision; being hard pressed by his sons and his cousins, he agreed to refit and reorganize the army under the command of the Hereditary Prince Nimur. The greatly strengthened expeditionary force left Torenth on the XVIIth of July in the year 984.

The II armies met on the Purple March at Grecotha on the afternoon of the IInd day of August, and fought a battle which continued until darkness. According to Hennique d'Archiac, "During the midnight Council of War held on the IIIrd day of August, the King advised against a direct attack on the city, saying, 'They must drive us out. They will come to us if we wait, and when they do, we will have them caught in the nutcracker. Then the shell of the nut will surely crack and break, leaving bare the fruit to be pluck'd.' But the Prince Nimur demurred, saying, 'We have II soldiers for every I of theirs, and they cannot retreat; we can crush them with I attack on the center of their line.' The King argued with his sons for several hours, but they would not relent, and so he agreed to allow the sally to go forward.

"But Jasher King of Gwynedd had redeployed his forces during the night, and when the Torenthis broke through the main gate of the city, they found no one there, for the Gwyneddans were attacking their supply train at the rear of their army. In the confusion the Princes Marek-Imre and Nimur and the King Malachy were killed and the Torenthi forces shattered and overrun. The Hereditary Prince Carolus assumed command and organized a retreat, but was himself severely wounded in the fighting; having taken the oath as King Károly II, he died V days later during the retreat to Torenth. The bodies of all IV Princes were brought to Torenthály, where they were buried in the family crypt of the House of Furstán with great honours. The King Malachy was XLIV years of age at the time of his passing." He was succeeded by his youngest son, the Prince Kyprian.

The Princess Arien says of this King that "...he was the handsomest of all the Kings of Torenth, gifted with a silver tongue and an aura of aristocracy, so that no one could ever mistake him for aught than he was. He was a natural commander of men. He always had a keen sense of his own destiny, and once boasted that he had never been defeated in battle. He collected scrolls of military histories and studied the campaigns of past kings and generals, regarding himself as an expert on strategy." *Non quello, che prende prima le armi, è cagione degli scandoli, ma colui che è primo a dar cagione che le si prendino.* R.I.P.

Malcolm Congal Aidan Julian *Haldane*, King of Gwynedd, Duke of Rhemuth. He was born on the Vth day of September in the Year of Our Lord 1008, being the third surviving son of Urien King of Gwynedd and the Princess Jaroni daughter of Bhair al-Salah King of R'Kassi. He intermarried firstly with the Princess Roisian eldest daughter of Jolyon II Sovereign Prince of Meara on the IXth day of August in the year 1025, intending with that union to join the Mearan state permanently and peacefully to Gwynedd, and by her he had children: the Princess Amalie Ovidia, who was betrothed to Tancrède King of Fallon at the time of her death at age XVII from the falling fits; the Princess Tiphaine Tallulah, later a nun of Saint Emerentiana's under the name of Sister Zita, who died at the age of LXXXII years, *sans postérité*, in the year 1110; the Hereditary Prince Donal Blaine later Donal Blaine II King of Gwynedd; the Princess Anaïs Alverossa Anastasia, who intermarried with Florestan Prince d'Uzès, leaving issue now extinct; the Prince Malcolm *Junior*, dead a day after his birth; the Princess Marfurca, dead of the yellow skin at age I.

After Queen Roisian's death of *la grippe* on the XXXth day of March in the year 1055 the King Malcolm intermarried secondly with Cecilia "Síle" Lady Calder of Sheele daughter of Rhupert Earl of Sheele and Prasanna Lady Fitz-Arthur Quinnell on the XIIIth day of May in the year 1055, and by her he had children: the Prince Richard later Duke of Carthmoor and Earl of Culdi; the Princess Tamelda, who took the veil under the name of Sister Symphorosa at the Abbey of Saint Perpetua in Carthmoor, and died unmarried at the age of LXI in the year 1119; the Princes Domnic and Kessoc, twin sons who both died within a few days of their birth; the Prince Julian, dead at age V of the black bile; the Princess Genèse, a twin with her brother, who, having renounced her titles in the year 1079, became a revered visionary and hermit near Shannis Meer in the Rheljan mountains, refusing to join any recognized order of the Holy Church, and dying unmarried and without issue at the age of LII in the year 1115; the Princess Hérone, dead at age VI of the typhoidous grippe. The King also acknowledged and legitimated several children by Glorvina Clonliff, but without dynastic rights: Jerome later Baron Drimeen; Brona, who intermarried with Gorry Lord Annamoe; Congal later Baron Bawnmore; Moreen, a well-known poet and artist, who painted several striking portraits in oils of her father and other relatives, and who was created a peeress in her own right as Baroness Doonreen.

The Prince Malcolm was created Duke of Rhemuth by his father on his coming of age in the year 1022, and was intended for a life in the Church, being sent in that year to the *Arx Fidei* seminary at Valoret. The Prince was called into military service in May of the year 1025, and never returned to the cloister. Following the debacle at Killingford on the XVIIth day of June in that year, in which Urien King of Gwynedd was killed together with many others, the Prince Malcolm helped to retrieve the wounded from the field and to organize the return of the army to Valoret. He succeeded his brother, King Cinhil II, at the latter's death on the XXIVth day instant, and was crowned on the battlefield by his uncle, Prince Jashan Bishop of Grecotha. He and his new wife were officially crowned King and Queen at Valoret by Archbishop Vespasian on the VIIth day of September, that being the feastday of Saint Bearand Haldane.

The difficulties facing this young Prince after Killingford were perhaps greater than the challenges met by any earlier King of Gwynedd save King Bearand his ancestor. The country was in ruins, the nobility decimated, the Principality of Meara in rebellion, the Kingdom of Torenth a continuing threat, and the Prince himself just XVI years of age, wholly untrained for his new responsibilities. To assist him the King appointed his uncle, the Prince Jashan Bishop of Grecotha, as High Chancellor of Gwynedd on the Ist day of July in the year 1025 to replace Tambert II Duke of Cassan, who had been killed in the fighting. In the month following, King Malcolm used the occasion of his Ist marriage to proclaim a new era for the Kingdom of Gwynedd, promising dowries to all of the unwed ladies in the Kingdom, and further urging the widows of Killingford to remarry as quickly as possible to secure the titles to their estates. He further announced a reform of the land laws, by which female heirs to the titles and estates of those killed in the recent war would be allowed to inherit and manage the lands entailed upon them. He reorganized the army into a smaller but more efficient force, and offered the younger sons of the nobility of the Côte d'Aurore across the Twin Rivers Strait grants of land and titles if they would emigrate to Gwynedd.

But the partisans of Meara were not satisfied with the marriage of the Princess Roisian to King Malcolm, and declaring that she had abdicated her throne by leaving Laas without the permission of the Great Lords, they made her sister the Princess Annalind Sovereign Prince in her place. However, the King Malcolm maintained his wife's right to the Throne of Meara, and despite all of his efforts to effect a peaceful settlement of the issue, he was forced to invade that province on the XXIXth day of May in the year 1027. On the XVIIIth day of June following he defeated and killed Loren Kincaid Earl of Kilarden near Ratharkin. The Princess Annalind and her mother the Dowager Princess Urracca fled from their capital of Laas into The Connait on the XXIIIrd day instant. The King Malcolm banned the Princesses from Meara under the pain of death, and placed them under the ægis of the law governing royal marriages in Gwynedd. He then appointed Ardal MacArdry Earl of Transha as the new Governor of Meara.

In the year 1041 the Princess Annalind married Rhiryd Earl of Kilarden, son of the late Loren Earl of Kilarden and Ayn Lady McLain daughter of Sir Roger McLain, in defiance of the Royal Marriages Act, and on the Ist day of December in the year 1044, she was again proclaimed Sovereign Prince of Meara by her supporters. The King Malcolm returned to Meara in July of the year 1045. The Pretender Annalind and her husband were captured and executed with several of her captains on the VIIIth day of August in the year 1045. *Desinit in piscem mulier formosa superne.*

Near the end of his life, on the VIIth day of October in the year 1070, the King commissioned from his daughter Moreen a large embroidered panel in the Great Hall of Rhemuth Palace displaying the arms of the House of Haldane, simultaneously creating her Baroness Doonreen. The masterpiece was not finally completed until the year 1078, being unveiled and dedicated on the XIIth day of July in that year by Malcolm's son and successor, King Donal Blaine II. The King Malcolm died in the fullness of his time on the IIIrd day of March in the year 1074, aged LXV years, and was buried with his ancestors in the family crypt at Rhemuth. R.I.P. [*The Bishop's Heir*; *The King's Justice*].

Malcolm "Mal" *Donalson*. This peasant supporter of Warin de Grey received a sword thrust in his leg at Jennan Vale in a skirmish with the forces of Nigel Duke of Carthmoor, and was found there by Royston Richardson. He was healed by Alaric Morgan Duke of Corwyn on the XVIIth day of June in the year 1121. [*High Deryni*].

Maldred, Earl Kirwan. He was born on the VIIIth day of June in the Year of Our Lord 859, being the eldest son and heir of Umfred Earl Kirwan and Ronat Lady Malwyn, and grandson of Solamh Earl Kirwan, who had fought with King Festil I during his invasion of Gwynedd in June of the year 822. He never married. The Earl Maldred was appointed to the High Council and Court of Commissioners by King Imre on the VIth day of January in the year 901. By September of the year 903 he was serving as a military commander and adviser to the King. He was assassinated by Coel Lord Howell on the XXXth day of November in that year, his death being made to implicate the innocent Cathan Hereditary Count of Culdi. He was aged XLIV years at his death, and was succeeded by his younger brother, Earl Uileos. He was a tall, florid man with the beginnings of a paunch, and had the reputation of being a cruel and uncompromising taskmaster. [*Camber of Culdi*].

Manfred Colquhoun Festil Tarquin *MacInnis*, Earl of Culdi, Baron Marlor, Earl Marshal, Vice Marshal, sometime Lord Regent of Gwynedd, Sir. He was born on the XVIth day of February in the Year of Our Lord 875, being the eldest son and heir of Sir Colquhoun Manfred MacInnis *de jure* Baron Marlor and Clayre Lady MacLanaghan, and brother to Hubert MacInnis Archbishop Primate of Valoret and All Gwynedd. He intermarried with Estellan Lady Buckleigh on the I[st] day of April in the year 895, and by her he had children: the Hereditary Count Iver later Earl of Culdi; the Lord Edward later Baron Arnham and Bishop of Grecotha.

The Lord Manfred was knighted on the VIth day of December in the year 893 by King Blaine I. He succeeded to his father's pretensions on the XXVIth day of December in the year 899, and was created Baron Marlor on the VIIth day of July in the year 905 by King Cinhil I in a reinstatement of his family's ancient lands and title; he then changed his IIIrd given name from "Festil" to "Cinhil" in the King's honour. He and his family were assaulted by rogue Deryni nobles on the XXXIst day of January in the year 917. He was appointed to the Royal Council on the IInd day of February following. He was named Earl of Culdi of the IInd creation by King Alroy on the I[st] day of October in that year. He brought news of the deaths of Archbishop Alister Cullen and Earl Jebediah to the state banquet held at Valoret on the Xth day of January in the year 918 to celebrate the joint nuptials of Rhun Earl of Sheele and Richard Lord Murdoch, and presented Cullen's personal pectoral cross as a wedding present to both couples.

He was named a Lord Regent and Earl Marshal of Gwynedd by the other Regents in place of Ewan I Duke of Claibourne on the XXVth day of May in the Year 918. On the IXth day of June following he witnessed the start of Revan's baptist ministry. He resigned as Earl Marshal at the time of King Alroy's coming of age on the XXVth day of May in the year 919, and was replaced by Lord Albertus formerly Peter Sinclair Earl of Tarleton. He was present at the death of King Alroy on the XXIIIrd day of June in the year 921, and carried the Sword of State in the funeral procession taking the King's body to Saint Hilary's Basilica on that same day. He returned to his estate at Culdi on the XXIIIrd day of August following.

He accompanied the Royal Expedition to Eastmarch which left on the XVth day of June in the year 928. After the death of Lord Albertus on the XXth day of that month, he assumed the title of Vice Marshal of Gwynedd. He was killed on the Vth day of July in that year by Rhun Earl of Sheele, who had been placed under a compulsion by King Rhys Michael to do so. Earl Manfred was LIII years of age at his death, and was succeeded by his son, Lord Iver.

According to the *Heirs*, he was "a more faded blond than his brother [Archbishop] Hubert, and slightly taller, but merely beefy where Hubert was undeniably fat. He held himself like the soldier he was, the blue eyes keen as flint above a sweeping pair of blond mustaches beginning to go grey. He had sunburned hands scarred and callused from years of wielding a sword." [*Camber the Heretic*; *The Harrowing of Gwynedd*; *King Javan's Year*; *The Bastard Prince*].

Marbury. This capital city of the Earldom of Marley is located in the far Northeastern part of Gwynedd at the foot of Lake Guitane where the River Glenkeen exits from it. The town serves as the seat of both the Earl of Marley and the Bishop of Marbury. Its placement on the major travel routes makes it the chief transit point for trade goods being shipped to and from the Duchy of Tolán in Torenth and the Kheldish Riding in Gwynedd.

Campbell de Broun once visited Marbury, and noted that: "We started this morning after sunrise in fine spirits, the weather pleasant and the roads good. In III leagues we arrived at Marbury, the weather by this time very cold. The road has been partly paved by the Earl of Marley at enormous expense. We crossed the Glenkeen on an excellent stone bridge with a single stone span nearly XX feet high across the stream. The foundation was a solid limestone rock; there were men there at work, blowing and breaking the rock to pave the road. Directly after crossing the bridge my team got frightened by the wagon's cloth catching on the limbs of a tree, and in spite of me, they ran off with III children in the wagon. They went a considerable distance before we stopped them when the off horse fell under the tongue." *Le silence est l'esprit des sots et l'une des vertus du sage.* [*King Javan's Year*; *The Bishop's Heir*].

Marcel Aymé Maxim *von Horthy*, Prince d'Orsal and Tralia. He was born on the XXVIth day of September in the Year of Our Lord 1113, being the third son of Létald Hort of Orsal and Prince of Tralia and Husniyya Sharifa of R'Kassi, and a twin of Princess Marcelline. [*King Kelson's Bride*].

Marcelline Aymée Maxime *von Horthy*, Princess d'Orsal and Tralia. She was born on the XXVIth day of September in the Year of Our Lord 1113, being the second daughter of Létald Hort of Orsal and Prince of Tralia and Husniyya Sharifa of R'Kassi, and a twin of Prince Marcel. She was considered as a possible bride for King Kelson in the year 1128. [*King Kelson's Bride*].

Marcus. He was serving as a lieutenant to Warin de Grey in June of the year 1121. [*High Deryni*].

Marcus *Concannon*, Chancellor General of the *Custodes Fidei*, Father. He was born on the Vth day of March in the Year of Our Lord 877. He was ordained priest on the XVIth day of May in the year 896. This well-known Deryni-hater was appointed Chancellor General of the newly formed Order, the *Custodes Fidei*, on the IInd day of February in the year 918, being put in charge of all seminaries and other institutions of education in Gwynedd. He was present at the Accession Council of King Javan on the XXIIIrd day of June in the year 921, and testified there that Javan's vows as a member of the *Custodes Fidei* Order were still binding. He was allowed to continue as Chancellor General of the *Custodes* after the accession of King Owain in June of the year 928, for he was a talented educator and administrator, but was charged by the new Synod of Bishops with the reformation of the Order. He died on the XXth day of November in the year 946, aged LXIX years. R.I.P. [*The Harrowing of Gwynedd*; *King Javan's Year*; *The Bastard Prince*].

Marek I, *i.e.*, **Mark I Imre Usbert *Furstán-Festil*, called "The Old Pretender," Hereditary Prince and Titular King of Gwynedd, Duke of Tolán *jure uxoris*, Duke of Imréaly.** This evil Prince was spawned of the Devil on the last day of January in the Year of Our Lord 905, being the posthumous natural son of an incestuous joining between Imre I King of Gwynedd and the Princess Ariella I his sister. He intermarried with his *cousine*, the Princess Charis daughter of Nimur I King of Torenth, on the XVIIth day of July in the year 927, and by her he had children: the Hereditary Prince and Duke Imre later Imre II Titular King of Gwynedd and Duke of Tolán; the Princess Imriella, who intermarried with her cousin, the Prince Ysarn Duke of Marluk and son of Arion I King of Torenth, on the XXIIIrd day of July in the year 944, leaving issue; the Princess Ysolte, born still; the Prince Arim-Miklós later Count of Moyrenc, dead at age XVI of the consumptive complaint, without issue; the Princess Chariella, who intermarried with her cousin, the Prince Rogan Hereditary Duke d'Arjenol, on the XIIth day of May in the year 949, leaving issue; the Princess Bernardine, who died a hydrophobe at age V; the Princess Ætherien, who took the veil under the name Sister Ragenfride of the Order of Saint Catulina and died in the year 978, aged XL years.

The Prince Marek succeeded to the pretensions of his parents on the death of his mother, the Titular Queen Ariella I, on the XXVth day of June in 905; and was girded with spur and sword and couped with *colée* in a manner inconsistent with the coronations of the Kings of Gwynedd, by the Torenthi Patriarch Antiochos I on New Year's Day in the year 920, for he sought throughout his life to acquire the legitimacy that he had not received from his parents. Although he was popularly believed to have gone into Arjenol at this time to continue his schooling, in reality he secretly served as aide to his cousin, the Torenthi Prince Miklós, on the latter's embassy to the Court of Gwynedd for the coronation of King Javan on the XXXIst day of July in the year 921.

He accompanied Prince Miklós to his meeting with Sudrey Countess of Eastmarch at Lochalyn Castle on the XIth day of March in the year 928, where she renounced her ties to Torenth, and the II Princes branded her traitor to the Furstáni Royal House. The pair then plotted together to restore Marek (the Torenthi form of his name) to the throne of Gwynedd, and the Prince Miklós occupied the Castle of Culliecairn on the VIIth day of June in that year, without securing permission from his brother the King. Miklós then sent a message to Rhys Michael King of Gwynedd demanding that he present himself at that Castle to honour the christening of Prince Marek's infant son, Prince Imre, and to show why Miklós should not give the fortress as a present to the young Prince. Marek had already promised the Prince Miklós the Duchy of Mooryn as a reward for his services when Marek should become King of Gwynedd. On the XXIInd day of June in that year Marek assumed the shape of the human Hombard of Tarkent and joined the parley of Prince Miklós with King Rhys Michael and Sudrey Countess of Eastmarch. Miklós abruptly attacked Sudrey and killed her with magic, but was himself killed by the King.

Following the death of Prince Miklós, Marek asked the Healer Cosim to alter Marek's memory, in order to keep the knowledge of the nature of his cousin's death from Arion I King of Torenth. Arion insisted that Marek secure his own succession before Arion would support a military incursion, and the King of Torenth was occupied with matters to the East for the next II decades. In the Spring of the year 948 the Prince Marek made a IInd attempt to capture Gwynedd, but although the King Arion provided mercenaries, money, and materiel to assist his efforts, the King utterly refused to invade Gwynedd, insisting that the Prince manage the affair himself. The battle was joined in Eastmarch in May of that year, and although Owain King of Gwynedd was killed shortly thereafter, the Toláni army was defeated by Owain's brother and successor the King Uthyr, and Prince Marek was forced back to his estates in Northern Torenth.

Following a stroke of paralysis that left him partially encrippled, the Prince Marek renounced his rights to the throne of Gwynedd in favour of his eldest son and heir, the Prince Imre II, on the IVth day of February in the year 975, and retired to his estates in Tolán. He was created Duke of Imréaly *ad personam* by Malachy II King of Torenth on the Ist day of December in that year. He died in Tolán on the XVIIIth day of April in the year 981, aged LXXVI years, just III months before his wife, and was buried with her in the family crypt at Torenthály. In his youth he was slender, with chestnut hair, fair skin, fine features, thin face, straight nose, and brown eyes.

The Princess Arien recalled that her great-grand-uncle Vidar Duke of Truvorsk and Prince-Bishop of Podébrad once said of this Prince that he was "sly and conniving, an orphan among men, who never took chances himself, but was always willing to risk other men's lives and fortunes with great abandon. He had all of the characteristics of the fox in the field, but he could not be trusted. My father King Arion disliked him all of his days, and never forgave him for Miklós's death. I met him on numerous occasions, and he would always flash me a smile and then touch my head or shoulder with apparent fondness and affection. Even as a lad, I remember, he sent chills down my back, for you could not trust the man." [*Saint Camber*; *The Harrowing of Gwynedd*; *King Javan's Year*; *The Bastard Prince*].

Marek II, *i.e.*, **Mark II Malachy Moyslav** *Furstán-Festil*, **Titular King of Gwynedd, Duke of Tolán.** He was born on the XVIth day of February in the Year of Our Lord 990, being the eldest son and heir of Imre III Titular King of Gwynedd and the Princess Torvalla daughter of Malachy II King of Torenth. He intermarried with Diadema Countess Nesbitt on the XXXth day of April in the year 1007, and by her he had children: the Hereditary Prince and Duke Festil (IV), killed with his father in the year 1025, who intermarried with Minerva Princess d'Estaing in the year 1024, leaving one son, the Prince Imre (IV) Alexander, dead of the colick at age VI months; the Hereditary Prince Marek later Duke of Valoret later Marek III Pretender of Gwynedd in succession to his father, *sans postérité*; the Princess Festilla, dead of chilblains at age VI. After the death of his first wife, the Prince Marek married secondly the Lady Pulcheria af Jutta, and by her he had one child: the Princess or Lady Salentina, who was said by her family to have had no dynastic rights, although such limitations were never imposed on her by her father while he still lived; and who was intermarried at the age of X years to the Prince Jaron Rhys Haldane, dying in childbirth in the year 1031, leaving one daughter, the Princess Tamarina, whose issue is believed extinct, but who was regarded by some few partisans as being the true Festillic pretender to the throne of Gwynedd while she was alive.

On the renunciation by his father of the throne of Gwynedd, the Prince Marek succeeded as Titular King of Gwynedd on the XXXIst day of December in the year 1024, and was girded with spur and sword and couped with *colée* on the following day by Patriarch Abraam IV. He then assumed command of the invasion force being assembled by Tolán and Torenth to invade Gwynedd. He was killed at the Great Battle of Killingford on the XVIIth day of June in that year, aged XXXV years, and was succeeded in his pretensions first by his younger son, Marek III, and then by his aunts, the Princesses Ariella II and Imriella.

Marek-Imre, *i.e.*, **Mark-Imre Cairill** *Furstán-Festil*, **Hereditary Prince of Gwynedd, Hereditary Duke of Tolán.** He was born on the last day of January in the Year of Our Lord 950, being the eldest son and heir of Imre II Titular King of Gwynedd and Tamara Countess of Netterhaven. He intermarried with the Countess Maryam daughter of Simon Count Tsérétéli on the XVIIth day of April in the year 970, and by her he had children: the Princess Ariella later Ariella II Titular Queen of Gwynedd and Duchess of Tolán, who intermarried with the Count Rogan younger son of Termöd II Duke d'Arjenol, and by him had one daughter, the Countess Charis-Tamara, dead of the *cholérique* at age X; the Prince Imre later Imre III Titular King of Gwynedd; the Princess Imriella Elizabeth later Titular Queen of Gwynedd and Duchess of Tolán, who intermarried with Swithven Count of Langendoss, *sans postérité*; the Prince Tamar, dead of the knobbish bones at age IV; the Princess Charsella, who assumed the veil at age XIV under the name Sister Hippolyte of the Little Mothers of Perpetual Sorrow, and died *consumptiva* at age XXXVIII.

In his father's campaign against Gwynedd in the Fall of the year 983, the Prince Mark-Imre commanded a IIIrd part of the invading forces, and was proclaimed Hereditary Prince of Gwynedd at Rengarth on the XXVIth day of October in that year. He was severely wounded several weeks later, and that Winter lost a foot to frostbite when the Festillic army was forced to encamp for III months on the plains North of Valoret. He recovered from his injuries and had a wooden leg mounted on his stump, returning to the field in the year 984. He was killed at the Battle of Grecotha on the IIIrd day of August in that year, aged XXXIV years, and was succeeded by his son, the Prince Imre. [*The Deryni Archives*].

Margaret *Sinclair* **McLain, Dowager Duchess of Cassan.** This widow of Raymond Sinclair intermarried with Jared McLain Duke of Cassan on the XXVIth day of September in the year 1116, but had no children by him. She became Dowager Duchess at his death on the Ist day of July in the year 1121. [*Deryni Checkmate*].

Margetan, Saint. This holy maiden is said to have been a native of Vth-century Antiyukh. She was condemned for her faith, but before she could be beheaded, she was swallowed by a fierce beast, who flew off with her. She is usually depicted as trampling or standing on a dragon, or issuing from its mouth, or piercing it with a cross-tipped spear. Her feastday is the XIIIth day of November. [*Camber of Culdi*].

Marian, Sister. She was serving as a companion to Princess Regent Rothana at the Court of Rhemuth in April of the year 1125. [*The Quest for Saint Camber*].

Marie Stephania *de Corwyn*. She was born on the I^st day of May in the Year of Our Lord 1071, being the younger daughter of Keryell Earl of Lendour and Stevana Heiress de Corwyn, and a twin sister to Ahern de Corwyn, Hereditary Duke of Corwyn. She was poisoned with *teinture du mercure* by Ser Parménide Le Frenais, acting on behalf of Walpurge, Maîtresse de Flémalle, Marie's jealous rival, and died unmarried and *sans postérité* on the IInd day of September in the year 1088, being buried in the Corwyn family vault at Coroth Cathedral. When he was finally entrapped at Gobet some II years later, Ser Parménide, by order of the King, was bound upright and unclothed in a tub of salt water that reached beyond his waist, and then spent several interesting days dancing with his bonny companions, a dozen crabs which had been introduced into the mix. The Lady Walpurge was disgraced from the nobility; her hands were then tied behind her back, and a noose placed around her neck, being stretched to the point where she could sustain her life only by rising upon her bare toes, dancing the *pas de mort*. Whenever she threatened to depart this life, the rope was loosened again. In this way did they both come to terms with their joint perfidy. R.I.P.

Maris. She was serving as a maidservant to Princess Ariella in the year 903. [*Camber of Culdi*].

Mark, Martyr and Saint. Of the many holy men of this name, he was the young man who ran away when our Lord was arrested. He accompanied the Saints Paul and Barnabas on their I^st missionary journey, and later he followed Saint Peter as his disciple and interpreter, "whose preaching he set down in writing in the gospel which bears his name." Saint Peter calls him "my son Mark." He afterwards died a martyr to the faith. His emblem is a winged lion; he is often shown writing or holding his gospel. Several churches and abbeys in Gwynedd honour his name. His feastday is the XXVth day of April.

Mark—SEE ALSO: Marek.

Marley. Originally called Northmarch or Normarch Ley, this coastal Earldom is located in the far North-eastern corner of Gwynedd, bordering on the Duchy of Tolán in Torenth to the East, the Northern Sea to the North, the Earldom of Rhendall to the West, and the Earldom of Eastmarch to the South. Marley has some of the richest farmland in the Eleven Kingdoms, and there has never been a famine recorded there in over D years of history. The seat of Marley is the quaint old town of Marbury.

Marley was founded on the IInd day of November in the year 592 by Count Ion, eldest son of Alöf Margrave of the Marches. His direct descendant, the Countess Ulrika, married Magnus I Count of Eastmarch on the XXXth day of April in the year 715, and their son, Count Yngvarr, inherited the combined countries, thereafter known as Eastmarch, on the Xth day of May in the year 744. The Counts and Earls of Eastmarch often used the title Count of Normarch Ley or Marley as a subsidiary title for their heirs. The section of Eastmarch known as Marley was annexed to Torenth on the XXIXth day of May in the year 755 by King Mátyás, but the Western part thereof was reconquered by Hrolf I Count of Eastmarch on the IInd day of September in the year 853. On the XVIIIth day of September in the year 905 Sighere Earl of Eastmarch and Marley conquered the old Principality of Kheldour, and in the year 906 he allied himself with Cinhil I King of Gwynedd. By the terms of the treaty he signed with Cinhil on the XXVIth day of August in that year, Sighere became Duke of Claibourne, and his youngest son, Sighere *Junior*, was created Earl of Marley, which was split off from old Eastmarch. Sighere *Junior*'s son Lord Sean Coris inherited the title, which continues in an unbroken chain in his family to this day.

The County is known for its fine shorthorn cattle and longhair goats, its barley, and its many varieties of beer. "Dark Marley" and "Coris Light" are quaffed at inns throughout the entire XI Kingdoms. [*Camber of Culdi*; *Saint Camber*; *The Harrowing of Gwynedd*; *The Bastard Prince*; *Deryni Rising*; *Deryni Checkmate*; *High Deryni*; *The Bishop's Heir*].

EARLS OF MARLEY

HOUSE OF CORIS

Sighere	906-935
Sean (son)	935-948
Brian (son)	948-983
Comyn (son)	983-1018
Becan (son)	1018-1025
Banan (brother)	1025-1044
Phelan (son)	1044-1070
Owen (son)	1070-1096
Michan (cousin)	1096-1101
Ryan (brother)	1101-1114
Bran (son)	1114-1121
Brendan (son)	1121-1130+

Marlor. This small Barony was situate in the central part of The Purple March, being partially flanked by Horthness in the East, Arnham in the South, Culdi in the West, and Transha in the North. Historically, the Barony belonged to the MacInnis family from as early as the year 704, when one Inis Lord Marlor is noted as title holder in a surviving tax record of Llarik King of Gwynedd. The title was attainted on VIth day of July in the year 822 after the invasion of Gwynedd by King Festil I. Sir Manfred MacInnis petitioned King Cinhil I for the restoration of his family Honour after the Restoration of the Haldanes, and his wish was granted on the VIIth day of July in the year 905. The estate was awarded as dowry to the Lady Janeltis MacInnis, who intermarried with Hrorik Ewan Earl of Rhendall on the IXth day of June in the year 940. [*The Harrowing of Gwynedd*].

BARONS OF MARLOR

HOUSE OF MACINNIS

Inis I mac Raphoe	704?-716
Manning (son)	716-744
Bannon (nephew)	744-775
Castor (usurper)	755-757
Iver I (son of Bannon)	775-793

Randall (son)	793-818
Dallan (son)	818-822

Pretenders of the House of MacInnis

Dallan (in exile)	822-839
Downe (son)	839-866
Colquhoun (son)	866-899
Manfred (son)	899-905

House of MacInnis (restored)

Manfred MacInnis	905-928
Iver II (son)	928-940
Janeltis (daughter)	940-970

House of MacEwan

Ewan (son)	970-984
Arran (son)	984-1025
Drummond (son)	1025-1037
Dainéal (son)	1037-1066
Innis II (son)	1066-1091
Darran (brother)	1091-1098
Odhran (son)	1098-1130+

Marluk. This Duchy of Torenth is situate South of Beldour City in the Mórmarlüky Mountains, being bounded on the North by the River Beldour and across that waterway by the Duchies of Csorna and Beldouria, on the West and South by the Principality of Tralia, and on the East by the Duchy of Lorsöl and the County of Vechta. The title was first granted by Arion I King of Torenth to his IInd son, the Prince Ysarn, on the VIth day of December in the year 934. It descended in Duke Ysarn's line until, at the death without issue of the Princess Charissa Festillic Pretender to the Throne of Gwynedd, the title became extinct on the XVth day of November in the year 1120, and escheated to the Torenthi Crown. The *prétendant* Teymuraz illegally revived the title in 1129. *Marlucca ventosa: sine vento venenosa; cum vento fastidiosa.* [*King Kelson's Bride*]. See also: Charissa, Hogan.

Dukes of Marluk

House of Furstán de Marluk

Ysarn I (son of Arion I of Torenth)	934-988
Darion (son)	988-1016
Kamien (son)	1016-1025
Bonica (daughter)	1025-1062
Ysarn II Furstán d'Avoine (son)	1062-1090
Larissa (daughter)	1090-1094
Clarissa (daughter)	1094
Charissa (sister)	1094-1120

Title Extinct

Martha, Lady. She was serving as a lady-in-waiting to Bronwyn Lady de Morgan in March of the year 1121. [*Deryni Checkmate*].

Martin. This soldier was healed by Warin de Grey at the Royal Tabard Inn in Kingslake on the XXVth day of March in the year 1121. [*Deryni Checkmate*].

Martin, Lord of Greystoke. He was born on the IXth day of August in the Year of Our Lord 1057, being the youngest son of Edgar Earl of Greystoke and Anaconda Lady Burrows. He intermarried with Jane Lady Lafonde on the IIIrd day of May in the year 1078, and by her he had children: the Lady Thuria; the Lady Raïce; the Lord Clayton; the Lord Danton; the Lord Hulbert. He was living near the town of Dhassa in June of the year 1121. His clerk was Master Thierry. [*High Deryni*].

Mary, Saint. She was the Blessed Mother of Our Lord Jesus Christ. Of the religious establishments dedicated to her name and memory, an isolated monastery, Saint Mary's in the Hills, was located in the highlands above Culdi. Father Joram MacRorie and Evaine Lady Thuryn took refuge there in January of the year 918. [*Camber the Heretic; The Harrowing of Gwynedd*].

Mary Elizabeth, Lady. She was serving as a lady-in-waiting to Bronwyn Lady de Morgan in March of the year 1121. [*Deryni Checkmate*].

Mary *Weaver*. She was one of the L human peasants executed in October of the year 903 at King Imre's command in retaliation for the murder of Lord Rannulf. R.I.P. [*Camber of Culdi*].

Maryse *MacArdry*. She was born on the IXth day of March in the Year of Our Lord 1091, being the eldest daughter of Caulay MacArdry Earl of Transha and Adreana Lady Calder of Sheele. She secretly intermarried with Duncan Lord McLain on the XXVth day of March in the year 1107, and died in childbirth on the IIIrd day of January in the year 1108, aged XVI years, having delivered I son: the Lord Dhugal, who was adopted and raised as the child of his grandparents, Caulay and Adreana. R.I.P. [*The Bishop's Heir; The King's Justice*].

Marywell. In this town in Northern Gwynedd a Deryni garrison ran amok in November of the year 903, killing many of the human residents. When the killers were not brought to justice, many humans expressed outrage. [*Camber of Culdi*].

Mathurin, Lord. This legendary Baron was commemorated in the "Ballad of Mathurin and Derverguille," which was composed by the troubadour Llewelyn in the early IXth century. He was supposedly killed by the cruel Lord Gerent. [*Deryni Checkmate*].

Matthew, Apostle and Saint. Levi, as he was originally named, was a tax collector in Galilee. After his conversion to Christianity, he penned the Ist Gospel of our Lord Jesus Christ. A city gate and a cathedral dedicated to his name are located in Coroth. It was at Saint Matthew's Gate in that city that the troubadour Gwydion learned one of the many songs that he sang for Alaric Morgan Duke of Corwyn. Saint Matthew's feastday is the XXIst day of September, and is often depicted in the glyphs as carrying the Holy Gospel under his arm. [*Deryni Checkmate*].

Matthew, son of Carlus, later Brother Benedict. He was born in the Year of Our Lord 857, and was received into the *Ordo Verbi Dei* under the name Benedict in the year 887. He was cloistered at the Priory of Saint Illtyd's in the year 903. [*Camber of Culdi*].

Matthias *MacArdry*. He was serving in the Cassani Army during its invasion of Meara in June of the year 1124. He assisted Dhugal MacArdry Earl of Transha in contacting King Kelson through psychic means after the debacle at Dorna Plain on the IInd day of July in that year. [*The King's Justice*].

Mátyás Imre *Furstán*, King of Torenth. He was born on the IIIrd day of June in the Year of Our Lord 734, being the only son and heir of Festil King of Torenth and the Princess Iphigénie daughter of Ursion I Roi de Bremagne. He intermarried with his IInd cousin, the Princess Jessandra daughter of François Thibaut Prince de Bremagne and Duc du Normande, on the XXXth day of October in the year 755, and by her he had children: the Hereditary Prince Káspár Karlóman, dead at the age of VIII months of the queasy quare; the Hereditary Prince Kálmán Imre later Kálmán II King of Torenth, a twin with his brother.

After his wife's death of the typhoidous grippe on the XVIIIth day of August in the year 756, the King Mátyás intermarried secondly with his Ist cousin the Countess Istvána, daughter of Prince Zsolt and grand-daughter of Imre I King of Torenth, on the XXIst day of June in the year 757, and by her he had further children: the Princess Maribeth, who intermarried with Damien Baron du Blais in Tralia; the Princess Kypriana, who intermarried with Kermit Count von Früghy in Lorsöl; the Princess Gillèse, who took the veil under the religious name Sister Stanislawa of the Venerable Virgins of Vézaire.

After his IInd wife's death on the XIXth day of January in the year 763, the King intermarried thirdly with Léonore Comtesse de Lillebonne on the VIIth day of July in the year 764, and by her he had further children: the Prince Imre Elgar later Count of Fathane, leaving issue, II daughters, the Princess Richardis and the Princess Tayce; the Prince Vaksos Ursión later Count of Truvorsk later Prince-Bishop of Frentz, *sans postérité*; the Prince Maksim Festil later Count of Arkadia and Commander of the East; the Prince Ottó Tamás later Count of Fajardô, who perished at the age of XXVI in a fight over a woman, leaving issue, Count Tamás Ottó.

After his IIIrd wife's death on the XIIth day of October in the year 770, the King intermarried fourthly with Landizábel Lady Ora'ash in Tuskanya on the IXth day of August in the year 772, and had further children: the Lady Carlotta, who intermarried with August Graf von Rhodrov; the Lady Berengaria, who intermarried with Núño Barón de la Cerda. The King also acknowledged and legitimated a son by the Lady Césky: the Lord Jolán Trugh later Graf Stánfürst, without dynastic rights.

The Prince Mátyás succeeded his father on the IInd day of January in the year 748, being placed under the Regency of his great-uncle, the Prince Wenzel Sylvist, for V months before being declared of age. He was girded with the sword on New Year's Day in the year 749 by Patriarch Theodotos I. He spent the next VI years training as a soldier and collecting and studying manuscripts on military strategy. On the XXIXth day of May in the year 755 he invaded and later annexed Marley in Eastmarch in a II-month campaign, and resisted all efforts by Yngvarr Count of Eastmarch to recover his lost territory. The King Mátyás also conducted raids in the years 762 and 766 against Eastmarch proper and Northern Gwynedd, striking as far West as the Purple March, although the King was never able to secure these lands on a permanent basis. The city of Grecotha was sacked on the IIIrd day of June in the year 767. In later years the King turned towards the East, attacking the Western fringes of Arjenol, particularly on the IInd day of June in the year 801, when his son and heir Prince Kálmán led an army deep into the Arjenoli Mountains. After killing Svarnik Prince d'Arjenol on the XIIth day instant, he withdrew his forces as Winter set in to avoid being trapped without supplies in a snowbound wilderness.

The Princess Arien calls this monarch "...the true founder of the Torenthi kingdom, who despite his preoccupation with things military was much loved by his people. For when the common folk went hungry in the great famine of the Winter of 772, he opened up the royal storehouses, and insisted that his own food be distributed free amongst them, saying, 'How can I ever meet my Maker if I cannot even feed my people when they cry out to me?' He insisted that the entire palace be put on limited rations, save only the very young, the very old, and those women who were expecting a child. 'We must set an example for the entire realm,' he said. At his funeral the people filled the streets of Beldour to honour his name."

The Great King Mátyás suffered terribly from paralysis and boils during the last III years of his life, finally expiring at Torenthály on the XVIIIth day of December in the year 808, after a lustrous reign of LX years, the longest in Torenthi history. He was aged LXXIV years at his death, and was succeeded by his eldest surviving son, Prince Kálmán. He is buried at Torenthály in the crypt of his forefathers. R.I.P.

Mátyás Torval Rikárd Karlman *Furstán d'Arjenol*, Duke d'Arjenol, Count of Komnéně, Amassy, and Brustarkia, Veliky Kniaz' of the Kingdom of Torenth. He was born posthumously on the IIIrd day of January in the Year of Our Lord 1101, being the youngest son of Mahael I Duke d'Arjenol and Daniela Grafina von Ryndziak. His godmother was Sofiana then Hereditary Princess of Andelon. He intermarried with the Lady Ophélie, daughter of Richard Duc du Joux, on the XXVth day of November in the year 1124, and by her he had children: the Hereditary Duke Lóránt Lajos Count Amassy; the Count Torval Trentán, who died several days after birth when his breath was stolen away in the night by an evil spirit; the Countess Lionella; the Count Kalinik Kelsón Ardrick Count of Komnéně.

This illustrious peer has rightly been accounted the saviour of his nation. He was fostered to the court of his godmother's father, Mikhail Sovereign Prince of Andelon, but after the latter's passing in December of the year 1112, and the succession of Princess Sofiana, Lord Mátyás was sent for training to the court of his cousin, Lóránt Duke of Truvorsk, an accomplished Deryni and a grandson of King Kyprian II, for it was not regarded as meet that a scion of the House of Furstán should be trained by a woman.

On his coming of age in the year 1115, he was created Lord of Komnénë, a small fief in the Duchy of Arjenol, but continued living with his cousin until the advancing illness of the latter made any further training impossible. The Lord Mátyás took possession of his lands in the year 1121, after the death of King Wencit. He was advanced to the rank of Count by King Liam Lajos II on the XVIth day of September in the year 1125.

In the year 1128, when the King attained his majority, Count Mátyás's elder brothers, Mahael II Duke d'Arjenol and Teymuraz Count of Brustarkia, plotted to murder their rightful monarch during the *killijálay* ceremony scheduled for mid-July, in order to seize power for themselves, and sought to involve their younger brother in their treasons; but the Count Mátyás believed that an oath was an oath, and on the XVIth day of that month, he helped to turn back the Duke's psychic attack on the King, joining with Kelson King of Gwynedd, Morag Dowager Duchess d'Arjenol, and Alpheios Patriarch of Torenth to defeat Duke Mahael.

Count Teymuraz betrayed the betrayer at the last moment, but he was ordered arrested by the King and held for questioning. However, he escaped his captors, and fled through a portal in the Nikolaseum. Later that same day, King Liam Lajos II gave Mahael's several honours and lands, including the Duchy d'Arjenol, to Count Mátyás, who also received the titles and estates of Count Teymuraz, after he was tried and condemned *in absentia*. Duke Mátyás was further honoured by being named the Chief Peer (Veliky Kniaz') of the Kingdom of Torenth, on the XIVth day of November in that year. According to *Bride*, he had a close-trimmed beard and pale eyes, and wore his black hair braided and neatly clubbed at the nape in a warrior's knot. He sported a fine miniature icon of the Blesséd Virgin on his breast, and dressed in the style of far Byzantyun. He was considered by Princess Sofiana as a candidate for the Camberian Council seat left vacant by the death of Lady Vivienne in the year 1128. *Nemo quam bene vivat, sed quamdiu, curat: quum omnibus possit contingere ut bene vivat.* [*King Kelson's Bride*].

McLain, House of. This cadet line of the ancient noble House of MacLean descends directly from Angus Lord MacLean, youngest son of Iain II Earl of Kierney. He was invested with the hereditary knighthood and lairdship of Léanshire by King Blaine I in the year 896. Sir Roger McLain married Lady Glorian MacInnis Heiress of Kierney on the XIth day of March in the year 990, and their son, Sir Arnall, inherited the County of Kierney on the XIth day of November in the year 1033. He married Lady Adelicia Heiress of Cassan, and their son, Lord Andrew, inherited the Duchy of Cassan at birth on the Ist day of December in the year 1034. The McLain arms include sleeping lions and roses: *argent*, III roses *gules*; in chief, *azure*, a lion dormant *argent*. [*The Bishop's Heir*]. See also: Cassan, Dhugal, Duncan, Elaine, Jared, Kevin, Kierney, Margaret, Vera, and the cognate House of MacLean.

HEREDITARY KNIGHTS & LAIRDS OF LÉANSHIRE

HOUSE OF MCLAIN

Angus McLain	896-904
Charles (son)	904-960
Arthur (son)	960-962
Duncan I (son)	962-983
Andrew I (son)	983-1003
Roger (son)	1003-1025
Tairchell (son)	1025-1060
Arnall (brother)	1060-1076
Andrew II (son)	1076
Jared (son)	1076-1121
Duncan II (son; abdicated)	1121-1125
Dhugal (son)	1125-1130+

Meara. This Principality is located in the far West of the XI Kingdoms, being situate on the Atalantic Ocean, and bordered by the Duchy of Cassan on the North, the Earldom of Kierney on the Northeast, the Earldom of Culdi on the East, Transflumenia or Travlum in the Kingdom of Gwynedd on the Southeast, and The Connaiti Federation on the South. The Mearans are a hardy people, accustomed to fending for themselves through subsistence farming and grazing. The land is mostly rocky and barely arable, filled with hills, tors, and scrub brush. Only the Culdi Highlands and the Cloome Mountains contain any natural beauty, being filled with streams, forests, and plenty of wild game.

The history of Meara has been the story of the constant struggle between the Great Lords and the ruling Prince for position and power, with the governance of the country being seriously weakened by the fierce independence of the border Barons and the inability of the government in Laas to handle them. Only the III main coastal cities of Meara remained under the certain control of the Princes throughout the centuries, and although some members of the House of Quinnell proved stronger than others, most faced an impossible task. The laws of the Principality disallowed a standing army, making the Princes of Meara no stronger militarily than the meanest Baron under them. Armies could be raised only in times of crisis, and were immediately disbanded afterwards, and the enforcement of taxes and other duties was almost nonexistent during many decades.

In ancient times Meara was a sovereign state that encompassed all of the present lands of Meara, Cassan, Kierney, and Transha, having been founded by Mear mac Quinnell, who proclaimed himself Sovereign Prince of Laas (later Meara) on the IInd day of August in the year 651. The state became known as Meara in his honour under his successors. The Eastern section of the Principality, Cassan, split from Meara on the XVIth day of November in the year 762 when Prince Janus died, leaving a young son, Prince Alphonse. Janus's younger brother, Prince Armon, seized the Mearan throne, while the young Alphonse fled with his mother, the Dowager Princess Ostrythe, to her native city of Ballymar in Cassan. There she raised the standard of revolt. After VIII years of intermittent warfare both parties signed a treaty on the VIth day of August in the year 770 recognizing the independent status of Cassan.

At the death of Prince Alban, the last ruler of Meara of the old line, on the XIV`th` day of April in the year 877, Meara became a vassal state of Gwynedd, and King Festil III included among his many titles that of Lord (*i.e.*, Overlord) of Meara. Alban's daughter and successor, Princess Jorianna, married her cousin, Lord Jubal mac Adam, in the year 880, and their descendants continued to govern the country until the XI`th` century. In the year 1024 the Prince Jolyon II, having no male heirs, allied himself with Kyprian II King of Torenth and Imre III Festillic Pretender to the Throne of Gwynedd, and precipated the Great War of the Three Kings. Prince Jolyon died on the XXIX`th` day of May in the year 1025, and his eldest daughter Princess Roisian was proclaimed his successor.

Roisian intermarried with Malcolm King of Gwynedd on the IX`th` day of August in that year, thereby ending the independence of her country, but her mother Dowager Princess Urracca and sister Princess Annalind refused to accept her marriage, declaring that she had abdicated the throne by leaving the country without the permission of the High Council of Meara. The Princess Annalind was proclaimed Sovereign Prince of Meara, and was able to maintain herself for II more years until King Malcolm invaded from Gwynedd. On the XVIII`th` day of June in the year 1027 the Mearan army was defeated near Ratharkin, and Loren Kincaid Earl of Kilarden and Commander of the Mearan forces was killed. Annalind, her mother Urracca, and her sister, the young Princess Magrette, then took refuge in The Connait. Subsequent expeditions were sent from Gwynedd in the years 1045, 1076, 1089, 1107, 1123, and 1124. The line of Princess Annalind was finally exterminated by King Kelson on the XII`th` day of July in the year 1124, save for the Princess Caitrin, who was exiled under close confinement to a nunnery. A cadet line, Ramsay of Cloome, inherited Caitrin's pretensions, but renounced all their claims in the year 1128, after Sir Jolyon Ramsay was created Duke of Laas by King Kelson.

The arms of Meara include a dancing bear *sable* and crimson *étoiles*. [*Camber of Culdi*; *Saint Camber*; *The Harrowing of Gwynedd*; *Deryni Rising*; *Deryni Checkmate*; *High Deryni*; *The Bishop's Heir*; *The King's Justice*; *King Kelson's Bride*].

SOVEREIGN PRINCES OF MEARA

HOUSE OF QUINNELL

Mear mac Quinnell	651-688
Archambald (son)	688-716
Jolyon I (son)	716-731
Aldebert (son)	731-755
Janus (son)	755-762
Armon (brother)	762-806
Judhael I (son)	806-822
Arturus (son)	822-845
Justin (son)	845-874
Alban (brother)	874-877
Jorianna (daughter)	877-892
Jubal mac Adam (husband and cousin)	880-906
Austin (son)	906-928
Jehan (brother)	928-948
Jordan mac Jonatan (nephew)	948-965
Ithel mac Judah mac Austin (cousin)	965-972
Joël (son)	972-976
Judhael II (son)	976-1001
Jolyon II (brother)	1001-1025
Roisian (daughter)	1025-1055

PRETENDERS OF MEARA OF THE HOUSE OF QUINNELL

Annalind (daughter of Jolyon II)	1025-1045
Judhael III (son)	1045-1109
Caitrin (daughter; deposed; died 1127)	1109-1124

PRETENDERS OF THE HOUSE OF RAMSAY OF CLOOME

Dafydd (cousin)	1124-1126
Jolyon III (son)	1126-1128

PRETENSIONS DISCLAIMED

Medras. The Torenthi city and County of this name are situate Northeast of Rengarth on the Eastern side of the Coamer Mountains, also called the Kómar Range in the Torenthi tongue, being bounded by the Counties of Fathane and Sostra to the South, the Duchy of Sasovna to the North, the Duchy of Altorf to the East, and the Gwyneddan Earldoms of Carcashale and Derry to the West.

The title of Count or Graf von Medras is first mentioned in the Annals of Torenth in the person of Count Vigil von Furstán, who occupied the fortress of Medras in about the year 650, and later called himself by that name. When his grandson, the Count Endre I, died without heirs male in the year 695, the County escheated to the Throne of Torenth, but was regranted in the year 702 to Prince Zsolt son of Imre I King of Torenth. The title again reverted to the Crown in the year 813, being granted as a Margraviate to Prince Festil the II`nd` son of Kálmán II King of Torenth in the year 818. The Margraf became King of Gwynedd in the year 822, and at his death in the year 839, the King Lajos I, King Festil's elder brother, claimed Medras for the Kingdom of Torenth, regranting it immediately to his youngest son, the Prince Endre. When Endre died without male issue in the year 869, the title again reverted, and was regranted by King Malachy I to his beloved daughter the Princess Mérode, whom he made Sovereign Countess. She was succeeded by her elder brother, Prince Miklós, in the year 897, in whose line the title has descended to this date. His son, Count Malachy, was forced to relinquish his sovereignty at his succession to the title in the year 911.

The city of Medras has often served as a staging area for invasions from Torenth into Gwynedd and Eastmarch, including an incursion by King Wencit's troops in March of the year 1121. [*Deryni Checkmate*].

COUNTS OF MEDRAS

HOUSE OF FURSTÁN-MEDRAS

Vigil von Furstán	650?-662
Oktar (son)	662-691
Endre I (son)	691-695
INTERREGNUM	
Zsolt (cousin)	702-760
Kopasz (son)	760-788
Béla (son)	788-813
INTERREGNUM	

Festil (cousin; Margraf)	818-839
Endre II (cousin; Count)	839-869
INTERREGNUM	
Mérode (cousin; Sovereign Countess)	871-897
Miklós (brother; Sovereign Count)	897-911
Malachy (son; Count)	911-944
Gejza (son)	944-969
Salamon (nephew)	969-1001
Otakar (son)	1001-1025
Zygmunt I (cousin)	1025-1034
Martel (son)	1034-1058
Kristóf I (son)	1058-1066
Endre III (son)	1066-1092
Kristóf II (son)	1092-1127
Zygmunt II (son)	1127-1130+

Megan Leonida *de Cameron*, Queen of Gwynedd, Lady. This beauteous lady was born on the XIIth day of January in the Year of Our Lord 888, being the only surviving child of Yorke Lord Farnham and Maia Lady Campbell. After her parents' death in a carriage accident on the XXIIIrd day of December in the year 891 she was made a ward of Camber Earl of Culdi, and was proposed by him as a potential bride for Prince Cinhil Haldane in December of the year 903. She intermarried with that Prince on the XXIVth day instant, and by him she had children: the Hereditary Prince Aidan Alroy Camber, murdered at the age of I month; the Hereditary Prince Alroy later King of Gwynedd; the Prince Javan later King of Gwynedd, a twin with his brother; the Prince Rhys Michael later Duke of Carthmoor later King of Gwynedd; the Prince Alister, dead at the age of III months. She was present on the Ist day of July in the year 905 when the victorious Gwyneddan army returned to Valoret. She died on the VIIIth day of August in the year 907 of the effects of childbirth, aged XIX years, and was buried in the family crypt of the Haldanes at Rhemuth.

According to Volumen I of *The Legends*, she was "...of medium height, willow slender, with wide, turquoise eyes spiced by a spray of freckles across the slightly tip-tilted nose. She even moved with an unaffected grace. Her wheaten hair was caught up in shining coils beneath a crown of holly and rosemary." She is also noted in the surviving chronicles as being a pious and dutiful Queen. *Chez elle un beau désordre, est un effet de l'art.* R.I.P. [*Camber of Culdi*; *Saint Camber*; *Camber the Heretic*].

Melissa *Howell*, Lady. She was born on the IVth day of May in the year 882, being the second daughter of Michael Lord Howell, but the first by his third wife Sheelin Lady MacKelworth. She was brought to Court at Valoret in November of the year 903 by her half-brother, Coel Lord Howell, to tempt King Imre. She died on the XIIth day of November in the year 917, aged XXXV years, mentioned in some accounts as being murdered by an anti-Deryni mob in Valoret. R.I.P. [*Camber of Culdi*].

Melwas, Father. He was ordained priest at the *Arx Fidei* Seminary with Father Denis Arilan on the IInd day of February in the year 1105. ["The Priesting of Arilan"].

merasha. This oft-misused drug was developed in the VIIIth century by the physician Junius Pollansus Magister as a sedative for medical use on patients whose minds had been tainted by the Devil. It was first obtained by boiling down the stalks of the *merash* bush which grows in the Anvil of the Lord, and then skimming off the residue. Its effect on Deryni was discovered accidentally by Junius when he attempted to quiet one of that race. It first came into extensive use under the Regency of King Alroy, when it was employed both to detect and to disable the regime's Deryni enemies. Originally administered orally, *merasha* could also be introduced directly into the bloodstream through the so-called "Deryni prickers," developed by certain *Custodes* physicians circa 917. Father Magan further refined this technique in the year 928 by inserting the drug directly into the navel, where it slowly leached into the victim's blood.

The fruit of the *merash* plant when fermented also produces a particularly potent distillation, the *liqueur* called *quinquet*, which is a favourite of seamen everywhere. It can be drunk by Deryni with no ill effects save those normally experienced when imbibing strong spirits. Campbell de Broun notes, "I have quaffed the *quinquet*, and I can vouch that *quatre quinquets* quell any qualms." [*The Bastard Prince*].

Meraude Mathilde Azæa *de Traherne*, Duchess of Carthmoor, Lady of Rhendall. She was born on the IInd day of August in the Year of Our Lord 1090, being the daughter of Ewan III Earl of Rhendall and Mellicent Lady MacEwan, and the sister of Saer de Traherne Earl of Rhendall. She intermarried with Nigel Prince of Gwynedd later Duke of Carthmoor on the VIIth day of June in the year 1106, and by him she had children: the Hereditary Duke Conall later Prince Regent of Gwynedd, executed for treason in the year 1125; the Prince Rory later Duke of Ratharkin; the Prince Payne later Duke of Travlum; the Princess Eirian betrothed of Liam Lajos II King of Torenth; the Princess Gloriana.

The Duchess Meraude lent her own wedding veil to the Lady Rothana Nabila of Nur Hallaj for the latter's marriage to Prince Regent Conall on the XIth day of April in the year 1125. In the year 1128 she worked with Dowager Queen Jehana to bring the late Prince Conall's natural daughter, Conalline Amelia, back to Court, and to reconcile both grandchildren with her husband, Duke Nigel. She introduced the young girl to Nigel on the XXVIth day of July in that year. Four days later, her grandson, Prince Albin, was reinstated by Nigel at the request of King Kelson as heir to the Duchy of Carthmoor. Conalline was legally adopted by Nigel on the VIIIth day of October following, in order to provide her with a name and standing in the Court, but without dynastic rights. [*The Bishop's Heir*; *The King's Justice*; *The Quest for Saint Camber*; *King Kelson's Bride*].

Merritt, Baron of Reider. He was born in Torenth on the IXth day of July in the Year of Our Lord 1075, being the eldest son and heir of Moseley Baron of Reider and Hedvig Lady Barcsay. He intermarried with Basta Lady Apaffy on the XXIst day of June in the year 1098, and by her he had children: the Hereditary Lord Báthor; the

Lady Zsófia; the Lord Boldiszár; the Lady Porga. He succeeded his father on the XVth day of March in the year 1119. This Deryni Lord was serving Wencit King of Torenth in the year 1121. He was one of the party of Lionel II Duke d'Arjenol, and offered himself as hostage to Bran Coris Earl of Marley on the XVIIIth day of June in that year while Coris met with King Wencit. He was given a sleeping potion so he could not use his Deryni powers against his human captors. His lands were located on the Torenthi side of the border between Marley and Tolán. [*High Deryni*].

Micah, Brother. He was a monk of the Servants of Saint Camber in the year 917. [*Camber the Heretic*].

Michael. He was serving as a Lieutenant for Warin de Grey in the year 1121. [*Deryni Rising*; *High Deryni*].

Michael. He was I of the children apprehended trying to steal the horse of Alaric Morgan Duke of Corwyn near Garwode in June of the year 1121. [*High Deryni*].

Michael, Brother. He was born about the year 1093, being the son of Walter the Smith and Elizabeth daughter of Andrew. He was a *Coisrigte* of the priestly caste of the hill folk of Saint Kyriell's in April of the year 1125, and acted as the spokesman for the Quorial of the village. He later became a member of the newly-founded Servants of Saint Camber, and with them came to Rhemuth on the XXXth day of July in the year 1128. His waist was thick during his middle years. [*The Quest for Saint Camber*; *King Kelson's Bride*].

Michael *DeForest*. He was serving as a guard at Rhemuth Castle in November of the year 1120. He was used as a medium by Ian Howell Earl of Eastmarch and then killed by him on the XIVth day instant, in order to implicate Alaric Morgan Duke of Corwyn. *On aime à deviner les austres, mais on n'aime pas à être deviné.* [*Deryni Rising*].

Michael II Cluim Kermit *Pirek-Haldane*, Earl of Carthane. He was born on the XIXth day of August in the year 1075, being the eldest son and heir of Quentin Pirek-Haldane Earl of Carthane and Ottilie Lady Shaugh. He intermarried with Paloma Lady de Valence on the IInd day of July in the year 1102, and by her he had children: the Hereditary Count Cluim; the Lady Quentina; the Lady Edwina; the Lord Garvin. He succeeded his father on the IXth day of November in the year 1100. His daughter Quentina elicited much interest among the young men at the Court of Kelson King of Gwynedd on the IIIrd day of March in the year 1125, at the celebration held following the knighting ceremony. Dhugal MacArdry Earl of Transha and Kierney is said to have flirted with her outrageously. [*The Quest for Saint Camber*].

Michael *MacArdry*, Tanist of Clan MacArdry, Hereditary Count of Transha. He was born on the IIIrd of January in the Year of Our Lord 1090, being the second son of Caulay MacArdry Earl of Transha and Adreana Lady Calder of Sheele. He never married. The Lord Michael succeeded his elder brother, the Lord Ardry, as Tanist and Hereditary Count on the XXIInd day of March in the year 1107. He died unmarried of the consumptive complaint on the XXIVth of October 1119, aged XXIX years, *sans postérité*, and was succeeded by his brother (actually nephew), the Lord Dhugal, as Tanist to the chieftainship and Hereditary Count and Master of Transha. R.I.P. [*The Bishop's Heir*].

Michael, Saint. This great Archangel, whose name means "who is like God," was also called "The Defender," and served as the patron saint of warriors. He was a favourite of Nigel Duke of Carthmoor. He was one of the protectors called upon to ward a magical circle in certain arcane ceremonies, his side of that circle being the South, and his sign a red glowing triangle. His element is fire. His Arabi name is Mik(h)ail, and his feastday is the XXIXth day of September, which is also called Michaelmas. An Order dedicated to his name, the Michaelines, was prominent in Gwynedd until suppressed by the Regents of King Alroy in the year 917. [*Saint Camber*; *Camber the Heretic*; *The Harrowing of Gwynedd*; *King Javan's Year*; *The King's Justice*; *The Bastard Prince*].

Michaela Jocelyne *Drummond*, called "Mika," Queen of Gwynedd. She was born on the XXIXth day of February in the Year of Our Lord 908, being the only daughter of James "Jamie" Lord Drummond and Elinor Lady Howell, and sister of Cathan Lord Drummond. She intermarried with Prince Rhys Michael Duke of Carthmoor later King of Gwynedd at Culdi on the XXth day of November in the year 921, and by him she had children: the Hereditary Prince Cinhil Javan Alroy, born still on the XIth day of May in the year 922; the Hereditary Prince Owain later King of Gwynedd; the Prince Uthyr later Duke of Carthmoor later King of Gwynedd. She had returned to Court with her parents and her younger brother by the Xth day of January in the year 918, and the powers of all IV were blocked by Tavis O'Neill on the XXIst day instant. She was questioned by the Regents on the next day about the events of the night before. By the IInd day of February in that year she had been made an attendant to Estellan Countess of Culdi.

Beginning in the Summer of the year 921, after the accession of King Javan, she was deliberately pushed by the Regents into a match with Prince Rhys Michael, in the hope that Javan could be set aside. After being caught by the King dallying with Prince Rhys Michael on the XXIst day of August in that year, she returned to Culdi with her guardian, Earl Manfred, II days later. She acted as a nurse to the injured Rhys Michael at Culdi on the XIth day of November in the same year, marrying him shortly thereafter, and quickly blossoming with child. But the *coup d'état* which brought her husband to the throne on the XIth day of May in the year 922 also cost her the life of her firstborn son, the Prince Cinhil, who was born still and dead, this being a great sorrow for both of his parents. Following the birth of her IInd son and heir, the Prince Owain, on her birthday in the year 924, she gave her husband a large brooch embossed with the golden lion of the House of Haldane to celebrate the occasion.

On the XIVth day of June in the year 928 she participated in enabling the Haldane potential of her husband, King Rhys Michael, together with Father Joram MacRorie and Rhysel and Tieg Thuryn. Her Deryni powers were unblocked and restored by Tieg at the same time, and she soon discovered that she had significant magical potential. Assisted by her brother Cathan, she became a strong Regent for her elder son, the young King Owain, and after his coming of age continued to serve the Crown of Gwynedd in an advisory capacity for the rest of her days.

According to the *Chronicles*, "She had sparkling blue eyes and waves of tawny hair cascading down her back to her hips, sometimes worn in a braid. She was a bright and lovely lady who, in spite of her youth and *naiveté*, remained courageous and utterly devoted to her husband to the end." The Dowager Queen Michaela died on the Xth of January in the year 989, aged LXXX years, and was buried with high honours in the crypt of the Haldanes beneath Saint George's Cathedral. R.I.P. *Prima caritas incipit a seipso.* [*Camber the Heretic*; *The Harrowing of Gwynedd*; *King Javan's Year*; *The Bastard Prince*].

Michaela Ryonsa Ambersine *Haldane*, Princess of Gwynedd. She was born on the VIIIth day of March in the year 821, being the second daughter of Ifor King of Gwynedd and Nuala Lady Udaut. She was murdered with her family by the soldiers of King Festil I on the XXIst day of June in the year 822, aged I year. R.I.P. [*Camber of Culdi*].

***Michaelines* (*Ordo Sancti Michaelis* or *Order of Saint Michael*).** This militant and teaching Order of priests, brothers, and laymen, predominantly Deryni, was founded during the reign of Bearand King of Gwynedd to hold the forts of the Anvil of the Lord against Moorish incursions, and to defend the sea-lanes from the Muslims and pirates. For its part in his campaign of the mid-VIIIth century the Order was granted extensive lands throughout Gwynedd, with its new Gwyneddan headquarters being located at Cheltham in the Lendour Highlands. After the destruction of that establishment by King Imre on the XVth day of December in the year 903, the Commanderie was moved to New Argoed at the Southern tip of Lendour. The Vicar General at this time was Father Alister Cullen, with Earl Jebediah of Alcara as Grand Master.

At the Battle of Iomaire on the XXVth day of June in the year 905 the Order suffered heavy losses; only CX knights of the CC who rode to war were reported as battle-ready at the Grand Chapter meeting in Valoret held on the IIIrd day of July following. Also noted at this meeting was the razing of X of the Order's XII major establishments of the Michaelines by King Imre since the year 903. The II surviving houses in July of the year 905 were Haut Eirial and Mollingford. Also at this meeting it was reported that the membership of the order then stood at CCC professed brothers and priests. However, the great service tendered by the Order to King Cinhil I was rewarded by the Crown with the grant of II new pieces of land at Cùilteine and New Argoed, the latter of which became the Michaelines' new Commanderie. Father Crevan Allyn was elected the new Vicar General on the VIth day of July in the year 905, and installed II days later.

The Order was suppressed in December of the year 917 by the Regents of King Alroy, but had already moved most of its surviving knights and lay brethren into outlying establishments in Torenth and Djellarda. In later centuries the Order gradually evolved into the Knights of the Anvil (*Equites Incudis*), the name being officially adopted on the I[st] day of January in the year 923, with the Mother House located at Djellarda in the Anvil of the Lord.

The priests of the Order of Saint Michael wore dark blue monastic robes or cassocks, with red cinctures or fringed red sashes, and dark blue mantles with the full Michaeline device on the left shoulder, and sported a token tonsure the size of a coin. Michaeline Knights were also tonsured, and wore dark blue surcoats with the full device on the front and back, white belts or fringed white sashes, and dark blue mantles. Lay brethren and military sergeants wore badges of a plain white cross moline fitchy. The Order's arms were: *azure*, a cross moline fitchy *argent*, issuing from a flame *gules* fimbriated *or*.

The many Abbeys of this Order included: Saint Liam's Abbey and School near Caerrorie (abandoned in the year 905), the Commanderie and Mother House near Cheltham (destroyed in the year 903), Haut Eirial in Lendour (given to another Order in the year 917), Mollingford in Haldane (given to another Order in the year 917), the Commanderie and Mother House at Argoed in Lendour (established in the year 905, abandoned in the year 917), Cùilteine on the border with Meara (established in the year 905, abandoned in the year 917), Saint Elderon in Tolán, Brustarkia in Arjenol, and the Commanderie and Mother House at Djellarda (established in the mid-700s, and serving as Mother House from the year 917).

The Order also established a secret underground Haven in the Lendour Mountains near Dhassa sometime prior to the year 903, and from that time through the Restoration of the Haldanes in the year 904 this facility served as the sanctuary of Prince Cinhil and his family and allies. The Haven was reopened by Father Joram MacRorie in the year 917, serving as home and headquarters of the Deryni there through at least the year 928. The Order also survived in exile. *Entre tard et trop tard, il y a, par la grâce de Dieu, une distance incommensurable.* [*Camber of Culdi*; *The Harrowing of Gwynedd*; *King Javan's Year*; *The King's Justice*].

***Michaelmas Plot*.** In this incident several minor Deryni noblemen attacked the Princes Javan and Rhys Michael on the XXVIIIth day of September in the year 917, but were quickly caught and punished. Davin MacRorie Earl of Culdi was fatally wounded protecting the Princes, and was posthumously and unjustly accused of participating in the plot. The Regents used this incident to increase their reprisals against the Deryni. [*Camber the Heretic*].

Michon Étienne Estèphe *de Courcy*, Baron de Courcy and Stanzar. He was born on the XIth day of May in the Year of Our Lord 1030, being the eldest son and heir of Guiscard Titular Baron de Courcy and

Stanzar and the Lady Lune daughter of Bonald Count of Trevalga. He intermarried with the Lady Sylphe MacAthan on the Ist day of May in the year 1055, and by her he had children: the Lady Charolys; the Hereditary Lord Aurélien later Titular Baron de Courcy and Stanzar; the Lord Jéhoram; the Lady Micheline; the Lord Fénelon; the Lady Chablys.

The Lord Michon succeeded his father as Titular Baron of de Courcy and Stanzar on the XXth day of November in the year 1056. He was trained in early life by the Deryni masters Norfal ap Ailfrid, Lewys ap Norfal, and Sayyid Nur al-Din Hajj ibn Shukr Allah al-Saif, a Knight of the Anvil. He was elected to the Camberian Council in the year 1067, and served with distinction until his death, secretly training many young Deryni in the magical arts.

The Lord Michon died on the XXXth day of October in the year 1097, aged LXVII years. He was secretly honoured at his funeral by a contingent of the Knights of the Anvil, VI of whom accompanied his coffin to the grave, floating it on a catafalque of golden fire to signify their respect. He was interred at night in the vaults at Valla de Courcy, since there could be no display that might reveal the Deryni nature of his line to the commonfolk. Barrett de Laney had fond memories of the man and his passing. [*King Kelson's Bride*].

Mikhail Maks *Vastouni*, Sovereign Prince of Andelon. He was born on the XIIth day of October in the Year of Our Lord 1055, being the eldest son and heir of Antun Sovereign Prince of Andelon and Callendra Shaikha of al-Qarrah. He intermarried with the Princess Ysabeau granddaughter of Yves Sovereign Prince of Jáca on the XIXth day of October in the year 1074, and by her he had children: the Princess Sofiana later Sovereign Princess of Andelon, who intermarried with Reyhan Lord Séchelles, leaving issue; the Princess Michendra, who intermarried with Richard Baron of Rheljan, leaving issue. After his first wife's death in childbirth on the XXIIIrd day of February in the year 1082, he intermarried secondly with Alinor Lady Cardiel sister of Father Thomas Lord Cardiel later Archbishop of Rhemuth on the Ist day of October in the year 1082, and by her he had further children: the Princess Claire, who died a cripple at the age of XXIII years, *sans postérité*; the Hereditary Prince Aliksandr, dead at the age of VII months when he would not wake.

The Prince Mikhail succeeded his father on the Vth day of May in the year 1081. He was well known as a Deryni scholar of the Ist order, making his lifelong work the discovery and restoration of ancient manuscripts relating to the Deryni race and powers. He died in the fullness of life on the XIIth day of December in the year 1112, aged LVII years, and was succeeded by his eldest daughter, the Princess Sofiana. *Sola iuvat virtus.* R.I.P.

Miklós Malachy Mátyás (*von*) *Furstán*, Prince of Torenth, Duke of Truvorsk. He was born on the XVIth day of August in the Year of Our Lord 904, being the second son of Nimur I King of Torenth and Katalin Countess of Festil-Mnata, and the younger brother of King Arion I. He never married, although he acknowledged II children sired on his mistress, Fatima Déodat, but without dynastic rights: the Lord Ivan; the Lady Fatimella. These infants were raised by King Arion in the royal household after Miklós's untimely passing, the son eventually being made Count Möneszélo and given a small fiefdom in the hinterlands of Southern Torenth, and the daughter being intermarried with Adnan Graf von Graïlle.

As a young man the Prince Miklós was known for his intelligence and charm, and was well schooled in the magical arts and in the science of diplomacy. His father intended him for a career in the Church, but after King Nimur's death he left the Monastery of Saint Tiridatés in the year 918 when he attained his majority, and never returned. He was then created Duke of Truvorsk by his brother on the XVIth day of August in the year 918 and appointed to the High Council of Torenth. King Arion soon began employing the Prince as a roving ambassador.

On the XXXIst day of July in the year 921 the Prince Miklós attended the coronation of King Javan in Rhemuth, serving as the official representative of his government together with his "aide," who was actually the Prince Marek, the disguised Festillic Pretender to the Throne of Gwynedd. He presented King Javan with a gift from his Royal brother, an ancient illuminated scroll detailing the life of King Bearand Haldane; in return, he asked for information on the fate of II Torenthi hostages and cousins, Sudrey Countess of Eastmarch and Kennet Count of Rhorau, taken by King Cinhil I in the year 906 and placed under the wardenship of Sighere then Earl of Eastmarch. The Prince returned to Beldour by ship several days later. Also at about this time, he arranged for his spy, the double agent Dimitri, to infiltrate the service of Paulin Sinclair Vicar General of the *Custodes Fidei*.

On the XIth of March in the year 928, after pressing for a meeting with Sudrey Countess of Eastmarch for some VII years, he and Marek were allowed to see her at Lochalyn Castle in the presence of her husband, Hrorik II Earl of Eastmarch; there she renounced her Torenthi allegiance to his face. On the VIIth day of June in that year his forces occupied Culliecairn Castle at the head of the Coldoire Pass, prompting an armed response from Earl Hrorik, who was killed in the skirmish that followed.

The Prince Miklós then sent an ultimatum to Rhys Michael King of Gwynedd, demanding that he appear at Culliecairn by Saint John's Eve for the christening of the Prince Imre II son of Marek the Pretender of Gwynedd, and demanding that Rhys Michael show why Miklós should not give the Castle to Imre as a present. For the Prince Miklós had been promised the Duchy of Mooryn as a reward for his services should the Prince Marek succeed in his quest to become King of Gwynedd.

On the XXIInd day of June in the year 928 the Prince arranged a parley between himself, Countess Sudrey, and Rhys Michael King of Gwynedd. After abruptly attacking and murdering Sudrey, he was himself killed by the King in an exchange of magic, aged XXIII years. His body was carried from the battlefield by Prince Marek, and was interred some days later with his ancestors at Torenthály. The King of Gwynedd was also injured, and eventually died from his wounds.

Concerning this Prince it was said by Péter von Mědvĕd that Miklós, "...like many great princes, looked somewhat better than he acted, and his impetuosity eventually cost him his life." According to Volumen II of the *Heirs*, "he was tall and graceful for his years, fair-haired and light-eyed, [with] languid Eastern manners masking a quick comprehension of all about him, quietly aglitter in tawny Eastern silks." In June of the year 928 "he had flaxen hair which was braided and clubbed at the back of his head in the soldier's knot. Other than some new lines around the dark eyes, Miklós looked scarcely older than when he had attended King Javan's coronation seven years before." *Primus in orbe deos fecit imor.* R.I.P. [*King Javan's Year*; *The Bastard Prince*].

Miles the Falconer. He was serving Alaric Morgan Duke of Corwyn as his falconer at Castle Coroth in March of the year 1121. Although mute, he could imitate the clicks and whistles of his birds, which he did all too frequently. [*Deryni Checkmate*].

minution. Originally intended as a voluntary aid for subduing the passions of the flesh, this method of blood-letting was introduced by Brother Serafin as a regular form of discipline for members of the *Custodes Fidei* from the founding of that Order on the IInd day of February in the year 918. Though the Rule of the Order prescribed the practice as voluntary, all brethren were required to submit to the procedure at least once during their novitiate, any resistance being quashed by force, if necessary. In practice, minution also became a means of intimidating and punishing dissident members. Typically, minution involved opening a vein in the postulant's arm, with the blood being allowed to drain into a special bowl with an indentation in the side to receive the arm. Afterward, depending on the severity of the treatment, partakers were allowed II or III days' rest in the Abbey's infirmary to recover their strength, with dietary restrictions relaxed. It was said that an Abbot who permitted such treatment IV to VI times per year was a great benefactor. [*King Javan's Year*; *The Bastard Prince*].

Mir de Kierney, Bishop. He was born on the Vth day of July in the Year of Our Lord 1066, being the son of Sir Montescue de Kierney and Rebecca Lady Lustnau. He was ordained priest on the XVIIth day of May in the year 1086, and was consecrated an itinerant Bishop of Gwynedd on the XXIIIrd day of March in the year 1117. On the XXIXth of November of 1123 he helped Edmund Loris ex-Archbishop Primate of Valoret and All Gwynedd to escape, and on the Vth day of December following he further supported the efforts of the Loris to restore himself as Primate of Gwynedd and establish a new Synod in Meara. After the failure and execution of Loris on the XIIth day of July in the year 1124, Bishop Mir was captured, and on the XVIIIth day of March in the year 1125 he was deprived of his rank as Bishop, but was allowed to continue functioning as a priest under close supervision. *Probitas verus honor.* [*The Bishop's Heir*; *The King's Justice*; *The Quest for Saint Camber*].

Moira. This native of the Anvil of the Lord was born on the Vth day of May in the Year of Our Lord 1106. Thorne Hagen found her wandering in a marketplace in Kharthat in the Anvil of the Lord in February of the year 1115. By June of the year 1121 she had become Hagen's mistress. [*High Deryni*].

Mollingford. Located in the central Gwyneddan plain on the Molling River, this Michaeline establishment was destroyed by King Imre in the year 904. It was partially rebuilt, but then given to the local Bishop in the Summer of the year 917 when the Michaelines withdrew from Gwynedd. The new house was mistakenly destroyed by Rhun the Ruthless on the XXIVth day of December in 917. On the IVth day of July in the year 928, Graham I Duke of Claibourne and Sighere Earl of Marley and their men changed horses here on their fast cross-country trek from Eastmarch to Rhemuth. *Les rivières sont des chemins qui marchent et qui portent où l'on veut aller.* [*Saint Camber*; *Camber the Heretic*; *The Bastard Prince*].

Moonwind. A small, dappled grey horse which served Cinhil I King of Gwynedd in his campaign against Ariella in June of the year 905. [*Saint Camber*].

Mooryn. This ancient Kingdom was situate to the Southeast of Gwynedd on the Southern Sea, and included the present-day Duchies of Corwyn and Carthmoor plus subsidiary Counties and Baronies. The region was occupied by the Byzantyun Empire by the year 249, being called by them Murianus Province. The Byzantyuns withdrew from the trading center at Caurus (later Coroth) in the year 486, and the last Governor, Maximianus, later declared himself *Comes Cauri*. The Kingdom was founded LXXV years later by Maxime I d'Estavaye Count of Coroth and great-grandson of Count Maximianus, on the Ist day of September in the year 561, and at that time consisted only of the coastal regions near Coroth. The Kings gradually extended their rule Westward between the Southern Sea and the River Lendour, and Northward towards Eastmarch. During the VIIIth century the Deryni-ruled Kingdom of Mooryn was a powerful ally of the Kings of Torenth.

On the XVIIth day of August in the year 826 Festil II August Hereditary Prince of Gwynedd married Brionne (later Briona) Heiress of Mooryn. Lord Dominic du Joux was created Duke of Corwyn later the same year to honour the contributions of his father, the Lord Richard, who had died helping to establish the King Festil I on his throne; for the Kingdom of Mooryn had now become a mere appendage of the Kingdom of Gwynedd, with King Nanthelme swearing allegiance to the House of Festil. The Queen Brionne died on the IVth day of October in the year 835, at which time the Kingdom of Mooryn was declared united with the Crown of Gwynedd, the Duchy of Carthmoor being established as a title reserved for members of the Royal family of Gwynedd. The Duchies of Corwyn and Carthmoor remained nominally autonomous regions of Gwynedd until the accession of King Cluim in the year 985. *Morranum hic, atavos et avorum antiqua sonantem nomina, per regesque actum genus omne*

Haldanos. [*Camber of Culdi*; *Saint Camber*; *King Javan's Year*; *The Bastard Prince*].

KINGS OF MOORYN

HOUSE OF ESTAVAYE

Maxime I d'Estavaye	561-565
Maximin (brother)	565-588
Maxell (brother)	588
Maxime II (son)	588-609
Prangins (son)	609-661
Godefroi (son)	661-664
Barthélemi (son)	664-672
Dominic I (brother)	672-674
Ottonin (cousin)	674-678
Ulrich I (son)	678-702
Prosper (son)	702-730
Ulrich II (son)	730-759
Alaric (son)	759-772
Maxime III (brother)	772-782
Melchionne (daughter)	782-783
Dominic II (grandson of Ulrich I)	783-799
Ulrich III (son)	799-824
Nanthelme (cousin)	824-833
Brionne (daughter)	833-835

MERGED WITH GWYNEDD

Morag Máriah Khadijah *Furstána*, Princess of Torenth, Dowager Duchess d'Arjenol, Duchess of Tolán, Titular Queen and Pretender of Gwynedd. This most powerful Lady in the history of the Torenthi Kingdom was born on the VIIth day of February in the Year of Our Lord 1080, being the only surviving daughter of Nimur II King of Torenth and Charis Rochelle Princess of Festil. She intermarried with her cousin, Lionel II Duke d'Arjenol, on the XXVIth day of September in the year 1107, and by him she had children: the Countess Jaïnette, dead at age VI months of the runny bowels; the Hereditary Duke Alroy later Arion II King of Torenth, dead at age XIV of a fall from his horse; the Prince Averil, drowned at age VI in the River Beldour; the Prince Liam later Duke of Nördmarcke later Lajos II King of Torenth; the Prince Ronal Rurik later Duke of Lorsöl later Heir Presumptive to the throne of Torenth; the Princess Stanisha, born VII months after the death of her father.

On the XXVIIIth day of November in the year 1119 the King Wencit of Torenth, the Duchess Morag's brother, lost his only grandchild, Prince Malachy Mátyás, and by letters testamentary signed on the IVth day of March in the year 1120, the King made Morag's III sons the next heirs to the throne of Torenth after any future heirs of his own flesh, and also removed them from succession to the Duchy of Arjenol, naming the Duke Lionel II's younger half-brother, Lord Mahael, as Hereditary Duke d'Arjenol. The King Wencit and Duke Lionel were killed on the IInd day of July in the year 1121, and Morag then succeeded her brother as the Festillic Pretender to the Throne of Gwynedd and as Duchess of Tolán; but was not installed as Pretender, that ceremony being forbidden to a woman.

Morag and Duke Mahael II also became co-Regents for Morag's underaged son, King Alroy Arion II, when he succeeded his uncle on the same date. Alroy died on the XIIth day of June in the year 1123, and was succeeded by his brother, Liam Duke of Nördmarcke, as King Lajos II, again under the joint Regency of Morag and Mahael, the Prince Ronal Rurik Duke of Lorsöl becoming Heir Presumptive to the Throne. Princess Morag traveled to Rhemuth with her son on the XIXth day of May in the year 1124 to swear homage to Kelson King of Gwynedd as Overlord of Torenth, and was detained at Court through the Mearan campaign in June and July of that year. By the time her son the King Liam was made squire to Nigel Duke of Carthmoor the following Spring, she had been moved secretly to Coroth Castle where she could be closely watched by Richenda Duchess of Corwyn. Negotiations began at Cardosa in the year 1125 to release her from her confinement.

The Princess Morag returned to Beldour on the IVth day of June in the year 1126. She discussed marriage candidates for her son, King Liam Lajos II, with her brothers-in-law, Mahael Duke d'Arjenol and Teymuraz Count of Brustarkia, on the XXVIIIth day of June in the year 1128. But she was not a participant in the treason which sought to kill King Liam and replace him with his younger brother, and defended him against the attack of Mahael and Teymuraz during the *killijálay* ceremony held on the XVIth day of July.

Later that day she used the scrolls and implements she had inherited from her late brother, King Wencit, to subvert the will of Sean Earl Derry, using him as her eyes and ears in the Gwyneddan Court. But over the next week she discovered, much to her surprise, that King Kelson was not the ogre she had imagined, but that he had the best interests of her son at heart, and she made no move against him. On the XXVIth day instant, she was abruptly attacked and strangled in her chambers by Count Teymuraz, who stole her magical knowledge by ripping her mind and taking with him her precious documents. She was buried with full honours at Torenthály on the IInd day of August.

Berrhones called this lady "svelte as a cobra and as charming; every word she speaks has more than one meaning, every move she makes more than one intent. One longs for the days when a dagger was a dagger and a sword a sword." Lord Callan once commented: "It should be interesting to see which of the Regents finishes the other first; whoever wins this race will become the true Master of Beldour. I would not wager a copper *centime* on the King Liam's chances of attaining his majority." Bubek Lord d'Ezdégë added: "It is the rare Queen who has the chance to crown each of her sons in turn. King, Queen, Knave, who can say which is the stronger suit?" At Morag's funeral, however, Count Berrhones was quoted as saying: "She was a great lady who ever maintained the welfare of her sons as the first priority in her life. She died defending their honour." According to *Bride*, she wore "tiny golden bells at her ear and throat, which chimed musically when she tossed her head." She had dark eyes. R.I.P. [*High Deryni*; *The Bishop's Heir*; *The King's Justice*; *The Quest for Saint Camber*; *King Kelson's Bride*].

Morgan, House of. The earliest known member of this House, Kai ap Morrin, was a Captain in the army of Festil I King of Gwynedd in the years following the latter's successful invasion of Gwynedd in the year 822. Kai's son, Captain Morgan ap Kai, was given the estate of Morganhall in Corwyn on the XVIth day of November in the year 844, together with an hereditary knighthood and the local lairdship. Sir Kenneth Kai Morgan married Lady Alyce Heiress of Corwyn, and their son, Lord Alaric, succeeded at birth both to the Duchy of Corwyn and the County of Lendour. The Morgans have been faithful servants to the House of Haldane since the Restoration. The arms of this House are: *sable*, a double tressure *or, argent* flory. See also: Alaric, Alyce, Briony, Bronwyn, Charlan, Kelric, Kenneth.

HEREDITARY KNIGHTS & LAIRDS OF MORGANHALL

HOUSE OF MORGAN

Morgan ap Kai	844-871
Kai I Lun (son)	871-897
Peregrine Kai (son)	897-917
Charlan Kai (son)	917-922
Kailan Alaric (brother)	922-948
Korun Kai (cousin)	948-953
Kai II Charlan (son of Kailan)	953-977
Anthony Peregrine (grandson)	977-1025
Richard Anthony (son)	1025-1044
Kai III Anthony (son)	1044-1076
Kenneth Kai (son)	1076-1100
Alaric Anthony (son)	1100-1130+

Morris, Bishop. He was born on the IIIrd day of March in the year 1059. He was ordained priest on the XXXth day of March in the year 1079, and was consecrated as an itinerant Bishop of Gwynedd on the VIIIth day of August in the year 1099. He initially supported Edmund Loris Archbishop Primate of Valoret and All Gwynedd in the Interdict Schism of the year 1121. He died of *la grippe* on the VIth day of November in the year 1121, aged LXII years, and was buried, in accordance with King Kelson's wishes, with full honours. R.I.P. [*High Deryni*; *The Bishop's Heir*].

Mortimer, Lord Pomarc, General. He was born on the XVth day of April in the Year of Our Lord 1067, being the second son of Dason Baron Pomarc and Vita Lady Mhin. He intermarried with Caroteen Lady Cathgils on the XXXth day of December in the year 1088, and by her he had children: the Lady Zinka; the Lord Flavin; the Lady Nyasyna; the Lord Thyamin; the Lady Beta. This military officer of the Gwyneddan Army was present at the Dhassa War Council on the XXIXth day of June in the year 1121. [*High Deryni*; *The Bishop's Heir*].

Murdoch, Earl and Baron of Carthane, sometime Lord Regent of Gwynedd. This evil Lord was born on the XVIIIth day of January in the Year of Our Lord 877, being the son of Sir Osmael *de jure* Baron of Carthane and Gwendola Lady Muckno, and the scion of an old human noble family of Gwynedd that had been dispossessed by King Festil I in the year 822. He intermarried with Elaine Lady de Fintan on the VIth day of March in the year 899, and by her he had children: the Lady Agnes, who intermarried as his IInd wife with Rhun Earl of Sheele; the Hereditary Lord Richard later Earl of Carthane; the Lord Jason, dead at age III of the shaking fits; the Lord Cashel *Senior*.

Master Murdoch was knighted on the XVIIth day of August in the year 898. On the VIth day of November in the year 905 he successfully petitioned King Cinhil I to restore his ancient lands and title of Baron of Carthane, and on the Ist day of December in the year 907 he was elevated to the rank of Earl. He conspired on the XVIth day of January in the year 917 to overthrow the will of King Cinhil I and to establish new procedures governing the functioning of the Regents. By the terms of the King's will he became one of the V Regents of the new King Alroy on the IInd day of February in that year, and was also appointed to the Royal Council. He was present at the trial of the Deryni assassins on the XXVIIIth day of September in that year.

It was the Earl Murdoch who devised the plan to strike at the Deryni noble houses on Christmas Eve of the year 917. He escorted his son and daughter-in-law back to Carthane on the VIth day of May in the following year. He was also directly responsible for the deposition and murder of the Regent Ewan I Duke of Claibourne on the XXVth day of May in that month; at the same time he also killed Ewan's aide, Sir Kennet, who tried to defend him. After having his own wounds healed by Oriel, he had the Deryni Declan Carmody killed on the very same day.

He attended the coronation of King Javan on the XXXIst day of July in the year 921, and in the procession bore the Haldane banner. At a banquet held later that evening he was accused by Hrorik II Earl of Eastmarch of murdering the latter's brother, the Duke Ewan, and Murdoch attacked Hrorik with his sword, the pair being separated by King Javan. However, when the Earl Hrorik challenged the Earl Murdoch to trial by combat, Murdoch was forced to accept or lose face, and was fatally injured by Hrorik in fair battle on the next day. He lingered for several hours before being given the *coup de grâce* by his friend, Rhun Earl of Sheele. His body was returned to Carthane for burial. He was aged XLIV years at his death, and was succeeded by his son, Lord Richard.

The Earl Murdoch is described in the *Legends* as having "a thin nasal voice, spider-like fingers, and narrow shoulders." King Javan called him "a smarmy little weasel with a bitch of a wife." According to the *Heirs*, "he was a tall man with a narrow gaunt face and a close-trimmed beard and prim, prissy lips drawn back in a grimace of distaste." His standard included black aurochs with curled silver horns on a crimson field. *Proprium humani ingenii est odisse quem læseris.* [*Saint Camber*; *The Harrowing of Gwynedd*; *King Javan's Year*; *The Bastard Prince*].

Murray, Captain. He was born on the XXth day of July in the Year of Our Lord 889, being the son of Wilburn a soldier and Mia his wife. He intermarried with Evangeline daughter of Caldus Master of Horse at Lochalyn Castle in about the year 907, and by her he had children: Tiarna, who intermarried with Jesse Hereditary Count of Ebor later Count of Trevalga; Frederick MacMurray later a knight in the service of his brother-in-law, Count Jesse; Tigris, who intermarried with Sir Bastian MacTeague in The Connait; Ferdinand

MacMurray later a wealthy hog farmer in The Connait. Murray followed his father's career by joining the service of Hrorik II Earl of Eastmarch, advancing to the rank of Captain under Corban Howell Earl of Eastmarch by June of the year 928. He was placed in command of Lochalyn Castle early that month when Corban rode for Marley; his eldest daughter, Tiarna MacMurray, was also briefly given the care of Kennet Hereditary Count of Eastmarch during this period of confusion. He was instructed by Sudrey Dowager Countess of Eastmarch on how to set up an infirmary for the wounded men. At his master's order he sent II messengers to the King at Rhemuth informing him of the situation. On the XXIVth day of June in that year he was given the banner of Eastmarch to hold at the formal investiture of Stacia and Corban, the new Countess and Earl of Eastmarch. He died on the XXXth day of November in the year 937, aged XLVIII years. R.I.P. [*The Bastard Prince*].

Mustafa ibn Husnak, Emir of Umm al-Zakkar. He was serving as one of the lieutenants of Charissa Pretender of Gwynedd in November of the year 1120. He had dark eyes, and wore a rich silver baldric indicating his rank. [*Deryni Rising*].

Nathan, Father. This Michaeline priest provided provisions for the exiles at the Haven during December of the year 903. On the IIIrd day of July in the year 905 he conducted Father Alister Cullen to the Abbatial throne in the Chapterhouse of the Michaelines at Valoret, and reported at the Grand Chapter Meeting on the current status of the Order's holdings. He had a scar running sleek and white along his chin. [*Camber of Culdi*; *Saint Camber*].

Nathan the Prophet, Saint. This Biblical seer was mentioned and invoked during the coronation of King Alroy on the XXVth day of May in the year 917 at Valoret and also at that of King Javan on the XXXIst day of July in the year 921. He was mentioned again at the ceremony which transferred the Haldane potential to Prince Regent Conall on the IVth day of April in the year 1125. [*Camber the Heretic*; *King Javan's Year*; *The Quest for Saint Camber*].

Ned. He was serving as a farrier at the Michaeline Haven in June of the year 921. [*King Javan's Year*].

Ned. This merchant appeared at Rhemuth to sell his wares in July of the year 1124. [*The King's Justice*].

Neela. Geordie Lord Drummond bought this brown filly for Beck in April of the year 905. [*Deryni Challenge*].

Nellwyn de Menville Draper. She was born on the last day of April in the Year of Our Lord 843, being the daughter of Raoul de Menville and Rosalia Copland. She intermarried with Royston Draper (Prince Alroy Haldane) on the XVth day of June in the year 859, and by him she had one child: the Prince Cinhil (also called Nicholas Draper). She died of the effects of childbirth on the XXVIIth day of April in the year 860, aged XVI years, and was buried at the parish Church of Saint John's in Valoret. R.I.P. [*Camber of Culdi*].

Neot, Saint. This Vth-century holy man was a choirmaster from Coroth who later tired of singing, took a vow of silence, and became a hermit in the Anvil of the Lord. There he thrived on dates and fried locusts and sour goat cheese, and wore the same tunic again and again until it had become mere rags, and never cleansed himself, for he wrote: "It is better to present oneself unto the Lord as pure as a newborn babe, unwashed and innocent of the sins of man, than to approach the throne of Heaven bowed down by the honours and fine clothing and riches of the world." He occasionally attracted followers to his holy way of life, but not for very long. His body was found perfectly preserved in the desert by Saint Illtyd, an event which is commemorated annually on Saint Neot's Day by the *Lavage de Saint-Néot* in Jáca, in which a procession of celebrants march to the basilica there to be cleansed symbolically of their sins. Located near the site of his cave is the *Bain de Saint-Néot*, a place considered most efficacious by the followers of this holy hermit, who are, however, instructed not to drink the water therein, it being sacred to his memory. Campbell de Broun once visited this site, noting that he was not particularly tempted to imbibe, but that he appreciated the symbolism of the memorial, "quaint tho' it might be."

An abbey of the Gabrilites, a Deryni esoteric religious order, was once devoted to his name, and was located in the Lendour highlands until its destruction by the Regents on the XXIVth day of December in the year 917. His feastday is the XXXIst day of July. [*Camber of Culdi*; *Camber the Heretic*; *The Harrowing of Gwynedd*; *Deryni Checkmate*; *High Deryni*].

Nesta. This Deryni seeress of the VIth century foretold the doom of Caeriesse in her *Liber Fati Caeriesse*, but no one believed her until the continent actually sank beneath the waves, at which point it was, perhaps, too late. Nonetheless, she is well remembered today for her admirable foresight. [*Camber the Heretic*].

Nesta *of* Erne, Lady. She was born on the XXIst day of November in the Year of Our Lord 878, being the daughter of Dothan Lord of Erne and Dulcie Lady Carrigaline. She tried to assassinate King Cinhil I with her blade on the XXIInd day of June in the year 905 in retaliation for the imprisonment of her father. Jebediah immediately killed her with his sword, and her brother Hywel, who had accompanied her, also died. She was XXVI years of age at her death. [*Saint Camber*].

Netterhaven. This Torenthi port is the capital city of the Duchy of Jándrich, being located East of Tolán on the coast of the Northern Sea. It serves as the major trading hub of Northern Torenth, providing access by land and sea to the Norselands as well as to the major ports of Gwynedd to the West.

The city was suddenly attacked and burnt by the barbarians of Eistenmark on the XVIth day of May in the year 997, and again put under siege on the XXXth day of May in the year 1003. It was eventually rebuilt by Torenthi Kings Kyprian II and Arkady II.

Campbell de Broun, who was once forced to winter here, had little good to say of it: "The weather is fine, but we are all here in a wretched situation; we don't know what to do. The season has long since arrived that we may expect winter; we have no place or kind of a shelter provided nor have we any prospect of getting any; some of the children are sick; our reserves are wasting fast; we are entirely amongst strangers and from the little acquaintance we have with them can not have any high opinion of them. Master Endre has been to see us again this morning; it was dark when he was here last night and I had not a view of him; he is a little onery-looking man and too insignificant to be a monster, yet I believe he is a sordid little wretch and a man without a heart. He has sort of given us grant of the place which is a little comfort.

"I have never thought seriously of home till now, and when I contrast our once-happy with our now-miserable condition, it awakes the most painful emotions. Nothing is so mortifying as being dependent on a wretch, and to solicit for this miserable hound. Whilst walking over the place and ruminating on the past in a kind of melancholy, I chanced to find a small piece of snake root which accidentally remained in my mantle pocket and on such trifling things depends man's happiness; that this had a wonderful effect on my mind when I consider where I got it, who I got it of, and the happy situation I was then in a thousand leagues from here; it awakes the keenest sensations I have ever yet experienced, reflecting too that they are fled forever makes them more so. Endre has been down to see us tonight and agrees to rent us this improvement. He asks an enormous price for it; he sees our necessity and takes advantage of it, which makes my conjecture true, that he is a man without a heart. We are obliged to agree to his terms." See also: Torval.

Nevan *d'Estrelldas*, Bishop. He was born on the IXth day of September in the Year of Our Lord 1065, being the third son of Sir Nevil d'Estrelldas in Bremagne and Leola Lady Bardenfleth. He was ordained priest on the VIIth day of June in the year 1083, came to Gwynedd in the year 1095, and was elected an itinerant Bishop in Kierney on the XIXth day of January in the year 1122. In the following year he supported Edmund Loris ex-Archbishop Primate of Valoret and All Gwynedd in his attempt to restore himself as Primate of Gwynedd. On the Ist day of December in the year 1123 he was captured by the soldiers of Dhugal MacArdry Earl of Transha, and was taken to Rhemuth for questioning by King Kelson on the VIth day instant. After Loris's capture and execution on the XIIth of July 1124, Nevan was suspended from his functions as a Bishop on the XVIIIth day of March in the year 1125, but was allowed to continue serving as a priest under close supervision. He is said to have retired to Bremagne later that year. [*The Bishop's Heir*; *The Quest for Saint Camber*].

Nevell. This soldier of the Rhemuth garrison "attacked" the Healer Oriel on the XXth day of March in the year 922, accompanied by one Baldwin. In reality, Nevell's will had been subverted by the Deryni Sitric at the instigation of the former Regents. He was questioned II days later by Lord Jerowen and the recovered Healer Oriel, but by then had only confused memories of the event. He was murdered by Master Dimitri on the day following, his death being made to look like that of a suicide, and was wrongly buried in potter's field. R.I.P. *Valeat quantum valere potest.* [*King Javan's Year*].

Niall *Estaban*. He was born on the IInd day of July in the Year of Our Lord 1117, being the son of Sir Maynard Estaban and the Demoiselle Parisis de Saint-Point. He served as a page to Kelson King of Gwynedd in the year 1128. He had dark eyes. [*King Kelson's Bride*].

Niallan *Trey*, Bishop of Dhassa. This Deryni prelate was born on the XVIIth day of September in the Year of Our Lord 866. He was early intended for the Church, joining the Michaeline Order in the year 881, and was ordained priest on the Xth day of May in the year 885. Niallan was elected Bishop of the Free City of Dhassa on the Vth day of October in the year 903. He attended the consecration of Father Alister Cullen as Bishop of Grecotha and Vicar General Robert Oriss as Archbishop of Rhemuth on the IXth day of July in the year 905 at Valoret. He became a friend and confidant of Father Joram MacRorie. He attended the Synod of Bishops held at Valoret in November and December of 917, but was attainted and outlawed by the Regents on the XXVIIth day of December. He met with Joram at Dhassa on the Xth day of January in the year 918.

Rhun Earl of Sheele put Dhassa under siege early in the year 918, and Niallan was forced to quit his see for good on the IIIrd day of February following. He was inducted into the Camberian Council on the XIIth day instant. At about this time he began a lengthy history of the Haldane family from its restoration to the Throne of Gwynedd in December of the year 904; included in this treatise was an eyewitness account transcribed by Tieg Lord Thuryn of Étienne Baron de Courcy's memories of the *coup d'état* conducted by the former Regents on the XIth day of May in the year 922.

He took up residence at the old Michaeline Haven in the year 918, and met there with the new King Javan on the XXIVth day of June in the year 921; later that day, he took him back through the portal to Rhemuth. On the XXIXth day of July in that year he transported to the newly established portal at Rhemuth Castle to question Father Lior and Brother Serafin. During the 920s he helped train Camlin Lord MacLean at the former Michaeline Haven. On the XIVth day of June in the year 928 he met with the Camberian Council to discuss Prince Miklós's demands of King Rhys Michael, and on the XXVth day instant he again met with the Council to discuss the death of Vicar General Paulin Sinclair and the King's injury. He died on the XXIst day of November in the year 942, aged LXXVI years. His neatly trimmed hair and beard were steely grey. *El saber y el valor alternan grandeza; porque lo son hacen immortales.* R.I.P. [*Saint Camber*; *Camber the Heretic*; *The Harrowing of Gwynedd*; *King Javan's Year*; *The Bastard Prince*].

Nicaret. This young Deryni widow, whose husband and baby had perished in a fire set by anti-Deryni zealots, was engaged as a wet nurse for Evaine Lady

Thuryn's infant daughter Jerusha in the Spring of the year 918. [*The Harrowing of Gwynedd*].

Nicholas. He was serving as a retainer at Lochalyn Castle in June of the year 928, and was instructed by Corban Howell Earl of Eastmarch to handle the provisioning of the fortress. [*The Bastard Prince*].

Nieve *O Nuallain Sinclair Fitz-Arthur*, Countess Fitz-Arthur. She was born on the XXIXth day of October in the Year of Our Lord 860, being the daughter of Gavin Lord O Nuallain and Quintilla Lady Templebredon. She intermarried with Bonner I Sinclair Earl of Tarleton on the IIIrd day of April in the year 876, and by him she had children: the Hereditary Count Peter later Earl of Tarleton later Lord Albertus Grand Master of the *Equites Custodum Fidei*; the Lord Paulin later Bishop of Stavenham later Vicar General of the *Custodes Fidei*; the Lady Quinna; the Lady Adelphia; the Lady Lauretta. Following her first husband's death of the leprous scurvy on the XXVIIIth day of December in the year 890, she intermarried secondly and secretly with Tammaron later Earl Fitz-Arthur on the XIIth day of August in the year 891, and by him she had further children: the Hereditary Count Eldon, dead at age XIV of the crimson pox; the Hereditary Count Fane later Regent of Cassan later Earl Fitz-Arthur, who intermarried with the Princess Anne Heiress of Cassan and daughter of Ambert Quinnell Sovereign Prince of Cassan, leaving issue; the Lord Fulk, who intermarried with Niamh Lady Ballymar, leaving issue; the Lord Quiric, who intermarried with the Lady Émeraude Baroness of Horthness in her own right and daughter of Rhun Earl of Sheele, leaving issue. She was present at the state banquet held in Valoret on the Xth day of January in the year 918 to celebrate the marriages of Richard Lord Murdoch with Lirin Lady Udaut and Rhun Earl of Sheele with Agnes Lady Murdoch. She was acting as a companion to Michaela Queen of Gwynedd by June of the year 928. She died on the IInd day of May in the year 945, aged LXXXIV years. R.I.P. [*The Harrowing of Gwynedd*; *The Bastard Prince*].

Nigel Cluim Gwydion Rhys *Haldane*, Prince of Gwynedd, Duke of Carthmoor, sometime Prince Regent of Gwynedd, Heir Presumptive to the Throne of Gwynedd. He was born on the XXth day of February in the Year of Our Lord 1087, being the second surviving son of Donal Blaine II King of Gwynedd and Richeldis Princess of Howicce and Llannedd, and brother of Brion King of Gwynedd. He intermarried with Meraude Lady of Rhendall on the VIIth day of June in the year 1106, and by her he had children: the Hereditary Duke Conall later Prince Regent of Gwynedd, executed on the IIIrd day of May in the year 1125 for high treason, aged XVIII years, leaving posthumous issue, the Prince and Hereditary Duke Albin, and a natural daughter, Conalline Amelia; the Prince Rory later Duke of Ratharkin, heir to Carthmoor from the year 1125 to the year 1128; the Prince Payne later Duke of Travlum; the Princess Eirian, betrothed in the year 1128 to Liam Lajos II King of Torenth; the Princess Gloriana Haldana Esmeralda. He also legally adopted the Lady (Conalline) Amelia, the natural daughter of Prince Conall, on the VIIIth day of October in the year 1128, who was created Baroness Whitney by King Kelson, but without dynastic rights.

In his youth the Prince Nigel was trained in the military arts by his uncle, Richard Duke of Carthmoor, and served as a military advisor and commander to several Kings of Gwynedd. On the XXIst day of June in the year 1105 he was present when Brion King of Gwynedd slew Hogan Gwernach the Marluk and Festillic Pretender, and was appointed Commander of the Royal Army when Duke Richard retired on the XVIth day of November in the year 1106. As Heir Presumptive to the throne of Gwynedd, his responsibilities included the training of the young pages of the Court.

The Prince Nigel was created Duke of Carthmoor by his brother in succession to their uncle, the Duke Richard, on the XXVth day of December in the year 1114. His Haldane potential was activated on the XVth day of May in the year 1124 so that he could serve as Prince Regent during the King's absence on the Mearan campaign. He again served briefly as Regent of Gwynedd from the IXth day of March in the year 1125 during Kelson's absence on his quest for Saint Camber, but refused to be proclaimed King when Kelson was swept away into the Grelder Creek on the XXIst day instant, saying he would not be crowned until a year and a day had passed. He was deposed and put into a magic-induced coma by his nefarious son, the Hereditary Duke Conall, on the XXVIth day following, and Conall then assumed the title of Prince Regent. He was revived by Alaric Morgan Duke of Corwyn and Bishop Duncan McLain Duke of Cassan on the XIXth day of April. He transferred the succession to the Duchy of Carthmoor to his IInd son, the Prince Rory, on the IIIrd day of May following, but at the instigation of King Kelson restored it to Prince Albin on the XXXth day of July in the year 1128.

In the latter year the Prince and Duke Nigel again served briefly as Regent of Gwynedd for II weeks during the absence of King Kelson in Torenth, beginning on the IIIrd day of July. On the XXIst day instant he arranged for a hawking expedition for Sir Jolyon Ramsay in the countryside near the City of Rhemuth. He met his granddaughter Conalline for the Ist time on the XXVIth day of July, and decided to bring her permanently to Court. He participated in the Royal weddings held over the succeeding weeks.

According to the *Chronicles*, he had black hair, grey eyes, and a wide smile, and was noted for his quick wit. He had an unconscious mannerism of occasionally brushing back a strand of his hair, which he wore short, cut to collar length. His arms are: *or*, a lion rampant guardant *gules*, within a bordure *gules*. ["Swords Against the Marluk"; "The Knighting of Derry"; *Deryni Rising*; *Deryni Checkmate*; *High Deryni*; *The Bishop's Heir*; *The King's Justice*; *The Quest for Saint Camber*; *King Kelson's Bride*].

Nikola Nimur Kassian Néstor Nándor *Furstán*, Prince of Torenth, Duke of Arkadia, Heir Presumptive to the Principality of Meara. He was born on the XXVIth day of July in the Year of Our Lord 998, being the second son of Kyprian II King of Torenth and Polyxena Grand Princess of Byzantyun. He was betrothed on the I^st day of January in the year 1025 to Princess Roisian of Meara, and created Heir Presumptive to the Amethyst Throne, but the marriage never actually took place.

Prince Nikola was created Duke of Arkadia on his coming of age in the year 1012. He was intended by his father for the life of a soldier, and was trained from an early age in all manner of weaponry and tactics. When hostilities broke out against Gwynedd in the Spring of the year 1025, he led the raiding party on the XVIth day of May that captured the fort at the head of the Magas Pass. He counseled his father to avoid the many impediments placed in the way of the Torenthi army during their invasion of Gwynedd, but his advice was not much heeded, to the ultimate detriment of Torenth.

During the great battle of Killingford he took an axe aimed at his beloved brother, the Prince Arkady, on the XVIth day of June, and perished most bravely, aged XXVI years. The Nikolaseum was later erected in his honour by King Arkady II. R.I.P. [*King Kelson's Bride*].

The Nikolaseum is the VII-tiered monument built in Torenthály to the memory of Prince Nikola by his brother, Arkady II King of Torenth. It was officially dedicated by the Patriarch Timotheos II on the XVIth day of June in the year 1030, and is considered one of the VII architectural wonders of the world. King Liam Lajos II and Mátyás Count of Komnénë showed Kelson King of Gwynedd and his entourage this great edifice on the Xth day of July in the year 1128. Six days later, Teymuraz Count of Brustarkia used the portal in the monument to escape his arrest for treason.

The Nikolaseum is described thusly in *Bride*: "They mounted seven pristine white steps to enter the building. Inside, the structure belied its external form of seven tiers, encompassing a single vaulted chamber clad with the same star-studded tiles of sacred blue that adorned the domes of ecclesiastical buildings. On a raised dais in the center, lit by a silvery glow, lay King Arkady's memorial to his slain brother. The prince's effigy, recumbent on a bier of black basalt, was slightly larger than life-sized, carved of a single block of rosy carrolan marble that gave the flesh a blush of seeming life, as if the slain prince only slept. The veining of the stone leant texture and contrast to the sculpted folds of the cloak in which he was wrapped from throat to ankles. The face was serene, handsome, even beautiful. Nikola had been only XXVI when he died. A carved stack of three battle drums guarded the foot of the bier, draped with a pair of crossed standards bearing the leaping hart device of Torenth, bright with paint-work on the carved alabaster. Beside the bier knelt a cloaked and hooded figure carved of tawny stone, its face buried in its hands, and a jeweled crown lying discarded beside it. A fine sword, ornately wrought of gold and silver, was leaned against the other side of the bier, so that its jewel-studded hilt projected as a sign of the Cross before the bowed head of the grieving Arkady." [*King Kelson's Bride*].

Nimur I Zsigmond *Furstán*, called "The Great," King of Torenth. This *Rex Notatus* was born on the XXIIIrd day of September in the Year of Our Lord 866, being the son and heir of Imre II King of Torenth and the Grand Princess Kónstantia daughter of Tiberios Grand Prince of Byzantyun. He intermarried with Margit Duchess of Baïan on the XIVth day of June in the year 887, and by her had I child: the Princess Lajosha, who was engaged to Imre I King of Gwynedd at the time of her death of the palsied paralysis on the I^st day of March in the year 904. After his first wife's death on the XXVIIIth day of April in the year 895, the King Nimur intermarried secondly with his *cousine*, Katalin Countess of Festil-Mnata, on the XXVIIth day of January in the year 899, and by her he had children: the Hereditary Prince Arion later Arion I King of Torenth; the Princess Charis later Duchess of Tolán in her own right, who intermarried with her cousin the Prince Marek I Festillic Pretender to the Throne of Gwynedd; the Prince Miklós later Duke of Truvorsk, who was killed by Rhys Michael King of Gwynedd on the XXIInd day of June in the year 928, *sans postérité légitime*; the Prince Torval later Torval I Duke d'Arjenol. The Queen Katalin dying of the effects of childbirth on the Xth day of July in the year 906, the King Nimur intermarried thirdly in his old age with one Mária Kosinsky, not of noble birth, on the XVth day of February in the year 912, and by her had a child, the Countess Hedvig, without dynastic rights, who later intermarried with Tamás Count Turjel.

The Prince Nimur succeeded his father on the Vth day of December in the year 891, and was girded with the sword at Iób by Patriarch Ióannés V on the New Year's Day following. In a series of military campaigns conducted in the years 892, 895, 899, and 904 the King Nimur doubled the size of Torenth, conquering many territories to the South, the East, and the Northeast, including the Principalities of Vorna, Lorsöl, and Vechta. Most notably, he defeated and killed Thrasarik Sovereign Prince d'Arjenol on the XVIIth day of July in the year 896, replacing him with a distant relative, the Prince Zdanik, who was forced to swear fealty to Nimur. When Zdanik himself revolted in the year 915, the King Nimur invaded a IInd time, defeating the Prince and executing all remaining members of the House of Arzh on the XXIst day of October in the year 916, save for Prince Zdanik's youngest daughter and surviving heir, the Princess Braïda, then aged I year, whom he intermarried with his X-year-old son, the Prince Torval, on the XXVth day instant. Torval was created I^st Duke d'Arjenol on that date.

The King Nimur I remained vigorous well into his old age. It is said that in his XXV-year reign the King spent no more than III months in his bed at Beldour, and only then because the capital was snowbound in the worst storm of the century. The major disappointment in his life was the loss in the year 904 of the Kingdom of Gwynedd, for which he was Overlord. He then established the policy later followed by most of his successors, of supporting the aspirations of his *cousine germaine*, the Queen Ariella I, her son, the Hereditary Prince Marek I, and their descendants to recover their lost throne; and he gave sanctuary to the infant Prince Marek when both of his parents were killed, treating the boy as if he were his own son.

Thoriswinth of Tütün has written the only surviving account of this King penned during his lifetime, stating that he "...was tall and muscular and very well built, though becoming somewhat stout in old age, with sleek black hair and bushy brows and mustachios, and eyes set like II black stones in his face, cold and calculating. When he smiled men feared for their lives, and when he laughed, men made testaments for the disposition of their estates." However, the Princess Arien, writing CL years later in her *Lives of the XII Kings of Torenth*, called Nimur I "a strong and capable King whose vision of expansion and aggression established the basis of the modern Torenthi state."

The Great King Nimur was wounded in the arm by an arrow during the siege of the minor Arjenoli fortress of Brustarkia, lingering for a week before dying of the rotting disease on the Ist day of April in the year 917, aged L years. He was succeeded by his eldest son, Prince Arion, and was buried with high honours in the crypt of his ancestors at Torentháÿ. R.I.P. [*Saint Camber*; *The Bastard Prince*].

Nimur II Dénes Kyprian Károly *Furstán*, called "The Old," King of Torenth. He was born on the VIth day of August in the Year of Our Lord 1035, being the fourth but eldest surviving son and heir of Arkady II King of Torenth and the Grafina Dura daughter of Arsieu II Sovereign Prince of Jáca. He intermarried with his *cousine germaine*, the Princess Charis Rochelle, called "Charchelle" even by those in Court, on the VIIIth day of June in the year 1060, and by her he had children: the Hereditary Prince Nimur, who was eaten up by a foul odor in the year 1095; the Prince Torval later Duke of Lorsöl, who, having been cursed by the Devil with imbecility, was excluded from the succession by his father on the VIth day of January in the year 1095 and sent to the cloister of Saint Simplicius, where he died in the year 1119, *sans postérité*; the Princess Nimurene, who fell in a hole and suffocated at age IV; the Princess Arkadene, dead of the phlegmatic grippe at age III; the Hereditary Prince Carolus later Duke of Nördmarcke later Károly III King of Torenth; the Prince Wencit later Duke of Vorna later Wenzel II King of Torenth; the Prince Bertóld, dead of the milk complaint at VI months; the Princess Jacéline, who died aquinsy at age IV; the Princess Morag later Pretender of Gwynedd, who intermarried with Lionel II Duke d'Arjenol, leaving issue.

King Nimur's Ist spouse having died in childbirth on the VIIth day of February in the year 1080, he intermarried secondly with a common seamstress, Cairbreana Olafsdottir, said by some to have been his mistress in previous years, whom he later created the Countess Perényi on the XIIIth day of May in the year 1081, and by her he had children, without dynastic rights: the Lord Termöd later Count Vechta; the Lady Ringgöld later a penitent of the Order of Saint Alix under the name Sister Zabel.

The Princes Arion and Sigard and István having died before him of the typhoidous grippe, the Prince Nimur succeeded his father on the XIIth day of May in the year 1080, and was girded with the sword at Hagios Iób on the New Year's Day following by Patriarch Bassos II. During the Ist decade of his reign, in the years 1082 and 1085, this King mounted several expeditions to secure the Southern and Eastern borders of his kingdom, and there built several notable fortifications to protect the land from the depredations of the desert folk, among them the grand castle of Mór Montarago, concerning which the poet Emilión has noted, in his list of his wonders of the world, "...the sun-drenched, serrated spires of Montarago." When Donal Blaine II King of Gwynedd made his expedition into Meara in the year 1089, the King Nimur took advantage of the absence of his brother monarch and the lack of a Duke in Corwyn to raid that Duchy, bringing home much booty to enrich his treasury.

In his IInd decade the King repulsed a counterforce sent by the King of Gwynedd in the year 1090, and II years later sent a message to every city and town in Torenth, requiring that copies be made of all extant scrolls and books in the land to enrich the Royal Library at Beldour. Many other manuscripts and arcane texts did he purchase of merchants and vendors from foreign lands, so that his Library grew to become the greatest in all the world save for that of Glorious Kónstantinopolis herself.

It is said by Count Ungnad that King Nimur "was short and somewhat pinched about the face, with bad teeth and thin, scraggled hair that quickly left his scalp not long after he succeeded to the throne. He was subject to frequent illness and ill temper during his life and looked strained and haggard even in middle age. He had much trouble with his bowels in later life. Although he was by all accounts well read and of quick mind and ready intelligence, he often expressed impatience with matters of state, leaving many of the lesser details and petty decisions of governing to the discretion of his councilors and later to his sons." But Lord Callan also notes that King Nimur was "fair and deliberate in his judgments," that "when a man appealed to the King, he knew that his petition would be carefully considered and a decision made based upon the merits of his case." Iwannés confirms that the King was "well respected among the people of Torenth."

In later years the King suffered from palsied hands and was often heard to lament his failing health, the contentiousness of his children, and the bickering of his councilors, and at times had to be restrained from wandering aimlessly through the corridors of his palace and onto the adjacent grounds. His daughter Morag cared for him after the death of his IInd wife on the XXXth day of November in the year 1101, and was by all accounts much devoted to him. He passed from this Earth at the XIth hour of the XXIInd day of November in the Year of Our Lord 1106, aged LXXI years, and was succeeded by his son, the Hereditary Prince Carolus. He was buried with great honours in the royal crypts at Torentháÿ.

Count Berrhones attended the inauguration of this King in the year 1081, describing it in his *Life of King Nimur II*: "The day dawned cool and clear in Beldour. For weeks the mages had laboured to produce the mild temperatures and cloudless skies that greeted us that New Year's morning. It was the Ist girding in more than half a century, and I looked forward to it with great anticipation, even though I still mourned the King Arkady, he who had raised me to the service of the Crown. The old King saved us from ourselves, but each one of his triumphs extracted from him an awful price, with God or mayhap the Devil taking away his children one by one, until only the Prince Nimur remained, who was destined to sit on his father's throne. What a curse to be a great man's son!

"The King-to-Be had been roused an hour before dawn, and escorted to the traditional milk bath to purify his body and soul for the events to come. No food or drink had passed his lips since the previous day. We were immediately called in to ward him in all his innocence, unprotected as he was, I and my III companions, the Counts Branyng, Ungnad, and Czalsky, for it was our privilege to be chosen as the King-to-Be's Moving Ward, and mine especially to hold the place of honour at the *Padishah*'s swordhand. I quickly donned the red tunic that signified my role as *Hagios Michaél*, who takes precedence over his III brethren in the *killijálay* as Captain of all the Hosts of Heaven. We took our stations surrounding the Great Nimur—Branyng in gold as Holy Raphaél in the front, Ungnad in blue as Holy Gabriél in the rear, Czalsky in green as Holy Ouriél to the left, and myself to the right—and began synchronizing our auras. This technique required a great deal of training to master, and was generally practiced only by those adepts of a certain age of life, in their IIIrd and IVth decades. Before that time one's control was insufficient to maintain a link for long, and the process used up so much energy if sustained for any length of time that only the relatively young had the stamina to continue the ward beyond a few minutes.

"'*Prótos*,' I said, setting my controls in place. '*Deuteros*,' replied young Branyng, linking his aura with mine. '*Tritos*,' added the gangly Ungnad. '*Tetartos*,' said Czalsky. Now came the difficult part. The King-to-Be, as the one being warded, had to center it on himself: '*Hé-nó-me-nos*,' he breathed, a syllable at a time, as he gathered together the IV strands of our souls one by one and wove them into a single unit. A faint, milky-white shadow suddenly popped into the air above us. I was young enough then to be impressed by the process.

"The King-to-Be's servants now covered his thin frame in a simple, lightly-woven white linen tunic and *shalvar*, covered by a white woolen *zuban* overcoat, its only decoration an embroidered Furstáni hart. A black silk sash was wrapped tightly about his waist, the fringed ends hanging free to the left. Finally, they brought in the pure white leather *stivalia* and harness and fitted them to the *Padishah* with silver clasps. A comb was run quickly through his wispy, greying hair. He looked at each of us somberly and nodded. We were ready.

"We proceeded very deliberately through the corridors of Furstánály Palace, moving at a steady, even pace so we would not lose contact with each other. We could in theory have maintained the link for a distance of about X paces apart, but the closer we were to each other and the more regular the spacing maintained, the easier it was for each of us to keep focused on our task. We had all practised this very delicate balancing act for many months. At the entrance awaited the great carriage of state, all gilded in gold and *lapis lazuli* and drawn by IV matched pairs of white R'Kassan stallions, with postilions astride the near IV. The steeds snorted and stamped their feet, tossing foam with each swing of their heads in anticipation of their activity. As was my privilege, I preceded the King-to-Be into the carriage and out the other door, there to perch precariously on the step as Czalsky took a like position on the left, and Branyng mounted the driver's box and Ungnad the rear of the carriage. And we were off!, moving down the *Avenue du Saint-Constantine* to Beldour-by-the-River, where the barge was waiting.

"The superbly fitted white *caïque* was decorated in silver and black and gold, topped by a raised canopy of scarlet velvet embroidered with Furstáni harts and fringed with golden tassels. Great Nimur took his seat upon the golden Throne, sitting straight and stolid and silent; below and beside him we flanked the King-to-Be on all IV quarters. As we moved upriver I could hear the 'swish-swish' of the XXVIII massive oars as they pulled through the brown waters of the River Beldour, the beat of the master's drum providing an almost hypnotic accompaniment to the barge's sensuous glide. Following us in procession were other craft containing the Hereditary Prince-to-Be and the lesser Princes of the House of Furstán, and all of the High Lords of State and their retinues. The air was scented with perfumes and with flowers specially grown for the occasion. As we passed under Saint Basil's Bridge, the Royal Guard stood rigidly at attention, bared *kiliç* held smartly in their right hands in salute to their Liege and Master. The cheers of the merchant sailors who lined the decks and perched in the high-flung, gaily-decorated yardarms of a multitude of ships moored on both sides of the Beldour River resounded again and again over the water, echoing off the walls and buildings on either side.

"Some V miles upriver we docked at the *Quai de l'Amirauté*, where the *Padishah* Nimur alighted with his escort and was welcomed by a band of trumpeters, their bronze instruments flashing in the light of the morning sun as they blew a glorious fanfare of exaltation. There awaited his favourite steed, a white Arabi stallion called *Karibajïl*, which had to be restrained by its handlers from rearing and plunging until the calming sphere of our Moving Ward enveloped it. The bridle seemed woven of liquid silver, and the heavy silver medallions adorned nearly every surface of the high-cantled saddle, gleaming in the sunlight against the perfection of a beautifully woven, red woolen blanket of intricate design. The *destrier* quieted immediately as its master mounted. Then the King-to-Be proceeded up the cobbled *Avenue des Rois*, still flanked on all sides by our Moving Ward, and closely accompanied by a squad of armed Circassian Guards. Tens of thousands of well-wishers lined the way, many of them waving black-and-silver pennants that had been distributed to them earlier in the day. I caught the whiff of freshly roasted lamb and my stomach growled in response, but I kept my concentration focused on the Moving Ward and the mounted figure within it.

"At Hagios Iób, the Chief of the *Hankyár Derviches* kissed the *Padishah* on his left shoulder, and the Most Holy Bassos welcomed us into his Church. We left our shoes at the entrance and slipped on cloth sandals, walking the prescribed XII paces forward in company with the *Hankyárar* of Konyály, whose privilege it was from time immemorial to gird the sword of

Furstán on each new monarch. The Grand Vizier greeted us with a salute, and in the name of the people bowed low to kiss the hem of the *Padishah*'s *zuban*.

"In the center of the church, directly beneath the great dome, I saw a black marble tomb covered with mosaics of onyx and a thin layer of fretted silver as delicate as the lace of a woman's gown, which contained the relick'd bones of Great Furstán, Founder of the House which bears his name. For the purposes of *killijálay*, the investment ceremony, the Patriarch and the XII Metropolitans of the Holy Synod had placed a ceremonial table of finely-polished walnut draped with a cloth of purple velvet at the head of the tomb. The sounding of a single clear note from Job's Complaint signaled that the hour of *hektë*, or *sext* in the Rûman tongue, had arrived and the girding should now commence.

"Six burly Albani guards slowly entered the Church bearing the sword of Furstán on his solid silver salver. Fashioned of a gold-bronze alloy, the scimitar was as long as a man is tall, curved at the end and weighing some XV stone, sheathed in black metal encrusted with rubies and emeralds and sapphires and opals and *lapis lazuli*. The hilt was cunningly wrought into an intricate twirl of metal; when passed in front of a light, it created a shadowy *tughra* spelling out the name Furstán. The Albanis carefully lowered the sword onto the table in front of the tomb, pointing towards the altar, then gently removed the sheath without touching the blade, and exited the Church. The Patriarch assumed a position between the table and the tomb, at the point of the sword, while the King-to-Be, the *Hankyárar*, and the Grand Vizier stood at the hilt. The Pillars of the Realm, that is to say, our Moving Ward, glided to each of the IV quarters—myself to the right of Great Furstán's tomb, Czalsky directly opposite in the North, Ungnad behind the *Padishah*, and Branyng at the far end of the tomb.

"The Most Holy Patriarch Bassos chanted: 'Glory be to Thee, God the Father, glory be to Thee, Eternal Son, glory be to Thee, Holy Spirit, by whom all is sanctified. World without end.' The congregation responded: 'Amen.' Incense began swirling above us in patches of strongly scented fog, making patterns knowable only to God. The Patriarch spoke again, lifting his hands toward the air above my head: 'I call upon thee, Holy Michaél, to stand rightly with us in joy and gladness at this *killijálay*, to sanctify thy servant, Nimouros.'

"A wind began to whine through the Church, lifting the hair of the men and the coverings of the women and stirring the solemn robes of the monks, and I felt a chill run up my spine, as if someone had lightly danced a cold finger there. I could see a glow forming in front of my eyes, and started with the realization of whence it came. My arms lifted involuntarily behind me and stretched into something else, light and feathery and almost weightless. My legs grew, my body lengthened, my face changed in ways I cannot describe. I saw and did not see, I felt and did not feel, I heard sounds that were not sounds, I breathed the air of another plane that had no air, I *knew* suddenly who I had become. Through eyes that were not my own I watched my brethren, the Archangels Gabriél, Raphaél, and Ouriél, take form, standing there X feet tall, as silent and strong as the Pillars they represented.

"And I knew that Holy Bassos spoke only to me: 'Lord and Master, Our God, who has established in Heaven the orders and armies of Angels and Archangels to minister to Thy Glory, grant that with us there may enter those holy Angels who serve and glorify Thy goodness. Shelter us under the shadow of their wings, drive away every foe and adversary.' Then he carefully pressed the tip of the sword with his right index finger, drawing a drop of blood: 'And the star came and stood above where the child was. Make beautiful, O Lord, this instrument of thy will. Thy glory has covered the heavens, and the earth is full of thy praises. Strengthen now Thy servant Nimouros, clothe him with beauty, remember him with Thy blessings. For when Thy servant Phourstanos did walk upon this earth, he promised to watch over his sons forever. Send down thy Holy Spirit to watch over us. Give us a sacrifice of Thy praise and bless thine inheritance.' Then he reached behind him with his right hand and touched the monument with his blood: 'Holy Deathless One, come thou forth from thy tomb!'

"The crowd gasped, for at that moment the tomb of Furstán rattled, and it seemed as if the lid slid back from the coffin. A shadowy, translucent figure garbed in strange robes seemed slowly to rise upwards and merge itself with the form of the Patriarch, who said: 'The grace of God, that always strengthens the weak and fills the empty, does here appoint Nimouros ho Phourstanos to be thy lawfully girded King. Let no man challenge the will of God. Let no man doubt the choice of Furstán. Prepare thou the girdle.'

"The *Hankyárar* brought forth an empty scabbard and belted it around the King-to-Be's waist, whispering in his ear, as was the custom: 'Remember, Lord, that thou art mortal.' Then the form of Furstán touched the great scimitar and a ripple of silver light flowed from his finger into the weapon. 'If thou hast the power,' he said, 'Then pick up thy sword!'

"In one smooth motion Nimur grasped the scimitar in both hands and pointed it straight up at the dome above. A beam of purplish light sprang from the tip of the weapon, penetrating through the roof into the sky where the crowds outside could see the proof of his empowerment, the beam slowing changing colours through the entire spectrum. Inside the church it seemed as if the colour spread from where it touched the inside of the onion-shaped dome slowly down around its skin, eventually coating the interior walls with a fine shimmering glow; and outside it was the sky itself that seemed to take on a range of pastel colours like the shimmering of the Northern Lights. '*Axios!*' shouted the Grand Vizier. 'He is worthy!' Three times the words echoed through the church and the crowds outside. '*Axios!*' The Princes and Lords shouted out a grand *huzzah* of acclamation. '*Axios!*'

"The light slowly died, and the tomb of Furstán seemed to close. I felt the power within me receding into dim memory, and I cried as it left, the tears streaming down my cheeks. Then the Holy Patriarch Bassos, filled with the glow of Jesus and all his Apostles, said: 'We do beseech thee Lord with humble mien to spare our Great King Nimur, the Second of that name, for III times XXX years, that with a clean and understanding heart he may rightly speak the word of faith as Guardian of the Realm. Preserve him in health, O Lord, in honour and in length of days, faithfully dispensing Thy word of truth. Fill him with the Holy Spirit and the grace and wisdom that he needs to govern the Realm.'

"The King Nimur responded: 'I will offer to Thee incense and rams; all my garments smell of myrrh, aloes, and cassia; let my prayer be as incense in Thy sight.' Then he carefully laid the Great Sword of Furstán back on its table. The Hereditary Prince approached with the smaller Sword of State, sinking to his knees and handing it to his father with these words: 'My Lord, accept this gift beyond price, given to us until the end of time.' The King sheathed the sword, replying: 'Peace be unto thee, my son, peace be to all the Lords of the land and to all the children of the Church. I do anoint thee my lawful successor. Lord, make him this day a sharer in Thy mystic supper. For I will not reveal Thy mysteries to Thine enemies, nor like Judas give Thee a kiss, but like the thief I say to Thee: Remember me, O Lord, in Thy kingdom. Remember me.' Finally, the Grand Vizier brought the Crown of State on its cushion of velvet, handing it to the Most Holy Bassos. The King bowed his head before the living symbol of God on earth, and received his temporal crown, the ancient diadem of hammered gold that has adorned the brows of Furstáni Kings since time immemorial. Then a choir of monks sang their song of rejoicing, and the newly-consecrated King and his entourage exited the Church, continuing up the Avenue to pay homage to the pyramids of his ancestors.

"I recall that time through the fog of my life as if I had seen it yesterday, I who have lived now some III score years and X. Seven Kings of Torenth I have known and VI I have buried, and several of that Festil lot. King Nimur was not the best of them and certainly not the worst, but he was a good and decent man to those around him. And so I add my prayers to all of theirs: 'Remember him, O Lord. Remember *me*.'" R.I.P. ["Legacy"; *The Deryni Archives*].

Nimur Miklós Ferencz Paval *Furstán*, called "The Younger," Hereditary Prince of Torenth, Duke of Beldouria. He was born on the XXIInd day of March in the Year of Our Lord 1061, being the eldest son and heir of Nimur II King of Torenth and Charis Rochelle Princess of Festil. He intermarried with the Countess Zsófia daughter of Boldiszár Count Sómlyö on the XXXth day of June in the year 1083, and by her he had children: the Princess Rhédenna, the eldest of his VI children and the only one to survive, who died of the streppèd throat at age XIV in the year 1098, *sans postérité*; the Princes Nimur Imre, Nimur Demagoy, Nimur Emrich, Nimur Tamás, and Nimur Miklós *Junior*, all of whom were born dead or died as infants of the blue blood.

This high and mighty Prince was educated by the greatest men of his time, and later served as Commander of the King's army. Berrhones says of him, "He was thin, well apportioned, quick to learn, a keen judge of men. His knowledge arcane exceeded that of any other member of the House of Furstán, before or after. I called him friend, and thought him the best of the Princes that I have met on this earth. His death was a great loss to Torenth, and also to me."

On the VIth day of December in the year 1094 an alchemical experiment which he was conducting went terribly awry, and he was found by his aides lying senseless on the floor of his *officina*. Lord Callan says: "He was removed to his bed, and although he regained his speech several days later, he could mumble only meaningless words and phrases and ofttimes glanced wildly around the room, as if looking for someone whom he knew to be present. His physique began to deteriorate, and a foul odor soon began to emanate from his bedclothes, causing his manservants to puke their breakfasts into the nightbucket near his bed. On the IInd day of January he gave a great cry, 'He comes,' and gave up his ghost, a look of terror still fixed on his face." He was buried by his grieving father and family in the crypt of his ancestors at Torenthály on the VIIth day of January in the year 1095, but his tomb was carefully sealed all around with dabs of lead and holy water. He was XXXIII years of age at his death, and was succeeded as Hereditary Prince by his younger brother, the Prince Carolus, the intervening brother the Prince Torval Duke of Lorsöl having been excluded from the succession by their father for imbecility. R.I.P.

Nimur Néstor Zsoltán *Furstán*, called "The Rash," Hereditary Prince of Torenth, Duke of Beldouria. He was born on the IVth day of August in the Year of Our Lord 965, being the eldest son and heir of Malachy II King of Torenth and Ianthe Princess of Salonique. He intermarried with Diavola Duchess d'Iméreth on the IInd day of May in the year 983, but she failed to conceive before she died. The Prince Nimur was sent by his father to the barracks at an early age to teach him the art and science of war, and he learned his lessons well. He was, according to Pribin van Quael, "A burly lad, who quickly mastered the sword and shield and spear and axe, and could beat any man in his army in hand-to-hand combat." He became friendly with the Prince Marek-Imre, the Festillic Pretender Imre II's eldest son, and encouraged his father to support the latter's aspirations.

In the year 983 the Prince Nimur joined the expeditionary force of Prince Imre II in its invasion of Gwynedd, leading a brigade of soldiers under his command which he called *Les Gardes Élites*, eventually retreating with Imre to the fortress of Rengarth. In the year 984 he returned to Torenth to take command of a relief force then being assembled at Beldour, which left that city on the XVIIIth day of June to join with his father's main army at Medras and the remnants of the Pretender Imre's army at Rengarth.

The combined force reached Carcashale on the XVIIth day of July, and moved West into Gwynedd. On the afternoon of the IInd day of August, the Torenthi force appeared before the walls of Grecotha and demanded the surrender of that city. That night the Princes Mark-Imre and Nimur urged a frontal assault on the Gwyneddan fortress, while the Pretender Imre II and King Malachy II counseled caution. However, the II young Princes carried the day, and at dawn the Festillic banners moved forward.

But Jasher the new King of Gwynedd had redeployed his forces during the night, and when the Torenthi army breached the Eastern gate of the city, they found no one inside, for the Gwyneddans were attacking them from the rear. The small cluster of Torenthi noblemen and officers directing the battle behind the lines was quickly overrun, the Princes Nimur and Marek-Imre and the King Malachy being killed almost immediately. He lacked one day of being XIX years of age at his death. His body was returned to Torenthály for honourable burial. R.I.P.

Ninian *de Piran*, Earl of Jenas. He was born on the XIVth day of December in the Year of Our Lord 1067, being the eldest son and heir of Rowan Earl of Jenas and Avril Lady Rogers. He intermarried with Thea Lady Mackey on the XXVIIth day of July in the year 1087, and by her he had children: the Hereditary Count Roger later Earl of Jenas; the Lord Mackey; the Lady Rowena; the Lady Maura. The Lord Ninian succeeded his father on the XIth day of October in the year 1101. He was captured by King Wencit at Rengarth with Jared McLain Duke of Cassan on the XXVIIIth day of June in the year 1121, and was then murdered by the King on the Ist day of July in the same year at Candor Rhea, aged LIII years. He was succeeded by his son, Roger Earl of Jenas. R.I.P. [*High Deryni*; *The Bishop's Heir*].

Niyyana. This flagship of the Hort of Orsal's fleet was a large *caïque* with a great green sail sporting a picture of the Hort of Orsal's emblem, the sea lion. It transported Létald Hort of Orsal, Kelson King of Gwynedd, and Liam Lajos II King of Torenth and their parties from Orsal to Beldour, leaving the former city on the IVth day of July, and arriving at the latter town on the VIIIth day instant. The *Niyyana* left Beldour on the XVIIth day of July under the command of Hereditary Prince Cyric, arriving back at Orsal III days later. Later that month the ship transported the wedding paraphernalia from Orsal to Desse, arriving there on the XXVIIth day instant. *Tabula ex naufragio*. [*King Kelson's Bride*].

Noelie Quintilla *Ramsay-Quinnell*, Duchess of Ratharkin. She was born on the XIth day of May in the Year of Our Lord 1108, being the eldest daughter of Sir Jolyon Ramsay later Duke of Laas and Oksana Lady d'Enghieux. She intermarried with the Prince Rory later Duke of Ratharkin on the XXXIst day of July in the year 1128, and by him she had a child: the Prince Bearand Bertald Ewan de Traherne Hereditary Duke of Ratharkin. She accompanied her parents to Rhemuth in the Summer of the year 1127, when she was introduced to Prince Rory. In the year 1128 her name was often paired with that of Kelson King of Gwynedd as a possible bride for that monarch, but she chose another. She had soulful eyes and masses of dark hair. [*King Kelson's Bride*].

Noirel. Geordie Lord Drummond was given this black stallion by Camber Earl of Culdi to ride on his quest to Stavenham in April of the year 905. He later sired the great stallion, Echidnaïs. *Nec scit qua sit iter, nec, si sciat, imperet illis*. [*Deryni Challenge*].

Norris. He was serving as a guard at Valoret Castle under the command of Rhun Earl of Sheele in January of the year 918, and was using the garde-robe on the Xth day of that month just before Tavis transported there. He was big, armed, and lightly armored, but was quickly put to sleep by Prince Javan. [*The Harrowing of Gwynedd*].

Norseland. This vast region lies to the North and East of the Duchies of Jándrich and Arjenol in Torenth, stretching from the Northern Sea on the West to the great inland Sea of Öst on the East, and is bordered on the North by impenetrable icelands and on the South by the Kingdom of Torenth, the Grand Duchy of Érskeburg, the Dual Principalities of West Veskitsa and East Veskitsa, the Kingdom of Szátmár, the Duchy of Mörovsky, the Free City of Sankt-Pöltán, the Republic of Záztrivá, the Duchy of Nova Suzhitsa, and the Empire of Byzantyun.

Now the tribes or states of the Norseland are these: Eistenmark, Tretelgia, Avarsland, Svålmark, Skågarrak, Filkermark, Skilfingsland, Kjölenmark, Galdhøpsland, Kristiansland, and Vesteråln, each having its own King or Jarl. The coastline along the Northern Sea, which is divided between Eistenmark, Tretelgia, and Avarsland, is fringed with islands, some under the control of Skågarrak, and deeply indented by numerous fjörds; the coast along the Sea of Öst, which is divided between Galdhøpsland, Kristiansland, and Vesteråln, is less rocky and more easily accessible. The land supports few crops, and the growing season is very short, but the vast mountain pastures support many sheep and domesticated deer, some of which are driven in huge flocks across the high plateau by the tribes of the interior. The coastal states have traditionally relied on fishing and pirating to provide much of their sustenance.

Northern Sea or *Great Northern Sea*. This great body of cold salt water connects with the Atalantic Ocean to the West, and flanks the coastlines of the Kheldish Riding, Marley, Tolán, Torenth, and the Norse countries of Eistenmark, Tretelgia, Avarsland, and Svålmark to the North, extending all the way to the impenetrable icelands. The principal ports situate on this sea are Netterhaven the capital of Jándrich in Torenth and Eistenfalla the capital of Eistenmark.

The Ancient Seamen of the Northlands (the "Norsemen") have long been respected for their maritime and fighting prowess, ofttimes sailing far to the South from their home ports, raiding and killing and ravaging other lands, and leaving nought but fear and fury in their wake. It has been said, with more truth than fiction, that the icy waters of the Northern Sea run as thick in the veins of its sons as does the blood of their fathers. In more recent centuries, however, the shipping lanes of the Great Northern Sea have been put to more peaceful pursuits. Trade and commerce are now pursued with as much persistence as pillaging and looting were in elden days. Fishing, too, has become a profitable employment, with hordes of crustacea and sea creatures of all shapes and kinds being pulled daily from the deep. The portside markets of Netterhaven and Eistenfalla along the Northern coast teem with the tasty and bountiful offerings of the modern-day descendents of the hardy Norsemen of yore.

As Campbell de Broun has observed: "On any given day one may take his leisure at the ubiquitous dockside *café*, chatting with the innkeeper or his obliging daughter, and imbibing freely of the bold, dark Norse ale whilst munching on a basketful of freshly-fried sea delicacies. If the sun is shining, one stretches his limbs out for Sol's ministrations; if the weather be glum, one moves indoors to the hearthside and the warming pine logs, where even more genial repasts may be found."

Nuala Nyana *Udaut*, Queen of Gwynedd. She was born on the XXIst day of June in the Year of Our Lord 790, being the daughter of Micah Lord Udaut and Maralicia Lady MacCathail. She intermarried with Ifor Haldane King of Gwynedd on the VIIIth day of November in the year 806, and by him she had children: the Hereditary Prince Jashan; the Prince Alroy; the Princess Maire; the Prince Donal; the Prince Aidan later called Daniel Draper; the Princess Michaela; the Princess Ysabeau. She was murdered with all of her family save for her son Aidan by King Festil I on the XXIst day of June in the year 822, aged XXXII years exactly. R.I.P.

Nur Hallaj. This sovereign Principality, considered by some to be one of the Forcinn Buffer States but by others as lying outside that jurisdiction, is bounded by Thuria on the Northeast, Vézaire on the Northwest, Logréine on the West, Andelon on the Southwest, and the Kingdom of R'Kassi on the East.

The Principality of Nur Hallaj was founded on the XXIInd day of August in the year 797 by Sheikh Aqaq ibn Yahya ar-Rafiq al-Hajj, who took the territory from the Duchy of Joux, re-establishing a state which had previously been called in olden days the Emirate of Sakistan. The Emir Hafiz was converted to the Christian faith in the year 866, taking the name Jabez when he was baptized.

Campbell de Broun describes thusly his Ist expedition into Nur Hallaj: "It was clear and cool in the morning; we started early across the prairie which was nearly level; the wind blew cold and the road was dusty. This prairie reminded me of the account I have read of the deserts of Arabi, being one extended plain and not a stick of timber to be seen; it was a dreary-looking prairie. We crossed II drains which had putrid water in them. We could, in some places, discover timber at a great distance on both sides of the road, which induced one to believe the road went through the prairie the longest way. It was XXIII leagues to the other side, and at the West end it was a considerable distance from any timber. On a smart eminence there was a well dug and there was some kind of shelter for the workmen made of tents and poles; on this hill, at the well (which could be seen at a very great distance on each side from the road), was a handsome site for building, but everything was inconvenient. On the West corner of this prairie there were a number of others; on leaving it we proceeded some distance to an oasis and spring surrounded by date palms, the first good water we had seen since entering this God-forsaken wilderness." The capital of Nur Hallaj is Khasifa. [*The King's Justice*; *The Quest for Saint Camber*; *King Kelson's Bride*].

PRINCES AND EMIRS OF NUR HALLAJ

HOUSE OF AR-RAFIQ

Aqaq bin Yahya ar-Rafiq (Acacius)	797-815
Hakim I (Joachim) (son)	815-846
Basiliyus (Basil) (nephew)	846-860
Hafiz (Jabez) (son)	860-892
Ayyub (Job) (son)	892-911
Ya'qub (Jacob) (brother)	911-916
Ilyas I (Elias) (son)	916-944
Afram (Ephrem) (son)	944-955
Jirjis (George) (nephew)	955-982
Ishaq (Isaac) (son)	982-1009
Ilyas II (Elias) (son)	1009-1038
Yunan (Jonah) (son)	1038
Shim'un (Simon) (brother)	1038-1044
Ibrahim (Abraham) (brother)	1044-1049
Dawud (David) (brother)	1049-1069
Yuhanna (John) (son)	1069-1091
Qais (Gaius) (nephew)	1091-1111
Hakim II (Joachim) (son)	1111-1130+

Nyford. Located in the Southernmost part of Carthane is the city of Nyford, which is situate at the point where the Lendour River enters the Eirian, on the Northern bank of the former. It was attacked, burned, and looted by Moorish invaders on the XXXIst day of May in the year 707. Formerly just a sleepy river port, consisting of little more than a dock and a warehouse, it was chosen by the new King Imre on the VIth day of January in the year 901 to become Gwynedd's new capital city, and a heavy tax was laid on every adult male in the realm to finance the construction. In November of the year 903 some C peasants died of exposure, and XXXII others were killed when an earthworks collapsed. Construction on the new capital was abandoned after the fall of King Imre on the IInd day of December in the year 904; however, both humans and Deryni moved into the abandoned building sites, and a thriving community sprang up. The water trade soon became firmly established, centered on Nyford's fine, well-sheltered harbour, the last Gwyneddan port in the mouth of the vast Eirian Estuary. A group of Forcinn Michaelines organized a sea-service out of Nyford, hiring on as pilots for the river ships which plied the waters North to Rhemuth and West into Llannedd and East into the Mooryn as well as on their native sea.

According to Volumen III of the *Legends*, in the Summer of the year 916, during "the heat of a particularly severe summer, tempers had seethed with the rising temperature and humidity of the Nyford Delta, and little was needed to spark the fire of violence. Rioting peasants led by local human barons had destroyed the town and slaughtered most of its inhabitants. Nyford had burned for a day and a night, but not before rampaging humans had put to death all the Deryni and Deryni sympathizers who could be found. Deryni-owned or -piloted ships were burned to the waterline where they lay at the quays, after being robbed of their cargoes. Deryni shops were vandalized and looted, their proprietors usually dying in the process. The *schola* was brought down stone by stone, after all its pupils and masters were put to the sword or clubbed to death, many no more than children. Saint Camber's-at-Nyford, church and school, was desecrated and torched, after the sacrilegious murder of the brothers and sisters of the Order which had founded it, most of them not even Deryni. The piles of bodies lining the streets fueled fires whose smoke besmirched the clean skies above the delta for most of the week."

Located just outside of town is the Cathedral of the Bishop of Nyford and the Palace of the Earls of Carthane. To the Northeast lies Saint Illtyd's Abbey. A weapon shop was located here in the XIth century. [*Camber of Culdi*; *Saint Camber*; *Camber the Heretic*; *King Javan's Year*; *High Deryni*; *King Kelson's Bride*]. See also: Mairi.

Nygel Rhys Owain *Haldane*, King of Gwynedd. He was born on the XXXth day of September in the Year of Our Lord 948, being the eldest son and heir of Uthyr King of Gwynedd and Grania MacInnis Countess of Culdi in her own right. He intermarried with Susanta Lady Eastmarch daughter of Kennet Howell Earl of Eastmarch and Tanya Lady Marley on the Vth day of August in the year 970, and by her he had children: the Hereditary Prince Corban Cinhil, dead at age X of the consumptive complaint; the Princess Bethanne, who intermarried with Keyne Prince of Llannedd, leaving issue; the Prince Quinnell later Duke of Carthmoor, dead at age II of the rosy rash; the Princess Venecia, who entered the convent of Saint Glaphyra under the name Sister Justyna; the Princess Mavourneen, who intermarried with Brynley Lord Cormine, leaving issue. The Princess Susanta died in childbirth on the XVth of October in the year 979. At the time of his death the King Nygel was betrothed to the Princess Cassia daughter of Lludd II King of Llannedd; she later intermarried with Hamon Sovereign Prince of Pardiac in The Connait.

The Prince Nygel succeeded his father on the XVIth day of September in the year 980, and was crowned at Valoret on Michaelmas by Halsten del Borgo Archbishop Primate of Valoret and All Gwynedd. On the XIIth day of August in the year 983 the Prince Imre II Pretender of Gwynedd attacked the city of Marbury, killing Brian Coris Earl of Marley. On the XVIIth day instant the King Nygel received news of Imre's invasion, and began assembling his Gwyneddan levies at Rhemuth. On the XXIVth day of the same month he set forth from Rhemuth with part of his army, arriving at Valoret III days later. Gathering additional soldiers from the local Barons, he proceeded North on the XXXth day of the month, using forced marches to move quickly through the Iomaire Plain. On the IIIrd day of September the II armies met just East of Old Argoed.

Historians differ on just what happened next. Rhuddlad ap Llanrhydd states: "The King Nygel moved too quickly to respond to the Festillic threat. His forces were uncoordinated and inexperienced. It had been more than a generation since the last incursion from Torenth, and none of his commanders had ever participated in anything more than minor skirmishes. Imre's levies were battle-hardened and well organized, and rested from their previous encounter with Marley's men; they picked the ground they wanted to defend even before the Gwynneddans arrived. King Nygel never had a chance."

However, Veranus of Thier, who was present at the battle, states: "It was the luck of the Devil. Good King Nygel had roused our spirits mightily, and we had all been blessed by Archbishop William before leaving Valoret. We were determined and ready to drive the bloody Festils from the field. But in the midst of the attack, when the sun was still high, King Nygel took a dart in his belly just twixt the slats of his mail, and had to be dragged to his tent. After that the heart just seemed to go out of the men. They fought till dusk, but the day was lost. We retreated during the night, and the King died that evening in his litter."

The King Nygel was XXXV years of age at his death, and was succeeded by his younger brother, the Prince Jasher Earl of Culdi. His body was returned to Rhemuth for burial in the crypt of the Haldanes beneath Saint George's Cathedral. R.I.P.

Oksana Urbane Adeléonore *Soubize Ramsay-Quinnell*, Duchess of Laas. She was born on the XXIst day of January in the year 1080, being the second daughter of Néron Sieur Grande-Grèce d'Enghieux in Fallon and the Lady Origène daughter of Réhon von Horthy Comte du Nouveau-Richemont in Tralia and Lady Chaville de Jordanet. She intermarried with Sir Jolyon Ramsay-Quinnell on the XXIInd day of May in the year 1102, and by him she had children: Sir Brecon Jolyon Jameson later Hereditary Duke of Laas and Earl of Kilarden and Culdi, who intermarried with the Princess Richelle Haldane Countess of Culdi; Judhael Jubal, dead at age V of the slimy slough; Noelie Quintilla, who intermarried with Prince Rory Haldane later Duke of Ratharkin; Dafydd Urban, who entered the Order of Saint Cyran in the year 1125 under the name Brother Christophle Urbanus; Taxila Oksana, who perished at age III of vescicance; Edwyn Colin, dead at age VI of the morning miasma. She traveled with her family to Rhemuth in the Summer of the year 1127 for the betrothal of her eldest son to Princess Richelle Haldane, and again in the year 1128 for the joint wedding of her son and daughter to Princess Richelle and Prince Rory Haldane, which event took place on the XXXIst day of July. She had dark hair and eyes, and was tall and graceful. [*King Kelson's Bride*].

Old Ones. They were the original gods of the pagan religion of Eistenmark and Tretelgia. Statues of the Old Ones are still displayed in the main temple of Eistenfalla. ["Trial"].

Oliver Ugo *de Nore*, Archbishop Primate of Valoret and All Gwynedd. This native of Nyford was born on the XIVth day of January in the Year of Our Lord 1041, being the son of Sir Marcus Eugenius de Nore and Flaura Lady Matin. He was ordained priest on the XXth day of May in the year 1060, and was consecrated an itinerant Bishop of Gwynedd on the IIIrd day of June in the year 1079. He spent most of the next II decades in his native Carthane, where he was known as a rabid burner of suspected Deryni heretics. He was elected

Archbishop Primate of Valoret and All Gwynedd on the Xth day of September in the year 1102 in succession to Paul Tollendal. On the I^st day of August in the year 1104 he appeared at the *Arx Fidei* Seminary near Valoret for the ordination of the seminarians there, and brought his own *merasha*-treated wine to be used in the ceremony. Father Jorian de Courcy, a Deryni, was thereby uncovered for what he was, and Archbishop Oliver presided over his trial on the I^st day of September in that year, condemning the young priest to death. Father Jorian was burned at the stake on the XIth day of November following.

The Archbishop Oliver had a discriminating palate for fine wines, often sending specimens of specific vintages to certain prelates as a sign of his personal favour. It was he who promoted the career of the like-minded priest, Father Edmund Loris, who eventually succeeded him, and also encouraged another young priest, Father Lawrence Gorony, whom he appointed Chaplain of his own establishment on the XIIIth day of February in the year 1104. The Archbishop Oliver died liverish from an overindulgence in spirits on the XXIInd day of December in the year 1114, aged LXXIII years.

In his later years he would often fall asleep during the longer sessions of important meetings and services, which events were wryly noted by some of the younger members of the clergy as a visitation of the "holy spirits" upon the Primate. *Successus improborum plures allicit.* ["The Priesting of Arilan"].

Ordo Verbi Dei (Order of the Word of God). Also known as the Order of Saint Jarlath, this cloistered contemplative Order was founded on the VIth day of January in the year 564, and spread rapidly throughout the Kingdom of Gwynedd, although not much beyond its borders. From the very beginning each of the monasteries of this Order was considered autonomous, with a Vicar General being elected at a general meeting to provide overall direction and leadership, and to adjudicate disputes between the local chapters. Thus, each abbey of this Order maintained its own local Rules and standards of dress, adhering only to the general principles written down by Saint Jarlath, the founder of the Order, plus any amendments to the Rule established by the agreement of all chapters at later general meetings.

The Order's many establishments included: the Mother House of Saint Jarlath's Abbey near Barwicke in the North Lendour Mountains, whose Abbot in the early 900s was Father Gregory of Arden, and whose habits featured burgundy for its Abbot, deep grey for its monks, and brown for its lay brothers; Saint Piran's Priory North of Saint Jarlath's and Valoret, whose Prior in the early 900s was Father Stephen, and whose habits featured white for its Prior, grey for its lay brothers, and black for its novices; Saint Foillan's Abbey in the Lendour Mountains Southeast of Valoret, whose Abbot in the early 900s was Father Zephram of Lorda and its Prior Father Patrick, and whose habits featured white for its Abbot and monks, and grey for its lay brothers; Saint Ultan's Priory on the Southwest coast of Mooryn; Saint Illtyd's Priory on the River Carthane Northeast of Nyford; and Saint Stefan's Priory near Carbury.

Vicars General of this Order in the early X^th century included: Robert Oriss later Archbishop of Rhemuth, and his successor, Zephram of Lorda later Bishop of Cashien. A choir drawn from different chapters of this Order provided the traditional hymn sung at the coronation of King Alroy on the XXVth day of May in the year 917, the monks wearing burgundy habits for the occasion. One of the best-known monks of this Order was Brother Benedict of Saint Foillan's Abbey, later known as Cinhil I King of Gwynedd. [*Camber of Culdi*; *Camber the Heretic*; *Deryni Challenge*; *The Harrowing of Gwynedd*].

Ordo Vox Dei (Order of the Voice of God). This religious group was founded by Brother Cyriac of Issel on the XXVIth day of May in the Year of Our Lord 1034 to foster the belief that individuals should each speak directly with God on both private and public occasions. The Order was not officially sanctioned until the rebellion of Theophylact Archbishop of Valoret in the year 1067, when the Grand Abbot of the Order, Michael of Kheldour, was instrumental in restoring the old Synod to power in the person of the new Archbishop Balthasar d'Archiac, and was rewarded for his devotion by being elevated to the See of Grecotha. The Order spread very rapidly thereafter, and had become popular in Gwynedd by the XIIth century. In March of the year 1125 an unknown member of this Order spoke out at the Synod of Valoret. One of the better-known members of this group was Father Bevan de Torigny, its Abbot in the year 1122, when he was elected itinerant Bishop. The monks of this Order wore black habits with blue girdles. [*The Quest for Saint Camber*].

Oriel *de Bourg*, Lord. This Deryni Healer was born on the XVth day of November in the Year of Our Lord 896, being the son of Osmer Lord de Bourg and Xenia Lady Greenlee. He intermarried with Alana Destaing on the IInd day of June in the year 916, and by her he had one daughter: the Lady Karis, who intermarried with Tieg Lord Thuryn. Lord Oriel was summoned to Valoret Castle on the XXVIIIth of May in the year 917 to heal Tavis's injured hand. Later that year he was impressed into the Regents' service through vile threats to his family, particularly from Bishop Hubert MacInnis and Tammaron Earl Fitz-Arthur; his wife and infant daughter were held hostage for his continued good behaviour. He was present at the trial of the Deryni assassins on the XXVIIIth day of September in the year 917.

He was ordered to make contact with Declan Carmody, the Deryni attached to Rhun Earl of Sheele's forces, on the XXIVth day of December in that same year, and to convey a mental message from the Regents. He attempted to heal Declan on the XXIInd day of January in the year 918. On the XXXth day of March following he interrupted Prince Javan while the latter was reading King Alroy's mind, and realized that Javan had shields and other mental powers; he pledged to support the Prince in whatever way he could.

The Lord Oriel was present at the death of King Alroy from consumption on the XXIIIrd day of June in the year 921, which he could delay but not prevent. The new King Javan arranged for a brief reunion between Oriel and his family in the Summer of that year. He attended the coronation of King Javan on the XXXIst day of July in the year 921. On the following day Javan ordered that Oriel not be compelled by the former Regents to heal the fatally injured Murdoch Earl of Carthane, but Oriel offered to give him relief from the pain anyway, the offer being refused.

He was attacked by the Deryni Sitric and others at the instigation of the former Regents on the XXth day of March in the year 922, but was saved by King Javan, Sir Guiscard, and Sir Charlan, and subsequently recovered from his wounds. This devoted practitioner of the Healer's Art was described as "having blond hair with a reddish beard framing a haunted visage. He was a tortured soul, forced by love for his family into using his powers in ways which were unacceptable to his creed. He made the most of an intolerable situation and soldiered on to the best of his abilities, easing pain where he could, and doing as little harm as possible, given his predicament." He was murdered by the former Regents during their *coup d'état* of the XIth day of May in the year 922, being aged XXV years at his death. However, his wife and child were saved by Étienne Baron de Courcy and taken by him to the old Michaeline Haven. R.I.P. [*Camber the Heretic*; *The Harrowing of Gwynedd*; *King Javan's Year*; *The Bastard Prince*].

Orin. This great Deryni adept and mystic is said to have been born on the IInd day of October in the Year of Our Lord 604; his parentage is unknown, although some Torenthi writers have suggested that he was descended from the Deryni mage Mahael through the latter's elder son Asahel, and thus distantly related to the House of Furstán in Torenth. He was perhaps best known as the author of *The Protocols of Orin* and the *Codex Orini*, the latter containing a collection of many potent spells of Deryni magic, including: "Holding off Death," "Conversation with the Holy Guardian Angel," "Preserving Life Beyond Death and Bringing Life Back Out of Death." The *Protocols* are arranged in V major sections, being The Black Protocol, The Vermillion Protocol, The Golden-Yellow Protocol, The Green Protocol, and The Royal Blue Protocol. He also penned several compelling works of religious poetry. A number of his works have apparently been lost, among them the *Organi Orini*, *Flexus Cæli*, *Silentium Agnorum*, and *Canis Mortuus Est*.

Orin was also known in ancient times as a teacher and adviser. He established the *Templum Archangelorum* in the year 634 to train Deryni masters and healers, following on the efforts of Saint Varnar, and is said by some scholars to have written the hymn *Adsum Domine*, although others state that he took an existing verse and made it an integral part of the practice of the healing arts. In the year 645 he supported the aspirations of Augarin Haldane to make himself King of Gwynedd and Aurel Haldane to establish a free and independent Church at Valoret. He later trained the well-known Deryni scholar and mystic, the Lady Jodotha. He died on the XVIIIth day of August in the year 675, aged LXX years, and was buried in an ancient chamber beneath Grecotha.

Camber Earl of Culdi proposed on the XXIInd day of June in the year 905 that the Gwyneddan Council of War use a kind of divination described in Orin's *Protocols* to determine the kind of magic being wrought by the Pretender Ariella. On the IInd day of July in that year The Yellow Protocol was used by Father Joram MacRorie, Evaine Lady Thuryn, and Rhys Lord Thuryn to help reintegrate Father Alister Cullen's memories with Camber Earl of Culdi's. Orin's *Protocols* were again consulted by Evaine Thuryn on the XVth day of June in the year 918 to find some method for releasing Camber's soul.

Orin's body was found covered with a net of *shiral* crystals on its bier beneath Grecotha by Father Joram, Lady Evaine, and Dom Queron on the XIXth day of April in the year 918, but passed to dust when touched by them, as did that of his disciple, Jodotha, which lay beside the bier. Beneath his body were II scrolls, one of them being the infamous Fifth Protocol, "The Scroll of Daring," and the other the *Codex Orini*. They also recovered II ivory wands and a ring owned by Orin. Orin's burial garments included a cloak of bird feathers stitched to a backing of scarlet silk over an ankle-length tunic of fine violet wool with a motif of solar crosses embroidered along the sleeve. His hands were holding a dower coin set in a locket which also contained a strand of Jodotha's hair and her portrait. He was a tall, well-made man. *Tuta scelera esse possunt; secura non possunt.* [*Saint Camber*; *Camber the Heretic*; *The Harrowing of Gwynedd*; *The King's Justice*; *King Kelson's Bride*].

Oriolt *de Jong*, Father. He was born on the XVIIth day of October in the Year of Our Lord 1083, being the son of Sir Bernin de Jong and Erica Lady Faustworthy. He was ordained at the *Arx Fidei* Seminary with Father Jorian de Courcy on the Ist day of August in the year 1104, and rescued the ciborium that Father Jorian nearly dropped when the *merasha* overtook him. Later that night Denis Arilan and others questioned him regarding the events surrounding Jorian's discovery by the Archbishop Oliver's men. ["The Priesting of Arilan"].

Orsal and Tralia. This sovereign Principality is situate South of Torenth on the Eastern shore of the Twin Rivers estuary, being bounded on the North by the County of Fathane and the Duchy of Marluk in Torenth, on the South by the River Thuria and across that waterway by the Duchy of Joux and the Principality of Thuria, on the East by the Duchy of Lorsöl and the County of Vechta in Torenth, and on the Southeast by the River Khabur and across that waterway by the Kingdom of R'Kassi. The capital of this state is the city of Orsalis, situate on the coast of Tralia at the mouth of the River Thuria.

The Isle of Orsal in the delta of the River Thuria was occupied in the IInd century by the Byzantyuns, who erected a trading station called Ouros and later Orsal, the site being easily defended with an excellent harbour, and accessible to all of the main trade routes of the Twin Rivers and the Southern Sea. The station was abandoned in the year 486 with the final withdrawal of the Empire from the West. The Rûman trader Horatius was established there by the year 500, and declared himself Comes Orsalis on the XIVth day of April in the year 506. His son, Quintus or Quint, began using the title Hort of Orsal after he succeeded his father in the year 518, and had soon adopted the surname Horthy.

By the mid-VIth century the Horts had established forts on both the Northern and Southern banks of the River Thuria, but were opposed in their efforts to extend their control inland by the Princes of East and West Tralia. The region now known as Joux was conquered in the year 588, but was given as a dowry in the year 661 to the Princess Romana von Horthy, who intermarried with Béraud Buyenne I[st] Duc du Joux. Thus was established the principle whereby V of the sovereign states of Forcinn—Joux, Vézaire, Thuria, Logréine, and Nur Hallaj—have continued to pledge their fealty to Orsal and Tralia.

On the IInd day of June in the year 603 His High-Highness Hewney von Horthy intermarried with the Princess Dorothea Heiress of West Tralia, and presented the Princess with a pair of ruby-encrusted slippers as a token of his undying thanks. The Duchy of Kormanant was conquered in the year 802, and East Tralia acceded to Orsal when the last ruler thereof, Prince Yordan de Vitry, died without heirs on the XIXth day of March in the year 847, and by his last will and testament left his nation to His Hortic Majesty. The Hort of Orsal then assumed the additional title of Prince of Tralia. Much of this Eastern part of Tralia consists of salt bush and scrub, being unfit for cultivation or even for grazing, but providing excellent hunting of the tri-antlered antelope and the lustrous lupesculus during the waning months of Autumn. The Princess Hortensia von Horthy wrote in her *Leme on a Lepine Leavetaking* that "nothing could be finer than a lambent Lepusiner," but Madame Stavroula notes in her *Commentary on Corolary* that "the Lady Hortensia had no sense of taste or smell in her latter years, making any invitations to her *soirées des lapins* eminently resistible."

On the XXVth day of May in the year 918 the Hort Uriel attended the birthday celebration of King Alroy in Rhemuth, presenting him with a bolt of gold-shot scarlet silk. The Duchy of Corwyn has always enjoyed good relations with Orsal, for together they control the Twin Rivers leading into the Torenthi heartland and into Gwynedd. However, the Hort's relations with the Kingdom of R'Kassi to the Southeast were sufficiently troubled in November of the year 1120 that the Hort did not attend the coronation of King Kelson on the XVth day instant, instead sending his eldest son and heir, Prince Cyric. The following year the Hort's IInd son, Prince Rogan, was squired to Alaric Morgan Duke of Corwyn on the XXVth day of March in the year 1121. It is said that the House of Horthy is related to all of the Royal families of the XI Regni. The banners of this nation feature a silver sea lion with tail raised, on a sea-green field. [*Deryni Rising*; *Deryni Checkmate*; *King Kelson's Bride*].

HORTS OF ORSAL AND PRINCES OF TRALIA

HOUSE OF HORTHY

Horatius I	506-518
Quintus (son)	518-542
Roybin I (son)	542-562
Trystan (son)	562-589
Hewney (nephew)	589-611
Wilfred (son)	611-630
Horthy (or Horatius) II (son)	630-655
Rogan (brother)	655-661
Raynulf (son)	661-698
Turpion (grandson)	698-731
Wulfram (uncle)	731-732
Waryn (son)	732-755
Ulick I (son)	755-788
Blandyn (cousin)	788-801
Cadenat (son)	801-831
Hungus (son)	831-833
Peador (nephew)	833-888
Ulick II (son)	888-893
Uriel (brother)	893-918
Udes (son)	918-962
Cyric I (cousin)	962-977
Erastus (son)	977-992
Makonnen (brother)	992-1008
Adémar (brother)	1008-1018
Roybin II (cousin)	1018
Olivier (grandson of Cyric I)	1018-1049
Cyric II (son)	1049-1074
Sobbon (son)	1074-1101
Létald (son)	1101-1130+

Östmarcke. This Duchy of Eastern Torenth is situate to the West of the Duchy d'Arjenol, South of the Duchy of Nördmarcke, East of the Duchy of Beldouria, and North of the Duchy of Vorna. The County of Östmarcke was created by King Lajos I for his son, Prince Tamás, in the year 813, and it passed to his nephew III years later. After the extinction of this line in the year 925, the King Arion I gave the Honour as a Grand Duchy *ad personam* to his brother, Prince Torval, who passed it to his youngest son, Prince Ringan. The capital of Östmarcke is Oldburg. [*King Kelson's Bride*].

DUKES OF ÖSTMARCKE

HOUSE OF FURSTÁN VON ÖSTMARCKE

Tamás (Count; son of King Lajos I)	813-816
Örs (nephew)	816-843
Zsíros (nephew)	843-876
Bolgár (son)	876-887
Borjú (brother)	887-893
Bánat (brother)	893-902
Borús (brother)	902-925
Torval I (Grand Duke; son of King Nimur I)	926-981
Ringan (Duke; son)	981-1007
Torval II (son)	1007-1029
Rollin (grandson)	1029-1060
Giscon (cousin)	1060-1066
Torval III (son)	1066-1091
Levi (son)	1091-1093
Torony (brother)	1093-1106
Václáv (nephew)	1106-1130+

Ostrythe, Dowager Princess of Meara, Princess of Cassan, Mother of the Convent of Saint Balbina, Saint. She was born at Ballymar on the XXIIIrd day of March in the Year of Our Lord 740, being the daughter of Oster Lord Ballymar and Rumona Lady ffoxx. She intermarried with Janus Sovereign Prince of Meara on the XIIth day of May in the year 758, and by him she had children: the Princess Janusine; the Hereditary Prince Alphonse later Sovereign Prince of Cassan.

Following the premature death of Prince Janus on the XVIth day of November in the year 762, the Prince Armon younger brother of Janus seized the Throne of Meara, and the Dowager Princess Ostrythe fled North to her native city of Ballymar, taking her young children with her. There she raised the standard of revolt, declaring her son Prince of Meara. But although she rallied the clans and clergy of Cassan behind her, she lacked the military strength to invade Meara proper; and Prince Armon was unable to dislodge his sister-in-law from her stronghold. On the VIth day of August in the year 770, after VIII years of intermittent fighting, the Princess Ostrythe and the Prince Armon agreed to recognize Cassan as a separate autonomous state, giving each family mutual rights of succession should the other line ever become extinct, a proviso which was later ignored.

After her son married, the Princess Ostrythe took the veil in the year 780 at the Convent of Saint Balbina, but its relaxed Rule did not suit her refined nature. She left this house in the year 783 to found her own Abbey, Saint Anastasia's, with a much stricter Rule under her own careful guidance, in which she sought to organize the ladies of the nobility into an establishment catering to the less fortunate members of society. For it is said that she believed in the efficacy of broth and bread to alleviate the hunger of the poor, and to meet this need she built a series of roadside shelters throughout Cassan, where her Ladies of the Lord would ladle out bowls of soup from the large cauldrons which were kept constantly a-boil there. Any poor soul who wandered by was fed for the asking, but in return they had to listen to the dear nuns preaching the Word of God. For as Saint Ostrythe was fond of saying, "There was none such thing as a free meal."

From this time forward she was constantly opening new houses and shelters everywhere in Cassan, smoothing away the difficulties for her sisters and placating those in power, who often opposed her and called her the most despicable of names, such as the "roving nun." She insisted upon eating always at her own establishments, supping only on broth and bread for II decades, and being favoured throughout this period with the most remarkable mystical experiences, which she described quite readily to anyone she met, and also recorded same in XLV volumes of iambic pentameter verse in the classic style, several of which have now, alas, been lost, but the surviving tomes of which are most heartily recommended for all demure young ladies everywhere. She died on the XVth day of October in the year 802, aged LXII years.

She is the patroness of cooks, tavern keepers, and poets, and is frequently depicted having her heart pierced by an arrow held by an angel, or holding a piercèd heart, book, and crucifix. A small convent dedicated to her name is located between Ebor and Sheele. King Rhys Michael sought refuge here in the year 928, and died of his wounds a few days later on the XXVIIIth day of June. Her feastday is the IVth day of August. *Dieu n'a créé les femmes que pour apprivoiser les hommes.* [*The Bastard Prince*]. See also: Saint Ostrythe's Convent.

Oswin Roybin Armin *von Horthy*, Prince d'Orsal and Tralia. He was born on the XVIth day of November in the Year of Our Lord 1124, being the fourth son of Létald Hort of Orsal and Prince of Tralia and Husniyya Sharifa of R'Kassi. [*King Kelson's Bride*].

Owain Javan Cinhil *Haldane*, King of Gwynedd. He was born on the XXIXth day of February in the Year of Our Lord 924, being the eldest surviving son and heir of Rhys Michael King of Gwynedd and Michaela Lady Drummond. He intermarried with Anne Lady Fitz-Arthur Quinnell on the IInd day of May in the year 947, and by her he had one child: the Princess Marisa, dead at the age of I week of the flux.

The Prince Owain succeeded his father on the XXVIIIth day of June in the year 928, being proclaimed King on the IInd day of July following, and his Haldane potential was set by Queen Michaela and Rhysel Thuryn on the next evening. He was crowned on the XXIXth day of September in the year 928 by Ailin Mac-Gregor Archbishop Primate of Valoret and All Gwynedd. As a boy, he had a set of toy knights made for him by his uncle, Cathan Lord Drummond. He attained his majority on the Ist day of March in the year 938, at which time the Regency Council was disbanded.

In the year 948 the King Owain was killed during the invasion of Gwynedd by Marek I Pretender of Gwynedd. He was XXIV years of age at his death, and was succeeded by his younger brother, the Prince Uthyr. His body was returned for burial in the crypt of his ancestors in Saint George's Cathedral in Rhemuth. R.I.P. [*The Bastard Prince*].

Owen *Mathisson*. This soldier was serving Warin de Grey in the year 1121. His legs were crushed in an accident, but his injuries were healed by Warin at Coroth in June of that year. [*High Deryni*].

Padrig *Udaut*, Lord Varagh. He was born on the XIVth day of February in the Year of Our Lord 1104, being the second but eldest surviving son and heir of Trevor Baron Varagh and Fathana Lady Carcashale, and a cousin of Sean Earl Derry, whom he was serving as page in May of the year 1115. ["The Knighting of Derry"].

Pargan *Howiccan*. This Deryni lyric poet who lived circa the year 800 is best known for his rousing epic sagas of the old High Gods of the Deryni, which are often cited as particularly fine examples of high adventure and declamation. Part of his work, *Canto IV: Being the Rise of the Lleassi and Johanan's Quest*, was being translated from the original dialect by Evaine Lady MacRorie and Camber Earl of Culdi on the XXVIIth day of September in the year 903 at Tor Caerrorie. With this manuscript, in the same repository, Camber also found a copy of the *Protocols of Orin*. [*Camber of Culdi; Saint Camber; Camber the Heretic; The Harrowing of Gwynedd*].

Patrick, Abbot of Saint Foillan's Abbey, Brother. In December of the year 903 Brother Patrick was Prior of Saint Foillan's Abbey and a subordinate of Abbot Zephram of Lorda. He reported to the Abbot on the Vth

day of that month that Brother Benedict (Prince Cinhil) was missing. He was later elected Abbot in succession to Zephram on the xv[th] day of April in the year 915. [*Camber of Culdi*; *Camber the Heretic*].

Patrick, Brother. He was one of Revan's reformed Deryni Willimite disciples in June of the year 918. [*The Harrowing of Gwynedd*].

Patrick II Pallascus *Corrigan*, **Archbishop of Rhemuth.** He was born on the xxii[nd] day of November in the Year of Our Lord 1055, being the son of Pallas Corrigan and Amy Fù. He was ordained priest on the ii[nd] day of January in the year 1073, consecrated an itinerant Bishop on the xix[th] day of October in the year 1088, and appointed Auxiliary Bishop to William MacCartney Archbishop of Rhemuth in the year 1105. He was elected successor to Alexander Darby Archbishop of Rhemuth on the xxiii[rd] day of March in the year 1117. With Edmund Loris Archbishop Primate of Valoret and All Gwynedd, he served as co-leader of the anti-Deryni faction of the Gwyneddan clergy. He and his supporters were defeated in their efforts to attaint Alaric Morgan Duke of Corwyn in the year 1121. He died of pains in the chest on the last day of October in the same year, aged LXV years, before action could be taken against him. King Kelson then decided that he should be buried with full honours together with his predecessors in the crypt of Saint George's Cathedral in Rhemuth. He is described as "a bear of a man— somewhat gruff, with bushy, grizzled brows and grasping pudgy hands. He was not particularly well-liked." R.I.P. [*Deryni Rising*; *Deryni Checkmate*; *High Deryni*; *The Bishop's Heir*].

Paul, Brother. He was serving as a monk at Saint Foillan's Abbey in November of the year 903. He assisted "Brother Benedict" when the latter fainted during Rhys Lord Thuryn and Camber Earl of Culdi's visit there on the xiv[th] day instant. [*Camber of Culdi*].

Paul *de Gendas*. He was serving as a lieutenant to Warin de Grey in the year 1121. [*Deryni Checkmate*; *High Deryni*].

Paulin *Sinclair* **of Ramos, Vicar General of the** ***Custodes Fidei*, sometime Bishop of Stavenham, sometime Vicar General of the Little Brothers of Saint Ercon, Lord.** He was born on the xth day of September in the Year of Our Lord 878, being the younger son of Bonner I Sinclair Earl of Tarleton and Nieve Lady O Nuallain, and the stepson of Tammaron Earl Fitz-Arthur, and the brother of Peter Sinclair Earl of Tarleton later Lord Albertus. He was early destined for the Church, and was ordained priest on the vii[th] day of March in the year 897; one of his classmates was Father Secorim, who was ordained on the same day. He founded the Little Brothers of Saint Ercon, an anti-Deryni teaching order, on the xxx[th] day of April in the year 912.

He was elected an itinerant Bishop of Gwynedd by the Synod of Bishops at Valoret on the xii[th] day of November in the year 917, and was translated as I[st] Bishop to the newly formed see of Stavenham on the xxvii[th] day instant. However, he never actually occupied his see, and resigned that office to found the *Custodes Fidei* on the ii[nd] day of February in the year 918, being named I[st] Vicar General of the Order. The Little Brothers of Saint Ercon were merged into the Order at this time. On the xi[th] day of June in the year 921 he recruited a rogue Deryni named Master Dimitri, whom he used to further his own ends and those of the former Regents. However, Dimitri later proved to be an agent of Prince Miklós of Torenth. Paulin attended the coronation of King Javan on the xxxi[st] day of July in that year. He ordered his brother Lord Albertus to murder Father Faelan on the xth day of October following.

Bishop Paulin accompanied the Royal Expedition to Eastmarch on the xv[th] day of June in the year 928, and was attacked by the devious Dimitri on the xx[th] day of that month. His mind was ripped and he severed his own tongue in his agony. He died without regaining his senses at Saint Cassian's Abbey on the xxiv[th] day of June, aged XLIX years, and was buried in the crypt there beside his brother, Lord Albertus. He was temporarily succeeded by Father Lior as Acting Vicar General. [*Camber the Heretic*; *The Harrowing of Gwynedd*; *King Javan's Year*; *The Bastard Prince*].

***Pax Romana* or *Rûmana*.** This complex network of treaties and protocols bound together the many kingdoms and other states of the ancient world for the purposes of communication, trade, and commerce amongst the signatory nations. The original document was proposed in the year 435 by Gaius Sempronius Gracchus, Grand Consul of Rûm, and was ratified by Etruskia, Byzantyun, Aigyptos, Asshyr, Samisrael, Grecia, and Kibris, with other states joining at later dates. Under this *détente* major roads and shipping lanes were vouchsafed, messengers and ambassadors were protected, and commerce was encouraged. The system began to fail in the late vii[th] century as the Moors and Norsemen grew active, and had broken down completely by the reign of Llarik King of Gwynedd. [*The Harrowing of Gwynedd*].

Payne Malcolm Saer Augarin *Haldane*, **Prince of Gwynedd, Duke of Travlum.** He was born on the xxx[th] day of August in the Year of Our Lord 1115, being the third son of Nigel Duke of Carthmoor and Meraude Lady de Treharne. He was betrothed to the Princess Stanisha daughter of Lionel II late Duke d'Arjenol on the xiv[th] day of November in the year 1128, the marriage to take place in the year 1136.

Prince Payne served as a page to the King at Rhemuth beginning in March of the year 1121. He was present at his brother Conall's wedding on the xi[th] day of April in the year 1125. He traveled with King Kelson on his trip to Torenth in the Summer of the Year 1128. On the xx[th] day of July, after returning to Orsal by ship downriver from Beldour, he was transported directly to Rhemuth by Duncan and Nivard. He was created Duke of Travlum by King Kelson when he attained his majority on the xxx[th] day of August in the year 1129. *Tu pol si sapis, Quod scis nescis.* [*Deryni Checkmate*; *High Deryni*; *The Bishop's Heir*; *The King's Justice*; *The Quest for Saint Camber*; *King Kelson's Bride*].

Pelagog. This Earldom is situate on the Western coast of the Duchy of Cassan. The Honour was first granted by King Uthyr to Glynway Lord Heavysege on the VIth day of January in the year 949, for services rendered in the recent war. Its banners were represented in the army of Kelson King of Gwynedd in June of the year 1121. Its capital is Porgonnedd. [*High Deryni*].

EARLS OF PELAGOG

HOUSE OF HEAVYSEGE

Glynway Heavysege	949-983
Abner (grandson)	983-1017
Almer (brother)	1017-1026
Carlin (uncle)	1026-1028
Garver (son)	1028-1033
Bodham (son)	1033-1067
Rodwell (son)	1067-1102
Conway (brother)	1102-1105
Albree (nephew)	1105-1130+

Perris, Lord Stard, General. He was born on the VIth day of December in the Year of Our Lord 1079, being the second son of Peleg Baron Stard and Bonaventura Lady Tallien. He intermarried with Elise Lady Idlewylde on the XXVth day of October in the year 1102, and by her he had children: the Lady Pelegra; the Lady Armentaria; the Lady Evanta; the Lady Justa; the Lady Perrisa. He was serving as I of the military advisers for Kelson King of Gwynedd during the war between Torenth and Gwynedd in the year 1121. He was also present at the Christmas Council which discussed the developing Mearan Crisis in the year 1123. [*High Deryni*; *The Bishop's Heir*].

Peter *Davency*. This soldier was serving Bran Coris Earl of Marley in June of the year 1121. He was killed by Sean O'Flynn Earl Derry at Llyndruth Meadows on the XXIst day instant. [*High Deryni*].

Peter *Sinclair*, sometime Earl of Tarleton, later called Lord Albertus, Grand Master of the *Equites Custodum Fidei*, Earl Marshal of Gwynedd, Sir. He was born on the XIth day of February in the Year of Our Lord 877, being the eldest son and heir of Bonner I Sinclair Earl of Tarleton and Nieve Lady O Nuallain, and the elder brother of Paulin Sinclair. He intermarried with Saskia Lady O'Conor on the I[st] day of March in the year 898, and by her he had children: the Hereditary Count Bonner later Bonner II Earl of Tarleton; the Lady Trilla; the Lady Neva.

The Lord Peter succeeded his father as Earl on the XXVIIIth day of December in the year 890. He was knighted by King Blaine I on the VIth day of January in the year 891. The Earl was present with Rhun Earl of Sheele at the sack of Saint Neot's Abbey on the XXIVth day of December in the year 917. He also attended the state banquet held in Valoret on the Xth day of January in the year 918 to celebrate the nuptials of Earl Rhun and Lord Richard Murdoch. On the XXIXth day instant he resigned his title in favour of his son, and assumed the religious name of Lord Albertus, being appointed Grand Master of the *Equites Custodum Fidei*, the military arm of the *Custodes Fidei*, when that suborder was established on the IInd day of February in that year. He was named Earl Marshal of Gwynedd on the XXVth day of May in the year 919, and in that guise inaugurated the Accession Council of King Javan on the XXIIIrd day of June in the year 921. He attended the coronation of King Javan on the XXXIst day of July following, and presided over the trial by combat between Hrorik II Earl of Eastmarch and Murdoch Earl of Carthane held on the next day. On the Xth day of October in that year he murdered Father Faelan at Paulin's orders.

He joined the Royal Expedition to Eastmarch on the XVth day of June in the year 928. On the XVIIIth day of that month, his horse was mysteriously spooked by a swarm of bees, and was driven into the River Eirian; one of his *Custodes* knights drowned, but Albertus was able to keep his seat and avoid injury. However, his suspicions were aroused, and II days later he commanded his Deryni double agent, Master Dimitri, to probe King Rhys Michael's mind, looking for signs of Deryni power there. Dimitri, acting under a compulsion placed in his mind by Father Joram MacRorie and his allies, abruptly turned on Lord Albertus and took over his mind, showing the King the many treacheries buried there. He then stopped the Grand Master's heart on the XXth day instant. Lord Albertus was aged LI years at his death, and was buried in the crypt at Saint Cassian's Abbey after being ritually exorcised; he was joined there V days later by his brother, Vicar General Paulin Sinclair. He was temporarily succeeded as Grand Master by Lord Joshua Delacroix, and as Earl Marshal of Gwynedd by Rhun Earl of Sheele. *Cursed be the man that trusteth in man, and maketh flesh his arm, and whose heart departeth from the Lord.* [*The Harrowing of Gwynedd*; *King Javan's Year*; *The Bastard Prince*].

Phineas, Brother. He was serving as gate-warder at Saint Foillan's Abbey on the XIVth day of November in the year 903. He assisted "Brother Benedict" when the latter fainted during the visit there of Camber Earl of Culid and Rhys Lord Thuryn. [*Camber of Culdi*].

Piedur, Sir. He was born on the XXIXth day of November in the Year of Our Lord 886, being the son of Sir Egan and Adina his wife. This knight helped guard the Princes Javan and Rhys Michael at the fair held in Valoret to celebrate King Alroy's coronation on the XXVIIIth of May in the year 917. By August of that year he was supervising the soldiers guarding the princes at Rhemuth. Davin MacRorie Earl of Culdi was assigned to Piedur's detail while wearing the guise of Eidiard the soldier. Sir Piedur was killed in a border skirmish with Torenth on the XIIth day of July in the year 919, aged XXXII years. R.I.P. [*Camber the Heretic*; *King Javan's Year*].

Piran, Saint. This worthy was born in Caurus (later the city of Coroth) in the Vth century. When pirates raided the coast near the city, he fled into the Lendour Mountains. There he established several Abbeys and restored another, building all III near mineral deposits which the monks worked. Thus, he is often venerated as the patron saint of miners and moneylenders. An *Ordo Verbi Dei* priory dedicated to his name is located a day's ride North of Saint Jarlath's; it was there that Father Joram MacRorie and Rhys Lord Thuryn interviewed the first II "Brothers Benedict." Saint Piran is supposedly the ancestor of the noble House of Piran, but few genealogists give this claim much credence. His feastday is the Vth day of March. [*Camber of Culdi*]. See also: *Ordo Verbi Dei*, Saint Piran's Priory.

Polidor, Constable. He was a white-haired local gendarme at Twilham Green in the Purple March in April of the year 905. [*Deryni Challenge*].

Polidorus, Brother. This *Custodes* monk was serving as infirmarian at Saint Cassian's Abbey in June of the year 928. He was present when Lord Albertus and Vicar General Paulin Sinclair were attacked by their Deryni double agent, Master Dimitri, and later tended the mind-ripped Paulin until his death. He indirectly caused the death of King Rhys Michael by bleeding him excessively during the return of the King's expedition from Eastmarch on the XXVIIth and XXVIIIth days instant. After the *coup d'état* of the Vth day of July in the year 928, he was tried and convicted as a regicide on the XVth day instant, and hanged by the neck until dead. [*The Bastard Prince*].

Porric *Lunal*, Father. This priest of the Order of Saint Michael was a candidate to succeed Father Alister Cullen as Vicar General of the Michaelines in the year 905, but was unsuccessful. At the Grand Chapter Meeting held on the IIIrd day of July in that year, he inquired about the Haut Eirial and Mollingford establishments of the Order. [*Saint Camber*].

Portals. The origins of these *nexus vis* are lost in the mists of obscurity. Some scholars believe that the art and science of portal creation was brought to the *XI Regni* by the earliest waves of Deryni immigrants from Caeriesse, while others, among them Sulien of R'Kassi, ascribe their inception to an otherwise unknown Deryni mage yclept Assaél, who supposedly lived in the East during the IIIrd century. The most ancient of the portals that is known to survive, situate in the Papiarchium in the city of Rûm, has a peculiar ambiance to its energy signature, either due to its age or to the archaic method of its construction.

According to the scholar Nivard, "in order to use a portal, one must learn its coordinates, the unique characteristics that make it different from any other portal. This is best done in person at the location, though occasionally it is possible for a skilled practitioner to show a portal location to another with sufficient clarity that the location could then be accessed. And, of course, one must also know the location of another portal where one wishes to go." Portals have occasionally been discovered by finding a detailed description of their energy signatures in surviving texts of the ancient mages; however, attempting to transport to a portal whose existence is only suspected is exceeding dangerous, and should not be attempted by anyone except the most experienced individuals.

Portals must be grounded in earth or stone or some other neutral medium to prevent a random discharge of energy when in use. There are many different kinds of portals, including those limited to the use of a single individual or group, trapped portals to prevent the intrusion of outsiders, large triports designed to facilitate the transport of many men and other materiel, and unidirectional portals, which can be used only to send or receive.

Portals require the coordinated efforts of several Deryni to create the proper focus of energy to imprint the portal signature, which is a unique record of that particular aperture, although especially vigorous adepts have been known to create small portals without assistance. The signature of an unused portal tends to fade over time, but can often be revived with a minimal influx of energy, even after many centuries of disuse. Sulien once noted: "Portals are forever."

In the chaos following the imposition of the Statutes of Ramos during the reign of King Alroy, many portals in Gwynedd were destroyed or disabled, with only a few being known to exist in that Kingdom during King Kelson's time. However, portals are relatively common in Torenth and the Forcinn States, being found with somewhat less frequency in the South and West. Many portal locations remain closely-guarded secrets, since they potentially provide access to friends and foes alike. However, even trapped portals can be breached by accomplished adepts under certain circumstances. [*King Kelson's Bride*].

Portree. This was the site of a long-vanished Healers' *schola* which included the adept Jodotha as an instructor in the VIIth century. [*The Harrowing of Gwynedd*].

Purple March. This region of lush meadowlands, so called for the peculiar purplish cast and shimmering quality of its native heathers and vetches, is located due North of Rhemuth and East of Kierney. The title "Lord of the Purple March" is one of the most valued appellations of the Crown of Gwynedd. Long cherished and coveted by its title-holders and their neighbours as both borderland and sanctuary, the Purple March provided a natural boundary between the Kingdom of Gwynedd and the Principality of Meara, being adjacent to the most sheltered harbours on the Gulf of Kheldour, and fronting the foothills of the Rhendall Mountains. The principal rivers of the Purple March are the Cleyde and the Slieven. The Battle of the Cleyde was fought here in the year 1025.

Campbell de Broun, who had cause to traverse the Purple March on more than one occasion, made note of the odd features of its grasslands: "We passed through some beautiful prairies today, the land rich and level. I observed in one place where it looked as if the grass had been mown, and drove the wagon out of the road to try if the ground was smooth, but found it uneven and lumpy, rather like tussocks, and had great difficulty pulling my cart back into the track. The eye can be greatly fooled here." [*Deryni Rising*; *Deryni Checkmate*; *High Deryni*; *The Bishop's Heir*].

Queen Sinead's Watch. This tower in the residence of the Bishop of Grecotha was named for the Consort of King Aidan Haldane, who threw herself from its ramparts in grief after learning of the death of her husband in battle on the VIIIth day of July in the year 698. A portal was located here in the year 917, and was used by Camber Earl of Culdi and Rhys Lord Thuryn to transfer to their meeting at Saint Neot's Abbey with Dom Emrys and Dom Queron on the XVIth day of April in that year. *Donne, pretti, e polli non son mai satolli.* [*Saint Camber*; *Camber the Heretic*].

Queron Kinevan, Dom and Abbot. He was born on the XXIVth day of August in the Year of Our Lord 872, being the son of Kinevan of Pwyllheli and Margerie daughter of Trezen de Yuste, and the brother of Parnell Kinevan, the great Deryni mage. This monk entered the Order of Saint Gabriel in the year 885 and trained as a Healer at Saint Neot's Abbey during the next decade. He was ordained priest on the XXIst day of May in the year 892. On the IInd day of May in the year 905 he witnessed the madness of the novice Ulric, who abruptly killed his teacher, Dom Calvagh. On the XXVIIIth day of October in that year he had a conversation with Guaire Lord d'Arliss at Grecotha which was partially overheard by Bishop Alister Cullen.

He resigned from the Gabrilite Order on the IInd day of April of the year 906, and helped found the Servants of Saint Camber in June of that year, buying a rundown manor called Dolban on the IVth day instant to use as the Mother House of the new Order. Later that year he visited Camber's tomb at Tor Caerrorie and discovered it empty, later testifying to that effect before the Council of Bishops held at Valoret on the XXIVth day of October in that same year. By January of the year 917 he was serving as Abbot of the Monastery at Dolban. Later that year he was enlisted by the Camberian Council to find additional Healers who could "block" Deryni powers, and met with Rhys Lord Thuryn, Cullen/Camber, Archbishop Jaffray, and others at Saint Neot's Abbey on the XVIth day of April. On the XXVIIIth day of December in that year he was sent by Evaine Lady Thuryn into the hills to find and warn Revan, and they both witnessed the sacking of Dolban by the Regents' men.

He arrived alone at Saint Mary's in the Hills on the Xth day of January in the year 918, used the newly-established portal there to transport to the Michaeline Haven, and burned his *g'dula* braid later that day. He was appointed to the Camberian Council on the morrow. He was sent to fetch Revan back to the Haven on the Vth day of February in the year 918, using the alias "Brother Aaron" for his trip to the Willimites. He was present at King Javan's empowerment at the Haven on the XXVIth day of June in the year 921. He witnessed the massacre of Revan, King Javan, and many others on the XIth day of May in the year 922, but managed to escape the slaughter. He helped train Camlin MacLean to use his Deryni powers during the 920s at the former Michaeline Haven.

On the XXVIth day of June in the year 928, at the behest of the Camberian Council, he transported to the ruins of Tor Caerrorie, taking a horse across country to seek the King's army, which was traveling South from Eastmarch with the gravely injured King Rhys Michael. He used the name "Father Donatus" and the guise of a monk of Saint Jarlath's to infiltrate the King's forces on the XXVIIIth day of that month, but was too late to save King Rhys, who perished later that day in his presence.

He is described in the *Legends* as being "a short, wiry man who affected the habit of the Gabrilite order, wearing the peculiar Gabrilite braid of reddish, auburn hair hanging almost to his cinctured waist, as thick as a man's wrist. He had the green healer's cloak underneath."

By the year 917 his hair had turned grey, and by the following year his braid had been cut, his ragged hair had covered his former tonsure, and his beard had grown out wiry and dark. In the year 921 his hair was white, and he was wearing it in a braid again by the year 928. In his later years he penned the *Annales Queroni*, a detailed chronicle of his life and times. His date of death has not been recorded, although Ailfrid ap Montag, in his *De Nassis Artium Magicarum*, stated that "...the Venerable Dom Queron wore himself out during the plague season attempting to heal the suffering of too many souls at once, and when he became ill himself, had no energy to fight against the pox. He died with a smile on his face, and his body was laid to rest in a hidden place where it would not be descrated by the Deryni-haters." R.I.P. ["The Examen"; *Camber the Heretic*; *The Harrowing of Gwynedd*; *King Javan's Year*; *The Bastard Prince*; *King Kelson's Bride*].

Quinnell. This royal House of Meara took its surname from Quinnell mac Diarmaid, the founder of the family, who is mentioned in the chronicles as a border Laird near the present-day city of Laas in the year 600. His son, Mear mac Quinnell, proclaimed himself Sovereign Prince of Laas (later Meara) on the IInd day of August in the year 651. The state became known as Meara in his honour under his successors. The Principality of Cassan split from Meara in the year 762 during the War of Succession, the division being recognized formally by a treaty signed by representatives of both branches of the House of Quinnell on the VIth day of August in the year 770, which agreement also provided that, in the event of the extinction of one branch of the family, the other would have succession rights to the other territory. The House of Quinnell-Cassan became extinct in the male line on the XXIst day of May in the year 921, and the Principality was annexed to Gwynedd, over the official protest of Austin Sovereign Prince of Meara. The House of Quinnell itself became extinct in the male line with the death of Jolyon II Sovereign Prince of Meara on the XXIXth day of May in the year 1025. [*King Javan's Year*; *The Bishop's Heir*; *The King's Justice*]. See also: Ambert, Annalind, Anne, Caitrin, Duvessa, Ithel, Jolyon, Judhael, Llewell, Magrette, Roisian, Sidana, Tambert.

Quiric *Fitz-Arthur*, Lord Fitz-Arthur, Baron of Horthness *jure uxoris*. He was born on the XVIIth day of September in the Year of Our Lord 909, being the fourth son of Tammaron Earl Fitz-Arthur and Nieve Lady O Nuallain, and a younger brother of Fane Deputy Regent of Kheldour. He intermarried with the Lady Émeraude daughter of Rhun Earl of Sheele and Baroness of Horthness in her own right on the XIVth day of June in the year 943, and by her he had children: the

Hereditary Lord Ulvar later Baron of Horthness; the Lady Fawna; the Lady Tammarona; the Lady Nievette; the Lord Merhun; the Lord Quire. He was serving as a junior squire at the Court of Rhemuth in the year 921, and was present at the death of King Alroy on the XXIIIrd day of June in that year. He accompanied the expedition of King Rhys Michael to Eastmarch on the XVth day of June in the year 928. He died of a shortness in his breath at a birthday *fête* given in his honour on the XVIIth day of September in the year 973, aged LXIV years exactly, and was succeeded by his son, Lord Ulvar. R.I.P. [*King Javan's Year*; *The Bastard Prince*].

Quorial. This VIII-person Council governed the long-hidden village of Saint Kyriell's in the North Lendour Mountains. Its spokesman in April of the year 1125 was Brother Michael, and other members then included Bened, Jilyan, Kylan, and Rhidian. [*The Quest for Saint Camber*].

Radan, Sir. He was serving as weapons master at Valoret Castle in February of the year 918, and later acted in the same capacity when the Court moved to Rhemuth. [*The Harrowing of Gwynedd*].

Radislaus Vakṣos *Furstán*, King of Torenth. He was born on the IXth day of November in the Year of Our Lord 666, being the eldest son and heir of László Vak King of Torenth and the Lady Charitóna daughter of Dionysios Despot of Morias. He intermarried with the Grand Princess Theophanó daughter of Bespasianos II Autokratór of Byzantyun on the IIIrd day of June in the year 685, and by her he had children: the Hereditary Prince László, killed with his father; the Princess Bónitas, who intermarried with Turpion the Hort of Orsal; the Princess Sibylla, sent to a nunnery by King Festil Ottó; the Prince Lipóld later Count of Hohensax, killed with his father.

The Prince Radislaus succeeded his first cousin, Imre I King of Torenth, who died at a banquet on the Vth day of December in the year 722. He then had King Imre's sons killed or banished from the kingdom for life on pain of death. He was girded with the sword at Iób by Patriarch Kosmas I on New Year's Day in the year 723. However, one of King Imre's younger sons, the Prince Festil Ottó, secretly returned to Beldour on the XVIth anniversary of his father's death, the Vth day of December in the year 738, and accused the King of murder at Christmas Court, challenging him to a duel arcane. When King Radislaus refused, being an old man of some LXXII years, the Prince Festil murdered him anyway without hesitation and sat himself upon his Throne, despite the better claim of Festil's II older brothers and their kin. He then killed the King Radislaus's sons and grandsons, and sent away his unmarried daughter Sibylla to a nunnery. All were buried in the family crypt of the Furstáns at Torenthály. R.I.P.

Radu, *i.e.*, Raduslav Lukiyán Berrhonidés Neilou von Shandis, Lord. This grandson of the great Torenthi statesman and chronicler, Count Berrhones, was born on the last day of February in the Year of Our Lord 1102, being the eldest son and heir of Neilos Ambrózy Hereditary Count Castlerodh and the Countess Liesse, who was the daughter of Radyslav Count Sympheropol and the sister of Erdödy Duke of Jándrich. He intermarried with the Lady Mariyana, daughter of Branyng I Count of Sostra, on the IInd day of August in the year 1124, and by her he had children: the Lord Berrhones; the Lord Branisláv; the Lady Neola. The Lord Radu entered into the service of the Torenthi government in the year 1126, joining the staff of the Grand Vizier a year later, and accompanying him to Beldour for the installation of Liam Lajos as King of Torenth. He announced the death of Count Czalsky on the afternoon of the XIth day of July in the year 1128, while meeting with the Royal uncles, King Kelson, Dhugal, and others at Furstánaly Palace. He is described in *Bride* as a "facile young man." [*King Kelson's Bride*].

Radulf *Donivald*, Baron d'Eirial, Sir. He was born on the IVth day of December in the year 917, being the eldest son and heir of Cyril Baron d'Eirial and Nohea Lady Middlemore. He intermarried with Eanswith Lady Fenwick on the Xth day of April in the year 956, and by her he had a child: the Hereditary Lord Gilrae later Baron d'Eirial. After his first wife's death in childbirth on the XIIth day of January in the year 957, he intermarried secondly with Zillah Lady Davison on the XVIIIth day of September in the 958, and by her he had children: the Lord Caprus later Baron d'Eirial; the Lady Cyrilla. He succeeded his father on the XIIth day of November in the year 952. He died on the XXIVth day of December in the year 977, aged LX years, being succeeded by his elder son, the Hereditary Lord Gilrae, who then resigned the title on the same day in favour of his half-brother, the Lord Caprus. R.I.P. ["Vocation"].

Raif *ibn Falun*. This Deryni scout from Nur Hallaj was serving in King Kelson's army during his invasion of Meara in May of the year 1124. He also acted as an agent for Sofiana Sovereign Princess of Andelon, and reported to her regularly on the King's progress into Meara. [*The King's Justice*].

Ralf *Tolliver*, Bishop of Coroth. He was born on the IVth day of April in the Year of Our Lord 1071. He was ordained priest on the XXVIIth day of June in the year 1092, and elected an itinerant Bishop of Gwynedd on the Xth day of May in the year 1108. On the XXIIIrd day of March in the year 1117 he was elected Bishop of Coroth in Corwyn. One of his fiefs is the port city of Kiltuin, situate on the Gwyneddan side of the Western River; it was here that he presided over the murder trial of the itinerant swordsmith Ferris on the XVIIth day of April in the year 1118; after the testimony of Alaric Morgan Duke of Corwyn proved the man innocent of any crime, Tolliver released him.

On the XXth day of March in the year 1121 he was sent a letter by the Archbishops of Gwynedd asking him to excommunicate Alaric and to place the Duchy of Corwyn under interdict. This he declined to do, as was his right under law, the Bishops of Coroth having autonomous ecclesiastical status within the Duchy of Corwyn, as they had once had in the ancient Kingdom of Mooryn. He then supported the Bishops Thomas

Cardiel and Denis Arilan during the Interdict Crisis which followed. In the year 1128 he was present at Coroth Castle when King Kelson visited there on the IInd day of July. Bishop Ralf had brown hair and wore polished riding boots with spurs protruding from beneath the hem of his purple cassock; he kept fit through regular outings in the open air. ["Trial"; *Deryni Checkmate*; *High Deryni*; *The Bishop's Heir*; *The King's Justice*; *King Kelson's Bride*].

Ramos. This small abbey town is located just West of Valoret on the South side of the River Eirian. It was here that the Mother Houses of the Little Brothers of Saint Ercon and its successor Order, the *Custodes Fidei*, were established in the early X^th century. It was also the site of the infamous Council of Ramos held in the years 917 and 918, which promulgated the I^st measures prohibiting Deryni from participating in the Church or holding noble titles or owning property. Lord Paulin Sinclair, the founder of both Orders, was born here. [*Camber the Heretic*; *The Harrowing of Gwynedd*; *The Bishop's Heir*].

Ramos Conventions or **Statutes of Ramos.** This repressive set of laws and practices specifically targeted the Deryni race. The measures were crafted by the Council of Ramos under the direction of Hubert MacInnis Archbishop Primate of Valoret and All Gwynedd beginning in December of the year 917, and continuing through the Spring of the following year. The initial body of regulations was ratified by the Regents of Gwynedd on the I^st day of January in the year 918. The Conventions forbade all Deryni from actively participating in the Church, from holding civil office or titles of nobility, from owning land, and from conducting any legal actions, including the rites of matrimony, without sanction of their Overlords.

The Ramos Conventions were partially repealed in the year 1125, at the instigation of King Kelson and Archbishops Cardiel and Bradene, with the remaining statutes either being discarded or rewritten during the following year, beginning on the XVth day of August. Central to the reforms were the recognition of the Deryni saints, including Camber of Culdi, and the recognition of the validity of Deryni holy orders. King Kelson issued a decree on the XVth day of August in the year 1126 restoring the civil and property rights of the Deryni, and on the VIth day of January in the year 1127 appointed a commission of scholars and judges to adjudicate the claims against the state made by former property and title holders and their legitimate male descendants. The first peerage to be restored was that of Barrett Lord de Laney in the year 1128. [*Camber the Heretic*; *The Quest for Saint Camber*; *King Kelson's Bride*].

Ramsay, Captain. He was serving as a member of Archbishop Hubert MacInnis's ecclesiastical cavalry in the year 918. He was "baptized" by Revan on the XIIth day of June in that year. [*The Harrowing of Gwynedd*].

Ramsay of Cloome, House of. This cadet House of the Earls of Cloome was founded by Lord Edward Ramsay of Cloome, younger son of James Earl of Cloome and Susana Lady Crewe, who intermarried with Magrette Princess of Meara in the year 1035. Their eldest son, Lord Colin, is the progenitor of this family, who are theoretically next in line to the Throne of Meara after the descendants of the Princess Annalind, Princess Magrette's elder sister. Lord Edward died on the XVIIth day of August in the year 1078, aged LXXIII years, and was deeply mourned by his family and retainers. His son Lord Colin died on the IIIrd day of November in the year 1101, aged LXIV years. The Lord Colin's son, Lord Dafydd, briefly inherited the pretensions of his *cousine germaine*, the Princess Caitrin, in the year 1124, but made no effort to assert any claims, himself dying on the XXXth day of January in the year 1126, aged LXX years. He was succeeded by his eldest son, the Lord Jolyon (III), who disclaimed any pretensions to the Throne of Meara for himself or his family in the year 1128, after being raised by King Kelson to the title of Duke of Laas. [*The King's Justice*; *King Kelson's Bride*].

Ranald, Lord Gilstrachan. He was born on the Vth day of January in the Year of Our Lord 878, being the third son of Hanald Baron Gilstrachan and Mena Lady Rouvre. He never married. This Deryni noble attempted to assassinate the Princes Javan and Rhys Michael on the XXVIIIth day of September in the year 917. He was captured, tried, attainted, and executed by the Regents on the same day, aged XXXIX years. [*Camber the Heretic*].

Randolph, Master. He was born on the IXth day of February in the Year of Our Lord 1080, and was trained as a physician. He was serving as surgeon to the Duke of Corwyn by the year 1115, when he treated Sean Earl Derry's wounds at Rhelledd on the I^st day of May. He later was present with the Duke's retinue during the Interdict Crisis, and reported to the Duke on the XXIVth day of March in the year 1121 regarding rumours abroad in the land. He cared for the Duke's wife, Lady Richenda, during her pregnancies in the years 1123 and 1125. ["The Knighting of Derry"; *Deryni Checkmate*; *The Bishop's Heir*; *The Quest for Saint Camber*].

Randolph of Fairhaven. He was serving as an officer in the guerrilla force of Ithel Hereditary Prince of Meara in June of the year 1124. [*The King's Justice*].

Rannulf, Lord Vaudemont. He was born on the Xth day of May in the Year of Our Lord 863, being the eldest son and heir of Rai Lord Vaudemont and Damienne Demoiselle de L'Eclerc in Vézaire. He intermarried with Augustina Lady Lévis on the IXth day of May in the year 884, and by her he had children: the Hereditary Lord Raimond later Lord Vaudemont; the Lord Damien; the Lady Éclaire; the Lord Auguste; the Lady Rannastine. This Deryni nobleman had a castle in Eastmarch and an estate near Tor Caerrorie. He succeeded his father on the XXXIst day of October in the year 893. He was known for his atrocities against the humans, and was nearly excommunicated in the year 902. On the XXVIth day of September in the year 903 he was drawn and quartered by Willimite terrorists; in retaliation, the King Imre's men took L hostages from among the local human peasantry, and had all but I executed over the next month. He was aged XL years at his death, and was succeeded by his eldest son, Lord Raimond. His family later relocated into Vézaire following the attainder of Deryni nobility in Gwynedd in the year 917. [*Camber of Culdi*].

Raphael, Saint. Also called "The Healer," this Archangel is I of the IV protecting spirits called upon to ward a magical circle in certain ceremonies; his quarter of the circle was the East and his sign a black circle. His element is air. His Arabi name is Rafael or Rafail, and his name means "God has healed." His feastday is the XXIVth day of October. [*Saint Camber*; *Camber the Heretic*; *The Harrowing of Gwynedd*; *King Javan's Year*; *The Bastard Prince*; *The King's Justice*].

al-Rasoul ibn Tarik *al-Buraini*, Lord. He was born in R'Kassi on the XXIst day of June in the Year of Our Lord 1081, being the son of Tarik ibn Mahmud al-Amin al-Buraini and Lellia bint Sardis al-Ruif. He intermarried with Duriye daughter of Genghiz al-Halki, on the IIIrd day of August in the year 1100, and by her he had children: the Lord Orhan; the Lord Abid; the Lady Ulviye; the Lady Neslishah; the Lord Neçmeddin; the Lady Biydâr; the Lord Rechad. He entered the foreign service of Wencit King of Torenth in the year 1107, serving primarily in the East until the accession of the Regent Mahael in the year 1121. This Moorish Deryni emissary from the Court of Torenth and the Regent Mahael II Duke d'Arjenol appeared at Rhemuth on the IIIrd day of March in the year 1125, following the knighting ceremony on that day. He wore a great live cheetah draped around his shoulders, and made a spectacular entrance. He was not happy at the news that King Liam Lajos II would be remaining at the Gwyneddan Court, but when he returned home he dutifully carried messages from King Kelson back to Duke Mahael.

In the year 1128 he journeyed to Gwynedd with Count Mátyás, arriving at Desse on the XXVIIIth day of June, and during the following week served as an escort for King Liam in his voyage home. On the IXth day of July he and Count Branyng gave King Kelson a tour of the city of Beldour. He supported the King against his uncles during the assassination attempt on the XVIth day of July in that year, and participated in the Ist Crown Council of King Liam Lajos II later that evening. He considered himself a master builder, and during his career had erected several castles and fortified towns in Southern Torenth and in the Northern regions of the Forcinn Buffer States. He had coal-black eyes and sported a close-trimmed beard. [*The Quest for Saint Camber*; *King Kelson's Bride*].

Ratharkin. This town in Eastern Meara was made the new capital of the Principality after the union of Meara and Gwynedd in the year 1027 and also became the seat of the Bishop of Meara, Prince Judhael. It was burned on the XXIXth day of June in the year 1124 by Brice Baron of Trurill and Ithel Hereditary Prince of Meara to keep it out of the hands of Kelson King of Gwynedd. A rebuilding program was begun in the following year. *A quien no mata puerco, no le dan morcilla.* [*The Bishop's Heir*; *The King's Justice*; *King Kelson's Bride*].

Rather *de Corbie*, Lord de Corbie. He was born on the Xth day of September in the Year of Our Lord 1065, being the son of Daniel Lord de Corbie and the Lady Rôtie de Côte-de-l'Or. He intermarried with the Lady Grenade de Machault on the XXth day of October in the Year 1092, and by her he had children: the Lord Jennings; the Lady Constantia; the Lady Christianne; the Lord Wolf; the Lord Brinkley. This Ambassador Extraordinaire was serving as the official representative of the Hort of Orsal at the Court of Duke of Corwyn in March of the year 1121, having been acquainted with Morgan for many years. He was present at Orsal when King Kelson and his party visited there on the IIIrd day of July in the year 1128. He is mentioned in the *Chronicles* as arriving "...in a contingent of men dressed in the sea green livery of the Hort of Orsal. He is a feisty old warrior, although his booming voice does not match his five-foot stature." [*Deryni Checkmate*; *King Kelson's Bride*].

Rathold, Lord d'Or. He was born on the XXIst day of February in the Year of Our Lord 1059, being the third son of Chrétien Sieur d'Or and Edythe Lady Channelle. He intermarried with Danna Lady Corin on the IIIrd day of July in the year 1079, and by her he had children: the Lord Berthold; the Lord Calvin; the Lord Oleg; the Lady Anne, who intermarried with Willim Lord Blass. He was serving as the Master of Wardrobe and Chamberlain for Alaric Morgan Duke of Corwyn at Coroth between the years 1121-1130. [*Deryni Checkmate*; *The Bishop's Heir*; *The Quest for Saint Camber*].

Raymer *de Valence*, Bishop. He was born on the IXth day of December in the Year of Our Lord 1069, being the third son of Sir Kilmer de Valence and Curtina Lady Draper. He was ordained priest on the XVIth day of June in the year 1089, and was elected an itinerant Bishop of Gwynedd on the XXIIIrd day of March in the year 1117. He supported Edmund Loris ex-Archbishop Primate of Valoret and All Gwynedd in his attempt to restore his position as Primate of Gwynedd in December of the year 1123. After Loris's execution on the XIIth day of July in the year 1124, he was arrested and suspended from office. On the XVIIIth day of March in the year 1125 he was deprived of his rank as Bishop by the Synod, but he was allowed to continue functioning as a priest under close supervision, but eventually returned to his ancestral home in Valentia. He died there on the IXth day of June in the year 1129, aged LXIX years, having repented his support of Loris. R.I.P. [*The Bishop's Heir*; *The King's Justice*; *The Quest for Saint Camber*].

Raymond *Eskill*, Sovereign Prince-Bishop of Dhassa. He was born on the XIIIth day of May in the Year of Our Lord 818, being the son of Alister Lord Eskill and Cosima Lady Braga, and the maternal uncle of Bishop Alister Cullen, whom he ordained on the IVth day of March in the year 877. He himself was ordained priest on the XVIIth day of August in the year 839. He was elected independent Prince-Bishop of Dhassa on the

XXXIst day of May in the year 862. On the XXIInd day of October in the year 879 he signed a treaty with Festil III King of Gwynedd, under the terms of which Dhassa would lose its independence when Bishop Raymond retired or died. He died on the IXth day of August in the year 903, aged LXXXV years, when Dhassa became part of Gwynedd. R.I.P. [*Saint Camber*].

Rechol. He was a blade merchant who appeared at Rhemuth in July of the year 1124. [*The King's Justice*].

Regina, Sister. She was a nun at Saint Ostrythe's Convent in June of the year 928. She helped treat Rhys Michael King of Gwynedd on the XXVIIth day of that month. [*The Bastard Prince*].

Remie, General. This Gwyneddan officer was present at the Dhassa War Council on the XXIXth day of June in the year 1121, and was assigned to hold the left flank of the army at Cardosa. He later participated in the Christmas Council of 1123 to discuss the developing Mearan Crisis, and served with the main Gwyneddan Army during the invasion of Meara in May of the year 1124. [*High Deryni*; *The Bishop's Heir*; *The King's Justice*].

Rengarth. This town and fortress is situate on the Western flank of the Coamer Mountains, about midway between Cardosa and Kingslake. The Bearncoill Pass to the East of the town provides access during the Summer months to the Torenthi city of Medras. On the XIIth day of October in the year 983 the Pretender Imre II occupied the city of Rengarth and proclaimed himself King of Gwynedd, establishing his Court here. He was able to maintain himself until the IInd day of July in the year 985, when Rengarth was besieged and captured by Jasher King of Gwynedd, who died in the battle. Imre then threw himself off the Palace wall to his death. Rengarth was also the site of the betrayal of the army of Jared McLain Duke of Cassan by Bran Coris Earl of Marley to Wencit King of Torenth on the XXVIIIth day of June in the year 1121. [*Camber of Culdi*; *Camber the Heretic*; *High Deryni*].

Rengarth Plain. This grassy area is located in the Glenwhirry Valley between the Coamer Mountains to the East and the Lendour Mountains to the West, and encompasses much of the territory of Carcashale, Derry, and several other Earldoms and Baronies. The River Coire or Curry traverses the plain. [*High Deryni*].

Revan, Master. This carpenter's apprentice was born on the IIth day of November in the Year of Our Lord 890. As a lad he was the brightest pupil at Evaine Lady MacRorie's village school near the MacRorie estate, Tor Caerrorie. He was one of L peasants taken by King Imre's men in revenge for the murder of Lord Rannulf in September of the year 903, but was saved from execution by Cathan MacRorie Hereditary Count of Culdi who, being allowed by the King to reprieve only I hostage, picked Revan. Following the death of Lord Cathan, Revan was taken under the protection of Cathan's sister, the Lady Evaine, who continued his education; by June of the year 905 he had become a valued clerk and trusted advisor in the Thuryn household. Between the years 915-917 he served as tutor to Rhys and Evaine Thuryn's children, Rhysel and Tieg.

The Camberian Council chose him on the VIth day of March in the year 917 to become the human agent for saving Deryni by blocking their magical powers. To convince skeptics of his "change of heart," he supposedly fell in love with Finella of Sheele, who "died" of the plague which only afflicted humans. Revan used her supposed passing as an excuse to leave the Thuryn household in disgust in order to join up with the Willimites, a radical anti-Deryni group.

By August of the year 917 he had become a charismatic preacher, patterning himself after the Biblical figure of John the Baptist, and urging all Deryni to be purged of the taint of their heritage by being baptized again. Humans would benefit from the cleansing by having their association with Deryni erased from their souls. Dom Queron was sent on the IXth day of February in the year 918 to find Revan. They both returned to the Haven on the XIIth day instant so that Revan could train the Healer Sylvan O'Sullivan as I of their team. He gradually acquired some Deryni-like abilities through his constant association with the race.

Revan began his formal ministry with Sylvan and others on the IXth day of June in that year, successfully "baptizing" Deryni and simultaneously blocking their powers, so that they could begin their lives anew somewhere else without the possibility of detection by the Regents' men. However, during an attack by the former Regents on his riverside ministry, he was slain by his own followers on the XIth day of May in the year 922, aged XXXI years. He is described in the *Legends* as "being blessed with a charismatic personality. He had long hair, a full beard which almost looked blond in the strong sunlight, pale brown eyes, and he was afflicted with a limp which did not deter him from his duty. In his role as 'baptizer' he customarily wore an ankle-length robe of some graying homespun stuff, threadbare and much patched, and cradled a twisted staff of what looked to be olivewood in the crook of his left arm." R.I.P. [*Camber of Culdi*; *Saint Camber*; *Camber the Heretic*; *The Harrowing of Gwynedd*; *King Javan's Year*; *The Bastard Prince*].

Reyhan Riel Raspail *de Jhelûme*, Lord Séchelles in Jáca. He was born on the XXIInd day of October in the Year of Our Lord 1074, being the eldest son and heir of Reval Lord Séchelles and the Lady Henriotte daughter of Mysore Sieur de Saint-Oléron in Fallon. He intermarried with the Princess Sofiana later Sovereign Princess of Andelon on the XXIst day of December in the year 1094, and by her he had children: the Hereditary Prince Kamil, who intermarried with Williama Nabila of Nur Hallaj; the Prince Taher, who intermarried with the Duchesse Ercille daughter of Centule V Grand Duc du Vézaire; the Prince Nephthys, who intermarried with the Princess Yussra daughter of Tahmasp II Great Khan of Khokanistan; the Princess Rohays, who intermarried with Sulen Hereditary Nabil of Nur Hallaj. He accompanied his wife to Beldour in July of the year 1128, and was present at a reception held at Furstánály Palace on the XIth day of that month. [*King Kelson's Bride*].

Reynald, Brother. He was serving as infirmarian at Saint Foillan's Abbey in December of the year 903. [*Camber of Culdi*; *Camber the Heretic*].

Rezza Élisabet Chemille *von Horthy*, Princess d'Orsal and Tralia. She often went by her second name in family circles. She was born on the last day of February in the Year of Our Lord 1108, being the eldest daughter of Létald Hort of Orsal and Prince of Tralia and Husniyya Sharifa of R'Kassi. She was a notable beauty of her time, being mentioned in the year 1128 as a potential bride for Kelson King of Gwynedd. [*King Kelson's Bride*].

Rhafallia. This flagship of the Caralighter Fleet of Alaric Morgan Duke of Corwyn was double-ended, clinker-built, and weighed L tons in the year 1121. According to Volumen II of the *Chronicles*, "Like most ships that plied the Southern Sea in trade, she carried a crew of thirty men and four officers, with room for perhaps half that many men-at-arms or passengers, in addition to cargo. When the wind blew from the right direction, she could make four to six knots with little difficulty. If the wind failed, there were always the oars. Recent rigging innovations copied from the Bremagni merchants to the South now made it possible to tack as close as forty degrees to the wind with a new forward sail called a jib. Even without the sail the narrow and high-riding *Rhafallia* could easily make the crossing to the Hort of Orsal's island port and back in less than a day...Although technically a merchant ship, she carried raised fighting platforms fore and aft. The helmsman steered the ship from the rear of the aft platform with a broad starboard steering oar, but the rest of the platform was ordinarily captain's country, used as a lounge and observation deck."

It was on this ship that an attempt against the life of Alaric was made on the XXVth day of March in the year 1121. The Duke later sailed with the *Rhafallia* from Desse, the main port of Rhemuth, on the Xth day of March in the year 1125 to return to his home port of Coroth.

The *Rhafallia* was used to bring the Torenthi ambassadors Rasoul and Count Mátyás to Desse on the XXVIIIth day of June in the year 1128, and II days later transported King Kelson and his party from Desse to Coroth, arriving there on the IInd day of July. On the next day, they sailed to Orsal, where they transferred to the Hort of Orsal's vessel. On the XVIIth day instant, the ship left Orsal at dawn, arriving at Coroth later the same day, and on the next day sailed for Desse, arriving there on the XXIst day of July. [*Deryni Checkmate*; *The Quest for Saint Camber*; *King Kelson's Bride*].

Rheljan. This Barony is situate on the Western flank of the Rheljan Mountains, being bordered on the East by the County of Gwernach in Torenth and on the West by the Earldom of Eastmarch, and includes the well-known lake region called Shannis Meer. The Honour was originally granted to Sir Richmond FitzEwan, a natural son of Ewan II Duke of Claibourne and Collotte Bas-Rhin. He was created Baron by King Cluim on the IInd day of December in the year 985 in recognition of his services during the recent war with Torenth. The title has continued to descend in his family to this day. Lady Richenda Duchess of Corwyn is the daughter of Richard Baron Rheljan. See also: Richenda.

BARONS OF RHELJAN

HOUSE OF FITZEWAN

Richmond FitzEwan	985-1004
Ewan (son)	1004-1031
Richmer (son)	1031-1066
Ewell (son)	1066-1069
Richton (brother)	1069-1092
Royce (brother)	1092-1096
Richard (son)	1096-1129
Murdo (son)	1129-1130+

Rheljan Mountains. This high range separates the Earldom of Eastmarch in Gwynedd from the Duchy of Tolán in Torenth, and extends Southward from the city of Marbury in Marley to the Torenthi city of Medras, where it changes direction and continues as the Coamer range. Major sites in the Rheljan Mountains include the towns of Cardosa, Medras, and Lochalyn, the Barony of Rheljan, and the Abbey of Saint Giles at Shannis Meer. Major peaks and ranges include Mount Melchisedek, Mount Gregory, Mount Benford, Mount Tópól, Mount Slüsser, Castlerók, the Westfalls, and the Spearheads. [*The Bishop's Heir*].

Rhelledd. This village is located in Northeastern Corwyn just South of Kingslake and North of Jennan Vale, West of the Torenthi border. It is known primarily for its annual Spring Horse Fair, usually held in late April or early May. Sean O'Flynn Earl Derry attended this Fair on the Ist day of May in the year 1115. It was to this town that Arnaud Sieur de Vali rode for help to repulse Warin de Grey's vandals in March of the year 1121. ["The Knighting of Derry"; *Deryni Checkmate*]. See also: Armaury.

***Rhemuth,* called "The Beautiful."** Originally named Rhombuticum by the Byzantyun Empire, the City of Rhemuth on the East bank of the River Eirian was settled from time immemorial, being occupied by the Byzantyuns about the year 249, who made the town capital of Carthanus Province. When the Easterners withdrew from the region in the year 444, Rhemuth became the capital of a new state of the same name, the Counts of Rhemuth being descended from Christian Rûman settlers who had moved there during the late IIIrd century. They resisted the expansionism of the Haldane Counts of Valoret, but gradually had their territory reduced to a small enclave on the Eastern side of the River Eirian. The last Count, Daunus, voluntarily relinquished his sovereignty to King Augarin on the IXth day of March in the year 655, and was made the chief peer of the realm during his lifetime. King Aidan Haldane moved his capital from Valoret to Rhemuth on the XVIIIth day of June in the year 674, a year after his accession.

Shortly after the conquest of Rhemuth by King Festil I on the XXIst day of June in the year 822, the center of government was returned to Valoret, and remained there during the Interregnum. During the next

XC years the population of the town was significantly reduced, and many of the old buildings deteriorated into ruin. On the XXth day of August in the year 885, shortly after the accession of King Blaine I, a revolt broke out in Rhemuth after the death of Archbishop Rudolf, a cousin of the King, when Cathyr Baron Carroch, a descendant in the female line of the old Haldane monarchy, declared himself King of Gwynedd. The insurrection was put down with great difficulty. Thereafter, the Archbishopric of Rhemuth was left vacant by the Festils as a deliberate policy of reducing the importance of the city.

King Cinhil I reinstated the see with the election of Archbishop Robert Oriss on the IXth day of July in the year 905, and King Alroy restored Rhemuth as the capital of Gwynedd on the XIVth day of July in the year 917. The city was extensively rebuilt during the Xth century, with the old Royal Palace and Saint George's Cathedral being completely restored. Lümin calls it "...regal Rhemuth, my one true love."

Campbell de Broun, who was profoundly interested in the architecture of such places, described the city when he passed through there in the year 1116: "We started after breakfast, and continued down the Mollingford Road to Rhemuth, which is situate on a plain North of the confluence of the Eirian and Molling Rivers. The Molling makes a great bend just before it reaches the city, bypassing it on the South and entering the Eirian at Desse, and the latter is much wider below the point where the II rivers join. We entered the town through the Eastern Gate, passing first under the New Wall built at the time of King Malcolm, and then through the Old Wall of King Alroy.

"The city is laid out on the same plan as Millflower in Bremagne, many of the older sections of the town having been deliberately swept away during the reconstruction of the past CC years. Rhemuth contains many good buildings of stone and brick. Among the major public buildings there are the Cathedral of Saint George and the Royal Palace. The commodious building called the Courthouse, wherein the King presides when hearing petitions and passing judgments, is an elegant structure some V storeys high flanked with a line of marble statues of the early monarchs of Gwynedd. A most stupendously large building of stone is likewise erected on the bank of the Eirian River for a huge water-driven gristmill to grind corn, and is designed to handle IV pairs of stones, more than I have ever seen employed elsewhere. There are III brick markethouses abundantly supplied, I of which has been recently built upon III rows of pillars and is CCC feet long; these are located near the docks where long barges containing goods are daily hauled upriver from Desse, using mules on a footpath. The *schola* consists of II oblong wings XXX feet apart, each LXXX feet deep, with a connecting building containing staircases leading to the IInd storey. The older parts of town have narrow, cobbled streets of stone in which it is easy to lose one's way.

"Late in the afternoon we saw the residence of the late majordomo, one Lord Rennick, some distance off to the lefthand side of the main avenue of the City, which street is called by the residents the Avenue of the Kings or Kings' Way. The dwelling is of stone and quite large, some III storeys high and flanked in front with pillars in the classical style; Lord Rennick at his death bequeathed it to his niece, the daughter of Robert Rennick, who has married a person of the exact same name, a distant relative, and who is the present owner of the place and Lord of the Manor. We stopped a short distance from there and took lodgings at the Boarshead Inn." [*Camber of Culdi*; *The Harrowing of Gwynedd*; *King Javan's Year*; *The Bishop's Heir*; *The Quest for Saint Camber*; *King Kelson's Bride*].

COUNTS OF RHEMUTH

HOUSE OF AMBROSIUS

Ambrosius	444-479
Fabius (son)	479-488
Cytorus (brother)	488-489
Clodius (son)	489-532
Ptolemæus (son)	532-558
Syrus (son)	558-571
Lycurgus (grandson)	571-611
Donatus (cousin)	611-629
Daunus (son)	629-659

ARCHBISHOPS OF RHEMUTH

Saint Paulus I de Bremagne	399-415
Saint Coelestinus	415-420
Theodosius	420-455
Saint Dulcitius	455-464
Eulogius	464-475
Scipio Romanistus	475
Florentinus	475-477
Euroldus	477-491
Antidius	491-501
Blessed Palladius	501-512
Gervasius Sementis	512-518
Ternatius Fatigo	518-542
Urbicus Merdus	544-559
Gemmus Inanis	560-562
Saint Patricius or Patrick I	562-569
Tetradius	569-575
Abbono	575-576
Gyrfredus	577-599
Salvius	599-603
Germesillus	603-619
Pancratius	619-645
Marcus I	645-651
Eusebius	651-667
Albinus I Grammont	668-673
Gaspard I Hébert	673-685
Ulric von Tolán	686-692
Gudin du Pont	692-699
Saint Antonius or Antony of Culdi	701-719
Leindrad of Kiltuin	719-734
Lantelm	734-739
Bonifacius de Tinseau	739-744
Robert I MacMain	744-759
Bernard Saquet	760-764
Symphorian of Rûm	764
Marcus II Ryons	765-800
William I of Gap	801-803
Alexander I Stewart	803-822
Gleb Rostovich	822-836

Pilgrin von Jutta	836-844
Adalbert von Beldour	845-867
Blaine Godomar Radislaus Furstán-Festil	867-868
INTERREGNUM	
Polemon Calboch	873-878
Rudolf Imre Eadgar von Furstán-Festil-Carthmoor	878-885
INTERREGNUM	
Robert II Oriss	905-928
Alfred of Woodbourne	928-948
Rostaing d'Ancézune	948
Piers Caradawg	948-963
Halsten del Borgo	963-976
Rosca MacImchadh	976-979
Claudius Alboni	979-995
Gilrae d'Eirial	995-998
Hieronymus (or Jérôme) Laurens	999-1000
Alexius of Medras	1000-1009
Gabriel de Tourre	1010-1021
Marcus III des Varreaux	1021-1025
Faustin MacArt	1025-1028
Gerald de Morgan	1028-1030
Briand of Meara	1030-1034
Jashan Nygel Ifor Eadwig Haldane	1034-1044
Thomas I Finnegan	1044-1055
Albin II MacDiarmaid	1055-1061
Paul II Faucon de La Forez	1061-1077
Gaspard II of Rengarth	1077-1079
William II MacCartney	1079-1092
Desmond MacCartney (brother of William)	1092-1099
James de Varagh	1100-1108
Alexander II Darby	1108-1117
Patrick II Corrigan	1117-1121
Thomas II Cardiel	1121-1130+

Rhendall or ***Rhenndall***. This successor peerage to the autonomous County of Rhorau was erected on the XXVIth day of August in the year 906 by King Cinhil I as a secondary title to the Duke of Claibourne, the Earldom being used at that time as a courtesy title by the eldest son and heir of the reigning Duke. At the death of Graham I Duke of Claibourne in the year 948, the County of Rhendall passed by virtue of his last will and testament to his granddaughter, Gillian MacEwan Countess of Rhendall, who intermarried with Sir Brion de Traherne.

Their son, Earl Braham, inherited the title on the XIIth day of October in the year 1008, and it passed down through his line to the present holder, Saer Earl of Rhendall, brother of Meraude Duchess of Carthmoor and brother-in-law to Prince Nigel Haldane. The banners of the Earldom were represented in the army of Kelson King of Gwynedd in the year 1121. *La lingua batte dove il dente duole.* [*Saint Camber*; *Camber the Heretic*; *The Harrowing of Gwynedd*; *The Bishop's Heir*; *King Kelson's Bride*].

EARLS OF RHENDALL

HOUSE OF MACEWAN

Ewan I	906-917
Graham I (son)	917-923
Hrorik Ewan II (son)	923-948
Gillian (daughter)	948-1008

HOUSE OF TRAHERNE

Brion I (husband)	957-997
Braham (son)	1008-1025
Gillis (son)	1025
Brion II (uncle)	1025-1028
Ghaire (son)	1028-1033
Graham II (brother)	1033-1040
Auben (brother)	1040-1051
Vere (son)	1051-1077
Hay (son)	1077-1091
Ewan III (cousin)	1091-1118
Saer (son)	1118-1130+

Rhendall Mountains. This range, located in Northwest Gwynedd, runs from the Gulf of Kheldour at the town of Carbury Northeast to the village of Woodbourne in the Duchy of Claibourne, encompassing the old County of Rhorau and the present Earldom of Rhendall. The region is known for its blue, clear mountain lakes and its fine hunting and fishing. Somewhere in the Southern part of this range is situate the hidden underground meeting place of the Camberian Council.

Rhennish Trace. This river flows from the twin lakes of Knockbrahe and Louisa in the Rhendall Mountains Southwest into the Gulf of Kheldour. It is well known for the purity of its waters and the fine trout fishing which can be found there. Campbell de Broun once fell into the Rhennish Trace, and opined that it was "too d---cold there even for the fish to swim. My bearskin and blanket were somewhat wet, as in crossing the Rhennish my mule mired in the sand and wet them some. I was forced to dismount and wade out, it being near waist-deep even along the banks. I laid down in my wet clothes, but did not experience any bad effects from it. Towards evening Molly brought me a letter that had been sent from Cloome some months or years ago. The paper was wet and some of the writing smeared. It seems my old Pa is finally gone and I can go home again. I do not know whether to laugh or to cry. I am much different from when I left. I have seen the great wide world and it has seen me. But I think I must go back and write of this. I wonder what my old Ma will make of Molly and the bairns."

***Rhetice Roxana Pætina* Haldane, Princess of Gwynedd**. She was born on the VIth day of April in the Year of Our Lord 1020, being the only surviving child of Cinhil II King of Gwynedd and Micole Lady of Dhassa. At her father's death in June of the year 1025, she was excluded from the succession in favour of her uncle, the Prince Malcolm, who was the next surviving male heir, for it is writ in Gwyneddan law that males shall succeed before females.

There is a great mystery concerning this Princess, who was made a ward of her uncle, the King Malcolm, at the age of V and raised by him as if she had been one of his own children. Abruzzès calls her "...handsome but not beautiful, dark-haired, with bright grey eyes that were short-sighted and often appeared to pinch together as she tried to see the features of those around her; she was very well-read, headstrong, and gifted with a great wit and intelligence that made her the center of any social gathering, for she could speak well on any subject of the day. She rejected all of the noble suitors proposed to her by her uncle, and also any of those who approached her on their own, including this personage, being utterly casual to their charms and to their titles, until the Yule Ball of the year 1039, when she was invited to dance by a curious gentleman—thin, dark, chin-bearded, and dressed all in grey. She danced no more with others that evening.

"I remember asking the majordomo who this man was and what were his estates, but the steward could not answer, nor could he tell me how this gentleman (for such he surely was) came to be present at the King's ball. When I asked her the next day who he was, she just smiled and said, 'An old friend I haven't seen in some time.' She continued to meet with him for several weeks, until the King discovered the liaison and put an end to it. I met the man just once, early in the new year, spying him in a little-traveled passageway of the palace; and stopping him, I introduced myself most graciously, saying how pleased I was that the Princess had found her old friend and that I hoped he would appreciate her company. He replied with a slight accent which I could not place that he was one Ælius Nemo, which is to say 'No One' in the Latin tongue, as I bethought afterwards, and that he hailed from faraway Rûm, which few men here have ever seen; and that he indeed considered the Princess a most gracious and special lady. His dress and aspect were noble yet exotic and seemed somehow familiar to me, but I could never identify in my mind where I had seen him or his like before, only that I had.

"But I put this swarthy gentleman out of my mind and saw him no more. In the month of April of the year 1040 a party was planned by the King for the Princess's XXth natal day, and the stranger had not been seen by anyone for the past III months, although methinks now that she had been meeting with him in some secret place. For when the ball had commenced, the King asked in a loud voice what she would have for her birthday, and she replied, 'What wouldst thou give me, Father?' and when he said, 'Anything that thou might wish, be it in my power,' she immediately stated, 'Then give me the hand of the noble Ælius as my weddèd husband.'

"Then there was a great silence fallen upon the multitude, as if someone of import had just died. I heard a woman trying not to cough in the background. And after a very long moment the King Malcolm finally spake with a great sigh, 'You know that I cannot!' The Princess Rhetice then turned her back on him, and very deliberately and slowly walked out of the room, back straight, looking at no one and seeing everyone, and she would not return, despite all the entreaties of the Queen and her handmaidens.

"That was the last anyone ever saw of her. The next morning she was not to be found, her room being vacant and her bed unslept, and a great hue and cry was made by the King, with every corner of the palace and even the city of Rhemuth being searched and searched and searched again. She was not there, nor has there been any word of her lo these XXX years. Yet I still recall those grave grey eyes and that dark hair, they still have the power to stir the blood in my veins to a boil, and I would give anything to know what has become of her."

Now it is true that no record mentions this Lady after her disappearance, save to speculate on her fate. No marriage record was ever found for her in the registers of Gwynedd. She is not buried with her family in the Haldane crypt in Saint George's Cathedral. Some say that her suitor was a Deryni, some say he was a spy, and some say both; and others hold that he was a commoner or a foreigner or a thief or an abductor or a foul creature of the night. These words are all romance and lies, for no one really knows. The King Malcolm wrote later that same month to the Grand Consul of Rûm, Septimus Pandarus, asking about this Ælius Nemo and his family; and the response, which he received some II years after, said that no such person or family dwelt in the VII Hills of Rûm or its environs, nor had ever been known to live there. Yet understand this, gentle-reader, that the reason why the Princess Rhetice is still mentioned by the tellers of tales, besides her great beauty, is that the progeny of this fair Lady, had she any, are the next heirs to the throne of Gwynedd after the families of Nigel Duke of Carthmoor and Richard late Duke of Carthmoor, for her uncle never had the heart to disinherit her, since he loved her so greatly. *Deux eftions et n'avions qu'ung cuer.*

Rhidian. This young Deryni woman was a member of the Quorial of Saint Kyriell's village. She may have joined with Kelson King of Gwynedd during his ordeal there on the XIth day of April in the year 1125. She accompanied the Servants of Saint Camber to Rhemuth in the year 1128, arriving on the XXXth day of July. [*The Quest for Saint Camber*; *King Kelson's Bride*].

Rhodri, Lord Pembroke, Lord Chamberlain of the Palace. He was born on the XXIXth day of December in the Year of Our Lord 1051, being the eldest son and heir of Kentigern Lord Pembroke and Palladia Lady Ahern. He intermarried with Kiara Lady Plegmund on the XXVIIth day of August in the year 1071, and by her he had children: the Hereditary Lord Paladin; the Lord Urban; the Lady Kybi; the Lord Meriadec; the Lady Lupa; the Lady Rhoda. He succeeded his father as Hereditary Lord Chamberlain of the Kingdom of Gwynedd on the XXth day of November in the year 1076. He was in charge of the musicians for the afternoon's entertainment following Sean O'Flynn Earl Derry's knighting on the XIth day of May in the year 1115. He woke the King Kelson on the XVth day of November in the year 1120 to prepare him for the coronation ceremony. He was present at the knighting of the King on the IIIrd day of March in the year 1125.

He is described in the *Chronicles* as a "...stately white-haired gentleman in deep burgundy velvet...He and Morgan were friends of long standing dating from the days shortly after Morgan first came to [King] Brion's court as a page; Rhodri had been chamberlain even then." ["The Knighting of Derry"; *Deryni Rising*; *The Bishop's Heir*; *The Quest for Saint Camber*].

Rhorau. This County was located in the lake region of the Rhendall Mountains, being part of the old Festillic Principality of Kheldour. On the XXVth day of April in the year 840 the title, which had been a subsidiary holding of the Princes of Kheldour, was ceded to the

Count Kálmán, IInd son of Termöd I Prince of Kheldour. Kálmán's son and successor, the Count Termöd, succeeded his uncle the Prince Tarquin as Sovereign Prince of Kheldour under the title Termöd II on the XIIIth day of December in the year 877, at which point the II honours merged. The Prince and Count Termöd II was murdered by Willimite terrorists on the IXth day of July in the year 904, and succeeded by his only son, the Prince and Count Tomlin, who was killed a year later on the XVIIIth day of September in the year 905 during the invasion of Sighere Earl of Eastmarch. At Tomlin's death his young Ist cousin, the Count Kennet son of the Count Kemal, succeeded in Rhorau only, and was able to maintain himself and his sister the Countess Sudrey in his fortress castle for a year before their capture by Sighere on the XVth day of August in the year 906.

Count Kennet's title was attained and re-erected into the Earldom of Rhendall as a subsidiary title of the Dukes of Claibourne. However, Kennet and his sister were given into the wardenship of Sighere's son Duke Ewan, who later knighted Kennet. Sir Kennet died unmarried and childless defending his master on the XXVth day of May in the year 918. His sister, Sudrey Heiress of Rhorau, married Hrorik II Earl of Eastmarch and younger brother to Ewan, and their only daughter Stacia Countess of Eastmarch married Corban Lord Howell. In Stacia's descendants is vested the right to petition for the re-establishment of this title. The senior representative of this line in the year 1130 is Rorik IV Titular Prince of Kheldour, Titular Earl of Eastmarch and Rhorau, and Baron Coldoire. [*Camber of Culdi*; *Saint Camber*; *High Deryni*].

COUNTS OF RHORAU

HOUSE OF FURSTÁN-KHELDOUR

Termöd I	823-840
Kálmán (son)	840-873
Termöd II (son)	873-904
Tomlin (son)	904-905
Kennet (cousin)	905-906

Rhorau Town. This capital of the old County of Rhorau is situate in the Rhendall Mountains between Lakes Knockbrahe and Louisa at the headwaters of the Rhennish Trace. It is generally regarded as one of the most beautiful towns in all of the Eleven Kingdoms, with broad, tree-lined boulevards and quaint houses of stone. After the Haldane Restoration it became the capital of the Earldom of Rhendall, the subsidiary title of the Dukes of Claibourne and later the independent holding of the House of Traherne.

Rhun *von Horthy*, called "The Ruthless," Earl of Sheele, Baron of Horthness, Earl Marshal, Vice-Marshal, sometime Lord Regent of Gwynedd. He was born on the IInd day of January in the Year of Our Lord 885, being the eldest surviving son and heir of Ulys Baron of Horthness and Ranalta Lady Rinville. He intermarried with Kristin Lady MacNeill on the XXXth day of August in the year 903, and by her he had children: the Lady Juliana, who intermarried with Sean Coris Earl of Marley; the Lady Adelicia, who intermarried with Tambert I Duke of Cassan. After his first wife's death on the VIIIth day of November in the year 913, he intermarried secondly with Agnes Lady Murdoch on the Xth day of January in the year 918, and by her he had children: the Hereditary Count Isarn later Earl of Sheele; the Lady Émeraude later Baroness of Horthness in her own right, who intermarried with Lord Quiric Fitz-Arthur.

The Lord Rhun succeeded his father as Baron of Horthness on the XXIInd day of March in the year 911. He conspired with Tammaron Earl Fitz-Arthur and Murdoch Earl of Carthane on the XVIth day of January in the year 917 to overthrow the will of King Cinhil I and to change the procedures governing the functioning of the Regency. He was appointed Regent to the young King Alroy on the IInd day of February in that year, which also gave him membership on the Royal Council. On the XXIVth day of December following, while on military maneuvers in the Lendour Highlands, he was ordered by the Regents to destroy Saint Neot's Abbey and the Michaeline establishment at Haut Eirial. He witnessed the death of the Abbot of Saint Neot's, Dom Emrys, who died destroying the portal there on that same day.

The Baron of Horthness was created Earl of Sheele by King Alroy on the XXVIth day of December in the year 917, and was also then named Vice-Marshal of Gwynedd. In January of the year 918 he laid siege to the city of Dhassa, his soldiers successfully taking that town on the IIIrd day of February following. After his marriage on the Xth day of January, he went on a trip with his new bride, but returned to Valoret by the IInd day of February. He formally took possession of his Sheele estates in the month of May.

Rhun was absent from Court at the death of King Alroy on the XXIIIrd day of June in the year 921, but had returned to Rhemuth by the time of Alroy's funeral III days later. He attended the coronation of King Javan on the XXXIst day of July in the year 921, and bore in the procession the Ring of Fire on a silver salver. On the following day he gave the *coup de grâce* to his friend Murdoch Earl of Carthane at the latter's specific request, after Murdoch was mortally wounded by Hrorik II Earl of Eastmarch. He then escorted Murdoch's son and successor, the Earl Richard, back to Carthane.

On the XVth day of June in the year 928 he accompanied the Royal Expedition to Eastmarch. After the death of Lord Albertus on the XXth day of that month, he assumed the title of Acting Earl Marshal, and also took command of the King's army. On the Vth day of July, acting under a compulsion previously set in place by the late King Rhys Michael, the Earl Rhun abruptly murdered his fellow co-conspirator, the Earl Manfred, and was himself killed by Sir Cathan Drummond a few minutes later. He was XLIII years of age at his death, and was succeeded as Earl by his only surviving son, Lord Isarn.

He is described in the *Legends* as "big-boned, well-muscled, solid but not fat. The sparse, wolfish grin was a feature which made friends and enemies alike refer to him as Rhun the Ruthless. He managed to look thoroughly dissipated in a long dressing gown of black wool and fur." His coat of arms featured a red ram's head. "*Populus me sibilat; at mihi plaudo.*" [*Camber the Heretic*; *The Harrowing of Gwynedd*; *King Javan's Year*; *The Bastard Prince*].

Rhydon, Baron Coldoire, Titular Earl of Eastmarch, Titular Regent of Kheldour and Rhorau. This noble Deryni Lord was born on the VIth day of June in the Year 1068, being the son of Emilian Baron Coldoire and Anastachia of Saint Elderon. He intermarried with the Countess Eulalia daughter and Heiress of Rorik III Earl of Eastmarch on the XVIIth day of May in the year 1104, and by her he had children: the Count Rorik IV Titular Prince of Kheldour, Titular Earl of Eastmarch and Rhorau, and Baron Coldoire; the Lord Sighere.

In May and June of the year 1105 he supported his father-in-law's moves against Ryan Coris Earl of Marley, and defied the King Brion when the latter attempted to intervene. He was left in command of the Eastmarch forces in Marley in early June when Rorik Earl of Eastmarch moved South to meet the King's army, and was not present when Rorik was captured by his cousin, Arban Howell Baron of Iomaire, on the XIIIth day instant. He was tried in absentia on the XXth day of June and banished from the Kingdom of Gwynedd on the pain of death, his titles being attainted and his right to the title of Eastmarch being specifically disallowed. He thereupon took his family to Tolán, where he proclaimed himself Earl of Eastmarch *jure uxoris* and Regent of Kheldour and Rhorau for his infant son. He had also served as a member of the Camberian Council from the XVIth day of November in the year 1091, but was forced to resign from that body in the year 1105 following his disgrace.

He later became an ally and adviser to Wencit King of Torenth after the latter's succession to the throne in the year 1110. Unbeknownst to his patron, the Lord Rhydon died of pains in the heart on the IIIrd day of March in the year 1116, his image and identity being then assumed by Stefan Coram, who sought to deceive the King in order to gain vengeance upon him. In this goal he was eventually successful some V years later. The Lord Rhydon was XLVII years of age at his death, and was eventually succeeded in his pretensions by his eldest son, the Lord Rorik.

The Lord Rhydon is described in the *Chronicles* in this light: "He was no longer a handsome man. A saber scar slashing across the bridge of his nose to the righthand corner of his mouth had forever rendered that an impossibility. But he was a striking man. Dark hair greying at the temples and a luxuriant salt-and-pepper mustache framed a lean, oval face; a small beard softened the pointed chin. The mouth was full and wide, but generally set in a firm line, with hints of predatory cruelty. In all, an almost sinister aura—one which the rapier mind behind the face cultivated and relished. A Deryni Lord of the first magnitude was Rhydon of Eastmarch; a man in every way Wencit's equal and complement; a man to be reckoned with." He was also reputed to be I of the most accomplished Deryni of his day.

His son Lord Rorik IV attached himself to the Torenthi royal Court after his father's death was revealed, calling himself Prince of Kheldour and Count of Eastmarch and Rhorau and Baron Coldoire, for he was the senior male representative of all these lines, but he was never acknowledged as such in the Kingdom of Gwynedd, nor was he ever allowed to return there. *La fiamma è poco lontana dal fumo.* [*High Deryni*; *The Bishop's Heir*; *The King's Justice*].

Rhys Malachy *Thuryn*, Lord. This distinguished Healer was born on the XVIIth day of February in the Year of Our Lord 877, being the only son of Malachy Lord Thuryn and Rosanagh Lady FitzWilliam, and a direct descendant in the male line of Émilien II last Comte du Thurie. He intermarried with Evaine Lady MacRorie daughter of Camber Earl of Culdi on the VIth day of January in the year 904, and by her he had children: the Lord Aidan Camber, murdered at age X by the Regents; the Lady Rhysel Jocelyn, who intermarried with Sir Robert Ainslie; the Lord Tieg Joram, who intermarried with Karis d'Oriel; the Lady Jerusha Evaine Jodotha, who intermarried with Sir Cathan Drummond.

When his parents died in the Great Plague of the year 878, the orphaned Rhys Thuryn was adopted by Camber Earl of Culdi, whose wife Jocelyn had been friendly with Rhys's mother. On the XIth day of October in the year 888 he was staying at Tor Caerrorie when he was seriously cut in the leg by bandits who invaded the manor. He was healed by Dom Sereld, Healer-surgeon to King Blaine I, who was then visiting with Earl Camber. Rhys's healing of his own pet cat on this occasion prompted the discovery of his own hitherto hidden talent. He was sent later that month with his foster brother Joram Lord MacRorie to attend school at Saint Liam's Abbey near Caerrorie. He subsequently pursued formal training as a Healer, eventually settling at an estate called Sheele North of Valoret, but also maintaining a residence within the city. One of his first patients was the elderly merchant, Daniel Draper.

On the XXVIIth day of September in the year 903 he was attending Draper when that ancient worthy revealed on his deathbed that his true identity was Prince Aidan Haldane, the last surviving child of Ifor King of Gwynedd. During the following year Rhys was instrumental in finding Prince Aidan's grandson, Prince Cinhil Haldane, and in proving Cinhil's connection with the old royal family. He acted as godfather to Cinhil's eldest son, Prince Aidan Haldane, on the VIth day of November in the year 904.

The Healer Rhys Thuryn was a founding member of the Camberian Council on the XVth day of April in the year 909. He participated in a special magical ceremony to baptize his own son, Tieg, on the I[st] day of August in the year 914. On the XXXIst day of January in the year 917, while attempting to heal Gregory Earl of Ebor, he discovered how to block a Deryni's powers.

He was drugged with *merasha* at Valoret by Tavis O'Neill on the XXIVth day of December in the year 917 in order to discover what had occurred at the empowering of the III Haldane Princes on the I[st] day of February in that year, and while still recovering from the influence of that drug, he was accidentally killed on the following day while helping Camber Earl of Culdi to escape from the Regents' trap at All Saints' Cathedral. Although deceased, he was attainted and outlawed by the Regents on the XXVIth day instant, and his family and estates were ordered to be seized; his manor,

Sheele, was appropriated and given to Rhun the Ruthless.

The Healer Rhys Thuryn was XL years of age at his death. His body was taken to the Michaeline Haven and was buried in the chapel there; on his tomb were engraved the words: "For of the most high cometh healing." He was principally remembered in later years as the discoverer of the Thuryn technique of concentration, by which a Deryni used a signet ring or some other device as a focal point for the beginning of a magical ritual. R.I.P. ["Catalyst"; *Camber of Culdi*; *Saint Camber*; "Healer's Song"; *Camber the Heretic*; *The Harrowing of Gwynedd*; *King Javan's Year*; *The Bastard Prince*; *Deryni Rising*; *Deryni Checkmate*; *High Deryni*].

Rhys Michael Alister *Haldane*, called "Rhysem," King of Gwynedd, Duke of Carthmoor. He was born on the XXIXth day of September in the Year of Our Lord 906, being the fourth son of Cinhil I King of Gwynedd and Megan Lady de Cameron. He intermarried with Michaela Lady Drummond at Culdi on the XXth day of November in the year 921, and by her he had children: the Hereditary Prince Cinhil Javan Alroy, dead at birth on the XIth day of May in the year 922; the Hereditary Prince Owain later King of Gwynedd; the Prince Uthyr later Duke of Carthmoor later King of Gwynedd.

The Prince Rhys Michael was created Duke of Carthmoor by his brother, the King Alroy, on his coming of age on the XXIXth day of September in the Year of Our Lord 920. The Haldane potential of this Prince had been set by his Royal father on the Ist day of February in the year 917. He was injured in an assassination attempt on the Princes outside Rhemuth on the XXVIIIth day of September in that year. By the Xth day of January in the year 918, when he attended the formal banquet in Valoret to celebrate the state weddings of Rhun Earl of Sheele and Lord Richard Murdoch, he had a tendency to imbibe over much.

The dying King Alroy asked to see him alone on the XXIIIrd day of June in the year 921, requesting that Prince Javan, their other brother, be fetched from the *Arx Fidei* Seminary North of Rhemuth; Rhys Michael then sent loyal knights to comply with the King's order. He supported the accession of his older brother, Prince Javan, to the throne on the same day. The former Regents soon began conspiring to marry him to Michaela Lady Drummond, and to have him replace King Javan his brother on the Throne of Gwynedd. He attended the coronation of King Javan on the XXXIst day of July in the year 921. On the XXIst day of August in that year, he was caught dallying with the Lady Michaela by the King, and admitted their betrothal. To keep the II lovers apart, the King appointed his brother Deputy Commissioner for Grecotha on the XIIth day of September in that year. The Prince left for that region on the XIXth day instant, but he was kidnapped by the former Regents on the XXXIst day of October in that year, although they blamed the outlawed Ansel MacRorie, and he was eventually taken to Culdi on the Xth day of November, where he was matched with Michaela Drummond.

He succeeded his brother, the King Javan, at the latter's murder on the XIth day of May in the year 922, but was kept drugged as a close prisoner during the early months of his reign. He was presented by his wife with a brooch embossed with the golden lion of the House of Haldane on the occasion of the birth of his IInd son and heir on the XXIXth day of February in the year 924. His brother, King Javan, had Ist noticed Prince Rhys Michael's development of shields in the Summer of the year 921; in the last II years of his reign Rhys Michael began to develop additional Deryni-like skills, including the ability to truth-read others.

On the XIVth day of June in the year 928 he received an ambassador from the Torenthi Prince Miklós, and accepted his challenge to go to Eastmarch; later that evening he was brought to his Haldane potential by Rhysel Thuryn, Tieg Thuryn, Queen Michaela, and Father Joram MacRorie. He led the King's Army out of Rhemuth on the XVth day instant, arriving at Lochalyn Castle VI days later. He defeated and killed the Prince Miklós through magic at their parley on the XXIInd day of that month, after Miklós had broken the truce and unilaterally attacked the Countess Sudrey, but was himself injured when his hand was crushed by a horse's hoof. *Das ist das Loos des Schönen auf der Erde.*

Two days later he secretly altered the terms of his will to change the makeup of a Regency Council for his underaged son, Prince Owain, in the event of his own death. His condition was worsened through bad treatment and excessive bleeding by the *Custodes Fidei*. He died on the return trip South at Saint Ostrythe's Convent on the XXVIIIth day of June in the year 928, aged XXI years, his body being returned to Rhemuth for burial in the crypt beneath Saint George's Cathedral. He was succeeded by his eldest surviving son, the Prince Owain, with his new will taking effect on the Vth day of July following, the day he was buried. R.I.P. *Ardir, che ai forti è brando, e mente, e scudo.* [*Camber of Culdi*; *Camber the Heretic*; *The Harrowing of Gwynedd*; *King Javan's Year*; *The Bastard Prince*; *The King's Justice*].

Rhysel Jocelyn *Thuryn*, Lady. She was born on the XVIIIth day of November in the Year of Our Lord 910, being the eldest daughter of Rhys Lord Thuryn and Evaine Lady MacRorie daughter of Camber Earl of Culdi. She intermarried with Sir Robert Ainslie on the XXIst day of August in the year 928, and by him she had children: the Lady Bethany, who intermarried with Alphard Baron Stanzar; Sir Javyl later Lord Argoed; the Lady Tiphane, who intermarried with Tammaron Duke of Cassan. On the VIIth day of January in the year 918 she went with her mother to the Michaeline Haven, and there assisted in the healing of Ansel Lord MacRorie on the XXIst day instant.

Under the name "Liesel," she was sent secretly to infiltrate the Court as a maid to Michaela Queen of Gwynedd by the year 928, where she became the chief contact between the Queen and Rhysel's uncle, Father Joram MacRorie, and his underground movement. She reported to Joram and his Deryni allies concerning the challenge sent by Prince Miklós to King Rhys Michael on the XIVth day of June in that year, and recommended that the monarch be brought to his Haldane potential that evening, with Rhysel, Joram, Tieg Thuryn, and Queen Michaela participating. She then interrupted the

King and Queen at their private dinner, and convinced them to allow the empowerment.

She died on the XXIInd day of October in the year 974, aged LXIII years. According to the *Heirs*, "she was pert and pretty, and shorter by a head than the Queen. She had rosy lips, hair a slightly paler shade of gold, braided and pinned close under the white kerchief that bound it. Her eyes were golden in the sunlight." R.I.P. [*Camber the Heretic*; *The Harrowing of Gwynedd*; *The Bastard Prince*].

Richard Bearand Rhupert Cinhil *Haldane*, Prince of Gwynedd, Duke of Carthmoor, Earl of Culdi, sometime Prince Regent of Gwynedd, Sir. He was born on the XXXIst day of December in the Year of Our Lord 1055, being the first child of Malcolm King of Gwynedd by his second wife, Cecilia "Síle" Lady Calder of Sheele. He intermarried with the Princess Sivorn daughter of Sobbon Hort of Orsal and Prince of Tralia and the Princess Maya daughter of Raimond Prince du Thuria on the XVth day of April in the year 1107, and by her he had children: the Princess Richelle Louise later Countess of Culdi in her own right, who intermarried with Sir Brecon Ramsay Earl of Kilarden; the Princess Araxie Léan, created Baroness Dunluce in her own right by King Brion on the XXVth day of December in the year 1114, who intermarried with Kelson King of Gwynedd on the VIIth day of August in the year 1128; the Prince and Hereditary Duke Cinric Sobbon Malcolm Earl of Culdi at birth by cession of his father, who was eaten up with fever at the age of III years on the XIVth day of September in the year 1114. After her husband's death in the year 1114, the Dowager Duchess Sivorn returned to Tralia with her II young daughters, and intermarried secondly with Savile Baron Kishknock on the XVIIth day of August in the year 1116, and by him she had further issue: the Lady Savilla; the Hereditary Lord Sivney; the Lady Siany; the Lord Sorley.

The Prince Richard was created Duke of Carthmoor and Earl of Culdi at birth in succession to his great-uncle, the Prince-Archbishop Jashan, who had recently died. From his youth he was trained as a soldier, and served as an officer in the Royal Army from the year 1073, being knighted on the VIth day of June in that year by King Malcolm his father. He participated in the expedition mounted by King Donal Blaine II into Meara on the IInd day of May in the year 1076. He was appointed Commander of the Gwyneddan army by his half-brother, Donal Blaine II King of Gwynedd, on the IInd day of March in the year 1085. He served as military leader of a IInd expedition into Meara on the XXXth day of April in the year 1089. On the XVIIIth day of May in the year 1090, the King ordered a raiding party sent into Sasovna in Torenth under the command of Duke Richard to retaliate for the Torenthi raids against Corwyn during the preceding year, but Richard was forced to withdraw back into Gwynedd after several weeks. He knighted King Brion on the VIth day of January in the year 1099. In the years 1102 and 1103 he served as Prince Regent of Gwynedd during the absences of King Brion Haldane in the East. He served with King Brion's forces during the Eastmarch Rebellion and incursion by Hogan Gwernach the Marluk in June of the year 1105.

Following the birth of the Hereditary Prince Kelson on the XIVth day of November in the year 1106, Duke Richard retired from active service to return to his estates in Dunluce, saying that he had had his fill of war. He married soon thereafter, and although he always welcomed visitors, rarely again ventured very far beyond the bounds of his own Duchy. Following the death of his only son and heir in the Fall of the year 1114, he took to making long rides by himself unto the furthest reaches of his lands. On one such occasion, on the XIth day of October in the year 1114, he fell from his horse during a storm, breaking his back, and died of his injuries IV days later, aged LVIII years. He was succeeded in the County of Culdi by his eldest daughter, the Princess Richelle, the Duchy of Carthmoor becoming extinct and escheating to the Crown. His body was returned to Rhemuth in the Spring of the following year for burial in the family crypt of the Haldanes beneath Saint George's Cathedral. His arms were: *gules*, III demi-lions guardant *or*, each engorged of a coronet *argent*. *Semper honos, nomenque tuum, laudesque manebunt.* R.I.P. ["Swords Against the Marluk"; *King Kelson's Bride*].

Richard, Bishop of Nyford. He was born of peasant stock on the XXVIIth day of February in the Year of Our Lord 1076. He was ordained priest on the XXXth day of August in the year 1096. On the XXIIIrd day of March in the year 1117 he was consecrated an itinerant Bishop of Gwynedd, and was elevated to the See of Nyford on the XIth day of April in the year 1119. He was captured with Jared McLain Duke of Cassan at Rengarth on the XXVIIIth day of June in the year 1121, and was executed with him by Wencit King of Torenth on the Ist day of July in that year, aged XLV years. His untimely passing was deeply felt by all. R.I.P. [*High Deryni*].

Richard, Hereditary Lord FitzWilliam, Sir. He was born on the XIXth day of November in the Year of Our Lord 1103, being the only son and heir of Fulk Baron FitzWilliam and Jemma Lady Behy. He never married. He was trained as a soldier by Alaric Morgan Duke of Corwyn, and was serving as a squire for the King of Gwynedd in November of the year 1120. He was present in March of the year 1121 when King Kelson received a copy of the interdict document penned by the Archbishops. He took a mortal blow from Andrew the helmsman during an assassination attempt against Morgan on the XXVth day of March in the year 1121 on board the Duke of Corwyn's good ship *Rhafallia*, and was knighted by him just before he died, aged XVII years. R.I.P. [*Deryni Rising*; *Deryni Checkmate*].

Richard *Murdoch*, Earl of Carthane, Lord Constable of Gwynedd, Sir. He was born on the Vth day of March in the Year of Our Lord 902, being the eldest son and heir of Murdoch Earl of Carthane and Elaine Lady de Fintan. He intermarried with Lirin Lady Udaut, daughter of Darius Lord Udaut Constable of Gwynedd, on the Xth day of January in the year 918, and by her he had children: the Hereditary Count Cashel *Junior* later Earl of Carthane, who died shortly after his father, *sans postérité*; the Lord Jason, killed in a border skirmish in the year 945, *sans postérité*; the

Lord Evert, who died young; the Lady Persephone; the Lady Elana, who died young; the Lord Ludovic, a monk of Saint Boniface's under the name Brother Gedeon; the Lady Margot, who intermarried with Flynn Fitz-Arthur Quinnell Earl Derry; the Lady Pemella, who died young; the Lord Murdoch *Junior*, who died young.

The Lord Richard was injured in a riding accident on the XXIXth day of April in the year 918, but was healed by the Deryni Oriel. With his father and new bride he returned to Carthane on the VIth day of May following, with the intention of taking up the governance of the Earldom. He was present at the death of King Alroy on the XXIIIrd day of June in the year 921. A month later he saw his father killed by Hrorik II Earl of Eastmarch on the Ist day of August, and succeeded him as Earl; his title was confirmed by King Javan on the next day, and he was allowed to take his father's seat on the Royal Council.

On the XVth day of June in the year 928 he was set to accompany the Royal Expedition to Eastmarch, but Lord Udaut suddenly died, and Richard was appointed Lord Constable of Gwynedd in his place, and was forced to remain behind at Rhemuth. He was dispossessed of that title by the Regents of King Owain later in that year. He died in the year 948, aged XLVI years, and was succeeded by his eldest son, Lord Cashel. He was described in the annals as randy and devious. [*The Harrowing of Gwynedd*; *King Javan's Year*; *The Bastard Prince*].

Richeldis Aoife Dionysia *MacFaolan-Gruffud*, Queen of Gwynedd, Princess of Howicce and Llannedd. She was born on the XIVth day of November in the year 1065, being the third daughter of Colman I King of Howicce and Gwenaël Sovereign Queen of Llannedd, and a sister to Illann II King of the United Kingdoms of Howicce and Llannedd. She intermarried as his second wife with Donal Blaine II King of Gwynedd on the IIIrd day of September in the year 1080, and by him she had children: the Hereditary Prince Brion later King of Gwynedd; the Prince Blaine Richard Colman Emanuel, dead at age X of the consumptive complaint; the Princess Xenia Iona Esmeralda Rosa, who intermarried with Sigismund Graf von Golzców, but died in childbirth on the XXVIth day of February in the year 1104 with her stillborn daughter, Dorothea Dulchesse; the Prince Nigel later Duke of Carthmoor; the Princess Silke Anne Gwenaël Lizabeth later Infirmarian of the Convent of Saint Dymphna at Grecotha and a great patroness of the arts and learning; the Prince Joachim Roy Walter Cinhil, who was trampled to death by a horse at age IV. On the XVIth day of May in the year 1099 she returned to Sirhowy in Howicce at the request of her young nephew, the new King Ronan IV, to act as *châtelaine* of his household, for he had neither wife nor children. She continued to maintain a household in Rhemuth, however, and returned there for extensive periods in later life, including the year 1105. The Lady Meraude served during this time in the household of the Queen. Richeldis died on the IVth day of February in the year 1118, aged LII years, and was buried in the Royal Pyramid at Sirhowy. R.I.P. *Gli uomini hanno gli anni che sentono, e le donne quelli che mostrano.* [*King Kelson's Bride*].

Richeldis Rixa *MacLean MacInnis*, Countess of Kierney and Culdi. She was born on the IXth day of January in the Year of Our Lord 904, being the eldest surviving daughter and heir of Lord Geoffrey MacLean and Laura Lady Wynford, and a niece of Iain II Earl of Kierney. When her father died on the XXIst day of November in the year 911, she was made a ward of her cousin, James Lord Drummond. At the death of her cousin, Adrian MacLean Hereditary Count of Kierney, and the presumed death of his son, Lord Camber MacLean, on the XXXIst day of December in the year 917, she and her surviving sister became co-heiresses to the Earldom of Kierney. She intermarried with Iver MacInnis Hereditary Count of Culdi on the Vth day of March in the Year 918 with Archbishop Hubert MacInnis presiding, and by him she had children: the Lady Janeltis later Baroness Marlor in her own right, who intermarried with Hrorik Ewan Hereditary Duke of Claibourne and Earl of Rhendall, leaving issue; the Hereditary Count Hobard later Earl of Kierney; the Lady Grania later Countess of Culdi in her own right, who intermarried with Uthyr King of Gwynedd, leaving issue.

She was introduced to her future husband at the state banquet held at Valoret on the Xth day of January in the year 918. Her sister the Lady Giesele was murdered by order of the Regents on the XXIst day instant, making Richeldis the sole heir to her uncle. Richeldis's Deryni powers were blocked by the Healer Tavis on this same day. She was questioned by the Regents on the XXIInd day instant regarding the events of the previous evening. She succeeded her uncle as Countess of Kierney on the XIXth day of March in the year 918.

Richeldis is described in the *Heirs* as looking in the year 918 "a good deal more grown up than the slightly plump adolescent who had attended the wedding feast not a week before. The black gown made her look slimmer, and her dark hair had been pulled back off her face and braided, the plaits pinned across the top of her head to show off a long graceful neck."

In her old age she became a great marvel at Court, for she had known personally all of the Kings and the Great Lords and Ladies and their relations from the earliest days of the Restoration, and even recalled old King Cinhil I himself, having sat on his knee as a girl; and in those twilight years of her life she delighted in gathering about her the young people of the Court, entertaining them with the stories of all the people she had known and all the events she had seen. Many would not believe the horrors that she related, even though everything she said was true; but the truest sorrow, she averred, was the premature loss of her parents and the murder of her beloved sister, Lady Giesele. She was proud of the fact that her descendants included V Kings of Gwynedd (for she counted King Uthyr her son-in-law among them), and as many Dukes and Earls, and predicted that within CC years all of the Great Lords of Gwynedd would count her as ancestress. At Christmas Court in the year 1000 she knew that she was failing, and she asked her great-grandson, the King Urien, to bless her one last time before she passed from this life into another. This wonderful old Lady died on the XXVIIIth day of December in the Millennium Year, aged XCVI years, and was buried by the special dispensation of the King in the Holy Crypt of the Haldanes beneath Saint George's Cathedral in Rhemuth. R.I.P. [*The Harrowing of Gwynedd*; *King Javan's Year*].

Richelle Louise *Haldane*, Princess of Gwynedd, Countess of Culdi and Kilarden. She was born on the XIth day of January in the Year of Our Lord 1108 to the Prince Richard Duke of Carthmoor and Earl of Culdi and Sivorn Princess of Orsal and Tralia. She was betrothed to Sir Brecon Ramsay later Earl of Kilarden in the Summer of the year 1127, and intermarried with him on the XXXIst day of July in the year 1128, and by him she had a child: the Lord Richard Albert Jolyon Hereditary Count of Kilarden and Culdi.

The Princess Richelle succeeded her father as Countess of Culdi on the XVth day of October in the year 1114, under the Regency of her mother. She was present at the marriage of her sister, Lady Araxie, to Kelson King of Gwynedd, which event was held just a week after her own wedding. She had dark hair, and wore a light veil in the Eastern fashion. [*King Kelson's Bride*].

Richenda Rayma Anisa *of Rheljan*, Dowager Countess and Regent of Marley, Duchess of Corwyn, Lady. She was born on the VIIth day of April in the Year of Our Lord 1099, being the eldest daughter of Richard FitzEwan Baron of Rheljan and the Princess Michendra daughter of Mikhail Sovereign Prince of Andelon, and a *cousine germaine* by marriage of Rothana Princess Regent of Gwynedd and Nabila of Nur Hallaj, and a great-niece by marriage of Thomas II Cardiel Archbishop of Rhemuth. She intermarried with Bran Coris Earl of Marley on the XIIth of June in the year 1116, and by him she had children: the Hereditary Count Brendan later Earl of Marley; the Lady Rhiannon Ysabeau, dead of the black mouth at age I. After her traitorous husband's ignominious death on the IInd day of July in the year 1121, she intermarried secondly with Alaric Morgan Duke of Corwyn on the I[st] day of May in the year 1122 in a ceremony conducted by Father Duncan McLain at Marley, and by him she had further issue: the Countess Briony Bronwyn; the Hereditary Duke Kelric Alain Earl of Lendour; the Countess Sophonisba Alyca Richenda.

She was sent to the safety of Dhassa by her first husband on the IInd day of March in the year 1121. On the XXIXth day of July in the year 1123 her innocent son was formally confirmed as Earl by King Kelson, and Richenda was made Regent of Marley in her son's name. After her IInd marriage she had difficulty in getting the Duke of Corwyn's men to accept her authority as Regent in Alaric's absence. On the XIXth day of December in the year 1124, being Deryni, she was given the task of keeping Morag Princess of Torenth and Dowager Duchess d'Arjenol closely confined at Coroth Castle.

In the year 1128 she was resident at Coroth Castle, and greeted her husband, King Kelson, King Liam, and their parties on their arrival on the IInd day of July. At a banquet held that evening, she discussed with others a list of possible brides for King Kelson. She then informed Kelson of Rothana's intention to establish a Deryni *schola* in Rhemuth. She sailed with her children from Coroth to Desse on the XVIIIth day of July, arriving there several days later. She dined with the King and his party in Rhemuth Palace on the evening of the XXIst day instant. She was among those who welcomed the Servants of Saint Camber on the XXXth day of July, and helped convince Rothana to allow Prince Albin to assume his birthright. She attended the Royal weddings there in late July and early August.

She is described in the *Chronicles* as having "...a reed slim figure, delicate, heart-shaped face framed by masses of reddish gold hair and eyes of a deep sea-blue shade." [*Deryni Checkmate*; *High Deryni*; *The Bishop's Heir*; *The King's Justice*; *The Quest for Saint Camber*; *Deryni Magic*; *King Kelson's Bride*].

Rickart, Dom. He was born on the IXth day of December in the Year of Our Lord 879. He entered the Gabrilite Order at an early age, was trained as a Healer, and was serving Bishop Niallan Trey in Dhassa early in the year 918. He became part of Niallan and Father Joram MacRorie's staff at the Michaeline Haven later that year. He prepared the sample *merasha* used by King Javan to experience the effects of that substance in August of the year 921. He helped train Camlin Lord MacLean to use his Deryni powers during the 920s at the former Michaeline Haven. He was included in the discussions by the Camberian Council on the XXVth day of June in the year 928 concerning the injury to the hand of King Rhys Michael and the new codicil to King's will. His date of death is unknown. According to Volumen I of *The Heirs of Saint Camber*, the "long hair drawn back in the tight single braid of his order was glossy chestnut." [*The Harrowing of Gwynedd*; *King Javan's Year*; *The Bastard Prince*].

Rimmell. He was born on the VIIIth day of May in the Year of Our Lord 1093. At the age of X his brown hair abruptly turned white during the night while he slept. He later trained as an architect, and took up service with Jared McLain Duke of Cassan. In the year 1121 he fell in love with Bronwyn Lady de Morgan, who was to be married to the Duke's son, Kevin McLain Earl of Kierney. To advance his suit and stop the wedding Rimmell purchased a love spell from Bethane, an old witch-woman of the hills, on the XXVIIth day of March in that year. However, the magic misfired and caused the accidental deaths of Bronwyn and her fiancé on the XXIXth day instant. The distraught Rimmell, then aged XXVII years, was immediately executed at Culdi by order of Duke Jared, and the architect's head was placed on a pike above the city gates to be eaten by the crows. "*Ci-gît Rimmelle, qui ne fut rien, pas même architecte.*" [*Deryni Checkmate*; *The Bishop's Heir*].

Ring of Fire. One of the items of state regalia belonging to the King of Gwynedd, it has been passed down from father to son since the time of Augarinus King of Gwynedd. [*Camber of Culdi*; *Camber the Heretic*; *King Javan's Year*; *Deryni Rising*; *The Quest for Saint Camber*].

Riordan, Father. He was Master of Novices at the *Arx Fidei* Seminary near Valoret in August of the year 1104.

He was very fond of Father Jorian de Courcy, and gave a gracious homily to the seminarians before Jorian's execution on the XIth day of November of that year, at great personal risk to himself and his own career. ["The Priesting of Arilan"].

R'Kassi. This ancient desert Kingdom is situate East of the Forcinn Buffer States, being framed by the River Thuria on the West and South and the River Khabur on the North, and bounded on the North by the Principality of Tralia, on the Northeast by the County of Vechta and Duchy of Vorna in Torenth, on the South and Southwest by the Anvil of the Lord, and on the East and Southeast by the Khanate of Khokanistan, the Kingdom of Libania, and the Holy Lands. R'Kassi was founded in the year 449 by the Sheikh Kasim al-Khojja, ruler of I of the many nomadic tribes in the region. The region converted to the Muslim faith during the time of the Prophet Muhammad, representing the Northernmost penetration of that heathen religion, other than by raiding parties. Three dynasties have ruled R'Kassi over the centuries. The capital city, Nabat', a collection of drab one- and two-storey mud brick buildings, is located at the confluence of the II major rivers.

The Kingdom of R'Kassi is famous for its blooded horses and for its archers, which are often hired out as mercenaries to the highest bidder. Its arms are: *azure, a pegasus passant or, wings elevated, mane and tail argent.* ["The Knighting of Derry"; *The Bishop's Heir*; *King Kelson's Bride*]. See also: Bahadur Khan, Sulien.

KINGS OF R'KASSI

HOUSE OF AL-KHOJJA

Kasim al-Khojja	449-481
Nu'man (son)	481-499
Aun al-Rafiq (son)	499-521
Sa'ud (son)	521-544
Talal (brother)	544
Zayid I (son)	544-577
Ali I (cousin)	577-579
Mubarak (son of Zayid)	579-588
Surur (son)	588-603
Yazid (son)	603-660
Ubaid (brother)	660-661
Umar (nephew)	661-666
Abd al-Malik (cousin)	666-669
Ali II (son)	669-702
Uthman (son)	702-706
Ja'afar (brother)	706-710
Abd al-Aziz (son)	710-742
Ismail (son)	742-760
Zayid II (son)	760-773
Faisal (cousin)	773-803

INTERREGNUM

HOUSE OF RHUPEN

Rhupen I	811-819
Timur (son)	819-832
Tigran (cousin)	832-855
Levon (son)	855-880
Rhupen II (son)	880-901
Thoros (brother)	901-903
Oshin (brother)	903-906
Levon (brother)	906-907
Hethum (brother)	907-909
Levon (restored)	909
Piran (brother)	909-913
Gosdantin (nephew)	913-922
Rhupen III (brother)	922-933

HOUSE OF AL-MUTTALIB

Hamdan al-Muttalib	933-945
Abu'l Fadl (son)	945-966
Bhair al-Salah (son)	966-999
Saif al-Din (brother)	999-1003
Abd al-Nasr (son)	1003-1033
Salah al-Din (brother)	1033-1049
Shihab al-Samani (son)	1049-1066
Abu'l Kasim (son)	1066
Jalal al-Din (cousin)	1066-1069
Qabus al-Duala (son)	1069-1089
Rauf al-Zaman (son)	1089-1100
Usman Khan (brother)	1100-1103
Arab Muhammad (brother)	1103-1107
Abd al-Ilah (brother)	1107-1112
Bahadur Khan (brother)	1112-1130+

Robard. He was serving as a scout in the party of Kelson King of Gwynedd during the latter's visit to Trurill on the XXIVth day of November in the year 1123. *Le nez de Robard, s'il eut été plus court, toute la face de la terre auroit changé.* [*The Bishop's Heir*].

Robear, Sir. He was born on the Vth day of August in the Year of Our Lord 883, being the son of Sir Roburn Reganson and Amaldie Lady MacInturff. He intermarried with Bova Lady Martano on the XXIIIrd day of July in the year 919, and by her he had children: the Lady Belva; the Lord Ross, both of whom used the surname MacRobar. He was the senior knight assigned to guard the Princes Javan and Rhys Michael during the great fair at Valoret on the XXVIIIth day of May in the year 917. He was also present at the assassination attempt on the Princes on the XXVIIIth day of September in that year. He remained loyal to King Javan when the latter succeeded to the throne, and paid homage to him at his accession on the XXIIIrd day of June in the year 921, bringing him a fresh tunic to wear. He was I of a group of loyal knights at Court who prepared a set of legal documents in anticipation of the accession of King Javan. He attended the coronation of the King on the XXXIst day of July in the year 921. Several days later, he was sent by the King to Nyford to report on conditions there. He was slain with his monarch by the former Regents on the XIth day of May in the year 922, aged XXXVIII years; his son was later ennobled by King Owain, partly out of respect for Robear's sacrifice. He was tall and fair, burly and bearded, and slightly greying, and enjoyed playing the lute. *Non domus hoc corpus sed hospitium et quidem breve.* R.I.P. [*Camber the Heretic*; *King Javan's Year*].

Robert *Ainslie*, called "Robin," Hereditary Lord Argoed, Lord Regent of Gwynedd, Sir. He was born on the I[st] day of April in the Year of Our Lord 901, being the eldest son and heir of Ainslie Lord Argoed and Eilidh Lady Ballingmore. He intermarried with

Rhysel Lady Thuryn on the XXIst day of August in the year 928, and by her he had children: the Lady Bethany, who intermarried with Alphard Baron Stanzar; Sir Javyl later Lord Argoed; the Lady Tiphane, who intermarried with Tammaron Duke of Cassan.

He was knighted on the IInd day of February in the year 919. He was sent by King Javan on the XXVth day of November in the year 921 with dispatches to Manfred Earl of Culdi and to the "rescued" Prince Rhys Michael. He accompanied the Royal Expedition to Eastmarch on the XVth day of June in the year 928. On the XXIVth day instant he was secretly ordered by King Rhys Michael to take I original copy of the new codicil to his will from Lochalyn Castle to the Queen Michaela in Rhemuth. He arrived there IV days later, and met his future wife, the Lady Rhysel Thuryn, to whom he gave the document to pass to the Queen. Sir Robert was later named to the new Regency Council of Owain King of Gwynedd on the IInd day of August in that same year. He died on the IIIrd day of February in the year 949, aged XLVII years, and was succeeded as Hereditary Lord by his son, Sir Javyl.

He is described in the *Heirs* as "a slim but well-built young man with curly brown hair and blue eyes, all but veiled by long lashes." His face was unmemorable. R.I.P. [*King Javan's Year*; *The Bastard Prince*].

Robert, Lord of Tendal[l], Hereditary Chancellor of the Duchy of Corwyn. He was born on the I^st day of December in the Year of Our Lord 1071, being the son of Jacob Lord of Tendal and Mabyn Lady Metras. He intermarried with Dulcibella Lady Comstock on the IVth day of January in the year 1092, and by her he had children: the Lady Dulcie; the Lady Bella, a twin with her sister; the Hereditary Lord Bobbin; the Lord Jacobus; the Lord Metras. He succeeded his father as Hereditary Chancellor of the Duchy of Corwyn on the IXth day of June in the year 1109, and served as a stalwart supporter of and adviser to Alaric Morgan Duke of Corwyn. [*Deryni Checkmate*; *The Bishop's Heir*; *The Quest for Saint Camber*].

Robert II *Oriss*, Archbishop of Rhemuth, sometime Vicar General of the *Ordo Verbi Dei*. He was born on the XXIXth day of February in the Year of Our Lord 848. In his youth he attended the monastery school at Saint Neot's Abbey, where he met and became friends with Anscom of Trevas later Archbishop Primate of Valoret and All Gwynedd. He joined the *Ordo Verbi Dei* in the year 869, being ordained priest on the XXth day of July in that year, and was elected Vicar General of the Order on the XIIth day of May in the year 898, residing at the Mother House of Saint Jarlath's Abbey in Barwicke. He was elected Archbishop of Rhemuth on the XIth day of June in the year 905, and was consecrated on the IXth day of July following. He was then named to the Royal Council on the VIth day of November. He was present at the coronation of King Alroy on the XXVth day of May in the year 917.

As the senior prelate present, he presided over the Synod of Bishops held at Valoret in November and December of 917. He abstained from the rigged vote of the XXVIth day of December which elected Bishop Hubert MacInnis Archbishop Primate of Valoret and All Gwynedd. He was present at the death of King Alroy on the XXIIIrd day of June in the year 921. He attended the coronation of King Javan on the XXXIst day of July in that year.

On the XVth day of June in the year 928 he blessed the King and army of Gwynedd as they departed Rhemuth on their Expedition to Eastmarch. A few days later, he became seriously ill, and was attended at his bedside by his colleagues, Archbishop Hubert and Secorim Abbot of the *Custodes* Chapter at Rhemuth. They were at his residence when Father Fabius arrived with the news of Lord Albertus's death and Brother Paulin's incapacitation on the XXVth day instant. He succumbed to the infirmities of old age and the shaking palsy on the XXIXth day of June in the year 928, within a day of the passing of Rhys Michael King of Gwynedd, a confluence which caused great comment at the time. He was LXXX years of age at his death, and was buried in the Crypt of Saint George's Cathedral. *Levia perpessæ sumus, si flenda patimur.* R.I.P. [*Camber of Culdi*; *Saint Camber*; *Camber the Heretic*; *The Harrowing of Gwynedd*; *King Javan's Year*; *The Bastard Prince*].

Robert, son of Peter, later Brother Benedict. He was born in the Year of Our Lord 864, and was received into the *Ordo Verbi Dei* and took the name Benedict in the year 883, being cloistered at the Priory of Saint Ultan's. [*Camber of Culdi*].

Rocail al-Din *al-Muttalib*, Grand Master of the Knights of the Anvil, Prince and Sharif of R'Kassi. He was born on the IInd day of March in the Year of Our Lord 1068, being the seventh son of Jalal al-Din King of R'Kassi and Raba'a Shaikha of al-Qarrah. He joined the Knights of the Anvil, the successors to the Michaelines, at Djellarda about the year 1100, and was elected Grand Master of the Order on the XXIVth day of July in the year 1113. He was still serving in that capacity in June of the year 1124. [*The King's Justice*].

Rogan Rufus Rehim *von Horthy*, Cadet d'Orsal and Prince of Tralia. He was born on the XVIIIth day of September in the Year of Our Lord 1110, being the second son and third child of Létald von Horthy Hort of Orsal and Prince of Tralia and Husniyya Princess and Sharifa of R'Kassi. He was sent to the Court of Alaric Morgan Duke of Corwyn on the XXVth day of March in the year 1121 to be trained as a squire and knight.

According to Father Duncan McLain Duke of Cassan, "He was a potential scholar or physician or monk if I ever saw one. It's a pity that he will never have the chance to pursue his true calling. Instead, he'll become some sort of minor functionary in his older brother's court when the time comes, never really happy, never knowing why, or perhaps knowing why but unable to do anything about it."

By the year 1128 he had achieved some of his ambitions, and was being trained as a scholar. He was stocky even as a youth. [*Deryni Checkmate*; *King Kelson's Bride*].

Roger *de Piran*, Earl of Jenas. He was born on the IVth day of June in the Year of Our Lord 1088, being the eldest son and heir of Ninian Earl of Jenas and Thea Lady Mackey. He intermarried with the Lady Mandana youngest daughter of Moncure Gillispie Earl of Danoc and Aidana Lady Perrin on the IIIrd day of March in the year 1105, and by her he had children: the Hereditary Lord Perrin; the Lady Moncura; the Lord Aidan; the Lord Gillispie; the Lady Nina. He succeeded his father on the Ist day of July in the year 1121, and was present at the Christmas Council of 1123 which discussed the developing Mearan Crisis. He later served with the main Gwyneddan Army during the invasion of Meara on the XXth day of May in the year 1124. It was he who discovered the sacrilegious desecration of Saint Brigid's Convent by Hereditary Prince Ithel on the XVIth day of June following. He stopped ex-Archbishop Edmund Loris from killing Father Duncan McLain Duke of Cassan on the field of Dorna on the IIIrd day of July. He accompanied the King on his quest for the relics of Saint Camber on the IXth day of March in the year 1125. [*The Bishop's Heir*; *The King's Justice*].

Rogier, Earl and Baron Fallon. He was born on the VIIth day of June in the Year of Our Lord 1080, being the son of Sir Rogain de Fallon and Aimone Lady Montvert. He intermarried with Béatrix Lady Thuriot on the XVIIth day of May in the year 1099, and by her he had children: the Hereditary Lord Rogier *Junior* later Rogier II Baron Fallon; the Lady Aimonette; the Lord Jean; the Lord César; the Lord Gauzbert; the Lady Emme. He was created Baron Fallon by King Brion on the Ist day of December in the year 1105, and was made an Earl *ad personam* on the last day of October in the year 1114. This member of the Royal Council of Gwynedd was a companion of Brion King of Gwynedd during his final hunt on the Ist day of November in the year 1120, when he was wearing dark green velvet and riding a grey stallion. Later that month he discovered Alaric Duke of Corwyn and the young King Kelson at the entrance to the royal crypt beneath Saint George's Cathedral. He was killed there a few moments later by Ian Howell Earl of Eastmarch on the XIVth day of November in the year 1120, aged XL years, and was found the next morning holding Duncan's crucifix in his hand. He was succeeded in the Barony of Fallon by his eldest son, Lord Rogier *Junior*. R.I.P. [*Deryni Rising*].

Rohays Ramona bint Reyhan *Vastouni*, Princess of Andelon and Nur Hallaj. She was born on the XXVIIth day of April in the Year of Our Lord 1105, being the youngest child of Reyhan Lord Séchelles of Jáca and Sofiana Sovereign Princess of Andelon. She intermarried with Sulen Hereditary Nabil of Nur Hallaj on the XXth day of June in the year 1120, and by him she had children: the Nabil Qais; the Nabila Athbissa; the Nabil Suleiman. She wrote to her *cousine germaine*, Richenda Duchess of Corwyn, on the XXXth day of June in the year 1124, using her husband's uncle, the Nabil Azim, as courier. *Der Stärkste hat Recht*. [*The King's Justice*].

Roisian Moira Faucona *Quinnell*, Sovereign Prince of Meara, Queen of Gwynedd. Her name is also spelled Rosheen in some accounts. She was born on the XXIIIrd day of January in the Year 1008, being the eldest daughter of Jolyon II Sovereign Prince of Meara and the Princess Urracca daughter of Faucon Hereditary Prince of Bremagne, and the elder twin sister of Princess Annalind. She was betrothed to Nikola Prince of Torenth and Duke of Arkadia on the Ist day of January in the year 1025, but the marriage never took place. She intermarried with Malcolm King of Gwynedd on the IXth day of August in the Year 1025, and by him she had children: the Princess Amalie, who was betrothed to Tancrède King of Fallon at the time of her death at age XVII from the falling fits; the Princess Tiphaine later a nun of Saint Emerentiana's under the name of Sister Zita, who died at the age of LXXXII years, *sans postérité*, in the year 1110; the Hereditary Prince Donal Blaine later Donal Blaine II King of Gwynedd; the Princess Anaïs, who intermarried with Florestan Prince d'Uzès, leaving issue now extinct; the Prince Malcolm *Junior*, dead a day after his birth; the Princess Marfurca, dead of the yellow skin at age I.

It is said that the Princess Roisian was her father's favourite child, that he stated on more than one occasion that had he been blessed with one carlin only, his choice would have been Roisian. But if her father loved her dearly, her mother favoured her sister, the Princess Annalind. Wags at Court were fond of noting that although Annalind and Roisian were born of the same parents, no one would have guessed them siblings. For where the Princess Roisian was tall and slender, Annalind was short and stocky, where Roisian had silky blonde tresses, her sister sported frizzy black curls that grew out wild and rough. The Princess Roisian had blue eyes, a low musical voice, was quiet and kind to servants and animals, and spent her time in the study of history, literature, music, and art. The Princess Annalind had dark eyes, her mother's sharp Bremagni tongue, a high voice, and preferred riding bareback across the moors, locks flying askew.

Following the death of Prince Jolyon II on the XXIXth day of May in the year 1025, the Princess Roisian succeeded her father as Sovereign Prince of Meara. However, she fled Laas shortly thereafter, and was declared by the High Council of State to have vacated the throne, although she never abdicated her rights or relinquished her claim. Her younger sister, Princess Annalind, succeeded her, but was herself dispossessed II years later by Malcolm King of Gwynedd and husband of Roisian. During the next II decades the Queen Roisian did all that she could to bring peace to the realm, but in Meara the partisans of her sister continued to resist, and were eventually declared outlaw, being banished from the Kingdom on pain of death. In August of the year 1045 the Princess Annalind was captured by King Malcolm, and the Queen saw her sister for the last time. On the VIIIth day of August the Princess Annalind and her kin were executed.

Then Queen Roisian took herself in sorrow off to the Convent of Saint Emerentiana in Fallon, never again to return to Gwynedd. She died there of *la grippe* on the IIIrd day of January in the year 1055, aged XLVI years, being returned for burial in the Crypt of the Haldanes beneath Saint George's Cathedral, Rhemuth. R.I.P. *Ma Rosanna si bella e ridente, mi si mostrò, che tra quelle vedute, si vuol lasciar che non seguir la mente*. [*The Bishop's Heir*; *The King's Justice*].

Roland, Auxiliary Bishop of Valoret. He was born on the XXXth day of August in the Year of Our Lord 847. He was ordained priest on the XVth day of July in the year 868, was consecrated an itinerant Bishop of Gwynedd on the XVIIth day of May in the year 889, and was named Auxiliary Bishop of Valoret on the Ist day of March in the year 901. He died on the Vth day of January in the year 916, aged LXVIII years. R.I.P. [*Camber of Culdi*; *Camber the Heretic*].

Rolf *MacPherson*, Lord. He was born on the IIIrd day of April in the Year of Our Lord 862, being the second son of Jamie Baron MacPherson and Ellie Lady Godwin. He never married. This Deryni Lord of the Xth century is said to have rebelled against the authority of the Camberian Council on the XIth day of May in the year 950. He died at an unknown date during the persecutions of the Deryni in Gwynedd, reportedly a bitter man, and is buried we know not where. [*High Deryni*; *The Bishop's Heir*; *The King's Justice*].

Rolf, son of Carrolan, later Brother Benedict. He was received into the *Ordo Verbi Dei* in the year 873, taking the name Benedict, being cloistered at the Priory of Saint Piran's by the year 903. [*Camber of Culdi*].

Romare. This blacksmith at Castle Derry treated Sean O'Flynn Earl Derry's injured horse on the Ist day of May in the year 1115. ["The Knighting of Derry"].

Romlin. This man from Twilham Green uncovered Geordie Lord Drummond's true identity in April of the year 905 by giving him *merasha*. [*Deryni Challenge*].

Ronal Rurik Radislaus Royse *Furstán d'Arjenol*, Hereditary Prince of Torenth, Duke of Lorsöl. He was born on the last day of February in the Year of Our Lord 1118, being the fourth son of Lionel II Duke d'Arjenol and Morag Princess of Torenth. He was created Duke of Lorsöl by King Wencit on the IVth day of March in the year 1120 in succession to his uncle, Prince Torval. At the death of his eldest brother, King Alroy Arion II, on the XIIth day of June in 1123, he became Heir Presumptive to the throne of Torenth. He was kept under the close supervision of his uncle, Mahael II Duke d'Arjenol and Regent of Torenth.

In the year 1128 he became a pawn in the conspiracy of Mahael Duke d'Arjenol and Teymuraz Count of Brustarkia against Ronal's elder brother, King Liam Lajos II, either as a supposed target for a later assassination, or as Liam's potential replacement on the throne. He was introduced to King Kelson at a reception held at Furstánály Palace in Beldour on the IXth day of July in that year. He is described in *Bride* as "an intense, wary ten-year-old, little resembling his elder sibling, bright-haired among the dark heads of his Furstáni kin. He is well shielded in his own right." [*High Deryni*; *The Bishop's Heir*; *The King's Justice*; *The Quest for Saint Camber*; *King Kelson's Bride*].

Rondel, Sir. He was born on the XIth day of November in the Year of Our Lord 888, being the son of one Radon a lieutenant for hire and Robine his wife. This knight was serving Manfred Earl of Culdi in the year 918. He was the only survivor of the encounter between Archbishop Alister Cullen and Earl Jebediah and the IV soldiers of Culdi on the VIth day of January of that year. He took Cullen's cross as proof of the encounter, and reported to his master on the day following. He then rode with him to Valoret, arriving at the state wedding banquet being held there on the Xth day of January; he was truth-read by Declan Carmody at the Regents' command to verify his account of events. At the order of Manfred he restrained Rhun Earl of Sheele from interfering with Brother Polidorus's treatment of the injured King Rhys Michael on the XXVIIth day of June in the year 928. He arrived in Rhemuth on the Ist day of July to report to the Council on the King's death. [*Camber the Heretic*; *The Harrowing of Gwynedd*; *The Bastard Prince*].

Rorik III Robur Berengar *Howell*, Earl of Eastmarch. He was born on the IVth day of May in the Year 1066, being the eldest son and heir of Corban II Earl of Eastmarch and Virgilia Lady MacEwan. He intermarried with Juliette Coris Lady Marley on the IVth day of August in the year 1086, and by her he had children: the Countess Eulalia Heiress of Eastmarch, who intermarried with Rhydon Baron Coldoire; the Hereditary Count Kennet, who was killed in the year 1105 by his cousin, the Lord Arban Howell, *sans postérité*.

The Lord Rorik succeeded his father on the IIIrd day of January in the year 1088. On the XXVIth day of November in the year 1104 he sent his soldiers into Arranal Canyon in Marley in defiance of royal writ, and refused to withdraw, saying that it was part of the ancient Earldom of Eastmarch and claiming it on behalf of his wife. He occupied the Western part of the Earldom of Marley on the XXIInd day of May in the following year. When he learned in June of that year that King Brion was mounting a force against him, he rallied his soldiers at Lochalyn Castle, and proceeded South. But his cousin, Arban Howell Baron of Iomaire, who supported the King and who was also next in line to the Earldom after Rorik's own children, abruptly attacked him on the XIIIth day of that month, capturing him and killing his son Kennet.

On the XXth day of June in the year 1105 he was tried by King Brion, and condemned, hanged, drawn, and quartered as a traitor, aged XXXIX years. Arban Baron Iomaire was named his successor on that same day, but Rorik's son-in-law, Rhydon Baron Coldoire, proclaimed himself Earl in the right of his wife. ["Swords Against the Marluk"].

Rory Werril Bertald Bearand *Haldane*, late Hereditary Duke of Carthmoor, Duke of Ratharkin, Prince of Gwynedd. He was born on the XIXth day of January in the Year of Our Lord 1110, being the second son of Prince Nigel Duke of Carthmoor and Meraude Lady de Traherne. He intermarried with the Lady Noelie Ramsay on the XXXIst day of July in the year 1128, and by her he had a child: the Prince Bearand Bertald Ewan de Traherne Hereditary Duke of Ratharkin.

The Prince Rory was trained as a squire at Court by his father, and was present at the marriage of his brother, Prince Regent Conall, to the Lady Rothana

Princess and Nabila of Nur Hallaj on the xi[th] day of April in the year 1125. After Conall's execution on the iii[rd] day of May in that year, the Prince Rory was named Hereditary Duke of Carthmoor by his father, bypassing the rights of Conall's unborn son, Prince Albin. He met his betrothed when the Ramsays visited Rhemuth in the Summer of the year 1127. He was created Duke of Ratharkin on the day of his marriage in the year 1128, at which time he relinquished all rights to the Honour of Carthmoor, which was thereupon restored to his nephew, Prince Albin. He had black hair worn in a neat border braid, and a rich tenor singing voice. [*High Deryni*; *The Bishop's Heir*; *The King's Justice*; *The Quest for Saint Camber*; *King Kelson's Bride*].

Ros. This follower of Warin de Grey led the band of brigands which burned out Arnaud Sieur de Vali in March of the year 1121. [*Deryni Checkmate*].

Rosane Marie Élisabeth Jaÿne *Haldane*, Princess of Gwynedd. She was born on the last day of October in the Year of Our Lord 1108, being the second child and only daughter of Brion King of Gwynedd and Queen Jehana Princess of Bremagne. She died of the blue skin on the iii[rd] day of November, and was buried in the Royal Crypt of the Haldanes beneath Saint George's Cathedral in Rhemuth. [*King Kelson's Bride*].

Rothana, *i.e.*, **R'thana Ayesha Kamila bint Hakim ar-Rafiq, Princess and Nabila of Nur Hallaj, sometime Princess Regent of Gwynedd, Sister and Lady.** She was born on the xx[th] day of October in the Year of Our Lord 1107, being the third daughter of Hakim II Sovereign Prince and Emir of Nur Hallaj and Fabrissa Princess of R'Kassi, and a *cousine germaine* by marriage of Richenda Duchess of Corwyn. She intermarried with Conall Hereditary Duke of Carthmoor and Prince Regent of Gwynedd on the xi[th] day of April in the year 1125, and by him she had a child: the Prince Albin Nigel Brion Hakim Hereditary Duke of Carthmoor, born posthumously.

The Princess Rothana was trained as a Deryni by her uncle Azim. She entered the Church in the year 1123. On the xv[th] day of June in the year 1124 she was serving as a novice at Saint Brigid's Abbey in Meara when that place was sacked by Brice Baron of Trurill and Ithel Hereditary Prince of Meara. She read the memories of Janniver Princess of Pardiac to provide King Kelson with the information that resulted in the execution of Ithel and Brice for their crimes. She returned to Rhemuth with Prince Conall on the xxvii[th] day of June, and remained at Court until her marriage. She was first seen in secular garb at a ball on the iii[rd] day of March the year 1125.

By the xxii[nd] day of that month she was entertaining thoughts of becoming King Kelson's bride. Before the King left on his quest for the relics of Saint Camber, the Princess Rothana told him that she had sent a letter to Thomas Cardiel Archbishop of Rhemuth asking for a release from her religious vows, and that the King was the cause. King Kelson received the news with joy. When Cardiel read the Princess's letter after Kelson's disappearance, he was wrongly convinced by Prince Regent Conall that Rothana had actually intended to marry him. On that same day, being the ii[nd] day of April, Conall approached the Lady Rothana concerning the political necessity of securing the succession to the Gwyneddan Throne, and asked her to marry him. She accepted her fate with hesitance. After Conall's execution as a traitor by the resurrected King Kelson, she entertained thoughts of re-entering the religious life, or of finding some other way to serve God and seek restitution for her late husband's sins. She took her son in the year after his birth to meet his grandparents in Nur Hallaj. She returned to Gwynedd by way of the Île d'Orsal, and then joined the Servants of Saint Camber about the year 1127.

In the year 1128 the Princess Rothana attended the wedding of Princess Janniver and Sir Jatham Kilshane on the xxviii[th] day of June, and told King Kelson later that evening that she could never marry him or anyone else. She then proposed that the King marry his cousin, Princess Araxie Haldane. She also proposed that Prince Albin be intended for the Church. She left Rhemuth later that night, and returned with the Servants of Saint Camber on the xxx[th] day of July. At this time the King proposed that Princess Rothana become a lay assistant to the Rector of the new Deryni *schola* being established in Rhemuth, which she ultimately accepted, together with the reinstatement of her son as heir to the Duchy of Carthmoor. She attended the double Royal wedding on the following day, and helped cleanse Sean Earl Derry of the longstanding compulsion originally inserted in his mind by Wencit King of Torenth. She was also present at Kelson and Araxie's marriage a week later.

She had long, blue-black hair and dark eyes. In the year 1128 she wore the simple, grey habit of the Servants of Saint Camber. [*The King's Justice*; *The Quest for Saint Camber*; *King Kelson's Bride*].

Rotrou II Gédéon Dragonet *de Mont-Volcan*, Sovereign Prince of Jáca. He was born on the xth day of September in the Year of Our Lord 1086, being the eldest son and heir of Dragonet Sovereign Prince of Jáca and the Princess Perpenna daughter of Bagrat Sovereign Prince of Autun. He intermarried with the Shaikha Kemala daughter of Rub'al Shaikh of al-Qarrah on the xvii[th] day of June in the year 1110, and by her he had children: the Princess Ekaterina Évariste Sisine; the Hereditary Prince Gédéon Rotrou Dragonet; the Princess Rubala Dragonette; the Prince Kemal Randon Yves; the Princess Eblesse Bagratine.

In the year 1128 the Prince Rotrou represented his father during the installation of Liam Lajos II King of Torenth, and attended a reception in the Hanging Gardens of Furstánály Palace on the xi[th] day of July in the year 1128. He succeeded his father on the xiii[th] day of January in the year 1129. [*King Kelson's Bride*].

Royal Haldane Lancers. This unit of the Gwyneddan Army marched North to Cardosa with the King's forces in June of the year 1121 to face the army of Wencit King of Torenth. [*High Deryni*].

Royal Tabard Inn. This CC-year-old hostel was located at Kingslake in Northern Corwyn. It was here that Sean

O'Flynn Earl Derry witnessed Warin de Grey's healing of Martin on the XXVth day of March in the year 1121. [*Deryni Checkmate*].

Royston *Richardson*. This peasant boy of X years found the injured Malcolm Donalson, his brother's friend, on the battlefield at Jennan Vale on the XVIIth day of June in the year 1121. He was sent to procure transport while Malcolm was healed by Alaric Morgan Duke of Corwyn and Father Duncan McLain Earl of Kierney. [*High Deryni*].

Ruadan *of Dhassa*, Saint. He was the ancient Deryni author of the *Liber Sancti Ruadan*, a mystic text. His feastday was the XXIst day of June, but his sainthood was rejected and disestablished by the Council of Ramos in 918. [*The Harrowing of Gwynedd*].

Rûm. This capital city of the ancient land of Etruskia is situate near the center of a peninsula surrounded by the Grand Canal of the Median Sea. Built upon VII hills, each with its own distinct architecture and culture, Rûm is connected by River Tyger, which weaves betwixt and among these mounds, tying them together inextricably. The natives speak a language called Latino, the older form of which is termed Latin, and is still being used by the Etruskian Church. The secular Republic of Etruskia is governed by a Grand Consul, who is elected by the Senate to rule for a single year only. Among the highlights of the city of Rûm are the Colossal Baths, the Grand Amphitorium, the Consulatorium, the great bronze statues of Rumulus and Romos, the colourfully plum'd aqui-ducks which swim playfully upon the Lake Pericomo, the Via Aeria and the Pia Zadoria, the Papiarchium or Seat of the Holy Papiarch and Pontifex Maximus, the Great Kitchens of the Coquus Boïardius, the Cloaca Dulcis, and the Ædicula Sistina, among many others. Tourism is a major industry here.

Rustán. This town and the Barony of the same name are located under the Rustán Cliffs in the Rheljan Mountains. The nearest city is Cardosa. ["Swords Against the Marluk"].

Rustán Cliffs. These sheer faces of rock are located in the Rheljan Mountains above Rustán Town and Castle not far from the city of Cardosa. It was here that King Brion agreed to meet Hogan Gwernach the Marluk on the XXIst day of June in the year 1105. ["Swords Against the Marluk"].

Ryons Gospatric *Haldane*, King of Gwynedd. He was born on the XVIIIth day of May in the Year of Our Lord 700, being the third surviving son of Llarik King of Gwynedd, but the first by his second wife, Sidonie Princess of Meara. He intermarried with the Princess Raphaela daughter of Imre I King of Torenth on the Xth day of June in the year 719, and by her he had children: the Hereditary Prince Bearand later King of Gwynedd; the Princess Asthore; the Princess Doireann; the Prince Phædrig Imre, who died young; the Princess Phiala Imretta, a twin with her brother.

The Prince Ryons succeeded his father on the XIth day of January in the year 719, and was crowned on the XXVIth day of March in the same year by Archbishop Marin. His whole reign consisted of a series of ongoing battles with the Muslim and Norse raiders and invaders. In the year 733 Moorish forces even besieged Rhemuth itself, before King Ryons marched South from Valoret with his army to relieve the city, arriving there on the VIth day of June. King Ryons was killed in battle against the Muslims at Nyford on the XIXth day of August the year 736, aged XXXVI years, and was succeeded by his son, Prince Bearand. His body was returned to Rhemuth for burial in the crypt of his ancestors. R.I.P.

Saer Sighere Tirso *de Traherne*, Earl of Rhendall, Sir. He was born on the XXIInd day of July in the Year of Our Lord 1093, being the eldest son and heir of Ewan III Earl of Rhendall and Mellicent Lady MacEwan, and brother of Meraude wife to Prince Nigel Duke of Carthmoor.

The Lord Saer came to Court in the year 1105, serving as a squire to Richard Haldane Duke of Carthmoor. He succeeded his father on the XIXth day of September in the year 1118. He was appointed to the High Council by King Kelson on the XIth day of July in the year 1122. He rode with the King to Trurill on the XXIVth day of November in the year 1123, and again several weeks later on Kelson's lightning raid to Ratharkin on the VIIIth day of December following. However, he stayed in Rhemuth during the Gwyneddan invasion of Meara in May of the year 1124.

He was present at the knighting of the King on the IIIrd day of March in the year 1125, and accompanied him on his quest for the relics of Saint Camber on the IXth day instant. He later informed the Bishops that the King was presumed dead on the XXIIIrd day of that month, and returned to Rhemuth. He attended his nephew Prince Regent Conall's wedding to Rothana Nabila of Nur Hallaj on the XIth day of April following.

In the year 1128 Earl Saer accompanied the Torenthi ambassadors, Rasoul and Count Mátyás, from Desse to Rhemuth on the XXIXth day of June. He was included in the Royal party of King Kelson that traveled to Beldour in July, and returned to Orsal from Beldour by ship, beginning on the XVIIth day of that month. On the XXIXth day instant he escorted the wedding finery overland from Desse to Rhemuth. He then attended the Royal weddings in late July and early August. He acted as Godfather to his niece, the Princess Gloriana, in the year 1129. *Ao bom amigo com teu pão, e com teu vinho.* [*The Bishop's Heir*; *The King's Justice*; *The Quest for Saint Camber*; *King Kelson's Bride*].

Sagart. This *coisrigte* or member of the priestly caste at Saint Kyriell's died there in March of the year 1125. On the Xth day of April in that year King Kelson and Dhugal MacArdry Earl of Transha accidentally defiled his tomb while exiting their underground prison. R.I.P. [*The Quest for Saint Camber*].

***Saint Andrew's Cathedral*—SEE: *Saint Senan's Cathedral*.**

***Saint Basil's Bridge*.** This massive structure, the largest bridge in the XI Kingdoms, spans the Beldour

River, uniting the new and old sections of Beldour, the capital of Torenth. Its construction was undertaken by the King Arkady II in the year 1031 and was completed and dedicated in a splendid ceremony held on the XVIth day of June in the year 1042. [*King Kelson's Bride*].

Saint Bearand's Abbey. This establishment, which honours the name of the Great King Bearand Haldane, is located at the foot of the High Grelder Pass Northeast of Caerrorie; the Pass leads from the Abbey into the Iomaire Plain. It was here that King Kelson and his party stopped on the XIXth and XXth days of March in the year 1125. [*The Quest for Saint Camber*].

Saint Brigid's Abbey. This convent, located on the Mearan side of the border between Meara and Gwynedd, was sacked by Brice Baron of Trurill and Ithel Hereditary Prince of Meara on the XVth day of June in the year 1124. Janniver Princess of Pardiac was staying here briefly on her way to Llannedd for her formal betrothal to Colman II King of Howicce and Llannedd, but she was violated by Prince Ithel during his attack on the Abbey. Although Janniver was rescued and escorted to safety by Prince Conall on the XVIIth day instant, she was rejected by both King Colman and by her own father, the Prince Pons, and forced into exile at the Court of Rhemuth. [*The King's Justice*; *The Quest for Saint Camber*].

Saint Camber's-at-Nyford Abbey. This *schola* and Abbey of the Servants of Saint Camber was burned to the ground on the Ist day of August in the year 916, with most of its postulants being killed. It was partially rebuilt later that year, but was finally abandoned in the Fall of the year 917. [*Camber the Heretic*].

Saint Camber's Basilica and Chapel. This facility was consecrated to the Honour of Saint Camber at Saint Hilary's Basilica within Rhemuth Palace on the XXXth day of July in the year 1128. The Chapel had walls of pale grey marble, a ribbed and vaulted ceiling supporting a soaring dome, and a mosaic depicting the crowning of King Cinhil I by Saint Camber. [*King Kelson's Bride*].

Saint Camber's Siege. This empty VIIIth seat in the Camberian Council was left vacant by Camber Earl of Culdi's death on the VIth day of January in the year 918. It was often, but not always, kept unfilled in his honour. The Council discovered that VII members somehow "balanced" better. [*The Harrowing of Gwynedd*].

Saint Cassian's Abbey. This *Custodes* House was located in the middle of the Plain of Iomaire Southwest of Lochalyn Castle. It was here that the Royal Expedition encamped overnight on its way to Eastmarch on the XXth day of June in the year 928. The bodies of Lord Albertus and his brother, Vicar General Paulin Sinclair, were buried side-by-side in the Abbey's crypt later that month. [*The Bastard Prince*].

Saint Constantine's Cathedral. This mighty edifice of Beldour in Torenth was originally completed as a small church in the year 232 and added to over the centuries, but was utterly destroyed by a great earthquake which struck the city at the XIth hour on the XIVth day of March in the year 1008. Reconstruction was begun immediately in even grander style than before, and this largest church in the Western world was consecrated anew after nearly II decades of construction on the XIVth day of March in the year 1022, the anniversary of the disaster, by the Patriarch Abraam IV. The nave of the Cathedral is exceeded in size only by that of Holy Sophia herself in Kónstantinopolis, and includes colourful icons depicting events in the lives of Saint Constantine and Saint Helena. The top of its gilded, onion-shaped dome stands some CCCL feet from the ground. [*King Kelson's Bride*].

Saint Dymphna's Convent. This Abbey is one of the XXXVII monasteries, *scholae*, and other religious establishments located in the city of Grecotha, having been established on the IXth day of September in the year 889 on the site of the old Rûman baths there by Mother Matilda Montesque du Breuil, founder of the Order of the Sisters of the Holy Water (*Ordo Sororum Aquae Sanctae*). For Mother Matilda believed that only through repeated immersions in the heated pools of *aqua vitae* and bubbling mud in the cisterns beneath the Abbey could transgressors be cleansed of their sins and the sick be cured of their ills, and she strongly recommended the procedure to one and all, it having proved most efficacious in her own situation. She also maintained an asylum on the site for the demented, the witless, and the confused.

In the year 918 Elinor Lady Drummond was sent here by the Regents to be closely confined against her will. The Princess Silke Haldane became a postulant of this Order in the year 1105, and was later appointed Infirmarian of the Convent on the XVIth day of May in the year 1125 to help oversee the rebuilding of the *lavabrum*, which had deteriorated and been allowed to fall into ruin. For it is obvious, she said, that "cleanliness is next to Godliness."

Saint Elderon's Abbey. This Michaeline House was located in the Duchy of Tolán in Northern Torenth, on the coast of the Northern Sea not far from the Eastmarch border. It was one of the III "outside" houses to which the Michaeline Order retreated from Gwynedd in August and September of the year 917. [*Camber the Heretic*].

Saint Ercon's Abbey. This Mother House of the Little Brothers of Saint Ercon was located in Ramos on the banks of the River Eirian. It was founded in the year 912 by Paulin of Ramos, who became the first Grand Master of the Order. The Little Brothers were merged into the *Custodes Fidei* on the IInd day of February in the year 918. [*Camber the Heretic*].

Saint Ethelburga's Shrine. This monument to I of the II patron saints of Dhassa guards the Northern approach to the holy city. [*The Bishop's Heir*].

Saint Foillan's Abbey. This cloistered establishment of the *Ordo Verbi Dei* was located about III days' ride Southeast of Valoret in the Lendour Mountains. It was here that Camber Earl of Culdi and Rhys Lord Thuryn found Prince Cinhil Haldane living under his religious name, Brother Benedict, on the XIVth day of November in the year 903. [*Camber of Culdi*].

Saint George's Cathedral. This great church, the seat of the Archbishop of Rhemuth, was rebuilt on the foundations of an earlier structure beginning in June of the year 905; its refurbishing was completed by April of the year 918. The church serves as the main place of worship for the royal family of Gwynedd, and is also the site where the Kings of Gwynedd are crowned. Its undercroft contains the tombs of the Kings and Queens and other members of the royal House of Haldane, as well as the Archbishops of Rhemuth. Adjoining the church is the Archbishop of Rhemuth's official residence. The structure is located in the Northern sector of Rhemuth, and features II bronze doors and a stubby bell tower housing "Great George," the largest bell in all of the Eleven Kingdoms. It was here that the Royal weddings were held in the year 1128. [*Camber the Heretic*; *The Harrowing of Gwynedd*; *Deryni Rising*; *Deryni Checkmate*; *King Kelson's Bride*].

Saint Giles's Abbey. This convent is located in the lake region of Shannis Meer in the Rheljan Mountains near the border of Eastmarch with Tolán; it was built in the year 809 by Sister Sigolena of Troclar, founder of the Little Mothers of Perpetua and Felicity, II early saints of Rûm. It was here that Jehana Queen of Gwynedd went into retreat on the Vth day of July in the year 1105 and again on the XIIIth day of March in the year 1121. Caitrin Pretender of Meara was exiled here under close confinement on the XIIth day of July in the year 1124. [*Deryni Checkmate*; *The Bishop's Heir*].

Saint Hilary's-Within-the-Walls Basilica. This ancient royal crypt and chapel is located within the outer wards of Rhemuth Castle, and is accessible both to the Court and to the citizens of Rhemuth. Father Boniface was associated with this facility in the year 918. The body of King Alroy lay in state here during the latter days of June in the year 921. Monsignor Duncan McLain was rector here during the early 1120s. [*The Harrowing of Gwynedd*; *King Javan's Year*; *The Bishop's Heir*; *King Kelson's Bride*].

Saint Hilda's Abbey. This convent is located a few miles from the ancient city of Grecotha, having been erected in the year 844 by Mother Fusca, founder of the *Soeurs des Sagesse et Culture*. Elspeth Lady MacRorie was elected Abbess here in the year 889, but was killed by the Regents' soldiers on the XIVth day of January in the year 918 during the anti-Deryni persecutions, her Abbey also being destroyed. [*King Javan's Year*].

Saint Illtyd's Abbey. This establishment of the *Ordo Verbi Dei* was located on the River Carthane Northeast of the town of Nyford. It was here that several of the Brothers Benedict were cloistered in the year 903. [*Camber of Culdi*].

Saint Ilona's Convent. This establishment was built in the early VIth century near Beldour at the behest of Kerkira, the daughter of a wealthy merchant, Demid Vonifatevich, who changed her name to Mother Lydwina and founded the *Ordo Sanctarum Nobilium*. It has long attracted the younger daughters of privileged houses who have a calling to devote their lives to the work of charity. The Princess Jessamyn, daughter of Kálmán II King of Torenth, took the veil here at the age of XIV years under the religious name of Sophia. *Canta la rana y no tiene pelo ni lana*.

Saint Iób's Church, also called Saint Job's. The oldest Christian site in Torenth, and the personal place of worship for the Kings of that land, this domed church is located in the small village of Torenthály, North of the City of Beldour. Here the Kings of Torenth are installed in the *killijálay* ceremony, and here the Kings of Torenth are buried.

This beauteous structure is described thusly in *Bride*: "The clustered onion domes were clad with burnished gold. Save for the covered entry porch, which was gilded like the domes, the rest of the building was covered with gold-starred blue tiles. The high, narrow windows set around the base of the principal dome were limned with gold. The structure itself was somewhat smaller than Kelson expected, though he reminded himself that Holy Iób was not a cathedral, but a memorial church and place of ceremony. Passing from the heat outside through Holy Iób's gold-cased double doors was like stepping into another world. The vestibule within was hushed and cool, welcome respite as servants there divested them of boots and shoes, and put upon them soft slippers of felt, for the inlaid floors and carpets within were too precious to walk upon shod. The walls and vaulted ceiling were clad with more of the blue tiles. Kelson could discern the shimmer of gold in the glazing, making the tiles almost glow in the light of handfire streaming from a pierced lantern. Beyond another set of even grander double doors lay a broad, long nave surmounted at the transept crossing with a vast and lofty space beneath a dome that seemed to stretch very near to Heaven. But it was not the dome to which the eye was immediately drawn, but what lay beneath it, the black tomb of Furstán, for which the great church had been built, final resting place of this almost legendary founder of the Torenthi royal house, whose black sarcophagus was the focal point for the transmission of Furstáni kingship." [*King Kelson's Bride*].

Saint Iveagh's Abbey. This Mother House of the *Fratres Silentii* (*Brothers of Silence*) is located on the Gulf of Kheldour on the Southwestern coast of Claibourne. It was here that Hubert MacInnis ex-Archbishop Primate of Valoret and All Gwynedd was sent on the XIth day of July in the year 928, following his trial and deposition, to be kept in close confinement and under a regimen of fasting and penance; he died there on the XXXth day of November in the year 929. Two hundred years later, Edmund Loris former Archbishop Primate of Valoret and All Gwynedd was sent into exile here following his deposition on the Xth day of January in the year 1122. However, he escaped captivity on the XXIXth day of November in the year 1123. [*The Bastard Prince*; *The Bishop's Heir*].

Saint Jarlath's Abbey. This Mother House of the *Ordo Verbi Dei* is located at Barwicke near the source of the River Eirian, II hours' ride Northeast of Saint Liam's Abbey on the Southwestern edge of the Plain of Iomaire. It was here that Father Joram MacRorie and Rhys Lord Thuryn traveled on the XXVIIIth day of September in the year 903 to discover the whereabouts of Brother Benedict, the religious name of Prince Cinhil Haldane. [*Camber of Culdi*; *The Bastard Prince*].

Saint John's Church. This parish church with adjoining cemetery was located near Fullers' Alley in the Textile District of the city of Valoret. It was in the official records of this church that the Draper family's births, deaths, and marriages were listed. Father Joram MacRorie consulted the registers here on the XXVIIIth day of November in the year 903. [*Camber of Culdi*].

Saint Kyriell's. This distant village is located in the hills Northeast of Caerrorie. It was here that some of the Servants of Saint Camber went into voluntary exile after the enforcement of the Statutes of Ramos in the early Xth century, and established a community to continue his veneration. The roughly LX inhabitants remaining in April of the year 1125 spoke a mountain dialect that was difficult for outsiders to understand. King Kelson and Dhugal MacArdry Earl of Transha and Kierney emerged here from a series of underground caverns on the Xth day of April in that year, and Kelson was put to the ordeal by the village Quorial, its governing body. Here was re-established the Servants of Saint Camber. In the year 1128 a contingent of the Servants traveled from this village to Rhemuth, arriving at the latter site on the XXXth day of July. [*The Quest for Saint Camber*; *King Kelson's Bride*].

Saint Liam's Abbey. This Michaeline Abbey school was located IV hours' ride Northeast of Valoret, on the River Eirian not far West from Tor Caerrorie. Father Alister Cullen attended this school as a boy, and Joram Lord MacRorie and Rhys Lord Thuryn were sent here to study in October of the year 888. By the year 903 Father Joram had become a schoolmaster at Saint Liam's. On the XXVIIIth day of September in that year Rhys Thuryn visited Saint Liam's and accompanied Father Joram home to Caerrorie. ["Catalyst"; *Camber of Culdi*; *Camber the Heretic*].

Saint Mark's Abbey. This religious establishment is located just East of Valoret on the South side of the Eirian River. It was here that the party of King Javan stayed on the evening of the Xth day of May in the year 922, this being his last night alive upon this earth. Two hundred years later, the bodies of Gérard Lord Ralson and Lord Colin of Fianna were taken here after their deaths from ambush on the VIIth day of November in the year 1120. King Kelson and his party passed through here on the XVIth day of March in the year 1125 on their way to Dolban. [*King Javan's Year*; *Deryni Rising*; *The Quest for Saint Camber*].

Saint Mark's Parish Church. This church was located near Saint Mark's Abbey East of Valoret. Assignment to this parish was generally regarded as a stepping-stone for ambitious clergymen who wished to move up quickly into the hierarchy. The pastor of Saint Mark's in August of the year 1104 was Father Alexander Darby later Archbishop of Rhemuth. ["The Priesting of Arilan"].

Saint Mary's in the Hills. This isolated monastery was located deep in the Culdi Highlands South of Trurill. Retainers of the MacRorie family established the Abbey about the year 800. It was here that Father Joram MacRorie and his sister Evaine Lady Thuryn and her family took refuge on the IInd day of January in the year 918. Camber, in his guise as Alister Cullen Bishop of Grecotha, expunged the official records of the Diocese of Grecotha to remove any mention of this place. [*Camber the Heretic*; *The Harrowing of Gwynedd*].

Saint Matthew's Cathedral. This seat of the Bishop of Coroth is located in the capital city of the Duchy of Corwyn.

Saint Matthew's Gate. This aperture in the Coroth city walls was where the troubadour Gwydion heard I of the songs he later sang for Alaric Morgan Duke of Corwyn in March of the year 1121. [*Deryni Checkmate*].

Saint Michael's Mount. This establishment of the Brethren of Saint Michael is said to have been situate at the tip of the Carthmoor peninsula, and slid into the sea, possibly as a result of abnormally high tides and storm activity. Concerning its fate the great Deryni master Orin cites a verse from Tanno's epic poem, *The Vengeance of Káthar Jolársson*, the body of which has, alas, been lost:

> Then cold, cave-bound Loryù,
> Driven mad by the deaths of her bairns
> Reached out her ice-rimed fingers
> Pulled back the cover of the sea
> And laughed whilst it rebounded
> O'er Mount Saint Michael's ley.

The surviving Brethren relocated to a new site near Kilchon in the Kingdom of Mooryn, where a local Deryni Baron, Barrlevin Graciano, gave them land and patronage.

Saint Neot's Abbey. Once the Mother House of the Order of Saint Gabriel the Archangel (the Gabrilites), a Deryni esoteric religious order specializing in the training of Healers, this monastery was located in the foothills of the Lendour Mountains on the Corwyn side of the border. It was founded on the XXIVth day of March in the year 745 by Brother Junius Pollansus. It was sacked and burned by Rhun the Ruthless and his confederates among the Regents on the XXIVth day of December in the year 917.

It was in the ruins of this establishment that the old hermit Simonn, once a Healer of Saint Neot's, cured the cancer of Gilrae Baron d'Eirial on the LXth anniversary of the monastery's destruction. Brion King of Gwynedd and Alaric Morgan Duke of Corwyn visited the site in November of the year 1106 when news arrived of the birth of the King's son and heir, the Prince Kelson.

Morgan and Father Duncan McLain stopped there on their way from Coroth to Dhassa on the XXVIIth day of March in the year 1121, returning there on the XIXth day of June following. [*Camber of Culdi*; *Camber the Heretic*; *The Harrowing of Gwynedd*; *Deryni Checkmate*; *High Deryni*].

Saint Ostrythe's Convent. This small religious house run by the *Matronae Domini* was located between Ebor and Sheele North of Valoret. It was here that Rhys Michael King of Gwynedd died on the XXVIIIth day of June in the year 928. A commemorative plaque dedicated to his memory was erected at Saint Ostrythe's in the year 945 by his son, King Owain. [*The Bastard Prince*].

Saint Piran's Priory. This establishment of the *Ordo Verbi Dei* was located a day's ride North of Saint Jarlath's Abbey. It was here that Father Joram MacRorie and Rhys Lord Thuryn interviewed the first II "Brothers Benedict" on the VIth day of November in the year 903 in their attempt to locate Prince Cinhil Haldane. [*Camber of Culdi*].

Saint-Sasile. A monastery in the Southern Torenthi town of Furstánán, on the Beldour River, the establishment features a great domed church and outbuildings. In the year 1128 the domes of Saint-Sasile were lit by Deryni fire to honour the arrival of King Liam Lajos II on the IVth day of July. The traitor Count Teymuraz took ship from here on the XVIth day instant. [*King Kelson's Bride*].

Saint Senan's Cathedral or Saint Andrew of Senon's Cathedral. This seat of the Bishop of Dhassa was named for Saint Andrew Senan, a holy martyr of the IVth century. It was here that the Curia of the Church of Gwynedd met on the XXVIIIth day of March in the year 1121 to pronounce a bull of excommunication against Alaric Morgan Duke of Corwyn and Father Duncan McLain. The Duke of Corwyn and Father McLain were received back into the communion of the Holy Church here some III months later, on the XXIst day of June. [*Deryni Checkmate*; *High Deryni*; *The Bishop's Heir*].

Saint Stefan's Monastery. This abbey is located on the coastal spires of the Atalantic Ocean North of the town of Stavenham. The Gryphon of God, a human rebel defeated by Geordie Lord Drummond, was resident here in April of the year 905. [*Deryni Challenge*].

Saint Stefan's Priory or Carbury Priory. This monastery is located on a hill overlooking the city of Carbury, on the edge of town. [*Deryni Checkmate*].

Saint Sviatoslav's Monastery, or Monastery of the Transubstantiation of the Silent Souls of Saint Sviatoslav. Located some XV miles West of Netterhaven on the coast of the Northern Sea, this isolated establishment of the Silent Souls of Saint Sviatoslav was built beginning in the year 805 by Ezzard à Hagyma as the Mother House of the newly-established Order. Although Ezzard later established another XI monasteries throughout Torenth and the Forcinn States, several of these were destroyed during the barbarian incursions which began in the year 997, and the Mother House itself was placed under siege in May of that year. Soon the Forcinn abbeys of the Order had established their own administrative structure, and by the end of the year 1025 the Silent Souls had only their original monastery remaining. It received the former Torenthi King Kyprian II as a postulant in the year 1033, and maintained him there as the monk Pantaleón until his death on the last day of the year 1037. Attached to the Monastery is the gilded Chapel of Saint Abél. The motto of the Silent Souls is "*Siópé chryseia.*"

Saint Teilo's Church. This parish church in Culdi is the burial place of Lady Alyce de Corwyn de Morgan, her daughter Lady Bronwyn de Corwyn, and Lord Kevin McLain Earl of Kierney. The latter II were to have been married here on the XXIXth day of March in the year 1121. [*Deryni Checkmate*].

Saint Torin's Shrine. This sacred establishment honours the patron saint of Dhassa, and is located Southeast of the city at the lower end of Lake Jashan, situate between the lake and the Gunury Pass on the road coming North from Coroth to Dhassa. All adult male travelers arriving from the South must stop and pay their respects (and an offering) to the Saint, and receive in return the burnished pewter capbadge identifying them as one of the faithful, or they will not be allowed to approach the ferryman who will take them across Lake Jashan. It was here that Alaric Morgan Duke of Corwyn and Father Duncan McLain were ambushed by Warin de Grey and Monsignor Lawrence Gorony on the XXVIIIth day of March in the year 1121. [*Deryni Checkmate*; *The Bishop's Heir*].

Saint Triduana's Convent. This religious house is located in the Forcinn Buffer States, and honours the memory of a maiden who accompanied Saint Sava on his mission to Thuria in the IVth century. Her convent was a center of devotion and pilgrimage from at least the year 550, when it was founded by Sister Polykarpa of the Daughters of the Burning Bush. It was destroyed by fire in the year 1103, but was rebuilt IV years later by Carolus III King of Torenth. The Countess Friederike became a nun at Saint Triduana's under the name Sister Thyra in the year 1109.

Saint Ultan's Priory. This establishment of the *Ordo Verbi Dei* was located in the year 903 toward the tip of the Carthmoor Peninsula, in the Southernmost part of Mooryn. [*Camber of Culdi*].

Saint Uriel and All Angels' Cathedral. This seat of the Bishop of Meara is located at Ratharkin in the Principality of Meara. Although badly damaged by fire when the city was burned on the XXIXth day of June in the year 1124, it was rebuilt a year later by King Kelson. [*The Bishop's Heir*].

Sam'l. This loyal old retainer of Camber Earl of Culdi was serving at Tor Caerrorie in September of the year 903. He was sent into the local village with Evaine Lady MacRorie to protect her. [*Camber of Culdi*].

Santare, Earl of Grand-Tellie. He was born on the XXVIth day of September in the Year of Our Lord 853, being the eldest surviving son and heir of Salzare Earl of Grand-Tellie and Kailyn Lady Drumkirk. He intermarried with Sinéidin Lady MacCaba on the XVIIIth day of July in the year 875, and by her he had children: the Lady Sarakay, a goddaughter of King Festil III, whose dark beauty and flashing eyes brightened the Court during the later years of King Blaine, and who intermarried with Amadeus Lord Weckesser in Torenth, leaving issue; the Hereditary Count Santray von Santare, a twin with his sister, who escaped to Torenth with the rest of his family after the death of his father, leaving descendants in whom are vested the right to petition for the restoration of the Earldom; the Lady Vivea; the Lady Azella; the Lord Lazare.

The Lord Santare succeeded his father on the XIth day of January in the year 898, was appointed to the High Council of Gwynedd by King Imre on the XXVth day of March in the year 900, and was added to the Court of Crown Commissioners on the VIth day of January in the year 901. He dismissed Guaire Lord d'Arliss from his service before the year 903. In early December of the year 903 he was named by the King to investigate the apparent MacRorie conspiracy to restore the Haldane heir. At the King's orders Earl Santare destroyed the Michaeline commanderie at Cheltham on the XVth day instant. He was arrested for his role in the destruction of Cheltham on the IInd day of December in the year 904, and was tried, convicted, attainted, and executed by King Cinhil I on the Xth day of January in the year 905, aged LI years. [*Camber of Culdi*].

Sardeux Forest. This secluded wooded region is located between Trurill and Transha Castle overlooking the Gulf of Kheldour. Bordered on the North by Meara and on the South by Gwynedd, the Sardeux has remained relatively unsettled into modern times, long being retained as a private game preserve by the various border clans. Its giant oaks and scented conifers provide ample refuge for the plentiful and varied game which roam these woods. The River Cùille runs through the center of the Sardeux on its way to the sea.

Campbell de Broun recalls his time in the Sardeux somewhat dismally: "In the evening I went out to hunt and was so unlucky as to mistake my dog for a deer, and leveling my bow with too fatal a certainty, I gave him a mortal wound. The poor fellow cry'd out most piteously and ran off a few paces and soon died, having been hit near the heart. This grieved me more, perhaps, than a more serious misfortune would have done; he was a faithful and good animal, and had follow'd me near 1000 leagues to die by the hand of his master. The next morning I went out a'hunting again, but killed nothing. I could not resist a desire to go and see my poor dog Teague, having left him before he died, as I could not bear to stay with him, and yet cherishing the hope, tho' vain, that the wound was not mortal; on coming to the place I found him stretched in the snow, dead and part of his entrails pressed out at the wound, a melancholy sight to me. I laid him by the side of a log in the snow as the last mournful tribute to a faithful friend and left him forever." *Cobra buena fama, y echate á dormir.* [*The Bishop's Heir*].

Sasovna or Westmarcke. This Duchy is located in the Western portion of the Kingdom of Torenth on its border with the Kingdom of Gwynedd, being situate South of the County of Kulnán and Duchy of Truvorsk, East of the Rheljan Mountains, North of the County of Medras, and West of the County of Vorarl and the Duchy of Altorf. It was first granted to Count Konrád son of Lajos I King of Torenth in the year 815 by King Kálmán II, and has passed to various branches of the House of Furstán ever since. Count Konrád III was elevated to the title of Duke by King Arion I. The title was regranted under the name of Sasovna by King Kyprian II in the year 986 to Philémón Lord Strugats', husband of the Duchess Mirra, in recognition of his services during the late war. The capital of Sasovna is Podébrad, which was itself an autonomous Prince-Bishopric under Prince Vidar from 984 until 1015.

COUNTS AND DUKES OF WESTMARCKE

HOUSE OF FURSTÁN VON WESTMARCKE

Konrád I (son of Lajos I of Torenth)	815-863
Malachy (son)	863-871
Konrád II (son)	871-880
Miklós (brother)	880-922
Konrád III (son; Duke)	922-938
Maksian (son)	938-960
Zakhar I (son)	960-984
Mirra (daughter)	984-1028

PRINCE-BISHOP OF PODÉBRAD

Vidar	984-1015

DUKES OF SASOVNA

HOUSE OF FURSTÁN-SASOVNA

Philémón (husband of Mirra)	986-1011
Konrád IV (son)	1011-1025
Issakhar (brother)	1025-1048
Zakhar II (son)	1048-1072
Konrád V (son)	1072-1103
Ignácz (son)	1103-1125
Zakhar III (nephew)	1125-1130+

Sava, Saint. This holy man of Jáca became known during the persecutions of Markos, a local Satrap, during which he ministered to the martyrs in prison and then interred their bodies after their executions. According to legend, he died while praying at their tombs, and it is said that his prayers were so powerful that many who had been given up for dead and prepared for burial were miraculously returned to life. Those emerging from their slumber were then released by the tyrant Markos, who trembled in terror for his immortal soul. Another saint often associated with his name was his follower, Saint Triduana. Saint Sava's feastday is the XXXth day of January, but it is often celebrated in conjunction with Twelfth Night as the beginning of the season of Spring and renewal. A shrine in his honour is located at Jachère.

Savile Saint-Pol *Perrache de Nieuport*, **Baron Kishknock in Tralia.** He was born on the VIIth day of June in the Year of Our Lord 1081, being the eldest surviving son of Lanfranc Baron Kishknock and Byrsa Lady Alvers. He intermarried with Josèphe Lady Sarralbe on the IInd day of May in the Year 1100, and by her he had children: the Lady Truyère, who intermarried with Yoánn Graf von Nolde later Count of Sostra; the Lady Félicité, who intermarried with Sir César du Crest; the Hereditary Lord René, who perished from *la peste pulmonaire* at age VI. After the death of his wife on the last day of November in the year 1113, the Baron Savile intermarried secondly with Sivorn Dowager Duchess of Carthmoor on the XVIIth day of August in the year 1116, and by her he had further children: the Lady Savilla; the Hereditary Lord Sivney; the Lady Siany; the Lord Sorley.

The Lord Savile succeeded his father on the XVIth day of February in the year 1115. In the year 1128 he traveled to Rhemeth with his family to participate in the Royal weddings there, and helped welcome the newly arrived Ramsays to Court on the XXth day of July. [*King Kelson's Bride*].

Savilla Héraute *Perrache de Nieuport*, Lady. She was born on the XXIst day of June in the Year of Our Lord 1117, being the daughter of Savile Baron Kishknock and Sivorn Dowager Duchess of Carthmoor. She traveled with her parents to Rhemuth in July of the year 1128 to participate in the Royal weddings there. [*King Kelson's Bride*].

Seamus Michael *O'Flynn*, Earl Derry. He was born on the XIIth day of December in the Year of Our Lord 1069, being the eldest son and heir of Airich Seamus O'Flynn Earl Derry and Petra Baroness de Lodovic. He intermarried with Moira Lady Udaut on the XVIIth day of March in the year 1094, and by her he had children: the Lady Elsavere Eurania, who intermarried with Justin Baron of Rhelledd; the Hereditary Count Sean Seamus later Earl Derry; the Lord Trevor Michael, dead at age III of the pox; the Lady Siobhanette Sostra, dead at age IV of the runny bowels; the Lord Airich Seamus *Junior*, dead at VI months when he could not wake; the Lady Elspeth Ethelgiva, who intermarried with Arnaud Sieur de Vali.

The Lord Derry succeeded his father as Earl on the IXth day of June in the year 1101. He participated in the campaign of Brion King of Gwynedd against Hogan Gwernach the Marluk on the XXIst day of June in the year 1105, and was severely wounded defending his King in the initial skirmish, losing his left leg to amputation. He died of the lingering effects of his injuries on the XXIXth day of April in the year 1106, aged XXXVI years, and was succeeded by his eldest son, Lord Sean. R.I.P. ["The Knighting of Derry"].

Sean Seamus *O'Flynn*, Earl Derry, Deputy Regent of Marley, Sir, called "Uncle Seandry." He was born on the XIXth day of April in the Year of Our Lord 1097, being the eldest son and heir of Seamus Michael O'Flynn Earl Derry and Moira Lady Udaut.

The Lord Sean succeeded his father on the XXIXth day of April in the year 1106, under the regency of his uncle, Trevor Udaut Baron Varagh. He attained his majority on the XIXth day of April in the year 1111. At the annual Horse Fair in Rhelledd on the Ist day of May in the year 1115 he was almost cheated by the sharp horse trader, Julius ben David, and was later kicked in the head by one of the stock, being treated by Master Randolph, the Duke of Corwyn's surgeon.

Sean Earl Derry was knighted by Brion King of Gwynedd on the XIth day of May in the year 1115, and became an aide and vassal to Alaric Morgan the Duke of Corwyn later that same day. He was with the Duke on his mission to Cardosa on the XVIth day of September in the year 1120, and was cut in the left wrist on their return trip on the VIIth day of November of that year. He was severely wounded on the XIVth day instant in Rhemuth Palace, but was healed and saved from imminent death by Duke Alaric.

The Earl Derry was appointed to the Royal Council of Gwynedd by King Kelson on the XIVth day of November in the year 1120. He was trained by the Duke of Corwyn to serve as the latter's agent in Torenth, and spent some time there in Fathane under the alias "John Banner" during March of the year 1121, attempting to uncover the military plans of King Wencit. His training included the transmission of short messages using the Thuryn trance technique. On the XIXth day of June in that year he scouted the area near Medras in Torenth searching for the Torenthi army. He was captured at Llyndruth Plain while scouting the forces of King Wencit II days later. He fled the enemy on the Ist day of July, but was hit by an arrow in his back, being healed by Warin de Grey. However, King Wencit had placed a *geas* on Sean which forced him to aid the traitor Bran Coris Earl of Marley in kidnapping the latter's young son, Hereditary Count Brendan. The spell was broken by Alaric Morgan Duke of Corwyn.

The Earl Derry was created Deputy Regent of Marley on the IInd day of December in the year 1121. He was present at the Christmas Council of the year 1123 to discuss the developing Mearan Crisis. In March of the year 1125 he was in Coroth with his master, the Duke of Corwyn.

In the year 1128 he was present at Coroth Castle when King Kelson and his party arrived from Rhemuth on the IInd day of July, and accompanied the King on his trip upriver to Beldour. After the installation of Torenthi King Liam Lajos II on the XVIth day instant, the young King's mother, the Dowager Duchess Morag, discovered among the treasury of magical implements and papers she had inherited from her brother, the late King Wencit, an iron ring that could be used to reinsert a *geas* over the will of the Earl. This she did accomplish that same evening, in order to use the Earl's eyes and ears to spy upon the Court of Rhemuth.

But when she saw that King Kelson intended nothing but good for her son, she softened her heart, and might have relinquished her control in due course, had not she been surprised by her brother, the traitor Count Teymuraz, and foully murdered by him. Teymuraz then bent his new power unto the destruction of Duke Mátyás and the Haldanes. At the dual Royal marriage held on the last day of July, he forced Earl Sean to strike Mátyás in the side with a knife, hoping to kill him; but through God's intervention, the Duke's life was spared. Then did Azim the Deryni master, with the aid of the Ladies Araxie and Rothana, cleanse Lord

Sean's mind of the foul stench of black magic, restoring it to health and sanity, so that he was made whole once again.

The heir to the Earldom in the year 1130 is Earl Sean's great-uncle, Sir Dashell O'Flynn. Lord Derry's arms are: *gules*, a naked arm in fess couped at the shoulder proper, holding a cross botonny in bend sinister *or*. He had blue eyes, and curly brown hair clubbed back in a warrior's knot. ["The Knighting of Derry"; *Deryni Rising*; *Deryni Checkmate*; *High Deryni*; *The Bishop's Heir*; *The King's Justice*; *The Quest for Saint Camber*; *King Kelson's Bride*].

Sean Sighere *Coris*, Earl of Marley. He began using the surname Coris in his youth, it being a Northern corruption of the Bremagni word "*coriace*," which is to say, "tough" or "stubborn." He was born on the IIIrd day of October in the Year of Our Lord 908, being the only surviving son and heir of Sighere Earl of Marley and Corissa Lady de Bruyn. He intermarried with Juliana Lady of Horthness on the VIth day of May in the year 929, and by her he had children: the Hereditary Count Brian later Earl of Marley; the Lady Tanya, who intermarried with her cousin, Kennet Howell Earl of Eastmarch; the Lord Daryl; the Lord Reiner; the Lady Artemis.

Lord Sean was a member of the welcoming party that greeted King Rhys Michael and his forces at Lochalyn Castle on the XXIst day of June in the year 928. He succeeded his father on the XXXth day of December in the year 935. He died in the year 948, aged XXXIX years, and was succeeded by his son, the Hereditary Count Brian. R.I.P. [*The Bastard Prince*].

Seanna *MacGregor*, Lady. She was born on the XIXth day of February in the Year of Our Lord 911, being the daughter of Gregory Earl of Ebor and Eloise Lady de Mauzé, and the younger sister of Jesse MacGregor later Count of Trevalga. In the year 921 she was given the task of regularly checking the pigeon roust at the former Michaeline Haven for incoming messages from the Camberian Council, and took a message to her brother on the XXIInd day of June in that year that King Alroy was dying. She is said to have intermarried with Sir Aldin McCarthy. She had dark eyes and a dark braid trailing down her back. [*King Javan's Year*].

Secorim, sometime Auxiliary Bishop of Rhemuth, sometime Abbot of the Valoret Chapter of the *Custodes Fidei*, Archbishop Primate of Valoret and All Gwynedd. He was born on the XIIIth day of September in the Year of Our Lord 878. He was ordained on the VIIth of March in the year 897; one of his classmates in seminary was Father Paulin Sinclair, and they remained friends until Paulin's death in the year 928. Father Secorim joined the *Custodes Fidei* on its founding by Paulin on the IInd day of February in the year 918, and was appointed Lord Abbot of the Rhemuth chapter of the Order on the XIIth day instant. Ten years later, he was present at the residence of the ailing Robert Oriss Archbishop of Rhemuth on the XXVth day of June in the year 928 when Hubert MacInnis Archbishop Primate of Valoret and All Gwynedd received news of the death of Lord Albertus and the incapacitation of Father Paulin. He was nominated as Archbishop of Rhemuth on the XXIXth day of June in the year 928 in succession to the deceased Oriss, but after the *coup d'état* of the Vth day of July following, was instead consecrated Auxiliary Bishop to the new Archbishop, Alfred of Woodbourne, VII days later. He was elected Archbishop Primate of Valoret and All Gwynedd in the year 948, but died later the same year, aged LXIX years. *Maledicus a malefico non distat nisi occasione.* [*The Harrowing of Gwynedd*; *The Bastard Prince*].

Selden. This ecclesiastical soldier of Thomas Cardiel Bishop of Dhassa assisted in the capture of Alaric Morgan Duke of Corwyn and Father Duncan McLain on the XIXth day of June in the year 1121. [*High Deryni*].

Selkirk, Master. Master-at-Arms to Imre King of Gwynedd in the year 903. [*Camber of Culdi*].

Serafin, Inquisitor General and Grand Inquisitor of the *Custodes Fidei*, Brother. He was born on the IVth day of March in the Year of Our Lord 875. One of the founding members of the *Custodes Fidei*, he was named the Order's first Inquisitor General (later Grand Inquisitor) on the IInd day of February in the year 918. He was partly responsible for securing the imprisonment of the families of the Deryni collaborators, and left standing orders that these "sniffers" could never visit their relatives. In June of the year 921 he began working with the Deryni spy Master Dimitri in Carthmoor, and sometime during that period Dimitri set a psychic "tell-tale" in his mind.

Brother Serafin was taken prisoner with Father Lior by King Javan and Sir Guiscard de Courcy on the XXIXth day of July in the year 921. He was then questioned and probed by Father Joram MacRorie and Bishop Niallan Trey, who discovered that Guiscard had triggered the "tell-tale" left in Serafin's mind by Master Dimitri. To prevent the Deryni spy from realizing that he had entered Serafin's mind, Guiscard killed Serafin later that night, making him suffer an apparent heart attack, aged XLVI years. Brother Serafin was succeeded as Inquisitor by his assistant, Father Lior.

Serafin was tall and gaunt and suffered from occasional fainting fits and a blood which ran high; thus, he bled himself regularly to keep his blood in check. From this practice—a common and previously voluntary monastic discipline of the time for relieving some of the physical tensions of close community living—Serafin derived a less benign application: the requirement that all *Custodes* postulants submit to *minution* at least once during their novitiate to demonstrate the absolute obedience they owed to the Order, even to the brink of death and beyond. By extension, *minution* became a means of intimidating and disciplining would-be dissidents within the Order.

Brother Serafin's death was the subject of much speculation by Lord Albertus, Vicar General Paulin Sinclair, and Archbishop Hubert MacInnis, but given his medical history, they ultimately decided that his passing was a natural act of God. *Dedit hanc contagio labem et dabit in plures.* [*The Harrowing of Gwynedd*; *King Javan's Year*; *The Bastard Prince*].

Sereld, Dom. This Healer was born about the year 838, and was serving as King Blaine's official surgeon in the year 888. On the XIth day of October in that year, when Rhys Lord Thuryn was wounded by bandits who had attacked Tor Caerrorie while the King was out hunting with Camber Earl of Culdi, Dom Sereld healed the child and discovered Rhys's hitherto unexpected talent for healing. Sereld had a receding hairline with freckles across his nose and cheeks, and reddish-brown, slightly greying hair, a neat grey beard and mustache, dark brown eyes, and a hearty laugh. He retired from Royal service after King Blaine's death in the year 900, and died a few years later. ["Catalyst"].

Servants of Saint Camber (Servi Sancti Camberi). This religious Order was founded by Guaire Lord d'Arliss on the IInd day of February in the year 906 to venerate the memory of Camber Earl of Culdi. On the XXIIIrd day of October in that year they petitioned the first consistory of Archbishop Jaffray for recognition as an Order and for the canonization of Camber MacRorie. After much investigation, the petition was granted on the XIVth day of November in that year. The Mother House of the Order was destroyed by the Regents on the XXVIIIth day of December in the year 917, with some LX followers being burned at the stake at Dolban.

After the Council of Ramos banished the Deryni and rescinded Camber's canonization, some of the Servants retreated into the hills Northeast of Caerrorie, where Camber had been buried, and established the village of Saint Kyriell's. They remained hidden and undiscovered there for some CC years, until King Kelson and Dhugal MacArdry Earl of Transha and Kierney emerged from their underground prison at this place on the Xth day of April in the year 1125.

The Servants were formally re-established and sanctioned by the Church of Gwynedd on the XVth day of August in the year 1126. On the XXXth day of July in the year 1128, the Servants traveled to Rhemuth, where they were officially welcomed by King Kelson and the Archbishops of Gwynedd. The Chapel of Saint Camber was established within Rhemuth Palace, and Bishop Duncan McLain was appointed Rector of the new *schola* of Deryni learning to be established there, with Princess Rothana as his assistant.

After they had been officially recognized by King and Church, the Servants wore simple grey robes girt at the waist with a cincture of knotted red and blue cord. Many of the men sported the *g'dula*, although this was not a requirement. The older women wore coifs and wimples covering their hair, reminiscent of religious habit; the younger ones favoured veils of fine gauzy white linen over hair neatly dressed in a knot at the back of the neck, bound across the brow with a braided torse of red and blue cord. "*Périsse l'univers pourvu que je me venge!*" [*Saint Camber*; *Camber the Heretic*; *The Quest for Saint Camber*; *King Kelson's Bride*].

Seven Wonders of the World. According to Campbell de Broun, these comprise the Nikolaseum and the Hanging Gardens in Torenth, the Crystalline Cathedral of Saint Mihiel in Llannedd, the Feu de Dieu in Bremagne, the Anvil of the Lord in the Anvil, the statue of the All-Father in Eistenfalla, the Colossus of Killingford. Other authors, however, include such wonders as the Castle of Mór Montarago in Torenth, the Octagon House of Howicce, the summer palace of the Hort of Orsal, and Saint Basil's Bridge in Torenth. *Atque aliquis posita monstrat fera prœlia mensa, pingit et exiguo Pergama tota mero. Hac ibat Simois: hic est Sigeïa tellus; hic steterat Priami regia celsa senis.*

Shandon, Father. This young chaplain was serving Bishop Duncan McLain at Rhemuth in March of the year 1125. [*The Quest for Saint Camber*].

Shannis Meer. This lake region is located in the Barony of Rheljan in the Rheljan Mountains near the Gwyneddan border with Torenth. Here can be found the Convent of Saint Giles, where Jehana Queen of Gwynedd went into retreat on the Vth day of July in the year 1105 and again on the XIIIth day of March in the year 1121. [*The Bishop's Heir*].

Shaw *Farquharson*, Lord. He was born on the IInd day of June in the Year of Our Lord 878, being the third son of Farquhar Baron Farquharson and Parisia Lady Trichinas. This Deryni Baron was killed in the attempted assassination of the Princes Javan and Rhys Michael on the XXVIIIth day of September in the year 917, aged XXXIX years. [*Camber the Heretic*].

Sheele. This comfortable manor house is located just North of Valoret. In the early Xth century it belonged to Lord Rhys and Lady Evaine Thuryn. Evaine abandoned the property following Rhys's death on the XXVth day of December in the year 917. She gave the deed to several of her trusted servants, and, before leaving, locked and sealed the portal there to all but blood relations. Shortly thereafter the manor was made the seat of the Earldom of Sheele, and given to Rhun the Ruthless. On the XXVIIIth day of January in the year 918, Evaine and her nephew Ansel Lord MacRorie returned to Sheele via the portal there in order to retrieve certain ancient papers and documents she had secreted before her retreat. In the year 948 the Earldom passed to Agnes daughter of Isarn Earl of Sheele and her husband Sir Edward Calder, who adopted by deed poll the surname and title Calder of Sheele. The title has remained in his family ever since. *Perfervidum ingenium Sheeletorum.* [*Camber the Heretic*; *The Harrowing of Gwynedd*; *The Bastard Prince*].

EARLS OF SHEELE

HOUSE VON HORTHY

Rhun	917-928
Isarn (son)	928-948
Agnes (daughter)	948-998

HOUSE OF CALDER OF SHEELE

Edward *Calder* (husband)	948-984
Richard (son)	998-1019
Edwy (son)	1019-1025
Rhupert (brother)	1025-1058
Thomas (son)	1058-1076
Kimball (son)	1076-1128
Kenward (son)	1128-1130+

Sholto *MacDhugal*, Lord. He was born on the VIth day of January in the Year of Our Lord 877, being the youngest son of Fechin Baron MacDhugal and Babilla Lady Pinnock. This Deryni bowman unsuccessfully attempted to assassinate the Princes Javan and Rhys Michael on the XXVIIIth day of September in the year 917; although several of his fellow conspirators were caught and executed, Sholto managed to escape into Torenth, where he ultimately attached himself to the entourage of the Pretender Marek I. He died in the year 948. [*Camber the Heretic*].

Siany Dihane *Perrache de Nieuport*, Lady. She was born on the XIth day of August in the Year of Our Lord 1121, being the daughter of Savile Baron Kishknock and Sivorn Dowager Duchess of Carthmoor. She traveled with her parents to Rhemuth in July of the year 1128 to participate in the Royal weddings there. [*King Kelson's Bride*].

Sicard Oswald *MacArdry*, Lord. He was born on the IVth day of April in the Year of Our Lord 1068, being the second surviving son of Arthur MacArdry Clan Chief and Earl of Transha and Alannah Lady O'Beirne, and great-uncle to Dhugal MacArdry later Earl of Transha and Kierney and Duke of Cassan. He intermarried with Isibeal Lady O'Keeffe on the Ist day of June in the year 1088, and by her he had children: the Lady Cauleen; the Lord Arthur, a twin with his sister, who died shortly after birth. After his first wife died of the effects of childbirth on the IIIrd day of March in the year 1089, the Lord Sicard intermarried secondly with the Princess Caitrin Pretender of Meara on the IXth day of March in the year 1107, and by her he had children: the Hereditary Prince Ithel, hanged for his crimes in the year 1124; the Prince Llewell, beheaded in the year 1124 for murdering his sister; the Princess Sidana, who intermarried with Kelson King of Gwynedd, and was foully murdered on the VIth day of January in the year 1124, her wedding day, by her brother Llewell.

The Lord Sicard was put in command of the main part of the Mearan Army in May of the year 1124, and sought to entrap and destroy the Cassani army moving South into Meara under command of Duncan McLain Duke of Cassan. He caught Lord Duncan at Dorna on the IInd day of July in the year 1124, but was defeated and killed by King Kelson on the following day, aged LVI years. His body was returned for burial in the family crypt of the Quinnells at Laas. R.I.P. [*The Bishop's Heir*; *The King's Justice*; *The Quest for Saint Camber*].

Sidana Salena Yolanda *MacArdry Quinnell*, Queen of Gwynedd, Princess of Meara. She was born on the VIIth day of July in the Year of Our Lord 1109, being the only daughter of Sicard Lord MacArdry and Caitrin Princess and Pretender of Meara. She was taken captive by Dhugal MacArdry Earl of Transha during his escape from Ratharkin on the IXth day of December in the year 1123, and after they met with the King's party coming from Rhemuth, was brought by him to Gwynedd. There she accepted the proposal of marriage made by Kelson King of Gwynedd on Christmas Day of that year, and was intermarried with him on the VIth day of January in the year 1124. Alas, she was murdered at the wedding ceremony by her brother, the Prince Llewell, and was buried as Queen of Gwynedd on the IXth day instant in the family vault of the Haldanes beneath Saint George's Cathedral in Rhemuth. She was XIV years of age at her death.

She is described in the *Chronicles* as being "...short, sapling-slender, with curling locks the colour of chestnut burrs escaping from beneath her travel hood..., [and] dark eyes holding the dreamy mystery of some creature from another realm: worldly yet innocent, wise but naive." R.I.P. [*The Bishop's Heir*; *The King's Justice*; *The Quest for Saint Camber*; *King Kelson's Bride*].

Sighere, Ist Duke of Claibourne, Viceroy of the Kheldish Riding, Warlord of Kheldour, Lord Regent of Gwynedd, sometime Earl of Eastmarch, sometime Earl of Rhendall. He was born on the XXXth day of August in the Year of Our Lord 861, being the second son of Ewan Earl of Eastmarch and Tacita Lady Faill. He intermarried with Synolda Lady de Lacey on the XIIth day of June in the year 880, and by her he had children: the Hereditary Count Ewan later Ewan I Duke of Claibourne and Earl of Rhendall; the Lord Hrorik later Hrorik II Earl of Eastmarch; the Lady Myfanwy; the Lord Sighere *Junior* later Earl of Marley; the Lady Eiddwen; the Lady Clodagh.

The Lord Sighere succeeded his brother, the Earl Hlodver, on the IVth day of July in the year 891. In June of the year 905, as the autonomous Earl of Eastmarch, he supported King Cinhil I against the Pretender Ariella I in the great Battle of Iomaire on the XXVth day of that month. He had conquered most of the Deryni Principality of Kheldour by the XVIIIth day of September in that year, with only the mountain fortresses still holding out under Kennet Count of Rhorau.

On the XVth day of March in the year 906 he came to Valoret to parley with King Cinhil I and offered to become the King's vassal; they exchanged mutual oaths to that effect. On the IInd day of July King Cinhil I went North to Kheldour to join Earl Sighere in pacifying that region. On the XVth day of August they captured Kennet Count of Rhorau and Countess Sudrey his sister, thereby reducing the last Festillic citadel in Rhendall. On the XXVIth day instant the Earl Sighere was created Duke of Claibourne and Viceroy of the Kheldish Riding, with his III sons being made Earls; he was also named to the Royal Council of Gwynedd on the same day, and also deeded his title of Eastmarch to his middle son, Lord Hrorik.

Duke Sighere was made a Regent of King Alroy on the IIIrd day of February in the year 917, substituting for Bishop Alister Cullen, but his failing health never permitted him to assume his duties. He died of the spotted plague on the IInd day of July in the year 917, aged LV years, and was succeeded by his eldest son, Earl Ewan. R.I.P. [*Saint Camber*; *Camber the Heretic*].

Sighere *Junior*, Earl of Marley, Lord Regent of Gwynedd. He was born on the XXIVth day of November in the Year of Our Lord 886, being the youngest son of Sighere Duke of Claibourne and Synolda Lady de

Lacey. He intermarried with Corissa Lady de Bruyn on the XVth day of September in the year 907, and by her he had children: the Hereditary Count Sean Sighere later Sean Coris Earl of Marley; the Lady Evana; the Lady Lacey; the Lord Ghere.

The Lord Sighere was created Earl of Marley by King Cinhil I on the XXVIth day of August in the year 906. He was present at Valoret for the coronation of King Alroy on the XXVth day of May in the year 917. He rode to Rhemuth on the IVth day of June in the year 918 with his brother and nephew to confirm Graham I Duke of Claibourne in his titles and estates. He attended the coronation of King Javan on the XXXIst day of July in the year 921. His assistance was sought by his nephew-in-law, Corban Howell Earl of Eastmarch, to push back the Torenthi invaders at Culliecairn on the VIIIth day of June in the year 928, and he was present to greet the arrival of King Rhys Michael and his army on the XXIst day instant. He was named to the new Regency Council of King Owain on the Vth day of July in the year 928. He died on the XXXth day of December in the year 935, aged XLIX years, and was succeeded by his son, Lord Sean. R.I.P. [*Saint Camber*; *Camber the Heretic*; *The Harrowing of Gwynedd*; *King Javan's Year*; *The Bastard Prince*].

Simeon. This Biblical priest took the child Jesus in his arms at the latter's presentation in the temple. He was mentioned in the Candlemas ceremony held to inaugurate the new Order, the *Custodes Fidei*, on the IInd day of February in the year 918. [*The Harrowing of Gwynedd*].

Simonn *de Beaumont*. This Deryni was born about the year 904. As a young boy he joined the Gabrilite Order at Saint Neot's Abbey, receiving some of his training as a Healer from Dom Kilian McShane during the years 915 through 917, until the Abbey was sacked by Rhun the Ruthless at the end of that year. He later lived as a hermit near the ruins of that establishment, tending sheep and acting as a Healer for the poor. It was on the XXIVth day of December in the year 977, the LXth anniversary of the destruction of Saint Neot's, that he cured the cancer of Gilrae Baron d'Eirial, encouraging the boy in his vocation to become a priest. He had kindly blue eyes and white hair. He is believed to have died in the 980s. R.I.P. ["First Session"; *Camber the Heretic*; "Vocation"].

Simplicius, Bishop of Autun, Saint. This simple man of God was born in Beldour in the VIth century. Although married at an early age, he lived as an unsullied virgin with his equally virginal wife. He sought to enter the church as a priest, and because of his evident innocence and the purity of his mind and body, was given a dispensation. He later became Bishop of Autun, where he worked zealously to promote chastity amongst the brethren, and to root out lust, lasciviousness, and licentiousness wherever he found them. He founded a thriving community of like-minded individuals, but alas, it eventually petered out. A monastery dedicated to his name was founded in Arjenol by the Brothers of Saint Simplicius (*Adelphoi Hagiou Simplikiou*), and it was here that the witless Torval Prince of Torenth and Duke of Lorsöl spent his final days tending his roses. Saint Simplicius is the patron of eunuchs and imbeciles; his feastday is the XIVth day of June.

Sinead, Queen of Gwynedd, Princess of Kheldour. She was born on the Vth day of August in the Year of Our Lord 635, being the daughter of Lulach Sovereign Prince of Kheldour and Sigrid Lady of Normarch Ley. She intermarried with Aidan King of Gwynedd on the I^st day of July in the year 659, and by him she had children: the Princess Bethany, who intermarried with Barghash ibn Hassan al-Khideri, Nabil of Salah Reis, and secondly with Imre I King of Torenth, leaving issue; the Prince Augustin, dead at age VI of flux; the Princess Moira Roselynn, who intermarried with Aleksy Prince of Torenth and Count of Altorf and Vorarl, and by him had a child, the Princess Rocasta, who intermarried with Lord Rhori Mór Prince of Kheldour and ancestor of the House of MacRorie; the Princess Usheen; the Princess Kiloran; the Hereditary Prince Kelvin, dead at age VIII of the bloody lungs; the Princess Hyacinthe; the Hereditary Prince Ifor, who was wounded in battle and died shortly thereafter.

This stately Queen, a Lady of great wit and wisdom, championed the cause of learning, and when the town of Grecotha, formerly a free city, was captured by King Aidan on the XIth day of July in the year 678, she amalgamated the *scholae* there into a university on the XXIXth day of May in the year 682. She had her own brother, Mogue Prince of Kheldour, appointed Bishop of Grecotha and Chancellor of the *Universitatis*, a charge which he undertook most vigorously.

When Queen Sinead's husband and surviving son rode off into battle against Torv Count of Eastmarch in the year 698, she took refuge with her brother in his residence at Grecotha, and, according to the *Legends*, "watched each day from the tower at dusk, praying for their safe return." King Aidan, however, died at the Battle of Ebor on the VIIth day of July in the year 698, his son, Hereditary Prince Ifor, being severely wounded at the same time.

King Aidan's Royal Guard returned to Grecotha at dusk on the evening of the VIIIth of July bearing the body of their slain Lord, laid out on a bier draped with his battle standard; his drummers marched alongside beating the dirge, and the litter bearers carrying the wounded Prince Ifor followed. Queen Sinead, upon seeing the funeral procession approach, was so distraught that she threw herself from the ramparts or perhaps fell from the parapet to her death below. "Her stricken kin renamed the tower in her memory, calling it Queen Sinead's Watch, an appellation which it bears to this very day." She was LXII years of age at her death, and was laid to rest by her brother in the Crypt beneath Grecotha Cathedral. R.I.P. [*Saint Camber*].

Sion *(de)* Benet (XXXVIII), Under-Chancellor to the Royal House of Llannedd, Sir. He was born on the IXth day of April in the Year of Our Lord 1086, being the eldest son and heir of Sir Sion Benet (XXXV) and Lady Pamphylie d'Enfantin. He intermarried with Dulcibelle Lady MacLaurin on the IVth day of May in the year 1109, and by her he had children: Sir Sion (XLII); the Lady Cythère; Sir Sion (XLIV); Sir Sion

(XLV); the Lady Cathay; the Lady Sionetta; the Lady Lémurie.

Sir Sion Benet, in accordance with the oath made by the founder of his house, received the same given name as all of the other male members of his family. He joined the service of the King of Howicce and Llannedd in the year 1111, and was appointed Under-Chancellor of the Royal House of Llannedd on the XXth day of November in the year 1125. He was elected to the Camberian Council on the IIIrd day of November in the year 1127, to fill the long-vacant seat of Tiercel de Claron, and was the youngest member of that body at the time of his appointment. According to *Bride*, he looked "like a perplexed lion, with his yellow eyes and beard and mane of tawny curls." [*King Kelson's Bride*].

Sitric. This Deryni was impressed into the service of Rhun Earl of Sheele as a "Deryni sniffer" in the year 917, his aged mother and young sister being held as hostages to his actions. He was present at the sacking of Saint Neot's Abbey on the XXIVth day of December in that year. He replaced Declan Carmody after the latter's death on the XXVth day of May in the year 918, but lacked his finesse and training. He went with Rhun and Richard Murdoch Earl of Carthane to the latter's estate on the IInd day of August in the year 921. In November of that year he was sent to Grecotha to help search for the "kidnapped" Prince Rhys Michael. He was ordered by the former Regents to murder Oriel, but only succeeded in wounding him; he was himself killed by Sir Guiscard de Courcy and King Javan on the XXth day of March in the year 922, being set aflame through sorcery. He was buried in Saint Hilary's Basilica, and his mother and sister were then released and allowed to join Ursin's family in cloister. He had the reputation of being as ambitious as his master, and was considered dangerous by the other Deryni at Court. [*The Harrowing of Gwynedd*; *King Javan's Year*].

Sivney de Saint-Élie *Perrache de Nieuport*, **Hereditary Lord Kishknock.** He was born on the XXXIst day of October in the Year of Our Lord 1119, being the eldest surviving son and heir of Savile Baron Kishknock and Sivorn Dowager Duchess of Carthmoor. He traveled with his parents to Rhemuth in July of the year 1128 to participate in the Royal weddings there. [*King Kelson's Bride*].

Sivorn Sorelle Nicée *von Horthy Perrache de Nieuport*, **Princess d'Orsal and Tralia, Dowager Duchess of Carthmoor, Baroness Kishknock.** She was born on the XXVIth day of January in the Year of Our Lord 1087, being the daughter of Sobbon Hort of Orsal and Prince of Tralia and the Princess Maya daughter of Prince du Thuria. She intermarried with Prince Richard Duke of Carthmoor on the XVth day of April in the year 1107, and by him she had children: the Princess Richelle Louise later Countess of Culdi in her own right, who intermarried with Sir Brecon Ramsay Earl of Kilarden; the Princess Araxie Léan, created Baroness Dunluce in her own right by King Brion on the XXVth day of December in the year 1114, who intermarried with Kelson King of Gwynedd on the VIIth day of August in the year 1128; the Prince and Hereditary Duke Cinric Sobbon Malcolm Earl of Culdi at birth by cession of his father, who was eaten up with fever at the age of III years on the XIVth day of September in the year 1114. After her husband's death in the year 1114, the Dowager Duchess Sivorn returned to Tralia with her II young daughters, and intermarried secondly with Savile Baron Kishknock on the XVIIth day of August in the year 1116, and by him she had further issue: the Lady Savilla; the Hereditary Lord Sivney; the Lady Siany; the Lord Sorley.

The Lady Sivorn met King Kelson and his party when they traveled to Orsal on the IIIrd day of July in the year 1128, and that night witnessed the betrothal of her daughter Araxie to the said King Kelson. When the King transported back to the island on the evening of the XVIth day instant, she had to be convinced by him that the danger posed by the traitor Count Teymuraz was sufficiently great to warrant the removal of the women from Orsal. She and her family arrived at Rhemuth on the XXth day of that month. On the XXVIth day of July, she formed part of the group that inspected the new Chapel of Saint Camber. She was also present at the Royal weddings conducted in Rhemuth at the end of July and the beginning of August. She had pale eyes and blonde hair. [*King Kelson's Bride*].

Siward, Bishop of Cardosa. He was born on the XXVth day of November in the year 1074. He was ordained priest on the IIIrd day of May in the year 1093, and was consecrated an itinerant Bishop of Gwynedd on the XXth day of February in the year 1115. He sided with Bishops Thomas Cardiel and Denis Arilan during the Interdict Crisis of the year 1121. As a reward for his support, he was elevated to the new see of Cardosa on the XVth day of January in the year 1122. At the Synod of Valoret on the XIXth day of March in the year 1125 he questioned Father Jodoc d'Armaine concerning his qualifications to be elected as an itinerant Bishop. [*Deryni Checkmate*; *High Deryni*; *The Bishop's Heir*; *The King's Justice*; *The Quest for Saint Camber*].

Sixtus, Father. This elderly priest was serving Hubert MacInnis Archbishop Primate of Valoret and All Gwynedd in November of the year 921. He brought mulled wine to the Archbishop and King Javan at their meeting in Hubert's quarters on the XIXth day of that month. [*King Javan's Year*].

Skenfor. He was an old farmer near Stavenham in April of the year 905. [*Deryni Challenge*].

Smalf the Miller. He loaned a donkey to Royston Richardson to carry the injured Malcolm from the battlefield at Jennan Vale on the XVIIth day of June in the year 1121. [*High Deryni*].

Sofiana Murranna Éliana Genève *Vastouni*, **Sovereign Princess of Andelon and Sultana of the Bhuttayriah.** She was born on the XVIIth day of July in the Year of Our Lord 1080, being the eldest daughter and heir of Mikhail Sovereign Prince of Andelon and the Princess Ysabeau granddaughter of Yves Sovereign Prince of Jáca, and an aunt to Richenda the Dowager Countess of Marley and Duchess of Corwyn, the daughter of Sofiana's deceased sister, Michendra Baroness of Rheljan. She intermarried with Reyhan Lord Séchelles of Jáca on the XXIst day of December in the year 1094, and by him she had children: the Hereditary Prince Kamil, who intermarried with Williama Nabila of Nur Hallaj; the Prince Taher, who intermarried with the Duchesse Ercille daughter of Centule V Grand Duc du Vézaire; the Prince Nephthys, who intermarried with the Princess Yussra daughter of Tahmasp II Great Khan of Khokanistan; the Princess Rohays, who intermarried with Sulen Hereditary Nabil of Nur Hallaj. She was appointed to the Camberian Council as a young woman, but felt compelled to resign that post shortly after she succeeded her father as Sovereign Princess of Andelon on the XIIth day of December in the year 1112. She accepted reappointment to the Council on the XIth day of August in the year 1123.

In the year 1128 she traveled to Beldour for the inauguration of King Liam Lajos II. On the XIth day of July in that year she was introduced to King Kelson at a reception held in the Hanging Garden of Furstánály Palace. On the XVth day instant, she transported from Beldour to the hideaway of the Camberian Council, to discuss recent developments with that group. Two days later, after the death of Vivienne, she was elected Co-Adjutor of the Council. She had dark hair and eyes. [*The King's Justice*; *The Quest for Saint Camber*; *King Kelson's Bride*].

Solomon, King of (Sam)Israel. This biblical monarch was mentioned during the coronation ceremony of King Alroy at Valoret on the XXVth day of May in the year 917, and also at the ceremony which transferred the Haldane potential to Prince Regent Conall on the IVth day of April in the year 1125. [*Camber the Heretic*; *The Quest for Saint Camber*].

Sophie *Smythe*. She was serving as a maid to Dowager Queen Jehana in the year 1128. [*King Kelson's Bride*].

Sorandor. This was the name used by the ancient Deryni scholar, Mahael, in his *Historia Kheldourias* to refer to Gwynedd. ["Lords of Sorandor"].

Sorle *Dalriada*, Sir. He was born on the XXVIth day of July in the Year of Our Lord 896. He was serving as squire to Cinhil I King of Gwynedd in June of the year 905, and went with him to the Battle of Iomaire on the XXVth day instant. He was knighted by the King on the VIth day of January in the year 917, being the last of that monarch's squires to be personally honoured by him. He later served as a tutor for Cinhil's III sons. He was I of a group of young knights who prepared a set of legal documents in anticipation of the succession of King Javan in June of the year 921. He attended the coronation of King Javan on the XXXIst day of July in the year 921. On the IInd day of August in that year he was given the responsibility by the King of watching over the Healer Oriel. He was made personal bodyguard to Oriel after Sitric's failed attack on the Healer on the XXth day of March in the year 922. He was murdered by the former Regents during their *coup d'état* of the XIth day of May in the year 922, aged XXV years. He was said to have been dark, quick, and handsome, and he had a penchant for the law. R.I.P. [*Saint Camber*; *Camber the Heretic*; *King Javan's Year*].

Sorley Rhadamanthe *Perrache de Nieuport*, Lord. He was born on the VIth day of November in the Year of Our Lord 1123, being the son of Savile Baron Kishknock and Sivorn Dowager Duchess of Carthmoor. He traveled with his parents to Rhemuth in July of the year 1128 to participate in the Royal weddings there. [*King Kelson's Bride*].

Sostra. This Torenthi town, capital of the County of the same name, is situate on the Eastern bank of the Western River in the Coamer Mountains East of Kingslake and North of Jennan Vale. The County of Sostra is bounded on the North by the County of Medras, on the Northeast by the Duchy of Altorf, on the East by the Duchy of Csorna, on the South by the County of Fathane, and on the West by the Duchy of Corwyn in Gwynedd.

The County was first granted by Furstán King of Torenth to his son, the Prince Kázmér, about the year 565, and passed through different branches of the House of Furstán down the centuries, briefly becoming a Duchy under Duke Mátyás. [*King Kelson's Bride*].

COUNTS OF SOSTRA

HOUSE OF FURSTÁN-SOSTRA

Kázmér (son of King Furstán)	565?-622
Thüring (son)	622-648
Bence (brother)	648-655
INTERREGNUM	
Wenzel Sylvist (son of King Aldred I)	683-755
Sylván I (son)	755-777
András (son)	777-812
Almos (son)	812-840
Folkus (nephew)	840-861
Jodok (brother)	861-889
Bernát (brother)	889-892
Lothár (cousin)	892-911
Valter (son)	911-952
INTERREGNUM	
Mátyás (Duke; son of Prince Károly)	960-977
INTERREGNUM	
Torval (son of Ringan IV Duke d'Arjenol)	1004-1025
Ringan (son)	1025-1068
Bertalan (brother)	1068-1075
Henrik (son)	1075-1082
Sylván II (uncle)	1082
Branyng I (grandson)	1082-1126
Branyng II (son)	1126-1128
Yoánn (cousin)	1128-1130+

Southern Sea. This region of the Great Atalantic Ocean encompasses the area between Howicce and Llannedd on the North and the Bremagni Kingdom to the South, and extends North and East to the Twin Rivers between Coroth in Corwyn and the island port of the Hort of Orsal. Into this Sea drain several major navigable waterways, including the Western River and the Eastern or Beldour River, the River Eirian, the

River Thuria, the River Laval, the River Llinmari, and the Eau-de-Vin.

The Great Southern Sea is well protected from the harsh winds and icy climes of the North, and thus provides a plethora of relatively secure ports and safe harbours which service a multitude of merchant and marine fleets traversing its waters year round. A great warm current from the South prevents the waters of the Great Southern from freezing over even during the severest of Winter storms. Ports of call include most, if not all, of the capital cities of the Kingdoms surrounding the Sea: Sirhowy at the mouth of the Llinmari River in Howicce; Pwyllheli at the mouth of the Eirian in Llannedd; Kilchon and Dunluce in Carthmoor; Coroth at the mouth of the Twin Rivers in Corwyn; Horthánthy on the Île d'Orsal; Trebaçeaux at the mouth of the Thuria River in Joux; Côte d'Alban in Vézaire and Lognac in Logréine, both on the Baie des Chameaux and the Fleuve Cèdre; Fianna the Capital of Fianna at the mouth of the Eau-de-Vin; Truyère in Fallon and Augusteville in Bremagne, both at the mouth of the Laval River on the Côte d'Aurore; and Millefleurs on the Baie des Fleurs in Bremagne.

In Gwynedd proper the cities of Nyford and Desse and the Free Port of Concaradine are all readily accessible from the Great Southern Sea up the Eirian River, and Rhemuth can be reached by flat barges; and, to a lesser degree, Kiltuin in Coroth and Fathane in Torenth may also be reached via the Western branch of the Twin Rivers. In addition, both the Northern and Southern coasts of the Great Southern Sea provide hundreds of inlets and quays wherein even the tiniest of its villages may have access to fishing and other forms of commerce. A brisk trade in contraband and pirated goods is engaged in by the occasional *entrepreneur*, a common practice not easily discouraged by even the most diligent of local Lords. As Campbell de Broun once quipped: "All ships on the Southern Sea are grey in the dark...." [*King Kelson's Bride*].

Stacia *Howell*, Countess of Eastmarch. She was born on the XXXth day of March in the Year of Our Lord 909, being the only surviving child and heir of Hrorik II Earl of Eastmarch and Sudrey Countess of Rhorau. She intermarried with Corban Howell later Earl of Eastmarch *jure uxoris* on the XXIInd day of May in the year 927, and by him she had children: the Hereditary Count Kennet later Earl of Eastmarch; the Lady Ferelithe; the Lord Jago; the Lady Joslin; the Lady Sudrette; the Lord Corbik.

The Lady Stacia succeeded her beloved father on the VIIth day of June in the year 928, and, though devastated by his death, she immediately began assisting her mother in preparing the defenses of Lochalyn Castle and in establishing an infirmary to receive the wounded. To free herself for these duties, she briefly gave over her infant son Kennet into the care of Captain Murray's daughter, Tiarna. She was present at Lochalyn on the XXIst day of that month to greet King Rhys Michael and his army. Her mother, the Dowager Countess Sudrey, was killed by Prince Miklós with magic on the XXIInd day instant, and was buried at Lochalyn. The King Rhys Michael then received the oaths of Stacia and Corban as new Countess and Earl of Eastmarch, and gave unto Stacia the symbols of her office on the XXIVth day of June. Later, she brought the old village midwife, Mother Angelica, to assist in treating the King's injuries, and attempted to make him as comfortable as possible before he returned to Rhemuth.

According to the *Heirs*, "her hair was a dark red, full and wild, where it escaped from her shawl. She had her mother's dark eyes. The beauteous Lady Stacia was renowned for her habit of keeping one or more pet wolfhounds at her side, both for their protection and for the companionship these faithful dogs provided her. She was a loving daughter, a faithful wife, and a devoted mother. She always saw her duty clearly, and never failed to support a just and rightful cause." She died on the IInd day of April in the year 967, aged LVIII years, and was succeeded by her son, Lord Kennet. R.I.P. [*King Javan's Year*; *The Bastard Prince*].

Stalker. This King's Ranger was based near Kiltuin, a port town on the Corwyn side of the border with Torenth. His fiancée, Lillas, was raped and killed by IV toughs on the XVIth day of April in the year 1118. Stalker accused an innocent man, Ferris, of the crime, but he was freed the next day based on testimony by Alaric Morgan Duke of Corwyn. Stalker was about XXX years of age, and wore the ciphered leather doublet and thigh-high boots that signified his office, plus a cockade of egret feathers jutting from the crown of his green leather hunt cap. ["Trial"].

Stanisha Lionella Ilona Konstancia *Furstána d'Arjenol*, Princess of Torenth. She was born posthumously on the XXth day of February in the Year of Our Lord 1122, being the youngest child of Lionel II late Duke d'Arjenol and Morag Princess of Torenth. She was betrothed to the Prince Payne son of Nigel Duke of Carthmoor on the XIVth day of November in the year 1128, the marriage to take place on her coming of age in the year 1136. She had blue-black hair worn in a braid. [*King Kelson's Bride*].

***Stavenham*.** Located in the far North of Kheldour on the Atalantic Ocean, this is the largest city of the Kheldish Riding, on the Claibourne side of the River Daffreen. It was near here that Geordie Lord Drummond was sent by Camber in April of the year 905 to find a renegade human priest, the Gryphon of God. The area was later erected into a Bishopric, being held briefly by Paulin Sinclair of Ramos in the year 917 before he founded the *Custodes Fidei* a few months later. Later primates included Bishop Conlan and Bishop Angelus de Lacey in the year 1121. [*Deryni Challenge*; *The Harrowing of Gwynedd*; *King Javan's Year*; *Deryni Checkmate*; *High Deryni*; *The Bishop's Heir*].

Stefan, Abbot and Saint. Born on the coast at Stavenham in the VIIIth century, this son of a sheep-shearer accompanied his father at the age of XII to the Abbey of Saint Elderon at Tolán. There he fell ill of the typhoidous grippe, but was miraculously cured of his flaming fever by being plunged repeatedly into the icy waters of the Northern Sea. Upon his recovery from this illness, he developed a lifelong stutter that forced him to remain encloistered there, but was adopted and educated by the kindly monks, who taught him to read, write, and occasionally to speak. On his return to Stavenham some XX years later, he founded a loose congregation of hermits, *The Isolates of Silence* (*Soli Silentii*), whom he ruled for some XLVI years without ever having been seen by them, although some questions have been raised by scholars over the matter of his ordination. Following his death a large group of his followers migrated to Carbury, where a priory was erected on a hill overlooking the Gulf of Kheldour, the better, they said, to contemplate the lessons of Saint Stefan's life. His feastday is the XXVIIIth day of May.

Stefan *Coram*. This illustrious and courageous seeker after truth was born in Torenth on the XXIInd day of June in the Year of Our Lord 1076, being the son, according to some accounts, of one Coram son of Leszek, a tanner, but according to others, of Khoram Ptolemaevich. He was well trained as a Deryni master in his youth, and was appointed to the Camberian Council before the year 1104; he was serving as Coadjutor of that body in the year 1121. He met with Sir Jamyl and Denis Arilan on the XVIIIth day of November in the year 1104 to discuss Denis's upcoming ordination, and how the *merasha* introduced by the Archbishops into the sacramental wine might be thwarted.

Between the years 1116 and 1121 he occasionally assumed the visage and name of the deceased Deryni Rhydon of Eastmarch in order to gain the confidence of Wencit King of Torenth, and ultimately to seek that monarch's death. In November of the year 1120 he warned Charissa Pretender of Gwynedd not to interfere in the politics of that country, an admonition which she ignored, to her ultimate destruction. He also took on the appearance of Camber Earl of Culdi on occasion to warn Alaric Morgan Duke of Corwyn and Father Duncan McLain of the dangers they faced from their Deryni challengers.

He had pale hair and pale blue-grey eyes, and spoke with a pleasant baritone. According to the *Chronicles*, "he had a habit of absently raking the fingers of one hand through a forelock of shortish white blond hair that kept slipping over one eye." His arms featured: chevrons and arrowheads on an *azure* field. He died with King Wencit, having poisoned all IV Torenthi participants in the duel arcane, including himself, on the IInd day of July in the year 1121, aged XLV years. R.I.P. ["The Priesting of Arilan"; *Deryni Rising*; *High Deryni*; *The Bishop's Heir*; *The King's Justice*].

stenrect crawler. This monstrous creature menaced King Kelson and Alaric Morgan Duke of Corwyn in the garden at Rhemuth Palace on the XIVth day of November in the year 1120, having been called from the nether places by Charissa Pretender of Gwynedd. It is described in the *Chronicles* as having a "bulbous orange body about the size of a man's head, spotted with blue, and many brittle legs, and two angrily gnashing pincers or stingers. There is no antidote for the sting."

The *stenrect* was supposedly a mythical creature of supernatural origin, spawned, it was said, of fire and acid-hatred before the world was born. Of all creatures real or imagined, there was none deadlier. They were things of the night, and it took a great deal of magical power to bring one into the light of day. [*Deryni Rising*].

Stephan, Father. He was serving as secretary to Bishop Creoda in November of the year 1123. [*The Bishop's Heir*].

Stephen. He was a student at Saint Neot's Abbey in Lendour in December of the year 917. [*Camber the Heretic*].

Stephen *de Longueville*. He was serving as a soldier for Bran Coris Earl of Marley in the year 1121. He was to have tested the physician Cordan's sleeping potion on the XVIIIth day of June in that year, but was rejected as a subject by Lionel II Duke d'Arjenol. [*High Deryni*].

Stephen, Father. He was serving as Prior of Saint Piran's Priory in the year 903. He gave permission to Father Joram MacRorie and Rhys Lord Thuryn to speak to Brother Benedict on the VIth day of November in that year. [*Camber of Culdi*].

Stephen, Father. This elderly priest was serving at Valoret Cathedral in February of the year 918. [*The Harrowing of Gwynedd*].

Stephen, Saint. He was the Ist martyr acknowledged by the Christian world, being stoned for his faith shortly after Christ's ascension into Heaven. He is usually depicted as a deacon. His feastday is the XXVIth day of December. [*King Javan's Year*].

Stevana *de Corwyn*, Heiress *de Corwyn*. This Deryni heiress was born on the XVIIIth day of October in the Year of Our Lord 1042, being the only surviving child and heir of Airlie Hereditary Duke of Corwyn and Grania d'Oriel. She intermarried as his IInd wife with Keryell Earl of Lendour on the XXVth day of May in the year 1069, and by him she had issue: the Lady Alyce Javana; the Lady Vera Laurela, a twin to her sister, who was said to have died young, but was secretly given to raise from infancy to the Lady Laurela Howell, who had just been delivered of a stillborn babe whose mouth was sewn shut by magic; the Hereditary Duke and Earl Ahern Jernian ap Keryell; the Lady Marie Stephania, a twin to her brother. The Lady Stevana died in the year 1075, aged XXXII years, and was buried in the Corwyn crypt beneath Coroth Cathedral. R.I.P. ["The Green Tower"; *King Kelson's Bride*].

Stevanus, Master. This *Custodes* battle surgeon was serving Manfred Earl of Culdi in the year 921. He treated Prince Rhys Michael after his "kidnapping" on the Xth day of November in that year. He accompanied the Royal expedition to Eastmarch on the XVth day of June in the year 928, and examined the body of Lord Albertus on the XXth day instant. He then stuck the double agent Master Dimitri with a Deryni "pricker." Two days later he tested the Torenthi envoy Hombard of Tarkent with *merasha*. On the XXIInd day of June, he treated the injured hand of King Rhys Michael after that monarch's battle with the Torenthi Prince Miklós at Coldoire; the King then took over Stevanus's mind, and made him his own man.

A few days later, at the former Regents' command, he was supplanted by the surgeon Polidorus, who bled the King repeatedly. On the XXXth day of June, II days after the King's death, Stevanus was sent under guard to the *Custodes* Mother House in Ramos for imprisonment and correction; he and IV of the knights accompanying him who knew the true circumstances of the King's passing died there before they could be rescued by the new Regents of King Owain. [*King Javan's Year*; *The Bastard Prince*].

Sudrey *Furstán-Kheldour*, Countess and Heiress of Rhorau, Dowager Countess of Eastmarch. She was born on the XIVth day of October in the Year of Our Lord 893, being the daughter of Kemal Count Iowerth and Bathsheba Lady of Claibourne, and the niece of Termöd II Prince of Kheldour and Count of Rhorau, who raised her after the early death of her parents; she was a direct descendant of the House of Furstán, although she renounced her ties to that family after her marriage. She was captured with her brother the Count Kennet at Rhorau on the XVth day of August in the year 906, and was given into the wardenship of Sighere Duke of Claibourne. She intermarried with Sighere's son, Hrorik II Earl of Eastmarch, on the XVth day of May in the year 908, and by him she had children: the Lady Stacia later Countess of Eastmarch; the Lady Swan, who died an infant; the Lady Shine, dead at age III of the rosy crawlies.

Prince Miklós of Torenth inquired about her fate at the coronation banquet of King Javan on the XXXIst day of July in the year 921. Late in the year 921 she received letters from Arion I King of Torenth, her cousin, but responded that she would not provide assistance to that monarch; she continued to receive periodical missives from Torenth for the next VII years. Finally, on the XIth day of March in the year 928 her husband, Hrorik II Earl of Eastmarch, arranged for a meeting at Lochalyn Castle between Sudrey and Miklós Prince of Torenth, on which occasion she formally rejected her ties with her relatives in Torenth. For this she was branded as traitor by the Prince.

After the occupation of Culliecairn Castle and the death of her husband in a skirmish with the Torenthi army on the VIIth day of June in that year, the Countess Sudrey established an infirmary at Lochalyn Castle and began organizing the defenses of the fortress. She was present there on the XXIst day of that month to help greet King Rhys Michael and his army. Later that evening she asked the King to accompany her to the chapel at Lochalyn Castle to offer up a prayer for Hrorik's soul; there she told him she still had Deryni powers, but remained loyal to the House of Haldane. She believed her feud with Prince Miklós was partly responsible for the latter's attack on Castle Culliecairn.

In a parley held the next day between Sudrey, Miklós, and Rhys Michael King of Gwynedd, she was abruptly attacked by Prince Miklós with magic, and died shortly thereafter, on the XXIInd day of June. She was XXXIV years of age at her death, and was returned to Lochalyn Castle for burial in the chapel there with her husband. As the sole surviving heir to the Honours of Rhorau and Kheldour, the Countess Sudrey was *de jure* Sovereign Princess of Kheldour and Countess of Rhorau, although she never used such titles after her marriage.

According to the *Heirs*, following her husband's death "she was still a handsome woman even in her grief, and with the air of brisk competence expected of Hrorik's wife. She died courageously in the service of her King." R.I.P. [*Saint Camber*; *King Javan's Year*; *The Bastard Prince*].

Sulien *of R'Kassi*. This ancient Deryni adept was best known as the author of *The Annales of Sulien*. Evaine Lady Thuryn consulted his works in the year 918. [*Camber the Heretic*; *The Harrowing of Gwynedd*; *King Javan's Year*; *The King's Justice*; *King Kelson's Bride*].

Supreme of Howicce. According to the *Chronicles of the Deryni*, this self-important *ministre premier* of Howicce was customarily escorted by an honour guard of XIII fierce Connaiti mercenary warriors, all VII feet tall, mailed in bronze and garbed garishly in the gaudy green and violet trappings of the United Kingdoms of Howicce and Llannedd. He was accustomed to having his own way, but his rudeness was put to an abrupt halt by Alaric Morgan Duke of Corwyn when he and his entourage made the mistake of confronting Morgan in the streets of Rhemuth. The Supreme served as the representative of his government at the coronation ceremony of Kelson King of Gwynedd on the XVth day of November in the year 1120. The Supreme resides in the curious Octagon House at Sirhowy in Howicce, with each of its VIII sides being painted a different colour. [*Deryni Rising*].

Sviatoslav, Saint. This worthy was a native of Netterhaven in the independent Principality of Jándrich. As a youth he was violent, insubordinate, disrespectful, and lazy, and after the death of his sainted father, Blessed Sviatopolk, he spent his time in debauchery and wasted his inheritance on gambling and wild women. To avoid prosecution for murder, he joined a band of brigands with whom his evil propensities reached full scope, and by middle age his excesses had ruined his health and more than once brought him close to death. When he was L years of age he suddenly lost his sight, and the shock of this deprivation occasioned a complete change in him.

He made a general confession of his sins and set out on a long and painful pilgrimage, barefooted and clothed in sackcloth, to the Old Cathedral of Saint Constantine in Beldour. While praying there the Holy Sviatoslav had a vision of Our Lady, and his blindness was miraculously cured. He was told by the Patriarch that he must make public restitution for the endless scandals that he had caused in Jándrich. So he returned to Netterhaven, where he went about the streets still clothed in sackcloth, scourging himself with a whip of switches until his back was streaming with blood. The whole city was amazed by his fervour and began to congregate around him. Visions were seen by many, and after his death from the rotting disease there was a spontaneous outpouring of affection for this curious conundrum, who was buried where he fell.

An austere monastery dedicated to Saint Sviatoslav is located on the coast of the Northern Sea near the border between Tolán and Jándrich. Here the former Torenthi King Kyprian II retired under the name Pantaleón in the year 1033. Saint Sviatoslav's feastday is the XIth day of December.

Sybaud, Sieur de Canlavay. He was born on the IXth day of December in the Year of Our Lord 1059, being the eldest surviving son and heir of Isoard Sieur de Canlavay and Sybille Demoiselle de Forcalquier. He intermarried with Anne-Louise Baronne d'Eyragues on the Xth day of July in the year 1080, but she proved barren. He succeeded his father on the XVIIIth day of March in the year 1103. He was serving with the Gwyneddan army when he was captured with Jared Duke of Cassan at Rengarth on the XXVIIIth day of June of the year 1121, and was executed with him on the Ist day of July following. He was LXI years of age at his death, and was succeeded by his younger brother, Lord Leger. [*High Deryni*].

Sylvan *O'Sullivan*. This Deryni Healer was born on the Ist day of January in the Year of Our Lord 885, being the second son of Owen Lord O'Sullivan and Sibéal Lady Joyce. He was schooled by the Varnarites in the healing arts, and later served as a battle-surgeon in the household of Gregory Earl of Ebor. On the XXIst day of January in the year 918 he helped Tavis heal the wounded Ansel MacRorie, and in the process Tavis discovered that Sylvan had the ability to block Deryni powers, being one of only III Deryni then known to possess this talent. He was brought by the Camberian Council into the Deryni underground movement at the Haven, and his training as both Healer and Deryni was substantially increased over the next few months. He met Prince Javan on the IXth day of February in that year, and later became part of Revan's "baptizing" team. He was slain by the former Regents with Revan and others on the XIth day of May in the year 922, aged XXXVII years. He had short brown hair and kindly-looking hazel eyes; his sparse beard and mustache had grown out by the year 918. *Sed difficulter continetur spiritus, integritatis qui sinceræ conscius a noxiorum premitur insolentiis*. R.I.P. [*The Harrowing of Gwynedd*; *King Javan's Year*].

Sylvie. This native of Jáca was serving as a maid to Rothana Princess Regent of Gwynedd in March of the year 1125. [*The Quest for Saint Camber*].

Tagas, Father. He was serving as chaplain to Alaric Morgan Duke of Corwyn at Coroth in March of the year 1125. [*The Quest for Saint Camber*].

Taher ibn Reyhan *Vastouni*, Prince of Andelon. He was born on the XXIVth day of November in the Year of Our Lord 1099, being the second son of Reyhan Lord Séchelles and Sofiana Sovereign Princess of Andelon. He intermarried with the Duchesse Ercille daughter of Centule V Grand Duc du Vézaire and Victoire Princess of Fianna, on the XXXth day of August in the year 1125, and by her he had children: the Princess Antonie; the Princess Xandra. The Prince Taher was the favourite child of his mother, and a Deryni adept in his own right. [*King Kelson's Bride*].

Talacara. This village in Northern Meara is situate near Ratharkin. Here Ithel Hereditary Prince of Meara and Brice Baron of Trurill were captured and executed by Kelson King of Gwynedd on the IInd day of July in the year 1124. [*The King's Justice*].

talacil. A *fébrifuge du médicin*, talacil is developed from the stalks of the talith weed, so-called because it produces elongated leaves that drape down on either side of the main stem like a tired old shawl. The leaves themselves are filled with a poisonous resin and must be discarded, together with the little yellow flowers and also the roots; but the stalks may be gathered together after the plant has gone to seed, boiled for several days, and then dried in the sun. The remnant must be ground between stones and leavened with parquat to achieve its maximum efficacy. *Temporis ars medicina fere est*.

Talbot *FitzGeoffrey*. He was the author of that well-known standard guide, *Lives of the Saints* (*Vitae Sanctorum*), which was consulted by Alaric Morgan Duke of Corwyn in November of the year 1120 to find a portrait of the banned Saint Camber. [*Deryni Rising*].

Talmud. This ancient Jewish code of law was cited by Bishop Denis Arilan on the XXVIIIth day of February in the year 1125 to support the claim before an ecclesiastical court of the Archbishops regarding the legitimate birth of Dhugal MacArdry later Earl of Transha to his parents, Maryse Lady MacArdry and Duncan Lord McLain. He was successful. [*The Quest for Saint Camber*].

Tal Traeth. This manor house in Valoret was the city residence of Cathan MacRorie Hereditary Count of Culdi and Minister to the Crown of Gwynedd in the year 903. [*Camber of Culdi*].

Tamás Termöd *Furstán*, called "The Fat," King of Torenth, sometime Count Vorarl and Count of Arkadia. He was born on the XXIInd day of December in the Year of Our Lord 620, being the second son of Aldred Count of Arkadia and Vorarl and Mariana Lady Hormizd, and a great-grandson of Arkady I King of Torenth. He intermarried with the Grand Princess Iouliana daughter of Kallistos Grand Prince of Byzantyun on the XIIth day of May in the year 644, and by her he had children: the Hereditary Prince Aldred later Aldred I King of Torenth; the Hereditary Prince László later King of Torenth; the Prince Aleksy later Count of Altorf later Count Vorarl by cession from his father, who intermarried with the Princess Moira Roselynn daughter of Aidan King of Gwynedd, and by her he had a child, the Princess Rocasta, who intermarried with Rhori Mór Prince of Kheldour and ancestor of the House of MacRorie; the Prince Melchior later Count of Arkadia by session of his father; the Princess Charlamayne, who intermarried with Markos

VI Autokratór of Byzantyun; the Princess Kypriona or Cipriona, who intermarried with Bearand Prince of Gwynedd; the Prince Ignaz Tamás later Count of Travejak, who intermarried with Agricola Countess de Spaur; the Prince Kassian Károly, whose fate is unknown.

The Lord Tamás was deeded the County of Arkadia by King István on the Vth day of December in the year 639, and succeeded his older twin brother Almár as Count Vorarl on the IInd day of July in the year 642. István King of Torenth was killed on the XVIIIth day of July in the year 652 in personal combat with Augarin King of Gwynedd. At the time of his death the King István's III sons were still minors. Therefore, the Count Károly, a grandson of Kálmán I King of Torenth, occupied Beldour with his small personal retinue, declared himself King, and was girded with the sword at Iób by the Patriarch Stylianos I on New Year's Day in the year 653. Several other Royal Princes, among them the Count Tamás and the Count Ulrich, opposed the new King, saying that the legitimate heir was the previous King's eldest son, the Prince Brecht. But King Károly seized Prince Brecht at Torenthály and executed him, declaring the boy bastard and imposter, and proscribing the lad's II little brothers, the Prince Kristóf (who died soon after of the ruby pox) and the young Prince Lipóld.

Within a year the flames of revolt had spread to all of the major cities and towns of Torenth outside Beldour, centering around the Count Tamás in the North at Arkadia, the Count Vigil in the far West at Medras, and the Count Ulrich, Champion of Prince Lipóld, at Termödy West of Beldour. By the Summer of the year 655 Beldour was under siege by the Count Ulrich. The disgruntled officers of the King opened the gates of the city to the Count and his army, and Károly was captured and executed and his head hung on a pike at the main gate. The Prince Lipóld was proclaimed King under the regency of Count Ulrich, who was now made Hereditary Prince; and the new King was girded with the sword at Iób by Patriarch Stylianos I on New Year's Day in the year 656.

But the Count Tamás had already been acclaimed King at Arkadia by his soldiers on the VIIIth day of June in the year 655, and he had soon been acknowledged by the Count Vigil and other members of the Royal family. He assembled an army at Medras, and marched on Beldour in the Spring of the year 657. He met his rivals on the plains West of the City on the XXIXth day of May in that year, and decisively defeated them in battle. Five thousand men were left on the field. The King Lipóld was blinded and deposed and sent to Saint Christodoulos's Monastery near Beldour, where he died X years later on the XXth day of February in the year 667; the Prince Ulrich was executed with all of his family.

The new King Tamás was girded with the sword at Iób by the Patriarch Stylianos I on New Year's Day in the year 658, but he himself always dated his reign from the VIIIth day of June in the year 655. In later years he grew most corpulent, but retained his great personal strength into old age. He died on the XVIIth day of June in the year 677, aged LVI years, and was buried with his ancestors at Torenthály; by terms of his testament, he left his throne jointly to the custody of his II eldest sons, I to become sole King only on the death of the other from natural causes. And so it was done according to his will. *Aurea nunc vere sunt sæcula; plurimus auro venit bonos: auro conciliatur amor.* R.I.P.

Tambert I *Fitz-Arthur Quinnell,* **Ist Duke of Cassan.** He was born on the IXth day of August in the Year of Our Lord 918, being the eldest son and heir of Fane Earl Fitz-Arthur and Anne Quinnell Princess of Cassan, and grandson of Tammaron Earl Fitz-Arthur and Ambert last Sovereign Prince of Cassan. He intermarried with Adelicia Lady of Horthness daughter of Rhun Earl of Sheele on the XXIst day of May in the year 929, and by her he had children: the Hereditary Duke Tammaron later Duke of Cassan; the Lord Flynn later Earl Derry; the Lady Eldona; the Lady Annetta. Duke Tambert's eldest son Tammaron Duke of Cassan married Tiphane Lady Ainslie on the XVIIth day of August in the year 950, and by her he had children: the Lady Swynbeth, who intermarried with Cluim King of Gwynedd; the Hereditary Duke Fane later Duke of Cassan, who intermarried with Ardana Lady de Courcy; the Lady Nerina, a twin to her brother, who intermarried with Sir Andrew McLain, father of Sir Roger McLain. Duke Tambert's second son Lord Flynn was created Earl Derry and intermarried with Margot Lady Murdoch on the IVth day of July in the year 953, and by her he had children: the Lady Blythe; the Hereditary Count Lanark later Earl Derry; the Lady Shelagh; the Lord Mellish later Earl Derry.

The Lord Tambert was created Hereditary Duke of Cassan in succession to his grandfather, Ambert Quinnell last Sovereign Prince of Cassan, and succeeded him on the XXIst day of May in the year 921. He was officially presented and acknowledged at Court in Rhemuth on the XXXth day of July in that year. He attended the coronation of young King Owain on the XXIXth day of September in the year 928, and became fast friends with the new monarch. He died in the year 948, aged XXIX years, and was succeeded by his son, Lord Tammaron. He had black hair and blue eyes. R.I.P. [*King Javan's Year*; *The Bastard Prince*].

Tammaron *Fitz-Arthur,* **Earl Fitz-Arthur, Lord Chancellor of Gwynedd, sometime Lord Regent of Gwynedd, Sir.** He was born on the VIth day of December in the Year of Our Lord 874, being the natural son of Sir Arthur Lennox and one Etilla or Tillie, a parlour maid. Fostered to the household of Bonner I Sinclair Earl of Tarleton at the age of VI years, he was educated for the knighthood alongside the Earl's II sons, Peter and Paulin, who were only a few years younger than he. Young Tammaron early demonstrated an astonishing aptitude for fiscal administration which he exercised increasingly on behalf of the ailing Earl from the age of XIV. Though only just reached XVI years at the death of his patron, on the XXVIIIth day of December in the year 890, the enterprising young Tammaron quickly exploited the affections long harboured for him by the Dowager Countess, who was some XIV years his senior, and secretly married her on the XIIth day of August in the year 891. By this marriage with Nieve Lady Sinclair he had children: the Hereditary Count Eldon, dead at age XIV of the pox; the Hereditary Count

Fane later Regent of Cassan later Earl Fitz-Arthur, who intermarried with the Princess Anne Heiress of Cassan and daughter of Ambert Quinnell Sovereign Prince of Cassan, leaving issue; the Lord Fulk, who intermarried with Niamh Lady Ballymar, leaving issue; the Lord Quiric, who intermarried with the Lady Émeraude Baroness of Horthness in her own right, daughter of Rhun Earl of Sheele, leaving issue.

The marriage was not revealed until after Tammaron's knighting by Blaine I King of Gwynedd on the Feast of Saint George (the XXIIIrd day of April) in the year 893, by which time his astute management of his stepson Peter's estates had defused any possible misgivings the new Earl might have entertained concerning some rival claim to his inheritance by this former foster brother now become his stepfather. The Earl's younger brother Paulin Sinclair had left home for seminary training well before their father's death, but likewise could find no fault with Tammaron's stewardship—and their mother seemed well content with the arrangement. The III men remained friends to the end of their days.

Sir Tammaron's rise at Court thereafter was meteoric. Although he was resented by some and admired by others for his audacity, his financial acumen was undeniable, for the fiscal reforms he put into place over the next VII years reaped unprecedented prosperity for the royal coffers. He was created an Earl *ad personam* by King Blaine I on the VIth day of January in the year 900 as one of the King's last official acts before his death. Earl Tammaron continued to serve Blaine's successor, King Imre, for another year, but he withdrew increasingly from government after the enactment of the so-called "Great Tariff" on the VIth day of January in the year 901, which typified that monarch's fiscal irresponsibility.

The Haldane Restoration on the IInd day of December in the year 904 returned Earl Tammaron to a position of influence. He affirmed his allegiance to the new King Cinhil I at the latter's coronation and again on the VIIth day of July in the year 905, when his title was made hereditary in the male line. He was appointed to the Royal Council by King Cinhil I on the VIth day of November in that same year. He was sent by King Cinhil I with Aquineas Earl Fintan on the IInd day of July in the year 906 to patrol the border between Eastmarch and Torenth in the Rheljan Mountains.

On the XVIth day of January in the year 917 the Earl Tammaron conspired with Rhun and Murdoch to overthrow the will of King Cinhil I and to establish new procedures governing the functioning of the Regency. He was named one of V Regents of Gwynedd for the young King Alroy on the IInd day of February in that year, and was created Lord Chancellor of Gwynedd on the next day following. He attended the trial of the Deryni assassins on the XXVIIIth day of September in that year.

He was present at the death of King Alroy on the XXIIIrd day of June in the year 921, and carried the State Crown of Gwynedd in the funeral procession to convey the King's body to Saint Hilary's Basilica later that same day. He attended the coronation of King Javan on the XXXIst day of July in that year, and again bore the State Crown of leaves and crosses intertwined. He conspired with his fellow former Regents to kill King Javan on the XIth day of May in the year 922.

Earl Tammaron remained behind in Rhemuth when King Rhys Michael's expedition to Eastmarch departed on the XVth day of June in the year 928. After that monarch's death on the XXVIIIth day instant and the institution of the new Regency for King Owain, the Earl Tammaron held the Queen Michaela to hostage in the crypt below Saint George's Cathedral and threatened to kill her, but was himself killed by Michaela through magic on the Vth day of July in the year 928, aged LIII years, being sent straight to Hell by the Devil for his sins. He was succeeded as Earl by his son, Lord Fane. He is described in the *Legends* as being "a stolid and expressionless shadow, overtowered by a head by the younger Rhun of Horthness." *Malum consilium consultori est pessimum*. [*Saint Camber*; *Camber the Heretic*; *The Harrowing of Gwynedd*; *King Javan's Year*; *The Bastard Prince*].

Tarkent. This town is located in the County of Vechta in Southeastern Torenth not far from its border with East Tralia. The Torenthi envoy Hombard derived from this place in the year 928. [*The Bastard Prince*]. See also: Hombard.

Tarleton. This guard captain negotiated with Barrett Lord de Laney on the Vth day of April in the year 1068 for release of a score of condemned Deryni children. ["Bethane"].

Tarleton. This County of Gwynedd was located in the Western part of the Iomaire plain near the Rhendall Mountains Northeast of the city of Carbury. King Festil I created the honour on the XXIInd day of July in the year 822 for his friend, the mercenary Philippe Cinq-Lorrons, who adopted the surname Sinclair. The title was attainted in the year 948, but Lord Tudur Sinclair eldest son of Bonner II was allowed to retain his subsidiary title of Baron Sinclair. In his descendants is vested the right to petition for the restoration of the earldom.

EARLS OF TARLETON

HOUSE OF SINCLAIR

Philippe Sinclair	822-844
Tudur (son)	844-871
Bonner I (son)	871-890
Peter (son; abdicated)	890-918
Bonner II (son)	918-948

Tarleville. This estate of Earl Tammaron was located on the great bend of River Eirian a few days' ride North of Rhemuth. [*The Harrowing of Gwynedd*].

Tavis O'Neill, Lord. He was born on the IVth day of October in the Year of Our Lord 879, being the eldest surviving son and heir of Tadleigh Lord O'Neill and Theo Lady Downs. He was trained briefly as a Healer by Dom Emrys at Saint Neot's Abbey and later by the Varnarites at Grecotha; but, having been injured psychically during his early training, he only in later life attained the potential that he had demonstrated as a young man. He succeeded his father on the XVIth day of December in the year 901.

By January of the year 917 Lord Tavis was serving as a Court-appointed Healer assigned to the crippled Prince Javan. He was drugged by Rhys Thuryn on the Ist day of February to prevent his interference in the ceremony during which the Haldane potential of the III royal Princes was set by their father, King Cinhil I. Princes Javan and Rhys Michael bought him a leather hunt cap in Healer's green at the great fair in Valoret on the XXVIIIth day of May in the year 917; later that day he was attacked in the city streets by masked Deryni, his hand being cut off to prevent him from aiding the human Haldanes with his healing powers.

On the XXIVth day of December in that same year he drugged Rhys Lord Thuryn to discover what had occurred on the night that King Cinhil I had died, and determined from his reading of Rhys's mind that he could himself learn to block Deryni powers; unfortunately, his tampering resulted in Rhys's accidental death on the next day. Five days later he took Prince Javan to Dhassa via the portal to meet with Archbishop Alister Cullen/Camber, who worked with Tavis for several hours to reduce his anxiety, guilt, and fear about using his ruined hand to heal, and who brought him into the circle of brave men and women who had been trying to save some of the Deryni. He soon became the main contact between the Camberian Council and Prince Javan.

He met with Father Joram MacRorie at Dhassa on the Xth day of January in the year 918. He participated in the expedition of the Camberian Council into Valoret Castle on the XXIst day instant, when he blocked the powers of the Drummond family. He was appointed to the Council on the XIIth day of February following. By Summer of that year he had become part of Revan's baptizer team, which had been organized by the Council to save Deryni from the Regents by blocking their powers. However, his continued concern and affection for the Haldane Princes earned the enmity of Murdoch Earl of Carthane, one of the V Regents of Gwynedd.

Tavis met with the new King Javan at the Haven on the XXVIth day of June in the year 921. He was slain on the XIth day of May in the year 922 by Revan's followers during the massacre by the former Regents' men at the River Eirian. He was XLII years of age at his death. He had dark red hair and aquamarine eyes; in later life some of his hair had turned grey, and he sported a rather bushy salt-and-pepper beard. R.I.P. [*Camber the Heretic*; *The Harrowing of Gwynedd*; *King Javan's Year*].

Tegan *O Daire*. His name is also spelled Tigan. This border chieftain was outlawed by Brion King of Gwynedd in the year 1107, and then became a brigand in the Marches of Northwestern Gwynedd. During the Rebellion of 1124 he supported Caitrin Princess of Meara, but was captured, tried, convicted, and executed on the XVIth day of September in that year. [*The King's Justice*].

Teilo, Abbot-Bishop of Llandaff, Saint. This companion of Saints David and Samson later served as Abbot-Bishop of Llandaff during the VIth century. One of this saint's most oft-quoted aphorisms is: "What is the supreme wisdom of man? Not to injure another when he has the power." A parish church dedicated to his name is located in Culdi; Bronwyn Lady de Morgan, Kevin Earl of Kierney, and Lady Alyce Lady de Corwyn de Morgan are all buried there. His feast-day is the IXth day of February; King Cinhil I's funeral was held on this date in the year 917. [*Camber the Heretic*; *Deryni Checkmate*].

Templum Archangelorum **(Temple of the Archangels)**. This long-destroyed Abbey is said to have been established by the great Deryni mage Orin in the year 634 as the first *schola* specifically intended for the training of Deryni masters and Healers. The mystic Jodotha studied here with Orin during the 670s. The establishment may have been destroyed at the command of the evil King Llarik Haldane circa the year 700. In any case, the location of the *Templum*'s ruins is now unknown. [*The Harrowing of Gwynedd*].

Tendal[l]. This Barony is located on the coast of the Duchy of Corwyn Southwest of the city of Coroth. Its title holders have traditionally served as Hereditary Chancellors of Corwyn and Mooryn since before the time of the Restoration. See also: Robert.

Termöd II Tamás *Furstán-Kheldour*, **Sovereign Prince of Kheldour, Count of Rhorau**. This Deryni prince was born on the XXVIIth day of February in the Year of Our Lord 851, being the eldest son and heir of Kálmán Count of Rhorau and Decla Lady Aghamore, and a grandson of Termöd I Prince of Kheldour son of Kálmán II King of Torenth, as well as a distant cousin of his contemporary, Imre I King of Gwynedd. He intermarried with Sheba Countess von Barstow on the Xth day of July in the year 870, and by her he had children: the Hereditary Prince Tomlin later Prince of Kheldour and Count of Rhorau; the Countess Frechette, who intermarried with Cumhai Lord Drumbarnet; the Count Tamás, who died young; the Count Kálmán, born still; the Countess Declara; the Count Festil, dead at age IV of the shaky fits.

The Count Termöd succeeded his father as Count on the XXIInd day of August in the year 873, and his uncle, the Prince Tarquin, as Prince of Kheldour on the XIIIth day of December in the year 877. He was murdered by Willimite terrorists on the IXth day of July in the year 904, aged LIII years, and was succeeded by his only surviving son, the Prince and Count Tomlin, who was killed a year later by Sighere Earl of Eastmarch on the XVIIIth day of September in the year 905, *sans postérité*. According to his niece, Lady Sudrey Countess of Eastmarch, he once commented that "Cinhil Haldane had called up something far outside the Deryni ability to defeat [Termöd's] cousin Imre." R.I.P. [*Camber of Culdi*; *Saint Camber*; *Camber the Heretic*; *The Bastard Prince*].

Tesselin, Lord Harkness. He was born on the XXth day of April in the Year of Our Lord 1062, being the only son and heir of Abner Lord Harkness and Tessalynne Lady Rethel. He intermarried with Callandra Lady Dampierre on the Ist day of June in the year 1083, and by her he had children: the Lady Salynne; the Hereditary Lord Regis later Lord Harkness; the Lord Philbin; the Lady Ophra; the Lord Donahue; the Lord Bryant; the Lady Barbe; the Lady Kathelea. He succeeded his father on the VIIth day of January in the year 1077. He was one of the Barons captured with Jared McLain Duke of Cassan at Rengarth on the XXVIIIth day of June in the year 1121. He was executed with Jared by King Wencit on the Ist day of July following, aged LIX years, and was succeeded by his eldest son, Lord Regis. R.I.P. [*High Deryni*].

Teymuraz Tivadar Termöd Theodorik *Furstán d'Arjenol-Brustarkia*, sometime Count of Brustarkia and Regent d'Arjenol, Grand Duke of Phourstania, Titular King of Toreth and Gwynedd, Sir. He was born on the Vth day of April in the Year of Our Lord 1095, being the third son of Mahael I Duke d'Arjenol by his second wife, Daniela Grafina von Ryndziak. He intermarried with the Grand Princess Justiniana, daughter of Grand Prince Alexios of Byzantyun, on the IXth day of December in the year 1128, and by her he had children: the Hereditary Grand Duke and Titular Hereditary Prince of Toreth and Gwynedd Iskander Károly Mahael Teymuraz; the Grand Duke and Titular Duke of Marluk Imre Alexios Wenzel Justinian, a twin to his brother. He also sired and acknowledged, in accordance with Torenthi law, a natural daughter, Lady Amabel les Gracques, by Zénobie Dame d'Éphèse in Thuria, in the year 1117; and a natural son, Lord Éon Teymurazovich, by Cosimina Lady Murat, in the year 1122, later ennobled as Baron Underwood.

Count Teymuraz was created Count of Brustarkia by King Carolus III on the Vth day of April in the year 1109, and placed under the tutelage of his cousin, Wencit Duke of Vorna, who undertook his instruction in all things Deryni. In the year 1110 Prince Wencit succeeded King Aldred II as King of Toreth under the name Wenzel II, and brought his young ward to court, where Teymuraz was introduced to the corruption that permeated the Beldouri Court during that decade.

When his elder brother, Mahael Count Amassy, succeeded to the Duchy of Arjenol on the IInd day of July in the year 1121, and simultaneously became co-Regent of Toreth for his young nephews, King Alroy Arion II and after him King Liam Lajos II, Count Teymuraz was appointed Regent d'Arjenol, a role he used to his own good advantage, increasing his wealth and power tenfold. Count Berrhones calls him "that sly snake, Teymuraz von Brustarkia, who wound his way through every unseemly cesspool in Beldour."

King Liam Lajos II attained his majority on the IIIrd day of April in the year 1128, and Duke Mahael and Count Teymuraz immediately began to plot treason against the state, seeking to supplant the monarch with his brother and then with Mahael. During the ceremony of *killijálay*, which took place on the XVIth day of July following, Mahael and Teymuraz attacked the King, but the former was overwhelmed by the joint forces of the Kings of Gwynedd and Torenth, the Patriarch Alpheios, and Princess Morag. Count Teymuraz was arrested by King Liam Lajos, but escaped his captors, fleeing through the portal in the Nikolaseum. He transported to Saint-Sasile, where he commandeered a war galley, and set sail towards Orsal.

Having been warned by his agent that the Hort had prepared for his arrival, he diverted his course, and landed some days later at Kharthat. He crossed the River Rampante to Alverville, and took refuge with Thorne Hagen in his castle in the Autuni Mountains. Then he transported to the private abode of his sister-in-law, Princess Morag, on the XXVIth day instant, seeking her assistance to gain the throne of Torenth. When she declined to participate in the proposed murder of her son, King Liam Lajos, the Count Teymuraz killed her where she stood, took the magical scrolls she had inherited from King Wencit, and also the iron ring that was bound to the will of Sean Earl Derry. This device he employed to see what Derry saw and to hear what Derry heard in Rhemuth.

He transported to the Cathedral there during the double Mearan wedding held on the last day of July, and forced Derry to attack Teymuraz's younger brother, Duke Mátyás; but his psychical assault being thwarted, he was forced once again to flee. He was attainted by a Torenthi court on the Xth day of August, deprived of his lands and titles, and condemned to death *in absentia*.

After stopping briefly again at Hagen's castle, Teymuraz took ship from Kharthat to the East, landing at Byzantyun some VI or VIII weeks later. There he was able to ingratiate himself into the Autokratórial Court, and soon had intermarried into the Royal Family itself, being created Grand Duke of Phourstania by the Autokratór Tiberios II on the IXth day of December. With the support of Byzantyun, Teymuraz issued a *tomos* on the IVth day of September in the year 1129, stating his claim to the Torenthi and Gwyneddan thrones. Although this broadside was circulated secretly throughout Torenth, it was not well received, either by the nobility or by the people. He had dark eyes and a black heart. *Wo der liebe Gott eine Kirche baut, da baut der Teufel eine Kapelle.* [*King Kelson's Bride*].

Thierry, Master. He was a clerk to Martin Lord of Greystoke. On the XIXth day of June in the year 1121 he was detained and interrogated by Alaric Morgan Duke of Corwyn and Father Duncan McLain on the Dhassa Road. [*High Deryni*].

Thomann, Brother. He was serving as a Healer novice at Saint Neot's Abbey on the IIIrd day of May in the year 905, when he assisted in the dissection of the bodies of Dom Calvagh and Brother Ulric. ["The Examen"].

Thomas. In the Summer of the year 906 he was a bailiff at Dolban working for the newly established order, the Servants of Saint Camber. [*Saint Camber*].

Thomas. He was a guard serving in Lord Rhys and Lady Evaine Thuryn's household in the year 917. He traveled with Evaine and her children from the manor of Sheele to Trurill on the XXIVth day of December in that same year. He was the Ist person to discover the massacre at Trurill Castle on the Ist day of January following. [*Camber the Heretic*].

Thomas d'Alver, Archbishop Primate of Valoret and All Gwynedd, sometime Bishop of Grecotha. He was born on the XVth day of December in the Year of Our Lord 825, being the third son of Alver I Sovereign Duc d'Alver and Rae Lady O'Dell. He was ordained priest in Alver on the XXIInd day of July in the year 844. He then took ship to study theology at the University of Grecotha, and soon began teaching there. He was elected Bishop of Grecotha on the IInd day of April in the year 859, and Archbishop Primate of Valoret and All Gwynedd on the XXIXth day of October in the year 862, and was known for his fiery sermons against the corruption and immortality at Court. He was struck by lightning while praying in the courtyard of the Archbishop's residence at Valoret, dying on the XXXIst day of October in the year 872, aged XLVI years, and was buried in the Crypt beneath All Saints' Cathedral. R.I.P. [*Camber the Heretic*].

Thomas, Earl Calder of Sheele, sometime Regent of Carthmoor. He was born on the Ist day of May in the Year of Our Lord 1029, being the eldest son and heir of Rhupert Earl Calder of Sheele and Aideen Lady Latteragh, and a brother of Cecilia "Síle" Lady Calder of Sheele, who intermarried as his second wife with Malcolm King of Gwynedd. He intermarried with Yvetta Lady Howard on the XIVth day of March in the year 1068, and by her he had children: the Hereditary Count Kimball later Earl Calder of Sheele; the Lady Adreana, who intermarried with Caulay MacArdry Earl of Transha; the Lord William later Sir William Calder of Sheele; the Lord Ian later an itinerant Bishop of Gwynedd; the Lady Vevina; the Lord Edward.

The Lord Thomas succeeded his father on the XXth day of November in the year 1058. Two years earlier he had been appointed Regent of Carthmoor by King Malcolm for Thomas's nephew, the Prince and Duke Richard Haldane, on Twelfth Night in the year 1056, and served in that capacity until his nephew came of age in the year 1069. He died on the IInd day of December in the year 1076, aged XLVII years, and was succeeded by his eldest son, Lord Kimball. R.I.P.

Thomas, Earl of Carcashale. He was born on the IVth day of November in the Year of Our Lord 1057, being the eldest son and heir of Theobald Earl of Carcashale and Breeda Lady Curtin. He intermarried with Maurya Lady MacKenna on the XIIth day of June in the year 1079, and by her he had children: the Lady Thomasina; the Hereditary Count Thibbot; the Lady Augusteen; the Lord Thady. He succeeded his elderly father on the XIIIth day of December in the year 1101. Earl Thomas is the present holder of the lands which include Camber's ruined manor house of Tor Caerrorie, but has placed his own seat further West near Dolban. King Kelson dined with the Earl of Carcashale on the XVIIth day of March in the year 1125, while on his quest for the relics of Saint Camber. [*The Quest for Saint Camber*].

Thomas II Linus Cardiel, Archbishop of Rhemuth, sometime Bishop of Dhassa. He was born at Cardiaque in Bremagne on the XXIInd day of March in the Year of Our Lord 1080, being the younger son and fifth child of Linus Lord Cardiel of Bremagne and Elleandor Lady Besmière, and brother of Alinor Cardiel who intermarried as his second wife with Mikhail Sovereign Prince of Andelon. His father served as Premier Ministre for Charibert King of Bremagne.

Thomas Lord Cardiel was ordained priest on the IIIrd day of April in the year 1098 by his uncle, Barthélemy Besmière Archevêque de Millefleurs, and removed himself to Coroth in the Kingdom of Gwynedd on the XIVth day of September in the year 1103, where he joined the staff of Hudriod du Mollard Bishop of Coroth, who had been his teacher and mentor in Bremagne. Shortly before the death of his patron in the year 1116, he was elected Bishop of Dhassa on the XXIst day of October in that year.

The Bishop Thomas Cardiel supported King Kelson and Alaric Morgan Duke of Corwyn during the Interdict Schism in March of the year 1121, becoming the leader of the King's party with Bishop Denis Arilan; and when his faction triumphed over Archbishop Edmund Loris and Archbishop Patrick Corrigan on the XXVIth day of June in that year, he was subsequently elected Archbishop of Rhemuth on the XIIIth day of January in the year 1122. He participated in the excommunication of Edmund Loris ex-Archbishop Primate of Valoret and All Gwynedd and his supporters on the XIIIth day of December in the year 1123.

Archbishop Cardiel presided over the marriage between Kelson King of Gwynedd and Sidana Princess of Meara on the VIth day of January in the year 1124. On the IInd day of April in the year 1125 he granted Rothana Princess and Nabila of Nur Hallaj's request to be released from her religious vows, being convinced by the lies of Prince Regent Conall that her petition was intended to facilitate their marriage. He crowned Princess Araxie Queen of Gwynedd on the VIIth day of August in the year 1128. He was determined to reform or eliminate the remaining anti-Deryni provisions of the Statutes of Ramos, and had achieved much of that goal by the year 1130. Τοῦ βίου καθάπερ ἀγάλματος πάντα τὰ μέρη καλὰ εἶναι δεῖ. [*Deryni Checkmate*; *High Deryni*; *The Bishop's Heir*; *The King's Justice*; *The Quest for Saint Camber*; *King Kelson's Bride*].

Thorne Hagen, Lord Saint-Stéphane. This Deryni adept was born on the XIIIth day of March in the Year of Our Lord 1070, being the son of Sir Thornton Hagen in Howicce and the Lady Emaline Montfort. He married Laloie de Saint-Étienne on the XIth day of April in the year 1105, and by her he had children: Thornette, born still; Cara Mia, dead of the pox at age X. His wife died of the effects of childbirth on the IInd day of August in the year 1106. He intermarried secondly with the Duchesse Henriette daughter of Alver XII Duc d'Alver and the Princess Giorgiana daughter of Irakli Prince of Autun, on the XIXth day of April in the year 1124, and by her he had children: the Lady Tibianna; the Hereditary Lord Thucydide.

Thorne Hagen was trained by the Deryni mage Muroran Urshili of Kharthat. He settled permanently in Alver in the year 1098, on Tophel Peak in the Southern Autuni Mountains. Thorne was appointed to the Camberian Council on the XXIInd day of February in the year 1113 to replace Sofiana Sovereign Princess of Andelon following her accession to the Throne, but was forced to resign from that body on the XVIth day of September in the year 1121, after conniving with Wencit King of Torenth to destroy Alaric Morgan Duke of Corwyn and King Kelson. By this time he had taken as mistress a XV-year-old girl called Moira, whom he had found wandering in the Kharthat marketplace. In July of the year 1128 he provided a refuge for his friend Teymuraz Count of Brustarkia, after the latter had fled the attempted assassination of King Liam Lajos II. [*High Deryni*; *The Bishop's Heir*; *The King's Justice*].

Thuria. This small sovereign Principality, one of the Forcinn Buffer States under the overall suzerainty of the Hort of Orsal, is bordered by the Principality of Tralia on the North, the Kingdom of R'Kassi on the East, the Principality of Nur Hallaj on the South, and the Duchy of Joux and Grand Duchy of Vézaire on the West. Its capital city is Kronburg, which lies on the South side of the River Thuria halfway between the junction of that mighty stream with the River Khabur and the Thurian Delta.

The autonomous Comté du Thurie was established on the IInd day of June in the year 688 by the Comte Thuris. His descendant, Émilien II, was forced to flee across the River Thuria into Tralia by the invading army of Joux on the XXth day of August in the year 812, his family eventually scattering into many different lands. On the XXXIst day of January in the year 931 Reynard III Duc du Joux died without heirs male, and by the terms of his will the Duchy of Joux went to his eldest daughter, the Lady Camille, and the Principauté du Thuria to his second daughter, the Lady Violette. The latter intermarried with Rhupen III King of R'Kassi on the XVIIIth day of May in the year 932, but he was deposed as King on the IIIrd day of September in the following year and had to content himself thereafter with the title of Prince of Thuria *jure uxoris*. The Princes of Thuria pay homage to the Hort of Orsal and Prince of Tralia as Overlord.

This Principality is noted primarily for its fat herds of cattle and goats and its many varieties of cheeses, which it exports throughout the lower reaches of the Eleven Kingdoms. Connoisseurs of *le fromage du Thurie* especially enjoy the *briquefort* variety, which sends a sharp bite to the palate and fills the nose with its pungent odor. Indeed, the citizens of this state take a particular pride in the excesses of the scent, celebrating the independence of Thuria each year with their Danse du Nez, in which huge pots of incense are burned throughout the city of Thuriféraire to scare away the minions of the Devil. Crowds of revelers dance in the streets until dawn, forming long chains of young men and women led by a masked harlequin swinging an incense burner from each hand. The celebration ends with the rising of the sun on the next day, when the exhausted dancers settle down to a hearty breakfast of *haricot* and *chou* which have been steaming all the night long, topped by shards of melted *briquefort* cheese. It is an experience that one will not long forget.

COMTES DU THURIE

HOUSE OF THURYN

Thuris	688-701
Fabien Chanteur (son)	701-729
Émilien I (son)	729-744
Jonque (brother)	744-777
Damien (son)	777-799
Michel (cousin)	799
Émilien II (son)	799-812

PRINCES DU THURIA

HOUSE OF RHUPEN

Violette (daughter of Reynard III of Joux)	931-975
Rhouben (husband; Rhupen III of R'Kassi)	932-959
Reynald (son)	975-984
Viol (brother)	984-999
Ezéchiel (son)	999-1018
Gédéon (son)	1018-1044
Esaïe (son)	1044
Pétremand (brother)	1044-1066
Juhel (brother)	1066-1088
Raimond (son)	1088-1101
Ysembard (son)	1101-1130+

Thuria River. This great waterway arises in the Jebel Khaibar in Eastern R'Kassi, and flows Northwest towards Djellarda, abruptly turning North there towards Thuria, where it again bends West, finally entering the Twin Rivers Strait at Orsal. Its main tributaries are the Khabur, which arises in the Sea of Karasal and forms the Northern boundary of R'Kassi; the Bhutti, which merges with it in Andelon; the Djell, which joins it at Djellarda; and the Bastul, which merges with it in Southern R'Kassi. The River Thuria is navigatible to the city of Nabat' in R'Kassi.

Thuryn, House of. This family of Healers originally derived from Comté du Thurie in the Forcinn Buffer States, claiming descent from Thuris the founder of that state. Comte Émilien II fled with his family before the invading army of Joux across the River Thuria into Tralia on the XXth day of August in the year 812, eventually receiving sanctuary in Mooryn. His eldest son and heir, the Hereditary Count Michel, settled at Dunluce in Carthmoor, and one of Michel's younger sons, Lord Malachy, died at Valoret in the Great Plague of 878. He was the father of the well-known Deryni Healer, Rhys Lord Thuryn. [*Camber of Culdi*]. See also: Aidan, Evaine, Jerusha, Rhys, Rhysel, Tieg.

Tibal Parménion *de Jordanet*, Sieur de Jordanet in Joux. He was born on the XVIth day of October in the Year of Our Lord 1073, being the eldest son and heir of Roker Sieur de Jordanet and the Countess Vivienne daughter of Émery Comte de Joux and Enna Lady Leix. He intermarried with Ernée Lady Dhulia on the XXVIIth day of March in the year 1105, and by her he had children: the Hereditary Lord Talière; the Lady Chanterelle; the Lady Topaze; the Lady Dahlia; the Lord Roquevaire. The Lord Tibal succeeded his father on the IXth day of December in the year 1109. He was present when his mother died on the XVIIth day of July in the year 1128. [*King Kelson's Bride*].

Tibald *MacErskine*. This border chieftain and brigand, who had been outlawed in the year 1107 by Brion

King of Gwynedd, supported Caitrin Princess of Meara during the Rebellion of 1123 and 1124. He was captured, tried, convicted, and executed by forces loyal to King Kelson on the XVIth day of September in the year 1124. [*The King's Justice*].

Tieg Joram *Thuryn*, Lord. He was born on the Ist day of August in the Year of Our Lord 914, being the third child and second son of Rhys Lord Thuryn and Evaine Lady MacRorie. He intermarried with Karis Lady d'Oriel on the XXVth day of August in the year 935, and by her he had children: the Lady Madelon, who intermarried with Jürgen Lord Leslie; the Lady Aine; the Lord Jacuth; the Lady Lassa. On the day of his birth he was baptized in a magical ceremony by his grandfather, Camber of Culdi, with the participation of his parents and Father Joram MacRorie. On the Ist day of January in the year 918 he helped to heal his cousin, Camlin Lord MacLean, who had been crucified by Manfred Earl of Culdi's men when they had burned Trurill Castle the day before. He was brought to the old Michaeline Haven by his mother on the IXth day instant, and helped heal Ansel Lord MacRorie on the XXIst day following, when it was discovered that little Tieg also had the ability to block Deryni powers.

On the XIth day of May in the year 922 he quickly read the memories of Étienne Baron de Courcy concerning the events leading up to the *coup d'état* by the former Regents on that day, and he later transcribed these fragments for Bishop Niallan Trey's lengthy history of the Haldane family since the Restoration of the year 904. He had become part of Father Joram MacRorie's underground band of Deryni by the year 928. On the XIVth day of June in that year he participated in enabling the Haldane potential of King Rhys Michael, together with Father Joram, Rhysel Lady Thuryn his sister, and Queen Michaela.

He died in the year 948, aged XXXIII years. He had hazel eyes and freckles, and was sporting a Gabrilite-style braid by the year 928, although he cut it before transporting to the library at Rhemuth Palace on the XIVth day of June in that year. R.I.P. ["*Healer's Song*"; *Camber the Heretic*; *The Harrowing of Gwynedd*; *The Bastard Prince*].

Tiercel *de Claron*. He was born on the Vth day of September in the Year of Our Lord 1098, being the son of Sir Tibur de Claron and Awdrey Lady Novell. He never married. He was appointed to the Camberian Council by the year 1121, being then the youngest member of that august body. He was one of IV arbiters of the duel arcane held between Wencit King of Torenth and Kelson King of Gwynedd and their followers at Llyndruth Meadows on the IInd day of July in that same year. He secretly began instructing Conall Prince of Gwynedd in attaining his Haldane potential in the Winter of the year 1124, intending to show the Council that more than one Haldane Prince could be empowered at the same time. However, the Prince Conall proved to be a willful student, and accidentally killed his master in a fit of temper on the VIIIth day of March in the year 1125. Tiercel's body was discovered on the XVth day instant by Bishop Duncan McLain. Tiercel was XXVI years of age at his death; his body was buried at his ancestral home of Claronette. R.I.P. [*High Deryni*; *The Bishop's Heir*; *The King's Justice*; *The Quest for Saint Camber*; *King Kelson's Bride*].

Tiernan, Brother. This monk was serving as gate-keeper at Saint Mary's in the Hills Abbey in January of the year 918. On the Xth day of that month he gave Dom Queron Kinevan a leather pouch left for him by Evaine Lady Thuryn. He was middle-aged, and garbed in a black habit and mantle. [*The Harrowing of Gwynedd*].

Tim *Sellar*. He was one of the L peasants executed in September of the year 903 at King Imre's command in retaliation for the murder of Lord Rannulf. R.I.P. [*Camber of Culdi*].

Tivar, Dom. He was serving as a Gabrilite priest and weapons master at Saint Neot's Abbey in April of the year 917. [*Camber the Heretic*].

Toban. This hospice page was serving Rhys Lord Thuryn at the Battle of Iomaire on the XXVth day of June in the year 905. He informed the Healer of Camber Earl of Culdi's supposed "death." [*Saint Camber*].

Tolán (-by-the-Sea). Bordered on the North by the Northern Sea, Tolán is the IInd largest fief in the Kingdom of Torenth, being exceeded in acreage only by the Duchy d'Arjenol, although the Duchy of Jándrich is comparable in size. It is bounded on the West by the Rheljan Mountains separating it from the Earldoms of Marley and Eastmarch in Gwynedd, by the Duchy of Nördmarcke to the South, the County of Tigre to the Southwest, and the Duchy of Jándrich on the East.

At one time an autonomous state under the independent Counts and Dukes von Tolán, it was annexed by the Kings of Torenth on the XXXth day of August in the year 677, when Aldred King of Torenth defeated and killed Zvonimir Herzog von Tolán at the Battle of Elderon. The title was awarded to Aldred's eldest son, the Prince Imre, who deeded it to his brother, Prince Nikon, on Imre's succession to the Throne in the year 701. The line of Nikon became extinct and the title escheated to the Crown in the year 888. The Duchy was presented as a dowry to Princess Charis sister of King Arion I on the XVIIth day of July in the year 927, on the occasion of her marriage to Hereditary Prince Marek I Festillic Pretender to the Throne of Gwynedd, and the title Duke or Duchess of Tolán was thereafter carried by each of the heirs of that family, whether male or female. It merged with the crown on the XVth day of November in the year 1120 with the death of the Duchess Charissa, who was succeeded in her pretensions by her *cousin germain*, Wencit King of Torenth. Upon his death a year later the title passed to his sister, Princess Morag Dowager Duchess d'Arjenol.

It is said of Tolán that its fishermen feed a IIIrd of the Kingdom of Torenth. The traveler Campbell de Broun noted in his diaries that "...I have been to Tolán. It is very cold there. The damp penetrates one's bones to the very core. The fog never lifts from the shore. Even the incessant blowing of the wind cannot take away the smell of rotting fish. The people are excessively rude. Their breaths stink of fish and garlic and rancid goat cheese. The women are fat and ugly and as cold as the clime. My spirits have never sunk lower. How I long for the sunny days and balmy nights of bonnie Cloome! I shall not go to Tolán again." *Era già l'ora che volge il disio a' naviganti, e internerisce il cuore lo dì c' han detto a' dolci amici addio; e che lo nuovo peregrin d'amore punge, se ode squilla di lontano, che paia il giorno pianger che si muore*. [*The Bastard Prince; Deryni Rising; The Bishop's Heir*].

HERZOGS VON TOLÁN

HOUSE OF MIR

Mirolyub	446-481
Miraks (son)	481-502
Miroslav (son)	502-516
Vladimir (brother)	516-538
Miron (son)	538-566
Kazimir (son)	566-590
Radomir (son)	590-622
Lyubomir (son)	622-649
Stanimir (son)	649-666
Zvonimir (brother)	666-677

COUNTS OF TOLÁN

HOUSE OF FURSTÁN-TOLÁN

Imre I (son of Torenthi King Aldred I)	677-701
Nikon I (brother)	701-732
Aldred (son)	732-755
Ilya (son)	755-789
Dimitrian (son)	789-811
Nikon II (nephew)	811-844
Imre II (grandson)	844-888

SEE PRETENDERS OF GWYNEDD FOR LATER DUKES

Tom *Weaver*. He was one of the L peasants executed at King Imre's command in retaliation for the murder of Lord Rannulf in September of the year 903. *Que messieurs les assassins commencent!* R.I.P. [*Camber of Culdi*].

Tomais. He was serving as a scout for Clan MacArdry on the XXIVth day of November in the year 1123. [*The Bishop's Heir*].

Tomais *d'Edergoll*, Sir. He was born on the XVIIIth day of January in the Year of Our Lord 901, being the son of Sir Thiou d'Edergoll and Viridiana Lady Arles. He was serving as a squire to Prince Rhys Michael in the year 917, and was present during the assassination attempt on the Princes on the XXVIIIth day of September in that year. He was knighted by King Alroy on the IIIrd day of December in the year 920. He became an aide to King Javan upon his accession on the XXIIIrd day of June in the year 921, and attended his coronation on the XXXIst day of July following. He was sent by the King to accompany the Royal Commission that went to Grecotha on the XIXth day of September in that year. After the attack on their party and the supposed "kidnapping" of Prince Rhys Michael, which occurred on the XXXIst day of October, he spent II days combing the region with the men at his disposal, assisted by a sizable troop of Bishop Edward MacInnis's men, but was unable to find any clue regarding the Prince's fate. He wrote to King Javan on the I[st] day of November following. He was slain at Rhemuth Castle on the XIth day of May in the year 922 during the *coup d'état* by the former Regents. He was XXI years of age at his death. R.I.P. [*Camber the Heretic; The Harrowing of Gwynedd; King Javan's Year; The Bastard Prince*].

Tophel Peak. This mountain in the Autuni Range was visible from Thorne Hagen's manor in Alver. [*High Deryni*].

Torcuill, Baron *de la Marche*, later Count of Marchmont in *The Connait*. This Deryni Lord was born on the VIIth day of April in the Year of Our Lord 861, being the eldest son and heir of Tomhas Baron de la Marche and Ovidée Lady Croix-Verte. He intermarried with Zaira Lady O Maolmhudaidh on the IXth day of May in the year 880, and by her he had children: the Lady Jocelynne; the Hereditary Lord Tomhar later Count of Marchmont; the Lady Ursula; the Lord Thadoir; the Lady Saira.

The Lord Torcuill succeeded his father on the XIXth day of May in the year 896. He was appointed to the Royal Council of King Imre on the VIth day of January in the year 901, when he was also named to the Court of Crown Commissioners. King Cinhil I appointed Baron Torcuill to his staff by June of the year 905; he was confirmed in his title on the VIIth day of July, and named to King Cinhil I's Royal Council on the VIth day of November. On the latter date he was sent by King Cinhil I to seek a treaty of alliance with Sighere Earl of Eastmarch and Warlord of Kheldour.

After the death of King Cinhil I, being Deryni, he was dismissed from the Royal Council on the IIIrd day of February in the year 917 by the Regents of King Alroy. He was present at the coronation of King Alroy on the XXVth day of May in that year, but later that Fall he moved his family out of Gwynedd into Trevalga in The Connait, staying temporarily at the estate owned there by Gregory Earl of Ebor. He returned to Gwynedd on the XIIth day of June in the year 918 to become Revan's first baptized "convert." He returned shortly thereafter to The Connait, where he bought an estate he called Marchmont, being awarded the title of autonomous Count Marchmont by Poncet Prince of Pardiac on the I[st] day of June in the year 923. He died there on the IXth day of September in the year 936, aged LXXV years, and was succeeded as Count by his son, Lord Tomhar. R.I.P. [*Camber of Culdi; Saint Camber; Camber the Heretic; The Harrowing of Gwynedd*].

Torenth. This mighty Kingdom, one of the largest in the known world, lies to the East of Gwynedd and to the North of Tralia, and encompasses VII once-independent principalities and duchies, including Tolán, Jándrich, Arjenol, Vorna, Lorsöl, Vechta, and Truvorsk. The region was conquered by the Empire of Byzantyun about the year 100. In the year 388 the Byzantyun Governor, Lord Phourstanos, was created Comes Beldouris. His descendant, Furstán III Duke of Beldouria, organized the Torenthi monarchy after conquering several of his neighbours, declaring himself King on the XXVIIth day of September in the Year of Our Lord 545, and being girded with the sword by the Archbishop Eudoxios I on the New Year's Day following. Thus, in the curious chronology of the Kingdom of Torenth, Anno Domini 545 was called the Accession Year of King Furstán I or the VIIIth Year of Duke Furstán III, and the year 546 was called the Ist Year in the reign of King Furstán I; hence, Anno Domini 566 became his XXIst Year, so that to the citizens of other lands the years of his reign and those of his successors might seem to be numbered I less than they ought.

Now it is true that the Great Mother Byzantyun had withdrawn from this region in the previous century, but still she coveted the steppes of Torenth, and so sent an army to the West in September of the year 566. The Byzantyuns were decisively defeated near Beldour on the IXth day of October in that year, but King Furstán the Founder was himself mortally wounded, and lingered little more than a week before expiring from the rotting disease. During the next century Torenth expanded but slowly, moving West and North into the fertile crescent. A Torenthi raiding force moved West out of Sostra in the year 648 and again in 652, penetrating Eastern Haldane, but withdrew after King István was killed in personal combat with Augarinus King of Gwynedd on the XVIIIth day of July. His defeat prompted a V-year civil war in Torenth over the succession, a struggle eventually won by Tamás the Fat, the descendant of the main line of the House of Furstán.

This King's son, Aldred the Great, extended his nation's boundaries to the Great Northern Sea, more than doubling the size of his territories and greatly enriching his family. King Aldred's great-grandson, Mátyás Imre, continued to march West and North, extending Torenthi rule as far as the Purple March in Northern Gwynedd. His son, King Kálmán II, gradually wore away at Gwynedd's defenses, and lived to see his younger son Prince Festil crowned King of that nation.

King Nimur I the Great lost his paramountcy over Gwynedd when his cousin, King Imre son of King Blaine I, was defeated and killed by the last of the Haldane line, King Cinhil I, but he expanded Torenth's boundaries far to the East, conquering Arjenol, Vorna, Lorsöl, and Vechta. His son Arion I again attempted to conquer Gwynedd for his Festil cousin, but failed, as did several of his descendants. King Kyprian II supported the Festillic Pretender and the Prince of Meara in the year 1025, but abdicated after the disaster at Killingford decimated his Kingdom's nobility. King Wenzel II, better known as Wencit, inherited the Festillic pretensions to the Gwyneddan throne in the year 1120, but lost his life on the IInd day of July in the year 1121 in another futile attempt to re-establish Torenth's paramountcy. At his death the male line of the Second House of Furstán became extinct, and the succession passed to the House of Furstán d'Arjenol.

The land of Torenth is filled with many wild places yet untamed, and with deserts and harsh steppes and desolate mountains. Interspersed throughout these barren places are beauteous stretches of dense forest and seemingly endless plains. And although the farming is very bad in the Eastern and Northern parts of the country, the Fertile Crescent created by the River Beldour in the central portion of Torenth feeds much of the country. Beasts of all kinds still roam the wild places of the land, especially boar and antelope and bear and lions, and much hunting occurs in the Summer and Fall months. Along the coast of the Northern Sea the fishermen of Jándrich and Tolán reap a rich harvest from the waters.

The Kingdom of Torenth lies at the nexus of the many roads and trails used by traders from the South and East to reach the markets of the West, including the ancient Great King's Way built by the potentates of Byzantyun, and the rulers of Torenth have not been lax in securing their tithe of this bounty. Then too, the River Beldour is navigable all the way to Kulnán in the foothills of the Rheljan Mountains, and serves as a broad passageway into Torenth from the Southern Sea, being continually plied by ships sailing upstream to Beldour Town, the capital. Also, there are numerous mines in the mountains of the East that supply iron and copper and gold and silver and many other ores and precious metals to the rest of the world. Thus, the nation prospers from its trade even during times of drought and famine.

The chief minister of the Kingdom is the Grand Vizier, although Torenth has numerous officials with equally grand titles whose functions are obscure to those not resident there. [*King Kelson's Bride*].

COUNTS AND DUKES OF BELDOURIA

HOUSE OF FURSTÁN

Furstán I (Phourstanos)	388-409
Bering (son)	409-421
Zsigmond (son; Duke 449)	421-455
Zudar (brother)	455-478
Zoltán (brother)	478
Furstán II (son)	478-502
Thüring (son)	502-537
Furstán III Torenthály (son)	537-545

KINGS OF TORENTH

HOUSE OF FURSTÁN

Furstán (III) Torenthály	545-566
Arkady I Bleda (son)	566-567
Miklós I Mózses (brother)	567-587
Rurik Toren (son)	587-588
Wenzel I Ardric (uncle; abdicated)	588-589
Kálmán I Gábor (son)	589-612
Kyprian I Arkady (nephew)	612-621
Miklós II Pál (brother)	621-638
István Zsolt (son)	638-652
Károly I Kálmán (grandson of Kálmán I)	652-655
Lipóld Demagoy (son of István)	655-657

HOUSE OF FURSTÁN TAMÁSY

Tamás Termöd "The Fat" (great-grandson of Arkady I)	655-677
Aldred I Arkady "The Great" (son)	677-701
László Vak (brother; joint king)	677-681
Imre I Zsolt (son of Aldred)	701-722
Radislaus Vaksos (son of László)	722-738

Festil Ottó (son of Imre)	738-748
Mátyás Imre (son)	748-808
Kálmán II Imre "The Carollan" (son)	808-822
Lajos I Kis (son)	822-845
Árpád Imre (grandson)	845-871
Malachy I Mihály (grandson of Lajos)	871-877
Imre II Tamás (son)	877-891
Nimur I Zsigmond "The Great" (son)	891-917
Arion I Mátyás (son)	917-972
Malachy II Miklós (grandson)	972-984
Károly II Káspár "Bold Carolus" (son)	984
Kyprian II Könyves "The Conqueror" (brother; abdicated)	984-1025
Arkady II Árpád (son)	1025-1080
Nimur II Dénes "The Old" (son)	1080-1106
Károly III Kyprian "Young Carolus" (son)	1106-1110
Aldred II Andre (son)	1110
Wenzel II Zsubit "Wencit" (uncle)	1110-1121

HOUSE OF FURSTÁN D'ARJENOL

Alroy Arion II (nephew)	1121-1123
Liam Lajos II (brother)	1123-1130+

Torenthály. Located V miles North of Beldour, this ancestral estate of the House of Furstán has belonged to the family from time immemorial. Here is situate the oldest Christian church in Torenth, Hagios Iób, and the LXXXVIII tombs of the Furstáns. [*King Kelson's Bride*].

Torin. He was serving as a guard in Bishop Cullen's household in January of the year 917. [*Camber the Heretic*].

Torin, Saint. He flourished circa Anno Domini 850, during the height of Festillic rule in Gwynedd. According to the *Chronicles*, "It was believed that he was the scion of a poor but noble family of great hunters whose males had always been hereditary wardens of the vast forest regions to the North. He was said to have had dominion over the beasts of the forests he guarded [and] to have performed many miracles. It was also rumoured that he had once saved the life of a legendary King of Gwynedd when that monarch was hunting in the royal forest preserves one stormy October morning, though no one could recall just how he managed to do this." He was adopted as the patron saint of Dhassa soon after his death, and a shrine dedicated to his name at the end of Lake Jashan is a required visit for any adult male to the region who approaches from the South. His feastday is the XIth day of February. [*Deryni Checkmate*; *High Deryni*].

Torval I Tamás *Furstán*, **Prince of Torenth, Duke d'Arjenol, Grand Duke of Östmarcke.** He was born on the VIIIth day of July in the Year of Our Lord 906, being the third son and fourth child of Nimur I King of Torenth and Katalin Countess of Festil-Mnata. At the age of X years, on the XXVth day of October in the year 916, he was intermarried by proxy to Braïda Princess and Heiress d'Arjenol, then aged I year, the ceremony being reaffirmed in person on the XIth day of January in the year 926, and by her he had children: the Countess Karela; the Hereditary Duke Rogan, who married the Princess Chariella daughter of Marek I Pretender of Gwynedd, and died before his father at the age of XXXIX years on the XXVIth day of October in the year 972, leaving issue, the Hereditary Duke Termöd II; the Countess Ratboda; the Countess Karlotta; the Countess Braidetta; the Count Ringan later Duke of Östmarcke.

The Prince Torval was created Ist Duke d'Arjenol by his father on the XXVth day of October in the year 916, with his uncle the Prince Dmitri serving as Regent until he came of age in the year 920; and Grand Duke of Östmarcke *ad personam* by his brother, King Arion I, on the XIth day of January in the year 926, for his services to Torenth. He passed from this world on the IInd day of December in 981, aged LXXV years, and was succeeded by his grandson, the Hereditary Duke Termöd. His direct descendant in the male line, the Hereditary Duke Alroy, became King of Torenth as Arion II on the IInd day of July in the year 1121. R.I.P.

Torval Termöd Toren *Furstán d'Arjenol-Netterhaven*, **Lord of Netterhaven.** He was born on the IVth day of October in the Year of Our Lord 1088, being the second son of Demagoy Dmitri Furstán Count von Netterhaven and Germana Lady von Furstánburg, and a direct descendant in the male line of Count Torval second son of Rogan, Hereditary Duke d'Arjenol. He intermarried with Phylandra Lady Gallarat on the XXIIrd day of April in the year 1110, and by her he had children: the Hereditary Lord Zsolt; the Lord Vak; the Lord German; the Lady Torvala. The Baron Torval was sent as hostage and messenger by King Wencit to King Kelson's camp at Llyndruth Meadows in July of the year 1121. When King Wencit killed C of his McLain prisoners on the Ist day of July in the year 1121, the Baron Torval was executed in return by Warin de Grey and Father Duncan McLain, aged XXXII years. He was succeeded by his eldest son, Lord Zsolt. R.I.P. [*High Deryni*].

Torval Zimri Arkady *Furstán*, **Prince of Torenth, Duke of Lorsöl.** He was born on the IXth day of August in the Year of Our Lord 1063, being the second son and second child of Nimur II King of Torenth and Charis Rochelle Princess of Festil. He was created Duke of Lorsöl in the year 1066 in succession to his uncle, Stephanos V Patriarch of Beldour. Having been cursed by the Devil with imbecility, he was excluded from the succession of Torenth by his father on the VIth day of January in the year 1095 following the death of his elder brother IV days earlier, and was sent to the Holy Icons Monastery of the Brothers of Saint Simplicius, where he became an expert gardener of roses. He was visited there frequently by his sister, Morag Duchess d'Arjenol, who loved him dearly. He died of the pustulant pox on the XVIth day of September in the year 1119, aged LVI years, and was buried with all honours with his ancestors at Torenthály. *Principibus placuisse viris non ultima laus est.* R.I.P.

Transha. The Earldom of Transha was created by writ of King Rhys Michael on the XIIth day of October in the year 926, when he elevated Egan Chief and Laird of Clan MacArdry to the peerage of Gwynedd. The Clan MacArdry has been consistently loyal to the House of Haldane ever since.

The town of Transha lies on the coast of the Gulf of Kheldour, not far from where the River Cùille enters the sea, and its County is bordered by Meara to the West, Kierney to the Northwest, the Purple March to the South and East, and the Gulf to the North. Castle Transha was designed to take advantage of its natural defenses: the entrance road spirals up to the left through a steep, narrow killing zone, while the seaward side sheers off in a straight drop to the surf far below. The keep itself rises XL feet above the rock, the gaps along the crenellated wall providing easy vantage points from which to bombard an approaching enemy. [*The Bishop's Heir*; *The King's Justice*; *King Kelson's Bride*]. See also: Ardry, Caball, Caulay, Dhugal, Michael.

EARLS OF TRANSHA

HOUSE OF MACARDRY

Egan	926-931
Donn (son)	931-955
Ardry (son)	955-966
Liam (brother)	966-1011
Naal (grandson)	1011-1022
Mael (son)	1022-1025
Ardal (cousin)	1025-1044
Arthur (son)	1044-1080
Caulay (son)	1080-1123
Dhugal (grandson)	1123-1130+

***Travlum* or *Transflumenia*.** This region is generally considered to be the land between the River Eirian, the River Llanarfon, the Mughdorna Mountains, and the city of Cùilteine. It was conquered by the Byzantyun Empire in the year 260, but was lost by them about XC years later. The Counts of Travlum ruled over part of the region for several centuries, before the last Count, Richthern II, fled in disgrace into The Connait following his unseemly actions during the events of the year 948. Later the title Duke of Travlum was awarded to several members of the House of Haldane, but remained in abeyance for many years before finally being regranted to Prince Payne in the year 1128.

DUKES OF TRAVLUM

HOUSE OF HALDANE

Alroy Uthyr (son of King Urien)	1000-1001
Ossian Albert (brother)	1017
Jaron Rhys (brother)	1025-1078
Tamarina (daughter)	1078
INTERREGNUM	
Payne (son of Prince Nigel)	1128-1130+

Tre-Arilan. This traditional seat of the Arilan family is located outside the city walls of Rhemuth. It has its own private portal. ["The Priesting of Arilan"].

Trefor, Lord of Morland. He was born on the IXth day of February in the Year of Our Lord 889, being the second son of Hannibal Baron of Morland and Ulrica Lady Biroc. This Deryni Baron was killed in the attempted assassination of the Princes Javan and Rhys Michael on the XXVIIIth day of September in the year 917, aged XXVIII years, with his cousin, Lord Amyot, also dying in the ambush. Trefor had organized the conspiracy to avenge the death of his foster brother, Dafydd Lord Leslie. [*Camber the Heretic*].

Trevalga. This estate is located in The Connait near its Eastern border with Gwynedd, and was purchased by Gregory Earl of Ebor in the Summer of the year 917 to provide a place of refuge for himself, his family, and other Deryni exiles, including Torcuill Baron de la Marche and Dom Aurelian. He removed his family there by the Ist day of October in that year to escape the persecution of the Deryni by the Regents of Gwynedd. A portal was established at Trevalga by January of the year 918. Gregory's title of Count was confirmed by the Council of Sovereign Princes of The Connait on the Ist day of December in the year 918. Two years later, on the XVIth day of November in the year 920, the Council admitted the sovereign County of Trevalga to its membership. Members of his family have continued to rule that small state unto this very day. In the year 1127 the reigning Count Saron petitioned the King of Gwynedd for restoration of the ancient title of Ebor, which request was granted a year later. [*Camber the Heretic*; *The Harrowing of Gwynedd*].

COUNTS OF TREVALGA

HOUSE OF MACGREGOR

Gregory (former Earl of Ebor)	918-932
Jesse (son)	932-981
Murray (son)	981-1002
Ebor (son)	1002-1029
Bonald (son)	1029-1055
Murrow (son)	1055-1066
Tristram (brother)	1066-1092
Grady (son)	1092-1114
Saron (son)	1114-1130+

Trevas. This village is located on the coast of Corwyn Southwest of the capital city of Coroth. It is primarily known for its tuna fishing and smuggling of goods across the Southern Sea to the Forcinn Buffer States. Its best-known citizen was Anscom Archbishop Primate of Valoret and All Gwynedd. *Imago animi vultus, indices oculi.* See also: Anscom.

Trevor *Udaut*, Baron Varagh, sometime Regent of Derry. He was born on the IInd day of June in the Year of Our Lord 1077, being the eldest son and heir of Lorenzo Udaut Baron Varagh and Camilla Lady Mentone. He intermarried with Fathana Lady Carcashale on the XIXth day of May in the year 1098, and by her he had children: the Hereditary Lord Absalom; the Lord Padrig, later a page to Sean O'Flynn Earl Derry; the Lady Charlotta; the Lord Rovert; the Lady Orsalla; the Lady Vye; the Lord Mentone; the Lord Lorenzo *Junior*; the Lady Phiala; the Lady Kalomine; the Lady Katherine, a twin to her sister; the Lady Mellie; the Lord Robuck; the Lady Unity; the Lord Eazé. He succeeded his father on the VIIth day of November in the year 1104. He served as Regent for his nephew, Sean Earl Derry, between the XXIXth day of April in the year 1106 and the XIXth day of April in the year 1111. On the I[st] day of May in the year 1115 he attended the annual Horse Fair at Rhelledd with his nephew, Sean Earl Derry, whom he sponsored on his knighting by King Brion on the XIth day instant. ["The Knighting of Derry"].

Triduana, Saint. This IVth-century maiden is connected with the legend of Saint Sava, who, it is said, raised her from the dead and awoke in her the first stirrings of her passion for her Lord. She followed him faithfully for the rest of his short career, pledging to raise him from the dead as he had once raised her. Alas, her ministrations, although devoted and persistent, failed in their attempts, and Saint Sava did not respond. She died by his side, consoling herself with the thought that she had tried, because, as she said, "A good man is hard to find." Some historians believe the latter comment to be apocryphal.

A convent devoted to her name was located in Thuria, and became a center of devotion and pilgrimage before its destruction by fire in the early XIIth century. The Countess Friederike became a nun at Saint Triduana's under the religious name of Sister Thyra. Saint Triduana's feastday is the XVIIIth day of August.

Trurill. This ancient marcher Barony lies on the border between Gwynedd and Meara West of Culdi, where the River Cùille joins the River Tharkane. The castle was held by Lord Adrian MacLean Master of Kierney in the year 917, and was sacked and burned by the Regents' men on the XXXIst day of December in that year. Lord Adrian was brutally tortured and slain, as was young Aidan Thuryn, who was being fostered by his cousins, along with many MacLean retainers. Adrian's son and heir, Lord Camber Allin, was crucified and left to die, but was rescued by Evaine Lady Thuryn; Adrian's grandmother, Lady Aislinn, sister to Camber MacRorie, also died. Three years later the fief was given by King Alroy to Bruce Baron of Trurill. By the year 1123 Trurill was held by his descendant, the Baron Brice, and the region was visited by Kelson King of Gwynedd on the XXIVth day of November in that year. After the execution of Brice on the IInd day of July in the year 1124, his title was attainted and Trurill reverted to the Crown. [*Camber the Heretic*; *The Harrowing of Gwynedd*; *The Bishop's Heir*].

Truvorsk. This Torenthi Duchy is situate North of the River Beldour, lying East of the Counties of Kulnán and Gwernach, South of the Duchy of Nördmarcke and County of Tigre, and North of the Duchies of Sasovna and Arkadia and County of Vorarl on the opposite side of the River Beldour. The last Sovereign Duke of Truvorsk, Bruno von Neumarck, acknowledged the suzerainty of Aldred I King of Torenth, but was deposed in the year 701 by Aldred's son, King Imre I, who gave it to a younger son, Count Porphyry. He died childless in the year 767. His nephew, King Mátyás, then gave the title to his own infant son, Prince Vaksos, who also died without issue in the year 832. The title was created anew for Count Vólmar son of King Lajos I. At the extinction of the honour in the year 915, it lay dormant for III years until being regranted by King Arion I as a Duchy to his younger brother, Prince Miklós. He died X years later without legitimate issue, when the title passed to his nephew, Prince Vidar, who chose a life in the Church. At his death in the year 1015 it was regranted by King Kyprian II to his son, Prince Zimri, and passed from him to his grandson, Hogan Pretender of Gwynedd, and thence to Duke Zimri's IInd son, Duke Lóránt. [*King Kelson's Bride*].

HERZOGS VON TRUVORSK

HOUSE OF NEUMARCK

Neumann	549-577
Aribert (son)	577-611
Joachim (son)	611-641
Anselm (brother)	641-644
Karl (son)	644-669
Bruno (son)	669-701

COUNTS AND DUKES OF TRUVORSK

HOUSE OF FURSTÁN-TRUVORSK

Porphyry (son of Imre I of Torenth)	701-767
Vaksos (great-nephew)	767-832
Vólmar I (great-nephew)	832-881
Lajos (son)	881-903
Vólmar II (brother)	903-915
Miklós (cousin; Duke)	918-928
Vidar (nephew)	928-1015
Zimri (great-nephew)	1015-1078
Hogan (grandson)	1078-1105
Lóránt (half-uncle)	1105-1122
Káspár (son)	1122-1130+

Turlough, Bishop of Marbury. He was born on the XXVIIIth day of December in the Year of Our Lord 855. He was ordained on the Vth day of May in the year 875, and consecrated an itinerant Bishop of Gwynedd on the XIIth day of September in the year 899. He attended the consecration of Father Alister Cullen as Bishop of Grecotha and Vicar General Robert Oriss as Archbishop of Rhemuth on the IXth day of July in the year 905 at Valoret. He participated in the Synod of Bishops held at Valoret in November and December of 917. He was elected the first Bishop of the newly created see of Marbury on the XXVth day of January in the year 918, and in that capacity attended the coronation of King Javan on the XXXIst day of July in the year 921. He died on the XXXIst day of January in the year 924, aged LXVIII years. R.I.P. [*Saint Camber*; *Camber the Heretic*; *King Javan's Year*].

Turstane, Dom. He was born on the XXIInd day of August in the Year of Our Lord 866. He worked as a stonecutter's apprentice before deciding to pursue his vocation as a Gabrilite priest, Healer, and philosopher at Saint Neot's Abbey. He participated in the dissection of the bodies of Brother Ulric and Dom Calvagh on the IIIrd day of May in the year 905. He was recommended by the venerable Dom Emrys for a position on the Camberian Council, taking his place on the XXIst day of December in 910, but was killed in an accidental fall on the XXIst day of May in the year 916, aged XLIX years. R.I.P. *Scribendi recte sapere est et principium et fons.* [*Camber the Heretic*].

Twilham Green. This village in the Purple March was visited by Geordie Lord Drummond in April of the year 905 after he rescued the boy Beck. The local constable was named Polidor. [*Deryni Challenge*].

Twin Rivers Strait*, or *Great Estuary. This waterway separates the Duchy of Joux, the Hort of Orsal, and the Principality of Tralia on the East from the Southeastern portion of the Duchy of Corwyn in Gwynedd on the West. The upper course of this sound eventually splits into the freshwaterway of the Western River, which serves as a natural border between Torenth and Northeastern Corwyn; and the Eastern or Beldour River, as it is known in Torenth, which arches into the form of a giant crescent encircling the lands which form the center of the old Kingdom of Torenth and Duchy of Beldouria, the so-called Fertile Crescent or the Heartlands. The Kings Kelson and Liam Lajos II traversed this waterway on their way to Beldour in early July of the year 1128. [*King Kelson's Bride*].

Uiskin. This town is located on the Northernmost promontory of the Duchy of Cassan. It is best known for its large fishing fleets, which regularly ply the Atalantic Ocean, and for the great lighthouse built there in the year 825 by Prince Amalric Quinnell.

Ulliam *ap Lugh*, Bishop of Nyford. He was born on the IIIrd day of January in the Year of Our Lord 849. He was ordained priest on the XXIVth day of September in the year 870, was consecrated an itinerant Bishop of Gwynedd on the XVIIth day of November in the year 894, and was elected Bishop of Nyford on the XIth day of August in the year 902. This human prelate attended the consecration of Father Alister Cullen as Bishop of Grecotha and Vicar General Robert Oriss as Archbishop of Rhemuth on the IXth day of July in the year 905 at Valoret. On the XXIVth day of October in the year 906 he supported the canonization of Camber MacRorie Earl of Culdi at the Council of Bishops in Valoret. He participated in the Synod of Bishops held in the same city in November and December of 917, where he was considered a possible candidate for the office of Archbishop Primate of Valoret. He attended the coronation of King Javan on the XXXIst day of July in the year 921. He died on the XXXth day of November in the year 933, aged LXXXIV years. R.I.P. [*Saint Camber*; *Camber the Heretic*; *King Javan's Year*].

Ulric, Brother. This novice Healer at Saint Neot's Abbey went berserk on the IInd day of May in the year 905 and killed his trainer, Dom Calvagh, while Dom Queron was still teaching there. He was himself killed with an arrow by the newly elected Abbot, Dom Emrys, and his body was then dissected on the next day to demonstrate the potential healing of war wounds. R.I.P. ["The *Examen*"; "First Session"; *Camber the Heretic*].

Ultan, Abbot and Saint. This brother of Saint Fursey and Saint Foillan succeeded the latter as Abbot in the Vth century, and also inherited his hives of bees, from which, it is said, he learned to hum like a bee. Indeed, from the study of these simple creatures he devised a completely new theory of harmonious chant, and founded an academy devoted to the promotion and study of coordinated, syncopated humming in ecclesiastical choirs. His theories caused a revolution in the development of vocal music. An *Ordo Verbi Dei* priory dedicated to his name is located on the Southwestern coast of Mooryn, although this Order resisted efforts by a minority of its brethren to change its name to the *Ordo Susurri Dei*. His feastday is the Ist day of May. [*Camber of Culdi*]. See also: *Ordo Verbi Dei*, Saint Ultan's Priory.

Umphred. This old carle was serving as bailiff to Camber Earl of Culdi at his Tor Caerrorie estates in the year 903. He later received Father Joram MacRorie and Rhys Lord Thuryn on the XVIth day of August in the year 906. [*Camber of Culdi*; *Saint Camber*].

Ungnad Isaiya *Lazarevic*, Count of Fajardô. He was born on the XXVth day of March in the Year of Our Lord 1060, being the eldest surviving son of Avram Count of Fajardô and the Countess Ibolya daughter of Levente Duke of Csorna. He intermarried with Lady Máriamnë Rufimovich on the Ist day of May in the year 1082, and by her he had children: the Lady Máribore; the Lady Hamâ; the Lady Thuine; the Lady Rózsa; the Lady Mátra; the Lady Tisza; the Hereditary Count Lazar.

The Lord Ungnad succeeded his father on the Vth day of October in the year 1068, under the regency of his uncle, Lord Maros, attaining his majority in the year 1074. He participated in the moving ward of King Nimur II at the *killijálay* of 1081, and attended every subsequent installation of a Torenthi monarch through King Liam Lajos II in the year 1128. [*King Kelson's Bride*].

University of Grecotha. This establishment is the preeminent institution of higher learning in the Kingdom of Gwynedd, having been founded by Sinead Queen of Gwynedd on the XXIXth day of May in the year 682, when she amalgamated several of the *scholae* there into one institution. She had her own brother, Mogue Prince of Kheldour, appointed Bishop of Grecotha and Chancellor of the *Universitatis*, a charge which he undertook most vigorously. The University has long served as the primary center for the higher training of priests and clergy in Gwynedd, and it mothered both the Gabrilite and Varnarite Orders. [*Saint Camber*].

Uriel, Saint. This archangel, also called "The Angel of Death," was one of the protectors called upon to ward a magical circle in certain ceremonies, his quarter being the North and his sign being a golden square. His Arabi name is Auriel and his Torenthi name is Ouriél, which in the old tongue means "Fire of God." His element is earth. A cathedral dedicated to his name and all the angels is the seat of the Bishop of Meara in Ratharkin. His feastday is the XXIst day of December. [*Saint Camber*; *Camber the Heretic*; *The Harrowing of Gwynedd*; *King Javan's Year*; *The Bastard Prince*; *The Bishop's Heir*; *The King's Justice*].

Urien Owain Rhys Michael *Haldane*, King of Gwynedd. He was born on the last day of March in the

Year of Our Lord 974, being the eldest son and heir of Cluim King of Gwynedd and Swynbeth Lady Fitz-Arthur Quinnell. He intermarried with the Princess Jaroni daughter of Bhair al-Salah King of R'Kassi on the VIIIth day of May in the year 988, and by her he had children: the Hereditary Prince Cinhil Aymeric Nygel later Cinhil II King of Gwynedd; the Prince Cluim Corwyn, dead at the age of III days; the Princess Suibhne, who intermarried with Turlough Lord Stainléigh; the Princess Bethra, who intermarried with Théofrid III Roi de Bremagne; the Prince Alroy Uthyr later Duke of Travlum, dead at age IV of the scarlet fever; the Prince Aidan Owain Jashan later Duke of Valoret, killed before his father, *sans postérité légitime*; the Princess Breida, who intermarried with Tancrède King of Fallon; the Prince Ossian Albert later Duke of Travlum in succession to his brother Prince Alroy, dead at age XIV of a misplaced lance through his spine; the Princess Rathnait, who intermarried with Onan *Junior* Prince of Jáca; the Prince Malcolm Congal Aidan Julian later Duke of Rhemuth later King of Gwynedd; the Prince Jaron Rhys later Duke of Travlum in succession to his brother Prince Ossian, who intermarried with the Lady Salentina daughter of Marek II Pretender of Gwynedd, and had one daughter, the Princess Tamarina later Duchess of Travlum, whose issue is believed extinct.

The Prince Urien succeeded his father on the XVIIIth day of December in the year 994. Within a few months he was forced to call up his levies to meet the planned invasion of Gwynedd by the forces of Imre III Pretender of Gwynedd and Imre's ally and friend, Kyprian II King of Torenth. However, the severe drought and heat which affected both Torenth and Gwynedd beginning in June of the year 995 eventually forced Kyprian to cancel his plans, and the Torenthi monarch soon had to face incursions by barbarian hordes in the East. Some historians have suggested that the King Urien used his connections to the R'Kassi royal family deliberately to create problems for the Torenthi on their Eastern borders.

On the I[st] day of December in the year 1000 King Urien graciously blessed his great-grandmother, Richeldis Dowager Countess of Kierney, at her specific request, for he loved her dearly, and when she died later that month he had her buried in the royal crypt of the Haldanes beneath Saint George's Cathedral. During his long reign the Kingdom of Gwynedd prospered greatly, being relieved of the necessity of fighting any wars on its borders, and the King Urien sought to increase that prosperity through deliberate alliances between his children and other royal houses.

War threatened the realm again in the year 1025, when the Festillic Pretender threatened an invasion from Torenth. King Urien gave his son the Hereditary Prince Cinhil complete authority to take whatever steps he deemed necessary to preserve the nation. Although the King took no active role in conducting the campaign that followed, he was visible before his troops at the major battles, and died fighting bravely at Killingford on the XVIIth day of June in the year 1025, aged LI years. King Urien was succeeded by his eldest son, the Prince Cinhil. His body was returned for burial in the family crypt of the Haldanes beneath Saint George's Cathedral in Rhemuth. R.I.P. *Si quis piorum manibus locus, si, ut sapientibus placet, non cum corpore extinguuntur magnæ animæ, placide quiescas, nosque domum tuam ab infirmo desiderio et muliebribus lamentis ad contemplationem virtutum tuarum voces, quas neque lugeri nequi plangi fas est.*

Urracca, *i.e.,* **Urracce-Ursine-Haÿte** *de Besançon* **Quinnell, Dowager Princess of Meara, Princess of Bremagne.** She was born on the XXVth day of November in the Year of Our Lord 990, being the daughter of Faucon Hereditary Prince of Bremagne and Adélaïde Comtesse de Joyeuse. She intermarried as his second wife with Jolyon II Sovereign Prince of Meara on the XXth day of April in the year 1007, and by him she had children: the Princess Roisian later Sovereign Prince of Meara, who intermarried with Malcolm King of Gwynedd; the Princess Annalind later Sovereign Prince and Pretender of Meara, a twin with her sister, who intermarried with Rhiryd Kincaid Earl of Kilarden, leaving issue; the Hereditary Prince Joël, dead at age II of the stoney relick; the Hereditary Prince Jubal, dead at age VI of a fall; the Princess Judit, tainted with cambique at the age of VIII; the Princess Jorianna, a twin with her sister, dead at age II of the frothing mouth; the Princess Magrette, who intermarried with Edward Lord Ramsay son of the Earl of Cloome; the Hereditary Prince Job, who died shortly after birth.

On the death of her husband in the year 1025, the Princess Urracca supported her IInd daughter the Princess Annalind for the throne, and was ultimately successful in advancing her cause. Two years later Malcolm King of Gwynedd invaded Meara with his army, and forced Annalind, Urracca, and Urracca's youngest daughter, the Princess Magrette, from their fortress of Laas into exile in The Connait. The Princess Urracca pleaded with her cousins in Bremagne to send her aid, but they saw no profit in involving themselves in what they regarded as a civil war.

On the XIIth day of May in the year 1035 the Princess Magrette left her mother and married the younger son of the Earl of Cloome against Urracca's will, but with the consent of Malcolm King of Gwynedd. On the XVth day of September in the year 1041 the Princess Annalind married Rhiryd Kincaid Earl of Kilarden, thereby securing the succession to the Mearan pretensions. When Annalind quickened with child, the Dowager Princess insisted that they return to the principality in the next year for the child's birth, for an old tradition required that all members of the House of Quinnell be born on the sacred soil of Meara. But the Royal Army of Gwynedd was waiting, and the Royals were forced into the hills. Princess Urracca sickened when the cold weather returned that Fall, dying worn and embittered of a cancer in her womb on the XXIst day of December in the year 1042, aged LII years. She was secretly buried in the hills above Ratharkin, but her body was later returned to Laas for reinterment in the family crypt of the Quinnells. *Vox tantum atque ossa supersunt. Vox manet.* R.I.P. [*The Deryni Archives*].

Ursin O'Carroll. He was born on the I[st] day of January in the Year of Our Lord 895, being the son of Carrollan O'Carroll and Cristin Browne. He intermarried with Birgit Subalter on the XIIth day of June in the year 916, and by her he had one son: Carrollan *Junior*. This former Varnarite classmate of Tavis was a failed Healer, but otherwise a powerful practitioner of Deryni magic. He was impressed into the service of Manfred Earl of Culdi by January of the year 918, with his human wife and son being held hostage to his actions. He was stripped of his powers by Revan's baptism at the River Eirian on the XIIth day of June in that year, and was then kept in solitary confinement by the *Custodes Fidei*, who tested him periodically with *merasha* to be certain that his powers had not returned.

He was still imprisoned there on the VIth day of March in the year 922, when he was visited by King Javan, who required that he be retested with the drug. Ursin was then taken to the cell of his wife and child, where his son was tested by Oriel and proved to be Deryni. Ursin was smothered in his bed by III unknown assailants on the XXth day of April in the same year, probably led by Master Dimitri at the instigation of the former Regents, and was buried at Saint Hilary's Basilica, aged XXVII years. Birgit and Carrollan O'Carroll were later spirited to safety from the massacre conducted at the River Eirian by the former Regents on the XIth day of May in that year. R.I.P. [*The Harrowing of Gwynedd*; *King Javan's Year*].

Ursula Yonne *MacFaolan-Gruffud*, Princess of Howicce. She was born on the XIIth day of November in the Year of Our Lord 1108, being the daughter of Prince Roen Count of Tirol, who was the son of Fergus Prince of Howicce, third son of King Colman I, and the Countess Photia daughter of Tallard Sovereign Duke of Llangan and the Lady Cotentine Countess of Cyby. She was considered as a possible bride for Kelson King of Gwynedd in the year 1128, being rich and accomplished. [*King Kelson's Bride*].

Uthyr Michael Richard *Haldane*, King of Gwynedd, Duke of Carthmoor. He was born posthumously on the XVth day of January in the Year of Our Lord 929, being the second surviving son of Rhys Michael King of Gwynedd and Michaela Lady Drummond. He intermarried with Grania MacInnis Countess of Culdi on the IInd day of May in the year 947, and by her he had children: the Hereditary Prince Nygel later King of Gwynedd; the Prince Cinhil Duke of Carthmoor, dead at age XIII of the palpitating palsy; the Prince Jasher later Earl of Culdi later King of Gwynedd; the Prince Cluim later Earl of Carthane later King of Gwynedd; the Princess Gesella, who intermarried with Erastus the Hort of Orsal and Prince of Tralia; the Princess Estella, a twin to her sister, dead at the age of II months of oversleeping; the Princess Graziana, who intermarried with Selvase Sieur de Broun, ancestor of the Broun family.

The Prince Uthyr was created Duke of Carthmoor at birth. He succeeded his brother, the King Owain, in the year 948, and shortly thereafter defeated the Festillic pretender, Prince Marek I. He was crowned King of Gwynedd by Bertrand de Tolbert Archbishop Primate of Valoret and All Gwynedd on the XXIXth day of September following. Much of his reign was spent in rebuilding the damage wrought by the Festils to the peerage and economy of Gwynedd. He attainted those houses who had taken an active role against the Haldanes, saying they could no longer be trusted in the circles of government, and executed the ringleaders of the great conspiracy. He encouraged the widows and daughters of the deceased noblemen to find suitable new husbands, stating that his own marriage during the previous year should set the example for the rest of the nation. He sent emissaries to Arion I King of Torenth urging peace between their II lands, and met with that monarch near Marbury on the VIth day of June in the year 955, receiving a personal pledge from King Arion that he would not again support the Festil during his own lifetime.

He knighted Gilrae Hereditary Lord d'Eirial at Easter Court in the year 977. He died on the XVIth day of September in the year 980, aged LI years, and was succeeded by his eldest son, Prince Nygel. He was buried with his ancestors in the crypt of the Haldanes beneath Saint George's Cathedral. R.I.P. [*The Bastard Prince*].

Valentin, Captain. He was serving as a senior officer to Marek I Hereditary Prince and Pretender of Gwynedd in June of the year 928. A seasoned veteran, Valentin had instructed both the Prince Marek and his cousin Prince Miklós on the art and science of swordplay during their earlier years. He defended his master against King Arion I's accusations on the XXVIth day of that month at Beldour. *Spem pretio non emam.* [*The Bastard Prince*].

Valerian, Brother. He was serving as the Latin tudor to the Princes Alroy, Javan, and Rhys Michael in the year 917. [*Camber the Heretic*].

Valla de Courcy. This estate of the de Courcy family in Gwynedd is situate in Western Travlum, near the border of the Kingdom with The Connait. [*King Kelson's Bride*].

Valoret. This ancient city was founded by the invading Byzantyun forces in the year 258 under the name Castrum Valloretum, being erected on the South bank of the River Erinys to guard the Northern frontiers of the Byzantyun territories in Carthanus Province. A town gradually formed around the walls of the old fort, and thrived over the next CC years as a major trading center between the South and the barbarian North. In the year 408 the Byzantyun armies withdrew to Carthanus Inferior, leaving behind a well-established political and religious organization that was easily subsumed III years later by Halbert the Dane, called Haldane, who proclaimed himself *Comes Valloreti* or *Haldani* on the XXXth day of June in the year 411. His successors called the new state Haldane in his honour. On the I[st] day of May in the year 645 the Count Augarin II proclaimed himself High King of Gwynedd, with his capital at Valoret. The capital was removed to Rhemuth by his son and successor, the King Aidan, on the XVIIIth day of June in the year 674. Following the successful invasion of Festil I on the XXIst day of June in the year 822, the capital was restored to Valoret, but at the restoration of the Haldanes on the IInd day of

December in the year 904, the capital returned again to Rhemuth on the XIVth day of July in the year 917.

The city of Valoret is situate on the South bank of the mighty River Eirian, and includes some of the finest examples of classical architecture in the Eleven Kingdoms. A site of particular interest is the magnificent All Saints' Cathedral, which was first commissioned by King Augarin Haldane and his brother, Archbishop Aurelius Haldane, in the year 646, being dedicated on the IIIrd day of September in the year 650. Additional structures were added to the Cathedral in the years 823 and 905. The old Royal Palace, which often serves as the residence of the King during the Summer months, has also been used in the last century as a seat of the government in the North. Here are buried the V Festillic Kings and their relatives, and the Archbishop Primates of Valoret and All Gwynedd.

Other notable structures include the Great Market, the Archbishop's residence, the Archbishop's offices, the Great Library of Valoret, the King Blaine Amphitheatre, the Archives of State, and the Hall of Kings. The *Cloaca Magna Valloreti* is considered to be among the engineering marvels of the Western World. [*Camber of Culdi*; *Saint Camber*; *Camber the Heretic*; *The Harrowing of Gwynedd*; *King Javan's Year*; *The Bastard Prince*; *Deryni Rising*; *Deryni Checkmate*; *High Deryni*; *The Bishop's Heir*; *The King's Justice*; *The Quest for Saint Camber*; *King Kelson's Bride*].

ARCHBISHOP PRIMATES OF VALORET AND ALL GWYNEDD

Saint Angelus Catho	258-272
Florentius Boötes	272-288
Otramnus Exesor	288-290
Saint Paulus I Serius	290-301
Nizerius Largificus	301-306
Leontius Decus	306-309
Agratus Insanus	309-311
Leon Edurus	311-325
Mamertus Postpartor	325-333
Lupicinus Serpens	333-340
Avitus Vetulus	340-364
Saint Deusdedit Adeodatus	364
Blessed Verus I Tyrius	364-371
Clarentius Pomosus	371-376
Simplides Bonus	377-386
Bertericus Caput	386-389
Isicius Antonius	390-400
Julianus Peniculus	400-417
Domninus Decus	417-419
Babolinus Honorius	419-431
Edictius Metrus	431-444
Verus II Defensor	444-454
Paracodes Semis	455-481
Blessed Anacletus Quietus	481-488
Sindulf Vetus	488-508
Saint Melchior Evidens	509-512
Blessed Palladius Decennis	512-522
Ceratus Coclea	522-553
Bernarr Cynewulf	554
Corbus Missus	555-575
Amicus Xystus	577-591
Artus Archetypus	591-603
Salvius Exemptus	603-615
Bonitus Chalybs	615-616
Gallus Vappa	616-633
Amadeus Fidicen	633-640
Marcellus Centaurus	640-642
Servilius Ops	642-645
Aurelius Haldanus	645-666
Higerius Intolerandus	666-673
Gisenod Cenelm	673-685
Gaspard Hebert	685-699
Blessed Jarente de Quint	699-701
Archideus Concursus	701-717
Marin MacTagh	717-719
Saint Lantelm	719-739
John I O'Conallin	739-764
Symphorian Auditòr	764-766
Edmond I Magistratus	766-777
Adon Interpunctio	777-780
Agilulfe Comprobator	780-792
Valatonius Præsutus	792-803
William I of Gap	803-821
Ennemond d'Escalle	821-822
Emerick von Tolán	822-834
Imre Ingwar Jöns Furstán-Festil	834-839
Mallenus of Beldour	839-845
Paul II de Dragonnet	845-848
Odilbert of Övaltin	848-862
Thomas d'Alver	862-872
Ursul von Isarn	872-888
William II of Howicce	888-890
Anscom of Trevas	891-906
Jaffray of Carbury	906-917
Alister Cullen	917
Hubert John William Valerian MacInnis	917-928
Ailin McGregor	928-941
Dermot O'Beirne	941-948
Secorim of Tiel	948
Bertrand de Tolbert	948-955
Soffred de Pons	955-976
Halsten del Borgo	976-981
William III d'Argenson	981-990
William IV Stephanis	990-999
Hieronymus (or Jérôme) Laurens	1000-1018
Ragenfrid de Hugues	1018-1020
John II of Benevent	1020-1025
Vespasian d'Aphienne	1025-1034
Briand of Meara	1034-1044
Jashan Nygel Ifor Eadwig Haldane	1044-1055
Léodegaire de Saint-Severin	1055-1066
Aymar von Weckesser	1066-1067
Theophylact (usurper)	1067
Balthasar d'Archiac	1067-1073
Michael of Kheldour	1073-1092
William V MacCartney	1092-1096
Paul III de Tolán (Tollendal)	1096-1102
Oliver de Nore	1102-1114
Edmund II Loris	1115-1122
Bradene of Grecotha	1122-1130+

Vanissa 't-Serclaes, called Maria. This country maid was born on the IInd day of January in the year 1108, being the daughter of one Indract 't-Serclaes, a farmhand, and Vanne Lurie. She became the kept woman of Conall Haldane Hereditary Duke of

Carthmoor later Prince Regent of Gwynedd in the year 1124, and by him she had one child: Conalline Amelia Haldana't-Serclaes later Haldane, who was born posthumously on the VIth day of August in the year 1125, but without dynastic rights. She was brought to Rhemuth Palace by the Duchess Meraude in July of the year 1128 and given a position there under the name Maria, so that Nigel Duke of Carthmoor could come to know his granddaughter. There she began learning the art of fine embroidery. She had brown eyes and hair and a sweet nature. [*The Quest for Saint Camber*; *King Kelson's Bride*].

Vantry, Lord Cerdagne. He was born on the IIIrd day of November in the Year of Our Lord 883, being the younger son of Junius Baron Cerdagne and Walerana Lady Debry. This *Custodes* knight carried a message from Lord Albertus to his brother Vicar General Paulin Sinclair on the Xth day of November in the year 921, and also reported to King Javan. He committed suicide on the XVIth day of July in the year 928, shortly after the disbanding of the *Equites* branch of the *Custodes* Order, aged XLIV years, and was buried in unhallowed ground. *Potius amicum quam dictum perdere.* [*King Javan's Year*].

Varian. The Barony of Varian was first granted by King Malcolm to Sir Vasco de Varian in the year 1025 to honour his service in the recent war with Torenth. The banners of this family were prominently displayed in the army of Kelson King of Gwynedd in June of the year 1121. Burchard Baron de Varian was created Earl of Eastmarch on the VIth day of January in the year 1122 by King Kelson to reward his service to the Crown during the preceding year. [*High Deryni*].

BARONS DE VARIAN

HOUSE OF DE VARIAN

Vasco or Basco de Varian	1025-1041
Balen (son)	1041-1079
Basil (brother)	1079-1082
Branson (usurper; cousin?)	1082
Boston (son)	1082-1101
Branwell (brother)	1101-1126
Burchard (son)	1126-1130+

Varnar *of Bassetdale*, Saint. This patron saint of Deryni learning and healing and of the hounds of the hunt is said to have been a natural son of Lord Alric Haldane, the younger brother of Jesric Count of Haldane; the name of Holy Varnar's mother has not, alas, survived. His date of birth also remains uncertain, some sources placing it in XVIIth year of Hansoc Count of Haldane, and others in the IInd year of his son, Count Guerric Haldane. The site of his birth no longer survives, but is believed to have been located near the small village of Schilling, north of Valoret.

About the year 480 he underwent a fast of XV days, and received the most miraculous visions from our Lord Jesus Christ, commanding him to minister to the sick and needy of the land. Soon he had become known throughout the County of Haldane as a healer and miracle-worker of the highest order.

But it was not until Aidan Hereditary Count of Haldane became ill with the spotted pox that Varnar gained the attention of Count Jesric, who promised to give Varnar whatever he wished, if only he would heal young Aidan. When the boy finally rose from his bed, the blemishes upon his face finally fading away, Varnar asked for a building in which he could establish a *schola* of learning for the Deryni, and the Count gratefully granted his request.

But about the year 500 a dispute arose over title to the property and the taxes owing thereupon, and Holy Varnar denounced his uncle, taking his teachers and implements and removing with them to the city of Grecotha, which was then governed by a council of free men. There Varnar established the *Schola Artis Salutaris* and many other places of Deryni learning, so that the young men of the XI Regni, and occasionally even the women, came from great distances to listen at the feet of the great *magister*.

He continued his teaching and the building of his *Conlegium Artium Derynianarum* for another XXIV years, before being assumed bodily into the bosom of Our Lord in the Year of Our Lord 524. He was canonized in the year 555 by Æmelius Patriarch of Bremagne, but his status as a saint was revoked in the Kingdom of Gwynedd by the Council of Ramos, and then restored again in the year 1127. The Ordo Sancti Varnari continued his work after his death. His feast-day is the XXVth day of August.

An image of Saint Varnar rising from the ground while surrounded by a pack of baying hounds was entiled into a superb mosaic by the Deryni master Vaél son of Amiél, and still commemorates his holy work in the Church of Saint Varnar in Sestos.

Varnarites (Ordo Sancti Varnari). This group of Deryni adepts and scholars split from the more conservative Gabrilites about the year 745, taking with them their library and records to new quarters in another part of the city of Grecotha. There they established the Varnarite University or *schola*, where they trained would-be Healers, although their approach to the subject tended to be somewhat pragmatic when compared to the philosophical teachings of the Gabrilites, and often ignored the more subtle nuances of the art. The lectures of Jodotha indicated that certain records of the Varnarites had been placed in a secret archive before the school moved to its new quarters in Grecotha. *Pone seram, cohibe; sed quis custodiet ipsos Custodes?* [*Saint Camber*; *Camber the Heretic*; *The Harrowing of Gwynedd*].

Vasilly *Dimitriades*, Lord Chief Chamberlain to the Hort of Orsal, Sir. He was born on the last day of December in the Year of Our Lord 1087, being the son of Sir Démyan Démétriadés of Vorna and Tamaris Lady Górash. He intermarried with Jeanne Demoiselle La Folle on the IVth day of May in the year 1116, and by her he had children: Sir Philogon; Lady Deya. He was appointed Deputy Chamberlain to the Hort of Orsal in the year 1111, and Chief Chamberlain in the year 1122, being awarded a barony *ad personam*. He officially welcomed the Kings Kelson and Liam Lajos II to Orsal on the IIIrd day of July in the year 1128. He wore sea-green robes and an office chain of golden cockle-shells. *Non domus hoc corpus sed hospitium et quidem breve.* [*King Kelson's Bride*].

Veldur Forests. This region of good hunting and trapping is located upriver from the Torenthi city of Fathane in the Southern Coamer Mountains on the Western River. [*Deryni Checkmate*].

Veneric, Saint. This author of the *Triads*, a group of pithy sayings penned about the year 650, is best known for his statement: "Three things there are which defy prediction: a woman's whims, the touch of the Devil's finger, and the weather of Gwynedd in March." He is said to have been a friend and counselor of King Augarin Haldane. His feastday is the Ist day of April. [*Deryni Checkmate*].

Vera Laurela *(de Corwyn) Howard McLain*, **Duchess of Cassan**. She was born on the IInd day of February in the Year of Our Lord 1070, being the second child of Keryell Earl of Lendour and Stevana Heiress de Corwyn, and the younger twin sister of Lady Alyce de Corwyn de Morgan. To shield her from the stigma of being Deryni, her mother gave her at birth to her close friend, Laurela Lady Howard, who had just been delivered of a stillborn child, and her supposed date of birth was adjusted accordingly to the previous day. Lady Laurela and her husband, Orban Lord Howard, then raised Vera as their own child. She intermarried as his IInd wife with Jared McLain Duke of Cassan on the IXth day of May in the year 1090, and by him she had children: the Lord Duncan Howard later Duke of Cassan later priest and Bishop, born on his mother's birthday; the Lady Isabet Anna, born still; the Lady Alicia Jesma Isabet, dead at age III of the roseola. She also fostered her deceased sister's children, Sir Alaric Morgan later Duke of Corwyn, and the Lady Bronwyn. She died of the wasting disease on the XXXIst day of January in the year 1115, just II days short of her XLVth birthday. *Candida, perpetuo reside, concordia, lecto, tamque pari semper sit Venus æqua jugo: diligat illa senem quondam; sed et ipsa marito, tunc quoque quum fuerit, non videatur anus.* R.I.P. [*Deryni Rising*; *Deryni Checkmate*; *The Deryni Archives*].

Vézaire. This small sovereign Grand Duchy, one of the Forcinn Buffer states, is situate between Joux and Logréine on the coast of the Southern Sea, and is bounded on the East by Thuria and on the Southeast by Nur Hallaj. Its capital city, Côte d'Alban, which lies on the East side of the Baie des Chameaux, is especially known for its quaint buildings and cobbled streets framed by the white chalk cliffs that ring the outer reaches of the harbour.

The Grand Duchy was founded by Nivelon I Vésan on the XVIth day of March in the year 813, when he declared his small estate, Mont Mouton, independent of Joux, and found, much to his surprise, that his nearby neighbours were joining with him in defying the tax collectors of that country. Soon he had gathered together a small army of men armed with pitchforks and scythes, and they defeated every attempt by Léonard Duc du Joux to put them down.

Finally, the Duc sent him an emissary, proposing a marriage between Léonard's spinster daughter, the Lady Hortense Zezayère, who had a slight speech impediment and several other minor defects, but who was quite suitable for a former sheep farmer, or so the Duc thought. He promptly knighted the young lad, giving him part of the land now called Vézaire as a dowry for his daughter, before introducing Nivelon to the lovely Hortense. After first spying his bride-to-be before the altar, and then giving her a somewhat closer examination, Sir Nivelon demanded the title of Grand Duc from his incipient father-in-law; the Duc Léonard shrugged his shoulders and gracefully agreed.

Allegedly, the Deryni spy Master Dimitri and his supposed brother Collos derived from this country, where Dimitri had once been an undersheriff in the Xth century, although this connection was later denied by Grand Duc Nivelon III. It was here that Donal Blaine II Hereditary Prince of Gwynedd married the Lady Dulchesse daughter of Nivelon IV late Grand Duc du Vézaire on the XVIIIth day of July in the year 1046. [*King Javan's Year*; *King Kelson's Bride*].

GRAND DUCS DU VÉZAIRE

HOUSE OF VÉSAN

Nivelon I Vésan	813-842
Centule I (son)	842-866
Nivelon II (son)	866-891
Centule II (son)	891-920
Nivelon III (son)	920-945
Centule III (son)	945-971
Centule IV (son)	971-1000
Nivelon IV (son)	1000-1039
Centulon I (brother)	1039-1041
Léonard (nephew)	1041-1055
Nivelon V (son)	1055-1072
Centulon II (brother)	1072-1088
Nivelon VI (son)	1088-1111
Centule V (son)	1111-1130+

Vivienne *(des Buyenne et Furstán) de Jordanet*, **Lady**. She was born on the XXIVth day of November in the Year of Our Lord 1052, being the daughter of Émery Comte du Joux and Enna Lady Leix, and a great-niece of Régnier I Duc du Joux through his younger brother, Comte Rémy. She intermarried with her second cousin, Roker Sieur de Jordanet in Joux, on the IXth day of May in the year 1070, and by him she had children: the Hereditary Lord Herculan Henriot, who died young of the febrile flurries; the Hereditary Lord Tibal Parménion later Sieur de Jordanet; the Lady Cirta, who was born still; the Lady Jacquette; the Lord Herculan Hastur; the Lord Riquet; the Lady Robertine; the Lord Virgile, a twin to his sister.

This conservative Deryni mage was appointed to the Camberian Council about the year 1080, and served several stints as Coadjutor of that body. She was one of IV arbiters of the duel arcane held between Wencit King of Torenth and Kelson King of Gwynedd and their followers at Llyndruth Meadows on the IInd day of July in the year 1121, which ended with the deaths of Wencit, Stefan Coram, Lionel Duke d'Arjenol, and Bran Earl of Marley. She was reappointed Coadjutor of the Council later in 1121 to replace Coram. She took an exceedingly dim view of the involvement of the Haldanes in matters magical. She died of paralysis at her estate on the XVIIth day of July in the year 1128, being attended by her son Tibal and by the physician Lord Laran ap Pardyce, and was buried with high honours at Alta Jorda II days later, next to her husband and daughter. *Gott macht gesund, und der Doktor bekommt das Geld.* R.I.P. [*High Deryni; The Bishop's Heir; The King's Justice; The Quest for Saint Camber; King Kelson's Bride*].

Wadi-Ghubrail. In the mid-1120s this oasis, located East of the Forcinn Buffer States in R'Kassi, was a shrine to Saint Gabriel the Archangel.

Warin de Grey. He believed himself to be a messiah divinely appointed to destroy all Deryni; his main center of operations was located in Southeastern Gwynedd in Dhassa and Corwyn. Although not Deryni, he demonstrated the ability to heal the sick. He was convinced on the XXVth day of June in the year 1121 by Kelson King of Gwynedd and the rebel Bishops to support the King's Party. He disappeared a year later.

According to Volumen II of the *Chronicles*, "Warin was not a large man. In fact, were it not for his regal bearing, he might have been considered short, but this was totally overshadowed by the fact that the man had presence, which radiated outward from his person like a living entity. The eyes were dark, almost black, with a wild, even reckless intensity which sent a shiver up Derry's spine. His hair was brown and crinkled, a dusty dun colour, closely cropped; and he wore a very short beard and mustache of the same dun hue. His uniform was a solid grey leather jerkin over tunic hose and high boots of the same shade, except that the falcon badge on his breast was large, covering most of his broad chest, and the cap badge on his close grey hat was silver rather than sewn. His grey leather riding cloak was full and long, almost brushing the floor." *Sic agitur censura et sic exempla parantur, quum vindex alios quod monet ipse facit.* [*Deryni Checkmate; High Deryni; The Bishop's Heir; The King's Justice*].

Warringham. This was the site of a shrine to Saint Camber in the year 917. [*Camber the Heretic*].

Wat. He was acting as a servant to Rhys Lord Thuryn in November of the year 903. [*Camber of Culdi*].

Wat Sellar. He was one of the L peasants executed at King Imre's command in retaliation for the murder of Lord Rannulf in September of the year 903. R.I.P. [*Camber of Culdi*].

Wenceslaus, Brother. He was a monk serving at Saint Iveagh's Abbey in Kheldour in November of the year 1123. [*The Bishop's Heir*].

Wencit, *i.e.*, **Wenzel II Zsubit Kyprian Nimur Furstán, King of Torenth, Titular King of Gwynedd, Duke of Vorna and Tolán, sometime Regent d'Arjenol.** He was born on the XVIIth day of January in the Year of Our Lord 1073, being the sixth child and third surviving son of Nimur II King of Torenth and Charis Rochelle Princess of Festil, and a brother to King Carolus III. From childhood he was known to his family as "Wencit," this being the name which his brother Torval called him. He intermarried with Euphrosine d'Yvreu Duchess of Térébol on the Ist day of March in the year 1098, and by her he had children: the Princess Nimura, dead at age II of the spotted pox; the Princess Eufemia, who intermarried with Mahael Count Amassy later Duke d'Arjenol and died abirthing on the XXVIth day of November in the year 1119, aged XVIII years, leaving I son, the Hereditary Prince Malachy Mátyás Mahael Nimur, who died II days after his mother of the sleeping scurvy.

Berrhones says that this Prince was "well-proportioned, well-mannered, the keenest of the sons of King Nimur II. He disagreed most frequently with his father and his brothers over matters of state, and although in many cases his was the better answer, his voice was not often heeded. When denied he could become harsh and condescending, and his manners did not well suit the sycophants of society. However, he carefully built up his own following at Court, including some of the ablest men of his time, and when his brother became King and the Prince was sent forth on various embassies to distant lands, solely for the purpose of removing him from the Palace, he was still able to know what was happening there within hours of its occurrence."

The Prince Wencit was created Duke of Vorna by his father upon attaining his majority in the year 1087. He was trained in the magical arts by the Deryni mage, Rodion Graf Budimirsky, and in turn trained Mahael II Duke d'Arjenol and his brother Teymuraz Count of Brustarkia, plus several others. He was appointed co-Regent d'Arjenol for his young cousin, Lionel II Duke d'Arjenol, on the XVIth day of May in the year 1100, together with Pépinot Count of Logréine, but relinquished this office when Lionel attained his majority on the VIIth day of August in the year 1101. Following the murder of Carolus III King of Torenth on the XIth day of February in the year 1110, which Nikolaos Lord Korbeil accuses the Prince of instigating (although Berrhones and Callan disagree), he was summoned back to the court of his nephew, the new King Aldred II. Many believe that the incident which precipitated the crisis was the beating of the Queen Charissa and her subsequent miscarriage on the XXXIst day of March following, but Doctor Marcus claims that infected with the madness of lust and power.

Several weeks later Charissa was well enough to seek her Uncle's help in removing the King, and he did so with the help of his noblemen friends on the XVth day of April. The King's body was thrown into the river, and Wencit's reign was predated to the XIth day of February. Abandoning her style as Dowager Queen of Torenth, the Princess Charissa immediately resumed her quest for her Gwyneddan Throne. Prince Wencit was girded with the sword at Iób as King Wenzel II on New Year's Day in the year 1111 by the Patriarch Gamalinos II, and, following Charissa's death in the year 1120, was again installed as Pretender of Gwynedd at Saint Constantine's Cathedral by the Patriarch Porphyrios II on the same date in the year 1121.

In return for Princess Charissa's support, the King Wencit renewed his niece's claim to Gwynedd, thereby ending the overtures that his brother had made to King Brion Haldane. According to Geoffroi Conde de Marisco, when Wencit's wife Queen Euphrosine died on the VIth day of February in the year 1115, "The King sought Princess Charissa's hand in matrimony, but she declined, saying that she had had enough of Furstáni men and their lies and little infidelities; however, she added, since she could no longer bear a child of her own flesh, she would make the King her sole heir and sign a testament to such effect, and he would have to be satisfied with that much. And so he was."

King Wencit's XI-year reign was notable for its peace and prosperity. Plans were laid for the creation of a standing military force, and an expedition was sent East into Thyrol in Kristiansland. The state bureaucracy was reformed and streamlined, new Councilors appointed, and border fortifications rebuilt and strengthened. Following the deaths of the King's only surviving child and grandchild in the year 1119, when it became evident that he was the last surviving male of the elder line of the House of Furstán, the King issued an edict on the IVth day of March in the year 1120 clarifying the succession to the throne, barring any future heirs of his own flesh, onto his nephews, the children of his sister the Princess Morag Duchess d'Arjenol, with further provisos should they die *sans postérité*.

When the Princess Charissa was killed by King Kelson on the XVth day of November in the year 1120, Wencit inherited her titles and proclaimed himself King of Gwynedd, a challenge that could not go unmet. He began assembling an army at Podébrad, and when the snows cleared from the passes, moved a force into Gwynedd the following summer, occupying Cardosa Castle. He also subverted the mind of Sean Earl Derry, binding the Gwyneddan's mind and will unto his own. He defeated and captured Jared Duke of Cassan at Rengarth on the XXVIIIth day of June in the year 1121, and executed him and his followers III days later at Llyndruth Meadows by impaling some on stakes and hanging the others.

The II monarchs finally clashed at Llyndruth on the IInd day of July instant. King Wencit was killed in a duel arcane at the age of XLVIII years through the treachery of Stefan Coram, who had assumed the visage and name of Rhydon late *soi-disant* Earl of Eastmarch and Baron Coldoire. His passing was greatly lamented in Torenth, for, according to Berrhones, "although he was not truly loved by the people, they welcomed the regimen which he brought to society, and feared for their future under a succession of minority kings dominated by Gwynedd." He was buried with his ancestors in the family crypt at Torenthály, and was succeeded by his sister Morag's son, the King Alroy Arion II, who, under the terms of King Wencit's agreement with King Kelson, was forced to acknowledge the latter monarch as overlord.

The *Chronicles* describe this Prince as "...tall, thin, almost angular, with hair of a brilliant rust-red, untouched by grey, and pale, almost colourless eyes. Wide, bushy sideburns and a sweeping mustache of the same fiery red emphasized the high cheekbones, the triangular shape of the face. When he moved, it was with an easy grace not usually associated with a man of his size and stature." ["Legacy"; *Deryni Rising*; *Deryni Checkmate*; *High Deryni*; *The Bishop's Heir*; *The King's Justice*; *The Quest for Saint Camber*; *King Kelson's Bride*].

Western or **Owenass** *River*. This lefthand branch of the Twin Rivers arises in the Kingslake Water in the Coamer Mountains; an Eastern branch, the River Medras, springs from the hills West of that place, and joins the main watercourse near Sostra Town in Torenth. From there the River flows South to the Twin Rivers Strait, forming the boundary line between Torenth and the Duchy of Corwyn. Located on its Eastern banks are the Torenthi burghs of Fathane and Sostra, and on the Western side the Gwyneddan towns of Kiltuin and Inishbofin. The Western River flows clear, cold, and fast all the way to the sea, and is a prime source of salmon and trout fishing in the region. It is impassable during flood season save for the rope ferry linking Fathane with Inishbofin on the River's opposite bank. In the elder tongue it was called Owenass.

Westmarcke— SEE: *Sasovna*.

Will *Weaver*. He was one of the L peasants executed at King Imre's command in retaliation for the murder of Lord Rannulf in September of the year 903. R.I.P. [*Camber of Culdi*].

William. He was a farrier at Grecotha in the year 905. [*Saint Camber*].

William. He was serving as Reeve of the Corwyn estates at Donneral in March of the year 1121; it was this land which was intended to become part of Bronwyn Lady de Morgan's dowry. After her death on the XXIXth day of March in the year 1121 it was placed in reserve for Alaric Morgan Duke of Corwyn's young daughter, Lady Briony. [*Deryni Checkmate*].

William, Baron du Chantal. He was born on the XXVIIIth day of April in the Year of Our Lord 1069, being the eldest surviving son and heir of Willibrord Baron du Chantal and Merryn Lady Montmorency. He intermarried with Febronia Lady Orgonne on the Xth day of June in the year 1088, and by her he had children: the Lady Argonia; the Hereditary Lord Willehad; the Lord Willeic, killed in the Mearan War; the Lord Willibald; the Lady Felixa; the Lady Baïna. He succeeded his father on the XVIIth day of October in the year 1119. This neighbour of Brice Baron of Trurill supported the pretender Caitrin Princess of Meara during the Rebellion of 1124. He was arrested, tried, attainted, and executed on the XIVth day of July in that same year, aged LV years. [*The King's Justice*].

William, Lord de Borgos. He was born posthumously on the VIth day of October in the Year of Our Lord 861, being the only son and heir of Edward Lord de Borgos and Margritt Lady Fewell. He intermarried with Yvesa Lady Porcien on the XIXth day of May in the year 880, and by her he had children: the Hereditary Lord Ysick later Lord de Borgos; the Lady Jovessa; the Lord Pasteur; the Lady Radona; the Lord Brulart. The Lord William succeeded his father at birth. He later became the proprietor of the finest racing stud farm in the Eleven Kingdoms in the year 918. As a birthday gift to King Alroy on the xxvth day of May in the year 918, Lord William promised the monarch a breeding of a coveted stallion he owned whose racing prowess was unsurpassed in the Eleven Kingdoms. He died on the xxxth day of September in the year 944, aged LXXXII years, and was succeeded by his son, Lord Ysick. R.I.P. [*The Harrowing of Gwynedd*].

William *of Desse*. This builder was serving as Royal Master of the Works in the year 921, being the person directly responsible for the restoration of the Palace at Rhemuth. He was introduced to the King by Sir Guiscard de Courcy in July of that year, and William suggested that King Javan inspect the new library complex. He was a slight, grey-haired man. [*King Javan's Year*].

Willibrord, Saint. This Gwyneddan monk was educated at the *schola* in Grecotha. He later traveled to the Forcinn Buffer States to train himself as a missionary in the East. His labours bore much fruit, for he founded in Andelon a monastery, the Abbey of Christ the King, on the IVth day of August in the year 719 to serve as the center of his operations; and thence he returned to die on the XIXth day of November in the year 738, after making XVII trips into R'Kassi and the Anvil of the Lord and converting thousands of Muslims to the faith. After his death his followers formed a religious community, the Order of the Penitents of Saint Willibrord (*Ordo Pœnitendum Sancti Willibrordi*), with the Mother House situate at the above-named establishment, to carry on his work. The Grand Master of the Order in the year 1130 is the Right Reverend Adelbert de Vaillant. The relics of this holy Saint repose in the altar of the Church of Saint Willibrord in the city of Rhanamé, and are greatly venerated by the faithful. His feastday is the VIIth day of November.

Willim, Saint. This younger brother of Saint Ercon was a child of XI years when he was murdered by Deryni ruffians on the XIIIth day of January in the year 795. He later became the patron saint of the anti-Deryni Willimite movement. His feastday is the XIIIth day of January. [*Camber of Culdi*; *Camber the Heretic*; *The Harrowing of Gwynedd*].

Willimites (Order of Saint Willim or Ordo Sancti Willimi). This human terrorist group, originally a lay Order, was devoted to the memory of the martyred Saint Willim, a young victim of Deryni ill use. The Order was sworn to punish any Deryni criminal who had escaped the reach of justice, a charge often expanded to include any Deryni they could find, whether guilty or innocent. The Willimites were popularly believed to have assassinated Lord Rannulf on the XXVIth day of September in the year 903 and Termöd II Prince of Kheldour on the IXth day of July in the year 904. King Imre then attempted to suppress the organization, capturing and executing some LXXX members of the group by the Fall of that year. The Willimites were revived during the latter half of the reign of King Cinhil I as a fundamentalist religious sect bent on forcing Deryni to renounce their evil powers and take up a life of penitence. Revan subverted the group in the year 917, using them as a base to begin his "baptisms" of Deryni to block their magical powers. Their main encampment in that year was located in the hills outside Valoret. *Contemnuntur ii, qui "nec sibi, nec alteri," ut dicitur: in quibus nullus labor, nulla industria, nulla cura est.* [*Camber of Culdi*; *Camber the Heretic*; *The Harrowing of Gwynedd*].

Willowen *of Treshire*, Dean of Grecotha Cathedral, Father. This human cleric was acting as Administrator of the Diocese of Grecotha during the vacancy in the office of Bishop that lasted between the years 900 through 905, and was immediately appointed Dean of Grecotha Cathedral by the new Bishop Alister Cullen on the XIIth day of July in the year 905. He was given the task of reorganizing the disarrayed diocesan records. By February of the year 906 he had completed the refurbishing of the episcopal residence and had re-established order in the library and its records. He was still serving Cullen in the year 917, but was retired early in the following year by the new Bishop, Edward MacInnis. [*Saint Camber*; *Camber the Heretic*].

Winifred, Sister. She was a junior nun at Saint Ostrythe's Convent in June of the year 928, and helped to tend the injuries of King Rhys Michael on the XXVIIth day of that month. She greeted Dom Queron on his arrival there on the next day, although unaware of his true identity; alas, Queron was too late to save the King's life. *Non est ad astra mollis e terris via.* [*The Bastard Prince*].

Wolfram *de Blanet*, Bishop of Grecotha. He was born on the XIth day of August in the Year of Our Lord 1053, being the fourth son of Sir Milton de Blanet and Archangela Lady Kinsaco. He was ordained priest on the Ist day of July in the year 1072, and was elected an itinerant Bishop of Gwynedd on the XIXth day of August in the year 1091. By March of the year 1121 he had become the dean and spokesman of the XII itinerant Bishops of Gwynedd. He sided with the Bishops Thomas Cardiel and Denis Arilan during the Interdict Schism. Soldiers loyal to Edmund Loris Archbishop Primate of Valoret and All Gwynedd attempted to assassinate him on the IIIrd day of June in that year. He was rewarded for his fidelity by being elected Bishop of Grecotha on the XIVth day of January in the year 1122. On the XXVIIIth day of February in the year 1125 he played the Devil's Advocate during the ecclesiastical trial of Dhugal MacArdry Earl of Transha's legitimacy before the Archbishops, and a few weeks later attended the Synod of Valoret. [*Deryni Checkmate*; *High Deryni*; *The Bishop's Heir*; *The Quest for Saint Camber*].

Woodbourne. This village is located at the far Northern end of the Rhendall Mountains in Claibourne. Its most famous citizen was Alfred Archbishop of Rhemuth.

Wulpher, Master. He was serving as steward at Tal Traeth for Cathan Hereditary Count of Culdi in the year 903. In September of that year he assisted his master at Court in Valoret. After Cathan's death on the Ist day of December following, he returned to Cor Culdi as a steward for Camber Earl of Culdi. He doubled for Father Joram MacRorie under a shape-changing spell on the next day. He brought a black horse to Geordie Lord Drummond at the beginning of the latter's quest to Stavenham in April of the year 905. [*Camber of Culdi*; *Deryni Challenge*; *Camber the Heretic*].

Yorel, Brother. He was serving as a monk of Saint Stefan's Abbey near Carbury in April of the year 905. [*Deryni Challenge*].

Yorke *de Cameron*, Lord Farnham. He was born on the IInd day of October in the Year of Our Lord 857, being the eldest son and heir of Gutor Lord Farnham and Leoline Lady MacTyre. He intermarried with Maia Lady Campbell on the XXth day of December in the year 886, and by her had one surviving child: the Lady Megan, who intermarried with Cinhil I King of Gwynedd. He succeeded his father on the IIIrd day of May in the year 881, and died on the XXIIIrd day of December in the year 891, aged XXXIV years, when he was succeeded by his younger brother, Lord Bayvel. His orphaned daughter was then made a ward of Camber Earl of Culdi. R.I.P. [*Camber of Culdi*].

Yousef ibn Zakka, Shaikh of Umm al-Zakkar. This mercenary from the Anvil of the Lord was serving as companion and bodyguard to Charissa Pretender of Gwynedd in November of the year 1120. He is described in the *Chronicles* as having "...slim brown hands, dressed in black robes, [with] black eyes beneath black silk." [*Deryni Rising*].

Ysabeau Nuala *Haldane*, Princess of Gwynedd. She was born on the XXth day of April in the Year of Our Lord 822, being the youngest child and daughter of Ifor King of Gwynedd and Nuala Lady Udaut. She was torn from her mother's arms and murdered with her family by the invading soldiers of King Festil I on the XXIst day of June in the year 822, aged II months. R.I.P. [*Camber of Culdi*].

Zachariah. The *Canticle of Zachariah* was read at the funeral service of Rhys Michael King of Gwynedd on the Vth day of July in the year 928. [*The Bastard Prince*].

Zadok. This Biblical priest was invoked during the coronation of King Alroy at Valoret on the XXVth day of May in the year 917, and at that of King Javan on the XXXIst day of July in the year 921, and also at the ceremony which transferred the Haldane potential to Prince Regent Conall on the IVth day of April in the year 1125. Ζωμεν γαρ ουχ 'ως θέλομεν, αλλ' 'ως δυνάμεθα. [*Camber the Heretic*; *King Javan's Year*; *The Quest for Saint Camber*].

Zephram *of Lorda*, Bishop of Cashien, sometime Abbot of Saint Foillan's Abbey. He was born at Lorda on the XXIVth day of February in the Year of Our Lord 860. He entered the *Ordo Verbi Dei* as a young man, and was ordained priest on the XXIInd day of July in the year 882. He was elected Abbot of Saint Foillan's Abbey Southeast of Valoret on the IIIrd day of May in the year 900, and an itinerant Bishop of Gwynedd on the VIIIth day of March in the year 915, being succeeded as Abbot by his assistant, Prior Patrick. He attended the Synod of Bishops held at Valoret in the Fall of 917, supporting the candidacy of Bishop Hubert MacInnis for the post of Archbishop of Valoret. He was elected Bishop of Cashien by the Council of Ramos on the XXVIIth day of December in the year 917. He attended the coronation of King Javan on the XXXIst day of July in the year 921.

Bishop Zephram was a firm supporter of the anti-Deryni policies of the Regents, and his own career rose with that of Hubert MacInnis Archbishop Primate of Valoret and All Gwynedd. After the fall of his mentor in July of the year 928, he was allowed to retire from his see of Cashien in the following year, ostensibly due to ill health and old age, and removed himself to a contemplative monastery in Carthmoor, where he died on a date unknown to this correspondent. *Inter arma leges silent*. [*Camber of Culdi*; *Camber the Heretic*; *King Javan's Year*].

Zimri Zsigmond Zacharias *Furstán*, Prince of Torenth, Duke of Truvorsk. He was born on the VIth day of January in the Millennium Year of Our Lord 1000, being the third son of Kyprian II King of Torenth and Grand Princess Polyxena daughter of Démétrios II Autokratór of Byzantyun. He intermarried with the Princess Chriselle Duchess of Tolán and Heiress Presumptive to the Festillic Pretensions to the Throne of Gwynedd, on the XIXth day of June in the year 1027, and by her he had children: the Princess Démétria, who died bilious at age III; the Princess Camille, who joined the Order of the Blessed Virgin under the name Mary Beatrice, and died in the year 1101; the Hereditary Duke and Prince Blaine, who was born still; the Princess Ariel, who died of the shaking disease at age V; the Princess Charis Rochelle, also called Charchelle, who intermarried with her cousin, Nimur II King of Torenth, leaving issue; the Hereditary Duke and Prince Marcus called Marek in Torenth, who intermarried with the Countess Jonelle Heiress of Gwernach and died at age XVIII of a pain in his belly, which was caused, according to popular belief, by poison supplied by the Haldanes, leaving issue, the Hereditary Prince Hogan later Duke of Tolán, Count of Gwernach, and Pretender of Gwynedd.

After his first wife's death on the XIth day of August in the year 1061, the Prince Zimri intermarried secondly with the Lady Dauphine natural daughter of Talière Duc du Joux on the Xth day of June in the year 1062, and by her he had surviving children, but without dynastic rights to the throne of Torenth: the Lord Lóránt later Duke of Truvorsk in succession to his nephew, Hogan Gwernach Pretender of Gwynedd, and a great Deryni mage; the Lady Talienne, born posthumously, who intermarried with Róry II Count Kulnán; and VI others who were born still or who died in infancy.

The Prince Zimri was created Duke of Truvorsk by his father on the XXVth day of December in the year 1015. His marriage with the Festillic Pretender cemented the ties between II of the main branches of the House of Furstán, but the Duke Zimri evinced little interest in politics. He retired to his estate on the Beldour River in central Torenth after the Duchess Chriselle's death, ostensibly to tend his bees, for he loved the taste of honey and experimented with obtaining differing flavours thereof by planting his fields with various kinds of flowers. He died on the XXIIIrd day of November in the year 1078, aged LXXVIII years, and was buried in the vault of his ancestors at Torentháły. *Barbarus hic ergo sum, quia non intelligor ulli: et rident stolidi verba Latina Getæ.* R.I.P.

Avia Pieridum peragro loca, nullius ante
Trita solo. Juvat integros accedere fontis
Atque haurire, juvatque novos decerpere flores,
Insignemque meo capiti petere inde coronam,
Unde prius nulli velarint tempora Musæ:
Primum quod magnis doceo de rebus et artis
Religionum animum nodis exsolvere pergo,
Deinde quod obscura de re tam lucida pango
Carmina, musæo contingens cuncta lepore.

De ta tige détachée
Pauvre feuille desséchée,
Où vas-tu? Je n'en sais rien.
L'orage a frappé le chêne
Qui seul était mon soutien.
De son inconstante haleine
Le zéphyr ou l'aquilon
Depuis ce jour me promène
De la forêt à la plaine,
De la montagne au vallon;
Je vais où le vent me mène
Sans me plaindre ou m'effrayer,
Je vais où va toute chose,
Où va la feuille de rose
Et la feuille de laurier.

Man is his own star, and the soul that can
Render an honest and a perfect man
Commands all light, all influence, all fate.
Nothing to him falls early, or too late.
Our acts our angels are, or good or ill,
Our fatal shadows that walk by us still.
Render me the grace, I do beg of thee
To listen, to reach, to touch, and to see.
Sanctus Camberus, ora pro nobis.

ORDO TEMPORUM

A CHRONOLOGY OF THE XI KINGDOMS

Virtus repulsæ nescia sordidæ
Intaminatis fulget honoribus;
Nec sumit aut ponit secures
Arbitrio popularis auræ

Pre Interregnum

9 B.C.
Byzantyun Autokratór Augoustos I conquers the coast of Britannia Magna (later Bremagne).

1 A.D.
December 25: Our Lord Jesus Christ is born in Galilee to the carpenter Joseph and Mary his wife.

33
Jesus Christ is crucified by the Rûman Pontius Pilatus. *Stabat mater dolorosa juxta crucem lacrymosa.*

100?
The area which will become Torenth is conquered and eventually Christianized by Byzantyun, with Greek as the official ecclesiastical language.

150?
The region which will become Gwynedd is Christianized by missionaries from Rûm, who speak the Latin tongue. Hereafter the Church of Gwynedd uses Latin as its ecclesiastical tongue.

200?
A fort called Caurus is established by Byzantyuni traders on the Twin Rivers.

249
The Byzantyuni Autokratór Basileios I, called "The Great," conquers the region later known as Mooryn and Haldane. Rhombuticum (later Rhemuth) on the River Erinys (later Eirian) becomes the capital city of Carthanus Exterior (Upper Carthane) Province.

253
The one attempt by the Byzantyun Empire to move Northwest of the River Erinys meets with disaster when Heldurnii tribes utterly destroy III legions and their auxiliaries, thereby halting any further expansion by the Empire in that direction.

258
Castrum Valloretum is erected on the South bank of the River Erinys to guard the Northern frontier of the Byzantyuni territories in Carthanus, and a town gradually forms around the walls. Valloretum becomes the capital of Provincia Quinta (the Fifth Province of the West).

260
August 8: Byzantyuni forces conquer Transflumenia (later Travlum), the region to the West of the River Erinys, with the Empire reaching its furthest extent in the West.

350?
Transflumenia is lost to barbarians from the North.

388
July 2: Furstán I Viceroy of Byzantyun declares himself Comes Beldouris, thereby founding the protostate that would eventually become the Kingdom of Torenth under his descendants.

408
The Empire of Byzantyun, which has expanded to include the states which will later become Torenth, Bremagne, Llannedd, Forcinn, and parts of Gwynedd, begins to disintegrate. The Byzantyuni armies, facing inexorable pressure from the barbarian tribes to the North, withdraw permanently from Fort Valloretum and Northern Haldane in 408, and Quinta (later Gwynedd) is abandoned. *Suspiciones, inimicitiæ, induciæ, bellum, pax rursus.*

411
June 30: Halbert surnamed the Dane establishes himself at Fort Valloretum, and proclaims himself Comes Valloreti (later called Haldane in his honour).

435
May 18: Gaius Sempronius Gracchus, Grand Consul of Rûm and Etruskia, proposes the *Pax Rûmanum* under the leadership of Rûm.

444
October 16: The final Byzantyun troops leave Rhombuticum and evacuate Southern Carthanus along the River Erinys, drawing a new line of defense at the River Lendurus (later Lendour), in Murianus (later Mooryn) Province. Lord Ambrosius proclaims himself Comes Rhombutici.

449
May 13: The Kingdom of R'Kassi is organized by Sheikh Kasim al-Khojja.

466
September 2: The last Byzantyun troops withdraw from the Province of Britannia Magna. Isik Lord Nyford conquers his neighbours and proclaims himself Count of Carthane.

468
Byzantyun completes its withdrawal from Murianus Province, save for Fort Caurus (later Coroth).

486
Byzantyun departs from Caurus, its last outpost in Murianus Province. The *Gubernator*, Maximianus, calls himself *Comes Cauri* by the year 500. Also abandoned in this year is the trading station at Ouros or Orsal (later Horthánthy).

500?
The *Airsid* is founded, being a fraternity of Deryni, many of them Healers, most of them in minor orders, with a liberal esoteric tradition. Also about this year, the Rûman trader Silvius Horatius establishes himself in the abandoned trading station at Ouros.

502
May 29: Furstán II Duke of Beldouria dies, aged XLVI years, and is succeeded by his son, Count Thüring.

506
April 14: Horatius declares himself Comes Orsalis.

508
September 14: Count Knut invades the Marches from the North, and proclaims himself Margrave.

509
January 9: Count Furstán is born to Thüring Duke of Beldouria and Cornelia Lady Arktoxidés. *Vixere fortes ante Furstanum.*

525?
A massive earthquake causes Caeriesse to sink beneath the sea. Tidal waves hit some of the coastlines of the XI Kingdoms.

537
June 5: Thüring Duke of Beldouria dies, aged LII years, and is succeeded by his eldest surviving son, Lord Furstán.

538
January 1: Furstán III Duke of Beldouria is anointed at Torenthály by Archbishop Stephanos I.

545
May 12: Furstán III Duke of Beldouria marries Judentha Lady d'Arzh.

September 27: Furstán III Duke of Beldouria declares himself King of Torenth.

546
January 1: Furstán I King of Torenth is girded with the sword at Iób by Archbishop Eudoxios I.
January 7: Archbishop Eudoxios I of Beldour is deposed by King Furstán and replaced by the King's 1st cousin, Héliadés I (formerly Ödön Count Fabinyi), under the new title of Patriarch.
June 9: Hereditary Prince Arkady is born to Furstán King of Torenth and Judentha Lady d'Arzh.

547
August 2: Count Hoël is born to Erispoé Count of Magne and Roschia Princess of Torenth. *Meminerunt omnia amantes.*

548
May 2: Prince Miklós is born to Furstán King of Torenth and Judentha Lady d'Arzh.

554
February 14: Prince Wenzel is born to Furstán King of Torenth and Judentha Lady d'Arzh.

555
June 3: Lord Cùnard invades the Claibourne coast from the sea, and proclaims himself Prince of Kheldour.
December 1: Erispoé Méen Count of Magne declares himself 1st King of Bremagne.

561
September 1: Maxime I d'Estavaye IVth Count of Coroth and great-grandson of Maximianus proclaims himself King of Mooryn.

564
January 6: Jarlath founds the *Ordo Verbi Dei*, a contemplative order.

566
October 9: An invading Byzantyun army led by Autokratór Klaudianos is defeated near Beldour and withdraws, but King Furstán is severely wounded.
October 19: Furstán King of Torenth dies of his injuries, aged LVII years, and is succeeded by his son, Prince Arkady.

567
January 1: Arkady I King of Torenth is girded with the sword at Iób by Patriarch Ióannés III.
March 22: Arkady I King of Torenth marries Mithrada Lady Báthory.
April 15: Arkady I King of Torenth is killed in a duel by his brother and heir, Prince Miklós, aged XX years.

568
January 1: Miklós I King of Torenth is girded with the sword at Iób by Patriarch Ióannés III.
January 3: Prince Kassian is born posthumously in Jándrich to Arkady I King of Torenth and Mithrada Lady Báthory.
June 11: Hoël Prince of Bremagne marries Ermessinde Comtesse du Bigerre.
July 8: Miklós I King of Torenth marries Doraï Grafina von Lorsöl.

569
April 29: Hereditary Prince Rurik is born to Miklós I King of Torenth and Doraï Grafina von Lorsöl. *C'est une fort mauvaise tête.*

573
September 19: Wenzel Prince of Torenth marries Noyanë Countess of Vechta.

574
July 1: Prince Kálmán is born to Wenzel Prince of Torenth and Noyanë Countess of Vechta.

575?
The Varnarite School is founded at Grecotha in conjunction with the Cathedral Chapter there, including a mixture of humans and Deryni. This proto-university features a curriculum of teaching both reading and writing, theology, philosophy, mathematics, and medicine. A section focusing on the healing arts is added at a later date. The *Airsid* associate both with the Chapter and with the Varnarites, offering specialized instruction in Healing and philosophy.

576
August 12: Prince Ulászló is born to Wenzel Prince of Torenth and Noyanë Countess of Vechta.

577
January 20: Erispoé Méen Roi de Bremagne dies, aged LVII years, and is succeeded by his son, Prince Hoël.

582
January 3: Prince Kassian comes of age, and is created Count Vorarl by Mstyslav Kniaz' of Jándrich.

587
July 11: Miklós I King of Torenth is killed through necromancy by his son and heir, Prince Rurik, aged XXXIX years.

588
January 1: Rurik King of Torenth is girded with the sword at Iób by Patriarch Euorkios I.
June 6: Jarlath, founder of the *Ordo Verbi Dei*, dies.
July 11: Rurik King of Torenth is found dead in bed without a mark on his body or any indication of why he has died, aged XIX years, and is succeeded by his uncle, Prince Wenzel.

589
January 1: Wenzel I King of Torenth is girded with the sword at Iób by Patriarch Euorkios I.
April 9: Wenzel I King of Torenth abdicates in favour of his eldest son, Prince Kálmán.

590
January 1: Kálmán I King of Torenth is girded with the sword at Iób by Patriarch Euorkios I.

591
February 22: Wenzel I former King of Torenth dies of the leprous scurvy, aged XXXVII years.

592
November 2: Alöf Margrave of the Marches dies, and his realm is split into IV pieces, I for each son: Ion Count of Northmarch, Thrond Count of Westmarch, Eirik I Count of Southmarch, and Einarr Count of Eastmarch.

594
October 29: Abnormally high tides inundate Saint Michael's Mount at the tip of the Mooryn Peninsula. The Brethren of Saint Michael, a precursor of the Order of that name, move to Kilchon, where a Deryni baron gives them land and patronage. *Le bon temps viendra.*

596
October 15: Ulászló Prince of Torenth marries Ielisavet Comtesse de Bosnie.

597
May 1: Prince-Bishop Fandilas declares the independence of Dhassa from Mooryn.

May 4: Kassian Count Vorarl marries Anna Lady Corvin.
July 31: Prince Kyprian is born to Ulászló Prince of Torenth and Ielisavet Comtesse de Bosnie.

598
November 25: Hoël Roi de Bremagne dies, aged LI years, and is succeeded by his son, Prince Meyric.

599
September 19: Prince Miklós is born to Ulászló Prince of Torenth and Ielisavet Comtesse de Bosnie.

600
January 9: Count Aldred is born to Kassian Count Vorarl and Anna Lady Corvin, and is created Count of Arkadia.

602
May 18: Kálmán I King of Torenth marries Izza Lady Könyves.

603
The Varnarite School is completed at the Bishop's residence in Grecotha. (The ledger stone in the *Templum* may actually read DIII, suggesting far earlier and stronger *Airsid* antecedents than generally supposed.)
June 2: Hewney Hort of Orsal marries the Princess Dorothea Heiress of West Tralia.

604
October 2: The great Deryni adept and mystic Orin is born. *Stat magni nominis umbra.*

605
August 29: Lord Aidan Kensell is born to Bearand Hereditary Count of Haldane and Gertrudis Princess of Mooryn.

609
August 8: Hereditary Prince Gábor is born to Kálmán I King of Torenth and Izza Lady Könyves.

611
July 27: Lord Augarin Alexander is born to Bearand II Count of Haldane and Gertrudis Princess of Mooryn.

612
August 28: Kálmán I King of Torenth dies in battle with Mstyslav Sovereign Kniaz' of Jándrich, aged XXXVIII years, being killed with his brother, the Prince Ulászló, and his cousin, Kassian Count Vorarl, who fights with Mstyslav. The King's nephew, the Prince Kyprian, puts away the III-year-old Hereditary Prince Gábor and assumes the throne himself.

613
January 1: Kyprian I King of Torenth is girded with the sword at Iób by Patriarch Gamalinos I.
August 18: Lord Aurel Albin is born to Bearand II Count of Haldane and Gertrudis Princess of Mooryn.

616
October 1: Kyprian I King of Torenth marries Ayya Grafina von Vorna.

619
June 16: Miklós Prince of Torenth marries Pakora Lady Hunyadi.

620
March 1: Aldred Count Vorarl marries Mariana Lady Hormizd.
May 12: Prince István is born to Miklós Prince of Torenth and Pakora Lady Hunyadi, who dies in childbirth.
December 22: Hereditary Count Almár and Lord Tamás (twins) are born to Aldred Count Vorarl and Mariana Lady Hormizd.

621
February 2: Kyprian I King of Torenth is poisoned by his wife, aged XXIII years, and is succeeded by his younger brother, Prince Miklós.
April 9: Miklós II King of Torenth marries his brother's widow, Queen Ayya.

622
January 1: Miklós II King of Torenth is girded with the sword at Iób by Patriarch Markos I.

625
June 12: The Brethren of Saint Michael, extending their burgeoning maritime activities in the Southern Sea, establish a land-based military arm at Djellarda in the Gate of the Anvil of the Lord, to guard against Moorish incursions.

626
May 24: Lord Augarin Haldane marries Rosemaryn Lady MacLean, some say contrary to the wishes of his father; the register recording the marriage is lost soon thereafter when the Church burns.

627
October 12: Lord Aidan is born to Lord Augarin Haldane and Rosemaryn Lady MacLean.

628
May 1: Lord Aurel Haldane enters the Church under the name Aurelius.
September 27: Gábor formerly Hereditary Prince of Torenth escapes from his prison and flees to Arjenol.

629
May 12: Gábor Prince of Torenth marries Ielena Lady Kreszimir.

630
February 14: Prince Károly is born to Gábor Prince of Torenth and Ielena Lady Kreszimir.

631
December 12: Bearand II Count of Haldane dies, and is succeeded by his eldest son, Hereditary Count Aidan.

632
June 8: Muhammad the Prophet dies in the Anvil of the Lord.
July 8: Lord Bearand is born to Augarin Hereditary Count of Haldane and Rosemaryn Lady MacLean, who dies giving birth.

633
June 12: Lord Aurelius Haldane is ordained priest.

634
May 2: Orin founds the *Templum Archangelorum* to train Deryni.

635
August 5: Princess Sinead is born to Lulach Sovereign Prince of Kheldour and Sigrid Lady of Normarch Ley. *Qui a des filles est toujours berger.*

637
May 11: Aidan II Count of Haldane marries Daphne Lady Buchan.

638
April 6: Lady Mooryna is born to Aidan II Count of Haldane and Daphne Lady Buchan.
October 30: Miklós II King of Torenth is poisoned by his wife, Queen Ayya, aged XXXIX years, and is succeeded by his son, Prince István.
November 1: Dowager Queen Ayya of Torenth is arrested, tried, and executed for murder by King István. *Böser Vogel, böses Ei.*

639
January 1: István King of Torenth is girded with the sword at Iób by Patriarch Patrikios I.
March 5: István King of Torenth marries Garma Lady Rákóczy.
December 5: Lord Tamás is deeded the County of Arkadia by István King of Torenth.
December 7: Hereditary Prince Brecht is born to István King of Torenth and Garma Lady Rákóczy.

640
March 11: Aidan II Count of Haldane, called "The Fat," dies of choking on a quail bone, aged XXXIV years, and is succeeded by his brother, Lord Augarin, as Regent.
July 24: Lady Ambrosine and Lord Ambrose (twins) are born posthumously to Aidan II Count of Haldane and Daphne Lady Buchan. The boy is said to have died later the same day.
July 26: The body of an infant boychild claimed to be that of Hereditary Count Ambrose Haldane is displayed at court in Valoret, and then buried with his father. The Countess Daphne protests, claiming the boy is still alive, and is sent away to a nunnery.
July 27: Lord Augarin Regent of Haldane is proclaimed Count under the title Augarin II.
November 13: Aldred Count Vorarl dies of the wilt, aged XL years, and is succeeded by his son, Hereditary Count Almár.

641
November 29: Prince Kristóf is born to István King of Torenth and Garma Lady Rákóczy.

642
March 18: Gábor Prince of Torenth invades Torenth with a raiding party from Arjenol, and dies in battle against King István, aged XXXII years, and is succeeded in his pretensions by his son, Prince Károly.
July 2: Almár Count Vorarl is accidentally killed during mock battle, aged XXI years, and is succeeded by his brother, Tamás Count of Arkadia.

643
August 19: Augarin II Count of Haldane defeats and kills Jamish Count of Lendour, occupying his territory.

644
May 12: Tamás Count Vorarl and Count of Arkadia marries Iouliana Grand Princess of Byzantyun.

645
January 27: Prince Lipóld is born to István King of Torenth and Garma Lady Rákóczy.
March 16: Father Aurelius Haldane is secretly consecrated Bishop by Sixtus Prince-Bishop of Dhassa and Honoratus Abbot-Bishop of Concaradine.
April 12: Bishop Aurelius and his colleagues from Dhassa and Concaradine declare their independence from Johannes III Patriarch of Bremagne.
April 20: Augarin II Count of Haldane defeats and kills Rubik Count of Carthane, and incorporates his territory into his own.
May 1: Augarin is proclaimed High King of Haldane by an assembly of Great Lords and clergy.
May 10: Aurelius Haldane, younger brother of the King, is elected first independent Archbishop Primate of Valoret and All Gwynedd by the assembled clergy, and is enthroned by Sixtus Prince-Bishop of Dhassa and Honoratus Abbot-Bishop of Concaradine. With the aid of these II autonomous prelates he immediately consecrates new titled Bishops for Nyford and Rhemuth, plus IV itinerant Bishops, including I who becomes his auxiliary and designated successor. *Wälzender Stein wird nicht moosig.*
May 20: King Augarin is crowned King of Haldane by his brother, Archbishop Aurelius.
June 1: Hereditary Count Aldred is born to Tamás Count Vorarl and Grand Princess Iouliana daughter of Kallistos Grand Prince of Byzantyun.
October 11: Lord Braïdik conquers the city of Arzh and proclaims the Sovereign Principality of Arjenol.

646
June 8: The cornerstone is laid for the construction of All Saints' Cathedral in Valoret. '*Οτι δύναται 'ο Θεος εκ των λίθων τούτων εγειραι τέκνα τω Αβραάμ.*
September 2: Augarin King of Haldane marries as his IInd wife Caldora Lady de la Marche, with the ceremony being conducted by the King's brother, Archbishop Aurelius.

647
January 1: King Augarin issues a proclamation changing the name of his state to Gwynedd, long the local name for the region.
November 6: Prince László is born to Tamás Prince of Torenth and Iouliana Grand Princess of Byzantyun.

649
August 19: Prince Donal is born to Augarin King of Gwynedd and Caldora Lady de la Marche.

650
September 3: All Saints' Cathedral in Valoret is completed and consecrated.

651
March 9: Prince Llarik is born to Augarin King of Gwynedd and Caldora Lady de la Marche.
June 1: Aed mac Faolan proclaims himself King of Howicce.
August 2: Mear mac Quinnell proclaims himself Sovereign Prince of Laas (later Meara).

652
July 18: István King of Torenth is killed in personal combat with Augarin King of Gwynedd, aged XXXII years, and is succeeded in a *coup d'état* at Beldour by his cousin, Prince Károly.
July 24: Brecht Hereditary Prince of Torenth, aged XII years, is murdered by King Károly.

653
January 1: Károly I King of Torenth is girded with the sword at Iób by Patriarch Stylianos I.
February 10: Kristóf Prince of Torenth dies of the ruby pox engendered by the poor conditions in the tower in which he is being held, aged XI years.

655
February 21: Jodotha is born at Carnedd.
March 9: The last Count of Rhemuth, Daunus, relinquishes his sovereignty to Augarin King of Gwynedd, and in turn is made the leading peer of the realm during his lifetime. *Sic transit gloria mundi.*
June 8: Beldour is captured by the army of Count Ulrich, and King Károly is executed, aged XXV years. Prince Lipóld is proclaimed King under the Regency of Count Ulrich, who is proclaimed Hereditary Prince of Torenth. However, Count Tamás is proclaimed King by his soldiers at Arkadia.

656
January 1: Lipóld King of Torenth is girded with the sword at Iób by Patriarch Stylianos I.

657
May 29: A great battle takes place on the plains West of the City of Beldour in Torenth between the armies of Lipóld King of Torenth and Tamás Pretender of Torenth. King Lipóld is captured, blinded, deposed, and sent into exile to Saint Christodoulos's Monastery near Beldour.

658
January 1: Tamás King of Torenth is girded with the sword at Iób by Patriarch Stylianos I.

659
July 1: Aidan Hereditary Prince of Gwynedd marries Sinead Princess of Kheldour.

661
November 11: Béraud Buyenne, a son-in-law of Rogan the Hort of Orsal, receives the Duchy of Joux as his wife's dowry.

663
August 19: Donal Prince of Gwynedd comes of age and is created Count of Desse.

665
March 9: Llarik Prince of Gwynedd comes of age and is created Count of Rhemuth.
September 15: László Prince of Torenth marries Lady Charitóna daughter of Dionysios Despot of Morias.

666
June 6: Aurelius Archbishop of Valoret and brother of King Augarin dies, aged LII years.
June 8: Aldred Hereditary Prince of Torenth marries the Princess Bertradis daughter of Augarin King of Gwynedd and Caldora Lady de la Marche.
November 9: Prince Radislaus is born to László Vak Hereditary Prince of Torenth and Charitona of Morias.

667
February 20: Lipóld former King of Torenth dies of ill treatment, aged XXII years.
November 8: Prince Imre is born to Aldred Hereditary Prince of Torenth and Bertradis Princess of Gwynedd.

673
February 28: Augarin King of Gwynedd dies, and is succeeded by his son, Prince Aidan. Prince Donal challenges the succession of his half-brother.
March 10: Prince Donal Count of Desse is found dead in the forest near Dolban, shot through the eye with an arrow, aged XXIII years. The mystery of his death is never solved, but his younger brother, Prince Llarik, blames the new King Aidan. *Le roi règne et ne gouverne pas.*
April 11: Prince Aidan is crowned King at Valoret as Aidan III by Archbishop Gisenod, the only occasion on which that style was used; he is commonly called Aidan I in the king lists of Gwynedd.

674
June 18: King Aidan transfers his capital from Valoret to Rhemuth.
June 30: Llarik Prince of Gwynedd and Count of Rhemuth marries Riona Countess of Carthane.

675
July 12: The city of Cashien is conquered by Aidan King of Gwynedd.

August 18: The great Deryni adept and mystic Orin dies, aged LXX years.
November 24: Prince Dolon Kensell is born to Llarik Prince of Gwynedd and Count of Rhemuth and Riona Countess of Carthane.

677
May 3: Lord Cadell ap Gruffud declares himself Ist Sovereign Prince of Llannedd.
June 17: Tamás King of Torenth dies, aged LVI years, and is succeeded jointly under the terms of his will by his elder sons, the Princes Aldred and László.
August 30: Aldred I King of Torenth defeats and kills Zvonimir Sovereign Herzog von Tolán at the Battle of Elderon, and Tolán is annexed to the Kingdom of Torenth. *Hochmut kommt vor dem Fall.*

678
January 1: King Aldred I and King László are jointly girded with the sword at Iób by Patriarch Meletios I.
July 11: The Free City of Grecotha is captured by Aidan King of Gwynedd.

679
August 24: Aidan King of Gwynedd conquers the town of Carbury.

680
September 8: Prince Jestyn is born to Llarik Prince of Gwynedd and Count of Rhemuth and Riona Countess of Carthane.

681
March 8: László King of Torenth dies, aged XXXIII years, and his brother, King Aldred I, becomes sole ruler.

682
May 29: The University of Grecotha is founded by Queen Sinead; Mogue Prince of Kheldour and Bishop of Grecotha, her brother, becomes the Ist Chancellor of the school. *Hoc lege, quod possit dicere vita, Meum est.*

683
June 12: Lord Rhori Mór is born to Mórolt Cùnard Prince of Kheldour and Paili Lady Tinnascart.

685
April 14: Imre Prince of Torenth marries Bethany Princess of Gwynedd.
June 3: Radilaus Prince of Torenth marries Theophanó Grand Princess of Byzantyun.

688
June 2: The autonomous Comté du Thurie is established by Comte Thuris.

693
March 3: Lord Rhori Mór of Kheldour is fostered to Aldred I King of Torenth.

697
November 16: Riona Princess of Gwynedd and Countess of Carthane dies, aged XXXIX years, and is succeeded in the latter title by her son, Prince Jestyn Haldane.

698
July 7: Aidan King of Gwynedd dies in the Battle of Ebor against Torv Earl of Eastmarch, aged LXX years; his only surviving son, the Hereditary Prince Ifor, is severely wounded in the same action, and is unable to assume the throne.
July 8: Sinead Queen of Gwynedd, upon learning her husband's fate, goes mad and throws herself from the ramparts at Grecotha, aged LXII years.

July 16: Prince Bearand Count of Haldane, the King's brother, declares himself Lord Protector of Gwynedd.
July 29: Jándrich is defeated by Aldred I King of Torenth, the Kniaz' Ulick falling on his sword in despair.
August 1: The High Council of Gwynedd meets to discuss the succession to the throne. Prince Ifor refuses to relinquish his rights.
August 2: Prince Bearand suffers an apoplectic attack at the Council meeting.
August 3: Prince Llarik, Bearand's half-brother, declares himself Lord Protector of Gwynedd.
September 2: Prince Llarik assumes the throne of Gwynedd. Prince Ifor, Prince Bearand, and Bearand's son, Prince Jashan, are dead by this date, although one report indicates that Jashan has escaped to Llannedd or Bremagne. Prince Llarik awards the County of Haldane to his younger brother, Prince Halbert.

699
May 25: Prince Festil is born to Imre I Hereditary Prince of Torenth and Bethany Lady Haldane.
August 2: Llarik King of Gwynedd marries Sidonie Princess of Meara.
October 6: The Hereditary Prince Kensell and Prince Jestyn are arrested by the order of their father, King Llarik of Gwynedd, and charged with treason.
October 16: Kensell Hereditary Prince of Gwynedd and Jestyn Count of Carthane are beheaded. According to legend the Lady Jodotha also perished on or about this date while attempting to save the II Princes. Prince Kensell is XXIII years of age at his death, and Count Jestyn is XIX years of age.

700
May 18: Hereditary Prince Ryons is born to Llarik King of Gwynedd and Sidonie Princess of Meara.

700-750
Dissention within the Grecotha Chapter of the Varnarites leads to the arch-conservative proto-Gabrilites forming their own group. The liberal *Airsid* also separate and go underground. *Hæc brevis est nostrorum summa malorum.*

701
October 22: Aldred I King of Torenth dies, aged LVI years, and is succeeded by his son, Prince Imre.

702
The *Pax Rûmanum* ceases by this date, when the barbarian hordes from the North and South begin attacking the Eleven Kingdoms. *Pax vel injusta utilior est quam justissimum bellum.*
January 1: Imre I King of Torenth is girded with the sword at Iób by Patriarch Antónios I.

705
July 12: Grecotha is sacked by Norsemen sailing down the Gulf of Kheldour.
September 16: Halbert II Count of Haldane dies, aged LII years, and is succeeded by his only son, Lord Aurelian.
October 2: Aurelian Count of Haldane is tried, attainted, and executed for treason by King Llarik.

707
May 31: Nyford is burned by Moorish raiders.

711
May 7: Lord Rhori Mór marries Rocasta Princess of Torenth.

712
March 2: Lord Siebert MacRhori is born to Lord Rhori Mór and Rocasta Princess of Torenth, and is created Count Cullanan at birth.

715
April 30: Ulrika Countess and Heiress of Northmarch marries Magnus I Count of Eastmarch, joining the II countries together.

719
January 11: Llarik King of Gwynedd falls from his window in the Palace at Rhemuth, aged LXVII years, and is succeeded by his son, Prince Ryons. *Tempus abire tibi est.*
March 26: Prince Ryons is crowned King of Gwynedd by Archbishop Marin.
June 10: Ryons King of Gwynedd marries Raphaela Princess of Torenth at Beldour. The II countries sign a formal treaty of alliance against the barbarians.
August 4: Saint Willibrord founds the Abbey of Christ the King in Andelon.

720
September 7: Hereditary Prince Bearand is born to Ryons King of Gwynedd and Raphaela Princess of Torenth.

722
December 5: Imre I King of Torenth dies, aged LV years, and is succeeded by his cousin, Prince Radislaus. Prince Aldred is arrested.
December 7: Aldred Hereditary Prince of Torenth is murdered by King Radislaus, aged XXXIV years.

723
January 1: Radislaus King of Torenth is girded with the sword at Iób by Patriarch Kosmas I. *Per Deum et ferrum obtinui.*

724
June 8: Festil Prince of Torenth marries Iphigénie Princess of Bremagne.

729
May 3: Cynan I Prince of Llannedd declares himself King of that country.
June 19: Siebert Count Cullanan marries Mhari Lady d'Arjenol.

730
June 19: Hereditary Count Maurin is born to Siebert Count Cullanan and Mhari Lady d'Arjenol.

733
May 30: Rhemuth is besieged by the Moors. *Solitudinem faciunt, pacem appellant.*
June 6: The city of Rhemuth is relieved by the army of King Ryons, brought by him from Valoret.

734
June 3: Prince Mátyás is born to Festil Prince of Torenth and Iphigénie Princess of Bremagne.

735
July 8: The County of Andelon is founded by Khoren.
August 11: Prince Bearand Haldane joins the Brothers of Saint Michael.

736
August 19: Ryons King of Gwynedd falls in battle to Moorish invaders at Nyford, aged XXXVI years, and is succeeded by his son, Prince Bearand.
September 29: Prince Bearand is crowned King of Gwynedd at Valoret by Archbishop Lantelm.

738
November 19: Saint Willibrord dies in Andelon.

December 5: Radislaus King of Torenth is killed, aged LXXII years, and is succeeded by his cousin, Prince Festil Ottó.

739
January 1: Festil Ottó King of Torenth is girded with the sword at Iób by Patriarch Theodotos I.

740
March 23: Lady Ostrythe is born to Oster Lord Ballymar and Rumona Lady ffoxx.

May 27: Bearand King of Gwynedd marries Iona Lady de Vali.

September 18: Lord Amaury is born to Siebert Count Cullanan and Mhari Lady d'Arjenol.

744
May 10: Yngvarr succeeds to the combined realms of Eastmarch and Northmarch.

745
March 24: The Order of Saint Gabriel is established at Saint Neot's Abbey by Brother Junius Pollansus. King Bearand, who as Prince had served briefly with the Brethren of Saint Michael in their maritime endeavors on the Southern Sea, recruits these warriors to assist in repelling the Moorish incursions.

748
January 2: Festil Ottó King of Torenth is killed, aged XLVIII years, and is succeeded by his son, Prince Mátyás, under the regency of Prince Wenzel.

749
January 1: Mátyás King of Torenth is girded with the sword at Iób by Patriarch Theodotos I.

July 10: Bearand King of Gwynedd defeats the Moorish armada at the Jamin Straits South of the Anvil of the Lord.

753
March 22: The Varnarite School formally splits from the Chapter over philosophical differences. The quarters located under the Bishop's residence, now small and decayed, are abandoned, although the above-ground buildings continue to be used by the Chapter as a cathedral school. *È facile far paura al toro dalla finestra.*

September 29: A Michaeline Commanderie is established at Cheltenham (later Cheltham), the gift of King Bearand.

755
May 29: Mátyás King of Torenth invades and annexes Marley from Eastmarch during a II-month campaign.

August 7: Flocon Lord d'Avoine declares himself Sovereign Prince of Logréine.

August 17: Bearand King of Gwynedd raids the Moorish port of Kharthat, destroying LIV enemy ships and burning the city; this battle forever ends the incursions of the Moors into Gwynedd. *C'est le commencement de la fin.*

September 29: The Order of Saint Michael is founded as an Order of religious knighthood in aftermath of the Moorish defeat, with strong Deryni representation within its ranks. Incorporating the Brethren of Saint Michael, its precursor, the new Order includes knights, priests, both vowed and lay brothers, and ancillary support members. The Order also retains a teaching function.

October 30: Mátyás King of Torenth marries Jessandra Princess of Bremagne.

756
August 18: The twin Princes Káspár and Kálmán are born to Mátyás King of Torenth and Jessandra Princess of Bremagne; she dies that same day of the complications of birth, aged XX years.

November 2: Káspár Hereditary Prince of Torenth dies, aged VIII months, and is succeeded by his brother, Prince Kálmán.

757
June 21: Mátyás King of Torenth marries Istvána Countess of Torenth.

758
May 12: Lady Ostrythe of Ballymar marries Janus Prince of Meara.

759
August 2: Amaury MacRhori Lord Cullanan marries Zarya Lady von Furstán-Altorf.

760
January 8: Sir Drummond Christopherson of Howicce is ennobled by King Bearand Haldane.

June 1: Lord Siebert is born to Amaury MacRhori Lord Cullanan and Zarya Lady von Furstán-Altorf.

762
June 7: Mátyás King of Torenth sends raiding parties into Eastmarch and Gwynedd.

November 16: Janus Sovereign Prince of Meara dies, aged XXV years, and is succeeded by his brother, Prince Armon, in Meara, and young his son, Prince Alphonse, in Cassan, with Dowager Princess Ostrythe as Regent.

763
January 19: Istvána Queen of Toreth dies, aged XXVII years.

764
July 7: Mátyás King of Torenth marries Léonore Comtesse de Lillebonne.

765
March 30: Lord Ballard later Earl of Culdi is born to Amaury MacRhori Lord Cullanan and Zarya Lady von Furstán-Altorf.

May 4: Prince Imre Elgar is born to Mátyás King of Torenth and Léonore Comtesse de Lillebonne.

766
August 1: Mátyás King of Torenth sends raiding parties into Eastmarch and Gwynedd.

November 21: Edmond Bishop of Grecotha is elected Archbishop Primate of Valoret and All Gwynedd.

767
June 3: Grecotha is sacked by Mátyás King of Torenth. *Justitia vacat.*

769
October 18: Siebert Count Cullanan dies, aged LVII years, and is succeeded by his son, Lord Maurin. Also on this day Siebert's grandson, Lord Angus later Earl of Culdi, is born to Amaury MacRhori Lord Cullanan and Zarya Lady von Furstán-Altorf.

770
August 6: Armon Sovereign Prince of Meara recognizes Alphonse as Sovereign Prince of Cassan.

October 12: Léonore Queen of Torenth dies, aged XXXIII years.

772
February 3: A great famine strikes Torenth; King Mátyás opens up the royal storehouses to feed his people. *Fabas indulcet fames.*

August 9: Mátyás King of Torenth marries Landizábel Lady Ora'ash.

773
February 11: Mátyás King of Torenth begins the construction of the Hanging Gardens of Furstánály Palace to please his new wife.

774
May 11: Kálmán Hereditary Prince of Torenth marries Démétria Grand Princess of Byzantyun.

775
February 17: Prince Lajos is born to Kálmán Hereditary Prince of Torenth and Démétria Grand Princess of Byzantyun.

776
November 14: Iona Queen of Gwynedd dies, aged LIV years.

777
May 5: Edmond I Archbishop Primate of Valoret and All Gwynedd dies, aged about LXXII years.
June 16: Bearand King of Gwynedd marries Aisling Lady Kincaid of Kilarden.
September 19: The Brotherhood of Saint Joric is founded by the newly elected Adon Archbishop Primate of Valoret and All Gwynedd.

778
April 9: Hereditary Prince Ifor is born to Bearand King of Gwynedd and Aisling Lady Kincaid.

779
May 4: Prince Imre Elgar is created Count of Fathane in Torenth by his father, Mátyás King of Torenth.

780
May 2: Lord Llewelyn ap Turlough is born.
June 8: Prince Festil is born to Kálmán Hereditary Prince of Torenth and Démétria Grand Princess of Byzantyun.

783
April 25: Ostrythe Princess of Cassan establishes Saint Anastasia's Convent.

786
April 30: Bellagh Lord Kilshane is created Earl by Alphonse Sovereign Prince of Cassan.

790
June 21: Lady Nuala is born to Micah Lord Udaut and Maralicia Lady MacCathail.
June 22: Angus MacRhori Lord Cullanan marries Fergie Lady Shinrone.

791
February 2: Maurin Count Cullanan dies, aged LX years, and is succeeded by his brother, Lord Amaury.

792
July 6: King Bresal I of Howicce conquers The Connait.

794
May 22: Lajos Prince of Torenth marries Amoena Grafina von Thys.
December 12: Bearand King of Gwynedd dies, aged LXXIV years, and is succeeded by his son, Prince Ifor.

795
January 13: Saint Willim is killed by Deryni ruffians.
January 20: Imre Elgar Count of Fathane dies, aged XXIX years, leaving II daughters, but in the absence of heirs male, the title escheats to the Crown.
March 8: Prince Ifor is crowned King of Gwynedd by Valatonius Archbishop Primate of Valoret. *Lupo affamato, mangia pan muffato.*

August 12: Prince Festil of Torenth is created Count of Fathane by Mátyás King of Torenth.

796
February 2: Lord Turlough ap Ladislas dies, aged about XL years, and is succeeded by his son, Lord Llewelyn.

797
May 14: Ifor King of Gwynedd makes an extended journey to the East under the name Niall Kincaid, in order to improve his learning.
August 22: The Principality of Nur Hallaj is established by Sheikh Aqaq ibn Yahya ar-Rafiq al-Hajj.

798
August 9: Lord Llewelyn ap Turlough is blinded by smallpox. While recovering, he takes up the wire-strung harp, and begins studying it under the master harpist, Breton ap Dhomhnaill.

799
April 14: Festil Count of Fathane marries Marie Duchess of Phtheus.
June 30: Ifor King of Gwynedd journeys to the East.

800
February 23: Prince Festil *Junior* is born to Festil Count of Fathane and Marie Duchess of Phtheus.
August 28: Lord Dominic is born to Richard Lord du Joux and Tayce Lady von Furstán.

801
April 1: Lord Llewelyn ap Turlough resigns his title to his younger brother, Lord Lludd ap Turlough, and sets out on the road as an itinerant musician.
April 14: Kálmán Hereditary Prince of Torenth is appointed Commander of the army.
June 2: Prince Kálmán leads an expedition into Arjenol, with his son Festil as Subcommander, in response to complaints from Torenthi settlers on the River Brust of harassment from the Prince of Arjenol.
June 12: Kálmán defeats and kills Svarnik Prince of Arjenol.
June 14: Kálmán loots and burns the city of Arzh, accompanied by mass executions of its citizens and all members of the House of Arzh that he can find; Svarnik's cousin Count Hernik escapes the slaughter.

802
October 15: Ostrythe Princess of Cassan dies, aged LXII years.

803
February 12: Count Hernik d'Arjenol proclaims himself Sovereign Prince of that country.

804
April 1: The Principality of Autun is founded by Giorgi Count of Nebroth.
September 15: King Bresal I of Howicce loses The Connait.

805
October 11: Lord Imre is born to Festil Count of Fathane and Marie Duchess of Phtheus.

806
November 8: Ifor King of Gwynedd marries Nuala Lady Udaut.

807
October 12: Hereditary Prince Jashan is born to Ifor King of Gwynedd and Nuala Lady Udaut.

808
July 11: Ifor King of Gwynedd makes a pilgrimage to the Holy Places near the Anvil of the Lord to give

thanks for the birth of his eldest son and heir. *Dominus illuminatio mea.*
October 5: Lord Ballard is born to Lord Adrian MacRorie and Jessamyn Lady de la Roché.
December 18: Mátyás King of Torenth dies, aged LXXIV years, and is succeeded by his son, Prince Kálmán.

809
January 1: Prince Kálmán is girded with the sword at Iób by Patriarch Ióannés IV.
October 9: Prince Alroy is born to Ifor King of Gwynedd and Nuala Lady Udaut.

811
November 30: Lady Ardis is born to David Lord Drummond and Anna Lady Cappell.

812
January 21: Princess Maire is born to Ifor King of Gwynedd and Nuala Lady Udaut.
August 20: Émilien II last Comte du Thurie is forced to flee across the River Thuria into Tralia by the invading forces of Léonard Duc du Joux. *Nihil eripit fortuna nisi quod et dedit.*

813
March 16: Nivelon I declares himself Grand Duc of Vézaire, which splits from the Duchy of Joux.
April 28: Lord John is born to David Lord Drummond and Anna Lady Cappell.

817
September 17: Prince Festil *Junior* of Torenth marries Chiara Marchesa de' Arabbia.

818
March 24: Prince Donal is born to Ifor King of Gwynedd and Nuala Lady Udaut.
May 13: Lord Raymond is born to Alister Lord Eskill and Cosima Lady Braga.
June 7: Prince Festil Count of Fathane is appointed Commander of the Torenthi Army and is created Margraf of Medras.
July 5: Prince Festil III is born to Prince Festil *Junior* of Torenth and Chiara Marchesa de' Arabbia; Princess Chiara dies of the effects of childbirth, aged XIX years. *Hé Dieu! Si j'eusse étudié au temps de ma jeunesse folle.*

819
July 8: Amaury Count Cullanan in Torenth dies, aged LXXVIII years, and is succeeded by his eldest son, Lord Siebert.

820
February 9: Prince Aidan is born to Ifor King of Gwynedd and Nuala Lady Udaut.
May 10: Master Festus is born to Sir Havil Legain and Artegalla Lady Moyle.
September 7: Bearand late King of Gwynedd is canonized by William I Archbishop of Valoret, and his feastday is established on this, the Cth anniversary of his birth.

821
March 8: Princess Michaela is born to Ifor King of Gwynedd and Nuala Lady Udaut.
June 6: Prince Árpád is born to Kyprian Prince of Torenth and Arabella Lady Miz'na.
July 16: The Duchy of Alver is founded by Alver Lord Firüz.
September 21: Lord Imre of Festil is ordained priest by Kyrión I Patriarch of Beldour and All Torenth.
October 12: Jashan Hereditary Prince of Gwynedd attains his majority, and is created Earl of Valoret by his father, King Ifor.

822
April 20: Princess Ysabeau Nuala is born to Ifor King of Gwynedd and Nuala Lady Udaut.

INTERREGNUM FESTILLIANUM

June 21: Prince Festil, younger son of the Deryni King of Torenth, successfully invades Gwynedd and accomplishes a sudden coup, massacring Ifor King of Gwynedd and all of his family at Rhemuth save the II-year-old Prince Aidan, who is saved by Jasper Draper. King Ifor is XLIV years of age at his death. *Expende Hannibalem; quot libras in duce summo invenies?*
July 1: Supporting forces from Torenth arrive to eliminate further resistance in Gwynedd.
July 3: Prince Festil of Torenth takes the oath as King of Gwynedd, and creates his eldest son, Prince Festil *Junior*, Earl of Lendour, and declares the rest of his family Princes and Princesses.
July 6: Several noble titles of Gwynedd are attainted, including that of Dallan Baron Marlor, who flees over the border to Cassan.
July 11: Ennemond d'Escalle Archbishop Primate of Valoret and All Gwynedd is deposed by the King, and his distant cousin, Emerick von Tolán, is nominated and elected in his place. *Mais priez Dieu que tous nous veuille absoudre.*
July 22: Prince Festil is crowned king at Valoret by Archbishop Emerick, and swears fealty to his father, King Kálmán II of Torenth. Valoret becomes the new capital of Gwynedd. Ballard MacRorie Lord Cullanan is created Earl of Culdi, Angus MacRorie Lord Cullanan is created Baron MacRorie, and Sir Philippe Cinq-Lorrons is created Earl of Tarleton by King Festil I.
August 12: Prince Imre is created Earl of Rhemuth.
September 12: Festil I King of Gwynedd conquers Kierney and gives it as an Earldom to his comrade-in-arms, Iolo Lord MacLean.
November 28: Kálmán II King of Torenth dies, aged LXVI years, and is succeeded by his eldest son, Prince Lajos.
December 6 : A number of Gwyneddan noble titles are attainted by King Festil I, including the Barony of Carthane (Lord Ursic).

823
January 1: Lajos I King of Torenth is girded with the sword at Iób by Patriarch Philoxenos I.
April 4: Festil I King of Gwynedd begins another campaign to eliminate all resistance to his regime.
May 29: Eirik III Count of Southmarch is defeated and killed by Festil I King of Gwynedd, and Eirik's territories are incorporated into the Kingdom.
June 8: Festil I King of Gwynedd erects part of Southmarch into the Earldom of Carcashale for his friend and supporter, Sir Valen Kanabos.
July 11: Father Imre Earl of Rhemuth is elected Bishop of Grecotha.
July 20: Dinan Sovereign Prince of Kheldour is defeated and killed by Festil I King of Gwynedd, aged XXXII years, but several of Dinan's minor children escape the massacre.

August 14: Termöd I Prince of Torenth is created Prince of Kheldour by Festil I King of Gwynedd, his elder brother, to whom he swears fealty.

September 29: Prince Malachy is born to Konrád Prince of Torenth and Graf von Westmarcke and Princess Richardis of Fathane.

824

August 2: Dominic Lord du Joux marries Angélique Countess of Jacance.

December 17: Ballard I Earl of Culdi dies, aged LIX years, and is succeeded by his brother, Angus Baron MacRorie.

825

June 22: Avis is born to Edward de Burgeys and Sari Hews.

December 6: Sir Martial de Fintan is created Baron by King Festil I.

December 15: Lord Thomas is born to Alver I Duc d'Alver and Rae Lady O'Dell.

826

March 12: Angus Earl of Culdi dies, aged LVI years, and is succeeded by his son, Lord Cathan.

August 17: Festil *Junior* Hereditary Prince of Gwynedd marries Brionne Hereditary Princess of Mooryn, and is created Duke of Carthmoor.

October 21: Dominic Lord du Joux is created Ist Duke of Corwyn by King Festil I.

827

August 4: Prince Kyprian, IInd son of Lajos I King of Torenth, dies of plague, aged XXX years, leaving children: Prince Árpád Imre, Prince Lajos Péter, and Princess Eufemia Avgusta.

September 29: Cathan Earl of Culdi dies of plague, aged XXXVI years, and is succeeded by his brother, Lord Joram. *Τον δε αποιχόμενον μνήμη τιματε, μη δάκρυσιν.*

828

January 2: Joram MacRorie Earl of Culdi dies of plague, aged XXXIV years, and is succeeded by his brother, Lord Adrian.

November 16: Prince Rudolf later Archbishop of Rhemuth and Duke of Carthmoor is born to Festil *Junior* Hereditary Prince of Gwynedd and Princess Brionne Heiress of Mooryn.

829

June 4: John Lord Drummond marries So-Domina Lady Dreenan.

831

April 12: Mátyás Hereditary Prince of Torenth dies fighting R'Kassi raiders, aged XXXV years, and is succeeded by his nephew, Prince Árpád Imre.

832

April 11: Lord Iain is born to Brennan Earl of Kierney and Ebora Lady of Transha.

July 17: Timur King of R'Kassi is killed in battle against Lajos I King of Torenth, and is succeeded by his cousin, Prince Tigran.

September 2: Lajos I King of Torenth takes up residence at the oasis of Kors in R'Kassi, and appoints his son Prince Konrád Prince Regent of Torenth.

833

October 2: Nanthelme last King of Mooryn dies, aged LIV years, and is succeeded by his only surviving child, Princess Brionne. *Mentre l'erba cresce, il cavallo muore di fame.*

834

May 23: Imre Earl of Rhemuth and Bishop of Grecotha is elected Archbishop Primate of Valoret and All Gwynedd.

835

September 5: Emrys later Abbot of Saint Neot's is born.

October 4: Brionne Queen of Mooryn dies, aged XXXVI years, and that Kingdom becomes part of Gwynedd.

836

June 23: Festil *Junior* Hereditary Prince of Gwynedd marries Agharat widow of Rhodri Kadell, and his son, Prince Festil III, marries Dionysia Lady Thópis.

837

January 3: Agharat Princess of Gwynedd dies, aged XXXII years.

March 12: Festil *Junior* Hereditary Prince of Gwynedd marries Jornanda Countess of Zrin.

March 17: Prince Festil Ferdinand is born to Festil III Prince of Gwynedd and Dionysia Lady Thópis.

838

March 29: Prince Festil Ferdinand dies, aged I year.

November 2: Adrian Earl of Culdi dies, aged XLIII years, and is succeeded by his son, Lord Ballard.

839

March 31: Prince Imre Lajos is born to Festil III Prince of Gwynedd and Dionysia Lady Thópis.

May 4: Ballard II Earl of Culdi marries Ardis Lady Drummond.

August 17: Raymond Lord Eskill is ordained priest. *La misa digala el cura.*

November 5: Festil I King of Gwynedd dies, aged LIX years, and is succeeded by his son, Prince Festil.

December 1: Imre Archbishop Primate of Valoret and All Gwynedd dies, aged XXXIV years.

December 12: Festil Hereditary Prince of Gwynedd is created Duke of Lendour, and Prince Rudolf is created Earl of Lendour by their father, King Festil II.

December 31: Bishop Mallenus of Beldour is elected Archbishop Primate of Valoret and All Gwynedd. *Rondinella pellegrina.*

840

March 16: Lady Elspeth is born to Ballard II Earl of Culdi and Ardis Lady Drummond.

April 1: Festil II King of Gwynedd is crowned by Mallenus Archbishop Primate of Valoret and All Gwynedd.

April 25: Prince Kálmán is ceded the County of Rhorau by his father, Termöd I Sovereign Prince of Kheldour.

May 1: Festil II King of Gwynedd travels to Beldour to acknowledge Lajos I King of Torenth as Overlord, but the latter monarch being absent in Kors, Festil gives his homage to Prince Regent Konrád.

May 9: Sir Festus Legain marries Redmonda Lady Teemore.

841

April 30: Princess Corinne is born to Festil III Hereditary Prince of Gwynedd and Dionysia Lady of Esclavonia. *Nemo quam bene vivat, sed quamdiu, curat: quum omnibus possit contingere ut bene vivat, ut diu nulli.*

July 14: Malachy Hereditary Count of Westmarcke marries Fabiana of Fallon.

842
January 15: Adrian Hereditary Count of Culdi is born to Ballard II Earl of Culdi and Ardis Lady Drummond.
May 30: Aidan Prince of Gwynedd (Daniel Draper) marries Avis de Burgeys.
July 18: Prince Imre is born to Malachy Hereditary Count of Westmarcke and Fabiana Princess of Fallon.
September 30: Lord Henry is born to James Lord Drummond and Afreca Lady MacCathal.
December 18: Prince Blaine is born to Festil III Hereditary Prince of Gwynedd and Dionysia Lady Thópis.

843
April 30: Nellwyn is born to Raoul de Menville and Rosalie Copland.
July 27: Fallon and Fianna declare their independence from the Kingdom of Bremagne, under the leadership of King Hennequin d'Albéric and Count Hervé d'Auxerre, respectively.
September 18: Lajos I King of Torenth returns to Beldour from Kors after an eleven-year absence, and resumes personal rule. *Parlez le loup, et vous verrez sa queue.*
December 28: Prince Alroy (Royston John Draper) is born to Aidan Prince of Gwynedd (Daniel Draper) and Avis de Burgeys.

844
April 5: Lord Angus is born to Ballard II MacRorie Earl of Culdi and Ardis Lady Drummond.
July 22: Thomas Lord d'Alver is ordained priest at Alverville.
November 16: Captain Morgan ap Kai is created Hereditary Knight and Laird of Morganhall in Corwyn by King Festil II.

845
March 20: Lajos I King of Torenth dies at Kors, aged LXX years, and is succeeded by his grandson, Prince Árpád.
March 26: Lord Frizell is born to Leofric Baron Lovat and Severa Lady Ludlow.

846
January 1: Árpád King of Torenth is girded with the sword at Iób by Patriarch Stephanos IV.
June 6: Sir Remig von Horthy is created Baron of Horthness by King Festil II.
August 3: Lord Camber Kyriell is born at Cor Culdi to Ballard II MacRorie Earl of Culdi and Ardis Lady Drummond.

847
March 19: Yordan de Vitry Prince of East Tralia dies, aged LXIII years, and by his last will and testament leaves his nation to the Hort of Orsal.
August 30: Roland later Auxiliary Bishop of Valoret is born.
November 17: Sir Festus Legain is created Earl by King Festil II.

848
February 22: Anscom later Archbishop of Valoret is born in Trevas.
February 29: Robert Oriss is born.
July 21: Lady Jocelyn is born to Evan Baron de la Marche and Brio Lady Gillaspie.

849
January 3: Ulliam ap Lugh is born.
April 22: A massive raid by pirates and Moors destroys the port of Nyford. *Furore.*
December 26: Lord Henricus is born to Festus Earl of Legain and Redmonda Lady Teemore.

850
By this year the Varnarite School is being run mostly by Deryni laymen. This period also includes the final days of Saint Torin of Dhassa.
April 16: Lord Llewelyn ap Turlough dies, aged about LXX years.
August 16: Festil II King of Gwynedd grants a petition by the Michaeline Order to exchange their establishment at Old Argoed for Mollingford.

851
February 26: Dionysia Princess of Gwynedd dies, aged XXXI years.
February 27: Count Termöd is born to Kálmán Count of Rhorau and Decla Lady Aghamore.
April 24: Lady Aislinn is born to Ballard II Earl of Culdi and Ardis Lady Drummond.
April 29: Festil II King of Gwynedd dies in an accident when his carriage overturns, aged LI years, and is succeeded by his son, Prince Festil III.
May 3: Hereditary Prince Imre is created Duke of Rhemuth by his father, King Festil III.
May 28: Festil III King of Gwynedd is crowned by Odilbert Archbishop Primate of Valoret and All Gwynedd.
July 18: Festil III King of Gwynedd travels to Beldour to acknowledge King Árpád as Overlord.

852
August 7: Festil III King of Gwynedd marries Hélène widow of Élias Kantakouz.

853
July 27: Festil III King of Gwynedd signs a treaty of alliance with Gérard Roi de Bremagne at Millefleurs.
September 2: Hrolf I Count of Eastmarch reconquers most of Marley from Torenth.
September 26: Lord Santare is born to Salzare Earl of Grand-Tellie and Kailyn Lady Drumkirk.
November 24: Prince Ambert is born to Audebert Prince of Cassan and Marianna Lady du Bois.

854
March 31: Princess Corinne dies, aged XII years.

855
April 9: Lord Aquineas is born to Virgil Baron de Fintan and Hebe Lady Clonmel.
November 5: Jerowen is born to Sir Jasper Reynolds and Alethea Lady Mexborough.
December 28: Turlough is born.

856
March 17: Lord Dothan is born to Anrai Lord of Erne and Cairbreanna Lady Arboe.
March 31: Adrian Hereditary Count of Culdi dies of the Black Death, aged XIV years, and is succeeded by his brother, Lord Angus.
April 3: Festil III King of Torenth meets with Lludd I King of Llannedd at Arrand to discuss their joint defense against the Moors.
July 5: Árpád King of Torenth marries Kadhloha Princess of Autun.
October 12: Darin Lord Kincaid is created Earl of Kilarden by Justin Sovereign Prince of Meara.
December 17: Cynfyn ap Dauyd is created Earl of Lendour by King Festil III.

857
October 2: Lord Yorke is born to Gutor Lord Farnham and Leoline Lady MacTyre.

858
May 1: The estate of (Old) Argoed is granted by King Festil III to Sir Philibert d'Argent.

August 9: Alister Cullen later Vicar General of the Order of Saint Michael later Bishop of Grecotha later Archbishop Primate of Valoret and All Gwynedd is born.

859
March 7: Kai Descantor is born.

April 2: Father Thomas d'Alver is elected Bishop of Grecotha. *Omnia ad Dei gloriam.*

June 8: Lord Maldred is born to Umfred Earl Kirwan and Ronat Lady Malwyn.

June 15: Prince Alroy Haldane (Royston Draper) marries Nellwyn de Menville.

July 27: Imre Lajos Hereditary Prince of Gwynedd marries Marie-Juhèle Comtesse du Charpigny.

860
February 24: Zephram later Bishop of Cashien is born at Lorda.

March 9: Blaine Prince of Gwynedd is ordained priest.

April 27: Prince Cinhil (Nicholas Draper) is born to Prince Alroy Haldane (Royston Draper) and Nellwyn de Menville, and is baptized by Father Edward. Nellwyn Draper dies in childbirth, aged XVI years. *Dominus illuminatio mea.*

October 29: Lady Nieve is born to Gavin Lord O Nuallain and Quintilla Lady Templebredon.

December 13: Brennan Earl of Kierney dies, aged LVI years, and is succeeded by his eldest son, Lord Iain.

861
April 7: Lord Torcuill is born to Tomhas Baron de la Marche and Ovidée Lady Croix-Verte.

July 18: Lord Jebediah is born to Obadiah Lord Alcara and Thamar Lady Mkheidze.

August 1: Edward Lord de Borgos dies, aged XXVII years.

August 30: Lord Sighere is born to Ewan Earl of Eastmarch and Tacita Lady Faill.

October 6: Lord William is born posthumously to Edward Lord de Borgos and Margritt Lady Fewell, succeeding his late father at birth.

October 16: Jaffray later Archbishop Primate of Valoret and All Gwynedd is born at Carbury.

December 29: Crevan Allyn later Vicar General of the Order of Saint Michael is born. *Al peso de los años lo eminente se rinde.*

862
February 1: Hereditary Lord Carloman is born to Carantock Lord Thornton and Mazota Lady Tay.

April 3: Lord Rolf is born to Jamie Baron MacPherson and Ellie Lady Godwin.

May 31: Father Raymond Eskill is elected Prince-Bishop of Dhassa, and Father Blaine Prince of Gwynedd is elected an itinerant Bishop of Gwynedd. *Rossor di sera buon tempo mena, rossor di mattina empie la marina.*

August 18: Angus Hereditary Count of Culdi dies of the Plague, aged XVIII years, and is succeeded as heir by his brother, Lord Camber.

October 29: Bishop Thomas d'Alver is elected Archbishop Primate of Valoret and All Gwynedd.

863
January 16: Konrád Graf von Westmarcke dies, aged LXI years, and is succeeded by his son, Count Malachy later King of Torenth.

May 10: Hereditary Lord Rannulf is born to Rai Lord Vaudemont and Damienne Demoiselle de L'Eclerc in Vézaire.

864
January 14: Virgil Baron de Fintan dies, aged XLII years, and is succeeded by his son, Lord Aquineas.

July 5: Henry Lord Drummond marries Amalia Lady MacNiall.

865
March 6: Hildred later Baron Nagapple is born to Aled, a horse trainer and breeder from Travlum, and his wife, Unity.

July 18: Imre Prince of Torenth marries Kónstantia Grand Princess of Byzantyun.

August 10: Lord Henry *Junior* is born to Henry Lord Drummond and Amalia Lady MacNiall.

866
January 5: Lady Lydia is born to Gordon Lord McBain and Louise Lady Reynnells.

April 1: The Emir Hafiz of Nur Hallaj is converted to Christianity.

August 22: Turstane is born.

September 17: Niallan fitz Rudolf is born in Trey.

September 23: Prince Nimur is born to Imre Prince of Torenth and Kónstantia Grand Princess of Byzantyun.

867
January 15: Carantock Lord Thornton dies, aged XXXIV years, and is succeeded by his son, Lord Carloman.

May 21: Bishop Blaine Prince of Gwynedd is elected Archbishop of Rhemuth.

868
June 3: Blaine Prince of Gwynedd and Archbishop of Rhemuth resigns, and is released from his priestly vows by Thomas d'Alver Archbishop Primate of Valoret and All Gwynedd.

July 15: Roland later Auxiliary Bishop of Valoret is ordained priest.

September 4: Blaine Prince of Gwynedd marries Pasqualetta Contessa di Barbarico di Torenti.

October 2: Lord Jowerth is born to Eoghan Lord Leslie and Poilina Lady Morchoe.

November 21: Davet is born to Sir Marius Nevan and Procla Lady Teltown.

869
January 8: Prince Festil is born to Blaine Prince of Gwynedd and Pasqualetta Contessa di Barbarico di Torenti.

February 4: Lady Maia is born to Hector Lord Campbell and Mirabel Lady O'Malley.

March 31: Lord Darius is born to Cyrus Lord Udaut and Philomena Lady Bourquin.

June 4: Iain I MacLean Earl of Kierney marries Aislinn Lady MacRorie.

July 20: Robert Oriss is ordained priest and joins the *Ordo Verbi Dei.*

870
February 14: Lady Duvessa is born to Tudur Earl of Tarleton and Paulina Lady Kilshane.

April 15: Lord Iain *Junior* is born to Iain I Earl of Kierney and Aislinn Lady MacRorie.

July 10: Termöd Hereditary Count of Rhorau marries Sheba Countess von Barstow.
September 24: Ulliam ap Lugh is ordained priest.
December 4: Leofric Baron Lovat dies, aged LXII years, and is succeeded by his son, Lord Frizell.

871
January 31: Lord Coel born to Michael Lord Howell and Gobinet of Vourney.
May 1: Árpád King of Torenth is deposed by the Council and the Church, and is succeeded by his cousin, Prince Malachy. Árpád is sent to the monastery of Sankt Pëtr in Arkadia. The County of Westmarcke is deeded to the new King's IInd son, Prince Konrád. *Quem sæpe transit casus aliquando invenit.*
May 17: Frizell Baron Lovat marries Germaine Lady Fezenze.
May 18: Camber Hereditary Count of Culdi marries Jocelyn Lady de la Marche, with Father Anscom presiding.
June 8: Ballard II Earl of Culdi dies, aged LXII years, and is succeeded by his son, Lord Camber.

872
January 1: Malachy I King of Torenth is girded with the sword at Iób by Patriarch Isidóros I.
February 3: Lord Dualta is born to Jeremias Lord Jarriot and Parca Lady Partridge.
April 4: Imre Lajos Hereditary Prince of Gwynedd is swept away and drowned in the River Slieven, aged XXXIII years, and is succeeded as Hereditary Prince by his brother, Prince Blaine.
April 10: Hereditary Prince Blaine is created Duke of Rhemuth by King Festil III.
May 13: Lord Geoffrey is born to Iain I Earl of Kierney and Aislinn Lady MacRorie.
June 6: Árpád former King of Torenth dies on his birthday, aged LI years.
August 24: Queron Kinevan is born.
October 31: Thomas d'Alver Archbishop Primate of Valoret and All Gwynedd is struck by lightning and killed, aged XLVI years. *E quindi uscimmo a riveder le stelle.*
November 16: Dominic Duke of Corwyn dies, aged LXXII years, and is succeeded by his grandson, Lord Artorius.

873
August 22: Kálmán Count of Rhorau dies, aged LI years, and is succeeded by his son, Count Termöd.
August 30: Hereditary Count and Master Cathan is born to Camber Earl of Culdi and Jocelyn Lady de la Marche.
October 19: Lord Ainslie is born to Philibert Lord Argoed and Jeronima Lady Corteskin.
November 22: Lord Étienne is born to Léopard Baron de Courcy and Duchesse Cygnette du Joux.

874
January 20: Prince Festil of Gwynedd dies, aged V years. *Après la pluie le beau temps.*
February 8: Lord Illan is born to Felician Baron Bourges and Elgiva Lady Birdsey.
June 16: Abel son of John the Goldsmith is received into the *Ordo Verbi Dei* as Brother Benedict, and is cloistered at the Priory of Saint Illtyd's.
September 8: Ailin MacGregor later Archbishop Primate of Valoret and All Gwynedd is born.
November 27: Alfred of Woodbourne later Archbishop of Rhemuth is born.
December 6: Tammaron is born out of wedlock to Sir Arthur Lennox and Etilla or Tillie, a parlour maid.

875
January 11: Lord Angus is born to Iain I Earl of Kierney and Aislinn Lady MacRorie.
January 16: Lord Gregory is born to Rhirid Earl of Ebor and Sibylla Lady Vansholt.
January 26: Lady Estellan is born to Sir Cyr Buckleigh and Engadine Lady Malreux.
February 16: Master Manfred is born to Sir Colquhoun MacInnis and Clayre Lady MacLanaghan.
March 4: Serafin is born.
March 21: Avis Draper dies, aged XLIX years.
May 5: Turlough later Bishop of Marbury is ordained priest. *Espérance en Dieu.*
May 8: Lord James is born to Henry Lord Drummond and Amalia Lady MacNiall.
May 24: Aquineas Baron de Fintan marries Lettice Lady Laughill.
July 18: Santare Hereditary Count of Grand-Tellie marries Sinéidin Lady MacCaba.
August 13: Lior is born.
October 9: Princess Ariella is born to Blaine Hereditary Prince of Gwynedd and Pasqualetta Contessa di Barbarico di Torenti.
October 26: Dermot O'Beirne later Archbishop Primate of Valoret and All Gwynedd is born to Sir Dionys O'Beirne and Lucretia Lady Sharpe.
December 1: Camber Earl of Culdi is appointed to the Royal Council of Gwynedd by King Festil III.

876
February 1: Lady Jerusha is born to Camber Earl of Culdi and Jocelyn Lady de la Marche.
April 3: Bonner I Earl of Tarleton marries Nieve Lady O Nuallain.
May 5: John Lord Drummond dies, aged LXIII years.
May 30: Sir Jerowen Reynolds marries Lepella Lady Joly.
August 12: Lady Ardis is born to Henry Lord Drummond and Amalia Lady MacNiall. *Al perro flaco, todas son pulgas.*
November 4: Master Hubert later Archbishop Primate of Valoret and All Gwynedd is born to Sir Colquhoun Manfred MacInnis *de jure* Baron Marlor and Clayre Lady MacLanaghan.

877
January 6: Lord Sholto is born to Fechin Baron MacDhugal and Babilla Lady Pinnock.
January 18: Master Murdoch is born to Sir Osmael *de jure* Baron of Carthane and Gwendola Lady Muckno.
February 11: Hereditary Lord Peter is born to Bonner I Sinclair Earl of Tarleton and Nieve Lady O Nuallain.
February 17: Lord Rhys is born to Malachy Lord Thuryn and Rosanagh Lady FitzWilliam.
March 4: Alister Cullen is ordained priest by his maternal uncle, Raymond Prince-Bishop of Dhassa.
March 5: Marcus Concannon is born.
April 14: Alban Sovereign Prince of Meara dies without heirs male, and Meara becomes a fief of Gwynedd.
August 15: Dothan Hereditary Lord of Erne marries Dulcie Lady Carrigaline.

September 12: Lord Ballard is born to Camber Earl of Culdi and Jocelyn Lady de la Marche.
November 2: Malachy I King of Torenth dies, aged LIV years, and is succeeded by his son, Prince Imre.
December 13: Tarquin Prince of Kheldour dies, aged LVII years, and is succeeded by his nephew, Termöd Count of Rhorau.

878

January 1: Imre II King of Torenth is girded with the sword at Iób by Patriarch Theodóritos I.
January 5: Lord Ranald is born to Hanald Baron Gilstrachan and Mena Lady Rouvre.
June 2: Lord Shaw is born to Farquhar Baron Farquharson and Parisia Lady Trichinas.
September 10: Lord Paulin is born to Bonner I Sinclair Earl of Tarleton and Nieve Lady O Nuallain.
September 13: Secorim is born.
September 22: Prince Alroy (Royston Draper) dies of plague, aged XXXIV years.
October 17: Festil III King of Gwynedd suffers a stroke of paralysis.
November 21: Lady Nesta is born to Dothan Lord of Erne and Dulcie Lady Carrigaline.
November 23: Lord Joram is born to Camber Earl of Culdi and Jocelyn Lady de la Marche.

879

March 11: Lord Dylan is born to Thomas Baron Coolhill and Buan Lady Laghy.
April 17: Nicholas Draper (Prince Cinhil Haldane) joins the *Ordo Verbi Dei*, and is sent to Saint Foillan's Abbey, taking the religious name, Brother Benedict.
June 12: Jaffray of Carbury is ordained priest. Lord Jebediah Alcara joins the Michaeline Order.
July 29: Kai Descantor is ordained priest.
October 4: Lord Tavis is born to Tadleigh Lord O'Neill and Theo Lady Downs.
October 22: Raymond Prince-Bishop of Dhassa signs a treaty with Festil III King of Gwynedd, under the terms of which Dhassa shall become part of Gwynedd at Raymond's death or resignation.
November 21: Master Dimitri is born.
December 9: Rickart later a Gabrielite Healer is born.

880

March 16: Kónstantia Queen of Torenth dies, aged XXXV years.
May 3: Imre II King of Torenth begins construction of an annex to and convent adjoining Saint Constantine's Cathedral in Beldour in memory of his late wife.
May 9: Torcuill Hereditary Lord de la Marche marries Zaira Lady O Maolmhudaidh.
May 13: Lady Elaine is born to Aquineas Baron de Fintan and Lettice Lady Laughill.
May 19: William Lord de Borgos marries Yvesa Lady Porcien. *Lauda la moglie e tienti donzello*.
June 1: Lady Elinor is born to Michael Lord Howell and Mary Lady MacLean.
June 5: Lord Guaire is born to Gui Lord d'Arliss and Minsmere Lady Adolphe.
June 12: Lord Sighere of Eastmarch marries Synolda Lady de Lacey.
December 11: Lord Hywel is born to Dothan Lord of Erne and Dulcie Lady Carrigaline.

881

April 14: Lord Ewan is born to Lord Sighere of Eastmarch and Synolda Lady de Lacey.
April 15: Imre II King of Torenth marries Chantal de Meulent widow of Gaspar Gorodnik.
May 3: Gutor Lord Farnham dies, aged XLVII years, and is succeeded by his son, Lord Yorke.
October 20: Crevan Allyn is ordained priest.
December 31: Prince Imre is born to Blaine Hereditary Prince of Gwynedd and Contessa Pasqualetta.

882

March 29: Ardis Dowager Countess of Culdi dies, aged LXX years.
May 4: Lady Melissa is born to Michael Lord Howell and Sheelin Lady MacKelworth.
June 10: Carloman Lord Thornton marries Foi Lady Mobeoc.
July 22: Zephram of Lorda is ordained priest.
October 6: Lady Evaine is born to Camber Earl of Culdi and Jocelyn Lady de la Marche.
October 8: Jason is born to Sir Jauncey Dunquin and Malise Lady Bantry.
December 27: Lord Hrorik is born to Lord Sighere of Eastmarch and Synolda Lady de Lacey.

883

August 5: Master Robear is born to Sir Roburn Reganson and Amaldie Lady MacInturff.
October 12: The new annex to Saint Constantine's Cathedral in Beldour is consecrated by Patriarch Theodóritos I.
November 3: Lord Vantry is born to Junius Baron Cerdagne and Walerana Lady Debry.

884

March 4: Cyrus Baron Udaut is killed in a duel, aged XLII years, and is succeeded by his son, Lord Darius.
April 21: Henry Lord Drummond *Junior* marries Lydia Lady McBain.
May 9: Rannulf Hereditary Lord Vaudemont marries Augustina Lady Lévis.

885

January 1: Lord Sylvan is born to Owen Lord O'Sullivan and Sibéal Lady Joyce.
January 2: Hereditary Lord Rhun is born to Ulys Baron of Horthness and Ranalta Lady Rinville.
March 6: Festil III King of Gwynedd dies, aged LXVI years, and is succeeded by his son, Prince Blaine.
March 16: King Blaine I deeds the Duchy of Rhemuth to his son and heir, Hereditary Prince Imre.
May 1: Blaine I King of Gwynedd is crowned by Ursul Archbishop Primate of Valoret and All Gwynedd.
May 10: Niallan Trey is ordained priest.
August 2: Blaine I King of Gwynedd travels to Beldour to pay homage to Imre II King of Torenth.
August 11: Rudolf Duke of Carthmoor and Archbishop of Rhemuth dies, aged LVI years, causing much unrest in Rhemuth and its environs.
August 20: Cathyr Baron Carroch declares himself King of Gwynedd as a direct descendant of Princess Aurora Haldane.
September 1: King Blaine I rushes back to Gwynedd to put down the rebellion of Cathyr Baron Carroch.
September 26: Cathyr Pretender of Gwynedd is captured by forces loyal to King Blaine I.
October 10: Cathyr Baron Carrach is tried, attainted, and executed with all of his family.

886

January 6: Camber MacRorie Earl of Culdi is appointed Lord Chancellor of Gwynedd by King Blaine.

February 6: Gallard is born to Sir August de Breffni and Celta Lady Fosseux.
September 30: Bayvel Lord de Cameron marries Ulicia Lady de Bonham.
November 24: Lord Sighere *Junior* is born to Lord Sighere of Eastmarch and Synolda Lady de Lacey.
November 29: Master Piedur is born to Sir Egan and Adina his wife.
December 20: Yorke Lord Farnham marries Maia Lady Campbell.

887
January 6: Lord Denzil is born to Avery Baron Carmichael and Pristeen Lady Gortnahù.
February 28: Lord Geordie is born to Henry Lord Drummond and Lydia Lady McBain.
June 14: Nimur Hereditary Prince of Torenth marries Margit Duchess of Baïan.
September 4: Declan Carmody is born.
October 3: Iain *Junior* Hereditary Count of Kierney marries Catriona Lady of Mar.

888
January 1: Festus Earl of Legain dies, aged LXVII years, and is succeeded by his eldest son, Lord Crispus. *Le cattive nuove sono le prime.*
January 12: Lady Megan is born to Yorke Lord Farnham and Maia Lady Campbell.
March 6: Lord Ballard MacRorie dies, aged X years, and Lady Jerusha MacRorie dies, aged XII years.
May 12: Lady Carrega is born to Carloman Lord Thornton and Foi Lady Mobeoc.
June 5: Davet Nevan is ordained priest.
July 3: Lord Fulbert is born to Jonah Baron de Morrisey and Frédérice Lady Bermond.
July 13: Dom Emrys is elected Abbot of Saint Neot's Abbey.

EVENTS OF "CATALYST" (FALL 888)

October 11: Cathan MacRorie Hereditary Count of Culdi, confined to his home with a cold, drives off bandits preying on the manor house of Tor Caerrorie, while Camber Earl of Culdi, his wife Jocelyn, and King Blaine I are away hunting. Rhys Lord Thuryn is injured by the ruffians, but is healed by Dom Sereld, King Blaine's surgeon. Rhys himself heals his first patient, his pet cat, thereby discovering his own new talent. *Ars varia vulpi, ast una echino maxima.*

* * * * * * *

November 11: Master Rondel is born to the soldier Radon and Robine his wife.
December 12: Rhirid Earl of Ebor dies, aged XLVI years, and is succeeded by his son, Lord Gregory.
December 21: Lord Adrian is born to Iain *Junior* Hereditary Count of Kierney and Catriona Lady of Mar.

889
February 9: Lord Trefor is born to Hannibal Baron of Morland and Ulrica Lady Biroc.
February 18: Lord Joshua is born to Averil Lord Delacroix and Tamsin Lady Firren.
May 17: Father Roland is elected an itinerant Bishop of Gwynedd.
June 27: Lady Elspeth MacRorie is elected Abbess of Saint Hilda's Convent.

July 20: Murray later a Captain in the service of the Earl of Eastmarch is born to Wilburn a soldier and Mia his wife.
September 2: Anrai Lord of Erne dies, aged LXI years, and is succeeded by his son, Lord Dothan.
September 9: Saint Dymphna's Convent is established in Grecotha.

890
July 27: Lady Mairi of Nyford is born to Cairbre Baron of Nyford and Oona Lady Chaplin.
November 2: Master Revan is born.
December 14: William II Archbishop Primate of Valoret and All Gwynedd dies, aged LI years.
December 28: Bonner I Earl of Tarleton dies, aged XXXV years, and is succeeded by his son, Lord Peter.

891
January 6: Peter Sinclair Earl of Tarleton is knighted by King Blaine I, who also confirms him in his new office. *El asno á la viheula.*
March 3: Bishop Anscom of Trevas is elected Archbishop Primate of Valoret and All Gwynedd in succession to Archbishop William II.
June 23: Étienne Baron de Courcy marries Kenza Lady Stiofan.
July 4: Hlodver Earl of Eastmarch dies, aged XL years, and is succeeded by his brother, Lord Sighere.
August 12: Tammaron Fitz-Arthur marries Nieve Dowager Countess of Tarleton.
December 5: Imre II King of Torenth dies, aged XLIX years, and is succeeded by his son, Prince Nimur.
December 12: Lord Kennet is born to Kemal Count Iorwerth and Bathsheba Lady of Claibourne.
December 23: Yorke Lord Farnham and Maia his wife die in a carriage accident, and he is succeeded by his younger brother, Lord Bayvel. Their only child, Lady Megan, is made a ward of Camber Earl of Culdi.

892
January 1: Nimur I King of Torenth is girded with the sword at Iób by Patriarch Ióannés V.
March 4: Hereditary Lord Guiscard is born to Étienne Baron de Courcy and Kenza Lady Stiofan.
May 21: Queron Kinevan is ordained a Gabrilite priest at Saint Neot's Abbey.
December 16: Lady Fiona is born to Iain *Junior* Hereditary Count of Kierney and Catriona Lady of Mar. *La verdad es hija de Dios.*

893
April 23: Tammaron Fitz-Arthur is knighted by King Blaine I, and his marriage is revealed.
May 15: Alfred of Woodbourne is ordained a priest.
May 31: Lord Angus MacLean marries Ardis Lady Drummond.
July 1: Jowerth Lord Leslie marries Siany Lady Taaffe.
October 14: Lady Sudrey is born to Kemal Count Iorwerth and Bathsheba Lady Claibourne.
October 20: Ailin MacGregor is ordained priest at All Saints' Cathedral in Valoret.
October 31: Rai Lord Vaudemont dies, aged LIV years, and is succeeded by his son, Lord Rannulf.
December 6: Master Manfred MacInnis is knighted by King Blaine I.

894
March 17: Lior is ordained priest.

April 1: Lord Charles is born to Angus Lord MacLean and Ardis Lady Drummond. He is the direct ancestor in the male line of the later McLain Earls of Kierney and Dukes of Cassan.
May 16: Lord Dafydd is born to Jonatan Lord Leslie and Rolanda Lady Healy.
November 17: Father Ulliam ap Lugh is consecrated an itinerant Bishop of Gwynedd.
December 4: Eoghan Lord Leslie dies, aged LI years, and is succeeded by his elder son, Lord Jowerth.

895
January 1: Ursin is born to Carrollan O'Carroll and Cristin Browne.
April 1: Sir Manfred MacInnis marries Estellan Lady Buckleigh.
April 28: Margit Queen of Torenth dies, aged XXV years.
August 12: Gregory Earl of Ebor marries Eloise Lady de Mauzé.
December 14: Master Fane is born to Sir Tammaron Fitz-Arthur and Nieve Lady O Nuaillain.
December 22: Iain I MacLean Earl of Kierney dies, aged LXIII years, and is succeeded by his son, Lord Iain *Junior*.

896
January 21: Master Iver is born to Sir Manfred MacInnis and Estellan Lady Buckleigh.
March 14: Master Hubert MacInnis is ordained priest by Archbishop Anscom.
May 16: Marcus Concannon is ordained priest.
May 19: Tomhas Baron de la Marche dies, aged LVIII years, and is succeeded by his son, Lord Torcuill.
July 17: Nimur I King of Torenth defeats and kills Thrasarik Sovereign Prince d'Arjenol, and replaces him with his cousin, Prince Zdanik, who is forced to swear fealty to the House of Furstán.
July 26: Sorle Dalriada is born.
November 15: The Deryni Oriel is born to Lord Osmer de Bourg and Xenia Lady Greenlee.
December 1: Lord Joram MacRorie is knighted by King Blaine I.
December 12: Jocelyn Countess of Culdi dies, aged XLVIII years.

897
March 7: Lord Paulin Sinclair and Secorim are ordained priests.
March 10: Birgit Subalter is born.
April 2: Suleiman Count of Andelon proclaims himself Sovereign Prince of that country.
April 8: Lord Joram MacRorie enters the Order of Saint Michael. *Esto peccator et pecca fortiter, sed fortius fide et gaude in Christo.*
May 26: Cathan Hereditary Count and Master of Culdi marries Elinor Lady Howell.
July 15: Ambert Prince of Cassan marries Duvessa Lady Sinclair.
August 4: Prince Aidan Haldane (Daniel Draper) becomes one of Rhys Thuryn's first patients.
December 3: Master Edward is born to Sir Manfred MacInnis and Estellan Lady Buckleigh.

898
January 11: Salzare Earl of Grand-Tellie dies, aged LXVI years, and is succeeded by his son, Lord Santare.
March 1: Peter Earl of Tarleton marries Saskia Lady O'Conor.
April 13: Lord Davin is born to Cathan Hereditary Count and Master of Culdi and Elinor Lady Howell.
May 12: Father Robert Oriss is elected Vicar General of the *Ordo Verbi Dei*, and takes up residence at Saint Jarlath's Abbey in Barwicke.
August 17: Master Murdoch is knighted.
October 31: Faelan is born.

899
January 27: Nimur I King of Torenth marries Katalin Countess of Festil-Mnata.
March 6: Sir Murdoch marries Elaine Lady de Fintan.
April 30: Geoffrey Lord MacLean marries Laura Lady Wynford.
May 3: The Princess Anne is born to Ambert Prince of Cassan and Duvessa Lady Sinclair.
May 15: Lord Joram MacRorie is ordained priest by Archbishop Anscom. *Dicta fides sequitur.*
September 6: Hereditary Count Bonner is born to Peter Sinclair Earl of Tarleton and Saskia Lady O'Conor.
September 12: Father Turlough is consecrated an itinerant Bishop of Gwynedd.
October 22: Alana Destaing is born.
December 18: Henry Lord Drummond dies, aged LVII years.
December 26: Sir Colquhoun MacInnis *de jure* Baron Marlor dies, aged LIX years, and is succeeded in his pretensions by his son, Sir Manfred.

900
January 4: Lady Agnes is born to Sir Murdoch later Earl of Carthane and Elaine Lady de Fintan.
January 6: Sir Tammaron Fitz-Arthur is created an Earl *ad personam* by King Blaine I.
February 14: Hereditary Prince Arion is born to Nimur I King of Torenth and Katalin Countess of Festil-Mnata.
February 28: Blaine I King of Gwynedd dies, and is succeeded by his only surviving son, Prince Imre. *Hæc brevis est nostrorum summa malorum.*
February 29: The *Fratres Silentii* (Brothers of Silence) are founded by Frater Felix Fortenoe.
March 23: Lord Ansel is born to Cathan Hereditary Count and Master of Culdi and Elinor Lady Howell.
March 25: Prince Imre is crowned King of Gwynedd by Anscom Archbishop Primate of Valoret and All Gwynedd, and appoints Cathan Hereditary Count and Master of Culdi, Dothan Lord of Erne, Jowerth Lord Leslie, Santare Earl of Grand-Tellie, and Coel Lord Howell to the Royal Council. Camber Earl of Culdi retires as Lord Chancellor of Gwynedd, and also resigns his seat on the Royal Council.
May 3: Father Zephram of Lorda is elected Abbot of Saint Foillan's Abbey of the *Ordo Verbi Dei*.
July 6: Ainslie Lord Argoed marries Eilidh Lady Ballingmore.
August 12: Father Davet Nevan is consecrated an itinerant Bishop of Gwynedd.
November 19: Lord Corban is born to Cellach Lord Howell and Phyllida Lady Rebais.

901
January 6: King Imre issues "The Great Tariff," taxing one-sixth of the property of all adult males in the realm, in order to finance the construction of a new capital of Gwynedd at Nyford. The King appoints the new Court of Crown Commissions to

oversee the collection of the duty, including Coel Lord Howell, Cathan Lord MacRorie, Maldred Earl Kirwan, Jowerth Lord Leslie, Torcuill Baron de la Marche, and Santare Earl Grand-Tellie.
January 18: Master Tomais is born to Sir Thiou d'Edergoll and Viridiana Lady Arles.
January 19: Hereditary Count Jesse is born to Gregory Earl of Ebor and Eloise Lady de Mauzé.
February 2: Tammaron Earl Fitz-Arthur tenders his resignation to King Imre.
February 18: Master Bertrand is born to Sir Bernard de Ville and Astoria Lady Sacheverell.
March 1: Bishop Roland is appointed Auxiliary Bishop of Valoret.
April 1: Hereditary Lord Robert is born to Ainslie Lord Argoed and Eilidh Lady Ballingmore.
April 20: Porphyrios I Patriarch of Torenth dies, aged LX years.
May 1: Arsieu Comte de Mont-Volcan declares the independence of the Principality of Jáca, with himself as first Prince.
July 11: Sergios Metropolitan of Medras is elected Patriarch of Torenth.
October 30: Father Alister Cullen is elected Vicar General of the Order of Saint Michael.
December 9: Princess Charis is born to Nimur I King of Torenth and Katalin Countess of Festil-Mnata.
December 16: Tadleigh Lord O'Neill dies, aged XLVIII years, and is succeeded by his son, Lord Tavis.

902

March 4: Master Gavin is born to Sir Godwin Lecarrow and Mathilde Lady Châlit.
March 5: Master Richard is born to Sir Murdoch later Earl of Carthane and Elaine Lady de Fintan.
March 30: Father Jaffray of Carbury and Father Kai Descantor, both Deryni, are elected itinerant Bishops of Gwynedd.
May 23: Imre King of Gwynedd travels to Beldour, where he pays homage to Nimur I King of Torenth.
June 7: Sir Jason Dunquin marries Gillian Lady Erskine. *Centum solatia curæ.*
June 12: Imre King of Gwynedd is betrothed to Lajosha Princess of Torenth.
August 3: Lord Jebediah is elected Grand Master of the Knights of the Order of Saint Michael.
August 11: Bishop Ulliam ap Lugh is elected Bishop of Nyford.
September 21: The scheduled marriage between King Imre and Lajosha Princess of Torenth is postponed when Imre delays his IInd trip to Beldour.
October 23: Master Charlan Kai is born to Sir Peregrine Kai Morgan and Charlandra Lady Dye.

903

May 13: Darius Lord Udaut marries Pema Lady MacInnis.
July 12: Father Dermot O'Beirne is elected Bishop of Cashien in succession to his uncle, Bishop Eacharn O'Beirne.
August 9: Raymond Prince-Bishop of Dhassa dies, aged LXXXV years, and Dhassa legally becomes part of the Kingdom of Gwynedd.
August 30: Rhun Baron of Horthness marries Kristin Lady MacNeill.
September 26: The widow Claret discovers the mutilated body of the Deryni Lord Rannulf on her land near Tor Caerrorie; he had been drawn and quartered by the Willimites. Lord Rannulf is aged XL years at his death, and is succeeded by his son, Lord Raimond.

EVENTS OF *CAMBER OF CULDI* (SEPTEMBER–DECEMBER 903)

September 27: Camber MacRorie Earl of Culdi and Lady Evaine his daughter attempt to translate an obscure passage from Pargan Howiccan's works. Jamie Lord Drummond visits Tor Caerrorie. In Valoret the Healer Rhys Lord Thuryn attends his elderly patient, Daniel Draper, who reveals to Rhys that he is really Prince Aidan Haldane, last child of King Ifor Haldane, and that he may still have a surviving grandson, Prince Cinhil. Prince Aidan dies of the infirmities of old age, aged LXXXIII years.
September 28: Rhys Thuryn rides to Saint Liam's Abbey East of Valoret to meet with his foster brother, Father Joram MacRorie; they discuss the secret that Rhys has uncovered, and leave that same day for Saint Jarlath's Abbey at Barwicke to examine the list of postulants there. Brother Egbert provides them with dry clothing at the monastery, and gives access to the records. They note several possible candidates for Prince Cinhil Haldane, and spend the night at the monastery.
September 29: The II men ride to Tor Caerrorie to report on their findings to Joram's father, Camber Earl of Culdi. They decide to investigate the V possible "Brothers Benedict" to see if Prince Cinhil is still alive and if he will make a suitable candidate for King of Gwynedd. Lord Jamie Drummond joins the group, and delivers a letter from Cathan Hereditary Count of Culdi stating that the King intends to initiate reprisals for the murder of Lord Rannulf. That night, at the Michaelmas Ball at court, Lord Cathan petitions the King for the lives of the L hostages, and Imre grants him I life only at his selection. Cathan picks the carpenter's apprentice, Master Revan.
September 30: Cathan joins the King on a royal hunting expedition, and notices II hostages hanging on the city walls as he leaves Valoret. The remaining hostages are executed II a day during the next XXIV days. Coel Lord Howell advises the King to increase his reprisals.
October 5: Father Niallan Trey is elected Bishop of Dhassa. *Afflavit Deus et dissapantur.*
October 20: The King and his entourage return to Valoret from their hunt. Lord Cathan leaves the same day for a retreat at Saint Liam's Abbey.
October 24: The final hostages are executed.
October 25: Cathan is depressed at receiving the news of the deaths of the hostages, and his brother Father Joram beseeches their father to come to Saint Liam's.
November 1 (All Souls' Eve): Cathan keeps vigil in the Abbey church throughout the night.
November 2 (All Souls' Day): Cathan, Camber, Joram, and Rhys return to Tor Caerrorie.
November 6 (Saint Illtyd's Day): Rhys and Joram leave for Saint Piran's Abbey to investigate the first II "Brothers Benedict."
November 14: Camber and Rhys visit Saint Foillan's Abbey, where they confirm the existence of Prince Cinhil Haldane, "Brother Benedict."

November 28: Cathan sees the King for the first time in III weeks. Joram and Rhys travel to Valoret to visit Cathan, and that evening secure evidence supporting the legitimacy of Prince Cinhil's descent.

November 29: Joram and Rhys return to Tor Caerrorie, and are followed there by Coel Lord Howell's spies, Bors and Fulk.

November 30: Howell's spies report back to him with accounts of Joram and Rhys's movements. Maldred Earl Kirwan is assassinated by an agent of Coel Howell in a plot to discredit Cathan MacRorie. Maldred is XLIV years of age at his death; he is succeeded by his brother, Lord Uileos.

December 1 (Beginning of Advent; White Winter Court): Lord Howell tells the King that Earl Maldred was killed by Cathan. Imre believes Howell and murders Lord Cathan before the opening of Yuletide Court. Cathan MacRorie is XXX years of age at his death, and is succeeded as Hereditary Count of Culdi by his eldest son, Lord Davin.

December 2: Cathan's body is returned to Caerrorie with a royal escort, and is buried that evening in the family crypt. Joram and Rhys ride for Saint Foillan's. Crinan and Wulpher are placed under shape-changing spells by Camber so that the King's soldiers will not be suspicious of the pair's absence. Camber takes Evaine via transfer portal to the Michaeline Commanderie at Cheltham, and makes plans with Vicar General Alister Cullen to evacuate Camber's family and the Michaeline priests.

December 4: Camber speaks with Guaire Lord d'Arliss and determines he is a friend. Coel Howell shows the King the documents he has found relating to the Draper family. King Imre orders the arrest of Camber and his family. Guaire warns and defends the family, and they escape, with Guaire being injured in the process. Rhys and Joram kidnap Brother Benedict (Prince Cinhil) from his monastery.

December 5: Cinhil is told why they have brought him out of his cloister, and asks to be returned to the Abbey. They reach Dhassa that evening, and use the transfer portal there to reach the Michaeline Haven in the nearby mountains. Cinhil is reported missing at the Abbey.

December 6: A mass is sung for Brother Benedict at Saint Foillan's. Brother Leviticus discovers II robes missing from the wardrobe. Abbot Zephram of Lorda questions his monks regarding the earlier visit by Rhys and Camber, and writes a letter to his superiors.

December 11: Zephram's letter reaches the eyes of Archbishop Anscom, who reports to the King.

December 14: Earl Santare and Coel Howell receive Anscom's letter, and continue their investigation. They report to the King, who notes that the Michaelines have disappeared throughout the Kingdom. Imre orders the suppression of the Michaeline Order and the destruction of its Commanderie at Cheltham; he also bans Camber and his supporters.

December 15: Earl Santare destroys the Michaeline establishment at Cheltham.

December 17: Camber discusses marriage candidates for Cinhil with Alister Cullen, and suggests his young ward, Megan Lady de Cameron, as a possibility. Camber discovers that Cinhil possesses some Deryni characteristics, even though he does not belong to that race, and discusses with Rhys the possibility that Cinhil's powers may be enhanced.

December 19: Imre's men capture Father Humphrey of Gallareaux, a Deryni Michaeline priest, at Saint Neot's Abbey.

December 22: Humphrey is interrogated by King Imre at Valoret; the monarch tampers with the priest's mind.

December 24: Prince Cinhil Haldane agrees to accept the burden of office. He is given a dispensation from his vows and marries Megan Lady de Cameron, the ward of Camber Earl of Culdi, at the Michaeline Haven, with Anscom Archbishop of Valoret presiding.

904

January 6: Evaine Lady MacRorie marries the Healer Rhys Lord Thuryn.

January 9: Lady Richeldis is born to Lord Geoffrey MacLean and Laura Lady Wynford.

January 26: Master Cashel is born to Sir Murdoch later Earl of Carthane and Elaine Lady de Fintan.

March 1: Lajosha Princess of Torenth and betrothed of Imre King of Gwynedd dies, aged XIX years, and the King begins a month of mourning.

March 12: Lord Angus MacLean dies, aged XXIX years.

March 17: Evaine gives Prince Cinhil a *shiral* crystal found near Kierney; he makes the crystal glow. Princess Megan is pregnant with her Ist child.

April 8: Artorius Duke of Corwyn dies, aged LIII years, and is succeeded by his son, Lord Taysan.

May 1 (Rudemas): Prince Cinhil is brought to his Haldane potential by Camber and his family.

May 28: Lady Juliana is born to Rhun Baron of Horthness and Kristin Lady MacNeill.

July 9: Termöd II Prince of Kheldour and Count of Rhorau is murdered by Willimite terrorists, aged LIII years, and is succeeded by his son, the Prince and Count Tomlin.

August 16: Prince Miklós is born to Nimur I King of Torenth and Katalin Countess of Festil-Mnata.

October 18: Hereditary Prince Aidan is born to Prince Cinhil Haldane and Megan Lady de Cameron.

November 6: Hereditary Prince Aidan is murdered at his baptism with poisoned salt administered by Father Humphrey, and Humphrey is killed by the magic of Prince Cinhil. Evaine and Rhys Thuryn serve as godparents to the child.

November 8: Prince Aidan is buried in the chapel at the Michaeline Haven.

November 9: Father Humphrey is buried in the chapel at the Haven.

December 1 (Advent): King Imre opens his Yule Court. Camber and his revolutionaries use the portals in Valoret Castle to transfer Michaeline knights into the city. One of the contingents is led by James Lord Drummond, and another by Lord Jebediah.

December 2: The Restoration. Imre goes to bed well after midnight. Two hours later Cinhil controls the castle with his forces. King Imre challenges Prince Cinhil to a duel arcane, but is defeated. The King dies by his own hand, aged XXII years, and Prince Cinhil is proclaimed the new monarch. Princess Ariella, pregnant with her brother's child, escapes through a secret passage. Later that day Coel Lord Howell and

Santare Earl Grand-Tellie are arrested for their crimes against the state. *Silent enim leges inter armes.*

* * * * * * *

POST INTERREGNUM

December 25: Cinhil I is officially crowned King of Gwynedd at Valoret by Anscom Archbishop Primate of Valoret and All Gwynedd.

905

January 3: Father Alfred of Woodbourne is appointed official Confessor to the King and Court.
January 6: Hildred Nagapple is knighted by King Cinhil I, along with other supporters of the new regime. Jowerth Lord Leslie is reaffirmed to the Royal Council.
January 10: Coel Lord Howell and Santare Earl of Grand-Tellie are tried, convicted, attainted, and executed for treason. Coel Howell is aged XXXIII years at his death, and Santare is aged LI years. Dothan Lord of Erne is arrested and held for trial.
January 16: A new Commanderie of the Order of Saint Michael is established at New Argoed in the Southern Lendour Mountains.
January 31: Prince Marek is born posthumously in Torenth to Imre King of Gwynedd and his sister, Ariella Princess of Gwynedd.
February 12: Henry Lord Drummond *Junior* dies, aged XXXIX years.
March 30: Sergios II Patriarch of Torenth dies, aged LXXIV years.

EVENTS OF *DERYNI CHALLENGE* (APRIL 905)

April 2: Geordie Lord Drummond, a kinsman of Camber Earl of Culdi, is sent on a mission to Kheldour to investigate the dealings of a rebel priest who calls himself the Gryphon of God.
April 30: Geordie successfully slays the Gryphon and returns to Culdi.

* * * * * * *

May 2: The Gabrilite novice Ulric goes berserk at Saint Neot's Abbey and kills the master Dom Calvagh; he himself is killed with an arrow shot through his heart by Dom Emrys.

EVENTS OF "THE *EXAMEN*" (MAY 905)

May 3: Dom Emrys uses the body of Ulric to demonstrate to the novices how to heal war wounds, and also dissects the body of Dom Calvagh, as is customary with the deceased brethren of Saint Neot's. Dom Juris and Dom Turstane assist Dom Emrys.

* * * * * * *

May 25: The twin Princes Alroy and Javan are born prematurely to Cinhil I King of Gwynedd and Megan Lady de Cameron; Hereditary Prince Alroy is sickly and frail, while Prince Javan is healthy but crippled by a deformed foot. Both survive.
June 9: The city of Cardosa in the Rheljan Mountains is occupied by the Pretender Ariella.
June 11: Father Robert Oriss, Vicar General of the *Ordo Verbi Dei*, is elected Archbishop of Rhemuth; Father Alister Cullen, Vicar General of the Order of Saint Michael, is elected Bishop of Grecotha.
June 12: Adrian Master of Kierney marries Mairi Lady of Nyford.

EVENTS OF *SAINT CAMBER* (JUNE 905-JANUARY 907)

June 19: Rain begins falling on Valoret through the magic of the Pretender Ariella I. The bad weather continues for VI straight days.
June 22: Cinhil, Camber, Jebediah, Rhys, Alister, and Guaire meet to discuss the forthcoming invasion of Gwynedd by the Pretender Ariella. Lord Hywel and Lady Nesta of Erne attempt to assassinate King Cinhil I, and injure Camber, who is healed by Rhys. The II would-be assassins are killed during the attack. Camber uses techniques described in the *Protocols of Orin* to scry how Ariella is deploying her forces.
June 23: Ariella brings DCCC of her soldiers through the Cardosa Defile. A War Council is convened by King Cinhil I in the Great Hall of Valoret Castle, and the Great Lords make their plans. Also present are Sighere Sovereign Earl of Eastmarch and his son and heir, Lord Ewan, and James Lord Drummond. The Gwyneddan army departs from Valoret that evening for Iomaire.
June 24: On a forced march the Gwyneddans reach Iomaire. The rain finally stops. Ariella's II armies merge and encamp at the other end of the Iomaire Ridge. Sighere's Eastmarch levies arrive late in the day to bolster Cinhil's army.
June 25: Ariella's army is engaged at Iomaire by King Cinhil I's forces. Father Alister Cullen dies while killing Princess Ariella, but his form and identity are assumed magically by Camber, who officially "dies" on this date. Camber is succeeded as Earl by his grandson, Davin MacRorie. Princess Ariella is XXIX years of age at her death, and is succeeded by her infant son, Hereditary Prince Marek. Father Alister Cullen is XLVI years of age at his death.
June 26: The victorious Gwyneddan army scours the Coldoire hills for fleeing elements of the Torenthi forces. Ariella's body is divided and parts are sent to various cities in the realm for display; her head is returned to Valoret.
June 27: Earl Sighere returns to Eastmarch, and King Cinhil I and his army return to Valoret. "Camber"'s body is carried in full state.
July 1: Camber's bier reaches Valoret with the Gwyneddan army, where they are received by Archbishop Anscom and others. Plans are made for his funeral and for the consecration of "Alister Cullen."
July 2: Camber uses the Yellow Protocol of Orin to integrate Alister Cullen's memories into his own with the assistance of Evaine (disguised as the Michaeline monk, "Brother John"), Joram, and Rhys. King Cinhil I accidentally interrupts the process and sees an image of Camber superimposed over that of Cullen, and interprets this as a miraculous intervention. Lord Dualta is also present, and sees what he believes is Camber's ghost.
July 3: Archbishop Anscom conducts a requiem mass with Joram and "Cullen" for Camber Earl of Culdi at All Saints' Cathedral in Valoret. Later that afternoon Cullen/Camber gathers the Michaelines together in a Grand Chapter Meeting to discuss the status of the

Order, and to begin the process of choosing a new Vicar General. Guaire sees the "ghost" of Camber.

July 4: "Camber"'s body is returned to Tor Caerrorie for burial. Cullen/Camber interviews candidates for the vacant post of Vicar General of the Michaelines.

July 5: Cullen/Camber continues his interviews.

July 6: Cullen/Camber picks Father Crevan Allyn as his successor as Vicar General of the Michaelines.

July 7: Eighteen heirs are confirmed by King Cinhil I, among them Camber's grandson, Davin MacRorie, as the new Earl of Culdi. Tammaron is created hereditary Earl Fitz-Arthur, Sir Manfred MacInnis is restored to his family's title of Baron Marlor, and Sir Torcuill is confirmed as Baron de la Marche. The King also creates a number of new peerages, among them: Aquineas Baron de Fintan as Earl de Fintan, and Hildred as Baron Nagapple.

July 8: Crevan Allyn is formally installed as Vicar General of the Order of Saint Michael. Cullen/Camber rides with King Cinhil I.

July 9: Camber admits his deception to Archbishop Anscom, who ordains him priest in the early hours of the morning at the Michaeline Haven in the presence of the former Earl's children. Later that day, in the guise of Father Alister Cullen, Camber is publicly consecrated Bishop of Grecotha at the Cathedral in Valoret at the same time that Vicar General Robert Oriss is consecrated as Archbishop of Rhemuth, the ceremony being witnessed by many prelates and dignitaries, including Theopompus, Vicar General of the Brotherhood of Saint Joric. King Cinhil I presents both Cullen and Oriss with special sets of vestments.

July 10: Cullen/Camber leaves Valoret to take up his new position at Grecotha.

July 12: Cullen/Camber arrives at Grecotha, and begins reorganizing his diocese; he appoints the acting administrator, Willowen of Treshire, Dean of Grecotha Cathedral.

July 15: Dothan Lord of Erne is tried, condemned, and executed, aged XLIX years.

August 22: Antiochos Metropolitan of Csorna is elected Patriarch of Torenth.

September 2: The body of Alister Cullen, clothed with the semblance of Camber Earl of Culdi, is moved to the Michaeline Haven for reburial next to Prince Aidan. *Θέλω, θέλω μανῆναι.*

September 18: Tomlin Prince of Kheldour and Count of Rhorau is captured and executed by Sighere Earl of Eastmarch, aged XXXIV years, and is succeeded as Count of Rhorau by his cousin, Lord Kennet *de jure* Prince of Kheldour.

October 19: Hildred Baron Nagapple marries Máda Lady de Léis.

October 28: Cullen/Camber speaks with Guaire and Queron.

October 31: Alister Cullen is summoned by King Cinhil I to attend him at early Winter Court, staying through Twelfth Night; he is also appointed to the Royal Council. Cullen/Camber shows Joram the ancient transfer portal he has discovered at Grecotha.

November 2: Cullen/Camber leaves Grecotha for Valoret. *Non omnia possumus omnes.*

November 4: Cullen/Camber arrives at Valoret.

November 6 (Saint Illtyd's Day): Cinhil opens his Winter Court and names Alister Cullen Chancellor of Gwynedd. Lord Jebediah is named Earl Marshal and Commander of the Royal Armies, with the life rank of Earl of Alcara. Also appointed to the new Royal Council are: Anscom Archbishop Primate of Valoret and All Gwynedd, Aquineas Earl de Fintan, Tammaron Earl Fitz-Arthur, Hildred Baron Nagapple, Torcuill Baron de la Marche, Robert Oriss Archbishop of Rhemuth, and Darius Lord Udaut as Lord Constable. Each member of the Council is given specific tasks, and asked to report back at the end of November. Torcuill and Udaut are sent to Eastmarch to seek an alliance with Earl Sighere. Hildred and Lord Dualta Jarriot are sent to survey the horse stud farms throughout Gwynedd. Sir Murdoch is restored to his Barony of Carthane.

November 30: The Royal Council reconvenes at Valoret. Lady Giesele is born to Geoffrey Lord MacLean and Laura Lady Wynford.

906

February 2: Cullen/Camber and Cinhil go stag hunting with Murdoch Baron of Carthane. Guaire petitions Cullen to found a new Order devoted to veneration of Camber and leaves the Bishop's service.

February 5: Cullen/Camber returns to Grecotha for I month. *Lumen in Cœlo.*

March 14: Cullen/Camber returns to Valoret. Ewan Hereditary Count of Eastmarch marries Mary Lady Graham.

March 15: Sighere Earl of Eastmarch and Warlord of Kheldour appears at Valoret with a modest escort to parley with the King. The Earl proposes to become a vassal of Gwynedd, and the II Lords exchange mutual oaths. *Frons prima decipit multos.*

March 20: Lord Camber Allin (Camlin) is born to Adrian MacLean Hereditary Count of Kierney and Mairi Lady of Nyford.

April 2: Dom Queron Kinevan resigns from the Gabrilite Order to join with Guaire.

June 4: Guaire Lord d'Arliss and Dom Queron Kinevan buy the ruined manor of Dolban to use as the Mother House of the newly established Order, The Servants of Saint Camber.

July 2: King Cinhil I goes North with Earl Jebediah in a joint campaign with Earl Sighere to pacify Kheldour and conquer Rhendall. Earl Tammaron is sent with Aquineas Earl Fintan to patrol the Eastmarch border with Torenth.

July 8: Prince Torval is born to Nimur I King of Torenth and Katalin Countess of Festil-Mnata.

July 10: Katalin Queen of Torenth dies of the effects of childbirth, aged XXVII years.

July 17: Elinor Lady Howell widow of Cathan MacRorie Hereditary Count of Culdi marries James "Jamie" Lord Drummond.

August 15: Kennet Count of Rhorau and titular Prince of Kheldour and Countess Sudrey his sister are captured by Sighere Earl of Eastmarch when the last Festillic stronghold in the North falls, and are placed into the wardenship of Sighere Sovereign Earl of Eastmarch and his son, Ewan Hereditary Count of Eastmarch.

August 16: Joram and Rhys pay a quick visit to Tor Caerrorie to check on Camber's tomb.

August 26: Eastmarch and Kheldour legally become part of Gwynedd on this day. Sighere Earl of Eastmarch is created Duke of Claibourne by King Cinhil I, his eldest son and heir Ewan Earl of Rhendall, and his youngest son Sighere *Junior* Earl of Marley; Sighere *Senior* cedes his original title of Eastmarch to his IInd son, Lord Hrorik. Kennet Count of Rhorau and titular Prince of Kheldour is attainted, and those titles are merged with the Crown.

September 1: Anscom Archbishop Primate of Valoret and All Gwynedd dies, aged LVIII years.

September 3: Archbishop Anscom is buried in the vault beneath the Cathedral floor, with Cullen performing the rites.

September 7: Jaffray of Carbury is elected Archbishop Primate of Valoret and All Gwynedd, and is officially enthroned.

September 17: King Cinhil I returns to Valoret.

September 29: Prince Rhys Michael is born to Cinhil I King of Gwynedd and Megan Lady de Cameron, and is named for Rhys Thuryn, the Queen's physician.

October 23: Archbishop Jaffray summons his first consistory, and receives a petition from Guaire Lord d'Arliss to recognize a new order, The Servants of Saint Camber, and to canonize Camber Earl of Culdi.

October 24: Dom Queron testifies that Camber's tomb is now empty, but Charles the Baker states that he originally saw Camber buried properly in his tomb. Lord Dualta testifies to the miraculous appearance of Camber the year before. King Cinhil I reluctantly testifies that he saw Camber's face superimposed over that of Alister Cullen after the former's "death," and that Cullen then recovered from his illness.

November 14: The canonization of Saint Camber is proclaimed throughout Gwynedd, and this date, the anniversary of Camber's discovery of Prince Cinhil Haldane III years before, is made his official feastday.

December 8: Lady Lirin is born to Darius Lord Udaut and Pema Lady MacInnis.

907

January 2: Cullen/Camber visits his new shrine at Valoret in the middle of the night, and speaks with King Cinhil I, who is also present.

* * * * * * *

January 6: Lord Aidan Camber is born to Rhys Lord Thuryn and Evaine Lady MacRorie.

January 30: Hereditary Count Graham is born to Ewan Earl of Rhendall and Mary Lady Graham.

July 18: Lord Fulk is born to Tammaron Earl Fitz-Arthur and Nieve Lady O Nuaillain.

August 1: Prince Alister is born to Cinhil I King of Gwynedd and Megan Lady de Cameron.

August 8: Queen Megan dies of the effects of childbirth, aged XIX years.

September 15: Sighere *Junior* Earl of Marley marries Corissa Lady de Bruyn.

November 13: Prince Alister dies, aged III months, and is buried in the family crypt at Rhemuth.

December 1: Murdoch Baron of Carthane is created Earl of Carthane by King Cinhil I.

908

February 29: Lady Michaela is born to James Lord Drummond and Elinor Lady Howell.

May 15: Hrorik II future Earl of Eastmarch marries Sudrey Lady of Rhorau.

August 30: Lydia Lady Drummond dies, aged XLII years.

October 3: Hereditary Lord Sean Sighere Coris is born to Sighere Earl of Marley and Corissa Lady de Bruyn.

909

March 12: Audebert Sovereign Prince of Cassan dies, aged LXXIX years, and is succeeded by his son, Prince Ambert.

March 30: Lady Stacia is born to Hrorik II future Earl of Eastmarch and Sudrey Lady of Rhorau.

April 15: The Camberian Council is founded by Cullen/Camber, Joram, Evaine, Rhys Thuryn, and Jebediah.

September 2: Declan Carmody marries Honoria Lettermore.

September 17: Lord Quiric is born to Tammaron Earl Fitz-Arthur and Nieve Lady O Nuallain.

October 13: Father Hubert MacInnis is elected an itinerant Bishop.

910

March 23: Lord Cathan is born to James Lord Drummond and Elinor Lady Howell.

August 2: Aquineas Earl de Fintan dies, aged LV years, and is succeeded by his son, Lord Ovid.

November 18: Lady Rhysel is born to Rhys Lord Thuryn and Evaine Lady MacRorie.

December 1: Bishop Kai Descantor is appointed to the Royal Council, succeeding Aquineas Earl de Fintan.

December 21: The Camberian Council adds the following new members: Archbishop Jaffray, Gregory Earl of Ebor, and Dom Turstane. Dom Emrys declines a position on the Council on account of age.

911

February 19: Lady Seanna is born to Gregory Earl of Ebor and Eloise de Mauzé.

March 22: Ulys Baron of Horthness dies, aged LV years, and is succeeded by his son, Lord Rhun. *Al raton que no tiene más que un agujero, presto le cogen.*

April 2: Lord Kennet of Rhorau is knighted by Ewan Earl of Rhendall.

August 21: Brother Benedict previously Henricus Lord Legain dies, aged LXI years.

November 21: Geoffrey Lord MacLean dies in a hunting accident, aged XXXIX years. Geoffrey's II surviving daughters, the Ladies Richeldis and Giesele, are made wards of their cousin, James Lord Drummond.

912

February 15: Nimur I King of Torenth marries Mária Kosinsky.

April 13: Davin Earl of Culdi attains his majority.

April 30: Father Paulin Sinclair founds the anti-Deryni teaching Order, the Little Brothers of Saint Ercon, at Ramos.

913

November 18: Lady Adelicia is born to Rhun Baron of Horthness and Kristin Lady MacNeill, who dies in childbirth, aged XXIX years.

EVENTS OF "HEALER'S SONG" (AUGUST 914)

914

August 1 (Lammas Night): Tieg Joram Lord Thuryn, a future Healer, is born to Healer Rhys Lord Thuryn and Evaine Lady MacRorie. Tieg is baptized in a magical ceremony conducted by his grandfather,

Camber former Earl of Culdi, with the assistance of his parents and his uncle, Father Joram MacRorie. *Der edle Mensch ist nur ein Bild von Gott.*

* * * * * * *

915

March 8: Abbot Zephram of Lorda is elected an itinerant Bishop of Gwynedd.

April 15: Brother Patrick is elected Abbot of Saint Foillan's Abbey, succeeding Zephram of Lorda.

August 8: Jowerth Lord Leslie dies, aged XLVI years, and is succeeded by his son, Lord Jambert.

December 2: Gregory Earl of Ebor is appointed Warden of the Western Marches by King Cinhil I.

916

January 5: Roland Auxiliary Bishop of Valoret dies, aged LXVIII years.

March 9: Father Ailin MacGregor is elected an itinerant Bishop of Gwynedd.

May 21: Dom Turstane is killed in a fall, aged XLIX years.

June 2: Oriel Lord de Bourg marries Alana Destaing.

June 12: Ursin O'Carroll marries Birgit Subalter.

August 1: Nyford is burned to the ground by a mob of peasants incited by local human Barons, especially Murdoch Earl of Carthane, with Deryni businesses, schools, and homes being specifically targeted. Saint Camber's-at-Nyford, an abbey of the Servants of Saint Camber, is one of the establishments destroyed. Hundreds of innocent civilians die.

September 12: Lord Edward MacInnis is ordained priest.

September 22: Anne Hereditary Princess of Cassan marries Fane Hereditary Count Fitz-Arthur. Ambert Sovereign Prince of Cassan signs a treaty with Cinhil I King of Gwynedd acknowledging the King as Overlord, and agreeing that at Ambert's death without heirs male the Principality of Cassan shall become a Duchy of Gwynedd under his daughter and son-in-law.

October 18: Bishop Hubert MacInnis is elected Auxiliary Bishop of Rhemuth.

October 21: Zdanik Sovereign Prince d'Arjenol is defeated and captured by Nimur I King of Torenth, and all of his family executed before his eyes except his I-year-old daughter, Princess Braïda.

October 25: The Prince Torval, youngest son of the King of Torenth, is created Duke d'Arjenol at the age of X years, with his uncle Prince Dmitri as Regent, and Duke Torval is married on that day by proxy to the Princess Braïda Heiress d'Arjenol, aged I year.

November 6: Zdanik last Sovereign Prince d'Arjenol dies from the effects of torture and privation, aged XLV years.

November 17: King Cinhil I, being terminally ill with the consumptive complaint, signs his last will and testament, naming (among others) Murdoch Earl of Carthane as I of V Regents for his underaged son, Hereditary Prince Alroy. *C'est pour l'achever de peindre.*

December 28: A group of Deryni toughs rapes and kills a farmer's wife, causing a public outcry.

917

January 6: The squire Sorle Dalriada is knighted by King Cinhil I.

EVENTS OF *CAMBER THE HERETIC* AND "FIRST SESSION" (JANUARY 917-JANUARY 918)

January 15: King Cinhil I sends Earl Jebediah to get Cullen/Camber back from Grecotha.

January 16: Three human peers, Tammaron Earl Fitz-Arthur, Murdoch Earl of Carthane, and Rhun Baron of Horthness, conspire to substitute a new document changing the terms of regency to favour them, and succeed in getting Cinhil to sign the alteration, which has been buried in a stack of other documents.

January 17: Jebediah arrives at Grecotha.

January 18: Cullen/Camber leaves Grecotha and arrives late that night at Valoret.

January 30: Gregory Lord of Ebor falls from his horse, suffering severe injuries; his son Jesse sends to the capital for the Healer, Rhys Lord Thuryn.

January 31: Cinhil sends Rhys to aid Earl Gregory at his estate North of Valoret. In trying to control the Deryni Gregory, Rhys discovers how to block Deryni powers. Rhys dispatches Jebediah to fetch Camber. Cullen/Camber and Joram go to Ebor to examine this new phenomenon. They start back towards Valoret and come upon the party of Manfred Baron Marlor, which has just been assaulted by a group of young Deryni noblemen. They provide assistance to Manfred, then stop briefly to report the assault at the Saint Camber shrine at Dolban, where they meet Abbot Queron. They then return to Valoret and report to King Cinhil I.

February 1: An ice storm ravages the Valoret plain. Evaine and Rhys return from Ebor in the afternoon. That night King Cinhil I sets the Haldane potential of his III surviving sons, with the aid of Cullen/Camber, Rhys, Joram, Evaine, and Earl Jebediah. Tavis and the squire Gavin are drugged to prevent their interference.

February 2: King Cinhil I dies in the early morning hours at his palace in Valoret, and is succeeded by his XII-year-old son, the Hereditary Prince Alroy. The V Regents assume power: Murdoch, Tammaron, Rhun, Bishop Hubert MacInnis, and Bishop Alister Cullen/Camber. *Functus officio.*

February 3: King Cinhil I's body lies in state in the main chapel of Valoret Castle. The Regency Council convenes its Ist meeting. Cullen/Camber is removed from the Regency and from his office as Lord Chancellor by vote of the other IV Regents, and is replaced by Sighere Duke of Claibourne, with Sighere's son Ewan Earl of Rhendall sitting in his chair as Acting Regent. Also dismissed from the Royal Council are: Jebediah, Bishop Kai, and Baron Torcuill. Jebediah is removed as Earl Marshal. Earl Tammaron is named Lord Chancellor of Gwynedd. Later that evening the Camberian Council assembles, together with Davin, Ansel, and Jesse, and is informed of Rhys's discovery of his blocking ability. Jesse identifies the young Deryni marauders of Manfred's party.

February 4: Cullen/Camber meets with Joram, Evaine, Rhys, and Jebediah in his own quarters. Rhys tests his new technique for blocking Deryni powers on Jebediah and Evaine, and over the next few days also tests many other Deryni. Constable Darius Baron Udaut is created Earl Udaut.

February 9: An official requiem mass is celebrated for the soul of the late King Cinhil I by Archbishop Jaffray. After having lain in state for a week, his body is buried temporarily in the crypt beneath All Saints Cathedral in Valoret. The Regents announce plans to relocate the Court and eventually Cinhil's body to the old capital at Rhemuth.

February 16: A mob of humans burns a Deryni school at Barwicke.

February 22: Rhys and Evaine are dismissed from Court, and take up residence at their townhouse in Valoret.

March 6: The Camberian Council makes plans to "block" Deryni powers if the persecutions continue, and begins to seek additional Healers who have this unique talent; Dom Emrys is specially requested to investigate the problem. The human Revan is selected as the agent by which the blocking will be presented to the public. Revan supposedly falls in love with a local Sheele girl, Finella, who appears to sicken and die.

March 20: Revan accuses Rhys Thuryn of not saving his "love," and uses this as an excuse to join the Willimites, an anti-Deryni group, where he can begin preaching the use of baptism to cleanse Deryni of their sins through the "blocking" of their powers.

March 25: The news of Revan leaving Rhys's service reaches Court, and becomes a topic of much discussion.

April 1: Nimur I King of Torenth dies, aged L years, and is succeeded by his eldest son, Prince Arion. *Il faut avoir pitié des morts*.

April 16: Jaffray meets at Saint Neot's Abbey with Rhys, Emrys, Cullen/Camber, and Queron, and Camber is given a tour of the facilities. Rhys demonstrates his blocking technique to Queron and Emrys. **"First Session":** the boy Simonn begins his training as a Gabrilite Healer at Saint Neot's by examining the workings of his own body under the tutelage of Dom Kilian. At about this time, the Regents begin reorganizing the Army of Gwynedd to exclude the Michaelines and other known Deryni officers.

May 15: Revan is now reported operating with a band of neo-Willimites in the hills East of Valoret. Bishop Hubert preaches a sermon on the conversion of Saul.

May 25: King Alroy is crowned at Valoret on his XIIth birthday. At the formal banquet which takes place that evening, the Regents imbibe rather overmuch. Jebediah leaves for New Argoed.

May 26: A great celebration opens at Valoret, lasting throughout the next week.

May 27: The King and his brothers are taken on a state visit to open the Town Fair. A tournament is held that afternoon, but Alroy is ill and cannot compete. Prince Javan receives a chaplet of wildflowers from Elaine Countess of Carthane. Arion I King of Torenth marries Kniazhna Pavela Heiress of Jándrich, in recognition whereof a treaty is signed on that date, with Ygor the Sovereign Kniaz' of Jándrich agreeing to cede that country to Torenth upon his death without heirs male.

May 28: King Alroy competes on the IInd day of the tournament. Javan and Rhys Michael go to the fair with Tavis disguised as pages, and buy gifts for their servants and guards. Tavis is attacked on the city streets by masked Deryni, who cut off his hand to keep him from functioning as a Healer/physician; the Healer Lord Oriel is brought in to assist the palace physicians. Camber and Rhys discover that Javan has shields. Tavis despairs of performing his healing functions in the future. Evaine discovers that her unborn child will be a rare female Healer. Tavis believes that Javan has called to him through magic; Javan tells Tavis that Rhys blocked his memory the night King Cinhil I died; they test each others' abilities.

May 29: Tavis's condition improves; he has healed his stump from within, with Javan's assistance. Rhys and Cullen/Camber arrive with the Healers Queron and Emrys to examine Tavis's injury. Queron mentions the story of the novice Ulric, who went berserk at Saint Neot's in the year 905. Javan asks his royal brothers about the events of the night their father, King Cinhil I, died.

June 1: Tammaron persuades the Regents to start hunting down the bands of Deryni renegades. The Camberian Council meets, with Emrys, Queron, Davin, Ansel, and Jesse also present. They discuss Tavis's healing. The Council decides to insert a spy into Court to report on events happening there. Davin volunteers to be blocked, shape-changed into a palace guard, and secretly sent to Valoret.

June 2: Davin begins a week of military training.

June 6: Sir Peregrine Kai Morgan dies, aged XLIX years, and is succeeded by his son, Sir Charlan.

June 8: Davin works for a week with Rhys and Evaine to practice his magical arts.

June 15: The Camberian Council gathers in the *keeill*. Davin has the shape of Eidiard the soldier placed upon him, his powers being blocked by Rhys. Davin is sent into the Palace at Valoret. The real Eidiard is taken back to New Argoed.

July 1: The Spotted Plague reaches Valoret, affecting humans far more than Deryni.

July 2: Sighere Duke of Claibourne dies of the Spotted Plague, aged LV years, and is succeeded by his son, Ewan, who is also named Lord Regent and Earl Marshal of Gwynedd, and Commander of the Royal Army.

July 3: Alroy and Javan finish their formal schooling. The Court of King Alroy begins its move to the refurbished Palace at Rhemuth.

July 9: Carrollan is born to Ursin O'Carroll and Birgit Subalter.

July 10: Ewan I Duke of Claibourne returns to Valoret with Rhun, and begins reorganizing the army of Gwynedd.

July 14: King Alroy and his court arrive at Rhemuth to take up official residence. Lady Karis is born to Lord Oriel and Alana Destaing.

July 18: Charis Princess of Torenth marries Ursion Graf von Brosswick.

August 4: Ewan calls up the Gwyneddan levies, and divides the army into II parts. The smaller section is sent to Rhemuth under the command of Murdoch and Tammaron, with assistance from Manfred; the larger part remains at Valoret, and holds military exercises on the plain West of the city.

August 16: The Camberian Council learns of the unusual movements of the army. The Regents begin sweeping the countryside for renegade Deryni bands. One of the Deryni that they arrest is Dafydd Lord Leslie.

August 21: Dafydd Lord Leslie dies of self-induced convulsions while being interrogated by Tavis under the orders of the Regents, aged XXIII years. Prince Javan questions Tavis about what happened on the night that King Cinhil I died, and Tavis regresses both of their memories to that time.

August 29: Rhys and Evaine travel to the Willimite encampment in the hills above Valoret, and speak with Revan.

September 2: The Michaelines begin moving surreptitiously out of Gwynedd. *O Domine Deus speravi in te. O care mi Iesu, nunc libera me!*

September 15: The Regents order Rhun to begin recruiting captive Deryni, particularly Healers, for service to the Regents. Deryni prisoners are allocated to individual units, both to provide communication and to "sniff out" other Deryni.

September 17: The Michaelines complete their withdrawal to their III external Abbeys, primarily in Djellarda.

September 28: An assassination attempt ("The Michaelmas Plot") is made on Princes Javan and Rhys Michael in the countryside outside Rhemuth. Davin Earl of Culdi is paralyzed and killed while protecting the Princes, aged XIX years, the illusion of his alter-ego Eidiard dissipating with his death. The Regents conduct a trial and interrogate the surviving conspirators; also present are the III Royal Princes and Oriel. The attackers are tried, convicted, and executed, their titles attainted, and their relatives outlawed; among them are Lords Amyot, Trefor, Denzil, Ranald, Shaw, Dylan, Ivo, Fulbert, and Ansel *de jure* Earl of Culdi, even though he had had no part in the ambush. The Cambrian Council gathers in the *keeill* at Rhendall. Cullen/Camber celebrates a mass for Davin's soul. Disguised as a monk, Ansel returns to Grecotha with Cullen/Camber and Joram.

September 29: Cullen/Camber, Joram, and Ansel celebrate Michaelmas. Rhys and Evaine return to Sheele. Jebediah returns to New Argoed and makes his farewells. Jaffray returns to Rhemuth and celebrates Michaelmas with Archbishop Robert Oriss; that evening he goes to Saint Neot's to inform the Gabrilites of recent events.

October 1: Gregory Earl of Ebor begins quietly moving his family to his newly purchased estate of Trevalga in The Connait. Manfred Baron Marlor is elevated to Earl of Culdi of the IInd creation by King Alroy.

October 6: The Cambrian Council meets to discuss possible human reprisals against the Deryni religious orders. *Αει γαρ ευ πιπτουσιν 'οι Διος κύβοι.*

October 14: The Spotted Plague returns to Gwynedd, and causes much unrest there.

October 15: Jaffray Archbishop Primate of Valoret and All Gwynedd is killed in the streets of Valoret while leading his ecclesiastical troops to put down an anti-Deryni riot by the townspeople of Valoret. He is LV years of age at his death. Lord Jebediah retrieves Jaffray's body. Over L individuals are killed in the unrest. Ewan I Duke of Claibourne restores order in the city. The Camberian Council assembles at the *keeill* to discuss the day's events. The Regents are notified and decide to put Bishop Hubert forward as their candidate for Jaffray's successor, and determine to return the Court to Valoret for the winter. Javan tells Tavis that evening that he can truth-read, and suggests drugging Rhys Thuryn to discover what had happened the night his father had died.

October 29: Cullen/Camber reaches Valoret with Ansel and Joram.

November 1: Jaffray's funeral is held at All Saints Cathedral Valoret, with requiem mass being sung by Bishop Alister Cullen. Jebediah and Rhys Thuryn attend.

November 2: The Regents, the Princes, and the Court return to Valoret I day too late for the funeral.

November 12: The Synod of Bishops assembles at Valoret to elect a successor to Archbishop Jaffray, under the presidency of Archbishop Robert Oriss. Three new itinerant Bishops are elected: Alfred of Woodbourne, Archer of Arrand, and Paulin Sinclair of Ramos. Melissa Lady Howell dies, aged XXXV years.

November 13: The III new Bishops are consecrated, making the Synod XV in number. The Synod continues to meet throughout the month except Sundays.

November 27: Bishop Paulin Sinclair is elected Bishop of the newly formed see of Stavenham. *Odero, si potero: si non, invitus amabo.*

December 2: The Synod begins discussing candidates for Archbishop of Valoret; King Alroy officially recommends Bishop Hubert MacInnis.

December 4: Master Radulf is born to Sir Cyril Donivald and Nohea Lady Middlemore.

December 6: Balloting begins for the selection of a new Archbishop, but the Synod is deadlocked between several candidates.

December 13: Carloman Lord Thornton is killed by an anti-Deryni mob at Stavenham, aged LV years, and his title is attainted.

December 23: Cullen/Camber is asked by Niallan, Kai, Dermot, and Robert Oriss to accept election as a compromise candidate for Archbishop. He reluctantly accepts. Camber sends Ansel to fetch Rhys Thuryn.

December 24: Cullen/Camber is elected Archbishop Primate of Valoret and All Gwynedd by two-thirds majority; Hubert, Zephram, and the III new Bishops dissent. Cullen/Camber asks Kai to contact Joram to summon Jebediah to assume direction of the household guard. Rhys Thuryn arrives at Valoret. The Regents decline to recognize the election, and order Rhun and Peter Sinclair Earl of Tarleton to destroy Saint Neot's Abbey and the Michaeline establishments at Mollingford and Haut Eirial, using the Healer Oriel to convey their orders mentally to Rhun's Deryni. Tavis learns of the plot, and warns Rhys Thuryn. Jebediah and Cullen/Camber try to alert the unsuspecting monks. Dom Emrys orders the evacuation of Saint Neot's, but Rhun attacks before they can be removed. Most escape, but Dom Emrys is killed destroying the portal, aged LXXXII years. Tavis uses Bertrand to call Rhys Thuryn to Javan's quarters; he captures and drugs Rhys to discover what had happened to Javan on the night King Cinhil I died. Tavis then realizes that he can also block Deryni powers. Evaine and her children and Ansel flee Sheele for

Saint Mary's in the Hills Abbey near Culdi. Murdoch devises a plan to strike at the Deryni noble houses of Gwynedd.

December 25: It is a snowy day in Valoret. Rhys is released by Tavis and Javan to warn Cullen/Camber. Murdoch, Tammaron, and Ewan with King Alroy surround the Cathedral with their troops. Alister Cullen is installed as Archbishop Primate of Valoret and All Gwynedd, but is interrupted illegally and deposed by the Regents. During the escape from the cathedral the Healer Rhys Thuryn and Bishops Davet and Kai are killed, the latter destroying the Cathredral portal. Bishops Niallan Trey and Dermot O'Beirne, Archbishop Cullen/ Camber, Father Joram MacRorie, and Earl Jebediah escape via portal to Dhassa. Bishops Turlough and Ulliam surrender to the soldiers.

December 26: Bishop Hubert MacInnis reopens the Synod of Bishops at Ramos, and VI new itinerant Bishops are named. In a rigged vote Hubert is elected Archbishop Primate of Valoret and All Gwynedd by a two-thirds majority, with III Bishops abstaining, among them Bishop Ailin MacGregor. Father Edward MacInnis Baron Arnham is elected an itinerant Bishop. King Alroy creates Rhun Earl of Sheele and Vice Marshal of Gwy-nedd. The Regents order the arrest of all MacRories and Thuryns.

December 27: Hubert MacInnis is enthroned as Archbishop Primate of Valoret and All Gwynedd. That afternoon convenes the infamous Council of Ramos, which repudiates Camber's sainthood and bars Deryni in Gwynedd from holding office or becoming clergy. Even speaking Camber's name is forbidden, and he is officially proclaimed a heretic. Magic is declared anathema, but Healers are still permitted to practice. The Council strips from office Bishops Alister, Dermot, and Niallan of their sees, and removes the priesthood from Alister, Niallan, and Joram. Abbot Zephram is elected Bishop of Cashien, Bishop Edward MacInnis is made Bishop of Grecotha, and Archer is named Bishop of Dhassa. Noble Deryni are attainted and Deryni landowners stripped of their estates. The deliberations of the Council continue through the Spring.

December 28: Dolban is sacked by the Regents' soldiers, and LX men and women of the Servants of Saint Camber are burned at the stake, among them Guaire Lord d'Arliss, aged XXXVII years. Revan and Queron witness the massacre from the hills above. Revan prevents Queron from interfering with the soldiers.

December 29: Javan and Tavis use a portal to reach Dhassa, where they confer with Alister Cullen, who tells them of Rhys Thuryn's death. Tavis demonstrates his newly found knowledge of "blocking" on Bishop Niallan, and is brought into the circle of men and women trying to save the Deryni. Prince Javan is coached concerning his own talents. Cullen/Camber sends Joram ahead via portal to Cor Culdi to meet Evaine at Saint Mary's in the Hills, and orders a portal constructed there.

December 31: Trurill Castle is sacked and burned by Manfred MacInnis's men, and Aidan Lord Thuryn, Adrian MacLean Hereditary Count and Master of Kierney, and Aislinn Dowager Countess of Kierney are brutally tortured and slain. Camber "Camlin" MacLean is left for dead by the Regents, but survives the ordeal.

918

January 1: Evaine and Ansel find the Trurill massacre at dawn. Camlin MacLean, although terribly injured, is found alive and is healed with the help of III-year-old Tieg Thuryn, but his survival is hidden from the Regents. Fiona and Mairi Lady MacLean also survive. The bodies of the slain are burned. Jerusha Thuryn is born to Evaine. Evaine and Ansel and their family leave for Saint Mary's in the Hills. Tavis reports to Cullen/Camber at Dhassa that the Regents have ratified the Ramos Conventions, and is persuaded to join Revan's baptizer group; he then returns via portal to Valoret. Arion I King of Torenth is girded with the sword at Iób by Patriarch Antiochos I.

January 2: Evaine realizes that her party is being trailed, and abandons their litter. She begins to hemmorhage. They arrive at Saint Mary's and meet Joram. Evaine is treated by Brother Dominic.

January 3: Camber and Jebediah contact Joram mentally, and are updated on events at Trurill; they use a portal to transport from Dhassa to Grecotha.

January 4: Camber and Jebediah steal II horses and leave Grecotha.

January 5: Camber and Jebediah spend the night at a small inn near Cor Culdi, where they are spotted by several knights of the Earl of Culdi.

January 6: Lord Jebediah is killed defending Camber; Cullen/Camber is apparently killed but manages to cast a spell which puts him into limbo. Sir Rondel is the only soldier who survives the encounter. Riders from the abbey find the bodies, and return them to Saint Mary's. James Lord Drummond and his family return to Court.

January 7: The portal at Saint Mary's is established by Joram, Evaine, Ansel, Fiona, Camlin, Rhysel, and Tieg. The bodies of Alister Cullen/Camber and Jebediah lie in the chapel at Saint Mary's, later to be taken to the Michaeline Haven.

****

January 8: Ansel MacRorie is inducted into the Camberian Council. Γνωθι σ'αυτόν.

EVENTS OF *THE HARROWING OF GWYNEDD* (JANUARY-AUGUST 918)

January 9: The bodies of Alister Cullen (Camber of Culdi) and Jebediah are brought from Saint Mary's to the Haven to their final resting spots, next to the real Cullen and the infant Prince Aidan. Jebediah is buried, but Camber's body is believed to be locked into a self-induced preservation or suspension spell, and is only laid out on a bier in a hidden chamber.

January 10: Joram goes to Dhassa, where he meets with Bishop Niallan, Bishop Dermot, Tavis, Rickart, and Ansel; he then travels to Rhendall. Queron arrives at Saint Mary's in the Hills, having cut his *g'dula* braid to reduce his public profile; he is given a pouch left by Evaine containing Rhys Thuryn's Healer's seal, which has been imprinted with a mental message summarizing the events of recent days. Evaine tries to find information in ancient Deryni scrolls regarding the spell used by Camber to preserve his body. Queron and Evaine transport to the Camberian Council, where they meet Joram, Gregory, Jesse, and Ansel; Queron informs the group of the destruction at Dolban. Queron and Joram return to the Haven. In a double state wedding ceremony at Valoret, Rhun Earl of Sheele marries Agnes Lady Murdoch and Richard Hereditary Count of Murdoch marries Lirin Lady Udaut, with a formal banquet following in the Great Hall at Valoret; all III Haldane Princes are required to be present. Manfred and Sir Rondel arrive from Culdi bringing the news of Alister's and Jebediah's deaths IV days earlier; Rondel is truth-read by Declan Carmody to verify his account. Manfred presents Cullen's pectoral cross to the couples as a personal wedding present. The Drummonds return to Court to attend the weddings; Lady Richeldis is introduced to her future husband, Lord Iver MacInnis. Queron meets Tavis at the chapel in the Haven, and Tavis tells him of Revan's efforts with the Willimites. Queron then burns his braid in a ritual ceremony. Tavis transports to Valoret, and brings Javan back to the Haven, where the Prince informs him of the Regents' banquet. Queron is able to read Javan's mind. Tavis returns the Prince to Valoret. Jesse Hereditary Count of Ebor is inducted into the Camberian Council.

January 11: The Camberian Council discusses sending an expedition to Valoret to block the Drummonds' powers. Tavis goes to Dhassa. Dom Queron Kinevan is inducted into the Camberian Council; he sees Camber's face.

January 12: Gregory and Jesse return to Travalga. Rhun takes his II Deryni "sniffers" with him on maneuvers. *Oublier je ne puis.*

January 14: Elspeth MacRorie Abbess of Saint Hilda's Convent is killed by the Regents' men, aged LXXVII years.

January 18: Javan tells Tavis and Ansel of recent events.

January 20: Hubert, Murdoch, Tammaron, and Oriel leave for Ramos for a continuation of the Council there.

January 21: Manfred and Iver leave Valoret for Culdi with their Deryni, Ursin. That night Tavis and Ansel mount an expedition into Valoret Castle to block the Deryni abilities of Lord James, Lady Elinor, Lady Michaela, and Cathan Lord Drummond, and are successful; however, they find Lady Giesele MacLean already smothered in her bed by the Regents' men, aged XII years; Giesele's death makes her sister Richeldis sole heir to her uncle, the Earl of Kierney. Ansel is wounded by a guard while leaving, but is healed by Tavis and Sylvan with the help of others, including Fiona and Rhysel and Tieg. Sylvan and young Tieg are found to have the ability to block Deryni powers.

January 22: The Regents return to Valoret and blame the Deryni for Giesele's death. They physically close up the last known portal in Valoret Castle. They question the Princes and the Drummonds about the events of the night before, but the latter are found to have no Deryni powers of their own, having had them blocked the day before. Declan objects and is forced to abase himself before Murdoch; he collapses from despair, and Oriel tries to heal him. The Regents decide to return to Rhemuth. They propose that Lord Iver MacInnis be engaged to marry Richeldis MacLean within the month.

January 25: Bishop Turlough is elected Bishop of the newly created see of Marbury.

January 28: Evaine and Ansel transport from the Haven to Sheele to retrieve the ancient manuscripts secreted there. They return to the Haven.

January 29: Peter Sinclair Earl of Tarleton resigns his title in favour of his only son, who becomes Bonner II Earl of Tarleton.

February 2: A new religious order, the *Custodes Fidei*, is promulgated at Candlemas by Archbishop Hubert, with a military suborder, the *Equites Custodum Fidei*; it incorporates the earlier Order, The Little Brothers of Saint Ercon. Appointed as new heads of the order are: Paulin as Vicar General, Lord Albertus (formerly Peter Earl of Tarleton) as Grand Master of the *Equites*, Marcus as Chancellor General, Serafin as Inquisitor General, and Father Lior as Serafin's assistant. A feast is held at the Archbishop's Palace. Michaela Lady Drummond is made an attendant to Lady Estellan Countess of Culdi.

February 3: Bishop Niallan Trey quits his see at Dhassa under pressure from Rhun's soldiers, and brings a number of scrolls and bound volumes of Deryni lore to the Haven. Bishop Archer takes possession of his new see at Dhassa.

February 5: Using the alias "Brother Aaron," Queron is sent to fetch Revan to the Haven with Ansel and Tavis, who will wait at the portal after blocking Queron's powers. They transport to a secondary portal at Tor Caerrorie.

February 9: Javan tries to read King Alroy's mind, putting him into a trance without difficulty. Javan also makes Father Stephen sleep, and then goes to Archbishop Hubert's quarters with Sir Charlan, where he confesses to Hubert that he may have a vocation. He then forces the Primate to sleep. He then finds and uses the portal in the Archbishop's quarters to transport to the Haven and make his report to the Camberian Council. He encounters Sylvan and briefly gives him a verbal and written message outlining events at Court since 21 January; Sylvan then reads him. Javan returns to Hubert's sleeping chambers, and amends the Archbishop's attitudes. Sylvan reports to Joram and Evaine at the Camberian Council chamber. Queron and Tavis arrive at the Willimite camp to meet Revan; they heal a little girl named Erena.

February 10: Javan leaves Hubert's chapel, and later serves in the mass that Hubert conducts there.

February 11: The Court leaves Valoret for Rhemuth. Queron sends a mental message to Jesse. They leave on a "retreat in the wilderness," but actually travel to Tor Caerrorie.

February 12: Queron and Tavis arrive at Tor Caerrorie, and transport to the Haven with Revan. The Camberian Council begins training Revan to work with Sylvan. Revan appears to develop Deryni-like affinities during this period. Tavis O'Neill and Bishop Niallan Trey are inducted into the Camberian Council. Father Secorim is appointed Abbot of the Rhemuth Chapter of the *Custodes Fidei*.

February 17: Members of the Court pause at Tarleville for several days.

February 21: Revan completes his preparations.

February 22: Revan meets with Torcuill Baron de la Marche, who will be the Ist of the prophet's "converts." Jesse transports Torcuill to Trevalga. Sylvan, Tavis, and Revan present themselves at the Haven's chapel to offer up their mission to God; they are blessed by Bishops Niallan and Dermot. Revan departs the Haven for the wilderness, for XL days of prayer and retreat with his chief followers.

February 24: Joram and Evaine discuss the location of the ancient Varnarite Library in the ruins under Grecotha; Joram is put into a trance and draws his recollection of the plans of the ruins originally unearthed by Camber. Queron is told of their plans to enter the ruins, and is informed of Camber's real history as Alister Cullen. The Court leaves Tarleville for Rhemuth.

February 25: Queron is told by Joram and Evaine of the rest of their plans, and all III leave for the ruins beneath Grecotha. They find a domed chamber that resembles the *keeill* at the Camberian Council.

February 26: The trio continue to search Grecotha.

February 27: The trio gain access to an area under the Bishop's residence.

February 28: The trio continue their researches in the daylight.

March 1: The trio spy the Varnarite Library being looted by Bishop Edward's men. They return to the Haven.

March 3: Members of the Court arrive at Rhemuth.

March 5: Iver Lord MacInnis marries Richeldis Lady MacLean; assisting at the ceremony is Iver's younger brother, Edward Bishop of Grecotha.

March 7: Hubert returns with Robert Oriss to Valoret to continue the Council of Ramos. Bishop Alfred is given the spiritual care of Prince Javan, but delegates much of the responsibility to Father Boniface.

March 19: Iain II Earl of Kierney meets with a "hunting accident" engineered by the Regents, aged XLVII years, and is succeeded by his niece, Richeldis wife of Iver MacInnis, the latter of whom becomes Earl by right of his wife.

March 20: Manfred and Edward return to Grecotha with Ursin to loot the Varnarite Schola, Ewan returns to Kheldour, Tammaron dismantles the castle at Caerrorie for his friend Manfred, and Murdoch and Rhun remain at Rhemuth, making frequent forays to the East.

March 25: Prince Javan uses Charlan to distract Rhys Michael's guards, and reads his brother's mind.

March 30: Javan speaks privately with his twin, King Alroy, and puts him to sleep. He reads Alroy's mind, and finds that the Regents keep the King constantly sedated. He is discovered by the Healer Oriel, who realizes Javan has shields and other Deryni-like powers. Oriel pledges to work with Javan. Lord Tammaron enters the room, but Oriel covers for the Prince.

April 3: Revan perfects his technique of "baptism" to remove Deryni powers.

April 10: Evaine travels to Rhemuth as the bearded "Brother John" of the *Ordo Verbi Dei* to meet Prince Javan.

April 13: Evaine contacts Javan and arranges a rendezvous. They transport briefly to the Haven, where Joram reads him, and then return to the Basilica at Rhemuth. Javan shows Evaine several rare Deryni manuscripts collected by Father Boniface.

April 14: Javan leaves several other Deryni manuscripts for Evaine at the Rhemuth Basilica portal.

April 15: Javan finds several additional manuscripts for Evaine.

April 19: The Camberian Council gathers in the *keeill*, where Evaine tells the assembled members of her findings. Queron shows Evaine and Joram an ancient purification ritual with the cubes. The altar in the *keeill* sinks into the floor, revealing an opening and stairs leading to a small, unfinished chamber. The III travel to the ruins beneath Grecotha to examine the older altar there. This altar also sinks when the ancient spell is uttered, and beneath it they find the preserved bodies of the ancient Deryni masters, Orin and Jodotha, plus a medallion containing a lock of hair of Jodotha and her portrait. Both bodies collapse into dust when disturbed, but they find II scrolls beneath Orin's body, plus II ivory wands, I belonging to each. Orin's ring is given to Joram.

April 20: The trio return to Grecotha to reinter the dust of Orin and Jodotha. They discover Jodotha's ring, and Evaine takes it.

April 21 (Easter): The King and his brothers celebrate in the Cathedral of Saint George in Rhemuth, together with the Regents and their families.

April 27: Ewan I Duke of Claibourne returns to Kheldour.

April 29: Richard Murdoch is injured while riding, and is healed by Oriel.

May 1: Archbishop Hubert makes an unexpected visit to Rhemuth.

May 4: Hubert leaves for Valoret, leaving Prince Javan's spiritual guidance in the hands of Father Lior and Father Secorim.

May 6: Earl Murdoch and his son Richard and daughter-in-law return to Carthane. *Id demum est homini turpe quod meruit pati.*

May 25: The Regents return to Valoret to celebrate King Alroy and Prince Javan's XIIIth birthday; they receive many fine and wonderful gifts. Later that day Ewan I Duke of Claibourne is deposed from his office by his fellow Regents, and then stabbed by Murdoch, whom he also wounds. Sir Kennet of Rhorau dies defending his master, aged XXVI years. While being healed by Oriel, Murdoch orders the Deryni Declan Carmody to rip Ewan's mind; instead, Declan gives Ewan the *coup de grâce* and slashes his own wrists. His family is executed by Murdoch before Declan's eyes before he too is allowed to die, aged XXX years. Manfred replaces Ewan as Regent and Earl Marshal. The Princes give their many presents away, regarding them tainted by blood. Duke Ewan is XXXVII years of age at his death, and is succeeded by his son, Lord Graham. *Asinus in unguento.*

June 4: Graham I Duke of Claibourne rides to Rhemuth to claim his title and his father's body, together with his uncles Sighere Earl of Marley and Hrorik Earl of Eastmarch, and L armed knights. The Viceregality of the Kheldish Riding is officially dismantled, and Fane Lord Fitz-Arthur is made Deputy Regent for Kheldour. Javan tells Oriel that he has no vocation, but intends to move closer to holy orders to protect himself.

June 7: Joram meets with Javan; the latter writes to Hubert in Valoret, informing him that the Prince will join him for several weeks of retreat. Archbishop Hubert agrees, and Manfred escorts Javan North.

June 8: Manfred leaves Javan at Valoret, and rides for Cor Culdi.

June 9 (Pentecost): Revan and Sylvan begin their public Willimite ministry at the River Eirian. Also present are Revan's close disciples: Flann, Geordie, Patrick, and Joachim, and Tavis. Gillebert is the first Deryni "cleansed" of his affliction. Earl Manfred, on his way to Culdi, witnesses the event, tests Gillebert, and confirms the loss of his powers by jabbing him with a Deryni "pricker." Manfred abruptly returns to Valoret and reports to his brother, Archbishop Hubert. *Aquila non mangia mosche.*

June 12: Hubert travels to the Willimite camp with Prince Javan, the Deryni "sniffer" Ursin, and Lior to witness Revan's baptisms for himself. Ursin is sent by Hubert to be cleansed as a test of Revan's ministry, and is stripped of his Deryni powers. Hubert doses him with *merasha*, to no effect. Javan goes down to the camp for purification by Revan. Lord Torcuill de la Marche appears and is also cleansed. Hubert attempts to arrest him, but is stymied by Torcuill's absence of any Deryni signs. Hubert has Revan tested with *merasha*, but he also shows no powers. The Archbishop's party returns to Valoret. Javan is punished by Hubert for his insolence, and is forced to kneel in darkness for hours; he is then given XX lashes. Javan dines that evening with Hubert and Abbot Secorim. Javan is asked to tell Secorim of the baptizer Revan and of the events that occurred that afternoon. Hubert decides to leave Revan alone for the present. Secorim returns to his quarters, and Javan volunteers to go on a XL-day retreat. Javan puts Hubert into a trance, adjusts his memory, and gives him mental suggestions that Revan is playing into their hands and that Javan is moving in the right direction. Hubert suggests that Javan become a lay brother for a few years, making temporary vows on Lammastide, when the ban on ordinations is lifted. Javan agrees. He returns to his quarters and Charlan treats the wounds on his back.

June 15: Jesse and Ansel report to the Camberian Council on Javan's actions at the Willimite Camp. Dozens of Deryni have been saved by Revan. Also present are Evaine, Joram, Queron, and Niallan. Ansel adds that Torcuill was spirited away and eventually restored to his powers. Evaine states that she had returned to Valoret as Brother John, and learned there of Javan's scourging and his forthcoming assumption of temporary vows. She also brings the Council current on her researches. She later examines the *Codex Orini* and its *Conversation of the Holy Guardian Angel*. She falls asleep and dreams of speaking to an angel who places Jodotha's ring in her hand. She then locks Orin's and Jodotha's rings together, and reads the inscription thus formed: *Domini, fac me vitrum ut tibi incendam* ("Lord, make me a lens that I may burn for thee"). Passing the joined rings over the manuscript, she reveals a paragraph of hitherto hidden writing by Orin that details the procedure for preserving life after death and then bringing it back again. She refuses to give Joram the complete document. Over the next weeks they make provisions for the working on Lammastide. Fiona offers to raise the Thuryn children if Evaine perishes in the attempt.

July 24: Hereditary Prince Károly is born to Arion I King of Torenth and Pavela Kniazhna of Jándrich.

July 29: Javan enters a III-day fast prior to his profession of vows.

July 30: Evaine transports to Valoret to meet Javan. She imparts to him subconsciously the knowledge that he will need to know to govern as King, should the eventuality ever arise. She returns to the Haven.

July 31: Evaine, Joram, and Queron transport Camber's body to the old chamber beneath Grecotha, where the working will occur, and where Camber's body will finally lie at rest on Orin's bier under the net of *shiral* crystals.

August 1 (Lammastide): Prince Javan makes his Ist profession of temporary vows in the *Custodes Fidei* in the chapel of the former refectory at Valoret, with the ceremony being conducted by Paulin, Secorim, and Hubert. King Alroy and Prince Rhys Michael are also present. Evaine confesses to Bishop Niallan, and goes to Grecotha with Joram and Queron. Sir Charlan leaves Javan's service, attaching himself to King Alroy's Court. While freeing her father from limbo, Evaine MacRorie Thuryn dies, aged XXXV years, but Joram and Queron both survive the ordeal. Ordinations resume in Gwynedd under supervision of the *Custodes Fidei*.

* * * * * * *

August 2: Immediately following his profession of vows, Prince Javan spends XXXVI days in solitary retreat within the episcopal apartments at Valoret under the direction of Hubert and Paulin: he must keep total silence, other than confession and spiritual direction once each day, prior to attendance at Mass, where he must prostrate himself before the altar except to receive holy communion. He can eat no meat whatsoever, but follows a fast of bread and water III days per week. He spends several hours daily prostrated in the *disciplinarium*, remembering his flogging, and wondering whether he will be required to submit to it again. Ζωμεν γαρ ουχ 'ως θέλομεν αλλ' 'ως δυνάμεθα.

August 9: Tambert Hereditary Duke of Cassan is born to Fane Hereditary Count Fitz-Arthur and Princess Anne Heiress of Cassan.

August 16: Miklós Prince of Torenth leaves the monastery and is created Duke of Truvorsk by his brother, King Arion I, who also appoints him to the High Council of Torenth.

September 1: The Council of Sovereign Princes in The Connait confirms Gregory Earl of Ebor's title.

September 2: Bonner II Earl of Tarleton marries Virbena Lady Spriggans.

September 21: Javan leaves for Rhemuth with Hubert and Paulin and an escort of *Custodes* knights for Prince Rhys Michael's birthday celebration.

September 25: Javan arrives in Rhemuth, and has a brief contact with Oriel, under the guise of tending to his crippled foot after the long ride. Oriel pronounces Javan's health good, other than the fact that he is thin from constant bouts of fasting. King Alroy, however, is not well: he has a persistent cough with wheezing, and is still kept slightly sedated on orders of the Regents. Javan practices archery with his brothers Alroy and Rhys Michael, with Charlan present. Charlan had been visited in the past week by a Deryni from the Camberian Council, and keyed so that he would not remember until he was alone with Javan that a message has come from Joram via Jesse regarding Evaine's death, with a promise to try to keep communication open. The message vanishes once Javan reads it. Javan reasserts his right to have letters sent back and forth from his brothers via Charlan, or he will not go back to the Abbey. Hubert agrees.

October 1: Hubert remains in Rhemuth for Council business; Paulin returns Javan to Ramos Abbey outside Valoret, and takes charge of his training.

October 23: James Lord Drummond is supposedly killed by highway robbers, aged XLII years, but is actually murdered by the Regents.

Fall/Winter: During this period the Prince Javan is subject to formal religious instruction under tight *Custodes* discipline. Meals and nights pass in silence, with III days of fasting weekly. Postulants are scourged for transgressions of the Rule, although the Prince is never disciplined in this way. The Rule permits *minution* every VI to VIII weeks, with III days of recovery in infirmary after each session and a relaxation of the dietary restrictions. Paulin insists that Javan submit once to this discipline to experience the benefits thereof, but Javan declines to volunteer thereafter, and he cannot be compelled to it on a regular basis. Letters continue to pass regularly between the III Haldane Princes, all vetted by the Regents, but with no chance of Deryni contact or support.

919

February 2: Robert Ainslie Hereditary Lord Argoed is knighted.

April 23: The bell called Great George on Saint George's Cathedral rings out for the Ist time across the city of Rhemuth.

May 25: King Alroy and Prince Javan attain their majorities, and the Regency Council is officially disbanded. Manfred Earl of Culdi resigns as Earl Marshal, and is replaced by Lord Albertus.

June 14: Sir Guiscard Hereditary Lord de Courcy marries Jael Lady Coanuy.

July 12: Sir Piedur dies in a border skirmish.

July 23: Sir Robear marries Bova Lady Martano.

October 10: Mairi Dowager Hereditary Countess of Kierney dies at Saint Mary's in the Hills, aged XXIX years.

920

January 1: Marek Hereditary Prince and Pretender of Gwynedd is installed at Saint Constantine's Cathedral by Patriarch Antiochos I.

March 2: Frizell former Baron Lovat dies in exile near Arrand in Llannedd, aged LXXIV years.

May 18: Prince Javan leaves for Rhemuth with Paulin for Javan and King Alroy's XVth birthday celebration.

May 22: Javan arrives at Rhemuth, but he has even less chance this time to make contact with his Deryni allies. Oriel gives a report on King Alroy's health, but the news only depresses Javan: the King continues to decline.

May 27: Hubert again remains behind, and Paulin takes Javan to the *Arx Fidei* Abbey North of Rhemuth, where he is to begin regular seminary training. Javan is compelled to take Minor Orders and to accept full tonsure, but the Rule is relaxed somewhat for seminarians who are good scholars such as Javan. Javan spends the next year here, with leave to spend III days at home each year for Rhys Michael's birthday, Christmas, and his own birthday.

July 18: Torval I Duke d'Arjenol attains his majority, and his uncle, Prince Dmitri, relinquishes his Regency of Arjenol.

August 9: Prince Ysarn is born to Arion I King of Torenth and Pavela Kniazhna of Jándrich.

September 29: Prince Rhys Michael comes of age, and is created Duke of Carthmoor by his brother, King Alroy.

November 6: Father Boniface dies, and is replaced by Father Ascelin.

November 16: The Council of Sovereign Princes of The Connait admits the County of Trevalga to its membership, with Gregory former Earl of Ebor as Count. *Juncta juvant*.

December 3: The squires Gavin, Charlan, and Tomais are knighted by King Alroy.

921

February 28: Lord Ithel is born to Judah Count of Castlethorn in Meara and Maybell Lady Styller.

May 21: Ambert Sovereign Prince of Cassan dies, aged LXVII years, and is succeeded by his grandson, Tambert I, as Duke of Cassan, with Princess Anne and her husband Fane Lord Fitz-Arthur as Co-Regents. *Fuimus*.

May 24: Javan rides to Rhemuth for his and Alroy's XVIth birthday celebration. King Alroy's health is poor, although he puts up a brave front.

May 26: Javan returns to *Arx Fidei*.

June 11: Master Dimitri is recruited as a Deryni "sniffer" by Paulin.

EVENTS OF *KING JAVAN'S YEAR* (JUNE 921-OCTOBER 922)

June 22: Jesse MacGregor receives a message at the Haven via carrier pigeon that King Alroy is dying of consumption. Joram suggests that Queron and Tavis move the projected *coup* against the Regents forward. The Great Lords of the Council begin gathering around the dying monarch. Prince Javan contemplates his future while praying at *Arx Fidei*.

June 23: Just after midnight King Alroy asks to see his brother, Prince Rhys Michael, and tells him that he must have the Regents send for Prince Javan. Rhys Michael orders Sir Charlan and Sir Bertrand to proceed to the *Arx Fidei* Abbey III hours North of Rhemuth with a troop of soldiers and return with Prince Javan, giving the knight his signet ring as a sign of his authority. Javan leaves the Abbey over the opposition of Abbot Halex and Sir Joshua Delacroix, and arrives at Court at dawn, where he is met by his brother, Prince Rhys Michael. The Healer Oriel has been keeping Alroy alive until Javan appears. Alroy gives Javan the Ring of Fire and the Eye of Rom, part of the regalia belonging to the King of Gwynedd. Javan gives Alroy the last sacraments and holy communion, with Hubert present but controlled by the Prince, and calls upon the IV archangels to witness his brother's passing. Prince Javan Haldane succeeds to the throne on the death of his brother, King Alroy, with the support of Étienne Baron de Courcy; Alroy is XVI years of age at his death. Javan announces that King Alroy will lie in state at Saint Hilary's for III days. Javan is secretly knighted by Sir Jason, I of a group of young knights and supporters of the new King who have drafted a set of legal documents for him to implement at the start of his reign; others of this group include Sir Sorle, Sir Guiscard de Courcy and his father, Lord Étienne, Sir Robear, and Lord Jerowen. The funeral procession forms to take Alroy's body to Saint Hilary's. Sir Tomais becomes an aide to King Javan. An Accession Council is held that afternoon, and Paulin calls upon Marcus Concannon to testify that Javan's religious vows were permanent, and he produces forged documents to bolster his statement. Étienne and Jerowen are summoned by Jason to counter with the actual transcripts of the vows. Javan orders the Healer Oriel brought forward to truth-read both parties. Marcus admits he did not make the transcriptions, but had been sent the records from the *Custodes* central office. Paulin is accused of preparing false documents. Javan swears that he never intended to become a cleric, and is now prepared to take up his dynastic duties. All of the members of the Council tender their resignations, as is customary, which Javan takes under advisement. He meets with some of his young supporters at Court. The former Regents meet that evening to discuss their options. Hubert mentions, in a breaking of the seal of the confessional, that Rhys Michael or his son might be a more malleable Prince, and that he has begun to fancy the Lady Michaela Drummond.

June 24: King Javan meets Étienne de Courcy to discuss appointments. Guiscard arrives with a message from Joram. Javan pays his respects to his brother's bier, and slips out the rear entrance of the basilica with Guiscard. They transport from the study there to the Michaeline Haven, where he meets Joram and Niallan. Jesse MacGregor is introduced to the King. Javan returns to Rhemuth. He meets with Murdoch Earl of Carthane, who has just returned to Court. Étienne Baron de Courcy is named the King's confidential secretary.

June 25: Javan reviews the briefing documents with his advisers, and dines with the Court in the Great Hall at Rhemuth.

June 26: Just after midnight Javan returns to the Haven to have his Haldane potential activated by Joram, Queron, and Tavis. Rhun the Ruthless returns to Court. That day King Alroy is buried in the crypt of his ancestors beneath Saint George's Cathedral at Rhemuth. After the funeral Javan attends a formal Court reception. Later that night Javan discusses with Oriel the threat of Sitric, Rhun's Deryni "sniffer."

June 27: The Royal Council meets for a IInd time, with all members present except Fane Lord Fitz-Arthur. Javan accepts the resignation of Fane, who is now Co-Regent of the new Duchy of Cassan. The King begins a program of exercises and military training: he is already an excellent archer. Baron Hildred will renew the King's skills as a rider.

July 2: Lord Jerowen is appointed to the empty seat on the Royal Council.

July 18: At the Council meeting held on this day Javan requests that Paulin provide him with a personal chaplain to use as a confessor. Father Faelan, whom he had known at *Arx Fidei*, is the priest Javan selects.

July 27: Javan secretly considers with Guiscard a possible site for a new portal at Rhemuth Palace, located in an area of the Castle that is now being restored, in a chamber adjoining the new library. At Guiscard's recommendation, the King tells Charlan the truth about his previous manipulations of the knight, and restores most of his memory, before again erasing it at Charlan's request. He names Charlan as his chief aide; Charlan recommends that Cathan Lord Drummond replace him as squire.

July 28: Guiscard introduces Javan to William of Desse, the Master of Works at Rhemuth Castle, who invites Javan to inspect the new library complex. Father Faelan is brought to Javan by Paulin; the priest shows obvious signs of torture and minution; the King orders Guiscard to give the priest an afternoon of rest. Javan participates in the grand rehearsal of the coronation ceremony. Later he tours the new portal site off the library. A state dinner is held following the rehearsal; the end of the official mourning period brings out the ladies of the court. Oriel reads and heals Faelan, but also discovers from Faelan's memories that Paulin has a new Deryni "sniffer." Jesse arrives disguised as a *Custodes* monk to examine the new portal site; Javan introduces him to Charlan. *Posse videor*.

July 29: Fane Lord Fitz-Arthur, his wife, Princess Anne, and their son, the III-year-old Duke Tambert I, arrive at Rhemuth. Javan talks with his brother, Rhys Michael, and questions him regarding Michaela Drummond; Rhys is discovered to have shields, and is noted to have a drinking problem. Javan and Faelan encounter Father Lior and Brother Serafin. Guiscard and Javan take the II men prisoner, and bring them under mental control. The new portal off the library in the Rhemuth Palace is established by Javan, Guiscard, Jesse, Étienne, and Oriel, with the assistance of the humans Faelan, Charlan, Lior, and Serafin, whose memories of the event are then wiped. Joram and Niallan transport through the new portal, and join Jesse in questioning Serafin and Lior; from Serafin they discover the name of Paulin's new "sniffer," Master Dimitri; the latter has left a tell-tale trigger buried deep in Serafin's mind that has been tripped by Guiscard, and the intrusion will be obvious to Dimitri when he examines the monk again. Joram has Javan take Joram back through the portal to the Haven as a test of the King's ability to transport, and gives him his blessing, with Camber making a spiritual appearance. Brother Serafin dies of an apparent heart attack, aged XLVI years, actually killed by Guiscard to prevent discovery of their probing by Dimitri, and is succeeded by Father Lior as Inquisitor General of the *Custodes Fidei*.

July 30 (Sunday): Fane Lord Fitz-Arthur, Princess Anne Quinnell, and Duke Tambert are officially received at Court, and young Tambert is confirmed as Ist Duke of Cassan, which is formally annexed to Gwynedd on that date. A delegation from Torenth headed by Prince Miklós, brother to King Arion I, arrives at Rhemuth, secretly accompanied by the Festillic Pretender, Marek, as the Prince's aide. Albertus, Paulin, and Hubert discuss the untimely death of Serafin, but decide that his passing was caused by heart failure.

July 31: The Earls of Eastmarch and Marley and the Duke of Claibourne arrive at Rhemuth. Prince Javan Haldane is crowned King of Gwynedd. The Torenthi Prince Miklós is surprised to notice a nimbus of power surrounding the King's head when Javan receives the crown from Archbishop Hubert. A banquet is held in the Great Hall at Rhemuth Palace that evening. Javan receives ambassadors from Llannedd, Mooryn, and Torenth. Prince Miklós presents a gift to the King, and asks a boon in return, that an account be made of the II hostages taken by King Cinhil I in 906; these individuals, Kennet and Sudrey of Rhorau, had been placed under the wardenship of Ewan I Earl of Rhendall and later Duke of Claibourne. Ewan's brother, Hrorik II Earl of Eastmarch, is called by the King to give his account. He accuses Earl Murdoch of the murder of Duke Ewan and Sir Kennet his aide, and challenges him to trial by combat, which Murdoch is forced to accept. The Lady Sudrey, Javan learns, is now Hrorik's wife.

August 1: Earl Hrorik fights and mortally wounds Earl Murdoch in fair battle, with the members of the Court and Council in attendance, and Lord Albertus presiding as Earl Marshal. Rhun Earl of Sheele gives his friend the *coup de grâce* when Oriel declines to end Murdoch's suffering. The Earl Murdoch is XLIV years of age at his death, and is succeeded by his son, Richard Lord Murdoch. The former Regents decide to take action against King Javan. The Great Tournament that had been planned for this day is cancelled.

August 2: Paulin escorts the body of Brother Serafin back to *Arx Fidei* for burial. Richard Lord Murdoch is confirmed by King Javan as the new Earl of Carthane, and immediately leaves for home with his father's body, accompanied by Rhun the Ruthless and his Deryni, Sitric. Javan meets Miklós alone, but refuses the latter's request to see Earl Hrorik and Sudrey his wife. Miklós returns to Torenth, leaving by ship from the port city of Desse. The King sends Robear and Gavin to Nyford to watch for Miklós's ship and to report on conditions there. Javan orders Oriel moved to quarters adjacent to Sir Sorle, and gives the latter the responsibility for Oriel's safety. *Privilegia paucorum non faciunt legem.*

August 5: Robear reports back to the King. Étienne de Courcy is moved into the chamber next to the new library to guard the new portal there, and becomes the King's main contact person with the Michaeline Haven.

August 6: Hrorik is well enough to return home with Graham and Sighere.

August 21: Javan sees Rhys Michael dallying with the Lady Michaela, and chastises both. Prince Rhys Michael claims that he and the Lady are betrothed; Javan forbids the marriage at this time. Rhys agrees to avoid Michaela for the present.

August 23: Earl Manfred returns to his estate at Culdi with his ward, Michaela Drummond. Javan transports to the Haven and informs Joram, Jesse, and Niallan of the incident involving Prince Rhys Michael. The latter is assigned by Javan to work with Lord Jerowen in the Chancery Office to prepare warrants regarding land holdings throughout the kingdom. *Grau, teurer Freund, ist allen Theorie, und grün des Lebens goldner Baum.*

August 26: Father Faelan returns to *Arx Fidei* for his monthly questioning by Paulin.

September 1: Ainslie Lord Argoed is appointed Deputy Commissioner for Grecotha by King Javan.

September 7: The new land warrants are given to Darius Earl Udaut to be dispatched immediately throughout the Kingdom. The King orders Lord Jerowen to compile a comprehensive index of the laws promulgated during the reigns of Kings Cinhil I and Alroy. That evening Javan *fêtes* Rhys Michael in their quarters, and briefs him about the practices of the *Custodes*.

September 8: Paulin and Faelan return to Rhemuth. Javan talks with Faelan that evening, and learns what had happened to him at *Arx Fidei*; he had been probed by Dimitri. Paulin and Hubert discuss Serafin's death, but again they decide that his passing was natural.

September 9: Paulin discusses the theology of the Statutes of Ramos and the inherent evil of the Deryni race at great length in a meeting of the Royal Council.

September 10: Paulin again brings up the question of the Deryni.

September 11: Rhys Michael makes a presentation to the Council regarding the codification of the laws.

September 12: Lord Udaut suggests that Rhys Michael be given additional responsibilities as a member of one of the King's traveling legal commissions; Rhys Michael is appointed the Deputy Commissioner for Grecotha.

September 19: Lord Ainslie, Prince Rhys Michael, Sir Jason, and Sir Tomais depart for Grecotha on Commission business, with Sir Jason being made specifically responsible for Prince Rhys Michael's safety.

September 23: Lord Ainslie's party arrives safely in Grecotha.

September 25: Javan experiments with the effects of *merasha*, with the help of Guiscard, Étienne, Jesse, and Charlan.

September 26: Javan awakes somewhat groggy.

September 27: Javan has fully recovered.

September 29: A feast is held at Rhemuth Castle.

October 2: Father Faelan is scheduled to return to *Arx Fidei* on this day, the first Monday of the month, but refuses to leave.

October 4: Paulin arrives back in Rhemuth, and summons the King, asking for an explanation of Faelan's absence. Javan supports the priest. Paulin indicates that he will excommunicate Faelan if he does not return. Later that evening, after the excommunication ceremony, Paulin meets with Hubert to discuss options. Father Daíthi is appointed successor to Father Faelan as King's Chaplain and Confessor.

October 5: The Council discusses Lord Jerowen's index to the laws, with special attention to the records of King Alroy's Regency period, which are delivered by Earl Tammaron that evening. *El ciego mal juzgará de colores.*

October 10: At Paulin's order, Lord Albertus strangles Father Faelan late that night, but makes his death look like a suicide by hanging. Faelan is XXII years of age at his death.

October 11: Father Faelan's body is discovered by the King and his men the next morning. They are convinced Faelan has been murdered, but without evidence are forced publicly to acknowledge his suicide. The priest's body is buried in a potter's field. Javan transports to the Haven with Guiscard and reports to Joram, Niallan, and Jesse; they discuss a plan to free the Deryni hostages.

October 31: Prince Rhys Michael is taken captive, supposedly by Deryni bandits, but actually by the Regents' men. Sir Jason is killed defending the Prince, aged XXXIX years, and Ainslie Lord Argoed is severely wounded and taken to Bishop Edward MacInnis's residence at Grecotha for recovery.

November 1: Sir Tomais sends a message from Grecotha to the King at Rhemuth.

November 4: Javan receives the message from Tomais.

November 8: During a "rescue" skirmish, Prince Rhys Michael is knocked unconscious.

November 10: Prince Rhys Michael awakens in Culdi, where he has been taken by the former Regents, and is being treated by Master Stevanus for "wounds" received during his rescue. Lord Manfred blames his kidnapping on the outlawed Ansel MacRorie and other Deryni. The King receives a letter from the alleged Deryni kidnappers, supposedly headed by Ansel MacRorie. Javan sends a report to Joram; Joram and Ansel reply that they know nothing of the attack. Lord Vantry delivers letters to Paulin and the King.

November 11: Rhys Michael is awakened by Master Stevanus, who introduces him to his new nurse, Michaela Lady Drummond.

November 13: King Javan receives a IInd note from the so-called kidnappers, including a severed toe purportedly (but not actually) belonging to Prince Rhys Michael.

November 15: Ansel sends a note to Court disavowing any involvement in Rhys's kidnapping.

November 19: Javan attends services at which Hubert officiates, and gets the Archbishop alone in his quarters. Javan takes over Hubert's mind and discovers that Paulin and Albertus, with Hubert's approval, have had Rhys Michael abducted by *Custodes* knights disguised as Ansel's men, and have had him rescued by Manfred's men, who have taken the Prince to Culdi. The real goal of the plot is to have Rhys Michael promptly married to Michaela Drummond, and an heir produced. He puts the thought into Hubert's mind that the King is enamored of Lady Juliana of Horthness, Rhun's daughter. Paulin interrupts the II men. Hubert relates the particulars to Paulin. Rhys Michael and Michaela consummate their union.

November 20: Manfred sends messages to Albertus at Grecotha and King Javan at Rhemuth. Rhys Michael Prince of Gwynedd marries Michaela Lady Drummond. Paulin sends instructions to Lior at *Arx Fidei*.

November 24: Javan receives Manfred's letter telling of Rhys Michael's rescue. The King asks Robert Oriss to sing a solemn *Te Deum* on the morrow in thanksgiving. Étienne reports to Joram. Paulin and Lior introduce Dimitri to Hubert. Dimitri reads Hubert and discovers Javan's interference with his memories. Paulin and Hubert determine to take steps to safeguard themselves.

November 25: A mass of thanksgiving is said at Rhemuth Cathedral. Sir Robert Ainslie is sent to Culdi with messages for Manfred and Rhys Michael. Hubert suggests at the Council meeting that afternoon that Oriel be sent to Culdi, but this is not done.

December 1: Manfred, Rhys Michael, Michaela, and others depart Culdi for Rhemuth. A troop of *Custodes* knights rides into the capital city with V bodies claimed to be Ansel's bandits, but these are actually the remains of peasants.

December 2: The V bodies of the "bandits" are ordered to be beheaded and quartered by Constable Udaut, and their parts distributed throughout the Kingdom. *Præfervidum ingenium dominorum*.

December 5: Manfred, Albertus, Rhys Michael, Robear, Tomais, and Michaela arrive at Rhemuth. The Prince announces his new wife, who is publicly accepted by Javan. A banquet of celebration is held at the Palace. The King has Oriel examine Rhys Michael, and discovers that several of his "wounds" were deliberately inflicted after his so-called kidnapping. Javan sees Sitric lurking at Court.

December 24: The Court keeps the Vigil of Christmas at Rhemuth.

December 25: Javan participates in an official stag hunt with Rhys, Michaela, and other young members of the Court. The King pretends to be amused by Juliana of Horthness.

December 26: Michaela is recognized and crowned as Princess of Gwynedd in an official pageant, with her hair unbound according to the usual custom for such ceremonies. She and Rhys renew their marriage vows. A banquet is held in their honour.

December 27: Javan again "confesses" to Hubert that he has romantic thoughts towards Lady Juliana, Earl Rhun's daughter.

922

January 6: Twelfth Night Court is held. Javan receives letters from young Tambert I Duke of Cassan and Graham I Duke of Claibourne. The King knights Cashel Lord Murdoch and other relatives of the great Lords, with Sir Robear assisting. *Noli equi dentes inspicere donati*.

January 9: Hrorik II Earl of Eastmarch sends the King letters forwarded from Arion I King of Torenth, with Countess Sudrey's reply to Arion: she will never return to Torenth or provide information to Arion. Michaela acknowledges that she is pregnant with a child due to be born in August or September.

March 6: Javan introduces the subject of the Deryni hostages into Council, and suggests that Ursin and his family be released, since they have tested negative for Deryniness. The King visits the captive, and again has him tested with *merasha*. He then goes to Ursin's wife and son, and Oriel tests the latter, proving his Deryniness. Javan proposes that Ursin's family be cleansed by Revan at Valoret, and that all III be sent to monasteries afterwards. Ursin, Hubert, and Paulin agree that Ursin will be sent to Ramos. Javan talks with Guiscard, Étienne, and Charlan to find a way to free Ursin and his family. Hubert, Paulin, and Albertus discuss the latest developments, and decide on the elimination of Oriel by Sitric.

March 18: Antiochos Patriarch of Torenth dies, aged LXII years.

March 20: At the instigation of the former Regents, Sitric attacks Oriel and his bodyguard, Sir Gavin. Gavin is killed, aged XX years, but Guiscard, Javan, and Charlan come to Oriel's rescue. Sitric is killed by Javan and Guiscard, who set the Deryni aflame through magic. Oriel has been wounded by *merasha*-tainted swords, but is saved. Rhun questions Albertus and Paulin regarding the attack, and is introduced to Dimitri, who had posed through shape-shifting as one of the battle surgeons treating Oriel.

March 22: Oriel questions Baldwin and Nevell, the II soldiers who had attacked him. Sir Sorle is assigned by Javan as Oriel's new bodyguard. Étienne reports to Joram.

March 23: Baldwin and Nevell are found dead, having been secretly murdered by Dimitri. Rhun implicates Oriel. Javan suspects Dimitri. Dimitri tells Paulin, Albertus, and Hubert that either the King or Guiscard or both have Deryni powers; he favours Javan as the chief suspect for the killing of Sitric.

April 20: Ursin is found dead in bed after one of his periodic testings with *merasha*, aged XXVII years, and his body is examined by Oriel, who determines that he had been smothered by III intruders, probably at the instigation of Dimitri.

April 21: Sir Bertrand is sent North by the King to confirm that Master Revan has returned to his baptizing on the River Eirian, and is baptized by him.

April 28: Sir Bertrand returns with news of Revan. Javan decides to make the trip to Valoret to see Revan.

May 3: Javan hands over command of Rhemuth Castle to Prince Rhys Michael, and departs for Valoret with his entourage and L Haldane lancers, plus Albertus, Rhun, Paulin, Lior, and the families of the deceased Deryni collaborators. They lay over at a priory of the *Ordo Verbi Dei*.

May 10: The King's party stops at Saint Mark's Abbey East of Valoret. Richard Murdoch Earl of Carthane returns to Court.

May 11: Javan and his group reach Revan's camp on the River Eirian. Tavis, Queron, and Sylvan are also present. Birgit and Carrollan are baptized. Paulin, Albertus, and Manfred attack Revan's group with forces disguised as Ansel's men, and start massacring the women and children there. Revan and Tavis are killed by a crowd of their former disciples. Queron escapes the massacre at the River, but the *Custodes* knights kill King Javan, Charlan, Robear, Guiscard, Bertrand, Sylvan, and the Haldane knights. King Javan is XVI years of age at his death. At the same time the former Regents in Rhemuth, including Hubert, Tammaron, Richard Murdoch, and Udaut, take over the Palace in a *coup d'état* with the help of Gideon. At the Royal Council being held in Rhemuth, Sir Tomais, Sir Sorle, Oriel, and Lord Jerowen are murdered, Hildred Baron Nagapple is severely wounded, and Prince Rhys Michael, Michaela, and Cathan are taken prisoner; Baron Étienne escapes through a portal, taking with him to safety Alana d'Oriel and her daughter Karis. Rhys Michael is drugged by Archbishop Hubert. Michaela goes into premature labour, producing a stillborn son, Prince Cinhil. Prince Rhys Michael Haldane succeeds his brother as King of Gwynedd. Étienne allows little Tieg Thuryn to read his memories of the events leading up to the *coup*, then courageously returns to Rhemuth Palace to avoid giving away the location of the portal there, and is promptly arrested and interrogated. Ansel MacRorie is blamed for King Javan's death.

May 13: Étienne Baron de Courcy is tortured and questioned by the Regents for the next week.

May 20: Étienne Baron de Courcy is executed, aged XLVIII years.

May 25: King Javan's body is brought back to Rhemuth on what would have been his XVIIth birthday.

May 27: King Javan is buried with his ancestors beneath the Cathedral at Rhemuth. King Rhys Michael is kept sedated by the former Regents.

May 31: Graham I Duke of Claibourne marries Nicola Lady Spenser.

September 29: King Rhys Michael is crowned at Rhemuth on his XVIth birthday. After this date the Council stops sedating Rhys Michael, and he is reunited with his Queen, in the hope that Michaela will become pregnant again.

September 30: Prince Sigard is born to Arion I King of Torenth and Pavela Kniazhna of Jándrich.

October 2: Eusebios Metropolitan of Sostra is elected Patriarch of Torenth.

October 15: Rhys Michael confesses to Michaela that he has become a puppet of the former Regents, and that she is expected by them to be the Royal brood mare. If they do not have additional children, one of the Council will force himself on Michaela.

****

923

January 1: The Order of Saint Michael, now located permanently in Djellarda, is renamed the Knights of the Anvil (*Equites Incudis*).

June 1: Torcuill Baron de la Marche is created Count Marchmont in The Connait by Poncet Sovereign Prince of Pardiac.

September 14: Hildred Baron Nagapple, formerly Master of Horse of Gwynedd, dies of his injuries, aged LVIII years, and is succeeded by his son, Lord DeLacey.

924

January 31: Turlough Bishop of Marbury dies, aged LXVIII years.

February 29: Hereditary Prince Owain is born to Rhys Michael King of Gwynedd and Michaela Lady Drummond. The Queen gives her husband a large fist-sized brooch embossed with the golden lion of Gwynedd to celebrate the occasion.

November 1: Princess Thomaïs is born to Arion I King of Torenth and Pavela Kniazhna of Jándrich. *El Bien nunca muere.*

926

January 11: Torval I Duke d'Arjenol marries Braïda Heiress d'Arjenol, and is created Grand Duke of Östmarcke *ad personam* by his brother, Arion I King of Torenth. *Les honneurs comptent.*

March 9: Bayvel de Cameron Lord Farnham dies, aged LXIV years, and is succeeded by his son, Lord Leonidas.
October 12: Egan Chief and Laird of Clan MacArdry is created Earl of Transha by King Rhys Michael.
November 24: Prince Vidar is born to Arion I King of Torenth and Pavela Kniazhna of Jándrich.
December 30: Lord Illan de Bourges is killed fighting Moors near Djellarda, aged LII years.

927

May 22: Corban Lord Howell marries Stacia Heiress of Eastmarch.
July 17: Prince Marek Pretender of Gwynedd marries Charis Princess of Torenth, and she is given the Duchy of Tolán as a dowry by her brother, Arion I King of Torenth.
Fall: The Royal Council receives reports of increased Torenthi troop movements along the Eastmarch border with Torenth.

928

January 6: Cathan Lord Drummond is knighted by King Rhys Michael, and is appointed his aide.
March 11: Prince Miklós and Prince Marek interview the Countess Sudrey at Lochalyn Castle in the presence of her husband, Hrorik II Earl of Eastmarch; she renounces her family ties to the House of Furstán.
May 23: Hereditary Duke and Prince Imre and Princess Imriella are born to Marek Pretender of Gwynedd and Charis Duchess of Tolán.

EVENTS OF *THE BASTARD PRINCE* (MAY-JULY 928)

May 30: Count Kennet is born to Stacia Heiress of Eastmarch and Corban Lord Howell. Hrorik II Earl of Eastmarch receives warning of an incursion by Torenthi forces into the Coldoire Pass, and he and Corban ride immediately with a troop of soldiers to investigate.
June 7: Prince Miklós occupies Culliecairn Castle at the head of the Coldoire Pass. Earl Hrorik agrees to parley with Prince Miklós, but is killed when the flag of truce is dishonoured, aged XLV years. His daughter, the Lady Stacia succeeds as Countess of Eastmarch, with her husband, Corban Lord Howell, becoming Earl *jure uxoris*.
June 8: Hrorik's body is returned to his Castle at Lochalyn by Corban, who has been slightly wounded. Corban puts Captain Murray in charge of Lochalyn Castle while the Earl rides for Marley. Messengers are sent to Graham I Duke of Claibourne, Sigehere Earl of Marley, and Rhys Michael King of Gwynedd.
June 14: The II messengers from Eastmarch arrive in Rhemuth, and report to the Council. The Council debates whether the King should be allowed to take part in the defense of the Kingdom. A herald from Prince Miklós arrives at Court and demands audience with the King. The Royal Council agrees to receive the ambassador, with the following members present: Rhys Michael, Hubert, Paulin, Robert Oriss, Tammaron, Rhun, Manfred, Albertus, and Richard Murdoch. Also present are Constable Udaut, Cathan, Dimitri, and Fulk. The herald, Eugen von Roslov, demands that Rhys Michael present himself at Culliecairn in X days to honour the christening of Prince Imre, Prince Marek's infant son and heir, and that he agree to the presentation of that fortress to Prince Imre. Eugen then throws down the gauntlet. After much discussion, Rhys Michael accepts the challenge, and decides to go North with his soldiers. Hubert consults with Paulin and Dimitri. The Council meets again to discuss the final arrangements for the expedition, and then summons the King. Rhysel Thuryn transports to the Haven to inform Joram, Ansel, Camlin MacLean, her brother Tieg, Niallan, Jesse, and Queron of the new developments; she recommends that Rhys Michael be brought to his Haldane potential that evening. After much discussion, they agree that Rhysel, Tieg, Joram, and Michaela will provide the catalyst for Rhys Michael's empowerment. Rhysel returns to Rhemuth. Michaela, Rhys Michael, and Sir Cathan Drummond dine in the King's quarters. Rhysel interrupts their dinner, and takes control of Michaela and Cathan. She tells Rhys Michael of their plans to enable his Haldane potential, and he agrees to let it proceed; she is the first Deryni to make contact with the Royal family in the VI years since King Javan's murder. They all swear on the Haldane brooch to help each other and to keep faith. Joram and Tieg transport to the library disguised as a Haldane man-at-arms and a squire; Tieg has trimmed his Gabrilite-style braid. They return to the King's quarters to find Fulk present, but Rhysel takes control of Fulk's mind, and makes certain that he will be the King's man in the future. Michaela and Cathan's Deryni powers are restored by Tieg, who removes the blocks that had been placed on them by Tavis years before. Rhys Michael receives his Haldane powers; he experiences the spiritual presence of both King Cinhil I and Camber Earl of Culdi. Joram and Tieg return to the Haven. In the cellar of Rhemuth Palace Master Dimitri encounters the young guard, Iosif, and uses him to transmit a message to his real master, Prince Miklós, at Culliecairn Castle. The Prince then tells his cousin Prince Marek that Rhys Michael will be riding North on the following day, and that he will himself challenge the King to a duel arcane. Marek promises Miklós the Duchy of Mooryn when Marek becomes King of Gwynedd. Dimitri unexpectedly meets Joram and Tieg as he returns to his quarters; they overpower his mind and read him, determining the true depth of his betrayal of Gwynedd. Joram takes the spy back to the Haven with them. Dimitri's mind is then altered to make him a weapon against the former Regents, and he is returned to Rhemuth Palace.
June 15: Rhysel communicates the news of Dimitri's entrapment to Michaela, who passes it to her husband. Archbishop Hubert offers a mass of dedication at the Cathedral for the success of the expedition. Rhys Michael and his hundred Haldane lancers and other levies assemble to depart Rhemuth for Eastmarch, together with the Lords Richard Murdoch, Manfred, Albertus, Paulin, Rhun, Fulk, Quiric, Cathan, Ainslie, and Cashel; more forces will be added along the way. Tammaron and Udaut will stay behind. Archbishop Robert Oriss blesses the troops as they file out, but Lord Udaut's horse is spooked by Dimitri, and the Constable is thrown to the ground, being instantly killed by a broken back. Richard Murdoch is appointed Lord Constable in his place, and is delegated to remain behind in Rhemuth. The expedition finally

departs the city. Lord Udaut is aged LXIX years at his death, being succeeded by his son, Lord Moray.

June 17: Jesse and Ansel collect XL former Michaeline knights to serve as an adjunct force available to take action on behalf of the Deryni underground movement. They depart for Lochalyn Castle to offer their services to Lady Sudrey, who accepts them. Graham I Duke of Claibourne and Sighere Earl of Marley assemble their levies at Lochalyn.

June 18: While riding along an embankment of the River Eirian, the lead riders of the Expedition are attacked by a swarm of bees. Lord Albertus and a companion *Custodes* knight are forced into the water; Albertus escapes, the other man drowns. The King and his party pass Valoret later that afternoon; LXXX *Custodes* knights under the command of Lord Joshua join them there. They camp near Sheele that night, and are joined by Rhun's XX-man levy, commanded by his castellan, Sir Drogo, who also provides new provisions for the growing army.

June 19: At Ebor the Expedition is joined by Manfred's levy of L Culdi lancers commanded by his son Iver Earl of Kierney. *Soliveau de la fable.*

June 20: The Expedition reaches the Iomaire plain. They encamp that evening near Saint Cassian's Abbey. Dispatches are received from Lady Sudrey. The King and his Lords dine at the Refectory. That evening, Rhys Michael is confronted by Lord Albertus, with the Deryni Dimitri, Fulk, and Cathan present. Albertus questions the King about Udaut's death. Dimitri confirms the truthfulness of the monarch's answers. Albertus then orders Dimitri to probe Rhys Michael's mind. Dimitri transmits a mental message to the King that he is compelled to help him whatever the cost to Dimitri, and that Rhys Michael should respond outwardly as a human. As Albertus continues to push his Deryni agent to extreme measures, Dimitri abruptly takes over Albertus's mind and confirms his suspicions about the latter's treachery, showing Rhys Michael how Albertus participated in the murder of King Javan. He then stops Albertus's heart; Albertus is LI years of age at his death. Cathan and Fulk make a token call for help, but Albertus cannot be revived. Paulin, Manfred, and Rhun respond, together with Father Ascelin and Master Stevanus, and Ascelin gives Albertus the last rites. Paulin asks very pointed questions of the King and particularly of Dimitri. Master Stevanus sticks Dimitri with a Deryni "pricker" tainted with *merasha*; before he loses control, Dimitri rips Paulin's mind, leaving him a mental vegetable. Dimitri is then tortured by Magan, Lior, and Gallard on the orders of Rhun, and dies a suicide when a mental trigger is tripped, aged XLVIII years, but not before reporting mentally to Prince Miklós at Culliecairn. Queron learns of Dimitri's death, and reports to Joram on the recent casualties. A brief War Council is held at Saint Cassian's Abbey: Rhun assumes the title of Earl Marshal, with Manfred as his Vice Marshal; Joshua becomes Acting Grand Master of the *Equites Custodum Fidei*, and Father Lior becomes Acting Vicar General of the *Custodes Fidei*.

June 21: Before Lord Albertus is buried in the crypt at Saint Cassian's, Dimitri's body is burned for heresy; and Albertus's body, the unconscious Paulin, the King, and the Great Lords are all exorcised by Father Kimball. The Expedition reaches Lochalyn Castle. The King is greeted by Sighere Earl of Marley, Sighere's son and heir Sean Coris, and Corban Howell Earl of Eastmarch. At the Castle the Lady Sudrey asks the King to accompany her to the chapel to pay his respects to the late Earl Hrorik, and she tells him that she is loyal to the House of Haldane, that she still has Deryni powers, and that she believes that her feud with Prince Miklós is partly responsible for the latter's incursion. Rhun threatens the King for meeting privately with Sudrey. Miklós requests a meeting with the King on the following day. Ansel, Jesse, and Tieg discuss their options in one of the outlying camps surrounding the Castle.

June 22: A joint command over the Eastmarch and Haldane forces is established, and a messenger is sent to Culliecairn, demanding that Miklós make his response via a human envoy only. The Torenthis send back Hombard of Tarkent, who is tested with *merasha* by Stevanus and Gallard, and then states that Miklós will withdraw from Culliecairn only if the King and Sudrey will meet privily with the Prince and Hombard. The War Council discusses the situation. Sudrey is asked to probe Rhys Michael's mind to see if he has been altered by Dimitri; in reality, they exchange thoughts in front of the Great Lords, without the Council being aware of their communication. At Culliecairn Miklós and Marek question Hombard regarding his meeting with Rhys Michael, and make their plans. That afternoon the King, accompanied by Lady Sudrey, parleys with Prince Miklós and "Hombard" in the Coldoire Pass; unbeknowst to the King, Prince Marek has assumed the shape of Hombard. Miklós suddenly brands Sudrey a traitor to her line and attacks her with magic, but is himself killed by King Rhys Michael, whose hand is injured when a horse tramples on it. Marek escapes, and Sudrey dies. Prince Miklós is XXIII years of age at his death; Sudrey is XXXIV years of age, and is publicly credited with Miklós's passing. Prince Marek and the Healer Cosim determine that Miklós was actually killed by Rhys Michael's magic; Cosim doctors Marek's memory to keep the knowledge from Arion I King of Torenth. Marek orders the Torenthi forces to withdraw from Culliecairn. He keeps a vigil beside his cousin's body through the night. Corban takes Sudrey's body back to Lochalyn Castle; Graham and Sighere remain with their forces in the Coldoire Pass. Stevanus treats the King's injured hand while Rhun begins closely questioning the monarch about the events of the day, which Rhun and Manfred could only see from a distance. Rhys Michael claims that Sudrey actually killed Miklós, and that the other man was Prince Marek masquerading as Hombard. Prince Marek sends Rhys Michael a message blaming him for the death of Miklós, but states that he is abandoning Culliecairn Castle. The King sends a mental message to Cathan advising him of his new plans. The pair seize control of Fulk and Stevanus, and Rhys makes the surgeon his own man for the future. Ansel, Tieg, and Jesse discuss the day's events in their camp outside Lochalyn. The King's tent is too well guarded to allow the Healer Tieg to enter it. Ansel reports mentally to Joram.

June 23: The Torenthi army leaves Culliecairn at dawn accompanying Prince Miklós's funeral cortège. Rhun, Manfred, Corban, and Joshua ride out after breakfast to observe the Torenthi withdrawal. Rhys Michael goes to Lochalyn with a *Custodes* escort to pay his respects to Stacia Countess of Eastmarch and the late Countess Sudrey. The King intervenes between Graham I Duke of Claibourne's men and Gallard's *Equites* to prevent an armed clash; the Church knights are left outside the Castle gates with Gallard and Lior. In the chapel Rhys Michael tells Graham and Stacia of the former Regents' murder of King Javan and of their imprisonment of and control over the King and Queen, and asks them to cooperate in setting up a new Regency dominated by the loyal Lords of Kheldour and Eastmarch, in the event that Rhys Michael does not survive. Iver Earl of Kierney interrupts their discussion, and announces that Culliecairn Castle has been vacated. Cathan is ordered to prepare a codicil to Rhys Michael's will, appointing Graham and Sighere to Owain's Regency Council, with Sighere's son Sean Coris as his potential replacement if Sighere dies, the appointments being irrevocable save by the King. The King rides to Culliecairn to inspect the reoccupation of that fortress. In Rhemuth Rhysel tells Michaela of the King's injury and of the deaths of Sudrey and Miklós. The Queen visits her son and heir, Hereditary Prince Owain. That evening Rhys Michael returns to Lochalyn, where he spends the night; he now has a fever, and his hand has swollen. The King tells Stevanus that he will not allow his hand to be amputated. Cathan shows Rhys Michael the new codicil to his will, which he approves; Cathan works through the night to prepare V original copies for signature the next day. *Über allen Gipfeln ist Ruh.*

June 24: Lady Sudrey is buried at Lochalyn. The King's fever continues. Rhys Michael takes the oaths of Stacia and Corban as new Countess and Earl of Eastmarch, giving Stacia symbols of her office, and also receives the renewed fealty of Graham I Duke of Claibourne and Sighere Earl of Marley, sealing their oaths man-to-man with a kiss to the hand. During the banquet held later that day in celebration, the new codicil to King Rhys Michael's will is signed by V persons who slip away from dinner I by I—Graham, Sighere, Stacia, Father Derfel, and the King—the document being witnessed by Father Derfel, the Castle chaplain. Rhun nearly interrupts the King as he is signing the documents, but Sighere, pretending to be drunk, distracts him. Rhys Michael completes his work, and is treated with the drug *tacil* by Mother Angelica, a midwife from the local village who is brought to him by Stacia. He orders Cathan to have copies of the codicil dispersed, retaining I for the King, and at the King's behest Sir Cathan commands Sir Robert Ainslie to take I original copy of the document to Queen Michaela in Rhemuth. The King then compels Fulk to write a document which he dictates, signs, and seals, in which Rhys Michael commands and authorizes the Duke of Claibourne and the Earl of Marley in the event of the King's death to appoint Sir Cathan Drummond to the Regency Council governing King Owain. Bishop Paulin Sinclair of Ramos dies at Saint Cassian's Abbey, aged XLIX years. *El que callar no puede, hablar no sabe.*

June 25: Paulin of Ramos is buried beside his brother in the crypt of Saint Cassian's. The King's fever seems improved by the *tacil*; he confirms that Robert Ainslie has left. The King and his army depart Lochalyn in mid-morning for Rhemuth; however, the levies of Caerrorie, Sheele, and Valoret will remain at Eastmarch for another week under the command of Joshua and Iver. Tieg and Jesse visit Stacia before they leave, inquiring about the extent of Rhys Michael's injuries and learning of the new codicil to his will; she allows Tieg to read her memories, briefly blocking her meager powers; he determines that the "*tacil*" used to treat the King is probably *talicil*, a mainstay of the Healer's pharmacopeia. Later Tieg reports to Queron at the Camberian Council, who calls the Council into session and shares the Healer's intelligence with Joram, Rickart, Queron, Niallan, and Camlin. Queron proposes to transport to Tor Caerrorie disguised as an intinerant hospitaller, and to travel thence to Valoret, Sheele, and Ebor, intercepting the army along the way and possibly healing the monarch's injury. Ansel, Jesse, and Tieg are ordered to shadow the army as it moves South. At the same time, Archbishop Hubert MacInnis and Father Secorim are attending Archbishop Robert Oriss in his final illness at his residence in Rhemuth when Brother Fabius, a monk of Saint Cassian's Abbey, arrives, handing them missives telling of the deaths of Albertus and Dimitri and the injury to Paulin's mind. Hubert summons the Royal Council, with the following present: Secorim, Fabius, Tammaron, Richard Murdoch, and Bonner Earl of Tarleton. The Council orders CC troops drawn from Carthane and *Arx Fidei* to defend Rhemuth against a possible invasion by Prince Marek. The King's Expedition reaches Saint Cassian's Abbey, where the army stays the night. Father Lior and Abbot Kimball request Rhys Michael's presence at a special prayer service for Paulin's soul. The King is examined by Brothers Polidorus, Stevanus, and Deiniol. Polidorus confiscates the remaining *tacil* as a Deryni drug, proposing cautery for the Monarch's hand, and recommending that he be bled. Rhys Michael tells Cathan to fetch Rhun and to inform him of the existence of the codicil. Rhun arrives and speaks to the King privily about his will. Rhys Michael gets Rhun to examine his hand and then controls him. He sets a series of irresistible commands in the soldier, and then blocks all memory of his actions. Stevanus is allowed to enter and dress his hand, but Polidorus is banned from the room. Queron continues riding to a rendezvous with the army.

June 26: The news of Prince Miklós's death and the King's injury reaches Rhemuth in early morning, and the Councilors are summoned from their beds. At the same time in Torenth, Prince Marek faces the wrath of Arion I King of Torenth, who examines him closely; Captain Valentin defends Marek's actions. Cosim assists in the mental probe of the Prince. Marek is ordered to bring Miklós's body to Beldour by land. The King's Expedition resumes its travel South, leaving Saint Cassian's that morning, accompanied by Brother Polidorus, and encamping on the Iomaire Plain that night. For his II sons the King implants in the Haldane brooch the key to the magical potential carried by his House, with mental instructions to Queen Michaela for its use. He then sets a last mental message in Cathan Drummond for his wife. Ansel, Jesse, and Tieg compare notes in a camp several miles away from the army. Queron transports to Tor Caerrorie, and emerges disguised as a common monk. He takes a horse from a nearby barn, and heads cross country.

June 27: Queron reaches an area just North of Valoret, hiding during the daylight hours. The army proceeds South, but the King continues to burn with fever. At midday his condition takes a dramatic turn for the worse when he has a convulsion. The convulsions continue to grow worse by the hour, and the doctors give him *merasha* as a sedative. The convoy returns to Saint Ostrythe's Convent an hour's ride back up the road, where the nuns again treat the King. Later that day Lior and Manfred assume control of the King's treatment, and have Brother Polidorus bleed the King over the protests of Stevanus and Rhun. Rhun is sedated and restrained. The King is bled IV times during the next day. *Après la mort le médicin*.

June 28: Queron, using the name "Father Donatus" and wearing the habit of Saint Jarlath's, reaches the Gwyneddan army at Saint Ostrythe's Convent. He probes a nun for news of the King's condition, and offers himself as a priest for the monarch's confession. Unable to reverse the King's failing condition, Dom Queron hears his final confession and gives him the last rites. The spirit of Camber makes an appearance. King Rhys Michael dies of his injuries and subsequent bad treatment by the *Custodes*, leaving a new will which names a completely different and favourable set of Regents for his son. The King is XXI years of age at his death. Cathan takes the Haldane brooch and the Eye of Rom from the King's body. Queron leaves the Abbey before he can be questioned, and successfully escapes. He contacts the Camberian Council and transmits the news of the King's death. Cathan and Fulk discover that the King's injured hand has been amputated to account for his extreme blood loss, and are ordered to give lip service to the story that Rhys Michael's wound had become gangrenous; they are drugged and bled to keep them docile. Prince Owain Haldane succeeds to the throne at the age of IV. Sir Robert Ainslie arrives at Rhemuth Castle with an original copy of the King's codicil to his will, and gives it and Rhys Michael's signet ring to Rhysel to pass along to Michaela. She reads his mind while kissing him, and allows him to retain the pleasant memories. She then contacts Joram, who tells her of the King's death and asks her to keep the news from Michaela for as long as possible. She hides the document and ring.

June 29: Robert Oriss Archbishop of Rhemuth dies during the early morning hours, aged LXXX years. A requiem mass is said in his honour at Saint George's Cathedral, presided over by Bishop Alfred of Woodbourne; Oriss's body will lie in state for two days. Rhysel meets Robert Ainslie and tells him the news; he must still return immediately to the army and save Cathan Drummond. She imprints in his mind a mental message for Cathan to read. Before leaving, he asks her to marry him. Tammaron receives a message from Rhun concerning the codicil to King Rhys Michael's will, and confirming Paulin's death. Hubert names Secorim as Archbishop-designate of Rhemuth, automatically making him a member of the Royal Council. Rhys Michael's funeral procession leaves Saint Ostrythe's Convent, with his coffined body born on a litter. Cathan Drummond follows behind the bier; he has been drugged by Brother Embert, his newly appointed physician. Stevanus reports to Cathan that Fulk has been sent under house arrest to his brother's court at Cassan, and confesses that the *Custodes* Order is hopelessly tainted; he himself has been ordered to Ramos because of the knowledge he possesses of the King's death.

June 30: Stevanus and a half dozen other *Custodes* leave the expedition for imprisonment and correction at Ramos, the Mother House of that order. Ansel and Tieg ride into Lochalyn Castle, and meet with Stacia, Graham, Sighere, and Corban, telling them of the King's death. The *Custodes* knights remaining under the command of Lord Joshua are sent North to Arranal Canyon with Iver MacInnis to remove them from Lochalyn Castle while the new Regents, Graham I Duke of Claiburne and Sighere Earl of Marley, ride South to Rhemuth. The Expedition encamps West of Ramos on the Eirian River. *Pendent opera interrupta*.

July 1: Sir Robert Ainslie returns to the Gwyneddan army and contacts Cathan, delivering the mental message implanted by Rhysel and receiving a message in return. Ainslie reports that night to Jesse MacGregor in a nearby camp, who passes it along to Joram. Robert Oriss Archbishop of Rhemuth is buried in the crypt beneath Saint George's Cathedral. Sir Rondel arrives from Rhun with a message to the Royal Council telling of King Rhys Michael's death, and of the new codicil to the King's will. He also relates the real circumstances of the monarch's death. Secorim, the newest member of the Council, agrees to support the fabricated story; he would have been killed otherwise. The Queen is told of her husband's death by Hubert.

July 2: Rhysel helps Michaela cope with Rhys Michael's passing. Prince Owain is informed of the news and is proclaimed King of Gwynedd by Earl Tammaron.

July 3: The funeral procession of King Rhys Michael reaches Rhemuth that afternoon. The body of the monarch lies in state for II days. Cathan tells Michaela about her husband's death and gives her the Eye of Rom and the Haldane brooch. Cathan and Manfred are questioned by the old Regency Council; also present are Hubert, Tammaron, Rhun, Lior, Richard Murdoch, and Secorim. Cathan testifies to the validity of the codicil to the late King's will. Hubert promises to kill Cathan once the Queen is delivered of her child, or to torture him if she loses it. Rhysel examines the brooch, and tells the Queen that it holds the Haldane potential and also contains a personal message to her from her late husband. They decide to set the potential in Owain that evening while keeping the boy asleep. Camber makes his presence felt during the ceremony. Rhysel reports to Joram about the day's events. Cathan is bled by Lior and Polidorus, and is then drugged and shackled to the wall of his cell. The old Council meets late at night to consider the Regency problem; they question Cathan about Father Donatus, the King's last confessor.

July 4: Cathan and Michaela sleep much of the day. Owain now has the mental aspect of a Deryni child. The Kheldour Lords pass through Valoret, and gain the aid of Ailin Auxiliary Bishop of Valoret, who joins their party. They stop briefly later that day at Mollingford to change horses. The old Regents meet again that evening; they dispatch CC knights to the North along the River Eirian under the command of Earl Richard Murdoch to meet any force coming South from Eastmarch.

July 5: Cathan is visited by Manfred, Gallard, and the *Custodes* physician Embert, who again drugs the Queen's brother. King Rhys Michael is buried with his ancestors in the crypt of Saint George's Cathedral next to his father, King Cinhil I, and his II royal brothers. The Duke of Claibourne and Earl of Marley arrive at Rhemuth with their forces and with Bishop Ailin, who gets them through the East Gate; with them are Tieg, Ansel, Queron, Father Derfel, and L knights. They surround Saint George's Cathedral and begin closing the trap, securing the interior of the building while the Great Lords, the Queen, the young King, and Sir Cathan are still in the crypt. Lord Ainslie and his men join forces with the border Lords. The new Regency Council then assumes power in a *coup d'état*, and declares Rhun and Manfred outlaw and their lives forfeit. Cathan is saved as he exits the crypt, and his captor Gallard is killed by Ansel. Rhun abruptly knifes Manfred in the chest while acting under a compulsion previously set in his mind by King Rhys Michael, and slashes the neck of Lior. Tammaron grabs Queen Michaela as a hostage and unjustly accuses her son of being Manfred's bastard, but is killed by her magic: she suddenly stops his heart. Rhun kidnaps King Owain, but is slain by Cathan. Cathan is immediately appointed to the new Council by Graham and Sighere. Archbishop Hubert is arrested by the new Regents. Tammaron is aged LIII years at his death, and is succeeded as Earl by his son, Fane Regent of Cassan. Manfred is aged LIII years at his death, and is succeeded as Earl by his son, Iver Earl of Kierney. Rhun is XLIII years of age at his death, and is succeeded by his son, Lord Isarn. Sir Gallard de Breffni is XLII years of age at his death.

July 7: Father Lior dies of his wounds, aged LII years.

July 9: Master Stevanus is killed at Ramos.

July 11: Archbishop Hubert is deposed from his office and from the Council, and is banished to confinement at Saint Iveagh's Abbey in Claibourne, where he must submit to a regimen of fasting and penance. Bishop Ailin MacGregor is elected his successor as Archbishop Primate of Valoret and All Gwynedd, and Bishop Alfred of Woodbourne is selected Archbishop of Rhemuth. Bishop Dermot is brought back by the new Archbishops from exile and named Auxiliary Bishop of Valoret. *Pone seram, cohibe; sed quis custodiet ipsos Custodes?*

July 12: The *Custodes* Abbey at Ramos is dissolved and given to the *Ordo Verbi Dei*. The *Custodes* Abbey at Rhemuth is also dissolved and the Order's ecclesiastical knights (the *Equites Custodum Fidei*) are disbanded. Brother Polidorus and Father Magan are stripped of their ecclesiastical offices and handed over to the secular courts for trial. Father Marcus Concannon is confirmed as head of the *Custodes* under his old title of Chancellor General, with the charge of reforming the Order. Father Secorim is elected Auxiliary Bishop of Rhemuth.

July 13: Some of the Statutes of Ramos are rescinded, although the rules forbidding Deryni participation in holy orders remain.

July 15: Brother Polidorus and Father Magan are tried, convicted, and hanged; their bodies are buried in a potter's field.

July 16: Vantry Lord Cerdagne and a former *Equis Custodum Fidei* commits suicide, aged XLIV years.

August 2: Lord Ainslie and his son Robert are appointed to the new Regency Council, which officially convenes on this date. The heirs of the old Great Lords are deposed from the Council, but allowed to retain their titles and estates.

August 10: Sir Fulk Fitz-Arthur is recalled from Cassan to testify against the King's murderers, and is appointed a Royal Equerry.

August 21: Sir Robert Ainslie marries Rhysel Lady Thuryn.

September 29: Prince Owain is crowned King of Gwynedd by Ailin MacGregor Archbishop Primate of Valoret and All Gwynedd. The young Tambert I Duke of Cassan swears fealty to the new King, beginning a long friendship that will later prove tragic. Richard Murdoch Earl of Carthane fails to attend the coronation, protesting ill health. *Quod semper, quod ubique, quod ab omnibus creditum est.*

December 26: Queen Michaela visits Rhemuth Cathedral with Cathan, Owain, and Archbishop Ailin. There they see the newly carved effigy of King Rhys Michael on his tomb. *Vixi! et, quem dederat cursum fortuna, peregi.*

****
929

January 15: Prince Uthyr is born posthumously to Rhys Michael King of Gwynedd and Michaela Lady Drummond, and is created Duke of Carthmoor.

March 7: Ygor Sovereign Kniaz' of Jándrich dies, aged LXIII years; by treaty his country becomes part of Torenth of this date. Prince Sigard of Torenth is created Duke of Jándrich by his father, King Arion I.

May 6: Sean Coris Hereditary Count of Marley marries Juliana Lady Horthness.

May 14: Ansel Lord MacRorie marries Fiona Lady MacLean.

May 21: Tambert I Duke of Cassan marries Adelicia Lady of Horthness.

November 30: Hubert MacInnis ex-Archbishop Primate of Valoret and All Gwynedd dies, aged LIII years.

930

April 12: Jesse Hereditary Count of Ebor and Trevalga marries Tiarna MacMurray; Sir Cashel Murdoch *Senior* disrupts the ceremony and challenges Jesse to a duel, but is defeated and killed in a fair fight, aged XXVI years. *Post prælia præmia.*

931

January 31: Reynard III Duc du Joux dies, and is succeeded in Joux by his elder daughter, Lady Camille, and in Thuria by his IInd daughter, Lady Violette.

932
February 10: Gregory Earl of Ebor and Sovereign Count of Trevalga dies, aged LVII years, and is succeeded in Trevalga by his son, Sir Jesse, in the latter title.
April 4: Sir Jesse MacGregor is confirmed as Sovereign Count of Trevalga by the Council of Sovereign Princes of The Connait. *Connaita locuta est; causa finita est.*
May 12: Crevan Allyn Vicar General of the Knights of the Anvil (formerly the Order of Saint Michael) dies in exile at Djellarda, aged LXX years.
May 18: Rhupen III King of R'Kassi marries Violette Sovereign Princess of Thuria.
October 2: Duvessa Princess of Cassan dies, aged LXII years.

933
June 16: Princess Chariella is born to Marek Pretender of Gwynedd and Charis Duchess of Tolán.
September 3: Rhupen III King of R'Kassi is deposed, and flees across the border into his wife's Principality of Thuria.
October 10: Hereditary Duke Rogan is born to Torval I Duke d'Arjenol and Princess Braïda Heiress d'Arjenol.
November 30: Ulliam ap Lugh Bishop of Nyford dies, aged LXXXIV years.

934
April 29: Hereditary Duke Tammaron is born to Tambert I Duke of Cassan and Adelicia Lady of Horthness.
December 6: Prince Ysarn is created Duke of Marluk by Arion I King of Torenth.

935
February 18: Eusebios I Patriarch of Torenth dies, aged LXXXI years.
May 11: Taysan Duke of Corwyn dies, aged LIX years, and is succeeded by his son, Lord Arion.
May 13: Eunomios Metropolitan of Ortenbourg is elected Patriarch of Torenth.
August 25: Tieg Lord Thuryn marries Karis Lady d'Oriel.
December 30: Sighere Earl of Marley dies, aged XLIX years, and is succeeded by his son, Hereditary Count Sean Coris.

936
May 17: Lord Flynn is born to Tambert I Duke of Cassan and Adelicia Lady of Horthness.
September 9: Torcuill Baron de la Marche and Count Marchmont dies at his estate in The Connait, aged LXXV years, and is succeeded by his son, Lord Tomhar, in the latter title.

937
April 30: Sir Cathan Drummond marries Jerusha Lady Thuryn.
November 30: Captain Murray dies, aged XLVIII years.

938
March 1: King Owain attains his majority and the Regency Council is disbanded. Ainslie Lord Argoed announces his retirement from the King's service.
April 16: Lord Joël is born to Ithel mac Judah Count of Castlethorn in Meara and Farrah Lady Henstridge.

939
March 11: Károly Hereditary Prince of Torenth marries Zubayda Nabila of Tôrtous.
November 16: Hobard Hereditary Count of Culdi marries Maud Lady Udaut.

940
January 9: Agnes Dowager Countess of Sheele dies, aged XL years.
April 19: Prince Malachy is born to Károly Hereditary Prince of Torenth and Zubayda Nabila of Tôrtous.
June 9: Hrorik Ewan Earl of Rhendall and Hereditary Duke of Claibourne marries Janeltis Lady MacInnis and Baroness Marlor, the latter title being deeded to her on this date as a dowry by her father Iver Earl of Culdi.
September 11: Lord Richard is born to Hobard Hereditary Count of Culdi and Maud Lady Udaut.
December 3: Lord Jován is born to Lord Nazár Csigály and Lady Ivanna Lélek.

941
October 20: Ailin MacGregor Archbishop Primate of Valoret and All Gwynedd dies in his sleep, aged LXVII years. *Quæ sint, quæ fuerint, quæ mox ventura trahantur.*
December 1: Bishop Dermot O'Beirne is elected Archbishop Primate of Valoret and All Gwynedd.

942
May 11: Prince Marek later Markos II Patriarch of Torenth is born to Károly Hereditary Prince of Torenth and Zubayda Nabila of Tôrtous. *God sufficeth me.*
November 18: Eunomios Patriarch of Torenth dies, aged LXI years.
November 21: Bishop Niallan Trey dies in exile, aged LXXVI years.

943
January 15: Prince Uthyr comes of age and the regency of the Duchy of Carthmoor is lifted by King Owain, his brother.
May 6: Loukas Abbot of Saint Sviatoslav is elected Patriarch of Torenth.
June 14: Lord Quiric Fitz-Arthur marries Émeraude Baroness of Horthness in her own right, and becomes Baron of Horthness *jure uxoris*.

944
March 11: Lord Quinn is born to Ithel mac Judah Count of Castlethorn in Meara and Lady Farrah.
March 12: Loukas Patriarch of Torenth dies, aged LXXIII years.
June 13: Princess Márisa is born to Károly Hereditary Prince of Torenth and Zubayda Nabila of Tôrtous.
July 11: Andreas Metropolitan of Tolán is elected Patriarch of Torenth.
July 23: Ysarn Prince of Torenth and Duke of Marluk marries the Princess Imriella daughter of Marek Pretender of Gwynedd and Charis Duchess of Tolán.
September 30: William Lord de Borgos dies, aged LXXXII years, and is succeeded by his son, Lord Ysick.

945
May 2: Nieve Dowager Countess of Tarleton and Fitz-Arthur dies, aged LXXXIV years.
May 7: Imre II King of Torenth is beatified at Beldour by Patriarch Andreas I.
December 23: Joshua Lord Delacroix dies, aged LVI years.

946
August 29: Estellan Dowager Countess of Culdi dies, aged LXXI years.

September 13: Prince Mátyás is born to Károly Hereditary Prince of Torenth and Zubayda Nabila of Tôrtous.
November 20: Father Marcus Concannon Chancellor General of the *Custodes Fidei* dies, aged LXIX years.

947

May 2: In a magnificent royal double wedding in Rhemuth, Owain King of Gwynedd marries Anne Lady Fitz-Arthur Quinnell, sister of Tambert I Duke of Cassan, and Prince Uthyr Duke of Carthmoor marries Grania Lady MacInnis.
June 9: Kennet Hereditary Count of Eastmarch marries Tanya Lady Marley.

948

March 11: Princess Marisa is born to Owain King of Gwynedd and Anne Lady Fitz-Arthur Quinnell.
March 19: Marisa Princess of Gwynedd dies of the flux, aged I week and I day.
April 4: Alfred Archbishop of Rhemuth dies of plague, aged LXXIII years, being among the Iˢᵗ victims of a new and widespread outbreak of the Black Death. Many humans blame the Deryni for the recurrence of the disease.
April 29: Rostaing d'Ancézune or Danson is elected Archbishop of Rhemuth.
April 30: An anti-Deryni riot breaks out in Rhemuth, and is suppressed with great difficulty.
May-July: The Festillic Pretender Prince Marek I, son of Imre and Ariella, attempts to retake the Gwyneddan throne, but is defeated and returns to his Duchy of Tolán; Károly Hereditary Prince of Torenth loses an arm in this engagement. King Owain dies, aged XXIV years, and is succeeded by his brother, Prince Uthyr Duke of Carthmoor. Also perishing during this period are: Andreas Patriarch of Torenth, aged LXII years; Ansel Lord MacRorie, aged XLVIII years; Ardis Lady MacLean, aged LXIX years; Banbhan Earl of Kilshane, aged XXVI years, when his title escheats to the Crown; Bonner II Sinclair Earl of Tarleton, aged XLVIII years; Camber Lord MacLean, aged XLII years; Cashel Murdoch *Junior* Earl of Carthane, aged XXV years, his title being attainted; Dermot O'Beirne Archbishop Primate of Valoret and All Gwynedd, aged LXXII years; Fane Earl Fitz-Arthur, aged LII years, who is succeeded by his son, Lord Eldon; Fiona Lady MacLean, aged LV years; Graham I MacEwan Duke of Claibourne, aged XLI years, who is succeeded by his grandson, Lord Ewan II; Hobard MacInnis Earl of Kierney, aged XXVI years, who is succeeded by his son, Lord Richard; Hrorik Ewan Earl of Rhendall and Hereditary Duke of Claibourne, aged XXV years, who is succeeded by his daughter, Gillian, as Countess of Rhendall, and by his son, Lord Ewan II, as Hereditary Duke; Iver MacInnis Earl of Culdi, aged LII years, who is succeeded by his son, Lord Hobard, as Earl of Kierney, and his daughter, Lady Grania, as Countess of Culdi; Father Joram MacRorie, aged LXIX years; Karis Lady Thuryn, aged XXXI years; Richard Murdoch Earl of Carthane, aged XLVI years, who is succeeded by his son, Lord Cashel; Rostaing d'Ancézune Archbishop of Rhemuth, aged XLVII years; Sean Coris Earl of Marley, aged XXXIX years, who is succeeded by his son, Lord Brian; Secorim Archbishop Primate of Valoret and All Gwynedd, aged LXIX years; Tambert I Fitz-Arthur Quinnell Duke of Cassan, aged XXIX years, who is succeeded by his son, Lord Tammaron; Tieg Lord Thuryn, aged XXXIII years.
September 15: Bertrand de Tolbert is elected Archbishop Primate of Valoret and All Gwynedd; Piers Caradawg is elected Archbishop of Rhemuth.
September 21: Princess Margitella is born to Károly Hereditary Prince of Torenth and Zubayda Nabila of Tôrtous.
September 29: Prince Uthyr is crowned King of Gwynedd by Bertrand de Tolbert Archbishop Primate of Valoret and All Gwynedd.
September 30: Hereditary Prince Nygel is born to Uthyr King of Gwynedd and Grania MacInnis Countess of Culdi.
October 16: Rhouphinos Metropolitan of Podébrad is elected Patriarch of Torenth. *Surely God wrongs not men, but themselves men wrong.*
November 15: The Earldoms of Carthane and Tarleton are attainted by King Uthyr and the High Council of Gwynedd. Tudur Hereditary Count of Tarleton is allowed to succeed to the lesser title of Baron Sinclair. Sir Ralson de Cosnac is created Baron d'Evering, and Lord Fulk Fitz-Arthur is created Baron Viskin. *Opinionum commenta delet dies, naturæ judicia confirmat.*
December 12: Imre Hereditary Prince of Festil marries Tamara Countess of Netterhaven. *Русская женщина, трижды женщина.*

949

January 6: Glynway Lord Heavysege is created Earl of Pelagog in Cassan by King Uthyr.
February 3: Sir Robert Ainslie dies, aged XLVII years.
May 12: Rogan Hereditary Duke d'Arjenol marries the Princess Chariella daughter of Marek I Prince and Pretender of Gwynedd and Charis Duchess of Tolán.

950

January 31: Prince Mark-Imre is born to Imre II Hereditary Prince of Festil and Tamara Countess of Netterhaven.
May 11: Rolf Lord MacPherson, a Deryni, rebels against the Camberian Council.
August 17: Tammaron Duke of Cassan marries Tiphane Lady Ainslie.
August 29: Count Termöd is born to Rogan Hereditary Duke d'Arjenol and Chariella Princess of Festil.
November 1: Princess Mikhailina is born to Károly Hereditary Prince of Torenth and Nabila Zubayda.

951

May 12: Lady Swynbeth is born to Tammaron Duke of Cassan and Tiphane Lady Ainslie.
October 2: Prince Jasher is born to Uthyr King of Gwynedd and Grania MacInnis Countess of Culdi.

952

April 17: Lord Duchad is born to Angus Mór Count of Tigre and Messalina Lady Rhorau.
November 12: Cyril Baron d'Eirial dies, aged LXIV years, and is succeeded by his son, Lord Radulf.
December 15: Hereditary Duke Fane and Lady Nerina (twins) are born to Tammaron Duke of Cassan and Tiphane Lady Ainslie.

953

January 3: Prince Miroslav is born to Károly Hereditary Prince of Torenth and Zubayda Nabila of Tôrtous.

April 24: Prince Cluim is born to Uthyr King of Gwynedd and Grania MacInnis Countess of Culdi, and is created Earl of Carthane.
July 4: Lord Flynn Fitz-Arthur Quinnell is created Earl Derry and marries Margot Lady Murdoch.

955
March 17: Adelicia Duchess of Cassan dies, aged XLI years.
June 6: Uthyr King of Gwynedd meets with Arion I King of Torenth near Marbury, and they exchange pledges of peace during their lifetimes.

956
April 10: Radulf Baron d'Eirial marries Eanswith Lady Fenwick.
July 23: Edward MacInnis Bishop of Grecotha dies, aged LVIII years.
August 31: Prince Menander is born to Károly Hereditary Prince of Torenth and Zubayda Nabila of Tôrtous.

957
January 12: Hereditary Lord Gilrae is born to Radulf Baron d'Eirial and Eanswith Lady Fenwick, who dies in childbirth.
October 18: Sir Cathan Drummond dies, aged XLVII years.
October 26: Elinor Lady Drummond dies of apoplexy after receiving the news of her son's death, aged LXXVII years.

958
September 18: Radulf Baron d'Eirial marries Zillah Lady Davison.

959
December 24: Arik Rufimovich, second son of Rufim Katunovich and Héliada his wife, is born in the village of Oberpfitzner in the Duchy of Nördmarcke in Torenth.

960
April 16: Lord Caprus is born to Radulf Baron d'Eirial and Zillah Lady Davison.
June 23: Princess Mösza is born to Károly Hereditary Prince of Torenth and Zubayda Nabila of Tôrtous.
November 23: Károly Hereditary Prince of Torenth dies, aged XLII years, and is succeeded by his son, Prince Malachy.

961
January 30: Rhouphinos Patriarch of Torenth dies, aged LIX years. *God charges not any soul save to its ability.*
March 7: Lord Judhael is born to Joël Count of Ithelthorn and Faustina Contessa di Cebà.
April 30: Eusebios Abbot of Saint-Sasile is elected Patriarch of Torenth.

963
November 18: Alana Destaing d'Oriel dies, aged LXIV years.

964
July 11: Malachy Hereditary Prince of Torenth marries Ianthe Princess of Salonique.

965
August 4: Prince Nimur is born to Malachy Hereditary Prince of Torenth and Ianthe Princess of Salonique.
August 5: Jordan Sovereign Prince of Meara is killed in ambush by bandits near Ratharkin, aged LIII years, and is succeeded by his cousin, Ithel Count of Castlethorn.

966
March 9: Angus MacEwan Hereditary Duke of Claibourne is created Earl of Kheldour by King Uthyr Haldane.
May 31: Duchad Mór Lord of Tigre marries Ariella Princess of Festil.
June 12: Eusebios II Patriarch of Torenth dies, aged LXIV years.
September 4: Abraam Metropolitan of Netterhaven is elected Patriarch of Torenth.
November 4: Prince Carolus is born to Malachy Hereditary Prince of Torenth and Ianthe Princess of Salonique.

967
March 22: Princess Ariella Countess of Tigre dies, aged XV years, giving birth to identical twin sons, Prince Festil and Prince Blaine.
April 2: Stacia Countess of Eastmarch dies, aged LVIII years, and is succeeded by her son, Lord Kennet. *Non Angli sed angeli.*
October 15: Duchad Mór Lord of Tigre marries Saraid Lady Aileach.

968
August 20: Termöd Count d'Arjenol marries Rupali Rani of Sinjh.
October 18: Princess Arien is born to Malachy Hereditary Prince of Torenth and Ianthe Princess of Salonique.
November 16: Lord Angus is born to Duchad Mór Lord of Tigre and Saraid Lady Aileach.
December 9: Corban Howell Earl of Eastmarch *jure uxoris* dies, aged LXVIII years.

969
March 14: Abraam II Patriarch of Torenth dies, aged LXXI years.
May 15: Count Ringan is born to Termöd Hereditary Duke d'Arjenol and Rupali Rani of Sinjh.
July 18: Abraam Metropolitan of Arjenol is elected Patriarch of Torenth.

970
January 26: Janeltis Baroness Marlor and Dowager Countess of Rhendall dies, aged L years, and is succeeded in her title of Marlor by her son, Ewan II Duke of Claibourne.
March 7: Prince Jolyon is born to Joël Prince of Meara and Count of Ithelthorn and Faustina Contessa di Cebà.
April 17: Mark-Imre Prince of Festil marries Maryam Countess Tsérétéli.
August 5: Nygel Hereditary Prince of Gwynedd marries Susanta Lady Howell.
September 29: Jasher Prince of Gwynedd becomes a lay knight of the Order of Saint Willibrord.
October 21: Elaine Dowager Countess of Carthane dies, aged XC years.
November 16: Princess Torvalla is born to Malachy Hereditary Prince of Torenth and Ianthe Princess of Salonique.

971
March 3: Princess Ariella is born to Mark-Imre Hereditary Festillic Prince of Gwynedd and Maryam Countess Tsérétéli.
May 30: Count Rogan is born to Termöd Hereditary Duke d'Arjenol and Rupali Rani of Sinjh. *C'est ainst qu'en partant je vous fais mes adieux.*

972

January 4: Prince Imre III is born to Mark-Imre Hereditary Festillic Prince of Gwynedd and Maryam Countess Tsérétéli.
March 2: Arion I King of Toreth dies at Beldour, aged LXXII years, and is succeeded by his grandson, Prince Malachy.
May 7: Lirin Dowager Countess of Carthane dies, aged LXV years.
May 9: Prince Cluim Earl of Carthane marries Swynbeth Lady Fitz-Arthur Quinnell.
August 18: Ithel Sovereign Prince of Meara dies, aged LI years, and is succeeded by his son, Prince Joël.
October 26: Rogan Hereditary Duke d'Arjenol dies, aged XXXIX years, and is succeeded by his son, Count Termöd.

973

January 1: Malachy II King of Toreth is girded with the sword at Iób by Patriarch Abraam III. *Tolle lege, tolle lege.*
January 4: Princess Genthia is born to Malachy II King of Toreth and Ianthe Princess of Salonique.
August 23: Kennet Earl of Eastmarch dies, aged XLV years, and is succeeded by his son, Lord Sighere.
September 17: Quiric Baron of Horthness dies, aged LXIV years exactly, and is succeeded by his son, Lord Ulvar.
October 24: Ainslie Lord Argoed dies at his estate in Old Argoed, aged C years and V days, an event which causes great comment at the time, and is succeeded by his grandson, Sir Javyl. *Celui qui à tâché de vivre de manière à n'avoir pas besoin de songer à la mort, la voit venir sans effroi.*
November 4: Ainslie Lord Argoed is buried at Old Argoed, with King Uthyr and all of his family and the Great Lords of Court in attendance.

974

March 31: Prince Urien is born to Cluim Earl of Carthane and Swynbeth Lady Fitz-Arthur Quinnell.
October 22: Rhysel Lady Ainslie dies, aged LXIII years.

975

February 4: Marek Hereditary Prince and Pretender of Gwynedd abdicates in favour of his son, Prince Imre II.
July 25: Princess Imriella is born to Mark-Imre Hereditary Festillic Prince of Gwynedd and Maryam Countess Tsérétéli.
October 13: Prince Kyprian is born to Malachy II King of Toreth and Ianthe Princess of Salonique.
December 1: Marek former Pretender of Gwynedd is created Duke of Imréaly *ad personam*.
December 31: Abraam III Patriarch of Toreth dies, aged XC years.

976

May 11: Archelaos Metropolitan of Sostra is elected Patriarch of Toreth. *Tutti fatti a sembianza d'un Solo, figli tutti d'un solo Riscatto.*
December 7: Joël Sovereign Prince of Meara is assassinated at his palace in Laas, aged XXXVIII years, and is succeeded by his eldest son, Prince Judhael.

977

January 1: Imre II Pretender of Gwynedd is installed at Saint Constantine's by Patriarch Archelaos I.
April 1: Gilrae Hereditary Lord d'Eirial is knighted by King Uthyr.
June 11: Mátyás Prince of Torenth and Duke of Sostra dies, aged XXX years.

EVENTS OF "VOCATION" (DECEMBER 977)

December 24: Radulf Baron d'Eirial dies, aged LX years, and is succeeded by his son, Lord Gilrae. Gilrae is cured of a cancer by the old Deryni hermit, Simonn, and then abdicates in favour of his half-brother, Lord Caprus, in order to enter holy orders. *Vox populi, vox Dei.*

* * * * * * *

978

July 10: Prince Jashan is born to Cluim Earl of Carthane and Swynbeth Lady Fitz-Arthur Quinnell.
August 18: Arion Duke of Corwyn dies, aged LXXIX years, and is succeeded by his son, Lord Jernian.
November 30: Sister Ragenfride of the Order of Saint Catulina formerly Aetherien Princess of Festil dies, aged XL years.
December 20: Ianthe Queen of Torenth dies, aged XXXVI years.

979

May 8: Angus Mór Count of Tigre dies, aged XLVIII years, and is succeeded by his son, Duchad.
June 1: Malachy II King of Torenth marries Brisquayne Baronne du Haut-Dossory in Fallon.
August 11: Sir Gilrae Donivald former Baron d'Eirial is ordained priest.
October 15: Princess Mavourneen is born to Nygel Prince of Gwynedd and Susanta Princess of Gwynedd, who dies in childbirth.
November 9: Juliana Dowager Countess of Marley dies, aged LXXV years.

980

April 6: Prince Marek-Rethel is born to Malachy II King of Torenth and Brisquayne Baronne du Haut-Dossory.
September 16: Uthyr King of Gwynedd dies, aged LI years, and is succeeded by his son, Prince Nygel.
September 29: Nygel King of Gwynedd is crowned at Valoret by Halsten del Borgo Archbishop Primate of Valoret and All Gwynedd.
November 4: Prince Carolus of Torenth is created Duke of Székaly on his coming of age.

981

April 18: Prince Marek I Duke of Imréaly and sometime Pretender of Gwynedd dies at Tolán, aged LXXVI years.
July 6: Charis Princess of Torenth and Duchess of Tolán widow of Marek Pretender of Gwynedd dies, aged LXXIX years, and is succeeded in Tolán by her son, Prince Imre.
September 15: Father Jován Csigály is chosen Abbot of Saint Sviatoslav's Monastery in Jándrich.
October 8: Jesse MacGregor *de jure* Earl of Ebor and Count of Trevalga in The Connait dies, aged LXXX years, and is succeeded by his son, Lord Murray. *Mirar las cosas con anteojos de larga vista.*
December 2: Torval I Duke d'Arjenol dies, aged LXXV years, and is succeeded by his grandson, the Hereditary Duke Termöd.

982

May 6: Princess Adeléonore and Princess Abyssinthe (twins) are born to Malachy II King of Torenth and Brisquayne Baronne du Haut-Dossory.

June 17: Caprus Baron d'Eirial marries Ardentia Lady d'Albi.

September 18: Anne Quinnell Fitz-Arthur Dowager Princess of Cassan dies, aged LXXXIII years.

November 30: Grania Dowager Queen of Gwynedd and Countess of Culdi dies, aged LII years, and by the terms of her will is succeeded by her IInd son, Prince Jasher, as Earl of Culdi.

983

May 2: Nimur Hereditary Prince of Torenth marries Diavola Duchess d'Iméreth.

August 12: Imre II Pretender of Gwynedd attacks Marbury, killing Brian Coris Earl of Marley. In the following days Marley is overrun. Brian Coris Earl of Marley is LIII years of age at his death, and is succeeded by his son, Lord Comyn.

August 17: Nygel King of Gwynedd is informed of Imre's invasion, and begins assembling a counterforce at Rhemuth.

August 24: The main body of the Gwyneddan army leaves from Rhemuth for Valoret.

August 27: King Nygel arrives with his army at Valoret and adds whatever local levies he can find.

August 30: King Nygel and his army are blessed by William d'Argenson Archbishop Primate of Valoret and All Gwynedd, and depart for the North.

September 3: The armies of Gwynedd and the Pretender Imre II meet just East of Old Argoed. King Nygel is defeated and killed, aged XXXV years, and is succeeded by his brother, Jasher Prince of Gwynedd and Earl of Culdi. Also killed is Pliny last Earl de Fintan, aged XLVII years, whose title becomes extinct at his death and escheats to the Crown. The remnants of the Gwyneddan army retreat South. During the following weeks most of Eastmarch is occupied by Imre's forces.

September 22: The Pretender Imre proclaims himself Imre II King of Gwynedd, and establishes his Court at Cardosa. Το δ' ευτυχειν, τοδ' εν βροτοις θεος τε και θεου πλέον.

October 10: Part of the army of the Pretender Imre is defeated at Shanbogh in The Purple March by King Jasher, and Imre retreats into Eastmarch.

October 12: Carchashale is occupied by Imre, and he shifts his Court to Rengarth in preparation for the Winter.

October 26: Mark-Imre is proclaimed Hereditary Prince of Gwynedd by his father at Rengarth; several Festillic followers are ennobled by the Pretender Imre II.

November 11: The Ist of a series of severe, early Winter storms strikes Gwynedd, paralyzing Imre's force and reducing military activities to a minimum on both sides.

December 1: Prince Jasher is crowned King of Gwynedd by William III d'Argenson Archbishop Primate of Valoret and All Gwynedd.

984

February 14: Half of Imre's debilitated army returns to Torenth through a momentary break in the weather. The rest of his forces remain in Rengarth.

April 15: Carolus Duke of Székaly marries Richardis Baroness de Kluwas.

June 18: Prince Nimur mounts a relief expedition from Beldour, joining his father, King Malachy II, at Medras where the expeditionary force is being refitted. Prince Kyprian is created Duke of Arkadia by his father, King Malachy.

July 17: The combined Torenthi armies depart from Rengarth for Iomaire and the Purple March; they are continually harassed by small groups of Gwyneddan soldiers.

August 2: Imre's forces appear outside the walls of Grecotha, where the Gwyneddans have taken a stand. King Jasher redeploys his forces.

August 3: A Council of War is held by the Torenthi Princes in the early hours of the morning. In an assault on Grecotha that noon Malachy II King of Torenth, Nimur Hereditary Prince of Torenth, Ewan II Duke of Claibourne, and Mark-Imre Hereditary Festillic Prince of Gwynedd are killed in battle. The remnants of the invading force withdraw into Eastmarch and Torenth. King Malachy is XLIV years of age at his death, and is succeeded by his IInd son, Carolus Duke of Székaly, as King Károly II. Prince Nimur is I day short of XIX years of age. Prince Mark-Imre is XXXIV years of age, and is succeeded by his son, Prince Imre III. Ewan II Duke of Claibourne is XLIII years of age at his death, and is succeeded in Claibourne by his eldest son, Lord Angus, and in the Barony of Marlor by his IInd son, Lord Arran.

August 8: Károly II King of Torenth dies of his wounds while returning to Torenth, aged XVII years, and is succeeded by his younger brother, Prince Kyprian, under the joint regency of his grandmother, Zubayda Dowager Princess of Torenth, and his great-uncle, Vidar Duke of Truvorsk and Prince-Bishop of Podébrad. The Pretender Imre II returns to his base in Rengarth.

December 7: Fulk Fitz-Arthur Baron Viskin dies, aged LXXVII years, and is succeeded by his eldest surviving son, Lord Redmond.

985

April 7: Lord Stiofan Anthony is born to Jernian Duke of Corwyn and Countess Procida daughter of Reynard IV Duc du Joux.

May 1: Imre III Hereditary Prince of Festil and grandson of the Pretender is declared of age a year ahead of time, is knighted and ennobled as Duke of Eastmarch, and is sent to Beldour to rally volunteers for the cause, and also to remove him in the case of disaster.

May 30: The Gwyneddan army is spotted near Rengarth.

June 2: Duchad Mór Count of Tigre and son-in-law of Imre II dies in battle against Jasher King of Gwynedd at Rengarth, aged XXXIII years, and is succeeded as Count by his son, Prince Festil. The Gwyneddans begin the siege of Rengarth.

June 29: A wholesale assault on the walls of Rengarth by the Gwyneddan army fails.

July 2: In the final battle of the war, Jasher King of Gwynedd dies while assaulting Rengarth, but the city falls. Rather than be captured, Imre II Pretender of Gwynedd throws himself from the walls of Rengarth Castle, aged LVII years, and is succeeded in his

pretensions by his grandson, Prince Imre III. Jasher King of Gwynedd is XXXIII years of age at his death, and is succeeded by his younger brother, Prince Cluim.
July 21: King Jasher is buried at Rhemuth.
September 6: Prisoners of war are exchanged in the Magas Pass between Gwynedd and Torenth.
September 7: King Cluim is crowned at Valoret by William III d'Argenson Archbishop Primate of Valoret and All Gwynedd.
September 24: Princess AriElinora is born to Blaine Prince of Festil and Corvina Lady Zevenden.
December 2: Sir Richmond FitzEwan is created Baron of Rheljan by King Cluim, who also confirms numerous successions to noble houses caused by the depredations of the war, and creates several other loyal retainers as barons.

986
January 1: Imre III Pretender of Gwynedd is installed at Saint Constantine's Cathedral by Patriarch Archelaos I.

987
May 17: Rogan Count d'Arjenol marries Ariella Princess of Festil.
September 2: Ringan Hereditary Duke d'Arjenol marries the Princess Genthia daughter of Malachy II King of Torenth.

988
May 8: Urien Hereditary Prince of Gwynedd marries Jaroni Princess of R'Kassi.
July 22: Count Averil is born to Ringan Hereditary Duke d'Arjenol and Genthia Princess of Torenth.
August 12: Archelaos Patriarch of Torenth dies, aged LVII years.
October 1: Olympios Metropolitan of Medras is elected Patriach of Torenth.

989
January 10: Michaela Dowager Queen of Gwynedd dies, aged LXXX years.
March 14: Prince Cinhil is born to Urien Hereditary Prince of Gwynedd and Jaroni Princess of R'Kassi.
May 31: Imre III Pretender of Gwynedd and Titular Duke of Eastmarch marries Torvalla Princess of Torenth.
October 13: Kyprian II King of Torenth comes of age, and the Regency Council is disbanded.

990
January 1: Kyprian II King of Torenth is girded with the sword at Iób by Patriarch Olympios I.
February 16: Hereditary Prince Marek is born to Imre III Pretender of Gwynedd and Princess Torvalla.
March 11: Sir Roger McLain marries Glorian Lady MacInnis Heiress of Kierney.
September 2: Count Sándor is born to Ringan Hereditary Duke d'Arjenol and Genthia Princess of Torenth.
November 25: Princess Urracca is born to Faucon Hereditary Prince of Bremagne and Adélaïde Comtesse de Joyeuse.
December 27: Lord Tairchell is born to Sir Roger McLain and Glorian Lady MacInnis.

991
April 18: Prince Cluim Corwyn is born to Urien Hereditary Prince of Gwynedd and Jaroni Princess of R'Kassi.
April 21: Cluim Corwyn Prince of Gwynedd dies, aged III days.

992
March 6: Termöd II Duke d'Arjenol dies, aged XLI years, and is succeeded by his son, the Hereditary Duke Ringan.
March 21: Prince Adolphus is born to Imre III Pretender of Gwynedd and Torvalla Princess of Torenth.
April 18: Lord Arnall is born to Sir Roger McLain Count of Kierney and Glorian Lady MacInnis Heiress of Kierney.
October 12: Count Torval is born to Ringan IV Duke d'Arjenol and Genthia Princess of Torenth.

993
January 21: Princess Suibhne is born to Urien Hereditary Prince of Gwynedd and Jaroni Princess of R'Kassi.
December 18: Princess Braïda Heiress d'Arjenol dies, aged LXXVIII years.

994
February 2: Olympios Patriarch of Torenth dies, aged LXVI years.
May 3: Prince Konstantiné is born to Imre III Pretender of Gwynedd and Torvalla Princess of Torenth.
May 12: Kyrión Metropolitan of Tolán is elected Patriarch of Torenth.
June 29: Kyprian II King of Torenth marries Polyxena Grand Princess of Byzantyun.
August 30: Festil Count of Tigre and his identical twin brother, Prince Blaine, are murdered at Marbury by Festil's jealous mistress, Lady Amandine, who first mistakes Blaine for his brother and then, realizing her error, kills Festil and herself in despair. The Princes Festil and Blaine are XXVII years of age at their death. The Prince Festil is succeeded as Count by his half-brother, Lord Angus II, and the Prince Blaine's rights to the throne of Gwynedd are transmitted to his daughter, the Lady AriElinora.
December 18: Cluim King of Gwynedd dies of the stytche, aged XLI years, and is succeeded by his son, Prince Urien.

995
February 2: Princess Bethra is born to Urien King of Gwynedd and Jaroni Princess of R'Kassi.
March 1: Imre III Pretender of Gwynedd and Kyprian II King of Torenth begin assembling a joint expeditionary force against Gwynedd, and Urien King of Gwynedd prepares a counterforce.
March 24: Father Gilrae Donivald is elected Archbishop of Rhemuth.
April 23: Urien King of Gwynedd is crowned at Valoret by William IV Stephanis Archbishop Primate of Valoret and All Gwynedd, with Gilrae d'Eirial the new Archbishop of Rhemuth assisting.
June-July: A severe heat wave and drought affects central Gwynedd and Torenth, causing the disbanding of the Festillic invasion force after disease strikes the encamped army.
November 30: Hereditary Prince Arkady is born to Kyprian II King of Torenth and Polyxena Grand Princess of Byzantyun.

996
May 30: Princess Agrafena is born to Imre III Pretender of Gwynedd and Torvalla Princess of Torenth.
Ya que no seas casto, se cauto.

December 1: Princess Arien is born to Kyprian II King of Torenth and Polyxena Grand Princess of Byzantyun.
December 14: Zubayda Dowager Hereditary Princess and ex-Regent of Torenth dies, aged LXXV years.

997
Winter: Dyggvi Bolverksson, a priest of the Old Ones in the Great Temple at Eistenfalla, hears the voice of the All-Father speaking to him of blood and iron and souls, and begins preaching a crusade against the heathens of the South. *Prorsus credibile est, quia ineptum est.*
March 18: Prince Alroy Uthyr is born to Urien King of Gwynedd and Jaroni Princess of R'Kassi.
Spring: Kyprian II and Imre III again begin assembling their army to invade Gwynedd.
May 16: The hordes of Eistenmark and Tretelgia attack the city of Netterhaven without warning, and put it to the torch. Thousands die in the slaughter.
May 17: A group of barbarians attacks the Monastery of Saint Sviatoslav and puts it under siege.
May 19: Brustarkia is overrun. King Kyprian receives a message at Medras concerning the invasion of Eastern Torenth. *Nihil est toto quod perstet in orbe. Cuncta fluunt, omnisque vagans, formatur imago, ipsa quoque assiduo labuntur tempora motu.*
May 20: Kyprian assumes control of the Toláni army and merges it with his own; he marches his force Northeast to face the Eistenmark pagans.
May 22: The city of Arzh is besieged.
May 25: Jován Csigály Abbot of Saint Sviatoslav Monastery in Jándrich is killed in the siege, aged LVI years, but the Abbey repulses the barbarians, who are unable to penetrate further West.
May 26: The Torenthi army relieves Arzh.
May 27: A battle is fought near Portis in Arjenol between the forces of Torenth and Eistenmark. No clear victor emerges.
May 30: Kyprian leaves part of his army to protect Arzh, and marches to Netterhaven.
June 2: Kyprian fights a IInd battle South of Netterhaven at Kálmár, defeating the horde of Tretelgia.
June 3: The Torenthi army enters the ruins of Netterhaven, and awaits resupply by ship.
June 7: The Torenthi army outside Arzh is massacred, and Arzh is overrun and burned. The Eistenmark horde leaves Arjenol for the East.
June 22: King Kyprian returns to Arzh, and begins rebuilding the city.

998
May 12: King Kyprian begins a campaign East of Arjenol to find and destroy the forces of Eistenmark.
July 8: Princess AriEmilia is born to Imre III Pretender of Gwynedd and Torvalla Princess of Torenth.
July 26: Prince Nikola is born to Kyprian II King of Torenth and Polyxena Grand Princess of Byzantyun.
August 4: Prince Jashan Duke of Carthmoor, brother of Urien King of Gwynedd, is ordained priest by Gilrae Archbishop of Rhemuth.
December 24: Gilrae Archbishop of Rhemuth dies of a growth, aged XLI years.

999
June 6: Jolyon Prince and Heir Presumptive to the throne of Meara marries Ysyllt Princess of Gwynedd. Ἥδιον ουδεν ερωτος.

December 31: Prince Aidan is born to Urien King of Gwynedd and Jaroni Princess of R'Kassi.

1000
January 1: Alroy Uthyr Prince of Gwynedd is created Duke of Travlum by his father.
January 6: Prince Zimri is born to Kyprian II King of Torenth and Polyxena Grand Princess of Byzantyun.
June 18: Faucon Hereditary Prince of Bremagne and Duc du Parmentier is killed in the tilts of the Millennium Fair being held at Millefleurs, aged XL years, and is succeeded as Hereditary Prince by his younger brother, Prince Théofrid.
December 1: Richeldis Dowager Countess of Kierney, being old and ill, seeks a final blessing from her great-grandson, King Urien.
December 28: Richeldis Dowager Countess of Kierney dies, aged XCVI years.

1001
January 7: Lady Jerusha Thuryn Drummond dies, aged LXXXIII years.
June 19: Princess Breida is born to Urien King of Gwynedd and Jaroni Princess of R'Kassi.
July 4: Alroy Uthyr Prince of Gwynedd and Duke of Travlum dies, aged IV years.
October 22: Judhael II Sovereign Prince of Meara dies of scales, aged XL years, and is succeeded by his younger brother, Prince Jolyon. Jolyon's uncle, Prince Quinn Count of Ithelthorn, becomes Heir Presumptive to the throne of Meara.

1002
March 2: Prince Kirill is born to Kyprian II King of Torenth and Polyxena Grand Princess of Byzantyun.
July 6: King Kyprian takes an army North into Eistenmark.
July 17: The Torenthi army is attacked from all sides near Roslow, and is forced to withdraw under heavy pressure; one-third of the army is lost.
August 4: Riots spring out in Beldour, Torenthály, and other Torenthi cities over the conduct of the war, and are put down by King Kyprian with great severity.

1003
April 18: Prince Ossian is born to Urien King of Gwynedd and Jaroni Princess of R'Kassi.
May 30: Netterhaven is attacked by hordes from Eistenmark, but the heathens are repulsed.
June 16: Kyrión II Patriarch of Torenth dies, aged LXXX years.
October 2: Markos Metropolitan of Medras formerly Prince Marek Duke of Arkadia is elected Patriarch of Beldour and All Torenth as Markos II. *Cur ergo hæc ipse non facis?*

1004
February 21: Princess Kónstanza is born to Kyprian II King of Torenth and Polyxena Grand Princess of Byzantyun.
July 24: Károly late Hereditary Prince of Torenth is beatified by his son, Markos II Patriarch of Beldour.

1005
March 31: Lord Edward is born to James Earl of Cloome and Susana Lady Crewe.
April 28: Princess Rathnait is born to Urien King of Gwynedd and Jaroni Princess of R'Kassi. *A mortos e a idos, não ha amigos.*
May 12: Manuel Graf von Spire marries Lady AriElinora of Festil.

1006
February 8: Prince Andruin later Stephanos V Patriarch of Beldour and All Torenth is born to Kyprian II King of Torenth and Polyxena Grand Princess of Byzantyun.
March 1: Hereditary Lord Blaine Manuel is born to Manuel Graf von Spire and AriElinora Countess of Festil.
October 12: Ysyllt Princess of Gwynedd and Meara dies, aged XXVI years.

1007
April 20: Jolyon II Sovereign Prince of Meara marries as his second wife Urracca Princess of Bremagne.
April 30: Marek II Hereditary Festillic Prince of Gwynedd marries Diadema Countess Nesbitt.

1008
January 23: The twin Princesses Roisian and Annalind are born to Jolyon II Sovereign Prince of Meara and Urracca Princess of Bremagne.
January 31: Princess Sachette is born to Kyprian II King of Torenth and Polyxena Grand Princess of Byzantyun.
February 22: Prince Festil is born to Marek II Festillic Prince of Gwynedd and Diadema Countess Nesbitt.
March 14: A great earthquake strikes Torenth and destroys much of the City of Beldour. A tidal wave on the Twin Rivers sweeps away Makonnen the Hort of Orsal and his children. *Вещи фантастически*.
April 22: Lady AriElandra is born to Manuel Graf von Spire and AriElinora Countess of Festil.
June 11: Dyggvi King of Eistenmark, proclaiming the earthquake as signifying the approval of the Gods, strikes South into Torenth, burning many farms and small towns over a II-week period.
September 5: Prince Malcolm is born to Urien King of Gwynedd and Jaroni Princess of R'Kassi.
October 12: Gillian Countess of Rhendall dies, aged LXVI years, and is succeeded by her son, Lord Braham.

1009
June 18: Kyprian II King of Torenth takes a large expedition North from Netterhaven into Eistenmark.
June 28: Kyprian defeats and kills Dyggvi King of Eistenmark. *Post bellum auxilium*.
June 30: Eistenfalla is occupied by Torenthi forces.
August 17: Michael Rhys Haldane Prince of Gwynedd and Earl of Carthane marries the Lady Mithradita Heiress of Pirek in Howicce, renounces his rights to the throne of Gwynedd, and becomes Duke *jure uxoris*.
September 3: King Kyprian withdraws his forces South from Eistenmark to Netterhaven before the snows set in.
September 28: Hereditary Prince Joël is born to Jolyon II Prince of Meara and Urracca Princess of Bremagne.

1010
February 22: Prince Marek *Junior* is born to Marek II Festillic Prince of Gwynedd and Diadema Countess Nesbitt.
May 15: Averil Hereditary Duke d'Arjenol marries the Princess Arien daughter of King Kyprian II.
July 5: Lady Chriselle is born to Manuel Graf von Spire and AriElinora Countess of Festil.
August 28: Angelos I Autokratór of Byzantyun is killed in battle fighting the barbarians of Avarsland, and is succeeded by his younger brother, Grand Prince Kónstas.
November 4: Averil Hereditary Duke d'Arjenol dies of consumption, aged XXII years, and is succeeded posthumously by his son, Lord Torval.

1011
January 2: Count Airlie is born to Stiofan Anthony Hereditary Duke of Corwyn and Lady Javana de Courcy.
February 14: Hereditary Duke Torval is born posthumously to Averil Hereditary Duke d'Arjenol and Arien Princess of Torenth.
August 16: Turlough Lord Stainléigh marries Suibhne Princess of Gwynedd.
September 27: Prince Jaron Rhys is born to Urien King of Gwynedd and Jaroni Princess of R'Kassi.
October 31: Joël Hereditary Prince of Meara dies, aged II years.

1012
February 14: Hereditary Prince Jubal is born to Jolyon II Prince of Meara and Urracca Princess of Bremagne.
March 8: Princess Festilla is born to Marek II Festillic Prince of Gwynedd and Diadema Countess Nesbitt.
May 1: Kyprian II King of Torenth travels East to Byzantyun, the first official visit from Torenth in hundreds of years.
June 22: Kyprian II meets with his wife's nephew, Kónstas Autokratór of Byzantyun. They agree on a treaty of defense against the Northern barbarians, who have been very active in recent decades.
July 22: Count Tayman is born to Stiofan Anthony Hereditary Duke of Corwyn and Lady Javana de Courcy.
November 6: Lady Markella is born to Manuel Graf von Spire and AriElinora Countess of Festil.

1013
June 4: The armies of Byzantyun and Torenth go North together against the heathen savages.
December 2: The twin Princesses Judit and Jorianna are born to Jolyon II Prince of Meara and Urracca Princess of Bremagne.

1014
January 1: Aidan Prince of Gwynedd is created Duke of Valoret by his father.
June 1: Théofrid III Roi de Bremagne marries Bethra Princess of Gwynedd.
June 16: A IInd campaign against the Northern hordes is conducted by Kyprian and Kónstas.
June 17: Tairchell McLain Hereditary Count of Kierney marries Rhetice Lady MacEwan.
November 15: Lady Salentina is born to Marek II Festillic Prince of Gwynedd and Lady Pulcheria af Jutta.

1015
March 2: Lord Lewys is born to Régnier I Duc de Joux and Jolanthe Princess of Fallon.
May 2: Arkady Hereditary Prince of Torenth marries the Grafina Dura daughter of Arsieu II Sovereign Prince of Jáca.
December 2: Vidar Duke of Truvorsk and Prince-Bishop of Podébrad and sometime Lord Regent of

Torenth dies, aged LXXXIX years, when the Duchy of Truvorsk escheats to the Crown.
December 23: Princess Magrette is born to Jolyon II Prince of Meara and Urracca Princess of Bremagne.
December 25: Zimri Prince of Torenth is created Duke of Truvorsk by his father, King Kyprian II.

1016
April 6: Jorianna Princess of Meara dies, aged II years. *Daffodils that come before the swallow dares.*
August 15: Princess Grigoryna is born to Arkady Hereditary Prince of Torenth and Dura Grafina von Jáca.
August 23: Konstantiné Prince of Festil and Earl of Cardosa is killed in a duel, aged XXII years.
September 9: Markos II Patriarch of Beldour and All Torenth dies, aged LXXIV years.
November 12: Abraam Metropolitan of Ortenbourg is elected Patriarch of Beldour and All Torenth.

1017
April 18: Ossian Prince of Gwynedd comes of age, and is created Duke of Travlum by his father.
June 28: Ossian Prince of Gwynedd and Duke of Travlum dies, aged XIV years, accidentally killed in a tournament.

1018
May 29: Byzantyun and Torenth again conduct joint operations against the Northern hordes.
May 30: Tancrède Hereditary Prince of Fallon marries Breida Princess of Gwynedd.
June 16: Aidan Duke of Valoret is named Subcommander of one-half of the Northern Army of Gwynedd.
July 5: Jubal Hereditary Prince of Meara dies, aged VI years.
July 6: Hereditary Prince Job is born to Jolyon II Prince of Meara and Urracca Princess of Bremagne, but dies later that day.
August 16: Kónstas Autokrátor of Byzantyun is killed at the Battle of Boldù against the Avarslanders, and is succeeded by his son, Angelos II. The Byzantyun army withdraws to Kónstantinopolis.
September 3: Festilla daughter of Marek II Festillic Prince of Gwynedd dies, aged VI years.
October 14: Prince Arion Nikola is born to Arkady Hereditary Prince of Torenth and Dura Grafina von Jáca.

1019
March 7: Father Jashan Haldane Duke of Carthmoor and brother of Urien King of Gwynedd is elected Bishop of Grecotha.
May 3: Cinhil Hereditary Prince of Gwynedd marries Micole Lady of Dhassa.

1020
April 6: Princess Rhetice is born to Cinhil Hereditary Prince of Gwynedd and Micole Lady of Dhassa.
April 21: Ringan IV Duke d'Arjenol dies, and is succeeded by his grandson, Lord Torval, under the Regency of Torval's mother, Princess Arien of Torenth. *Homem apercebido, meio combatido.*
June 18: Prince Aidan Haldane Duke of Valoret dies at Grecotha, aged XX years.

1021
January 28: Prince Sigard is born to Arkady Hereditary Prince of Torenth and Dura Grafina von Jáca.
February 11: Master Perrin is born posthumously to the Prince Aidan Haldane late Duke of Valoret and Étiennette Countess du Roringe.
June 12: Prince Onan *Junior* of Jáca marries Rathnait Princess of Gwynedd.

1022
February 20: Arnall McLain Hereditary Count of Kierney marries Adelicia Fitz-Arthur Quinnell Heiress of Cassan.
March 14: The great Cathedral of Saint Constantine is reconsecrated at Beldour in Torenth by Patriarch Abraam IV.
March 30: Prince Aldan is born to Cinhil Hereditary Prince of Gwynedd and Micole Lady of Dhassa, but dies that same day.
June 16: Judit Princess of Meara dies, aged VIII years.
September 5: Malcolm Prince of Gwynedd comes of age and is created Duke of Rhemuth by his father.
October 9: Malcolm Duke of Rhemuth enters the *Arx Fidei* seminary near Valoret.

1023
April 2: Princess Nummela is born to Arkady Hereditary Prince of Torenth and Dura Grafina von Jáca.
August 3: The barbarians of Avarsland are destroyed at Avargorod by Kyprian II King of Torenth.
September 30: A great celebration to mark the end of the war with the Norsemen is held at Beldour in Torenth. *Nemo tam divos habuit faventes, crastinum ut possit sibi polliceri.*
November 22: Prince Quinn mac Ithel Quinnell, bachelor Count of Ithelthorn and Heir Presumptive to the throne of Meara, dies childless at Cloome, aged LXXIX years.

1024
April 14: Jolyon II Prince of Meara declares before the Mearan Council of State that Princess Roisian is now heir presumptive to the throne of Meara, barring any further male issue from his body.
August 2: Princess Micole, wife of Cinhil Hereditary Prince of Gwynedd, dies aged XXII years while giving birth to Princess Albina.
December 31: Imre III Prince of Festil and Duke of Tolán abdicates his pretensions to the throne of Gwynedd in favour of his son, Prince Marek II.

1025
January 1: Marek II Pretender of Gwynedd is installed at St. Constantine's Cathedral by Patriarch Abraam IV and is named Commander of the Festillic army. Princess Roisian of Meara is betrothed to Prince Nikola of Torenth, and Princess Annalind of Meara is betrothed to Prince Adolphus of Festil.
January 30: Adolphus Prince of Festil and Titular Duke of Eastmarch dies at Beldour, aged XXXII years.
February 4: Cinhil Hereditary Prince of Gwynedd is named Commander of the Royal Army.
February 14: Torval II Duke d'Arjenol attains his majority; his mother, Princess Arien, relinquishes her position as Regent and returns to Beldour.
May 25: Malcolm Duke of Rhemuth is recalled from the *Arx Fidei* seminary to enter the army of Gwynedd.
May 29: Prince Cinhil defeats and kills Jolyon II Prince of Meara at the Cleyde; Jolyon is aged LV years at his death, and is succeeded by his daughter, Princess Roisian.

June 15: The Battle of Killingford begins North of Valoret on a ford of the Falling Water River near the village of Schilling.

June 17: The Battle of Killingford concludes with the Torenthi forces withdrawing from Gwynedd. Marek II Pretender of Gwynedd is killed, aged XXXV years, together with Urien King of Gwynedd, aged LI years, Imre III Duke of Tolán and Eastmarch, aged LIII years, John II Archbishop Primate of Valoret and All Gwynedd, aged LXI years, and Beldouri Patriarch Abraam IV, aged LXVII years. *"Hath his bellyful of fighting."*

June 24: Cinhil II King of Gwynedd dies, aged XXXVI years, and is succeeded by his brother, the Prince Malcolm Duke of Rhemuth.

July 6: Timotheos Metropolitan of Ortenbourg is elected Patriarch of Beldour and All Torenth as Timotheos II.

July 10: Princess Annalind is declared Sovereign Prince of Meara in contravention of the late Prince Jolyon's will.

July 21: Kyprian II King of Torenth abdicates his throne, and is succeeded by his eldest son, Hereditary Prince Arkady.

August 9: Malcolm King of Gwynedd marries Roisian Sovereign Prince of Meara, and his brother Prince Jaron Rhys, Heir Presumptive to the throne of Gwynedd, marries Salentina Lady Festil, the marriages being conducted by Prince Jashan Haldane Bishop of Grecotha; Jaron Rhys is declared of age on this date by King Malcolm and is created Duke of Travlum.

August 21: Itinerant Bishop Vespasian d'Aphienne is elected Archbishop Primate of Valoret and All Gwynedd.

September 7: On the feast of Saint Bearand Haldane Prince Malcolm and Princess Roisian are crowned King and Queen of Gwynedd and Meara by Vespasian d'Aphienne Archbishop Primate of Valoret and All Gwynedd.

October 18: Carbury is established as a new episcopal see under Bishop Heber.

November 19: King Malcolm creates XIV new peers, including: Lord Gillis Gillispie as Earl of Danoc; Lord Kennet Howell as Baron of Iomaire; Sir Piran ap Coran as Earl of Jenas. He also confirms XLVI new titleholders in their ranks.

1026

January 1: Arkady II King of Torenth is girded with the sword at Iób by Patriarch Timotheos II.

March 17: Princess Amalie is born to Malcolm King of Gwynedd and Roisian Princess of Meara.

June 24: Five hundred couples are joined in matrimony at Beldour by Patriarch Timotheos II.

November 11: Prince István is born to Arkady II King of Torenth and Dura Grafina von Jáca.

December 2: Jernian Duke of Corwyn dies, aged LXV years, and is succeeded by his son, Lord Stiofan.

December 25: Imriella Duchess of Tolán and Pretender of Gwynedd marries Swithven Count of Langendoss.

1027

May 29: King Malcolm leads an expedition into Meara to capture the Princess Annalind and her relatives. *La silence du peuple est la leçon des rois.*

June 18: King Malcolm kills Loren Kincaid Earl of Kilarden and Danvan Lord Kincaid his younger son, Dowager Princess Urracca's captains, in a minor skirmish near Ratharkin, but fails to locate the main body of the rebels, who flee to The Connait. Loren Earl of Kilarden is L years of age at his death, and is succeeded by his elder son, Lord Rhiryd; Lord Danvan is XXVI years of age at his death, and is succeeded by his son, Lord Robert.

June 19: Zimri Prince of Torenth and Duke of Truvorsk marries Chriselle Lady von Spire daughter of AriElinora Heiress Presumptive of Tolán and Festil.

June 23: Annalind Princess of Meara abandons her capital of Laas.

June 30: King Malcolm appoints Ardal MacArdry Earl of Transha as Lord Regent of Meara and then returns to Rhemuth.

1028

May 3: Princess Tiphaine is born to Malcolm King of Gwynedd and Roisian Princess of Meara.

1029

March 20: Princess Mladena is born to Arkady II King of Torenth and Dura Grafina von Jáca.

May 1: Lord Thomas is born to Rhupert Earl Calder of Sheele and Aideen Lady Latteragh.

October 4: Princess Demetria is born to Zimri Duke of Truvorsk and Chriselle Lady of Festil and Tolán.

1030

May 7: Hereditary Prince Donal Blaine is born to Malcolm King of Gwynedd and Roisian Princess of Meara.

June 4: Torval II Duke d'Arjenol marries Markella Lady von Spire daughter of AriElinora Heir Presumptive of Festil.

June 16: The great VII-tiered tomb, the Nikolaseum, is dedicated by King Arkady II of Torenth to the memory of his deceased brother, Prince Nikola.

1031

February 5: Lady Tamarina is born to Jaron Rhys Duke of Travlum and Salentina Lady Festil, who dies that same day in childbirth, aged XVI years.

November 14: Princess Camille is born to Zimri Duke of Truvorsk and Chriselle Lady of Festil and Tolán.

1032

July 3: Sigard Prince of Torenth dies of the typhoidous grippe, aged XI years.

July 4: Arion Nikola Hereditary Prince of Torenth dies of the typhoidous grippe, aged XIII years.

July 6: Mladena Princess of Torenth dies of the typhoidous grippe, aged III years.

July 16: István Hereditary Prince of Torenth dies of the typhoidous grippe, aged V years.

July 20: Nummela Princess of Torenth dies of the typhoidous grippe, aged IX years.

August 11: Princess Anaïs is born to Malcolm King of Gwynedd and Roisian Princess of Meara.

1033

June 1: Timotheos II Patriarch of Beldour and All Torenth dies, aged LXXI years.

August 18: Athanasios Metropolitan of Netterhaven is elected Patriarch of Beldour and All Torenth as Athanasios II.

November 11: Glorian MacInnis Countess of Kierney dies, aged LXXIII years, and is succeeded by her son, Lord Arnall McLain.

1034
January 2: Prince Blaine is born still to Zimri Duke of Truvorsk and Chriselle Lady of Festil and Tolán.
January 4: Vespasian d'Aphienne Archbishop Primate of Valoret and All Gwynedd dies, aged LIV years.
April 15: Briand of Meara Bishop of Dhassa is elected Archbishop Primate of Valoret and All Gwynedd; Jashan Duke of Carthmoor and Bishop of Grecotha is elected Archbishop of Rhemuth.
May 26: Brother Cyriac of Issel founds the *Ordo Vox Dei*. *You shall see in him the triple pillar of the world transformed.*
August 18: Prince Malcolm *Junior* is born to Malcolm King of Gwynedd and Roisian Princess of Meara.
December 1: Lord Andrew is born to Arnall McLain Hereditary Count of Kierney and Adelicia Fitz-Arthur Quinnell Heiress of Cassan, and becomes Duke of Cassan at birth.

1035
March 3: Hereditary Duke Mahael is born to Torval II Duke d'Arjenol and Markella Lady von Spire.
May 12: Magrette Princess of Meara marries Lord Edward Ramsay of Cloome with the permission of King Malcolm.
August 6: Hereditary Prince Nimur is born to Arkady II King of Torenth and Dura Grafina von Jáca.

1036
January 28: Princess Ariel is born to Zimri Duke of Truvorsk and Chriselle Lady of Festil and Tolán.
August 17: Master Perrin du Roringe natural son of the Prince Aidan late Duke of Valoret is created Baron Kilchon by King Malcolm.
September 28: Princess Marfurca is born to Malcolm King of Gwynedd and Roisian Princess of Meara.

1037
June 1: Sir Colin is born to Lord Edward Ramsay of Cloome and Magrette Princess of Meara.
June 24: Princess Grigoryna of Torenth, being forced by her father King Arkady II to marry a man not of her choosing, Balthazar Count von Maultasche, throws herself off the battlements of her father's castle, aged XX years, on the anniversary of the Great Marriage Feast of 1026. *"I am dying, Torenth, dying, only I here importune death awhile."*
December 31: The monk Pantaleón sometime Kyprian II King of Torenth dies, aged LXII years.

1038
February 14: Princess Imriella Duchess of Tolán and Pretender of Gwynedd dies, aged LXII years, and is succeeded by her *cousine germain*, Lady AriElinora.
May 7: Lewys ap Norfal Sieur du Joux marries Ilde Countess d'Arjenol.

1039
February 28: Princess Charis Rochelle is born to Zimri Duke of Truvorsk and Chriselle Hereditary Princess of Festil and Tolán.
December 25: At the Yule Ball given by Malcolm King of Gwynedd, his niece, Rhetice Princess of Gwynedd, is captivated by one Ælius Nemo.

1040
April 6: At a party held on the XXth birthday of Rhetice Princess of Gwynedd, she petitions the King Malcolm for the hand of Ælius Nemo, and is refused. *De bons propositos está o Inferno cheio, e o Ceo de boas obras.*
April 7: The Princess Rhetice of Gwynedd disappears from her rooms in Rhemuth Castle, never to be heard from again. *Nulla nuova, buona nuova.*

1041
January 14: Master Oliver later Archbishop Primate of Gwynedd is born to Sir Marcus Eugenius de Nore and Flaura Lady Matin.
February 7: Sister Vibiana formerly Princess Sachette of Torenth dies of the consumptive complaint, aged XXXIII years.
September 15: Annalind Princess and Pretender of Meara marries Rhiryd Kincaid Earl of Kilarden in contravention of the Royal Marriages Act of Gwynedd. *Les hommes font les lois, les femmes font les mœurs.*
November 30: Madawc King of Llannedd dies without male heirs, aged XLIII years, and is succeeded by his elder daughter, Princess Gwenaël.

1042
January 30: Prince Marcus is born to Zimri Duke of Truvorsk and Chriselle Hereditary Princess of Festil and Tolán.
June 16: Saint Basil's Bridge is dedicated by King Arkady II as a permanent link between Old and New Beldour in Torenth. *Exegi monumentum ære perennius regalique situ pyramidum altius; quod non imber edax, non Aquilo impotens possit diruere, et innumerabilis annorum series, et fuga temporum.*
June 19: Hereditary Prince and Count Judhael is born to Rhiryd Earl of Kilarden and Annalind Princess and Pretender of Meara.
October 18: Stevana de Corwyn is born to Airlie Hereditary Duke of Corwyn and Grania d'Oriel.
December 21: Urracca Dowager Princess of Meara dies of a cancer in her womb at her stronghold in the Ratharkin Mountains, aged LII years.

1043
January 18: Angelus de Lacey, later Bishop of Stavenham, is born.

1044
February 1: Carsten, later Bishop of Meara, is born.
August 11: Briand of Meara Archbishop Primate of Valoret and All Gwynedd dies, aged LXXXI years.
October 26: Alexander Darby, later Archbishop of Rhemuth, is born.
October 30: Jashan Duke of Carthmoor and Archbishop of Rhemuth is elected Archbishop Primate of Valoret and All Gwynedd.
December 1: Annalind Princess of Meara is again proclaimed Sovereign Prince of Meara at Laas, and commences her IInd reign.

1045
July 22: King Malcolm leads a IInd expedition into Meara.
August 6: Princess Annalind and her husband are captured after a pitched battle near Laas. Her son and heir, the III-year-old Prince Judhael, is hidden away by the Earl of Cloome; Annalind's infant daughter, Princess Jorice, dies of malnutrition.
August 8: Princess Annalind, her husband Rhiryd Earl of Kilarden, and his nephew, Robert Lord Kincaid son of Danvan Lord Kincaid, are tried and executed for treason. Prince Judhael succeeds his mother as Pretender of Meara and his father as Earl of Kilarden. Princess Annalind is aged XXXVII years at her death;

Rhiryd Earl of Kilarden is aged XLVI years; Robert Lord Kincaid is aged XX years, and is succeeded by his infant son, Lord Robard.

August 13: Prince Judhael is proclaimed Sovereign Prince of Meara by his supporters under the title Judhael III.

August 25: After completing the pacification of Meara, King Malcolm returns to Rhemuth.

December 9: Ariella II Princess of Festil and by some considered rightful Queen of Gwynedd dies at Trebaçeaux in Joux, aged LXXIV years, when the elder branch of the House of Festil becomes extinct.

1046

July 18: Donal Blaine Hereditary Prince of Gwynedd marries Dulchesse Duchesse du Vézaire.

September 18: Roisian Queen of Gwynedd and Princess of Meara enters the Convent of Saint Emerentiana in Fallon.

October 7: Sir Kenneth Kai is born to Sir Kai Morgan and Madonna Lucinda Lady McLain.

1048

February 16: Athanasios II Patriarch of Beldour and All Torenth dies, aged LXIII years.

April 16: Philoxenos Metropolitan of Sostra is elected Patriarch of Torenth.

October 30: Philoxenos II Patriarch of Beldour and All Torenth dies, aged LVIII years.

1049

March 3: Symeón Metropolitan of Tolán is elected Patriarch of Torenth.

November 10: Lewys ap Norfal Sieur du Joux, an infamous Deryni mage, rejects the authority of the Camberian Council. *Qui à deux maîtres servira a un de ceux il mentira.*

1050

September 30: AriElinora Duchess of Tolán and Pretender of Gwynedd dies, aged LXV years, and is succeeded by her daughter, Princess Chriselle.

November 16: Lord Barrett is born to Barstowe Lord de Laney and Modesta Lady Bannock.

1051

December 29: Hereditary Lord Rhodri is born to Kentigern Lord Pembroke and Palladia Lady Ahern.

1052

March 21: Lewys ap Norfal Sieur du Joux vanishes, aged XXXVII years, when an occult experiment goes seriously awry at the Green Tower in Castle Coroth.

November 24: Lady Vivienne is born to Émery Comte du Joux and Enna Lady Leix.

1053

August 11: Master Wolfram de Blanet, later Bishop of Grecotha, is born to Sir Milton de Blanet and Archangela Lady Kinsaco.

1054

July 17: Creoda, later Bishop of Carbury and Culdi, is born.

August 15: Sir Colin Ramsay of Cloome marries Corea Lady Fursey.

December 11: Symeón II Patriarch of Beldour and All Torenth dies, aged LXVII years.

1055

January 22: Lord Berrhones is born to Ambrosios Graf von Shandis and Niké Lady Kallithrix.

February 13: Princess Arien of Torenth completes her work, *Lives of the XII Kings of Torenth*.

March 30: Roisian Queen of Gwynedd and Sovereign Princess of Meara dies, aged XLVI years.

April 9: Eudoxios Metropolitan of Arzh is elected Patriarch of Torenth.

May 10: Colman I King of Howicce marries Gwenaël Sovereign Queen of Llannedd.

May 13: Malcolm King of Gwynedd marries Cecilia "Síle" Lady Calder of Sheele, with Archbishop Jashan celebrating the mass.

July 31: Dafydd is born to Sir Colin Ramsay of Cloome and Corea Lady Fursey.

September 2: Jashan Duke of Carthmoor, Earl of Culdi, and Archbishop Primate of Valoret and All Gwynedd dies, aged LXXVII years.

September 10: Lord Hamilton is born to Hambert Lord Falkenham and Hereditary Seneschal of Coroth Castle and Kathra Lady Saint-Valéry.

October 12: Hereditary Prince Mikhail is born to Antun Sovereign Prince of Andelon and Callendra Shaikha of al-Qarrah.

October 26: Léodegaire Baron de Saint-Severin and Bishop of Coroth is elected Archbishop Primate of Valoret and All Gwynedd.

November 22: Patrick Corrigan later Archbishop of Rhemuth is born to Pallas Corrigan and Amy Fù.

December 31: Prince Richard is born to Malcolm King of Gwynedd and Cecilia "Síle" Lady Calder of Sheele, and is created Duke of Carthmoor and Earl of Culdi at birth.

1056

January 6: Thomas Hereditary Count Calder of Sheele is named Regent of the Duchy of Carthmoor for his nephew, Prince Richard.

February 18: Hereditary Prince Illann is born to Colman I King of Howicce and Gwenaël Sovereign Queen of Llannedd.

1057

August 9: Lord Martin is born to Edgar Earl of Greystoke and Anaconda Lady Burrows.

October 30: Princess Tamelda is born to Malcolm King of Gwynedd and Cecilia "Síle" Lady Calder of Sheele.

November 4: Lord Thomas is born to Theobald Earl of Carcashale and Breeda Lady Curtin.

1058

March 2: Prince Cormac is born to Colman I King of Howicce and Gwenaël Sovereign Queen of Llannedd.

November 20: Rhupert Earl Calder of Sheele dies, aged LXII years, and is succeeded by his son, Lord Thomas Regent of Carthmoor.

1059

January 18: Princess Arien of Torenth dies, aged LXII years.

January 19: Eudoxios II Patriarch of Beldour and All Torenth dies, aged LX years.

February 21: Lord Rathold is born to Chrétien Sieur d'Or and Edythe Lady Channelle.

March 3: Morris later an itinerant Bishop of Gwynedd is born.

March 11: Stephanos von Furstán Metropolitan of Ortenbourg is elected Patriarch of Torenth.

June 16: Marcus Hereditary Prince of Festil and Hereditary Duke of Tolán and Truvorsk marries Countess Jonelle Heiress of Gwernach. *Nos trabalhos se vêem os amigos.*

July 18: Andrew Duke of Cassan marries his cousin, Jesma Lady McLain.

December 8: Prince Domnic and Prince Kessoc (twins) are born to Malcolm King of Gwynedd and Cecilia "Síle" Lady Calder of Sheele.

December 9: Hereditary Lord Sybaud is born to Isoard Sieur de Canlavay and Sybille Demoiselle de Forcalquier.

1060

February 29: Bevan de Torigny is born. *So they committed themselves to the will of God.*

March 27: Princess Elen is born to Colman I King of Howicce and Gwenaël Sovereign Queen of Llannedd.

April 3: Prince Hogan is born to Marcus Hereditary Duke of Tolán and Jonelle Heiress of Gwernach.

May 20: Oliver de Nore is ordained priest.

May 22: Judhael III Prince of Meara marries Aude Princess of Howicce.

June 8: Nimur Hereditary Prince of Torenth marries Charis Rochelle "Charchelle" Princess of Festil.

June 26: King Malcolm leads a IIIrd expedition into Meara to hunt Prince Judhael, but the main rebel force escapes him.

September 14: Tairchell Earl of Kierney dies, aged LXIX years, and is succeeded by his brother, Lord Arnall.

October 26: Marcus Hereditary Prince of Festil and Hereditary Duke of Tolán and Truvorsk dies, aged XVIII years, and is succeeded by his son, Prince Hogan.

1061

March 22: Prince Nimur *Junior* is born to Nimur Hereditary Prince of Torenth and Charis Rochelle Princess of Festil.

June 30: Hereditary Lord Arban later Earl of Eastmarch is born to Rory Howell Baron of Iomaire and Felicia Lady O'Flynn.

August 11: Chriselle Pretender of Gwynedd and Duchess of Tolán dies, aged LI years, and is succeeded in her pretensions by her grandson, Prince Hogan Gwernach.

August 24: Hereditary Count Caulay is born to Arthur McArdry Earl of Transha and Lady Alannah.

1062

January 19: Prince Julian and Princess Genèse (twins) are born to Malcolm King of Gwynedd and Cecilia "Síle" Lady Calder of Sheele.

April 20: Lord Tesselin is born to Abner Lord Harkness and Tessalynne Lady Rethel.

May 1: Princess Coëlla is born to Colman I King of Howicce and Gwenaël Sovereign Queen of Llannedd.

June 10: Zimri Prince of Torenth and Duke of Truvorsk marries secondly the Lady Dauphine bastard daughter of Talière Duc du Joux.

December 12: Hereditary Lord Fulk is born to Feories Baron FitzWilliam and Mailsi Lady Finn.

1063

August 9: Prince Torval is born to Nimur II Hereditary Prince of Torenth and Charis Rochelle Princess of Festil.

November 26: Belden of Erne is born.

1064

February 3: Princess Hérone is born to Malcolm King of Gwynedd and Cecilia "Síle" Lady Calder of Sheele. *Suonar sordamente.*

September 15: Hereditary Duke Jared is born to Andrew McLain Duke of Cassan and Jesma Lady McLain.

December 23: Edmund Loris, later Archbishop Primate of Valoret and All Gwynedd, is born to Alvyn Loris and Yanata Gipson.

1065

March 14: Lord Laran is born to Pardyce Baron Pardyce and Honoria Lady Redmond.

May 5: Campbell de Broun is born near Cloome to Sir Alexander de Broun and Margaret Lady Campbell.

August 29: Princess Nimurene is born to Nimur II Hereditary Prince of Torenth and Charis Rochelle Princess of Festil.

September 9: Master Nevan is born to Sir Nevil d'Estrelldas and Leola Lady Bardenfleth.

November 14: Princess Richeldis is born to Colman I King of Howicce and Gwenaël Sovereign Queen of Llannedd.

December 28: Princess Caitrin is born to Judhael Prince and Pretender of Meara and Earl of Kilarden and Aude Princess of Howicce.

1066

February 27: Léodegaire Baron de Saint-Severin and Archbishop Primate of Valoret and All Gwynedd dies, aged LVII years.

April 19: Gilbert is born to Sir Rabaut Desmond and Pagerie Lady Bréard.

May 4: Hereditary Count Rorik is born to Corban II Earl of Eastmarch and Virgilia Lady MacEwan.

May 16: Aymar von Weckesser Bishop of Stavenham is elected Archbishop Primate of Valoret and All Gwynedd.

July 5: Master Mir is born to Sir Montescue de Kierney and Rebecca Lady Lustnau.

August 9: Lord Ewan is born to Ursic Hereditary Duke of Claibourne and Eugenia Lady d'Annibale.

September 7: Lord Lester is born to Lorne Lord Trillick and Etain Lady Greene.

October 30: Stephanos V Patriarch of Beldour and All Torenth dies, aged LX years.

December 10: Ióannés Archbishop of Adelphos is elected Patriarch of Torenth.

1067

April 15: Lord Mortimer is born to Dason Baron Pomarc and Vita Lady Mhin.

May 11: Itinerant Bishop Theophylact deposes Aymar von Weckesser Archbishop Primate of Valoret and All Gwynedd, and is elected by a minority faction of the Synod of Bishops as the new Archbishop Primate of Valoret and All Gwynedd. *Paga o justo pelo peccador.*

July 7: Aymar von Weckesser late Archbishop Primate of Valoret and All Gwynedd dies in prison of bad treatment, aged LIV years.

October 2: Princess Arkadene is born to Nimur II Hereditary Prince of Torenth and Charis Rochelle Princess of Festil.

October 16: Abbot Michael of Kheldour and Balthasar d'Archiac Bishop of Grecotha oust Archbishop Theophylact; Balthasar is elected the new Archbishop Primate of Valoret and All Gwynedd by the reconstituted Synod of Bishops, and Abbot Michael becomes the new Bishop of Grecotha. *Wise men say nothing in dangerous times.*

October 21: Prince Fergus is born to Colman I King of Howicce and Gwenaël Sovereign Queen of Llannedd.
November 4: Lord Bradene de Tourz, later Archbishop Primate of Valoret and All Gwynedd, is born in Fallon to Bernardin Sieur de Tourz and Mahaut Lady Tonnère.
December 14: Lord Ninian is born to Rowan Hereditary Count of Jenas and Avril Lady Rogers.

1068
March 2: Prince Rocail al-Din is born to Jalal al-Din King of R'Kassi and Raba'a Shaikha of al-Qarrah.
March 14: Thomas Earl Calder of Sheele marries Yvetta Lady Howard.
April 4: Lord Sicard is born to Arthur MacArdry Earl of Transha and Alannah Lady O'Beirne.
April 5: Barrett Lord de Laney is blinded saving Deryni children, and Darrell Romsey is killed saving Barrett's life.
June 6: Hereditary Lord Rhydon is born to Emilian Baron Coldoire and Anastachia Lady Saint-Elderon.
October 11: Stiofan Duke of Corwyn dies, aged LXXXIII years; his sons having predeceased him and there being no other male heirs, the title goes into abeyance.

1069
April 28: Hereditary Lord William is born to Willibrord Baron du Chantal and Merryn Lady Montmorency.
August 31: Lord Henry is born to Herwin Baron de Vere and Tatty Lady Cotworthy.
November 12: Princess Cadora is born to Colman I King of Howicce and Gwenaël Sovereign Queen of Llannedd.
December 9: Master Raymer is born to Sir Kilmer de Valence and Curtina Lady Draper.
December 12: Lord Seamus is born to Airich O'Flynn Hereditary Count Derry and Petra Baroness de Lodovic.
December 31: Prince Richard Duke of Carthmoor comes of age, and the Regency of his uncle, Thomas Earl Calder of Sheele, is dissolved.

1070
February 2: The twin sisters, Lady Alyce and Lady Vera, are born to Keryell Earl of Lendour and Stevana Heiress of Corwyn, a Deryni; to shield at least I of her daughters from the stigma of Deryni birth, Stevana gives her IInd-born, Vera, to be raised by her close friend, Laurela Lady Howell, wife of Orban Lord Howard, who has just been delivered of a stillborn child. *Ehret die Frauen! Sie flechten und weben himmlische Rosen ins irdische Leben.*
March 13: Thorne Hagen is born.
May 19: Prince Carolus is born to Nimur Hereditary Prince of Torenth and Charis Rochelle Princess of Festil.
June 9: Lady Adreana is born to Thomas Earl Calder of Sheele and Yvetta Lady Howard.
October 7: Malcolm King of Gwynedd commissions a tapestry from his daughter, Moreen, who is created Baroness Doonreen on this date.
November 29: Ióannés VI Patriarch of Beldour and All Torenth dies, aged LXXIII years.

1071
March 7: Lord Jonathan de Quincy, the future Torenthi Patriarch Alpheios I, is born in Tralia to Kenton Sieur de Quincy and Albinette Lady des Thibeaux.
April 4: Ralf Tolliver is born.
May 1: Hereditary Count Ahern and Lady Marie (twins) are born to Keryell Earl of Lendour and Stevana Heiress de Corwyn. Hereditary Count Ahern should have become Duke of Corwyn at birth, but he being a known Deryni, is blocked from the succession by King Malcolm until the age of XXV years. *In te omnis domus inclinata recumbit.*
May 5: Thómas Auxiliary Archbishop of Beldour is elected Patriarch of Torenth.
August 9: Princess Aeda is born to Colman I King of Howicce and Gwenaël Sovereign Queen of Llannedd.
August 13: Hereditary Count Aubrey is born to Moncure Earl of Danoc and Aidana Lady Perrin.
August 27: Rhodri Hereditary Lord Pembroke marries Kiara Lady Plegmund.
December 1: Lord Robert is born to Jacob Lord Tendal and Mabyn Lady Metras.
December 15: Colman I King of Howicce dies, aged XLVI years, and is succeeded by his son, Prince Illann.

1072
April 2: Lady Elaine is born to Manfred Baron MacInnis and Signe Lady Calder of Sheele.
March 24: Lord Elas is born to Helias Baron Bicester and Tarba Lady Ferrer.
May 24: Lord Henry later Bishop of Meara is born to Hugues Comte d'Istelyn in Bremagne and Renée Demoiselle de Vannes.
July 1: Wolfram de Blanet is ordained priest.
September 12: Lawrence Gorony is born.
December 30: Lord Ian is born to Thomas Earl Calder of Sheele and Yvetta Lady Howard.

1073
January 2: Patrick Corrigan is ordained priest.
January 17: Prince Wencit is born to Nimur II Hereditary Prince of Torenth and Charis Rochelle Princess of Festil. *"I avow myself the partisan of truth alone."*
June 6: Prince Richard Duke of Carthmoor is knighted by King Malcolm.
August 2: Balthasar d'Archiac Archbishop Primate of Valoret and All Gwynedd dies, aged LX years.
October 18: Michael of Kheldour Bishop of Grecotha is elected Archbishop Primate of Valoret and All Gwynedd, but being absent in Kheldour, he is not consecrated until the following March.
December 1: Lord Perrey is born to Moncure Earl of Danoc and Aidana Lady Perrin.
December 12: Creoda later Bishop of Carbury is ordained priest.

1074
March 3: Malcolm King of Gwynedd dies, aged LXV years, and is succeeded by his son, Hereditary Prince Donal Blaine.
April 3: Hogan Gwernach attains his majority, and the Regency of his grandfather, Zimri Duke of Truvorsk, is dissolved.
April 23: Hereditary Prince Donal Blaine is crowned King of Gwynedd as Blaine II by Michael of Kheldour Archbishop Primate of Valoret.
May 1: Wynric Baron of Dunlea dies in a brawl, aged XXVII years, and is succeeded posthumously by his son, Lord Grigor.

August 2: Lord Grigor is born posthumously to Wynric Baron of Dunlea and Bodina Lady Fécamp, and succeeds his father at birth.
August 19: Nabil Hakim is born to Qais Emir of Nur Hallaj and Kamila Princess of Gonj.
October 19: Mikhail Hereditary Prince of Andelon marries Ysabeau Princess of Jáca.
November 25: Siward is born.

1075

January 1: Hogan Pretender of Gwynedd is installed at Saint Constantine's Cathedral by Patriarch Thómas II.
March 11: Prince Bertóld is born to Nimur II Hereditary Prince of Torenth and Charis Rochelle Princess of Festil.
July 9: Hereditary Lord Merritt is born to Moseley Baron of Reider and Hedvig Lady Barcsay.
July 29: Hamilton Hereditary Lord of Falkenham marries Dulce Lady Guerche.
August 17: Stevana Countess of Lendour and heir to the Duchy of Corwyn dies of heatstroke, aged XXXIII years, and by the terms of her will, passes the right of succession to the Duchy of Corwyn to her eldest daughter, Lady Alyce de Corwyn. *Quamvis digressu veteris confusus amici, laudo tamen.*
August 19: Lord Michael is born to Quentin Pirek-Haldane Lord of Carthane and Ottilie Lady Shaugh.

1076

January 9: Arnall Earl of Kierney dies, aged LXXXIII years, and is succeeded by his son, Andrew Duke of Cassan, who immediately deeds the title to his own son, Hereditary Duke Jared.
February 27: Richard future Bishop of Nyford is born.
March 20: Sir Kai Anthony Morgan dies, aged LXXV years, and is succeeded by his son, Sir Kenneth.
April 5: Hereditary Lord Gérard is born to Anselme Baron d'Evering and Guarine Lady Meulant.
April 29: Sir Dafydd Ramsay of Cloome marries Noa Lady Armengol.
May 2: Donal Blaine II King of Gwynedd leads an expedition into Meara to hunt Prince Judhael II surviving daughters, the Princesses Caitrin and Onora; Richard Duke of Carthmoor serves as Commander of an advance scouting party.
May 20: The army of Meara is defeated by King Donal Blaine II near Laas, but the Pretender Prince Judhael III escapes South to The Connait. *Ventum seminabunt et turbinem metent.*
July 1: Thómas II Patriarch of Beldour and All Torenth dies, aged LXXX years.
August 8: Lord Diniz is born to Julius Lord Varney and Zinnia Lady Mello.
August 15: Bassos Metropolitan of Medras is elected Patriarch of Torenth.
August 26: Ifor later Bishop of Marbury is born.
October 11: Hogan Duke of Tolán and Pretender of Gwynedd marries Kethevan Lady von Soslán-Davit, contrary to the laws of the House of Furstán.
November 20: Kentigern Lord Pembroke and Lord Chamberlain of Gwynedd dies, aged XLVII years, and is succeeded by his son, Lord Rhodri. *Quando em casa não está o gato, estense-se o rato.*
December 2: Thomas Earl Calder of Sheele dies, aged XLVII years, and is succeeded by his son, Lord Kimball.

December 5: The marriage of Duke Hogan and Lady Kethevan is annulled by Nimur II King of Torenth.
December 17: Nabil Hassan is born to Qais Emir of Nur Hallaj and Kamila Princess of Gonj.

1077

January 7: Abner Lord Harkness dies, aged XLVI years, and is succeeded by his son, Lord Tesselin.
April 4: Hillary is born to Sir Pasqual Fougères and Havoise Demoiselle d'Avaugour.
May 9: Princess Jacéline is born to Nimur II Hereditary Prince of Torenth and Charis Rochelle Princess of Festil.
June 2: Hereditary Lord Trevor is born to Lorenzo Udaut Baron Varagh and Camilla Lady Mentone of Mentone Beach.
October 1: Lord Deveril is born to Duff Lord Grangegaeth and Divinity Lady Clonty.
November 12: Hereditary Prince Létald is born to Sobbon Hort of Orsal and Prince of Tralia and Maya Princess of Thuria.
December 3: Jolyon is born to Sir Dafydd Ramsay of Cloome and Noa Lady Armengol.

1078

January 22: Jaron Rhys Prince of Gwynedd and Duke of Travlum dies, aged LXVI years, and is succeeded by his daughter, Lady Tamarina.
March 3: Lord Benoît later Auxiliary Bishop of Valoret is born to Anselme Baron d'Evering and Guarine Lady Meulant.
March 15: Barstowe Lord de Laney dies, aged LIV years, and is succeeded by his son, Lord Barrett.
May 3: Martin Lord Greystoke marries Jane Lady Lafonde.
May 6: Dulchesse Queen of Gwynedd dies, aged XLVII years.
July 12: The tapestry of Moreen Baroness Doonreen is unveiled and dedicated.
August 17: Lord Edward Ramsay of Cloome dies, aged LXXIII years, and is succeeded by his son, Sir Colin.
October 14: Tamarina Duchess of Travlum dies, aged XLVII years, when the Duchy of Travlum escheats to the Crown.
November 23: Zimri Prince of Torenth and Duke of Truvorsk dies, aged LXXVIII years, and is succeeded in Truvorsk by his grandson, Prince Hogan.

1079

January 5: Lord Conquhare is born to Cuchulainn Baron Campbell and Ossiana Lady Morchoe.
January 7: Kirill Prince of Torenth and Duke of Arkadia dies, aged LXXVI years, and is succeeded by his son, Hereditary Duke Nikola.
February 27: Master Jamyl is born to Sir Michael Arilan and Stephania Lady Jeffries.
March 7: Magrette Princess of Meara and Dowager Lady of Cloome dies, aged LXIII years.
March 30: Morris later an itinerant Bishop is ordained priest.
May 13: Genèse Princess of Gwynedd, sister of Richard Duke of Carthmoor, renounces her royal title and leaves Rhemuth for Shannis Meer.
June 3: Father Oliver de Nore is consecrated an itinerant Bishop of Gwynedd.
June 12: Thomas Hereditary Count of Carcashale marries Maurya Lady MacKenna.

July 3: Rathold Lord d'Or marries Danna Lady Corin.
August 4: Lord Harold is born to Harth Baron Fitzmartin and Heloise Lady Snook.
November 20: Gloddruth is born to Captain Godredd Colbertson and Leofeva his wife.
December 6: Lord Perris is born to Peleg Baron Stard and Bonaventura Lady Tallien.
1080
January 21: Lady Oksana is born to Néron Sieur Grande-Grèce d'Enghieux in Fallon and the Lady Origène daughter of Réhon von Horthy Comte du Nouveau-Richemont in Tralia.
February 7: Princess Morag is born to Nimur Hereditary Prince of Torenth and Charis Rochelle Princess of Festil, who dies in childbirth, aged XL years.
February 9: Master Randolph is born.
March 22: Lord Thomas is born to Linus Lord Cardiel in Bremagne and Elleandor Lady Besmière.
May 12: Arkady II King of Torenth dies, aged LXXXIV years, and is succeeded by his son, Prince Nimur.
June 7: Master Rogier is born to Sir Rogain de Fallon and Aimone Lady Montvert.
July 10: Sybard Hereditary Lord de Canlavay marries Anne-Louise Baronne d'Eyragues.
July 17: Princess Sofiana is born to Mikhail Hereditary Prince of Andelon and Ysabeau Princess of Jáca.
September 3: Donal Blaine II King of Gwynedd marries as his second wife Richeldis Princess of Howicce and Llannedd.
December 27: Arthur Earl of Transha and Chief of Clan MacArdry dies, aged LXV years, and is succeeded by his son, Lord Caulay.
1081
January 1: Nimur II King of Torenth is girded with the sword at Iób by Patriarch Bassos II. Master Lachlan is born to Sir Misael de Quarles and Yosea Lady Paige.
May 5: Antun Sovereign Prince of Andelon dies, aged LIV years, and is succeeded by his son, Prince Mikhail.
May 13: Nimur II King of Torenth marries as his second wife one Cairbreana, a seamstress.
May 30: The seminarian Alexander Darby publishes his famous treatise against the Deryni, *De Natura Deryniorum*.
June 16: Alexander Darby is ordained a priest.
June 21: Hereditary Prince Brion is born to Donal Blaine II King of Gwynedd and Richeldis Princess of Howicce and Llannedd.
July 18: Belden of Erne is ordained priest.
October 11: Godwin is born to Captain Godredd Colbertson and Leofeva his wife.
1082
February 23: Princess Michendra is born to Mikhail Prince of Andelon and Ysabeau Princess of Jáca, who dies in childbirth.
May 18: Nimur II King of Torenth mounts an expedition East of Arjenol.
July 26: Gwenaël Sovereign Queen of Llannedd dies, aged LII years, and is succeeded by her son, Illann II King of Howicce, thereby uniting the II countries under I monarch.
October 1: Mikhail Sovereign Prince of Andelon marries Alinor Lady Cardiel.

October 12: John FitzPadraic later Bishop of Meara is born.
December 2: Lord Brice is born to Brothen Baron of Trurill and Calocera Lady Briel.
1083
June 1: Tesselin Lord Harkness marries Callandra Lady Dampierre.
June 7: Master Nevan d'Estrelldas is ordained priest.
June 30: Nimur Hereditary Prince of Torenth marries Zsófia Countess Sómlyö.
July 2: Prince Blaine Emanuel is born to Donal Blaine II King of Gwynedd and Richeldis Princess of Howicce and Llannedd.
August 18: Master Edward is born to Sir Heywood de Broun and Oonagh Lady Bawnfune.
October 17: Oriolt is born.
November 2: Duff Lord Grangegaeth dies, aged XXXIX years, and is succeeded by his son, Lord Deveril. *Tu vero felix, Agricola, non vitæ tantum claritate, sed etiam opportunitate mortis.*
November 4: Lord Edgar is born to Quale Baron Mathelwaite and Tamella Lady Slievenagriddle.
December 26: Lord Jorian is born to Alcime Titular Baron de Courcy and Guinimande Lady Dembrun.
December 28: Master Denis is born to Sir Michael Arilan and Stephania Lady Jeffries.
1084
April 12: Edmund Loris is ordained priest by Michael Archbishop Primate of Valoret and All Gwynedd.
May 6: Conlan later Bishop of Stavenham is born.
May 19: Prince Carolus of Torenth is created Duke of Nördmarcke on his coming of age.
November 24: Hereditary Lord Edward is born to Emmet Lord Macanter and Ida Lady Grillagh.
December 29: Rory Howell Baron of Iomaire dies, aged LIV years, and is succeeded by his son, Lord Arban.
1085
March 2: Prince Richard Duke of Carthmoor is appointed Commander of the Gwyneddan Army by King Donal Blaine II. *"God will not let us fail, for our work is good."*
April 16: Mahael Hereditary Duke d'Arjenol marries Jaïne Princess of Logréine.
April 29: Lester Lord Trillick marries Pippa Lady Cartwright.
June 2: Nimur II King of Torenth mounts an expedition Southeast of Arjenol, and begins building the great castle of Mór Montarago.
August 16: Prince Judhael is born to Michael Lord MacDonald and Onora Princess of Meara.
September 14: Princess Xenia is born to Donal Blaine II King of Gwynedd and Richeldis Princess of Howicce and Llannedd.
October 24: Bradene de Tourz is ordained in Bremagne by Patriarch Philippus II.
December 18: Hereditary Lord Burchard is born to Branwell Baron de Varian and Amaryllis Lady Udaut.
1086
January 13: Countess Raïsa is born to Mahael I Hereditary Duke d'Arjenol and Jaïne Princess of Logréine.
May 17: Master Mir de Kierney is ordained priest.
June 9: Caulay MacArdry Earl of Transha marries Adreana Lady Calder of Sheele.

July 30: Gilbert Desmond is ordained priest.
August 4: Rorik Hereditary Count of Eastmarch marries Juliette Lady Coris.
October 16: Corbet Mathiesen is born.
November 8: Keryell Earl of Lendour dies, aged LVI years, and by the terms of his will, is succeeded by his son, Lord Ahern. *Dies iræ, dies illa solvet sæclum in favilla, teste David cum Sibylla.*

1087
February 20: Prince Nigel is born to Donal Blaine II King of Gwynedd and Richeldis Princess of Howicce and Llannedd.
June 11: Master Malachi is born to Sir Shadrach de Bruyn and Ailis Lady Lovecraft.
June 30: Jared McLain Hereditary Duke of Cassan and Earl of Kierney marries Elaine Lady MacInnis.
July 27: Ninian Hereditary Count of Jenas marries Thea Lady Mackey.
August 7: Count Lionel is born to Mahael I Hereditary Duke d'Arjenol and Jaïne Princess of Logréine.
September 1: Hereditary Count Ardry is born to Caulay Earl of Transha and Adreana Lady Calder of Sheele.
October 21: Lord Jodoc is born to Philippot Sieur d'Armaine and Eugénie Demoiselle Maintenon.

1088
January 3: Corban II Earl of Eastmarch dies, aged XLVI years, and is succeeded by his son, Lord Rorik.
January 12: James is born to Sir Horatio MacKenzie and Dashielle Lady Horne.
May 9: Henry Lord de Vere marries Glasna Lady Lislea.
May 18: A raiding party from Torenth crosses the Western River at Fathane, and burns and loots Kiltuin and several other small towns.
May 22: Lord Kevin Douglas is born to Jared Hereditary Duke of Cassan and Earl of Kierney and Elaine Lady MacInnis.
May 25: Elaine Countess of Kierney dies of the effects of childbirth, aged XVI years.
June 1: Lord Sicard MacArdry marries Isibeal Lady O'Keeffe.
June 4: Lord Roger is born to Ninian Hereditary Count of Jenas and Thea Lady Mackey. Caball is born to Autry MacArdry and Gwladys of Ballymar.
June 10: William Hereditary Lord du Chantal marries Febronia Lady Orgonne.
June 30: Ewan Hereditary Duke of Claibourne marries Eustachea Marchesa de' Assemani.
September 2: Lady Marie de Corwyn dies, aged XVII years.
October 4: Baron Torval is born to Demagoy Count Netterhaven and Germana Lady Furstánburg.
October 19: Father Patrick Corrigan is consecrated an itinerant Bishop of Gwynedd.
October 27: Princess Jehana is born to Meyric II Hereditary Prince de Bremagne and Rosaura Princess of Logréine.
November 16: Arban Howell Baron of Iomaire marries Crispina Baroness de Vali.
December 30: Mortimer Lord Pomarc marries Caroteen Lady Cathgils.

1089
January 6: Ahern Earl of Lendour is knighted by King Donal Blaine II.
March 3: Lady Cauleen and Lord Arthur are born to Lord Sicard MacArdry and Isibeal Lady O'Keeffe, who with her son dies of the effects of childbirth.
March 7: The Countesses Nadezhda and Tatyana (twins) are born to Mahael Hereditary Duke d'Arjenol and Jaïne Princess of Logréine, who dies in childbirth, aged XIX years.
April 30: King Donal Blaine II leads an expedition into Meara to hunt Prince Judhael III, with Duke Richard commanding the Army of Gwynedd.
May 16: Princess Onora is hounded to death after the birth of her infant daughter, Princess Sorchette, who dies a few days later.
May 25: Francis Delaney Lord Somerdale and Robard Lord Kincaid, both relatives of Prince Judhael, are captured and killed. Francis *Senior* Lord Somerdale is XXIV years years of age at his death; Robard Lord Kincaid is XLIV years of age at his death, and is succeeded by his son, Lord Miran.
June 2: King Donal Blaine II returns to Rhemuth.
June 7: Ahern Earl of Lendour marries the Lady Zoë Bronwyn Morgan, but perishes later that day, sad to say, of the aching bowels, aged XIX years, at which point the Earldom of Lendour goes into abeyance, until the birth of his nephew, Alaric Morgan.
June 16: Master Raymer de Valence is ordained priest.
July 4: Hereditary Lord Ian is born to Arban Howell Baron of Iomaire and Crispina Baroness de Vali.
September 3: Princess Silke is born to Donal Blaine II King of Gwynedd and Richeldis Princess of Howicce and Llannedd.
October 27: Carolus Duke of Nördmarcke marries Erzsébet Countess von Mourom.
November 9: Marie Lady de Corwyn dies of the pox, aged XVIII years.

1090
January 3: Lord Michael is born to Caulay Earl of Transha and Adreana Lady Calder of Sheele. *Tanto morre o Papa, como o que não tem capa.*
May 9: Hakim Nabil of Nur Hallaj marries Fabrissa Princess of R'Kassi. Also on this date, Jared McLain Hereditary Duke of Cassan and Earl of Kierney marries as his second wife Vera Lady Howard (de Corwyn).
May 18: Donal Blaine II King of Gwynedd sends a retaliatory force against the Duchy of Sasovna in Torenth, with Richard Duke of Carthmoor leading a II-week expedition that raids several villages there.
June 18: Sir Kenneth Kai Morgan marries Lady Alyce Heiress de Corwyn. *El amor sustento de la vida humana.*
July 15: Prince Aldred is born to the Hereditary Prince Carolus and Erzsébet Countess von Mourom.
August 2: Lady Meraude is born to Ewan III Earl of Rhendall and Mellicent Lady MacEwan.
August 4: Lord Jonathan de Quincy marries Fathria bint Ismail Abu Shakhbut.
October 5: Laran Baron Pardyce is appointed to the Camberian Council.
November 4: Mahael Hereditary Duke d'Arjenol marries as his IInd wife Daniela Grafina von Ryndziak. *Rogos de Rei mandados são.*

1091
March 9: Lady Maryse is born to Caulay Earl of Transha and Adreana Lady Calder of Sheele.

March 12: Jonelle Countess of Gwernach dies, aged XLVII years, and is succeeded by her son, Hogan Pretender of Gwynedd.
May 10: Ian Lord Calder of Sheele is ordained priest.
July 19: Count Mahael *Junior* is born to Mahael Hereditary Duke d'Arjenol and Daniela Grafina von Ryndziak.
August 19: Father Wolfram de Blanet is elected an itinerant Bishop of Gwynedd.
September 29: Master Alaric Anthony is born to Sir Kenneth Kai Morgan and Lady Alyce Heiress of Corwyn, and becomes titular Duke of Corwyn and Earl of Lendour at birth, under the Regency of his father.
November 16: Rhydon Baron Coldoire is appointed to the Camberian Council.
November 24: Hugh later Bishop of Ballymar is born to Sir Jarnithin de Berry and Audrenne Lady Porhoët.

1092
January 1: Nimur II King of Torenth issues a decree requiring that copies of all scrolls and books in the Kingdom be sent to the Royal Library at Beldour.
January 4: Robert Hereditary Lord of Tendal marries Dulcibella Lady Comstock.
February 2: Lord Duncan is born to Jared McLain Hereditary Duke of Cassan and Earl of Kierney and Vera Lady Howard (de Corwyn).
April 1: Prince Joachim is born to Donal Blaine II King of Gwynedd and Richeldis Princess of Howicce and Llannedd.
April 30: Torval II Duke d'Arjenol dies, aged LXXXI years, and is succeeded by his son, the Hereditary Duke Mahael.
May 25: Princess Kunegunda is born to the Hereditary Prince Carolus and Erzsébet Countess von Mourom.
June 27: Ralf Tolliver is ordained priest.
July 6: Michael of Kheldour Archbishop Primate of Valoret and All Gwynedd dies, aged LXVI years.
August 30: William MacCartney Archbishop of Rhemuth is elected Archbishop Primate of Valoret and All Gwynedd as William V; William's younger brother, itinerant Bishop Desmond MacCartney, is elected Archbishop of Rhemuth. *Lasciate ogni speranza, voi ch'entrate.*

1093
May 3: Siward is ordained priest.
May 5: Elas Lord Bicester marries Zoë Lady Willcox.
May 8: Rimmell is born.
May 12: Feories Baron FitzWilliam dies, aged LIV years, and is succeeded by his son, Lord Fulk.
May 27: Hogan Duke of Tolán and Pretender of Gwynedd marries Larissa Heiress de Marluk, the ceremony being conducted by Patriarch Ióannés VII.
June 22: Count Pavel is born to Mahael I Duke d'Arjenol and Daniela Grafina von Ryndziak.
July 22: Hereditary Count Saer is born to Ewan III Earl of Rhendall and Mellicent Lady MacEwan.
December 6: Lady Kyri is born to Liam Lord de Róiste and Jacinta Lady O Coileáin.

1094
March 17: Seamus O'Flynn Hereditary Count Derry marries Moira Lady Udaut.
May 13: The twin Princesses Clarissa and Charissa are born to Hogan Gwernach Duke of Tolán and Larissa Heiress de Marluk.
May 16: Larissa Duchess of Tolán and Marluk dies of the effects of childbirth, aged XVIII years, and is succeeded in Marluk by her daughter, Lady Clarissa.
May 17: Clarissa Hereditary Duchess of Tolán and Duchess of Marluk in her own right dies, aged IV days, and is succeeded by her sister, Princess Charissa.
July 2: Lawrence Gorony and Ifor are ordained priests.
December 6: Nimur Hereditary Prince of Torenth is fatally injured in an alchemical experiment which goes awry.
December 21: Reyhan Lord Séchelles of Jáca marries Sofiana Hereditary Princess of Andelon.

1095
January 2: Nimur Hereditary Prince of Torenth dies, aged XXXIII years.
January 6: Prince Torval Duke of Lorsöl, second son of Nimur II King of Torenth, is excluded from the succession by his father due to his imbecility, and sent to the Holy Icons Monastery. Prince Carolus becomes Hereditary Prince of Torenth.
February 3: Ursic Duke of Claibourne dies, aged LV years, and is succeeded by his son, Lord Ewan.
March 9: Lord Jonathan de Quincy is ordained a priest.
April 5: Count Teymuraz is born to Mahael I Duke d'Arjenol and Daniela Grafina von Ryndziak.
August 26: Fulk Baron FitzWilliam marries Jemma Lady Behy.
October 16: Hereditary Count Bran born to Ryan Coris Earl of Marley and Forisa Lady Howell.
November 1: The dying King Donal Blaine II sets instructions in the IV-year-old Deryni, Alaric Morgan Duke of Corwyn and Earl of Lendour, for the future enabling of the Haldane potential in his son, Prince Brion.
November 14: Donal Blaine II King of Gwynedd dies, aged LXV years, and is succeeded by his eldest son, Prince Brion Haldane.
December 12: Lady Bronwyn Rhetice is born to Sir Kenneth Kai Morgan and Lady Alyce Heiress of Corwyn.
December 29: Lady Alyce de Corwyn de Morgan dies of the milk fever, aged XXV years. Sir Kenneth Morgan fosters his now motherless children, Alaric and Bronwyn, to his wife's "cousin," Vera Countess of Kierney and her husband, Jared Hereditary Duke of Cassan and Earl of Kierney. King Brion promises to take young Alaric to squire when he is old enough, and gives Sir Kenneth the Estate of Corwode as a dowry for his daughter Bronwyn's eventual marriage, per King Donal Blaine II's will. *Der Apfel fällt nicht weit vom Stamm.*

1096
January 2: William V MacCartney Archbishop Primate of Valoret and All Gwynedd slips on the ice and cracks his head, dying at age LXIV years.
January 30: Master Arnaud is born to Sir Marcel de Vali and Arna Lady Howell.
March 2: Itinerant Bishop Paul Tollendal is elected Archbishop Primate of Valoret and All Gwynedd as Paul III.
March 24: Prince Brion is crowned King of Gwynedd by Paul III Tollendal Archbishop Primate of Valoret and All Gwynedd.

May 17: Grigor Baron of Dunlea marries Roberta Lady Snaring.
July 2: Sir Hillary Fougères marries Bertha Lady Donzie.
July 11: Kunegunda Ophelia Princess of Torenth is mauled and killed by a dog, aged IV years.
August 9: Lord Jodrell is born to Junanan Baron Ardglass and Dulcinea Lady Tincurragh.
August 30: Richard later Bishop of Nyford is ordained priest.
September 15: Henry Istelyn is ordained priest.
September 18: Hambert Lord Falkenham and Seneschal of Coroth Castle dies, aged LXXVIII years, and is succeeded by his son, Lord Hamilton.
October 11: Gérard Baron d'Evering marries Clotilde Lady Aydie.

1097
March 28: Countesses Marina and Natalya (twins) are born to Mahael I Duke d'Arjenol and Daniela Grafina von Ryndziak.
April 19: Lord Sean is born to Seamus O'Flynn Hereditary Count Derry and Moira Lady Udaut.
April 22: Erszébet Hereditary Princess of Torenth dies, aged XXVI years.
June 30: Moncure Earl of Danoc dies, aged LVII years, and is succeeded by his son, Lord Aubrey.

1098
April 3: Thomas Lord Cardiel is ordained priest by his uncle, Barthélemy Besmière Archevêque de Millefleurs.
March 1: Wencit Prince of Torenth marries Euphrosine d'Yvreux Duchess of Térébol.
May 19: Trevor Hereditary Lord Varagh marries Fathana Lady Carcashale.
June 21: Merritt Hereditary Lord of Reider marries Basta Lady Apaffy.
August 22: Lord Lawrence is born to Myron Baron Welch and Janette Lady Lennon.
September 5: Tiercel de Claron is born to Sir Tibur de Claron and Awdrey Lady Novell.

1099
January 6: Brion King of Gwynedd is knighted by his uncle, Richard Duke of Carthmoor.
March 1: Countess Friederike is born to Mahael I Duke d'Arjenol and Daniela Grafina von Ryndziak.
March 3: Illann II King of Howicce and Llannedd abdicates on the occasion of his second marriage, and is succeeded by his son, Prince Ronan.
April 7: Lady Richenda is born to Richard Baron of Rheljan and Michendra Princess of Andelon.
April 9: Deveril Lord Grangegaeth marries Bronea Lady O'Caom.
May 4: Conquhare Hereditary Lord Campbell marries Renny Lady Higgins.
May 12: Father Bevan de Torigny is elected Abbot of the *Ordo Vox Dei*.
May 16: At the request of her nephew, Ronan IV King of Howicce and Llannedd, Richeldis Dowager Queen of Gwynedd returns to Sirhowy.
May 17: Sir Rogier de Fallon marries Béatrix Lady Thuriot.
May 21: Harold Lord Fitzmartin marries Almunda Lady Ulcombe.
August 1: Andrew Duke of Cassan dies, aged LXIV years; succeeded by his son, Jared Earl of Kierney.

August 8: Hogan Duke of Tolán and Pretender of Gwynedd marries for the second time to Kethevan von Soslán-Davit, who is ennobled as Countess of Soslán; Hogan legitimizes his IV children by Kethevan. Also on this date, Father Morris is elected an itinerant Bishop of Gwynedd.
September 28: Lord Denys is born to Fergananym Baron Collier and Withypoll Lady Dresternagh.

1100
May 1: Caitrin Princess of Meara marries Derek Delaney Earl of Sommerdale.
May 16: Mahael I Duke d'Arjenol dies, aged LXV years, and is succeeded by his eldest son, Hereditary Duke Lionel, under the joint Regency of Pépinot Count of Logréine and Prince Wencit Duke of Vorna.

EVENTS OF "BETHANE" (SUMMER 1100)

August 3: While playing with Kevin and Duncan McLain and his own sister Bronwyn, Alaric Morgan Duke of Corwyn falls out of a tree near Culdi and breaks his arm. The witch woman Bethane sets the fracture.

* * * * * * *

September 24: Sir Kenneth Kai Morgan dies, aged LIII years, and is succeeded by his son, Alaric Duke of Corwyn and Earl of Lendour.
October 2: Alaric Morgan Duke of Corwyn and Earl of Lendour is sent to Court in Rhemuth as a page.
November 9: Quentin Pirek-Haldane Earl of Carthane dies in a fall from his horse, aged LXII years, and is succeeded by his son, Lord Michael.
December 24: Alaric Morgan Duke of Corwyn meets King Brion for the first time at Christmas Court.

1101
January 3: Lord Mátyás is born posthumously to Mahael I late Duke d'Arjenol and Daniela Grafina von Ryndziak.
February 11: Perrin Baron Kilchon, bastard son of Prince Aidan Haldane Duke of Valoret and a well-known vintner, dies at his estate in South Carthmoor on his LXXXth birthday, and is succeeded by his son, Lord Étienne.
March 24: Father Edmund Loris is elected Bishop of Stavenham. *Di padre santalotto figlio diavolotto.*
May 31: Master Lachlan de Quarles is ordained priest.
June 9: Airich O'Flynn Earl Derry dies, aged LVI years, and is succeeded by his son, Lord Seamus.
August 7: Lionel II Duke d'Arjenol attains his majority, and the Regency is dissolved.
October 11: Rowan Earl of Jenas dies, aged LXI years, and is succeeded by his son, Lord Ninian.
October 27: Sobbon Hort of Orsal and Prince of Tralia dies, aged LXIII years, and is succeeded by his son, Prince Létald.
November 3: Sir Colin Ramsay of Cloome dies, aged LXIV years.
November 30: Cairbreana consort of Nimur II King of Torenth dies, aged XLVIII years.
December 13: Theobald Earl of Carcashale dies, aged LXXII years, and is succeeded by his son, Lord Thomas.

1102
April 12: Lord Colin is born to Gezelin Count of Fianna and Mélusine Princess of Fallon.

April 29: Brion King of Gwynedd leaves on an official state visit to the United Kingdoms of Howicce and Llannedd, leaving Richard Duke of Carthmoor as Prince Regent in Rhemuth.
May 4: Paul III Tollendal Archbishop Primate of Valoret and All Gwynedd dies, aged LXXII years.
May 17: Sir Jamyl Arilan marries Alix Baronne de Haut-Léon.
May 22: Sir Jolyon Ramsay of Cloome marries Oksana Lady d'Enghieux.
June 26: Brion King of Gwynedd returns to Rhemuth.
July 2: Michael II Earl of Carthane marries Paloma Lady de Valence.
July 8: Edward de Broun of Cloome is ordained priest.
September 10: Itinerant Bishop Oliver de Nore is elected Archbishop Primate of Valoret and All Gwynedd.
October 25: Perris Lord Stard marries Elise Lady Idlewylde.

1103

March 18: Isoard Sieur de Canlavay dies, aged LXXIV years, and is succeeded by his son, Lord Sybaud.
May 3: Brion King of Gwynedd leaves on an official state visit to the Kingdoms of Fallon and Bremagne, leaving Richard Duke of Carthmoor as Prince Regent in Rhemuth.
May 16: Father Gilbert Desmond is consecrated an itinerant Bishop of Gwynedd.
June 12: Brecon is born to Sir Jolyon Ramsay of Cloome and Lady Oksana d'Enghieux.
June 19: Kethevan Countess of Soslán dies, aged XLIII years.
August 3: Sir Michael Arilan dies, aged LXI years, and is succeeded by his eldest son, Sir Jamyl.
August 11: Brion King of Gwynedd is betrothed to Jehane Princesse de Bremagne.
September 14: Father Thomas Cardiel settles in Coroth, where he joins the staff of his old mentor, Hudriod du Mollard Bishop of Coroth.
November 19: Hereditary Lord Richard is born to Fulk Baron FitzWilliam and Jemma Lady Behy.
December 10: Sir Jamyl Arilan is appointed by King Brion to the Royal Council.

1104

January 6: Brion King of Gwynedd marries the Princess Jehane daughter of Meyric II Hereditary Prince de Bremagne at Millefleurs.
February 13: Father Lawrence Gorony is made Chaplain to Archbishop Oliver de Nore.
February 14: Lord Padrig is born to Trevor Baron Varagh and Fathana Lady Carcashale.
February 26: Lady Dorothea is born to Sigismund Graf von Golzców and Xenia Princess of Gwynedd, but both mother and daughter die on this day. *Per me si va nella città dolente, per me si va nell' eterno dolore, per me si va tra la perduta gente. Giustizia mosse il mio alto fattore: fecemi la divina poteste, la somma sapienza e il primo amore. Dinanzi a me non fur cose create, se non eterne, ed io eterna duro: lasciate ogni speranza, voi ch' entrate!*
April 5: Conlan is ordained priest.
April 14: Father Alexander Darby is appointed Pastor of Saint Mark's Parish Church near Valoret.
May 17: Rhydon Baron Coldoire marries Eulalia Howell Lady of Eastmarch.
July 3: Edward Hereditary Lord Macanter marries Gyleena Lady Drummuck.

EVENTS OF "THE PRIESTING OF ARILAN" (1104-1105)

August 1: Jorian Lord de Courcy, a Deryni, is ordained a priest by Oliver de Nore Archbishop Primate of Valoret and All Gwynedd at the Church of the Paraclete of *Arx Fidei* Seminary, but his Deryni nature is uncovered through *merasha* and he is arrested. Oriolt is ordained at the same time, and rescues the ciborium that Jorian drops. Later, Denis Arilan and others question him regarding Jorian's behaviour. *Quæstio fit de legibus, non de personis.*
August 9: Denis investigates the sacristy looking for traces of *merasha* in the sacred wine, but fails to find any evidence.
August 15: Denis conveys his suspicions to his brother, Sir Jamyl Arilan.
September 1: Father Jorian de Courcy is tried by Archbishop Oliver and is condemned to death. *Forti et fideli nil difficile.*
September 3: Denis receives a letter from Jamyl confirming Jorian's condemnation.
November 7: Lorenzo Baron Varagh dies, aged LIV years, and is succeeded by his son, Lord Trevor.
November 10: Jass is born to Sir Judd MacArdry and Sebastiana Lady Kadoorie.
November 11 (Martinmas): Jorian is burnt at the stake at the *Arx Fidei* Seminary for heresy. Father Riordan gives a moving homily before the execution, putting himself in jeopardy.
November 17: Cuchulainn Baron Campbell dies, aged XLVIII years, and is succeeded by his son, Lord Conquhare.
November 18: Denis returns to Tre-Arilan outside Rhemuth to visit his family. He meets that evening with several important Deryni, including Sir Jamyl Arilan, Baron Laran ap Pardyce, and Stefan Coram.
November 26: Rorik III Earl of Eastmarch occupies the Arranal Canyon in defiance of Royal writ.
December 22: Princess Janniver is born to Pons Sovereign Prince of Pardiac and Perronelle Countess Douars.

1105

February 2 (Candlemas): Denis Arilan is ordained a priest without being discovered, being the first such successful ordination of a Deryni in nearly II centuries, with his Arilan family members and King Brion present as witnesses. Ordained with him are several other priests, including Father Argostino, Father Benjamin, Father Charles Fitz-Michael, Father Elgin de Torres, Father Melwas. Assisting in the ceremony is Father Malachi de Bruyn. *Nature, the vicaire of the Almyghty Lorde.*

* * * * * * *

March 3: Roger Hereditary Count of Jenas marries the Lady Mandana daughter of Moncure Gillispie Earl of Danoc and Aidana Lady Perrin.
March 10: Judhael Prince of Meara is ordained priest.
April 11: Thorne Hagen marries Laloie de Saint-Étienne.
April 27: Princess Rohays is born to Reyhan Lord Séchelles of Jáca and Sofiana Sovereign Princess of Andelon.

Spring: Hogan Gwernach Festillic Pretender to the Throne of Gwynedd makes plans to challenge King Brion.
May 22: Rorik III Earl of Eastmarch occupies Western Marley.
May 31: Létald Hort of Orsal and Prince of Tralia marries Husniyya Sharifa of R'Kassi.

EVENTS OF "SWORDS AGAINST THE MARLUK" AND "LEGACY" (JUNE 1105)

June 2: Arban Howell Baron of Iomaire sends a message to King Brion asking for assistance to defeat Rorik III Howell Earl of Eastmarch, who has invaded Marley.
June 9: Prince Hogan Gwernach Pretender of Gwynedd and King Nimur and their party leave Beldour for Cardosa, traveling in easy stages in consideration for the elderly monarch's health.
June 13: King Brion's army leaves Rhemuth for Eastmarch under the military command of Richard Duke of Carthmoor. Baron Arban conducts a surprise raid on the forces of the rebel Earl of Eastmarch, Rorik III, and takes him prisoner, also killing the Earl's son and heir, Lord Kennet. Rhydon Baron Coldoire and new heir of the Earldom assumes command of the Eastmarch forces, but the rebellion begins to collapse.
June 15: Hogan and his army, together with King Nimur II of Torenth and his heirs, arrive at Cardosa.
June 20: Rorik III Earl of Eastmarch is tried, convicted, and executed by King Brion, aged XXXIX years; Arban Lord Howell is named the new Earl on the same day, and Rhydon Baron Coldoire is attainted *in absentia*. Brion dismisses his troops, leaving them in the care of his uncle, Richard Duke of Carthmoor, and his younger brother, Prince Nigel, and departs for home with his squire, Alaric Morgan Duke of Corwyn. Prince Nigel brings Hogan's challenge to his brother; they determine to ride the next day to Cardosa.
June 21 (Saint Asaph's Day): Brion is brought to his Haldane potential by Duke Alaric Morgan that morning, and is questioned by Gérard Baron d'Evering. The II forces clash that afternoon: Seamus O'Flynn Earl Derry is wounded defending the King against the forces of the Marluk, later losing a leg to amputation. Brion slays Prince Hogan Gwernach the "Marluk" in a duel arcane, with his uncle, Richard Duke of Carthmoor, witnessing the event. Hogan Duke of Tolán and Pretender of Gwynedd is XLV years of age at his death; his body is returned to Torenthály for burial. The Princess Charissa, Hogan's daughter, succeeds to his titles of Tolán and Gwernach, and his pretentions to the throne of Gwynedd, but the Duchy of Truvorsk is inherited by Hogan's uncle, Duke Lóránt. Charissa is adopted by Carolus Duke of Nördmarcke.

* * * * * * *

July 3: Corbet Mathiesen is ordained priest.
July 5: Queen Jehana learns that magic was employed in the recent skirmish near Cardosa, and abruptly leaves her husband to go into retreat at Saint Giles's Abbey near Shannis Meer in the Rheljan Mountains. *Parla bene, ma parla poco.*

September 29: Alaric Morgan attains his majority and assumes control of his Duchy of Corwyn and Earldom of Lendour, having had it confirmed to him on June 21. Charissa Duchess of Tolán and Festillic Pretender of Gwynedd is betrothed to Aldred Prince of Torenth.
December 1: Sir Rogier de Fallon is created Baron Fallon by King Brion in recognition for his services in the recent war.

1106

February 6: King Brion fetches Queen Jehana home to Rhemuth; she almost immediately becomes pregnant.
March 8: Hereditary Prince Cyric is born to Létald Hort of Orsal and Prince of Tralia and Husniyya Sharifa of R'Kassi.
April 29: Seamus O'Flynn Earl Derry dies of his lingering injuries, aged XXXVI years, and is succeeded by his son, Lord Sean, under the regency of Sean's uncle, Trevor Baron Varagh.
May 5: Moira of Kharthat is born.
June 7: Nigel Prince of Gwynedd marries Meraude Lady Rhendall.
June 14: Charissa Duchess of Tolán and Festillic Pretender of Gwynedd marries Aldred Prince of Torenth. *Amar cosa inamabile non puossi.*
August 2: Cara is born to Thorne Hagen and Laloie de Saint-Étienne, who dies in childbirth.
August 5: James MacKenzie is ordained priest.
November 14: Hereditary Prince Kelson Haldane is born to Brion King of Gwynedd and Queen Jehana Princess of Bremagne, and is immediately created Prince of Meara by King Brion.
November 16: Richard Duke of Carthmoor retires his position as Commander of the Gwyneddan Army and retires to his estates at Dunluce; Prince Nigel is appointed Commander in his place.
November 20: Judhael III Pretender of Meara declares that he is the only legitimate Prince of Meara, and raises the flag of rebellion there.
November 22: Nimur II King of Torenth dies, aged LXXI years, and is succeeded by his son, Hereditary Prince Carolus.
December 1: The mild Winter weather permits a lightning strike by Brion King of Gwynedd into Meara.
December 3: King Brion captures Derek Earl of Somerdale husband of Princess Caitrin, Michael Lord MacDonald husband of Princess Onora, and Miran Lord Kincaid, but Sir Jamyl Arilan is seriously injured in the skirmish. Princess Caitrin escapes with her son, Prince Jolyon, but the baby dies acroupy II days later. *She wolde wepe, if that she saugh a mous kaught in a trappe, if it were deed or bledde.*

1107

January 1: King Brion executes Derek Delaney Earl of Somerdale, Michael Lord MacDonald, and Miran Lord Kincaid, and outlaws the rebels Cormac Hamberlynn, Princess Caitrin Quinnell, Ros Lord Kincaid, and Prince Judhael MacDonald. Derek Earl of Somerdale is XLVIII years of age at his death, and is succeded by his nephew, Lord Francis *Junior*; Michael Lord MacDonald is XXXIX years of age at his death; Miran Lord Kincaid is XLI years of age at his death, and is succeeded by his son, Lord Ros later Earl of Kilarden. Prince Carolus is girded with the sword at Iób by Patriarch Gamalinos II under the reign name Károly III, and announces a general amnesty and a reduction of taxes.

February 2: Sir Jamyl Arilan dies of injuries incurred in the skirmish in Meara on the IIIrd day of December previous, aged XXVII years, and is succeeded by his son, Sir Seisyll.

March 3: Prince Conall is born to Nigel Prince of Gwynedd and Meraude Lady Rhendall.

March 9: Caitrin Princess of Meara secretly marries Sicard Lord MacArdry.

March 22: Ardry Hereditary Count of Transha and Tanist of Clan MacArdry dies in a brawl with a McLain retainer, aged XIX years, and is succeeded by his brother, Lord Michael.

March 25: Upon learning that the II families are to part to avoid bloodfeud over Ardry's death, Duncan Lord McLain secretly handfasts with the slain Ardry's sister, Lady Maryse. Clan McArdry leaves on the next morning, but Maryse has conceived a son.

April 12: Father Alexander Darby is elected an itinerant Bishop of Gwynedd.

April 13: Princess Marcissa is born to Aldred Hereditary Prince of Torenth and Charissa Duchess of Tolán and Pretender of Gwynedd.

April 15: Richard Duke of Carthmoor marries Sivorn Princess of Orsal and Tralia.

April 30: Brice Hereditary Lord of Trurill marries Merwenna Lady MacThorlac.

May 16: Burchard Baron de Varian marries Maire Lady of Eastmarch.

September 26: Lionel II Duke d'Arjenol marries Morag Princess of Torenth.

October 11: Master Jatham is born to Sir Manus Kilshane and Amaryllis Lady Macosquin.

October 20: Nabila (Lady) Rothana is born to Hakim Emir of Nur Hallaj and Fabrissa Princess of R'Kassi.

November 4: Lord Jodoc d'Armaine is ordained priest.

December 2: Prince Ithel is born to Caitrin Hereditary Princess of Meara and Sicard Lord MacArdry.

1108

January 1: Lady Caldreana is born to Caulay Earl of Transha and Adreana Lady Calder of Sheele. Her birthdate is recorded in the baptismal register as January 3 to make her birth coincide with that of her supposed twin brother, Dhugal.

January 2: Vanissa is born to Indract 't-Serclaes and Vanne his wife.

January 3: Lord Dhugal is born to Duncan Lord McLain and Maryse Lady MacArdry. Lady Maryse dies of the complications of birth, aged XVI years; her mother, Lady Adreana, conceals the circumstances of Dhugal's birth and raises him as a twin to her own daughter, Lady Caldreana, who was born II days earlier.

January 11: Princess Richelle is born to Richard Duke of Carthmoor and Sivorn Princess of Orsal and Tralia.

February 29: Princess Rezza Elisabet is born to Létald Hort of Orsal and Prince of Tralia and Husniyya Sharifa of R'Kassi.

March 21: Father Alpheios is elected an itinerant Bishop of Torenth.

March 28: Duncan hears that Maryse has died of a winter fever and puts all thoughts of her aside, pursuing his earlier inclinations toward the priesthood, never dreaming that he has a son.

May 10: Bishop Alexander Darby is elected Archbishop of Rhemuth in succession to Archbishop James de Varagh; Fathers Bradene de Tourz, Creoda, and Ralf Tolliver are elected itinerant Bishops. *Homo proponet et Deus disponit.*

May 11: Noelie is born to Sir Jolyon Ramsay of Cloome and Lady Oksana d'Enghieux.

September 9: Prince Llewell is born to Caitrin Princess of Meara and Sicard Lord MacArdry.

October 31: Princess Rosane Marie Élisabeth Jaÿne is born to Brion King of Gwynedd and Queen Jehana Princess of Bremagne.

November 3: Rosane Princess of Gwynedd dies of the blue skin, aged III days.

1109

February 14: Judhael III Prince and Pretender of Meara dies, aged LXVI years, and is succeeded in his pretentions by his daughter, Princess Caitrin.

May 12: Hereditary Duke Alroy later Arion II King of Torenth is born to Lionel II Duke d'Arjenol and Morag Princess of Torenth.

June 9: Jacob Lord of Tendal and Hereditary Chancellor of Corwyn dies, aged LXVII years, and is succeeded by his son, Lord Robert.

July 7: Princess Sidana is born to Caitrin Princess and Pretender of Meara and Sicard Lord MacArdry.

October 19: Father Ifor is consecrated an itinerant Bishop of Gwynedd.

November 16: Marcissa Princess of Torenth dies in a fall, aged II years.

December 11: Torenthi guards at the border town of Fathane clash with a patrol of Alaric Morgan Duke of Corwyn.

December 18: Princess Araxie is born to Richard Duke of Carthmoor and Sivorn Princess of Orsal and Tralia.

1110

January 2: Carolus III King of Torenth sends an emissary to Brion King of Gwynedd proposing a personal meeting to discuss a possible peace treaty and a permanent settlement of the Festillic claims to Gwynedd.

January 19: Prince Rory is born to Nigel Prince of Gwynedd and Meraude Lady de Traherne.

February 11: Carolus III King of Torenth dies, aged XXXIX years, allegedly killed through poison, and is succeeded by his only son, Prince Aldred. *Beinahe bringt keine Mücke um.*

March 3: Alaric Morgan Duke of Corwyn and Earl of Lendour is knighted by King Brion.

March 31: Hereditary Prince Gejza Taksóny is born to Aldred II King of Torenth and Charissa Duchess of Tolán, but dies later that same day.

April 4: Dafydd is born to Sir Jolyon Ramsay of Cloome and Lady Oksana d'Enghieux.

April 15: King Aldred II is deposed by his uncle, Prince Wencit, who succeeds to the throne.

April 18: Former King Aldred II of Torenth is tried, condemned, and executed for his crimes; he is XIX years of age at his death. *Ego sum Rex Torenthus et super grammaticam.*

April 23: Torval Baron of Netterhaven marries Phylandra Lady Gallarat.

June 21: Brothen Baron of Trurill dies, aged XLIX years, and is succeeded by his eldest surviving son, Lord Brice.
June 22: Dolfin is born.
July 20: John FitzPadraic is ordained priest.
September 18: Prince Rogan is born to Létald Hort of Orsal and Prince of Tralia and Husniyya Sharifa of R'Kassi.
October 1: Mahael *Junior* Count d'Arjenol is betrothed to Eufemia Princess of Torenth.

1111

January 1: King Wencit is girded with the sword at Iób by Patriarch Gamalinos II under the reign name of Wenzel II.
January 7: Charissa Duchess of Tolán and Pretender of Gwynedd signs a last will and testament naming as next heir to her pretensions after any issue of her own body her cousin Wencit King of Torenth and after him the Princess Morag his sister, their heirs and assigns.
April 19: Sean O'Flynn Earl Derry attains his majority, and the Regency of Trevor Baron Varagh is dissolved.
June 3: Qais Emir of Nur Hallaj dies, aged LXIII years, and is succeeded by his son, Nabil Hakim.
September 1: Prince and Hereditary Duke Cinric is born to Richard Duke of Carthmoor and Earl of Culdi and Sivorn Princess of Orsal and Tralia, and is ceded his father's title of Culdi.

1112

February 2: Luther Lord Trillick dies, aged LXXIV years, and is succeeded by his cousin, Lord Lester.
March 16: Father Denis Arilan, anticipating Duncan McLain's ordination, has himself transferred to Rhemuth to facilitate it. *Humanum amare est, humanum autem ignoscere est.*
June 10: Father Belden of Erne is elected Bishop of Cashien.
June 13: Illann II Duke of Lusk and sometime King of Howicce and Llannedd dies, aged LVI years.
December 12: Mikhail Sovereign Prince of Andelon dies, aged LVII years, and is succeeded by his elder daughter, Princess Sofiana; she soon resigns from the Camberian Council.

1113

February 22: Thorne Hagen is appointed to the Camberian Council to replace Sofiana Sovereign Princess of Andelon.
April 10: Duncan Lord McLain and Hugh de Berry are ordained priests at Saint George's Cathedral in Rhemuth by Alexander Darby Archbishop of Rhemuth, under the watchful eye of Father Denis Arilan. Duncan is assigned to a parish at Culdi near his family's estate, and Hugh becomes personal secretary to Bishop Patrick Corrigan.
July 24: Rocail al-Din Prince of R'Kassi is elected Grand Master of the Knights of the Anvil at Djellarda.
September 26: Prince Marcel and Princess Marcelline (twins) are born to Létald Hort of Orsal and Prince of Tralia and Husniyya Sharifa of R'Kassi.
December 15: Emmet Lord Macanter dies, aged LIX years, and is succeeded by his son, Lord Edward.

1114

January 3: Ryan Coris Earl of Marley dies, aged LVI years, and is succeeded by his son, Lord Bran.
April 3: Lord Liam is born to Lionel II Duke d'Arjenol and Morag Princess of Torenth.
September 12: Father Duncan is sent to the University at Grecotha for II years' further study.
September 14: Prince Cinric Hereditary Duke of Carthmoor and Earl of Culdi dies of a fever, aged III years.
October 11: Richard Duke of Carthmoor is injured in a fall from his horse.
October 15: Richard Haldane Duke of Carthmoor dies, aged LVIII years, and is succeeded by his elder daughter, Lady Richelle, as Countess of Culdi in her own right, the Duchy of Carthmoor becoming extinct and escheating to the Crown.
October 31: Rogier Baron Fallon is created Earl Fallon *ad personam* by King Brion.
December 22: Oliver de Nore Archbishop Primate of Valoret and All Gwynedd dies, aged LXXIII years.
December 25: Nigel Prince of Gwynedd is created Duke of Carthmoor by Brion King of Gwynedd, who also makes the Princess Araxie, second daughter of Richard late Duke of Carthmoor, Baroness Dunluce in her own right.

1115

January 31: Vera Duchess of Cassan, Father Duncan McLain's mother, dies, aged XLIV years, thus ending Duncan and Morgan's only source of Dernyi training.
February 6: Euphrosine Queen of Torenth dies, aged XXXV years.
February 20: Edmund Loris Bishop of Stavenham is elected Archbishop Primate of Valoret and All Gwynedd. Father Ian Calder of Sheele, Father Lachlan de Quarles, and Father Siward are elected itinerant Bishops. Loris appoints Father Lawrence Gorony as his principal aide.
February 28: Quale Baron Mathelwaite dies, aged LV years, and is succeeded by his son, Lord Edgar.
March 18: Father Denis Arilan becomes Confessor to King Brion, and is promoted to Monsignor.

EVENTS OF "THE KNIGHTING OF DERRY" (MAY 1115)

May 1: Sean O'Flynn Earl Derry attends the Spring Horse Fair at Rhelledd in Corwyn with his uncle, Trevor Udaut Baron Varagh. Sean has dealings with the Jewish horsetrader Julius ben David, but is injured when he rescues a child from a horse fight, and is treated by Master Randolph. Alaric Morgan Duke of Corwyn helps treat one of the injured steeds and also Sean Derry, who returns to Castle Derry in a litter.
May 7: Sean and his family leave for Rhemuth.
May 10: Sean arrives in Rhemuth for his knighting, and spends that night in a vigil with other candidates for knighthood, including Arnaud Sieur de Vali.
May 11: Sean O'Flynn Earl Derry is knighted at Rhemuth by Brion King of Gwynedd, along with Arnaud Sieur de Vali and others, and becomes the liege man of Alaric Morgan Duke of Corwyn. Lord Rhodri handles the entertainment at Rhemuth Palace.

* * * * * * *

June 10: Mahael *Junior* Count d'Arjenol marries Eufemia Princess of Torenth.
August 30: Prince Payne is born to Nigel Duke of Carthmoor and Meraude Lady de Treharne.
December 15: Arban Howell Earl of Eastmarch dies, aged LIV years, and is succeeded by his son, Lord Ian.

1116

March 3: Rhydon Baron Coldoire dies, aged XLVII years; however, Stefan Coram, who is present at his death, assumes his image and identity, and hides Rhydon's body.

May 4: Monsignor Denis Arilan brings Father Duncan McLain to Rhemuth as his secretary and assistant.

June 12: Bran Coris Earl of Marley marries Richenda Lady of Rheljan.

June 21: Father Duncan becomes a tutor to Prince Kelson.

August 17: Sivorn Dowager Duchess of Carthmoor returns with her daughters to Tralia and marries Savile Baron Kishknock.

September 26: Jared McLain Duke of Cassan marries Margaret Neuve widow of Raymond Sinclair.

October 17: Bishop Alpheios is elected Metropolitan of Netterhaven.

October 19: Cara Hagen dies of the pox, aged X years.

October 21: Father Thomas Cardiel is elected Bishop of Dhassa.

December 2: Hudriod du Mollard Bishop of Coroth dies.

1117

February 3: Alexander Darby Archbishop of Rhemuth dies, aged LXXII years.

March 23: At a Synod held at Valoret, Bishop Patrick Corrigan is elected Archbishop of Rhemuth, itinerant Bishop Bradene de Tourz is elected Bishop of Grecotha, itinerant Bishop Ralf Tolliver is elected Bishop of Coroth, Father Creoda is elected Auxiliary Bishop of Rhemuth, and Father Raymer de Valence, Father Henry Istelyn, Father Richard of Nyford, and Father Mir de Kierney are elected itinerant Bishops. Father Lawrence Gorony is promoted to Monsignor. *Horror ubique animos, simul ipsa silentia terrent.*

June 2: Hereditary Count Brendan is born to Bran Coris Earl of Marley and Richenda Lady of Rheljan.

December 1: Father Duncan McLain becomes Confessor and Chaplain to Hereditary Prince Kelson.

1118

January 6: Father Duncan McLain is promoted to Monsignor. *"For the proverbe seith that 'manye smale maken a greet.'"*

February 4: Richeldis Dowager Queen of Gwynedd dies at Sirhowy, aged LII years.

February 28: Prince Ronal Rurik is born to Lionel II Duke d'Arjenol and Morag Princess of Torenth.

EVENTS OF "TRIAL" (APRIL 1118)

April 16: Lillas, the fiancée of Stalker, is raped and murdered in Kiltuin in the Duchy of Corwyn. An itinerant Eistenmark swordsmith named Ferris is arrested and accused of the crime.

April 17: Ferris is tried by Bishop Ralf Tolliver. Alaric Morgan Duke of Corwyn examines him and declares him innocent, then discovers the guilty parties. Ferris is released, and pledges to make a special sword for Duke Alaric. *Fiat justitia, ruat cœlum.*

* * * * * * *

May 22: Monsignor Denis Arilan is elected Auxiliary Bishop of Rhemuth and is appointed to King Brion's High Council. *Di meliora piis, erroremque hostibus illum.*

July 3: Lawrence Lord Welch marries Roberta Lady Floren.

September 19: Ewan III Earl of Rhendall dies, aged LII years, and is succeeded by his son, Lord Saer.

November 4: Adreana Countess of Transha dies, aged XLVIII years.

1119

February 3: Proulx Sieur de Vali dies, aged LVI years, and is succeeded by his cousin, Sir Arnaud de Vali.

February 28: Sister Symphorosa of the Abbey of Saint Perpetua in Carthmoor, formerly Tamelda Princess of Gwynedd, dies unmarried, aged LX years. Φοβου το γηρας, ου γαρ ερχεται μόνον.

March 15: Moseley Baron of Reider in Torenth dies, aged LXXV years, and is succeeded by his son, Lord Merritt.

April 11: At a Synod held in Rhemuth, Bishop Creoda is elected Bishop of Carbury, and Bishop Richard is elected Bishop of Nyford.

July 2: Lady Rhiannon is born to Bran Coris Earl of Marley and Richenda Lady of Rheljan.

September 16: Torval Prince of Torenth and Duke of Lorsöl dies at the Holy Icons Monastery, aged LVI years.

October 17: Willibrord Baron du Chantal dies, aged LXXV years, and is succeeded by his son, Lord William.

October 24: Michael Hereditary Count of Transha dies, aged XXIX years, and is succeeded as Tanist by his brother (actually nephew), Dhugal Lord MacArdry.

November 24: Sir Hillary Fougères is ennobled *ad personam* by Alaric Morgan Duke of Corwyn with the sanction of King Brion.

November 26: Hereditary Prince Malachy Mátyás Mahael Nimur is born to Mahael *Junior* Count Amassy and Eufemia Princess and Heiress of Torenth, who dies giving birth, aged XVIII years. Prince Malachy is created Duke of Beldouria by King Wencit.

November 28: Malachy Mátyás Hereditary Prince of Torenth and Duke of Beldouria dies, aged II days.

December 8: Ronan IV King of Howicce and Llannedd dies of fits, aged XXX years, and is succeeded by his brother, Prince Colman.

1120

March 4: Wencit King of Torenth makes a new last will and testament, naming his nephews, the III sons of Lionel II Duke d'Arjenol, heirs to the throne of Gwynedd after any heirs of his own body, and Lionel's younger brother, Mahael Count Amassy, Lionel's heir to the Duchy of Arjenol. On this date Prince Alroy Arion is created Duke of Beldouria, Prince Liam Lajos is created Duke of Nördmarcke, and Prince Ronal Rurik Duke of Lorsöl.

March 12: Bishop Ifor is elected Bishop of Marbury.

June 8: King Brion signs a new border treaty with Wencit King of Torenth, but believes that war is imminent.

June 20: Sulen Hereditary Nabil of Nur Hallaj marries Rohays Princess of Andelon.

August 19: Father Conlan is elected an itinerant Bishop of Gwynedd.

September 16: Alaric Morgan Duke of Corwyn goes to the border town of Cardosa in the Rheljan

Mountains with Sean O'Flynn Earl Derry to observe the activities of the Torenthi forces gathering there.

October 31: The night is unseasonably cold in Rhemuth.

EVENTS OF *DERYNI RISING* (NOVEMBER 1120)

November 1: King Brion goes stag hunting on the plain of Candor Rhea directly North of Rhemuth, accompanied by his son, the Hereditary Prince Kelson, Ewan III Duke of Claibourne, Rogier Earl Fallon, Bishop Denis Arilan, Kevin Earl of Kierney, Colin Lord of Fianna, Prince Nigel Duke of Carthmoor and his III sons, and Jared McLain Duke of Cassan. The King and his son discuss the current political situation, and especially the military threat from Wencit King of Torenth and Charissa Duchess of Tolán. Brion tells his son to send for Alaric Morgan Duke of Corwyn should anything happen to him. Colin gives the King a flask of wine tainted with *merasha*. The Duchess of Tolán observes the scene from afar with her III Moorish aides, and confers with Ian Howell Earl of Eastmarch, one of her co-conspirators. Ian rejoins the hunting party, but his right stirrup conveniently gives way, providing an excuse to drop behind with Colin. Made vunerable by the drugged wine, the King is murdered through the magic of the Festillic Pretender Charissa, who stops his heart. Bishop Denis Arilan gives him the last rites. King Brion is aged XXXIX years at his death, and is succeeded by his only son, Hereditary Prince Kelson Haldane. Kelson sends Ralson and Colin to Cardosa to fetch Alaric Morgan. The body of the late King lies in state for the next II days. Queen Jehana becomes Regent for her underaged son, Prince Kelson.

November 4: King Brion is buried in the crypt of Saint George's Cathedral at Rhemuth. *Our plesance here is all vain glory, this false world is but transitory.*

November 5: Lords Ralson and Colin inform Alaric Morgan Duke of Corwyn of the death of King Brion, and that he has been summoned to Rhemuth by the new King, Kelson. Alaric starts from Cardosa for the capital.

November 7: Morgan's party is ambushed near Valoret, and Gérard Ralson Baron d'Evering and V others are killed; Colin is severely wounded, and Sean O'Flynn Earl Derry is cut on his left wrist. Gérard is XLIV years of age at his death, and is succeeded by his son, Lord Torsin.

November 8: Colin Lord of Fianna dies of his wounds, aged XVIII years. Ralson's and Colin's bodies are held at Saint Mark's Abbey, to be retrieved later. *Audacem fecerat ipse timor.*

November 14: Alaric Morgan Duke of Corwyn returns to Rhemuth with his aide, Sean O'Flynn Earl Derry. They are forced to move off the street by the Connaiti mercenaries guarding the passage of the Supreme of Howicce, who has come to Rhemuth to attend the new King's coronation. Morgan greets the Lord High Chancellor, Ewan III Duke of Claibourne, and Bran Earl of Marley, Ian Earl of Eastmarch, Jared Duke of Cassan, and Kevin Earl of Kierney. Richard Lord FitzWilliam warns Morgan of a plot against him by the Regency Council, which will meet later that afternoon. Morgan discusses recent events with Prince Nigel, who tells him that Dowager Queen Jehana plans to charge the Duke with treason and heresy; Morgan asks the Prince to intercede with Jehana. Morgan talks with Kelson in the garden. Kevin meets Sean outside the Council doors. Jehana considers her options in the Sun Room, and is determined to take Morgan's life. She meets with Nigel, but is not persuaded by him. Kelson and Morgan are threatened by a stenrect crawler, which is killed by the Duke. They are summoned by Lady Esther to the Council meeting. The Regency Council meets to discuss the fate of the Duke of Corwyn, who is popularly believed to have had a hand in King Brion's death. Members in attendance include: Dowager Queen Jehana, Prince Nigel Duke of Carthmoor, Jared Duke of Cassan, Kevin Earl of Kierney, Ewan III Duke of Claibourne and Hereditary Marshal of Gwynedd, Bran Earl of Marley, Rogier Earl Fallon, Bishop Denis Arilan, Ian Earl of Eastmarch, Archbishop Patrick Corrigan, and Sean Earl Derry, occupying the place of his master, Alaric Morgan Duke of Corwyn, plus several dozen other Lords who join this special meeting without voting privileges. Ewan as Hereditary Lord Marshal calls the session to order at Jehana's command before the King arrives. Jehana addresses the Council and accuses Morgan of being a traitor and blasphemer. Morgan and Kelson meet with Father Duncan McLain: Morgan shows them the Ring of Fire, which Brion had entrusted to him before Morgan went on his mission to Cardosa. Duncan reveals to Kelson that he and Morgan are distant cousins in the paternal line, but 1st cousins through their mothers. Duncan retrieves a flat box hidden in a secret compartment in the altar of the basilica, which includes a parchment written by King Brion describing the steps needed to empower Kelson. They discover that the Eye of Rom, which is needed in the ceremony, was buried with Brion's body in the crypt of the Cathedral, and determine to secure it that evening. They see Archbishop Edmund Loris arriving outside the church. Morgan sends Kelson to the Council meeting, and then surrenders to Loris's ecclesiastical soldiers, who arrest him. Kelson and Morgan arrive at the Council chamber. Loris surrenders Morgan's sword to Kelson at the King's request. Kelson asks for a reprise of the Council's vote against Morgan; IV vote to acquit (Nigel, Denis, Kevin, Jared), V to convict (Bran, Ian, Rogier, Ewan, Corrigan). Kelson interjects that Derry was not allowed to vote, but Jehana objects that Sean is not a member; Kelson says that Derry was substituting for Morgan, who has a right to vote as a Council member even though he is the person being tried. Jehana then insists on her right to vote, making the total VI to V against the Duke of Corwyn. To delay the issue Kelson asks that the full writ of attainder be read out by the Lord Marshal Ewan Duke of Claibourne. Kelson knows that he will achieve his majority on the IIIrd hour of that afternoon when he reaches his XIVth birthday. Taking control of the Council, he appoints Sean Earl Derry to the seat vacated by the death of Lord Ralson. Sean votes to acquit, and the King then breaks the VI to VI tie by voting himself, thereby defeating Jehana's measure. Ian uses the body of the guard Michael DeForest to communicate mentally with Charissa, and then kills him. Morgan wards Kelson, and conducts research in Brion's library at Rhemuth Palace. While seeking further guidance regarding Kelson's Haldane empowerment, Morgan conjures up an image of Saint Camber, which he checks against a portrait in Talbot's *Lives of the Saints*, and discovers that they are the same. Charissa abruptly enters the room through the portal in the antechamber, and speaks to Morgan; she denies any participation in the death of Brion, but will challenge Kelson on the morrow. Morgan returns to the King's quarters. Sean has posted the guard around the area. Morgan shows Kelson a secret passage from the room, and they use it to exit to the square opposite Saint Hilary's Basilica. Duncan meets them inside, and they transport to Saint George's Cathedral. Lord Rogier discovers the III Lords at the entrance to the crypt, but is abruptly put to sleep by Duncan, together with the II guards there. Kelson and his II companions enter the crypt where the Kings of Gwynedd are buried, and open Brion's casket. Inside is the body of an old man whose identity is unknown. They begin searching for the dead King's corpse by opening the other sarcophagi. However, Morgan comes to suspect that the "old man" is actually the shape-changed body of the deceased monarch, whose soul has been bound and ensorcelled by Charissa in an unholy bond. Duncan releases King Brion from his bondage, allowing him finally to achieve the peace of death. Morgan takes the Eye of Rom, and leaves behind Duncan's crucifix in exchange. Rogier is released from his spell, and they return to Duncan's study at the basilica. King Kelson is brought to his Haldane potential by Duncan McLain and Alaric Morgan. Kelson is returned unconscious to his apartments in the Palace, but the party is attacked by III would-be assassins, all vassals of the Duke of Corwyn: Edgar Baron of Mathelwaite, Lord Harold Fitzmartin, and Lord Lawrence. Edgar commits suicide under a magical compusion, Harold is killed by Duncan, and Lawrence is captured. Edgar is XXXVII years of age at his death, and is succeeded by his brother, Lord Edwin. Harold is XLI years of age at his death. Morgan finds the guards outside the King's chambers lying there either dead or wounded, with Sean Earl Derry dying of his injuries. Morgan heals Derry and saves his life, the Ist time in his life that he has performed this act. Bran, Ewan, Nigel, Ian, and Jehana arrive and accuse Morgan of treason. The King orders them to leave Morgan in peace, and retires for the night, but not before telling Morgan and Duncan that he saw Saint Camber during his empowerment. Morgan and Duncan speculate on the King's parentage, and particularly that Jehana might be Deryni. Ian Earl of Eastmarch communicates with Charissa, and tells her that Kelson is wearing the Eye of Rom. The Pretender mentions that she has been warned by Stefan Coram and the Camberian Council. Ian rides to the hills North of Rhemuth, where he meets Charissa in her underground hideaway.

November 15: Lord Rhodri wakes the King to prepare him for the coronation. Alaric Morgan Duke of Corwyn is created King's Champion, a title which has been hereditary in the past, and is dressed in his special livery. Ian steals the chain of office of the King's Champion and substitutes an ensorcelled copy. Nigel reports that Rogier has been found dead next to King Brion's casket; in Rogier's hand was Duncan's crucifix. Rogier Earl Fallon is XL years of age at his death, and is succeeded only in the Barony of Fallon by his eldest son, Lord Rogier *Junior*. Jehana accuses them of heresy and desecration, and denounces her son. Morgan tells Jehana that she is Deryni, and that she must attend the coronation. The procession begins. Charissa views the events through the large ensorcelled stone in the Duke's badge of office. Awaiting the King at the Cathedral are Archbishops Loris and Corrigan and Bishop Arilan. Sean is posted to the Belltower next to the Cathedral to watch for Charissa. Loris and Corrigan are chided by Kelson, and threatened with exile and banishment if they take action against Duncan or Morgan. Also present are Duncan, Morgan, Jehana, Ian, Bran, Ewan, Nigel, Jared, Kevin, and others. The coronation ceremony begins. Sean reports that Charissa is approaching. Kelson worries that the empowerment ritual specified by his father has not been completed; he has no power. Charissa enters with her soldiers, and stops Corrigan from crowning the King. Her Champion, Ian Howell Earl of Eastmarch, challenges Alaric Morgan Duke of Corwyn, but is severely wounded by him; Ian throws a dagger which wounds Morgan after his chain of office twists around his neck. Ian is given the *coup de grâce* by the Pretender; he is aged XXXI years at his death. Morgan is treated by Duncan. Jehana challenges Charissa but is defeated and placed in a binding spell. Kelson determines that the final symbol empowering him is the seal of Saint Camber, the "Defender of Humankind," embedded in the Cathedral floor, and accepts the Pretender's challenge. He walks to Camber's seal, and steps on it: his power comes to him. Morgan heals himself with Duncan's assistance. King Kelson defeats Charissa Pretender of Gwynedd in a duel arcane in Saint George's Cathedral in Rhemuth, and is then crowned King there. The figure of Camber appears to the eyes of the Deryni to help validate the coronation. The Great Lords give their homage to the new King. Charissa Duchess of Tolán is XXVI years of age at her death, and is succeeded in her pretensions by her *cousin germain*, Wencit King of Torenth, the Duchy of Marluk becoming extinct and escheating to the Torenthi throne, and the County of Gwernach going into abeyance between II co-heiresses. *Meno era chi si promette variazione nelle cose del mondo, che chi se le persuade ferme e stabili.*

* * * * * * *

December 13: Lawrence Lord Welch is tried, convicted, and executed for his attack on Alaric Morgan Duke of Corwyn.
December 14: Lady Rhiannon Coris dies, aged I year.

1121
January 1: Wencit King of Torenth is installed at Saint Constantine's Cathedral as Pretender of Gwynedd by Patriarch Porphyrios II.
March 2: Richenda Countess of Marley is sent for safety with her young son to Dhassa by her husband, Bran Coris Earl of Marley.
March 13: Jehana Dowager Queen of Gwynedd withdraws herself for retreat at Saint Giles's Abbey at Shannis Meer. *Aus den Augen, aus dem Sinn.*

March 16: Heremon Baron de Vere is killed by rebels in the Duchy of Corwyn, aged LXI years, and is succeeded by his younger brother, Lord Henry.

EVENTS OF *DERYNI CHECKMATE* (MARCH 1121)

March 20: The Archbishops Loris and Corrigan send a message to Ralf Tolliver Bishop of Corwyn, asking him to excommunicate Alaric Morgan Duke of Corwyn unless he "recants," and placing his Duchy under interdict if he does not. Father Duncan McLain is also suspended from his priestly functions, and called before the ecclesiastical court. Loris relates that a rebellion has broken out in Northern Corwyn under the leadership of Warin de Grey. Monsignor Lawrence Gorony departs for the Free Port of Concaradine, and there takes a merchant ship to Corwyn in order to deliver the interdict document to Bishop Tolliver. Kelson dines that evening with Duncan and Nigel. Father Hugh de Berry secretly brings a copy of the interdict document to the King. Kelson and Duncan discuss the situation. Kelson sends Duncan to warn Morgan, and the priest rides out that night, before the warrant against him can be delivered. *Tout est perdu fors l'honneur.*

March 22: Duncan arrives in Coroth to warn Morgan of the Archbishops' plot. Gorony arrives III hours later. Derry is sent to spy on Torenthi movements in the border region between Corwyn and Torenth. Duncan is sent to Bishop Tolliver with a letter from Morgan.

March 23: Duncan is sent by Morgan back to Bishop Tolliver to determine what message has been sent to him by the Archbishops.

March 24: Morgan is apprised by Master Randolph of a scurrilous rhyme that is circulating in his Duchy. Sean Lord Derry does some spying in Fathane in Torenth, and is beaten for his troubles.

March 25: Duncan and Morgan board the *Rhafallia*, Morgan's flagship, to sail to the Island of Orsal to meet with Létald Hort of Orsal and Sovereign Prince of Tralia. Richard FitzWilliam dies while thwarting an assassination attempt on the Duke by Andrew. The King and the rest of the wedding party arrive at Culdi for the nuptials of Hereditary Duke Kevin McLain and Lady Bronwyn de Corwyn. Derry leaves Fathane and comes upon a raiding party of Warin's North of the town which has burned the manor house of Arnaud Sieur de Vali; he sees Warin heal one of his injured men. Rogan Prince of Tralia IInd son of the Hort of Orsal, returns with Duke Alaric to be trained as his squire and a knight.

March 26: Derry reports to Morgan that Warin can indeed heal and may possibly be Deryni.

March 27: Morgan and Duncan leave Coroth for Dhassa; that evening they explore the ruins of Saint Neot's Abbey in the Southern Lendour Mountains, discovering the psychic message left in the destroyed portal there by the last Abbot, Dom Emrys. In Culdi the architect Rimmell secures a love charm from the witch woman Bethane to use on Bronwyn Lady de Corwyn. *Il soverchio dolor t' ha fatto insano.*

March 28: Duncan and Morgan are trapped by Father Gorony and Warin at Saint Torin's Shrine near Dhassa, and Morgan is drugged and captured. Duncan manages a rescue, but only with the assistance of his Deryni powers, thus publicly revealing the priest's nature for the Ist time. The Synod then excommunicates the pair for having desecrated the holy shrine.

March 29: Lady Bronwyn Morgan and Kevin Earl of Kierney are killed by the misguided love charm of Bethane, which had been purchased by the architect Rimmell; Bronwyn is aged XXV years and Kevin is aged XXXII years at their deaths. Rimmell is immediately executed for his crimes. Father Duncan McLain becomes Earl of Kierney and Hereditary Duke of Cassan at Kevin's death. Cardiel, Arilan, and IV other Bishops break permanently with the ruling Synod of Gwynedd, in effect forming their own rival group, and splitting the Church of Gwynedd. Cardiel's group supports King Kelson and his Deryni allies.

March 31: Morgan and Duncan arrive at Culdi, and are informed of the deaths of Bronwyn and Kevin and of their own excommunications. Duncan conducts a mass of the dead for the pair. Kelson learns of the split in the Curia.

* * * * * * *

May 6: Wencit King of Torenth occupies the walled city of Cardosa in the Rheljan Mountains.

June 3: Rebels loyal to Archbishop Edmund Loris attempt to assassinate itinerant Bishop Wolfram.

EVENTS OF *HIGH DERYNI* (JUNE-JULY 1121)

June 17: Duke Nigel's army is ambushed by the rebels of Warin de Grey at Jennan Vale. Duncan and Morgan heal a wounded partisan, Mal Donalson, who had been found on the field by Royston Richardson, and then leave to meet the King at Dol Shaia.

June 18: King Kelson, encamped at Dol Shaia, receives documents from the Archbishops Loris and Corrigan excommunicating him and placing Gwynedd under interdict until he submits. Lionel II Duke d'Arjenol and Merritt Baron of Reider give themselves as hostage to Bran Coris Earl of Marley, who agrees to meet with King Wencit. Wencit seduces Bran into joining the Torenthi cause, promising him a Dukedom. The Camberian Council votes to let Morgan and Duncan be liable to magical challenge. Duncan and Morgan arrive at Dol Shaia, and persuade the King that they must go to Dhassa. *L'amico mio, e non della ventura.*

June 19: Morgan and Duncan leave Dol Shaia via Saint Neot's. After interrogating Master Thierry on the Dhassa Road, they take a back trail around Lake Jashan to reach the city of Dhassa. There they submit themselves to the rebel Bishops. The Bishops announce that they will accept Morgan and Duncan's petition to be reinstated in the Church's good grace. Bishop Denis Arilan reveals to Bishop Thomas Cardiel that he is Deryni. Sean leaves to scout the Torenthi armies near Medras.

June 21: Morgan and Duncan are absolved of sin by the rebel Bishops, and their excommunication is lifted. Arilan admits he is Deryni to Alaric Morgan. Derry is captured at Llyndruth Plain and is taken to Esgair Ddu at Cardosa, where he is questioned and tortured by King Wencit.

June 23: The rebel faction of Bishops pays homage to the King at Dol Shaia, and absolves him of any sin of consorting with excommunicants and heretics. *An nescis, mi fili, quantilla prudentia mundus regatur?*

June 25: The King and his army assemble before the gates of Coroth; Prince Conall is sent under a flag of truce to seek a meeting with Warin. Kelson and his Lords parley with Warin de Grey and Archbishop Loris, who hold the city, but the latter refuses to obey the King's commands to open the gates. Kelson and his friends swim through an underground passage to enter Coroth Palace unobserved. Warin is persuaded to support the King after Duncan is healed by Morgan; however, Warin is tested and proves not to be Deryni.

June 26: Kelson deposes and arrests Archbishop Loris, and secures victory for the King's supporters in the Interdict Crisis. Cardiel is appointed acting Primate of Gwynedd until an election can be held by the new Curia. Those Bishops who cannot support the new regime are sent home. King Kelson's forces leave Coroth in the late afternoon for Dhassa.

June 28: The Gwyneddan army arrives at Dhassa, where it is reunited with the rest of the expedition. Jared Duke of Cassan arrives with his army at Rengarth, where he is treacherously attacked by Bran Earl of Marley and King Wencit. Duke Jared and many of his officers are captured and taken to Llyndruth, but Generals Burchard Baron de Varian and Gloddruth escape. *C'est magnifique, mais ce n'est pas la guerre.*

June 29: The King receives a messenger telling of the defeat of Duke Jared and treachery of Bran Coris. Richenda, Bran's wife, convinces Kelson to let her accompany the army. A War Council is held to make final battle plans.

June 30: The Gwyneddan army departs Dhassa before dawn, and proceeds by forced march. On Llyndruth Plain near Cardosa Kelson's army finds the grisly remains of Jared's force, the bodies and armor having been propped up by the Torenthi on stakes. That night they finally see the enemy soldiers, and set up camp opposite them.

July 1: The II armies array themselves on Llyndruth Meadow. One hundred hostages are hanged by Wencit, including Jared Duke of Cassan, Ninian Earl of Jenas, Sybaud Sieur de Canlavay, Denys Lord Collier, Tesselin Lord Harkness, Lester Lord Trillick, and Bishop Richard of Nyford. Jared Duke of Cassan is aged LVI years at his death, and is succeeded by his son, Father Duncan McLain Earl of Kierney; Ninian Earl of Jenas is LIII years of age at his death, and is succeeded by his son, Lord Roger. Sybaud Sieur de Canlavay is LXI years of age at his death, and is succeeded by his brother, Lord Leger. Torval of Netterhaven, the hostage sent by King Wencit to the Gwyneddan army, is killed by Warin de Grey and Father Duncan, aged XXXII years. Tesselin Lord Harkness is LIX years of age at his death, and is succeeded by his son, Lord Regis. Lester Lord Trillick is aged LIV years at his death, and is succeeded by his son, Lord Adam. Sean O'Flynn Earl Derry is rescued. King Wencit parleys with Kelson and presents the King with an ultimatum, suggesting a duel between the leaders instead of a large-scale battle. With Arilan's assistance, King Kelson visits the Camberian Council, and asks for their help in making the coming contest with Wencit a fair one. They agree to supervise the duel arcane. Morgan expresses his love for Richenda, wife of Bran Coris. Brendan is stolen by his father Bran with the aid of Sean Earl Derry, who has been ensorceled by Wencit. Derry's spell is broken by Morgan and Duncan.

July 2: Four members of the Camberian Council—Barrett Lord de Laney, Lord Laran ap Pardyce, Tiercel de Claron, and Vivienne Lady de Jordanet—arrive to adjudicate the conflict between Gwynedd and Torenth. Wencit, Lionel, Bran, and Stefan Coram (masquerading as Rhydon) participate in a duel arcane with King Kelson, Duncan, Arilan, and Morgan. Kelson wins the day when Coram poisons himself and the III Torenthi sorcerors, and he becomes Overlord of Torenth for the new King, XII-year-old Prince Alroy. Princess Morag and her brother-in-law, Mahael II the new Duke d'Arjenol, become Regents of Torenth. Morag also succeeds as the next Festillic claimant to Gwynedd, since that title can pass to (and not just through) a female heir. King Wencit is XLVIII years of age at his death, Earl Bran is XXV years of age, Duke Lionel is XXXIII years of age, and Stefan Coram is XLV years of age.

* * * * * * *

September 1: Junanan Baron Ardglass dies of wounds suffered during the recent war with Torenth, aged XLVII years, and is succeeded by his son, Lord Jodrell.

September 16: Thorne Hagen resigns under pressure from the Camberian Council.

October 31: Patrick Corrigan Archbishop of Rhemuth dies, aged LXV years; Princess Aynbeth is born to Létald Hort of Orsal and Prince of Tralia and Husniyya Sharifa of R'Kassi.

November 6: Itinerant Bishop Morris dies of *la grippe*, aged LXII years.

December 2: Morgan sends Derry to Marley with Richenda to help her establish a Regency in her son's name.

Winter: King Kelson's Court is consolidated at Rhemuth, with details of Kelson's administration being planned. Morgan spends most of the Winter going back and forth between Rhemuth and Coroth, counseling Kelson and reestablishing his own hold in Corwyn. Father Duncan winters in Cassan and Kierney, attending to his affairs and getting his new inheritance in order, but privately settling back into his priestly vocation.

1122

January 1: Alroy King of Torenth is girded with the sword at Iób by the Patriarch Aristarchos I under the reign name of Arion II.

January 6: Burchard Baron de Varian husband of Maire Heiress of Eastmarch is created Earl of Eastmarch by King Kelson as a reward for his valor in the recent war, and because Kelson needs a capable General to guard that frontier.

January 10: At a Church Council held at Rhemuth, the Synod of Bishops officially censures Edmund Loris Archbishop Primate of Valoret and All Gwynedd, relieves him of his rank, and sentences him to perpetual exile at Saint Iveagh's Abbey in Rhendall.

January 12: Bradene Bishop of Grecotha is elected Archbishop Primate of Valoret and All Gwynedd.

January 13: Thomas Cardiel Bishop of Dhassa is elected Archbishop of Rhemuth as Thomas II.
January 14: Denis Arilan Auxiliary Bishop of Rhemuth is elected Bishop of Dhassa, and itinerant Bishop Wolfram de Blanet is elected Bishop of Grecotha.
January 15: The Bishopric of Carbury is abolished, and Bishop Creoda is transferred to the reactivated See of Culdi. Itinerant Bishop Siward is elected Bishop of Cardosa, and Father Lachlan de Quarles is created Bishop of Ballymar, a new see.
January 16: Angelus de Lacey Bishop of Stavenham dies of pneumonia in the midst of the Synod, aged LXXVIII years.
January 17: Two days of mourning are held for the repose of the soul of Bishop de Lacey.
January 19: Itinerant Bishop Conlan is elected Bishop of Stavenham to replace Angelus de Lacy. Itinerant Bishop Henry Istelyn is elected Auxiliary Bishop of Valoret under Bradene. Fathers Hugh de Berry, Corbet Mathiesen, Edward de Broun, James MacKenzie, John FitzPadraic, Nevan d'Estrelldas, Bevan de Torigny, and Amaury of Rhelledd are elected itinerant Bishops.
February 20: Princess Stanisha is born posthumously to Lionel II late Duke d'Arjenol and Morag Princess of Torenth.
April 14: Jodrell Baron Ardglass is appointed to the High Council by King Kelson.
May 1: Alaric Morgan Duke of Corwyn marries Richenda Dowager Countess of Marley in Marbury, with Father Duncan McLain officiating in the presence of the King. Sean Earl Derry remains in Marley as Deputy Regent for the young Earl Brendan, while Morgan takes his bride and new young stepson to Corwyn for the Summer. For the next few months he continues to reform his government and spend time with his new wife; his presence there guards against possible Torenthi encroachments on his side of the frontier between Gwynedd and Torenth.
June 30: From Marley, Kelson heads North with Father Duncan McLain Duke of Cassan to progress through his Kheldish lands and evaluate the military readiness of the realm, while keeping a wary eye on Torenth.
July 11: Saer de Traherne Earl of Rhendall and brother of Meraude Duchess of Carthmoor, is appointed to the Royal Council by King Kelson, her nephew.
July 18: Arnaud Sieur de Vali marries Elspeth Lady Derry.
July 23: Duncan continues on to Kierney and Cassan and spends the rest of the Summer touring his own lands and establishing a structure for governing mostly *in absentia*. By the end of this period Meara is beginning to rumble once again, sparked by dissatisfaction with the Deryni Duke and priest who now rules part of Old Meara. Rumours begin to surface that supporters of the old royal line are again agitating for Mearan independence.
Fall/Winter: Kelson makes plans to progress through Cassan, Kierney, and Meara the following Summer and squelch the separatist rumblings with a show of his royal presence. Courts of justice are held through the Winter. Morgan goes back and forth between Rhemuth and Coroth during this period, since Richenda is expecting their 1st child.

1123

January 23: Alaric Morgan Duke of Corwyn is named Lord Protector of the South by King Kelson.
January 31: Countess Briony Bronwyn is born at Coroth to Alaric Morgan Duke of Corwyn and Richenda Lady of Rheljan.
May 12: King Alroy Arion II of Torenth comes of age, and his Regency Council is disbanded. The regirding ceremony at Iób to transfer power formally from Duke Mahael II to King Alroy is set for Saint Vladimir's day (July 15).
June 1: King Alroy is invited on a hunting expedition by his uncle, Mahael II Duke d'Arjenol, to celebrate his coming-of-age.
June 9: While riding alone in the woods King Alroy of Torenth falls from his horse when his cinch snaps and breaks his neck; he declines healing, since his paralysis cannot be cured. Πέρας μεν γαρ ‘άπασιν ανθρώποις εστι του βίου θάνατος.
June 12: King Alroy of Torenth dies of the injuries he suffered III days earlier, aged XIV years. Rumours begin almost immediately in Torenth that King Kelson has engineered the accident, fearing the power of a Torenthi king in his majority. The IX-year-old Prince Liam becomes King of Torenth, with Princess Morag and Duke Mahael II again serving as co-Regents, and with various Torenthi Lords vying for her hand in marriage.
June 30: Alroy Arion II King of Torenth is buried in Torenthály.
July 20: Carsten Bishop of Meara dies, aged LXXIX years, precipitating the Mearan Crisis of 1124.
July 29: Kelson turns his attention toward the worsening Mearan situation, progressing through Meara, Cassan and Kierney with Duncan, as previously planned. Morgan spends most of the Summer in Corwyn to make certain there will be no Torenthi threat from the East, but joins Kelson in Culdi after the ailing Carsten leaves the important See of Meara to be filled. Brendan Coris is formally confirmed as Earl of Marley on this date and Richenda officially ratified as Regent of Marley.
August 8: Aristarchos Patriarch of Torenth dies, aged LXXIII years.
August 11: Sofiana Sovereign Princess of Andelon is reappointed to the Camberian Council. *Ben fiorisce negli nomini il volere; ma la pioggia continua converte in bozzacchioni le susine vere.*
September 12: Alpheios Metropolitan of Netterhaven is elected Patriarch of Beldour and All Torenth.
September 30: Alpheios I Patriarch of Beldour is enthroned.
November 2: Ithel Prince of Meara is knighted by his father, Lord Sicard MacArdry.
November 14: Kelson celebrates his XVIIth birthday. *Unter den Blinden ist der Einäugige König.*
November 20: The Synod of Bishops meets in Culdi to choose a new Mearan Primate, but before beginning deliberations elects several new itinerant Bishops, among them Father Duncan McLain as Auxiliary Bishop of Rhemuth and assistant to Archbishop Thomas Cardiel.

EVENTS OF *THE BISHOP'S HEIR* (NOVEMBER 1123-JANUARY 1124)

November 23: The Bishops of Gwynedd meet in consistory at Culdi to elect a successor to Carsten late Bishop of Meara. King Kelson and his councilors are present to speak to the assembly.

November 24: Kelson comes to the aid of a party of Trurill men fighting border outlaws, and discovers his foster brother Dhugal MacArdry Hereditary Count of Transha among them; they ride to Transha.

November 25: Kelson and his party reach Castle Transha, where he is introduced once again by Dhugal to the latter's presumed father, the aged Caulay MacArdry Clan Chief and Earl of Transha, and the King pays his respects. Prince Conall causes some embarrassment to the King by objecting to the austere accomodations.

November 26: Auxiliary Bishop Henry Istelyn is elected to the See of Meara by the consistory of Bishops assembled at Culdi. Father Judhael Prince of Meara is considered for this office, but is passed over due to the developing political crisis there.

November 28: The King returns to Culdi, where he ratifies the selection of Istelyn.

November 29: Edmund Loris sometime Archbishop Primate of Valoret and All Gwynedd escapes from his prison cell in St. Iveagh's Abbey with the help of Jeroboam and Monsignor Lawrence Gorony. *Other sins only speak; murder shrieks out.*

November 30: Bishop Henry Istelyn is consecrated as Bishop of Meara in Ratharkin.

December 1: Loris lands near Transha. Dhugal MacArdry Heir of Transha is captured by Brice Baron of Trurill and taken to Ratharkin; the news of his capture kills his grandfather, Caulay Earl of Transha, who suffers a heart attack, aged LXII years, making his foster son, Lord Dhugal, the new Earl and Clan Chief. In Dhugal's absence, Caball MacArdry, the new Tanist, assumes control of Castle Transha. Bishop Nevan is captured by Dhugal's soldiers, and is sent to Rhemuth.

December 4: Loris arrives at Ratharkin.

December 5: Edmund Loris deposes Henry Istelyn as Bishop of Meara and has him arrested. Loris illegally declares himself Primate of Meara, and creates Prince Judhael Bishop of Ratharkin, with the support of several renegade Bishops, including Creoda, Ian Calder of Sheele, Belden of Erne, and Lachlan de Quarles. King Kelson arrives at Rhemuth.

December 6: Morgan interrogates Bishop Nevan, who has been brought as a prisoner from Kierney. Kelson holds a Council of war, and decides to take an armed party of C knights to Ratharkin to rescue Dhugal and Istelyn.

December 8: Kelson's expedition to Meara departs Rhemuth with Alaric Morgan Duke of Corwyn and others. Princess Caitrin of Meara arrives at Ratharkin with her entourage.

December 9: Prince Judhael is consecrated Bishop of Ratharkin by Edmund Loris and his illegal "Synod." Dhugal escapes from Ratharkin, taking Princess Sidana with him as captive. He is pursued by Sicard Lord MacArdry and his knights, but meets Kelson's party coming up from Cùilteine; in the ensuing *mêlée*, Prince Llewell of Meara is also taken prisoner by Prince Conall. The King and his raiding party return to Rhemuth.

December 12: The King arrives at Rhemuth with his prisoners.

December 13: The King receives a letter of defiance from Loris and convenes the High Council at Rhemuth. The assembled Bishops and Archbishops excommunicate Loris, Caitrin, and their followers in Meara. *La vérité est cachée au fond du puits.*

December 16: Monsignor Duncan McLain is consecrated Auxiliary Bishop of Rhemuth.

December 17: The bull of excommunication reaches Ratharkin, and a formal response of defiance is made by the Pretender of Meara, who declares herself Sovereign Queen.

December 18: Bishop Henry Istelyn is degraded from his offices and executed by Caitrin and Loris.

December 25: The Great Lords and Generals gather at Rhemuth for Christmas observances. Kelson receives the letter of defiance from Meara and begins planning a Spring campaign against that province. Dhugal is invested as Earl of Transha. Kelson proposes a marriage of political expediency to Sidana Princess of Meara, who reluctantly accepts.

1124

January 1: Liam King of Torenth is girded with the sword at Iób by Patriarch Alpheios I under the reign name of Lajos II.

January 6: Duncan realizes that Dhugal MacArdry is actually his son. Sidana Princess of Meara marries Kelson King of Gwynedd, the ceremony being conducted by Archbishop Thomas Cardiel, but she is murdered most foully at the ceremony by her brother, the Prince Llewell, aged XIV years. *Erst bessin's, dann beginn's.*

* * * * * * *

January 9: Sidana Queen of Gwynedd and Princess of Meara is buried in the royal crypt of the Haldanes at Rhemuth.

January 31: Fulk Baron FitzWilliam dies, aged LXI years, and is succeeded by his younger brother, Lord Finn.

February 2: Llewell Prince of Meara is tried and executed for the murder of his sister, aged XV years.

April 4: Janniver Princess of Pardiac is betrothed to Colman II King of the United Kingdoms of Howicce and Llannedd.

EVENTS OF *THE KING'S JUSTICE* (MAY-JULY 1124)

May 15: Dowager Queen Jehana returns to Rhemuth. Preparatory to the departure of Kelson King of Gwynedd to put down the growing Mearan Rebellion, Nigel Duke of Carthmoor is made Prince Regent and is brought to his Haldane power with the aid of Morgan and others.

May 16: Duncan Duke of Cassan and Dhugal Earl of Transha depart Rhemuth to raise their army to invade Meara from the North.

May 19: Liam Lajos II King of Torenth arrives at Rhemuth with his mother Princess Morag to pay homage to King Kelson as his Overlord, and is ordered to remain in Rhemuth for VI months under the guard of Richenda Duchess of Corwyn. The latter

shows Kelson an interesting scroll from the East detailing the last days of Camber Earl of Culdi.
May 20: An expedition to quell the Mearan Rebellion leaves Rhemuth under the command of King Kelson.
May 26: The Pretender Caitrin's army leaves Ratharkin.
June 15: Ithel Hereditary Prince of Meara and Brice Baron of Trurill ravage the Convent of Saint Brigid, assaulting and violating the Princess Janniver of Pardiac, among others.
June 16: Kelson, Roger Earl of Jenas, and the Gwyneddan army discover the ruins of Saint Brigid's Abbey, and learn that it was ravaged by Brice and Ithel. Kelson meets Rothana Nabila of Nur Hallaj, a novice nun, who also proves to be a Deryni Princess and cousin of Morgan's wife, Richenda.
June 17: Prince Conall is sent by the King to Rhemuth to safeguard the refugee nuns and ladies of Saint Brigid's Abbey, including Rothana and Princess Janniver. Princess Eirian is born to Nigel Duke of Carthmoor and Meraude Lady de Traherne.
June 27: Prince Conall returns to Rhemuth with the refugees from Saint Brigid's; he meets there with Nigel and later with Tiercel. Richenda and Rothana talk with Jehana.
June 29: Richenda sets controls in Conall to prevent interference by the Deryni Morag, so that he may be privy to future high-level discussions of war strategy. Prince Ithel reports to his mother Caitrin in Ratharkin about the advance of the Gwyneddan army. Princess Caitrin and her Bishops retreat to the coastal fortress of Laas, and Ratharkin is burned by Brice Baron of Trurill and Ithel Hereditary Prince of Meara. Kelson and Morgan see the fire. Duncan and Dhugal encamp far to the North.
June 30: Richenda and Rothana meet in the solar in Rhemuth Castle, where Jehana hears Orin's verses. Azim, using the name "Ludolphus the Peddler," delivers a coded message to Richenda from Princess Rohays, Richenda's cousin, detailing a plot against Duke Nigel. Conall secretly meets the Deryni Tiercel de Claron in a clearing outside of Rhemuth, and tells Tiercel about Azim.
July 1: Kelson "reads" a scout and pursues Prince Ithel's forces. Dowager Queen Jehana confronts Father Ambros, her chaplain, concerning certain sermons he has been preaching to her.
July 2: Ithel Hereditary Prince of Meara and Brice Baron of Trurill are captured at Talacara near Ratharkin, and are tried, convicted, and hanged for their war crimes. The Cassani army of Duncan McLain Duke of Cassan, invading Meara from the North, is trapped at Dorna by Sicard Lord MacArdry husband of Caitrin the Pretender; Duncan is captured and tortured by Loris. Dhugal escapes from the battlefield and makes mental contact with Kelson. Jehana discovers a plot against Nigel and warns him; Nigel captures the potential assassins. Brice Baron of Trurill is XLI years of age at his death, and Prince Ithel is XVI years of age, and is succeeded as Hereditary Prince by his *cousin germain*, Prince-Bishop Judhael.
July 3: Lord Sicard MacArdry is defeated and killed by King Kelson, aged LVI years. Roger Earl of Jenas stops Loris from killing Duncan: Loris and Gorony are captured, and Duncan is rescued. Raif uses the soldier Hoag as a medium to contact Princess Sofiana on the Camberian Council. Bishop Denis Arilan meets with the Council to discuss the events of the last several days.
July 4: Gorony and Loris are questioned by the King.
July 5: Kelson's army leaves Dorna for Laas.
July 12: King Kelson and his soldiers arrive at Laas, and Dhugal approaches the Pretender with a harsh offer of a truce. The Mearans finally surrender unconditionally. Edmund Loris sometime Archbishop Primate of Valoret and All Gwynedd, Monsignor Lawrence Gorony, and Prince Judhael Bishop of Ratharkin and nephew of Caitrin, are tried, convicted, and executed by Kelson. The Pretender Caitrin is deposed and cloistered at Saint Giles's Abbey, where Jehana took sojourn so many years before. Dhugal is named Lord Lieutenant of Meara, and Duncan Viceroy of Meara. Loris is LIX years of age at his death, Gorony is LI years, and Prince Judhael is XXXVIII years. The Princess Caitrin is succeeded in her pretensions by her *cousin germain*, Sir Dafydd Ramsay of Cloome, a descendant of Princess Magrette. *Principis est virtus maxima, nosse suos.*
* * * * * * *
July 14: William Baron du Chantal is arrested, tried, convicted, attainted, and executed, aged LV years.
August 2: Morgan takes his levies home via Rhemuth, where Richenda and the children remain there so that she can supervise Torenthi Princess Morag. Before he leaves, Richenda is with child again—a boy due the coming May.
September 16: Tegan O Daire and Tibald MacErskine are captured, tried, convicted, and executed by forces loyal to King Kelson.
Fall: Morgan is back and forth between Rhemuth and Coroth all Autumn, taking Richenda, the children, and Princess Morag back to Coroth. All are present to celebrate Christmas Court, including Duncan and Dhugal. King Liam has been fostered to Duke Nigel's household, and remains in Rhemuth. Morag's presence at Coroth is not widely known or talked about, since they do not want Torenth to get her back; but Kelson hopes to be able to release her at the end of the following Summer. Duncan and Dhugal spend Fall and much of the Winter in Meara reestablishing a Gwyneddan administration there. Gloddruth and Godwin remain in Kierney and Cassan maintain order.
October 12: John Nivard, a Deryni, is ordained priest by Bishop Denis Arilan.
November 14: Kelson celebrates his XVIIIth birthday.
November 16: Prince Oswin is born to Létald Hort of Orsal and Prince of Tralia and Husniyya Sharifa of R'Kassi.
November 25: Mátyás Lord Komnéné marries Lady Ophélie daughter of Richard Duc du Joux.
December 19: Morag Princess of Torenth and Duchess of Tolán is confined at Coroth Castle under the guardianship of Richenda Duchess of Corwyn.

1125

January 1: Torenthi Patriarch Alpheios I blesses an enameled cross to be presented to King Kelson at Rhemuth in March.
February 25: Duncan and Dhugal travel to Rhemuth to attend the latter's knighting. Morgan also returns to Rhemuth for the knightings.

EVENTS OF *THE QUEST FOR SAINT CAMBER* (FEBRUARY-JULY 1125)

February 28: It is raining in Gwynedd. Prince Conall meets again with Tiercel. Dhugal's relationship with his father is argued before the Archbishops in Valoret, with Bishop Wolfram acting as Devil's Advocate in the proceedings. That night, in the presence of Morgan, Duncan, Arilan, and Nigel, Kelson and Dhugal are administered *merasha* so they will be prepared for its effects. *Absentem lædit, cum ebrio qui litigat.*

March 1: Kelson is ill from the effects of *merasha*, but attends mass. The Archbishops announce that Dhugal MacArdry Earl of Transha has been confirmed as a legitimate son and heir of Bishop Duncan McLain. The Ladies Meraude, Jehana, Richenda, Rothana, the infant Eirian, and Janniver gather to talk in the solar at Rhemuth Palace. Jatham and Janniver make eyes at each other. Kelson argues with his mother, Dowager Queen Jehana.

March 2: The more than XX candidates for knighthood keep a night-long vigil at Saint Hilary's Basilica.

March 3: Kelson, Dhugal, Conall, Jatham, Duncan, Jass, and others are knighted, the King and Conall by Duke Nigel and Dhugal by Bishop Duncan after his own knighting by Kelson, with Ewan III Duke of Claibourne as witness. Duncan publicly reveals himself and his son to be Deryni. Al-Rasoul ibn Tarik, official ambassador from the Kingdom of Torenth and the Regent Mahael II Duke d'Arjenol, inquires about the status of King Liam and his mother, the Princess Morag. The former has been made a squire to Nigel Duke of Carthmoor, and is brought forward for his inspection. A banquet and dance are held that evening, at which Dhugal flirts with Lady Quentina daughter of Michael II Earl of Carthane. Lady Rothana wears secular garb for the first time in Kelson's presence. Rasoul takes ship from Desse, being escorted there by Morgan and Duncan.

March 4 (Ash Wednesday): Bishop Duncan is celebrating mass with Father Shandon, but is avoided by some penitents while he is dispensing ashes to mark the onset of Lent, and argues with Arilan. Bishop Arilan transports to the Camberian Council, which discusses the situation. Kelson calls a meeting of the Gwyneddan High Council. Arilan, Cardiel, and Duncan meet later that day, and the latter is later asked by Cardiel to refrain from publicly saying mass or performing other priestly duties until the Synod addresses the issue of Deryni priests.

March 8: Morgan presents Dhugal and Kelson with Saint Camber medals, which Duncan blesses. Kelson meets Rothana in the garden and pledges his love, and she admits that she feels something for him as well, and that she is considering leaving her Order. He asks her to marry him when he returns at the end of the Summer, and gives her Sidana's ring. Conall spies on the pair from the window above. That evening, after being taught by Tiercel how to use the transfer portals from and to the library in Rhemuth Castle, Prince Conall kills the Deryni in a fit of temper and hides the body in a secret passage there.

March 9: King Kelson, Dhugal, Conall, Jass, Jatham, Saer, Roger, Father Lael, VIII Haldane Lancers, III MacArdry men, and others depart Rhemuth on the King's quest for the relics of Saint Camber. Duke Nigel discusses current events with Morgan. Duke Nigel again becomes Prince Regent of Gwynedd in King Kelson's absence. Morgan rides to Desse to spend the night on the *Rhafallia*.

March 10: Alaric Morgan Duke of Corwyn takes the *Rhafallia* from Desse to return to his capital city of Coroth.

March 11: A steady rain begins, and continues for the next IV days. Kelson's expedition seeks refuge with a local Lord.

March 14: The King's party arrives at Valoret.

March 15: The day is wet and cold. Father Elroy announces King Kelson to the Synod. The King addresses the General Synod called by Archbishop Bradene at the Chapter House in Valoret, urging those gathered to elect qualified candidates for the III empty sees, and to repeal some of the more restrictive edicts of the Council of Ramos, thereby allowing Deryni legally to participate in priestly functions. Kelson has a cold. In Rhemuth, Bishop Duncan has been transcribing paperwork for Prince Regent Nigel. He accidentally discovers the decomposing body of Tiercel de Claron while traversing a little-used secret passageway at Rhemuth Castle. Nigel and Duncan investigate.

March 16: The weather is finally clearing. King Kelson and his party depart Valoret for Dolban via Saint Mark's Abbey on the Eirian River. Duncan rides from Rhemuth to bring the news of Tiercel's passing to Bishop Arilan at Valoret. The King and his party stay at Saint Dolban's that evening.

March 17: Kelson dines with Thomas Earl of Carcashale, and spends the night at his estate.

March 18: Duncan arrives at Valoret with dispatches from Duke Nigel, and tells Arilan and Cardiel of Tiercel's death. Arilan and Duncan transport to Rhemuth to examine the body of Tiercel; Arilan then reports to the Camberian Council, returning to Valoret via portal, with messages from Duke Nigel, who writes to Kelson informing him of Tiercel's death. Duncan remains at Rhemuth. Creoda Bishop of Culdi, Belden of Erne Bishop of Cashien, and Lachlan de Quarles Bishop of Ballymar are degraded from their sees and imprisoned for life. Five other Bishops are deprived of rank but allowed to continue functioning as priests under close supervision: Gilbert Desmond, Mir de Kierney, Raymer de Valence, Ian Calder of Sheele, and Nevan d'Estrelldas. The Synod elects Father Hugh de Berry as Bishop of Ballymar, itinerant Bishop Bevan de Torigny as Bishop of Culdi, Father John FitzPadraic as Bishop of Meara, and Father James MacKenzie as Bishop of Cashien.

March 19: Bishop Arilan sends dispatches from Valoret to Kelson, and then attends the deliberations of the Bishops. The Synod begins questioning candidates for the V vacant itinerant Bishoprics of Gwynedd. Kelson's expedition spends the night at Saint Bearand's Abbey at the foot of the High Grelder Pass. Morgan arrives at Coroth via ship.

March 20: Jatham and Jass organize a hunting party, but Kelson, Dhugal, Saer, and Dolfin decide to explore the ruins of old Tor Caerrorie, being guided by brother Arnold, a local monk, and specifically examining the tombs of Ballard II MacRorie Earl of

Culdi, Camber's father, and several of Camber's siblings. Arilan's messenger reaches Saint Bearand's Abbey, but the courier turns over the dispatch pouch to Prince Conall. Conall reads the letter from Nigel regarding the discovery of Tiercel de Claron's body, and uses 1 of Tiercel's drugs to taint a flask of Dhugal's wine with *merasha*. The King spends another night at Saint Bearand's. In Valoret, Father Jodoc d'Armaine is elected an itinerant Bishop of Gwynedd.

March 21: The day is cold and clear, but rain begins soon thereafter. The King's party leaves Saint Bearand's Abbey to traverse the High Grelder Pass. Kelson, Dhugal, Dolfin, Jowan, and Brother Gelric fall from the disintegrating muddy trail winding its way up the cliff down into the Grelder Creek, and are swept away by the torrent. Prince Conall nearly follows them over the edge, but manages to save himself at the last minute. Jowan and Brother Gelric are found drowned; only Dolfin is recovered alive. Kelson and Dhugal disappear, being carried away underground by the water. Dhugal awakes in a dark cavern next to the flooding river, having badly sprained his wrist and ankle. He finds the barely-conscious body of the King, and discovers that he has suffered a serious blow to his head, fracturing the skull. Back at Valoret, Father Benoît Lord d'Evering is elected Auxiliary Bishop of Valoret.

March 22: The survivors of the King's party conduct a thorough search of the stream and the area, but discover no additional bodies. Part of the group returns to Saint Bearand's that evening.

March 23: The survivors of the King's expedition ride out from Saint Bearand's early that morning and reach Valoret at dusk. Saer de Traherne informs the Bishops that the King is presumed dead. The remnants of the expedition leave Valoret that evening with the Archbishops for Rhemuth.

March 24: In the underground cavern, Dhugal uses his Deryni power to alleviate the pressure on Kelson's skull by mentally lifting the piece of depressed bone.

March 25 (Lady Day): The King's party returns to Rhemuth late in the day. Nigel refuses to be proclaimed King, but will continue as Prince Regent until a year and a day have passed. Duncan and Arilan transport to Dhassa via portal, where Duncan is introduced to Deryni priest John Nivard, Arilan's *protégé*. Duncan travels to Coroth by horse to tell Morgan.

March 26: In Coroth, a messenger arrives by ship at Coroth to tell Morgan of Tiercel's death. Morgan argues with his wife Richenda regarding her potential appointment as Regent of Corwyn in his absence, saying his soldiers do not trust her. The Camberian Council is called into session by Denis Arilan to consider Kelson's presumed death. At Rhemuth, the High Council meets to discuss proclaiming Nigel King, with attendance by Nigel, Arilan, Conall, Saer, Bradene, and Cardiel. Conall presses Rothana for marriage now that Kelson is gone, but she neither accepts nor refuses him. Later he confronts his father. Duke Nigel becomes suspicious of his son's activities, and Conall puts him into a magic-induced coma when Nigel guesses his son's association with Tiercel. Nigel is examined by physicians and judged to have had a stroke.

March 27: Duncan arrives at Coroth and informs Morgan of Dhugal and Kelson's supposed deaths. Duncan and Morgan promptly leave for Dhassa to give their support to Nigel. Richenda is made Regent of Corwyn in Morgan's absence. In the cavern, Dhugal and Kelson slowly follow the underground river downward, feeding themselves from the carcass of a horse and the fish they catch. In Rhemuth, Conall consolidates his power, being named Prince Regent of Gwynedd in his father's place.

March 29: Duncan and Morgan arrive at Dhassa, and try with Father Nivard to locate Kelson and Dhugal through a mind link. They fail. They then transport to Rhemuth via portal, and examine Nigel, but can do nothing to help. They discuss the situation with Arilan, who wants Prince Conall confirmed as the Haldane heir.

April 2: Conall is told by Bishop Denis Arilan that his Haldane potential will be activated by Duncan, Morgan, and Arilan in 11 days. The Prince Regent asks Archbishop Thomas Cardiel to grant Rothana's request for release from her religious vows to allow her to marry, stating falsely that the letter she had earlier sent to Cardiel actually refers to Conall. Later that same day he convinces Rothana to marry him in the interests of state.

April 4: Prince Conall's Haldane potential is activated with the assistance of Morgan, Duncan, and Arilan.

April 5: Duncan and Morgan transport to Valoret, there to leave for Saint Bearand's to hunt for Kelson and Dhugal or their bodies.

April 8: Kelson and Dhugal discover a manmade wall at the end of the series of underground caverns they have been traversing. Duncan and Morgan investigate the High Grelder Pass, and begin dowsing to find the course of the underground part of the river.

April 9: Dhugal breaks through the wall into a burial chamber, but finds the other end blocked by a door latched from the outside. He draws energy from the King to open the lock, and they slowly make their way through a series of such chambers, each newer than the last.

April 10: Kelson and Dhugal continue moving through chambers, and finally emerge from the last tomb. They are captured by Bened and the villagers of Saint Kyriell's, a long-lost enclave still venerating the memory of Saint Camber. Dhugal discovers he can heal, and cures his own wounds and those of the King. In Rhemuth, Rothana is released from her vows. *A cruce salus.*

April 11: Conall Prince Regent of Gwynedd marries Rothana Nabila of Nur Hallaj in a private ceremony at Rhemuth Palace; Meraude gives Rothana her own wedding veil as a present. Kelson and Dhugal are questioned by the Quorial (governing Council) of Saint Kyriell's, and that night Kelson is put to the ordeal to test his vision. Duncan and Morgan lose track of the underground stream they are following. Dhugal makes mental contact with his father while Kelson undergoes his test.

April 12 (Palm Sunday): Kelson emerges successfully from his ordeal. With the assistance of the villagers, the pair depart Saint Kyriell's, meeting Duncan and Morgan late that night. Kelson is told of all the changes to his kingdom. Dhugal wonders if Kelson has inadvertently mated with the girl Rhidian during his ordeal.

April 14: Kelson, Dhugal, and the others leave for Valoret.

April 16: Kelson's party reaches Valoret.

April 17: The King reviews the decisions of the Synod: all of the vacant sees have now been filled, and VI new itinerant Bishops have been elected, with IV positions yet to be chosen. The canonization of Henry Istelyn has been unanimously approved. The Statutes of Ramos have been almost completely rewritten.

April 18: Bishop Hugh de Berry speaks in Duncan's defense before the Synod, and Bishop Duncan McLain is formally reinstated to his rank at the King's request.

April 19 (Easter Sunday): Rothana tells Conall that she is pregnant with his son. The King and his party return via portal to Rhemuth Cathedral and depose the Prince Regent Conall. Duke Nigel is revived from his coma by Duncan and Morgan. Prince Conall takes Jass MacArdry hostage and demands a duel arcane with the King, but is defeated when the image of Saint Camber appears. He is dosed with *merasha* and bound over for future trial. *Acta deos nunquam mortalia fallunt.*

May 3: Prince Conall is tried, convicted, and beheaded for his crimes, aged XVIII years, and Prince Rory is made new heir to the Duchy of Carthmoor by his father, Conall's unborn son being specifically disinherited by Nigel. Hereditary Duke and Earl Kelric Alain is born to Alaric Morgan Duke of Corwyn and Richenda Lady of Rheljan.

May 16: Lady Silke Haldane is named Infirmarian of Saint Dymphna's Convent.

May 21: Dhugal becomes Duke of Cassan by cession from his father, Bishop Duncan McLain.

June 10: The King visits Morgan at his palace in Coroth, where Kelric Alain Morgan Hereditary Duke of Corwyn and Earl of Lendour is baptized by Duncan, with Kelson serving as godfather. Rothana will establish a new religious Order at Saint Kyriell's. Dhugal and Kelson meet a stranger on the beach, who shows them a vision of Camber's body lying in its burial chamber.

* * * * * * *

August 6: The natural child Conalline Amelia Haldana't-Serclaes is born posthumously to Conall Prince Regent of Gwynedd and Vanissa 't-Serclaes, his former mistress.

September 4: Hereditary Lord Lóránt Lajos is born to Mátyás Lord Komnéné and Ophélie Lady du Joux.

September 16: Mátyás Lord Komnéné is elevated to the rank of Count Komnéné by King Liam Lajos II.

November 14: King Kelson celebrates his XIXth birthday.

December 5: Étienne Baron Kilchon dies, aged LXXXIV years, and is succeeded by his son, Lord Caidin.

1126

January 29: Branwell Baron de Varian dies, aged LXVI years, and is succeeded by his son, Burchard Earl of Eastmarch *jure uxoris*. With the approval of King Kelson, Burchard declares his IInd son, Lord Bassey, heir to the subsidiary title of Varian.

January 30: Sir Dafydd Ramsay of Cloome dies, aged LXIX years, and is succeeded as Pretender of Meara by his son, Sir Jolyon III.

February 3: Prince Albin Nigel Brion Hakim Haldane is born posthumously to Conall Prince Regent of Gwynedd and Rothana Princess of Gwynedd and Nabila of Nur Hallaj, his widow. *"What, nephew,"* said the king, *"is the wind in that door?"*

May 1 (Mayday): On this day that grate boke yclept *Ye Codex Derynianus* is made compleat, and a copy is sent to King Kelson.

June 4: Princess Morag is released from her captivity in Corwyn and returns to Beldour.

June 15: Branyng I Count of Sostra dies, aged LXVIII years, and is succeeded by his son, Branyng II.

August 15: The lords spiritual of Gwynedd meet at Grecotha to further amend the Statutes of Ramos. The Deryni saints are restored to their official status in the Church, although the celebration of their feasts is made optional throughout the land. The final restrictions on Deryni serving as higher clergy are also removed, with King Kelson giving his sanction. The King also issues a decree on this date, specifically revoking certain acts of his predecessors that were aimed against the Deryni, and providing a mechanism whereby descendants of those illegally deprived of title or property can seek legal redress, without, however, the displacement of any current owners of such lands or honours. The Servants of Saint Camber are formally recognized and sanctioned. *Thou shalt make castels thanne in Spayne, and dreme of joye, all but in vayne.*

November 14: King Kelson celebrates his XXth birthday.

1127

January 6: King Kelson announces the appointment of a commission to adjudicate the claims of descendants of former Deryni title holders and property owners. Alaric Morgan Duke of Corwyn will chair the group.

February 9: Ros Earl of Kilarden dies of the wasting sickness, aged XLIII years; his only son, the Hereditary Count Rossan, having perished before him *sans postérité* in the recent Mearan conflict, the title goes into abeyance among the descendants of several female co-heiresses, among them descendants of the House of Ramsay.

July 29: Lady Kyri marries Martel Lord Nykorik, a scion of the House of Furstán-Medras.

August 2: Sir Jolyon Ramsay and his family arrive in Rhemuth for the betrothal of his eldest son, Brecon Ramsay, to Princess Richelle Haldane.

September 11: Lord Torval is born to Mátyás Lord Komnéné and Ophélie Lady du Joux, but dies later that day.

October 11: Ewan Duke of Claibourne leaves Claibourne Town for Rhemuth.

October 21: Princess Caitrin, ex-Pretender of Meara, dies, aged LXI years.

November 1: Ewan Duke of Claibourne arrives at Rhemuth.

November 3: At a meeting of the Camberian Council, Sir Sion Benet is elected to fill the seat of the late Tiercel de Claron. Lady Kyri announces her retirement from the Council, since she is expecting a child the following summer.

November 14: King Kelson celebrates his XXIst birthday.
November 16: Dhugal leaves for Transha, where he intends to spend the winter.

1128

January 6: Prince Rory Haldane, second son of Nigel Duke of Carthmoor, and Angus Lord MacEwan, son and heir of Graham Earl of Kheldour, are knighted by King Kelson.
February 11: Azim is elected to the Camberian Council, replacing the Lady Kyri.
April 3: Liam Lajos II King of Torenth attains his majority, and the regency of Mahael II Duke d'Arjenol and Morag Dowager Duchess d'Arjenol is dissolved. *Il faut hurler avec les loups.*
June 26: Dowager Queen Jehana returns to court with her entourage to take up duties as part of the Regency Council to govern Gwynedd during her son's pending absence.

EVENTS OF *KING KELSON'S BRIDE* (JUNE-AUGUST 1128)

June 28: In Beldour, Mahael Duke d'Arjenol, Teymuraz Count of Brustarkia, and the Princess Morag Queen Mother of Torenth meet to discuss suitable brides for King Liam Lajos II. Six of the seven members of the Camberian Council also meet in its mountain aerie to discuss possible brides for King Kelson. Al-Rasoul ibn Tarik and Mátyás Count of Komnénë, emissaries from the court of Torenth, arrive in their war galley at the port of Desse south of Rhemuth, accompanied by Duke Alaric Morgan in his ship *Rhafallia*. In Rhemuth, Janniver Princess of Pardiac marries Sir Jatham Kilshane, Father John Nivard conducting the ceremony, with King Kelson, Torenthi King Liam, Princess Rothana, Bishop Duncan McLain, Dhugal Duke of Cassan, Prince Rory, Prince Payne, and many other friends in attendance. Kelson announces that he intends to make Jatham Baron of Kilshane, thereby reviving an ancient extinct title. Afterwards, Kelson and Rothana have a private conversation, discussing the construction of the new chapel of the Servants of Saint Camber, and the future of Rothana's son, Prince Albin, whom Rothana wishes to enter a religious establishment. The King reaffirms his love for Rothana and asks for her hand in marriage, but she irrevocably rejects him. Rothana tells Kelson that Prince Rory and Lady Noelie Ramsay are in love. She then proposes that Kelson marry his first cousin, Araxie Haldane, Baroness Dunluce, who is popularly believed to be betrothed to Prince Cuan, heir presumptive to the throne of Howicce. Rothana tells the King that, on the contrary, Cuan loves his cousin, Princess Gwenlian, heiress to the throne of Llannedd. Araxie, Rothana states, has been trained by Azim, who approves of a potential liaison between the girl and Kelson. Late that night, the women take Janniver to the wedding chamber. Kelson and his comrades celebrate, and then take Jatham to his new wife, singing various wedding songs. Dhugal accompanies Kelson to the library, where the King wishes to check some family history. Kelson then shows Dhugal the access to the secret annex next door, the only entrance to which is disguised as a garde-robe, and which is warded by a "veil" from egress (in either direction) by anyone save those of Haldane blood and their guests. The library annex contains shelves of magical texts and books on the history of the Deryni, and a portal to which the Camberian Council has been given access. Rothana and her son leave during the night for Saint Kyriell's.

June 29: Kelson meets privily with Prince Rory Haldane, who confesses his attraction for Lady Noelie. After mass, Kelson discusses recent developments with his uncle, Duke Nigel, and Duke Dhugal, and advises them of Rory's attraction to Noelie Ramsay, of which he approves. But if Rory settles in Meara, then the succession to Carthmoor must be adjusted, perhaps back to Prince Albin Haldane, Nigel's grandson by Prince Conall and Rothana. Duke Alaric Morgan, Saer Earl de Traherne, and Brendan Earl of Marley, Morgan's page, accompany al-Rasoul ibn Tarik and Count Mátyás, emissaries from the Court of Torenth, from the port of Desse overland to Rhemuth, where they are met by Prince Rory and Lord Pemberly the Deputy-Chamberlain. They observe from the back of the Great Hall the creation by King Kelson of Sir Jatham as new Baron of Kilshane. The two Torenthi visitors are formally introduced to King Kelson, and King Liam also receives them. The emissaries present several gifts, including robes of state and an ancient Torenthi crown. They withdraw to a private audience, where Kelson comforts Liam, who is reluctant to leave Rhemuth. The King tells Liam he must return and accept his responsibilities, or Mahael will become ruler of Torenth. But Liam will remain a squire until he leaves Gwyneddan soil. Kelson tells Mátyás about his concern over the intentions of Mahael and Teymuraz, the Count's older brothers. Later, the King talks with Morgan about future wedding plans for himself and developments in Meara. That evening, Kelson hosts a banquet in honour of their guests, including members of the Regency Council that will take over when he leaves for Torenth. Afterwards, Kelson meets with his mother Jehana, who gives him a letter to carry to his aunt, Sivorn, in Orsal, plus a set of coral prayer-beads cum gold amulet for his protection in Torenth.

June 30: After morning mass, Kelson, Liam, and the Torenthis depart by ship from Desse for Coroth, capital of Corwyn.

July 2: Around noon, Duke Morgan's ship *Rhafallia* and the Torenthi galley carrying the foreign emissaries approach Coroth Harbour. They are met at the dock by Sean Earl Derry and Lady Briony de Morgan, and at Castle Coroth by the Duchess Richenda, Bishop Arilan, and Bishop Tolliver. Kelson discusses his pending journey to Beldour with Derry, who desires to accompany the King. Sean acknowledges that the nightmares that had plagued him many years earlier, after the late King Wencit's mental intrusion, have now returned. That evening, a private banquet for their foreign guests is held in Morgan's ducal chambers. Afterwards, Kelson withdraws to discuss recent developments privily with Richenda, Dhugal, Morgan, and Bishop Arilan. The latter takes issue with several of the King's opinions. Then the talk turns to possible brides for Kelson, with Arilan leading the discussion. Richenda tells the King of

Rothana's intention to establish a new Deryni *schola* with the assistance of the Servants of Saint Camber.

July 3: Kelson and his party take ship to the Île d'Orsal, lying across the Twin River Straits. A row of Torenthi war galleys awaits them there to provide an official escort for Liam. Vasily Dimitriades, the Hort's Chief Chamberlain, welcomes them at the dock of Horthánthy. On the steep, winding road leading to the Palace at the top of the hill, Kelson and Liam are attacked near the summit by two mind-warped assassins. Both commit suicide when their assault fails. Kelson is slightly wounded, but will survive intact. Létald Hort of Orsal apologizes for the outrage, and conducts the party to a private reception room, where they discuss the reasons for the attack and other matters of the day. That afternoon, Dhugal heals Kelson's bruise, and the travelers retire to their private quarters to rest. Later, Kelson and Liam and their entourages attend a banquet in their honour given by the Hort of Orsal. Kelson talks with Azim, an accomplished Deryni and uncle of Rothana; he tells the King that he has arranged a private rendezvous with Princess Araxie. That night, Kelson tells Morgan of his pending engagement to Araxie. Azim appears, and discusses the political situation in Torenth with Kelson, Morgan, and Dhugal. Azim suspects that Mahael is plotting against King Liam's life. Then Azim takes Kelson to meet privily with Araxie. Kelson and Araxie come to an agreement that they will be married after his return from his forthcoming trip to Beldour. Later, Kelson takes off Sidana's wedding ring, and with Dhugal's aid melts it down with magic; he gives the residue to Arilan. He selects a different ring to give to Araxie as a token of their engagement. The King and Araxie announce their betrothal before a handful of close friends, and plight their troth before Bishop Arilan. Arilan later meets Azim privily, and complains over Azim's lack of consultation with the Camberian Council.

July 4: In Rhemuth, Meraude and Jehana discuss possible bridal candidates for Kelson, as well as Nigel's disclosure to them that morning that Prince Rory may marry Lady Noelie Ramsay. They recall their early lives, the courting of their husbands, and the war with the Marluk in 1105. They retire to the palace library to check the blood lines of the Ramsay family. Jehana discovers the entrance to the secret library annex. After the ladies depart, Father Nivard emerges briefly from the annex to make certain none of his work has been disturbed. Later, Meraude and Jehana go to the royal gardens, where Meraude suggests that they visit Vanissa and Conalline, the late Prince Conall's natural daughter, in a few days. That evening, Queen Jehana returns to the library, where she wishes further to explore the hidden doorway at the garde-robe. First, however, she must use her own magic to open the locked main library entrance, since she does not have a key. She enters the annex, and discovers a number of forbidden magical texts lining the shelves. There is also a transfer portal, the parameters of which she explores. Then she suddenly realizes that a bald-headed man is present with her in the darkened room. Barrett de Laney tells her that he is a scholar given leave by the King to use the library, and that he fell asleep. She sees that he is blind. Another old man, Laran ap Pardyce, abruptly joins them, and then both men depart through the portal. The Queen returns to her own quarters. That same day, King Kelson, King Liam, Létald the Hort of Orsal, and their parties leave for Beldour on the *Niyyana*, one of the Hort's fleet of coastal vessels, accompanied by six black Torenthi galleys. They head north along the coast of Tralia to the River Beldour, anchoring that evening near the domed city of Furstánán. Rasoul and Mátyás join the Hort on his vessel for dinner. Liam discusses recent and current political events with Kelson, blaming Mahael for his older brother's death. As darkness falls, lights appear on the dome over the Church of Saint-Sasile in Furstánán, generated by the Deryni monks of that establishment to honour their young King's return to his homeland. Mátyás and Kelson discuss the history of their nations, the former suggesting that the Festillic claims to the Gwyneddan throne are now *passés*. That night, Kelson, Morgan, and Dhugal link together, and the King relates to them his earlier conversations with the Torenthis.

July 5: The three Tralian vessels and six Torenthi galleys continue their journey, entering the mouth of the river proper. In Rhemuth, Jehana confronts Father Nivard, and demands to know details about the annex to the library and its doorway, and the man Barrett de Laney whom she had encountered there. Nivard explains the restrictions that the King has set on the use of the annex, to prevent unauthorized access to the rest of the palace. That afternoon, the Queen, Meraude, and Rory visit Vanissa and her daughter Conalline in the countryside near Rhemuth. Meraude offers Vanissa a place in the royal household, so that the little girl will have a future appropriate to the great-granddaughter of a king. Meraude suggests that Conalline be called by her second name, Amelia, until Nigel can be reconciled to her presence, and Vanissa will be called Maria, Mary being her confirmation name. Vanissa agrees to everything. *Il più forte ha sempre ragione.*

July 6: The party reaches the borders of Marluk.

July 7: The prevailing winds die down, and they are forced to resort to rowers to keep the ships moving upriver. Hereditary Prince Cyric of Orsal and Tralia talks to Kelson about the Prince's own marriage prospects, and suggests Lady Noelie as a possible bride. They anchor off a walled town, Südmarcke, that issues forth a fleet of small boats filled with locals singing paeans to their lawful king.

July 8: In the afternoon Kelson and Liam's party reaches the great City of Beldour, where they are welcomed with a grand celebration. They land at the Quai du Saint-Basile, where they are officially welcomed. That evening, Mahael, Teymuraz, Mátyás, Branyng II Count of Sostra, and László Count of Czalsky, who will be participating in the enthronement of King Liam a week hence, meet to discuss current events. Mátyás informs them of the assassination attempt, and all seem surprised. They talk about Kelson's and Liam's abilities. Branyng indicates that he is courting Dowager Queen Morag, King Liam's mother.

July 9: Rasoul and Count Branyng give Kelson a tour of the City of Beldour, while Létald meets with official observers from the Forcinn States. Liam remains with his uncles, mother, and brother. Kelson returns to the Hanging Gardens of Furstánály Palace, where he joins a reception to honour King Liam's guests, among them Bahadur Khan King of R'Kassi, Isarn II Sovereign Prince of Logréine, and Gron III Sovereign Grand Duke of Calam. Kelson also meets several members of the Torenthi royal family, including Duke Mahael, Count Teymuraz, and Hereditary Prince Ronal Rurik, Liam's heir presumptive. Liam tells Kelson that Count Berrhones, Master of Ceremonies, has asked both kings to begin rehearsals on the morrow at Sankt Ióbʼs Church for the *killijálay* ceremony. They dine together a little later, accompanied by Mátyás and several other Torenthi nobles, Káspár Duke of Truvorsk, Erdödy Duke of Jándrich, and Amaury Makróry Hereditary Count of Kulnán.

July 10: Kelson, Liam, and the designated celebrants travel to the church of Hagios Iób at Torenthály north of Beldour, to rehearse the enthronement ceremony of King Liam. Other participants include Alpheios, the Patriarch of Beldour and All Torenth; Count Berrhones, the Master of Ceremonies; Father Károly, who will explain to Kelson what is happening in the ceremony, including the moving wards to shield the unprotected King. Later that afternoon, Liam and Mátyás show Kelson, Morgan, and Dhugal the Nikolaseum, the architectural marvel built by King Arkady II to honour the memory of his younger brother Nikola, who saved the Kingʼs life at the Battle of Killingford a hundred years earlier. There Mátyás and Liam ask Kelson to accompany them through the portal in the monument to a place where they can talk privily. At Mátyásʼs private chapel, the Count tells Kelson of the plot being perpetrated by Mahael and Teymuraz to mind-rip King Liam and kill Prince Ronal Rurik during the enthronement ceremony, when Mátyás, Teymuraz, László, and Branyng serve at Liamʼs moving ward. Mátyás proposes to stop his two brothers, but needs the help of Kelson during the *killijálay*. Mátyás will remove László, and Liam will demand that Kelson be appointed his substitute. Kelson agrees. That evening, after a state dinner, Kelson shares the events of the afternoon with Dhugal.

July 11: Kelson and his party attend a reception in one of the tiered gardens for Prince Centule of Vézaire and Rotrou Hereditary Prince of Jáca. Kelson is also introduced to Sofiana Sovereign Princess of Andelon. The body of László Count Czalsky is found floating in the river; he has been strangled. Czalsky is XXVII years of age at his death, and is succeeded by his younger brother, Lord Bertil. Lord Radu meets with Kelson, Dhugal, Morgan, Derry, and the Royal uncles, and announces Count Czalskyʼs death. Later that afternoon, Kelson, Azim, Dhugal, and Derry ride out into the nearby hills. Azim tells the King that Liam has asked for Kelson to replace Czalsky in the moving ward. Azim offers his assistance.

July 12: Kelson receives a summons from Duke Mahael. In the presence of the chief officers of court, Patriarch Alpheios asks him formally to participate in the *killijálay*. Kelson accepts the charge. That afternoon Kelson begins private instruction with Azim, who tells the King that he will represent the western quarter of the ward, or Saint Gabriel. Mátyás will represent the north, or Saint Uriel. Teymuraz will represent the south, or Saint Michael. Branyng will represent the east, or Saint Raphael. Lady Vivienne suffers a paralytic seizure.

July 13: Kelson continues his training with Azim, gradually lengthening his period of concentration to over an hour. Father Irenæus, Father Károly, and János Sokrat assist Azim in strengthening the training techniques. *Ευτυχία πολύφιλος.*

July 14: Kelson begins rehearsing the *killijálay* with the Furstáns, practicing moving along corridors and over obstacles. Then they practice shifting the ward to and from a carriage. Liam is pleased with the progress. That evening, a state banquet is held in Beldour to celebrate new arrivals of official visitors.

July 15: The rehearsals with the Furstáns continue, with a full-scale practice to set a moving ward around both a carriage and then a *caïque* to Torenthály, and finally around a stallion from the quay to Holy Iób. Then they practice the ceremony itself within the church. That evening, Sofiana, Azim, and Arilan transport from Beldour to the Camberian Council, where they meet Barrett and Sion. Barrett says that Laran is with Vivienne, who is dying. Arilan reveals that Kelson is betrothed to Araxie. They discuss other recent events.

July 16: Arilan tells Kelson that Azim is a member of the Camberian Council, and warns him that the Council believes that a plot involving Mahael, Teymuraz, and Branyng is aimed at King Liam, but that Mátyás can be trusted. King Kelson then joins Mátyás, Teymuraz, and Branyng in the moving ward protecting King Liam for the *killijálay*, the formal empowerment of the Torenthi monarch. The procession proceeds from Furstánály Palace by carriage to the river, thence by caïque upriver to Torenthály, and then by horse to Holy Iób. At the church, Patriarch Alpheios and the XII metropolitans of the Holy Synod of Torenth welcome them, and the ceremony begins. Mahael, with the help of Teymuraz and Branyng, attacks Liam, but Mátyás, Alpheios, Morag, and Kelson fight back to protect the young king. Liam reaches for the great sword of Furstán, the ultimate source of his power. Branyng crumbles, Liam grabs the hilt of the sword, and absorbs its power. Teymuraz then turns traitor, and Mahael is mind-ripped and his power taken. He is dragged out and impaled on a stake. Duke Mahael is XXXVI years of age at his death; his honours are attainted and given to his youngest brother, Count Mátyás. Branyng II Count of Sostra also perishes of his psychic injuries, aged XXX years, and his dead body impaled on a stake; he is succeeded by his cousin, Count Yoánn. Teymuraz disclaims any responsibility for the attack, but is arrested and held for later judgment; he is ordered to attend the two impaled traitors until Liam indicates otherwise. Then the ceremony is brought to its appropriate conclusion, and the lords temporal and spiritual begin to make their individual homages to their lawfully-inaugurated king. Liam also offers fealty to Kelson as his overlord, but Kelson releases him from his vassaldom. Then the patriarch offers a celebratory mass. Teymuraz escapes his guards, bolts into the Nikolaseum, and uses the portal there to flee to safety. The participants in the ceremony return to Beldour, where they are received by the cheering crowds. At the palace, a feast of celebration is held in the Hanging Gardens. Liam then begins receiving petitioners. When night falls, the domes light up over Beldour in a grand display of Deryni magic. Mátyás arranges for the King's first Crown Council with a dozen supporters of the new king, including himself, Liam, Alpheios, Rasoul, Azim, Kelson, Morgan, Dhugal, and Arilan. Liam formally creates Mátyás Duke d'Arjenol, leaving him Komnéné as well, and then outlines a plan for the first year of his reign. Afterwards, Kelson and his companions, including Azim, Dhugal, and Arilan, meet privily with Liam and Mátyás. Mátyás requests that Arilan and Morgan remain for a time in Beldour to provide Liam with their counsel, or at least to return periodically. The two sides agree to establish reciprocal portal locations in Rhemuth and Beldour to facilitate communication back and forth. They discuss the Mearan situation, and Kelson reveals the impending marriage between Noelie and Rory. A servant interrupts the meeting to report that Teymuraz has been sighted at Saint-Sasile earlier that day, where he commandeered a war galley and crew, and put out to sea. He may be heading for the Île d'Orsal to kidnap one of the Haldane princesses. Létald must be informed immediately. Azim reveals that the Hort may have a portal in his island Palace. The ladies could be moved out of danger, and transported to Dhassa. Létald joins their discussions, and finally agrees to allow them access to his private portal at Horthánthy, in order to evacuate the families. His condition is that both Torenth and Gwynedd provide him reciprocal access to a portal in those countries. Elsewhere in Beldour, Princess Morag orders her servant to contact Sean Earl Derry. She has discovered the psychic connection that her brother King Wencit had established with Derry, and has refocused it so that she now has the control. All she has to do is to have the magical finger ring delivered to Derry. King Kelson and his party are brought to a staff room in Furstánály Palace, where they are introduced to the portal there. They transport to the portal at Horthánthy, and then memorize the portal's coordinates. Létald orders the womenfolk awakened and prepared for departure, but Sivorn objects. Kelson then announces to the assembled personages that he and Araxie are betrothed, and the ladies reluctantly agree to leave. Kelson has a private conversation with Araxie. In Beldour, Sean receives a message from King Liam (but actually from Princess Morag), asking for an audience, and is entrapped by her when he responds to her invitation. She reawakens the compulsions previously set in his mind by King Wencit. At Horthánthy, Liam returns to Beldour with Arilan. Kelson and Morgan discuss the King's impending marriage and its political consequences. They then transport to the library of Rhemuth Castle, where they abruptly meet Jehana, Barrett, and Nivard. The Queen has been meeting with them for the past week to discuss the ancient Deryni texts. Kelson informs them of recent events, and Barrett leaves to inform the Camberian Council. The King asks Nivard to rouse the other members of the royal family. Kelson tells his mother of his impending marriage, and then informs the rest of his family; Jehana tells him of the new developments with Albin and Conalline. *Ἡ γλωσσ᾽ ὀμώμοχ᾽, ἡ δε φρὴν ἀνώμοτος.*

July 17: Lady Vivienne de Jordanet dies of paralysis in the early hours of the morning, aged LXXV years. Araxie and her family are transported from Orsal to Rhemuth, where they are lodged in quarters appropriate to them. Morgan and Dhugal are back sent to Létald, with instructions to transport again to Beldour and report to Liam and Mátyás, and to oversee the departure of the remaining Gwyneddan contingent from Torenth. Azim also departs for Horthánthy; he will share the location of the library portal with the Torenthis. At dawn, the *Rhafallia* departs the Île d'Orsal for Coroth. Iddin de Vesca, one of the Hort's servants and a spy for Teymuraz, notes that the women have departed. He takes over the guard Luric's mind, and then discovers the Hort's portal. He transmits the information to Teymuraz, who is thus warned from landing at Horthánthy. In Rhemuth, Kelson meets with Nigel and Rory to discuss strategy. Morgan and Dhugal return from Beldour. An hour later, at noon, the King meets the Privy Council of Gwynedd, and brings them up to date on recent developments at home and abroad, including his own engagement to Araxie Haldane, and the proposed betrothal between Prince Rory and Lady Noelie. A dispensation will be granted to allow Kelson to marry his cousin. At the same hour, the Camberian Council meets, and Lady Vivienne's death is announced. Princess Sofiana is chosen as Coadjutor in Vivienne's place; she will be installed several days later, after the funeral. Azim brings the Council up-to-date on recent developments, including the King's marriage plans and Jehana's change of heart. Arilan returns to Beldour, where he becomes Gwynedd's ambassador. In Beldour, Létald's ships depart Beldour, heading downriver to the Île d'Orsal, under the command of Prince Cyric; included in the entourage are Derry, Saer, Payne, Brendan, and Ivo. Létald transports directly to Horthánthy. Morag watches the departure from a window in the Palace, and uses her magic to see what Derry sees and to hear what Derry hears.

July 18: The *Rhafallia* leaves Coroth for Rhemuth with Richenda and children. The bodies of Branyng and Mahael are removed from their stakes for burial.

July 19: Vivienne's funeral is held on her estate of Alta Jorda; the ceremony is attended by the Camberian Council. *Prima inter pares.*

July 20: Morgan rides to Desse with Sir Angus MacEwan and Davoran to meet the *Rhafallia*, which is carrying Richenda and party from Coroth, and is expected to arrive within the day. The Mearan wedding party arrives at Rhemuth in the late afternoon, and the Ramsays are welcomed by the Court, including Lord Savile and Sivorn and their family, Jehana, Meraude, and King Kelson. Létald's ships arrive at the Île d'Orsal. Kelson sups privily with Dhugal, and then meets Duncan and party in the library; Duncan and Nivard have transported Derry, Brendan, and Payne from Horthánthy to Rhemuth. Derry shows obvious signs of strain. Kelson discusses the matter with Duncan. Later that night, while Derry sleeps, Morag retrieves images from the Earl's mind telling her of the events of the day. Also on this day, Teymuraz's galley is spotted off the horn of Bremagne, heading south; the report of this sighting does not reach Rhemuth until July XXXth.

July 21: Rory tells Kelson that Noelie has accepted his proposition of marriage. That afternoon, Nigel arranges a hawking expedition for Jolyon, while his wife Oksana retreats to the solar with the Haldane ladies. Kelson broaches the idea of a possible marriage between Rory and Noelie to the latter's father, who grants his permission, but notes that his wife Oksana may be less agreeable. Morgan returns from Desse with his wife and children. Kelson dines that evening with Morgan, Richenda, Duncan, and Dhugal. Jolyon retires early to discuss marriage plans with his wife. Later that night, Kelson meets with Araxie, who recommends that Kelson give Jolyon a major title, and make his son Brecon the Earl of Kilarden, thereby resolving the abeyancy. Afterwards, Kelson discusses the future of Albin Haldane with his grandfather, Duke Nigel, and asks him to restore Albin to the Carthmoor succession, and Nigel says he will agree if Rothana agrees.

July 22: Kelson offers a Dukedom to Jolyon to sweeten the connection between their families, and Jolyon accepts. The ship filled with wedding paraphernalia leaves the Île d'Orsal for Desse.

July 23: Hereditary Lord Karloman is born to Martel Lord Nykorik and Lady Kyri de Róiste.

July 24: Meraude invites Oksana and her daughter to join the ladies of the royal family in the solar. Later, Jehana goes to the library, where she meets Barrett and gives him the most recent wedding news. He then invites her to see the lovely gardens at his own residence, and with her permission, transports her there. She shows him the gardens through her eyes.

July 26: Prince Rory is formally betrothed to Lady Noelie. Kelson reveals that he will bestow the titles of Duke of Ratharkin and Viceroy of Meara on Rory Haldane on his wedding day, the title of Earl of Kilarden on Brecon Ramsay on his wedding day, and the title of Duke of Laas on Jolyon Ramsay on the weddings' eve. Albin is restored to his rightful position as Hereditary Duke of Carthmoor. Kelson asks Duncan to become the ecclesiastical visitor or Rector of the new *schola*. Shortly after the noon hour, Kelson, Dhugal, Morgan, Nigel, and the two archbishops inspect the new Chapel of Saint Camber in the basilica of the Royal Palace, which will be the center of the new Deryni *schola* to be established by Rothana. Duncan is already present, and they meet Meraude, Jehana, Sivorn, and the Mearan brides on the way, together with some of the children of the Royal Court. The little girls accompany the inspection team to Saint Camber's. Nigel meets and acknowledges his granddaughter, Conalline Amelia, for the first time; their introduction has been deliberately arranged by the ladies of the court, including his own wife Meraude, Jehana, and Araxie. In Torenthály, Princess Morag continues to view events in Gwynedd through her psychic link with Sean Earl Derry. Suddenly she is confronted by Teymuraz, who uses the private portal in her chambers. He attempts to persuade her to assassinate her own son and put Ronal Rurik on the throne. Teymuraz also proposes that she take over Gwynedd as heir to the Festillic claim, while he becomes ruler of Torenth. Morag refuses. He then seizes her and breaks her neck. He discovers her secret control over Derry (an iron ring), and also takes with him her private collection of scrolls and magical implements, many of them previously gathered by Wencit. Morag is XLVIII years of age at her death.

July 27: Morag's body is discovered in Torenthály, and news of her death is immediately sent by Mátyás to King Liam and Bishop Arilan. Morag was mind-ripped; Teymuraz's complicity is soon revealed. Mátyás orders János and Amaury to ward all of the portals in Torenthály and Beldour against Teymuraz. Kelson receives news of Morag's passing at noon, Arilan and Azim having transported to the palace library in Rhemuth. Teymuraz may now have access to all of the training given to Morag by her brother Wencit, but he will have to have time to sift through her memories in order to make use of them. Arilan and Azim then return to Torenth by portal. Kelson orders Father Nivard to offer masses for Morag's soul. The Tralian wedding ship finally arrives at Desse that afternoon. In the evening, the King welcomes the newly-arrived wedding guests.

July 29: Saer brings the baggage train containing the Tralian wedding finery up from Desse. The Servants of Saint Camber, including Rothana and Albin, arrive at Rhemuth that evening from Saint Kyriell's, and are housed in the abbey adjoining the basilica. Brother Christophle Ramsay arrives for the wedding.

July 30: Kelson, Morgan, Dhugal, Araxie, Richenda, Meraude, Jehana, and Richelle welcome the XIII Servants of Saint Camber that morning, among them the *Ban-aba* Jilyan, Michael, Rhidian, and Rothana. Duncan has now been officially appointed Provost of the Basilica Chapter, and is soon to be named Rector of the *schola*. Kelson, Dhugal, Duncan, Morgan, Richenda, and Araxie then meet privately with the Servants. The King proposes that a Royal *schola* or *conlegium* be established at Rhemuth to educate Deryni under the guidance of the Servants; the Crown is prepared to grant the lands and facilities. There are three conditions: first, that the institution be housed within Rhemuth Castle and that sufficient numbers of the Servants relocate there to help manage the school; second, that Bishop Duncan McLain be appointed Rector of the facility; and three, that Rothana remain in Rhemuth as lay assistant to the Rector. She objects, but he asks her to suspend any decision until later. Richenda and Araxie discuss the matter with Rothana, revealing that Albin has been reinstated as Nigel's heir to the Duchy of Carthmoor. Rothana finally agrees to accept the King's appointment and her son's new status. Saint Camber's Chapel is formally consecrated at noon. Afterward, Richenda tells Kelson of Rothana's acquiescence. Later, Kelson meets with Rothana and Araxie. At a brief court held that evening, Kelson formally creates Sir Jolyon Ramsay Duke of Laas. Later that night, Mátyás meets with Kelson in the Palace library, and asks permission for himself and Liam to attend the weddings on the morrow. Kelson and Morgan give Mátyás the coordinates of the Cathedral portal. Mátyás reports that Teymuraz was last seen sailing around the horn of Bremagne, far to the south. In distant Alver, Teymuraz observes some of the proceedings through Derry's eyes, having taken over Morag's iron ring. The Count is gradually extending control over his unsuspecting spy.

July 31: The double weddings of Brecon and Richelle and of Rory and Noelie are held at noon in Saint George's Cathedral at Rhemuth, amid great pomp and circumstance. King Liam and Duke Mátyás quietly transport to the Cathedral, and unobtrusively join King Kelson as part of the wedding party, veiled against the eyes of others. Kelson introduces Liam and Mátyás to Araxie, his future Queen. Sean Earl Derry, acting under a *géas* placed on him by Count Teymuraz, attacks Mátyás with a dagger, but Araxie saves the life of the Torenthi Duke, who is wounded. Count Teymuraz, who has been lurking behind a pillar, is attacked by Morgan, but manages to escape. Morgan and Dhugal heal the Duke's knife wound. Azim, Araxie, and Rothana cleanse Derry's mind of its longstanding compulsion, under Azim's guidance, while Kelson observes. Liam and Mátyás return to Beldour, and Azim goes back to his brethren, hoping to use Derry's iron ring to find Teymuraz. A feast of celebration takes place that evening at Rhemuth Palace. The King's formal engagement to Princess Araxie is announced to universal joy. Sir Brecon Ramsay is created Earl of Kilarden, and Prince Rory Haldane is created Duke of Ratharkin.

August 2: Morag's funeral is held at Sankt Iób's Church in Torenthály.

August 7: King Kelson weds Princess Araxie on the west steps of Saint George's Cathedral in Rhemuth, with Bishop Duncan presiding, and Liam and Mátyás in attendance. Inside the Cathedral Princess Araxie is annointed Queen of Gwynedd by Archbishop Bradene. Archbishop Thomas Cardiel then sets the Crown of Gwynedd upon her head, and Kelson espies a brief image of Saint Camber conjoining his hands with those of the primate in blessing and approbation. A feast is held that evening in Rhemuth Palace to celebrate the nuptials. Afterwards, the bride and groom are sung to the bridal chamber. This date marks the beginning of the era known as the *Pax Kelsona*.

* * * * * * *

August 10: Count Teymuraz is attainted and charged with treason, deprived of his lands and titles, and sentenced to death in absentia.

August 14: Lady Lionella is born to Mátyás Duke d'Arjenol and Ophélie Lady du Joux.

September 1: The surviving nobility of Meara all gather at Laas to witness the declaration of Jolyon Duke of Laas, who irrevocably renounces all claims to the Throne of Meara for himself and all his descendants. Brecon Earl of Kilarden makes his own renunciation, as do Brother Christophle Ramsay and Lady Noelie. The assembly ratifies his statement, and its members swear mighty oaths never again to take up arms against their lawful king, on pain of eternal damnation. *Jucundi acti labores*.

September 22: Lord Kelliam and Lady Péadora (twins) are born to Létald Hort of Orsal and Prince of Tralia and Husniyya Sharifa of R'Kassi.

October 8: Nigel Duke of Carthmoor legally adopts Conalline Amelia, natural daughter of his late son, Prince Conall, who is created Baroness Whitney by King Kelson, but without dynastic rights.

October 15: Dowager Queen Jehana marries Barrett Titular Baron de Laney, who is created Earl Barstowe on the same day by King Kelson, with remainder to any heirs of his body whatsoever; his former title of Lord de Laney is also confirmed by the King, the Ist such Deryni peerage to be restored. *My library was dukedom large enough*.

November 14: King Kelson celebrates his XXIInd birthday by announcing that an agreement has been reached with King Liam Lajos II, whereby, in order to further the peace and amity now existing between the ruling families of Haldane and Furstán, a betrothal has been arranged between King Liam and Princess Eirian daughter of Duke Nigel, the marriage to take place when she comes of age in the year 1138; and Prince Payne son of Duke Nigel will be betrothed to Princess Stanisha, sister of King Liam, marrying her when she comes of age in the year 1136. The alliance of families is greatly celebrated in both Rhemuth and Beldour, as is the King's announcement that the Queen is with child. Mátyás Duke d'Arjenol is named Veliky Kniaz' (Chief Peer) of Torenth by King Liam Lajos II. King Kelson grants the petition of Saron Count of Trevalga in The Connait for the restoration of the ancient Earldom of Ebor, giving him an estate in Travlum. In recognition of the injustice done to the de Courcy family by depriving it of the de Courcy estate for over CC years, Barnabé Titular Baron de Courcy and Stanzar is created Earl de Courcy on this date. The petition of Sir Lyon MacAthan for the restoration of the Earldom of Culdi is denied, on the grounds that that title has become an appendage of the Royal Family of Gwynedd; however, Sir Lyon is created Earl MacRorie on this date. The petition of Rorik Baron Coldoire for restoration of the ancient Principality of Kheldour is denied for cause. The petition of Sir Rodney Lovat for the restoration of the Barony of that name is denied for lack of documentation, pending further investigation.

December 9: Teymuraz late Count of Brustarkia marries Justiniana Grand Princess of Byzantyun, daughter of Grand Prince Alexios, and is created Grand Duke of Phourstania by the Autokratór Tiberios II. *Mais où sont les neiges d'antan?*

1129

January 13: Dragonet Sovereign Prince of Jáca dies, aged LXIX years, and is succeeded by his son, Prince Rotrou II.

March 22: Princess Gloriana Haldana Esmeralda is born to Nigel Duke of Carthmoor and Meraude Lady Rhendall. *Spem gregis*.

April 12: Lady Grania Marie Araxelle is born to Alaric Duke of Corwyn and Richenda Lady of Rheljan.

April 14: Hereditary Lord Aldus is born to Jatham Baron Kilshane and Janniver Princess of Pardiac.

May 31: Lord Richard Albert Jolyon is born to Brecon Earl of Kilarden and Richelle Countess of Culdi.

June 2: The Princesses Araxandra Louise Sivorn Cécile and Rhuÿs Jehane Silvé Richelle (twins) are born to Kelson King of Gwynedd and Araxie Baroness Dunluce.

July 30: Lady Arÿole Rosaura Modeste is born to Barrett Earl Barstowe and Jehana former Queen of Gwynedd.

August 30: Prince Payne attains his majority, and is created Duke of Travlum by King Kelson.

September 4: The Grand Dukes Iskander Károly Mahael Teymuraz and Imre Alexios Wenzel Justinian (twins) are born to Teymuraz Grand Duke of Phourstania and Justiniana Valeria Grand Princess of Byzantyun. Teymuraz issues a *tomos* claiming the thrones of Torenth and Gwynedd, with Grand Duke Iskander being created Hereditary Prince of Torenth and Imre Duke of Marluk.

November 14: King Kelson celebrates his XXIIIrd birthday by announcing that Queen Araxie is expecting their third child in May.

December 13: Ewan III Duke of Claibourne dies of *la grippe*, aged LXIII years, and is succeeded by his son, Graham Earl of Kheldour. Graham is succeeded in the Earldom by his eldest son, Lord Angus. *Ita missa est.*

1130

February 2: Count Kalinik is born to Mátyás Duke d'Arjenol and Ophélie Lady du Joux, and is deeded the County of Komnénë by his father.

March 11: Gezelin Sovereign Count of Fianna dies, aged LXXI years, and is succeeded by his eldest son, Count Antoine II.

May 5: Hereditary Prince Javan Uthyr Richard Urien is born to Kelson King of Gwynedd and Araxie his Queen, and is created Prince of Meara at birth, thereby securing the succession in the senior Haldane line. *Gaudeamus!*

May 15: On this ye fifteenthe daye of the monthe of Maye, ye greate booke yclepte *Ye Codex Derynianus, Editio Secunda*, is once again made compleat. *Nihil obstat. Si monumentum requiris, amice, circumspice.*

+Theophilus Frater, O.S.C.

'Οταν αγαθον πράσσης, Θεους, μη σαυτον, αιτιω

CALENDARIUM LITURGICUM

January

1st: Blessed Virgin Mary.
2nd: Saint Basil the Great, the Holy Hierarch, and Saint Abel.
6th: Epiphany or Twelfth Night; the Monday following is called Plough Monday, and marks the beginning of field work after Christmas.
9th: Saint Alix, patroness of teachers of the poor. *Il buono è buono, ma il meglio vince.*
13th: Saint Willim, Martyr.
16th: Saint Fursey, Abbot.
21st: Saint Agnes.
23rd: Saint Emerentiana.
26th: Saint Timothy, disciple of Saint Paul
30th: Saint Sava of the East, patron of the bereaved.
31st: Saint Elderon.

Chiaro mi fu allor com' ogni dove in cielo è paradiso.

February

1st: Saint Severus.
2nd: Saint Brigid, patroness of those who are engaged in dairy work; Candlemas, the feast of the Purification of the Blessed Virgin Mary and her presentation at the Temple; candles are blessed on this day.
9th: Saint Teilo.
10th: Saint Hyacinth.
11th: Saint Torin.
14th: Saint Catulina, patroness of virtuous maidens.
15th: Saint Lucius.
22nd: Saint John, Abbot.
29th: Saint Iveagh, patron of those who cannot speak.

Dovunque il guardo io giro
Immenso Dio ti vedo;
Nelle opre tue t'ammiro,
Ti riconosco in me.

March

1st: Saint David or Dewi.
4th: Saint Leonard of Avranches.
5th: Saint Piran, patron of miners.
8th: Saint Andrew Senan, Abbot and Bishop, patron of bakers and stokers.
12th: Saint Theophanés.
15th: Saint Matrona.
16th: Saint Agapitus, Archbishop, and Saint Abraham Kidunaia.
17th: Saint Joseph of Arimathea.
19th: Saint Joseph the Father of Jesus.
21st: Vernal Equinox.
24th: Saint Gabriel the Archangel.
25th: Lady Day; the second Monday and Tuesday following Easter are called Hock Days; manorial courts are held at this time.

April

1st: Saint Veneric.
2nd: Saint Urban.
12th: Saint Zeno.
13th: Saint Ursus.
23rd: Saint George, patron of soldiers.
25th: Saint Mark, patron of scribes.
26th: Saint Exuperantia.
27th: Saint Maccul, Bishop, patron of fishermen.
30th: Saint Ercon.

May

1st: Beltane, the old Scottish New Year; Rudemas; Saint Ultán.
2nd: Saints Hesperius, Zoë, Cyriacus, and Theodulus.
3rd: Holy Rood Day.
5th: Saint Hilary, Bishop.
8th: Apparition of Saint Michael.
10th: Saint Job.
12th: Saint Pancras.
14th: Saint Mathias.
15th: Saints Dymphna and Ctesiphon.
16th: Saint Peregrine.
19th: Saint Pudentiana.
20th: Saints Basilla and Plautilla.
21st: Saint Constantine.
28th: Saint Stefan, patron of wanderers.
29th: Saint Alexander.
30th: Saint Alver.
31st: Saint Petronilla.

La terra, il mar, le sfere
Parlan del tuo potere
Tue sei per tutto, e noi
Tutti viviamo in te.

June

1st: Saint Justin of Nablus, the Philosopher.
3rd: Saint Genesius.
6th: Saint Jarlath.
8th: Saint Médard.
11th: Saint Barnabas.
14th: Saint Simplicius, patron of imbeciles. *Fede ed innocenza son reperte solo nei parvoletti.*
15th: Saint Vitus (Ouitos).
16th: Saints Quiricus and Tychon.
17th: Saint Botulf.
21st: Saint Ruadan of Dhassa; Summer Solstice; and Saint Asaph, patron of coppersmiths.
22nd: Saint Acacius the Martyr.
23rd: Saint Moelray or Mölray.
24th: Saint John the Baptist, Saint John's Day; Midsummer Day.
25th: Saint Maximus.
26th: Saints Salvius and Superius.
27th: Saints Zoilus and László.
28th: Saint Irenæus.
29th: Saint Peter and Saint Paul, Apostles; and Saint Casdoe.
30th: Saint Joric the Gardener.

July

1st: Saint Julius the Martyr.
2nd: Saints Processus and Martinian.
3rd: Saint Germanus.
4th: Saint Liam, patron of teachers.

5th: Saint Numerian.
6th: Saint Monenna.
7th: Saint Palladius.
8th: Saint Kilian.
9th: Saint Averil.
10th: Feast of the Seven Brothers.
11th: Saint Benedict, Abbot.
13th: Saint Silas.
15th: Saint Vladimir, Prince.
16th: Saint Hélier.
17th: Saint Alexius.
18th: Saint Theneva.
19th: Saints Justa and Rufina.
20th: Saint Wulmar.
21st: Saint Praxedes.
22nd: Saint Vandrille.
23rd: Saint Liborius.
25th: Saint Christopher, patron of travellers.
27th: Saint Panteleimon.
30th: Saints Abdon and Sennen.
31st: Saint Neot.

In un giorno non si fe' Roma.

AUGUST

1st: Lammastide, a harvest festival at which loaves of bread are consecrated.
3rd: Saint Gamaliel.
4th: Saint Ostrythe, Princess of Meara.
5th: Saint Cassian of Autun.
6th: Feast of the Transfiguration.
9th: Saint Emygdius.
10th: Saint Laurence.
16th: Saint Ambrose the Base.
18th: Saints Triduana and Helena.
23rd: Saint Apollinaris.
24th: Saint Aurea.
25th: Saint Varnar.
28th: Saint Augustine.
30th: Saint Yabhalaha bar Qayyuma.

SEPTEMBER

1st: Saint Giles, patron of cripples and the indigent.
4th: Saint Moses the Prophet.
5th: Saint Bertin the Abbot.
6th: Saint Eleutherius.
7th: Saint Bearand, King of Gwynedd.
8th: Saint Adrian.
11th: Saint Paphnytius.
21st: Saint Matthew the Apostle; Autumn Equinox.
23rd: Saint Xantilla; Saint Polyxena.
24th: Saint Thecla.
25th: Saint Finnbarr.
28th: Saint Wenceslas.
29th: Saint Michael the Archangel, Michaelmas.
30th: Saint Jerome, patron of scholars and students.

Le miel est doux, mais l'abeille pique.

OCTOBER

1st: Saint Rémy.
3rd: Saint Faustus.

8th: Saint Demetrius.
12th: Saint Ethelburga, Abbess.
16th: Saint Eloff or Eliphius, the Martyr of Howicce.
17th: Saint Ignatius.
18th: Saint Luke the Evangelist, patron of Healers.
19th: Saint Ptolemy. *Il timor di Dio facilita qualunque impresa.*
24th: Saint Raphael the Archangel.
28th: Saint Jude, patron of lost causes.
31st: All Hallows' Eve; Saint Foillan and Saint Stachys.

Se d' alcuno s' intende, o legge, che, senza alcuno suo commodo, o interesse, ami più il male, che il bene, si deve chiamare bestia, e non uomo, poichè manca dell' appetito naturale.

NOVEMBER

1st: All Saints' Day or Samhain.
2nd: All Souls' Day.
6th: Saint Illtyd.
7th: Saint Willibrord, Bishop.
8th: Feast of the Four Crowned Ones *or Quatuor Coronati*, patrons of stone masons.
11th: Saint Martin, Martinmas: this day marks the traditional start of Winter slaughtering.
13th: Saint Margetan.
14th: Saint Camber of Culdi or Saint Kyriell, Cambermasl. *O somma Sapienza, quanta è l'arte che mostri in cielo, in terra e nel mal mondo.*
15th: Saint Edmund.
17th: Saint Hilda.
22nd: Saint Cecilia.
28th: Saint Stylianus.
30th: Saint Andrew the Apostle.

Ninna cosa fa morir tanto contento, quanto ricordarsi di non aver mai offeso alcuno, anzi piuttosto beneficato ognuno.

DECEMBER

1st: Saint Eloi.
9th: Saint Leocadia.
10th: Saint Eulalia.
11th: Saint Sviatoslav, patron of those who cannot see.
18th: Saint Henry Istelyn, Bishop and Martyr.
21st: Saint Uriel the Archangel, also known as St. Auriel, the Angel of Death; Winter Solstice.
24th: Vigil of Christmas; Saint Ilona, patroness of almsgivers.
25th: The Birth of Christ (Christmas).
26th: Saint Stephen the First Martyr.
28th: Feast of the Holy Innocents (Childermas).
30th: Saint Leander.
31st: Saint Sylvester.

Les grands hommes qui ne doivent ce titre qu'à certainese actions d'éclat, n'ont quelquefois de grand que le spectacle. C'est que, dans les occasions d'éclat l'homme est comme sur le théâtre; il représente: mais, dans le cours ordinaire des actions de la vie, il est, pour ainsi dire, rendu à lui-même; c'est lui qu'on voit; il quitte le personnage, et ne montre plus que sa personne.

DE AUCTORIBUS

ET

BIBLIOGRAPHIA LIBRORUM

DE AUCTORIBUS

KATHERINE KURTZ

KATHERINE KURTZ published her 1st novel, *Deryni Rising*, in 1970, and has since written IV trilogies set in the Deryni universe, plus a collection of short stories, *The Deryni Archives*, and a grimoire, *Deryni Magic*. Her *Lammas Night* (Ballantine, 1983) began a fantasy sequence set in modern times that loosely encompasses THE ADEPT series (Ace Books, V volumes); she also edited III historical fantasy anthologies for Warner Books based around the Knights Templar. Ms. Kurtz received a Balrog Award in 1982 for Best Fantasy Novel of the Year for *Camber the Heretic*. Her latest Deryni novel, *In the King's Service*, the beginning of the Childe Morgan Trilogy, was published by Ace in 2003. She lives in a CL-year-old manor house in County Wicklow, Ireland. *Justiciæ fundamentum est fides; justicia regnorum fundamentum.*

ROBERT REGINALD

ROBERT REGINALD published his 1st book, *Stella Nova: The Contemporary Science Fiction Authors*, in 1970, and will surpass *Opus C* in 2005. In 1993 he received the XXIVth annual Pilgrim Award and the 1st annual Lifetime Collector's Award for his contributions to SF criticism, bibliography, and publishing. His fiction includes a collection of short stories, *Katydid & Other Critters: Tales of Fantasy and Mystery* (2001), II historical fantasy novels set in Nova Europa, *The Dark-Haired Man; or, The Hieromonk's Tale* (2004) and *The Exiled Prince; or, The Archquisitor's Tale* (2004), II science fiction novels, *War of the Worlds I: Invasion!* (2005) and *War of the Worlds II: Operation Crimson Storm* (2005), III historical mystery novellas, and several forthcoming books, including *Quæstiones; or, The Protopresbyter's Tale* (a Nova Europa novel) and *War of the Worlds III: The Martians Strike Back!* He lives in San Bernardino, California. *Principibus placuisse viris non ultima laus est.*

BIBLIOGRAPHIA LIBRORUM

The Bastard Prince. New York: Ballantine/Del Rey, 1994.
"Bethane," in *The Deryni Archives*, p. 77-98.
The Bishop's Heir. New York: Ballantine/Del Rey, 1984.
Camber of Culdi. New York: Ballantine/Del Rey, 1976.
Camber the Heretic. New York: Ballantine/Del Rey, 1981.
"Catalyst," in *The Deryni Archives*, p. 10-27.
Codex Derynianus. San Bernardino, CA: Borgo Press; Grass Valley, CA: Underwood Books, 1998.
The Deryni Archives. New York: Ballantine/Del Rey, 1986.
Deryni Challenge, by Stephen Billias. New York: Tor, 1988.
Deryni Checkmate. New York: Ballantine, 1972.
Deryni Magic: A Grimoire. New York: Ballantine/Del Rey, 1990.
Deryni Rising. New York: Ballantine, 1970.
Deryni Tales: An Anthology, edited by Katherine Kurtz. New York: Ace Books, 2002; includes "The Green Tower," by Katherine Kurtz, p. 243-265.
"The *Examen*," in *Deryni Magic*, p. 213-224.
"First Session," in *Deryni Magic*, p. 202-210.
The Harrowing of Gwynedd. New York: Ballantine/Del Rey, 1989.
"Healer's Song," in *The Deryni Archives*, p. 28-44.
High Deryni. New York: Ballantine, 1973.
In the King's Service. New York: Ace Books, 2003.
King Javan's Year. New York: Ballantine/Del Rey, 1992.
King Kelson's Bride. New York: Ace Books, 2000.
The King's Justice. New York: Ballantine/Del Rey, 1985.
"The Knighting of Derry," in *The Deryni Archives*, p. 173-204.
"Legacy," in *The Deryni Archives*, p. 158-172.
"The Priesting of Arilan," in *The Deryni Archives*, p. 99-157.
The Quest for Saint Camber. New York: Ballantine/Del Rey, 1986.
Saint Camber. New York: Ballantine/Del Rey, 1978.
"Swords Against the Marluk," in *Flashing Swords! #4: Barbarians and Black Magicians*, edited by Lin Carter. New York: Dell, 1977, p. 161-201.
"Trial," in *The Deryni Archives*, p. 205-230.
Venture in Vain: A Tale of the Deryni. San Bernardino, CA: Millefleurs, 2001.
"Vocation," in *The Deryni Archives*, p. 45-76.

Nobilitas sola est atque unica virtus.

GENEALOGIÆ FAMILIARUM REGIARUM XI REGNORUM

GENEALOGIES OF THE ROYAL FAMILIES OF THE XI KINGDOMS

Vixere fortes ante Agamemnona
Multi; sed omnes illacrimabiles
Urgentur ignotique longa
Nocte, carent quia vate sacro

Kings of Torenth

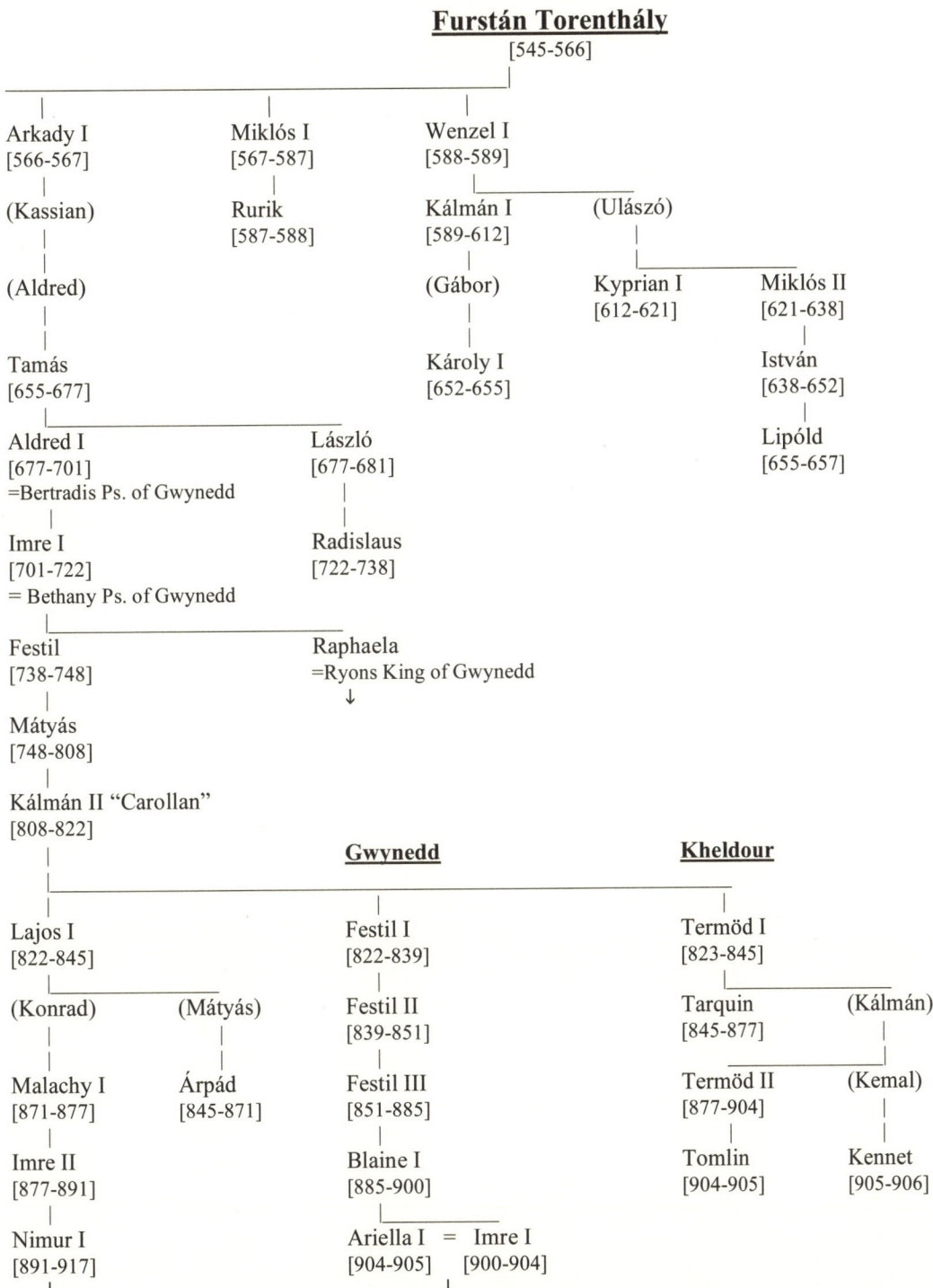

Kings of Torenth (cont.)

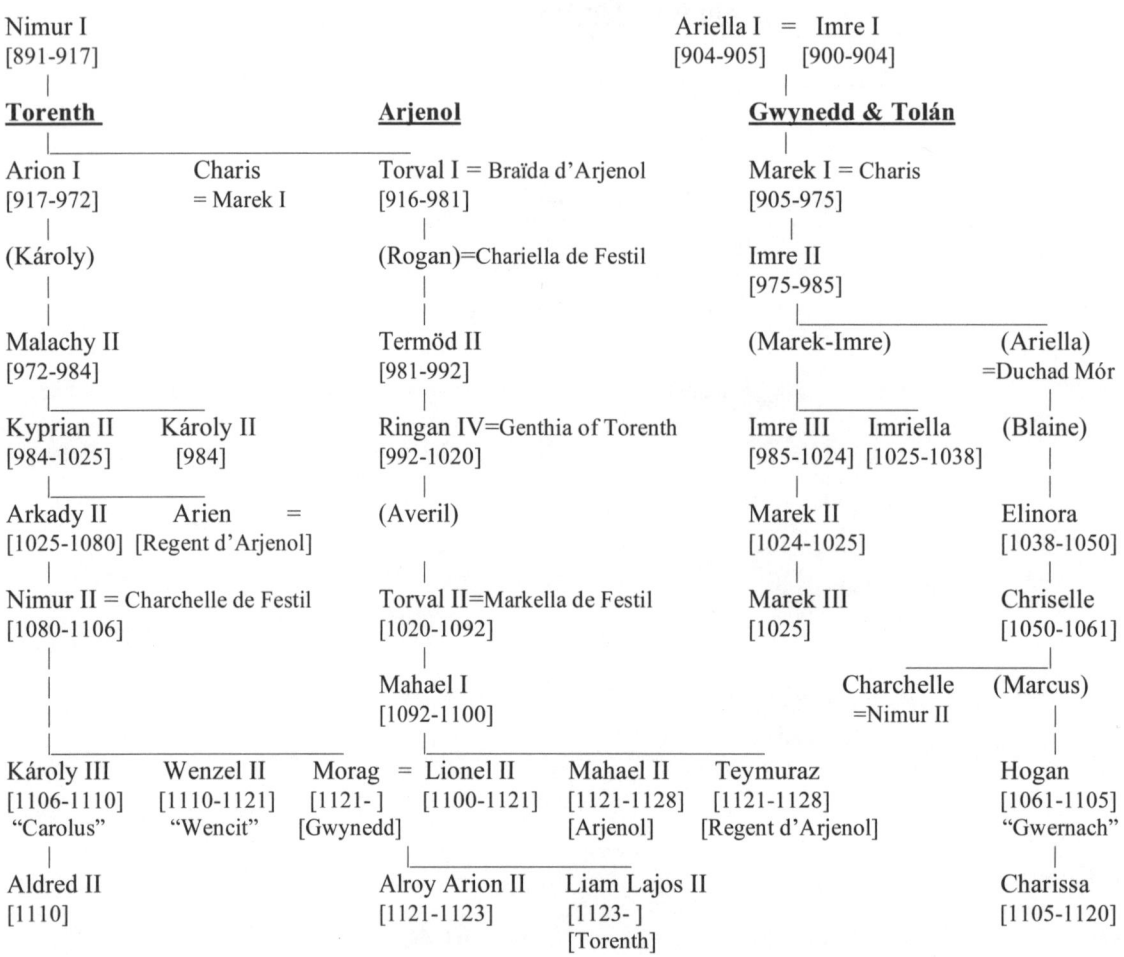

Counts of Haldane

Halbert the Dane
[411-433]

- Hansoc [433-461]
  - Guerric [461-465]
  - Jestyn [465-466]
  - Jesric [466-506]
    - Aidan I [506-522]
      - Cinhil I [522-544]
      - (Haldin)
        - Bearand I [544-559]
        - Cinhil II [559-572]
          - Augarin I [572-601]
            - Kensell [601-609]
              - Bearand II [609-631]
                - Aidan II [631-640]
                - Augarin II [640-645] King of Gwynedd

Kings of Gwynedd

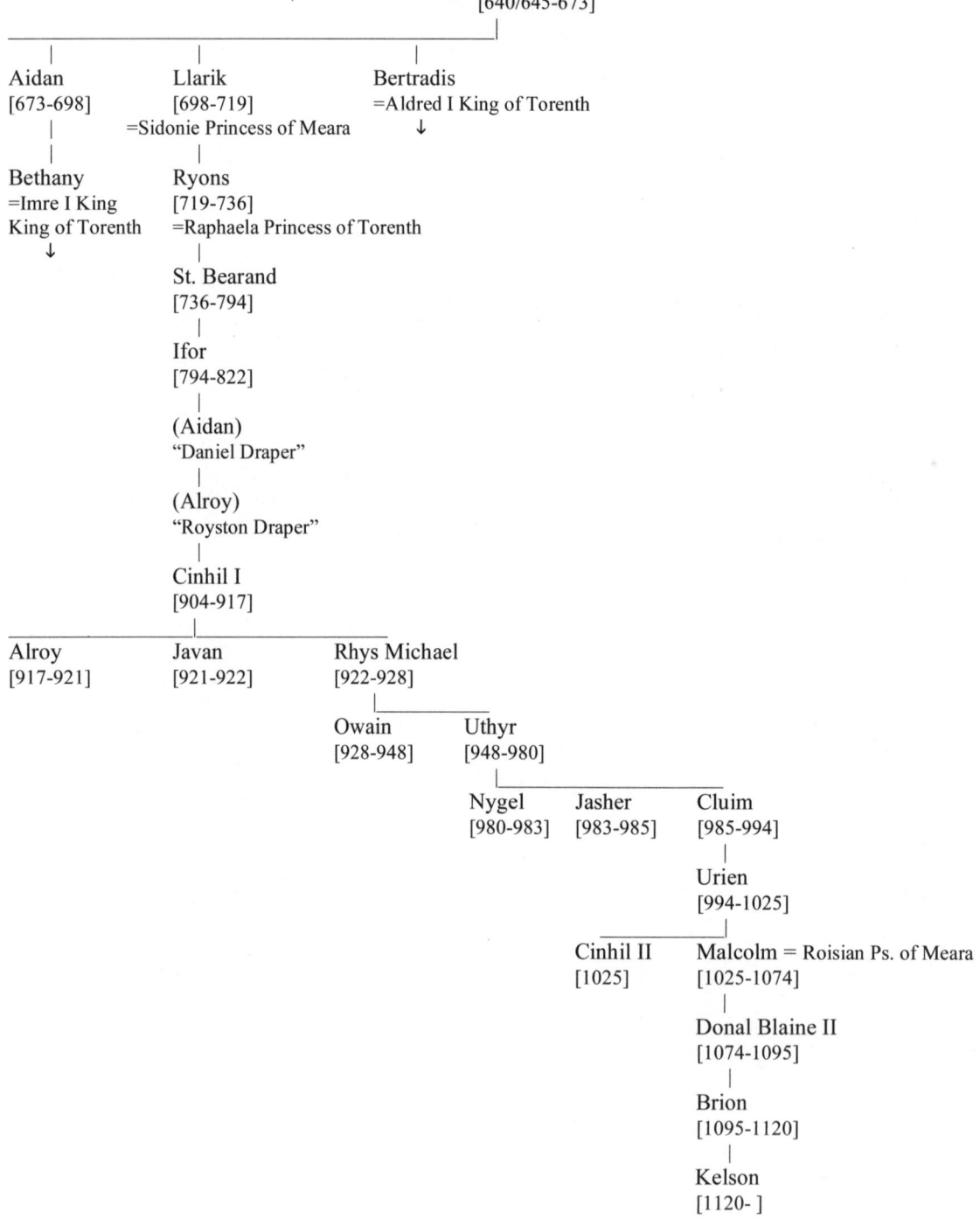

Princes of Meara

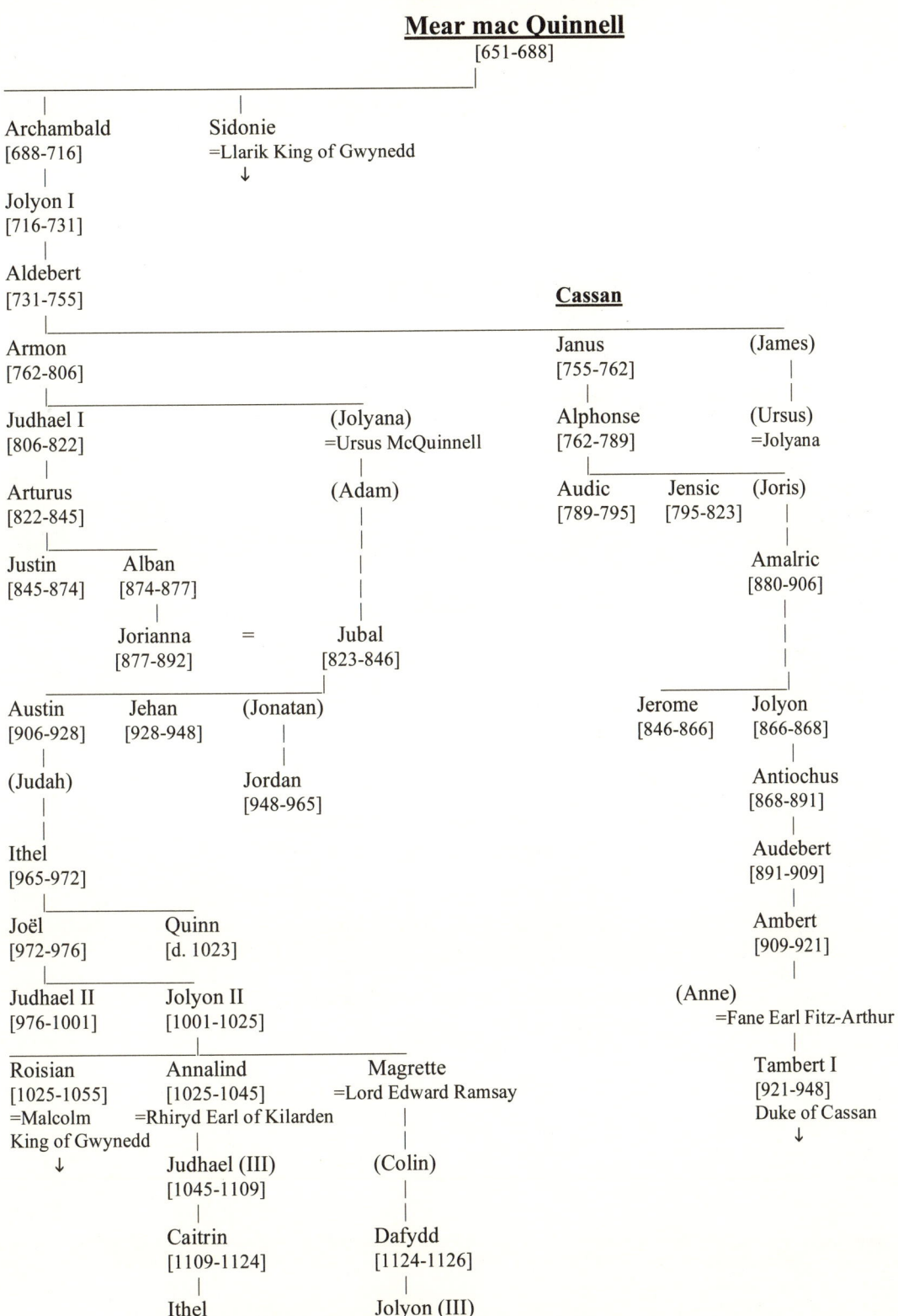

TABULÆ XI REGNORUM

MAPS OF THE XI KINGDOMS

by

Amy Harlib

Beatus ille, qui procul negotiis,
Ut prisca gens mortalium,
Paterna rura bubus exercet suis,
Solutus omni fenore;

Neque excitatur classico miles truci,
Neque horret iratum mare;
Forumque vitat, et superba civium
Potentiorum limina.